THE MODERN LIBRARY
of the World's Best Books

>>

QUENTIN DURWARD
IVANHOE
KENILWORTH

>>

*The publishers will be pleased to send, upon
request, an illustrated folder setting forth
the purpose and scope of* THE MODERN
LIBRARY, *and listing each volume in the
series. Every reader of books will find titles
he has been looking for, handsomely printed,
in unabridged editions, and at an
unusually low price.*

>>

QUENTIN DURWARD
IVANHOE · KENILWORTH

BY

SIR WALTER SCOTT

THE MODERN LIBRARY

NEW YORK

THE MODERN LIBRARY

IS PUBLISHED BY

RANDOM HOUSE, INC.

BENNETT A. CERF · DONALD S. KLOPFER · ROBERT K. HAAS

Manufactured in the United States of America
By H. Wolff

CONTENTS

QUENTIN DURWARD

La guerre est ma patrie,
Mon harnois ma maison,
Et en toute saison
Combattre c'est ma vie.

CONTENTS

CONTENTS

4

INTRODUCTION

THE scene of this romance is laid in the fifteenth century, when the feudal system, which had been the sinews and nerves of national defence, and the spirit of chivalry, by which, as by a vivifying soul, that system was animated, began to be innovated upon and abandoned by those grosser characters, who centred their sum of happiness in procuring the personal objects on which they had fixed their own exclusive attachment. The same egotism had indeed displayed itself even in more primitive ages; but it was now for the first time openly avowed as a professed principle of action. The spirit of chivalry had in it this point of excellence, that, however overstrained and fantastic many of its doctrines may appear to us, they were all founded on generosity and self-denial, of which, if the earth were deprived, it would be difficult to conceive the existence of virtue among the human race.

Among those who were the first to ridicule and abandon the self-denying principles in which the young knight was instructed, and to which he was so carefully trained up, Louis the XIth of France was the chief. That Sovereign was of a character so purely selfish—so guiltless of entertaining any purpose unconnected with his ambition, covetousness, and desire of selfish enjoyment, that he almost seems an incarnation of the devil himself, permitted to do his utmost to corrupt our ideas of honour in its very source. Nor is it to be forgotten, that Louis possessed to a great extent that caustic wit which can turn into ridicule all that a man does for any other person's advantage but his own, and was, therefore, peculiarly qualified to play the part of a cold-hearted and sneering fiend.

In this point of view, Goethe's conception of the character and reasoning of Mephistopheles, the tempting spirit in the singular play of "Faust," appears to me more happy than that which has been formed by Byron, and even than the Satan of Milton. These last great authors have given to the Evil Principle something which elevates and dignifies his wickedness; a sustained and unconquerable resistance against Omnipotence itself—a lofty scorn of suffering compared with submission, and all those points of attraction in the Author of Evil, which have induced Burns and others to consider him as the Hero of the "Paradise Lost." The great German poet has, on the contrary, rendered his seducing spirit a being who, otherwise totally unimpassioned, seems only to have existed for the purpose of increasing, by his persuasions and temptations, the mass of moral evil, and who calls forth by his seductions those slumbering passions which otherwise might have allowed the human being who was the object of the Evil Spirit's operations to pass the tenor of his life in tran-

5

quillity. For this purpose Mephistopheles is, like Louis XI., endowed with an acute and depreciating spirit of caustic wit, which is employed incessantly in undervaluing and vilifying all actions, the consequences of which do not lead certainly and directly to self-gratification.

Even an author of works of mere amusement may be permitted to be serious for a moment, in order to reprobate all policy, whether of a public or private character, which rests its basis upon the principles of Machiavel, or the practice of Louis XI.

The cruelties, the perjuries, the suspicions of this prince, were rendered more detestable, rather than amended, by the gross and debasing superstition which he constantly practised. The devotion to the heavenly saints, of which he made such a parade, was upon the miserable principle of some petty deputy in office, who endeavours to hide or atone for the malversations of which he is conscious, by liberal gifts to those whose duty it is to observe his conduct, and endeavours to support a system of fraud, by an attempt to corrupt the incorruptible. In no other light can we regard his creating the Virgin Mary a countess and colonel of his guards, or the cunning that admitted to one or two peculiar forms of oath the force of a binding obligation, which he denied to all others, strictly preserving the secret, which mode of swearing he really accounted obligatory, as one of the most valuable of State mysteries.

To a total want of scruple, or, it would appear, of any sense whatever of moral obligation, Louis XI. added great natural firmness and sagacity of character, with a system of policy so highly refined, considering the times he lived in, that he sometimes overreached himself by giving way to its dictates.

Probably there is no portrait so dark as to be without its softer shades. He understood the interests of France, and faithfully pursued them so long as he could identify them with his own. He carried the country safe through the dangerous crisis of the war termed "for the public good;" in thus disuniting and dispersing this grand and dangerous alliance of the great crown vassals of France against the Sovereign, a King of a less cautious and temporising character, and of a more bold and less crafty disposition than Louis XI., would, in all probability, have failed. Louis had also some personal accomplishments not inconsistent with his public character. He was cheerful and witty in society; caressed his victim like the cat, which can fawn when about to deal the most bitter wound; and none was better able to sustain and extol the superiority of the coarse and selfish reasons by which he endeavoured to supply those nobler motives for exertion, which his predecessors had derived from the high spirit of chivalry.

In fact, that system was now becoming ancient, and had, even while in its perfection, something so overstrained and fantastic in its principles as rendered it peculiarly the object of ridicule, whenever, like other old fashions, it began to fall out of repute, and the weapons of raillery could be employed against it, without exciting the disgust and horror with which they would have been rejected at an early period, as a species of blasphemy. In the fourteenth century a tribe of scoffers had arisen, who pretended to supply what was naturally useful in chivalry by other resources, and threw ridicule upon the extravagant and exclusive principles of honour and virtue, which were openly treated as absurd, because, in fact, they were cast in a mould of perfection too lofty for the practice of fallible beings. If an ingenuous and high-spirited youth proposed to frame himself on his father's principles of honour, he was vulgarly derided as if he had brought to the field the good old knight's Durindarte or two-handed sword, ridiculous from its antique make and fashion, although its blade might be the Ebro's temper, and its ornaments of pure gold.

In like manner, the principles of chivalry were cast aside, and their aid supplied by baser stimulants. Instead of the high spirit which pressed every man forward in the defence of his country, Louis XI. substituted the exertions of the ever ready mercenary soldier, and persuaded his subjects, among whom the mercantile class began to make a figure, that it was better to leave to mercenaries the risks and labours of war, and to supply the Crown with the means of paying them, than to peril themselves in defence of their own substance. The merchants were easily persuaded by this reasoning. The hour did not arrive, in the days of Louis XI., when the landed gentry and nobles could be in like manner excluded from the ranks of war; but the wily monarch commenced that system, which, acted upon by his successors, at length threw the whole military defence of the State into the hands of the Crown.

He was equally forward in altering the principles which were wont to regulate the intercourse of the sexes. The doctrines of chivalry had established, in theory at least, a system in which Beauty was the governing and remunerating divinity—Valour her slave, who caught his courage from her eye, and gave his life for her slightest service. It is true, the system here, as in other branches, was stretched to fantastic extravagance, and cases of scandal not unfrequently arose. Still they were generally such as those mentioned by Burke, where frailty was deprived of half its guilt, by being purified from all its grossness. In Louis XIth's practice, it was far otherwise. He was a low voluptuary, seeking pleasure without sentiment, and despising the sex from whom he desired to obtain it; his mistresses were of inferior rank, as little to be compared with the elevated though faulty character of Agnes Sorel, as Louis was to his heroic father, who freed France from the threatened yoke of England. In like manner, by selecting his favourites and ministers from among the dregs of the people, Louis showed the slight regard which he paid to eminent station and high birth; and although this might be not only excusable but meritorious, where the monarch's fiat promoted obscure talent, or called forth modest worth, it was very different when the King made his favourite associates of such men as Tristan l'Hermite, the Chief of his Marshalsea, or police; and it was evident that such a prince could no longer be, as his descendant Francis elegantly designed himself, "the first gentleman in his dominions."

Nor were Louis's sayings and actions in private or public, of a kind which could redeem such gross offences against the character of a man of honour. His word, generally accounted the most sacred test of a man's character, and the least impeachment of which is a capital offence by the code of honour, was forfeited without scruple on the slightest occasion, and often accompanied by the perpetration of the most enormous crimes. If he broke his own personal and plighted faith, he did not treat that of the public with more ceremony. His sending an inferior person disguised as a herald to Edward IV., was in those days, when heralds were esteemed the sacred depositaries of public and national faith, a daring imposition, of which few save this unscrupulous prince would have been guilty.[1]

In short, the manners, sentiments, and actions of Louis XI. were such as were inconsistent with the principles of chivalry, and his caustic wit was sufficiently disposed to ridicule a system adopted on what he considered as the most absurd of all bases, since it was founded on the principle of devoting toil, talents, and time, to the accomplishment of objects, from which no personal advantage could, in the nature of things, be obtained.

It is more than probable that, in thus renouncing almost openly the ties of religion, honour, and morality, by which mankind at large feel themselves influenced, Louis sought to obtain great advantages in his negotiations with parties who might esteem themselves bound, while he himself enjoyed liberty. He started from the goal, he might suppose, like the racer who has got rid of the weights with which his competitors are still encumbered, and expects to succeed of course. But Providence seems always to unite the existence of peculiar danger, with some circumstance which may put those exposed to the peril upon their guard. The constant suspicion attached to any public person who becomes badly eminent for breach of faith, is to him what the rattle is to the poisonous serpent; and men come at last to calculate, not so much on what their antagonist says, as upon that which he is likely to do; a degree of mistrust which tends to counteract the intrigues of such a faithless character, more than his freedom from the scruples of conscientious men can afford him advantage. The example of Louis XI. raised disgust and suspicion rather than a desire of imitation among other nations in Europe, and the circumstances of his outwitting more than one of his contemporaries, operated to put others on their guard. Even the system of chivalry, though much less generally extended than heretofore, survived this profligate monarch's reign, who did so much to sully its lustre, and long after the death of Louis XI. it inspired the Knight without Fear and Reproach, and the gallant Francis I.

Indeed, although the reign of Louis had been as successful in a political

[1] See Note XII. Disguised Herald.

point of view as he himself could have desired, the spectacle of his death-bed might of itself be a warning-piece against the seduction of his example. Jealous of every one, but chiefly of his own son, he immured himself in his Castle of Plessis, entrusting his person exclusively to the doubtful faith of his Scottish mercenaries. He never stirred from his chamber; he admitted no one into it, and wearied Heaven and every saint with prayers, not for the forgiveness of his sins, but for the prolongation of his life. With a poverty of spirit totally inconsistent with his shrewd worldly sagacity, he importuned his physicians, until they insulted as well as plundered him. In his extreme desire of life, he sent to Italy for supposed relics, and the yet more extraordinary importation of an ignorant crack-brained peasant, who, from laziness probably, had shut himself up in a cave, and renounced flesh, fish, eggs, or the produce of the dairy. This man, who did not possess the slightest tincture of letters, Louis reverenced as if he had been the Pope himself, and to gain his goodwill founded two cloisters.

It was not the least singular circumstance of this course of superstition, that bodily health and terrestrial felicity seemed to be his only objects. Making any mention of his sins when talking on the state of his health, was strictly prohibited; and when at his command a priest recited a prayer to Saint Eutropius, in which he recommended the King's welfare both in body and soul, Louis caused the two last words to be omitted, saying it was not prudent to importune the blessed saint by too many requests at once. Perhaps he thought by being silent on his crimes, he might suffer them to pass out of the recollection of the celestial patrons, whose aid he invoked for his body.

So great were the well-merited tortures of this tyrant's death-bed, that Philip des Comines enters into a regular comparison between them and the numerous cruelties inflicted on others by his order; and, considering both, comes to express an opinion, that the worldly pangs and agony suffered by Louis were such as might compensate the crimes he had committed, and that, after a reasonable quarantine in purgatory, he might in mercy be found duly qualified for the superior regions.

Fénélon also has left his testimony against this prince, whose mode of living and governing he has described in the following remarkable passage:—

"Pygmalion, tourmenté par une soif insatiable des richesses, se rend de plus en plus misérable et odieux à ses sujets. C'est un crime à Tyr que d'avoir de grands biens; l'avarice le rend défiant, soupçonneux, cruel; il persécute les riches, et il craint les pauvres.

"C'est un crime encore plus grand à Tyr d'avoir de la vertu; car Pygmalion suppose que les bons ne peuvent souffrir ses injustices et ses infamies; la vertu le condamne, il s'aigrit et s'irrite contre elle. Tout l'agite, l'inquiète, le ronge; il a peur de son ombre; il ne dort ni nuit ni jour; les Dieux, pour le confondre, l'accablent de trésors dont il n'ose jouir. Ce qu'il cherche pour être heureux est précisément ce qui l'empêche de l'être. Il regrette tout ce qu'il donne, et craint toujours de perdre; il se tourmente pour gagner.

"On ne le voit presque jamais; il est seul, triste, abattu, au fond de son palais; ses amis mêmes n'osent l'aborder, de peur de lui devenir suspects. Une garde terrible tient toujours des épées nues et des piques levées autour de sa maison. Trente chambres qui communiquent les unes aux autres, et dont chacune a une porte de fer avec six gros verroux, sont le lieu où il se renferme; on ne sait jamais dans laquelle de ces chambres il couche; et on assure qu'il ne couche jamais deux nuits de suite dans le même, de peur d'y être égorgé. Il ne connoît ni les doux plaisirs, ni l'amitié encore plus douce. Si on lui parle de chercher la joie, il sent qu'elle fuit loin de lui, et qu'elle refuse d'entrer dans son cœur. Ses yeux creux sont pleins d'un feu âpre et farouche; ils sont sans cesse errans de tous cotés; il prête l'oreille au moindre bruit, et se sent tout ému; il est pâle, défait, et les noirs soucis sont peints sur son visage toujours ridé. Il se tait, il soupire, il tire de son cœur de profonds gémissemens, il ne peut cacher les remords qui déchirent ses entrailles. Les mets les plus exquis de dégoûtent. Ses enfans, loin d'être son espérance, sont le sujet de sa terreur: il en a fait ses plus dangereux ennemis. Il n'a eu toute sa vie aucun moment d'assuré: il ne se conserve qu'à force de répandre le sang de tous ceux qu'il craint. Insensé, qui ne voit pas que sa cruauté, à laquelle il se confine, le fera périr! Quelqu'un de ses domestiques, aussi défiant que lui, se hâtera de délivrer le monde de ce monstre."

The instructive but appalling scene of the tyrant's sufferings, was at length closed by death, 30th August, 1485.

The selection of this remarkable person as the principal character in the romance—for it will be easily comprehended, that the little love intrigue of Quentin is only employed as the means of bringing out the story—afforded considerable facilities to the author. The whole of Europe was, during the fifteenth century, convulsed with dissensions from such various causes, that it would have required almost a dissertation to have brought the English reader with a mind perfectly alive and prepared to admit the possibility of the strange scenes to which he was introduced.

In Louis XI.'s time, extraordinary commotions existed throughout all Europe. England's civil wars were ended rather in appearance than reality, by the short-lived ascendency of the House of York. Switzerland was asserting that freedom which was afterwards so bravely defended. In the Empire, and in France, the great vassals of the Crown were endeavouring to emancipate themselves from its control, while Charles of Burgundy, by main force, and Louis more artfully by indirect means, laboured to subject them to subservience to their respective sovereignties. Louis, while with one hand he circumvented and subdued his own rebellious vassals, laboured secretly with the other to aid and encourage the large trading towns of Flanders to rebel against the Duke of Burgundy, to which their wealth and irritability naturally disposed them.

In the more woodland districts of Flanders, the Duke of Gueldres, and William de la Marck, called from his ferocity the Wild Boar of Ardennes, were throwing off the habits of knights and gentlemen, to practise the violences and brutalities of common bandits.

A hundred secret combinations existed in the different provinces of France and Flanders; numerous private emissaries of the restless Louis, Bohemians, pilgrims, beggars, or agents disguised as such, were everywhere spreading the discontent which it was his policy to maintain in the dominions of Burgundy.

Amidst so great an abundance of materials, it was difficult to select such as should be most intelligible and interesting to the reader; and the author had to regret, that though he made liberal use of the power of departing from the reality of history, he felt by no means confident of having brought his story into a pleasing, compact, and sufficiently intelligible form. The mainspring of the plot is that which all who know the least of the feudal system can easily understand, though the facts are absolutely fictitious. The right of a feudal superior was in nothing more universally acknowledged than in his power to interfere in the marriage of a female vassal. This may appear to exist as a contradiction both of the civil and canon law, which declare that marriage shall be free, while the feudal or municipal jurisprudence, in case of a fief passing to a female, acknowledges an interest in the superior of the fief to dictate the choice of her companion in marriage. This is accounted for on the principle that the superior was, by his bounty, the original granter of the fief, and is still interested that the marriage of the vassal shall place no one there who may be inimical to his liege lord. On the other hand, it might be reasonably pleaded that this right of dictating to the vassal to a certain extent in the choice of a husband, is only competent to the superior, from whom the fief is originally derived. There is therefore no violent improbability in a vassal of Burgundy flying to the protection of the King of France, to whom the Duke of Burgundy himself was vassal; nor is it a great stretch of probability to affirm, that Louis, unscrupulous as he was, should have formed the design of betraying the fugitive into some alliance which might prove inconvenient, if not dangerous, to his formidable kinsman and vassal of Burgundy.

I may add, that the romance of QUENTIN DURWARD, which acquired a popularity at home more extensive than some of its predecessors, found also unusual success on the Continent, where the historical allusions awakened more familiar ideas.

ABBOTSFORD, 1st December 1831.

INTRODUCTION [1]

And one who hath had losses—go to.
Much Ado About Nothing.

WHEN honest Dogberry sums up and recites all the claims which he had
to respectability, and which, as he opined, ought to have exempted him
from the injurious appellation conferred on him by Master Gentleman
Conrade, it is remarkable that he lays not more emphasis even upon his
double gown (a matter of some importance in a certain ci-devant capital
which I wot of), or upon his being "a pretty piece of flesh as any in
Messina," or even upon the conclusive argument of his being "a *rich* fellow enough," than upon his being *one that hath had losses.*

Indeed, I have always observed your children of prosperity, whether
by way of hiding their full glow of splendour from those whom fortune
has treated more harshly, or whether that to have risen in spite of calamity
is as honourable to their fortune as it is to a fortress to have undergone
a siege,—however this be, I have observed that such persons never fail
to entertain you with an account of the damage they sustain by the
hardness of the times. You seldom dine at a well-supplied table, but
the intervals between the Champagne, the Burgundy, and the Hock, are
filled, if your entertainer be a moneyed man, with the fall of interest and
the difficulty of finding investments for cash, which is therefore lying idle
on his hands; or, if he be a landed proprietor, with a woeful detail of
arrears and diminished rents. This hath its effects. The guests sigh and
shake their heads in cadence with their landlord, look on the sideboard
loaded with plate, sip once more the rich wines which flow around them
in quick circulation, and think of the genuine benevolence, which, thus
stinted of its means, still lavishes all that it yet possesses on hospitality;
and, what is yet more flattering, on the wealth, which, undiminished by
these losses, still continues, like the inexhaustible hoard of the generous
Aboulcasem, to sustain, without impoverishment, such copious drains.

This querulous humour, however, hath its limits, like to the coining
of grievances, which all valetudinarians know is a most fascinating
pastime, so long as there is nothing to complain of but chronic complaints. But I never heard a man whose credit was actually verging to
decay talk of the diminution of his funds; and my kind and intelligent
physician assures me, that it is a rare thing with those afflicted with a
good rousing fever, or any such active disorder, which

[1] It is scarcely necessary to say, that all that follows is imaginary.

12

With mortal crisis doth pretend
His life to appropinque an end,

to make their agonies the subject of amusing conversation.

Having deeply considered all these things, I am no longer able to disguise from my readers, that I am neither so unpopular nor so low in fortune, as not to have any share in the distresses which at present afflict the moneyed and landed interest of the realms. Your authors who live upon a mutton chop may rejoice that it has fallen to threepence per pound, and, if they have children, gratulate themselves that the peck-loaf may be had for sixpence; but we who belong to the tribe which is ruined by peace and plenty—we who have lands and beeves, and sell what these poor gleaners must buy—we are driven to despair by the very events which would make all Grub Street illuminate its attics, if Grub Street could spare candle-ends for the purpose. I therefore put in my proud claim to share in the distresses which only affect the wealthy; and write myself down, with Dogberry, "a rich fellow enough," but still "one who hath had losses."'

With the same generous spirit of emulation, I have had lately recourse to the universal remedy for the brief impecuniosity of which I complain —a brief residence in a southern climate, by which I have not only saved many cart-loads of coals, but have also had the pleasure to excite general sympathy for my decayed circumstances among those, who, if my revenue had continued to be spent among them, would have cared little if I had been hanged. Thus, while I drink my *vin ordinaire,* my brewer finds the sale of his small-beer diminished—while I discuss my flask of *cinq francs,* my modicum of port hangs on my wine-merchant's hands— while my *côtelette à la Maintenon* is smoking on my plate, the mighty sirloin hangs on its peg in the shop of my blue-aproned friend in the village. Whatever, in short, I spend here is missed at home; and the few sous gained by the *garçon perruquier,* nay, the very crust I give to his little bare-bottomed, red-eyed poodle, are *autant de perdu* to my old friend the barber, and honest Trusty, the mastiff-dog in the yard. So that I have the happiness of knowing at every turn, that my absence is both missed and moaned by those, who would care little were I in my coffin, were they sure of the custom of my executors. From this charge of self-seeking and indifference, however I solemnly except Trusty, the yard-dog, whose courtesies towards me, I have reason to think, were of a more disinterested character than those of any other person who assisted me to consume the bounty of the Public.

Alas! the advantage of exciting such general sympathies at home cannot be secured without incurring considerable personal inconvenience. "If thou wishest me to weep, thou must first shed tears thyself," says Horace; and, truly, I could sometimes cry myself at the exchange I have made of the domestic comforts which custom had rendered necessaries, for the foreign substitutes which caprice and love of change had ren-

dered fashionable. I cannot but confess with shame, that my home-bred
stomach longs for the genuine steak, after the fashion of Dolly's, hot
from the gridiron, brown without, and scarlet when the knife is applied;
and that all the delicacies of Very's *carte*, with its thousand various
orthographies of *Bifticks de Mouton*, do not supply the vacancy. Then
my mother's son cannot learn to delight in thin potations; and, in these
days when malt is had for nothing, I am convinced that a double *straick*
of John Barleycorn must have converted "the poor domestic creature,
small beer," into a liquor twenty times more generous than the acid
unsubstantial tipple, which here bears the honoured name of wine, though,
in substance and qualities, much similar to your Seine water. Their
higher wines, indeed, are well enough—there is nothing to except against
in their Château Margout, or Sillery; yet I cannot but remember the
generous qualities of my sound old Oporto. Nay, down to the *garçon* and
his poodle, though they are both amusing animals, and play ten thousand
monkey-tricks which are diverting enough, yet there was more sound
humour in the wink with which our village Packwood used to communicate the news of the morning, than all Antoine's gambols could have
expressed in a week, and more of human and doglike sympathy in the
wag of old Trusty's tail, than if his rival, Touton, had stood on his hind-
legs for a twelvemonth.

These signs of repentance come perhaps a little late, and I own (for I
must be entirely candid with my dear friend the Public) that they have
been somewhat matured by the perversion of my niece Christy to the
ancient Popish faith by a certain whacking priest in our neighbourhood,
and the marriage of my Aunt Dorothy to a *demi-solde* captain of horse, a
ci-devant member of the Legion of Honour, and who would, he assures
us, have been a Field-Marshal by this time, had our old friend Bona-
parte continued to live and to triumph. For the matter of Christy, I must
own her head had been so fairly turned at Edinburgh with five routs a
night, that, though I somewhat distrusted the means and medium of her
conversion, I was at the same time glad to see that she took a serious
thought of any kind;—besides, there was little loss in the matter, for the
Convent took her off my hands for a very reasonable pension. But Aunt
Dorothy's marriage on earth was a very different matter from Christian's
celestial espousals. In the first place, there were two thousand three-per-
cents as much lost to my family as if the sponge had been drawn over
the national slate—for who the deuce could have thought Aunt Dorothy
would have married? Above all, who would have thought a woman of
fifty years' experience would have married a French anatomy, his lower
branch of limbs corresponding with the upper branch, as if one pair of
half-extended compasses had been placed perpendicularly upon the top
of another, while the space on which the hinges revolved, quite sufficed
to represent the body? All the rest was moustache, pelisse, and calico
trouser. She might have commanded a Polk of real Cossacks in 1815,
for half the wealth which she surrendered to this military scarecrow.

However, there is no more to be said upon the matter, especially as she had come the length of quoting Rousseau for sentiment—and so let that pass.

Having thus expectorated my bile against a land, which is, notwith standing, a very merry land, and which I cannot blame, because I sought it, and it did not seek me, I come to the more immediate purpose of this Introduction, and which, my dearest Public, if I do not reckon too much on the continuance of your favours (though to say truth, consistency and uniformity of taste are scarce to be reckoned upon by those who court your good graces), may perhaps go far to make me amends for the loss and damage I have sustained by bringing Aunt Dorothy to the country of thick calves, slender ankles, black moustaches, bodiless limbs (I assure you the fellow is, as my friend Lord L—— said, a complete giblet-pie, all legs and wings), and fine sentiments. If she had taken from the half-pay list, a ranting Highlandman, ay, or a dashing son of Erin, I would never have mentioned the subject; but as the affair has happened, it is scarce possible not to resent such a gratuitous plundering of her own lawful heirs and executors. But "be hushed my dark spirit!" and let us invite our dear Public to a more pleasing theme to us, a more interesting one to others.

By dint of drinking acid tiff, as above mentioned, and smoking cigars, in which I am no novice, my Public are to be informed, that I gradually sipp'd and smoked myself into a certain degree of acquaintance with *un homme comme il faut,* one of the few fine old specimens of nobility who are still to be found in France; who, like mutilated statues of an anti-quated and obsolete worship, still command a certain portion of awe and estimation in the eyes of those by whom neither one nor other are volun tarily rendered.

On visiting the coffee-house of the village, I was, at first, struck with the singular dignity and gravity of this gentleman's manners, his sedu lous attachment to shoes and stockings, in contempt of half-boots and pantaloons, the *croix de Saint Louis* at his buttonhole, and a small white cockade in the loop of his old-fashioned *shakoo.* There was something interesting in his whole appearance; and besides, his gravity among the lively group around him, seemed like the shade of a tree in the glare of a sunny landscape, more interesting from its rarity. I made such advances towards acquaintance as the circumstances of the place, and the manners of the country, authorised—that is to say, I drew near him, smoked my cigar by calm and intermitted puffs, which were scarcely visible, and asked him those few questions which good-breeding everywhere, but more especially in France, permits strangers to put, without hazarding the imputation of impertinence. The Marquis de Hautlieu, for such was his rank, was as short and sententious as French politeness permitted —he answered every question, but proposed nothing, and encouraged no farther inquiry.

The truth was, that, not very accessible to foreigners of any nation, or even to strangers among his own countrymen, the Marquis was peculiarly shy towards the English. A remnant of ancient national prejudice might dictate this feeling; or it might arise from his idea that they are a haughty, purse-proud people, to whom rank, united with straitened circumstances, affords as much subject for scorn as for pity; or, finally, when he reflected on certain recent events, he might perhaps feel mortified as a Frenchman, even for those successes, which had restored his master to the throne, and himself to a diminished property and dilapidated château. His dislike, however, never assumed a more active form than that of alienation from English society. When the affairs of strangers required the interposition of his influence in their behalf, it was uniformly granted with the courtesy of a French gentleman, who knew what is due to himself and to national hospitality.

At length, by some chance, the Marquis made the discovery, that the new frequenter of his ordinary was a native of Scotland, a circumstance which told mightily in my favour. Some of his own ancestors, he informed me, had been of Scottish origin, and he believed his house had still some relations in what he was pleased to call the province of Hanguisse, in that country. The connection had been acknowledged early in the last century on both sides, and he had once almost determined, during his exile (for it may be supposed that the Marquis had joined the ranks of Condé, and shared all the misfortunes and distresses of emigration), to claim the acquaintance and protection of his Scottish friends. But, after all, he said, he cared not to present himself before them in circumstances which could do them but small credit, and which they might think entailed some little burden, perhaps even some little disgrace; so that he thought it best to trust in Providence, and do the best he could for his own support. What that was I never could learn; but I am sure it inferred nothing which could be discreditable to the excellent old man, who held fast his opinions and his loyalty, through good and bad repute, till time restored him, aged, indigent, and broken-spirited, to the country which he had left in the prime of youth and health, and sobered by age into patience, instead of that tone of high resentment, which promised speedy vengeance upon those who expelled him. I might have laughed at some points of the Marquis's character, at his prejudices, particularly, both of birth and politics, if I had known him under more prosperous circumstances; but, situated as he was, even if they had not been fair and honest prejudices, turning on no base or interested motive, one must have respected him as we respect the confessor or the martyr of a religion which is not entirely our own.

By degrees we became good friends, drank our coffee, smoked our cigar, and took our *bavaroise* together, for more than six weeks, with little interruption from avocations on either side. Having, with some difficulty, got the key-note of his inquiries concerning Scotland, by a fortunate conjecture that the province d'Hanguisse could only be our shire of Angus, I was enabled to answer the most of his queries concerning his allies there in a manner more or less satisfactory, and was much surprised to find the Marquis much better acquainted with the genealogy of some of the distinguished families in that country, than I could possibly have expected.

On his part, his satisfaction at our intercourse was so great, that he at length wound himself to such a pitch of resolution, as to invite me to dine at the Château de Hautlieu, well deserving the name, as occupying a commanding eminence on the banks of the Loire. This building lay about three miles from the town at which I had settled my temporary establishment; and when I first beheld it, I could easily forgive the mortified feelings which the owner testified, at receiving a guest in the asylum which he had formed out of the ruins of the palace of his fathers. He gradually, with much gaiety, which yet evidently covered a deeper feeling, prepared me for the sort of place I was about to visit; and for this he had full opportunity whilst he drove me in his little cabriolet, drawn by a large heavy Norman horse, towards the ancient building.

Its remains run along a beautiful terrace overhanging the river Loire, which had been formerly laid out with a succession of flights of steps, highly ornamented with statues, rockwork, and other artificial embellishments, descending from one terrace to another, until the very verge of the river was attained. All this architectural decoration, with its accompanying parterres of rich flowers and exotic shrubs, had, many years since, given place to the more profitable scene of the vine-dresser's labours; yet the remains, too massive to be destroyed, are still visible, and, with the various artificial slopes and levels of the high bank, bear perfect evidence how actively Art had been here employed to decorate Nature.

Few of these scenes are now left in perfection; for the fickleness of fashion has accomplished in England the total change which devastation and popular fury have produced in the French pleasure-grounds. For my part, I am contented to subscribe to the opinion of the best qualified judge of our time,[1] who thinks we have carried to an extreme our taste for simplicity, and that the neighbourhood of a stately mansion requires some more ornate embellishments than can be derived from the meagre accompaniments of grass and gravel. A highly romantic situation may be degraded, perhaps, by an attempt at such artificial ornaments; but then, in by far the greater number of sites, the intervention of more architectural decoration than is now in use, seems necessary to redeem the naked tameness of a large house, placed by itself in the midst of a lawn, where it looks as much unconnected with all around, as if it had walked out of town upon an airing.

How the taste came to change so suddenly and absolutely, is rather

[1] See Price's "Essay on the Picturesque," in many passages: but I would particularise the beautiful and highly poetical account which he gives of his own feelings on destroying, at the dictate of an improver, an ancient sequestrated garden, with its yew hedges, ornamented iron gates, and secluded wilderness.

a singular circumstance, unless we explain it on the same principle on which the three friends of the father in Molière's comedy recommend a cure for the melancholy of his Daughter—that he should furnish her apartments, viz. with paintings—with tapestry—or with china, according to the different commodities in which each of them was a dealer. Tried by this scale, we may perhaps discover, that, of old, the architect laid out the garden and the pleasure-grounds in the neighbourhood of the mansion, and, naturally enough, displayed his own art there in statues and vases, and paved terraces and flights of steps, with ornamented balustrades; while the gardener, subordinate in rank, endeavoured to make the vegetable kingdom correspond to the prevailing taste, and cut his evergreens into verdant walls, with towers and battlements, and his detached trees into a resemblance of statuary. But the wheel has since revolved, so as to place the landscape gardener, as he is called, upon almost a level with the architect; and hence a liberal and somewhat violent use is made of spade and pick-axe, and a conversion of the ostentatious labours of the architect into a *ferme ornée,* as little different from the simplicity of Nature, as displayed in the surrounding country, as the comforts of convenient and cleanly walks, imperiously demanded in the vicinage of a gentleman's residence, can possibly admit.

To return from this digression, which has given the Marquis's cabriolet (its activities greatly retarded by the downward propensities of Jean Roast-beef, which I suppose the Norman horse cursed as heartily as his countrymen of old time execrated the stolid obesity of a Saxon slave) time to ascend the hill by a winding causeway, now much broken, we came in sight of a long range of roofless buildings, connected with the western extremity of the castle, which was totally ruinous. "I should apologise," he said, "to you, as an Englishman, for the taste of my ancestors, in connecting that row of stables with the architecture of the château. I know in your country it is usual to remove them to some distance; but my family had an hereditary pride in horses, and were fond of visiting them more frequently than would have been convenient if they had been kept at a greater distance. Before the Revolution, I had thirty fine horses in that ruinous line of buildings."

This recollection of past magnificence escaped from him accidentally, for he was generally sparing in alluding to his former opulence. It was quietly said, without any affectation either of the importance attached to early wealth, or as demanding sympathy for its having passed away. It awakened unpleasing reflections, however, and we were both silent, till, from a partially repaired corner of what had been a porter's lodge, a lively French *paysanne,* with eyes as black as jet, and as brilliant as diamonds, came out with a smile, which showed a set of teeth that duchesses might have envied, and took the reins of the little carriage.

"Madelon must be groom to-day," said the Marquis, after graciously nodding in return for her deep reverence to Monsieur, "for her husband is gone to market; and for La Jeunesse, he is almost distracted with his various occupations.—Madelon," he continued, as we walked forward under the entrance-arch, crowned with the mutilated armorial bearings of former lords, now half-obscured by moss and rye-grass, not to mention the vagrant branches of some unpruned shrubs,—"Madelon was my wife's god-daughter, and was educated to be fille-de-chambre to my daughter."

This passing intimation, that he was a widowed husband and childless father, increased my respect for the unfortunate nobleman, to whom every particular attached to his present situation brought doubtless its own share of food for melancholy reflection. He proceeded, after the pause of an instant, with something of a gayer tone,—"You will be entertained with my poor La Jeunesse," he said, "who, by the way, is ten years older than I am"—(the Marquis is above sixty)—"he reminds me of the player in the *Roman Comique,* who acted a whole play in his own proper person—he insists on being maître d'hotel, maître de cuisine, valet-de-chambre, a whole suite of attendants in his own poor individuality. He sometimes reminds me of a character in the Bridle of Lammermore, which you must have read, as it is the work of one of your *gens de lettres, qu'on appelle, je crois, le Chevalier Scott."* [1]

"I presume you mean Sir Walter?"

"Yes—the same—the same," answered the Marquis.

We are now led away from more painful recollections; for I had to put my French friend right in two particulars. In the first I prevailed with difficulty; for the Marquis, though he disliked the English yet, having been three months in London, piqued himself on understanding the most intricate difficulties of our language, and appealed to every dictionary, from Florio downwards, that *la Bride* must mean the Bridle. Nay, so sceptical was he on this point of philology, that, when I ventured to hint that there was nothing about a bridle in the whole story, he with great composure, and little knowing to whom he spoke, laid the whole blame of that inconsistency on the unfortunate author. I had next the common candour to inform my friend, upon grounds which no one could know so well as myself, that my distinguished literary countryman, of whom I shall always speak with the respect his talents deserve, was not responsible for the slight works which the humour of the public had too generously, as well as too rashly, ascribed to him. Surprised by the impulse of the moment, I might even have gone farther, and clenched the negative by positive evidence, owning to my entertainer that no one else could possibly have written these works, since I myself was the author, when I was saved from so rash a commitment of myself by the calm reply of the Marquis, that he was glad to hear these sort of trifles were not written by a person of condition. "We read them," he said, "as we listen to the pleasantries of a comedian, or as our ancestors did to those of a professed family-jester, with a good deal of amusement, which,

---

[1] It is scarce necessary to remind the reader that this passage was published during the author's incognito; and, as Lucio expresses it, spoken "according to the trick."

however, we should be sorry to derive from the mouth of one who has better claims to our society."

I was completely recalled to my constitutional caution by this declaration; and became so much afraid of committing myself, that I did not even venture to explain to my aristocratic friend, that the gentleman whom he had named owed his advancement, for aught I had ever heard, to certain works of his, which may, without injury, be compared to romances in rhyme.

The truth is, that, amongst some other unjust prejudices, at which I have already hinted, the Marquis had contracted a horror, mingled with contempt, for almost every species of author-craft, slighter than that which compounds a folio volume of law or of divinity, and looked upon the author of a romance, novel, fugitive poem, or periodical piece of criticism, as men do on a venomous reptile, with fear at once and with loathing. The abuse of the press, he contended, especially in its lighter departments, had poisoned the whole morality of Europe, and was once more gradually regaining an influence which had been silenced amidst the voice of war. All writers, except those of the largest and heaviest calibre, he conceived to be devoted to this evil cause, from Rousseau and Voltaire down to Pigault le Brun and the author of the Scotch Novels; and although he admitted he read them *pour passer le temps,* yet, like Pistol eating his leek, it was not without execrating the tendency, as he devoured the story, of the work with which he was engaged.

Observing this peculiarity, I backed out of the candid confession which my vanity had meditated, and engaged the Marquis in farther remarks on the mansion of his ancestors. "There," he said, "was the theatre where my father used to procure an order for the special attendance of some of the principal actors of the Comedie Françoise, when the King and Madame Pompadour more than once visited him at this place;—yonder, more to the centre, was the Baron's hall, where his feudal jurisdiction was exercised when criminals were to be tried by the Seigneur or his bailiff; for we had, like your old Scottish nobles, the right of pit and gallows, or *fossa cum furca,* as the civilians term it; beneath that lies the question-chamber, or apartment for torture; and, truly, I am sorry a right so liable to abuse should have been lodged in the hands of any living creature. But," he added, with a feeling of dignity derived even from the atrocities which his ancestors had committed beneath the grated windows to which he pointed, "such is the effect of superstition, that, to this day, the peasants dare not approach the dungeons, in which, it is said, the wrath of my ancestors had perpetrated, in former times, much cruelty."

As we approached the window, while I expressed some curiosity to see this abode of terror, there arose from its subterranean abyss a shrill shout of laughter, which we easily detected as produced by a group of playful children, who had made the neglected vaults a theatre, for a joyous romp at Colin Maillard.

The Marquis was somewhat disconcerted, and had recourse to his *tabatière;* but, recovering in a moment, observed, these were Madelon's children, and familiar with the supposed terrors of the subterranean recesses. "Besides," he added, "to speak the truth, these poor children have been born after the period of supposed illumination, which dispelled our superstition and our religion at once; and this bids me to remind you, that this is a *jour maigre.* The Curé of the parish is my only guest, besides yourself, and I would not voluntarily offend his opinions. Besides," he continued, more manfully, and throwing off his restraint, "adversity has taught me other thoughts on these subjects than those which prosperity dictated; and I thank God I am not ashamed to avow, that I follow the observances of my Church."

I hastened to answer, that, though they might differ from those of my own I had every possible respect for the religious rules of every Christian community, sensible that we addressed the same Deity, on the same grand principle of salvation, though with different forms; which variety of worship, had it pleased the Almighty not to permit, our observances would have been as distinctly prescribed to us as they are laid down under the Mosaic law.

The Marquis was no shaker of hands, but upon the present occasion he grasped mine, and shook it kindly—the only mode of acquiescence in my sentiments which perhaps a zealous Catholic could, or ought consistently to have given upon such an occasion.

This circumstance of explanation and remark, with others which arose out of the view of the extensive ruins, occupied us during two or three turns upon the long terrace, and a seat of about a quarter of an hour's duration in a vaulted pavilion of freestone, decorated with the Marquis's armorial bearings, the roof of which, though disjointed in some of its groined arches, was still solid and entire. "Here," said he, resuming the tone of a former part of his conversation, "I love to sit, either at noon, when the alcove affords me shelter from the heat, or in the evening, when the sun's beams are dying on the broad face of the Loire—here, in the words of your great poet, whom, Frenchman as I am, I am more intimately acquainted with than most Englishmen, I love to rest myself,

'Showing the code of sweet and bitter fancy.' "

Against this various reading of a well-known passage in Shakespeare I took care to offer no protest; for I suspect Shakespeare would have suffered in the opinion of so delicate a judge as the Marquis, had I proved his having written "chewing the cud," according to all other authorities. Besides, I had had enough of our former dispute, having been long convinced (though not till ten years after I had left Edinburgh College), that the pith of conversation does not consist in exhibiting your own superior knowledge on matters of small consequence, but in enlarging, improving, and correcting the information you possess, by the authority of others. I therefore let the Marquis *show* his *code* at his pleasure, and was rewarded by his entering into a learned and well-informed disquisition on the florid style of architecture introduced into France during the seventeenth century. He pointed out its merits and its defects with considerable taste; and having touched on topics similar to those upon which I have formerly digressed, he made an appeal of a different kind in their favour, founded on the associations with which they were combined. "Who," he said, "would willingly destroy the terraces of the château of Sully, since we cannot tread them without recalling the image of that statesman, alike distinguished for severe integrity and for strong and unerring sagacity of mind? Were they an inch less broad, a ton's weight less massive, or were they deprived of their formality by the slightest inflections, could we suppose them to remain the scene of his patriotic musings? Would an ordinary root-house be a fit scene for the Duke occupying an arm-chair, and his Duchess a *tabouret*—teaching from thence lessons of courage and fidelity to his sons,—of modesty and submission to his daughters,—of rigid morality to both; while the circle of young noblesse listened with ears attentive, and eyes modestly fixed on the ground, in a standing posture, neither replying nor sitting down, without the express command of their prince and parent?—No, Monsieur," he said with enthusiasm; "destroy the princely pavilion in which this edifying family-scene was represented, and you remove from the mind the vraisemblance, the veracity, of the whole representation. Or can your mind suppose this distinguished peer and patriot walking in a *jardin Anglois?* Why, you might as well fancy him dressed with a blue frock and white waistcoat, instead of his Henri Quatre coat and *chapeau-à-plumes*—Consider how he could have moved in the tortuous maze of what you have called a *ferme ornée* with his usual attendants of two files of Swiss guards preceding, and the same number following him. To recall his figure, with his beard—*haut-de-chausses à canon,* united to his doublet by ten thousand *aiguilettes* and knots of ribbon, you could not, supposing him in a modern *jardin Anglois,* distinguish the picture in your imagination, from the sketch of some mad old man, who has adopted the humour of dressing like his great-great-grandfather, and whom a party of gens-d'armes were conducting to the *Hôpital des Fous.* But look on the long and magnificent terrace, if it yet exists, which the loyal and exalted Sully was wont to make the scene of his solitary walk twice a day, while he pondered over the patriotic schemes which he nourished for advancing the glory of France; or, at a later, and more sorrowful period of life, brooded over the memory of his murdered master, and the fate of his distracted country;—throw in that noble background of arcades, vases, images, urns, and whatever could express the vicinity of a ducal palace, and the landscape becomes consistent at once. The *factionnaires,* with their harquebuses ported, placed at the extremities of the long and level walk, intimate the presence of the feudal prince; while the same is more clearly shown by the guard of honour which precede and follow him, their halberds carried upright, their mien martial and stately, as if in the presence of an enemy, yet moved, as it were, with the same soul as their princely superior—teaching their steps to attend upon his, marching as he marches, halting as he halts, accommodating their pace even to the slight irregularities of pause and advance dictated by the fluctuations of his reverie, and wheeling with military precision before and behind him, who seems the centre and animated principle of their armed files, as the heart gives life and energy to the human body. Or, if you smile," added the Marquis, looking doubtfully on my countenance, "at a promenade so inconsistent with the light freedom of modern manners, could you bring your mind to demolish that other terrace trod by the fascinating Marchioness de Sevigne, with which are united so many recollections connected with passages in her enchanting letters?"

A little tired of this disquisition, which the Marquis certainly dwelt upon to exalt the natural beauties of his own terrace, which, dilapidated as it was, required no such formal recommendation, I informed my companion, that I had just received from England a journal of a tour made in the south of France by a young Oxonian friend of mine, a poet, a draughtsman, and a scholar,—in which he gives such an animated and interesting description of the Château Grignan, the dwelling of Madame de Sevigné's beloved daughter, and frequently the place of her own residence, that no one who ever read the book would be within forty miles of the same, without going a pilgrimage to the spot. The Marquis smiled, seemed very much pleased, and asked the title at length of the work in question; and writing down to my dictation, "An Itinerary of Provence and the Rhone, made during the year 1819; by John Hughes, A.M., of Oriel College, Oxford."—observed, he could now purchase no books for the château, but would recommend that the Itineraire should be commissioned for the library to which he was *abonné* in the neighbouring town. "And here," he said, "comes the Curé, to save us farther disquisition; and I see La Jeunesse gliding round the old portico on the terrace, with the purpose of ringing the dinner-bell—a most unnecessary ceremony for assembling three persons, but which it would break the old man's heart to forego. Take no notice of him at present, as he wishes to perform the duties of the inferior departments incognito; when the bell has ceased to sound, he will blaze forth on us in the character of major-domo."

As the Marquis spoke, we had advanced towards the eastern extremity of the château, which was the only part of the edifice that remained still habitable.

"The *Bande Noire*," said the Marquis, "when they pulled the rest of the house to pieces, for the sake of the lead, timber, and other materials, have, in their ravages, done me the undesigned favour to reduce it to dimensions better fitting the circumstances of the owner. There is enough of the leaf left for the caterpillar to coil up his chrysalis in, and what needs he care though reptiles have devoured the rest of the bush?"

As he spoke thus, we reached the door, at which La Jeunesse appeared, with an air at once of prompt service and deep respect, and a countenance, which, though puckered by a thousand wrinkles, was ready to answer the first good-natured word of his master with a smile, which showed his white set of teeth firm and fair, in despite of age and suffering. His clean silk stockings, washed till their tint had become yellowish—his cue tied with a rosette—the thin grey curl on either side of his lank cheek—the pearl-coloured coat, without a collar—the solitaire, the *jabot*, the ruffles at the wrist, and the *chapeau-bras*—all announced that La Jeunesse considered the arrival of a guest at the château as an unusual event, which was to be met with a corresponding display of magnificence and parade on his part.

As I looked at the faithful though fantastic follower of his master, who doubtless inherited his prejudices as well as his cast-clothes, I could not but own, in my own mind, the resemblance pointed out by the Marquis betwixt him and my own Caleb, the trusty squire of the Master of Ravenswood. But a Frenchman, a Jack-of-all-trades by nature, can, with much more ease and suppleness, address himself to a variety of services, and suffice in his own person to discharge them all, than is possible for the formality and slowness of a Scottishman. Superior to Caleb in dexterity, though not in zeal, La Jeunesse seemed to multiply himself with the necessities of the occasion, and discharged his several tasks with such promptitude and assiduity that farther attendance than his was neither missed nor wished for.

The dinner, in particular, was exquisite. The soup, although bearing the term of *maigre*, which Englishmen use in scorn, was most delicately flavoured, and the matelot of pike and eels reconciled me, though a Scottishman, to the latter. There was even a *petit plat* of *bouilli* for the heretic, so exquisitely dressed as to retain all the juices, and at the same time, rendered so thoroughly tender, that nothing could be more delicate. The *potage*, with another small dish or two, were equally well arranged. But what the old maître d'hotel valued himself upon as something superb, smiling with self-satisfaction, and in enjoyment of my surprise, as he placed it on the table, was an immense *assiétte* of spinage, not smoothed into a uniform surface, as by our uninaugurated cooks upon your side of the water, but swelling into hills, and declining into vales, over which swept a gallant stag, pursued by a pack of hounds in full cry, and a noble field of horsemen with bugle-horns, and whips held upright, and brandished after the manner of broadswords—hounds, huntsmen, and stag, being all very artificially cut out of toasted bread. Enjoying the praises which I failed not to bestow on this *chef-d'œuvre*, the old man acknowledged it had cost the best part of two days to bring it to perfection; and added, giving honour where honour was due, that an idea so brilliant was not entirely his own, but that Monsieur himself had taken the trouble to give him several valuable hints, and even condescended to assist in the execution of some of the most capital figures.

The Marquis blushed a little at this *éclaircissement,* which he might probably have wished to suppress, but acknowledged he had wished to surprise me with a scene from a popular poem of my country, Miladi Lac. I answered, that so splendid a cortège much more resembled a grand *chasse* of Louis Quatorze than of a poor King of Scotland, and that the *paysage* was rather like Fontainebleau than the wilds of Callender. He bowed graciously in answer to this compliment, and acknowledged that recollections of the costume of the old French Court, when in its splendour, might have misled his imagination—and so the conversation passed on to other matters.

Our dessert was exquisite—the cheese, the fruits, the salad, the olives, the *cerneaux,* and the delicious white wine, each in their way were *impayables;* and the good Marquis, with an air of great satisfaction, observed, that his guest did sincere homage to their merits. "After all," he said, "and yet it is but confessing a foolish weakness—but, after all, I cannot but rejoice in feeling myself equal to offering a stranger a sort of hospitality which seems pleasing to him. Believe me, it is not entirely out of pride that we *pauvres revenants* live so very retired, and avoid the duties of hospitality. It is true, that too many of us wander about the halls of our fathers, rather like ghosts of their deceased proprietors, than like living men restored to their own possessions—yet it is rather on your account, than to spare our own feelings, that we do not cultivate the society of our foreign visitors. We have an idea that your opulent nation is particularly attached to *faste* and to *grande chère*—to your ease and enjoyment of every kind; and the means of entertainment left to us are, in most cases, so limited, that we feel ourselves totally precluded from such expense and ostentation. No one wishes to offer his best where he has reason to think it will not give pleasure; and, as many of you publish your journals, Monsieur le Marquis would not probably be much gratified, by seeing the poor dinner which he was able to present to Milord Anglois put upon permanent record."

I interrupted the Marquis, that, were I to wish an account of my entertainment published, it would be only in order to preserve the memory of the very best dinner I ever had eaten in my life. He bowed in return, and presumed "that I either differed much from the national taste, or the accounts of it were greatly exaggerated. He was particularly obliged to me for showing the value of the possessions which remained to him. The useful," he said, "had no doubt survived the sumptuous at Hautlieu as elsewhere. Grottoes, statues, curious conservatories of exotics, temple and tower, had gone to the ground; but the vineyard, the *potager,* the orchard, the *étang,* still existed;" and once more he expressed himself "happy to find, that their combined productions could make what even a Briton accepted as a tolerable meal. I only hope," he continued, "that you will convince me your compliments are sincere, by accepting the hospitality of the Château de Hautlieu as often as better engagements will permit during your stay in this neighbourhood."

I readily promised to accept an invitation offered with such grace, as to make the guest appear the person conferring the obligation.

The conversation then changed to the history of the château and its vicinity—a subject which was strong ground to the Marquis, though he was no great antiquary, and even no very profound historian, when other topics were discussed. The Curé, however, chanced to be both, and withal a very conversable pleasing man, with an air of *prévenance*, and ready civility of communication, which I have found a leading characteristic of the Catholic clergy, whether they are well-informed or otherwise. It was from him that I learned there still existed the remnant of a fine library in the Château de Hautlieu. The Marquis shrugged his shoulders as the Curé gave me this intimation, looked to the one side and the other, and displayed the same sort of petty embarrassment which he had been unable to suppress when La Jeunesse blabbed something of his interference with the arrangements of the *cuisine*. "I should be happy to show the books," he said, "but they are in such a wild condition, so dismantled, that I am ashamed to exhibit them to any one."

"Forgive me, my dear sir," said the Curé, "you know you permitted the great English bibliomaniac, Dr. Dibdin, to consult your curious reliques, and you know how highly he spoke of them."

"What could I do, my dear friend?" said the Marquis; "the good Doctor had heard some exaggerated account of these remnants of what was once a library—he had stationed himself in the *auberge* below, determined to carry his point or die under the walls. I even heard of his taking the altitude of the turret, in order to provide scaling-ladders. You would not have had me reduce a respectable divine, though of another Church, to such an act of desperation? I could not have answered it in conscience."

"But you know, besides, Monsieur le Marquis," continued the Curé, "that Dr. Dibdin was so much grieved at the dilapidation your library had sustained, that he avowedly envied the powers of our Church, so much did he long to launch an anathema at the heads of the perpetrators."

"His resentment was in proportion to his disappointment, I suppose," said our entertainer.

"Not so," said the Curé; "for he was so enthusiastic on the value of what remains, that I am convinced nothing but your positive request to the contrary prevented the Château of Hautlieu occupying at least twenty pages in that splendid work of which he sent us a copy, and which will remain a lasting monument of his zeal and erudition."

"Dr. Dibdin is extremely polite," said the Marquis; "and, when we have had our coffee—here it comes—we will go to the turret; and I hope, as Monsieur has not despised my poor fare, so he will pardon the state of my confused library, while I shall be equally happy if it can afford anything which can give him amusement. Indeed," he added, "were it otherwise, you, my good father, have every right over books, which, without your intervention, would never have returned to the owner."

Although this additional act of courtesy was evidently wrested by the importunity of the Curé from his reluctant friend, whose desire to conceal the nakedness of the land, and the extent of his losses, seemed always to struggle with his disposition to be obliging, I could not help accepting an offer, which, in strict politeness, I ought perhaps to have refused. But then the remains of a collection of such curiosity as had given to our bibliomaniacal friend the desire of leading the forlorn hope in an escalade—it would have been a desperate act of self-denial to have declined an opportunity of seeing it. La Jeunesse brought coffee, such as we only taste on the Continent, upon a salver, covered with a napkin, that it might be *censé* for silver; and *chasse-caffé* from Martinique on a small waiter, which was certainly so. Our repast thus finished, the Marquis led me up an *escalier derobé*, into a very large and well-proportioned saloon, of nearly one hundred feet in length; but so waste and dilapidated, that I kept my eyes on the ground, lest my kind entertainer feel himself called upon to apologise for tattered pictures and torn tapestry; and, worse than both, for casements that had yielded, in one or two instances, to the boisterous blast.

"We have contrived to make the turret something more habitable," said the Marquis, as he moved hastily through this chamber of desolation. "This," he said, "was the picture gallery in former times, and in the boudoir beyond, which we now occupy as a book-closet, were preserved some curious cabinet paintings, whose small size required that they should be viewed closely."

As he spoke, he held aside a portion of the tapestry I have mentioned, and we entered the room of which he spoke.

It was octangular, corresponding to the external shape of the turret whose interior it occupied. Four of the sides had latticed windows, commanding each, from a different point, the most beautiful prospect over the majestic Loire, and the adjacent country through which it winded; and the casements were filled with stained glass, through two of which streamed the lustre of the setting sun, showing a brilliant assemblage of religious emblems and armorial bearings, which it was scarcely possible to look at with an undazzled eye, but the other two windows, from which the sunbeams had passed away, could be closely examined, and plainly showed that the lattices were glazed with stained glass, which did not belong to them originally, but, as I afterwards learned, to the profaned and desecrated chapel of the Castle. It had been the amusement of the Marquis, for several months, to accomplish this *rifacciamento,* with the assistance of the curate and the all-capable La Jeunesse; and though they had only patched together fragments, which were in many places very minute, yet the stained glass, till examined very closely, and with the eye of an antiquary, produced, on the whole, a very pleasing effect.

The sides of the apartment, not occupied by the lattices, were (except the space for the small door) fitted up with presses and shelves, some of walnut-tree, curiously carved, and brought to a dark colour by time, nearly resembling that of a ripe chestnut, and partly of common deal, employed to repair and supply the deficiencies occasioned by violence and devastation. On these shelves were deposited the wrecks, or rather the precious relics, of a most splendid library.

The Marquis's father had been a man of information, and his grandfather was famous, even in the Court of Louis XIV., where literature was in some degree considered as the fashion, for the extent of his acquirements. Those two proprietors, opulent in their fortunes, and liberal in the indulgence of their taste, had made such additions to a curious old Gothic library, which had descended from their ancestors, that there were few collections in France which could be compared to that of Hautlieu. It had been completely dispersed, in consequence of an ill-judged attempt of the present Marquis, in 1790, to defend his château against a revolutionary mob. Luckily, the Curé, who, by his charitable and moderate conduct, and his evangelical virtues, possessed much interest among the neighbouring peasantry, prevailed on many of them to buy, for the petty sum of a few sous, and sometimes at the vulgar rate of a glass of brandy, volumes which had cost large sums, but which were carried off in mere spite by the ruffians who pillaged the castle. He himself also had purchased as many of the books as his funds could possibly reach, and to his care it was owing that they were restored to the turret in which I found them. It was no wonder, therefore, that the good Curé had some pride and pleasure in showing the collection to strangers.

In spite of odd volumes, imperfections, and all the other mortifications which an amateur encounters in looking through an ill-kept library, there were many articles in that of Hautlieu, calculated, as Bayes says, "to elevate and surprise" the bibliomaniac. There were—

The small rare volume, dark with tarnish'd gold,

as Dr. Ferrier feelingly sings—curious and richly painted missals, manuscripts of 1380, 1320, and even earlier, and works in Gothic type, printed in the fifteenth and sixteenth centuries. But of these I intend to give a more detailed account, should the Marquis grant his permission.

In the meantime, it is sufficient to say, that, delighted with the day I had spent at Hautlieu, I frequently repeated my visit, and that the key of the octangular tower was always at my command. In those hours I became deeply enamoured of a part of French history, which, although most important to that of Europe at large, and illustrated by an inimitable old historian, I had never sufficiently studied. At the same time, to gratify the feelings of my excellent host, I occupied myself occasionally with some family memorials, which had fortunately been preserved, and which contained some curious particulars respecting the connection with Scotland, which first found me favour in the eyes of the Marquis de Hautlieu.

I pondered on these things, *more meo,* until my return to Britain, to beef and sea-coal fires, a change of residence which took place since I drew up these Gallic reminiscences. At length, the result of my meditations took the form of which my readers, if not startled by this preface, will presently be enabled to judge. Should the Public receive it with favour, I shall not regret having been for a short time an Absentee.

QUENTIN DURWARD

CHAPTER I

THE CONTRAST

Look here upon this picture and on this,
The counterfeit presentment of two brothers.
Hamlet.

THE latter part of the fifteenth century prepared a train of future events, that ended by raising France to that state of formidable power, which has ever since been, from time to time, the principal object of jealousy to the other European nations. Before that period she had to struggle for her very existence with the English, already possessed of her fairest provinces; while the utmost exertions of her King, and the gallantry of her people, could scarcely protect the remainder from a foreign yoke. Nor was this her sole danger. The princes who possessed the grand fiefs of the crown, and, in particular, the Dukes of Burgundy and Bretagne, had come to wear their feudal bonds so lightly, that they had no scruple in lifting the standard against their liege and sovereign lord, the King of France, on the slightest pretence. When at peace, they reigned as absolute princes in their own provinces; and the House of Burgundy, possessed of the district so called, together with the fairest and richest part of Flanders, was itself so wealthy, and so powerful, as to yield nothing to the crown, either in splendour or in strength.

In imitation of the grand feudatories, each inferior vassal of the crown assumed as much independence as his distance from the sovereign power, the extent of his fief, or the strength of his château, enabled him to maintain; and these petty tyrants, no longer amenable to the exercise of the law, perpetrated with impunity the wildest excesses of fantastic oppression and cruelty. In Auvergne alone, a report was made of more than three hundred of these independent nobles, to whom incest, murder, and rapine, were the most ordinary and familiar actions.

Besides these evils, another, springing out of the long-continued wars betwixt the French and English, added no small misery to this distracted kingdom. Numerous bodies of soldiers, collected into bands, under officers chosen by themselves, from among the bravest and most successful adventurers, had been formed in various parts of France out of the refuse of all other countries. These hireling combatants sold their swords for a time to the best bidder; and, when such service was not to be had, they made war on their own account, seizing castles and towers, which they used as the places of their retreat,—making prisoners and ransoming them,—exacting tribute from the open villages, and the country around them,—and acquiring, by every species of rapine, the appropriate epithets of *Tondeurs* and *Ecorcheurs*, that is, *Clippers* and *Flayers*.

In the midst of the horrors and miseries arising from so distracted a state of public affairs, reckless and profuse expense distinguished the courts of the lesser nobles, as well as of the superior princes; and their dependants, in imitation, expended in rude but magnificent display, the wealth which they extorted from the people. A tone of romantic and chivalrous gallantry (which, however, was often disgraced by unbounded licence) characterised the intercourse between the sexes; and the language of knight-errantry was yet used, and its observances followed, though the pure spirit of honourable love, and benevolent enterprise which it inculcates, had ceased to qualify and atone for its extravagances. The jousts and tournaments, the entertainments and revels, which each petty court displayed, invited to France every wandering adventurer; and it was seldom that, when arrived there, he failed to employ his rash courage, and headlong spirit of enterprise, in actions for which his happier native country afforded no free stage.

At this period, and as if to save their fair realm from the various woes with which it was menaced, the tottering throne was ascended by Louis XI., whose character, evil as it was in itself, met, combated, and in a great degree neutralised, the mischiefs of the time—as poisons of opposing qualities are said, in ancient books of medicine, to have the power of counteracting each other.

Brave enough for every useful and political purpose, Louis had not a spark of that romantic valour, or of the pride generally associated with it, which fought on for the point of honour, when the point of utility had been long gained. Calm, crafty, and profoundly attentive to his own interest, he made every sacrifice, both of pride and passion, which could interfere with it. He was careful in disguising his real sentiments and purposes from all who approached him, and frequently used the expressions "that the king knew not how to reign, who knew not how to dissemble; and that, for himself, if he thought his very cap knew his secrets, he would throw it into the fire." No man of his own, or of any other time, better understood how to avail himself of the frailties of others, and when to avoid giving any advantage by the untimely indulgence of his own.

He was by nature vindictive and cruel, even to the extent of finding pleasure in the frequent executions which he commanded. But, as no touch of mercy ever induced him to spare, when he could with safety condemn, so no sentiment of vengeance ever stimulated him to a premature violence. He seldom sprung on his prey till it was fairly within his grasp, and till all hope of rescue was vain; and his movements were so studiously disguised, that his success was generally what first announced to the world the object he had been manœuvring to attain.

In like manner, the avarice of Louis gave way to apparent profusion, when it was necessary to bribe the favourite or minister of a rival prince for averting any impending attack, or to break up any alliance confederated against him. He was fond of licence and pleasure; but neither beauty nor the chase, though both were ruling passions, ever withdrew him from the most regular attendance to public business and the affairs of his kingdom. His knowledge of mankind was profound, and he had sought it in the private walks of life, in which he often personally mingled; and, though naturally proud and haughty, he hesitated not, with an inattention to the arbitrary divisions of society which was then thought something portentously unnatural, to raise from the lowest rank men whom he employed on the most important duties, and knew so well how to choose them, that he was rarely disappointed in their qualities.

Yet there were contradictions in the character of this artful and able monarch; for human nature is rarely uniform. Himself the most false and insincere of mankind, some of the greatest errors of his life arose from too rash a confidence in the honour and integrity of others. When these errors took place, they seem to have arisen from an over-refined system of policy, which induced Louis to assume the appearance of un-doubting confidence in those whom it was his object to overreach; for, in his general conduct, he was as jealous and suspicious as any tyrant who ever breathed.

Two other points may be noticed, to complete the sketch of this formidable character, by which he rose among the rude chivalrous sovereigns of the period to the rank of a keeper among wild beasts, who, by superior wisdom and policy, by distribution of food, and some discipline by blows, comes finally to predominate over those, who, if unsubjected by his arts, would by main strength have torn him to pieces.

The first of these attributes was Louis's excessive superstition, a plague with which Heaven often afflicts those who refuse to listen to the dictates of religion. The remorse arising from his evil actions, Louis never endeavoured to appease by any relaxation in his Machiavellian stratagems, but laboured, in vain, to soothe and silence that painful feeling by superstitious observances, severe penance, and profuse gifts to the ecclesiastics. The second property, with which the first is sometimes found strangely united, was a disposition to low pleasures and obscure debauchery. The wisest, or at least the most crafty sovereign of his time, he was fond of low life, and, being himself a man of wit, enjoyed the jests and repartees of social conversation more than could have been expected from other points of his character. He even mingled in the comic adventures of obscure intrigue, with a freedom little consistent with the habitual and guarded jealousy of his character; and he was so fond of this species of humble gallantry, that he caused a number of its gay and licentious anecdotes to be enrolled in a collection well known to book-collectors, in whose eyes (and the work is unfit for any other) the *right* edition is very precious.[1]

By means of this monarch's powerful and prudent, though most un-amiable character, it pleased Heaven, who works by the tempest as well as by the soft small rain, to restore to the great French nation the benefits of civil government, which, at the time of his accession, they had nearly lost.

Ere he succeeded to the crown, Louis had given evidence of his vices rather than of his talents. His first wife, Margaret of Scotland, "was done to death by slanderous tongues" in her husband's Court, where, but for the encouragement of Louis himself, not a word would have been breathed against that amiable and injured princess. He had been an ungrateful and a rebellious son, at one time conspiring to seize his father's person, and at another, levying open war again him. For the first offence, he was banished to his appanage of Dauphiné, which he governed with much sagacity—for the second, he was driven into abso-lute exile, and forced to throw himself on the mercy, and almost on the charity, of the Duke of Burgundy and his son, where he enjoyed hospi-tality, afterwards indifferently requited, until the death of his father in 1461.

In the very outset of his reign, Louis was almost overpowered by a league formed against him by the great vassals of France, with the Duke of Burgundy, or rather his son, the Count de Charalois, at its head. They levied a powerful army, blockaded Paris, fought a battle of doubt-ful issue under its very walls, and placed the French monarchy on the brink of actual destruction. It usually happens in such cases, that the more sagacious general of the two gains the real fruit, though perhaps not the martial fame, of the disputed field. Louis, who had shown great personal bravery during the battle of Montl'héry, was able, by his prudence, to avail himself of its undecided character, as if it had been a victory on his side. He temporised until the enemy had broken up their leaguer, and showed so much dexterity in sowing jealousies among those great powers, that their alliance "for the public weal," as they termed it, but, in reality, for the overthrow of all but the external appearance of the French monarchy, dissolved itself, and was never again renewed in a manner so formidable. From this period, Louis, relieved of all danger from England, by the Civil Wars of York and Lancaster, was engaged for several years, like an unfeeling but able physician, in curing the wounds of the body politic, or rather in stopping, now by gentle remedies, now by the use of fire and steel, the progress of those mortal gangrenes with which it was then infected. The *brigandage* of the Free

---

[1]This *editio princeps,* which, when in good preservation, is much sought after by connoisseurs, is entitled, *Les Cent Nouvelles Nouvelles, contenant Cent Histoires Nouveaux, qui sont moult plaisans à raconter en toutes bonnes compagnies par manière de joyeuxeté. Paris, Antoine Verard. Sans date d'année d'impression; in-folio gotique.* See DE BURE.

Companies, and the unpunished oppressions of the nobility, he laboured to lessen, since he could not actually stop them; and, by dint of unrelaxed attention, he gradually gained some addition to his own regal authority, or effected some diminution of those by whom it was counterbalanced.

Still the King of France was surrounded by doubt and danger. The members of the league "for the public weal," though not in unison, were in existence, and, like a scotched snake, might reunite and become dangerous again. But a worse danger was the increasing power of the Duke of Burgundy, then one of the greatest Princes of Europe, and little diminished in rank by the very slight dependence of his duchy upon the crown of France.

Charles, surnamed the Bold, or rather the Audacious, for his courage was allied to rashness and frenzy, then wore the ducal coronet of Burgundy, which he burned to convert into a royal and independent regal crown. The character of this Duke was in every respect the direct contrast to that of Louis XI.

The latter was calm, deliberate, and crafty, never prosecuting a desperate enterprise, and never abandoning one likely to be successful, however distant the prospect. The genius of the Duke was entirely different. He rushed on danger because he loved it, and on difficulties because he despised them. As Louis never sacrificed his interest to his passion, so Charles, on the other hand, never sacrificed his passion, or even his humour, to any other consideration. Notwithstanding the near relationship that existed between them, and the support which the Duke and his father had afforded to Louis in his exile when Dauphin, there was mutual contempt and hatred betwixt them. The Duke of Burgundy despised the cautious policy of the King, and imputed to the faintness of his courage, that he sought by leagues, purchases, and other indirect means, those advantages, which, in his place, the Duke would have snatched with an armed hand. He likewise hated the King, not only for the ingratitude he had manifested for former kindnesses, and for personal injuries and imputations which the ambassadors of Louis had cast upon him, when his father was yet alive, but also, and especially, because of the support which he afforded in secret to the discontented citizens of Ghent, Liege, and other great towns in Flanders. These turbulent cities, jealous of their privileges, and proud of their wealth, were frequently in a state of insurrection against their liege lords the Dukes of Burgundy, and never failed to find underhand countenance at the Court of Louis, who embraced every opportunity of fomenting disturbance within the dominions of his overgrown vassal.

The contempt and hatred of the Duke were retaliated by Louis with equal energy, though he used a thicker veil to conceal his sentiments. It was impossible for a man of his profound sagacity not to despise the stubborn obstinacy which never resigned its purpose, however fatal perseverance might prove, and the headlong impetuosity, which commenced its career without allowing a moment's consideration for the obstacles to be encountered. Yet the King hated Charles even more than he contemned him, and his scorn and hatred were the more intense, that they were mingled with fear; for he knew that the onset of the mad bull, to whom he likened the Duke of Burgundy, must ever be formidable, though the animal makes it with shut eyes. It was not alone the wealth of the Burgundian provinces, the discipline of the warlike inhabitants, and the mass of their crowded population, which the King dreaded, for the personal qualities of their leader had also much in them that was dangerous. The very soul of bravery, which he pushed to the verge of rashness, and beyond it—profuse in expenditure—splendid in his court, his person, and his retinue, in all which he displayed the hereditary magnificence of the house of Burgundy, Charles the Bold drew into his service almost all the fiery spirits o' the age whose tempers were congenial; and Louis saw too clearly what might be attempted and executed by such a train of resolute adventurers, following a leader of a character as ungovernable as their own.

There was yet another circumstance which increased the animosity of Louis towards his overgrown vassal; he owed him favours which he never meant to repay, and was under the frequent necessity of temporising with him, and even of enduring bursts of petulant insolence, injurious to the regal dignity, without being able to treat him otherwise than as his "fair cousin of Burgundy."

It was about the year 1468, when their feuds were at the highest, though a dubious and hollow truce, as frequently happened, existed for the time betwixt them, that the present narrative opens. The person first introduced on the stage will be found indeed to be of a rank and condition, the illustration of whose character scarcely called for a dissertation on the relative position of two great princes; but the passions of the great, their quarrels, and their reconciliations, involve the fortunes of all who approach them; and it will be found, on proceeding farther in our story, that this preliminary chapter is necessary for comprehending the history of the individual whose adventures we are about to relate.

CHAPTER II

THE WANDERER

Why then the world is my oyster, which I with sword will open.
Ancient Pistol.

IT was upon a delicious summer morning, before the sun had assumed its scorching power, and while the dews yet cooled and perfumed the air, that a youth, coming from the northeastward, approached the ford of a small river, or rather a large brook, tributary to the Cher, near to the royal Castle of Plessis-les-Tours, whose dark and multiplied battlements rose in the background over the extensive forest with which they were surrounded. These woodlands comprised a noble chase, or royal park, fenced by an enclosure, termed, in the Latin of the middle ages, *Plexitium*, which gives the name of Plessis to so many villages in France. The castle and village of which we particularly speak, was called Plessis-les-Tours, to distinguish it from others, and was built about two miles to the southward of the fair town of that name, the capital of ancient Touraine, whose rich plain has been termed the Garden of France.

On the bank of the above-mentioned brook, opposite to that which the traveller was approaching, two men, who appeared in deep conversation, seemed, from time to time, to watch his motions; for, as their station was much more elevated, they could remark him at considerable distance.

The age of the young traveller might be about nineteen, or betwixt that and twenty, and his face and person, which were very prepossessing, did not, however, belong to the country in which he was now a sojourner. His short grey cloak and hose were rather of Flemish than of French fashion, while the smart blue bonnet, with a single sprig of holly and an eagle's feather, was already recognised as the Scottish headgear. His dress was very neat, and arranged with the precision of a youth conscious of possessing a fine person. He had at his back a satchel, which seemed to contain a few necessaries, a hawking gauntlet on his left hand, though he carried no bird, and in his right a stout hunter's pole. Over his left shoulder hung an embroidered scarf which sustained a small pouch of scarlet velvet, such as was then used by fowlers of distinction to carry their hawks' food, and other matters belonging to that much-admired sport. This was crossed by another shoulder-belt, to which was hung a hunting knife, or *couteau de chasse*. Instead of the boots of the period, he wore buskins of half-dressed deer's-skin.

Although his form had not yet attained its full strength, he was tall and active, and the lightness of the step with which he advanced, showed that his pedestrian mode of travelling was pleasure rather than pain to him. His complexion was fair, in spite of a general shade of darker hue, with which the foreign sun, or perhaps constant exposure to the atmosphere in his own country, had, in some degree, embrowned it.

His features, without being quite regular, were frank, open, and pleasing. A half smile, which seemed to arise from a happy exuberance of animal spirits, showed, now and then, that his teeth were well set, and as pure as ivory; whilst his bright blue eye, with a corresponding gaiety, had an appropriate glance for every object which it encountered, expressing good humour, lightness of heart, and determined resolution.

He received and returned the salutation of the few travellers who frequented the road in those dangerous times, with the action which suited each. The strolling spearman, half soldier, half brigand, measured the youth with his eye, as if balancing the prospect of booty with the chance of desperate resistance; and read such indications of the latter in the fearless glance of the passenger, that he changed his ruffian purpose for a surly "Good-morrow, comrade," which the young Scot answered with as martial, though a less sullen tone. The wandering pilgrim, or the begging friar, answered his reverend greeting with a paternal benedi-cite; and the dark-eyed peasant girl looked after him for many a step after they had passed each other, and interchanged a laughing good-morrow. In short, there was an attraction about his whole appearance not easily escaping attention, and which was derived from the combination of fearless frankness and good-humour, with sprightly looks, and a handsome face and person. It seemed, too, as if his whole demeanour bespoke one who was entering on life with no apprehension of the evils with which it is beset, and small means for struggling with its hardships, except a lively spirit and a courageous disposition; and it is with such tempers that youth most readily sympathises, and for whom chiefly age and experience feel affectionate and pitying interest.

The youth whom we have described, had been long visible to the two persons who loitered on the opposite side of the small river which divided him from the park and the castle; but as he descended the rugged bank to the water's edge, with the light step of a roe which visits the fountain, the younger of the two said to the other, "It is our man—it is the Bohemian! If he attempts to cross the ford, he is a lost man—the water is up, and the ford impassable."

"Let him make that discovery himself, gossip," said the elder personage; "it may, perchance, save a rope, and break a proverb."

"I judge him by the blue cap," said the other, "for I cannot see his face.—Hark, sir—he halloes to know whether the water be deep."

"Nothing like experience in this world," answered the other—"let him try."

The young man, in the meanwhile, receiving no hint to the contrary, and taking the silence of those to whom he applied as an encouragement to proceed, entered the stream without farther hesitation than the delay necessary to take off his buskins. The elder person, at the same moment, hallooed to him to beware, adding, in a lower tone, to his companion, "*Mortdieu*—gossip—you have made another mistake—this is not the Bohemian chatterer."

But the intimation to the youth came too late. He either did not hear or could not profit by it, being already in the deep stream. To one less alert and practised in the exercise of swimming, death had been certain, for the brook was both deep and strong.

"By Saint Anne! but he is a proper youth," said the elder man—"Run, gossip, and help your blunder, by giving him aid, if thou canst. He belongs to thine own troop—if old saws speak truth, water will not drown him."

Indeed, the young traveller swam so strongly, and buffeted the waves so well, that, notwithstanding the strength of the current, he was carried but a little way down from the ordinary landing-place.

By this time the younger of the two strangers was hurrying down to the shore to render assistance, while the other followed him at a graver pace, saying to himself as he approached, "I knew water would never drown that young fellow.—By my halidome, he is ashore, and grasps his pole!—If I make not the more haste, he will beat my gossip for the only charitable action which I ever saw him perform, or attempt to perform, in the whole course of his life."

There was some reason to augur such a conclusion of the adventure, for the bonny Scot had already accosted the younger Samaritan, who was hastening to his assistance, with these ireful words—"Discourteous dog! why did you not answer when I called to know if the passage was fit to be attempted? May the foul fiend catch me, but I will teach you the respect due to strangers on the next occasion!"

This was accompanied with that significant flourish with his pole, which is called *le moulinet*, because the artist, holding it in the middle, brandishes the two ends in every direction, like the sails of a windmill in motion. His opponent, seeing himself thus menaced, laid hand upon his sword, for he was one of those who on all occasions are more ready for action than for speech; but his more considerate comrade, who came up, commanded him to forbear, and, turning to the young man, accused him in turn of precipitation in plunging into the swollen ford, and of intemperate violence in quarrelling with a man who was hastening to his assistance.

The young man, on hearing himself thus reproved by a man of advanced age and respectable appearance, immediately lowered his weapon, and said he would be sorry if he had done them injustice; but, in reality, it appeared to him as if they had suffered him to put his life in peril for want of a word of timely warning, which could be the part neither of honest men nor of good Christians, far less of respectable burgesses, such as they seemed to be.

"Fair son," said the elder person, "you seem, from your accent and complexion, a stranger; and you should recollect your dialect is not so easily comprehended by us, as perhaps it may be uttered by you."

"Well, father," answered the youth, "I do not care much about the ducking I have had, and I will readily forgive your being partly the cause, provided you will direct me to some place where I can have my clothes dried; for it is my only suit, and I must keep it somewhat decent."

"For whom do you take us, fair son?" said the elder stranger, in answer to this question.

"For substantial burgesses, unquestionably," said the youth; "or, hold—you, master, may be a money-broker, or a corn-merchant; and this man a butcher, or grazier."

"You have hit our capacities rarely," said the elder, smiling. "My business is indeed to trade in as much money as I can; and my gossip's dealings are somewhat of kin to the butcher's. As to your accommodation, we will try to serve you; but I must first know who you are, and whither you are going; for, in these times, the roads are filled with travellers on foot and horseback, who have anything in their head but honesty and the fear of God."

The young man cast another keen and penetrating glance on him who spoke, and on his silent companion, as if doubtful whether they, on their part, merited the confidence they demanded; and the result of his observation was as follows.

The eldest, and most remarkable of these men, in dress and appearance resembled the merchant or shopkeeper of the period. His jerkin, hose, and cloak, were of a dark uniform colour, but worn so threadbare, that the acute young Scot conceived that the wearer must be either very rich or very poor, probably the former. The fashion of the dress was close and short—a kind of garments which were not then held decorous among gentry, or even the superior class of citizens, who generally wore loose gowns which descended below the middle of the leg.

The expression of this man's countenance was partly attractive, and partly forbidding. His strong features, sunk cheeks, and hollow eyes, had, nevertheless, an expression of shrewdness and humour congenial to the character of the young adventurer. But then, those same sunken eyes, from under the shroud of thick black eyebrows, had something in them that was at once commanding and sinister. Perhaps this effect was increased by the low fur cap, much depressed on the forehead, and adding to the shade from under which those eyes peered out; but it is certain that the young stranger had some difficulty to reconcile his looks with the meanness of his appearance in other respects. His cap, in particular, in which all men of any quality displayed either a brooch of gold or of silver, was ornamented with a paltry image of the Virgin, in lead, such as the poorer sort of pilgrims bring from Loretto.

His comrade was a stout-formed, middle-sized man, more than ten years younger than his companion, with a down-looking visage, and a very ominous smile, when by chance he gave way to that impulse, which was never, except in reply to certain secret signs that seemed to pass between him and the elder stranger. This man was armed with a sword and dagger; and, underneath his plain habit, the Scotsman observed that he concealed a *jazeran,* or flexible shirt of linked mail, which, as being often worn by those, even of peaceful professions, who were called upon at that perilous period to be frequently abroad, confirmed the young man in his conjecture, that the wearer was by profession a butcher, grazier, or something of that description, called upon to be much abroad.

The young stranger, comprehending in one glance the result of the observation which has taken us some time to express, answered, after a moment's pause, "I am ignorant whom I may have the honour to address," making a slight reverence at the same time, "but I am indifferent who knows that I am a cadet of Scotland; and that I come to seek my fortune in France, or elsewhere, after the custom of my countrymen."

"*Pasques-dieu!* and a gallant custom it is," said the elder stranger. "You seem a fine young springald, and at the right age to prosper, whether among men or women. What say you? I am a merchant, and want a lad to assist in my traffic—I suppose you are too much a gentleman to assist in such mechanical drudgery?"

"Fair sir," said the youth, "if your offer be seriously made—of which I have my doubts—I am bound to thank you for it, and I thank you accordingly; but I fear I should be altogether unfit for your service."

"What!" said the senior, "I warrant thou knowest better how to draw the bow, than how to draw a bill of charges,—canst handle a broadsword better than a pen—ha!"

"I am, master," answered the young Scot, "a braeman, and therefore, as we say, a bowman. But besides that, I have been in a convent, where the good fathers taught me to read and write, and even to cipher."

"*Pasques-dieu!* that is too magnificent," said the merchant. "By our Lady of Embrun, thou art a prodigy, man!"

"Rest you merry, fair master," said the youth, who was not much pleased with his new acquaintance's jocularity, "I must go dry myself, instead of standing dripping here, answering questions."

The merchant only laughed louder as he spoke, and answered, "*Pasques-dieu!* the proverb never fails—*fier comme un Ecossois*—but come, youngster, you are of a country I have a regard for, having traded in Scotland in my time—an honest poor set of folks they are; and, if you will come with us to the village, I will bestow on you a cup of burnt sack and a warm breakfast, to atone for your drenching.—But, *tête-bleau!* what do you with a hunting-glove on your hand? Know you not there is no hawking permitted in a royal chase?"

"I was taught that lesson," answered the youth, "by a rascally forester of the Duke of Burgundy. I did but fly the falcon I had brought with me from Scotland, and that I reckoned on for bringing me into some note, at a heron near Peronne, and the rascally schelm shot my bird with an arrow."

"What did you do?" said the merchant.

"Beat him," said the youngster, brandishing his staff, "as near to death as one Christian man should belabour another—I wanted not to have his blood to answer for."

"Know you," said the burgess, "that had you fallen into the Duke of Burgundy's hands, he would have hung you up like a chestnut?"

"Ay, I am told he is as prompt as the King of France for that sort of work. But, as this happened near Peronne, I made a leap over the frontiers, and laughed at him. If he had not been so hasty, I might perhaps have taken service with him."

"He will have a heavy miss of such a paladin as you are, if the truce should break off," said the merchant, and threw a look at his own companion, who answered him with one of the downcast lowering smiles, which gleamed along his countenance, enlivening it as a passing meteor enlivens a winter sky.

The young Scot suddenly stopped, pulled his bonnet over his right eyebrow, as one that would not be ridiculed, and said firmly, "My masters, and especially you, sir, the elder, and who should be the wiser, you will find, I presume, no sound or safe jesting at my expense. I do not altogether like the tone of your conversation. I can take a jest with any man, and a rebuke, too, from my elder, and say thank you, sir, if I know it to be deserved; but I do not like being borne in hand as if I were a child, when, God wot, I find myself man enough to belabour you both, if you provoke me too far."

The eldest man seemed like to choke with laughter at the lad's demeanour—his companion's hand stole to his sword-hilt, which the youth observing, dealt him a blow across the wrist, which made him incapable of grasping it; while his companion's mirth was only increased by the incident. "Hold, hold," he cried, "most doughty Scot, even for thine own dear country's sake; and you, gossip, forbear your menacing look. *Pasques-dieu!* let us be just traders, and set off the wetting against the knock on the wrist, which was given with so much grace and alacrity.— And hark ye, my young friend," he said to the young man with a grave sternness, which, in spite of all the youth could do, damped and overawed him, "no more violence. I am no fit object for it, and my gossip, as you may see, has had enough of it. Let me know your name."

"I can answer a civil question civilly," said the youth; "and will pay fitting respect to your age, if you do not urge my patience with mockery. Since I have been here in France and Flanders, men have called me, in their fantasy, the Varlet with the Velvet Pouch, because of this hawk-purse which I carry by my side; but my true name, when at home, is Quentin Durward."

"Durward!" said the querist; "is it a gentleman's name?"

"By fifteen descents in our family," said the young man; "and that makes me reluctant to follow any other trade than arms."

"A true Scot! Plenty of blood, plenty of pride, and right great scarcity of ducats, I warrant thee.—Well, gossip," he said to his companion, "go before us, and tell them to have some breakfast ready yonder at the Mulberry-grove; for this youth will do as much honour to it as a starved mouse to a housewife's cheese. And for the Bohemian—hark in thy ear——"

His comrade answered by a gloomy, but intelligent smile, and set forward at a round pace, while the elder man continued, addressing young Durward,—"You and I will walk leisurely forward together, and we may take a mass at Saint Hubert's Chapel in our way through the forest; for it is not good to think of our fleshly before our spiritual wants."

Durward, as a good Catholic, had nothing to object against this proposal, although he might probably have been desirous, in the first place, to have dried his clothes and refreshed himself. Meanwhile, they soon lost sight of their downward-looking companion, but continued to follow the same path which he had taken, until it led them into a wood of tall trees, mixed with thickets and brushwood, traversed by long avenues, through which were seen, as through a vista, the deer trotting in little herds with a degree of security which argued their consciousness of being completely protected.

"You asked me if I were a good bowman," said the young Scot—"Give me a bow and a brace of shafts, and you shall have a piece of venison in a moment."

"*Pasques-dieu!* my young friend," said his companion, "take care of that; my gossip yonder hath a special eye to the deer; they are under his charge, and he is a strict keeper."

"He hath more the air of a butcher, than of a gay forester," answered Durward. "I cannot think yon hang-dog look of his belongs to any one who knows the gentle rules of woodcraft."

"Ah, my young friend," answered his companion, "my gossip hath somewhat an ugly favour to look upon at the first; but those who become acquainted with him, never are known to complain of him."

Quentin Durward found something singularly and disagreeably significant in the tone with which this was spoken; and, looking suddenly at the speaker, thought he saw in his countenance, in the slight smile that curled his upper lip, and the accompanying twinkle of his keen dark eye, something to justify his unpleasing surprise. "I have heard of robbers," he thought to himself, "and of wily cheats and cut-throats—what if yonder fellow be a murderer, and this old rascal his decoy-duck? I will be on my guard—they will get little by me but good Scottish knocks."

While he was thus reflecting, they came to a glade, where the large forest trees were more widely separated from each other, and where the ground beneath, cleared of underwood and bushes, was clothed with a carpet of the softest and most lovely verdure, which, screened from the scorching heat of the sun, was here more beautifully tender than it is usually to be seen in France. The trees in this secluded spot were chiefly beeches and elms of huge magnitude, which rose like great hills of leaves into the air. Amidst these magnificent sons of the earth, there peeped out, in the most open spot of the glade, a lowly chapel, near which trickled a small rivulet. Its architecture was of the rudest and most simple kind; and there was a very small lodge beside it, for the accommodation of a hermit or solitary priest, who remained there for regularly discharging the duty of the altar. In a small niche, over the arched doorway, stood a stone image of Saint Hubert, with the bugle-horn around his neck, and a leash of greyhounds at his feet. The situation of the chapel in the midst of a park or chase, so richly stocked with game, made the dedication to the Sainted Huntsman peculiarly appropriate.[1]

Towards this little devotional structure the old man directed his steps, followed by young Durward; and, as they approached, the priest, dressed in his sacerdotal garments, made his appearance, in the act of proceeding from his cell to the chapel, for the discharge, doubtless, of his holy office. Durward bowed his body reverently to the priest, as the respect due to his sacred office demanded; whilst his companion, with an appearance of still more deep devotion, kneeled on one knee to receive the holy man's blessing, and then followed him into church, with a step and manner expressive of the most heart-felt contrition and humility.

The inside of the chapel was adorned in a manner adapted to the occupation of the patron-saint while on earth. The richest furs of such animals as are made the objects of the chase in different countries, supplied the place of tapestry and hangings around the altar and elsewhere, and the characteristic emblazonments of bugles, bows, quivers, and other emblems of hunting, surrounded the walls, and were mingled with the heads of deer, wolves, and other animals considered beasts of sport. The whole adornments took an appropriate and silvan character; and the mass itself, being considerably shortened, proved to be of that sort which is called a *hunting-mass,* because in use before the noble and powerful, who while assisting at the solemnity, are usually impatient to commence their favourite sport.

Yet, during this brief ceremony, Durward's companion seemed to pay the most rigid and scrupulous attention; while Durward, not quite so much occupied with religious thoughts, could not forbear blaming himself in his own mind, for having entertained suspicions derogatory to the character of so good and so humble a man. Far from now holding him as a companion and accomplice of robbers, he had much to do to forbear regarding him as a saint-like personage.

When mass was ended, they retired together from the chapel, and the elder said to his young comrade, "It is but a short walk from hence to the village—you may now break your fast with an unprejudiced conscience—follow me."

Turning to the right, and proceeding along a path which seemed gradually to ascend, he recommended to his companion by no means to

[1] Every vocation had, in the middle ages, its protecting saint. The chase, with its fortunes and its hazards, the business of so many, and the amusement of all, was placed under the direction of Saint Hubert.

This silvan saint was the son of Bertrand, Duke of Acquitaine, and, while in the secular state, was a courtier of King Pepin. He was passionately fond of the chase, and used to neglect attendance on divine worship for this amusement. While he was once engaged in this pastime, a stag appeared before him, having a crucifix bound betwixt his horns, and he heard a voice which menaced him with eternal punishment if he did not repent of his sins. He retired from the world and took orders, his wife having also retreated into the cloister. Hubert afterwards became Bishop of Maestrecht and Liege; and from his zeal in destroying remnants of idolatry, is called the Apostle of Ardennes and of Brabant. Those who were descended of his race were supposed to possess the power of curing persons bitten by mad dogs.

quit the track, but, on the contrary, to keep the middle of it as nearly as he could. Durward could not help asking the cause of this precaution.

"You are now near the Court, young man," answered his guide; "and, *Pasques-dieu!* there is some difference betwixt walking in this region and on your own heathy hills. Every yard of this ground, excepting the path which we now occupy, is rendered dangerous, and well-nigh impracticable, by snares and traps, armed with scythe-blades, which shred off the unwary passenger's limb as sheerly as a hedge-bill lops a hawthorn-sprig—and calthrops that would pierce your foot through, and pit-falls deep enough to bury you in them for ever; for you are now within the precincts of the royal demesne, and we shall presently see the front of the Château."

"Were I the King of France," said the young man, "I would not take so much trouble with traps and gins, but would try instead to govern so well, that no man should dare to come near my dwelling with a bad intent; and for those who came there in peace and goodwill, why, the more of them the merrier we should be."

His companion looked round affecting an alarmed gaze, and said "Hush, hush, Sir Varlet with the Velvet Pouch! for I forgot to tell you, that one great danger of these precincts is, that the very leaves of the trees are like so many ears, which carry all which is spoken to the King's own cabinet."

"I care little for that," answered Quentin Durward; "I bear a Scottish tongue in my head, bold enough to speak my mind to King Louis's face, God bless him—and, for the ears you talk of, if I could see them growing on a human head, I would crop them out of it with my wood-knife."

CHAPTER III

THE CASTLE

Full in the midst a mighty pile arose,
Where iron-grated gates their strength oppose
To each invading step—and, strong and steep,
The battled walls arose, the fosse sunk deep.
Slow round the fortress roll'd the sluggish stream,
And high in middle air the warder's turrets gleam.
Anonymous.

WHILE Durward and his new acquaintance thus spoke, they came in sight of the whole front of the Castle of Plessis-les-Tours, which, even in those dangerous times, when the great found themselves obliged to reside within places of fortified strength, was distinguished for the extreme and jealous care with which it was watched and defended.

From the verge of the wood where young Durward halted with his companion, in order to take a view of this royal residence, extended, or rather arose, though by a very gentle elevation, an open esplanade, devoid of trees and bushes of every description, excepting one gigantic and half-withered old oak. This space was left open, according to the rules of fortification in all ages, in order that an enemy might not approach the walls under cover, or unobserved from the battlements, and beyond it arose the Castle itself.

There were three external walls, battlemented and turreted from space to space, and at each angle, the second enclosure rising higher than the first, and being built so as to command the exterior defence in case it was won by the enemy; and being again, in the same manner, itself commanded by the third and innermost barrier. Around the external wall, as the Frenchman informed his young companion (for, as they stood lower than the foundation of the wall, he could not see it), was sunk a ditch of about twenty feet in depth, supplied with water by a dam-head on the river Cher, or rather on one of its tributary branches. In front of the second enclosure, he said, there ran another fosse, and a third, both of the same unusual dimensions, was led between the second and the innermost enclosure. The verge, both of the outer and inner circuit of this triple moat, was strongly fenced with palisades of iron, serving the purpose of what are called *chevaux-de-frise* in modern fortification, the top of each pale being divided into a cluster of sharp spikes, which seemed to render any attempt to climb over an act of self-destruction.

From within the innermost enclosure arose the Castle itself, containing buildings of different periods, crowded around, and united with the ancient and grim-looking donjon-keep, which was older than any of them, and which rose, like a black Ethiopian giant, high into the air, while the absence of any windows larger than shot-holes, irregularly disposed for defence, gave the spectator the same unpleasant feeling which we experience on looking at a blind man. The other buildings seemed scarcely better adapted for the purposes of comfort, for the windows opened to an inner and enclosed courtyard; so that the whole external front looked much more like that of a prison than a palace. The reigning King had even increased this effect; for, desirous that the additions which he himself had made to the fortifications should be of a character not easily distinguished from the original building (for, like many jealous persons, he loved not that his suspicions should be observed), the darkest-coloured brick and freestone were employed, and soot mingled with the lime, so as to give the whole Castle the same uniform tinge of extreme and rude antiquity.

This formidable place had but one entrance, at least Durward saw none along the spacious front, except where, in the centre of the first and outward boundary, arose two strong towers, the usual defences of a gateway; and he could observe their ordinary accompaniments, portcullis and drawbridge—of which the first was lowered, and the last raised. Similar entrance-towers were visible on the second and third bounding wall, but not in the same line with those on the outward circuit; because the passage did not cut right through the whole three enclosures at the same point, but, on the contrary, those who entered had to proceed nearly thirty yards betwixt the first and second wall, exposed, if their purpose were hostile, to missiles from both; and again, when the second boundary was passed, they must make a similar digression from the straight line, in order to attain the portal of the third and innermost enclosure; so that before gaining the outer court, which ran along the front of the building, two narrow and dangerous defiles were to be traversed, under a flanking discharge of artillery, and three gates, defended in the strongest manner known to the age, were to be successively forced.

Coming from a country alike desolated by foreign war and internal feuds,—a country, too, whose unequal and mountainous surface, abounding in precipices and torrents, affords so many situations of strength,— young Durward was sufficiently acquainted with all the various contrivances by which men, in that stern age, endeavoured to secure their dwellings; but he frankly owned to his companion, that he did not think it had been in the power of art to do so much for defence, where nature had done so little; for the situation, as we have hinted, was merely the summit of a gentle elevation ascending upwards from the place where they were standing.

To enhance his surprise, his companion told him that the environs of the Castle, except the single winding-path by which the portal might be safely approached, were, like the thickets through which they had passed, surrounded with every species of hidden pit-fall, snare, and gin, to entrap the wretch who should venture thither without a guide; that upon the walls were constructed certain cradles of iron, called *swallows' nests,* from which the sentinels, who were regularly posted there, could, without being exposed to any risk, take deliberate aim at any who should attempt to enter without the proper signal or pass-word of the day; and that the Archers of the Royal Guard performed that duty day and night, for which they received high pay, rich clothing, and much honour and profit at the hands of King Louis. "And now tell me, young man," he continued, "did you ever see so strong a fortress, and do you think there are men bold enough to storm it?"

The young man looked long and fixedly on the place, the sight of which interested him so much, that he had forgotten, in the eagerness of youthful curiosity, the wetness of his dress. His eye glanced, and his colour mounted to his cheek like that of a daring man who meditates an honourable action, as he replied, "It is a strong castle, and strongly guarded; but there is no impossibility to brave men."

"Are there any in your country who could do such a feat?" said the elder, rather scornfully.

"I will not affirm that," answered the youth; "but there are thousands that, in a good cause, would attempt as bold a deed."

"Umph!" said the senior, "perhaps you are yourself such a gallant?"

"I should sin if I were to boast where there is no danger," answered young Durward; "but my father has done as bold an act, and I trust I am no bastard."

"Well," said his companion, smiling, "you might meet your match, and your kindred withal in the attempt; for the Scottish Archers of King Louis's Life-guards stand sentinels on yonder walls—three hundred gentlemen of the best blood in your country."

"And were I King Louis," said the youth, in reply, "I would trust my safety to the faith of the three hundred Scottish gentlemen, throw down my bounding walls to fill up the moat, call in my noble peers and paladins, and live as became me, amid breaking of lances in gallant tournaments, and feasting of days with nobles, and dancing of nights with ladies, and have no more fear of a foe than I have of a fly."

His companion again smiled, and turning his back on the Castle, which, he observed, they had approached a little too nearly, he led the way again into the wood, by a more broad and beaten path than they had yet trodden. "This," he said, "leads us to the village of Plessis, as it is called, where you, as a stranger, will find reasonable and honest accommodation. About two miles onward lies the fine city of Tours, which gives name to this rich and beautiful earldom. But the village of Plessis, or Plessis of the Park, as it is sometimes called, from its vicinity to the royal residence, and the chase with which it is encircled, will yield you nearer, and as convenient hospita'ity."

"I thank you, kind master, for your information," said the Scot; "but my stay will be so short here, that, if I fail not in a morsel of meat, and a drink of something better than water, my necessities in Plessis, be it of the park or the pool, will be amply satisfied."

"Nay," answered his companion, "I thought you had some friend to see in this quarter."

"And so I have—my mother's own brother," answered Durward; "and as pretty a man, before he left the braes of Angus, as ever planted brogue on heather."

"What is his name?" said the senior; "we will inquire him out for you; for it is not safe for you to go up to the Castle, where you might be taken for a spy."

"Now, by my father's hand!" said the youth, "I taken for a spy!— By Heaven, he shall brook cold iron that brands me with such a charge! —But for my uncle's name, I care not who knows it—it is Lesly. Lesly— an honest and noble name."

"And so it is, I doubt not," said the old man; "but there are three of the name in the Scottish Guard."

"My uncle's name is Ludovic Lesly," said the young man.

"Of the three Leslys," answered the merchant, "two are called Ludovic."

"They call my kinsman Ludovic with the Scar," said Quentin.—"Our

family names are so common in a Scottish house, that, where there is no
land in the case, we always give a *to-name*."

"A *nom de guerre*, I suppose you to mean," answered his companion;
"and the man you speak of, we, I think, call *Le Balafré*, from that scar
on his face—a proper man, and a good soldier. I wish I may be able to
help you to an interview with him, for he belongs to a set of gentlemen
whose duty is strict, and who do not often come out of garrison, unless
in the immediate attendance on the King's person.—And now, young
man, answer me one question. I will wager you are desirous to take
service with your uncle in the Scottish Guard. It is a great thing, if you
propose so; especially as you are very young, and some years' experience
is necessary for the high office which you aim at."

"Perhaps I may have thought on some such thing," said Durward
carelessly; "but if I did, the fancy is off."

"How so, young man?" said the Frenchman, something sternly—"Do
you speak thus of a charge which the most noble of your countrymen
feel themselves emulous to be admitted to?"

"I wish them joy of it," said Quentin composedly.—"To speak plain,
I should have liked the service of the French King full well; only, dress
me as fine, and feed me as high as you will, I love the open air better
than being shut up in a cage or a swallow's nest yonder, as you call
these same grated pepper-boxes. Besides," he added, in a lower voice, "to
speak truth, I love not the Castle when the covin-tree [1] bars such acorns
as I see yonder."

"I guess what you mean," said the Frenchman; "but speak yet more
plainly."

"To speak more plainly, then," said the youth, "there grows a fair
oak some flight-shot or so from yonder Castle—and on that oak hangs
a man in a grey jerkin, such as this which I wear."

"Ay and indeed!" said the man of France—"*Pasques-dieu!* see what
it is to have youthful eyes! Why, I did see something, but only took
it for a raven among the branches. But the sight is no way strange, young
man; when the summer fades into autumn, and moonlight nights are
long, and roads become unsafe, you will see a cluster of ten, ay of twenty
such acorns, hanging on that old doddered oak.—But what then?—they
are so many banners displayed to scare knaves; and for each rogue that
hangs there, an honest man may reckon that there is a thief, a traitor,
a robber on the highway, a *pilleur* and oppressor of the people, the
fewer in France. These, young man, are signs of our Sovereign's justice."

"I would have hung them farther from my palace, though, were I King
Louis," said the youth.—"In my country, we hang up dead corbies where
living corbies haunt, but not in our gardens or pigeon-houses. The very

---

[1] The large tree in front of a Scottish Castle was sometimes called so. It is difficult
to trace the derivation; but at that distance from the castle, the laird received guests
of rank, and thither he convoyed them on their departure.

scent of the carrion—faugh—reached my nostrils at the distance where we stood."

"If you live to be an honest and loyal servant of your Prince, my good youth," answered the Frenchman, "you will know there is no perfume to match the scent of a dead traitor."

"I shall never wish to live till I lose the scent of my nostrils or the sight of my eyes," said the Scot.—"Show me a living traitor, and here are my hand and my weapon; but when life is out, hatred should not live longer.—But here, I fancy, we come upon the village; where I hope to show you that neither ducking nor disgust have spoiled mine appetite for my breakfast. So, my good friend, to the hostelrie, with all the speed you may.—Yet, ere I accept of your hospitality, let me know by what name to call you."

"Men call me Maitre Pierre," answered his companion.—"I deal in no titles. A plain man, that can live on mine own good—that is my designation."

"So be it, Maitre Pierre," said Quentin, "and I am happy my good chance has thrown us together; for I want a word of seasonable advice, and can be thankful for it."

While they spoke thus, the tower of the church, and a tall wooden crucifix, rising above the trees, showed that they were at the entrance of the village.

But Maitre Pierre, deflecting a little from the road, which had now joined an open and public causeway, said to his companion, that the inn to which he intended to introduce him stood somewhat secluded, and received only the better sort of travellers.

"If you mean those who travel with the better-filled purses," answered the Scot, "I am none of the number, and will rather stand my chance of your flayers on the highway, than of your flayers in the hostelrie!"

"*Pasques-dieu!*" said his guide, "how cautious your countrymen of Scotland are! An Englishman, now, throws himself headlong into a tavern, eats and drinks of the best, and never thinks of the reckoning till his belly is full. But you forget, Master Quentin, since Quentin is your name, you forget I owe you a breakfast for the wetting which my mistake procured you—It is the penance of my offence towards you."

"In truth," said the light-hearted young man, "I had forgot wetting, offence, and penance and all. I have walked my clothes dry, or nearly so, but I will not refuse your offer in kindness; for my dinner yesterday was a light one, and supper I had none. You seem an old and respectable burgess, and I see no reason why I should not accept your courtesy."

The Frenchman smiled aside, for he saw plainly that the youth, while he was probably half famished, had yet some difficulty to reconcile himself to the thoughts of feeding at a stranger's cost, and was endeavouring to subdue his inward pride by the reflection, that, in such slight obligations, the acceptor performed as complaisant a part as he by whom the courtesy was offered.

In the meanwhile, they descended a narrow lane, overshadowed by tall elms, at the bottom of which a gateway admitted them into the court-yard of an inn of unusual magnitude, calculated for the accommodation of the nobles and suitors who had business at the neighbouring Castle, where very seldom, and only when such hospitality was altogether un-avoidable, did Louis XI. permit any of his Court to have apartments. A scutcheon, bearing the *fleur-de-lys,* hung over the principal door of the large irregular building; but there was about the yard and the offices little or none of the bustle which in those days, when attendants were maintained both in public and in private houses, marked that business was alive, and custom plenty. It seemed as if the stern and unsocial character of the royal mansion in the neighbourhood had communicated a portion of its solemn and terrific gloom even to a place designed, according to universal custom elsewhere, for the temple of social in-dulgence, merry society, and good cheer.

Maitre Pierre, without calling any one, and even without approaching the principal entrance, lifted the latch of a side door, and led the way into a large room, where a faggot was blazing on the hearth, and arrange-ments made for a substantial breakfast.

"My gossip has been careful," said the Frenchman to the Scot—"You must be cold, and I have commanded a fire; you must be hungry, and you shall have breakfast presently."

He whistled, and the landlord entered,—answered Maitre Pierre's *bon jour* with a reverence,—but in no respect showed any part of the prating humour properly belonging to a French publican of all ages.

"I expected a gentleman," said Maitre Pierre, "to order breakfast— Hath he done so?"

In answer, the landlord only bowed; and while he continued to bring, and arrange upon the table, the various articles of a comfortable meal, omitted to extol their merits by a single word. And yet the breakfast merited such eulogiums as French hosts are wont to confer upon their regales, as the reader will be informed in the next chapter.

CHAPTER IV

THE DÉJEUNER

Sacred heaven! what masticators! what bread!
Yorick's Travels.

WE left our young stranger in France situated more comfortably than he had found himself since entering the territories of the ancient Gauls. The breakfast, as we hinted in the conclusion of the last chapter, was admirable. There was a *pâté de Perigord,* over which a gastronome would have wished to live and die, like Homer's lotus-eaters, forgetful of kin, native country, and all social obligations whatever. Its vast walls of magnificent crust seemed raised like the bulwarks of some rich metro-

politan city, an emblem of the wealth which they designed to protect.
There was a delicate ragout, with just that *petit point de l'ail* which
Gascons love, and Scottishmen do not hate. There was, besides, a delicate
ham, which had once supported a noble wild boar in the neighbouring
wood of Mountrichart. There was the most exquisite white bread, made
into little round loaves called *boules* (whence the bakers took their
French name of *boulangers*), of which the crust was so inviting, that, even
with water alone, it would have been a delicacy. But the water was not
alone, for there was a flask of leather called *bottrine,* which contained
about a quart of exquisite *Vin de Beaulne.* So many good things might
have created appetite under the ribs of death. What effect, then, must
they have produced upon a youngster of scarce twenty, who (for the
truth must be told) had eaten little for the two last days, save the scarcely
ripe fruit which chance afforded him an opportunity of plucking, and
a very moderate portion of barley-bread? He threw himself upon the
ragout, and the plate was presently vacant—he attacked the mighty pasty,
marched deep into the bowels of the land, and, seasoning his enormous
meal with an occasional cup of wine, returned to the charge again and
again, to the astonishment of mine host, and the amusement of Maitre
Pierre.

The latter, indeed, probably because he found himself the author
of a kinder action than he had thought of, seemed delighted with the
appetite of the young Scot; and when, at length, he observed that his
exertions began to languish, endeavoured to stimulate him to new efforts,
by ordering confections, *darioles,* and any other light dainties he could
think of, to entice the youth to continue his meal. While thus engaged,
Maitre Pierre's countenance expressed a kind of good-humour almost
amounting to benevolence, which appeared remote from its ordinary
sharp, caustic, and severe character. The aged almost always sympathise
with the enjoyments of youth, and with its exertions of every kind,
when the mind of the spectator rests on its natural poise, and is not disturbed by inward envy or idle emulation.

Quentin Durward also, while thus agreeably employed, could do no
otherwise than discover that the countenance of his entertainer, which
he had at first found so unprepossessing, mended when it was seen
under the influence of the *Vin de Beaulne,* and there was kindness in the
tone with which he reproached Maitre Pierre, that he amused himself
with laughing at his appetite, without eating anything himself.

"I am doing penance," said Maitre Pierre, "and may not eat anything before noon, save some comfiture and a cup of water.—Bid yonder
lady," he added, turning to the innkeeper, "bring them hither to me."

The innkeeper left the room, and Maitre Pierre proceeded,—"Well,
have I kept faith with you concerning the breakfast I promised you?"

"The best meal I have eaten," said the youth, "since I left Glen-
houlakin."

"Glen—what?" demanded Maitre Pierre; "are you going to raise the devil, that you use such long-tailed words?"

"Glen-houlakin," answered Quentin good-humouredly, "which is to say the Glen of the Midges, is the name of our ancient patrimony, my good sir. You have bought the right to laugh at the sound, if you please."

"I have not the least intention to offend," said the old man; "but I was about to say, since you like your present meal so well, that the Scottish Archers of the guard eat as good a one, or a better, every day."

"No wonder," said Durward, "for if they be shut up in the *swallows' nests* all night, they must needs have a curious appetite in the morning."

"And plenty to gratify it upon," said Maitre Pierre. "They need not. like the Burgundians, choose a bare back, that they may have a full belly—they dress like counts, and feast like abbots."

"It is well for them," said Durward.

"And wherefore will you not take service here, young man? Your uncle might, I dare say, have you placed on the file when there should a vacancy occur. And, hark in your ear, I myself have some little interest, and might be of some use to you. You can ride, I presume, as well as draw the bow?"

"Our race are as good horsemen as ever put a plated shoe into a steel stirrup; and I know not but I might accept of your kind offer. Yet, look you, food and raiment are needful things, but, in my case, men think of honour, and advancement, and brave deeds of arms. Your King Louis—God bless him, for he is a friend and ally of Scotland—but he lies here in this castle, or only rides about from one fortified town to another; and gains cities and provinces by politic embassies, and not in fair fighting. Now, for me, I am of the Douglasses' mind, who always kept the fields, because they loved better to hear the lark sing than the mouse squeak."

"Young man," said Maitre Pierre, "do not judge too rashly of the actions of sovereigns. Louis seeks to spare the blood of his subjects, and cares not for his own. He showed himself a man of courage at Montl'héry."

"Ay, but that was some dozen years ago or more," answered the youth. —"I should like to follow a master that would keep his honour as bright as his shield, and always venture foremost in the very throng of the battle."

"Why did you not tarry at Brussels, then, with the Duke of Burgundy? He would put you in the way to have your bones broken every day; and, rather than fail, would do the job for you himself—especially if he heard that you had beaten his forester."

"Very true," said Quentin; "my unhappy chance has shut that door against me."

"Nay, there are plenty of dare-devils abroad, with whom mad youngsters may find service," said his adviser. "What think you, for example, of William de la Marck?"

"What!" exclaimed Durward, "serve Him with the Beard—serve the

Wild Boar of Ardennes—a captain of pillagers and murderers, who would take a man's life for the value of his gaberdine, and who slays priests and pilgrims as if they were so many lance-knights and men-at-arms? It would be a blot on my father's scutcheon for ever."

"Well, my young hot-blood," replied Maitre Pierre, "if you hold the *Sanglier* too unscrupulous, wherefore not follow the young Duke of Gueldres?"[1]

"Follow the foul fiend as soon," said Quentin. "Hark in your ear—he is a burden too heavy for earth to carry—hell gapes for him! Men say that he keeps his own father imprisoned, and that he has even struck him— Can you believe it?"

Maitre Pierre seemed somewhat disconcerted with the naïve horror with which the young Scotsman spoke of filial ingratitude, and he answered, "You know not, young man, how short a while the relations of blood subsist amongst those of elevated rank;" then changed the tone of feeling in which he had begun to speak, and added gaily, "besides, if the Duke has beaten his father, I warrant you his father hath beaten him of old, so it is but a clearing of scores."

"I marvel to hear you speak thus," said the Scot, colouring with indignation; "grey hairs such as yours ought to have fitter subjects for jesting. If the old Duke did beat his son in childhood, he beat him not enough; for better he had died under the rod, than have lived to make the Christian world ashamed that such a monster had ever been baptized."

"At this rate," said Maitre Pierre, "as you weigh the characters of each prince and leader, I think you had better become a captain yourself; for where will one so wise find a chieftain fit to command him?"

"You laugh at me, Maitre Pierre," said the youth good-humouredly, "and perhaps you are right; but you have not named a man who is a gallant leader, and keeps a brave party up here, under whom a man might seek service well enough."

"I cannot guess whom you mean."

"Why, he that hangs like Mahomet's coffin (a curse be upon Mahomet!) between the two loadstones—he that no man can call either French or Burgundian, but who knows to hold the balance between them both, and makes both of them fear and serve him, for as great princes as they be."

---

[1] This was Adolphus, son of Arnold and of Catherine de Bourbon. The present story has little to do with him, though one of the most atrocious characters of his time. He made war against his father; in which unnatural strife he made the old man prisoner, and used him with the most brutal violence, proceeding, it is said, even to the length of striking him with his hand. Arnold, in resentment of this usage, disinherited the unprincipled wretch, and sold to Charles of Burgundy whatever rights he had over the duchy of Gueldres and earldom of Zutphen. Mary of Burgundy, daughter of Charles, restored these possessions to the unnatural Adolphus, who was slain in 1477.

"I cannot guess whom you mean," said Maitre Pierre thoughtfully.

"Why, whom should I mean but the noble Louis de Luxembourg, Count of Saint Paul, the High Constable of France? Yonder he makes his place good, with his gallant little army, holding his head as high as either King Louis or Duke Charles, and balancing between them, like the boy who stands on the midst of a plank, while two others are swinging on the opposite ends." [1]

"He is in danger of the worst fall of the three," said Maitre Pierre. "And hark ye, my young friend, you who hold pillaging such a crime, do you know that your politic Count of Saint Paul was the first who set the example of burning the country during the time of war? and that before the shameful devastation which he committed, open towns and villages, which made no resistance, were spared on all sides?"

"Nay, faith," said Durward, "if that be the case, I shall begin to think no one of these great men is much better than another, and that a choice among them is but like choosing a tree to be hung upon. But this Count de Saint Paul, this Constable, hath possessed himself by clean conveyance of the town which takes its name from my honoured saint and patron, Saint Quentin" [2] (here he crossed himself), "and methinks, were I dwelling there, my holy patron would keep some look-out for me—he has not so many named after him as your more popular saints—and yet he must have forgotten me, poor Quentin Durward, his spiritual god-son, since he lets me go one day without food, and leaves me the next morning to the harbourage of Saint Julian, and the chance courtesy of a stranger, purchased by a ducking in the renowned river Cher, or one of its tributaries."

"Blaspheme not the saints, my young friend," said Maitre Pierre. "Saint Julian is the faithful patron of travellers; and, peradventure, the blessed Saint Quentin hath done more and better for thee than thou art aware of."

As he spoke, the door opened, and a girl, rather above than under fifteen years old, entered with a platter, covered with damask, on which was placed a small saucer of the dried plums which have always added to the reputation of Tours, and a cup of the curiously chased plate which the goldsmiths of that city were anciently famous for executing with a delicacy of workmanship that distinguishes them from the other cities of France, and even excelled the skill of the metropolis. The form of the

---

[1] This part of Louis XIth's reign was much embarrassed by the intrigues of the Constable Saint Paul, who affected independence, and carried on intrigues with England, France, and Burgundy, at the same time. According to the usual fate of such variable politicians, the Constable ended by drawing upon himself the animosity of all the powerful neighbours whom he had in their turn amused and deceived. He was delivered up by the Duke of Burgundy to the King of France, tried, and hastily executed for treason, A.D. 1475.

[2] It was by his possession of this town of Saint Quentin that the Constable was able to carry on those political intrigues, which finally cost him so dear.

goblet was so elegant, that Durward thought not of observing closely
whether the material was of silver, or, like what had been placed before
himself, of a baser metal, but so well burnished as to resemble the richer
ore.

But the sight of the young person by whom this service was executed,
attracted Durward's attention far more than the petty minutiæ of the
duty which she performed.

He speedily made the discovery, that a quantity of long black tresses,
which, in the maiden fashion of his own country, were unadorned by any
ornament, except a single chaplet lightly woven out of ivy leaves, formed
a veil around a countenance, which, in its regular features, dark eyes,
and pensive expression, resembled that of Melpomene, though there was
a faint glow on the cheek, and an intelligence on the lips and in the eye,
which made it seem that gaiety was not foreign to a countenance so expressive, although it might not be its most habitual expression. Quentin
even thought he could discern that depressing circumstances were the
cause why a countenance so young and so lovely was graver than belongs
to early beauty; and as the romantic imagination of youth is rapid in
drawing conclusions from slight premises, he was pleased to infer, from
what follows, that the fate of this beautiful vision was wrapped in silence
and mystery.

"How now, Jacqueline!" said Maitre Pierre, when she entered the
apartment—"Wherefore this? Did I not desire that Dame Perette should
bring what I wanted?—*Pasques-dieu!*—Is she, or does she think herself,
too good to serve me?"

"My kinswoman is ill at ease," answered Jacqueline, in a hurried yet
a humble tone; "ill at ease, and keeps her chamber."

"She keeps it *alone,* I hope?" replied Maitre Pierre, with some emphasis; "I am *vieux routier,* and none of those upon whom feigned disorders
pass for apologies."

Jacqueline turned pale, and even tottered at the answer of Maitre
Pierre; for it must be owned, that his voice and looks, at all times harsh,
caustic, and unpleasing, had, when he expressed anger or suspicion, an
effect both sinister and alarming.

The mountain chivalry of Quentin Durward was instantly awakened,
and he hastened to approach Jacqueline, and relieve her of the burden
she bore, and which she passively resigned to him, while, with a timid
and anxious look, she watched the countenance of the angry burgess. It
was not in nature to resist the piercing and pity-craving expression of her
looks, and Maitre Pierre proceeded, not merely with an air of diminished
displeasure, but with as much gentleness as he could assume in countenance and manner, "I blame not thee, Jacqueline, and thou art too
young to be—what it is pity to think thou must be one day—a false and
treacherous thing, like the rest of thy giddy sex. No man ever lived to

man's estate, but he had the opportunity to know you all.[1] Here is a Scottish cavalier will tell you the same."

Jacqueline looked for an instant on the young stranger, as if to obey Maitre Pierre, but the glance, momentary as it was, appeared to Durward a pathetic appeal to him for support and sympathy; and with the promptitude dictated by the feelings of youth, and the romantic veneration for the female sex inspired by his education, he answered hastily, "That he would throw down his gage to any antagonist, of equal rank and equal age, who should presume to say such a countenance, as that which he now looked upon, could be animated by other than the purest and the truest mind."

The young woman grew deadly pale, and cast an apprehensive glance upon Maitre Pierre, in whom the bravado of the young gallant seemed only to excite laughter, more scornful than applausive. Quentin, whose second thoughts generally corrected the first, though sometimes after they had found utterance, blushed deeply at having uttered what might be construed into an empty boast, in presence of an old man of a peaceful profession; and, as a sort of just and appropriate penance, resolved patiently to submit to the ridicule which he had incurred. He offered the cup and trencher to Maitre Pierre with a blush in his cheek, and a humiliation of countenance, which endeavoured to disguise itself under an embarrassed smile.

"You are a foolish young man," said Maitre Pierre, "and know as little of women as of princes,—whose hearts," he said, crossing himself devoutly, "God keeps in His right hand."

"And who keeps those of the women, then?" said Quentin, resolved, if he could help it, not to be borne down by the assumed superiority of this extraordinary old man, whose lofty and careless manner possessed an influence over him of which he felt ashamed.

"I am afraid you must ask of them in another quarter," said Maitre Pierre composedly.

Quentin was again rebuffed, but not utterly disconcerted. "Surely," he said to himself, "I do not pay this same burgess of Tours all the deference which I yield him, on account of the miserable obligation of a breakfast, though it was a right good and substantial meal. Dogs and hawks are attached by feeding only—man must have kindness, if you would bind him with the cords of affection and obligation. But he is an extraordinary person; and that beautiful emanation that is even now vanishing—surely a thing so fair belongs not to this mean place, belongs not even to the money-gathering merchant himself, though he seems to exert authority over her, as doubtless he does over all whom chance brings within his little circle. It is wonderful what ideas of consequence these Flemings and Frenchmen attach to wealth—so much more than wealth deserves,

---

[1] It was a part of Louis's very unamiable character, and not the best part of it, that he entertained a great contempt for the understanding, and not less for the character, of the fair sex.

that I suppose this old merchant thinks the civility I pay to his age is given to his money—I, a Scottish gentleman of blood and coat-armour, and he a mechanic of Tours!"

Such were the thoughts which hastily traversed the mind of young Durward; while Maitre Pierre said, with a smile, and at the same time patting Jacqueline's head, from which hung down her long tresses, "This young man will serve me, Jacqueline—thou mayst withdraw. I will tell thy negligent kinswoman she does ill to expose thee to be gazed on unnecessarily."

"It was only to wait on you," said the maiden. "I trust you will not be displeased with my kinswoman, since—"

"*Pasques-dieu!*" said the merchant, interrupting her, but not harshly, "do you not bandy words with me, you brat, or stay you to gaze upon the youngster here?—Begone—he is noble, and his services will suffice me."

Jacqueline vanished; and so much was Quentin Durward interested in her sudden disappearance, that it broke his previous thread of reflection, and he complied mechanically, when Maitre Pierre said, in the tone of one accustomed to be obeyed, as he threw himself carelessly upon a large easy-chair, "Place that tray beside me."

The merchant then let his dark eyebrows sink over his keen eyes, so that the last became scarce visible, or but shot forth occasionally a quick and vivid ray, like those of the sun setting behind a dark cloud, through which its beams are occasionally darted, but singly, and for an instant.

"That is a beautiful creature," said the old man at last, raising his head, and looking steadily and firmly at Quentin, when he put the question—"a lovely girl to be the servant of an *auberge?*—she might grace the board of an honest burgess; but 'tis a vile education, a base origin."

It sometimes happens that a chance shot will demolish a noble castle in the air, and the architect on such occasions entertains little goodwill towards him who fires it, although the damage on the offender's part may be wholly unintentional. Quentin was disconcerted, and was disposed to be angry—he himself knew not why—with this old man, for acquainting him that this beautiful creature was neither more nor less than what her occupation announced—the servant of the *auberge*—an upper servant, indeed, and probably a niece of the landlord, or such like; but still a domestic, and obliged to comply with the humour of the customers, and particularly of Maitre Pierre, who probably had sufficiency of whims, and was rich enough to ensure their being attended to.

The thought, the lingering thought, again returned on him, that he ought to make the old gentleman understand the difference betwixt their conditions, and call on him to mark, that, how rich soever he might be, his wealth put him on no level with a Durward of Glen-houlakin. Yet, whenever he looked on Maitre Pierre's countenance with such a purpose, there was, notwithstanding the downcast look, pinched features, and mean and miserly dress, something which prevented the young man from asserting the superiority over the merchant which he conceived himself to possess. On the contrary, the oftener and more fixedly Quentin looked at him, the stronger became his curiosity to know who or what this man actually was; and he set him down internally for at least a Syndic or high magistrate of Tours, or one who was, in some way or other, in the full habit of exacting and receiving deference.

Meantime, the merchant seemed again sunk into a reverie, from which he raised himself only to make the sign of the cross devoutly, and to eat some of the dried fruit, with a morsel of biscuit. He then signed to Quentin to give him the cup, adding, however, by way of question, as he presented it—"You are noble, you say?"

"I surely am," replied the Scot, "if fifteen descents can make me so— So I told you before. But do not constrain yourself on that account, Maitre Pierre—I have always been taught it is the duty of the young to assist the more aged."

"An excellent maxim," said the merchant, availing himself of the youth's assistance in handing the cup, and filling it from a ewer which seemed of the same materials with the goblet, without any of those scruples in point of propriety which, perhaps, Quentin had expected to excite.

"The devil take the ease and familiarity of this old mechanical burgher," said Durward once more to himself; "he uses the attendance of a noble Scottish gentleman with as little ceremony as I would that of a gillie from Glen-Isla."

The merchant, in the meanwhile, having finished his cup of water, said to his companion, "From the zeal with which you seemed to relish the *Vin de Beaulne*, I fancy you would not care much to pledge me in this elemental liquor. But I have an elixir about me which can convert even the rock water into the richest wines of France."

As he spoke, he took a large purse from his bosom, made of the fur of the sea-otter, and streamed a shower of small silver pieces into the goblet, until the cup, which was but a small one, was more than half full.

"You have reason to be more thankful, young man," said Maitre Pierre, "both to your patron Saint Quentin, and to Saint Julian, than you seemed to be but now. I would advise you to bestow alms in their name. Remain in this hostelry until you see your kinsman, Le Balafré, who will be relieved from guard in the afternoon. I will cause him to be acquainted that he may find you here, for I have business in the Castle."

Quentin Durward would have said something to have excused himself from accepting the profuse liberality of his new friend; but Maitre Pierre, bending his dark brows, and erecting his stooping figure into an attitude of more dignity than he had yet seen him assume, said, in a tone of authority, "No reply, young man, but do what you are commanded."

With these words, he left the apartment, making a sign, as he departed, that Quentin must not follow him.

The young Scotsman stood astounded, and knew not what to think of the matter. His first most natural, though perhaps not most dignified impulse, drove him to peep into the silver goblet, which assuredly was more than half full of silver pieces, to the number of several scores, of which perhaps Quentin had never called twenty his own at one time during the course of his whole life. But could he reconcile it to his dignity as a gentleman, to accept the money of this wealthy plebeian?— This was a trying question; for, though he had secured a good breakfast, it was no great reserve upon which to travel either back to Dijon, in case he chose to hazard the wrath, and enter the service, of the Duke of Burgundy, or to Saint Quentin, if he fixed on that of the Constable Saint Paul; for to one of those powers, if not to the King of France, he was determined to offer his services. He perhaps took the wisest resolution in the circumstances, in resolving to be guided by the advice of his uncle; and, in the meantime, he put the money into his velvet hawking-pouch, and called for the landlord of the house, in order to restore the silver cup—resolving, at the same time, to ask him some questions about this liberal and authoritative merchant.

The man of the house appeared presently; and, if not more communicative, was at least more loquacious, than he had been formerly. He positively declined to take back the silver cup. It was none of his, he said, but Maitre Pierre's, who had bestowed it on his guest. He had, indeed, four silver *hanaps* of his own, which had been left him by his grandmother, of happy memory, but no more like the beautiful carving of that in his guest's hand, than a peach was like a turnip,—that was one of the famous cups of Tours, wrought by Martin Dominique, an artist who might brag all Paris.

"And pray, who is this Maitre Pierre," said Durward, interrupting him, "who confers such valuable gifts on strangers?"

"Who is Maitre Pierre?" said the host, dropping the words as slowly from his mouth as if he had been distilling them.

"Ay," said Durward, hastily and peremptorily, "who is this Maitre Pierre, and why does he throw about his bounties in this fashion? And who is the butcherly-looking fellow whom he sent forward to order breakfast?"

"Why, fair sir, as to who Maitre Pierre is, you should have asked the question of himself; and for the gentleman who ordered breakfast to be made ready, may God keep us from his closer acquaintance!"

"There is something mysterious in all this," said the young Scot. "This Maitre Pierre tells me he is a merchant."

"And if he told you so," said the innkeeper, "surely he is a merchant."

"What commodities does he deal in?"

"Oh, many a fair matter of traffic," said the host; "and especially he has set up silk manufactories here, which match those rich bales that the Venetians bring from India and Cathay. You might see the rows of mulberry-trees as you came thither, all planted by Maitre Pierre's commands, to feed the silk-worms."

"And that young person who brought in the confections, who is she, my good friend?" said the guest.

"My lodger, sir, with her guardian, some sort of aunt or kinswoman, as I think," replied the innkeeper.

"And do you usually employ your guests in waiting on each other?" said Durward; "for I observed that Maitre Pierre would take nothing from your hand, or that of your attendant."

"Rich men may have their fancies, for they can pay for them," said the landlord; "this is not the first time that Maitre Pierre has found the true way to make gentlefolks serve at his beck."

The young Scotsman felt somewhat offended at the insinuation; but, disguising his resentment, he asked whether he could be accommodated with an apartment at this place for a day, and perhaps longer.

"Certainly," the innkeeper replied; "for whatever time he was pleased to command it."

"Could he be permitted," he asked, "to pay his respects to the ladies, whose fellow-lodger he was about to become?"

The innkeeper was uncertain. "They went not abroad," he said, "and received no one at home."

"With the exception, I presume, of Maitre Pierre?" said Durward.

"I am not at liberty to name any exceptions," answered the man, firmly but respectfully.

Quentin, who carried the notions of his own importance pretty high considering how destitute he was of means to support them, being somewhat mortified by the innkeeper's reply, did not hesitate to avail himself of a practice common enough in that age. "Carry to the ladies," he said, "a flask of *vernât*, with my humble duty; and say, that Quentin Durward, of the house of Glen-houlakin, a Scottish cavalier of honour, and now their fellow-lodger, desires the permission to dedicate his homage to them in a personal interview."

The messenger departed, and returned, almost instantly, with the thanks of the ladies, who declined the proffered refreshment, and with their acknowledgments to the Scottish cavalier, regretted that, residing there in privacy, they could not receive his visit.

Quentin bit his lip, took a cup of the rejected *vernât*, which the host had placed on the table. "By the mass, but this is a strange country," said he to himself, "where merchants and mechanics exercise the manners and munificence of nobles, and little travelling damsels, who hold their court in a *cabaret*, keep their state like disguised princesses! I will see that black-browed maiden again, or it will go hard, however;" and having formed this prudent solution, he demanded to be conducted to the apartment which he was to call his own.

The landlord presently ushered him up a turret staircase, and from thence along a gallery, with many doors opening from it, like those of cells in a convent; a resemblance which our young hero, who recollected, with much ennui, an early specimen of a monastic life, was far from admiring. The host paused at the very end of the gallery, selected a key from the large bunch which he carried at his girdle, opened the door, and showed his guest the interior of a turret-chamber, small, indeed, but which, being clean and solitary, and having the pallet bed, and the few articles of furniture, in unusually good order, seemed, on the whole, a little palace.

"I hope you will find your dwelling agreeable here, fair sir," said the landlord.—"I am bound to pleasure every friend of Maitre Pierre."

"Oh, happy ducking!" exclaimed Quentin Durward, cutting a caper on the floor, so soon as his host had retired: "Never came good luck in a better or a wetter form. I have been fairly deluged by my good fortune."

As he spoke thus, he stepped towards the little window, which, as the turret projected considerably from the principal line of the building, not only commanded a very pretty garden, of some extent, belonging to the inn, but overlooked, beyond its boundary, a pleasant grove of those very mulberry-trees, which Maitre Pierre was said to have planted for the support of the silk-worm. Besides, turning the eye from these more remote objects, and looking straight along the wall, the turret of Quentin was opposite to another turret, and the little window at which he stood commanded a similar little window, in a corresponding projection of the building. Now, it would be difficult for a man twenty years older than Quentin, to say why this locality interested him more than either the pleasant garden or the grove of mulberry-trees; for, alas! eyes which have been used for forty years and upwards, look with indifference on little turret-windows, though the lattice be half open to admit the air, while the shutter is half closed to exclude the sun, or perhaps a too curious eye—nay, even though there hang on the one side of the casement a lute, partly mantled by a light veil of sea-green silk. But, at Durward's happy age, such *accidents,* as a painter would call them, form sufficient foundation for a hundred airy visions and mysterious conjectures, at recollection of which the fullgrown man smiles while he sighs, and sighs while he smiles.

As it may be supposed that our friend Quentin wished to learn a little more of his fair neighbour, the owner of the lute and veil,—as it may be supposed he was at least interested to know whether she might not prove the same whom he had seen in humble attendance on Maitre Pierre, it must of course be understood, that he did not produce a broad staring visage and person in full front of his own casement. Durward knew better the art of bird-catching; and it was to his keeping his person skilfully withdrawn on one side of his window, while he peeped through the lattice, that he owed the pleasure of seeing a white, round, beautiful arm, take down the instrument, and that his ears had presently after their share in the reward of his dexterous management.

The maid of the little turret, of the veil, and of the lute, sung exactly such an air as we are accustomed to suppose flowed from the lips of the high-born dames of chivalry, when knights and troubadours listened and languished. The words had neither so much sense, wit, or fancy, as to withdraw the attention from the music, nor the music so much of art, as to drown all feeling of the words. The one seemed fitted to the other; and if the song had been recited without the notes, or the air played without the words, neither would have been worth noting. It is, therefore, scarcely fair to put upon record lines intended not to be said or read, but only to be sung. But such scraps of old poetry have always had a sort of fascination for us; and as the tune is lost for ever—unless Bishop happens to find the notes, or some lark teaches Stephens to warble the air—we will risk our credit, and the taste of the Lady of the Lute, by preserving the verses, simple and even rude as they are:

> "Ah! County Guy, the hour is nigh,
>   The sun has left the lea,
> The orange flower perfumes the bower,
>   The breeze is on the sea.
> The lark, his lay who thrill'd all day,
>   Sits hush'd his partner nigh;
> Breeze, bird, and flower, confess the hour,
>   But where is County Guy?
>
> The village maid steals through the shade,
>   Her shepherd's suit to hear;
> To beauty shy, by lattice high,
>   Sings high-born Cavalier.
> The star of Love, all stars above,
>   Now reigns o'er earth and sky;
> And high and low the influence know—
>   But where is County Guy?"

Whatever the reader may think of this simple ditty, it had a powerful effect on Quentin, when married to heavenly airs, and sung by a sweet and melting voice, the notes mingling with the gentle breezes which wafted perfumes from the garden, and the figure of the songstress being so partially and obscurely visible, as threw a veil of mysterious fascination over the whole.

At the close of the air, the listener could not help showing himself more boldly than he had yet done, in a rash attempt to see more than he had yet been able to discover. The music instantly ceased—the casement was closed, and a dark curtain, dropped on the inside, put a stop to all further observation on the part of the neighbour in the next turret.

Durward was mortified and surprised at the consequence of his precipitance, but comforted himself with the hope, that the Lady of the Lute could neither easily forego the practice of an instrument which seemed so familiar to her, nor cruelly resolve to renounce the pleasures of fresh air and an open window, for the churlish purpose of preserving for her own exclusive ear the sweet sounds which she created. There

came, perhaps, a little feeling of personal vanity to mingle with these
consolatory reflections. If, as he shrewdly suspected, there was a beautiful dark-tressed damsel inhabitant of the one turret, he could not but
be conscious that a handsome, young, roving, bright-locked gallant, a
cavalier of fortune, was the tenant of the other; and romances, those
prudent instructors, had taught his youth, that if damsels were shy, they
were yet neither void of interest nor of curiosity in their neighbour's
affairs.

Whilst Quentin was engaged in these sage reflections, a sort of attendant or chamberlain of the inn informed him that a cavalier desired
to speak with him below.

CHAPTER V

THE MAN-AT-ARMS

—Full of strange oaths, and bearded like the pard,
Seeking the bubble reputation
Even in the cannon's mouth.

As You Like It.

THE cavalier who awaited Quentin Durward's descent into the apartment
where he had breakfasted, was one of those of whom Louis XI. had long
since said, that they held in their hands the fortune of France, as to them
were entrusted the direct custody and protection of the royal person.

Charles the Sixth had instituted this celebrated body, the Archers, as
they were called, of the Scottish Body-Guard, with better reason than
can generally be alleged for establishing round the throne a guard of
foreign and mercenary troops. The divisions which tore from his side
more than half of France, together with the wavering and uncertain
faith of the nobility who yet acknowledged his cause, rendered it impoli-
tic and unsafe to commit his personal safety to their keeping. The Scottish nation was the hereditary enemy of the English, and the ancient,
and, as it seemed, the natural allies of France. They were poor, courageous, faithful—their ranks were sure to be supplied from the super-
abundant population of their own country, than which none in Europe
sent forth more or bolder adventurers. Their high claims of descent, too,
gave them a good title to approach the person of a monarch more closely
than other troops, while the comparative smallness of their numbers
prevented the possibility of their mutinying, and becoming masters
where they ought to be servants.

On the other hand, the French monarchs made it their policy to conciliate the affections of this select band of foreigners, by allowing them
honorary privileges and ample pay, which last most of them disposed of
with military profusion in supporting their supposed rank. Each of them
ranked as a gentleman in place and honour; and their near approach to
the King's person gave them dignity in their own eyes, as well as im-

portance in those of the nation of France. They were sumptuously armed, equipped and mounted; and each was entitled to allowance for a squire, a valet, a page, and two yeomen, one of whom was termed *coutelier*, from the large knife which he wore to despatch those whom in the *mêlée* his master had thrown to the ground. With these followers, and a corresponding equipage, an Archer of the Scottish Guard was a person of quality and importance; and vacancies being generally filled up by those who had been trained in the service as pages or valets, the cadets of the best Scottish families were often sent to serve under some friend and relation in those capacities, until a chance of preferment should occur.

The coutelier and his companion, not being noble or capable of this promotion, were recruited from persons of inferior quality; but as their pay and appointments were excellent, their masters were easily able to select from among their wandering countrymen the strongest and most courageous to wait upon them in these capacities.

Ludovic Lesly, or, as we shall more frequently call him, Le Balafré, by which name he was generally known in France, was upwards of six feet high, robust, strongly compacted in person, and hard-favoured in countenance, which latter attribute was much increased by a large and ghastly scar, which, beginning on his forehead, and narrowly missing his right eye, had laid bare the cheek-bone, and descending from thence almost to the tip of his ear, exhibiting a deep seam, which was some-times scarlet, sometimes purple, sometimes blue, and sometimes approaching to black; but always hideous, because at variance with the complexion of the face in whatever state it chanced to be, whether agitated or still, flushed with unusual passion, or in its ordinary state of weatherbeaten and sunburnt swarthiness.

His dress and arms were splendid. He wore his national bonnet, crested with a tuft of feathers, and with a Virgin Mary of massive silver for a brooch. These brooches had been presented to the Scottish Guard, in consequence of the King, in one of his fits of superstitious piety, having devoted the swords of his guard to the service of the Holy Virgin, and, as some say, carried the matter so far as to draw out a commission to Our Lady as their Captain-General. The Archer's gorget, arm-pieces, and gauntlets, were of the finest steel, curiously inlaid with silver, and his hauberk, or shirt of mail, was as clear and bright as the frostwork of a winter morning upon fern or brier. He wore a loose surcoat, or cassock, of rich blue velvet, open at the sides like that of a herald, with a large white St. Andrew's cross of embroidered silver bisecting it both before and behind—his knees and legs were protected by hose of mail and shoes of steel—a broad strong poniard (called the *Mercy of God*) hung by his right side—the baldric for his two-handed sword, richly embroidered, hung upon his left shoulder; but, for convenience, he at present carried in his hand that unwieldy weapon, which the rules of his service forbade him to lay aside.

Quentin Durward, though, like the Scottish youth of the period, he had been early taught to look upon arms and war, thought he had never seen a more martial-looking, or more completely equipped and accomplished man-at-arms, than now saluted him in the person of his mother's brother, called Ludovic with the Scar or Le Balafré; yet he could not but shrink a little from the grim expression of his countenance, while, with its rough moustaches, he brushed first the one and then the other cheek of his kinsman, welcomed his nephew to France, and, in the same breath, asked what news from Scotland.

"Little good tidings, dear uncle," replied young Durward; "but I am glad that you know me so readily."

"I would have known thee, boy, in the *landes* of Bordeaux, had I met thee marching there like a crane on a pair of stilts.[1] But sit thee down—sit thee down—if there is sorrow to hear of, we will have wine to make us bear it.—Ho! old Pinch-Measure, our good host, bring us of thy best, and that in an instant."

The well-known sound of the Scottish-French was as familiar in the taverns near Plessis, as that of the Swiss-French in the modern *gûinguettes* of Paris; and promptly—ay, with the promptitude of fear and precipitation, was it heard and obeyed. A flagon of champagne stood before them, of which the elder took a draught, while the nephew helped himself only to a moderate sip, to acknowledge his uncle's courtesy, saying, in excuse, that he had already drunk wine that morning.

"That had been a rare good apology in the mouth of thy sister, fair nephew," said Le Balafré; "you must fear the wine-pot less if you would wear beard on your face, and write yourself soldier. But come—come—unbuckle your Scottish mail-bag—give us the news of Glen-houlakin—How doth my sister?"

"Dead, fair uncle," answered Quentin sorrowfully.

"Dead!" echoed his uncle, with a tone rather marked by wonder than sympathy—"why, she was five years younger than I, and I was never better in my life. Dead! the thing is impossible. I have never had so much as a headache, unless after revelling out my two or three days' furlough with the brethren of the joyous science—and my poor sister is dead!—And your father, fair nephew, hath he married again?"

And ere the youth could reply, he read the answer in his surprise at the question, and said, "What! no?—I would have sworn that Allan Durward was no man to live without a wife. He loved to have his house in order—loved to look on a pretty woman too; and was somewhat strict in life withal—matrimony did all this for him. Now, I care little about these comforts; and I can look on a pretty woman without thinking on the sacrament of wedlock—I am scarce holy enough for that."

"Alas! dear uncle, my mother was left a widow a year since, when

---

[1] The crutches or stilts, which in Scotland are used to pass rivers. They are employed by the peasantry of the country near Bordeaux, to traverse those deserts of loose sand called Landes.

Glen-houlakin was harried by the Ogilvies. My father, and my two uncles, and my two elder brothers, and seven of my kinsmen, and the harper, and the tasker, and some six more of our people, were killed in defending the castle; and there is not a burning hearth or a standing stone in all Glen-houlakin."

"Cross of Saint Andrew!" said Le Balafré; "that is what I call an onslaught! Ay, these Ogilvies were ever but sorry neighbours to Glen-houlakin—an evil chance it was; but fate of war—fate of war.—When did this mishap befall, fair nephew?" With that he took a deep draught of wine, and shook his head with much solemnity, when his kinsman replied, that his family had been destroyed upon the festival of Saint Jude last by-past.

"Look ye there," said the soldier; "I said it was all chance—on that very day I and twenty of my comrades carried the Castle of Roche-noir by storm, from Amaury Bras-de-fer, a captain of free lances, whom you must have heard of. I killed him on his own threshold, and gained as much gold as made this fair chain, which was once twice as long as it now is—and that minds me to send part of it on an holy errand.—Here, Andrew—Andrew!"

Andrew, his yeoman, entered, dressed like the Archer himself in the general equipment, but without the armour for the limbs,—that of the body more coarsely manufactured—his cap without a plume, and his cassock made of serge, or ordinary cloth, instead of rich velvet. Un-twining his gold chain from his neck, Balafré twisted off, with his firm and strong-set teeth, about four inches from the one end of it, and said to his attendant, "Here, Andrew, carry this to my gossip, jolly Father Boniface, the monk of Saint Martin's—greet him well from me, by the same token that he could not say God save ye when we last parted at midnight—Tell my gossip that my brother and sister, and some others of my house, are all dead and gone, and I pray him to say masses for their souls as far as the value of these links will carry him, and to do on trust what else may be necessary to free them from Purgatory. And hark ye, as they were just-living people, and free from all heresy, it may be that they are well-nigh out of limbo already, so that a little matter may have them free of the fetlocks; and in that case, look ye, ye will say I desire to take out the balance of the gold in curses upon a genera-tion called the Ogilvies of Angus-shire, in what way soever the Church may best come at them. You understand all this, Andrew?"

The coutelier nodded.

"Then look that none of the links find their way to the wine-house ere the Monk touches them; for if it so chance, thou shalt taste of saddle-girth and stirrup-leather, till thou art as raw as Saint Bartholomew.—Yet hold, I see thy eye has fixed on the wine measure, and thou shalt not go without tasting."

So saying, he filled him a brimful cup, which the coutelier drank off, and retired to do his patron's commission.

"And now, fair nephew, let us hear what was your own fortune in this unhappy matter."

"I fought it out among those who were older and stouter than I was, till we were all brought down," said Durward, "and I received a cruel wound."

"Not a worse slash than I received ten years since myself," said Le Balafré.—"Look at this now, my fair nephew," tracing the dark crimson gash which was imprinted on his face—"An Ogilvy's sword never ploughed so deep a furrow."

"They ploughed deep enough," answered Quentin sadly; "but they were tired at last, and my mother's entreaties procured mercy for me, when I was found to retain some spark of life; but although a learned monk of Aberbrothick, who chanced to be our guest at the fatal time, and narrowly escaped being killed in the fray, was permitted to bind my wounds, and finally to remove me to a place of safety, it was only on promise, given both by my mother and him, that I should become a monk."

"A monk!" exclaimed the uncle—"Holy Saint Andrew! that is what never befell me. No one, from my childhood upwards, ever so much as dreamed of making me a monk—And yet I wonder when I think of it; for you will allow that, bating the reading and writing, which I could never learn, and the psalmody, which I could never endure, and the dress, which is that of a mad beggar—Our Lady forgive me!—[here he crossed himself]—and their fasts, which do not suit my appetite, I would have made every whit as good a monk as my little gossip at Saint Martin's yonder. But I know not why, none ever proposed the station to me.— Oh so, fair nephew, you were to be a monk, then—and wherefore, I pray you?"

"That my father's house might be ended, either in the cloister or in the tomb," answered Quentin, with deep feeling.

"I see," answered his uncle—"I comprehend. Cunning rogues—very cunning! They might have been cheated, though; for, look ye, fair nephew, I myself remember the canon Robersart who had taken the vows, and afterwards broke out of cloister, and became a captain of Free Companions. He had a mistress, the prettiest wench I ever saw, and three as beautiful children—There is no trusting monks, fair nephew, —no trusting them—they may become soldiers and fathers when you least expect it—but on with your tale."

"I have little more to tell," said Durward, "except that, considering my poor mother to be in some degree a pledge for me, I was induced to take upon me the dress of a novice, and conformed to the cloister rules, and even learned to read and write."

"To read and write!" exclaimed Le Balafré, who was one of that sort of people who think all knowledge is miraculous which chances to exceed their own—"To write, say'st thou, and to read! I cannot believe it— never Durward could write his name that ever I heard of, nor Lesly either. I can answer for one of them—I can no more write than I can fly. Now, in Saint Louis's name, how did they teach it you?"

"It was troublesome at first," said Durward, "but became more easy by use; and I was weak with my wounds and loss of blood, and desirous to gratify my preserver, Father Peter, and so I was the more easily kept to my task. But after several months' languishing, my good kind mother died, and as my health was now fully restored, I communicated to my benefactor, who was also Sub-Prior of the Convent, my reluctance to take the vows; and it was agreed between us, since my vocation lay not to the cloister, that I should be sent out into the world to seek my fortune, and that, to save the Sub-Prior from the anger of the Ogilvies, my departure should have the appearance of flight; and to colour it, I brought off the Abbot's hawk with me. But I was regularly dismissed, as will appear from the hand and seal of the Abbot himself."

"That is right—that is well," said his uncle. "Our King cares little what other theft thou mayst have made, but hath a horror at anything like a breach of the cloister. And, I warrant thee, thou hast no great treasure to bear thy charges?"

"Only a few pieces of silver," said the youth; "for to you, fair uncle, I must make a free confession."

"Alas!" replied Le Balafré, "that is hard. Now, though I am never a hoarder of my pay, because it doth ill to bear a charge about one in these perilous times, yet I always have (and I would advise you to follow my example) some odd gold chain, or bracelet, or carcanet, that serves for the ornament of my person, and can at need spare a superfluous link or two, or it may be a superfluous stone, for sale, that can answer any immediate purpose.—But you may ask, fair kinsman, how you are to come by such toys as this?"—(he shook his chain with complacent triumph)—"They hang not on every bush—they grow not in the fields like the daffodils, with whose stalks children make knights' collars. What then?—you may get such where I got this, in the service of the good King of France, where there is always wealth to be found, if a man has but the heart to seek it, at the risk of a little life or so."

"I understand," said Quentin, evading a decision to which he felt himself as yet scarcely competent, "that the Duke of Burgundy keeps a more noble state than the King of France, and that there is more honour to be won under his banners—that good blows are struck there, and deeds of arms done; while the most Christian King, they say, gains his victories by his ambassadors' tongues."

"You speak like a foolish boy, fair nephew," answered he with the Scar; "and yet, I bethink me, when I came hither I was nearly as simple: I could never think of a King but what I supposed him either sitting under the high deas, and feasting amid his higher vassals and Paladins, eating *blancmanger,* with a great gold crown upon his head, or else charging at the head of his troops like Charlemagne in the romaunts, or like Robert Bruce or William Wallace in our own true histories, such as

Barbour and the Minstrel. Hark in thine ear, man—it is all moonshine in
the water. Policy—policy does it all. But what is policy, you will say?
It is an art this French King of ours has found out, to fight with other
men's swords, and to wage his soldiers out of other men's purses. Ah! it
is the wisest Prince that ever put purple on his back—and yet he weareth
not much of that neither—I see him often go plainer than I would think
befitted me to do."

"But you meet not my exception, fair uncle," answered young Durward; "I would serve, since serve I must in a foreign land, somewhere
where a brave deed, were it my hap to do one, might work me a name."

"I understand you, my fair nephew," said the royal man-at-arms, "I
understand you passing well; but you are unripe in these matters. The
Duke of Burgundy is a hot-brained, impetuous, pudding-headed, iron-
ribbed dare-all. He charges at the head of his nobles and native knights,
his liegemen of Artois and Hainault; think you, if you were there, or if I
were there myself, that we could be much farther forward than the
Duke and all his brave nobles of his own land? If we were not up with
them, we had a chance to be turned on the Provost-Marshal's hands for
being slow in making to; if we were abreast of them, all would be called
well, and we might be thought to have deserved our pay; and grant that
I was a spear's-length or so in the front, which is both difficult and
dangerous in such a *mêlée* where all do their best, why, my lord duke
says, in his Flemish tongue, when he sees a good blow struck, 'Ha! *gut
getroffen!* a good lance—a brave Scot—give him a florin to drink our
health;' but neither rank, nor lands, nor treasures, come to the stranger
in such a service—all goes to the children of the soil."

"And where should it go, in Heaven's name, fair uncle?" demanded
young Durward.

"To him that protects the children of the soil," said Balafré, drawing
up his gigantic height. "Thus says King Louis:—'My good French peasant
—mine honest Jacques Bonhomme—get you to your tools, your plough
and your harrow, your pruning-knife and your hoe—here is my gallant
Scot that will fight for you, and you shall only have the trouble to pay
him—And you, my most serene duke, my illustrious count, and my most
mighty marquis, e'en rein up your fiery courage till it is wanted, for it is
apt to start out of the course, and to hurt its master; here are my companies of ordnance—here are my French Guards—here are, above all,
my Scottish Archers, and mine honest Ludovic with the Scar, who will
fight, as well or better than you, with all that undisciplined valour,
which, in your father's time, lost Cressy and Azincour.' Now, see you
not in which of these states a cavalier of fortune holds the highest rank,
and must come to the highest honour?"

"I think I understand you, fair uncle," answered the nephew; "but, in
my mind, honour cannot be won where there is no risk. Sure, this is—I
pray you pardon me—an easy and almost slothful life, to mount guard
round an elderly man whom no one thinks of harming, to spend summer-

day and winter-night up in yonder battlements, and shut up all the while in iron cages, for fear you should desert your posts—uncle, uncle, it is but the hawk upon his perch, who is never carried out to the fields!"

"Now by Saint Martin of Tours, the boy has some spirit! a right touch of the Lesly in him; much like myself, though always with a little more folly in it. Hark ye, youth—Long live the King of France!—scarce a day but there is some commission in hand, by which some of his followers may win both coin and credit. Think not that the bravest and most dangerous deeds are done by daylight. I could tell you of some, as scaling castles, making prisoners, and the like, where one who shall be nameless hath run higher risk, and gained greater favour, than any desperado in the train of desperate Charles of Burgundy. And if it please his Majesty to remain behind, and in the background, while such things are doing, he hath the more leisure of spirit to admire, and the more liberality of hand to reward the adventurers, whose dangers, perhaps, and whose feats of arms, he can better judge of than if he had personally shared them. Oh, 'tis a sagacious and most politic monarch!"

His nephew paused, and then said, in a low but impressive tone of voice, "The good Father Peter used often to teach me there might be much danger in deeds by which little glory was acquired. I need not say to you, fair uncle, that I do in course suppose that these secret commissions must needs be honourable."

"For whom or for what take you me, fair nephew?" said Balafré, somewhat sternly; "I have not been trained, indeed, in the cloister, neither can I write nor read. But I am your mother's brother; I am a loyal Lesly. Think you that I am like to recommend you to anything unworthy? The best knight in France, Du Guesclin himself, if he were alive again, might be proud to number my deeds among his achievements."

"I cannot doubt your warranty, fair uncle," said the youth; "you are the only adviser my mishap has left me. But is it true, as fame says, that this King keeps a meagre Court here at his Castle of Plessis? No repair of nobles or courtiers, none of his grand feudatories in attendance, none of the high officers of the crown; half solitary sports, shared only with the menials of his household; secret councils, to which only low and obscure men are invited; rank and nobility depressed, and men raised from the lowest origin to the kingly favour—all this seems unregulated, resembles not the manners of his father, the noble Charles, who tore from the fangs of the English lion this more than half conquered kingdom of France."

"You speak like a giddy child," said Le Balafré; "and even as a child, you harp over the same notes on a new string. Look you: if the King employs Oliver Dain, his barber, to do what Oliver can do better than any peer of them all, is not the kingdom the gainer? If he bids his stout Provost-Marshal, Tristan, arrest such or such a seditious burgher, take off such or such a turbulent noble, the deed is done and no more of it;

when, were the commission given to a duke or peer of France, he might perchance send the King back a defiance in exchange. If, again, the King pleases to give to plain Ludovic le Balafré a commission which he will execute, instead of employing the High Constable, who would perhaps betray it, doth it not show wisdom? Above all, doth not a monarch of such conditions best suit cavaliers of fortune, who must go where their services are most highly prized, and most frequently in demand?—no, no, child, I tell thee Louis knows how to choose his confidants, and what to charge them with; suiting, as they say, the burden to each man's back. He is not like the King of Castile, who choked of thirst because the great butler was not beside to hand his cup.—But hark to the bell of Saint Martin's! I must hasten back to the Castle.— Farewell—make much of yourself, and at eight to-morrow morning present yourself before the drawbridge, and ask the sentinel for me. Take heed you step not off the straight and beaten path in approaching the portal! There are such traps and snap-haunches as may cost you a limb, which you will sorely miss. You shall see the King, and learn to judge him for yourself—farewell."

So saying, Balafré hastily departed, forgetting, in his hurry, to pay for the wine he had called for, a shortness of memory incidental to persons of his description, and which his host, overawed, perhaps, by the nodding bonnet and ponderous two-handed sword, did not presume to use any efforts for correcting.

It might have been expected that, when left alone, Durward would have again betaken himself to his turret, in order to watch for the repetition of those delicious sounds which had soothed his morning reverie. But that was a chapter of romance, and his uncle's conversation had opened to him a page of the real history of life. It was no pleasing one, and for the present the recollections and reflections which it excited, were qualified to overpower other thoughts, and especially all of a light and soothing nature.

Quentin resorted to a solitary walk along the banks of the rapid Cher, having previously inquired of his landlord for one which he might traverse without fear of disagreeable interruption from snares and pitfalls, and there endeavoured to compose his turmoiled and scattered thoughts, and consider his future motions, upon which his meeting with his uncle had thrown some dubiety.

CHAPTER VI

THE BOHEMIANS

Sae rantingly, sae wantonly,
Sae dauntingly gaed he,
He play'd a spring and danced a round
Beneath the gallows-tree!

Old Song.

THE manner in which Quentin Durward had been educated, was not of a kind to soften the heart, or perhaps to improve the moral feeling. He, with the rest of his family, had been trained to the chase as an amusement, and taught to consider war as their only serious occupation, and that it was the great duty of their lives stubbornly to endure, and fiercely to retaliate, the attacks of their feudal enemies, by whom their race had been at last almost annihilated. And yet there mixed with these feuds a spirit of rude chivalry, and even courtesy, which softened their rigour; so that revenge, their only justice, was still prosecuted with some regard to humanity and generosity. The lessons of the worthy old monk, better attended to, perhaps, during a long illness and adversity, than they might have been in health and success, had given young Durward still farther insight into the duties of humanity towards others; and, considering the ignorance of the period, the general prejudices entertained in favour of a military life, and the manner in which he himself had been bred, the youth was disposed to feel more accurately the moral duties incumbent on his station than was usual at that time.

He reflected on his interview with his uncle with a sense of embarrassment and disappointment. His hopes had been high; for although intercourse by letters was out of the question, yet a pilgrim, or an adventurous trafficker, or a crippled soldier, sometimes brought Lesly's name to Glen-houlakin, and all united in praising his undaunted courage, and his success in many petty enterprises which his master had entrusted to him. Quentin's imagination had filled up the sketch in his own way, and assimilated his successful and adventurous uncle (whose exploits probably lost nothing in the telling) to some of the champions and knights-errant of whom minstrels sang, and who won crowns and kings' daughters, by dint of sword and lance. He was now compelled to rank his kinsman greatly lower in the scale of chivalry; but blinded by the high respect paid to parents, and those who approach that character—moved by every early prejudice in his favour—inexperienced besides, and passionately attached to his mother's memory, he saw not, in the only brother of that dear relation, the character he truly held, which was that of an ordinary mercenary soldier, neither much worse nor greatly better than many of the same profession whose presence added to the distracted state of France.

Without being wantonly cruel, Le Balafré was, from habit, indifferent to human life and human suffering; he was profoundly ignorant, greedy of booty, unscrupulous how he acquired it, and profuse in expending it on the gratification of his passions. The habit of attending exclusively to his own wants and interests, had converted him into one of the most selfish animals in the world; so that he was seldom able, as the reader may have remarked, to proceed far in any subject without considering how it applied to himself, or, as it is called, making the case his own, though not upon feelings connected with the golden rule, but such as were very different. To this must be added, that the narrow round of his duties and his pleasures had gradually circumscribed his thoughts, hopes, and wishes, and quenched in a great measure the wild spirit of honour, and desire of distinction in arms, by which his youth had been once animated. Balafré was, in short, a keen soldier, hardened, selfish, and narrow-minded; active and bold in the discharge of his duty, but acknowledging few objects beyond it, except the formal observance of a careless devotion, relieved by an occasional debauch with brother Boniface, his comrade and confessor. Had his genius been of a more extended character he would probably have been promoted to some important command, for the King, who knew every soldier of his bodyguard personally, reposed much confidence in Balafré's courage and fidelity; and, besides, the Scot had either wisdom or cunning enough perfectly to understand, and ably to humour, the peculiarities of that sovereign. Still, however, his capacity was too much limited to admit of his rising to higher rank, and though smiled on and favoured by Louis on many occasions, Balafré continued a mere Lifeguardsman, or Scottish Archer.

Without seeing the full scope of his uncle's character, Quentin felt shocked at his indifference to the disastrous extirpation of his brother-in-law's whole family, and could not help being surprised, moreover, that so near a relative had not offered him the assistance of his purse, which, but for the generosity of Maitre Pierre, he would have been under the necessity of directly craving from him. He wronged his uncle, however, in supposing that this want of attention to his probable necessities was owing to avarice. Not precisely needing money himself at that moment, it had not occurred to Balafré that his nephew might be in exigencies; otherwise, he held a near kinsman so much a part of himself, that he would have provided for the weal of the living nephew, as he endeavoured to do for that of his deceased sister and her husband. But whatever was the motive, the neglect was very unsatisfactory to young Durward, and he wished more than once he had taken service with the Duke of Burgundy before he quarrelled with his forester. "Whatever had then become of me," he thought to himself, "I should always have been able to keep up my spirits with the reflection, that I had, in case of the worst, a stout back-friend in this uncle of mine. But now I have seen him, and, woe worth him, there has been more help in a mere mechanical stranger, than I have found in my own mother's brother, my countryman, and a cavalier! One would think the slash, that has carved all comeliness out of his face, had let at the same time every drop of gentle blood out of his body."

Durward now regretted he had not had an opportunity to mention Maitre Pierre to Le Balafré, in the hope of obtaining some farther account of that personage; but his uncle's questions had followed fast on each other, and the summons of the great bell of Saint Martin of Tours had broken off their conference rather suddenly. That old man, he thought to himself, was crabbed and dogged in appearance, sharp and scornful in language, but generous and liberal in his actions; and such a stranger is worth a cold kinsman—"What says our old Scotch proverb? —'Better kind fremit, than fremit kindred.'[1] I will find out that man, which, methinks, should be no difficult task, since he is so wealthy as mine host bespeaks him. He will give me good advice for my governance, at least; and if he goes to strange countries, as many such do, I know not but his may be as adventurous a service as that of those Guards of Louis."

As Quentin framed this thought, a whisper from those recesses of the heart in which lies much that the owner does not know of, or will not acknowledge willingly, suggested that, perchance, the lady of the turret, she of the veil and lute, might share that adventurous journey.

As the Scottish youth made these reflections, he met two grave-looking men, apparently citizens of Tours, whom, doffing his cap with the reverence due from youth to age, he respectfully asked to direct him to the house of Maitre Pierre.

"The house of whom, my fair son?" said one of the passengers.

"Of Maitre Pierre, the great silk merchant, who planted all the mulberry-trees in the park yonder," said Durward.

"Young man," said one of them who was nearest to him, "you have taken up an idle trade a little too early."

"And have chosen wrong subjects to practise your fooleries upon," said the farther one, still more gruffly. "The Syndic of Tours is not accustomed to be thus talked to by strolling jesters from foreign parts."

Quentin was so much surprised by the causeless offence which these two decent-looking persons had taken at a very simple and civil question, that he forgot to be angry at the rudeness of their reply, and stood staring after them as they walked on with amended pace, often looking back at him, as if they were desirous to get as soon as possible out of his reach.

He next met a party of vine-dressers, and addressed to them the same question; and, in reply, they demanded to know whether he wanted Maitre Pierre, the schoolmaster? or Maitre Pierre, the carpenter? or Maitre Pierre, the beadle? or half-a-dozen of Maitre Pierres besides. When none of these corresponded with the description of the person after

---

[1] *Better kind strangers than estranged kindred.* The motto is engraved on a dirk, belonging to a person who had but too much reason to choose such a device. It was left by him to my father, and is connected with a strange course of adventures, which may one day be told. The weapon is now in my possession.

whom he inquired, the peasants accused him of jesting with them impertinently, and threatened to fall upon him and beat him, in guerdon of his
raillery. The oldest among them, who had some influence over the rest,
prevailed on them to desist from violence.

"You see by his speech and his fool's cap," said he, "that he is one
of the foreign mountebanks who are come into the country, and whom
some call magicians and soothsayers, and some jugglers, and the like,
and there is no knowing what tricks they have amongst them. I have
heard of such a one paying a liard to eat his bellyful of grapes in a poor
man's vineyard; and he ate as many as would have loaded a wain, and
never undid a button of his jerkin—and so let him pass quietly, and
keep his way, as we will keep ours.—And you, friend, if you would shun
worse, walk quietly on, in the name of God, our Lady of Marmoutier,
and Saint Martin of Tours, and trouble us no more about your Maitre
Pierre, which may be another name for the devil, for aught we know."

The Scot, finding himself much the weaker party, judged it his wisest
course to walk on without reply; but the peasants, who at first shrank
from him in horror, at his supposed talents for sorcery and grape-
devouring, took heart of grace as he got to a distance, and having uttered
a few cries and curses, finally gave them emphasis with a shower of
stones, although at such a distance as to do little or no harm to the
object of their displeasure. Quentin, as he pursued his walk, began to
think, in his turn, either that he himself lay under a spell, or that the
people of Touraine were the most stupid, brutal, and inhospitable of
the French peasants. The next incident which came under his observation did not tend to diminish his opinion.

On a slight eminence, rising above the rapid and beautiful Cher, in
the direct line of his path, two or three large chestnut trees were so
happily placed as to form a distinguished and remarkable group; and
beside them stood three or four peasants, motionless, with their eyes
turned upwards, and fixed, apparently, upon some object amongst the
branches of the tree next to them. The meditations of youth are seldom
so profound as not to yield to the slightest impulse of curiosity, as easily
as the lightest pebble, dropped casually from the hand, breaks the
surface of a limpid pool. Quentin hastened his pace, and ran lightly up
the rising ground, time enough to witness the ghastly spectacle which
attracted the notice of these gazers—which was nothing less than the
body of a man, convulsed by the last agony, suspended on one of the
branches.

"Why do you not cut him down?" said the young Scot, whose hand
was as ready to assist affliction, as to maintain his own honour when he
deemed it assailed.

One of the peasants, turning on him an eye from which fear had
banished all expression but its own, and a face as pale as clay, pointed
to a mark cut upon the bark of the tree, having the same rude resemblance
to a *fleur-de-lys* which certain talismanic scratches, well known to our

revenue officers, bear to a *broad arrow*. Neither understanding nor heeding to the import of this symbol, young Durward sprung lightly as the
ounce up into the tree, drew from his pouch that most necessary implement of a Highlander or woodsman, the trusty *skene dhu*,[1] and, calling
to those below to receive the body on their hands, cut the rope asunder
in less than a minute after he had perceived the exigency.

But his humanity was ill seconded by the bystanders. So far from
rendering Durward any assistance, they seemed terrified at the audacity
of his action, and took to flight with one consent, as if they feared their
merely looking on might have been construed into accession to his daring
deed. The body, unsupported from beneath, fell heavily to earth, in
such a manner, that Quentin, who presently afterwards jumped down,
had the mortification to see that the last sparks of life were extinguished.
He gave not up his charitable purpose, however, without farther efforts.
He freed the wretched man's neck from the fatal noose, undid the
doublet, threw water on the face, and practised the other ordinary
remedies resorted to for recalling suspended animation.

While he was thus humanely engaged, a wild clamour of tongues,
speaking a language which he knew not, arose around him; and he had
scarcely time to observe that he was surrounded by several men and
women of a singular and foreign appearance, when he found himself
roughly seized by both arms, while a naked knife, at the same moment,
was offered to his throat.

"Pale slave of Eblis!" said a man, in imperfect French, "are you robbing him you have murdered?—But we have you—and you shall abye
it."

There were knives drawn on every side of him as these words were
spoken, and the grim and distorted countenances which glared on him,
were like those of wolves rushing on their prey.

Still the young Scot's courage and presence of mind bore him out.
"What mean ye, my masters?" he said; "if that be your friend's body,
I have just now cut him down, in pure charity, and you will do better to
try to recover his life, than to misuse an innocent stranger to whom he
owes his chance of escape."

The women had by this time taken possession of the dead body, and
continued the attempts to recover animation which Durward had been
making use of, though with the like bad success; so that, desisting from
their fruitless efforts, they seemed to abandon themselves to all the
Oriental expressions of grief; the women making a piteous wailing, and
tearing their long black hair, while the men seemed to rend their garments, and to sprinkle dust upon their heads. They gradually became so
much engaged in their mourning rites, that they bestowed no longer any
attention on Durward, of whose innocence they were probably satisfied

---

[1] Black knife; a species of knife without a clasp or hinge, formerly much used by
the Highlanders, who seldom travelled without such an ugly weapon, though it is
now rarely used.

from circumstances. It would certainly have been his wisest plan to have left these wild people to their own courses, but he had been bred in almost reckless contempt of danger, and felt all the eagerness of youthful curiosity.

The singular assemblage, both male and female, wore turbans and caps, more similar, in general appearance, to his own bonnet, than to the hats commonly worn in France. Several of the men had curled black beards, and the complexion of all was nearly as dark as that of Africans. One or two, who seemed their chiefs, had some tawdry ornaments of silver about their necks and in their ears, and wore showy scarfs of yellow, or scarlet, or light green; but their legs and arms were bare, and the whole troop seemed wretched and squalid in appearance. There were no weapons among them that Durward saw, except the long knives with which they had lately menaced him, and one short crooked sabre, or Moorish sword, which was worn by an active-looking young man, who often laid his hand upon the hilt, while he surpassed the rest of the party in his extravagant expressions of grief, and seemed to mingle with them threats of vengeance.

The disordered and yelling group were so different in appearance from any beings whom Quentin had yet seen, that he was on the point of concluding them to be a party of Saracens, of those "heathen hounds," who were the opponents of gentle knights and Christian monarchs, in all the romances which he had heard or read, and was about to withdraw himself from a neighbourhood so perilous, when a galloping of horse was heard, and the supposed Saracens, who had raised by this time the body of their comrade upon their shoulders, were at once charged by a party of French soldiers.

This sudden apparition changed the measured wailing of the mourners into regular shrieks of terror. The body was thrown to the ground in an instant, and those who were around it showed the utmost and most dexterous activity in escaping, under the bellies as it were of the horses, from the point of the lances which were levelled at them, with exclamations of "Down with the accursed heathen thieves—take and kill—bind them like beasts—spear them like wolves!"

These cries were accompanied with corresponding acts of violence; but such was the alertness of the fugitives, the ground being rendered unfavourable to the horsemen by thickets and bushes, that only two were struck down and made prisoners, one of whom was the young fellow with the sword, who had previously offered some resistance. Quentin, whom fortune seemed at this period to have chosen for the butt of her shafts, was at the same time seized by the soldiers, and his arms, in spite of his remonstrances, bound down with a cord; those who apprehended him showing a readiness and despatch in the operation, which proved them to be no novices in matters of police.

Looking anxiously to the leader of the horsemen, from whom he hoped to obtain liberty, Quentin knew not exactly whether to be pleased or alarmed upon recognising in him the down-looking and silent companion of Maitre Pierre. True, whatever crime these strangers might be accused of, this officer might know, from the history of the morning, that he, Durward, had no connection with them whatever; but it was a more difficult question, whether this sullen man would be either a favourable judge or a willing witness in his behalf, and he felt doubtful whether he would mend his condition by making any direct application to him.

But there was little leisure for hesitation. "Trois-Eschelles and Petit-André," said the down-looking officer to two of his band, "these same trees stand here quite convenient. I will teach these misbelieving, thieving sorcerers to interfere with the King's justice, when it has visited any of their accursed race. Dismount, my children, and do your office briskly."

Trois-Eschelles and Petit-André were in an instant on foot, and Quentin observed that they had each, at the crupper and pommel of his saddle, a coil or two of ropes, which they hastily undid, and showed that, in fact, each coil formed a halter, with the fatal noose adjusted, ready for execution. The blood ran cold in Quentin's veins, when he saw three cords selected, and perceived that it was proposed to put one around his own neck. He called on the officer loudly, reminded him of their meeting that morning, claimed the right of a free-born Scotsman, in a friendly and allied country, and denied any knowledge of the persons along with whom he was seized, or of their misdeeds.

The officer whom Durward thus addressed, scarce deigned to look at him while he was speaking, and took no notice whatever of the claim he preferred to prior acquaintance. He barely turned to one or two of the peasants who were now come forward, either to volunteer their evidence against the prisoners, or out of curiosity, and said gruffly, "Was yonder young fellow with the vagabonds?"

"That he was, sir, and it please your noble Provostship," answered one of the clowns; "he was the very first blasphemously to cut down the rascal whom his Majesty's justice most deservedly hung up, as we told your worship."

"I'll swear by God, and Saint Martin of Tours, to have seen him with their gang," said another, "when they pillaged our *métairie*."

"Nay, but, father," said a boy, "yonder heathen was black, and this youth is fair; yonder one had short curled hair, and this hath long fair locks."

"Ay, child," said the peasant, "and perhaps you will say yonder one had a green coat and this a grey jerkin. But his worship, the Provost, knows that they can change their complexions as easily as their jerkins, so that I am still minded he was the same."

"It is enough that you have seen him intermeddle with the course of the King's justice, by attempting to recover an executed traitor," said the officer.—"Trois-Eschelles and Petit-André, despatch."

"Stay, signior officer!" exclaimed the youth, in mortal agony—"hear me speak—let me not die guiltlessly—my blood will be required of you

by my countrymen in this world, and by Heaven's justice in that which
is to follow."

"I will answer for my actions in both," said the Provost, coldly; and
made a sign with his left hand to the executioners; then, with a smile
of triumphant malice, touched with his forefinger his right arm, which
hung suspended in a scarf, disabled probably by the blow which Durward
had dealt him that morning.

"Miserable, vindictive wretch!" answered Quentin, persuaded by that
action that private revenge was the sole motive of this man's rigour, and
that no mercy whatever was to be expected from him.

"The poor youth raves," said the functionary; "speak a word of comfort to him ere he make his transit, Trois-Eschelles; thou art a comfortable man in such cases, when a confessor is not to be had. Give him
one minute of ghostly advice, and despatch matters in the next. I must
proceed on the rounds.—Soldiers, follow me!"

The Provost rode on, followed by his guard, excepting two or three who
were left to assist in the execution. The unhappy youth cast after him
an eye almost darkened by despair, and thought he heard, in every tramp
of his horse's retreating hoofs, the last slight chance of his safety vanish.
He looked around him in agony, and was surprised, even in that moment,
to see the stoical indifference of his fellow-prisoners. They had previously
testified every sign of fear, and made every effort to escape; but now,
when secured, and destined apparently to inevitable death, they awaited
its arrival with the utmost composure. The scene of fate before them
gave, perhaps, a more yellow tinge to their swarthy cheeks; but it neither
agitated their features, nor quenched the stubborn haughtiness of their
eye. They seemed like foxes, which, after all their wiles and artful attempts at escape are exhausted, die with a silent and sullen fortitude,
which wolves and bears, the fiercer objects of the chase, do not exhibit.

They were undaunted by the conduct of the fatal executioners, who
went about their work with more deliberation than their master had
recommended, and which probably arose from their having acquired by
habit a kind of pleasure in the discharge of their horrid office. We pause
an instant to describe them, because, under a tyranny, whether despotic
or popular, the character of the hangman becomes a subject of great
importance.

These functionaries were essentially different in their appearance and
manners. Louis used to call them Democritus and Heraclitus, and their
master, the Provost, termed them, *Jean-qui-pleure* and *Jean-qui-rit*.

Trois-Eschelles was a tall, thin, ghastly man, with a peculiar gravity
of visage, and a large rosary round his neck, the use of which he was
accustomed piously to offer to those sufferers on whom he did his duty.
He had one or two Latin texts continually in his mouth on the nothing-
ness and vanity of human life; and, had it been regular to have enjoyed
such a plurality, he might have held the office of confessor to the jail
in commendam with that of executioner. Petit-André, on the contrary,

was a joyous-looking, round, active, little fellow, who rolled about in execution of his duty as if it were the most diverting occupation in the world. He seemed to have a sort of fond affection for his victims, and always spoke of them in kindly and affectionate terms. They were his poor honest fellows, his pretty dears, his gossips, his good old fathers, as their age or sex might be; and as Trois-Eschelles endeavoured to inspire them with a philosophical or religious regard to futurity, Petit-André seldom failed to refresh them with a jest or two, as if to induce them to pass from life as something that was ludicrous, contemptible, and not worthy of serious consideration.

I cannot tell why or wherefore it was, but these two excellent persons, notwithstanding the variety of their talents, and the rare occurrence of such among persons of their profession, were both more utterly detested than, perhaps, any creatures of their kind, whether before or since; and the only doubt of those who knew aught of them was, whether the grave and pathetic Trois-Eschelles, or the frisky, comic, alert Petit-André, was the object of the greatest fear or of the deepest execration. It is certain they bore the palm in both particulars over every hangman in France, unless it were perhaps their master, Tristan l'Hermite, the renowned Provost-Marshal, or *his* master, Louis XI.[1]

It must not be supposed that these reflections were of Quentin Durward's making. Life, death, time, and eternity, were swimming before his eyes—a stunning and overwhelming prospect, from which human nature recoiled in its weakness, though human pride would fain have borne up. He addressed himself to the God of his fathers; and when he did so, the little rude and unroofed chapel, which now held almost all his race but himself, rushed on his recollection. "Our feudal enemies gave my kindred graves in our own land," he thought, "but I must feed the ravens and kites of a foreign land, like an excommunicated felon!" The tears gushed involuntarily from his eyes. Trois-Eschelles, touching one shoulder, gravely congratulated him on his heavenly disposition for death, and pathetically exclaiming, *Beati qui in Domino moriuntur,* remarked the soul was happy that left the body while the tear was in the eye. Petit-André, slapping the other shoulder, called out, "Courage, my fair son! since you must begin the dance, let the ball open gaily, for all the rebecs are in tune," twitching the halter at the same time, to give point to his joke. As the youth turned his dismayed looks, first on one and then on the other, they made their meaning plainer by gently urging him forward to the fatal tree, and bidding him be of good courage, for it would be over in a moment.

---

[1] One of these two persons, I learned from the Chronique de Jean de Troyes, but too late to avail myself of the information, might with more accuracy have been called Petit-Jean than Petit-André. This was actually the name of the son of Henry de Cousin, master executioner of the High Court of Justice. The Constable Saint Paul was executed by him with such dexterity, that the head, when struck off, struck the ground at the same time with the body. This was in 1475.

In this fatal predicament, the youth cast a distracted look around him. "Is there any good Christian who hears me," he said, "that will tell Ludovic Lesly of the Scottish Guard, called in this country Le Balafré, that his nephew is here basely murdered?"

The words were spoken in good time, for an Archer of the Scottish Guard, attracted by the preparations for the execution, was standing by, with one or two other chance-passengers, to witness what was passing.

"Take heed what you do," he said to the executioners; "if this young man be of Scottish birth, I will not permit him to have foul play."

"Heaven forbid, Sir Cavalier," said Trois-Eschelles; "but we must obey our orders," drawing Durward forward by one arm.

"The shortest play is ever the fairest," said Petit-André, pulling him onward by the other.

But Quentin had heard words of comfort, and, exerting his strength, he suddenly shook off both the finishers of the law, and, with his arms still bound, ran to the Scottish Archer. "Stand by me, countryman," he said in his own language, "for the love of Scotland and Saint Andrew! I am innocent—I am your own native landsman. Stand by me, as you shall answer at the last day!"

"By Saint Andrew! they shall make at you through me," said the Archer, and unsheathed his sword.

"Cut my bonds, countryman," said Quentin, "and I will do something for myself."

This was done with a touch of the Archer's weapon; and the liberated captive, springing suddenly on one of the Provost's guard, wrested from him a halberd with which he was armed; "And now," he said, "come on, if you dare!"

The two officers whispered together.

"Ride thou after the Provost-Marshal," said Trois-Eschelles, "and I will detain them here, if I can.—Soldiers of the Provost's guard, stand to your arms."

Petit-André mounted his horse and left the field, and the other Marshals-men in attendance drew together so hastily at the command of Trois-Eschelles, that they suffered the other two prisoners to make their escape during the confusion. Perhaps they were not very anxious to detain them; for they had of late been sated with the blood of such wretches, and, like other ferocious animals, were, through long slaughter, become tired of carnage. But the pretext was, that they thought themselves immediately called upon to attend to the safety of Trois-Eschelles; for there was a jealousy, which occasionally led to open quarrels, betwixt the Scottish Archers and the Marshal-guards, who executed the order of their Provost.

"We are strong enough to beat the proud Scots twice over, if it be your pleasure," said one of these soldiers to Trois-Eschelles.

But that cautious official made a sign to him to remain quiet, and addressed the Scottish Archer with great civility. "Surely, sir, this is a great insult to the Provost-Marshal, that you should presume to interfeie with the course of the King's justice, duly and lawfully committed to his charge; and it is no act of justice to me, who am in lawful possession of my criminal. Neither is it a well-meant kindness to the youth himself, seeing that fifty opportunities of hanging him may occur, without his being found in so happy a state of preparation as he was before your ill-advised interference."

"If my young countryman," said the Scot, smiling, "be of opinion I have done him an injury, I will return him to your charge without a word more dispute."

"No, no!—for the love of Heaven, no!" exclaimed Quentin. "I would rather you swept my head off with your long sword—it would better become my birth, than to die by the hands of such a foul churl."

"Hear how he revileth!" said the finisher of the law. "Alas! how soon our best resolutions pass away!—he was in a blessed frame for departure but now, and in two minutes he has become a contemner of authorities."

"Tell me at once," said the Archer, "what has this young man done?"

"Interfered," answered Trois-Eschelles, with some earnestness, "to take down the dead body of ⸱⸱ criminal, when the *fleur-de-lys* was marked on the tree where he hung with my own proper hand."

"How is this, young man?" said the Archer; "how came you to have committed such an offence?"

"As I desire your protection," answered Durward, "I will tell you the truth as if I were at confession. I saw a man struggling on the tree, and I went to cut him down out of mere humanity. I thought neither of *fleur-de-lys* nor of clove-gilliflower, and had no more idea of offending the King of France than our Father the Pope."

"What a murrain had you to do with the dead body, then?" said the Archer. "You'll see them hanging, in the rear of this gentleman, like grapes on every tree, and you will have enough to do in this country if you go a-gleaning after the hangman. However, I will not quit a countryman's cause if I can help it.—Hark ye, Master Marshals-man, you see this is entirely a mistake. You should have some compassion on so young a traveller. In our country at home he has not been accustomed to see such active proceedings as yours and your master's."

"Not for want of need of them, Signior Archer," said Petit-André, who returned at this moment. "Stand fast, Trois-Eschelles, for here comes the Provost-Marshal; we shall presently see how he will relish having his work taken out of his hand before it is finished."

"And in good time," said the Archer, "here come some of my comrades."

Accordingly, as the Provost Tristan rode up with his patrol on one side of the little hill which was the scene of the altercation, four or five Scottish Archers came as hastily up on the other, and at their head the Balafré himself.

Upon this urgency, Lesly showed none of that indifference towards his nephew of which Quentin had in his heart accused him; for he no sooner saw his comrade and Durward standing upon their defence, than he exclaimed, "Cunningham, I thank thee.—Gentlemen—comrades, lend me your aid—It is a young Scottish gentleman—my nephew—Lindesay —Guthrie—Tyrie, draw, and strike in!"

There was now every prospect of a desperate scuffle between the parties, who were not so disproportioned in numbers, but that the better arms of the Scottish cavaliers gave them an equal chance of victory. But the Provost-Marshal, either doubting the issue of the conflict, or aware that it would be disagreeable to the King, made a sign to his followers to forbear from violence, while he demanded of Balafré, who now put himself forward as the head of the other party, "What he, a cavalier of the King's Body Guard, purposed by opposing the execution of a criminal?"

"I deny that I do so," answered the Balafré. "Saint Martin! there is, I think, some difference between the execution of a criminal, and the slaughter of my own nephew?"

"Your nephew may be a criminal as well as another, Signior," said the Provost-Marshal; "and every stranger in France is amenable to the laws of France."

"Yes, but we have privileges, we Scottish Archers," said Balafré; "have we not, comrades?"

"Yes, yes," they all exclaimed together. "Privileges—privileges! Long live King Louis—long live the bold Balafré—long live the Scottish Guard—and death to all who would infringe our privileges!"

"Take reason with you, gentlemen cavaliers," said the Provost-Marshal; "consider my commission."

"We will have no reason at your hand," said Cunningham; "our own officers shall do us reason. We will be judged by the King's grace, or by our own Captain, now that the Lord High Constable is not in presence."

"And we will be hanged by none," said Lindesay, "but Sandie Wilson, the auld Marshals-man of our ain body."

"It would be a positive cheating of Sandie, who is as honest a man as ever tied noose upon hemp, did we give way to any other proceeding," said the Balafré. "Were I to be hanged myself, no other should tie tippet about my craig."

"But hear ye," said the Provost-Marshal, "this young fellow belongs not to you, and cannot share what you call your privileges."

"What we *call* our privileges, all shall admit to be such," said Cunningham.

"We will not hear them questioned!" was the universal cry of the Archers.

"Ye are mad, my masters," said Tristan l'Hermite—"No one disputes your privileges; but this youth is not one of you."

"He is *my* nephew," said the Balafré, with a triumphant air.

"But no Archer of the Guard, I think," retorted Tristan l'Hermite.

The Archers looked at each other in some uncertainty.

"Stand to it yet, comrade," whispered Cunningham to Balafré—"Say he is engaged with us."

"Saint Martin! you say well, fair countryman," answered Lesly; and, raising his voice, swore that he had that day enrolled his kinsman as one of his own retinue.

This declaration was a decisive argument.

"It is well, gentlemen," said the Provost Tristan, who was aware of the King's nervous apprehension of disaffection creeping in among his Guards.—"You know, as you say, your privileges, and it is not my duty to have brawls with the King's Guards, if it is to be avoided. But I will report this matter for the King's own decision; and I would have you to be aware, that, in doing so, I act more mildly than perhaps my duty warrants me."

So saying, he put his troop into motion, while the Archers, remaining on the spot, held a hasty consultation what was next to be done.

"We must report the matter to Lord Crawford, our Captain in the first place, and have the young fellow's name put on the roll."

"But, gentlemen, and my worthy friends and preservers," said Quentin, with some hesitation, "I have not yet determined whether to take service with you or no."

"Then settle in your own mind," said his uncle, "whether you choose to do so, or be hanged—for I promise you, that, nephew of mine as you are, I see no other chance of your 'scaping the gallows."

This was an unanswerable argument, and reduced Quentin at once to acquiesce in what he might have otherwise considered as no very agreeable proposal; but the recent escape from the halter, which had been actually around his neck, would probably have reconciled him to a worse alternative than was proposed.

"He must go home with us to our caserne," said Cunningham; "there is no safety for him out of our bounds, whilst these man-hunters are prowling about."

"May I not then abide for this night at the hostelry where I breakfasted, fair uncle?" said the youth—thinking, perhaps, like many a new recruit, that even a single night of freedom was something gained.

"Yes, fair nephew," answered his uncle ironically, "that we may have the pleasure of fishing you out of some canal or moat, or perhaps out of a loop of the Loire, knit up in a sack, for the greater convenience of swimming—for that is like to be the end on't.—The Provost-Marshal smiled on us when we parted," continued he, addressing Cunningham, "and that is a sign his thoughts were dangerous."

"I care not for his danger," said Cunningham; "such game as we are beyond his bird-bolts. But I would have thee tell the whole to the Devil's Oliver, who is always a good friend to the Scottish Guard, and will see Father Louis before the Provost can, for he is to shave him to-morrow."

"But hark you," said Balafré, "it is ill going to Oliver empty-handed, and I am as bare as the birch in December."

"So are we all," said Cunningham—"Oliver must not scrupe to take our Scottish words for once. We will make up something handsome among us against the next pay-day; and if *he* expects to share, let me tell you, the pay-day will come about all the sooner."

"And now for the Château," said Balafré; "and my nephew shall tell us by the way how he brought the Provost-Marshal on his shoulders, that we may know how to frame our report both to Crawford and Oliver." [1]

CHAPTER VII

THE ENROLMENT

Justice of Peace.—Here, hand me down the Statute—read the articles—
Swear, kiss the book—subscribe, and be a hero;
Drawing a portion from the public stock
For deeds of valour to be done hereafter—
Sixpence per day, subsistence and arrears.
                                        The Recruiting Officer.

An attendant upon the Archers having been dismounted, Quentin Durward was accommodated with his horse, and, in company of his martial countrymen, rode at a round pace towards the Castle of Plessis, about to become, although on his own part involuntarily, an inhabitant of that gloomy fortress, the outside of which had, that morning, struck him with so much surprise.

In the meanwhile, in answer to his uncle's repeated interrogations, he gave him an exact account of the accident which had that morning brought him into so much danger. Although he himself saw nothing in his narrative save what was affecting, he found it was received with much laughter by his escort.

"And yet it is no good jest either," said his uncle, "for what, in the devil's name, could lead the senseless boy to meddle with the body of a cursed misbelieving Jewish Moorish pagan?"

"Had he quarrelled with the Marshals-men about a pretty wench, as Michael of Moffat did, there had been more sense in it," said Cunningham.

"But I think it touches our honour, that Tristan and his people pretend to confound our Scottish bonnets with these pilfering vagabonds' *tocques and turbands*, as they call them," said Lindesay—"If they have not eyes to see the difference, they must be taught by rule of hand. But it's my belief, Tristan but pretends to mistake, that he may snap up the kindly Scots that come over to see their kinsfolks."

"May I ask, kinsman," said Quentin, "what sort of people these are of whom you speak?"

"In troth you may ask," said his uncle, "but I know not, fair nephew

[1] Note I.—Gipsies or Bohemians.

who is able to answer you. Not I, I am sure, although I know, it may be, as much as other people; but they have appeared in this land within a year or two, just as a flight of locusts might do." [1]

"Ay," said Lindesay, "and Jacques Bonhomme (that is our name for the peasant, young man,—you will learn our way of talk in time),—honest Jacques, I say, cares little what wind either brings them or the locusts, so he but knows any gale that would carry them away again."

"Do they do so much evil?" asked the young man.

"Evil?—why, boy, they are heathens, or Jews, or Mahommedans at the least, and neither worship Our Lady nor the Saints"—(crossing himself)—"and steal what they can lay hands on, and sing, and tell fortunes," added Cunningham.

"And they say there are some goodly wenches amongst these women," said Guthrie; "but Cunningham knows that best."

'How, brother!" said Cunningham; "I trust ye mean me no reproach?"

"I am sure I said ye none," answered Guthrie.

"I will be judged by the company," said Cunningham.—"Ye said as much as that I, a Scottish gentleman, and living within pale of holy Church, had a fair friend among these off-scourings of Heathenesse."

"Nay, nay," said Balafré, "he did but jest—We will have no quarrels among comrades."

"We must have no such jesting then," said Cunningham, murmuring as if he had been speaking to his own beard.

"Be there such vagabonds in other lands than France?" said Lindesay.

"Ay, in good sooth, are there—tribes of them have appeared in Germany, and in Spain, and in England," answered Balafré. "By the blessing of good Saint Andrew, Scotland is free of them yet."

"Scotland," said Cunningham, "is too cold a country for locusts, and too poor a country for thieves."

"Or perhaps John Highlander will suffer no thieves to thrive there but his own," said Guthrie.

"I let you all know," said Balafré, "that I come from the braes of Angus, and have gentle Highland kin in Glen-Isla, and I will not have the Highlanders slandered."

"You will not deny that they are cattle-lifters?" said Guthrie.

"To drive a spreagh, or so, is no thievery," said Balafré, "and that I will maintain when and how you dare."

"For shame, comrade," said Cunningham, "who quarrels now?—the young man should not see such mad misconstruction.—Come, here we are at the Château. I will bestow a runlet of wine to have a rouse in friendship, and drink to Scotland, Highland and Lowland both, if you will meet me at dinner at my quarters."

"Agreed—agreed," said Balafré, "and I will bestow another, to wash

[1] See Note I. on the Gipsies or Bohemians.

away unkindness, and to drink a health to my nephew on his first entrance to our corps."

At their approach, the wicket was opened, and the drawbridge fell. One by one they entered; but when Quentin appeared, the sentinels crossed their pikes, and commanded him to stand, while bows were bent, and harquebusses aimed at him from the walls—a rigour of vigilance used, notwithstanding that the young stranger came in company of a party of the garrison, nay, of the very body which furnished the sentinels who were then upon duty.

Le Balafré, who had remained by his nephew's side on purpose, gave the necessary explanations, and, after some considerable hesitation and delay, the youth was conveyed under a strong guard to the Lord Crawford's apartment.

This Scottish nobleman was one of the last relics of the gallant band of Scottish lords and knights who had so long and so truly served Charles VI. in those bloody wars which decided the independence of the French crown, and the expulsion of the English. He had fought, when a boy, abreast with Douglas and with Buchan, had ridden beneath the banner of the Maid of Arc, and was perhaps one of the last of those associates of Scottish chivalry who had so willingly drawn their swords for the *fleur-de-lys,* against their "auld enemies of England." Changes which had taken place in the Scottish kingdom, and perhaps his having become habituated to French climate and manners, had induced the old Baron to resign all thoughts of returning to his native country, the rather that the high office which he held in the household of Louis, and his own frank and loyal character, had gained a considerable ascendency over the King, who, though in general no ready believer in human virtue or honour, trusted and confided in those of the Lord Crawford, and allowed him the greater influence, because he was never known to interfere excepting in matters which concerned his charge.

Balafré and Cunningham followed Durward and the guard to the apartment of their officer, by whose dignified appearance, as well as with the respect paid to him by these proud soldiers, who seemed to respect no one else, the young man was much and strongly impressed.

Lord Crawford was tall, and through advanced age had become gaunt and thin; yet retaining in his sinews the strength, at least, if not the elasticity, of youth, he was able to endure the weight of his armour during a march as well as the youngest man who rode in his band. He was hard-favoured, with a scarred and weather-beaten countenance, and an eye that had looked upon death as his playfellow in thirty pitched battles, but which nevertheless expressed a calm contempt of danger, rather than the ferocious courage of a mercenary soldier. His tall erect figure was at present wrapped in a loose chamber-gown, secured around him by his buff belt, in which was suspended his richly-hilted poniard. He had round his neck the collar and badge of the order of Saint Michael. He sat upon a couch covered with deer's hide, and with spectacles on his nose (then a recent invention), was labouring to read a huge manuscript, called the *Rosier de la Guerre,* a code of military and civil policy which Louis had compiled for the benefit of his son the Dauphin, and upon which he was desirous to have the opinion of the experienced Scottish warrior.

Lord Crawford laid his book somewhat peevishly aside upon the entrance of these unexpected visitors, and demanded, in his broad national dialect, "What, in the foul fiend's name, they lacked now?"

Le Balafré, with more respect than perhaps he would have shown to Louis himself, stated at full length the circumstances in which his nephew was placed, and humbly requested his Lordship's protection. Lord Crawford listened very attentively. He could not but smile at the simplicity with which the youth had interfered in behalf of the hanged criminal, but he shook his head at the account which he received of the ruffle betwixt the Scottish Archers and the Provost-Marshal's guard.[1]

"How often," he said, "will you bring me such ill-winded pirns to ravel out? How often must I tell you, and especially both you, Ludovic Lesly, and you, Archie Cunningham, that the foreign soldier should bear himself modestly and decorously towards the people of the country, if you would not have the whole dogs of the town at your heels? However, if you must have a bargain, I would rather it were with that loon of a Provost than any one else; and I blame you less for this onslaught than for other frays that you have made, Ludovic, for it was but natural and kindlike to help your young kinsman. This simple bairn must come to no skaith neither; so give me the roll of the company yonder down from the shelf, and we will even add his name to the troop, that he may enjoy the privileges."

"May it please your Lordship"—said Durward——

"Is the lad crazed!" exclaimed his uncle—"Would you speak to his Lordship, without a question asked?"

"Patience, Ludovic," said Lord Crawford, "and let us hear what the bairn has to say."

"Only this, if it may please your Lordship," replied Quentin, "that I told my uncle formerly I had some doubts about entering this service. I have now to say that they are entirely removed, since I have seen the noble and experienced commander under whom I am to serve; for there is authority in your look."

"Weel said, my bairn," said the old Lord, not insensible to the compliment; "we have had some experience, had God sent us grace to improve by it, both in service and in command. There you stand, Quentin, in our

---

[1] Such dispute between the Scots Guards, and the other constituted authorities of the ordinary military corps, often occurred. In 1474, two Scotsmen had been concerned in robbing John Pensart, a fishmonger, of a large sum of money. They were accordingly apprehended by Philip du Four, Provost, with some of his followers. But ere they could lodge one of them, called Mortimer, in the prison of the Chastellet, they were attacked by two Archers of the King's Scottish Guard, who rescued the prisoner.—See Chronique de Jean de Troyes, at the said year, 1474.

honourable corps of Scottish Body-Guards, as esquire to your uncle, and serving under his lance. I trust you will do well, for you should be a right man-at-arms, if all be good that is upcome,[1] and you are come of a gentle kindred.—Ludovic, you will see that your kinsman follow his exercise diligently, for we will have spears breaking one of these days."

"By my hilts, and I am glad of it, my Lord—this peace makes cowards of us all. I myself feel a sort of decay of spirit, closed up in this cursed dungeon of a Castle."

"Well, a bird whistled in my ear," continued Lord Crawford, "that the old banner will be soon dancing in the field again."

"I will drink a cup the deeper this evening to that very tune," said Balafré.

"Thou wilt drink to any tune," said Lord Crawford; "and I fear me, Ludovic, you will drink a bitter browst of your own brewing one day."

Lesly, a little abashed, replied, "that it had not been his wont for many a day; but his Lordship knew the use of the company, to have a carouse to the health of a new comrade."

"True," said the old leader, "I had forgot the occasion. I will send a few stoups of wine to assist your carouse; but let it be over by sunset. And, hark ye—let the soldiers for duty be carefully pricked off; and see that none of them be more or less partakers of your debauch."

"Your Lordship shall be lawfully obeyed," said Ludovic; "and your health duly remembered."

"Perhaps," said Lord Crawford, "I may look in myself upon your mirth—just to see that all is carried decently."

"Your Lordship shall be most dearly welcome," said Ludovic; and the whole party retreated in high spirits to prepare for their military banquet, to which Lesly invited about a score of his comrades, who were pretty much in the habit of making their mess together.

A soldier's festival is generally a very extempore affair, providing there is enough of meat and drink to be had; but on the present occasion, Ludovic bustled about to procure some better wine than ordinary; observing, that the "old Lord was the surest gear in their aught, and that, while he preached sobriety to them, he himself, after drinking at the royal table as much wine as he could honestly come by, never omitted any creditable opportunity to fill up the evening over the wine-pot; so you must prepare, comrades," he said, "to hear the old histories of the battles of Vernoil and Beaugé."[2]

The Gothic apartment in which they generally met was, therefore, hastily put into the best order; their grooms were despatched to collect green rushes to spread upon the floor; and banners, under which the Scot-

---

[1] That is, if your courage corresponds with your personal appearance.
[2] In both these battles, the Scottish auxiliaries of France, under Stewart, Earl of Buchan, were distinguished. At Beaugé they were victorious, killing the Duke of Clarence, Henry Vth's brother, and cutting off his army. At Vernoil they were defeated, and nearly extirpated.

tish Guard had marched to battle, or which they had taken from the enemies' ranks, were displayed, by way of tapestry, over the table, and around the walls of the chamber.

The next point was, to invest the young recruit as hastily as possible with the dress and appropriate arms of the Guard, that he might appear in every respect the sharer of its important privileges, in virtue of which, and by the support of his countrymen, he might freely brave the power and the displeasure of the Provost-Marshal—although the one was known to be as formidable, as the other was unrelenting.

The banquet was joyous in the highest degree; and the guests gave vent to the whole current of their national partiality on receiving into their ranks a recruit from their beloved fatherland. Old Scottish songs were sung, old tales of Scottish heroes told—the achievements of their fathers, and the scenes in which they were wrought, were recalled to mind: and, for a time, the rich plains of Touraine seemed converted into the mountainous and sterile regions of Caledonia.

When their enthusiasm was at high flood, and each was endeavouring to say something to ennance the dear remembrance of Scotland, it received a new impulse from the arrival of Lord Crawford, who, as Le Balafré had well prophesied, sat as it were on thorns at the royal board, until an opportunity occurred of making his escape to the revelry of his own countrymen. A chair of state had been reserved for him at the upper end of the table; for, according to the manners of the age, and the constitution of that body, although their leader and commander under the King and High Constable, the members of the corps (as we should now say, the privates) being all ranked as noble by birth, their Captain sat with them at the same table without impropriety, and might mingle when he chose in their festivity, without derogation from his dignity as commander.

At present, however, Lord Crawford declined occupying the seat prepared for him, and bidding them "hold themselves merry," stood looking on the revel with a countenance which seemed greatly to enjoy it.

"Let him alone," whispered Cunningham to Lindesay, as the latter offered the wine to their noble Captain, "let him alone—hurry no man's cattle—let him take it of his own accord."

In fact, the old Lord, who at first smiled, shook his head, and placed the untasted wine-cup before him, began presently, as if it were in absence of mind, to sip a little of the contents, and in doing so, fortunately recollected that it would be ill-luck did he not drink a draught to the health of the gallant lad who had joined them this day. The pledge was filled, and answered, as may be well supposed, with many a joyous shout, when the old leader proceeded to acquaint them that he had possessed Master Oliver with an account of what had passed that day: "And as," he said, "the scraper of chins hath no great love for the stretcher of throats, he has joined me in obtaining from the King an order, commanding the Provost to suspend all proceedings, under whatever pretence, against Quentin Durward; and to respect, on all occasions, the privileges of the Scottish Guard."

Another shout broke forth, the cups were again filled till the wine sparkled on the brim, and there was an acclaim to the health of the noble Lord Crawford, the brave conservator of the privileges and rights of his countrymen. The good old Lord could not but in courtesy do reason to this pledge also, and gliding into the ready chair, as it were, without reflecting what he was doing, he caused Quentin to come up beside him, and assailed him with many more questions concerning the state of Scotland, and the great families there, than he was well able to answer; while ever and anon, in the course of his queries, the good Lord kissed the wine-cup by way of parenthesis, remarking, that sociality became Scottish gentlemen, but that young men, like Quentin, ought to practise it cautiously, lest it might degenerate into excess; upon which occasion he uttered many excellent things, until his own tongue, although employed in the praises of temperance, began to articulate something thicker than usual. It was now that, while the military ardour of the company augmented with each flagon which they emptied, Cunningham called on them to drink the speedy hoisting of the *Oriflamme* (the royal banner of France).

"And a breeze of Burgundy to fan it!" echoed Lindesay.

"With all the soul that is left in this worn body do I accept the pledge, bairns," echoed Lord Crawford; "and as old as I am, I trust I may see it flutter yet. Hark ye, my mates" (for wine had made him something communicative), "ye are all true servants to the French crown, and wherefore should ye not know there is an envoy come from Duke Charles of Burgundy, with a message of an angry favour."

"I saw the Count of Crèvecœur's equipage, horses and retinue," said another of the guests, "down at the inn yonder, at the Mulberry Grove. They say the King will not admit him into the Castle."

"Now, Heaven send him an ungracious answer!" said Guthrie; "but what is it he complains of?"

"A world of grievances upon the frontier," said Lord Crawford; "and latterly, that the King hath received under his protection a lady of his land, a young Countess, who hath fled from Dijon, because, being a ward of the Duke, he would have her marry his favourite, Campo-basso."

"And hath she actually come hither alone, my Lord?" said Lindesay.

"Nay, not altogether alone, but with the old Countess, her kinswoman, who hath yielded to her cousin's wishes in this matter."

"And will the King," said Cunningham, "he being the Duke's feudal sovereign, interfere between the Duke and his ward, over whom Charles hath the same right, which, were he himself dead, the King would have over the heiress of Burgundy?"

"The King will be ruled, as he is wont, by rules of policy; and you know," continued Crawford, "that he hath not publicly received these ladies, nor placed them under the protection of his daughters, the Lady of Beaujeau, or the Princess Joan, so, doubtless, he will be guided by circumstances. He is our master—but it is no treason to say, he will chase with the hounds, and run with the hare, with any Prince in Christendom."

"But the Duke of Burgundy understands no such doubling," said Cunningham.

"No," answered the old Lord; "and, therefore, it is likely tc mak ; work between them."

"Well—Saint Andrew further the fray!" said Le Balafré. "I had iṫ foretold me ten, ay, twenty years since, that I was to make the fortune of my house by marriage. Who knows what may happen, if once we come to fight for honour and ladies' love, as they do in the old romaunts?"

"*Thou* name ladies' love, with such a trench in thy visage!" said Guthrie.

"As well not love at all, as love a Bohemian woman of Heathenesse," retorted Le Balafré.

"Hold there, comrades," said Lord Crawford; "no tilting with sharp weapons, no jesting with keen scoffs—friends all. And for the lady, she is too wealthy to fall to a poor Scottish lord, or I would put in my own claim, fourscore years and all, or not very far from it. But here is her health, nevertheless, for they say she is a lamp of beauty."

"I think I saw her," said another soldier, "when I was upon guard this morning at the inner barrier; but she was more like a dark lantern than a lamp, for she and another were brought into the Château in close litters."

"Shame! shame! Arnot!" said Lord Crawford; "a soldier on duty should say nought of what he sees. Besides," he added after a pause, his own curiosity prevailing over the show of discipline which he had thought it necessary to exert, "why should these litters contain this very same Countess Isabelle de Croye?"

"Nay, my lord," replied Arnot, "I know nothing of it save this, that my coutelier was airing my horses in the road to the village, and fell in with Doguin the muleteer, who brought back the litters to the inn, for they belong to the fellow of the Mulberry Grove yonder—he of the Fleur-de-Lys, I mean—and so Doguin asked Saunders Steed to take a cup of wine, as they were acquainted, which he was no doubt willing enough to do——"

"No doubt—no doubt," said the old Lord; "it is a thing I wish were corrected among you, gentlemen; but all your grooms and couteliers, and jackmen, as we should call them in Scotland, are but too ready to take a cup of wine with any one—It is a thing perilous in war, and must be amended. But, Andrew Arnot, this is a long tale of yours, and we will cut it with a drink; as the Highlander says, *Skeoch doch nan skial;* [1] and that's good Gaelic.—Here is to the Countess Isabelle of Croye, and a better husband to her than Campo-basso, who is a base Italian cullion!—

---

[1] "Cut a tale with a drink;" an expression used when a man preaches over his liquor, as *bons vivants* say in England.

And now, Andrew Arnot, what said the muleteer to this yeoman of thine?"

"Why, he told him in secrecy, if it please your Lordship," continued Arnot, "that these two ladies whom he had presently before convoyed up to the Castle in the close litters, were great ladies, who had been living in secret at his master's house for some days, and that the King had visited them more than once very privately, and had done them great honour; and that they had fled up to the Castle, as he believed, for fear of the Count de Crèvecœur, the Duke of Burgundy's ambassador, whose approach was just announced by an advanced courier."

"Ay, Andrew, come you there to me?" said Guthrie; "then I will be sworn it was the Countess whose voice I heard singing to the lute, as I came even now through the inner court—the sound came from the bay-windows of the Dauphin's Tower; and such melody was there as no one ever heard before in the Castle of Plessis of the Park. By my faith, I thought it was the music of the Fairy Melusina's making. There I stood —though I knew your board was covered, and that you were all impatient—there I stood, like——"

"Like an ass, Johnny Guthrie," said his commander; "thy long nose smelling the dinner, thy long ears hearing the music, and thy short discretion not enabling thee to decide which of them thou didst prefer.— Hark! is not the Cathedral bell tolling to vespers?—Sure it cannot be that time yet?—The mad old sexton has toll'd even-song an hour too soon."

"In faith, the bell rings but too justly the hour," said Cunningham; "yonder the sun is sinking on the west side of the fair plain."

"Ay," said the Lord Crawford, "is it even so?—Well, lads, we must live within compass—Fair and soft goes far—slow fire makes sweet malt— to be merry and wise is a sound proverb.—One other rouse to the weal of old Scotland, and then each man to his duty."

The parting-cup was emptied, and the guests dismissed—the stately old Baron taking the Balafré's arm, under pretence of giving him some instructions concerning his nephew, but, perhaps, in reality, lest his own lofty pace should seem in the public eye less steady than became his rank and high command. A serious countenance did he bear as he passed through the two courts which separated his lodging from the festal chamber, and solemn as the gravity of a hogshead was the farewell caution, with which he prayed Ludovic to attend his nephew's motions, especially in the matters of wenches and wine-cups.

Meanwhile, not a word that was spoken concerning the beautiful Countess Isabelle had escaped the young Durward, who, conducted into a small cabin, which he was to share with his uncle's page, made his new and lowly abode the scene of much high musing. The reader will easily imagine that the young soldier should build a fine romance on such a foundation as the supposed, or rather the assumed, identification of the Maiden of the Turret, to whose lay he had listened with so much interest, and the fair cup-bearer of Maitre Pierre, with a fugitive Countess of rank and wealth, flying from the pursuit of a hated lover, the favourite of an oppressive guardian, who abused his feudal power. There was an interlude in Quentin's vision concerning Maitre Pierre, who seemed to exercise such authority even over the formidable officer from whose hands he had that day, with much difficulty, made his escape. At length the youth's reveries, which had been respected by little Will Harper, the companion of his cell, were broken in upon by the return of his uncle, who commanded Quentin to bed, that he might arise betimes in the morning, and attend him to his Majesty's antechamber, to which he was called by his hour of duty, along with five of his comrades.

CHAPTER VIII

THE ENVOY

Be thou as lightning in the eyes of France;
For ere thou canst report I will be there,
The thunder of my cannon shall be heard—
So, hence! Be thou the trumpet of our wrath.
King John.

HAD sloth been a temptation by which Durward was easily beset, the noise with which the *caserne* of the guards resounded after the first toll of primes, had certainly banished the syren from his couch; but the discipline of his father's tower, and of the convent of Aberbrothick, had taught him to start with the dawn; and he did on his clothes gaily, amid the sounding of bugles and the clash of armour, which announced the change of the vigilant guards—some of whom were returning to barracks after their nightly duty, whilst some were marching out to that of the morning—and others, again, amongst whom was his uncle, were arming for immediate attendance upon the person of Louis. Quentin Durward soon put on, with the feelings of so young a man on such an occasion, the splendid dress and arms appertaining to his new situation; and his uncle, who looked with great accuracy and interest to see that he was completely fitted out in every respect, did not conceal his satisfaction at the improvement which had been thus made in his nephew's appearance. "If thou dost prove as faithful and bold as thou art well-favoured, I shall have in thee one of the handsomest and best esquires in the Guard, which cannot but be an honour to thy mother's family. Follow me to the presence-chamber; and see thou keep close at my shoulder."

So saying, he took up a partisan, large, weighty, and beautifully inlaid and ornamented, and directing his nephew to assume a lighter weapon of a similar description, they proceeded to the inner-court of the palace, where their comrades, who were to form the guard of the interior apartments, were already drawn up, and under arms—the squires each standing behind their masters, to whom they thus formed a second rank. Here were also in attendance many yeomen-prickers, with gallant horses and noble dogs, on which Quentin looked with such inquisitive delight, that his uncle was obliged more than once to remind him that the animals were not there for his private amusement, but for the King's, who had a strong passion for the chase, one of the few inclinations which he indulged, even when coming in competition with his course of policy; being so strict a protector of the game in the royal forests, that it was currently said, you might kill a man with greater impunity than a stag.

On a signal given, the Guards were put into motion by the command of Le Balafré, who acted as officer upon the occasion; and, after some minutiæ of word and signal, which all served to show the extreme and punctilious jealousy with which their duty was performed they marched into the hall of audience, where the King was immediately expected.

New as Quentin was to scenes of splendour, the effect of that which was now before him rather disappointed the expectations which he had formed of the brilliancy of a Court. There were household officers, indeed, richly attired; there were guards gallantly armed, and there were domestics of various degrees: But he saw none of the ancient counsellors of the kingdom, none of the high officers of the crown, heard none of the names which in those days sounded an alarum to chivalry; saw none either of those generals or leaders, who, possessed of the full prime of manhood, were the strength of France, or of the more youthful and fiery nobles, those early aspirants after honour, who were her pride. The jealous habits —the reserved manners—the deep and artful policy of the King, had estranged this splendid circle from the throne, and they were only called around it upon certain stated and formal occasions, when they went reluctantly, and returned joyfully, as the animals in the fable are supposed to have approached and left the den of the lion.

The very few persons who seemed to be there in the character of counsellors, were mean-looking men, whose countenances sometimes expressed sagacity, but whose manners showed they were called into a sphere for which their previous education and habits had qualified them but indifferently. One or two persons, however, did appear to Durward to possess a more noble mien, and the strictness of the present duty was not such as to prevent his uncle communicating the names of those whom he thus distinguished.

With the Lord Crawford, who was in attendance, dressed in the rich habit of his office, and holding a leading staff of silver in his hand, Quentin, as well as the reader, was already acquainted. Among others who seemed of quality, the most remarkable was the Count de Dunois, the son of the celebrated Dunois, known by the name of the Bastard of Orleans, who, fighting under the banner of Jeanne d'Arc, acted such a distinguished part in liberating France from the English yoke. His son well supported the high renown which had descended to him from such an honoured source; and, notwithstanding his connection with the royal family, and his hereditary popularity both with the nobles and the people, Dunois had, upon all occasions, manifested such an open, frank loyalty of character, that he seemed to have escaped all suspicion, even on the part of the jealous Louis, who loved to see him near his person, and sometimes even called him to his councils. Although accounted complete in all the exercises of chivalry, and possessed of much of the character of what was then termed a perfect knight, the person of the Count was far from being a model of romantic beauty. He was under the common size, though very strongly built, and his legs rather curved outwards, into that make which is more convenient for horseback, than elegant in a pedestrian. His shoulders were broad, his hair black, his complexion swarthy, his arms remarkably long and nervous. The features of his countenance were irregular, even to ugliness; yet, after all, there was an air of conscious worth and nobility about the Count de Dunois, which stamped, at the first glance, the character of the high-born nobleman, and the undaunted soldier. His mien was bold and upright, his step free and manly, and the harshness of his countenance was dignified by a glance like an eagle, and a frown like a lion. His dress was a hunting suit, rather.sumptuous than gay, and he acted on most occasions as Grand Huntsman, though we are not inclined to believe that he actually held the office.

Upon the arm of his relation Dunois, walking.with a step so slow and melancholy, that he seemed to rest on his kinsman and supporter, came Louis Duke of Orleans, the first Prince of the blood royal (afterwards King, by the name of Louis XII.), and to whom the guards and attendants rendered their homage as such. The jealously-watched object of Louis's suspicions, this Prince, who, failing the King's offspring, was heir to the kingdom, was not suffered to absent himself from Court, and, while residing there, was alike denied employment and countenance. The dejection which his degraded and almost captive state naturally impressed on the deportment of this unfortunate Prince, was at this moment greatly increased, by his consciousness that the King meditated, with respect to him, one of the most cruel and unjust actions which a tyrant could commit, by compelling him to give his hand to the Princess Joan of France, the younger daughter of Louis, to whom he had been contracted in infancy, but whose deformed person rendered the insisting upon such an agreement an act of abominable rigour.

The exterior of this unhappy Prince was in no respect distinguished by personal advantages; and in mind, he was of a gentle, mild, and beneficent disposition, qualities which were visible even through the veil of extreme dejection, with which his natural character was at present obscured. Quentin observed that the Duke studiously avoided even looking at the Royal Guards, and when he returned their salute, that he kept his eyes bent on the ground, as if he feared the King's jealousy might have construed that gesture of ordinary courtesy, as arising from the purpose of establishing a separate and personal interest among them.

Very different was the conduct of the proud Cardinal and Prelate, John of Balue, the favourite minister of Louis for the time, whose rise and character bore as close a resemblance to that of Wolsey, as the

difference betwixt the crafty and politic Louis, and the headlong and
rash Henry VIII. of England, would permit. The former had raised his
minister from the lowest rank, to the dignity, or at least to the emolu-
ments, of Grand Almoner of France, loaded him with benefices, and
obtained for him the hat of a cardinal; and although he was too cautious
to repose in the ambitious Balue the unbounded power and trust which
Henry placed in Wolsey, yet he was more influenced by him than by
any other of his avowed counsellors. The Cardinal, accordingly, had not
escaped the error incidental to those who are suddenly raised to power
from an obscure situation, for he entertained a strong persuasion, dazzled
doubtless by the suddenness of his elevation, that his capacity was equal
to intermeddling with affairs of every kind, even those most foreign to
his profession and studies. Tall and ungainly in his person, he affected
gallantry and admiration of the fair sex, although his manners rendered
his pretensions absurd, and his profession marked them as indecorous.
Some male or female flatterer had, in evil hour, possessed him with the
idea that there was much beauty of contour in a pair of huge substantial
legs, which he had derived from his father, a carman of Limoges, or,
according to other authorities, a miller of Verdun; and with this idea he
had become so infatuated, that he always had his cardinal's robes a little
looped up on one side, that the sturdy proportion of his limbs might not
escape observation. As he swept through the stately apartment in his
crimson dress and rich cope, he stopped repeatedly to look at the arms
and appointments of the cavaliers on guard, asked them several questions
in an authoritative tone, and took upon him to censure some of them for
what he termed irregularities of discipline, in language to which these
experienced soldiers dared no reply, although it was plain they listened
to it with impatience and with contempt.

"Is the King aware," said Dunois to the Cardinal, "that the Burgundian
Envoy is peremptory in demanding an audience?"

"He is," answered the Cardinal; "and here, as I think, comes the all-
sufficient Oliver Dain,[1] to let us know the royal pleasure."

As he spoke, a remarkable person, who then divided the favour of
Louis with the proud Cardinal himself, entered from the inner apartment
but without any of that important and consequential demeanour which
marked the full-blown dignity of the churchman. On the contrary, this
was a little, pale, meagre man, whose black silk jerkin and hose, without
either coat, cloak, or cassock, formed a dress ill-qualified to set off to
advantage a very ordinary person. He carried a silver basin in his hand,
and a napkin flung over his arm indicated his menial capacity. His
visage was penetrating and quick, although he endeavoured to banish
such expression from his features, by keeping his eyes fixed on the ground,
while, with the stealthy and quiet pace of a cat, he seemed modestly rather

---

[1] Oliver's name, or nickname, was Le Diable, which was bestowed on him by
public hatred, in exchange for Le Daim, or Le Dain. He was originally the King's
barber, but afterwards a favourite counsellor.

to glide than to walk through the apartment. But though modesty may easily obscure worth, it cannot hide court-favour; and all attempts to steal unperceived through the presence-chamber were in vain, on the part of one known to have such possession of the King's ear, as had been attained by his celebrated barber and groom of the chamber, Oliver le Dain, called sometimes Oliver le Mauvais, and sometimes Oliver le Diable, epithets derived from the unscrupulous cunning with which he assisted in the execution of the schemes of his master's tortuous policy. At present he spoke earnestly for a few moments with the Count de Dunois, who instantly left the chamber, while the tonsor glided quietly back towards the royal apartment whence he had issued, every one giving place to him; which civility he only acknowledged by the most humble inclination of the body, excepting in a very few instances, where he made one or two persons the subject of envy to all the other courtiers by whispering a single word in their ear; and at the same time muttering something of the duties of his place, he escaped from their replies, as well as from the eager solicitations of those who wished to attract his notice. Ludovic Lesly had the good fortune to be one of the individuals who, on the present occasion, were favoured by Oliver with a single word, to assure him that his matter was fortunately terminated.

Presently afterwards, he had another proof of the same agreeable tidings; for Quentin's old acquaintance, Tristan l'Hermite, the Provost-Marshal of the Royal Household, entered the apartment, and came straight to the place where Le Balafré was posted. This formidable officer's uniform, which was very rich, had only the effect of making his sinister countenance and bad mien more strikingly remarkable, and the tone which he meant for conciliatory, was like nothing so much as the growling of a bear. The import of his words, however, was more amicable than the voice in which they were pronounced. He regretted the mistake which had fallen between them on the preceding day, and observed it was owing to the Sieur Le Balafré's nephew, not wearing the uniform of his corps, or announcing himself as belonging to it, which had led him into the error for which he now asked forgiveness.

Ludovic Lesly made the necessary reply, and as soon as Tristan had turned away, observed to his nephew, that they had now the distinction of having a mortal enemy from henceforward in the person of this dreaded officer. "But we are above his *volée*—a soldier," said he, "who does his duty, may laugh at the Provost-Marshal."

Quentin could not help being of his uncle's opinion, for, as Tristan parted from them, it was with the look of angry defiance which the bear casts upon the hunter whose spear has wounded him. Indeed, even when less strongly moved, the sullen eye of this official expressed a malevolence of purpose which made men shudder to meet his glance; and the thrill of the young Scot was the deeper and more abhorrent, that he seemed to himself still to feel on his shoulders the grasp of the two death-doing functionaries of this fatal officer.

Meanwhile, Oliver, after he had prowled around the room in the stealthy manner which we have endeavoured to describe,—all, even the highest officers, making way for him, and loading him with their ceremonious attentions, which his modesty seemed desirous to avoid,—again entered the inner apartment, the doors of which were presently thrown open, and King Louis entered the presence-chamber.

Quentin, like all others, turned his eyes upon him; and started so suddenly, that he almost dropt his weapon, when he recognised in the King of France that silk-merchant, Maitre Pierre, who had been the companion of his morning walk. Singular suspicions respecting the real rank of this person had at different times crossed his thoughts; but this, the proved reality, was wilder than his wildest conjecture.

The stern look of his uncle, offended at this breach of the decorum of his office, recalled him to himself; but not a little was he astonished when the King, whose quick eye had at once discovered him, walked straight to the place where he was posted, without taking notice of any one else.—"So," he said, "young man, I am told you have been brawling on your first arrival in Touraine; but I pardon you, as it was chiefly the fault of a foolish old merchant, who thought your Caledonian blood required to be heated in the morning with *Vin de Beaulne*. If I can find him, I will make him an example to those who debauch my Guards.— Balafré," he added, speaking to Lesly, "your kinsman is a fair youth, though a fiery. We love to cherish such spirits, and mean to'make more than ever we did of the brave men who are around us. Let the year, day, hour, and minute of your nephew's birth be written down, and given to Oliver Dain."

Le Balafré bowed to the ground, and re-assumed his erect military position, as one who would show by his demeanour his promptitude to act in the.King's quarrel or defence. Quentin, in the meantime, recovered rom his first surprise, studied the King's appearance more attentively, and was surprised to find how differently he now construed his deportment and features than he had done at their first interview.

These were not much changed in exterior, for Louis, always a scorner of outward show, wore, on the present occasion, an old dark-blue hunting-dress, not much better than the plain burgher-suit of the preceding day, and garnished with a huge rosary of ebony, which had seen sent to him by no less a personage than the Grand Seignior, with an attestation that it had been used by a Coptic hermit on Mount Lebanon, a personage of profound sanctity. And instead of his cap with a single image, he now wore a hat, the band of which was garnished with at least a dozen of little paltry figures of saints stamped in lead. But those eyes, which, according to Quentin's former impression, only twinkled with the love of gain, had, now that they were known to be the property of an able and powerful monarch, a piercing and majestic glance; and those wrinkles on the brow, which he had supposed were formed during a long series of petty schemes of commerce, seemed now the furrows which sagacity had worn while toiling in meditation upon the fate of nations.

Presently after the King's appearance, the Princesses of France, with the ladies of their suite, entered the apartment. With the eldest, afterwards married to Peter of Bourbon, and known in French history by the name of the Lady of Beaujeau, our story has but little to do. She was tall, and rather handsome, possessed eloquence, talent, and much of her father's sagacity, who reposed great confidence in her, and loved her as well perhaps as he loved any one.

The younger sister, the unfortunate Joan, the destined bride of the Duke of Orleans, advanced timidly by the side of her sister, conscious of a total want of those external qualities which women are most desirous of possessing, or being thought to possess. She was pale, thin, and sickly in her complexion; her shape visibly bent to one side, and her gait so unequal that she might be called lame. A fine set of teeth, and eyes which were expressive of melancholy, softness, and resignation, with a quantity of light brown locks, were the only redeeming points which flattery itself could have dared to number, to counteract the general homeliness of her face and figure. To complete the picture, it was easy to remark, from the Princess's negligence in dress, and the timidity of her manner, that she had an unusual and distressing consciousness of her own plainness of appearance, and did not dare to make any of those attempts to mend by manners or by art what nature had left amiss, or in any other way to exert a power of pleasing. The King (who loved her not) stepped hastily to her as she entered.—"How now!" he said, "our world-contemning daughter—Are you robed for a hunting-party, or for the convent, this morning? Speak—answer."

"For which your highness pleases, sire," said the Princess, scarce raising her voice above her breath.

"Ay, doubtless, you would persuade me, it is your desire to quit the Court, Joan, and renounce the world and its vanities.—Ha! maiden, wouldst thou have it thought that we, the first-born of Holy Church, would refuse our daughter to heaven?—Our Lady and Saint Martin forbid we should refuse the offering, were it worthy of the altar, or were thy vocation in truth thitherward!"

So saying, the King crossed himself devoutly, looking, in the meantime, as appeared to Quentin, very like a cunning vassal, who was depreciating the merit of something which he was desirous to keep to himself, in order that he might stand excused for not offering it to his chief or superior. "Dares he thus play the hypocrite with Heaven," thought Durward, "and sport with God and the Saints, as he may safely do with men, who dare not search his nature too closely?"

Louis meantime resumed, after a moment's mental devotion—"No, fair daughter, I and another know your real mind better—Ha! fair cousin of Orleans, do we not? Approach, fair sir, and lead this devoted vestal of ours to her horse."

Orleans started when the King spoke, and hastened to obey him; but with such precipitation of step, and confusion, that Louis called out, "Nay, cousin, rein your gallantry, and look before you.—Why, what a headlong matter a gallant's haste is on some occasions!—You had well-nigh taken Anne's hand instead of her sister's.—Sir, must I give Joan's to you myself?"

The unhappy Prince looked up, and shuddered like a child, when forced to touch something at which it has instinctive horror—then making an effort, took the hand which the Princess neither gave nor yet withheld. As they stood, her cold damp fingers enclosed in his trembling hand, with their eyes looking on the ground, it would have been difficult to say which of these two youthful beings was rendered more utterly miserable—the Duke, who felt himself fettered to the object of his aversion by bonds which he durst not tear asunder, or the unfortunate young woman, who too plainly saw that she was an object of abhorrence to him, to gain whose kindness she would willingly have died.

"And now to horse, gentlemen and ladies—We will ourselves lead forth our daughter of Beaujeau," said the King; "and God's blessing and Saint Hubert's be on our morning sport!"

"I am, I fear, doomed to interrupt it, sire," said the Compte de Dunois —"the Burgundian Envoy is before the gates of the Castle, and demands an audience."

"*Demands* an audience, Dunois?" replied the King—"Did you not answer him, as we sent you word by Oliver, that we were not at leisure to see him to-day,—and that to-morrow was the festival of Saint Martin, which, please Heaven, we would disturb by no earthly thoughts,—and that on the succeeding day we were designed for Amboise—but that we would not fail to appoint him as early an audience, when we returned, as our pressing affairs would permit?"

"All this I said," answered Dunois; "but yet, sire——"

"*Pasques-dieu!* man, what is it that thus sticks in thy throat?" said the King. "This Burgundian's terms must have been hard of digestion."

"Had not my duty, your Grace's commands, and his character as an Envoy, restrained me," said Dunois, "he should have tried to digest them himself; for, by our Lady of Orleans, I had more mind to have made him eat his own words, than to have brought them to your Majesty."

"Body of me, Dunois," said the King, "it is strange that thou, one of the most impatient fellows alive, shouldst have so little sympathy with the like infirmity in our blunt and fiery cousin, Charles of Burgundy. Why, man, I mind his blustering messages no more than the towers of this Castle regard the whistling of the north-east wind, which comes from Flanders, as well as this brawling Envoy."

"Know then, sire," replied Dunois, "that the Count of Crèvecœur tarries below, with his retinue of pursuivants and trumpets, and says, that, since your Majesty refuses him the audience which his master has instructed him to demand, upon matters of most pressing concern, he will remain there till midnight, and accost your Majesty at whatever hour you are pleased to issue from your Castle, whether for business, exercise, or devotion; and that no consideration, except the use of absolute force, shall compel him to desist from this resolution."

"He is a fool," said the King, with much composure. "Does the hot-headed Hainaulter think it any penance for a man of sense to remain for twenty-four hours quiet within the walls of his Castle, when he hath the affairs of a kingdom to occupy him? These impatient coxcombs think that all men, like themselves, are miserable, save when in saddle and stirrup. Let the dogs be put up, and well looked to, gentle Dunois— We will hold council to-day, instead of hunting."

"My Liege," answered Dunois, "you will not thus rid yourself of Crèvecœur; for his master's instructions are, that if he hath not this audience which he demands, he shall nail his gauntlet to the palisades before the Castle, in token of mortal defiance on the part of his master, shall renounce the Duke's fealty to France, and declare instant war."

"Ay," said Louis, without any perceptible alteration of voice, but frowning until his piercing dark eyes became almost invisible under his shaggy eyebrows, "is it even so?—will our ancient vassal prove so masterful—our dear cousin treat us thus unkindly?—Nay then, Dunois, we must unfold the *Oriflamme,* and cry *Dennis Montjoye!*"

"Marry and amen, and in a most happy hour!" said the martial Dunois; and the guards in the hall, unable to resist the same impulse, stirred each upon his post, so as to produce a low but distinct sound of clashing arms. The King cast his eye proudly round, and, for a moment, thought and looked like his heroic father.

But the excitement of the moment presently gave way to the host of political considerations, which, at that conjuncture, rendered an open breach with Burgundy so peculiarly perilous. Edward IV., a brave and victorious king, who had in his own person fought thirty battles, was now established on the throne of England, was brother to the Duchess of Burgundy, and it might well be supposed, waited but a rupture between his near connection and Louis, to carry into France, through the ever-open gate of Calais, those arms which had been triumphant in the English civil wars, and to obliterate the recollection of internal dissensions by that most popular of all occupations amongst the English, an invasion of France. To this consideration was added the uncertain faith of the Duke of Bretagne, and other weighty subjects of reflection. So that, after a deep pause, when Louis again spoke, although in the same tone, it was with an altered spirit. "But God forbid," he said, "that aught less than necessity should make us, the Most Christian King, give cause to the effusion of Christian blood, if anything short of dishonour may avert such a calamity. We tender our subjects' safety dearer than the ruffle which our own dignity may receive from the rude breath of a

malapert ambassador, who hath perhaps exceeded the errand with which
he was charged.—Admit the Envoy of Burgundy to our presence."

"*Beati pacifici,*" said the Cardinal Balue.

"True; and your eminence knoweth that they who humble themselves
shall be exalted," added the King.

The Cardinal spoke an amen, to which few assented; for even the pale
cheek of Orleans kindled with shame, and Balafré suppressed his feelings
so little, as to let the butt-end of his partisan fall heavily on the floor,—
a movement of impatience for which he underwent a bitter reproof from
the Cardinal, with a lecture on the mode of handling his arms when in
presence of the Sovereign. The King himself seemed unusually embarrassed at the silence around him. "You are pensive, Dunois," he said—
"You disapprove of our giving way to this hot-headed Envoy."

"By no means," said Dunois; "I meddle not with matters beyond my
sphere. I was but thinking of asking a boon of your Majesty."

"A boon, Dunois—what is it?—You are an unfrequent suitor, and
may count on our favour."

"I would, then, your Majesty would send me to Evreux to regulate
the clergy," said Dunois, with military frankness.

"That were indeed beyond thy sphere," replied the King, smiling.

"I might order priests as well," replied the Count, "as my Lord Bishop
of Evreux, or my Lord Cardinal, if he likes the title better, can exercise
the soldiers of your Majesty's guard."

The King smiled again, and more mysteriously, while he whispered
Dunois, "The time may come when you and I will regulate the priests
together—But this is for the present a good conceited animal of a
Bishop. Ah, Dunois! Rome, Rome put him and other burdens upon us—
But patience, cousin, and shuffle the cards, till our hand is a stronger
one."[1]

The flourish of trumpets in the courtyard now announced the arrival
of the Burgundian nobleman. All in the presence-chamber made haste

---

[1] Dr. Dryasdust here remarks, that cards, said to have been invented in a preceding reign, for the amusement of Charles V. during the intervals of his mental
disorder, seem speedily to have become common among the courtiers, since they
already furnished Louis XI. with a metaphor. The same proverb was quoted by
Durandarte, in the enchanted cave of Montesinos. The alleged origin of the invention of cards produced one of the shrewdest replies I have ever heard given in
evidence. It was made by the late Dr. Gregory of Edinburgh to a counsel of great
eminence at the Scottish bar. The Doctor's testimony went to prove the insanity
of the party whose mental capacity was the point at issue. On a cross-interrogation,
he admitted that the person in question played admirably at whist. "And do you
seriously say, doctor," said the learned counsel, "that a person having a superior
capacity for a game so difficult, and which requires in a pre-eminent degree, memory,
judgment, and combination, can be at the same time deranged in his understanding?"—"I am no card player," said the doctor, with great address, "but I have
read in history that cards were invented for the amusement of an insane king." The
consequences of this reply were decisive.

to arrange themselves according to their proper places of precedence, the King and his daughters remaining in the centre of the assembly.

The Count of Crèvecœur, a renowned and undaunted warrior, entered the apartment; and, contrary to the usage among the envoys of friendly powers, he appeared all armed, excepting his head, in a gorgeous suit of the most superb Milan armour, made of steel, inlaid and embossed with gold, which was wrought into the fantastic taste called the Arabesque. Around his neck, and over his polished cuirass, hung his master's order of the Golden Fleece, one of the most honoured associations of chivalry then known in Christendom. A handsome page bore his helmet behind him, a herald preceded him, bearing his letters of credence, which he offered on his knee to the King; while the ambassador himself paused in the midst of the hall, as if to give all present time to admire his lofty look, commanding stature, and undaunted composure of countenance and manner. The rest of his attendants waited in the antechamber, or court-yard.

"Approach, Seignior Count de Crèvecœur," said Louis, after a moment's glance at his commission; "we need not our Cousin's letters of credence, either to introduce to us a warrior so well known, or to assure us of your highly deserved credit with your master. We trust that your fair partner, who shares some of our ancestral blood, is in good health. Had you brought her in your hand, Seignior Count, we might have thought you wore your armour, on this unwonted occasion, to maintain the superiority of her charms against the amorous chivalry of France. As it is, we cannot guess the reason of this complete panoply."

"Sire," replied the ambassador, "the Count of Crèvecœur must lament his misfortune, and entreat your forgiveness, that he cannot, on this occasion, reply with such humble deference as is due to the royal courtesy with which your Majesty has honoured him. But, although it is only the voice of Philip Crèvecœur de Cordès which speaks, the words which he utters must be those of his gracious Lord and Sovereign the Duke of Burgundy."

"And what has Crèvecœur to say in the words of Burgundy?" said Louis, with an assumption of sufficient dignity. "Yet hold—remember, that in this presence, Philip Crèvecœur de Cordès speaks to him who is his Sovereign's Sovereign."

Crèvecœur bowed, and then spoke aloud:—"King of France, the mighty Duke of Burgundy once more sends you a written schedule of the wrongs and oppressions committed on his frontiers by your Majesty's garrisons and officers; and the first point of inquiry is, whether it is your Majesty's purpose to make him amends for these injuries?"

The King, looking slightly at the memorial which the herald delivered to him upon his knee, said, "These matters have been already long before our Council. Of the injuries complained of, some are in requital of those sustained by my subjects, some are affirmed without any proof, some have been retaliated by the Duke's garrisons and soldiers; and if there remain any which fall under none of those predicaments, we are not, as a Christian prince, averse to make satisfaction for wrongs actually sustained by our neighbour, though committed not only without our countenance, but against our express order."

"I will convey your Majesty's answer," said the ambassador, "to my most gracious master; yet, let me say, that, as it is in no degree different from the evasive replies which have already been returned to his just complaints, I cannot hope that it will afford the means of re-establishing peace and friendship betwixt France and Burgundy."

"Be that at God's pleasure," said the King. "It is not for dread of thy Master's arms, but for the sake of peace only, that I return so temperate an answer to his injurious reproaches. Proceed with thine errand."

"My Master's next demand," said the ambassador, "is, that your Majesty will cease your secret and underhand dealings with his towns of Ghent, Liege, and Malines. He requests that your Majesty will recall the secret agents, by whose means the discontents of his good citizens of Flanders are inflamed; and dismiss from your Majesty's dominions, or rather deliver up to the condign punishment of their liege lord, those traitorous fugitives, who, having fled from the scene of their machinations, have found too ready a refuge in Paris, Orleans, Tours, and other French cities."

"Say to the Duke of Burgundy," replied the King, "that I know of no such indirect practices as those with which he injuriously charges me; that my subjects of France have frequent intercourse with the good cities of Flanders, for the purpose of mutual benefit by free traffic, which it would be as much contrary to the Duke's interest as mine to interrupt; and that many Flemings have residence in my kingdom, and enjoy the protection of my laws, for the same purpose; but none, to our knowledge, for those of treason or mutiny against the Duke. Proceed with your message—you have heard my answer."

"As formerly, Sire, with pain," replied the Count of Crèvecœur; "it not being of that direct or explicit nature which the Duke, my master, will accept, in atonement for a long train of secret machinations, not the less certain, though now disavowed by your Majesty. But I proceed with my message. The Duke of Burgundy farther requires the King of France to send back to his dominions without delay, and under a secure safe-guard, the persons of Isabelle Countess of Croye, and of her relation and guardian the Countess Hameline, of the same family, in respect the said Countess Isabelle, being, by the law of the country, and the feudal tenure of her estates, the ward of the said Duke of Burgundy, hath fled from his dominions, and from the charge which he, as a careful guardian, was willing to extend over her, and is here maintained in secret by the King of France, and by him fortified in her contumacy to the Duke, her natural lord and guardian, contrary to the laws of God and man, as they ever have been acknowledged in civilised Europe.—Once more I pause for your Majesty's reply."

"You did well, Count de Crèvecœur," said Louis scornfully, "to begin your embassy at an early hour; for if it be your purpose to call on me to account for the flight of every vassal whom your master's heady passion may have driven from his dominions, the bead-roll may last till sunset. Who can affirm that these ladies are in my dominions? who can presume to say, if it be so, that I have either countenanced their flight hither, or have received them with offers of protection? Nay, who is it will assert, that, if they are in France, their place of retirement is within my knowledge?"

"Sire," said Crèvecœur, "may it please your Majesty, I *was* provided with a witness on this subject—one who beheld these fugitive ladies in the inn called the Fleur-de-Lys, not far from this Castle—one who saw your Majesty in their company, though under the unworthy disguise of a burgess of Tours—one who received from them, in your royal presence, messages and letters to their friends in Flanders—all which he conveyed to the hand and ear of the Duke of Burgundy."

"Bring him forward," said the King; "place the man before my face who dares maintain these palpable falsehoods."

"You speak in triumph, Sire; for you are well aware that this witness no longer exists. When he lived, he was called Zamet Maugrabin, by birth one of those Bohemian wanderers. He was yesterday, as I have learned, executed by a party of your Majesty's Provost-Marshal, to prevent, doubtless, his standing here, to verify what he said of this matter to the Duke of Burgundy, in presence of his Council, and of me, Philip Crèvecœur de Cordès."

"Now, by our Lady of Embrun!" said the King, "so gross are these accusations, and so free of consciousness am I of aught that approaches them, that, by the honour of a King, I laugh, rather than am wroth at them. My Provost-guard daily put to death, as is their duty, thieves and vagabonds; and is my crown to be slandered with whatever these thieves and vagabonds may have said to our hot cousin of Burgundy and his wise counsellors? I pray you, tell my kind cousin, if he loves such companions, he had best keep them in his own estates; for here they are like to meet short shrift and a tight cord."

"My master needs no such subjects, Sir King," answered the Count, in a tone more disrespectful than he had yet permitted himself to make use of; "for the noble Duke uses not to inquire of witches, wandering Egyptians, or others, upon the destiny and fate of his neighbours and allies."

"We have had patience enough, and to spare," said the King, interrupting him; "and since thy sole errand here seems to be for the purpose of insult, we will send some one in our name to the Duke of Burgundy— convinced, in thus demeaning thyself towards us, thou hast exceeded thy commission, whatever that may have been."

"On the contrary," said Crèvecœur, "I have not yet acquitted myself of it.—Hearken, Louis of Valois, King of France—Hearken, nobles and gentlemen, who may be present—Hearken, all good and true men—And thou, Toison d'Or," addressing the herald, "make proclamation after me.—I, Philip Crévecœur of Cordès, Count of the Empire, and Knight of the honourable and princely Order of the Golden Fleece, in the name of the most puissant Lord and Prince, Charles, by the Grace of God, Duke of Burgundy and Lotharingia, of Brabant and Limbourg, of Luxembourg and of Gueldres; Earl of Flanders and of Artois; Count Palatine of Hainault, of Holland, Zealand, Namur, and Zutphen; Marquis of the Holy Empire; Lord of Friezeland, Salines, and Malines, do give you, Louis, King of France, openly to know, that you having refused to remedy the various griefs, wrongs, and offences, done and wrought by you, or by and through your aid, suggestion, and instigation, against the said Duke and his loving subjects, he, by my mouth, renounces all allegiance and fealty towards your crown and dignity—pronounces you false and faithless; and defies you as a Prince, and as a man. There lies my gage, in evidence of what I have said."

So saying, he plucked the gauntlet off his right hand, and flung it down on the floor of the hall.

Until this last climax of audacity, there had been a deep silence in the royal apartment during the extraordinary scene; but no sooner had the clash of the gauntlet, when cast down, been echoed by the deep voice of Toison d'Or, the Burgundian herald, with the ejaculation, "Vive Bourgogne!" than there was a general tumult. While Dunois, Orleans, old Lord Crawford, and one or two others, whose rank authorised their interference, contended which should lift up the gauntlet, the others in the hall exclaimed, "Strike him down! Cut him to pieces! Comes he here to insult the King of France in his own palace!"

But the King appeased the tumult by exclaiming, in a voice like thunder, which overawed and silenced every other sound, "Silence, my lieges! lay not a hand on the man, not a finger on the gage!—And you, Sir Count, of what is your life composed, or how is it warranted, that you thus place it on the cast of a die so perilous? Or is your Duke made of a different metal from other princes, since he thus asserts his pretended quarrel in a manner so unusual?"

"He is indeed framed of a different and more noble metal than the other princes of Europe," said the undaunted Count of Crèvecœur; "for, when not one of them dared to give shelter to you—to *you*, I say, King Louis—when you were yet only Dauphin, an exile from France, and pursued by the whole bitterness of your father's revenge, and all the power of his kingdom, you were received and protected like a brother by my noble master, whose generosity of disposition you have so grossly misused. Farewell, Sire, my mission is discharged."

So saying, the Count de Crèvecœur left the apartment abruptly, and without farther leave-taking.

"After him—after him—take up the gauntlet and after him!" said the King.—"I mean not you, Dunois, nor you, my Lord of Crawford, who, methinks, may be too old for such hot frays; nor you, cousin of Orleans, who are too young for them.—My Lord Cardinal—my Lord Bishop of Auxerre—it is your holy office to make peace among princes;—do you lift the gauntlet, and remonstrate with Count Crèvecœur on the sin he has committed, in thus insulting a great monarch in his own Court, and forcing us to bring the miseries of war upon his kingdom and that of his neighbour."

Upon this direct personal appeal, the Cardinal Balue proceeded to lift the gauntlet, with such precaution as one would touch an adder,—so great was apparently his aversion to this symbol of war,—and presently left the royal apartment to hasten after the challenger.

Louis paused and looked round the circle of his courtiers, most of whom, except such as we have already distinguished, being men of low birth, and raised to their rank in the King's household for other gifts than courage or feats of arms, looked pale on each other, and had obviously received an unpleasant impression from the scene which had been just acted. Louis gazed on them with contempt, and then said aloud, "Although the Count of Crèvecœur be presumptuous and overweening, it must be confessed that in him the Duke of Burgundy hath as bold a servant as ever bore message for a prince. I would I knew where to find as faithful an Envoy to carry back my answer."

"You do your French nobles injustice, Sire," said Dunois; "not one of them but would carry a defiance to Burgundy on the point of his sword."

"And, Sire," said old Crawford, "you wrong also the Scottish gentlemen who serve you. I, or any of my followers, being of meet rank, would not hesitate a moment to call yonder proud Count to a reckoning; my own arm is yet strong enough for the purpose, if I have but your Majesty's permission."

"But your Majesty," continued Dunois, "will employ us in no service through which we may win honour to ourselves, to your Majesty, or to France."

"Say, rather," said the King, "that I will not give way, Dunois, to the headlong impetuosity, which, on some punctilio of chivalry, would wreck yourselves, the throne, France, and all. There is not one of you who knows not how precious every hour of peace is at this moment, when so necessary to heal the wounds of a distracted country; yet there is not one of you who would not rush into war on account of the tale of a wandering gipsy, or of some errant demosel, whose reputation, perhaps, is scarce higher.—Here comes the Cardinal, and we trust with more pacific tidings.—How now, my Lord—have you brought the Count to reason and to temper?"

"Sire," said Balue, "my task hath been difficult. I put it to yonder proud Count, how he dared to use towards your Majesty, the presumptuous reproach with which his audience had broken up, and which must be understood as proceeding, not from his master, but from his own insolence, and as placing him therefore in your Majesty's discretion, for what penalty you might think proper."

"You said right," replied the King; "and what was his answer?"

"The Count," continued the Cardinal, "had at that moment his foot in the stirrup, ready to mount; and, on hearing my expostulation, he turned his head without altering his position. 'Had I,' said he, 'been fifty leagues distant, and had heard by report that a question vituperative of my Prince had been asked by the King of France, I had, even at that distance, instantly mounted, and returned to disburden my mind of the answer which I gave him but now.' "

"I said, sirs," said the King, turning around, without any show of angry emotion, "that in the Count Philip of Crèvecœur, our cousin the Duke possesses as worthy a servant as ever rode at a prince's right hand. —But you prevailed with him to stay?"

"To stay for twenty-four hours; and in the meanwhile to receive again his gage of defiance," said the Cardinal: "he has dismounted at the Fleur-de-Lys."

"See that he be nobly attended and cared for, at our charges," said the King; "such a servant is a jewel in a prince's crown.—Twenty-four hours?" he added, muttering to himself, and looking as if he were stretching his eyes to see into futurity; "twenty-four hours?—'tis of the shortest. Yet twenty-four hours, ably and skilfully employed, may be worth a year in the hand of indolent or incapable agents.—Well.—To the forest—to the forest, my gallant lords!—Orleans, my fair kinsman, lay aside that modesty, though it becomes you; mind not my Joan's coyness. The Loire may as soon avoid mingling with the Cher, as she from favouring your suit, or you from preferring it," he added, as the unhappy prince moved slowly on after his betrothed bride. "And now for your boar-spears, gentlemen; for Allegre, my pricker, hath harboured one that will try both dog and man.—Dunois, lend me your spear,—take mine, it is too weighty for me; but when did *you* complain of such a fault in your lance?—To horse—to horse, gentlemen."

And all the chase rode on.

CHAPTER IX

THE BOAR-HUNT

> I will converse with unrespective boys
> And iron-witted fools. None are for me
> That look into me with suspicious eyes.
> *King Richard.*

ALL the experience which the Cardinal had been able to collect of his master's disposition, did not, upon the present occasion, prevent his falling into a great error of policy. His vanity induced him to think that he had been more successful in prevailing upon the Count of Crèvecœur

to remain at Tours, than any other moderator whom the King might
have employed, would, in all probability, have been. And as he was well
aware of the importance which Louis attached to the postponement of a
war with the Duke of Burgundy, he could not help showing that he
conceived himself to have rendered the King great and acceptable service.
He pressed nearer to the King's person than he was wont to do, and
endeavoured to engage him in conversation on the events of the morning.

This was injudicious in more respects than one; for princes love not
to see their subjects approach them with an air conscious of deserving,
and thereby seeming desirous to extort acknowledgment and recompense
for their services; and Louis, the most jealous monarch that ever lived,
was peculiarly averse and inaccessible to any one who seemed either to
presume upon service rendered, or to pry into his secrets.

Yet, hurried away, as the most cautious sometimes are, by the self-
satisfied humour of the moment, the Cardinal continued to ride on the
King's right hand, turning the discourse, whenever it was possible, upon
Crèvecœur and his embassy; which, although it might be the matter at
that moment most in the King's thoughts, was nevertheless precisely
that which he was least willing to converse on. At length Louis, who had
listened to him with attention, yet without having returned any answer
which could tend to prolong the conversation, signed to Dunois, who rode
at no great distance, to come up on the other side of his horse.

"We came hither for sport and exercise," said he, "but the reverend
Father here would have us hold a council of state."

"I hope your Highness will excuse my assistance," said Dunois; "I am
born to fight the battles of France, and have heart and hand for that,
but I have no head for her councils."

"My Lord Cardinal hath a head turned for nothing else, Dunois,"
answered Louis; "he hath confessed Crèvecœur at the Castle-gate, and
he hath communicated to us his whole shrift—Said you not the *whole?*"
he continued, with an emphasis on the word, and a glance at the Cardinal,
which shot from betwixt his long dark eyelashes, as a dagger gleams
when it leaves the scabbard.

The Cardinal trembled, as, endeavouring to reply to the King's jest,
he said, "That though his order were obliged to conceal the secrets of
their penitents in general, there was no *sigillum confessionis,* which could
not be melted at his Majesty's breath."

"And as his Eminence," said the King, "is ready to communicate the
secrets of others to us, he naturally expects that we should be equally
communicative to him; and, in order to get upon this reciprocal footing,
he is very reasonably desirous to know if these two ladies of Croye be
actually in our territories. We are sorry we cannot indulge his curiosity,
not ourselves knowing in what precise place errant damsels, disguised
princesses, distressed countesses, may lie leaguer within our dominions,
which are, we thank God and our Lady of Embrun, rather too extensive
for us to answer easily his Eminence's most reasonable inquiries. But

supposing they were with us, what say you, Dunois, to our cousin's peremptory demand?"

"I will answer you, my Liege, if you will tell me in sincerity, whether you want war or peace," replied Dunois, with a frankness which, while it arose out of his own native openness and intrepidity of character, made him from time to time a considerable favourite with Louis, who, like all astucious persons, was as desirous of looking into the hearts of others, as of concealing his own.

"By my halidome," said he, "I should be as well contented as thyself, Dunois, to tell thee my purpose, did I myself but know it exactly. But say I declared for war, what should I do with this beautiful and wealthy young heiress, supposing her to be in my dominions?"

"Bestow her in marriage on one of your own gallant followers, who has a heart to love and an arm to protect her," said Dunois.

"Upon thyself, ha!" said the King. "*Pasques-dieu!* thou art more politic than I took thee for, with all thy bluntness."

"Nay, Sire," answered Dunois, "I am aught except politic. By our Lady of Orleans, I come to the point at once, as I ride my horse at the ring. Your Majesty owes the house of Orleans at least one happy marriage."

"And I will pay it, Count. *Pasques-dieu,* I will pay it!—See you not yonder fair couple?"

The King pointed to the unhappy Duke of Orleans and the Princess, who, neither daring to remain at a greater distance from the King, nor in his sight appear separate from each other, were riding side by side, yet with an interval of two or three yards betwixt them, a space which timidity on the one side, and aversion on the other, prevented them from diminishing, while neither dared to increase it.

Dunois looked in the direction of the King's signal, and as the situation of his unfortunate relative and the destined bride reminded him of nothing so much as of two dogs, which, forcibly linked together, remain nevertheless as widely separated as the length of their collars will permit, he could not help shaking his head, though he ventured not on any other reply to the hypocritical tyrant. Louis seemed to guess his thoughts.

"It will be a peaceful and quiet household they will keep—not much disturbed with children, I should augur.[1] But these are not always a blessing."

It was, perhaps, the recollection of his own filial ingratitude that made the King pause as he uttered the last reflection, and which converted the

---

[1] Here the King touches on the very purpose for which he pressed on the match with such tyrannic severity, which was, that as the Princess's personal deformity admitted little chance of its being fruitful, the branch of Orleans, which was next in succession to the crown, might be, by the want of heirs, weakened or extinguished. In a letter to the Compte de Dammarten, Louis, speaking of his daughter's match, says, "Qu'ils n'auroient pas beaucoup d'ambarras a nourrir les enfans que naitroient de leur union; mais cependant elle aura lieu, quelque chose qu'on en puisse dire."— WRAXALL's *History of France,* vol. i. p. 143, note.

sneer that trembled on his lip into something resembling an expression
of contrition. But he instantly proceeded in another tone.

"Frankly, my Dunois, much as I revere the holy sacrament of matrimony" (here he crossed himself), "I would rather the house of Orleans
raised for me such gallant soldiers as thy father and thyself, who share
the blood-royal of France without claiming its rights, than that the
country should be torn to pieces, like to England, by wars arising from
the rivalry of legitimate candidates for the crown. The lion should never
have more than one cub."

Dunois sighed and was silent, conscious that contradicting his arbitrary
Sovereign might well hurt his kinsman's interests, but could do him no
service; yet he could not forbear adding, in the next moment—

"Since your Majesty has alluded to the birth of my father, I must
needs own, that, setting the frailty of his parents on one side, he might
be termed happier, and more fortunate, as the son of lawless love, than
of conjugal hatred."

"Thou art a scandalous fellow, Dunois, to speak thus of holy wedlock," answered Louis jestingly. "But to the devil with the discourse,
for the boar is unharboured.—Lay on the dogs, in the name of the holy
Saint Hubert!—Ha! ha! tra-la-la-lira-la!"—And the King's horn rung
merrily through the woods as he pushed forward on the chase, followed
by two or three of his guards, amongst whom was our friend Quentin
Durward. And here it was remarkable, that, even in the keen prosecution
of his favourite sport, the King, in indulgence of his caustic disposition,
found leisure to amuse himself by tormenting Cardinal Balue.

It was one of that able statesman's weaknesses, as we have elsewhere
hinted, to suppose himself, though of low rank and limited education,
qualified to play the courtier and the man of gallantry. He did not, indeed,
actually enter the lists of chivalrous combat, like Becket, or levy soldiers
like Wolsey. But gallantry, in which they also were proficients, was his
professed pursuit; and he likewise affected great fondness for the martial
amusement of the chase. Yet, however well he might succeed with certain
ladies, to whom his power, his wealth, and his influence as a statesman,
might atone for deficiencies in appearance and manners, the gallant horses,
which he purchased at almost any price, were totally insensible to the
dignity of carrying a Cardinal, and paid no more respect to him than
they would have done to his father, the carter, miller, or tailor, whom
he rivalled in horsemanship. The King knew this, and, by alternately
exciting and checking his own horse, he brought that of the Cardinal,
whom he kept close by his side, into such a state of mutiny against his
rider, that it became apparent they must soon part company; and then,
in the midst of its starting, bolting, rearing, and lashing out, alternately,
the royal tormentor rendered the rider miserable, by questioning him
upon many affairs of importance, and hinting his purpose to take that

opportunity of communicating to him some of those secrets of state, which the Cardinal had but a little while before seemed so anxious to learn.[1]

A more awkward situation could hardly be imagined, than that of a privy-councillor forced to listen to and reply to his sovereign, while each fresh gambade of his unmanageable horse placed him in a new and more precarious attitude—his violet robe flying loose in every direction, and nothing securing him from an instant and perilous fall, save the depth of the saddle, and its height before and behind. Dunois laughed without restraint; while the King, who had a private mode of enjoying his jest inwardly, without laughing aloud, mildly rebuked his minister on his eager passion for the chase, which would not permit him to dedicate a few moments to business. "I will no longer be your hindrance to a course," continued he, addressing the terrified Cardinal, and giving his own horse the rein at the same time.

Before Balue could utter a word by way of answer or apology, his horse, seizing the bit with his teeth, went forth at an uncontrollable gallop, soon leaving behind the King and Dunois, who followed at a more regulated pace, enjoying the statesman's distressed predicament. If any of our readers has chanced to be run away with in his time (as we ourselves have in ours), he will have a full sense at once of the pain, peril, and absurdity of the situation. Those four limbs of the quadruped, which, no way under the rider's control, nor sometimes under that of the creature they more properly belong to, fly at such a rate as if the hindermost meant to overtake the foremost—those clinging legs of the biped which we so often wish safely planted on the green sward, but which now only augment our distress by pressing the animal's sides—the hands which have forsaken the bridle for the mane—the body which, instead of sitting upright on the centre of gravity, as old Angelo used to recommend, or stooping forward like a jockey's at Newmarket, lies, rather than hangs, crouched upon the back of the animal, with no better chance of saving itself than a sack of corn—combine to make a picture more than sufficiently ludicrous to spectators, however uncomfortable to the exhibitor. But add to this some singularity of dress or appearance on the part of the unhappy cavalier—a robe of office, a splendid uniform, or any other peculiarity of costume,—and let the scene of action be a

---

[1] A friendly, though unknown correspondent, has pointed out to me that I have been mistaken in alleging that the Cardinal was a bad rider. If so, I owe his memory an apology; for there are few men who, until my latter days, have loved that exercise better than myself. But the Cardinal may have been an indifferent horseman, though he wished to be looked upon as equal to the dangers of the chase. He was a man of assumption and ostentation, as he showed at the siege of Paris in 1465, where, contrary to the custom and usage of war, he mounted guard during the night with an unusual sound of clarions, trumpets, and other instruments. In imputing to the Cardinal a want of skill in horsemanship, I recollected his adventure in Paris when attacked by assassins, on which occasion his mule, being scared by the crowd, ran away with the rider, and taking its course to a monastery, to the abbot of which he formerly belonged, was the means of saving his master's life.—See Jean de Troyes' *Chronicle*.

racecourse, a review, a procession, or any other place of concourse and
public display, and if the poor wight would escape being the object of a
shout of inextinguishable laughter, he must contrive to break a limb or
two, or, which will be more effectual, to be killed on the spot; for on no
slighter condition will his fall excite anything like serious sympathy.
On the present occasion, the short violet-coloured gown of the Cardinal,
which he used as a riding-dress (having changed his long robes before
he left the Castle), his scarlet stockings and scarlet hat, with the long
strings hanging down, together with his utter helplessness, gave infinite
zest to his exhibition of horsemanship.

The horse, having taken matters entirely into his own hand, flew rather
than galloped up a long green avenue, overtook the pack in hard pursuit
of the boar, and then, having overturned one or two yeomen prickers,
who little expected to be charged in the rear,—having ridden down several
dogs, and greatly confused the chase,—animated by the clamorous expostulations and threats of the huntsman, carried the terrified Cardinal
past the formidable animal itself, which was rushing on at a speedy
trot, furious and embossed with the foam which he churned around his
tusks. Balue, on beholding himself so near the boar, set up a dreadful
cry for help, which, or perhaps the sight of the boar, produced such an
effect on his horse, that the animal interrupted its headlong career by
suddenly springing to one side; so that the Cardinal, who had long kept
his seat only because the motion was straight forward, now fell heavily
to the ground. The conclusion of Balue's chase took place so near the
boar, that, had not the animal been at that moment too much engaged
about his own affairs, the vicinity might have proved as fatal to the
Cardinal, as it is said to have done to Favila, King of the Visigoths, of
Spain. The powerful churchman got off, however, for the fright, and,
crawling as hastily as he could out of the way of hounds and huntsmen,
saw the whole chase sweep by him without affording him assistance; for
hunters in those days were as little moved by sympathy for such misfortunes as they are in our own.

The King, as he passed, said to Dunois, "Yonder lies his Eminence low
enough—he is no great huntsman, though for a fisher (when a secret is
to be caught) he may match Saint Peter himself. He has, however, for
once, I think, met with his match."

The Cardinal did not hear the words, but the scornful look with
which they were spoken led him to suspect their general import. The devil
is said to seize such opportunities of temptation as was now afforded
by the passions of Balue, bitterly moved as they had been by the scorn
of the King. The momentary fright was over so soon as he had assured
himself that his fall was harmless; but mortified vanity, and resentment
against his Sovereign, had a much longer influence on his feelings.

After all the chase had passed him, a single cavalier, who seemed rather
to be a spectator than a partaker of the sport, rode up with one or two
attendants, and expressed no small surprise to find the Cardinal upon

the ground, without a horse or attendants, and in such a plight as plainly showed the nature of the accident which had placed him there. To dismount, and offer his assistance in this predicament,—to cause one of his attendants resign a staid and quiet palfrey for the Cardinal's use—to express his surprise at the customs of the French Court, which thus permitted them to abandon to the dangers of the chase, and forsake in his need, their wisest statesman, were the natural modes of assistance and consolation which so strange a rencontre supplied to Crèvecœur; for it was the Burgundian ambassador who came to the assistance of the fallen Cardinal.

He found the minister in a lucky time and humour for essaying some of those practices on his fidelity, to which it is well known that Balue had the criminal weakness to listen. Already in the morning, as the jealous temper of Louis had suggested, more had passed betwixt them than the Cardinal durst have reported to his master. But although he had listened with gratified ears to the high value, which, he was assured by Crèvecœur, the Duke of Burgundy placed upon his person and talents, and not without a feeling of temptation, when the Count hinted at the munificence of his master's disposition, and the rich benefices of Flanders, it was not until the accident, as we have related, had highly irritated him, that, stung with wounded vanity, he resolved, in a fatal hour, to show Louis XI., that no enemy can be so dangerous as an offended friend and confidant.

On the present occasion, he hastily requested Crèvecœur to separate from him, lest they should be observed, but appointed him a meeting for the evening in the Abbey of Saint Martin's at Tours, after vesper service; and that in a tone which assured the Burgundian that his master had obtained an advantage hardly to have been hoped for, except in such a moment of exasperation.

In the meanwhile, Louis, who, though the most politic Prince of his time, upon this, as on other occasions, had suffered his passions to interfere with his prudence, followed contentedly the chase of the wild boar, which was now come to an interesting point. It had so happened that a sounder (*i.e.* in the language of the period, a boar of only two years old) had crossed the track of the proper object of the chase, and withdrawn in pursuit of him all the dogs (except two or three couple of old stanch hounds), and the greater part of the huntsmen. The King saw, with internal glee, Dunois, as well as others, follow upon this false scent, and enjoyed in secret the thought of triumphing over that accomplished knight, in the art of venerie, which was then thought almost as glorious as war. Louis was well mounted, and followed close on the hounds; so that, when the original boar turned to bay in a marshy piece of ground, there was no one near him but the King himself.

Louis showed all the bravery and expertness of an experienced huntsman; for, unheeding the danger, he rode up to the tremendous animal, which was defending itself with fury against the dogs, and struck him with his boar-spear; yet, as the horse shyed from the boar, the blow was not so effectual as either to kill or disable him. No effort could prevail on the horse to charge a second time; so that the King, dismounting, advanced on foot against the furious animal, holding naked in his hand one of those short, sharp, straight, and pointed swords, which huntsmen used for such encounters. The boar instantly quitted the dogs to rush on his human enemy, while the King, taking his station, and posting himself firmly, presented the sword, with the purpose of aiming it at the boar's throat, or rather chest, within the collar-bone; in which case the weight of the beast and the impetuosity of its career, would have served to accelerate its own destruction. But, owing to the wetness of the ground, the King's foot slipped, just as this delicate and perilous manœuvre ought to have been accomplished, so that the point of the sword encountering the cuirass of bristles on the outside of the creature's shoulder, glanced off without making any impression, and Louis fell flat on the ground. This was so far fortunate for the Monarch, because the animal, owing to the King's fall, missed his blow in his turn, and in passing only rent with his tusk the King's short hunting-cloak, instead of ripping up his thigh. But when, after running a little ahead in the fury of his course, the boar turned to repeat his attack on the King at the moment when he was rising, the life of Louis was in imminent danger. At this critical moment, Quentin Durward, who had been thrown out in the chase by the slowness of his horse, but who, nevertheless, had luckily distinguished and followed the blast of the King's horn, rode up, and transfixed the animal with his spear.

The King, who had by this time recovered his feet, came in turn to Durward's assistance, and cut the animal's throat with his sword. Before speaking a word to Quentin, he measured the huge creature not only by paces, but even by feet—then wiped the sweat from his brow, and the blood from his hands—then took off his hunting-cap, hung it on a bush, and devoutly made his orisons to the little leaden images which it contained—and at length, looking upon Durward, said to him, "Is it thou, my young Scot?—thou hast begun thy woodcraft well, and Maitre Pierre owes thee as good entertainment as he gave thee at the Fleur-de-Lys yonder.—Why dost thou not speak? Thou hast lost thy forwardness and fire, methinks, at the Court, where others find both."

Quentin, as shrewd a youth as ever Scottish breeze breathed caution into, had imbibed more awe than confidence towards his dangerous master, and was far too wise to embrace the perilous permission of familiarity which he seemed thus invited to use. He answered in very few and well-chosen words, that if he ventured to address his Majesty at all, it could be but to crave pardon for the rustic boldness with which he had conducted himself when ignorant of his high rank.

"Tush! man," said the King; "I forgive thy sauciness for thy spirit and shrewdness. I admired how near thou didst hit upon my gossip Tristan's occupation. You have nearly tasted of his handiwork since, as I am given to understand. I bid thee beware of him; he is a merchant who deals in rough bracelets and tight necklaces. Help me to my horse—I like thee, and will do thee good. Build on no man's favour but mine—not even on thine uncle's or Lord Crawford's—and say nothing of thy timely aid in this matter of the boar; for if a man makes boast that he has served a King in such a pinch, he must take the braggart humour for its own recompense."

The King then winded his horn, which brought up Dunois and several attendants, whose compliments he received on the slaughter of such a noble animal, without scrupling to appropriate a much greater share of merit than actually belonged to him; for he mentioned Durward's assistance as slightly as a sportsman of rank, who, in boasting of the number of birds which he has bagged, does not always dilate upon the presence and assistance of the gamekeeper. He then ordered Dunois to see that the boar's carcase was sent to the brotherhood of Saint Martin, at Tours, to mend their fare on holydays, and that they might remember the King in their private devotions.

"And," said Louis, "who hath seen his Eminence my Lord Cardinal? Methinks it were but poor courtesy, and cold regard to Holy Church, to leave him afoot here in the forest."

"May it please you, Sire," said Quentin, when he saw that all were silent, "I saw his Lordship the Cardinal accommodated with a horse, on which he left the forest."

"Heaven cares for its own," replied the King. "Set forward to the Castle, my lords; we'll hunt no more this morning.—You, Sir Squire," addressing Quentin, "reach me my wood-knife—it has dropped from the sheath beside the quarry there. Ride on, Dunois—I follow instantly."

Louis, whose lightest motions were often conducted like stratagems, thus gained an opportunity to ask Quentin privately, "My bonny Scot, thou hast an eye, I see—Canst thou tell me who helped the Cardinal to a palfrey?—Some stranger, I should suppose; for, as *I* passed without stopping, the courtiers would likely be in no hurry to do him such a timely good turn."

"I saw those who aided his Eminence but an instant, Sire," said Quentin; "it was only a hasty glance, for I had been unluckily thrown out, and was riding fast, to be in my place; but I think it was the Ambassador of Burgundy and his people."

"Ha!" said Louis.—"Well, be it so—France will match them yet."

There was nothing more remarkable happened, and the King, with his retinue, returned to the Castle.

CHAPTER X

THE SENTINEL

Where should this music be? i' the air, or the earth?
The Tempest.

————I was all ear,
And took in strains that might create a soul
Under the ribs of death.
Comus.

QUENTIN had hardly reached his little cabin, in order to make some necessary changes in his dress, when his worthy relative required to know the full particulars of all that had befallen him at the hunt.

The youth, who could not help thinking that his uncle's hand was probably more powerful than his understanding, took care, in his reply, to leave the King in full possession of the victory which he had seemed desirous to appropriate. Le Balafré's reply was a boast of how much better he himself would have behaved in the like circumstances, and it was mixed with a gentle censure of his nephew's slackness, in not making in to the King's assistance, when he might be in imminent peril. The youth had prudence, in answer, to abstain from all farther vindication of his own conduct, except that, according to the rules of woodcraft, he held it ungentle to interfere with the game attacked by another hunter, unless he was specially called upon for his assistance. This discussion was scarcely ended, when occasion was afforded Quentin to congratulate himself for observing some reserve towards his kinsman. A low tap at the door announced a visitor—it was presently opened, and Oliver Dain, or Mauvais, or Diable, for by all these names he was known, entered the apartment.

This able but most unprincipled man has been already described, in so far as his exterior is concerned. The aptest resemblance of his motions and manners might perhaps be to those of the domestic cat, which, while couching in seeming slumber, or gliding through the apartment with slow, stealthy, and timid steps, is now engaged in watching the hole of some unfortunate mouse, now in rubbing herself with apparent confidence and fondness against those by whom she desires to be caressed, and presently after, is flying upon her prey, or scratching, perhaps, the very object of her former cajolements.

He entered with stooping shoulders, a humble and modest look, and threw such a degree of civility into his address to the Seignior Balafré, that no one who saw the interview could have avoided concluding that he came to ask a boon of the Scottish Archer. He congratulated Lesly on the excellent conduct of his young kinsman in the chase that day, which, he observed, had attracted the King's particular attention. He here paused for a reply; and with his eyes fixed on the ground, save just when once or twice they stole upwards to take a side glance at Quentin, he heard

Balafré observe, "That his Majesty had been unlucky in not having himself by his side instead of his nephew, as he would questionless have made in, and speared the brute, a matter which he understood Quentin had left upon his Majesty's royal hands, so far as he could learn the story. But it will be a lesson to his Majesty," he said, "while he lives, to mount a man of my inches on a better horse; for how could my great hill of a Flemish dray-horse keep up with his Majesty's Norman runner? I am sure I spurred till his sides were furrowed. It is ill considered, Master Oliver, and you must represent it to his Majesty."

Master Oliver only replied to this observation by turning towards the bold bluff speaker one of those slow, dubious glances, which, accompanied by a slight motion of the hand, and a gentle depression of the head to one side, may be either interpreted as a mute assent to what is said, or as a cautious deprecation of farther prosecution of the subject. It was a keener, more scrutinising glance, which he bent on the youth, as he said, with an ambiguous smile, "So, young man, is it the wont of Scotland to suffer your Princes to be endangered for the lack of aid, in such emergencies as this of to-day?"

"It is our custom," answered Quentin, determined to throw no farther light on the subject, "not to encumber them with assistance in honourable pastimes, when they can aid themselves without it. We hold that a Prince in a hunting-field must take his chance with others, and that he comes there for the very purpose. What were woodcraft without fatigue and without danger?"

"You hear the silly boy," said his uncle; "that is always the way with him; he hath an answer or a reason ready to be rendered to every one. I wonder whence he hath caught the gift; I never could give a reason for anything I have ever done in my life, except for eating when I was a-hungry, calling the muster-roll, and such points of duty as the like."

"And pray, worthy Seignior," said the royal tonsor, looking at him from under his eyelids, "what might your reason be for calling the muster-roll on such occasions?"

"Because the Captain commanded me," said Le Balafré. "By Saint Giles, I know no other reason! If he had commanded Tyrie or Cunningham, they must have done the same."

"A most military final cause!" said Oliver.—"But, Seignior Le Balafré, you will be glad, doubtless, to learn, that his Majesty is so far from being displeased with your nephew's conduct, that he hath selected him to execute a piece of duty this afternoon."

"Selected *him?*" said Balafré, in great surprise;—"Selected *me,* I suppose, you mean?"

"I mean precisely as I speak," replied the barber, in a mild but decided tone; "the King hath a commission with which to entrust your nephew."

"Why, wherefore, and for what reason?" said Balafré; "why doth he choose the boy, and not me?"

"I can go no farther back than your own ultimate cause, Seignior Le

Balafré; such are his Majesty's commands. But," said he, "if I might use the presumption to form a conjecture, it may be his Majesty hath work to do, fitter for a youth like your nephew, than for an experienced warrior like yourself, Seignior Balafré.—Wherefore, young gentleman, get your weapons and follow me. Bring with you a harquebuss, for you are to mount sentinel."

"Sentinel!" said the uncle. "Are you sure you are right, Master Oliver? The inner guards of the Castle have ever been mounted by those only who have (like me) served twelve years in our honourable body."

"I am quite certain of his Majesty's pleasure," said Oliver, "and must no longer delay executing it."

"But," said Le Balafré, "my nephew is not even a free Archer, being only an Esquire, serving under my lance."

"Pardon me," answered Oliver, "the King sent for the register not half-an-hour since, and enrolled him among the Guard.—Have the goodness to assist to put your nephew in order for the service."

Balafré, who had no ill-nature, or even much jealousy, in his disposition, hastily set about adjusting his nephew's dress, and giving him directions for his conduct under arms, but was unable to refrain from larding them with interjections of surprise at such luck chancing to fall upon the young man so early.

"It had never taken place before in the Scottish Guard," he said, "not even in his own instance. But doubtless his service must be to mount guard over the popinjays and Indian peacocks, which the Venetian ambassador had lately presented to the King—it could be nothing else; and such duty being only fit for a beardless boy" (here he twirled his own grim moustaches), "he was glad the lot had fallen on his fair nephew."

Quick, and sharp of wit, as well as ardent in fancy, Quentin saw visions of higher importance in this early summons to the royal presence, and his heart beat high at the anticipation of rising into speedy distinction. He determined carefully to watch the manners and language of his conductor, which he suspected must, in some cases at least, be interpreted by contraries, as soothsayers are said to discover the interpretation of dreams. He could not but hug himself on having observed strict secrecy on the events of the chase, and then formed a resolution, which, for so young a person, had much prudence in it, that while he breathed the air of this secluded and mysterious Court, he would keep his thoughts locked in his bosom, and his tongue under the most careful regulation.

His equipment was soon complete, and, with his harquebuss on his shoulder (for though they retained the name of Archers, the Scottish Guard very early substituted fire-arms for the long-bow, in the use of which their nation never excelled), he followed Master Oliver out of the barrack.

His uncle looked long after him, with a countenance, in which wonder was blended with curiosity; and though neither envy nor the malignant feelings which it engenders, entered into his honest meditations, tnere was yet a sense of wounded or diminished self-importance, which mingled with the pleasure excited by his nephew's favourable commencement of service.

He shook his head gravely, opened a privy cupboard, took out a large *bottrine* of stout old wine, shook it to examine how low the contents had ebbed, filled and drank a hearty cup; then took his seat, half reclining, on the great oaken settle, and having once again slowly shaken his head, received so much apparent benefit from the oscillation, that, like the toy called a mandarin, he continued the motion until he dropped into a slumber, from which he was first roused by the signal to dinner.

When Quentin Durward left his uncle to these sublime meditations, he followed his conductor, Master Oliver, who, without crossing any of the principal courts, led him partly through private passages exposed to the open air, but chiefly through a maze of stairs, vaults, and galleries, communicating with each other by secret doors, and at unexpected points, into a large and spacious latticed gallery, which, from its breadth, might have been almost termed a hall, hung with tapestry more ancient than beautiful, and with a very few of the hard, cold, ghastly-looking pictures, belonging to the first dawn of the arts, which preceded their splendid sunrise. These were designed to represent the Paladins of Charlemagne, who made such a distinguished figure in the romantic history of France; and as the gigantic form of the celebrated Orlando constituted the most prominent figure, the apartment acquired from him the title of Roland's Hall, or Roland's Gallery.[1]

"You will keep watch here," said Oliver, in a low whisper, as if the hard delineations of monarchs and warriors around could have been offended at the elevation of his voice, or as if he had feared to awaken the echoes that lurked among the groined-vaults and Gothic drop-work on the ceiling of this huge and dreary apartment.

"What are the orders and signs of my watch?" answered Quentin, in the same suppressed tone.

"Is your harquebuss loaded?" replied Oliver, without answering his query.

"That," answered Quentin, "is soon done;" and proceeded to charge his weapon, and to light the slow-match (by which when necessary it was discharged) at the embers of a wood fire, which was expiring in the huge hall chimney—a chimney itself so large, that it might have been called a Gothic closet or chapel appertaining to the hall.

When this was performed, Oliver told him that he was ignorant of one of the high privileges of his own corps, which only received orders from the King in person, or the High Constable of France, in lieu of their own officers. "You are placed here by his Majesty's command, young

---

[1] Charlemagne, I suppose on account of his unsparing rigour to the Saxons and other heathens, was accounted a saint during the dark ages; and Louis XI., as one of his successors, honoured his shrine with peculiar observance.

man," added Oliver, "and you will not be long here without knowing
wherefore you are summoned. Meantime your walk extends along this
gallery. You are permitted to stand still while you list, but on no account
to sit down. or quit your weapon. You are not to sing aloud, or whistle,
upon any account; but you may, if you list, mutter some of the Church's
prayers, or what else you list that has no offence in it, in a low voice.
Farewell, and keep good watch."

"Good watch!" thought the youthful soldier as his guide stole away
from him with that noiseless gliding step which was peculiar to him,
and vanished through a side-door behind the arras—"Good watch! but
upon whom, and against whom?—for what, save bats or rats, are there
here to contend with, unless these grim old representatives of humanity
should start into life for the disturbance of my guard? Well, it is my
duty, I suppose, and I must perform it."

With the vigorous purpose of discharging his duty, even to the very
rigour, he tried to while away the time with some of the pious hymns
which he had learned in the convent in which he had found shelter after
the death of his father—allowing in his own mind, that, but for the
change of a novice's frock for the rich military dress which he now wore,
his soldierly walk in the royal gallery of France resembled greatly those
of which he had tired excessively in the cloistered seclusion of Aberbrothick.

Presently, as if to convince himself he now belonged not to the cell but
to the world, he chanted to himself, but in such tone as not to exceed the
licence given to him, some of the ancient rude ballads which the old family
harper had taught him, of the defeat of the Danes at Aberlemno and
Forres, the murder of King Duffus at Forfar, and other pithy sonnets
and lays, which appertained to the history of his distant native country,
and particularly of the district to which he belonged. This wore away a
considerable space of time, and it was now more than two hours past noon,
when Quentin was reminded by his appetite, that the good fathers of
Aberbrothick, however strict in demanding his attendance upon the hours
of devotion, were no less punctual in summoning him to those of refection; whereas here, in the interior of a royal palace, after a morning
spent in exercise, and a noon exhausted in duty, no man seemed to consider it as a natural consequence that he must be impatient for his dinner.

There are, however, charms in sweet sounds which can lull to rest
even the natural feelings of impatience, by which Quentin was now
visited. At the opposite extremities of the long hall or gallery, were two
large doors, ornamented with heavy architraves, probably opening into
different suites of apartments, to which the gallery served as a medium
of mutual communication. As the sentinel directed his solitary walk
betwixt these two entrances, which formed the boundary of his duty,
he was startled by a strain of music, which was suddenly waked near one
of those doors, and which, at least in his imagination, was a combination
of the same lute and voice by which he had been enchanted on the pre-

ceding day. All the dreams of yesterday morning, so much weakened
by the agitating circumstances which he had since undergone, again rose
more vivid from their slumber, and, planted on the spot where his ear
could most conveniently drink in the sounds, Quentin remained, with his
harquebuss shouldered, his mouth half open, ear, eye, and soul directed
to the spot, rather the picture of a sentinel than a living form,—without
any other idea than that of catching, if possible, each passing sound of
the dulcet melody.

These delightful sounds were but partially heard—they languished,
lingered, ceased entirely, and were from time to time renewed after uncertain intervals. But, besides that music, like beauty, is often most delightful, or at least most interesting to the imagination, when its charms are
but partially displayed, and the imagination is left to fill up what is
from distance but imperfectly detailed, Quentin had matter enough to
fill up his reverie during the intervals of fascination. He could not doubt,
from the report of his uncle's comrades, and the scene which had passed
in the presence-chamber that morning, that the syren who thus delighted
his ears, was not, as he had profanely supposed, the daughter or kinswoman of a base *cabaretier,* but the same disguised and distressed
Countess, for whose cause kings and princes were now about to buckle
on armour, and put lance in rest. A hundred wild dreams, such as romantic and adventurous youth readily nourished in a romantic and
adventurous age, chased from his eyes the bodily presentment of the
actual scene, and substituted their own bewildering delusions, when at
once, and rudely, they were banished by a rough grasp laid upon his
weapon, and a harsh voice which exclaimed, close to his ear, "Ha!
Pasques-dieu, Sir Squire, methinks you keep sleepy ward here!"

The voice was the tuneless, yet impressive and ironical tone of Maitre
Pierre, and Quentin, suddenly recalled to himself, saw, with shame and
fear, that he had, in his reverie, permitted Louis himself—entering
probably by some secret door, and gliding along by the wall, or behind
the tapestry—to approach him so nearly, as almost to master his weapon.

The first impulse of his surprise was to free his harquebuss by a violent
exertion, which made the King stagger backward into the hall. His next
apprehension was, that in obeying the animal instinct, as it may be
termed, which prompts a brave man to resist an attempt to disarm him,
he had aggravated, by a personal struggle with the King, the displeasure
produced by the negligence with which he had performed his duty upon
guard; and, under this impression, he recovered his harquebuss without
almost knowing what he did, and, having again shouldered it, stood
motionless before the Monarch, whom he had reason to conclude he had
mortally offended.

Louis, whose tyrannical disposition was less founded on natural ferocity
or cruelty of temper, than on cold-blooded policy and jealous suspicion,
had, nevertheless, a share of that caustic severity which would have made
him a despot in private conversation, and always seemed to enjoy the

pain which he inflicted on occasions like the present. But he did not push his triumph far, and contented himself with saying,—"Thy service of the morning hath already overpaid some negligence in so young a soldier— Hast thou dined?"

Quentin, who rather looked to be sent to the Provost-Marshal, than greeted with such a compliment, answered humbly in the negative.

"Poor lad," said Louis in a softer tone than he usually spoke in, "hunger hath made him drowsy.—I know thine appetite is a wolf," he continued; "and I will save thee from one wild beast as thou didst me from another; —thou hast been prudent too in that matter, and I thank thee for it.— Canst thou yet hold out an hour without food?"

"Four-and-twenty, Sire," replied Durward, "or I were no true Scot."

"I would not for another kingdom be the pasty which should encounter thee after such a vigil," said the King; "but the question now is, not of thy dinner, but of my own. I admit to my table this day, and in strict privacy, the Cardinal Balue and this Burgundian—this Count de Crève-cœur, and something may chance—the devil is most busy when foes meet on terms of truce."

He stopped, and remained silent, with a deep and gloomy look. As the King was in no haste to proceed, Quentin at length ventured to ask what his duty was to be in these circumstances.

"To keep watch at the beauffet, with thy loaded weapon," said Louis; "and if there is treason, to shoot the traitor dead."

"Treason, Sire! and in this guarded Castle!" exclaimed Durward.

"You think it impossible," said the King, not offended, it would seem, by his frankness; "but our history has shown that treason can creep into an auger-hole.—Treason excluded by guards! Oh, thou silly boy!— *quis custodiat ipsos custodes*—who shall exclude the treason of those very warders?"

"Their Scottish honour," answered Durward boldly.

"True; most right—thou pleasest me," said the King cheerfully; "the Scottish honour was ever true, and I trust it accordingly. But treason!"— Here he relapsed into his former gloomy mood, and traversed the apartment with unequal steps—"She sits at our feasts, she sparkles in our bowls, she wears the beard of our counsellors, the smiles of our courtiers, the crazy laugh of our jesters—above all, she lies hid under the friendly air of a reconciled enemy. Louis of Orleans trusted John of Burgundy— he was murdered in the Rue Barbette. John of Burgundy trusted the faction of Orleans—he was murdered on the Bridge of Montereau.—I will trust no one—no one. Hark ye; I will keep my eye on that insolent Count; ay, and on the Churchman too, whom I hold not too faithful. When I say, *Ecosse, en avant,*[1] shoot Crèvecœur dead on the spot."

"It is my duty," said Quentin, "your Majesty's life being endangered."

"Certainly—I mean it no otherwise," said the King.—"What should I

[1] Forward, Scotland.

get by slaying this insolent soldier?—Were it the Constable Saint Paul indeed"—Here he paused, as if he thought he had said a word too much, but resumed, laughing, "There's our brother-in-law, James of Scotland—your own James, Quentin—poniarded the Douglas when on a hospitable visit, within his own royal castle of Skirling."

"Of Stirling," said Quentin, "and so please your highness.—It was a deed of which came little good."

"Stirling call you the castle?" said the King, overlooking the latter part of Quentin's speech—"Well, let it be Stirling—the name is nothing to the purpose. But I meditate no injury to these men—none.—It would serve me nothing. They may not purpose equally fair by me.—I rely on thy harquebuss."

"I shall be prompt at the signal," said Quentin, "but yet——"

"You hesitate," said the King. "Speak out—I give thee full leave. From such as thou art, hints may be caught that are right valuable."

"I would only presume to say," replied Quentin, "that your Majesty having occasion to distrust this Burgundian, I marvel that you suffer him to approach so near your person, and that in privacy."

"Oh, content you, Sir Squire," said the King. "There are some dangers, which, when they are braved, disappear, and which yet, when there is an obvious and apparent dread of them displayed, become certain and inevitable. When I walk boldly up to a surly mastiff, and caress him, it is ten to one I soothe him to good temper; if I show fear of him, he flies on me and rends me. I will be thus far frank with thee—it concerns me nearly that this man returns not to his headlong master in a resentful humour. I run my risk, therefore. I have never shunned to expose my life for the weal of my kingdom.—Follow me."

Louis led his young Life-guards-man, for whom he seemed to have taken a special favour, through the side-door by which he had himself entered, saying, as he showed it him, "He who would thrive at Court must know the private wickets and concealed staircases—ay, and the traps and pitfalls of the palace, as well as the principal entrances, folding-doors, and portals."

After several turns and passages, the King entered a small vaulted room, where a table was prepared for dinner with three covers. The whole furniture and arrangements of the room were plain almost to meanness. A beauffet, or folding and movable cupboard, held a few pieces of gold and silver plate, and was the only article in the chamber which had, in the slightest degree, the appearance of royalty. Behind this cupboard, and completely hidden by it, was the post which Louis assigned to Quentin Durward; and after having ascertained, by going to different parts of the room, that he was invisible from all quarters, he gave him his last charge—"Remember the word, *Ecosse, en avant;* and so soon as ever I utter these sounds, throw down the screen—spare not for cup or goblet, and be sure thou take good aim at Crèvecœur—If thy piece fail, cling to him, and use thy knife—Oliver and I can deal with the Cardinal."

Having thus spoken, he whistled aloud, and summoned into the apartment Oliver, who was premier-valet of the chamber as well as barber, and who, in fact, performed all offices immediately connected with the King's person, and who now appeared, attended by two old men, who were the only assistants or waiters at the royal table. So soon as the King had taken his place, the visitors were admitted; and Quentin, though himself unseen, was so situated as to remark all the particulars of the interview.

The King welcomed his visitors with a degree of cordiality, which Quentin had the utmost difficulty to reconcile with the directions which he had previously received, and the purpose for which he stood behind the beauffet with his deadly weapon in readiness. Not only did Louis appear totally free from apprehension of any kind, but one would have supposed that those visitors whom he had done the high honour to admit to his table, were the very persons in whom he could most unreservedly confide, and whom he was most willing to honour. Nothing could be more dignified and at the same time more courteous, than his demeanour. While all around him, including even his own dress, was far beneath the splendour which the petty princes of the kingdom displayed in their festivities, his own language and manners were those of a mighty Sovereign in his most condescending mood. Quentin was tempted to suppose, either that the whole of his previous conversation with Louis had been a dream, or that the dutiful demeanour of the Cardinal, and the frank, open, and gallant bearing of the Burgundian noble, had entirely erased the King's suspicion.

But whilst the guests, in obedience to the King, were in the act of placing themselves at the table, his Majesty darted one keen glance on them, and then instantly directed his look to Quentin's post. This was done in an instant; but the glance conveyed so much doubt and hatred towards his guests, such a peremptory injunction on Quentin to be watchful in attendance, and prompt in execution, that no room was left for doubting that the sentiments of Louis continued unaltered, and his apprehensions unabated. He was, therefore, more than ever astonished at the deep veil under which that Monarch was able to conceal the movements of his jealous disposition.

Appearing to have entirely forgotten the language which Crèvecœur had held towards him in the face of his Court, the King conversed with him of old times, of events which had occurred during his own exile in the territories of Burgundy, and inquired respecting all the nobles with whom he had been then familiar, as if that period had indeed been the happiest of his life, and as if he retained towards all who had contributed to soften the terms of his exile, the kindest and most grateful sentiments.

"To an ambassador of another nation," he said, "I would have thrown something of state into our reception; but to an old friend, who often shared my board at the Castle of Genappes,[1] I wished to show myself, as I love best to live, old Louis of Valois, as simple and plain as any of his Parisian *badauds*. But I directed them to make some better cheer than ordinary for you, Sir Count, for I know your Burgundian proverb, *'Mieux vault bon repas que bel habit;'* and therefore I bid them have some care of our table. For our wine, you know well it is the subject of an old emulation betwixt France and Burgundy, which we will presently reconcile; for I will drink to you in Burgundy, and you, Sir Count, shall pledge me in Champagne.—Here, Oliver, let me have a cup of *Vin d'Auxerre;"* and he hummed gaily a song then well known—

"Auxerre est le boisson des Rois."

"Here, Sir Count, I drink to the health of the noble Duke of Burgundy, our kind and loving cousin.—Oliver, replenish yon golden cup with *Vin de Rheims*, and give it to the Count on your knee—he represents our loving brother.—My Lord Cardinal, we will ourself fill your cup."

"You have already, Sire, even to overflowing," said the Cardinal, with the lowly mien of a favourite towards an indulgent master.

"Because we know that your Eminence can carry it with a steady hand," said Louis. "But which side do you espouse in the great controversy—Sillery or Auxerre—France or Burgundy?"

"I will stand neutral, Sire," said the Cardinal, "and replenish my cup with Auvernat."

"A neutral has a perilous part to sustain," said the King; but as he observed the Cardinal colour somewhat, he glided from the subject, and added, "But you prefer the Auvernat, because it is so noble a wine it endures not water.—You, Sir Count, hesitate to empty your cup. I trust you have found no national bitterness at the bottom."

"I would, Sire," said the Count de Crèvecœur, "that all national quarrels could be as pleasantly ended as the rivalry betwixt our vineyards."

"With time, Sir Count," answered the King, "with time—such time as you have taken to your draught of Champagne.—And now that it is finished, favour me by putting the goblet in your bosom, and keeping it as a pledge of our regard. It is not to every one that we would part with it. It belonged of yore to that terror of France, Henry V. of England, and was taken when Rouen was reduced, and those islanders expelled from Normandy by the joint arms of France and Burgundy. It cannot be better bestowed than on a noble and valiant Burgundian, who well knows that on the union of these two nations depends the continuance of the freedom of the continent from the English yoke."

The Count made a suitable answer, and Louis gave unrestrained way to the satirical gaiety of disposition which sometimes enlivened the darker shades of his character. Leading, of course, the conversation, his remarks, always shrewd and caustic, and often actually witty, were

[1] During his residence in Burgundy, in his father's lifetime, Genappes was the usual abode of Louis. This period of exile is often alluded to in the novel.

seldom good-natured, and the anecdotes with which he illustrated them were often more humorous than delicate; but in no one word, syllable, or letter, did he betray the state of mind of one who, apprehensive of assassination, hath in his apartment an armed soldier, with his piece loaded, in order to prevent or anticipate an attack on his person.

The Count of Crèvecœur gave frankly in to the King's humour; while the smooth Churchman laughed at every jest, and enhanced every ludicrous idea, without exhibiting any shame at expressions which made the rustic young Scot blush even in his place of concealment.[1] In about an hour and a half the tables were drawn; and the King, taking courteous leave of his guests, gave the signal that it was his desire to be alone.

So soon as all, even Oliver, had retired, he called Quentin from his place of concealment; but with a voice so faint, that the youth could scarce believe it to be the same which had so lately given animation to the jest, and zest to the tale. As he approached, he saw an equal change in his countenance. The light of assumed vivacity had left the King's eyes, the smile had deserted his face, and he exhibited all the fatigue of a celebrated actor, when he has finished the exhausting representation of some favourite character, in which, while upon the stage, he had displayed the utmost vivacity.

"Thy watch is not yet over," said he to Quentin—"refresh thyself for an instant—yonder table affords the means—I will then instruct thee in thy farther duty. Meanwhile, it is ill talking between a full man and a fasting."

He threw himself back on his seat, covered his brow with his hand, and was silent.

CHAPTER XI

THE HALL OF ROLAND

Painters show Cupid blind—Hath Hymen eyes?
Or is his sight warp'd by those spectacles
Which parents, guardians, and advisers, lend him,
That he may look through them on lands and mansions,
On jewels, gold, and all such rich dotations,
And see their value ten times magnified?—
Methinks 'twill brook a question.
                    The Miseries of Enforced Marriage.

Louis the XIth of France, though the sovereign in Europe who was fondest and most jealous of power, desired only its substantial enjoyment; and though he knew well enough, and at times exacted strictly, the observances due to his rank, was in general singularly careless of show.

[1] The nature of Louis XIth's coarse humour may be guessed at by those who have perused the "Cent Nouvelles," which are grosser than most similar collections of the age.

In a prince of sounder moral qualities, the familiarity with which he invited subjects to his board—nay, occasionally sat at theirs—must have been highly popular; and even such as he was, the King's homeliness of manners atoned for many of his vices with that class of his subjects who were not particularly exposed to the consequences of his suspicion and jealousy. The *tiers état*, or commons of France, who rose to more opulence and consequence under the reign of this sagacious Prince, respected his person, though they loved him not; and it was resting on their support that he was enabled to make his party good against the hatred of the nobles, who conceived that he diminished the honour of the French crown, and obscured their own splendid privileges, by that very neglect of form which gratified the citizens and commons.

With patience, which most other princes would have considered as degrading, and not without a sense of amusement, the Monarch of France waited till his Life-guards-man had satisfied the keenness of a youthful appetite. It may be supposed, however, that Quentin had too much sense and prudence to put the royal patience to a long or tedious proof; and indeed he was repeatedly desirous to break off his repast ere Louis would permit him. "I see it in thine eye," he said good-naturedly, "that thy courage is not half abated. Go on—God and Saint Dennis!—charge again. I tell thee that meat and mass" (crossing himself) "never hindered the work of a good Christian man. Take a cup of wine; but mind thou be cautious of the wine-pot—it is the vice of thy countrymen as well as of the English, who, lacking that folly, are the choicest soldiers ever wore armour. And now wash speedily—forget not thy *bénédicité*, and follow me."

Quentin obeyed, and, conducted by a different, but as mazelike an approach as he had formerly passed, he followed Louis into the Hall of Roland.

"Take notice," said the King imperatively, "thou hast never left this post—let that be thine answer to thy kinsman and comrades—and, hark thee, to bind the recollection on thy memory, I give thee this gold chain" (flinging on his arm one of considerable value). "If I go not brave myself, those whom I trust have ever the means to ruffle it with the best. But, when such chains as these bind not the tongue from wagging too freely, my gossip, L'Hermite, hath an amulet for the throat, which never fails to work a certain cure. And now attend.—No man, save Oliver or I myself, enters here this evening; but ladies will come hither, perhaps from the one extremity of the hall, perhaps from the other, perhaps one from each. You may answer if they address you, but, being on duty, your answer must be brief; and you must neither address them in your turn, nor engage in any prolonged discourse. But hearken to what they say. Thine ears, as well as thy hands, are mine—I have bought thee, body and soul. Therefore, if thou hearest aught of their conversation, thou must retain it in memory until it is communicated to me, and then forget it. And, now I think better on it, it will be best that thou pass for a Scottish recruit, who hath come straight down from his mountains, and hath not yet acquired our most Christian language.—Right.—So, if they speak to thee, thou wilt *not* answer—this will free you from embarrassment, and lead them to converse without regard to your presence. You understand me.—Farewell. Be wary, and thou hast a friend."

The King had scarce spoken these words ere he disappeared behind the arras, leaving Quentin to meditate on what he had seen and heard. The youth was in one of those situations from which it is pleasanter to look forward than to look back; for the reflection that he had been planted like a marksman in a thicket who watches for a stag, to take the life of the noble Count of Crèvecœur, had in it nothing ennobling. It was very true, that the King's measures seemed on this occasion merely cautionary and defensive; but how did the youth know but he might be soon commanded on some offensive operation of the same kind? This would be an unpleasant crisis, since it was plain, from the character of his master, that there would be destruction in refusing, while his honour told him there would be disgrace in complying. He turned his thoughts from this subject of reflection, with the sage consolation so often adopted by youth when prospective dangers intrude themselves on their mind, that it was time enough to think what was to be done when the emergence actually arrived, and that sufficient for the day was the evil thereof.

Quentin made use of this sedative reflection the more easily, that the last commands of the King had given him something more agreeable to think of than his own condition. The Lady of the Lute was certainly one of those to whom his attention was to be dedicated; and well in his mind did he promise to obey one part of the King's mandate, and listen with diligence to every word that might drop from her lips, that he might know if the magic of her conversation equalled that of her music. But with as much sincerity did he swear to himself, that no part of her discourse should be reported by him to the King, which might affect the fair speaker otherwise than favourably.

Meantime, there was no fear of his again slumbering on his post. Each passing breath of wind, which, finding its way through the open lattice, waved the old arras, sounded like the approach of the fair object of his expectation. He felt, in short, all that mysterious anxiety, and eagerness of expectation, which is always the companion of love, and sometimes hath a considerable share in creating it.

At length, a door actually creaked and jingled (for the doors even of palaces did not in the fifteenth century turn on their hinges so noiseless as ours); but, alas! it was not at that end of the hall from which the lute had been heard. It opened, however, and a female figure entered, followed by two others, whom she directed by a sign to remain without, while she herself came forward into the hall. By her imperfect and unequal gait, which showed to peculiar disadvantage as she traversed this long gallery, Quentin at once recognised the Princess Joan, and, with the respect which became his situation, drew himself up in a fitting attitude of silent vigilance, and lowered his weapon to her as she passed. She acknowledged the courtesy by a gracious inclination of her head, and he had an opportunity of seeing her countenance more distinctly than he had in the morning.

There was little in the features of this ill-fated Princess to atone for the misfortune of her shape and gait. Her face was, indeed, by no means disagreeable in itself, though destitute of beauty; and there was a meek expression of suffering patience in her large blue eyes, which were commonly fixed upon the ground. But besides that she was extremely pallid in complexion, her skin had the yellowish discoloured tinge which accompanies habitual bad health; and though her teeth were white and regular, her lips were thin and pale. The Princess had a profusion of flaxen hair, but it was so light-coloured, as to be almost of a bluish tinge; and her tire-woman, who doubtless considered the luxuriance of her mistress's tresses as a beauty, had not greatly improved matters, by arranging them in curls around her pale countenance, to which they added an expression almost corpse-like and unearthly. To make matters still worse, she had chosen a vest or cymar of a pale green silk, which gave her, on the whole, a ghastly and even spectral appearance.

While Quentin followed this singular apparition with eyes in which curiosity was blended with compassion, for every look and motion of the Princess seemed to call for the latter feeling, two ladies entered from the upper end of the apartment.

One of these was the young person, who, upon Louis's summons, had served him with fruit, while Quentin made his memorable breakfast at the Fleur-de-Lys. Invested now with all the mysterious dignity belonging to the nymph of the veil and lute, and proved, besides (at least in Quentin's estimation), to be the high-born heiress of a rich earldom, her beauty made ten times the impression upon him which it had done when he beheld in her one whom he deemed the daughter of a paltry innkeeper, in attendance upon a rich and humorous old burgher. He now wondered what fascination could ever have concealed from him her real character. Yet her dress was nearly as simple as before, being a suit of deep mourning, without any ornaments. Her head-dress was but a veil of crape, which was entirely thrown back, so as to leave her face uncovered; and it was only Quentin's knowledge of her actual rank, which gave in his estimation new elegance to her beautiful shape, a dignity to her step which had before remained unnoticed, and to her regular features, brilliant complexion, and dazzling eyes, an air of conscious nobleness, that enhanced their beauty.

Had death been the penalty, Durward must needs have rendered to this beauty and her companion the same homage which he had just paid to the royalty of the Princess. They received it as those who were accustomed to the deference of inferiors, and returned it with courtesy; but he thought—perhaps it was but a youthful vision—that the young lady coloured slightly, kept her eyes on the ground, and seemed embarrassed, though in a trifling degree, as she returned his military salutation. This must have been owing to her recollection of the audacious stranger in the neighbouring turret at the Fleur-de-Lys; but did that discomposure express displeasure? This question he had no means to determine.

The companion of the youthful Countess, dressed like herself simply, and in deep mourning, was at the age when women are apt to cling most closely to that reputation for beauty which has for years been diminishing. She had still remains enough to show what the power of her charms must once have been, and, remembering past triumphs, it was evident from her manner that she had not relinquished the pretensions to future conquests. She was tall and graceful, though somewhat haughty in her deportment, and returned the salute of Quentin with a smile of gracious condescension, whispering, the next instant, something into her companion's ear, who turned towards the soldier, as if to comply with some hint from the elder lady, but answered, nevertheless, without raising her eyes. Quentin could not help suspecting that the observation called on the young lady to notice his own good mien; and he was (I do not know why) pleased with the idea, that the party referred to did not choose to look at him, in order to verify with her own eyes the truth of the observation. Probably he thought there was already a sort of mysterious connection beginning to exist between them, which gave importance to the slightest trifle.

This reflection was momentary, for he was instantly wrapped up in attention to the meeting of the Princess Joan with these stranger ladies. She had stood still upon their entrance, in order to receive them, conscious, perhaps, that motion did not become her well; and as she was somewhat embarrassed in receiving and repaying their compliments, the elder stranger, ignorant of the rank of the party whom she addressed, was led to pay her salutation in a manner, rather as if she conferred than received an honour through the interview.

"I rejoice, madam," she said, with a smile, which was meant to express condescension at once and encouragement, "that we are at length permitted the society of such a respectable person of our own sex as you appear to be. I must say, that my niece and I have had but little for which to thank the hospitality of King Louis—Nay, niece, never pluck my sleeve—I am sure I read in the looks of this young lady, sympathy for our situation.—Since we came hither, fair madam, we have been used little better than mere prisoners; and after a thousand invitations to throw our cause and our persons under the protection of France, the Most Christian King has afforded us at first but a base inn for our residence, and now a corner of this moth-eaten palace, out of which we are only permitted to creep towards sunset, as if we were bats or owls, whose appearance in the sunshine is to be held matter of ill omen."

"I am sorry," said the Princess, faltering with the awkward embarrassment of the interview, "that we have been unable, hitherto, to receive you according to your deserts.—Your niece, I trust, is better satisfied?"

"Much—much better than I can express," answered the youthful Countess—"I sought but safety, and I have found solitude and secrecy besides. The seclusion of our former residence, and the still greater solitude of that now assigned to us, augment, in my eye, the favour which the King vouchsafed to us unfortunate fugitives."

"Silence, my silly cousin," said the elder lady, "and let us speak according to our conscience, since at last we are alone with one of our own sex—I say alone, for that handsome young soldier is a mere statue, since he seems not to have the use of his limbs, and I am given to understand he wants that of his tongue, at least in civilised language—I say, since no one but this lady can understand us, I must own there is nothing I have regretted equal to taking this French journey. I looked for a splendid reception, tournaments, carousals, pageants, and festivals; and instead of which, all has been seclusion and obscurity! and the best society whom the King introduced to us, was a Bohemian vagabond, by whose agency he directed us to correspond with our friends in Flanders.—Perhaps," said the lady, "it is his politic intention to mew us up here until our lives' end, that he may seize on our estates, after the extinction of the ancient house of Croye. The Duke of Burgundy was not so cruel; he offered my niece a husband, though he was a bad one."

"I should have thought the veil preferable to an evil husband," said the Princess, with difficulty finding opportunity to interpose a word.

"One would at least wish to have the choice, madam," replied the voluble dame. "It is, Heaven knows, on account of my niece that I speak; for myself, I have long laid aside thoughts of changing my condition. I see you smile, but, by my halidome, it is true—yet that is no excuse for the King, whose conduct, like his person, hath more resemblance to that of old Michaud, the money-changer of Ghent, than to the successor of Charlemagne."

"Hold!" said the Princess with some asperity in her tone; "remember you speak of my father."

"Of your father!" replied the Burgundian lady in surprise.

"Of my father," repeated the Princess, with dignity. "I am Joan of France.—But fear not, madam," she continued, in the gentle accent which was natural to her, "you designed no offence, and I have taken none. Command my influence to render your exile, and that of this interesting young person, more supportable. Alas! it is but little I have in my power; but it is willingly offered."

Deep and submissive was the reverence with which the Countess Hameline de Croye, so was the elder lady called, received the obliging offer of the Princess's protection. She had been long the inhabitant of Courts, was mistress of the manners which are there acquired, and held firmly the established rule of courtiers of all ages, who, although their usual private conversation turns upon the vices and follies of their patrons, and on the injuries and neglect which they themselves have sustained, never suffer such hints to drop from them in the presence of the Sovereign or those of his family. The lady was, therefore, scandalised to the last degree at the mistake which had induced her to speak so indecorously in presence of the daughter of Louis. She would have exhausted herself in expressing regret and making apologies, had she not been put to silence and restored to equanimity by the Princess, who requested, in the most gentle manner, yet which, from a Daughter of France, had the weight of a command, that no more might be said in the way either of excuse or of explanation.

The Princess Joan then took her own chair with a dignity which became her, and compelled the two strangers to sit, one on either hand, to which the younger consented with unfeigned and respectful diffidence, and the elder with an affectation of deep humility and deference, which was intended for such. They spoke together, but in such a low tone that the sentinel could not overhear their discourse, and only remarked, that the Princess seemed to bestow much of her regard on the younger and more interesting lady; and that the Countess Hameline, though speaking a great deal more, attracted less of the Princess's attention by her full flow of conversation and compliment, than did her kinswoman by her brief and modest replies to what was addressed to her.

The conversation of the ladies had not lasted a quarter of an hour, when the door at the lower end of the hall opened, and a man entered shrouded in a riding-cloak. Mindful of the King's injunction, and determined not to be a second time caught slumbering, Quentin instantly moved towards the intruder, and, interposing between him and the ladies, requested him to retire instantly.

"By whose command?" said the stranger, in a tone of contemptuous surprise.

"By that of the King," said Quentin firmly, "which I am placed here to enforce."

"Not against Louis of Orleans," said the Duke, dropping his cloak.

The young man hesitated a moment; but how enforce his orders against the first Prince of the blood, about to be allied, as the report now generally went, with the King's own family?

"Your Highness," he said, "is too great that your pleasure should be withstood by me. I trust your Highness will bear me witness that I have done the duty of my post, so far as your will permitted."

"Go to—you shall have no blame, young soldier," said Orleans; and passing forward, paid his compliments to the Princess, with that air of constraint which always marked his courtesy when addressing her.

"He had been dining," he said, "with Dunois, and understanding there was society in Roland's Gallery, he had ventured on the freedom of adding one to the number."

The colour which mounted into the pale cheek of the unfortunate Joan, and which for the moment spread something of beauty over her features, evinced that this addition to the company was anything but indifferent to her. She hastened to present the Prince to the two ladies of Croye, who received him with the respect due to his eminent rank; and the Princess, pointing to a chair, requested him to join their conversation party.

The Duke declined the freedom of assuming a seat in such society; but taking a cushion from one of the settles, he laid it at the feet of the beautiful young Countess of Croye, and so seated himself, that, without appearing to neglect the Princess, he was enabled to bestow the greater share of his attention on her lovely neighbour.

At first, it seemed as if this arrangement rather pleased than offended his destined bride. She encouraged the Duke in his gallantries towards the fair stranger, and seemed to regard them as complimentary to herself. But the Duke of Orleans, though accustomed to subject his mind to the stern yoke of his uncle when in the King's presence, had enough of princely nature to induce him to follow his own inclinations whenever that restraint was withdrawn; and his high rank giving him a right to overstep the ordinary ceremonies, and advance at once to familiarity, his praises of the Countess Isabelle's beauty became so energetic, and flowed with such unrestrained freedom, owing perhaps to his having drunk a little more wine than usual—for Dunois was no enemy to the worship of Bacchus—that at length he seemed almost impassioned, and the presence of the Princess appeared well-nigh forgotten.

The tone of compliment which he indulged was grateful only to one individual in the circle; for the Countess Hameline already anticipated the dignity of an alliance with the first Prince of the blood, by means of her whose birth, beauty, and large possessions, rendered such an ambitious consummation by no means impossible, even in the eyes of a less sanguine projector, could the views of Louis XI. have been left out of the calculation of chances. The younger Countess listened to the Duke's gallantries with anxiety and embarrassment, and ever and anon turned an entreating look towards the Princess, as if requesting her to come to her relief. But the wounded feelings, and the timidity of Joan of France, rendered her incapable of an effort to make the conversation more general; and at length, excepting a few interjectional civilities of the Lady Hameline, it was maintained almost exclusively by the Duke himself, though at the expense of the younger Countess of Croye, whose beauty formed the theme of his high-flown eloquence.

Nor must I forget that there was a third person, the unregarded sentinel, who saw his fair visions melt away like wax before the sun, as the Duke persevered in the warm tenor of his passionate discourse. At length the Countess Isabelle de Croye made a determined effort to cut short what was becoming intolerably disagreeable to her, especially from the pain to which the conduct of the Duke was apparently subjecting the Princess.

Addressing the latter, she said, modestly, but with some firmness, that the first boon she had to claim from her promised protection was "that her Highness would undertake to convince the Duke of Orleans, that the ladies of Burgundy, though inferior in wit and manners to those of

France, were not such absolute fools, as to be pleased with no other conversation than that of extravagant compliment."

"I grieve, lady," said the Duke, preventing the Princess's answer, "that you will satirise, in the same sentence, the beauty of the dames of Burgundy, and the sincerity of the knights of France. If we are hasty and extravagant in the expression of our admiration, it is because we love as we fight, without letting cold deliberation come into our bosoms, and surrender to the fair with the same rapidity with which we defeat the valiant."

"The beauty of our countrywomen," said the young Countess, with more of reproof than she had yet ventured to use towards the high-born suitor, "is as unfit to claim such triumphs, as the valour of the men of Burgundy is incapable of yielding them."

"I respect your patriotism, Countess," said the Duke; "and the last branch of your theme shall not be impugned by me, till a Burgundian knight shall offer to sustain it with lance in rest. But for the injustice which you have done to the charms which your land produces, I appeal from yourself to yourself.—Look there," he said, pointing to a large mirror, the gift of the Venetian republic, and then of the highest rarity and value, "and tell me, as you look, what is the heart that can resist the charms there represented?"

The Princess, unable to sustain any longer the neglect of her lover, here sunk backwards on her chair, with a sigh, which at once recalled the Duke from the land of romance, and induced the Lady Hameline to ask whether her Highness found herself ill.

"A sudden pain shot through my forehead," said the Princess, attempting to smile; "but I shall be presently better."

Her increasing paleness contradicted her words, and induced the Lady Hameline to call for assistance, as the Princess was about to faint.

The Duke, biting his lip, and cursing the folly which could not keep guard over his tongue, ran to summon the Princess's attendants, who were in the next chamber; and when they came hastily, with the usual remedies, he could not but, as a cavalier and gentleman, give his assistance to support and to recover her. His voice, rendered almost tender by pity and self-reproach, was the most powerful means of recalling her to herself, and just as the swoon was passing away, the King himself entered the apartment.

CHAPTER XII

THE POLITICIAN

This is a lecturer so skill'd in policy,
That (no disparagement to Satan's cunning)
He well might read a lesson to the devil,
And teach the old seducer new temptations.
Old Play.

As Louis entered the Gallery, he bent his brows in the manner we have formerly described as peculiar to him, and sent, from under his gathered and gloomy eyebrows, a keen look on all around; in darting which, as Quentin afterwards declared, his eyes seemed to turn so small, so fierce, and so piercing, as to resemble those of an aroused adder looking through the bush of heath in which he lies coiled.

When, by this momentary and sharpened glance, the King had reconnoitred the cause of the bustle which was in the apartment, his first address was to the Duke of Orleans.

"You here, my fair cousin?" he said;—and turning to Quentin, added sternly, "Had you not charge?"

"Forgive the young man, Sire," said the Duke; "he did not neglect his duty; but I was informed that the Princess was in this gallery."

"And I warrant you would not be withstood when you came hither to pay your court," said the King, whose detestable hypocrisy persisted in representing the Duke as participating in a passion which was felt only on the side of his unhappy daughter; "and it is thus you debauch the sentinels of my guard, young man?—But what cannot be pardoned to a gallant who only lives *par amours!*"

The Duke of Orleans raised his head, as if about to reply, in some manner which might correct the opinion conveyed in the King's observation; but the instinctive reverence, not to say fear, of Louis, in which he had been bred from childhood, chained up his voice.

"And Joan hath been ill?" said the King; "but do not be grieved, Louis; it will soon pass away; lend her your arm to her apartment, while I will conduct these strange ladies to theirs."

The order was given in a tone which amounted to a command, and Orleans accordingly made his exit with the Princess at one extremity of the gallery, while the King, ungloving his right hand, courteously handed the Countess Isabelle and her kinswoman to their apartment, which opened from the other. He bowed profoundly as they entered, and remained standing on the threshold for a minute after they had disappeared; then, with great composure, shut the door by which they had retired, and turning the huge key, took it from the lock and put it into his girdle,—an appendage which gave him still more perfectly the air of some old miser, who cannot journey in comfort unless he bear with him the key of his treasure closet.

With slow and pensive step, and eyes fixed on the ground, Louis now paced towards Quentin Durward, who, expecting his share of the royal displeasure, viewed his approach with no little anxiety.

"Thou hast done wrong," said the King, raising his eyes, and fixing them firmly on him when he had come within a yard of him,—"thou hast done foul wrong, and deservest to die.—Speak not a word in defence!—What hadst thou to do with Dukes or Princesses?—what with *any* thing but my order?"

"So please your Majesty," said the young soldier, "what could I do?"

"What couldst thou do when thy post was forcibly passed?" answered the King scornfully,—"What is the use of that weapon on thy shoulder? Thou shouldst have levelled thy piece, and if the presumptuous rebel did not retire on the instant, he should have died within this very hall! Go—pass into these farther apartments. In the first thou wilt find a large staircase, which leads to the inner Bailley; there thou wilt find Oliver Dain. Send him to me—do thou begone to thy quarters.—As thou dost value thy life, be not so loose of thy tongue as thou hast been this day slack of thy hand."

Well pleased to escape so easily, yet with a soul which revolted at the cold-blooded cruelty which the King seemed to require from him in the execution of his duty, Durward took the road indicated, hastened downstairs, and communicated the royal pleasure to Oliver, who was waiting in the court beneath. The wily tonsor bowed, sighed, and smiled, as, with a voice even softer than ordinary, he wished the youth a good evening; and they parted, Quentin to his quarters, and Oliver to attend the King.

In this place, the Memoirs which we have chiefly followed in compiling this true history, were unhappily defective; for, founded chiefly on information supplied by Quentin, they do not convey the purport of the dialogue which, in his absence, took place between the King and his secret counsellor. Fortunately, the Library of Hautlieu contains a manuscript copy of the *Chronique Scandaleuse* of Jean de Troyes, much more full than that which has been printed; to which are added several curious memoranda, which we incline to think must have been written down by Oliver himself after the death of his master, and before he had the happiness to be rewarded with the halter which he had so long merited. From this we have been able to extract a very full account of the obscure favourite's conversation with Louis upon the present occasion, which throws a light upon the policy of that Prince, which we might otherwise have sought for in vain.

When the favourite attendant entered the Gallery of Roland, he found the King pensively seated upon the chair which his daughter had left some minutes before. Well acquainted with his temper, he glided on with his noiseless step until he had just crossed the line of the King's sight, so as to make him aware of his presence, then shrank modestly backward and out of sight, until he should be summoned to

speak or to listen. The Monarch's first address was an unpleasant one:—
"So, Oliver, your fine schemes are melting like snow before the south
wind!—I pray to our Lady of Embrun that they resemble not the ice-
heaps of which the Switzer churls tell such stories, and come rushing
down upon our heads."

"I have heard with concern that all is not well, Sire," answered Oliver.

"Not well!" exclaimed the King, rising and hastily marching up and
down the gallery,—"All is ill, man—and as ill nearly as possible;—so
much for thy fond romantic advice, that I, of all men, should become
a protector of distressed damsels! I tell thee Burgundy is arming, and on
the eve of closing an alliance with England. And Edward, who hath
his hands idle at home, will pour his thousands upon us through that
unhappy gate of Calais. Singly, I might cajole or defy them; but united,
united—and with the discontent and treachery of that villain Saint Paul!
--All thy fault, Oliver, who counselled me to receive the women, and to
use the services of that damned Bohemian to carry messages to their
vassals."

"My liege," said Oliver, "you know my reasons. The Countess's
domains lie between the frontiers of Burgundy and Flanders—her castle
is almost impregnable—her rights over neighbouring estates are such as,
if well supported, cannot but give much annoyance to Burgundy, were
the lady but wedded to one who should be friendly to France."

"It is, it *is* a tempting bait," said the King; "and could we have concealed her being here, we might have arranged such a marriage for
this rich heiress, as would have highly profited France.—But that cursed
Bohemian, how couldst thou recommend such a heathen hound for a
commission which required trust?"

"Please you," said Oliver, "to remember, it was your Majesty's self
who trusted him too far—much farther than I recommended. He would
have borne a letter trustily enough to the Countess's kinsman, telling him
to hold out her castle, and promising speedy relief; but your Highness
must needs put his prophetic power to the test; and thus he became
possessed of secrets which were worth betraying to Duke Charles."

"I am ashamed, I am ashamed,"—said Louis. "And yet, Oliver, they
say that these heathen people are descended from the sage Chaldeans,
who did read the mysteries of the stars in the plains of Shinar."

Well aware that his master, with all his acuteness and sagacity, was
but the more prone to be deceived by soothsayers, astrologers, diviners,
and all that race of pretenders to occult science, and that he even conceived himself to have some skill in these arts, Oliver dared to press
this point no farther; and only observed that the Bohemian had been
a bad prophet on his own account, else he would have avoided returning
to Tours, and saved himself from the gallows he had merited.

"It often happens that those who are gifted with prophetic knowledge,"
answered Louis, with much gravity, "have not the power of foreseeing
those events in which they themselves are personally interested."

"Under your Majesty's favour," replied the confidant, "that seems as if a man could not see his own hand by means of the candle which he holds, and which shows him every other object in the apartment."

"He cannot see his own features by the light which shows the faces of others," replied Louis; "and that is the more faithful illustration of the case.—But this is foreign to my purpose at present. The Bohemian hath had his reward, and peace be with him.—But these ladies—Not only does Burgundy threaten us with war for harbouring them, but their presence is like to interfere with my projects in my own family. My simple cousin of Orleans hath barely seen this damsel, and I venture to prophesy that the sight of her is like to make him less pliable in the matter of his alliance with Joan."

"Your Majesty," said the counsellor, "may send the ladies of Croye back to Burgundy, and so make your peace with the Duke. Many might murmur at this as dishonourable; but if necessity demands the sacrifice——"

"If profit demanded the sacrifice, Oliver, the sacrifice should be made without hesitation," answered the King. "I am an old experienced salmon, and use not to gulp the angler's hook because it is busked up with a feather called honour. But what is worse than a lack of honour, there were, in returning those ladies to Burgundy, a forfeiture of those views of advantage which moved us to give them an asylum. It were heart-breaking to renounce the opportunity of planting a friend to ourselves, and an enemy to Burgundy, in the very centre of his dominions, and so near to the discontented cities of Flanders. Oliver, I cannot relinquish the advantages which our scheme of marrying the maiden to a friend of our own seems to hold out to us."

"Your Majesty," said Oliver, after a moment's thought, "might confer her hand on some right trusty friend, who would take all blame on himself, and serve your Majesty secretly, while in public you might disown him."

"And where am I to find such a friend?" said Louis. "Were I to bestow her upon any one of our mutinous and ill-ruled nobles, would it not be rendering him independent? and hath it not been my policy for years to prevent them from becoming so?—Dunois indeed—him, and him only, I might perchance trust.—He would fight for the crown of France, whatever were his condition. But honours and wealth change men's natures—Even Dunois I will not trust."

"Your Majesty may find others," said Oliver, in his smoothest manner, and in a tone more insinuating than that which he usually employed in conversing with the King, who permitted him considerable freedom; "men dependent entirely on your own grace and favour, and who could no more exist without your countenance than without sun or air—men rather of head than of action—men who——"

"Men who resemble thyself, ha!" said King Louis.—"No, Oliver, by my faith that arrow was too rashly shot!—What! because I indulge thee with my confidence, and let thee, in reward, poll my lieges a little now and then, dost thou think it makes thee fit to be the husband of that beautiful vision, and a Count of the highest class to the boot?—thee— thee, I say, low-born and lower bred, whose wisdom is at best a sort of cunning, and whose courage is more than doubtful?"

"Your Majesty imputes to me a presumption of which I am not guilty, in supposing me to aspire so highly," said Oliver.

"I am glad to hear it, man," replied the King; "and truly, I hold your judgment the healthier that you disown such a reverie. But methinks thy speech sounded strangely in that key.—Well, to return.—I dare not wed this beauty to one of my subjects.—I dare not return her to Burgundy—I dare not transmit her to England, or to Germany, where she is likely to become the prize of some one more apt to unite with Burgundy than with France, and who would be more ready to discourage the honest malcontents in Ghent and Liege, than to yield them that wholesome countenance which might always find Charles the Hardy enough to exercise his valour on, without stirring from his own domains —and they were in so ripe a humour for insurrection, the men of Liege in especial, that they alone, well heated and supported, would find my fair cousin work for more than a twelvemonth;—and backed by a warlike Count of Croye,—Oh, Oliver! the plan is too hopeful to be resigned without a struggle.—Cannot thy fertile brain devise some scheme?"

Oliver paused for a long time—then at last replied, "What if a bridal could be accomplished betwixt Isabelle of Croye, and young Adolphus, the Duke of Gueldres?"

"What!" said the King, in astonishment; "sacrifice her, and she, too, so lovely a creature, to the furious wretch who deposed, imprisoned, and has often threatened to murder, his own father!—No, Oliver, no—that were too unutterably cruel even for you and me, who look so steadfastly to our excellent end, the peace and the welfare of France, and respect so little the means by which it is attained. Besides, he lies distant from us, and is detested by the people of Ghent and Liege.—No, no—I will none of Adolphus of Gueldres—think on some one else."

"My invention is exhausted, Sire," said the counsellor; "I can remember no one who, as husband to the Countess of Croye, would be likely to answer your Majesty's views. He must unite such various qualities—a friend to your Majesty—an enemy to Burgundy—of policy enough to conciliate the Gauntois and Liegeois, and of valour sufficient to defend his little dominions against the power of Duke Charles—Of noble birth besides—that your Highness insists upon; and of excellent and most virtuous character, to the boot of all."

"Nay, Oliver," said the King, "I leaned not so much—that is, so very much, on character; but methinks Isabelle's bridegroom should be something less publicly and generally abhorred than Adolphus of Gueldres.— For example, since I myself must suggest some one,—why not William de la Marck?"

"On my halidome, Sire," said Oliver, "I cannot complain of your demanding too high a standard of moral excellence in the happy man, if the Wild Boar of Ardennes can serve your turn. De la Marck?—why, he is the most notorious robber and murderer on all the frontiers—excommunicated by the Pope for a thousand crimes."

"We will have him released from the sentence, friend Oliver—Holy Church is merciful."

"Almost an outlaw," continued Oliver, "and under the ban of the Empire, by an ordinance of the chamber at Ratisbon."

"We will have the ban taken off, friend Oliver," continued the King, in the same tone; "the Imperial Chamber will hear reason."

"And admitting him to be of noble birth," said Oliver, "he hath the manners, the face, and the outward form, as well as the heart, of a Flemish butcher—She will never accept of him."

"His mode of wooing, if I mistake him not," said Louis, "will render it difficult for her to make a choice."

"I was far wrong indeed, when I taxed your Majesty with being over scrupulous," said the counsellor. "On my life, the crimes of Adolphus are but virtues to those of De la Marck!—And then how is he to meet with his bride?—Your Majesty knows he dare not stir far from his own Forest of Ardennes."

"That must be cared for," said the King; "and, in the first place, the two ladies must be acquainted privately that they can be no longer maintained at this Court, except at the expense of a war between France and Burgundy, and that, unwilling to deliver them up to my fair cousin of Burgundy, I am desirous they should secretly depart from my dominions."

"They will demand to be conveyed to England," said Oliver; "and we shall have her return to Flanders with an island lord, having a round fair face, long brown hair, and three thousand archers at his back."

"No—no," replied the King; "we dare not (you understand me) so far offend our fair cousin of Burgundy as to let her pass to England—It would bring his displeasure as certainly as our maintaining her here. No, no—to the safety of the Church alone we will venture to commit her; and the utmost we can do is to connive at the Ladies Hameline and Isabelle de Croye departing in disguise, and with a small retinue, to take refuge with the Bishop of Liege, who will place the fair Isabelle for the time under the safeguard of a convent."

"And if that convent protect her from William de la Marck, when he knows of your Majesty's favourable intentions, I have mistaken the man."

"Why, yes," answered the King, "thanks to our secret supplies of money, De la Marck hath together a handsome handful of as unscrupulous soldiery as ever were outlawed; with which he contrives to maintain himself among the woods, in such a condition as makes him formidable both to the Duke of Burgundy and the Bishop of Liege. He lacks nothing but some territory which he may call his own; and this being so fair an opportunity to establish himself by marriage, I think that, *Pasques-dieu!* he will find means to win and wed, without more than a hint on our part. The Duke of Burgundy will then have such a thorn in his side, as no lancet of our time will easily cut out from his flesh. The Boar of Ardennes, whom he has already outlawed, strengthened by the possession of that fair lady's lands, castles, and seigniory, with the discontented Liegeois to boot, who, by my faith, will not be in that case unwilling to choose him for their captain and leader—let Charles then think of wars with France when he will, or rather let him bless his stars if she war not with him.—How dost thou like the scheme, Oliver, ha?"

"Rarely," said Oliver, "save and except the doom which confers that lady on the Wild Boar of Ardennes.—By my halidome, saving in a little outward show of gallantry, Tristan, the Provost-Marshal, were the more proper bridegroom of the two."

"Anon thou didst propose Master Oliver the barber," said Louis; "but friend Oliver and gossip Tristan, though excellent men in the way of counsel and execution, are not the stuff that men make Counts of. Know you not that the burghers of Flanders value birth in other men, precisely because they have it not themselves?—A plebeian mob ever desire an aristocratic leader. Yonder Ked, or Cade, or—how called they him?— in England, was fain to lure his rascal rout after him, by pretending to the blood of the Mortimers. William de la Marck comes of the blood of the princes of Sedan, as noble as mine own.—And now to business. I must determine the ladies of Croye to a speedy and secret flight, under sure guidance. This will be easily done—we have but to hint the alternative of surrendering them to Burgundy. Thou must find means to let William de la Marck know of their motions, and let him choose his own time and place to push his suit. I know a fit person to travel with them."

"May I ask to whom your Majesty commits such an important charge?" asked the tonsor.

"To a foreigner, be sure," replied the King; "one who has neither kin nor interest in France, to interfere with the execution of my pleasure; and who knows too little of the country, and its factions, to suspect more of my purpose than I choose to tell him—in a word, I design to employ the young Scot who sent you hither but now."

Oliver paused in a manner which seemed to imply a doubt of the prudence of the choice, and then added, "Your Majesty has reposed confidence in that stranger boy earlier than is your wont."

"I have my reasons," answered the King.—"Thou knowest" (and he crossed himself) "my devotion for the blessed Saint Julian. I had been saying my orisons to that holy Saint late in the night before last, wherein (as he is known to be the guardian of travellers) I made it my humble petition that he would augment my household with such wandering foreigners as might best establish throughout our kingdom unlimited devotion to our will; and I vowed to the good Saint in guerdon, that I would, in his name, receive, and relieve, and maintain them."

"And did Saint Julian," said Oliver, "send your Majesty this long-legged importation from Scotland in answer to your prayers?"

Although the barber, who well knew that his master had superstition in a large proportion to his want of religion, and that on such topics nothing was more easy than to offend him—although, I say, he knew the royal weakness, and therefore carefully put the preceding question in the softest and most simple tone of voice, Louis felt the innuendo which it contained, and regarded the speaker with high displeasure.

"Sirrah," he said, "thou art well called Oliver the Devil, who darest thus to sport at once with thy master and with the blessed Saints. I tell thee, wert thou one grain less necessary to me, I would have thee hung up on yonder oak before the Castle, as an example to all who scoff at things holy!—Know, thou infidel slave, that mine eyes were no sooner closed, than the blessed Saint Julian was visible to me, leading a young man, whom he presented to me, saying, that his fortune should be to escape the sword, the cord, the river, and to bring good fortune to the side which he should espouse, and to the adventures in which he should be engaged. I walked out on the succeeding morning, and I met with this youth, whose image I had seen in my dream. In his own country he hath escaped the sword, amid the massacre of his whole family, and here, within the brief compass of two days, he hath been strangely rescued from drowning and from the gallows, and hath already, on a particular occasion, as I but lately hinted to thee, been of the most material service to me. I receive him as sent hither by Saint Julian, to serve me in the most difficult, the most dangerous, and even the most desperate services."

The King, as he thus expressed himself, doffed his hat, and selecting from the numerous little leaden figures with which the hat-band was garnished that which represented Saint Julian, he placed it on the table, as was often his wont when some peculiar feeling of hope, or perhaps of remorse, happened to thrill across his mind, and, kneeling down before it, muttered, with an appearance of profound devotion, *"Sancte Juliane, adsis precibus nostris! Ora, ora, pro nobis!"*

This was one of the ague-fits of superstitious devotion which often seized on Louis in such extraordinary times and places, that they gave one of the most sagacious Monarchs who ever reigned, the appearance of a madman, or at least of one whose mind was shaken by some deep consciousness of guilt.

While he was thus employed, his favourite looked at him with an expression of sarcastic contempt, which he scarce attempted to disguise. Indeed it was one of this man's peculiarities, that, in his whole intercourse with his master, he laid aside that fondling, purring affectation of officiousness and humility, which distinguished his conduct to others; and if he still bore some resemblance to a cat, it was when the animal is on its guard,—watchful, animated, and alert for sudden exertion. The cause of this change was probably Oliver's consciousness, that his master was himself too profound a hypocrite not to see through the hypocrisy of others.

"The features of this youth, then, if I may presume to speak," said Oliver, "resemble those of him whom your dream exhibited?"

"Closely and intimately," said the King, whose imagination, like that of superstitious people in general, readily imposed upon himself—"I have had his horoscope cast, besides, by Galeotti Martivalle, and I have plainly learned, through his art and mine own observation, that, in many respects, this unfriended youth has his destiny under the same constellation with mine."

Whatever Oliver might think of the causes thus boldly assigned for the preference of an inexperienced stripling, he dared make no farther objections, well knowing that Louis, who, while residing in exile, had bestowed much of his attention on the supposed science of judicial astrology, would listen to no raillery of any kind which impeached his skill. He therefore only replied, that he trusted the youth would prove faithful in the discharge of a task so delicate.

"We will take care he hath no opportunity to be otherwise," said Louis; "for he shall be privy to nothing, save that he is sent to escort the ladies of Croye to the residence of the Bishop of Liege. Of the probable interference of William de la Marck, he shall know as little as they themselves. None shall know that secret but the guide; and Tristan or thou must find one fit for our purpose."

"But in that case," said Oliver, "judging of him from his country and his appearance, the young man is like to stand to his arms so soon as the Wild Boar comes on them, and may not come off so easily from the tusks as he did this morning."

"If they rend his heart-strings," said Louis composedly, "Saint Julian, blessed be his name! can send me another in his stead. It skills as little that the messenger is slain after his duty is executed, as that the flask is broken when the wine is drunk out.—Meanwhile, we must expedite the ladies' departure, and then persuade the Count de Crèvecœur that it has taken place without our connivance; we having been desirous to restore them to the custody of our fair cousin, which their sudden departure has unhappily prevented."

"The Count is perhaps too wise, and his master too prejudiced. to believe it."

"Holy Mother!" said Louis, "what unbelief would that be in Christian men! But, Oliver, they *shall* believe us. We will throw into our whole conduct towards our fair cousin, Duke Charles, such thorough and unlimited confidence, that, not to believe we have been sincere with him in every respect, he must be worse than an infidel. I tell thee, so convinced am I that I could make Charles of Burgundy think of me in every respect as I would have him, that, were it necessary for silencing his doubts, I would ride unarmed, and on a palfrey, to visit him in his tent, with no better guard about me than thine own simple person, friend Oliver."

"And I," said Oliver, "though I pique not myself upon managing steel in any other shape than that of a razor, would rather charge a Swiss battalion of pikes, than I would accompany your Highness upon such a visit of friendship to Charles of Burgundy, when he hath so many grounds to be well assured that there is enmity in your Majesty's bosom against him."

"Thou art a fool, Oliver," said the King, "with all thy pretensions to wisdom—and art not aware that deep policy must often assume the appearance of the most extreme simplicity, as courage occasionally shrouds itself under the show of modest timidity. Were it needful, full surely would I do what I have said—the Saints always blessing our purpose, and the heavenly constellations bringing round, in their course, a proper conjuncture for such an exploit."

In these words did King Louis XI. give the first hint of the extraordinary resolution which he afterwards adopted, in order to dupe his great rival, the subsequent execution of which had very nearly proved his own ruin.

He parted with his counsellor, and presently afterwards went to the apartment of the Ladies of Croye. Few persuasions beyond his mere licence would have been necessary to determine their retreat from the Court of France, upon the first hint that they might not be eventually protected against the Duke of Burgundy; but it was not so easy to induce them to choose Liege for the place of their retreat. They entreated and requested to be transferred to Bretagne or Calais, where, under protection of the Duke of Bretagne, or King of England, they might remain in a state of safety, until the Sovereign of Burgundy should relent in his rigorous purpose towards them. But neither of these places of safety at all suited the plans of Louis, and he was at last successful in inducing them to adopt that which did coincide with them.

The power of the Bishop of Liege for their defence was not to be questioned, since his ecclesiastical dignity gave him the means of protecting the fugitives against all Christian princes; while, on the other hand, his secular forces, if not numerous, seemed at least sufficient to defend his person, and all under his protection, from any sudden violence. The difficulty was to reach the little Court of the Bishop in safety; but for this Louis promised to provide, by spreading a report that the Ladies of Croye had escaped from Tours by night, under fear of being delivered up to the Burgundian Envoy, and had taken their flight towards Bretagne. He also promised them the attendance of a small, but faithful retinue, and letters to the commanders of such towns and fortresses as they might pass, with instructions to use every means for protecting and assisting them on their journey.

The Ladies of Croye, although internally resenting the ungenerous and discourteous manner in which Louis thus deprived them of the

promised asylum in his Court, were so far from objecting to the hasty
departure which he proposed, that they even anticipated his project, by
entreating to be permitted to set forward that same night. The Lady
Hameline was already tired of a place where there were neither admiring
courtiers, nor festivities to be witnessed; and the Lady Isabelle thought
she had seen enough to conclude, that were the temptation to become a
little stronger, Louis XI., not satisfied with expelling them from his
Court, would not hesitate to deliver her up to her irritated Suzerain, the
Duke of Burgundy. Lastly, Louis himself readily acquiesced in their
hasty departure, anxious to preserve peace with Duke Charles, and
alarmed lest the beauty of Isabelle should interfere with and impede the
favourite plan which he had formed, for bestowing the hand of his daughter Joan upon his cousin of Orleans.

CHAPTER XIII

THE JOURNEY

> Talk not of kings—I scorn the poor comparison;
> I am a SAGE, and can command the elements—
> At least men think I can; and on that thought
> I found unbounded empire.
>
> ALBUMAZAR.

OCCUPATION and adventure might be said to crowd upon the young
Scottishman with the force of a spring-tide; for he was speedily
summoned to the apartment of his Captain, the Lord Crawford,
where, to his astonishment, he again beheld the King. After a few
words respecting the honour and trust which were about to be reposed
in him, which made Quentin internally afraid that they were again
about to propose to him such a watch as he had kept upon the
Count of Crèvecœur, or perhaps some duty still more repugnant to
his feelings, he was not relieved merely, but delighted, with hearing
that he was selected, with the assistance of four others under his
command, one of whom was a guide, to escort the Ladies of Croye to
the little Court of their relative, the Bishop of Liege, in the safest and
most commodious, and, at the same time, in the most secret manner
possible. A scroll was given him, in which were set down directions for his
guidance, for the places of halt (generally chosen in obscure villages,
solitary monasteries, and situations remote from towns), and for the
general precautions which he was to attend to, especially on approaching
the frontier of Burgundy. He was sufficiently supplied with instructions
what he ought to say and do to sustain the personage of the Maitre
d'Hotel of two English ladies of rank, who had been on a pilgrimage to
Saint Martin of Tours, and were about to visit the holy city of Cologne,
and worship the relics of the sage Eastern Monarchs, who came to adore
the nativity of Bethlehem; for under that character the Ladies of Croye
were to journey.

Without having any defined notions of the cause of his delight, Quentin Durward's heart leapt for joy at the idea of approaching thus nearly to the person of the Beauty of the Turret, and in a situation which entitled him to her confidence, since her protection was in so great a degree entrusted to his conduct and courage. He felt no doubt in his own mind, that he should be her successful guide through the hazards of her pilgrimage. Youth seldom thinks of dangers, and bred up free, and fearless, and self-confiding, Quentin, in particular, only thought of them to defy them. He longed to be exempted from the restraint of the Royal presence, that he might indulge the secret glee with which such unexpected tidings filled him, and which prompted him to bursts of delight which would have been totally unfitting for that society.

But Louis had not yet done with him. That cautious Monarch had to consult a counsellor of a different stamp from Oliver le Diable, and who was supposed to derive his skill from the superior and astral intelligences, as men, judging from their fruits, were apt to think the counsels of Oliver sprung from the Devil himself.

Louis therefore led the way, followed by the impatient Quentin, to a separate tower of the Castle of Plessis, in which was installed, in no small ease and splendour, the celebrated astrologer, poet, and philosopher, Galeotti Marti, or Martius, or Martivalle, a native of Narni, in Italy, the author of the famous Treatise, *De Vulgo Incognitis*,[1] and the subject of his age's admiration, and of the panegyrics of Paulus Jovius. He had long flourished at the Court of the celebrated Matthias Corvinus, King of Hungary, from whom he was in some measure decoyed by Louis, who grudged the Hungarian Monarch the society and the counsels of a sage, accounted so skilful in reading the decrees of Heaven.

Martivale was none of those ascetic, withered, pale professors of mystic learning of those days, who bleared their eyes over the midnight furnace, and macerated their bodies by outwatching the polar bear. He indulged in all courtly pleasures, and, until he grew corpulent, had excelled in all martial sports and gymnastic exercises, as well as in the use of arms; insomuch, that Janus Pannonius has left a Latin epigram, upon a wrestling match betwixt Galeotti and a renowned champion of that art, in the presence of the Hungarian King and Court, in which the Astrologer was completely victorious.

The apartments of this courtly and martial sage were far more splendidly furnished than any which Quentin had yet seen in the royal palace; and the carving and ornamented woodwork of his library, as well as the magnificence displayed in the tapestries, showed the elegant taste of the learned Italian. Out of his study one door opened to his sleeping-apartment, another led to the turret which served as his observatory. A large oaken table, in the midst of the chamber, was covered with a rich Turkey carpet, the spoils of the tent of a Pacha after the great battle of Jaiza,

[1] Concerning things unknown to the generality of mankind.

where the Astrologer had fought abreast with the valiant champion of Christendom, Matthias Corvinus. On the table lay a variety of mathematical and astrological instruments, all of the most rich materials and curious workmanship. His astrolabe of silver was the gift of the Emperor of Germany, and his Jacob's staff of ebony, jointed with gold, and curiously inlaid, was a mark of esteem from the reigning Pope.

There were various other miscellaneous articles disposed on the table, or hanging around the walls; amongst others, two complete suits of armour, one of mail, the other of plate, both of which, from their great size, seemed to call the gigantic Astrologer their owner; a Spanish toledo, a Scottish broadsword, a Turkish scimitar, with bows, quivers, and other warlike weapons; musical instruments of several different kinds; a silver crucifix, a sepulchral antique vase, and several of the little brazen Penates of the ancient heathens, with other curious nondescript articles, some of which, in the superstitious opinions of that period, seemed to be designed for magical purposes. The library of this singular character was of the same miscellaneous description with his other effects. Curious manuscripts of classical antiquity lay mingled with the voluminous labours of Christian divines, and of those painstaking sages who professed the chemical science, and proffered to guide their students into the most secret recesses of nature, by means of the Hermetical Philosophy. Some were written in the Eastern character, and others concealed their sense or nonsense under the veil of hieroglyphics and cabalistic characters. The whole apartment, and its furniture of every kind, formed a scene very impressive on the fancy, considering the general belief then indisputably entertained, concerning the truth of the occult sciences; and that effect was increased by the manners and appearance of the individual himself, who, seated in a huge chair, was employed in curiously examining a specimen, just issued from the Frankfort press, of the newly invented art of printing.

Galeotti Martivalle was a tall, bulky, yet stately man, considerably past his prime, and whose youthful habits of exercise, though still occasionally resumed, had not been able to contend with his natural tendency to corpulence, increased by sedentary study, and indulgence in the pleasures of the table. His features, though rather overgrown, were dignified and noble, and a Santon might have envied the dark and downward sweep of his long-descending beard. His dress was a chamber-robe of the richest Genoa velvet, with ample sleeves, clasped with frogs of gold, and lined with sables. It was fastened round his middle by a broad belt of virgin parchment, round which were represented, in crimson characters, the signs of the zodiac. He rose and bowed to the King, yet with the air of one to whom such exalted society was familiar, and who was not at all likely, even in the royal presence, to compromise the dignity then especially affected by the pursuers of science.

"You are engaged, father," said the King, "and, as I think, with this new-fashioned art of multiplying manuscripts, by the intervention of machinery. Can things of such mechanical and terrestrial import interest the thoughts of one, before whom Heaven has unrolled her own celestial volumes?"

"My brother," replied Martivalle,—"for so the tenant of this cell must term even the King of France, when he deigns to visit him as a disciple,— believe me that, in considering the consequences of this invention, I read with as certain augury, as by any combination of the heavenly bodies, the most awful and portentous changes. When I reflect with what slow and limited supplies the stream of science hath hitherto descended to us; how difficult to be obtained by those most ardent in its search; how certain to be neglected by all who regard their ease; how liable to be diverted, or altogether dried up, by the invasions of barbarism; can I look forward without wonder and astonishment, to the lot of a succeeding generation, on whom knowledge will descend like the first and second rain, uninterrupted, unabated, unbounded; fertilising some grounds, and overflowing others; changing the whole form of social life; establishing and overthrowing religions; erecting and destroying kingdoms——"

"Hold, Galeotti," said Louis,—"shall these changes come in our time?"

"No, my royal brother," replied Martivalle; "this invention may be likened to a young tree, which is now newly planted, but shall, in succeeding generations, bear fruit as fatal, yet as precious, as that of the Garden of Eden; the knowledge, namely, of good and evil."

Louis answered, after a moment's pause, "Let futurity look to what concerns them—we are men of this age, and to this age we will confine our care. Sufficient for the day is the evil thereof.—Tell me, hast thou proceeded farther in the horoscope which I sent to thee, and of which you made me some report? I have brought the party hither, that you may use palmistry, or chiromancy, if such is your pleasure. The matter is pressing."

The bulky Sage arose from his seat, and, approaching the young soldier, fixed on him his keen large dark eyes, as if he were in the act of internally spelling and dissecting every lineament and feature.—Blushing and borne down by this close examination on the part of one whose expression was so reverent at once and commanding, Quentin bent his eyes on the ground, and did not again raise them, till in the act of obeying the sonorous command of the Astrologer, "Look up and be not afraid, but hold forth thy hand."

When Martivalle had inspected his palm, according to the form of the mystic arts which he practised, he led the King some steps aside.—"My royal brother," he said, "the physiognomy of this youth, together with the lines impressed on his hand, confirm, in a wonderful degree, the report which I founded on his horoscope, as well as that judgment which your own proficiency in our sublime arts induced you at once to form of him. All promises that this youth will be brave and fortunate."

"And faithful?" said the King; "for valour and fortune square not with fidelity."

"And faithful also," said the Astrologer; "for there is manly firmness in look and eye, and his *linea vitæ* is deeply marked and clear, which indicates a true and upright adherence to those who do benefit or lodge trust in him. But yet——"

"But what?" said the King; "Father Galeotti, wherefore do you now pause?"

"The ears of Kings," said the Sage, "are like the palates of those dainty patients, which are unable to endure the bitterness of the drugs necessary for their recovery."

"My ears and my palate have no such niceness," said Louis; "let me hear what is useful counsel, and swallow what is wholesome medicine. I quarrel not with the rudeness of the one, or the harsh taste of the other. I have not been cockered in wantonness or indulgence; my youth was one of exile and suffering. My ears are used to harsh counsel and take no offence at it."

"Then plainly, Sire," replied Galeotti, "if you have aught in your purposed commission, which—which, in short, may startle a scrupulous conscience—entrust it not to this youth—at least, not till a few years' exercise in your service has made him as unscrupulous as others."

"And is this what you hesitated to speak, my good Galeotti? and didst thou think thy speaking it would offend me?" said the King. "Alack, I know that thou art well sensible, that the path of royal policy cannot be always squared (as that of private life ought invariably to be) by the abstract maxims of religion and of morality. Wherefore do we, the Princes of the earth, found churches and monasteries, make pilgrimages, undergo penances, and perform devotions, with which others may dispense, unless it be because the benefit of the public, and the welfare of our kingdoms, force us upon measures which grieve our consciences as Christians? But Heaven has mercy—the Church, an unbounded stock of merits, and the intercession of Our Lady of Embrun, and the blessed saints, is urgent, everlasting, and omnipotent."—He laid his hat on the table, and devoutly kneeling before the images stuck into the hat-band repeated, in an earnest tone, *"Sancte Huberte, Sancte Juliane, Sancte Martine, Sancte Rosalia, Sancti quotquot adestis, orate pro me peccatore!"* He then smote his breast, arose, reassumed his hat, and continued:—"Be assured, good father, that whatever there may be in our commission, of the nature at which you have hinted, the execution shall not be entrusted to this youth, nor shall he be privy to such part of our purpose."

"In this," said the Astrologer, "you, my royal brother, will walk wisely. Something may be apprehended likewise from the rashness of this your young commissioner; a failing inherent in those of sanguine complexion. But I hold that, by the rules of art, this chance is not to be weighed against the other properties discovered from his horoscope and otherwise."

"Will this next midnight be a propitious hour in which to commence a perilous journey?" said the King.—"See, here is your Ephemerides—you see the position of the moon in regard to Saturn, and the ascendence of Jupiter—That should argue, methinks, in submission to your better art, success to him who sends forth the expedition at such an hour."

"To him who *sends forth* the expedition," said the Astrologer, after a pause, "this conjunction doth indeed promise success; but, methinks, that Saturn being combust, threatens danger and infortune to the party *sent;* whence I infer that the errand may be perilous, or even fatal, to those who are to journey. Violence and captivity, methinks, are intimated in that adverse conjunction."

"Violence and captivity to those who are sent," answered the King, "but success to the wishes of the sender—Runs it not thus, my learned father?"

"Even so," replied the Astrologer.

The King paused, without giving any further indication how far this presaging speech (probably hazarded by the Astrologer from his conjecture that the commission related to some dangerous purpose) squared with his real object, which, as the reader is aware, was to betray the Countess Isabelle of Croye into the hands of William de la Marck, a nobleman indeed of high birth, but degraded by his crimes into a leader of banditti, distinguished for his turbulent disposition and ferocious bravery.

The King then pulled forth a paper from his pocket, and ere he gave it to Martivalle, said, in a tone which resembled that of an apology— "Learned Galeotti, be not surprised, that, possessing in you an oracular treasure, superior to that lodged in the breast of any now alive, not excepting the great Nostradamus himself, I am desirous frequently to avail myself of your skill in those doubts and difficulties which beset every Prince who hath to contend with rebellion within his land, and with external enemies, both powerful and inveterate."

"When I was honoured with your request, Sire," said the philosopher, "and abandoned the Court of Buda for that of Plessis, it was with the resolution to place at the command of my royal patron whatever my art had, that might be of service to him."

"Enough, good Martivalle—I pray thee attend to the import of this question."—He proceeded to read from the paper in his hand:—"A person having on hand a weighty controversy, which is like to draw to debate either by law or by force of arms, is desirous, for the present, to seek accommodation by a personal interview with his antagonist. He desires to know what day will be propitious for the execution of such a purpose; also what is likely to be the success of such a negotiation, and whether his adversary will be moved to answer the confidence thus reposed in him, with gratitude and kindness, or may rather be likely to abuse the opportunity and advantage which such meeting may afford him?"

"It is an important question," said Martivalle, when the King had done reading, "and requires that I should set a planetary figure, and give it instant and deep consideration."

"Let it be so, my good father in the sciences, and thou shalt know what it is to oblige a King of France. We are determined, if the constellations forbid not,—and our own humble art leads us to think that they approve our purpose,—to hazard something, even in our own person, to stop these anti-Christian wars."

"May the Saints forward your Majesty's pious intent," said the Astrologer, "and guard your sacred person!"

"Thanks, learned father.—Here is something, the while, to enlarge your curious library."

He placed under one of the volumes a small purse of gold; for, economical even in his superstitions, Louis conceived the Astrologer sufficiently bound to his service by the pensions he had assigned him, and thought himself entitled to the use of his skill at a moderate rate, even upon great exigencies.

Louis, having thus, in legal phrase, added a refreshing fee to his general retainer, turned from him to address Durward.—"Follow me," he said, "my bonny Scot, as one chosen by Destiny and a Monarch to accomplish a bold adventure. All must be got ready, that thou mayst put foot in stirrup the very instant the bell of Saint Martin's tolls twelve. One minute sooner, one minute later, were to forfeit the favourable aspect of the constellations which smile on your adventure."

Thus saying, the King left the apartment, followed by his young guardsman; and no sooner were they gone, than the Astrologer gave way to very different feelings from those which seemed to animate him during the royal presence.

"The niggardly slave!" he said, weighing the purse in his hand,—for, being a man of unbounded expense, he had almost constant occasion for money,—"The base sordid scullion!—A coxswain's wife would give more to know that her husband had crossed the narrow seas in safety. *He* acquire any tincture of humane letters!—yes, when prowling foxes and yelling wolves become musicians. *He* read the glorious blazoning of the firmament!—ay, when sordid moles shall become lynxes.—*Post tot promissa*—after so many promises made, to entice me from the Court of the magnificent Matthias, where Hun and Turk, Christian and Infidel, the Czar of Muscovia and the Cham of Tartary themselves contended to load me with gifts,—doth he think I am to abide in this old Castle, like a bullfinch in a cage, fain to sing as oft as he chooses to whistle, and all for seed and water?—Not so—*aut inveniam viam, aut faciam*—I will discover or contrive a remedy. The Cardinal Balue is politic and liberal— this query shall to him, and it shall be his Eminence's own fault if the stars speak not as he would have them."

He again took the despised guerdon, and weighed it in his hand. "It may be," he said, "there is some jewel, or pearl of price, concealed in this paltry case—I have heard he can be liberal even to lavishness, when it suits his caprice or interest."

He emptied the purse, which contained neither more nor less than ten gold pieces. The indignation of the Astrologer was extreme.—"Thinks he that for such paltry rate of hire I will practise that celestial science which I have studied with the Armenian Abbot of Istrahoff, who had not seen the sun for forty years,—with the Greek Dubravius, who is said to have raised the dead,—and have even visited the Scheik Ebn Hali in his cave in the deserts of Thebais?—No, by Heaven!—he that contemns art shall perish through his own ignorance. Ten pieces!—a pittance which I am half ashamed to offer to Toinette, to buy her new breast-laces."

So saying, the indignant Sage nevertheless plunged the contemned pieces of gold into a large pouch which he wore at his girdle, which Toinette, and other abettors of lavish expense, generally contrived to empty fully faster than the philosopher, with all his art, could find the means of filling.[1]

CHAPTER XIV

THE JOURNEY

> I see thee yet, fair France—thou favour'd land
> Of art and nature—thou art still before me;
> Thy sons, to whom their labour is a sport,
> So well thy grateful soil returns its tribute;
> Thy sunburnt daughters, with their laughing eyes
> And glossy raven-locks. But, favour'd France,
> Thou hast had many a tale of woe to tell,
> In ancient times as now.
>
> *Anonymous.*

AVOIDING all conversation with any one (for such was his charge). Quentin Durward proceeded hastily to array himself in a strong but plain cuirass, with thigh and arm-pieces, and placed on his head a good steel cap without any visor. To these was added a handsome cassock of shamois leather, finely dressed, and laced down the seams with some embroidery, such as might become a superior officer in a noble household.

These were brought to his apartment by Oliver, who, with his quiet, insinuating smile and manner, acquainted him that his uncle had been summoned to mount guard, purposely that he might make no inquiries concerning these mysterious movements.

"Your excuse will be made to your kinsman," said Oliver, smiling again; "and, my dearest son, when you return safe from the execution of this pleasing trust, I doubt not you will be found worthy of such promotion as will dispense with your accounting for your motions to any one, while it will place you at the head of those who must render an account of theirs to you."

[1] Note II.—Galeotti.

So spoke Oliver le Diable, calculating, probably, in his own mind, the great chance there was that the poor youth whose hand he squeezed affectionately as he spoke, must necessarily encounter death or captivity in the commission entrusted to his charge. He added to his fair words a small purse of gold, to defray necessary expenses on the road, as a gratuity on the King's part.

At a few minutes before twelve at midnight, Quentin, according to his directions, proceeded to the second courtyard, and paused under the Dauphin's Tower, which, as the reader knows, was assigned for the temporary residence of the Countesses of Croye. He found, at this place of rendezvous, the men and horses appointed to compose the retinue, leading two sumpter mules already loaded with baggage, and holding three palfreys for the two Countesses and a faithful waiting-woman, with a stately war-horse for himself, whose steel-plated saddle glanced in the pale moonlight. Not a word of recognition was spoken on either side. The men sat still in their saddles, as if they were motionless; and by the same imperfect light Quentin saw with pleasure that they were all armed, and held long lances in their hands. They were only three in number; but one of them whispered to Quentin, in a strong Gascon accent, that their guide was to join them beyond Tours.

Meantime, lights glanced to and fro at the lattices of the tower, as if there was bustle and preparation among its inhabitants. At length, a small door, which led from the bottom of the tower to the court, was unclosed, and three females came forth, attended by a man wrapped in a cloak. They mounted in silence the palfreys which stood prepared for them, while their attendant on foot led the way, and gave the pass-words and signals to the watchful guards, whose posts they passed in succession. Thus they at length reached the exterior of these formidable barriers. Here the man on foot, who had hitherto acted as their guide, paused, and spoke low and earnestly to the two foremost females.

"May Heaven bless you, Sire," said a voice which thrilled upon Quentin Durward's ear, "and forgive you, even if your purposes be more interested than your words express! To be placed in safety under the protection of the good Bishop of Liege, is the utmost extent of my desire."

The person whom she thus addressed, muttered an inaudible answer, and retreated back through the barrier-gate, while Quentin thought, that, by the moon-glimpse, he recognised in him the King himself, whose anxiety for the departure of his guests had probably induced him to give his presence, in case scruples should arise on their part, or difficulties on that of the guards of the Castle.

When the riders were beyond the Castle, it was necessary for some time to ride with great precaution, in order to avoid the pitfalls, snares, and similar contrivances, which were placed for the annoyance of strangers. The Gascon was, however, completely possessed of the clew to this labyrinth, and in a quarter of an hour's riding, they found themselves beyond the limits of Plessis le Parc, and not far distant from the city of Tours.

The moon, which had now extricated herself from the clouds through which she was formerly wading, shed a full sea of glorious light upon a landscape equally glorious. They saw the princely Loire rolling his majestic tide through the richest plain in France, and sweeping along between banks ornamented with towers and terraces, and with olives and vineyards. They saw the walls of the city of Tours, the ancient capital of Touraine, raising their portly towers and embattlements white in the moonlight, while, from within their circle, rose the immense Gothic mass which the devotion of the sainted Bishop Perpetuus erected as early as the fifth century, and which the zeal of Charlemagne and his successors had enlarged with such architectural splendour, as rendered it the most magnificent church in France. The towers of the church of Saint Gatien were also visible, and the gloomy strength of the Castle, which was said to have been, in ancient times, the residence of the Emperor Valentinian.

Even the circumstances in which he was placed, though of a nature so engrossing, did not prevent the wonder and delight with which the young Scottishman, accustomed to the waste though impressive landscape of his own mountains, and the poverty even of his country's most stately scenery, looked on a scene, which art and nature seemed to have vied in adorning with their richest splendour. But he was recalled to the business of the moment by the voice of the elder lady (pitched at least an octave higher than those soft tones which bid adieu to King Louis), demanding to speak with the leader of the band. Spurring his horse forward, Quentin respectfully presented himself to the ladies in that capacity, and thus underwent the interrogatories of the Lady Hameline.

"What was his name, and what his degree?"

He told both.

"Was he perfectly acquainted with the road?"

"He could not," he replied, "pretend to much knowledge of the route, but he was furnished with full instructions, and he was, at their first resting-place, to be provided with a guide, in all respects competent to the task of directing their farther journey; meanwhile, a horseman who had just joined them, and made the number of their guard four, was to be their guide for the first stage."

"And wherefore were you selected for such a duty, young gentleman?" said the lady—"I am told you are the same youth who was lately upon guard in the gallery in which we met the Princess of France. You seem young and inexperienced for such a charge—a stranger, too, in France, and speaking the language as a foreigner."

"I am bound to obey the commands of the King, madam, but am not qualified to reason on them," answered the young soldier.

"Are you of noble birth?" demanded the same querist.

"I may safely affirm so, madam," replied Quentin.

"And are you not," said the younger lady, addressing him in her turn, but with a timorous accent, "the same whom I saw when I was called to wait upon the King at yonder inn?"

Lowering his voice, perhaps from similar feelings of timidity, Quentin answered in the affirmative.

"Then, methinks, my cousin," said the Lady Isabelle, addressing the Lady Hameline, "we must be safe under this young gentleman's safeguard; he looks not, at least, like one to whom the execution of a plan of treacherous cruelty upon two helpless women could be with safety entrusted."

"On my honour, madam," said Durward, "by the fame of my House, by the bones of my ancestry, I could not, for France and Scotland laid into one, be guilty of treachery or cruelty towards you!"

"You speak well, young man," said the Lady Hameline; "but we are accustomed to hear fair speeches from the King of France and his agents. It was by these that we were induced, when the protection of the Bishop of Liege might have been attained with less risk than now, or when we might have thrown ourselves on that of Wencesiaus of Germany, or of Edward of England, to seek refuge in France. And in what did the promises of the King result? In an obscure and shameful concealing of us, under plebeian names, as a sort of prohibited wares, in yonder paltry hostelry, when we,—who, as thou knowest, Marthon" (addressing her domestic), "never put on our head-tire save under a canopy, and upon a daïs of three degrees,—were compelled to attire ourselves, standing on the simple floor, as if we had been two milkmaids."

Marthon admitted that her lady spoke a most melancholy truth.

"I would that had been the sorest evil, dear kinswoman," said the Lady Isabelle; "I could gladly have dispensed with state."

"But not with society," said the elder Countess; "that, my sweet cousin, was impossible."

"I would have dispensed with all, my dearest kinswoman," answered Isabelle, in a voice which penetrated to the very heart of her young conductor and guard, "with all, for a safe and honourable retirement. I wish not—God knows, I never wished—to occasion war betwixt France and my native Burgundy, or that lives should be lost for such as I am. I only implored permission to retire to the Convent of Marmoutier, or to any other holy sanctuary."

"You spoke then like a fool, my cousin," answered the elder lady, "and not like a daughter of my noble brother. It is well there is still one alive, who hath some of the spirit of the noble House of Croye. How should a high-born lady be known from a sunburnt milkmaid, save that spears are broken for the one, and only hazel-poles shattered for the other? I tell you, maiden, that while I was in the very earliest bloom, scarcely older than yourself, the famous Passage of Arms at Haflinghem was held in my honour; the challengers were four, the assailants so many as twelve. It lasted three days; and cost the lives of two adventurous knights, the fracture of one back-bone, one collar-bone, three legs and two arms, besides flesh-wounds and bruises beyond the heralds' counting; and thus have the ladies of our House ever been honoured. Ah! had you but half

the heart of your noble ancestry, you would find means at some Court,
where ladies' love and fame in arms are still prized, to maintain a tournament, at which your hand should be the prize, as was that of your great-
grandmother of blessed memory, at the spear-running of Strasbourg;
and thus should you gain the best lance in Europe, to maintain the
rights of the House of Croye, both against the oppression of Burgundy
and the policy of France."

"But, fair kinswoman," answered the younger Countess, "I have been
told by my old nurse, that although the Rhinegrave was the best lance
at the great tournament at Strasbourg, and so won the hand of my respected ancestor, yet the match was no happy one, as he used often to
scold, and sometimes even to beat, my great-grandmother of blessed
memory."

"And wherefore not?" said the elder Countess, in her romantic enthusiasm for the profession of chivalry; "why should those victorious
arms, accustomed to deal blows when abroad, be bound to restrain their
energies at home? A thousand times rather would I be beaten twice a
day, by a husband whose arm was as much feared by others as by me,
than be the wife of a coward, who dared neither to lift hand to his wife,
nor to any one else!"

"I should wish you joy of such an active mate, fair aunt," replied
Isabelle, "without envying you; for if broken bones be lovely in tour-
neys, there is nothing less amiable in ladies' bower."

"Nay, but the beating is no necessary consequence of wedding with a
knight of fame in arms," said the Lady Hameline; "though it is true
that our ancestor of blessed memory, the Rhinegrave Gottfried, was
something rough-tempered, and addicted to the use of Rheinwein.—The
very perfect knight is a lamb among ladies, and a lion among lances.
There was Thibault of Montigni—God be with him!—he was the kindest
soul alive, and not only was he never so discourteous as to lift hand
against his lady, but, by our good dame, he who beat all enemies without doors, found a fair foe who could belabour him within.—Well, 'twas
his own fault—he was one of the challengers at the Passage of Haflinghem, and so well bestirred himself, that, if it had pleased Heaven, and
your grandfather, there might have been a lady of Montigni, who had
used his gentle nature more gently."

The Countess Isabelle, who had some reason to dread this Passage of
Haflinghem, it being a topic upon which her aunt was at all times very
diffuse, suffered the conversation to drop; and Quentin, with the natural
politeness of one who had been gently nurtured, dreading lest his presence
might be a restraint on their conversation, rode forward to join the guide,
as if to ask him some questions concerning their route.

Meanwhile, the ladies continued their journey in silence, or in such
conversation as is not worth narrating, until day began to break; and
as they had then been on horseback for several hours, Quentin, anxious

lest they should be fatigued, became impatient to know their distance from the nearest resting-place.

"I will show it you," answered the guide, "in half-an-hour."

"And then you leave us to other guidance?" continued Quentin.

"Even so, Seignior Archer," replied the man; "my journeys are always short and straight.—When you and others, Seignior Archer, go by the bow, I always go by the cord."

The moon had by this time long been down, and the lights of dawn were beginning to spread bright and strong in the east, and to gleam on the bosom of a small lake, on the verge of which they had been riding for a short space of time. This lake lay in the midst of a wide plain, scattered over with single trees, groves, and thickets; but which might be yet termed open, so that objects began to be discerned with sufficient accuracy. Quentin cast his eye on the person whom he rode beside, and, under the shadow of a slouched overspreading hat, which resembled the sombrero of a Spanish peasant, he recognised the facetious features of the same Petit-André, whose fingers, not long since, had, in concert with those of his lugubrious brother, Trois-Eschelles, been so unpleasantly active about his throat.—Impelled by aversion, not altogether unmixed with fear (for in his own country the executioner is regarded with almost superstitious horror), which his late narrow escape had not diminished, Durward instinctively moved his horse's head to the right, and pressing him at the same time with the spur, made a demi-volte, which separated him eight feet from his hateful companion.

"Ho, ho, ho, ho!" exclaimed Petit-André; "by our Lady of the Grève, our young soldier remembers us of old.—What! comrade, you bear no malice, I trust?—every one wins his bread in this country. No man need be ashamed of having come through my hands, for I will do my work with any that ever tied a living weight to a dead tree.—And God hath given me grace to be such a merry fellow withal—Ha! ha! ha!—I could tell you such jests I have cracked between the foot of the ladder and the top of the gallows, that, by my halidome, I have been obliged to do my job rather hastily, for fear the fellows should die with laughing, and so shame my mystery!"

As he thus spoke, he edged his horse sideways, to regain the interval which the Scot had left between them, saying at the same time, "Come, Seignior Archer, let there be no unkindness betwixt us!—For my part, I always do my duty without malice, and with a light heart, and I never love a man better than when I have put my scant-of-wind collar about his neck, to dub him Knight of the Order of Saint Patibularius, as the Provost's Chaplain, the worthy Father Vaconeldiablo, is wont to call the Patron Saint of the Provostry."

"Keep back, thou wretched object!" exclaimed Quentin, as the finisher of the law again sought to approach him closer, "or I will be tempted to teach you the distance that should be betwixt men of honour and such an outcast."

"La you there, how hot you are!" said the fellow; "had you said men of *honesty*, there had been some savour of truth in it;—but for men of *honour*, good lack, I have to deal with them every day, as nearly and closely as I was about to do business with you.—But peace be with you, and keep your company to yourself. I would have bestowed a flagon of Auvernât upon you to wash away every unkindness—but 'tis like you scorn my courtesy.—Well. Be as churlish as you list—I never quarrel with my customers—my jerry-come-tumbles, my merry dancers, my little playfellows, as Jacques Butcher says to his lambs—those, in fine, who, like your seigniorship, have H. E. M. P. written on their foreheads— No, no, let them use me as they list, they shall have my good service at last—and yourself shall see, when you next come under Petit-André's hands, that he knows how to forgive an injury."

So saying, and summing up the whole with a provoking wink, and such an interjectional *tchick* as men quicken a dull horse with, Petit-André drew off to the other side of the path, and left the youth to digest the taunts he had treated him with, as his proud Scottish stomach best might. A strong desire had Quentin to have belaboured him while the staff of his lance could hold together; but he put a restraint on his passion, recollecting that a brawl with such a character could be creditable at no time or place, and that a quarrel of any kind, on the present occasion, would be a breach of duty, and might involve the most perilous consequences. He therefore swallowed his wrath at the ill-timed and professional jokes of Mons. Petit-André, and contented himself with devoutly hoping that they had not reached the ears of his fair charge, on which they could not be supposed to make an impression in favour of himself, as one obnoxious to such sarcasms. But he was speedily aroused from such thoughts by the cry of both the ladies at once, "Look back—look back!—For the love of Heaven look to yourself, and us—we are pursued!"

Quentin hastily looked back, and saw that two armed men were in fact following them, and riding at such a pace as must soon bring them up with their party. "It can," he said, "be only some of the Provostry making their rounds in the forest.—Do thou look," he said to Petit-André, "and see what they may be."

Petit-André obeyed; and rolling himself jocosely in the saddle after he had made his observations, replied, "These, fair sir, are neither your comrades nor mine—neither Archers nor Marshalmen—for I think they wear helmets, with visors lowered, and gorgets of the same.—A plague upon these gorgets, of all other pieces of armour!—I have fumbled with them an hour before I could undo the rivets."

"Do you, gracious ladies," said Durward, without attending to Petit-André, "ride forward—not so fast as to raise an opinion of your being in flight, and yet fast enough to avail yourself of the impediment which I shall presently place between you and these men who follow us."

The Countess Isabelle looked to their guide, and then whispered to her aunt, who spoke to Quentin thus—"We have confidence in your care, fair Archer, and will rather abide the risk of whatever may chance in your company, than we will go onward with that man, whose mien is, we think, of no good augury."

"Be it as you will, ladies," said the youth—"There are but two who come after us; and though they be knights, as their arms seem to show, they shall, if they have any evil purpose, learn how a Scottish gentleman can do his devoir in the presence and for the defence of such as you.— Which of you there," he continued, addressing the guards whom he commanded, "is willing to be my comrade, and to break a lance with these gallants?"

Two of the men obviously faltered in resolution; but the third, Bertrand Guyot, swore, "that *cap de diou,* were they Knights of King Arthur's Round Table, he would try their mettle, for the honour of Gascony."

While he spoke, the two knights—for they seemed of no less rank— came up with the rear of the party, in which Quentin, with his sturdy adherent, had by this time stationed himself. They were fully accoutred in excellent armour of polished steel, without any device by which they could be distinguished.

One of them, as they approached, called out to Quentin, "Sir Squire, give place—we come to relieve you of a charge which is above your rank and condition. You will do well to leave these ladies in our care, who are fitter to wait upon them, especially as we know that in yours they are little better than captives."

"In return to your demand, sirs," replied Durward, "know, in the first place, that I am discharging the duty imposed upon me by my present Sovereign; and next, that however unworthy I may be, the ladies desire to abide under my protection."

"Out, sirrah!" exclaimed one of the champions; "will you, a wandering beggar, put yourself on terms of resistance against belted knights?"

"They are indeed terms of resistance," said Quentin, "since they oppose your insolent and unlawful aggression; and if there be difference of rank between us, which as yet I know not, your discourtesy has done it away. Draw your sword, or, if you will use the lance, take ground for your career."

While the knights turned their horses, and rode back to the distance of about a hundred and fifty yards, Quentin, looking to the ladies, bent low on his saddle-bow, as if desiring their favourable regard, and as they streamed towards him their kerchiefs, in token of encouragement, the two assailants had gained the distance necessary for their charge.

Calling to the Gascon to bear himself like a man, Durward put his steed into motion; and the four horsemen met in full career in the midst of the ground which at first separated them. The shock was fatal to the poor Gascon; for his adversary, aiming at his face, which was undefended by a visor, ran him through the eye into the brain, so that he fell dead from his horse.

On the other hand, Quentin, though labouring under the same disadvantage, swayed himself in the saddle so dexterously, that the hostile lance, slightly scratching his cheek, passed over his right shoulder; while his own spear, striking his antagonist fair upon the breast, hurled him to the ground. Quentin jumped off, to unhelm his fallen opponent; but the other knight (who had never yet spoken), seeing the fortune of his companion, dismounted still more speedily than Durward, and bestriding his friend, who lay senseless, exclaimed, "In the name of God and Saint Martin, mount, good fellow, and get thee gone with thy woman's ware!—Ventre Saint Gris, they have caused mischief enough this morning."

"By your leave, Sir Knight," said Quentin, who could not brook the menacing tone in which this advice was given, "I will first see whom I have had to do with and learn who is to answer for the death of my comrade."

"That shalt thou never live to know or to tell," answered the knight. "Get thee back in peace, good fellow. If we were fools for interrupting your passage, we have had the worst, for thou hast done more evil than the lives of thou and thy whole band could repay.—Nay, if thou *wilt* have it" (for Quentin now drew his sword, and advanced on him), "take it with a vengeance!"

So saying, he dealt the Scot such a blow on the helmet, as, till that moment (though bred where good blows were plenty), he had only read of in romance. It descended like a thunderbolt, beating down the guard which the young soldier had raised to protect his head, and, reaching his helmet of proof, cut it through so far as to touch his hair, but without further injury; while Durward, dizzy, stunned, and beaten down on one knee, was for an instant at the mercy of the knight, had it pleased him to second his blow. But compassion for Quentin's youth, or admiration of his courage, or a generous love of fair play, made him withhold from taking such advantage; while Durward, collecting himself, sprung up and attacked his antagonist with the energy of one determined to conquer or die, and at the same time with the presence of mind necessary for fighting the quarrel out to the best advantage. Resolved not again to expose himself to such dreadful blows as he had just sustained, he employed the advantage of superior agility, increased by the comparative lightness of his armour, to harass his antagonist, by traversing on all sides, with a suddenness of motion and rapidity of attack, against which the knight, in his heavy panoply, found it difficult to defend himself without much fatigue.

It was in vain that this generous antagonist called aloud to Quentin, "that there now remained no cause of fight betwixt them, and that he was loath to be constrained to do him injury." Listening only to the suggestions of a passionate wish to redeem the shame of his temporary defeat, Durward continued to assail him with the rapidity of lightning—now menacing him with the edge, now with the point of his sword—and ever keeping such an eye on the motions of his opponent, of whose superior strength he had had terrible proof, that he was ready to spring backward, or aside, from under the blows of his tremendous weapon.

"Now the devil be with thee for an obstinate and presumptuous fool," muttered the knight, "that cannot be quiet till thou art knocked on the head!" So saying, he changed his mode of fighting, collected himself as if to stand on the defensive, and seemed contented with parrying, instead of returning, the blows which Quentin unceasingly aimed at him, with the internal resolution, that the instant when either loss of breath, or any false or careless pass of the young soldier, should give an opening, he would put an end to the fight by a single blow. It is likely he might have succeeded in this artful policy, but Fate had ordered it otherwise.

The duel was still at its hottest, when a large party of horse rode up, crying, "Hold, in the King's name!" Both champions stepped back—and Quentin saw, with surprise, that his Captain, Lord Crawford, was at the head of the party who had thus interrupted their combat. There was also Tristan l'Hermite, with two or three of his followers; making, in all, perhaps twenty horse.

CHAPTER XV

THE GUIDE

He was a son of Egypt, as he told me,
And one descended from those dread magicians,
Who waged rash war, when Israel dwelt in Goshen,
With Israel and her Prophet—matching rod
With his the sons of Levi's—and encountering
Jehovah's miracles with incantations,
Till upon Egypt came the avenging Angel,
And those proud sages wept for their first-born,
As wept the unletter'd peasant.

Anonymous.

THE arrival of Lord Crawford and his guard put an immediate end to the engagement which we endeavoured to describe in the last chapter; and the Knight, throwing off his helmet, hastily gave the old lord his sword, saying, "Crawford, I render myself—But hither—and lend me your ear—a word, for God's sake—save the Duke of Orleans!"

"How?—what?—the Duke of Orleans!" exclaimed the Scottish commander,—"How came this, in the name of the foul fiend? It will ruin the callant with the King, for ever and a day."

"Ask no questions," said Dunois—for it was no other than he—"it was all my fault.—See, he stirs. I came forth but to have a snatch at yonder damsel, and make myself a landed and a married man—and see what is come on't. Keep back your canaille—let no man look upon him." So saying, he opened the visor of Orleans, and threw water on his face, which was afforded by the neighbouring lake.

Quentin Durward, meanwhile, stood like one planet-struck; so fast did new adventures pour in upon him. He had now, as the pale features of his first antagonist assured him, borne to the earth the first Prince of the blood in France, and had measured swords with her best champion, the celebrated Dunois;—both of them achievements honourable in themselves; but whether they might be called good service to the King, or so esteemed by him, was a very different question.

The Duke had now recovered his breath, and was able to sit up and give attention to what passed betwixt Dunois and Crawford, while the former pleaded eagerly, that there was no occasion to mention in the matter the name of the most noble Orleans, while he was ready to take the whole blame on his own shoulders; and to avouch that the Duke had only come thither in friendship to him.

Lord Crawford continued listening, with his eyes fixed on the ground, and from time to time he sighed and shook his head. At length he said, looking up, "Thou knowest, Dunois, that for thy father's sake, as well as thine own, I would full fain do thee a service."

"It is not for myself I demand anything," answered Dunois. "Thou hast my sword, and I am your prisoner—what needs more?—But it is for this noble Prince, the only hope of France, if God should call the Dauphin. He only came hither to do me a favour—in an effort to make my fortune—in a matter which the King had partly encouraged."

"Dunois," replied Crawford, "if another had told me thou hadst brought the noble Prince into this jeopardy to serve any purpose of thine own, I had told him it was false. And now, that thou dost pretend so thyself, I can hardly believe it is for the sake of speaking the truth."

"Noble Crawford," said Orleans, who had now entirely recovered from his swoon, "you are too like in character to your friend Dunois, not to do him justice. It was indeed I that dragged him hither, most unwillingly, upon an enterprise of harebrained passion, suddenly and rashly undertaken.—Look on me all who will," he added, rising up and turning to the soldiery—"I am Louis of Orleans, willing to pay the penalty of my own folly. I trust the King will limit his displeasure to me, as is but just.—Meanwhile, as a child of France must not give up his sword to any one—not even to you, brave Crawford—fare thee well, good steel."

So saying, he drew his sword from its scabbard, and flung it into the lake. It went through the air like a stream of lightning, and sunk in the flashing waters, which speedily closed over it. All remained standing in irresolution and astonishment, so high was the rank, and so much esteemed was the character, of the culprit; while, at the same time, all were conscious that the consequences of his rash enterprise, considering the views which the King had upon him, were likely to end in his utter ruin.

Dunois was the first who spoke, and it was in the chiding tone of an offended and distrusted friend:—"So! your Highness hath judged it fit to cast away your best sword, in the same morning when it was your

pleasure to fling away the King's favour, and to slight the friendship of
Dunois?"

"My dearest kinsman," said the Duke, "when or how was it in my
purpose to slight your friendship, by telling the truth, when it was due
to your safety and my honour?"

"What had you to do with my safety, my most princely cousin,
I would pray to know?" answered Dunois gruffly;—"What, in God's
name, was it to you, if I had a mind to be hanged, or strangled, or flung
into the Loire, or poniarded, or broke on the wheel, or hung up alive in
an iron cage, or buried alive in a castle-fosse, or disposed of in any
other way in which it might please King Louis to get rid of his faithful
subject?—(you need not wink and frown, and point to Tristan l'Hermite
—I see the scoundrel as well as you do). But it would not have stood
so hard with me—And so much for my safety. And then for your own
honour—by the blush of Saint Magdalene, I think the honour would
have been to have missed this morning's work, or kept it out of sight.
Here has your Highness got yourself unhorsed by a wild Scottish boy."

"Tut, tut!" said Lord Crawford; "never shame his Highness for that.
It is not the first time a Scottish boy hath broke a good lance—I am glad
the youth hath borne him well."

"I will say nothing to the contrary," said Dunois; "yet, had your
Lordship come something later than you did, there might have been
a vacancy in your band of Archers."

"Ay, ay," answered Lord Crawford; "I can read your handwriting
in that cleft morion.—Some one take it from the lad, and give him a
bonnet, which, with its steel lining, will keep his head better than that
broken loom.—And let me tell your Lordship, that your own armour of
proof is not without some marks of good Scottish handwriting.—But,
Dunois, I must now request the Duke of Orleans and you take horse and
accompany me, as I have power and commission to convey you to a place
different from that which my good-will might assign you."

"May I not speak one word, my Lord of Crawford, to yonder fair
ladies?" said the Duke of Orleans.

"Not one syllable," answered Lord Crawford; "I am too much a
friend of your Highness to permit such an act of folly."—Then, addressing Quentin, he added, "You, young man, have done your duty. Go on
to obey the charge with which you are entrusted."

"Under favour, my Lord," said Tristan, with his usual brutality of
manner, "the youth must find another guide. I cannot do without Petit-
André, when there is so like to be business on hand for him."

"The young man," said Petit-André, now coming forward, "has only
to keep the path which lies straight before him, and it will conduct him
to a place where he will find the man who is to act as his guide.—I would
not for a thousand ducats be absent from my Chief this day! I have
hanged knights and squires many a one, and wealthy Echevins, and
burgomasters to boot—even counts and marquisses have tasted of my

handywork—but, a-humph——" He looked at the Duke, as if to intimate that he would have filled up the blank, with "a prince of the blood!"—"Ho, ho, ho! Petit-André, thou wilt be read of in Chronicle!"

"Do you permit your ruffians to hold such language in such a presence?" said Crawford, looking sternly to Tristan.

"Why do you not correct him yourself, my Lord?" said Tristan sullenly.

"Because thy hand is the only one in this company that can beat him, without being degraded by such an action."

"Then rule your own men, my Lord, and I will be answerable for mine," said the Provost-Marshal.

Lord Crawford seemed about to give a passionate reply; but, as if he had thought better of it, turned his back short upon Tristan, and, requesting the Duke of Orleans and Dunois to ride one on either hand of him, he made a signal of adieu to the ladies, and said to Quentin, "God bless thee, my child; thou hast begun thy service valiantly, though in an unhappy cause." He was about to go off—when Quentin could hear Dunois whisper to Crawford, "Do you carry us to Plessis?"

"No, my unhappy and rash friend," answered Crawford, with a sigh; "to Loches."

"To Loches!" The name of a castle, or rather prison, yet more dreaded than Plessis itself, fell like a death-toll upon the ear of the young Scotchman. He had heard it described as a place destined to the workings of those secret acts of cruelty with which even Louis shamed to pollute the interior of his own residence. There were in this place of terror dungeons under dungeons, some of them unknown even to the keepers themselves; living graves, to which men were consigned, with little hope of farther employment during the rest of their life, than to breathe impure air, and feed on bread and water. At this formidable castle were also those dreadful places of confinement called *cages*, in which the wretched prisoner could neither stand upright, nor stretch himself at length, an invention, it is said, of the Cardinal Balue.[1] It is no wonder that the name of this place of horrors, and the consciousness that he had been partly the means of despatching thither two such illustrious victims, struck so much sadness into the heart of the young Scot, that he rode for some time with his head dejected, his eyes fixed on the ground, and his heart filled with the most painful reflections.

As he was now again at the head of the little troop, and pursuing the road which had been pointed out to him, the Lady Hameline had an opportunity to say to him,—

"Methinks, fair sir, you regret the victory which your gallantry has attained in our behalf?"

There was something in the question which sounded like irony, but Quentin had tact enough to answer simply and with sincerity.

[1] Who himself tenanted one of these dens for more than eleven years.

"I can regret nothing that is done in the service of such ladies as you are; but, methinks, had it consisted with your safety, I had rather have fallen by the sword of so good a soldier as Dunois, than have been the means of consigning that renowned knight and his unhappy chief, the Duke of Orleans, to yonder fearful dungeons."

"It *was*, then, the Duke of Orleans," said the elder lady, turning to her niece. "I thought so, even at the distance from which we beheld the fray.—You see, kinswoman, what we might have been, had this sly avaricious monarch permitted us to be seen at his Court. The first Prince of the blood of France, and the valiant Dunois, whose name is known as wide as that of his heroic father—This young gentleman did his devoir bravely and well; but methinks 'tis pity that he did not succumb with honour, since his ill-advised gallantry has stood betwixt us and these princely rescuers."

The Countess Isabelle replied in a firm and almost a displeased tone; with an energy, in short, which Quentin had not yet observed her use.

"Madam," she said, "but that I know you jest, I would say your speech is ungrateful to our brave defender, to whom we owe more, perhaps, than you are aware of. Had these gentlemen succeeded so far in their rash enterprise as to have defeated our escort, is it not still evident, that, on the arrival of the Royal Guard, we must have shared their captivity? For my own part, I give tears, and will soon bestow masses, on the brave man who has fallen, and I trust" (she continued, more timidly) "that he who lives will accept my grateful thanks."

As Quentin turned his face towards her, to return the fitting acknowledgments, she saw the blood which streamed down on one side of his face, and exclaimed, in a tone of deep feeling, "Holy Virgin, he is wounded! he bleeds!—Dismount, sir, and let your wound be bound up."

In spite of all that Durward could say of the slightness of his hurt, he was compelled to dismount, and to seat himself on a bank, and unhelmet himself, while the ladies of Croye, who, according to a fashion not as yet antiquated, pretended to some knowledge of leech-craft, washed the wound, stanched the blood, and bound it with the kerchief of the younger Countess, in order to exclude the air, for so their practice prescribed.

In modern times, gallants seldom or never take wounds for ladies' sake, and damsels on their side never meddle with the cure of wounds. Each has a danger the less. That which the men escape will be generally acknowledged; but the peril of dressing such a slight wound as that of Quentin's, which involved nothing formidable or dangerous, was perhaps as real in its way as the risk of encountering it.

We have already said the patient was eminently handsome; and the removal of his helmet, or, more properly, of his morion, had suffered his fair locks to escape in profusion, around a countenance in which the hilarity of youth was qualified by a blush of modesty at once and pleasure. And then the feelings of the younger Countess, when compelled to hold the kerchief to the wound, while her aunt sought in their baggage for some vulnerary remedy, were mingled at once with a sense of delicacy and embarrassment; a thrill of pity for the patient, and of gratitude for his services, which exaggerated, in her eyes, his good mien and handsome features. In short, this incident seemed intended by Fate to complete the mysterious communication which she had, by many petty and apparently accidental circumstances, established betwixt two persons, who, though far different in rank and fortune, strongly resembled each other in youth, beauty, and the romantic tenderness of an affectionate disposition. It was no wonder, therefore, that from this moment the thoughts of the Countess Isabelle, already so familiar to his imagination, should become paramount in Quentin's bosom, nor that if the maiden's feelings were of a less decided character, at least so far as known to herself, she should think of her young defender, to whom she had just rendered a service so interesting, with more emotion than of any of the whole band of high-born nobles who had for two years past besieged her with their adoration. Above all, when the thought of Campo-Basso, the unworthy favourite of Duke Charles, with his hypocritical mien, his base, treacherous spirit, his wry neck, and his squint, occurred to her, his portrait was more disgustingly hideous than ever, and deeply did she resolve no tyranny should make her enter into so hateful a union.

In the meantime, whether the good Lady Hameline of Croye understood and admired masculine beauty as much as when she was fifteen years younger (for the good Countess was at least thirty-five, if the records of that noble house speak the truth), or whether she thought she had done their young protector less justice than she ought, in the first view she had taken of his services, it is certain that he began to find favour in her eyes.

"My niece," she said, "has bestowed on you a kerchief for the binding of your wound; I will give you one to grace your gallantry, and to encourage you in your farther progress in chivalry."

So saying, she gave him a richly embroidered kerchief of blue and s lver, and pointing to the housing of her palfrey, and the plumes in her riding-cap, desired him to observe that the colours were the same.

The fashion of the time prescribed one absolute mode of receiving such a favour, which Quentin followed accordingly, by tying the napkin round his arm; yet his manner of acknowledgement had more of awkwardness, and less of gallantry in it, than perhaps it might have had at another time, and in another presence for though the wearing of a lady's favour, given in such a manner, was merely matter of general compliment, he would much rather have preferred the right of displaying on his arm that which bound the wound inflicted by the sword of Dunois.

Meantime they continued their pilgrimage, Quentin now riding abreast of the ladies, into whose society he seemed to be tacitly adopted. He did not speak much, however, being filled by the silent consciousness of happiness, which is afraid of giving too strong vent to its feelings. The

Countess Isabelle spoke still less, so that the conversation was chiefly
carried on by the Lady Hameline, who showed no inclination to let it
drop; for, to initiate the young Archer, as she said, into the principles
and practice of chivalry, she detailed to him, at full length, the Passage
of Arms at Haflinghem, where she had distributed the prizes among the
victors.

Not much interested, I am sorry to say, in the description of this
splendid scene, or in the heraldic bearings of the different Flemish and
German knights, which the lady blazoned with pitiless accuracy, Quentin
began to entertain some alarm lest he should have passed the place where
his guide was to join him—a most serious disaster, and from which, should
it really have taken place, the very worst consequences were to be
apprehended.

While he hesitated whether it would be better to send back one of his
followers, to see whether this might not be the case, he heard the blast
of a horn, and looking in the direction from which the sound came,
beheld a horseman riding very fast towards them. The low size, and
wild, shaggy, untrained state of the animal, reminded Quentin of the
mountain breed of horses in his own country; but this was much more
finely limbed, and, with the same appearance of hardiness, was more
rapid in its movements. The head particularly, which, in the Scottish
pony, is often lumpish and heavy, was small and well placed in the neck
of this animal, with thin jaws, full sparkling eyes, and expanded nostrils.

The rider was even more singular in his appearance than the horse
which he rode, though that was extremely unlike the horses of France.
Although he managed his palfrey with great dexterity, he sat with his feet
in broad stirrups, something resembling shovels, so short in the leathers,
that his knees were well-nigh as high as the pommel of his saddle. His
dress was a red turban of small size, in which he wore a sullied plume,
secured by a clasp of silver; his tunic, which was shaped like those of the
Estradiots (a sort of troops whom the Venetians at that time levied in
the provinces, on the eastern side of their gulf), was green in colour,
and tawdrily laced with gold; he wore very wide drawers or trousers of
white, though none of the cleanest, which gathered beneath the knee,
and his swarthy legs were quite bare, unless for the complicated laces
which bound a pair of sandals on his feet; he had no spurs, the edge of
his large stirrups being so sharp as to serve to goad the horse in a very
severe manner. In a crimson sash this singular horseman wore a dagger
on the right side, and on the left a short crooked Moorish sword; and
by a tarnished baldric over the shoulder hung the horn which announced
his approach. He had a swarthy and sunburnt visage, with a thin beard,
and piercing dark eyes, a well-formed mouth and nose, and other features which might have been pronounced handsome, but for the black
elf-locks which hung around his face, and the air of wildness and emaciation, which rather seemed to indicate a savage than a civilised man.

"He also is a Bohemian!" said the ladies to each other; "Holy Mary, will the King again place confidence in these outcasts?"

"I will question the man, if it be your pleasure," said Quentin, "and assure myself of his fidelity as I best may."

Durward, as well as the ladies of Croye, had recognised in this man's dress and appearance, the habit and the manners of those vagrants with whom he had nearly been confounded by the hasty proceedings of Trois-Eschelles and Petit-André, and he, too, entertained very natural apprehensions concerning the risk of reposing trust in one of that vagrant race.

"Art thou come hither to seek us?" was his first question.

The stranger nodded.

"And for what purpose?"

"To guide you to the palace of him of Liege."

"Of the Bishop?"

The Bohemian again nodded.

"What token canst thou give me, that we should yield credence to thee?"

"Even the old rhyme, and no other," answered the Bohemian,—

> "The page slew the boar,
> The peer had the gloire."

"A true token," said Quentin; "lead on, good fellow—I will speak further with thee presently." Then falling back to the ladies, he said, "I am convinced this man is the guide we are to expect, for he hath brought me a pass-word, known, I think, but to the King and me. But I will discourse with him further, and endeavour to ascertain how far he is to be trusted."

CHAPTER XVI

THE VAGRANT

I am as free as Nature first made man,
Ere the base laws of servitude began,
When wild in woods the noble savage ran.
The Conquest of Grenada.

WHILE Quentin held the brief communication with the ladies, necessary to assure them that this extraordinary addition to their party was the guide whom they were to expect on the King's part, he noticed (for he was as alert in observing the motions of the stranger, as the Bohemian could be on his part), that the man not only turned his head as far back as he could, to peer at them, but that, with a singular sort of agility, more resembling that of a monkey than of a man, he had screwed his whole person around on the saddle, so as to sit almost sidelong upon the horse, for the convenience, as it seemed, of watching them more attentively.

Not greatly pleased with this manœuvre, Quentin rode up to the

Bohemian, and said to him, as he suddenly assumed his proper position on the horse, "Methinks, friend, you will prove but a blind guide, if you look at the tail of your horse rather than his ears."

"And if I were actually blind," answered the Bohemian, "I could not the less guide you through any country in this realm of France, or in those adjoining to it."

"Yet you are no Frenchman born," said the Scot.

"I am not," answered the guide.

"What countryman, then, are you?" demanded Quentin.

"I am of no country," answered the guide.

"How! of no country?" repeated the Scot.

"No," answered the Bohemian, "of none. I am a Zingaro, a Bohemian, an Egyptian, or whatever the Europeans, in their different languages, may choose to call our people; but I have no country."

"Are you a Christian?" asked the Scotchman.

The Bohemian shook his head.

"Dog!" said Quentin (for there was little toleration in the spirit of Catholicism in those days), "dost thou worship Mahoun?"

"No," was the indifferent and concise answer of the guide, who neither seemed offended nor surprised at the young man's violence of manner.

"Are you a Pagan, then, or what are you?"

"I have no religion," [1] answered the Bohemian.

Durward started back; for though he had heard of Saracens and Idolaters, it had never entered into his ideas or belief, that any body of men could exist who practised no mode of worship, whatever. He recovered from his astonishment, to ask his guide where he usually dwelt.

"Wherever I chance to be for the time," replied the Bohemian. "I have no home."

"How do you guard your property?"

"Excepting the clothes which I wear, and the horse I ride on, I have no property."

"Yet you dress gaily, and ride gallantly," said Durward. "What are your means of subsistence?"

"I eat when I am hungry, drink when I am thirsty, and have no other means of subsistence than chance throws in my way," replied the vagabond.

"Under whose laws do you live?"

"I acknowledge obedience to none, but as it suits my pleasure or my necessities," said the Bohemian.

"Who is your leader, and commands you?"

"The Father of our tribe—if I choose to obey him," said the guide—"otherwise I have no commander."

"You are then," said the wondering querist, "destitute of all that other men are combined by—you have no law, no leader, no settled means of subsistence, no house or home. You have, may Heaven compassionate you, no country—and, may Heaven enlighten and forgive you, you have no God! What is it that remains to you, deprived of government, domestic happiness, and religion?"

"I have liberty," said the Bohemian—"I crouch to no one—obey no one—respect no one.—I go where I will—live as I can—and die when my day comes."

"But you are subject to instant execution, at the pleasure of the Judge?"

"Be it so," returned the Bohemian; "I can but die so much the sooner."

"And to imprisonment also," said the Scot; "and where, then, is your boasted freedom?"

"In my thoughts," said the Bohemian, "which no chains can bind; while yours, even when your limbs are free, remain fettered by your laws and your superstitions, your dreams of local attachment, and your fantastic visions of civil policy. Such as I are free in spirit when our limbs are chained—You are imprisoned in mind, even when your limbs are most at freedom."

"Yet the freedom of your thoughts," said the Scot, "relieves not the pressure of the gyves on your limbs."

"For a brief time that may be endured," answered the vagrant; "and if within that period I cannot extricate myself, and fail of relief from my comrades, I can always die, and death is the most perfect freedom of all."

There was a deep pause of some duration, which Quentin at length broke by resuming his queries.

"Yours is a wandering race, unknown to the nations of Europe—whence do they derive their origin?"

"I may not tell you," answered the Bohemian.

"When will they relieve this kingdom from their presence, and return to the land from whence they came?" said the Scot.

"When the day of their pilgrimage shall be accomplished," replied his vagrant guide.

"Are you not sprung from those tribes of Israel, which were carried into captivity beyond the great river Euphrates?" said Quentin, who had not forgotten the lore which had been taught him at Aberbrothick.

"Had we been so," answered the Bohemian, "we had followed their faith, and practised their rites."

"What is thine own name?" said Durward.

"My proper name is only known to my brethren—The men beyond our tents call me Hayraddin Maugrabin, that is, Hayraddin the African Moor."

"Thou speakest too well for one who hath lived always in thy filthy horde," said the Scot.

"I have learned some of the knowledge of this land," said Hayraddin.—"When I was a little boy, our tribe was chased by the hunters after human flesh. An arrow went through my mother's head, and she died. I was entangled in the blanket on her shoulders, and was taken by the pursuers. A priest begged me from the Provost's archers, and trained me up in Frankish learning for two or three years."

"How came you to part with him?" demanded Durward.

"I stole money from him—even the God which he worshipped," answered Hayraddin, with perfect composure; "he detected me, and beat me—I stabbed him with my knife, fled to the woods, and was again united to my people."

"Wretch!" said Durward, "did you murder your benefactor?"

"What had he to do to burden me with his benefits?—The Zingaro boy was no house-bred cur, to dog the heels of his master, and crouch beneath his blows, for scraps of food—He was the imprisoned wolf-whelp, which at the first opportunity broke his chain, rended his master, and returned to his wilderness."

There was another pause, when the young Scot, with a view of still farther investigating the character and purpose of this suspicious guide, asked Hayraddin, "Whether it was not true that his people, amid their ignorance, pretended to a knowledge of futurity, which was not given to the sages, philosophers, and divines, of more polished society?"

"We pretend to it," said Hayraddin, "and it is with justice."

"How can it be, that so high a gift is bestowed on so abject a race?" said Quentin.

"Can I tell you?" answered Hayraddin—"Yes, I may indeed; but it is when you shall explain to me why the dog can trace the footsteps of a man, while man, the nobler animal, hath not power to trace those of the dog. These powers, which seem to you so wonderful, are instinctive in our race. From the lines on the face and on the hand, we can tell the future fate of those who consult us, even as surely as you know from the blossom of the tree in spring, what fruit it will bear in the harvest."

"I doubt of your knowledge, and defy you to the proof."

"Defy me not, Sir Squire," said Hayraddin Maugrabin—"I can tell you, that, say what you will of your religion, the Goddess whom you worship rides in this company."

"Peace!" said Quentin, in astonishment; "on thy life, not a word farther, but in answer to what I ask thee.—Canst thou be faithful?"

"I can—all men can," said the Bohemian.

"But *wilt* thou be faithful?"

"Wouldst thou believe me the more should I swear it?" answered Maugrabin, with a sneer.

"Thy life is in my hand," said the young Scot.

"Strike, and see whether I fear to die," answered the Bohemian.

"Will money render thee a trusty guide?" demanded Durward.

"If I be not such without it, No," replied the heathen.

"Then what will bind thee?" asked the Scot.

"Kindness," replied the Bohemian.

"Shall I swear to show thee such, if thou art true guide to us on this pilgrimage?"

"No," replied Hayraddin, "it were extravagant waste of a commodity so rare. To thee I am bound already."

"How!" exclaimed Durward, more surprised than ever.

"Remember the chestnut-trees on the banks of the Cher! The victim, whose body thou didst cut down, was my brother, Zamet, the Maugrabin."

"And yet," said Quentin, "I find you in correspondence with those very officers by whom your brother was done to death; for it was one of them who directed me where to meet with you—the same, doubtless, who procured yonder ladies your services as a guide."

"What can we do?" answered Hayraddin gloomily—"These men deal with us as the sheep-dogs do with the flock; they protect us for a while, drive us hither and thither at their pleasure, and always end by guiding us to the shambles."

Quentin had afterwards occasion to learn that the Bohemian spoke truth in this particular, and that the Provost-guard, employed to suppress the vagabond bands by which the kingdom was infested, entertained correspondence among them, and forbore, for a certain time, the exercise of their duty, which always at last ended in conducting their allies to the gallows. This is a sort of political relation between thief and officer, for the profitable exercise of their mutual professions, which has subsisted in all countries, and is by no means unknown to our own.

Durward, parting from the guide, fell back to the rest of the retinue, very little satisfied with the character of Hayraddin, and entertaining little confidence in the professions of gratitude which he had personally made to him. He proceeded to sound the other two men who had been assigned him for attendants, and he was concerned to find them stupid, and as unfit to assist him with counsel, as in the rencounter they had shown themselves reluctant to use their weapons.

"It is all the better," said Quentin to himself, his spirit rising with the apprehended difficulties of his situation; "that lovely young lady shall owe all to me.—What one hand—ay, and one head can do,—methinks I can boldly count upon. I have seen my father's house on fire, and he and my brothers lying dead amongst the flames—I gave not an inch back, but fought it out to the last. Now I am two years older, and have the best and fairest cause to bear me well, that ever kindled mettle within a brave man's bosom."

Acting upon this resolution, the attention and activity which Quentin bestowed during the journey, had in it something that gave him the appearance of ubiquity. His principal and most favourite post was of course by the side of the ladies; who, sensible of his extreme attention to their safety, began to converse with him in almost the tone of familiar friendship, and appeared to take great pleasure in the _naïveté_, yet shrewd.

ness, of his conversation. Yet Quentin did not suffer the fascination of this intercourse to interfere with the vigilant discharge of his duty.

If he was often by the side of the Countesses, labouring to describe to the natives of a level country the Grampian mountains, and, above all, the beauties of Glen-houlakin,—he was as often riding with Hayraddin, in the front of the cavalcade, questioning him about the road, and the resting-places, and recording his answers in his mind, to ascertain whether upon cross-examination he could discover anything like meditated treachery. As often again he was in the rear, endeavouring to secure the attachment of the two horsemen, by kind words, gifts, and promises of additional recompense, when their task should be accomplished.

In this way they travelled for more than a week, through by-paths and unfrequented districts, and by circuitous routes, in order to avoid large towns. Nothing remarkable occurred, though they now and then met strolling gangs of Bohemians, who respected them, as under the conduct of one of their tribe,—straggling soldiers, or perhaps banditti, who deemed their party too strong to be attacked,—or parties of the Mare-chaussée, as they would now be termed, whom Louis, who searched the wounds of the land with steel and cautery, employed to suppress the dis-orderly bands which infested the interior. These last suffered them to pursue their way unmolested, by virtue of a pass-word, with which Quen-tin had been furnished for that purpose by the King himself.

Their resting-places were chiefly the monasteries, most of which were obliged by the rules of their foundation to receive pilgrims, under which character the ladies travelled, with hospitality, and without any trouble-some inquiries into their rank and character, which most persons of distinction were desirous of concealing while in the discharge of their vows. The pretence of weariness was usually employed by the Countesses of Croye, as an excuse for instantly retiring to rest, and Quentin, as their Major Domo, arranged all that was necessary betwixt them and their entertainers, with a shrewdness which saved them all trouble, and an alacrity that failed not to excite a corresponding degree of goodwill on the part of those who were thus sedulously attended to.

One circumstance gave Quentin peculiar trouble, which was the char-acter and nation of his guide; who, as a heathen, and an infidel vagabond, addicted besides to occult arts (the badge of all his tribe), was often looked upon as a very improper guest for the holy resting-places at which the company usually halted, and was not in consequence admitted within even the outer circuit of their walls, save with extreme reluctance. This was very embarrassing; for, on the one hand, it was necessary to keep in good humour a man who was possessed of the secret of their expedition; and on the other, Quentin deemed it indispensable to maintain a vigilant though secret watch on Hayraddin's conduct, in order that, as far as might be, he should hold no communication with any one without being observed. This of course was impossible, if the Bohemian was lodged without the precincts of the convent at which they stopped, and Durward

could not help thinking that Hayraddin was desirous of bringing about
this latter arrangement; for, instead of keeping himself still and quiet in
the quarters allotted to him, his conversation, tricks, and songs, were, at
the same time, so entertaining to the novices and younger brethren, and
so unedifying in the opinion of the seniors of the fraternity, that, in more
cases than one, it required all the authority, supported by threats, which
Quentin could exert over him, to restrain his irreverent and untimeous
jocularity, and all the interest he could make with the Superiors, to prevent the heathen hound from being thrust out of doors. He succeeded,
however, by the adroit manner in which he apologised for the acts of
indecorum committed by their attendant, and the skill with which he
hinted the hope of his being brought to a better sense of principles and
behaviour, by the neighbourhood of holy relics, consecrated buildings,
and, above all, of men dedicated to religion.

But upon the tenth or twelfth day of their journey, after they had
entered Flanders, and were approaching the town of Namur, all the
efforts of Quentin became inadequate to suppress the consequences of the
scandal given by his heathen guide. The scene was a Franciscan convent,
and of a strict and reformed order, and the Prior a man who afterwards
died in the odour of sanctity. After rather more than the usual scruples
(which were indeed in such a case to be expected) had been surmounted,
the obnoxious Bohemian at length obtained quarters in an out-house
inhabited by a lay brother, who acted as gardener. The ladies retired to
their apartment, as usual, and the Prior, who chanced to have some distant alliances and friends in Scotland, and who was fond of hearing
foreigners tell of their native countries, invited Quentin, with whose mien
and conduct he seemed much pleased, to a slight monastic refection in his
own cell. Finding the Father a man of intelligence, Quentin did not
neglect the opportunity of making himself acquainted with the state of
affairs in the country of Liege, of which, during the last two days of their
journey, he had heard such reports, as made him very apprehensive for
the security of his charge during the remainder of their route, nay, even of
the Bishop's power to protect them, when they should be safely conducted to his residence. The replies of the Prior were not very consolatory.

He said, that "the people of Liege were wealthy burghers, who, like
Jeshurun of old, had waxed fat and kicked—that they were uplifted in
heart because of their wealth and their privileges—that they had divers
disputes with the Duke of Burgundy, their liege lord, upon the subject of
imposts and immunities—and that they had repeatedly broken out into
open mutiny, whereat the Duke was so much incensed, as being a man of
a hot and fiery nature, that he had sworn, by Saint George, on the next
provocation, he would make the city of Liege like to the desolation of
Babylon, and the downfall of Tyre, a hissing and a reproach to the whole
territory of Flanders."

"And he is a prince, by all report, likely to keep such a vow," said

Quentin; "so the men of Liege will probably beware how they give him occasion."

"It were to be so hoped," said the Prior; "and such are the prayers of the godly in the land, who would not that the blood of the citizens were poured forth like water, and that they should perish, even as utter cast-aways, ere they make their peace with Heaven. Also the good Bishop labours night and day to preserve peace, as well becometh a servant of the altar; for it is written in holy scripture, *Beati pacifici*. But——" here the good Prior stopped, with a deep sigh.

Quentin modestly urged the great importance of which it was to the ladies whom he attended, to have some assured information respecting the internal state of the country, and what an act of Christian charity it would be, if the worthy and reverend Father would enlighten them upon that subject.

"It is one," said the Prior, "on which no man speaks with willingness; for those who speak evil of the powerful, *etiam in cubiculo*, may find that a winged thing shall carry the matter to his ears. Nevertheless, to render you, who seem an ingenuous youth, and your ladies, who are devout votaresses accomplishing a holy pilgrimage, the little service that is in my power, I will be plain with you."

He then looked cautiously round, and lowered his voice, as if afraid of being overheard.

"The people of Liege," he said, "are privily instigated to their frequent mutinies by men of Belial, who pretend, but, as I hope, falsely, to have commission to that effect from our most Christian King; whom, however, I hold to deserve that term better than were consistent with his thus disturbing the peace of a neighbouring state. Yet so it is, that his name is freely used by those who uphold and inflame the discontents at Liege. There is, moreover, in the land, a nobleman of good descent, and fame in warlike affairs; but otherwise, so to speak, *Lapis offensionis et petra scandali*,—a stumbling-block of offence to the countries of Burgundy and Flanders. His name is William de la Marck."

"Called William with the Beard," said the young Scot, "or the Wild Boar of Ardennes?"

"And rightly so called, my son," said the Prior; "because he is as the wild boar of the forest, which treadeth down with his hoofs, and rendeth with his tusks. And he hath formed to himself a band of more than a thousand men, all, like himself, contemners of civil and ecclesiastical authority, and holds himself independent of the Duke of Burgundy, and maintains himself and his followers by rapine and wrong, wrought without distinction, upon churchmen and laymen. *Imposuit manus in Christos Domini,*—he hath stretched forth his hand upon the anointed of the Lord, regardless of what is written,—'Touch not mine anointed, and do my prophets no wrong.'—Even to our poor house did he send for sums of gold and sums of silver, as a ransom for our lives, and those of our brethren; to which we returned a Latin supplication, stating our inability to answer his demand, and exhorting him in the words of the preacher, *Ne moliaris amico tuo malum, cum habet in te fiduciam*. Nevertheless, this Gulielmus Barbatus, this William de la Marck, as completely ignorant of humane letters as of humanity itself, replied, in his ridiculous jargon, '*Si non payatis, brulabo monasterium vestrum.*' " [1]

"Of which rude Latin, however, you, my good father," said the youth, "were at no loss to conceive the meaning?"

"Alas, my son," said the Prior, "Fear and Necessity are shrewd interpreters; and we were obliged to melt down the silver vessels of our altar to satisfy the rapacity of this cruel chief—May Heaven requite it to him seven-fold! *Pereat improbus—Amen, amen, anathema esto!*"

"I marvel," said Quentin, "that the Duke of Burgundy, who is so strong and powerful, doth not bait this boar to purpose, of whose ravages I have already heard so much."

"Alas! my son," said the Prior, "the Duke Charles is now at Peronne, assembling his captains of hundreds and his captains of thousands, to make war against France; and thus, while Heaven hath set discord between the hearts of those great princes, the country is misused by such subordinate oppressors. But it is in evil time that the Duke neglects the cure of these internal gangrenes; for this William de la Marck hath of late entertained open communication with Rouslaer and Pavillon, the chiefs of the discontented at Liege, and it is to be feared he will soon stir them up to some desperate enterprise."

"But the Bishop of Liege," said Quentin, "he hath still power enough to subdue this disquieted and turbulent spirit— hath he not, good father? —Your answer to this question concerns me much."

"The Bishop, my child," replied the Prior, "hath the sword of Saint Peter, as well as the keys. He hath power as a secular prince, and he hath the protection of the mighty House of Burgundy; he hath also spiritual authority as a prelate, and he supports both with a reasonable force of good soldiers and men-at-arms. This William de la Marck was bred in his household, and bound to him by many benefits. But he gave vent, even in the court of the Bishop, to his fierce and bloodthirsty temper, and was expelled thence for a homicide, committed on one of the Bishop's chief domestics. From thenceforward, being banished from the good Prelate's presence, he hath been his constant and unrelenting foe; and now, I grieve to say, he hath girded his loins, and strengthened his horn against him."

"You consider, then, the situation of the worthy Prelate as being dangerous?" said Quentin, very anxiously.

"Alas! my son," said the good Franciscan, "what or who is there in this weary wilderness, whom we may not hold as in danger? But Heaven forefend, I should speak of the reverend Prelate as one whose peril is

---

[1] A similar story is told of the Duke of Vendome, who answered in this sort of macaronic Latin the classical expostulations of a German convent against the imposition of a contribution.

imminent. He has much treasure, true counsellors, and brave soldiers; and, moreover, a messenger who passed hither to the eastward yesterday, saith that the Duke of Burgundy hath despatched, upon the Bishop's request, an hundred men-at-arms to his assistance. This reinforcement, with the retinue belonging to each lance, are enough to deal with William de la Marck, on whose name be sorrow!—Amen."

At this crisis their conversation was interrupted by the Sacristan, who, in a voice almost inarticulate with anger, accused the Bohemian of having practised the most abominable arts of delusion among the younger brethren. He had added to their nightly meal cups of a heady and intoxicating cordial, of ten times the strength of the most powerful wine, under which several of the fraternity had succumbed,—and indeed, although the Sacristan had been strong to resist its influence, they might yet see, from his inflamed countenance and thick speech, that even he, the accuser himself, was in some degree affected by this unhallowed potation. Moreover, the Bohemian had sung songs of worldly vanity and impure pleasures; he had derided the cord of Saint Francis, made jest of his miracles, and termed his votaries fools and lazy knaves. Lastly, he had practised palmistry, and foretold to the young Father Cherubin, that he was beloved by a beautiful lady, who should make him father to a thriving boy.

The Father Prior listened to these complaints for some time in silence, as struck with mute horror by their enormous atrocity. When the Sacristan had concluded, he rose up, descended to the court of the convent, and ordered the lay brethren, on pain of the worst consequences of spiritual disobedience, to beat Hayraddin out of the sacred precincts, with their broom-staves and cart-whips.

This sentence was executed accordingly, in the presence of Quentin Durward, who, however vexed at the occurrence, easily saw that his interference would be of no avail.

The discipline inflicted upon the delinquent, notwithstanding the exhortations of the Superior, was more ludicrous than formidable. The Bohemian ran hither and thither through the court, amongst the clamour of voices, and noise of blows, some of which reached him not, because purposely misaimed; others, sincerely designed for his person, were eluded by his activity; and the few that fell upon his back and shoulders, he took without either complaint or reply. The noise and riot was the greater, that the inexperienced cudgel-players, among whom Hayraddin ran the gauntlet, hit each other more frequently than they did him; till at length, desirous of ending a scene which was more scandalous than edifying, the Prior commanded the wicket to be flung open, and the Bohemian, darting through it with the speed of lightning, fled forth into the moonlight.

During this scene, a suspicion which Durward had formerly entertained, recurred with additional strength. Hayraddin had, that very morning, promised to him more modest and discreet behaviour than he was wont to exhibit, when they rested in a convent on their journey; yet he had broken his engagement, and had been even more offensively obstreperous than usual. Something probably lurked under this; for whatever were the Bohemian's deficiencies, he lacked neither sense, nor, when he pleased, self-command; and might it not be probable that he wished to hold some communication, either with his own horde or some one else, from which he was debarred in the course of the day, by the vigilance with which he was watched by Quentin, and had recourse to this stratagem in order to get himself turned out of the convent?

No sooner did this suspicion dart once more through Quentin's mind, than, alert as he always was in his motions, he resolved to follow his cudgelled guide, and observe (secretly if possible) how he disposed of himself. Accordingly, when the Bohemian fled, as already mentioned, out at the gate of the convent, Quentin, hastily explaining to the Prior the necessity of keeping sight of his guide, followed in pursuit of him.

CHAPTER XVII

THE ESPIED SPY

What, the rude ranger? and spied spy?—hands off—
You are for no such rustics.
                    BEN JONSON's *Tale of Robin Hood*.

WHEN Quentin sallied from the convent, he could mark the precipitate retreat of the Bohemian, whose dark figure was seen in the far moonlight, flying with the speed of a flogged hound quite through the street of the little village, and across the level meadow that lay beyond.

"My friend runs fast," said Quentin to himself; "but he must run faster yet, to escape the fleetest foot that ever pressed the heather of Glen-houlakin."

Being fortunately without his cloak and armour, the Scottish mountaineer was at liberty to put forth a speed which was unrivalled in his own glens, and which, notwithstanding the rate at which the Bohemian ran, was likely soon to bring his pursuer up with him. This was not, however, Quentin's object; for he considered it more essential to watch Hayraddin's motions, than to interrupt them. He was the rather led to this, by the steadiness with which the Bohemian directed his course; and which continuing, even after the impulse of the violent expulsion had subsided, seemed to indicate that his career had some more certain goal for its object than could have suggested itself to a person unexpectedly turned out of good quarters when midnight was approaching, to seek a new place of repose. He never even looked behind him; and consequently Durward was enabled to follow him unobserved. At length the Bohemian, having traversed the meadow, and attained the side of a little stream, the banks of which were clothed with alders and willows, Quentin observed that he stood still, and blew a low note on his horn, which was answered by a whistle at some little distance.

"This is a rendezvous," thought Quentin; "but how shall I come near enough to overhear the import of what passes? the sound of my steps, and the rustling of the boughs through which I must force my passage, will betray me, unless I am cautious—I will stalk them, by Saint Andrew, as if they were Glen-isla deer—they shall learn that I have not conned woodcraft for nought. Yonder they meet, the two shadows—and two of them there are—odds against me if I am discovered, and if their purpose be unfriendly, as is much to be doubted. And then the Countess Isabelle loses her poor friend!—Well—and he were not worthy to be called such, if he were not ready to meet a dozen in her behalf.—Have I not crossed swords with Dunois, the best knight in France, and shall I fear a tribe of yonder vagabonds?—Pshaw—God and Saint Andrew to friend, they will find me both stout and wary."

Thus resolving, and with a degree of caution taught him by his silvan habits, our friend descended into the channel of the little stream, which varied in depth, sometimes scarce covering his shoes, sometimes coming up to his knees, and so crept along, his form concealed by the boughs overhanging the bank, and his steps unheard amid the ripple of the water. (We have ourselves, in the days of yore, thus approached the nest of the wakeful raven.) In this manner, the Scot drew near unperceived, until he distinctly heard the voices of those who were the subject of his observation, though he could not distinguish the words. Being at this time under the drooping branches of a magnificent weeping willow, which almost swept the surface of the water, he caught hold of one of its boughs, by the assistance of which, exerting at once much agility, dexterity, and strength, he raised himself up into the body of the tree, and sat, secure from discovery, among the central branches.

From this situation he could discover that the person with whom Hayraddin was now conversing was one of his own tribe, and, at the same time, he perceived, to his great disappointment, that no approximation could enable him to comprehend their language, which was totally unknown to him. They laughed much; and as Hayraddin made a sign of skipping about, and ended by rubbing his shoulder with his hand, Durward had no doubt that he was relating the story of the bastinading which he had sustained previous to his escape from the convent.

On a sudden, a whistle was again heard in the distance, which was once more answered by a low tone or two of Hayraddin's horn. Presently afterwards, a tall, stout, soldierly-looking man, a strong contrast in point of thews and sinews to the small and slender-limbed Bohemians, made his appearance. He had a broad baldric over his shoulder, which sustained a sword that hung almost across his person; his hose were much slashed, through which slashes was drawn silk or tiffany, of various colours; they were tied by at least five hundred points or strings, made of ribbon, to the tight buff-jacket which he wore, and the right sleeve of which displayed a silver boar's head, the crest of his Captain. A very small hat sat jauntily on one side of his head, from which descended a quantity of curled hair, which fell on each side of a broad face, and mingled with as broad a beard, about four inches long. He held a long lance in his hand; and his whole equipment was that of one of the German adventurers, who were known by the name of lanzknechts, in English, spearmen, who constituted a formidable part of the infantry of the period. These mercenaries were, of course, a fierce and rapacious soldiery, and having an idle tale current among themselves, that a lanzknecht was refused admittance into heaven on account of his vices, and into hell on the score of his tumultuous, mutinous, and insubordinate disposition, they manfully acted as if they neither sought the one, nor eschewed the other.

"Donner and blitz!" was his first salutation, in a sort of German-French, which we can only imperfectly imitate, "Why have you kept me dancing in attendance dis dree nights?"

"I could not see you sooner, Meinherr," said Hayraddin, very submissively; "there is a young Scot, with as quick an eye as the wild-cat, who watches my least motions. He suspects me already, and, should he find his suspicion confirmed, I were a dead man on the spot, and he would carry back the women into France again."

"Was henker!" said the lanzknecht; "we are three—we will attack them to-morrow, and carry the women off without going farther. You said the two valets were cowards—you and your comrade may manage them, and the Teufel sall hold me, but I match your Scots wild-cat."

"You will find that foolhardy," said Hayraddin; "for, besides that we ourselves count not much in fighting, this spark hath matched himself with the best knight in France, and come off with honour—I have seen those who saw him press Dunois hard enough."

"Hagel and sturmwetter! It is but your cowardice that speaks," said the German soldier.

"I am no more a coward than yourself," said Hayraddin; "but my trade is not fighting.—If you keep the appointment where it was laid, it is well—if not, I guide them safely to the Bishop's Palace, and William de la Marck may easily possess himself of them there, provided he is half as strong as he pretended a week since."

"Poz tausend!" said the soldier, "we are as strong and stronger; but we hear of a hundreds of the lances of Burgund,—das ist,—see you,—five men to a lance do make five hundreds, and then hold me the devil, they will be fainer to seek for us, than we to seek for them; for der Bischoff hath a goot force on footing—ay, indeed!"

"You must then hold to the ambuscade at the Cross of the Three Kings, or give up the adventure," said the Bohemian.

"Geb up—geb up the adventure of the rich bride for our noble hauptman—Teufel! I will charge through hell first.—Mein soul, we will be all princes and hertzogs, whom they call dukes, and we will hab a snab at the wein-kellar, and at the mouldy French crowns, and it may be at the pretty garces too, when He with de beard is weary on them."

"The ambuscade at the Cross of the Three Kings then still holds?" said the Bohemian.

"Mein Got, ay,—you will swear to bring them there; and when they are on their knees before the cross, and down from off their horses, which all men do, except such black heathens as thou, we will make in on them, and they are ours."

"Ay; but I promised this piece of necessary villainy only on one condition," said Hayraddin.—"I will not have a hair of the young man's head touched. If you swear this to me, by your Three Dead Men of Cologne, I will swear to you, by the Seven Night Walkers, that I will serve you truly as to the rest. And if you break your oath, the Night Walkers shall wake you seven nights from your sleep, between night and morning, and, on the eighth, they shall strangle and devour you."

"But, donner and hagel, what need you be so curious about the life of this boy, who is neither your bloot nor kin?" said the German.

"No matter for that, honest Heinrick; some men have pleasure in cutting throats, some in keeping them whole—So swear to me, that you will spare him life and limb, or, by the bright star Aldeboran, this matter shall go no further—Swear, and by the Three Kings, as you call them, of Cologne—I know you care for no other oath."

"Du bist ein comische man," said the lanzknecht, "I swear——"

"Not yet," said the Bohemian—"Faces about, brave lanzknecht, and look to the east, else the Kings may not hear you."

The soldier took the oath in the manner prescribed, and then declared that he would be in readiness, observing the place was quite convenient, being scarce five miles from their present leaguer.

"But, were it not making sure work to have a fahnlein of riders on the other road, by the left side of the inn, which might trap them if they go that way?"

The Bohemian considered a moment, and then answered, "No—the appearance of their troops in that direction might alarm the garrison of Namur, and then they would have a doubtful fight, instead of assured success. Besides, they shall travel on the right bank of the Maes, for I can guide them which way I will; for, sharp as this same Scottish mountaincr is, he hath never asked any one's advice, save mine, upon the direction of their route.—Undoubtedly, I was assigned to him by an assured friend, whose word no man mistrusts till they come to know him a little."

"Hark ye, friend Hayraddin," said the soldier, "I would ask you somewhat.—You and your bruder were, as you say yourself, gross sternendeuter, that is, star-lookers and geister-seers—Now, what henker was it made you not foresee him, your bruder Zamet, to be hanged?"

"I will tell you, Heinrick," said Hayraddin;—"if I could have known my brother was such a fool as to tell the counsel of King Louis to Duke Charles oi Burgundy, I could have foretold his death as sure as I can foretell fair weather in July. Louis hath both ears and hands at the Court of Burgundy, and Charles's counsellors love the chink of French gold as well as thou dost the clatter of a wine-pot.—But fare thee well, and keep appointment—I must await my early Scot a bow-shot without the gate of the den of the lazy swine yonder, else will he think me about some excursion which bodes no good to the success of his journey."

"Take a draught of comfort first," said the lanzknecht, tendering him a flask,—"but I forget; thou art beast enough to drink nothing but water, like a vile vassal of Mahound and Termagund."

"Thou art thyself a vassal of the wine-measure and the flagon," said the Bohemian,—"I marvel not that thou art only trusted with the blood-thirsty and violent part of executing what better heads have devised.—He must drink no wine, who would know the thoughts of others, or hide his own. But why preach to thee, who hast a thirst as eternal as a sand-bank in Arabia?—fare thee well.—Take my comrade Tuisco with thee—his appearance about the monastery may breed suspicion."

The two worthies parted, after each had again pledged himself to keep the rendezvous at the Cross of the Three Kings.

Quentin Durward watched until they were out of sight, and then descended from his place of concealment, his heart throbbing at the narrow escape which he and his fair charge had made—if, indeed, it could yet be achieved—from a deep-laid plan of villainy. Afraid, on his return to the monastery, of stumbling upon Hayraddin, he made a long detour, at the expense of traversing some very rough ground, and was thus enabled to return to his asylum on a different point from that by which he left it.

On the route, he communed earnestly with himself concerning the safest plan to be pursued. He had formed the resolution, when he first heard Hayraddin avow his treachery, to put him to death as soon as the conference broke up, and his companions were at a sufficient distance; but when he heard the Bohemian express so much interest in saving his own life, he felt it would be ungrateful to execute upon him, in its rigour, the punishment his treachery had deserved. He therefore resolved to spare his life, and even, if possible, still to use his services as a guide, under such precautions as should ensure the security of the precious charge, to the preservation of which his own life was internally devoted.

But whither were they to turn—the Countesses of Croye could neither obtain shelter in Burgundy, from which they had fled, nor in France, from which they had been in a manner expelled. The violence of Duke Charles in the one country, was scarcely more to be feared than the cold and tyrannical policy of King Louis in the other. After deep thought, Durward could form no better or safer plan for their security, than that, evading the ambuscade, they should take the road to Liege by the left hand of the Maes, and throw themselves, as the ladies originally designed, upon the protection of the excellent Bishop. That Prelate's will to protect them could not be doubted. and, if reinforced by this Burgundian party or men-at-arms, he might be considered as having the power. At any rate, if the dangers to which he was exposed from the hostility of William de la Marck, and from the troubles in the city of Liege, appeared imminent, he would still be able to protect the unfortunate ladies until they could be despatched to Germany with a suitable escort.

To sum up this reasoning—for when is a mental argument conducted without some reference to selfish considerations?—Quentin imagined that the death or captivity to which King Louis had, in cold blood, consigned him, set him at liberty from his engagements to the Crown of France; which, therefore, it was his determined purpose to renounce. The Bishop of Liege was likely, he concluded, to need soldiers, and he thought that, by the interposition of his fair friends, who now, especially the elder Countess, treated him with much familiarity, he might get some command, and perhaps might have the charge of conducting the Ladies of Croye to some place more safe than the neighbourhood of Liege. And, to conclude, the ladies had talked, although almost in a sort of jest, of raising the Countess's own vassals, and, as others did in those stormy times, fortifying her strong castle against all assailants whatever; they had jestingly asked Quentin, whether he would accept the perilous office of their Seneschal; and, on his embracing the office with ready glee and devotion, they had, in the same spirit, permitted him to kiss both their hands on that confidential and honourable appointment. Nay, he thought that the hand of the Countess Isabelle, one of the best formed and most beautiful to which true vassal ever did such homage, trembled when his lips rested on it a moment longer than ceremony required, and that some confusion appeared on her cheek and in her eye as she withdrew it. Something might come of all this; and what brave man, at Quentin Durward's age, but would gladly have taken the thoughts which it awakened, into the considerations which were to determine his conduct?

This point settled, he had next to consider in what degree he was to use the further guidance of the faithless Bohemian. He had renounced his first thought of killing him in the wood, and, if he took another guide, and dismissed him alive, it would be sending the traitor to the camp of William de la Marck, with intelligence of their motions. He thought of taking the Prior into his counsels, and requesting him to detain the Bohemian by force, until they should have time to reach the Bishop's castle; but, on reflection, he dared not hazard such a proposition to one who was timid both as an old man and a friar, who held the safety of his convent the most important object of his duty, and who trembled at the mention of the Wild Boar of Ardennes.

At length Durward settled a plan of operation, on which he could better reckon, as the execution rested entirely upon himself; and, in the cause in which he was engaged, he felt himself capable of everything. With a firm and bold heart, though conscious of the dangers of his situation, Quentin might be compared to one walking under a load, of the weight of which he is conscious, but which yet is not beyond his strength and power of endurance. Just as his plan was determined, he reached the convent.

Upon knocking gently at the gate, a brother, considerately stationed for that purpose by the Prior, opened it, and acquainted him that the brethren were to be engaged in the choir till daybreak, praying Heaven to forgive to the community the various scandals which had that evening taken place among them.

The worthy friar offered Quentin permission to attend their devo- tions; but his clothes were in such a wet condition, that the young Scot was obliged to decline the opportunity, and request permission, instead, to sit by the kitchen fire, in order to his attire being dried before morn- ing; as he was particularly desirous that the Bohemian, when they should next meet, should observe no traces of his having been abroad during the night. The friar not only granted his request, but afforded him his own company, which fell in very happily with the desire which Durward had to obtain information concerning the two routes which he had heard mentioned by the Bohemian in his conversation with the lanzknecht. The friar, entrusted upon many occasions with the business of the convent abroad, was the person in the fraternity best qualified to afford him the information he requested, but observed, that, as true pilgrims, it became the duty of the ladies whom Quentin escorted, to take the road on the right side of the Maes, by the Cross of the Kings, where the blessed relics of Caspar, Melchior, and Balthasar (as the Catholic Church has named the eastern Magi who came to Bethlehem with their offerings), had rested as they were transported to Cologne, and on which spot they had wrought many miracles.

Quentin replied, that the ladies were determined to observe all the holy stations with the utmost punctuality, and would certainly visit that of the Cross, either in going to or returning from Cologne, but they had heard reports that the road by the right side of the river was at present rendered unsafe by the soldiers of the ferocious William de la Marck.

"Now may Heaven forbid," said Father Francis, "that the Wild Boar of Ardennes should again make his lair so near us!—Nevertheless, the broad Maes will be a good barrier betwixt us, even should it so chance."

"But it will be no barrier between my ladies and the marauder, should we cross the river, and travel on the right bank," answered the Scot.

"Heaven will protect its own, young man," said the friar; "for it were hard to think that the Kings of yonder blessed city of Cologne, who will not endure that a Jew or infidel should even enter within the walls of their town, could be oblivious enough to permit their worshippers, coming to their shrine as true pilgrims, to be plundered and misused by such a miscreant dog as this Boar of Ardennes, who is worse than a whole desert of Saracen heathens, and all the ten tribes of Israel to boot."

Whatever reliance Quentin, as a sincere Catholic, was bound to rest upon the special protection of Melchior, Caspar, and Balthasar, he could not but recollect, that the pilgrim habits of the ladies being assumed out of mere earthly policy, he and his charge could scarcely expect their countenance on the present occasion; and therefore resolved, as far as possible, to avoid placing the ladies in any predicament where miraculous interposition might be necessary; whilst, in the simplicity of his good faith, he himself vowed a pilgrimage to the Three Kings of Cologne in his own proper person, provided the simulate design of those over whose safety he was now watching, should be permitted by those reasonable and royal, as well as sainted personages, to attain the desired effect.

That he might enter into this obligation with all solemnity, he requested the friar to show him into one of the various chapels which opened from the main body of the church of the convent, where, upon his knees, and with sincere devotion, he ratified the vow which he had made internally. The distant sound of the choir, the solemnity of the deep and dead hour which he had chosen for this act of devotion, the effect of the glimmering lamp with which the little Gothic building was illuminated— all contributed to throw Quentin's mind into the state when it most readily acknowledges its human frailty, and seeks that supernatural aid and protection, which, in every worship, must be connected with repentance for past sins, and resolutions of future amendment. That the object of his devotion was misplaced, was not the fault of Quentin; and, its purpose being sincere, we can scarce suppose it unacceptable to the only true Deity, who regards the motives, and not the forms of prayer, and in whose eyes the sincere devotion of a heathen is more estimable than the specious hypocrisy of a Pharisee.

Having commended himself and his helpless companions to the Saints, and to the keeping of Providence, Quentin at length retired to rest, leaving the friar much edified by the depth and sincerity of his devotion.

CHAPTER XVIII

PALMISTRY

When many a merry tale and many a song
Cheer'd the rough road, we wish'd the rough road long.
The rough road, then, returning in a round,
Mock'd our enchanted steps, for all was fairy ground.
                                        SAMUEL JOHNSON.

By peep of day Quentin Durward had forsaken his little cell, had roused the sleepy grooms, and, with more than his wonted care, seen that everything was prepared for the day's journey. Girths and bridles, the horse-furniture, and the shoes of the horses themselves, were carefully inspected with his own eyes, that there might be as little chance as possible of the occurrence of any of those casualties, which, petty as they seem, often interrupt or disconcert travelling. The horses were also, under his own inspection, carefully fed, so as to render them fit for a long day's journey, or, if that should be necessary, for a hasty flight.

Quentin then betook himself to his own chamber, armed himself with unusual care, and belted on his sword with the feeling at once of approaching danger, and of stern determination to dare it to the uttermost.

These generous feelings gave him a loftiness of step, and a dignity of manner, which the Ladies of Croye had not yet observed in him, though they had been highly pleased and interested by the grace, yet, *naïveté*, of his general behaviour and conversation, and the mixture of shrewd intelligence which naturally belonged to him, with the simplicity arising from his secluded education and distant country. He let them understand, that it would be necessary that they should prepare for their journey this morning rather earlier than usual; and, accordingly, they left the convent immediately after a morning repast, for which, as well as the other hospitalities of the House, the ladies made acknowledgment by a donation to the altar, befitting rather their rank than their appearance. But this excited no suspicion, as they were supposed to be Englishwomen; and the attribute of superior wealth attached at that time to the insular character as strongly as in our own day.

The Prior blessed them as they mounted to depart, and congratulated Quentin on the absence of his heathen guide; "for," said the venerable man, "better stumble in the path, than be upheld by the arm of a thief or robber."

Quentin was not quite of his opinion; for, dangerous as he knew the Bohemian to be, he thought he could use his services, and, at the same time, baffle his treasonable purpose, now that he saw clearly to what it tended. But his anxiety upon this subject was soon at an end, for the little cavalcade was not an hundred yards from the monastery and the village before Maugrabin joined it, riding as usual on his little active and wild-looking jennet. Their road led them along the side of the same brook where Quentin had overheard the mysterious conference of the preceding evening, and Hayraddin had not long rejoined them, ere they passed under the very willow-tree which had afforded Durward the means of concealment, when he became an unsuspected hearer of what then passed betwixt that false guide and the lanzknecht.

The recollections which the spot brought back stirred Quentin to enter abruptly into conversation with his guide, whom hitherto he had scarce spoken to.

"Where hast thou found night-quarter, thou profane knave?" said the Scot.

"Your wisdom may guess, by looking on my gaberdine," answered the Bohemian, pointing to his dress, which was covered with the seeds of hay.

"A good haystack," said Quentin, "is a convenient bed for an astrologer, and a much better than a heathen scoffer at our blessed religion, and its ministers, ever deserves."

"It suited my Klepper better than me, though," said Hayraddin, patting his horse on the neck; "for he had food and shelter at the same time. The old bald fools turned him loose, as if a wise man's horse could

have infected with wit or sagacity a whole convent ŏf asses. Lucky that
Klepper knows my whistle, and follows me as truly as a hound, or we
had never met again, and you in your turn might have whistled for
a guide."

"I have told thee more than once," said Durward sternly, "to restrain
thy ribaldry when thou chancest to be in worthy men's company, a thing
which, I believe, hath rarely happened to thee in thy life before now;
and I promise thee, that, did I hold thee as faithless a guide as I esteem
thee a blasphemous and worthless catiff, my Scottish dirk and thy
heathenish heart had ere now been acquainted, although the doing such
a deed were as ignoble as the sticking of swine."

"A wild boar is near akin to a sow," said the Bohemian, without flinch-
ing from the sharp look with which Quentin regarded him, or altering,
in the slightest degree, the caustic indifference which he affected in his
language; "and many men," he subjoined, "find both pride, pleasure,
and profit, in sticking them."

Astonished at the man's ready confidence, and uncertain whether he
did not know more of his own history and feelings than was pleasant for
him to converse upon, Quentin broke off a conversation in which he had
gained no advantage over Maugrabin, and fell back to his accustomed
post beside the ladies.

We have already observed, that a considerable degree of familiarity
had begun to establish itself between them. The elder Countess treated
him (being once well assured of the nobility of his birth) like a favoured
equal; and though her niece showed her regard to their protector less
freely, yet, under every disadvantage of bashfulnss and timidity, Quentin
thought he could plainly perceive, that his company and conversation
were not by any means indifferent to her.

Nothing gives such life and soul to youthful gaiety as the consciousness that it is successfully received; and Quentin had accordingly, during
the former period of their journey, amused his fair charge with the liveliness of his conversation, and the songs and tales of his country, the
former of which he sung in his native language, while his efforts to
render the latter into his foreign and imperfect French, gave rise to a
hundred little mistakes and errors of speech, as diverting as the narratives
themselves. But on this anxious morning, he rode beside the ladies of
Croye without any of his usual attempts to amuse them, and they could
not help observing his silence as something remarkable.

"Our young companion has seen a wolf," said the Lady Hameline,
alluding to an ancient superstition, "and he has lost his tongue in consequence." [1]

> [1] "Vox quoque Mœrim
> Jam fugit ipsa; lupi Mœrim videre priores."
>   VIRGILII, ix. ecloga.

The commentators add, in explanation of this passage, the opinion of Pliny: "The
being beheld by a wolf in Italy is accounted noxious, and is supposed to take away
the speech of a man, if these animals behold him ere he sees them."

"To say I had tracked a fox were nearer the mark," thought Quentin, but gave the reply no utterance.

"Are you well, Seignior Quentin?" said the Countess Isabelle, in a tone of interest at which she herself blushed, while she felt that it was something more than the distance between them warranted.

"He hath sat up carousing with the jolly friars," said the Lady Hameline; "the Scots are like the Germans, who spend all their mirth over the Rheinwein, and bring only their staggering steps to the dance of the evening, and their aching heads to the ladies' bower in the morning."

"Nay, gentle ladies," said Quentin, "I deserve not your reproach. The good friars were at their devotions almost all night; and for myself, my drink was barely a cup of their thinnest and most ordinary wine."

"It is the badness of his fare that has put him out of humour," said the Countess Isabelle. "Cheer up, Seignior Quentin; and should we ever visit my ancient Castle of Bracquemont together, if I myself should stand your cup-bearer, and hand it to you, you shall have a generous cup of wine, that the like never grew upon the vines of Hochheim or Johannisberg."

"A glass of water, noble lady, from *your* hand"—Thus far did Quentin begin, but his voice trembled; and Isabelle continued, as if she had been insensible of the tenderness of the accentuation upon the personal pronoun.

"The wine was stocked in the deep vaults of Bracquemont, by my great-grandfather the Rhinegrave Godfrey," said the Countess Isabelle.

"Who won the hand of her great-grandmother," interjected the Lady Hameline, interrupting her niece, "by proving himself the best son of chivalry, at the great tournament of Strasbourg—ten knights were slain in the lists. But those days are over, and no one now thinks of encountering peril for the sake of honour, or to relieve distressed beauty."

To this speech, which was made in the tone in which a modern beauty, whose charms are rather on the wane, may be heard to condemn the rudeness of the present age, Quentin took upon him to reply, "that there was no lack of that chivalry which the Lady Hameline seemed to consider as extinct, and that, were it eclipsed everywhere else, it would still glow in the bosoms of the Scottish gentlemen."

"Hear him!" said the Lady Hameline; "he would have us believe, that in his cold and bleak country still lives the noble fire which has decayed in France and Germany! The poor youth is like a Swiss mountaineer, mad with partiality to his native land—he will next tell us of the vines and olives of Scotland."

"No, madam," said Durward; "of the wine and the oil of our mountains I can say little, more than that our swords can compel these rich productions, as tribute from our wealthier neighbours. But for the unblemished faith and unfaded honour of Scotland, I must now put to the proof how far you can repose trust in them, however mean the individual who can offer nothing more as a pledge of your safety."

"You speak mysteriously—you know of some pressing and present danger," said the Lady Hameline.

"I have read it in his eye for this hour past!" exclaimed the Lady Isabelle, clasping her hands. "Sacred Virgin, what will become of us?"

"Nothing, I hope, but what you would desire," answered Durward. "And now I am compelled to ask—Gentle ladies, can you trust me?"

"Trust you?" answered the Countess Hameline—"certainly—But why the question? Or how far do you ask our confidence?"

"I, on my part," said the Countess Isabelle, "trust you implicitly, and without condition. If you can deceive us, Quentin, I will no more look for truth, save in Heaven."

"Gentle lady," replied Durward, highly gratified, "you do me but justice. My object is to alter our route, by proceeding directly by the left bank of the Maes to Liege, instead of crossing at Namur. This differs from the order assigned by King Louis, and the instructions given to the guide. But I heard news in the monastery of marauders on the right bank of the Maes, and of the march of Burgundian soldiers to suppress them. Both circumstances alarm me for your safety. Have I your permission so far to deviate from the route of your journey?"

"My ample and full permission," answered the younger lady.

"Cousin," said the Lady Hameline, "I believe with you, that the youth means us well;—but bethink you—we transgress the instructions of King Louis, so positively iterated."

"And why should we regard his instructions?" said the Lady Isabelle. "I am, I thank Heaven for it, no subject of his; and, as a suppliant, he has abused the confidence he induced me to repose in him. I would not dishonour this young gentleman by weighing his word for an instant against the injunctions of yonder crafty and selfish despot."

"Now, may God bless you for that very word, lady," said Quentin joyously; "and if I deserve not the trust it expresses, tearing with wild horses in this life, and eternal tortures in the next, were e'en too good for my deserts."

So saying, he spurred his horse, and rejoined the Bohemian. This worthy seemed of a remarkably passive, if not a forgiving temper. Injury or threat never dwelt, at least seemed not to dwell, on his recollection; and he entered into the conversation which Durward presently commenced, just as if there had been no unkindly word betwixt them in the course of the morning.

"The dog," thought the Scot, "snarls not now, because he intends to clear scores with me at once and for ever, when he can snatch me by the very throat; but we will try for once whether we cannot foil a traitor at his own weapons.—Honest Hayraddin," he said, "thou hast travelled with us for ten days, yet hast never shown us a specimen of your skill in fortune-telling; which you are, nevertheless, so fond of practising, that you must needs display your gifts in every convent at which we stop, at the risk of being repaid by a night's lodging under a haystack."

"You have never asked me for a specimen of my skill," said the gipsy. "You are like the rest of the world, contented to ridicule those mysteries which they do not understand."

"Give me then a present proof of your skill," said Quentin; and, ungloving his hand, he held it out to the Zingaro.

Hayraddin carefully regarded all the lines which crossed each other on the Scotchman's palm, and noted, with equally scrupulous attention, the little risings or swellings at the roots of the fingers, which were then believed as intimately connected with the disposition, habits, and fortunes of the individual, as the organs of the brain are pretended to be in our own time.

"Here is a hand," said Hayraddin, "which speaks of toils endured, and dangers encountered. I read in it an early acquaintance with the hilt of the sword; and yet some acquaintance also with the clasps of the massbook."

"This of my past life you may have learned elsewhere," said Quentin; "tell me something of the future."

"This line from the hill of Venus," said the Bohemian, "not broken off abruptly, but attending and accompanying the line of life, argues a certain and large fortune by marriage, whereby the party shall be raised among the wealthy and the noble by the influence of successful love."

"Such promises you make to all who ask your advice," said Quentin; "they are part of your art."

"What I tell you is as certain," said Hayraddin, "as that you shall in a brief space be menaced with mighty danger; which I infer from this bright blood-red line cutting the table-line transversely, and intimating stroke of sword, or other violence, from which you shall only be saved by the attachment of a faithful friend."

"Thyself, ha?" said Quentin, somewhat indignant that the chiromantist should thus practise on his credulity, and endeavour to found a reputation by predicting the consequences of his own treachery.

"My art," replied the Zingaro, "tells me nought that concerns myself."

"In this, then, the seers of my land," said Quentin, "excel your boasted knowledge; for their skill teaches them the dangers by which they are themselves beset. I left not my hills without having felt a portion of the double vision with which their inhabitants are gifted; and I will give thee a proof of it, in exchange for thy specimen of palmistry. Hayraddin, the danger which threatens me lies on the right bank of the river—I will avoid it by travelling to Liege on the left bank."

The guide listened with an apathy, which, knowing the circumstances in which Maugrabin stood, Quentin could not by any means comprehend. "If you accomplish your purpose," was the Bohemian's reply, "the dangerous crisis will be transferred from your lot to mine."

"I thought," said Quentin, "that you said but now, that you could not presage your own fortune?"

"Not in the manner in which I have but now told you yours," answered Hayraddin; "but it requires little knowledge of Louis of Valois, to presage that he will hang your guide, because your pleasure was to deviate from the road which he recommended."

"The attaining with safety the purpose of the journey, and ensuring its happy termination," said Quentin, "must atone for a deviation from the exact line of the prescribed route."

"Ay," replied the Bohemian, "if you are sure that the King had in his own eye the same termination of the pilgrimage which he insinuated to you."

"And of what other termination is it possible that he could have been meditating? or why should you suppose he had any purpose in his thought, other than was avowed in his direction?" inquired Quentin.

"Simply," replied the Zingaro, "that those who know aught of the Most Christian King, are aware, that the purpose about which he is most anxious, is always that which he is least willing to declare. Let our gracious Louis send twelve embassies, and I will forfeit my neck to the gallows a year before it is due, if in eleven of them there is not something at the bottom of the ink-horn more than the pen has written in the letters of credence."

"I regard not your foul suspicions," answered Quentin; "my duty is plain and peremptory—to convey these ladies in safety to Liege; and I take it on me to think that I best discharge that duty in changing our prescribed route, and keeping the left side of the river Maes. It is likewise the direct road to Liege. By crossing the river, we should lose time, and incur fatigue, to no purpose—Wherefore should we do so?"

"Only because pilgrims, as they call themselves, destined for Cologne," said Hayraddin, "do not usually descend the Maes so low as Liege; and that the route of the ladies will be accounted contradictory of their professed destination."

"If we are challenged on that account," said Quentin, "we will say that alarms of the wicked Duke of Gueldres, or of William de la Marck, or of the *Ecorcheurs* and lanzknechts, on the right side of the river, justify our holding by the left, instead of our intended route."

"As you will, my good seignior," replied the Bohemian—"I am, for my part, equally ready to guide you down the left as down the right side of the Maes—Your excuse to your master you must make out for yourself."

Quentin, although rather surprised, was at the same time pleased with the ready, or at least the unrepugnant acquiescence of Hayraddin in their change of route, for he needed his assistance as a guide, and yet had feared that the disconcerting of his intended act of treachery would have driven him to extremity. Besides, to expel the Bohemian from their society, would have been the ready mode to bring down William de la Marck, with whom he was in correspondence, upon their intended route; whereas if Hayraddin remained with them, Quentin thought he could manage to prevent the Moor from having any communication with strangers, unless he was himself aware of it.

Abandoning, therefore, all thoughts of their original route, the little party followed that by the left bank of the broad Maes, so speedily and successfully, that the next day early brought them to the purposed end of their journey. They found that the Bishop of Liege, for the sake of his health, as he himself alleged, but rather, perhaps, to avoid being surprised by the numerous and mutinous population of the city, had established his residence in his beautiful Castle of Schonwaldt, about a mile without Liege.

Just as they approached the Castle, they saw the Prelate returning in long procession from the neighbouring city, in which he had been officiating at the performance of High Mass. He was at the head of a splendid train of religious, civil, and military men, mingled together, or, as the old ballad-maker expresses it,

> "With many a cross-bearer before,
> And many a spear behind."

The procession made a noble appearance, as, winding along the verdant banks of the broad Maes, it wheeled into, and was as it were devoured by, the huge Gothic portal of the Episcopal residence.

But when the party came more near, they found that circumstances around the Castle argued a doubt and sense of insecurity, which contradicted that display of pomp and power which they had just witnessed. Strong guards of the Bishop's soldiers were heedfully maintained all around the mansion and its immediate vicinity; and the prevailing appearances in an ecclesiastical residence, seemed to argue a sense of danger in the reverend Prelate, who found it necessary thus to surround himself with all the defensive precautions of war. The ladies of Croye, when announced by Quentin, were reverently ushered into the great hall, where they met with the most cordial reception from the Bishop, who met them there at the head of his little court. He would not permit them to kiss his hand, but welcomed them with a salute, which had something in it of gallantry on the part of a prince to fine women, and something also of the holy affection of a pastor to the sisters of his flock.

Louis of Bourbon, the reigning Bishop of Liege, was in truth a generous and kind-hearted prince; whose life had not indeed been always confined, with precise strictness, within the bounds of his clerical profession; but who, notwithstanding, had uniformly maintained the frank and honourable character of the House of Bourbon, from which he was descended.

In later times, as age advanced, the Prelate had adopted habits more beseeming a member of the hierarchy than his early reign had exhibited, and was loved among the neighbouring princes, as a noble ecclesiastic, generous and magnificent in his ordinary mode of life, though preserving no very ascetic severity of character, and governing with an easy indifference, which, amid his wealthy and mutinous subjects, rather encouraged than subdued rebellious purposes.

The Bishop was so fast an ally of the Duke of Burgundy, that the latter claimed almost a joint sovereignty in his bishopric, and repaid the good-natured ease with which the Prelate admitted claims which he might easily have disputed, by taking his part on all occasions, with the determined and furious zeal which was a part of his character. He used to say, he considered Liege as his own, the Bishop as his brother (indeed they might be accounted such, in consequence of the Duke having married for his first wife, the Bishop's sister), and that he who annoyed Louis of Bourbon, had to do with Charles of Burgundy; a threat which, considering the character and the power of the prince who used it, would have been powerful with any but the rich and discontented city of Liege, where much wealth had, according to the ancient proverb, made wit waver.

The Prelate, as we have said, assured the Ladies of Croye of such intercession as his interest at the Court of Burgundy, used to the uttermost, might gain for them, and which, he hoped, might be the more effectual, as Campo-Basso, from some late discoveries, stood rather lower than formerly in the Duke's personal favour. He promised them also such protection as it was in his power to afford; but the sigh with which he gave the warrant, seemed to allow that his power was more precarious than in words he was willing to admit.

"At every event, my dearest daughters," said the Bishop, with an air in which, as in his previous salute, a mixture of spiritual unction qualified the hereditary gallantry of the House of Bourbon, "Heaven forbid I should abandon the lamb to the wicked wolf, or noble ladies to the oppression of faitours. I am a man of peace, though my abode now rings with arms; but be assured I will care for your safety as for my own; and should matters become yet more distracted here, which, with our Lady's grace, we trust will be rather pacified than inflamed, we will provide for your safe conduct to Germany; for not even the will of our brother and protector, Charles of Burgundy, shall prevail with us to dispose of you in any respect contrary to your own inclinations. We cannot comply with your request of sending you to a convent; for, alas! such is the influence of the sons of Belial among the inhabitants of Liege, that we know no retreat to which our authority extends, beyond the bounds of our own castle and the protection of our soldiery. But here you are most welcome, and your train shall have all honourable entertainment; especially this youth, whom you recommend so particularly to our countenance, and on whom in especial we bestow our blessing."

Quentin kneeled, as in duty bound, to receive the Episcopal benediction.

"For yourselves," proceeded the good Prelate, "you shall reside here with my sister Isabelle, a Canoness of Triers, and with whom you may dwell in all honour, even under the roof of so gay a bachelor as the Bishop of Liege."

He gallantly conducted the ladies to his sister's apartment, as he concluded the harangue of welcome; and his Master of the Household, an officer, who, having taken Deacon's orders, held something between a secular and ecclesiastical character, entertained Quentin with the hospitality which his master enjoined, while the other personages of the retinue of the Ladies of Croye were committed to the inferior departments.

In this arrangement Quentin could not help remarking, that the presence of the Bohemian, so much objected to in country convents, seemed, in the household of this wealthy, and perhaps we might say worldly prelate, to attract neither objection nor remark.

CHAPTER XIX

THE CITY

Good friends, sweet friends, let me not stir you up
To any sudden act of mutiny!

Julius Cæsar.

SEPARATED from the Lady Isabelle, whose looks had been for so many days his load-star, Quentin felt a strange vacancy and chillness of the heart, which he had not yet experienced in any of the vicissitudes to which his life had subjected him. No doubt the cessation of the close and unavoidable intercourse and intimacy betwixt them was the necessary consequence of the Countess having obtained a place of settled residence; for, under what pretext could she, had she meditated such an impropriety, have had a gallant young squire, such as Quentin, in constant attendance upon her?

But the shock of the separation was not the more welcome that it seemed unavoidable, and the proud heart of Quentin swelled at finding he was parted with like an ordinary postillion, or an escort whose duty is discharged; while his eyes sympathised so far as to drop a secret tear or two over the ruins of all those airy castles, so many of which he had employed himself in constructing during their too interesting journey. He made a manly, but, at first, a vain effort, to throw off this mental dejection; and so, yielding to the feelings he could not suppress, he sat him down in one of the deep recesses formed by a window which lighted the great Gothic hall of Schonwaldt, and there mused upon his hard fortune, which had not assigned him rank or wealth sufficient to prosecute his daring suit.

Quentin tried to dispel the sadness which overhung him by despatching Charlet, one of the valets, with letters to the court of Louis, announcing the arrival of the Ladies of Croye at Liege. At length his natural buoyancy of temper returned, much excited by the title of an old *romaunt*

which had been just printed at Strasbourg, and which lay beside him
in the window, the title of which set forth,

> How the Squire of lowe degree,
> Loved the King's daughter of Hongarie.

While he was tracing the "letters blake" of the ditty so congenial to
his own situation, Quentin was interrupted by a touch on the shoulder,
and, looking up, beheld the Bohemian standing by him.

Hayraddin, never a welcome sight, was odious from his late treachery,
and Quentin sternly asked him, why he dared take the freedom to touch
a Christian and a gentleman?

"Simply," answered the Bohemian, "because I wished to know if the
Christian gentleman had lost his feeling as well as his eyes and ears.
I have stood speaking to you these five minutes, and you have stared
on that scrap of yellow paper, as if it were a spell to turn you into a
statue, and had already wrought half its purpose."

"Well, what dost thou want? Speak, and begone!"

"I want what all men want, though few are satisfied with it," said
Hayraddin; "I want my due; my ten crowns of gold for guiding the
ladies hither."

"With what face darest thou ask any guerdon beyond my sparing thy
worthless life?" said Durward fiercely; "thou knowest that it was thy
purpose to have betrayed them on the road."

"But I did *not* betray them," said Hayraddin; "if I had, I would have
asked no guerdon from you or from them, but from him whom their
keeping upon the right-hand side of the river might have benefited. The
party that I have served is the party who must pay me."

"Thy guerdon perish with thee, then, traitor!" said Quentin, telling
out the money. "Get thee to the Boar of Ardennes, or to the devil! but
keep hereafter out of my sight, lest I send thee thither before thy time."

"The Boar of Ardennes!" repeated the Bohemian, with a stronger
emotion of surprise than his features usually expressed; "it was then
no vague guess—no general suspicion—which made you insist on changing the road?—Can it be—are there really in other lands arts of prophecy
more sure than those of our wandering tribes? The willow-tree under
which we spoke could tell no tales. But no—no—no—Dolt that I was!—
I have it—I have it!—The willow by the brook near yonder convent—I
saw you look towards it as you passed it, about half a mile from yon
hive of drones—that could not indeed speak, but it might hide one who
could hear! I will hold my councils in an open plain henceforth; not a
bunch of thistles shall be near me for a Scot to shroud amongst—Ha! ha!
the Scot hath beat the Zingaro at his own subtle weapons. But know,
Quentin Durward, that you have foiled me to the marring of thine own
fortune—Yes! the fortune I told thee of, from the lines on thy hand,
had been richly accomplished but for thine own obstinacy."

"By Saint Andrew," said Quentin, "thy impudence makes me laugh in spite of myself—How, or in what, should thy successful villainy have been of service to me? I heard, indeed, that you did stipulate to save my life, which condition your worthy allies would speedily have forgotten, had we once come to blows—but in what thy betrayal of these ladies could have served me, but by exposing me to death or captivity, is a matter beyond human brains to conjecture."

"No matter of thinking of it, then," said Hayraddin, "for I mean still to surprise you with my gratitude. Had you kept back my hire, I should have held that we were quit, and had left you to your own foolish guidance. As it is, I remain your debtor for yonder matter on the banks of the Cher."

"Methinks I have already taken out the payment in cursing and abusing thee," said Quentin.

"Hard words, or kind ones," said the Zingaro, "are but wind, which make no weight in the balance. Had you struck me, indeed, instead of threatening——"

"I am likely enough to take out payment in that way, if you provoke me longer."

"I would not advise it," said the Zingaro; "such payment, made by a rash hand, might exceed the debt, and unhappily leave a balance on your side, which I am not one to forget or forgive. And now farewell, but not for a long space—I go to bid adieu to the Ladies of Croye."

"Thou?" said Quentin in astonishment—"*thou* be admitted to the presence of the ladies, and here, where they are in a manner recluses under the protection of the Bishop's sister, a noble canoness? It is impossible."

"Marthon, however, waits to conduct me to their presence," said the Zingaro, with a sneer; "and I must pray your forgiveness if I leave you something abruptly."

He turned as if to depart, but instantly coming back, said, with a tone of deep and serious emphasis, "I know your hopes—they are daring, yet not vain if I aid them. I know your fears—they should teach prudence, not timidity. Every woman may be won. A count is but a nickname, which will befit Quentin as well as the other nickname of duke befits Charles, or that of King befits Louis."

Ere Durward could reply, the Bohemian had left the hall. Quentin instantly followed; but, better acquainted than the Scot with the passages of the House, Hayraddin kept the advantage which he had gotten; and the pursuer lost sight of him as he descended a small back staircase. Still Durward followed, though without exact consciousness of his own purpose in doing so. The staircase terminated by a door opening into the alley of a garden, in which he again beheld the Zingaro hastening down a pleached walk.

On two sides, the garden was surrounded by the buildings of the castle —a huge old pile, partly castellated, and partly resembling an ecclesiastical building; on the other two sides, the enclosure was a high embattled wall. Crossing the alleys of the garden to another part of the building, where a postern-door opened behind a large massive buttress, overgrown with ivy, Hayraddin looked back, and waved his hand in signal of an exulting farewell to his follower, who saw that in effect the postern-door was opened by Marthon, and that the vile Bohemian was admitted into the precincts, as he naturally concluded, of the apartment of the Countesses of Croye. Quentin bit his lips with indignation, and blamed himself severely that he had not made the ladies sensible of the full infamy of Hayraddin's character, and acquainted with his machinations against their safety. The arrogating manner in which the Bohemian had promised to back his suit, added to his anger and his disgust; and he felt as if even the hand of the Countess Isabelle would be profaned, were it possible to attain it by such patronage. "But it is all a deception," he said— "a turn of his base juggling artifice. He has procured access to these ladies upon some false pretence, and with some mischievous intention. It is well I have learned where they lodge. I will watch Marthon, and solicit an interview with them, were it but to place them on their guard. It is hard that I must use artifice and brook delay, when such as he have admittance openly and without scruple. They shall find, however, that though I am excluded from their presence, Isabelle's safety is still the chief subject of my vigilance."

While the young lover was thus meditating, an aged gentleman of the Bishop's household approached him from the same door by which he had himself entered the garden, and made him aware, though with the greatest civility of manner, that the garden was private, and reserved only for the use of the Bishop, and guests of the very highest distinction.

Quentin heard him repeat this information twice ere he put the proper construction upon it; and then starting as from a reverie, he bowed and hurried out of the garden, the official person following him all the way, and overwhelming him with formal apologies for the necessary discharge of his duty. Nay, so pertinacious was he in his attempts to remove the offence which he conceived Durward to have taken, that he offered to bestow his own company upon him, to contribute to his entertainment; until Quentin, internally cursing his formal foppery, found no better way of escape, than pretending a desire of visiting the neighbouring city, and setting off thither at such a round pace as speedily subdued all desire in the gentleman-usher to accompany him farther than the drawbridge. In a few minutes, Quentin was within the walls of the city of Liege, then one of the richest in Flanders, and of course in the world.

Melancholy, even love-melancholy, is not so deeply seated, at least in minds of a manly and elastic character, as the soft enthusiasts who suffer under it are fond of believing. It yields to unexpected and striking impressions upon the senses, to change of place, to such scenes as create new trains of association, and to the influence of the busy hum of mankind. In a few minutes, Quentin's attention was as much engrossed by the variety of objects presented in rapid succession by the busy streets of Liege, as if there had neither been a Countess Isabelle, nor a Bohemian. in the world.

The lofty houses,—the stately, though narrow and gloomy streets,—the splendid display of the richest goods and most gorgeous armour in the warehouses and shops around,—the walks crowded by busy citizens of every description, passing and repassing with faces of careful importance or eager bustle,—the huge wains, which transported to and fro the subjects of export and import, the former consisting of broad cloths and serge, arms of all kinds, nails and iron work, while the latter comprehended every article of use or luxury, intended either for the consumption of an opulent city, or received in barter, and destined to be transported elsewhere,—all these objects combined to form an engrossing picture of wealth, bustle, and splendour, to which Quentin had been hitherto a stranger. He admired also the various streams and canals, drawn from and communicating with the Maes, which, traversing the city in various directions, offered to every quarter the commercial facilities of water-carriage, and he failed not to hear a mass in the venerable old Church of Saint Lambert, said to have been founded in the eighth century.

It was upon leaving this place of worship that Quentin began to observe, that he, who had been hitherto gazing on all around him with the eagerness of unrestrained curiosity, was himself the object of attention to several groups of substantial-looking burghers, who seemed assembled to look upon him as he left the church, and amongst whom arose a buzz and whisper, which spread from one party to another; while the number of gazers continued to augment rapidly, and the eyes of each who added to it were eagerly directed to Quentin, with a stare which expressed much interest and curiosity, mingled with a certain degree of respect.

At length he now formed the centre of a considerable crowd, which yet yielded before him while he continued to move forward; while those who followed or kept pace with him, studiously avoided pressing on him, or impeding his motions. Yet his situation was too embarrassing to be long endured, without making some attempt to extricate himself, and to obtain some explanation.

Quentin looked around him, and fixing upon a jolly, stout-made, respectable man, whom, by his velvet cloak and gold chain, he concluded to be a burgher of eminence, and perhaps a magistrate, he asked him, "Whether he saw anything particular in his appearance, to attract public attention in a degree so unusual? or whether it was the ordinary custom of the people of Liege thus to throng around strangers who chanced to visit their city?"

"Surely not, good seignior," answered the burgher; "the Liegeois are neither so idly curious as to practise such a custom, nor is there anything in your dress or appearance, saving that which is most welcome to this city, and which our townsmen are both delighted to see, and desirous to honour."

"This sounds very polite, worthy sir," said Quentin; "but by the Cross of Saint Andrew, I cannot even guess at your meaning."

"Your oath, sir," answered the merchant of Liege, "as well as your accent, convinces me that we are right in our conjecture."

"By my patron St. Quentin!" said Durward, "I am farther off from your meaning than ever."

"There again now," rejoined the Liegeois, looking, as he spoke, most provokingly, yet most civilly, politic and intelligent.—"It is surely not for us to see that which you, worthy seignior, deem it proper to conceal. But why swear by Saint Quentin, if you would not have me construe your meaning?—We know the good Count of Saint Paul, who lies there at present, wishes well to our cause."

"On my life," said Quentin, "you are under some delusion—I know nothing of Saint Paul."

"Nay, we question you not," said the burgher; "although, hark ye— I say, hark in your ear—my name is Pavillon."

"And what is my business with that, Seignior Pavillon?" said Quentin.

"Nay, nothing—only methinks it might satisfy you that I am trust-worthy—Here is my colleague Rouslaer, too."

Rouslaer advanced, a corpulent dignitary, whose fair round belly, like a battering-ram, "did shake the press before him," and who, whis-pering caution to his neighbour, said, in a tone of rebuke—"You forget, good colleague, the place is too open—the seignior will retire to your house or mine, and drink a glass of Rhenish and sugar, and then we shall hear more of our good friend and ally, whom we love with all our honest Flemish hearts."

"I have no news for any of you," said Quentin impatiently; "I will drink no Rhenish; and I only desire of you, as men of account and respectability, to disperse this idle crowd, and allow a stranger to leave your town as quietly as he came into it."

"Nay, then, sir," said Rouslaer, "since you stand so much on your incognito, and with us, too, who are men of confidence, let me ask you roundly, wherefore wear you the badge of your company if you would remain unknown in Liege?"

"What badge, and what order?" said Quentin; "you look like reverend men and grave citizens, yet, on my soul, you are either mad yourselves, or desire to drive me so."

"Sapperment!" said the other burgher, "this youth would make Saint Lambert swear! Why, who wear bonnets with the Saint Andrew's cross and *fleur-de-lys*, save the Scottish Archers of King Louis's Guards?"

"And supposing I am an Archer of the Scottish Guard, why should you make a wonder of my wearing the badge of my company?" said Quentin impatiently.

"He has avowed it, he has avowed it!" said Rouslaer and Pavillon, turning to the assembled burghers in attitudes of congratulation, with waving arms, extended palms, and large round faces radiating with glee. "He hath avowed himself an Archer of Louis's Guard—of Louis, the guardian of the liberties of Liege!"

A general shout and cry now arose from the multitude, in which were mingled the various sounds of "Long live Louis of France! Long live the Scottish Guard! Long live the valiant Archer! Our liberties, our privileges, or death! No imposts! Long live the valiant Boar of Ardennes! Down with Charles of Burgundy! and confusion to Bourbon and his bishopric!"

Half-stunned by the noise, which began anew in one quarter so soon as it ceased in another, rising and falling like the billows of the sea, and augmented by thousands of voices which roared in chorus from distant streets and market-places, Quentin had yet time to form a conjecture concerning the meaning of the tumult, and a plan for regulating his own conduct.

He had forgotten that, after his skirmish with Orleans and Dunois, one of his comrades had, at Lord Crawford's command, replaced the morion, cloven by the sword of the latter, with one of the steel-lined bonnets, which formed a part of the proper and well-known equipment of the Scotch Guards. That an individual of this body, which was always kept very close to Louis's person, should have appeared in the streets of a city, whose civil discontents had been aggravated by the agents of that King, was naturally enough interpreted by the burghers of Liege into a determination on the part of Louis openly to assist their cause; and the apparition of an individual archer was magnified into a pledge of immediate and active support from Louis—nay, into an assurance that his auxiliary forces were actually entering the town at one or other, though no one could distinctly tell which, of the city-gates.

To remove a conviction so generally adopted, Quentin easily saw was impossible—nay, that any attempt to undeceive men so obstinately prepossessed in their belief, would be attended with personal risk, which, in this case, he saw little use of incurring. He therefore hastily resolved to temporise, and to get free the best way he could; and this resolution he formed while they were in the act of conducting him to the Stadt-house, where the notables of the town were fast assembling, in order to hear the tidings which he was presumed to have brought, and to regale him with a splendid banquet.

In spite of all his opposition, which was set down to modesty, he was on every side surrounded by the donors of popularity, the unsavoury side of which now floated around him. His two burgomaster friends, who were *Schoppen*, or Syndics of the city, had made fast both his arms. Before him Nikkel Blok, the chief of the butchers' incorporation, hastily summoned from his office in the shambles, brandished his death-doing axe, yet smeared with blood and brains, with a courage and grace which *brantwein* alone could inspire. Behind him came the tall, lean, raw-boned,

very drunk, and very patriotic figure of Claus Hammerlein, president of
the mystery of the workers in iron, and followed by at least a thousand
unwashed artificers of his class. Weavers, nailers, ropemakers, artisans
of every degree and calling, thronged forward to join the procession from
every gloomy and narrow street. Escape seemed a desperate and impossible adventure.

In this dilemma, Quentin appealed to Rouslaer, who held one arm,
and to Pavillon, who had secured the other, and who were conducting
him forward at the head of the ovation, of which he had so unexpectedly become the principal object. He hastily acquainted them "with his
having thoughtlessly adopted the bonnet of the Scottish Guard, on an
accident having occurred to the head-piece in which he had proposed
to travel; he regretted that, owing to this circumstance, and the sharp
wit with which the Liegeois drew the natural inference of his quality
and the purpose of his visit, these things had been publicly discovered;
and he intimated, that, if just now conducted to the Stadthouse, he might
unhappily feel himself under the necessity of communicating to the assembled notables certain matters, which he was directed by the King to
reserve for the private ears of his excellent gossips, Meinheers Rouslaer
and Pavillon of Liege."

This last hint operated like magic on the two citizens, who were the
most distinguished leaders of the insurgent burghers, and were, like all
demagogues of their kind, desirous to keep everything within their own
management, so far as possible. They therefore hastily agreed that Quentin should leave the town for the time, and return by night to Liege,
and converse with them privately in the house of Rouslaer, near the
gate opposite to Schonwaldt. Quentin hesitated not to tell them, that
he was at present residing in the Bishop's palace, under pretence of
bearing despatches from the French Court, although his real errand
was, as they had well conjectured, designed to the citizens of Liege; and
this tortuous mode of conducting a communication, as well as the character and rank of the person to whom it was supposed to be entrusted,
was so consonant to the character of Louis, as neither to excite doubt
nor surprise.

Almost immediately after this *éclaircissement* was completed, the
progress of the multitude brought them opposite to the door of Pavillon's
house, in one of the principal streets, but which communicated from
behind with the Maes, by means of a garden, as well as an extensive
manufactory of tanpits and other conveniences for dressing hides; for
the patriotic burgher was a felt-dresser, or currier.

It was natural that Pavillon should desire to do the honours of his
dwelling to the supposed envoy of Louis, and a halt before his house
excited no surprise on the part of the multitude; who, on the contrary,
greeted Meinheer Pavillon with a loud *vivat*, as he ushered in his distinguished guest. Quentin speedily laid aside his remarkable bonnet, for
the cap of a felt-maker, and flung a cloak over his other apparel. Pavillon

then furnished him with a passport to pass the gates of the city, and to return by night or day as should suit his convenience; and, lastly, committed him to the charge of his daughter, a fair and smiling Flemish lass, with instructions how he was to be disposed of, while he himself hastened back to his colleague, to amuse their friends at the Stadthouse, with the best excuses which they could invent for the disappearance of King Louis's envoy. We cannot, as the footman says in the play, recollect the exact nature of the lie which the belwethers told the flock; but no task is so easy as that of imposing upon a multitude whose eager prejudices have more than half done the business, ere the impostor has spoken a word.

The worthy burgess was no sooner gone, than his plump daughter, Trudchen, with many a blush, and many a wreathed smile, which suited very prettily with lips like cherries, laughing blue eyes, and a skin transparently pure, escorted the handsome stranger through the pleached alleys of the Sieur Pavillon's garden, down to the water-side, and there saw him fairly embarked in a boat, which two stout Flemings, in their trunk-hose, fur caps, and many-buttoned jerkins, had got in readiness with as much haste as their low-country nature would permit.

As the pretty Trudchen spoke nothing but German, Quentin,—no disparagement to his loyal affection to the Countess of Croye,—could only express his thanks by a kiss on those same cherry lips, which was very gallantly bestowed, and accepted with all modest gratitude; for gallants with a form and face like our Scottish Archer, were not of everyday occurrence among the *bourgeoisie* of Liege.[1]

While the boat was rowed up the sluggish waters of the Maes, and passed the defences of the town, Quentin had time enough to reflect what account he ought to give of his adventure in Liege, when he returned to the Bishop's palace of Schonwaldt; and disdaining alike to betray any person who had reposed confidence in him, although by misapprehension, or to conceal from the hospitable Prelate the mutinous state of his capital, he resolved to confine himself to so general an account as might put the Bishop upon his guard, while it should point out no individual to his vengeance.

He was landed from the boat, within half a mile of the castle, and rewarded his rowers with a guilder, to their great satisfaction. Yet, short as was the space which divided him from Schonwaldt, the castle-bell had tolled for dinner, and Quentin found, moreover, that he had approached the castle on a different side from that of the principal entrance, and that to go round would throw his arrival considerably

[1] The adventure of Quentin at Liege may be thought over-strained, yet it is extraordinary what slight circumstances will influence the public mind in a moment of doubt and uncertainty. Most readers must remember, that, when the Dutch were on the point of rising against the French yoke, their zeal for liberation received a strong impulse from the landing of a person in a British volunteer uniform, whose presence, though that of a private individual, was received as a guarantee of succours from England.

later. He, therefore, made straight towards the side that was nearest him, as he discerned that it presented an embattled wall, probably that of the little garden already noticed, with a postern opening upon the moat, and a skiff moored by the postern, which might serve, he thought, upon summons, to pass him over. As he approached, in hopes to make his entrance this way, the postern opened, a man came out, and, jumping into the boat, made his way to the farther side of the moat, and then with a long pole, pushed the skiff back towards the place where he had embarked. As he came near, Quentin discerned that this person was the Bohemian, who, avoiding him, as was not difficult, held a different path towards Liege, and was presently out of his ken.

Here was a new subject for meditation. Had this vagabond heathen been all this while with the Ladies of Croye, and for what purpose should they so far have graced him with their presence? Tormented with this thought, Durward became doubly determined to seek an explanation with them, for the purpose at once of laying bare the treachery of Hayraddin, and announcing to them the perilous state in which their protector, the Bishop, was placed, by the mutinous state of his town of Liege.

As Quentin thus resolved, he entered the castle by the principal gate, and found that part of the family who assembled for dinner in the great hall, including the Bishop's attendant clergy, officers of the household, and strangers below the rank of the very first nobility, were already placed at their meal. A seat at the upper end of the board had, however, been reserved beside the Bishop's domestic chaplain, who welcomed the stranger with the old college jest of, *Sero venientibus ossa,* while he took care so to load his plate with dainties, as to take away all appearance of that tendency to reality, which, in Quentin's country, is said to render a joke either no joke, or at best an unpalatable one.[1]

In vindicating himself from the suspicion of ill-breeding, Quentin briefly described the tumult which had been occasioned in the city by his being discovered to belong to the Scottish Archer-guard of Louis, and endeavoured to give a ludicrous turn to the narrative by saying, that he had been with difficulty extricated by a fat burgher of Liege and his pretty daughter.

But the company were too much interested in the story to taste the jest. All operations of the table were suspended while Quentin told his tale; and when he had ceased, there was a solemn pause, which was only broken by the Major-Domo saying, in a low and melancholy tone, "I would to God that we saw those hundred lances of Burgundy!"

"Why should you think so deeply on it?" said Quentin—"You have many soldiers here, whose trade is arms; and your antagonists are only the rabble of a disorderly city, who will fly before the first flutter of a banner with men-at-arms arrayed beneath it."

---

[1] "A sooth boord [true joke] is no boord," says the Scot.

"You do not know the men of Liege," said the Chaplain, "of whom it may be said, that, not even excepting those of Ghent, they are at once the fiercest and the most untameable in Europe. Twice has the Duke of Burgundy chastised them for their repeated revolts against their Bishop, and twice hath he suppressed them with much severity, abridged their privileges, taken away their banners, and established rights and claims to himself, which were not before competent over a free city of the Empire—Nay, the last time he defeated them with much slaughter near Saint Tron, where Liege lost nearly six thousand men, what with the sword, what with those drowned in the flight; and, thereafter, to disable them from farther mutiny, Duke Charles refused to enter at any of the gates which they had surrendered, but, beating to the ground forty cubits breadth of their city wall, marched into Liege as a conqueror, with visor closed, and lance in rest, at the head of his chivalry, by the breach which he had made. Nay, well were the Liegeois then assured, that, but for the intercession of his father, Duke Philip the Good, this Charles, then called Count of Charalois, would have given their town up to spoil. And yet, with all these fresh recollections, with their breaches unrepaired, and their arsenals scarcely supplied, the sight of an Archer's bonnet is sufficient again to stir them to uproar. May God amend all! but I fear there will be bloody work between so fierce a population and so fiery a Sovereign; and I would my excellent and kind master had a see of lesser dignity and more safety, for his mitre is lined with thorns instead of ermine. This much I say to you, Seignior stranger, to make you aware, that, if your affairs detain you not at Schonwaldt, it is a place from which each man of sense should depart as speedily as possible. I apprehend that your ladies are of the same opinion; for one of the grooms who attended them on the route, has been sent back by them to the Court of France, with letters which, doubtless, are intended to announce their going in search of a safer asylum."

CHAPTER XX

THE BILLET

Go to—thou art made, if thou desirest to be so—If not, let
me see thee still the fellow of servants, and not fit to touch
Fortune's fingers.

Twelfth Night.

WHEN the tables were drawn, the Chaplain, who seemed to have taken a sort of attachment to Quentin Durward's society, or who perhaps desired to extract from him farther information concerning the meeting of the morning, led him into a withdrawing apartment, the windows of which, on one side, projected into the garden; and as he saw his companion's eye gaze rather eagerly upon the spot, he proposed to Quentin to go down and take a view of the curious foreign shrubs with which the Bishop had enriched its parterres.

Quentin excused himself, as unwilling to intrude, and therewithal communicated the check which he had received in the morning. The Chaplain smiled, and said, "That there was indeed some ancient prohibition respecting the Bishop's private garden; but this," he added, with a smile, "was when our reverend father was a princely young prelate of not more than thirty years of age, and when many fair ladies frequented the Castle for ghostly consolation. Need there was," he said, with a downcast look, and a smile, half simple and half intelligent, "that these ladies, pained in conscience, who were ever lodged in the apartments now occupied by the noble Canoness, should have some space for taking the air, secure from the intrusion of the profane. But of late years," he added, "this prohibition, although not formally removed, has fallen entirely out of observance, and remains but as the superstition which lingers in the brain of a superannuated gentleman-usher. If you please," he added, "we will presently descend, and try whether the place be haunted or no."

Nothing could have been more agreeable to Quentin than the prospect of a free entrance into the garden, through means of which, according to a chance which had hitherto attended his passion, he hoped to communicate with, or at least obtain sight of, the object of his affections, from some such turret or balcony-window, or similar "coign of vantage," as at the hostelry of the *Fleur-de-lys*, near Plessis, or the Dauphin's Tower, within that Castle itself. Isabelle seemed still destined, wherever she made her abode, to be the Lady of the Turret.

When Durward descended with his new friend into the garden, the latter seemed a terrestrial philosopher, entirely busied with the things of the earth; while the eyes of Quentin, if they did not seek the heavens, like those of an astrologer, ranged at least all around the windows, balconies, and especially the turrets, which projected on every part from the inner front of the old building, in order to discover that which was to be his cynosure.

While thus employed, the young lover heard with total neglect, if indeed he heard at all, the enumeration of plants, herbs, and shrubs, which his reverend conductor pointed out to him; of which this was choice, because of prime use in medicine; and that more choice for yielding a rare flavour to pottage; and a third, choicest of all, because possessed of no merit but its extreme scarcity. Still it was necessary to preserve some semblance at least of attention; which the youth found so difficult, that he fairly wished at the devil the officious naturalist and the whole vegetable kingdom. He was relieved at length by the striking of a clock, which summoned the Chaplain to some official duty.

The reverend man made many unnecessary apologies for leaving his new friend, and concluded by giving him the agreeable assurance, that he might walk in the garden till supper, without much risk of being disturbed.

"It is," said he, "the place where I always study my own homilies, as being most sequestered from the resort of strangers. I am now about to deliver one of them in the chapel, if you please to favour me with your audience.—I have been thought to have some gift—But the glory be where it is due!"

Quentin excused himself for this evening, under pretence of a severe headache, which the open air was likely to prove the best cure for; and at length the well-meaning priest left him to himself.

It may be well imagined, that in the curious inspection which he now made, at more leisure, of every window or aperture which looked into the garden, those did not escape which were in the immediate neighbourhood of the small door by which he had seen Marthon admit Hayraddin, as he pretended, to the apartment of the Countesses. But nothing stirred or showed itself, which could either confute or confirm the tale which the Bohemian had told, until it was becoming dusky; and Quentin began to be sensible, he scarce knew why, that his sauntering so long in the garden might be subject of displeasure or suspicion.

Just as he had resolved to depart, and was taking what he had destined for his last turn under the windows which had such attraction for him, he heard above him a slight and cautious sound, like that of a cough, as intended to call his attention, and to avoid the observation of others. As he looked up in joyful surprise, a casement opened—a female hand was seen to drop a billet, which fell into a rosemary bush that grew at the foot of the wall. The precaution used in dropping this letter, prescribed equal prudence and secrecy in reading it. The garden, surrounded, as we have said, upon two sides, by the buildings of the palace, was commanded, of course, by the windows of many apartments; but there was a sort of grotto of rock-work, which the Chaplain had shown Durward with much complacency. To snatch up the billet, thrust it into his bosom, and hie to this place of secrecy, was the work of a single minute. He there opened the precious scroll, and blessed, at the same time, the memory of the Monks of Aberbrothick, whose nurture had rendered him capable of deciphering its contents.

The first line contained the injunction, "Read this in secret,"—and the contents were as follows: "What your eyes have too boldly said, mine have perhaps too rashly understood. But, unjust persecution makes its victims bold, and it were better to throw myself on the gratitude of one, than to remain the object of pursuit to many. Fortune has her throne upon a rock; but brave men fear not to climb. If you dare do aught for one that hazards much, you need but pass into this garden at prime to-morrow, wearing in your cap a blue-and-white feather; but expect no farther communication. Your stars have, they say, destined you for greatness, and disposed you to gratitude.—Farewell—be faithful, prompt, and resolute, and doubt not thy fortune." Within this letter was enclosed a ring with a table diamond, on which were cut, in form of a lozenge, the ancient arms of the House of Croye.

The first feeling of Quentin upon this occasion was unmingled ecstasy —a pride and joy which seemed to raise him to the stars,—a determination to do or die, influenced by which he treated with scorn the thousand obstacles that placed themselves betwixt him and the goal of his wishes.

In this mood of rapture, and unable to endure any interruption which might withdraw his mind, were it but for a moment, from so ecstatic a subject of contemplation, Durward, retiring to the interior of the castle, hastily assigned his former pretext of a headache for not joining the household of the Bishop at the supper-meal, and, lighting his lamp, betook himself to the chamber which had been assigned him, to read, and to read again and again, the precious billet, and to kiss a thousand times the no less precious ring.

But such high-wrought feelings could not remain long in the same ecstatic tone. A thought pressed upon him, though he repelled it as ungrateful—as even blasphemous—that the frankness of the confession implied less delicacy, on the part of her who made it, than was consistent with the high romantic feeling of adoration with which he had hitherto worshipped the Lady Isabelle. No sooner did this ungracious thought intrude itself, than he hastened to stifle it, as he would have stifled a hissing and hateful adder, that had intruded itself into his couch. Was it for him—him the Favoured—on whose account she had stooped from her sphere, to ascribe blame to her for the very act of condescension, without which he dared not have raised his eyes towards her? Did not her very dignity of birth and of condition, reverse, in her case, the usual rules which impose silence on the lady until her lover shall have first spoken? To these arguments, which he boldly formed into syllogisms, and avowed to himself, his vanity might possibly suggest one which he cared not to embody even mentally with the same frankness—that the merit of the party beloved might perhaps warrant, on the part of the lady, some little departure from common rules; and, after all, as in the case of Malvolio, there was example for it in chronicle. The Squire of low degree, of whom he had just been reading, was, like himself, a gentleman void of land and living, and yet the generous Princess of Hungary bestowed on him, without scruple, more substantial marks of her affection, than the billet he had just received:—

> "Welcome," she said, "my swete Squyre,
> My heartis roote, my soule's desire;
> I will give thee kisses three,
> And als five hundrid poundis in fee."

And again the same faithful history made the King of Hongrie himself avouch,

"I have yknown many a page
Come to be Prince by marriage."

So that, upon the whole, Quentin generously and magnanimously reconciled himself to a line of conduct on the Countess's part, by which he
was likely to be so highly benefited.

But this scruple was succeeded by another doubt, harder of digestion. The traitor Hayraddin had been in the apartments of the ladies,
for aught Quentin knew, for the space of four hours, and, considering
the hints which he had thrown out, of possessing an influence of the
most interesting kind over the fortunes of Quentin Durward, what should
assure him that this train was not of his laying? and if so, was it not
probable that such a dissembling villain had set it on foot to conceal
some new plan of treachery—perhaps to seduce Isabelle out of the protection of the worthy Bishop? This was a matter to be closely looked into,
for Quentin felt a repugnance to this individual proportioned to the
unabashed impudence with which he had avowed his profligacy, and
could not bring himself to hope, that anything in which he was concerned
could ever come to an honourable or happy conclusion.

These various thoughts rolled over Quentin's mind like misty clouds,
to dash and obscure the fair landscape which his fancy had at first drawn,
and his couch was that night a sleepless one. At the hour of prime—
ay, and an hour before it, was he in the castle-garden, where no one
now opposed either his entrance or his abode, with a feather of the
assigned colour, as distinguished as he could by any means procure
in such haste. No notice was taken of his appearance for nearly two
hours; at length he heard a few notes of the lute, and presently the
lattice opened right above the little postern-door at which Marthon
had admitted Hayraddin, and Isabelle, in maidenly beauty, appeared at
the opening, greeted him half-kindly, half-shyly, coloured extremely at
the deep and significant reverence with which he returned her courtesy
—shut the casement, and disappeared.

Daylight and champaign could discover no more! The authenticity
of the billet was ascertained—it only remained what was to follow;
and of this the fair writer had given him no hint. But no immediate
danger impended—The Countess was in a strong castle, under the protection of a Prince, at once respectable for his secular, and venerable
for his ecclesiastical authority. There was neither immediate room nor
occasion for the exulting Squire interfering in the adventure; and it
was sufficient if he keep himself prompt to execute her commands whenever they should be communicated to him. But Fate purposed to call
him into action sooner than he was aware of.

It was the fourth night after his arrival at Schonwaldt, when Quentin
had taken measures for sending back on the morrow, to the Court of
Louis, the remaining groom who had accompanied him on his journey,
with letters from himself to his uncle and Lord Crawford, renouncing

the service of France, for which the treachery to which he had been
exposed by the private instructions of Hayraddin gave him an excuse,
both in honour and prudence; and he betook himself to his bed with
all the rosy-coloured ideas around him which flutter about the couch
of a youth when he loves dearly, and thinks his love as sincerely repaid.

But Quentin's dreams, which at first partook of the nature of those
happy influences under which he had fallen asleep, began by degrees
to assume a more terrific character.

He walked with the Countess Isabelle, beside a smooth and inland
lake, such as formed the principal characteristic of his native glen; and
he spoke to her of his love, without any consciousness of the impediments which lay between them. She blushed and smiled when she listened
—even as he might have expected from the tenor of the letter, which,
sleeping or waking, lay nearest to his heart. But the scene suddenly
changed from summer to winter—from calm to tempest; the winds and
the waves rose with such a contest of surge and whirlwind, as if the
demons of the water and of the air had been contending for their roaring empires in rival strife. The rising waters seemed to cut off their
advance and their retreat—the increasing tempest, which dashed them
against each other, seemed to render their remaining on the spot impossible; and the tumultuous sensations produced by the apparent
danger awoke the dreamer.

He awoke; but although the circumstances of the vision had disappeared, and given place to reality, the noise, which had probably suggested them, still continued to sound in his ears.

Quentin's first impulse was to sit erect in bed, and listen with astonishment to sounds, which, if they had announced a tempest, might have
shamed the wildest that ever burst down from the Grampians; and again
in a minute he became sensible, that the tumult was not excited by the
fury of the elements, but by the wrath of men.

He sprung from bed, and looked from the window of his apartment;
but it opened into the garden, and on that side all was quiet, though the
opening of the casement made him still more sensible, from the shouts
which reached his ears, that the outside of the castle was beleaguered and
assaulted, and that by a numerous and determined enemy. Hastily collecting his dress and arms, and putting them on with such celerity as
darkness and surprise permitted, his attention was solicited by a knocking at the door of his chamber. As Quentin did not immediately answer,
the door, which was a slight one, was forced open from without, and
the intruder, announced by his peculiar dialect to be the Bohemian,
Hayraddin Maugrabin, entered the apartment. A phial, which he held
in his hand, touched by a match, produced a dark flash of ruddy fire,
by means of which he kindled a lamp, which he took from his bosom.

"The horoscope of your destinies," he said energetically to Durward,
without any farther greeting, "now turns upon the determination of a
minute."

"Caitiff!" said Quentin, in reply, "there is treachery around us; and where there is treachery, thou *must* have a share in it."

"You are mad," answered Maugrabin—"I never betrayed any one but to gain by it—and wherefore should I betray you, by whose safety I can take more advantage than by your destruction? Hearken for a moment, if it be possible for you, to one note of reason, ere it is sounded into your ear by the death-shot of ruin. The Liegeois are up—William de la Marck with his band leads them—Were there means of resistance, their numbers, and his fury, would overcome them; but there are next to none. If you would save the Countess and your own hopes, follow me, in the name of her who sent you a table-diamond, with three leopards engraved on it!"

"Lead the way," said Quentin hastily—"In that name, I dare every danger!"

"As I shall manage it," said the Bohemian, "there is no danger, if you can but withhold your hand from strife which does not concern you; for, after all, what is it to you whether the Bishop, as they call him, slaughters his flock, or the flock slaughters the shepherd?—Ha! ha! ha! Follow me, but with caution and patience; subdue your own courage, and confide in my prudence—and my debt of thankfulness is paid, and you have a Countess for your spouse.—Follow me."

"I follow," said Quentin, drawing his sword; "but the moment in which I detect the least sign of treachery, thy head and body are three yards separate!"

Without more conversation, the Bohemian, seeing that Quentin was now fully armed and ready, ran down the stairs before him, and winded hastily through various side-passages, until they gained the little garden. Scarce a light was to be seen on that side, scarce any bustle was to be heard; but no sooner had Quentin entered the open space, than the noise on the opposite side of the castle became ten times more stunningly audible, and he could hear the various war-cries of "Liege! Liege! Sang-lier! Sanglier!" shouted by the assailants, while the feebler cry of "Our Lady for the Prince Bishop!" was raised in a faint and faltering tone, by those of the prelate's soldiers who had hastened, though surprised and at disadvantage, to the defence of the walls.

But the interest of the fight, notwithstanding the martial character of Quentin Durward, was indifferent to him in comparison of the fate of Isabelle of Croye, which, he had reason to fear, would be a dreadful one, unless rescued from the power of the dissolute and cruel freebooter, who was now, as it seemed, bursting the gates of the castle. He reconciled himself to the aid of the Bohemian, as men in a desperate illness refuse not the remedy prescribed by quacks and mountebanks, and followed across the garden, with the intention of being guided by him until he should discover symptoms of treachery, and then piercing him through the heart, or striking his head from his body. Hayraddin seemed himself conscious that his safety turned on a feather-weight, for he forbore, from the moment he entered the open air, all his wonted gibes and quirks, and seemed to have made a vow to act at once with modesty, courage, and activity.

At the opposite door, which led to the ladies' apartments, upon a low signal made by Hayraddin, appeared two women, muffled in the black silk veils which were then, as now, worn by the women in the Netherlands. Quentin offered his arm to one of them, who clung to it with trembling eagerness, and indeed hung upon him so much, that had her weight been greater, she must have much impeded their retreat. The Bohemian, who conducted the other female, took the road straight for the postern which opened upon the moat, through the garden wall, close to which the little skiff was drawn up, by means of which Quentin had formerly observed Hayraddin himself retreating from the castle.

As they crossed, the shouts of storm and successful violence seemed to announce that the castle was in the act of being taken; and so dismal was the sound in Quentin's ears, that he could not help swearing aloud, "But that my blood is irretrievably devoted to the fulfilment of my present duty, I would back to the wall, take faithful part with the hospitable Bishop, and silence some of those knaves whose throats are full of mutiny and robbery!"

The lady, whose arm was still folded in his, pressed it lightly as he spoke, as if to make him understand that there was a nearer claim on his chivalry than the defence of Schonwaldt; while the Bohemian exclaimed, loud enough to be heard, "Now, that I call right Christian frenzy, which would turn back to fight, when love and fortune both demand that we should fly.—On, on—with all the haste you can make—Horses wait us in yonder thicket of willows."

"There are but two horses," said Quentin, who saw them in the moonlight.

"All that I could procure without exciting suspicion—and enough, besides," replied the Bohemian. "You two must ride for Tongres ere the way becomes unsafe—Marthon will abide with the women of our horde, with whom she is an old acquaintance. Know, she is a daughter of our tribe, and only dwelt among you to serve our purpose as occasion should fall."

"Marthon!" exclaimed the Countess, looking at the veiled female with a shriek of surprise; "is not this my kinswoman?"

"Only Marthon," said Hayraddin—"Excuse me that little piece of deceit. I dared not carry off *both* the Ladies of Croye from the Wild Boar of Ardennes."

"Wretch!" said Quentin, emphatically—"but it is not—shall not be too late—I will back to rescue the Lady Hameline."

"Hameline," whispered the lady, in a disturbed voice, "hangs on thy arm, to thank thee for her rescue."

"Ha! what!—How is this?" said Quentin, extricating himself from her hold, and with less gentleness than he would at any other time have used towards a female of any rank—"Is the Lady Isabelle then left behind!—Farewell—farewell."

As he turned to hasten back to the castle, Hayraddin laid hold of him—"Nay, hear you—hear you—you run upon your death! What the foul fiend did you wear the colours of the old one for?—I will never trust blue and white silk again. But she has almost as large a dower—has jewels and gold—hath pretensions, too, upon the earldom."

While he spoke thus, panting on in broken sentences, the Bohemian struggled to detain Quentin, who at length laid his hand on his dagger, in order to extricate himself.

"Nay, if that be the case," said Hayraddin, unloosing his hold, "go—and the devil, if there be one, go along with you!"—And, soon as freed from his hold, the Scot shot back to the castle with the speed of the wind.

Hayraddin then turned round to the Countess Hameline, who had sunk down on the ground, between shame, fear, and disappointment.

"Here has been a mistake," he said, "up, lady, and come with me—I will provide you, ere morning comes, a gallanter husband than this smock-faced boy; and if one will not serve, you shall have twenty."

The Lady Hameline was as violent in her passions, as she was vain and weak in her understanding. Like many other persons, she went tolerably well through the ordinary duties of life; but in a crisis like the present, she was entirely incapable of doing aught, save pouring forth unavailing lamentations, and accusing Hayraddin of being a thief, a base slave, an impostor, a murderer.

"Call me Zingaro," returned he composedly, "and you have said all at once."

"Monster! you said the stars had decreed our union, and caused me to write—Oh wretch that I was!" exclaimed the unhappy lady.

"And so they *had* decreed your union," said Hayraddin, "had both parties been willing—but think you the blessed constellations can make any one wed against his will?—I was led into error with your accursed Christian gallantries, and fopperies of ribbons and favours—and the youth prefers veal to beef, I think—that's all.—Up, and follow me; and take notice, I endure neither weeping nor swooning."

"I will not stir a foot," said the Countess obstinately.

"By the bright welkin, but you shall, though!" exclaimed Hayraddin. "I swear to you, by all that ever fools believed in, that you have to do with one, who would care little to strip you naked, bind you to a tree, and leave you to your fortune!"

"Nay," said Marthon, interfering, "by your favour, she shall not be misused. I wear a knife as well as you, and can use it.—She is a kind woman, though a fool.—And you, madam, rise up and follow us—Here has been a mistake; but it is something to have saved life and limb. There are many in yonder castle would give all the wealth in the world to stand where we do now."

As Marthon spoke, a clamour, in which the shouts of victory were mingled with screams of terror and despair, was wafted to them from the Castle of Schonwaldt.

"Hear that, lady!" said Hayraddin, "and be thankful you are not adding your treble pipe to yonder concert. Believe me, I will care for you honestly, and the stars shall keep their words, and find you a good husband."

Like some wild animal, exhausted and subdued by terror and fatigue, the Countess Hameline yielded herself up to the conduct of her guides, and suffered herself to be passively led whichever way they would. Nay, such was the confusion of her spirits and the exhaustion of her strength, that the worthy couple, who half bore, half led her, carried on their discourse in her presence without her even understanding it.

"I ever thought your plan was folly," said Marthon. "Could you have brought the *young* people together, in deed, we might have had a hold on their gratitude, and a footing in their castle. But what chance of so handsome a youth wedding this old fool?"

"Rizpah," said Hayraddin, "you have borne the name of a Christian, and dwelt in the tents of those besotted people, till thou hast become a partaker in their follies. How could I dream that he would have made scruples about a few years, youth or age, when the advantages of the match were so evident? And thou knowest, there would have been no moving yonder coy wench to be so frank as this coming Countess here, who hangs on our arms as dead a weight as a wool-pack. I loved the lad too, and would have done him a kindness: to wed him to this old woman, was to make his fortune: to unite him to Isabelle, were to have brought on him De la Marck, Burgundy, France,—every one that challenges an interest in disposing of her hand. And this silly woman's wealth being chiefly in gold and jewels, we should have had our share. But the bow-string has burst, and the arrow failed. Away with her—we will bring her to William with the Beard. By the time he has gorged himself with wassail, as is his wont, he will not know an old Countess from a young one. Away, Rizpah—bear a gallant heart. The bright Aldeboran still influences the destinies of the Children of the Desert!"

CHAPTER XXI

THE SACK

The gates of mercy shall be all shut up,
And the flesh'd soldier, rough and hard of heart,
In liberty of bloody hand shall range,
With conscience wide as hell.
                                        Henry V.

THE surprised and affrighted garrison of the Castle of Schonwaldt had, nevertheless, for some time. made good the defence of the place against the assailants; but the immense crowds which, issuing from the city of Liege, thronged to the assault like bees, distracted their attention, and abated their courage.

There was also disaffection at least, if not treachery, among the defenders; for some called out to surrender, and others, deserting their posts, tried to escape from the castle. Many threw themselves from the walls into the moat, and such as escaped drowning, flung aside their distinguishing badges, and saved themselves by mingling among the motley crowd of assailants. Some few, indeed, from attachment to the Bishop's person, drew around him, and continued to defend the great keep, to which he had fled; and others, doubtful of receiving quarter, or from an impulse of desperate courage, held out other detached bulwarks and towers of the extensive building. But the assailants had got possession of the courts and lower parts of the edifice, and were busy pursuing the vanquished, and searching for spoil, while one individual, as if he sought for that death from which all others were flying, endeavoured to force his way into the scene of tumult and horror, under apprehensions still more horrible to his imagination, than the realities around were to his sight and senses. Whoever had seen Quentin Durward that fatal night, not knowing the meaning of his conduct, had accounted him a raging madman; whoever had appreciated his motives, had ranked him nothing beneath a hero of romance.

Approaching Schonwaldt on the same side from which he had left it, the youth met several fugitives making for the wood, who naturally avoided him as an enemy, because he came in an opposite direction from that which they had adopted. When he came nearer, he could hear, and partly see, men dropping from the garden-wall into the castle fosse, and others who seemed precipitated from the battlements by the assailants. His courage was not staggered, even for an instant. There was not time to look for the boat, even had it been practicable to use it, and it was in vain to approach the postern of the garden, which was crowded with fugitives, who ever and anon, as they were thrust through it by the pressure behind, fell into the moat which they had no means of crossing.

Avoiding that point, Quentin threw himself into the moat, near what was called the little gate of the castle, and where there was a drawbridge, which was still elevated. He avoided with difficulty the fatal grasp of more than one sinking wretch, and, swimming to the drawbridge, caught hold of one of the chains which was hanging down, and, by a great exertion of strength and activity, swayed himself out of the water, and attained the platform from which the bridge was suspended. As with hands and knees he struggled to make good his footing, a lanzknecht, with his bloody sword in his hand, made towards him, and raised his weapon for a blow, which must have been fatal.

"How now, fellow!" said Quentin, in a tone of authority—"Is that the way in which you assist a comrade?—Give me your hand."

The soldier in silence, and not without hesitation, reached him his arm, and helped him upon the platform, when, without allowing him time for reflection, the Scot continued in the same tone of command— "To the western tower, if you would be rich—the Priest's treasury is in the western tower."

These words were echoed on every hand: "To the western tower—the treasure is in the western tower!" And the stragglers who were within hearing of the cry, took, like a herd of raging wolves, the direction opposite to that which Quentin, come life, come death, was determined to pursue.

Bearing himself as if he were one, not of the conquered, but of the victors, he made a way into the garden, and pushed across it, with less interruption than he could have expected; for the cry of "To the western tower!" had carried off one body of the assailants, and another was summoned together, by war-cry and trumpet-sound, to assist in repelling a desperate sally, attempted by the defenders of the Keep, who had hoped to cut their way out of the castle, bearing the Bishop along with them. Quentin, therefore, crossed the garden with an eager step and throbbing heart, commending himself to those heavenly powers which had protected him through the numberless perils of his life, and bold in his determination to succeed, or leave his life in this desperate undertaking. Ere he reached the garden, three men rushed on him with levelled lances, crying, "Liege, Liege!"

Putting himself in defence, but without striking, he replied, "France, France, friend of Liege!"

"Vivat France!" cried the burghers of Liege, and passed on. The same signal proved a talisman to avert the weapons of four or five of La Marck's followers, whom he found straggling in the garden, and who set upon him, crying, "Sanglier!"

In a word, Quentin began to hope that his character as an emissary of King Louis, the private instigator of the insurgents of Liege, and the secret supporter of William de la Marck, might possibly bear him through the horrors of the night.

On reaching the turret, he shuddered when he found the little side-door, through which Marthon and the Countess Hameline had shortly before joined him, was now blockaded with more than one dead body.

Two of them he dragged hastily aside, and was stepping over the third body, in order to enter the portal, when the supposed dead man laid hand on his cloak, and entreated him to stay and assist him to rise. Quentin was about to use rougher methods than struggling to rid himself of this untimely obstruction, when the fallen man continued to exclaim, "I am stifled here, in mine own armour!—I am the Syndic Pavillon of Liege! If you are for us, I will enrich you—if you are for the other side, I will protect you; but do not—do not leave me to die the death of a smothered pig!"

In the midst of this scene of blood and confusion, the presence of mind of Quentin suggested to him, that this dignitary might have the means of protecting their retreat. He raised him on his feet, and asked him if he was wounded.

"Not wounded—at least I think not"—answered the burgher; "but much out of wind."

"Sit down then on this stone, and recover your breath," said Quentin; "I will return instantly."

"For whom are you?" said the burgher, still detaining him.

"For France—for France," answered Quentin, studying to get away.

"What! my lively young Archer?" said the worthy Syndic. "Nay, if it has been my fate to find a friend in this fearful night, I will not quit him, I promise you. Go where you will, I follow; and, could I get some of the tight lads of our guildry together, I might be able to help you in turn; but they are all squandered abroad like so many pease.— Oh, it is a fearful night!"

During this time, he was dragging himself on after Quentin, who, aware of the importance of securing the countenance of a person of such influence, slackened his pace to assist him, although cursing in his heart the encumbrance that retarded him.

At the top of the stair was an anteroom, with boxes and trunks, which bore marks of having been rifled, as some of the contents lay on the floor. A lamp, dying in the chimney, shed a feeble beam on a dead or senseless man, who lay across the hearth.

Bounding from Pavillon, like a greyhound from his keeper's leash, and with an effort which almost overthrew him, Quentin sprung through a second and a third room, the last of which seemed to be the bedroom of the Ladies of Croye. No living mortal was to be seen in either of them. He called upon the Lady Isabelle's name, at first gently, then more loudly, and then with an accent of despairing emphasis; but no answer was returned. He wrung his hands, tore his hair, and stamped on the earth with desperation. At length, a feeble glimmer of light, which shone through a crevice in the wainscoting of a dark nook in the bedroom, announced some recess or concealment behind the arras. Quentin hasted to examine it. He found there was indeed a concealed door, but it resisted his hurried efforts to open it. Heedless of the personal injury he might sustain, he rushed at the door with his whole force and weight of his body; and such was the impetus of an effort made betwixt hope and despair, that it would have burst much stronger fastenings.

He thus forced his way, almost headlong, into a small oratory, where a female figure, which had been kneeling in agonising supplication before the holy image, now sunk at length on the floor, under the new terrors implied in this approaching tumult. He hastily raised her from the ground, and, joy of joys! it was she whom he sought to save—the Countess Isabelle. He pressed her to his bosom—he conjured her to awake —entreated her to be of good cheer—for that she was now under the protection of one who had heart and hand enough to defend her against armies.

"Durward!" she said, as she at length collected herself, "is it indeed you?—then there is some hope left. I thought all living and mortal friends had left me to my fate—Do not again abandon me!"

"Never—never!" said Durward. "Whatever shall happen—whatever danger shall approach, may I forfeit the benefits purchased by yonder blessed sign, if I be not the sharer of your fate until it is again a happy one!"

"Very pathetic and touching, truly," said a rough, broken, asthmatic voice behind—"A love affair, I see; and, from my soul, I pity the tender creature, as if she were my own Trudchen."

"You must do more than pity us," said Quentin, turning towards the speaker; "you must assist in protecting us, Meinheer Pavillon. Be assured this lady was put under my especial charge by your ally the King of France; and, if you aid me not to shelter her from every species of offence and violence, your city will lose the favour of Louis of Valois. Above all, she must be guarded from the hands of William de la Marck."

"That will be difficult," said Pavillon, "for these schelms of lanz-knechts are very devils at rummaging out the wenches; but I'll do my best—We will to the other apartment, and there I will consider—It is but a narrow stair, and you can keep the door with a pike, while I look from the window, and get together some of my brisk boys of the curriers' guildry of Liege, that are as true as the knives they wear in their girdles. —But first undo me these clasps—for I have not worn this corslet since the battle of Saint Tron; [1] and I am three stone heavier since that time, if there be truth in Dutch beam and scale."

The undoing of the iron enclosure gave great relief to the honest man, who, in putting it on, had more considered his zeal to the cause of Liege, than his capacity of bearing arms. It afterwards turned out, that being, as it were, borne forward involuntarily, and hoisted over the walls by his company as they thronged to the assault, the magistrate had been carried here and there, as the tide of attack and defence flowed or ebbed, without the power, latterly, of even uttering a word; until, as the sea casts a log of driftwood ashore in the first creek, he had been ultimately thrown down in the entrance to the Ladies of Croye's apart-ments, where the encumbrance of his own armour, with the superin-cumbent weight of two men slain in the entrance, and who fell above him, might have fixed him down long enough, had he not been relieved by Durward.

The same warmth of temper, which rendered Hermann Pavillon a hot-headed and intemperate zealot in politics, had the more desirable con-sequence of making him, in private, a good-tempered, kind-hearted man,

[1] Fought by the insurgents of Liege against the Duke of Burgundy, Charles the Bold, when Count of Charalois, in which the people of Liege were defeated with great slaughter.

who, if sometimes a little misled by vanity, was always well-meaning and benevolent. He told Quentin to have an especial care of the poor pretty *yung frau;* and, after this unnecessary exhortation, began to halloo from the window, "Liege, Liege, for the gallant skinners' guild of curriers!"

One or two of his immediate followers collected at the summons, and at the peculiar whistle with which it was accompanied (each of the crafts having such a signal among themselves), and, more joining them, established a guard under the window from which their leader was bawling, and before the postern-door.

Matters seemed now settling into some sort of tranquillity. All opposition had ceased, and the leaders of the different classes of assailants were taking measures to prevent indiscriminate plunder. The great bell was tolled, as summons to a military council, and its iron tongue communicating to Liege the triumphant possession of Schonwaldt by the insurgents, was answered by all the bells in that city; whose distant and clamorous voices seemed to cry, Hail to the victors! It would have been natural, that Meinheer Pavillon should now have sallied from his fastness; but, either in reverent care of those whom he had taken under his protection, or perhaps for the better assurance of his own safety, he contented himself with despatching messenger on messenger, to command his lieutenant, Peterkin Geislaer, to attend him directly.

Peterkin came at length, to his great relief, as being the person upon whom, on all pressing occasions, whether of war, politics, or commerce, Pavillon was most accustomed to repose confidence. He was a stout, squat figure, with a square face, and broad black eyebrows, that announced him to be opinionative and disputatious,—an advice-giving countenance, so to speak. He was endued with a buff jerkin, wore a broad belt and cutlass by his side, and carried a halberd in his hand.

"Peterkin, my dear lieutenant," said his commander, "this has been a glorious day—night, I should say—I trust thou art pleased for once?"

"I am well enough pleased that you are so," said the doughty lieutenant; "though I should not have thought of your celebrating the victory, if you call it one, up in this garret by yourself, when you are wanted in council."

"But *am* I wanted there?" said the Syndic.

"Ay, marry are you, to stand up for the rights of Liege, that are in more danger than ever," answered the Lieutenant.

"Pshaw, Peterkin," answered his principal, "thou art ever such a frampold grumbler——"

"Grumbler? not I," said Peterkin; "what pleases other people, will always please me. Only I wish we have not got King Stork, instead of King Log, like the fabliau that the Clerk of Saint Lambert's used to read us out of Meister Æsop's book."

"I cannot guess your meaning, Peterkin," said the Syndic.

"Why then, I tell you, Master Pavillon, that this Boar, or Bear, is

like to make his own den of Schonwaldt, and 'tis probable to turn
out as bad a neighbour to our town as ever was the old Bishop, and
worse. Here has he taken the whole conquest in his own hand, and is
only doubting whether he should be called Prince or Bishop;—and it
is a shame to see how they have mishandled the old man among them."

"I will not permit it, Peterkin," said Pavillon, bustling up; "I dislike
the mitre, but not the head that wore it. We are ten to one in the field,
Peterkin, and will not permit these courses."

"Ay, ten to one in the field, but only man to man in the castle;
besides that Nikkel Blok the butcher, and all the rabble of the suburbs,
take part with William de la Marck, partly for *saus* and *braus* (for he
has broached all the ale-tubs and wine-casks), and partly for old envy
towards us, who are the craftsmen, and have privileges."

"Peter," said Pavillon, "we will go presently to the city. I will stay
no longer in Schonwaldt."

"But the bridges of this castle are up, master," said Geisler—"the
gates locked, and guarded by these lanzknechts: and, if we were to try
to force our way, these fellows, whose everyday business is war, might
make wild work of us, that only fight of a holyday."

"But why has he secured the gates?" said the alarmed burgher; "or
what business hath he to make honest men prisoners?"

"I cannot tell—not I," said Peter. "Some noise there is about the
Ladies of Croye, who have escaped during the storm of the Castle. That
first put the Man with the Beard beside himself with anger, and now
he's beside himself with drink also."

The Burgomaster cast a disconsolate look towards Quentin, and
seemed at a loss what to resolve upon. Durward, who had not lost a
word of the conversation, which alarmed him very much, saw nevertheless that their only safety depended on his preserving his own presence
of mind, and sustaining the courage of Pavillon. He struck boldly into
the conversation, as one who had a right to have a voice in the deliberation.—"I am ashamed," he said, "Meinheer Pavillon, to observe you hesitate what to do on this occasion. Go boldly to William de la Marck,
and demand free leave to quit the castle, you, your lieutenant, your
squire, and your daughter. He can have no pretence for keeping you
prisoner."

"For me and my lieutenant—that is myself and Peter?—good—but
who is my squire?"

"I am, for the present," replied the undaunted Scot.

"You!" said the embarrassed burgess; "but are you not the envoy
of King Louis of France?"

"True, but my message is to the magistrates of Liege—and only in
Liege will I deliver it.—Were I to acknowledge my quality before
William de la Marck, must I not enter into negotiations with him? ay,
and, it is like, be detained by him. You must get me secretly out of the
Castle in the capacity of your squire."

"Good—my squire;—but you spoke of my daughter—my daughter is, I trust, safe in my house in Liege—where I wish her father was, with all my heart and soul."

"This lady," said Durward, "will call you father while we are in this place."

"And for my whole life afterwards," said the Countess, throwing herself at the citizen's feet, and clasping his knees.—"Never shall the day pass in which I will not honour you, love you, and pray for you as a daughter for a father, if you will but aid me in this fearful strait—Oh, be not hard-hearted! think your own daughter may kneel to a stranger, to ask him for life and honour—think of this, and give *me* the protection you would wish *her* to receive!"

"In troth," said the good citizen, much moved with her pathetic appeal—"I think, Peter, that this pretty maiden hath a touch of our Trudchen's sweet look,—I thought so from the first; and that this brisk youth here, who is so ready with his advice, is somewhat like Trudchen's bachelor—I wager a groat, Peter, that this is a true love matter, and it is a sin not to further it."

"It were a shame and sin both," said Peter, a good-natured Fleming, notwithstanding all his self-conceit; and as he spoke, he wiped his eyes with the sleeve of his jerkin.

"She *shall* be my daughter, then," said Pavillon, "well wrapped up in her black silk veil; and if there are not enough of true-hearted skinners to protect her, being the daughter of their Syndic, it were pity they should ever tug leather more.—But hark ye,—questions must be answered—How if I am asked what should my daughter make here at such an onslaught?"

"What should half the women in Liege make here when they followed us to the Castle?" said Peter; "they had no other reason, sure, but that it was just the place in the world that they should *not* have come to. Our *yung frau* Trudchen has come a little farther than the rest—that is all."

"Admirably spoken," said Quentin: "only be bold, and take this gentleman's good counsel, noble Meinheer Pavillon, and, at no trouble to yourself, you will do the most worthy action since the days of Charlemagne.—Here, sweet lady, wrap yourself close in this veil" (for many articles of female apparel lay scattered about the apartment),— "be but confident, and a few minutes will place you in freedom and safety. —Noble sir," he added, addressing Pavillon, "set forward."

"Hold—hold—hold a minute," said Pavillon, "my mind misgives me! —This De la Marck is a fury; a perfect boar in his nature as in his name; what if the young lady be one of those of Croye?—and what if he discover her, and be addicted to wrath?"

"And if I were one of those unfortunate women," said Isabelle, again attempting to throw herself at his feet, "could you for that reject me in this moment of despair? Oh, that I had been indeed your daughter, or the daughter of the poorest burgher!"

"Not so poor—not so poor neither, young lady—we pay as we go," said the citizen.

"Forgive me, noble sir," again began the unfortunate maiden.

"Not noble, nor sir neither," said the Syndic; "a plain burgher of Liege, that pays bills of exchange in ready guilders.—But that is nothing to the purpose.—Well, say you *be* a countess, I will protect you nevertheless."

"You are bound to protect her, were she a duchess," said Peter, "having once passed your word."

"Right, Peter, very right," said the Syndic; "it is our old Low Dutch fashion, *ein wort, ein man;* and now let us to this gear.—We must take leave of this William de la Marck; and yet I know not, my mind misgives me when I think of him; and were it a ceremony which could be waived, I have no stomach to go through it."

"Were it not better, since you have a force together, make for the gate and force the guard?" said Quentin.

But with united voice, Pavillon and his adviser exclaimed against the propriety of such an attack upon their ally's soldiers, with some hints concerning its rashness, which satisfied Quentin that it was not a risk to be hazarded with such associates. They resolved, therefore, to repair boldly to the great hall of the castle, where, as they understood, the Wild Boar of Ardennes held his feast, and demand free egress for the Syndic of Liege and his company, a request too reasonable, as it seemed, to be denied. Still the good Burgomaster groaned when he looked on his companions, and exclaimed to his faithful Peter,—"See what it is to have too bold and too tender a heart! Alas! Peterkin, how much have courage and humanity cost me! and how much may I yet have to pay for my virtues, before Heaven makes us free of this damned Castle of Schonwaldt!"

As they crossed the courts, still strewed with the dying and dead, Quentin, while he supported Isabelle through the scene of horrors, whispered to her courage and comfort, and reminded her that her safety depended entirely on her firmness and presence of mind.

"Not on mine—not on mine," she said, "but on yours—on yours only. —Oh, if I but escape this fearful night, never shall I forget him who saved me! One favour more only, let me implore at your hand, and I conjure you to grant it, by your mother's fame and your father's honour!"

"What is it you can ask that I could refuse?" said Quentin, in a whisper.

"Plunge your dagger in my heart," said she, "rather than leave me captive in the hands of these monsters."

Quentin's only answer was a pressure of the young Countess's hand, which seemed as if, but for terror, it would have returned the caress.

And, leaning on her youthful protector, she entered the fearful hall, preceded by Pavillon and his Lieutenant, and followed by a dozen of the Kurschenschaft, or skinner's trade, who attended, as a guard of honour, on the Syndic.

As they approached the hall, the yells of acclamation, and bursts of wild laughter, which proceeded from it, seemed rather to announce the revel of festive demons, rejoicing after some accomplished triumph over the human race, than of mortal beings, who had succeeded in a bold design. An emphatic tone of mind, which despair alone could have inspired, supported the assumed courage of the Countess Isabelle; undaunted spirits, which rose with the extremity, maintained that of Durward; while Pavillon and his lieutenants made a virtue of necessity, and faced their fate like bears bound to a stake, which must necessarily stand the dangers of the course.

CHAPTER XXII

THE REVELLERS

Cade. Where's Dick, the butcher of Ashford?
Dick. Here, sir.
Cade. They fell before thee like sheep and oxen; and thou behavedst thyself as if thou hadst been in thine own slaughter-house.
Second Part of King Henry VI.

THERE could hardly exist a more strange and horrible change than had taken place in the castle-hall of Schonwaldt since Quentin had partaken of the noontide meal there; and it was indeed one which painted, in the extremity of their dreadful features, the miseries of war—more especially when waged by those most relentless of all agents, the mercenary soldiers of a barbarous age—men who, by habit and profession, had become familiarised with all that was cruel and bloody in the art of war, while they were devoid alike of patriotism and of the romantic spirit of chivalry.

Instead of the orderly, decent, and somewhat formal meal, at which civil and ecclesiastical officers had, a few hours before, sat mingled in the same apartment, where a light jest could only be uttered in a whisper, and where, even amid superfluity of feasting and of wine, there reigned a decorum which almost amounted to hypocrisy, there was now such a scene of wild and roaring debauchery, as Satan himself, had he taken the chair as founder of the feast, could scarcely have improved.

At the head of the table sat, in the Bishop's throne and state, which had been hastily brought thither from his great council-chamber, the redoubted Boar of Ardennes himself, well deserving that dreaded name, in which he affected to delight, and which he did as much as he could think of to deserve. His head was unhelmeted, but he wore the rest of his ponderous and bright armour, which indeed he rarely laid aside.

Over his shoulders hung a strong surcoat, made of the dressed skin of a huge wild boar, the hoofs being of solid silver, and the tusks of the same. The skin of the head was so arranged, that, drawn over the casque, when the Baron was armed, or over his bare head, in the fashion of a hood, as he often affected when the helmet was laid aside, and as he now wore it, the effect was that of a grinning, ghastly monster; and yet the countenance which it overshadowed scarce required such horrors to improve those which were natural to its ordinary expression.

The upper part of De la Marck's face, as Nature had formed it, almost gave the lie to his character; for though his hair, when uncovered, resembled the rude and wild bristles of the hood he had drawn over it, yet an open, high, and manly forehead, broad ruddy cheeks, large, sparkling, light-coloured eyes, and a nose hooked like the beak of the eagle, promised something valiant and generous. But the effect of these more favourable traits was entirely overpowered by his habits of violence and insolence, which, joined to debauchery and intemperance, had stamped upon the features a character inconsistent with the rough gallantry which they would otherwise have exhibited. The former had, from habitual indulgence, swollen the muscles of the cheeks, and those around the eyes, in particular the latter; evil practices and habits had dimmed the eyes themselves, reddened the part of them that should have been white, and given the whole face a hideous likeness of the monster, which it was the terrible Baron's pleasure to resemble. But from an odd sort of contradiction, De la Marck, while he assumed in other respects the appearance of the Wild Boar, and even seemed pleased with the name, yet endeavoured, by the length and growth of his beard, to conceal the circumstance that had originally procured him that denomination. This was an unusual thickness and projection of the mouth and upper jaw, which, with the large projecting side teeth, gave that resemblance to the bestial creation, which, joined to the delight that De la Marck had in haunting the forest so called, originally procured for him the name of the Boar of Ardennes. The beard, broad, grisly, and uncombed, neither concealed the natural horrors of the countenance, nor dignified its brutal expression.

The soldiers and officers sat around the table, intermixed with the men of Liege, some of them of the very lowest description; among whom Nikkel Blok the butcher, placed near De la Marck himself, was distinguished by his tucked-up sleeves, which displayed arms smeared to the elbows with blood, as was the cleaver which lay on the table before him. The soldiers wore, most of them, their beards long and grisly, in imitation of their leader; had their hair plaited and turned upwards, in the manner that might best improve the natural ferocity of their appearance; and intoxicated, as many of them seemed to be, partly with the sense of triumph, and partly with the long libations of wine which they had been quaffing, presented a spectacle at once hideous and disgusting. The language which they held, and the songs which they sung, without even pretending to pay each other the compliment of listening, were so full of licence and blasphemy, that Quentin blessed God that the extremity of the noise prevented them from being intelligible to his companion.

It only remains to say, of the better class of burghers who were associated with William de la Marck's soldiers in this fearful revel, that the wan faces and anxious mien of the greater part, showed that they either disliked their entertainment, or feared their companions; while some of lower education, or a nature more brutal, saw only in the excesses of the soldier a gallant bearing, which they would willingly imitate, and the tone of which they endeavoured to catch so far as was possible, and stimulated themselves to the task, by swallowing immense draughts of wine and *schwarz bier*—indulging a vice which at all times was too common in the Low Countries.

The preparations for the feast had been as disorderly as the quality of the company. The whole of the Bishop's plate—nay, even that belonging to the service of the Church, for the Boar of Ardennes regarded not the imputation of sacrilege—was mingled with black-jacks, or huge tankards made of leather, and drinking-horns of the most ordinary description.

One circumstance of horror remains to be added and accounted for; and we willingly leave the rest of the scene to the imagination of the reader. Amidst the wild licence assumed by the soldiers of De la Marck, one who was excluded from the table (a lanzknecht, remarkable for his courage and for his daring behaviour during the storm of the evening), had impudently snatched up a large silver goblet, and carried it off, declaring it should atone for his loss of the share of the feast. The leader laughed till his sides shook at a jest so congenial to the character of the company; but when another, less renowned, it would seem, for audacity in battle, ventured on using the same freedom, De la Marck instantly put a check to a jocular practice, which would soon have cleared his table of all the more valuable decorations.—"Ho! by the spirit of the thunder!" he exclaimed, "those who dare not be men when they face the enemy, must not pretend to be thieves among their friends. What! thou frontless dastard, thou—thou who didst wait for opened gate and lowered bridge, when Comrade Horst forced his way over moat and wall, must *thou* be malapert?—Knit him up to the stanchions of the hall-window! He shall beat time with his feet, while we drink a cup to his safe passage to the devil."

The doom was scarce sooner pronounced than accomplished; and in a moment the wretch wrestled out his last agonies, suspended from the iron bars. His body still hung there when Quentin and the others entered the hall, and intercepting the pale moonbeam, threw on the castle-floor an uncertain shadow, which dubiously, yet fearfully, intimated the nature of the substance that produced it.

When the Syndic Pavillon was announced from mouth to mouth in this tumultuous meeting, he endeavoured to assume in right of his authority and influence, an air of importance and equality, which a glance at the fearful object at the window, and at the wild scene around him, rendered it very difficult for him to sustain, notwithstanding the exhortations of Peter, who whispered in his ear, with some perturbation, "Up heart, master, or we are but gone men!"

The Syndic maintained his dignity, however, as well as he could, in a short address, in which he complimented the company upon the great victory gained by the soldiers of De la Marck and the good citizens of Liege.

"Ay," answered De la Marck sarcastically, "we have brought down the game at last, quoth my lady's brach to the wolf-hound. But ho! Sir Burgomaster, you come like Mars, with Beauty by your side. Who is this fair one?—Unveil, unveil—no woman calls her beauty her own to-night."

"It is my daughter, noble leader," answered Pavillon; "and I am to pray your forgiveness for her wearing a veil. She has a vow for that effect to the Three Blessed Kings."

"I will absolve her of it presently," said De la Marck; "for here, with one stroke of a cleaver, will I consecrate myself Bishop of Liege; and I trust one living bishop is worth three dead kings."

There was a shuddering and murmur among the guests; for the community of Liege, and even some of the rude soldiers, reverenced the Kings of Cologne, as they were commonly called, though they respected nothing else.

"Nay, I mean no treason against their defunct majesties," said De la Marck; "only bishop I am determined to be. A prince both secular and ecclesiastical, having power to bind and loose, will best suit a band of reprobates such as you, to whom no one else would give absolution.— But come hither, noble Burgomaster—sit beside me, when you shall see me make a vacancy for my own preferment.—Bring in our predecessor in the holy seat."

A bustle took place in the hall, while Pavillon, excusing himself from the proffered seat of honour, placed himself near the bottom of the table, his followers keeping close behind him, not unlike a flock of sheep which, when a stranger dog is in presence, may be sometimes seen to assemble in the rear of an old bell-wether, who is, from office and authority, judged by them to have rather more courage than themselves. Near the spot sat a very handsome lad, a natural son, as was said, of the ferocious De la Marck, and towards whom he sometimes showed affection, and even tenderness. The mother of the boy, a beautiful concubine, had perished by a blow dealt her by the ferocious leader in a fit of drunkenness or jealousy; and her fate had caused her tyrant as much remorse as he was capable of feeling. His attachment to the surviving orphan might be partly owing to these circumstances. Quentin, who had learned this point of the leader's character from the old priest, planted himself as close as he could to the youth in question; determined to make him, in some way or other, either a hostage or a protector, should other means of safety fail them.

While all stood in a kind of suspense, waiting the event of the orders which the tyrant had issued, one of Pavillon's followers whispered Peter, "Did not our master call this wench his daughter?—Why, it cannot be our Trudchen. This strapping lass is taller by two inches; and there is a black lock of hair peeps forth yonder from under her veil. By Saint Michael of the Market-place, you might as well call a black bullock's hide a white heifer's!"

"Hush! hush!" said Peter, with some presence of mind—"What if our master hath a mind to steal a piece of doe-venison out of the Bishop's park here without our good dame's knowledge? And is it for thee or me to be a spy on him?"

"That will not I, brother," answered the other, "though I would not have thought of his turning deer-stealer at his years. Sapperment— what a shy fairy it is! See how she crouches down on yonder seat, behind folk's backs, to escape the gaze of the Marckers.—But hold, hold; what are they about to do with the poor old Bishop?"

As he spoke, the Bishop of Liege, Louis of Bourbon, was dragged into the hall of his own palace by the brutal soldiery. The dishevelled state of his hair, beard, and attire, bore witness to the ill-treatment he had already received; and some of his sacerdotal robes hastily flung over him, appeared to have been put on in scorn and ridicule of his quality and character. By good fortune, as Quentin was compelled to think it, the Countess Isabelle, whose feelings at seeing her protector in such an extremity might have betrayed her own secret and compromised her safety, was so situated as neither to hear nor see what was about to take place; and Durward sedulously interposed his own person before her, so as to keep her from observing alike, and from observation.

The scene which followed was short and fearful. When the unhappy Prelate was brought before the footstool of the savage leader, although in former life only remarkable for his easy and good-natured temper, he showed in this extremity a sense of his dignity and noble blood, well becoming the high race from which he was descended. His look was composed and undismayed; his gesture, when the rude hands which dragged him forward were unloosed, was noble, and at the same time resigned, somewhat between the bearing of a feudal noble and of a Christian martyr; and so much was even De la Marck himself staggered by the firm demeanour of his prisoner, and recollection of the early benefits he had received from him, that he seemed irresolute, cast down his eyes, and it was not until he had emptied a large goblet of wine, that, resuming his haughty insolence of look and manner, he thus addressed his unfortunate captive:—"Louis of Bourbon," said the truculent soldier, drawing hard his breath, clenching his hands, setting his teeth, and using the other mechanical actions to rouse up and sustain his native ferocity of temper—"I sought your friendship, and you rejected mine,

What would you now give that it had been otherwise?—Nikkel, be ready."

The butcher rose, seized his weapon, and stealing round behind De la Marck's chair, stood with it uplifted in his bare and sinewy arms.

"Look at that man, Louis of Bourbon," said De la Marck again— "What terms wilt thou now offer to escape this dangerous hour?"

The Bishop cast a melancholy but unshaken look upon the grisly satellite, who seemed prepared to execute the will of the tyrant, and then he said with firmness, "Hear me, William de la Marck; and good men all, if there be any here who deserve that name, hear the only terms I can offer to this ruffian.—William de la Marck, thou hast stirred up to sedition an imperial city—hast assaulted and taken the palace of a Prince of the Holy German Empire—slain his people—plundered his goods—maltreated his person; for this thou art liable to the Ban of the Empire—hast deserved to be declared outlawed and fugitive, landless and rightless. Thou hast done more than all this. More than mere human laws hast thou broken—more than mere human vengeance hast thou deserved. Thou hast broken into the sanctuary of the Lord—laid violent hands upon a Father of the Church—defiled the house of God with blood and rapine, like a sacrilegious robber—"

"Hast thou yet done?" said De la Marck, fiercely interrupting him, and stamping with his foot.

"No," answered the Prelate, "for I have not yet told thee the terms which you demanded to hear from me."

"Go on," said De la Marck; "and let the terms please me better than the preface, or woe to thy grey head!" And flinging himself back in his seat, he grinded his teeth till the foam flew from his lips, as from the tusks of the savage animal whose name and spoils he wore.

"Such are thy crimes," resumed the Bishop, with calm determination; "now hear the terms, which, as a merciful Prince and a Christian Prelate, setting aside all personal offence, forgiving each peculiar injury, I condescend to offer. Fling down thy leading-staff—renounce thy command —unbind thy prisoners—restore thy spoil—distribute what else thou hast of goods, to relieve those whom thou hast made orphans and widows— array thyself in sackcloth and ashes—take a palmer's staff in thy hand, and go barefooted on pilgrimage to Rome, and we will ourselves be intercessors for thee with the Imperial Chamber at Ratisbon for thy life, with our Holy Father the Pope for thy miserable soul."

While Louis of Bourbon proposed these terms, in a tone as decided as if he still occupied his episcopal throne, and as if the usurper kneeled a suppliant at his feet, the tyrant slowly raised himself in his chair, the amazement with which he was at first filled giving way gradually to rage, until, as the Bishop ceased, he looked to Nikkel Blok, and raised his finger, without speaking a word. The ruffian struck, as if he had been doing his office in the common shambles, and the murdered Bishop sunk, without a groan, at the foot of his own episcopal throne.[1] The Liegeois, who were not prepared for so horrible a catastrophe, and who had expected to hear the conference end in some terms of accommodation, started up unanimously, with cries of execration, mingled with shouts of vengeance.

But William de la Marck, raising his tremendous voice above the tumult, and shaking his clenched hand and extended arm, shouted aloud, "How now, ye porkers of Liege! ye wallowers in the mud of the Maes!— do ye dare to mate yourselves with the Wild Boar of Ardennes?—Up, ye Boar's brood!" (an expression by which he himself, and others, often designated his soldiers), "let these Flemish hogs see your tusks!"

Every one of his followers started up at the command, and mingled as they were among their late allies, prepared too for such a surprisal, each had, in an instant, his next neighbour by the collar, while his right hand brandished a broad dagger, that glimmered against lamplight and moonshine. Every arm was uplifted, but no one struck; for the victims were too much surprised for resistance, and it was probably the object of De la Marck only to impose terror on his civic confederates.

But the courage of Quentin Durward, prompt and alert in resolution beyond his years, and stimulated at the moment by all that could add energy to his natural shrewdness and resolution, gave a new turn to the scene. Imitating the action of the followers of De la Marck, he sprung on Carl Eberson, the son of their leader, and mastering him with ease, held his dirk at the boy's throat, while he exclaimed, "Is that your game? then here I play my part."

"Hold! hold!" exclaimed De la Marck, "it is a jest—a jest—Think you I would injure my good friends and allies of the city of Liege?— Soldiers, unloose your holds; sit down; take away the carrion" (giving the Bishop's corpse a thrust with his foot) "which hath caused this strife among friends, and let us drown unkindness in a fresh carouse."

All unloosened their holds, and the citizens and soldiers stood gazing on each other, as if they scarce knew whether they were friends or foes. Quentin Durward took advantage of the moment.

"Hear me," he said, "William de la Marck, and you, burghers and citizens of Liege;—and do you, young sir, stand still" (for the boy Carl was attempting to escape from his gripe), "no harm shall befall you, unless another of these sharp jests shall pass round."

"Who art thou, in the fiend's name," said the astonished De la Marck, "who art come to hold terms and take hostages from us in our own lair —from us, who exact pledges from others, but yield them to no one?"

"I am a servant of King Louis of France," said Quentin boldly; "an Archer of the Scottish Guard, as my language and dress may partly tell you. I am here to behold and to report your proceedings; and I see with wonder, that they are those of heathens, rather than Christians—

[1] Note IV.—Murder of the Bishop of Liege.

of madmen, rather than men possessed of reason. The hosts of Charles of Burgundy will be instantly in motion against you all; and if you wish assistance from France, you must conduct yourselves in a different manner.—For you, men of Liege, I advise your instant return to your own city; and if there is any obstruction offered to your departure, I denounce those by whom it is so offered, foes to my master, his most gracious Majesty of France."

"France and Liege! France and Liege!" cried the followers of Pavillon, and several other citizens, whose courage began to rise at the bold language held by Quentin.

"France and Liege, and long live the gallant Archer! We will live and die with him!"

William de la Marck's eyes sparkled, and he grasped his dagger as if about to launch it at the heart of the audacious speaker; but glancing his eye around, he read something in the looks of his soldiers, which even *he* was obliged to respect. Many of them were Frenchmen, and all of them knew the private support which William had received, both in men and in money, from that Kingdom; nay, some of them were rather startled at the violent and sacrilegious action which had been just committed. The name of Charles of Burgundy, a person likely to resent to the utmost the deeds of that night, had an alarming sound, and the extreme impolicy of at once quarrelling with the Liegeois and provoking the Monarch of France, made an appalling impression on their minds, confused as their intellects were. De la Marck, in short, saw he would not be supported, even by his own band, in any farther act of immediate violence, and relaxing the terrors of his brow and eye, declared that "he had not the least design against his good friends of Liege, all of whom were at liberty to depart from Schonwaldt at their pleasure; although he had hoped they would revel one night with him, at least, in honour of their victory." He added, with more calmness than he commonly used, that "he would be ready to enter into negotiations concerning the partition of spoil, and the arrangement of measures for their mutual defence, either the next day, or as soon after as they would. Meantime, he trusted that the Scottish gentleman would honour his feast by remaining all night at Schonwaldt."

The young Scot returned his thanks, but said, his motions must be determined by those of Pavillon, to whom he was directed particularly to attach himself; but that, unquestionably, he would attend him on his next return to the quarters of the valiant William de la Marck.

"If you depend on my motions," said Pavillon, hastily and aloud, "you are likely to quit Schonwaldt without an instant's delay; and, if you do not come back to Schonwaldt, save in my company, you are not likely to see it again in a hurry."

This last part of the sentence the honest citizen muttered to himself, afraid of the consequences of giving audible vent to feelings, which, nevertheless, he was unable altogether to suppress.

"Keep close about me, my brisk Kurschner lads," he said to his body-guard, "and we will get as fast as we can out of this den of thieves."

Most of the better classes of the Liegeois seemed to entertain similar opinions with the Syndic, and there had been scarce so much joy amongst them at the obtaining possession of Schonwaldt, as now seemed to arise from the prospect of getting safe out of it. They were suffered to leave the castle without opposition of any kind; and glad was Quentin when he turned his back on those formidable walls.

For the first time since they had entered that dreadful hall, Quentin ventured to ask the young Countess how she did.

"Well, well," she answered, in feverish haste, "excellently well—do not stop to ask a question; let us not lose an instant in words—Let us fly—let us fly!"

She endeavoured to mend her pace as she spoke; but with so little success, that she must have fallen from exhaustion, had not Durward supported her. With the tenderness of a mother, when she conveys her infant out of danger, the young Scot raised his precious charge in his arms; and, while she encircled his neck with one arm, lost to every other thought save the desire of escaping, he would not have wished one of the risks of the night unencountered, since such had been the con-clusion.

The honest Burgomaster was, in his turn, supported and dragged forward by his faithful counsellor Peter, and another of his clerks; and thus, in breathless haste, they reached the banks of the river, encoun-tering many strolling bands of citizens, who were eager to know the event of the siege, and the truth of certain rumours already afloat, that the conquerors had quarrelled among themselves.

Evading their curiosity as they best could, the exertions of Peter and some of his companions at length procured a boat for the use of the company, and with it an opportunity of enjoying some repose, equally welcome to Isabelle, who continued to lie almost motionless in the arms of her preserver, and to the worthy Burgomaster, who, after delivering a broken string of thanks to Durward, whose mind was at the time too much occupied to answer him, began a long harangue, which he addressed to Peter, upon his own courage and benevolence, and the dangers to which these virtues had exposed him, on this and other occasions.

"Peter, Peter," he said, resuming the complaint of the preceding evening, "if I had not had a bold heart, I would never have stood out against paying the burghers-twentieths, when every other living soul was willing to pay the same.—Ay, and then a less stout heart had not seduced me into that other battle of Saint Tron, where a Hainault man-at-arms thrust me into a muddy ditch with his lance, which neither heart nor hand that I had could help me out of, till the battle was over.—Ay, and then, Peter, this very night my courage seduced me, moreover, into too strait a corslet, which would have been the death of me, but for the aid of this gallant young gentleman, whose trade is fighting, whereof I wish him heartily joy. And then for my tenderness of heart, Peter, it has made a poor man of me—that is, it would have made a poor man of me, if I had not been tolerably well to pass in this wicked world;—and Heaven knows what trouble it is like to bring on me yet, with ladies, countesses, and keeping of secrets, which, for aught I know, may cost me half my fortune, and my neck into the bargain!"

Quentin could remain no longer silent, but assured him, that whatever danger or damage he should incur on the part of the young lady now under his protection, should be thankfully acknowledged, and, as far as was possible, repaid.

"I thank you, young Master Squire Archer, I thank you," answered the citizen of Liege; "but who was it told you that I desired any repayment at your hand for doing the duty of an honest man? I only regretted that it might cost me so and so; and I hope I may have leave to say so much to my lieutenant, without either grudging my loss or my peril."

Quentin accordingly concluded that his present friend was one of the numerous class of benefactors to others, who take out their reward in grumbling, without meaning more than, by showing their grievances, to exalt a little the idea of the valuable service by which they have incurred them, and therefore prudently remained silent, and suffered the Syndic to maunder on to his lieutenant concerning the risk and the loss he had encountered by his zeal for the public good, and his disinterested services to individuals, until they reached his own habitation.

The truth was, that the honest citizen felt that he had lost a little consequence, by suffering the young stranger to take the lead at the crisis which had occurred at the castle-hall of Schonwaldt; and, however delighted with the effect of Durward's interference at the moment, it seemed to him, on reflection, that he had sustained a diminution of importance, for which he endeavoured to obtain compensation, by exaggerating the claims which he had upon the gratitude of his country in general, his friends in particular, and more especially still, on the Countess of Croye, and her youthful protector.

But when the boat stopped at the bottom of his garden, and he had got himself assisted on shore by Peter, it seemed as if the touch of his own threshold had at once dissipated those feelings of wounded self-opinion and jealousy, and converted the discontented and obscured demagogue into the honest, kind, hospitable, and friendly host. He called loudly for Trudchen, who presently appeared; for fear and anxiety would permit few within the walls of Liege to sleep during that eventful night. She was charged to pay the utmost attention to the care of the beautiful and half-fainting stranger; and, admiring her personal charms, while she pitied her distress, Gertrude discharged the hospitable duty with the zeal and affection of a sister.

Late as it now was, and fatigued as the Syndic appeared, Quentin, on his side, had difficulty to escape a flask of choice and costly wine, as old as the battle of Azincour; and must have submitted to take his share, however unwilling, but for the appearance of the mother of the family, whom Pavillon's loud summons for the key of the cellar brought forth from her bedroom. She was a jolly little roundabout woman, who had been pretty in her time, but whose principal characteristics for several years had been a red and sharp nose, a shrill voice, and a determination that the Syndic, in consideration of the authority which he exercised when abroad, should remain under the rule of due discipline at home.

So soon as she understood the nature of the debate between her husband and his guest, she declared roundly, that the former, instead of having occasion for more wine, had got too much already; and, far from using, in furtherance of his request, any of the huge bunch of keys which hung by a silver chain at her waist, she turned her back on him without ceremony, and ushered Quentin to the neat and pleasant apartment in which he was to spend the night, amid such appliances to rest and comfort as probably he had till that moment been entirely a stranger to; so much did the wealthy Flemings excel, not merely the poor and rude Scots, but the French themselves, in all the conveniences of domestic life.

CHAPTER XXIII

THE FLIGHT

————Now bid me run,
And I will strive with things impossible;
Yet, get the better of them.

. . . .

————Set on your foot;
And, with a heart new fired, I follow you,
To do I know not what.
Julius Cæsar.

In spite of a mixture of joy and fear, doubt, anxiety, and other agitating passions, the exhausting fatigues of the preceding day were powerful enough to throw the young Scot into a deep and profound repose, which lasted until late on the day following; when his worthy host entered the apartment, with looks of care on his brow.

He seated himself by his guest's bedside, and began a long and complicated discourse upon the domestic duties of a married life, and especially upon the awful power and right supremacy which it became married men to sustain in all differences of opinion with their wives. Quentin listened with some anxiety. He knew that husbands, like other belligerent powers, were sometimes disposed to sing *Te Deum*, rather to conceal a defeat than to celebrate a victory; and he hastened to probe the matter more closely, "by hoping their arrival had been attended with no inconvenience to the good lady of the household."

"Inconvenience!—no," answered the Burgomaster—"No woman can be less taken unawares than Mother Mabel—always happy to see her friends—always a clean lodging and a handsome meal ready for them, with God's blessing on bed and board—No woman on earth so hospitable —only 'tis pity her temper is something particular."

"Our residence here is disagreeable to her, in short?" said the Scot, starting out of bed, and beginning to dress himself hastily. "Were I but sure the Lady Isabelle were fit for travel after the horrors of the last night, we would not increase the offence by remaining here an instant longer."

"Nay," said Pavillon, "that is just what the young lady herself said to Mother Mabel; and truly I wish you saw the colour that came to her face as she said it—a milkmaid that has skated five miles to market against the frost-wind is a lily compared to it—I do not wonder Mother Mabel may be a little jealous, poor dear soul."

"Has the Lady Isabelle then left her apartment?" said the youth, continuing his toilette operations with more despatch than before.

"Yes," replied Pavillon; "and she expects your approach with much impatience, to determine which way you shall go—since you are both determined on going.—But I trust you will tarry breakfast?"

"Why did you not tell me this sooner?" said Durward impatiently.

"Softly—softly," said the Syndic; "I have told it you too soon, I think, if it puts you into such a hasty fluster. Now I have some more matter for your ear, if I saw you had some patience to listen to me."

"Speak it, worthy sir, as soon and as fast as you can—I listen devoutly."

"Well, then," resumed the Burgomaster, "I have but one word to say, and that is, that Trudchen, who is as sorry to part with yonder pretty lady as if she had been some sister of hers, wants you to take some other disguise; for there is word in the town that the Ladies of Croye travel the country in Pilgrim's dresses, attended by a French life-guardsman of the Scottish Archers; and it is said one of them was brought into Schonwaldt last night by a Bohemian after we had left it; and it was said still farther, that this same Bohemian had assured William de la Marck that you were charged with no message either to him or to the good people of Liege, and that you had stolen away the young Countess, and travelled with her as her paramour. And all this news hath come from Schonwaldt this morning; and it has been told to us and the other counsellors, who know not well what to advise; for though our own opinion is that William de la Marck has been a thought too rough both with the Bishop and with ourselves, yet there is a great belief that he is a goodnatured soul at bottom—that is, when he is sober—and that he is the only leader in the world to command us against the Duke of Burgundy; —and, in truth, as matters stand, it is partly my own mind that we must keep fair with him, for we have gone too far to draw back."

"Your daughter advises well," said Quentin Durward, abstaining from reproaches or exhortations, which he saw would be alike unavailing to sway a resolution, which had been adopted by the worthy magistrate in compliance at once with the prejudices of his party and the inclination of his wife—"Your daughter counsels well—We must part in disguise, and that instantly. We may, I trust, rely upon you for the necessary secrecy, and for the means of escape?"

"With all my heart—with all my heart," said the honest citizen, who, not much satisfied with the dignity of his own conduct, was eager to find some mode of atonement. "I cannot but remember that I owed you my life last night, both for unclasping that accursed steel doublet, and helping me through the other scrape, which was worse; for yonder Boar and his brood look more like devils than men. So I will be true to you as blade to haft, as our cutlers say, who are the best in the whole world. Nay, now you are ready, come this way—you shall see how far I can trust you."

The Syndic led him from the chamber in which he had slept to his own counting-room, in which he transacted his affairs of business; and after bolting the door, and casting a piercing and careful eye round him, he opened a concealed and vaulted closet behind the tapestry, in which stood more than one iron chest. He proceeded to open one which was full of guilders, and placed it at Quentin's discretion, to take whatever sum he might think necessary for his companion's expenses and his own.

As the money with which Quentin was furnished on leaving Plessis was now nearly expended, he hesitated not to accept the sum of two hundred guilders; and by doing so took a great weight from the mind of Pavillon, who considered the desperate transaction in which he thus voluntarily became the creditor, as an atonement for the breach of hospitality which various considerations in a great measure compelled him to commit.

Having carefully locked his treasure-chamber, the wealthy Fleming next conveyed his guest to the parlour, where, in full possession of her activity of mind and body, though pale from the scenes of the preceding night, he found the Countess attired in the fashion of a Flemish maiden of the middling class. No other was present excepting Trudchen, who was sedulously employed in completing the Countess's dress, and instructing her how to bear herself. She extended her hand to him, which, when he had reverently kissed, she said to him, "Seignior Quentin, we must leave our friends here, unless I would bring on them a part of the misery which has pursued me ever since my father's death. You must change your dress and go with me, unless you also are tired of befriending a being so unfortunate."

"I!—I tired of being your attendant!—To the end of the earth will I guard you! But you—you yourself—are you equal to the task you undertake?—Can you, after the terrors of last night—"

"Do not recall them to my memory," answered the Countess; "I remember but the confusion of a horrid dream.—Has the excellent Bishop escaped?"

"I trust he is in freedom," said Quentin, making a sign to Pavillon, who seemed about to enter on the dreadful narrative, to be silent.

"Is it possible for us to rejoin him?—Hath he gathered any power?" said the lady.

"His only hopes are in Heaven," said the Scot; "but wherever you wish to go, I stand by your side, a determined guide and guard."

"We will consider," said Isabelle; and after a moment's pause, she added, "A convent would be my choice, but that I fear it would prove a weak defence against those who pursue me."

"Hem! hem!" said the Syndic; "I could not well recommend a convent within the district of Liege; because the Boar of Ardennes, though in the main a brave leader, a trusty confederate, and a well-wisher to our city, has, nevertheless, rough humours, and payeth, on the whole, little regard to cloisters, convents, nunneries, and the like. Men say that there are a score of nuns—that is, such as were nuns—who march always with his company."

"Get yourself in readiness hastily, Seignior Durward," said Isabelle, interrupting this detail, "since to your faith I must needs commit myself."

No sooner had the Syndic and Quentin left the room, than Isabelle began to ask of Gertrude various questions concerning the roads, and so forth, with such clearness of spirit and pertinence, that the latter could not help exclaiming, "Lady, I wonder at you!—I have heard of masculine firmness, but yours appears to me more than belongs to humanity."

"Necessity," answered the Countess—"necessity, my friend, is the mother of courage, as of invention. No long time since, I might have fainted when I saw a drop of blood shed from a trifling cut—I have since seen life-blood flow around me, I may say, in waves, yet I have retained my senses and my self-possession.—Do not think it was an easy task," she added, laying on Gertrude's arm a trembling hand, although she still spoke with a firm voice; "the little world within me is like a garrison besieged by a thousand foes, whom nothing but the most determined resolution can keep from storming it on every hand, and at every moment. Were my situation one whit less perilous than it is—were I not sensible that my only chance to escape a fate more horrible than death, is to retain my recollection and self-possession—Gertrude, I would at this moment throw myself into your arms, and relieve my bursting bosom by such a transport of tears and agony of terror, as never rushed from a breaking heart!"

"Do not do so, lady!" said the sympathising Fleming; "take courage, tell your beads, throw yourself on the care of Heaven; and surely, if ever Heaven sent a deliverer to one ready to perish, that bold and adventurous young gentleman must be designed for yours. There is one, too," she added, blushing deeply, "in whom I have some interest. Say nothing to my father; but I have ordered my bachelor, Hans Glover, to wait for you at the eastern gate, and never to see my face more, unless he brings word that he has guided you safe from the territory."

To kiss her tenderly was the only way in which the young Countess could express her thanks to the frank and kindhearted city-maiden, who returned the embrace affectionately, and added, with a smile, "Nay, if two maidens and their devoted bachelors cannot succeed in a disguise and an escape, the world is changed from what I am told it wont to be."

A part of this speech again called the colour into the Countess's pale cheeks, which was not lessened by Quentin's sudden appearance. He entered completely attired as a Flemish boor of the better class, in the holyday suit of Peter, who expressed his interest in the young Scot by the readiness with which he parted with it for his use; and swore, at the same time, that, were he to be curried and tugged worse than ever was bullock's hide, they should make nothing out of him, to the betraying of the young folks. Two stout horses had been provided by the activity of Mother Mabel, who really desired the Countess and her attendant no harm, so that she could make her own house and family clear of the dangers which might attend upon harbouring them. She beheld them mount and go off with great satisfaction, after telling them that they would find their way to the east gate by keeping their eye on Peter, who was to walk in that direction as their guide, but without holding any visible communication with them.

The instant her guests had departed, Mother Mabel took the opportunity to read a long practical lecture to Trudchen upon the folly of reading romances, whereby the flaunting ladies of the Court were grown so bold and venturous, that, instead of applying to learn some honest housewifery, they must ride, forsooth, a damsel-erranting through the country, with no better attendant than some idle squire, debauched page, or rake-helly archer from foreign parts, to the great danger of their health, the impoverishing of their substance, and the irreparable prejudice of their reputation.

All this Gertrude heard in silence, and without reply; but, considering her character, it might be doubted whether she derived from it the practical inference which it was her mother's purpose to enforce.

Meantime, the travellers had gained the eastern gate of the city, traversing crowds of people, who were fortunately too much busied in the political events and rumours of the hour to give any attention to a couple who had so little to render their appearance remarkable. They passed the guards in virtue of a permission obtained for them by Pavillon, but in the name of his colleague Rouslaer, and they took leave of Peter Geislaer with a friendly though brief exchange of good wishes on either side. Immediately afterwards, they were joined by a stout young man, riding a good grey horse, who presently made himself known as Hans Glover, the bachelor of Trudchen Pavillon. He was a young fellow with a good Flemish countenance—not, indeed, of the most intellectual cast, but arguing more hilarity and good-humour than wit, and, as the Countess could not help thinking, scarce worthy to be bachelor to the generous Trudchen. He seemed, however, fully desirous to second the views which she had formed in their favour; for, saluting them respectfully, he asked of the Countess in Flemish, on which road she desired to be conducted?

"Guide me," said she, "towards the nearest town on the frontiers of Brabant."

"You have then settled the end and object of your journey?" said Quentin, approaching his horse to that of Isabelle, and speaking French, which their guide did not understand.

"Surely," replied the young lady; "for, situated as I now am, it must be of no small detriment to me if I were to prolong a journey in my present circumstances, even though the termination should be a rigorous prison."

"A prison!" said Quentin.

"Yes, my friend, a prison; but I will take care that you shall not share it."

"Do not talk—do not think of me," said Quentin. "Saw I you but safe, my own concerns are little worth minding."

"Do not speak so loud," said the Lady Isabelle; "you will surprise our guide—you see he has already rode on before us;"—for, in truth, the good-natured Fleming, doing as he desired to be done by, had removed from them the constraint of a third person, upon Quentin's first motion towards the lady.—"Yes," she continued, when she noticed they were free from observation, "to you, my friend, my protector—why should I be ashamed to call you what Heaven has made you to me?—to you it is my duty to say, that my resolution is taken to return to my native country, and to throw myself on the mercy of the Duke of Burgundy. It was mistaken, though well-meant advice, which induced me ever to withdraw from his protection, and place myself under that of the crafty and false Louis of France."

"And you resolve to become the bride, then, of the Count of Campo-basso, the unworthy favourite of Charles?"

Thus spoke Quentin, with a voice in which internal agony struggled with his desire to assume an indifferent tone, like that of the poor condemned criminal, when, affecting a firmness which he is far from feeling, he asks if the death-warrant be arrived.

"No, Durward, no," said the Lady Isabelle, sitting up erect in her saddle, "to that hated condition all Burgundy's power shall not sink a daughter of the House of Croye. Burgundy may seize on my lands and fiefs, he may imprison my person in a convent; but that is the worst I have to expect; and worse than that I will endure ere I give my hand to Campo-basso."

"The worst!" said Quentin; "and what worse can there be than plunder and imprisonment?—Oh, think, while you have God's free air around you, and one by your side who will hazard life to conduct you to England, to Germany, even to Scotland, in all of which you shall find generous protectors—Oh, while this is the case, do not resolve so rashly to abandon the means of liberty, the best gift that Heaven gives!—Oh, well sung a poet of my own land—

> 'Ah, freedom is a noble thing—
> Freedom makes man to have liking—
> Freedom the zest to pleasure gives—
> He lives at ease who freely lives.
> Grief, sickness, poortith, want, are all
> Summ'd up within the name of thrall.' "

She listened with a melancholy smile to her guide's tirade in praise of liberty; and then answered after a moment's pause, "Freedom is for man alone—woman must ever seek a protector, since nature made her incapable to defend herself. And where am I to find one?—In that voluptuary Edward of England—in the inebriated Wenceslaus of Germany—in Scotland?—Ah, Durward, were I your sister, and could you promise me shelter in some of those mountain-glens which you love to describe, where, for charity, or for the few jewels I have preserved, I might lead an unharassed life, and forget the lot I was born to—Could you promise me the protection of some honoured matron of the land—of some baron whose heart was as true as his sword—that were indeed a prospect, for which it were worth the risk of farther censure to wander farther and wider!"

There was a faltering tenderness of voice with which the Countess Isabelle made this admission, that at once filled Quentin with a sensation of joy, and cut him to the very heart. He hesitated a moment ere he made an answer, hastily reviewing in his mind the possibility there might be that he could procure her shelter in Scotland; but the melancholy truth rushed on him, that it would be alike base and cruel to point out to her a course, which he had not the most distant power or means to render safe. "Lady," he said at last, "I should act foully against my honour and oath of chivalry, did I suffer you to ground any plan upon the thoughts that I have the power in Scotland to afford you other protection than that of the poor arm which is now by your side. I scarce know that my blood flows in the veins of an individual who now lives in my native land. The Knight of Innerquharity stormed our castle at midnight, and cut off all that belonged to my name. Were I again in Scotland, our feudal enemies are numerous and powerful, I single and weak; and even had the King a desire to do me justice, he dared not, for the sake of redressing the wrongs of a poor individual, provoke a chief who rides with five hundred horse."

"Alas!" said the Countess, "there is then no corner of the world safe from oppression, since it rages as unrestrained amongst those wild hills which afford so few objects to covet, as in our rich and abundant Lowlands!"

"It is a sad truth, and I dare not deny it," said the Scot, "that, for little more than the pleasure of revenge and the lust of bloodshed, our hostile clans do the work of executioners on each other; and Ogilvies and the like act the same scenes in Scotland, as De la Marck and his robbers do in this country."

"No more of Scotland, then," said Isabelle, with a tone of indifference, either real or affected—"no more of Scotland,—which indeed I mentioned but in jest, to see if you really dared recommend to me, as a place of rest, the most distracted kingdom in Europe. It was but a trial of your sincerity, which I rejoice to see may be relied on, even when your partialities are most strongly excited. So, once more, I will think of no other protection than can be afforded by the first honourable baron holding of Duke Charles, to whom I am determined to render myself."

"And why not rather betake yourself to your own estates, and to your own strong castle, as you designed when at Tours?" said Quentin. "Why not call around you the vassals of your father, and make treaty with Burgundy, rather than surrender yourself to him? Surely there must be many a bold heart that would fight in your cause; and I know at least of one, who would willingly lay down his life to give example."

"Alas!" said the Countess, "that scheme, the suggestion of the crafty Louis, and, like all which he ever suggested, designed more for his advantage than for mine, has become impracticable, since it was betrayed to Burgundy by the double traitor Zamet Maugrabin. My kinsman was then imprisoned, and my houses garrisoned. Any attempt of mine would but expose my dependants to the vengeance of Duke Charles; and why should I occasion more bloodshed than has already taken place on so worthless an account? No, I will submit myself to my Sovereign as a dutiful vassal, in all which shall leave my personal freedom of choice uninfringed; the rather that I trust my kinswoman, the Countess Hameline, who first counselled, and indeed urged my flight, has already taken this wise and honourable step!"

"Your kinswoman!" repeated Quentin, awakened to recollections to which the young Countess was a stranger, and which the rapid succession of perilous and stirring events had, as matters of nearer concern, in fact banished from his memory.

"Ay—my aunt—the Countess Hameline of Croye—know you aught of her?" said the Countess Isabelle; "I trust she is now under the protection of the Burgundian banner.—You are silent! Know you aught of her?"

The last question, urged in a tone of the most anxious inquiry, obliged Quentin to give some account of what he knew of the Countess's fate. He mentioned that he had been summoned to attend her in a flight from Liege, which he had no doubt the Lady Isabelle would be partaker in— he mentioned the discovery that had been made after they had gained the forest—and finally, he told his own return to the castle, and the circumstances in which he found it. But he said nothing of the views with which it was plain the Lady Hameline had left the Castle of Schon-

waldt, and as little about the floating report of her having fallen into
the hands of William de la Marck. Delicacy prevented him even hinting at the one, and regard for the feelings of his companion, at a moment
when strength and exertion were most demanded of her, prevented him
from alluding to the latter, which had, besides, only reached him as a
mere rumour.

This tale, though abridged of those important particulars, made a
strong impression on the Countess Isabelle, who, after riding some time
in silence, said at last, with a tone of cold displeasure: "And so you
abandoned my unfortunate relative in a wild forest, at the mercy of a
vile Bohemian and a traitorous waiting-woman?—Poor kinswoman, thou
wert wont to praise this youth's good faith!"

"Had I not done so, madam," said Quentin, not unreasonably offended at the turn thus given to his gallantry, "what had been the fate
of one to whose service I was far more devoutly bound? Had I *not*
left the Countess Hameline of Croye to the charge of those whom she
had herself selected as counsellors and advisers, the Countess Isabelle
had been ere now the bride of William de la Marck, the Wild Boar of
Ardennes."

"You are right," said the Countess Isabelle, in her usual manner; "and
I, who have the advantage of your unhesitating devotion, have done you
foul and ungrateful wrong. But oh, my unhappy kinswoman! and the
wretch Marthon, who enjoyed so much of her confidence, and deserved
it so little—it was she that introduced to my kinswoman the wretched
Zamet and Hayraddin Maugrabin, who, by their pretended knowledge
in soothsaying and astrology, obtained a great ascendency over her
mind; it was she who, strengthening their predictions, encouraged her
in—I know not what to call them—delusions concerning matches and
lovers, which my kinswoman's age rendered ungraceful and improbable.
I doubt not that, from the beginning, we had been surrounded by these
snares by Louis of France, in order to determine us to take refuge at his
Court, or rather to put ourselves into his power; after which rash act on
our part, how unkingly, unknightly, ignobly, ungentlemanlike, he hath
conducted himself towards us, you, Quentin Durward, can bear witness.
But alas! my kinswoman—what think you will be her fate?"

Endeavouring to inspire hopes which he scarce felt, Durward answered,
that the avarice of these people was stronger than any other passion;
that Marthon, even when he left them, seemed to act rather as the Lady
Hameline's protectress; and, in fine, that it was difficult to conceive any
object these wretches could accomplish by the ill usage or murder of the
Countess, whereas they might be gainers by treating her well, and putting
her to ransom.

To lead the Countess Isabelle's thoughts from this melancholy subject, Quentin frankly told her the treachery of the Maugrabin, which he
had discovered in the night-quarter near Namur, and which appeared
the result of an agreement betwixt the King and William de la Marck.

Isabelle shuddered with horror, and then recovering herself, said, "I am ashamed, and I have sinned in permitting myself so far to doubt of the saints' protection, as for an instant to have deemed possible the accomplishment of a scheme so utterly cruel, base, and dishonourable, while there are pitying eyes in Heaven to look down on human miseries. It is not a thing to be thought of with fear or abhorrence, but to be rejected as such a piece of incredible treachery and villainy, as it were atheism to believe could ever be successful. But I now see plainly why that hypocritical Marthon often seemed to foster every seed of petty jealousy or discontent betwixt my poor kinswoman and myself, whilst she always mixed with flattery, addressed to the individual who was present, whatever could prejudice her against her absent kinswoman. Yet, never did I dream she could have proceeded so far as to have caused my once affectionate kinswoman to have left me behind in the perils of Schonwaldt, whilst she made her own escape."

"Did the Lady Hameline not mention to you, then," said Quentin, "her intended flight?"

"No," replied the Countess, "but she alluded to some communication which Marthon was to make to me. To say truth, my poor kinswoman's head was so turned by the mysterious jargon of the miserable Hayraddin, whom that day she had admitted to a long and secret conference, and she threw out so many strange hints, that—that—in short, I cared not to press on her, when in that humour, for any explanation. Yet it was cruel to leave me behind her."

"I will excuse the Lady Hameline from intending such unkindness," said Quentin; "for such was the agitation of the moment, and the darkness of the hour, that I believe the Lady Hameline as certainly conceived herself accompanied by her niece, as I at the same time, deceived by Marthon's dress and demeanour, supposed I was in the company of both the Ladies of Croye:—and of *her* especially," he added, with a low but determined voice, "without whom the wealth of worlds would not have tempted me to leave Schonwaldt."

Isabelle stooped her head forward, and seemed scarce to hear the emphasis with which Quentin had spoken. But she turned her face to him again when he began to speak of the policy of Louis; and it was not difficult for them, by mutual communication, to ascertain that the Bohemian brothers, with their accomplice Marthon, had been the agents of that crafty monarch, although Zamet, the elder of them, with a perfidy peculiar to his race, had attempted to play a double game, and had been punished accordingly. In the same humour of mutual confidence, and forgetting the singularity of their own situation, as well as the perils of the road, the travellers pursued their journey for several hours, only stopping to refresh their horses at a retired dorff, or hamlet, to which they were conducted by Hans Glover, who, in all other respects, as well as in leaving them much to their own freedom in conversation, conducted himself like a person of reflection and discretion.

Meantime, the artificial distinction which divided the two lovers (for such we may now term them), seemed dissolved, or removed, by the circumstances in which they were placed; for if the Countess boasted the higher rank, and was by birth entitled to a fortune incalculably larger than that of the youth, whose revenue lay in his sword, it was to be considered that, for the present, she was as poor as he, and for her safety, honour, and life, exclusively indebted to his presence of mind, valour, and devotion. They *spoke* not indeed of love, for though the young lady, her heart full of gratitude and confidence, might have pardoned such a declaration, yet Quentin, on whose tongue there was laid a check, both by natural timidity and by the sentiments of chivalry, would have held it an unworthy abuse of her situation had he said anything which could have the appearance of taking undue advantage of the opportunities which it afforded them. They *spoke* not then of love, but the thoughts of it were on both sides unavoidable; and thus they were placed in that relation to each other, in which sentiments of mutual regard are rather understood than announced, and which, with the freedoms which it permits, and the uncertainties that attend it, often forms the most delightful hours of human existence, and as frequently leads to those which are darkened by disappointment, fickleness, and all the pains of blighted hope and unrequited attachment.

It was two hours after noon, when the travellers were alarmed by the report of the guide, who, with paleness and horror in his countenance, said that they were pursued by a party of De la Marck's *Schwarz-reiters*. These soldiers, or rather banditti, were bands levied in the lower circles of Germany, and resembled the lanzknechts in every particular, except that the former acted as light cavalry. To maintain the name of Black Troopers, and to strike additional terror into their enemies, they usually rode on black chargers, and smeared with black ointment their arms and accoutrements, in which operation their hands and faces often had their share. In morals, and in ferocity these Schwarz-reiters emulated their pedestrian brethren the lanzknechts.[1]

On looking back, and discovering along the long level road which they had traversed a cloud of dust advancing, with one or two of the headmost troopers riding furiously in front of it, Quentin addressed his companion—"Dearest Isabelle, I have no weapon left save my sword; but since I cannot fight for you, I will fly with you. Could we gain yonder wood that is before us ere they come up, we may easily find means to escape."

"So be it, my only friend," said Isabelle, pressing her horse to the gallop; "and thou, good fellow," she added, addressing Hans Glover, "get thee off to another road, and do not stay to partake our misfortune and danger."

The honest Fleming shook his head, and answered her generous ex-

[1] Note V.—Schwarz-reiters.

hortation, with *Nein, nein! das geht nichts,*[1] and continued to attend them, all three riding towards the shelter of the wood as fast as their jaded horses could go, pursued, at the same time, by the Schwarz-reiters, who increased their pace when they saw them fly. But notwithstanding the fatigue of the horses, still the fugitives, being unarmed, and riding lighter in consequence, had considerably the advantage of the pursuers, and were within about a quarter of a mile of the wood, when a body of men-at-arms, under a knight's pennon, was discovered advancing from the cover, so as to intercept their flight.

"They have bright armour," said Isabelle; "they must be Burgundians. Be they who they will, we must yield to them, rather than to the lawless miscreants who pursue us."

A moment later, she exclaimed, looking on the pennon, "I know the cloven heart which it displays! It is the banner of the Count of Crève-cœur, a noble Burgundian—to him I will surrender myself."

Quentin Durward sighed; but what other alternative remained? and how happy would he have been but an instant before, to have been certain of the escape of Isabelle, even under worse terms! They soon joined the band of Crèvecœur, and the Countess demanded to speak to the leader, who had halted his party till he should reconnoitre the Black Troopers; and as he gazed on her with doubt and uncertainty, she said, "Noble Count,—Isabelle of Croye, the daughter of your old companion in arms, Count Reinold of Croye, renders herself, and asks protection from your valour for her and hers."

"Thou shalt have it, fair kinswoman, were it against a host—always excepting my liege Lord of Burgundy. But there is little time to talk of it. These filthy-looking fiends have made a halt, as if they intended to dispute the matter.—By Saint George of Burgundy, they have the insolence to advance against the banner of Crèvecœur!—What! will not the knaves be ruled?—Damian, my lance—Advance banner—Lay your spears in the rest—Crèvecœur to the Rescue!"

Crying his war-cry, and followed by his men-at-arms, he galloped rapidly forward to charge the Schwarz-reiters.

CHAPTER XXIV

THE SURRENDER

Rescue or none, Sir Knight, I am your captive;
Deal with me what your nobleness suggests—
Thinking the chance of war may one day place you
Where I must now be reckon'd—i' the roll
Of melancholy prisoners.

Anonymous.

THE skirmish betwixt the Schwarz-reiters and the Burgundian men-at-arms lasted scarcely five minutes, so soon were the former put to the

---

[1] "No, no! that must not be."

rout by the superiority of the latter, in armour, weight of horse, and military spirit. In less than the space we have mentioned, the Count of Crèvecœur, wiping his bloody sword upon his horse's mane ere he sheathed it, came back to the verge of the forest, where Isabelle had remained a spectator of the combat. One part of his people followed him, while the other continued to pursue the flying enemy for a little space along the causeway.

"It is shame," said the Count, "that the weapons of knights and gentlemen should be soiled by the blood of those brutal swine."

So saying, he returned his weapon to the sheath, and added, "This is a rough welcome to your home, my pretty cousin, but wandering princesses must expect such adventures. And well I came up in time, for, let me assure you, the Black Troopers respect a countess's coronet as little as a country-wench's coif, and I think your retinue is not qualified for much resistance."

"My Lord Count," said the Lady Isabelle, "without farther preface, let me know if I am a prisoner, and where you are to conduct me."

"You know, you silly child," answered the Count, "how I would answer that question, did it rest on my own will. But you and your foolish match-making, marriage-hunting aunt, have made such wild use of your wings of late, that I fear you must be contented to fold them up in a cage for a little while. For my part, my duty, and it is a sad one, will be ended when I have conducted you to the Court of the Duke, at Peronne; for which purpose, I hold it necessary to deliver the command of this reconnoitring party to my nephew, Count Stephen, while I return with you thither, as I think you may need an intercessor—And I hope the young giddy-pate will discharge his duty wisely."

"So please you, fair uncle," said Count Stephen, "if you doubt my capacity to conduct the men-at-arms, even remain with them yourself, and I will be the servant and guard of the Countess Isabelle of Croye."

"No doubt, fair nephew," answered his uncle, "this were a goodly improvement on my scheme; but methinks I like it as well in the way I planned it. Please you, therefore, to take notice, that your business here is not to hunt after and stick these black hogs, for which you seemed but now to have felt an especial vocation, but to collect and bring to me true tidings what is going forward in the country of Liege, concerning which we hear such wild rumours. Let some half-score of lances follow me, and the rest remain with my banner, under your guidance."

"Yet one moment, cousin of Crèvecœur," said the Countess Isabelle, "and let me, in yielding myself prisoner, stipulate at least for the safety of those who have befriended me in my misfortunes. Permit this good fellow, my trusty guide, to go back unharmed to his native town of Liege."

"My nephew," said Crèvecœur, after looking sharply at Glover's honest breadth of countenance, "shall guard this good fellow, who seems indeed, to have little harm in him, as far into the territory as he himself advances, and then leave him at liberty."

"Fail not to remember me to the kind Gertrude," said the Countess to her guide, and added, taking a string of pearls from under her veil, "Pray her to wear this in remembrance of her unhappy friend."

Honest Glover took the string of pearls, and kissed, with clownish gesture, but with sincere kindness, the fair hand which had found such a delicate mode of remunerating his own labours and peril.

"Umph! signs and tokens!" said the Count; "any farther bequests to make, my fair cousin?—It is time we were on our way."

"Only," said the Countess, making an effort to speak, "that you will be pleased to be favourable to this—this young gentleman."

"Umph!" said Crèvecœur, casting the same penetrating glance on Quentin which he had bestowed on Glover, but apparently with a much less satisfactory result, and mimicking, though not offensively, the embarrassment of the Countess—"Umph!—Ay,—this is a blade of another temper.—And pray, my cousin, what has this—this *very* young gentleman done, to deserve such intercession at your hands?"

"He has saved my life and honour," said the Countess, reddening with shame and resentment.

Quentin also blushed with indignation, but wisely concluded, that to give vent to it might only make matters worse.

"Life and honour?—Umph!" said again the Count Crèvecœur, "methinks it would have been as well, my cousin, if you had not put yourself in the way of lying under such obligations to this very young gentleman.—But let it pass. The young gentleman may wait on us, if his quality permit, and I will see he has no injury—only I will myself take in future the office of protecting your life and honour, and may perhaps find for him some fitter duty than that of being a squire of the body to damosels errant."

"My Lord Count," said Durward, unable to keep silence any longer, "lest you should talk of a stranger in slighter terms than you might afterwards think becoming, I take leave to tell you, that I am Quentin Durward, an Archer of the Scottish Body-guard, in which, as you well know, none but gentlemen and men of honour are enrolled."

"I thank you for your information, and I kiss your hands, Seignior Archer," said Crèvecœur, in the same tone of raillery. "Have the goodness to ride with me to the front of the party."

As Quentin moved onward at the command of the Count, who had now the power, if not the right, to dictate his motions, he observed that the Lady Isabelle followed his motions with a look of anxious and timid interest, which amounted almost to tenderness, and the sight of which brought water into his eyes. But he remembered that he had a man's part to sustain before Crèvecœur, who, perhaps of all the chivalry in France or Burgundy, was the least likely to be moved to anything but laughter by a tale of true-love sorrow. He determined, therefore, not to wait his addressing him, but to open the conversation in a tone which should assert his claim to fair treatment, and to more respect than the Count, offended perhaps at finding a person of such inferior note placed so near the confidence of his high-born and wealthy cousin, seemed disposed to entertain for him.

"My Lord Count of Crèvecœur," he said, in a temperate but firm tone of voice, "may I request of you, before our interview goes farther, to tell me if I am at liberty, or am to account myself your prisoner?"

"A shrewd question," replied the Count, "which, at present, I can only answer by another—Are France and Burgundy, think you, at peace or war with each other?"

"That," replied the Scot, "you, my lord, should certainly know better than I. I have been absent from the Court of France, and have heard no news for some time."

"Look you there," said the Count; "you see how easy it is to ask questions, but how difficult to answer them. Why, I myself, who have been at Peronne with the Duke for this week and better, cannot resolve this riddle any more than you; and yet, Sir Squire, upon the solution of that question depends the said point, whether you are prisoner or free man; and, for the present, I must hold you as the former—Only, if you have really and honestly been of service to my kinswoman, and if you are candid in your answers to the questions I shall ask, affairs shall stand the better with you."

"The Countess of Croye," said Quentin, "is best judge if I have rendered any service, and to her I refer you on that matter. My answers you will yourself judge of when you ask me your questions."

"Umph!—haughty enough," muttered the Count of Crèvecœur, "and very like one that wears a lady's favour in his hat, and thinks he must carry things with a high tone, to honour the precious remnant of silk and tinsel.—Well, sir, I trust it will be no abatement of your dignity, if you answer me, how long you have been about the person of the Lady Isabelle of Croye?"

"Count of Crèvecœur," said Quentin Durward, "if I answer questions which are asked in a tone approaching towards insult, it is only lest injurious inferences should be drawn from my silence respecting one to whom we are both obliged to render justice. I have acted as escort to the Lady Isabelle since she left France to retire into Flanders."

"Ho! ho!" said the Count; "and that is to say, since she fled from Plessis-les-Tours?—You, an Archer of the Scottish Guard, accompanied her, of course, by the express orders of King Louis?"

However little Quentin thought himself indebted to the King of France, who, in contriving the surprisal of the Countess Isabelle by William de la Marck, had probably calculated on the young Scotchman being slain in her defence, he did not yet conceive himself at liberty to betray any trust which Louis had reposed, or had seemed to repose in him, and therefore replied to Count Crèvecœur's inference, "that it was sufficient for him to have the authority of his superior officer for what he had done, and he inquired no farther."

"It is quite sufficient," said the Count. "We know the King does not permit his officers to send the Archers of his Guard to prance like paladins by the bridle-rein of wandering ladies, unless he hath some politic purpose to serve. It will be difficult for King Louis to continue to aver so boldly, that he knew not of the Ladies of Croye's having escaped from France, since they were escorted by one of his own Life-guard.—And whither, Sir Archer, was your retreat directed?"

"To Liege, my lord," answered the Scot; "where the ladies desired to be placed under the protection of the late Bishop."

"The *late* Bishop!" exclaimed the Count of Crèvecœur; "is Louis of Bourbon dead?—Not a word of his illness had reached the Duke—Of what did he die?"

"He sleeps in a bloody grave, my lord—that is, if his murderers have conferred one on his remains."

"Murdered!" exclaimed Crèvecœur again—"Holy Mother of Heaven! —young man, it is impossible!"

"I saw the deed done with my own eyes, and many an act of horror besides."

"Saw it! and made not in to help the good Prelate!" exclaimed the Count, "or to raise the Castle against his murderers?—Know'st thou not, that even to look on such a deed, without resisting it, is profane sacrilege?"

"To be brief, my lord," said Durward, "ere this act was done, the Castle was stormed by the bloodthirsty William de la Marck, with help of the insurgent Liegeois."

"I am struck with thunder!" said Crèvecœur. "Liege in insurrection! —Schonwaldt taken!—the Bishop murdered!—Messenger of sorrow, never did one man unfold such a packet of woes!—Speak—knew you of this assault—of this insurrection—of this murder?—Speak—thou art one of Louis's trusted Archers, and it is he that has aimed this painful arrow.—Speak, or I will have thee torn with wild horses!"

"And if I *am* so torn, my lord, there can be nothing rent out of me, that may not become a true Scottish gentleman. I know no more of these villainies than you,—was so far from being partaker in them, that I would have withstood them to the uttermost, had my means, in a twentieth degree, equalled my inclination. But what could I do?—they were hundreds, and I but one. My only care was to rescue the Countess Isabelle, and in that I was happily successful. Yet, had I been near enough when the ruffian deed was so cruelly done on the old man, I had saved his grey hairs, or I had avenged them; and as it was, my abhorrence was spoken loud enough to prevent other horrors."

"I believe thee, youth," said the Count; "thou art neither of an age nor nature to be trusted with such bloody work, however well fitted to be the squire of dames. But alas! for the kind and generous Prelate, to be murdered on the hearth where he so often entertained the stranger with Christian charity and princely bounty—and that by a wretch, a monster! a portentous growth of blood and cruelty!—bred up in the very hall where he has imbrued his hands in his benefactor's blood! But I know not Charles of Burgundy—nay, I should doubt of the justice of Heaven, if vengeance be not as sharp, and sudden, and severe, as this villainy has been unexampled in atrocity. And, if no other shall pursue the murderer,"—here he paused, grasped his sword, then quitting his bridle, struck both gauntleted hands upon his breast, until his corslet clattered, and finally held them up to heaven, as he solemnly continued—"I—I, Philip Crèvecœur of Cordès, make a vow to God, Saint Lambert, and the Three Kings of Cologne, that small shall be my thought of other earthly concerns, till I take full revenge on the murderers of the good Louis of Bourbon, whether I find them in forest or field, in city or in country, in hill or plain, in King's court, or in God's church! and thereto I pledge lands and living, friends and followers, life and honour. So help me God and Saint Lambert of Liege, and the Three Kings of Cologne!"

When the Count of Crèvecœur had made his vow, his mind seemed in some sort relieved from the overwhelming grief and astonishment with which he had heard the fatal tragedy that had been acted at Schonwaldt, and he proceeded to question Durward more minutely concerning the particulars of that disastrous affair, which the Scot, nowise desirous to abate the spirit of revenge which the Count entertained against William de la Marck, gave him at full length.

"But those blind, unsteady, faithless, fickle beasts, the Liegeois," said the Count, "that they should have combined themselves with this inexorable robber and murderer, to put to death their lawful Prince!"

Durward here informed the enraged Burgundian that the Liegeois, or at least the better class of them, however rashly they had run into the rebellion against their Bishop, had no design, so far as appeared to him, to aid in the execrable deed of De la Marck; but, on the contrary, would have prevented it if they had had the means, and were struck with horror when they beheld it.

"Speak not of the faithless, inconstant, plebeian rabble!" said Crèvecœur. "When they took arms against a Prince, who had no fault, save that he was too kind and too good a master for such a set of ungrateful slaves—when they armed against him, and broke into his peaceful house, what could there be in their intention but murder?—when they banded themselves with the Wild Boar of Ardennes, the greatest homicide in the marches of Flanders, what else could there be in their purpose *but* murder, which is the very trade he lives by? And again, was it not one of their own vile rabble who did the very deed, by thine own account?—I hope to see their canals running blood by the light of their burning houses. Oh, the kind, noble, generous lord, whom they have slaughtered! —Other vassals have rebelled under the pressure of imposts and penury;

but the men of Liege, in the fulness of insolence and plenty."—He again abandoned the reins of his war-horse, and wrung bitterly the hands, which his mail-gloves rendered untractable. Quentin easily saw that the grief which he manifested was augmented by the bitter recollection of past intercourse and friendship with the sufferer, and was silent accordingly; respecting feelings which he was unwilling to aggravate, and at the same time felt it impossible to soothe.

But the Count of Crèvecœur returned again and again to the subject —questioned him on every particular of the surprise of Schonwaldt, and the death of the Bishop; and then suddenly, as if he had recollected something which had escaped his memory, demanded what had become of the Lady Hameline, and why she was not with her kinswoman? "Not," he added contemptuously, "that I consider her absence as at all a loss to the Countess Isabelle; for, although she was her kinswoman, and upon the whole a well-meaning woman, yet the Court of Cocagne never produced such a fantastic fool; and I hold it for certain, that her niece, whom I have always observed to be a modest and orderly young woman, was led into the absurd frolic of flying from Burgundy to France, by that blundering, romantic, old, match-making and match-seeking idiot!"

What a speech for a romantic lover to hear! and to hear, too, when it would have been ridiculous in him to attempt what it was impossible for him to achieve,—namely, to convince the Count, by force of arms, that he did foul wrong to the Countess—the peerless in sense as in beauty —in terming her a modest and orderly young woman; qualities which might have been predicated with propriety of the daughter of a sunburnt peasant, who lived by goading the oxen, while her father held the plough. And, then, to suppose her under the domination and supreme guidance of a silly and romantic aunt—the slander should have been repelled down the slanderer's throat. But the open, though severe, physiognomy of the Count of Crèvecœur, the total contempt which he seemed to entertain for those feelings which were uppermost in Quentin's bosom, overawed him; not for fear of the Count's fame in arms—that was a risk which would have increased his desire of making out a challenge—but in dread of ridicule, the weapon of all others most feared by enthusiasts of every description, and which, from its predominance over such minds, often checks what is absurd, and fully as often smothers that which is noble.

Under the influence of this fear, of becoming an object of scorn rather than resentment, Durward, though with some pain, confined his reply to a confused account of the Lady Hameline having made her escape from Schonwaldt before the attack took place. He could not, indeed, have made his story very distinct, without throwing ridicule on the near relation of Isabelle, and perhaps incurring some himself, as having been the object of her preposterous expectations. He added to his embarrassed detail, that he had heard a report, though a vague one, of the

Lady Hameline having again fallen into the hands of William de la Marck.

"I trust in Saint Lambert that he will marry her," said Crèvecœur, "as, indeed, he is likely enough to do, for the sake of her money-bags; and equally likely to knock her on the head, so soon as these are either secured in his own grasp, or, at farthest, emptied."

The Count then proceeded to ask so many questions concerning the mode in which both ladies had conducted themselves on the journey, the degree of intimacy to which they admitted Quentin himself, and other trying particulars, that, vexed and ashamed and angry, the youth was scarce able to conceal his embarrassment from the keen-sighted soldier and courtier, who seemed suddenly disposed to take leave of him, saying, at the same time, "Umph—I see it as I conjectured, on one side at least; I trust the other party has kept her senses better.—Come, Sir Squire, spur on, and keep the van, while I fall back to discourse with the Lady Isabelle. I think I have learned now so much from you, that I can talk to her of these sad passages without hurting her nicety, though I have fretted yours a little.—Yet stay, young gallant—one word ere you go. You have had, I imagine, a happy journey through Fairy-land—all full of heroic adventure, and high hope and wild minstrel-like delusion, like the gardens of Morgaine la Fée. Forget it all, young soldier," he added, tapping him on the shoulder; "remember yonder lady only as the honoured Countess of Croye—forget her as a wandering and adventurous damsel: And her friends—one of them I can answer for—will remember, on their part, only the services you have done her, and forget the unreasonable reward which you have had the boldness to propose to yourself."

Enraged that he had been unable to conceal from the sharp-sighted Crèvecœur feelings which the Count seemed to consider as the object of ridicule, Quentin replied indignantly, "My Lord Count, when I require advice of you, I will ask it; when I demand assistance of you, it will be time enough to grant or refuse it; when I set peculiar value on your opinion of me, it will not be too late to express it."

"Heyday!" said the Count; "I have come between Amadis and Oriana, and must expect a challenge to the lists!"

"You speak as if that were an impossibility," said Quentin—"When I broke a lance with the Duke of Orleans, it was against a breast in which flowed better blood than that of Crèvecœur—When I measured swords with Dunois, I engaged a better warrior."

"Now Heaven nourish thy judgment, gentle youth!" said Crèvecœur, still laughing at the chivalrous inamorato. "If thou speak'st truth, thou hast had singular luck in this world; and, truly, if it be the pleasure of Providence exposes thee to such trials, without a beard on thy lip, thou wilt be mad with vanity ere thou writest thyself man. Thou canst not move me to anger, though thou mayest to mirth. Believe me, though thou mayest have fought with Princes, and played the champion for

Countesses, by some of those freaks which Fortune will sometimes exhibit, thou art by no means the equal of those of whom thou hast been either the casual opponent, or more casual companion. I can allow thee, like a youth who hath listened to romances till he fancied himself a Paladin, to form pretty dreams for some time; but thou must not be angry at a well-meaning friend, though he shake thee something roughly by the shoulders to awake thee."

"My Lord of Crèvecœur," said Quentin, "my family——"

"Nay, it is not utterly of family that I spoke," said the Count; "but of rank, fortune, high station, and so forth, which place a distance between various degrees and classes of persons. As for birth, all men are descended from Adam and Eve."

"My Lord Count," repeated Quentin, "my ancestors, the Durwards of Glen-houlakin——"

"Nay," said the Count, "if you claim a farther descent for them than from Adam, I have done! Good-even to you."

He reined back his horse, and paused to join the Countess, to whom, if possible, his insinuations and advices, however well meant, were still more disagreeable than to Quentin, who, as he rode on, muttered to himself, "Cold-blooded, insolent, overweening coxcomb!—Would that the next Scottish Archer who has his harquebuss pointed at thee, may not let thee off so easily as I did!"

In the evening they reached the town of Charleroi, on the Sambre, where the Count of Crèvecœur had determined to leave the Countess Isabelle, whom the terror and fatigue of yesterday, joined to a flight of fifty miles since morning, and the various distressing sensations by which it was accompanied, had made incapable of travelling farther, with safety to her health. The Count consigned her, in a state of great exhaustion, to the care of the Abbess of the Cistercian convent in Charleroi, a noble lady, to whom both the families of Crèvecœur and Croye were related, and in whose prudence and kindness he could repose confidence.

Crèvecœur himself only stopped to recommend the utmost caution to the governor of a small Burgundian garrison who occupied the place, and required him also to mount a guard of honour upon the convent during the residence of the Countess Isabelle of Croye,—ostensibly to secure her safety, but perhaps secretly to prevent her attempting to escape. The Count only assigned as a cause for the garrison being vigilant, some vague rumours which he had heard of disturbances in the Bishopric of Liege. But he was determined himself to be the first who should carry the formidable news of the insurrection and the murder of the Bishop, in all their horrible reality, to Duke Charles; and for that purpose, having procured fresh horses for himself and suite, he mounted with the resolution of continuing his journey to Peronne without stopping for repose; and informing Quentin Durward that he must attend him, he made, at the same time, a mock apology for parting fair company, but hoped, that to so devoted a squire of dames a night's journey by moonshine would be more agreeable, than supinely to yield himself to slumber like an ordinary mortal.

Quentin, already sufficiently afflicted by finding that he was to be parted from Isabelle, longed to answer this taunt with an indignant defiance; but aware that the Count would only laugh at his anger, and despise his challenge, he resolved to wait some future time, when he might have an opportunity of obtaining some amends from this proud lord, who, though for very different reasons, had become nearly as odious to him as the Wild Boar of Ardennes himself. He therefore assented to Crèvecœur's proposal, as to what he had no choice of declining, and they pursued in company, and with all the despatch they could exert, the road between Charleroi and Peronne.

CHAPTER XXV

THE UNBIDDEN GUEST

No human quality is so well wove
In warp and woof, but there's some flaw in it:
I've known a brave man fly a shepherd's cur,
A wise man so demean him, drivelling idiocy
Had well-nigh been ashamed on't. For your crafty,
Your worldly-wise man, he, above the rest,
Weaves his own snares so fine, he's often caught in them.
                                                    Old Play.

QUENTIN, during the earlier part of the night journey, had to combat with that bitter heart-ache, which is felt when youth parts, and probably for ever, with her he loves. As, pressed by the urgency of the moment, and the impatience of Crèvecœur, they hastened on through the rich lowlands of Hainault, under the benign guidance of a rich and lustrous harvest-moon, she shed her yellow influence over rich and deep pastures, woodland, and corn-fields, from which the husbandmen were using her light to withdraw the grain, such was the industry of the Flemings, even at that period; she shone on broad, level, and fructifying rivers, where glided the white sail in the service of commerce, uninterrupted by rock or torrent, beside lively [?] quiet villages, whose external decency and cleanliness expressed the ease and comfort of the inhabitants;—she gleamed upon the feudal castle of many a gallant Baron and Knight, with its deep moat, battlemented court, and high belfry,—for the chivalry of Hainault was renowned among the nobles of Europe;—and her light displayed at a distance, in its broad beam, the gigantic towers of more than one lofty minster.

Yet all this fair variety, however differing from the waste and wilderness of his own land, interrupted not the course of Quentin's regrets and sorrows. He had left his heart behind him, when he departed from Charleroi; and the only reflection which the farther journey inspired was, that every step was carrying him farther from Isabelle. His imagination was taxed to recall every word she had spoken, every look she had directed towards him; and, as happens frequently in such cases, the impression made upon his imagination by the recollection of these particulars, was even stronger than the realities themselves had excited.

At length, after the cold hour of midnight was past, in spite alike of love and of sorrow, the extreme fatigue which Quentin had undergone the two preceding days began to have an effect on him, which his habits of exercise of every kind, and his singular alertness and activity of character, as well as the painful nature of the reflections which occupied his thoughts, had hitherto prevented his experiencing. The ideas of his mind began to be so little corrected by the exertions of his senses, worn-out and deadened as the latter now were by extremity of fatigue, that the visions which the former drew superseded or perverted the information conveyed by the blunted organs of seeing and hearing; and Durward was only sensible that he was awake, by the exertions which, sensible of the peril of his situation, he occasionally made, to resist falling into a deep and dead sleep. Every now and then, a strong consciousness of the risk of falling from or with his horse roused him to exertion and animation; but ere long his eyes again were dimmed by confused shades of all sorts of mingled colours, the moonlight landscape swam before them, and he was so much overcome with fatigue, that the Count of Crèvecœur, observing his condition, was at length compelled to order two of his attendants, one to each rein of Durward's bridle, in order to prevent the risk of his falling from his horse.

When at length they reached the town of Landrecy, the Count, in compassion to the youth, who had now been in a great measure without sleep for three nights, allowed himself and his retinue a halt of four hours, for rest and refreshment.

Deep and sound were Quentin's slumbers, until they were broken by the sound of the Count's trumpet, and the cry of his Fouriers and harbingers, "Débout! débout!—Ha! Messires, en route, en route!"— Yet, unwelcomely early as the tones came, they awaked him a different being in strength and spirits from what he had fallen asleep. Confidence in himself and his fortunes returned with his reviving spirits, and with the rising sun. He thought of his love no longer as a desperate and fantastic dream, but as a high and invigorating principle, to be cherished in his bosom, although he might never propose to himself, under all the difficulties by which he was beset, to bring it to any prosperous issue. —"The pilot," he reflected, "steers his bark by the polar star, although he never expects to become possessor of it; and the thoughts of Isabelle of Croye shall make me a worthy man-at-arms, though I may never see her more. When she hears that a Scottish soldier, named Quentin Durward, distinguished himself in a well-fought field, or left his body on the breach of a disputed fortress, she will remember the companion of her journey, as one who did all in his power to avert the snares and misfortunes which beset it, and perhaps will honour his memory with a tear, his coffin with a garland."

In this manly mood of bearing his misfortune, Quentin felt himself more able to receive and reply to the jests of the Count of Crèvecœur, who passed several on his alleged effeminacy and incapacity of undergoing fatigue. The young Scot accommodated himself so good-humouredly to the Count's raillery, and replied at once so happily and so respectfully, that the change of his tone and manner made obviously a more favourable impression on the Count than he had entertained from his prisoner's conduct during the preceding evening, when, rendered irritable by the feelings of his situation, he was alternately moodily silent or fiercely argumentative.

The veteran soldier began at length to take notice of his young companion, as a pretty fellow, of whom something might be made; and more than hinted to him, that, would he but resign his situation in the Archer Guard of France, he would undertake to have him enrolled in the household of the Duke of Burgundy in an honourable condition, and would himself take care of his advancement. And although Quentin, with suitable expressions of gratitude, declined this favour at present, until he should find out how far he had to complain of his original patron, King Louis, he, nevertheless, continued to remain on good terms with the Count of Crèvecœur; and, while his enthusiastic mode of thinking, and his foreign and idiomatical manner of expressing himself, often excited a smile on the grave cheek of the Count, that smile had lost all that it had of sarcastic and bitter, and did not exceed the limits of good humour and good manners.

Thus travelling on with much more harmony than on the preceding day, the little party came at last within two miles of the famous and strong town of Peronne, near which the Duke of Burgundy's army lay encamped, ready, as was supposed, to invade France; and, in opposition to which, Louis XI. had himself assembled a strong force near Saint Maxence, for the purpose of bringing to reason his over-powerful vassal.

Peronne, situated upon a deep river, in a flat country, and surrounded by strong bulwarks and profound moats, was accounted in ancient, as in modern times, one of the strongest fortresses in France.[1] The Count of Crèvecœur, his retinue, and his prisoner, were approaching the fortress about the third hour after noon; when, riding through the pleasant glades of a large forest, which then covered the approach to the town on the east side, they were met by two men of rank, as appeared from the number of their attendants, dressed in the habits worn in the time of peace; and who, to judge from the falcons which they carried on their wrists, and the number of spaniels and greyhounds led by their followers,

---

[1] Indeed, though lying on an exposed and warlike frontier, it was never taken by an enemy, but preserved the proud name of Peronne la Pucelle, until the Duke of Wellington, a great destroyer of that sort of reputation, took the place in the memorable advance upon Paris in 1815.

were engaged in the amusement of hawking. But on perceiving Crèvecœur, with whose appearance and liveries they were sufficiently intimate,
they quitted the search which they were making for a heron along the
banks of a long canal, and came galloping towards him.

"News, news, Count of Crèvecœur!" they cried both together;—"will
you give news, or take news? or will you barter fairly?"

"I would barter fairly, Messires," said Crèvecœur, after saluting them
courteously, "did I conceive you had any news of importance sufficient
to make an equivalent for mine."

The two sportsmen smiled on each other; and the elder of the two,
a fine baronial figure, with a dark countenance, marked with that sort
of sadness which some physiognomists ascribe to a melancholy temperament, and some, as the Italian statuary augured of the visage of Charles
I., consider as predicting an unhappy death,[1] turning to his companion,
said, "Crèvecœur has been in Brabant, the country of commerce, and
he has learned all its artifices—he will be too hard for us if we drive
a bargain."

"Messires," said Crèvecœur, "the Duke ought in justice to have the
first of my wares, as the Seigneur takes his toll before open market begins.
But tell me, are your news of a sad or a pleasant complexion?"

The person whom he particularly addressed was a lively-looking man,
with an eye of great vivacity, which was corrected by an expression of
reflection and gravity about the mouth and upper lip—the whole physiognomy marking a man who saw and judged rapidly, but was sage and
slow in forming resolutions or in expressing opinions. This was the
famous Knight of Hainault, son of Collart, or Nicolas de l'Elite, known
in history, and amongst historians, by the venerable name of Philip des
Comines, at this time close to the person of Duke Charles the Bold,[2] and
one of his most esteemed counsellors. He answered Crèvecœur's question
concerning the complexion of the news of which he and his companion,
the Baron d'Hymbercourt, were the depositaries.—"They were," he said,
"like the colours of the rainbow, various in hue, as they might be viewed
from different points, and placed against the black cloud or the fair sky
—Such a rainbow was never seen in France or Flanders since that of
Noah's ark."

"My tidings," replied Crèvecœur, "are altogether like the comet;
gloomy, wild, and terrible in themselves, yet to be accounted the fore-
runners of still greater and more dreadful evils which are to ensue."

"We must open our bales," said Comines to his companion, "or our
market will be forestalled by some new-comers, for ours are public news.

---

[1] D'Hymbercourt, or Imbercourt, was put to death by the inhabitants of Ghent
with the Chancellor of Burgundy, in the year 1477. Mary of Burgundy, daughter
of Charles the Bold, appeared in mourning in the marketplace, and with tears
besought the life of her servants from her insurgent subjects, but in vain.

[2] Note VI.—Philip des Comines.

—In one word, Crèvecœur—listen, and wonder—King Louis is at Peronne!"

"What!" said the Count in astonishment; "has the Duke retreated without a battle? and do you remain here in your dress of peace, after the town is besieged by the French?—for I cannot suppose it taken."

"No, surely," said D'Hymbercourt, "the banners of Burgundy have not gone back a foot; and still King Louis is here."

"Then Edward of England must have come over the seas with his bowmen," said Crèvecœur, "and, like his ancestors, gained a second field of Poictiers."

"Not so," said Comines—"Not a French banner has been borne down, not a sail spread from England—where Edward is too much amused among the wives of the citizens of London, to think of playing the Black Prince. Hear the extraordinary truth. You know, when you left us, that the conference between the commissioners on the parts of France and Burgundy was broken up, without apparent chance of reconciliation?"

"True; and we dreamt of nothing but war."

"What has followed has been indeed so like a dream," said Comines, "that I almost expect to awake, and find it so. Only one day since, the Duke had in council protested so furiously against farther delay, that it was resolved to send a defiance to the King, and march forward instantly into France. Toison d'Or, commissioned for the purpose, had put on his official dress, and had his foot in the stirrup to mount his horse, when lo! the French herald Mont-joie rode into our camp. We thought of nothing else than that Louis had been beforehand with our defiance; and began to consider how much the Duke would resent the advice, which had prevented him from being the first to declare war. But a council being speedily assembled, what was our wonder when the herald informed us, that Louis, King of France, was scarce an hour's riding behind, intending to visit Charles, Duke of Burgundy, with a small retinue, in order that their differences might be settled at a personal interview!"

"You surprise me, Messires," said Crèvecœur; "and yet you surprise me less than you might have expected; for, when I was last at Plessis-les-Tours, the all-trusted Cardinal Balue, offended with his master, and Burgundian at heart, did hint to me, that he could so work upon Louis's peculiar foibles, as to lead him to place himself in such a position with regard to Burgundy, that the Duke might have the terms of peace of his own making. But I never suspected that so old a fox as Louis could have been induced to come into the trap of his own accord. What said the Burgundian counsellors?"

"As you may guess," answered D'Hymbercourt; "talked much of faith to be observed, and little of advantage to be obtained, by such a visit; while it was manifest they thought almost entirely of the last, and were only anxious to find some way to reconcile it with the necessary preservation of appearances."

"And what said the Duke?" continued the Count of Crèvecœur.

"Spoke brief and bold, as usual," replied Comines. " 'Which of you was it,' he asked, 'who witnessed the meeting of my cousin Louis and me after the battle of Montl'hery,[1] when I was so thoughtless as to accompany him back within the intrenchments of Paris with half a score of attendants, and so put my person at the King's mercy?' I replied, that most of us had been present; and none could ever forget the alarm which it had been his pleasure to give us. 'Well,' said the Duke, 'you blamed me for my folly, and I confessed to you that I had acted like a giddy-pated boy; and I am aware, too, that my father of happy memory being then alive, my kinsman, Louis, would have had less advantage by seizing on my person than I might now have by securing his. But, nevertheless, if my royal kinsman comes hither on the present occasion, in the same singleness of heart, under which I then acted, he shall be royally welcome. If it is meant by this appearance of confidence, to circumvent and to blind me, till he execute some of his politic schemes, by Saint George of Burgundy, let him look to it!' And so, having turned up his moustaches, and stamped on the ground, he ordered us all to get on our horses, and receive so extraordinary a guest."

"And you met the King accordingly?" replied the Count of Crèvecœur—"Miracles have not ceased!—How was he accompanied?"

"As slightly as might be," answered D'Hymbercourt; "only a score or two of the Scottish Guard, and a few knights and gentlemen of his household—among whom his astrologer, Galeotti, made the gayest figure."

"That fellow," said Crèvecœur, "holds some dependence on the Cardinal Balue—I should not be surprised that he has had his share in determining the King to this step of doubtful policy. Any nobility of higher rank?"

"There are Monsieur of Orleans and Dunois," replied Comines.

"I will have a rouze with Dunois," said Crèvecœur, "wag the world as it will. But we heard that both he and the Duke had fallen into disgrace, and were in prison?"

"They were both under arrest in the Castle of Loches, that delightful place of retirement for the French nobility," said D'Hymbercourt; "but Louis has released them, in order to bring them with him—perhaps because he cared not to leave Orleans behind. For his other attendants, faith, I think his gossip, the Hangman Marshal, with two or three of his retinue, and Oliver, his barber, may be the most considerable—and the whole bevy so poorly arrayed, that, by my honour, the King resembles most an old usurer going to collect desperate debts, attended by a body of catchpolls."

"And where is he lodged?" said Crèvecœur.

"Nay, that," replied Comines, "is the most marvellous of all. Our Duke offered to let the King's Archer Guard have a gate of the town, and a bridge of boats over the Somme, and to have assigned to Louis

---

[1] Note VII.—Meeting of Louis and Charles after the battle of Montl'hery.

himself the adjoining house, belonging to a wealthy burgess, Giles Orthen; but, in going thither, the King espied the banners of De Lau and Pencil de Rivière, whom he had banished from France; and scared, at it would seem, with the thought of lodging so near refugees and malcontents of his own making, he craved to be quartered in the Castle of Peronne, and *there* he hath his abode accordingly."

"Why, God ha' mercy!" exclaimed Crèvecœur, "this is not only venturing into the lion's den, but thrusting his head into his very jaws—Nothing less than the very bottom of the rat-trap would serve the crafty old politician!"

"Nay," said Comines, "D'Hymbercourt hath not told you the speech of Le Glorieux [1]—which, in my mind, was the shrewdest opinion that was given."

"And what said *his* most illustrious wisdom?" asked the Count.

"As the Duke," replied Comines, "was hastily ordering some vessels and ornaments of plate, and the like, to be prepared as presents for the King and his retinue, by way of welcome on his arrival, 'Trouble not thy small brain about it, my friend Charles,' said Le Glorieux, 'I will give thy cousin Louis a nobler and a fitter gift than thou canst; and that is my cap and bells, and my bauble to boot; for, by the mass, he is a greater fool than I am, for putting himself in thy power.'—'But if I give him no reason to repent it, sirrah, how then?' said the Duke. 'Then, truly, Charles, thou shalt have cap and bauble thyself, as the greatest fool of the three of us.' I promise you this knavish quip touched the Duke closely—I saw him change colour and bite his lip.—And now, our news are told, noble Crèvecœur, and what think you they resemble?"

"A mine full-charged with gunpowder," answered Crèvecœur, "to which, I fear, it is my fate to bring the kindled linstock. Your news and mine are like flax and fire, which cannot meet without bursting into flame, or like certain chemical substances which cannot be mingled without an explosion. Friends,—gentlemen,—ride close by my rein; and when I tell you what has chanced in the bishopric of Liege, I think you will be of opinion, that King Louis might as safely have undertaken a pilgrimage to the infernal regions, as this ill-timed visit to Peronne."

The two nobles drew up close on either hand of the Count, and listened, with half-suppressed exclamations, and gestures of the deepest wonder and interest, to his account of the transactions at Liege and Schonwaldt. Quentin was then called forward, and examined and re-examined on the particulars of the Bishop's death, until at length he refused to answer any farther interrogatories, not knowing wherefore they were asked, or what use might be made of his replies.

They now reached the rich and level banks of the Somme, and the ancient walls of the little town of Peronne la Pucelle, and the deep green meadows adjoining, now whitened with the numerous tents of the Duke of Burgundy's army, amounting to about fifteen thousand men.

[1] The jester of Charles of Burgundy, of whom more hereafter.

CHAPTER XXVI

THE INTERVIEW

When Princes meet, Astrologers may mark it
An ominous conjunction, full of boding,
Like that of Mars with Saturn.

Old Play.

ONE hardly knows whether to term it a privilege or a penalty annexed to the quality of princes, that, in their intercourse with each other, they are required, by the respect which is due to their own rank and dignity, to regulate their feelings and expressions by a severe etiquette, which precludes all violent and avowed display of passion, and which, but that the whole world are aware that this assumed complaisance is a matter of ceremony, might justly pass for profound dissimulation. It is no less certain, however, that the overstepping of these bounds of ceremonial, for the purpose of giving more direct vent to their angry passions, has the effect of compromising their dignity with the world in general; as was particularly noted when those distinguished rivals, Francis the First, and the Emperor Charles, gave each other the lie direct, and were desirous of deciding their differences hand to hand, in single combat.

Charles of Burgundy, the most hasty and impatient, nay, the most imprudent prince of his time, found himself, nevertheless, fettered within the magic circle which prescribed the most profound deference to Louis, as his Suzerain and liege Lord, who had deigned to confer upon him, a vassal of the crown, the distinguished honour of a personal visit. Dressed in his ducal mantle, and attended by his great officers, and principal knights and nobles, he went in gallant cavalcade, to receive Louis XI. His retinue absolutely blazed with gold and silver; for the wealth of the Court of England being exhausted by the wars of York and Lancaster, and the expenditure of France limited by the economy of the Sovereign, that of Burgundy was for the time the most magnificent in Europe. The *cortège* of Louis, on the contrary, was few in number, and comparatively mean in appearance, and the exterior of the King himself, in a threadbare cloak, with his wonted old high-crowned hat stuck full of images, rendered the contrast yet more striking; and as the Duke, richly attired with the coronet and mantle of state, threw himself from his noble charger, and, kneeling on one knee, offered to hold the stirrup while Louis dismounted from his little ambling palfrey, the effect was almost grotesque.

The greeting between the two potentates was, of course, as full of affected kindness and compliment, as it was totally devoid of sincerity. But the temper of the Duke rendered it much more difficult for him to preserve the necessary appearances, in voice, speech, and demeanour; while in the King, every species of simulation and dissimulation seemed so much a part of his nature, that those best acquainted with him could not have distinguished what was feigned from what was real.

Perhaps the most accurate illustration, were it not unworthy two such high potentates, would be, to suppose the King in the situation of a stranger, perfectly acquainted with the habits and dispositions of the canine race, who, for some purpose of his own, is desirous to make friends with a large and surly mastiff, that holds him in suspicion, and is disposed to worry him on the first symptoms either of diffidence or of umbrage. The mastiff growls internally, erects his bristles, shows his teeth, yet is ashamed to fly upon the intruder, who seems at the same time so kind and so confiding, and therefore the animal endures advances which are far from pacifying him, watching at the same time the slightest opportunity which may justify him in his own eyes for seizing his friend by the throat.

The King was no doubt sensible, from the altered voice, constrained manner, and abrupt gestures of the Duke, that the game he had to play was delicate, and perhaps he more than once repented having ever taken it in hand. But repentance was too late, and all that remained for him was that inimitable dexterity of management, which the King understood equally at least with any man that ever lived.

The demeanour which Louis used towards the Duke, was such as to resemble the kind overflowing of the heart in a moment of sincere reconciliation with an honoured and trusty friend, from whom he had been estranged by temporary circumstances now passed away, and forgotten as soon as removed. The King blamed himself for not having sooner taken the decisive step, of convincing his kind and good kinsman by such a mark of confidence as he was now bestowing, that the angry passages which had occurred betwixt them were nothing in his remembrance, when weighed against the kindness which received him when an exile from France, and under the displeasure of the King his father. He spoke of the good Duke of Burgundy, as Philip the father of Duke Charles was currently called, and remembered a thousand instances of his paternal kindness.

"I think, cousin," he said, "your father made little difference in his affection, betwixt you and me; for I remember, when by an accident I had bewildered myself in a hunting-party, I found the good Duke upbraiding you with leaving me in the forest, as if you had been careless of the safety of an elder brother."

The Duke of Burgundy's features were naturally harsh and severe; and when he attempted to smile, in polite acquiescence to the truth of what the King told him, the grimace which he made was truly diabolical.

"Prince of dissemblers," he said, in his secret soul, "would that it stood with my honour to remind you *how* you have requited all the benefits of our House!"

"And then," continued the King, "if the ties of consanguinity and gratitude are not sufficient to bind us together, my fair cousin, we have those of spiritual relationship; for I am godfather of your fair daughter

Mary, who is as dear to me as one of my own maidens; and when the Saints (their holy name be blessed!) sent me a little blossom which withered in the course of three months, it was your princely father who held it at the font, and celebrated the ceremony of baptism, with richer and prouder magnificence than Paris itself could have afforded. Never shall I forget the deep, the indelible impression, which the generosity of Duke Philip, and yours, my dearest cousin, made upon the half-broken heart of the poor exile!"

"Your Majesty," said the Duke, compelling himself to make some reply, "acknowledged that slight obligation in terms which overpaid all the display which Burgundy could make, to show due sense of the honour you had done its Sovereign."

"I remember the words you mean, fair cousin," said the King, smiling; "I think they were, that in guerdon of the benefit of that day, I, poor wanderer, had nothing to offer, save the persons of myself, of my wife, and of my child.—Well, and I think I have indifferently well redeemed my pledge."

"I mean not to dispute what your Majesty is pleased to aver," said the Duke; "but——"

"But you ask," said the King, interrupting him, "how my actions have accorded with my words—Marry thus: the body of my infant child Joachim rests in Burgundian earth—my own person I have this morning placed unreservedly in your power—and, for that of my wife.—truly, cousin, I think, considering the period of time which has passed, you will scarce insist on my keeping my word in that particular. She was born on the day of the Blessed Annunciation" (he crossed himself, and muttered an *Ora pro nobis*), "some fifty years since; but she is no farther distant than Rheims, and if you insist on my promise being fulfilled to the letter, she shall presently wait your pleasure."

Angry as the Duke of Burgundy was at the barefaced attempt of the King to assume towards him a tone of friendship and intimacy, he could not help laughing at the whimsical reply of that singular monarch, and his laugh was as discordant as the abrupt tones of passion in which he often spoke. Having laughed longer and louder than was at that period, or would now be, thought fitting the time and occasion, he answered in the same tone, bluntly declining the honour of the Queen's company, but stating his willingness to accept that of the King's eldest daughter, whose beauty was celebrated.

"I am happy, fair cousin," said the King, with one of those dubious smiles of which he frequently made use, "that your gracious pleasure has not fixed on my younger daughter Joan. I should otherwise have had spear-breaking between you and my cousin of Orleans; and, had harm come of it, I must on either side have lost a kind friend and affectionate cousin."

"Nay, nay, my royal sovereign," said Duke Charles, "the Duke of Orleans shall have no interruption from me in the path which he has chosen *par amours*. The cause in which I couch my lance against Orleans, must be fair and straight."

Louis was far from taking amiss this brutal allusion to the personal deformity of the Princess Joan. On the contrary, he was rather pleased to find, that the Duke was content to be amused with broad jests, in which he was himself a proficient, and which (according to the modern phrase) spared much sentimental hypocrisy. Accordingly, he speedily placed their intercourse on such a footing, that Charles, though he felt it impossible to play the part of an affectionate and reconciled friend to a monarch whose ill offices he had so often encountered, and whose sincerity on the present occasion he so strongly doubted, yet had no difficulty in acting the hearty landlord towards a facetious guest; and so the want of reciprocity in kinder feelings between them was supplied by the tone of good fellowship which exists between two boon companions,—a tone natural to the Duke from the frankness, and, it might be added, the grossness of his character, and to Louis, because, though capable of assuming any mood of social intercourse, that which really suited him best was mingled with grossness of ideas, and caustic humour in expression.

Both Princes were happily able to preserve, during the period of a banquet at the town-house of Peronne, the same kind of conversation, on which they met as on a neutral ground, and which, as Louis easily perceived, was more available than any other to keep the Duke of Burgundy in that state of composure which seemed necessary to his own safety.

Yet he was alarmed to observe, that the Duke had around him several of those French nobles, and those of the highest rank, and in situations of great trust and power, whom his own severity or injustice had driven into exile; and it was to secure himself from the possible effects of their resentment and revenge, that (as already mentioned) he requested to be lodged in the Castle or Citadel of Peronne, rather than in the town itself.[1] This was readily granted by Duke Charles, with one of those grim smiles, of which it was impossible to say, whether it meant good or harm to the party whom it concerned.

But when the King, expressing himself with as much delicacy as he could, and in the manner he thought best qualified to lull suspicion asleep, asked, whether the Scottish Archers of his Guard might not maintain the custody of the Castle of Peronne during his residence there, in lieu

[1] The arrival of three brothers, Princes of the House of Savoy, of Monseigneur de Lau, whom the King had long detained in prison, of Sire Poncet de Rivière, and the Seigneur de Urfé,—who, by the way, as a romance writer of a peculiar turn, might have been happily enough introduced into the present work, but the fate of the Euphuist was a warning to the author—all of these nobles bearing the emblem of Burgundy, the cross, namely, of Saint Andrew, inspired Louis with so much suspicion, that he very impolitically demanded to be lodged in the old Castle of Peronne, and thus rendered himself an absolute captive.—See COMINES' *Memoirs for the year* 1468.

of the gate of the town which the Duke had offered to their care, Charles replied, with his wonted sternness of voice, and abruptness of manner, rendered more alarming by his habit, when he spoke, of either turning up his moustaches or handling his sword or dagger, the last of which he used frequently to draw a little way, and then return to the sheath,[1]— "Saint Martin! No, my liege. You are in your vassal's camp and city—so men call me in respect to your Majesty—my castle and town are yours, and my men are yours; so it is indifferent whether my men-at-arms or the Scottish Archers guard either the outer gate or defences of the Castle.— No, by Saint George! Peronne is a virgin fortress—she shall not lose her reputation by any neglect of mine. Maidens must be carefully watched, my royal cousin, if we would have them continue to live in good fame."

"Surely, fair cousin, and I altogether agree with you," said the King, "I being in fact more interested in the reputation of the good little town than you are—Peronne being, as you know, fair cousin, one of those upon the same river Somme, which, pledged to your father of happy memory for redemption of money, are liable to be redeemed upon repayment. And, to speak truth, coming, like an honest debtor, disposed to clear off my obligations of every kind, I have brought here a few sumpter mules loaded with silver for the redemption—enough to maintain even your princely and royal establishment, fair cousin, for the space of three years."

"I will not receive a penny of it," said the Duke, twirling his moustaches; "the day of redemption is past, my royal cousin; nor was there ever serious purpose that the right should be exercised, the cession of these towns being the sole recompense my father ever received from France, when, in a happy hour for your family, he consented to forget the murder of my grandfather, and to exchange the alliance of England for that of your father. Saint George! if he had not so acted, your royal self, far from having towns on the Somme, could scarce have kept those beyond the Loire. No—I will not render a stone of them, were I to receive for every stone so rendered its weight in gold. I thank God, and the wisdom and valour of my ancestors, that the revenues of Burgundy, though it be but a duchy, will maintain my state, even when a King is my guest, without obliging me to barter my heritage."

"Well, fair cousin," answered the King, with the same mild and placid manner as before, and unperturbed by the loud tone and violent gestures of the Duke, "I see that you are so good a friend to France, that you are unwilling to part with aught that belongs to her. But we shall need some moderator in these affairs when we come to treat of them in council —What say you to Saint Paul?"

"Neither Saint Paul, nor Saint Peter, nor e'er a Saint in the Calendar,"

[1] This gesture, very indicative of a fierce character, is also by stage-tradition a distinction of Shakespeare's Richard III.

said the Duke of Burgundy, "shall preach me out of the possession of Peronne."

"Nay, but you mistake me," said King Louis, smiling; "I mean Louis de Luxembourg, our trusty Constable, the Count of Saint Paul.—Ah! Saint Mary of Embrun! we lack but his head at our conference! the best head in France, and the most useful to the restoration of perfect harmony betwixt us."

"By Saint George of Burgundy!" said the Duke, "I marvel to hear your Majesty talk thus of a man, false and perjured both to France and Burgundy—one, who hath ever endeavoured to fan into a flame our frequent differences, and that with the purpose of giving himself the airs of a mediator. I swear by the Order I wear, that his marshes shall not be long a resource for him!"

"Be not so warm, cousin," replied the King, smiling, and speaking under his breath; "when I wished for the Constable's *head*, as a means of ending the settlement of our trifling differences, I had no desire for his *body*, which might remain at Saint Quentin's with much convenience."

"Ho! ho! I take your meaning, my royal cousin," said Charles, with the same dissonant laugh which some other of the King's coarse pleasantries had extorted, and added, stamping with his heel on the ground, "I allow, in that sense, the head of the Constable *might* be useful at Peronne."

These, and other discourses, by which the King mixed hints at serious affairs amid matters of mirth and amusement, did not follow each other consecutively; but were adroitly introduced during the time of the banquet at the Hôtel de Ville, during a subsequent interview in the Duke's own apartments, and, in short, as occasion seemed to render the introduction of such delicate subjects easy and natural.

Indeed, however rashly Louis had placed himself in a risk, which the Duke's fiery temper, and the mutual subjects of exasperated enmity which subsisted between them, rendered of doubtful and perilous issue, never pilot on an unknown coast conducted himself with more firmness and prudence. He seemed to sound, with the utmost address and precision, the depths and shallows of his rival's mind and temper, and manifested neither doubt nor fear, when the result of his experiments discovered much more of sunken rocks, and of dangerous shoals, than of safe anchorage.

At length a day closed, which must have been a wearisome one to Louis, from the constant exertion, vigilance, precaution, and attention, which his situation required, as it was a day of constraint to the Duke, from the necessity of suppressing the violent feelings to which he was in the general habit of giving uncontrolled vent.

No sooner had the latter retired into his own apartment, after he had taken a formal leave of the King for the night, than he gave way to the explosion of passion which he had so long suppressed; and many an oath and abusive epithet, as his jester, Le Glorieux, said, "fell that night upon heads which they were never coined for,"—his domestics reaping the benefit of that hoard of injurious language, which he could not in decency bestow on his royal guest, even in his absence, and which was yet become too great to be altogether suppressed. The jests of the clown had some effect in tranquillising the Duke's angry mood;—he laughed loudly, threw the jester a piece of gold, caused himself to be disrobed in tranquillity, swallowed a deep cup of wine and spices, went to bed, and slept soundly.

The _couchée_ of King Louis is more worthy of notice than that of Charles; for the violent expression of exasperated and headlong passion, as indeed it belongs more to the brutal than the intelligent part of our nature, has little to interest us, in comparison to the deep workings of a vigorous and powerful mind.

Louis was escorted to the lodgings he had chosen in the Castle, or Citadel of Peronne, by the chamberlains and harbingers of the Duke of Burgundy, and received at the entrance by a strong guard of archers and men-at-arms.

As he descended from his horse to cross the drawbridge, over a moat of unusual width and depth, he looked on the sentinels, and observed to Comines, who accompanied him, with other Burgundian nobles, "They wear Saint Andrew's crosses—but not those of my Scottish Archers."

"You will find them as ready to die in your defence, Sire," said the Burgundian, whose sagacious ear had detected in the King's tone of speech a feeling, which doubtless Louis would have concealed if he could. "They wear the Saint Andrew's Cross as the appendage of the collar of the Golden Fleece, my master the Duke of Burgundy's Order."

"Do I not know it?" said Louis, showing the collar which he himself wore in compliment to his host; "It is one of the dear bonds of fraternity which exist between my kind brother and myself. We are brothers in chivalry, as in spiritual relationship; cousins by birth, and friends by every tie of kind feeling and good neighbourhood.—No farther than the base-court, my noble lords and gentlemen! I can permit your attendance no farther—you have done me enough of grace."

"We were charged by the Duke," said D'Hymbercourt, "to bring your Majesty to your lodging.—We trust your Majesty will permit us to obey our master's command."

"In this small matter," said the King, "I trust you will allow my command to outweigh his, even with you his liege subjects.—I am something indisposed,—my lords, something fatigued. Great pleasure hath its toils, as well as great pain. I trust to enjoy your society better to-morrow.— And yours too, Seignior Philip of Comines—I am told you are the annalist of the time—we that desire to have a name in history, must speak you fair, for men say your pen hath a sharp point, when you will.—Good-night, my lords and gentles, to all and each of you."

The Lords of Burgundy retired much pleased with the grace of Louis's manner, and the artful distribution of his attentions; and the King was left with only one or two of his own personal followers, under the arch-way of the base-court of the Castle of Peronne, looking on the huge tower which occupied one of the angles, being in fact the Donjon, or principal Keep, of the place. This tall, dark, massive building, was seen clearly by the same moon which was lighting Quentin Durward betwixt Charle-roi and Peronne, which, as the reader is aware, shone with peculiar lustre. The great Keep was in form nearly resembling the White Tower in the Citadel of London, but still more ancient in its architecture, deriving its date, as was affirmed, from the days of Charlemagne. The walls were of a tremendous thickness, the windows very small, and grated with bars of iron, and the huge clumsy bulk of the building cast a dark and portentous shadow over the whole of the courtyard.

"I am not to be lodged *there!*" the King said, with a shudder, that had something in it ominous.

"No," replied the grey-headed seneschal, who attended upon him un-bonneted.—"God forbid!—Your Majesty's apartments are prepared in these lower buildings which are hard by, and in which King John slept two nights before the battle of Poictiers."

"Hum—that is no lucky omen neither"—muttered the King; "but what of the Tower, my old friend? and why should you desire of Heaven that I may not be there lodged?"

"Nay, my gracious liege," said the seneschal, "I know no evil of the Tower at all—only that the sentinels say lights are seen, and strange noises heard in it, at night; and there are reasons why that may be the case, for anciently it was used as a state prison, and there are many tales of deeds which have been done in it."

Louis asked no farther questions; for no man was more bound than he to respect the secrets of a prison-house. At the door of the apartments destined for his use, which, though of later date than the Tower, were still both ancient and gloomy, stood a small party of the Scottish Guard, which the Duke, although he declined to concede the point to Louis, had ordered to be introduced, so as to be near the person of their master. The faithful Lord Crawford was at their head.

"Crawford—my honest and faithful Crawford," said the King, "where hast thou been to-day?—Are the Lords of Burgundy so inhospitable as to neglect one of the bravest and most noble gentlemen that ever trode a court?—I saw you not at the banquet."

"I declined it, my liege," said Crawford—"times are changed with me. The day has been that I could have ventured a carouse with the best man in Burgundy, and that in the juice of his own grape; but a matter of four pints now flusters me, and I think it concerns your Majesty's service to set in this an example to my callants."

"Thou art ever prudent," said the King; "but surely your toil is less when you have so few men to command?—and a time of festivity requires not so severe self-denial on your part as a time of danger."

"If I have few men to command," said Crawford, "I have the more need to keep the knaves in fitting condition; and whether this business be like to end in feasting or fighting, God and your Majesty know better than old John of Crawford."

"You surely do not apprehend any danger?" said the King hastily, yet in a whisper.

"Not I," answered Crawford; "I wish I did; for, as old Earl Tine-man [1] used to say, apprehended dangers may be always defended dangers. —The word for the night, if your Majesty pleases?"

"Let it be Burgundy, in honour of our host and of a liquor that you love, Crawford."

"I will quarrel with neither Duke nor drink, so called," said Crawford, "provided always that both be sound. A good night to your Majesty!"

"A good night, my trusty Scot," said the King, and passed on to his apartments.

At the door of his bedroom Le Balafré was placed sentinel. "Follow me hither," said the King, as he passed him; and the Archer accordingly, like a piece of machinery put in motion by an artist, strode after him into the apartment, and remained there fixed, silent, and motionless, attending the royal command.

"Have you heard from that wandering Paladin, your nephew?" said the King; "for he hath been lost to us, since, like a young knight who had set out upon his first adventures, he sent us home two prisoners, as the first fruits of his chivalry."

"My lord, I heard something of that," said Balafré; "and I hope your Majesty will believe, that if he hath acted wrongfully, it was in no shape by my precept or example, since I never was so bold as to unhorse any of your Majesty's most illustrious house, better knowing my own condition, and——"

"Be silent on that point," said the King; "your nephew did his duty in the matter."

"There indeed," continued Balafré, "he had the cue from me.— 'Quentin,' said I to him, 'whatever comes of it, remember you belong to the Scottish Archer-Guard, and do your duty whatever comes on't.'"

"I guessed he had some such exquisite instructor," said Louis; "but it concerns me that you answer my first question—Have you heard of your nephew of late?—Stand aback, my masters," he added, addressing the gentlemen of his chamber, "for this concerneth no ears but mine."

"Surely, please your Majesty," said Balafré, "I have seen this very evening the groom Charlot, whom my kinsman despatched from Liege, or some castle of the Bishop's which is near it, and where he hath lodged the Ladies of Croye in safety."

"Now our Lady of Heaven be praised for it!" said the King. "Art thou sure of it?—sure of the good news?"

"As sure as I can be of aught," said Le Balafré; "the fellow, I think, hath letters for your Majesty from the Ladies of Croye."

[1] An Earl of Douglas, so called.

"Haste to get them," said the King—"Give thy harquebuss to one of these knaves—to Oliver—to any one.—Now our Lady of Embrun be praised; and silver shall be the screen that surrounds her high altar!"

Louis, in this fit of gratitude and devotion, doffed, as usual, his hat, selected from the figures with which it was garnished that which represented his favourite image of the Virgin, placed it on a table, and, kneeling down, repeated reverently the vow he had made.

The groom, being the first messenger whom Durward had despatched from Schonwaldt, was now introduced with his letters. They were addressed to the King by the Ladies of Croye, and barely thanked him in very cold terms for his courtesy while at his court, and, something more warmly, for having permitted them to retire, and sent them in safety from his dominions; expressions at which Louis laughed very heartily, instead of resenting them. He then demanded of Charlot, with obvious interest, whether they had not sustained some alarm or attack upon the road? Charlot, a stupid fellow, and selected for that quality, gave a very confused account of the affray in which his companion, the Gascon, had been killed, but knew of no other. Again Louis demanded of him, minutely and particularly, the route which the party had taken to Liege; and seemed much interested when he was informed, in reply, that they had, upon approaching Namur, kept the more direct road to Liege, upon the right bank of the Maes, instead of the left bank, as recommended in their route. The King then ordered the man a small present, and dismissed him, disguising the anxiety he had expressed, as if it only concerned the safety of the Ladies of Croye.

Yet the news, though they inferred the failure of one of his own favourite plans, seemed to imply more internal satisfaction on the King's part than he would have probably indicated in a case of brilliant success. He sighed like one whose breast has been relieved from a heavy burden, muttered his devotional acknowledgments with an air of deep sanctity, raised up his eyes, and hastened to adjust newer and surer schemes of ambition.

With such purpose, Louis ordered the attendance of his astrologer, Martius Galeotti, who appeared with his usual air of assumed dignity, yet not without a shade of uncertainty on his brow, as if he had doubted the King's kind reception. It was, however, favourable, even beyond the warmest which he had ever met with at any former interview. Louis termed him his friend, his father in the sciences—the glass by which a king should look into distant futurity—and concluded by thrusting on his finger a ring of very considerable value. Galeotti, not aware of the circumstances which had thus suddenly raised his character in the estimation of Louis, yet understood his own profession too well to let that ignorance be seen. He received with grave modesty the praises of Louis, which he contended were only due to the nobleness of the science which he practised, a science the rather more deserving of admiration on account of its working miracles through means of so feeble an agent as himself; and he and the King took leave, for once much satisfied with each other.

On the Astrologer's departure, Louis threw himself into a chair, and appearing much exhausted, dismissed the rest of his attendants, excepting Oliver alone, who, creeping around with gentle assiduity and noiseless step, assisted him in the task of preparing for repose.

While he received this assistance, the King, unlike to his wont, was so silent and passive, that his attendant was struck by the unusual change in his deportment. The worst minds have often something of good principle in them—banditti show fidelity to their captain, and sometimes a protected and promoted favourite has felt a gleam of sincere interest in the monarch to whom he owed his greatness. Oliver le Diable, le Mauvais (or by whatever other name he was called expressive of his evil propensities), was, nevertheless, scarcely so completely identified with Satan as not to feel some touch of grateful feeling for his master in this singular condition, when, as it seemed, his fate was deeply interested, and his strength seemed to be exhausted. After for a short time rendering to the King in silence the usual services paid by a servant to his master at the toilet, the attendant was at length tempted to say, with the freedom which his Sovereign's indulgence had permitted him in such circumstances, "*Tête-dieu*, Sire, you seem as if you had lost a battle; and yet I, who was near your Majesty during this whole day, never knew you fight a field so gallantly."

"A field!" said King Louis, looking up, and assuming his wonted causticity of tone and manner; "*Pasques-dieu*, my friend Oliver, say I have kept the arena in a bull-fight; for a blinder, and more stubborn, untameable, uncontrollable brute, than our cousin of Burgundy, never existed, save in the shape of a Murcian bull, trained for the bull-feasts.— Well, let it pass—I dodged him bravely. But, Oliver, rejoice with me that my plans in Flanders have not taken effect, whether as concerning those two rambling Princesses of Croye, or in Liege—you understand me?"

"In faith, I do not, Sire," replied Oliver; "it is impossible for me to congratulate your Majesty on the failure of your favourite schemes, unless you tell me some reason for the change in your own wishes and views."

"Nay," answered the King, "there is no change in either, in a general view. But, *Pasques-dieu*, my friend, I have this day learned more of Duke Charles than I before knew. When he was Count de Charalois, in the time of the old Duke Philip and the banished Dauphin of France, we drank, and hunted, and rambled together—and many a wild adventure we have had. And in those days I had a decided advantage over him— like that which a strong spirit naturally assumes over a weak one. But he has since changed—has become a dogged, daring, assuming, disputatious dogmatist, who nourishes an obvious wish to drive matters to extremities, while he thinks he has the game in his own hands. I was compelled to glide as gently away from each offensive topic, as if I touched red-hot iron. I did but hint at the possibility of those erratic Countesses of Croye ere they attained Liege (for thither I frankly confessed that, to the best of my belief, they were gone), falling into the hands of some wild snapper upon the frontiers, and, *Pasques-dieu!* you would have thought I had spoken of sacrilege. It is needless to tell you what he said, and quite enough to say, that I would have held my head's safety very insecure, if, in that moment, accounts had been brought of the success of thy friend, William with the Beard, in his and thy honest scheme of bettering himself by marriage."

"No friend of *mine,* if it please your Majesty," said Oliver—"neither friend nor plan of mine."

"True, Oliver," answered the King; "thy plan had not been to wed, but to shave such a bridegroom. Well, thou didst wish her as bad a one, when thou didst modestly hint at thyself. However, Oliver, lucky the man who has her not; for hang, draw, and quarter, were the most gentle words which my gentle cousin spoke of him who should wed the young Countess, his vassal, without his most ducal permission."

"And he is, doubtless, as jealous of any disturbances in the good town of Liege?" asked the favourite.

"As much, or much more so," replied the King, "as your understanding may easily anticipate; but, ever since I resolved on coming hither, my messengers have been in Liege, to repress, for the present, every movement to insurrection; and my very busy and bustling friends, Rouslaer and Pavillon, have orders to be quiet as a mouse until this happy meeting between my cousin and me is over."

"Judging, then, from your Majesty's account," said Oliver dryly, "the utmost to be hoped from this meeting is, that it should not make your condition worse?—Surely this is like the crane that thrust her head into the fox's mouth, and was glad to thank her good fortune that it was not bitten off. Yet your Majesty seemed deeply obliged even now to the sage philosopher who encouraged you to play so hopeful a game."

"No game," said the King sharply, "is to be despaired of until it is lost, and that I have no reason to expect it will be in my own case. On the contrary, if nothing occurs to stir the rage of this vindictive madman, I am sure of victory; and surely, I am not a little obliged to the skill which selected for my agent, as the conductor of the Ladies of Croye, a youth whose horoscope so far corresponded with mine, that he hath saved me from danger, even by the disobedience of my own commands, and taking the route which avoided De la Marck's ambuscade."

"Your Majesty," said Oliver, "may find many agents who will serve you on the terms of acting rather after their own pleasure than your instructions."

"Nay, nay, Oliver," said Louis impatiently, "the heathen poet speaks of *Vota diis exaudita malignis,*—wishes, that is, which the saints grant to us in their wrath; and such, in the circumstances, would have been the success of William de la Marck's exploit, had it taken place about this time, and while I am in the power of this Duke of Burgundy.—And this my own art foresaw—fortified by that of Galeotti; that is, I foresaw not the miscarriage of De la Marck's undertaking, but I foresaw that the expedition of yonder Scottish Archer should end happily for me—and such has been the issue, though in a manner different from what I expected; for the stars, though they foretell general results, are yet silent on the means by which such are accomplished, being often the very reverse of what we expect, or even desire.—But why talk I of these mysteries to thee, Oliver, who art in so far worse than the very devil, who is thy namesake, since he believes and trembles; whereas thou art an infidel both to religion and to science, and wilt remain so till thine own destiny is accomplished, which, as thy horoscope and physiognomy alike assure me, will be by the intervention of the gallows!"

"And if it indeed shall be so," said Oliver, in a resigned tone of voice, "it will be so ordered, because I was too grateful a servant to hesitate at executing the commands of my royal master."

Louis burst into his usual sardonic laugh.—"Thou hast broke thy lance on me fairly, Oliver; and, by Our Lady, thou art right, for I defied thee to it. But, prithee, tell me in sadness, dost thou discover anything in these men's measures towards us, which may argue any suspicion of ill-usage?"

"My liege," replied Oliver, "your Majesty, and yonder learned philosopher, look for augury to the stars and heavenly host—I am an earthly reptile, and consider but the things connected with my vocation. But, methinks, there is a lack of that earnest and precise attention on your Majesty, which men show to a welcome guest of a degree so far above them. The Duke, to-night, pleaded weariness, and saw your Majesty not farther than to the street, leaving to the officers of his household the task of conveying you to your lodgings. The rooms here are hastily and carelessly fitted up—the tapestry is hung up awry—and, in one of the pieces, as you may observe, the figures are reversed, and stand on their heads, while the trees grow with their roots uppermost."

"Pshaw! accident, and the effect of hurry," said the King. "When did you ever know me concerned about such trifles as these?"

"Not on their own account are they worth notice," said Oliver; "but as intimating the degree of esteem in which the officers of the Duke's household observe your Grace to be held by him. Believe me, that had his desire seemed sincere that your reception should be in all points marked by scrupulous attention, the zeal of his people would have made minutes do the work of days—And when," he added, pointing to the basin and ewer, "was the furniture of your Majesty's toilet of other substance than silver?"

"Nay," said the King, with a constrained smile, "that last remark upon the shaving utensils, Oliver, is too much in the style of thine own peculiar occupation to be combated by any one.—True it is, that when

I was only a refugee, and an exile, I was served upon gold-plate by order of the same Charles, who accounted silver too mean for the Dauphin, though he seems to hold that metal too rich for the King of France. Well, Oliver, we will to bed—Our resolution has been made and executed; there is nothing to be done but to play manfully the game on which we have entered. I know that my cousin of Burgundy, like other wild bulls, shuts his eyes when he begins his career. I have but to watch that moment, like one of the tauridors whom we saw at Burgos, and his impetuosity places him at my mercy."

CHAPTER XXVII

THE EXPLOSION

'Tis listening fear, and dumb amazement all,
When to the startled eye, the sudden glance
Appears far south, eruptive through the cloud.
                    THOMSON's *Summer*.

THE preceding chapter, agreeable to its title, was designed as a retrospect, which might enable the reader fully to understand the terms upon which the King of France and the Duke of Burgundy stood together, when the former, moved, partly perhaps by his belief in astrology, which was represented as favourable to the issue of such a measure, and in a great measure doubtless by the conscious superiority of his own powers of mind over those of Charles, had adopted the extraordinary, and upon any other ground altogether inexplicable, resolution of committing his person to the faith of a fierce and exasperated enemy—a resolution also the more rash and unaccountable, as there were various examples in that stormy time to show, that safe-conducts, however solemnly plighted, had proved no assurance for those in whose favour they were conceived; and indeed the murder of the Duke's grandfather, at the Bridge of Montereau, in presence of the father of Louis, and at an interview solemnly agreed upon for the establishment of peace and amnesty, was a horrible precedent, should the Duke be disposed to resort to it.

But the temper of Charles, though rough, fierce, headlong, and unyielding, was not, unless in the full tide of passion, faithless or ungenerous, faults which usually belong to colder dispositions. He was at no pains to show the King more courtesy than the laws of hospitality positively demanded; but, on the other hand, he evinced no purpose of overleaping their sacred barriers.

On the following morning after the King's arrival, there was a general muster of the troops of the Duke of Burgundy, which were so numerous and so excellently appointed, that, perhaps, he was not sorry to have an opportunity of displaying them before his great rival. Indeed, while he paid the necessary compliment of a vassal to his Suzerain, in declaring that these troops were the King's, and not his own, the curl of his upper lip, and the proud glance of his eye, intimated his consciousness, that the words he used were but empty compliment, and that his fine army, at his own unlimited disposal, was as ready to march against Paris as in any other direction. It must have added to Louis's mortification, that he recognised, as forming part of this host, many banners of French nobility, not only of Normandy and Bretagne, but of provinces more immediately subjected to his own authority, who, from various causes of discontent, had joined and made common cause with the Duke of Burgundy.

True to his character, however, Louis seemed to take little notice of these malcontents, while, in fact, he was revolving in his mind the various means by which it might be possible to detach them from the banners of Burgundy and bring them back to his own, and resolved for that purpose, that he would cause those to whom he attached the greatest importance to be secretly sounded by Oliver and other agents.

He himself laboured diligently, but at the same time cautiously, to make interest with the Duke's chief officers and advisers, employing for that purpose the usual means of familiar and frequent notice, adroit flattery and liberal presents; not, as he represented, to alienate their faithful services from their noble master, but that they might lend their aid in preserving peace betwixt France and Burgundy,—an end so excellent in itself, and so obviously tending to the welfare of both countries, and of the reigning Princes of either.

The notice of so great and so wise a King was in itself a mighty bribe; promises did much, and direct gifts, which the customs of the time permitted the Burgundian courtiers to accept without scruple, did still more. During a boar-hunt in the forest, while the Duke, eager always upon the immediate object, whether business or pleasure, gave himself entirely up to the ardour of the chase, Louis, unrestrained by his presence, sought and found the means of speaking secretly and separately to many of those who were reported to have most interest with Charles, among whom D'Hymbercourt and Comines were not forgotten; nor did he fail to mix up the advances which he made towards those two distinguished persons with praises of the valour and military skill of the first, and of the profound sagacity and literary talents of the future historian of the period.

Such an opportunity of personally conciliating, or, if the reader pleases, corrupting, the ministers of Charles, was perhaps what the King had proposed to himself, as a principal object of his visit, even if his art should fail to cajole the Duke himself. The connection betwixt France and Burgundy was so close, that most of the nobles belonging to the latter country had hopes or actual interests connected with the former, which the favour of Louis could advance, or his personal displeasure destroy. Formed for this and every other species of intrigue, liberal to profusion when it was necessary to advance his plans, and skilful in putting the most plausible colour upon his proposals and presents, the King contrived to reconcile the spirit of the proud to their profit, and to hold out to the real or pretended patriot the good of both France and Burgundy, as the ostensible motive; whilst the party's own private interest, like the concealed wheel of some machine, worked not the less powerfully that its operations were kept out of sight. For each man he had a suitable bait, and a proper mode of presenting it; he poured the guerdon into the sleeve of those who were too proud to extend their hand, and trusted that his bounty, though it descended like the dew without noise and imperceptibly, would not fail to produce, in due season, a plentiful crop of goodwill at least, perhaps of good offices, to the donor. In fine, although he had been long paving the way by his ministers for an establishment of such an interest in the Court of Burgundy, as should be advantageous to the interests of France, Louis's own personal exertions, directed doubtless by the information of which he was previously possessed, did more to accomplish that object in a few hours, than his agents had effected in years of negotiation.

One man alone the King missed, whom he had been particularly desirous of conciliating, and that was the Count de Crèvecœur, whose firmness, during his conduct as Envoy at Plessis, far from exciting Louis's resentment, had been viewed as a reason for making him his own if possible. He was not particularly gratified when he learnt that the Count, at the head of an hundred lances, was gone towards the frontiers of Brabant, to assist the Bishop, in case of necessity, against William de la Marck and his discontented subjects; but he consoled himself, that the appearance of this force, joined with the directions which he had sent by faithful messengers, would serve to prevent any premature disturbances in that country, the breaking out of which might, he foresaw, render his present situation very precarious.

The Court upon this occasion dined in the forest when the hour of noon arrived, as was common in those great hunting-parties; an arrangement at this time particularly agreeable to the Duke, desirous as he was to abridge that ceremonious and deferential solemnity with which he was otherwise, under the necessity of receiving King Louis. In fact, the King's knowledge of human nature had in one particular misled him on this remarkable occasion. He thought that the Duke would have been inexpressibly flattered to have received such a mark of condescension and confidence from his liege lord; but he forgot that the dependence of this Dukedom upon the Crown of France was privately the subject of galling mortification to a Prince so powerful, so wealthy, and so proud as Charles, whose aim it certainly was to establish an independent kingdom. The presence of the King at the Court of the Duke of Burgundy, imposed on that prince the necessity of exhibiting himself in the subordinate character of a vassal, and of discharging many rites of feudal observance and deference, which, to one of his haughty disposition, resembled derogation from the character of a Sovereign Prince, which on all occasions he affected as far as possible to sustain.

But although it was possible to avoid much ceremony by having the dinner upon the green turf, with sound of bugles, broaching of barrels, and all the freedom of a sylvan meal, it was necessary that the evening repast should, even for that very reason, be held with more than usual solemnity.

Previous orders for this purpose had been given, and, upon returning to Peronne, King Louis found a banquet prepared with such a profusion of splendour and magnificence, as became the wealth of his formidable vassal, possessed as he was of almost all the Low Countries, then the richest portion of Europe. At the head of the long board, which groaned under plate of gold and silver, filled to profusion with the most exquisite dainties, sat the Duke, and on his right hand, upon a seat more elevated than his own, was placed his royal guest. Behind him stood on one side the son of the Duke of Gueldres, who officiated as his grand carver—on the other, Le Glorieux, his jester, without whom he seldom stirred; for, like most men of his hasty and coarse character, Charles carried to extremity the general taste of that age for court-fools and jesters—experiencing that pleasure in their display of eccentricity and mental infirmity, which his more acute, but not more benevolent rival, loved better to extract from marking the imperfections of humanity in its nobler specimens, and finding subject for mirth in the "fears of the brave, and follies of the wise." And indeed, if the anecdote related by Brantome be true, that a court-fool, having overheard Louis, in one of his agonies of repentant devotion, confess his accession to the poisoning of his brother, Henry Count of Guyenne, divulged it next day at dinner before the assembled court, that monarch might be supposed rather more than satisfied with the pleasantries of professed jesters for the rest of his life.

But, on the present occasion, Louis neglected not to take notice of the favourite buffoon of the Duke, and to applaud his repartees; which he did the rather, that he thought he saw that the folly of Le Glorieux, however grossly it was sometimes displayed, covered more than the usual quantity of shrewd and caustic observation proper to his class.

In fact, Tiel Wetzweiler, called Le Glorieux, was by no means a jester of the common stamp. He was a tall, fine-looking man, excellent at many exercises, which seemed scarce reconcilable with mental imbecility, because it must have required patience and attention to attain them. He usually followed the Duke to the chase and to the fight; and at Montl'hery, when Charles was in considerable personal danger, wounded in the throat, and likely to be made prisoner by a French knight who had hold of his horse's rein, Tiel Wetzweiler charged the assailant so forcibly, as to overthrow him and disengage his master. Perhaps he was afraid of this being thought too serious a service for a person of his condition, and that it might excite him enemies among those knights and nobles, who had left the care of their master's person to the court-fool. At any rate, he chose rather to be laughed at than praised for his achievement, and made such gasconading boasts of his exploits in the battle, that most men thought the rescue of Charles was as ideal as the rest of his tale; and it was on this occasion he acquired the title of Le Glorieux (or the boastful), by which he was ever afterwards distinguished.

Le Glorieux was dressed very richly, but with little of the usual distinction of his profession; and that little rather of a symbolical than a very literal character. His head was not shorn; on the contrary, he wore a profusion of long curled hair, which descended from under his cap, and joining with a well-arranged, and handsomely trimmed beard, set off features, which, but for a wild lightness of eye, might have been termed handsome. A ridge of scarlet velvet carried across the top of his cap, indicated, rather than positively represented, the professional cockscomb, which distinguished the headgear of a fool in right of office. His bauble, made of ebony, was crested, as usual, with a fool's head, with ass's ears formed of silver; but so small, and so minutely carved, that, till very closely examined, it might have passed for an official baton of a more solemn character. These were the only badges of his office which his dress exhibited. In other respects, it was such as to match with that of the most courtly nobles. His bonnet displayed a medal of gold; he wore a chain of the same metal around his neck; and the fashion of his rich garments was not much more fantastic than those of young gallants who have their clothes made in the extremity of the existing fashion.

To this personage Charles, and Louis, in imitation of his host, often addressed themselves during the entertainment; and both seemed to manifest, by hearty laughter, their amusement at the answers of Le Glorieux.

"Whose seats be those that are vacant?" said Charles to the jester.

"One of those at least should be mine by right of succession, Charles," replied Le Glorieux.

"Why so, knave?" said Charles.

"Because they belong to the Sieur D'Hymbercourt and Des Comines, who are gone so far to fly their falcons, that they have forgot their supper. They who would rather look at a kite on the wing than a pheasant on the board, are of kin to the fool, and he should succeed to the stools, as a part of their movable estate."

"That is but a stale jest, my friend Tiel," said the Duke; "but, fools or wise men, here come the defaulters."

As he spoke, Comines and D'Hymbercourt entered the room, and, after having made their reverence to the two Princes, assumed in silence the seats which were left vacant for them.

"What ho! sirs," exclaimed the Duke, addressing them, "your sport has been either very good or very bad, to lead you so far and so late. Sir Philip des Comines, you are dejected—hath D'Hymbercourt won so heavy a wager on you?—You are a philosopher, and should not grieve at bad fortune.—By Saint George! D'Hymbercourt looks as sad as thou dost.—How now, sirs? Have you found no game? or have you lost your

falcons? or has a witch crossed your way? or has the Wild Huntsman [1]
met you in the forest? By my honour, you seem as if you were come
to a funeral, not a festival."

While the Duke spoke, the eyes of the company were all directed
towards D'Hymbercourt and Des Comines, and the embarrassment and
dejection of their countenances, neither being of that class of persons to
whom such expression of anxious melancholy was natural, became so
remarkable, that the mirth and laughter of the company, which the rapid
circulation of goblets of excellent wine had raised to a considerable height,
was gradually hushed; and, without being able to assign any reason
for such a change in their spirits, men spoke in whispers to each other,
as on the eve of expecting some strange and important tidings.

"What means this silence, Messires?" said the Duke, elevating his
voice, which was naturally harsh. "If you bring these strange looks, and
this stranger silence, into festivity, we shall wish you had abode in the
marshes seeking for herons, or rather for woodcocks and howlets."

"My gracious lord," said Des Comines, "as we were about to return
hither from the forest, we met the Count of Crèvecœur."

"How!" said the Duke; "already returned from Brabant?—but he
found all well there, doubtless?"

"The Count himself will presently give your Grace an account of his
news," said D'Hymbercourt, "which we have heard but imperfectly."

"Body of me, where is the Count?" said the Duke.

"He changes his dress, to wait upon your Highness," answered D'Hym-
bercout.

"His dress? *Saint-bleu!*" exclaimed the impatient Prince, "what care
I for his dress? I think you have conspired with him to drive me mad!"

"Or rather, to be plain," said Des Comines, "he wishes to communicate these news at a private audience."

"*Teste-dieu!* my Lord King," said Charles, "this is ever the way our
counsellors serve us—If they have got hold of aught which they consider as important for our ear, they look as grave upon the matter, and
are as proud of their burden as an ass of a new pack-saddle.—Some one
bid Crèvecœur come to us directly!—He comes from the frontiers of
Liege, and *we*, at least" (he laid some emphasis on the pronoun), "have
no secrets in that quarter which we would shun to have proclaimed before
the assembled world."

All perceived that the Duke had drunk so much wine as to increase the
native obstinacy of his disposition; and though many would willingly
have suggested that the present was neither a time for hearing news, nor
for taking counsel, yet all knew the impetuosity of his temper too well to
venture on farther interference, and sat in anxious expectation of the
tidings which the Count might have to communicate.

A brief interval intervened, during which the Duke remained looking

---

[1] The famous apparition, sometimes called le Grand Veneur. Sully gives some
account of this hunting spectre.

eagerly to the door, as if in a transport of impatience, whilst the guests sat with their eyes bent on the table, as if to conceal their curiosity and anxiety. Louis alone maintaining perfect composure, continued his conversation alternately with the grand carver and with the jester.

At length Crèvecœur entered, and was presently saluted by the hurried question of his master, "What news from Liege and Brabant, Sir Count? —the report of your arrival has chased mirth from our table—we hope your actual presence will bring it back to us."

"My liege and master," answered the Count, in a firm, but melancholy tone, "the news which I bring you are fitter for the council board than the feasting table."

"Out with them, man, if they were tidings from Antichrist!" said the Duke, "but I can guess them—the Liegeois are again in mutiny."

"They are, my lord," said Crèvecœur, very gravely.

"Look there, man," said the Duke, "I have hit at once on what you have been so much afraid to mention to me—the harebrained burghers are again in arms. It could not be in better time, for we may at present have the advice of our own Suzerain," bowing to King Louis, with eyes which spoke the most bitter, though suppressed resentment, "to teach us how such mutineers should be dealt with.—Hast thou more news in thy packet? Out with them, and then answer for yourself why you went not forward to assist the Bishop."

"My lord, the farther tidings are heavy for me to tell, and will be afflicting to you to hear.—No aid of mine, or of living chivalry, could have availed the excellent Prelate. William de la Marck, united with the insurgent Liegeois, has taken his Castle of Schonwaldt, and murdered him in his own hall."

"*Murdered him!*" repeated the Duke, in a deep and low tone, but which nevertheless was heard from the one end of the hall in which they were assembled to the other; "thou hast been imposed upon, Crèvecœur, by some wild report—it is impossible!"

"Alas! my lord!" said the Count, "I have it from an eyewitness, an archer of the King of France's Scottish Guards, who was in the hall when the murder was committed by William de la Marck's order."

"And who was doubtless aiding and abetting in the horrible sacrilege!" exclaimed the Duke, starting up and stamping with his foot with such fury, that he dashed in pieces the footstool which was placed before him. "Bar the doors of this hall, gentlemen—secure the windows—let no stranger stir from his seat, upon pain of instant death!—Gentlemen of my chamber, draw your swords." And turning upon Louis, he advanced his own hand slowly and deliberately to the hilt of his weapon, while the King, without either showing fear or assuming a defensive posture, only said,

"These news, fair cousin, have staggered your reason."

"No!" replied the Duke, in a terrible tone, "but they have awakened a just resentment, which I have too long suffered to be stifled by trivial

considerations of circumstance and place. Murderer of thy brother!—
rebel against thy parent!—tyrant over thy subjects!—treacherous ally!
—perjured King!—dishonoured gentleman!—thou art in my power,
and I thank God for it."

"Rather thank my folly," said the King; "for when we met on equal
terms at Montl'hery, methinks you wished yourself farther from me
than you are now."

The Duke still held his hand on the hilt of his sword, but refrained
to draw his weapon, or to strike a foe, who offered no sort of resistance
which could in anywise provoke violence.

Meanwhile, wild and general confusion spread itself through the hall.
The doors were now fastened and guarded by order of the Duke; but
several of the French nobles, few as they were in number, started from
their seats, and prepared for the defence of their Sovereign. Louis had
spoken not a word either to Orleans or Dunois since they were liberated
from restraint at the Castle of Loches, if it could be termed liberation,
to be dragged in King Louis's train, objects of suspicion evidently, rather
than of respect and regard; but, nevertheless, the voice of Dunois was
first heard above the tumult, addressing himself to the Duke of Burgundy.—"Sir Duke, you have forgotten that you are a vassal of France,
and that we, your guests, are Frenchmen. If you lift a hand against our
Monarch, prepare to sustain the utmost effects of our despair; for, credit
me, we shall feast as high with the blood of Burgundy as we have done
with its wine.—Courage, my Lord of Orleans—and you, gentlemen of
France, form yourselves round Dunois, and do as he does!"

It was in that moment when a King might see upon what tempers
he could certainly rely. The few independent nobles and knights who
attended Louis, most of whom had only received from him frowns of
discountenance, unappalled by the display of infinitely superior force,
and the certainty of destruction in case they came to blows, hastened
to array themselves around Dunois, and, led by him, to press towards
the head of the table where the contending Princes were seated.

On the contrary, the tools and agents whom Louis had dragged forward out of their fitting and natural places, into importance which was
not due to them, showed cowardice and cold heart, and, remaining still
in their seats, seemed resolved not to provoke their fate by intermeddling,
whatever might become of their benefactor.

The first of the more generous party was the venerable Lord Crawford,
who, with an agility which no one would have expected at his years,
forced his way through all opposition (which was the less violent, as many
of the Burgundians, either from a point of honour, or a secret inclination to prevent Louis's impending fate, gave way to him), and threw
himself boldly between the King and the Duke. He then placed his
bonnet, from which his white hair escaped in dishevelled tresses, upon
one side of his head—his pale cheek and withered brow coloured, and
his aged eye lightened with all the fire of a gallant who is about to dare

some desperate action. His cloak was flung over one shoulder, and his action intimated his readiness to wrap it about his left arm, while he unsheathed his sword with his right.

"I have fought for his father and his grandsire," that was all he said, "and, by Saint Andrew, end the matter as it will, I will not fail him at this pinch."

What has taken some time to narrate, happened, in fact, with the speed of light; for so soon as the Duke assumed his threatening posture, Crawford had thrown himself betwixt him and the object of his vengeance; and the French gentlemen, drawing together as fast as they could, were crowding to the same point.

The Duke of Burgundy still remained with his hand on his sword, and seemed in the act of giving the signal for a general onset, which must necessarily have ended in the massacre of the weaker party, when Crèvecœur rushed forward, and exclaimed, in a voice like a trumpet,—"My liege Lord of Burgundy, beware what you do! This is *your* hall—you are the King's vassal—do not spill the blood of your guest on your hearth, the blood of your Sovereign on the throne you have erected for him, and to which he came under your safeguard. For the sake of your house's honour, do not attempt to revenge one horrid murder by another yet worse!"

"Out of my road, Crèvecœur," answered the Duke, "and let my vengeance pass!—Out of my path!—The wrath of Kings is to be dreaded like that of Heaven."

"Only when, like that of Heaven, it is *just*," answered Crèvecœur firmly—"Let me pray of you, my lord, to rein the violence of your temper, however justly offended.—And for you, my Lords of France, where resistance is unavailing, let me recommend you to forbear whatever may lead towards bloodshed."

"He is right," said Louis, whose coolness forsook him not in that dreadful moment, and who easily foresaw, that if a brawl should commence, more violence would be dared and done in the heat of blood, than was likely to be attempted if peace were preserved.—"My cousin Orleans—kind Dunois—and you, my trusty Crawford—bring not on ruin and bloodshed by taking offence too hastily. Our cousin the Duke is chafed at the tidings of the death of a near and loving friend, the venerable Bishop of Liege, whose slaughter we lament as he does. Ancient, and, unhappily, recent subjects of jealousy, lead him to suspect us of having abetted a crime which our bosom abhors. Should our host murder us on this spot—us, his King and his kinsman, under a false impression of our being accessory to this unhappy accident, our fate will be little lightened, but, on the contrary, greatly aggravated, by your stirring. —Therefore, stand back, Crawford—Were it my last word, I speak as a King to his officer, and demand obedience.—Stand back, and, if it is required, yield up your sword. I command you to do so, and your oath obliges you to obey."

"True, true, my lord," said Crawford, stepping back, and returning to the sheath the blade he had half drawn.—"It may be all very true; but, by my honour, if I were at the head of threescore and ten of my brave fellows, instead of being loaded with more than the like number of years, I would try whether I could have some reason out of these fine gallants, with their golden chains and looped-up bonnets, with braw-warld dyes and devices on them."

The Duke stood with his eyes fixed on the ground for a considerable space, and then said, with bitter irony, "Crèvecœur, you say well; and it concerns our honour, that our obligations to this great King, our honoured and loving guest, be not so hastily adjusted, as in our hasty anger we had at first proposed. We will so act, that all Europe shall acknowledge the justice of our proceedings.—Gentlemen of France, you must render up your arms to my officers! Your master has broken the truce, and has no title to take farther benefit of it. In compassion, however, to your sentiments of honour, and in respect to the rank which he hath disgraced, and the race from which he hath degenerated, we ask not our cousin Louis's sword."

"Not one of us," said Dunois, "will resign our weapon, or quit this hall, unless we are assured of at least our King's safety, in life and limb."

"Nor will a man of the Scottish Guard," exclaimed Crawford, "lay down his arms, save at the command of the King of France, or his High Constable."

"Brave Dunois," said Louis, "and you, my trusty Crawford, your zeal will do me injury instead of benefit.—I trust," he added with dignity, "in my rightful cause, more than in a vain resistance, which would but cost the lives of my best and bravest.—Give up your swords—the noble Burgundians, who accept such honourable pledges, will be more able than you are to protect both you and me.—Give up your swords —It is I who command you."

It was thus that, in this dreadful emergency, Louis showed the promptitude of decision and clearness of judgment, which alone could have saved his life. He was aware, that until actual blows were exchanged, he should have the assistance of most of the nobles present to moderate the fury of their Prince; but that were a *mêlée* once commenced, he himself and his few adherents must be instantly murdered. At the same time, his worst enemies confessed, that his demeanour had in it nothing either of meanness, or cowardice. He shunned to aggravate into frenzy the wrath of the Duke; but he neither deprecated nor seemed to fear it, and continued to look on him with the calm and fixed attention with which a brave man eyes the menacing gestures of a lunatic, whilst conscious that his own steadiness and composure operate as an insensible and powerful check on the rage even of insanity.

Crawford, at the King's command, threw his sword to Crèvecœur, saying, "Take it! and the devil give you joy of it.—It is no dishonour to the rightful owner who yields it, for we have had no fair play."

"Hold, gentlemen," said the Duke, in a broken voice, as one whom passion had almost deprived of utterance, "retain your swords; it is sufficient you promise not to use them.—And you, Louis of Valois, must regard yourself as my prisoner, until you are cleared of having abetted sacrilege and murder. Have him to the Castle—Have him to Earl Herbert's Tower. Let him have six gentlemen of his train to attend him, such as he shall choose.—My Lord of Crawford, your guard must leave the Castle, and shall be honourably quartered elsewhere. Up with every drawbridge, and down with every portcullis—Let the gates of the town be trebly guarded—Draw the floating-bridge to the right-hand side of the river—Bring round the Castle my band of Black Walloons, and treble the sentinels on every post!—You, D'Hymbercourt, look that patrols of horse and foot make the round of the town every half-hour during the night, and every hour during the next day,—if indeed such ward shall be necessary after daybreak, for it is like we may be sudden in this matter.—Look to the person of Louis, as you love your life!"

He started from the table in fierce and moody haste, darted a glance of mortal enmity at the King, and rushed out of the apartment.

"Sirs," said the King, looking with dignity around him, "grief for the death of his ally hath made your Prince frantic. I trust you know better your duty, as knights and noblemen, than to abet him in his treasonable violence against the person of his liege Lord."

At this moment was heard in the streets the sound of drums beating, and horns blowing, to call out the soldiery in every direction.

"We are," said Crèvecœur, who acted as the Marshal of the Duke's household, "subjects of Burgundy, and must do our duty as such. Our hopes and prayers, and our efforts, will not be wanting to bring about peace and union between your Majesty and our liege Lord. Meantime, we must obey his commands. These other lords and knights will be proud to contribute to the convenience of the illustrious Duke of Orleans, of the brave Dunois, and the stout Lord Crawford. I myself must be your Majesty's chamberlain, and bring you to your apartments in other guise than would be my desire, remembering the hospitality of Plessis. You have only to choose your attendants, whom the Duke's commands limit to six."

"Then," said the King, looking around him, and thinking for a moment,—"I desire the attendance of Oliver le Dain, of a private of my Life-Guard, called Balafré, who may be unarmed if you will—of Tristan l'Hermite, with two of his people—and my right loyal and trusty philosopher, Martius Galeotti."

"Your Majesty's will shall be complied with in all points," said the Count de Crèvecœur. "Galeotti," he added, after moment's inquiry, "is, I understand, at present supping in some buxom company, but he shall instantly be sent for; the others will obey your Majesty's command upon the instant."

"Forward, then, to the new abode, which the hospitality of our cousin provides for us," said the King. "We know it is strong, and have only to hope it may be in a corresponding degree safe."

"Heard you the choice which King Louis has made of his attendants?" said Le Glorieux to Count Crèvecœur apart, as they followed Louis from the hall.

"Surely, my merry gossip," replied the Count,—"What hast thou to object to them?"

"Nothing, nothing—only they are a rare election!—A panderly barber—a Scottish hired cut-throat—a chief hangman and his two assistants, and a thieving charlatan.—I will along with you, Crèvecœur, and take a lesson in the degrees of roguery, from observing your skill in marshalling them. The devil himself could scarce have summoned such a synod, or have been a better president amongst them."

Accordingly, the all-licensed jester, seizing the Count's arm familiarly, began to march along with him, while, under a strong guard, yet forgetting no semblance of respect, he conducted the King towards his new apartment." [1]

CHAPTER XXVIII

UNCERTAINTY

——Then happy low, lie down;
Uneasy lies the head that wears a crown.
Henry IV.—Part Second.

FORTY men-at-arms, carrying alternately naked swords and blazing torches, served as the escort, or rather the guard, of King Louis, from the town-hall of Peronne to the Castle; and as he entered within its darksome and gloomy strength, it seemed as if a voice screamed in his ear that warning which the Florentine has inscribed over the portal of the infernal regions, "Leave all hope behind!"

At that moment, perhaps, some feeling of remorse might have crossed the King's mind, had he thought on the hundreds, nay thousands, whom, without cause, or on light suspicion, he had committed to the abysses of his dungeons, deprived of all hope of liberty, and loathing even the life to which they clung by animal instinct.

The broad glare of the torches outfacing the pale moon, which was more obscured on this than on the former night, and the red smoky light which they dispersed around the ancient buildings, gave a darker shade to that huge donjon, called the Earl Herbert's Tower. It was the same that Louis had viewed with misgiving presentiment on the preceding evening, and of which he was now doomed to become an inhabitant, under the terror of what violence soever the wrathful temper of his overgrown vassal might tempt him to exercise in those secret recesses of despotism.

[1] Note VIII.

To aggravate the King's painful feelings, he saw, as he crossed the courtyard, several bodies, over each of which had been hastily flung a military cloak. He was not long of discerning that they were corpses of slain archers of the Scottish Guard, who having disputed, as the Count Crèvecœur informed him, the command given them to quit the post near the King's apartments, a brawl had ensued between them and the Duke's Walloon body-guards, and before it could be composed by the officers on either side, several lives had been lost.

"My trusty Scots!" said the King, as he looked upon this melancholy spectacle; "had they brought only man to man, all Flanders, ay, and Burgundy to boot, had not furnished champions to mate you."

"Yes, an it please your Majesty," said Balafré, who attended close behind the King, "Maistery mows the meadow—few men can fight more than two at once. I myself never care to meet three, unless it be in the way of special duty, when one must not stand to count heads."

"Art thou there, old acquaintance?" said the King, looking behind him; "then I have one true subject with me yet."

"And a faithful minister, whether in your councils, or in his offices about your royal person," whispered Oliver le Dain.

"We are all faithful," said Tristan l'Hermite gruffly; "for should they put to death your Majesty, there is no one of us whom they would suffer to survive you, even if we would."

"Now, that is what I call good corporal bail for fidelity," said Le Glorieux, who, as already mentioned, with the restlessness proper to an infirm brain, had thrust himself into their company.

Meanwhile, the Seneschal, hastily summoned, was turning with laborious effort the ponderous key which opened the reluctant gate of the huge Gothic Keep, and was at last fain to call for the assistance of one of Crèvecœur's attendants. When they had succeeded, six men entered with torches, and showed the way through a narrow and winding passage, commanded at different points by shot-holes from vaults and casements constructed behind, and in the thickness of the massive walls. At the end of this passage arose a stair of corresponding rudeness, consisting of huge blocks of stone, roughly dressed with the hammer, and of unequal height. Having mounted this ascent, a strong iron-clenched door admitted them to what had been the great hall of the donjon, lighted but very faintly even during the daytime (for the apertures, diminished in appearance by the excessive thickness of the walls, resembled slits rather than windows), and now, but for the blaze of the torches, almost perfectly dark. Two or three bats, and other birds of evil presage, roused by the unusual glare, flew against the lights, and threatened to extinguish them; while the Seneschal formally apologised to the King, that the State-hall had not been put in order, such was the hurry of the notice sent to him; and adding, that, in truth, the apartment had not been in use for twenty years, and rarely before that time, so far as ever he had heard, since the time of King Charles the Simple.

"King Charles the Simple!" echoed Louis; "I know the history of the Tower now.—He was here murdered by his treacherous vassal, Herbert, Earl of Vermandois—So say our annals. I knew there was something concerning the Castle of Peronne which dwelt on my mind, though I could not recall the circumstance.—*Here,* then, my predecessor was slain?"

"Not here, not exactly here, and please your Majesty," said the old Seneschal, stepping with the eager haste of a cicerone, who shows the curiosities of such a place—"Not *here,* but in the side-chamber a little onward, which opens from your Majesty's bedchamber."

He hastily opened a wicket at the upper end of the hall, which led into a bedchamber, small, as is usual in such old buildings; but, even for that reason, rather more comfortable than the waste hall through which they had passed. Some hasty preparations had been here made for the King's accommodation. Arras had been tacked up, a fire lighted in the rusty grate, which had been long unused, and a pallet laid down for those gentlemen who were to pass the night in his chamber, as was then usual.

"We will get beds in the hall for the rest of your attendants," said the garrulous old man; "but we have had such brief notice, if it please your Majesty—And if it please your Majesty to look upon this little wicket behind the arras, it opens into the little old cabinet in the thickness of the wall where Charles was slain; and there is a secret passage from below, which admitted the men who were to deal with him. And your Majesty, whose eyesight I hope is better than mine, may see the blood still on the oak-floor, though the thing was done five hundred years ago."

While he thus spoke, he kept fumbling to open the postern of which he spoke, until the King said, "Forbear, old man—forbear but a little while, when thou mayst have a newer tale to tell, and fresher blood to show.—My Lord of Crèvecœur, what say you?"

"I can but answer, Sire, that these two interior apartments are as much at your Majesty's disposal as those in your own Castle at Plessis, and that Crèvecœur, a name never blackened by treachery or assassination, has the guard of the exterior defences of it."

"But the private passage into that closet, of which the old man speaks?" This King Louis said in a low and anxious tone, holding Crèvecœur's arm fast with one hand, and pointing to the wicket-door with the other.

"It must be some dream of Mornay's," said Crèvecœur, "or some old and absurd tradition of the place;—but we will examine."

He was about to open the closet door, when Louis answered, "No, Crèvecœur, no—Your honour is sufficient warrant.—But what will your Duke do with me, Crèvecœur? He cannot hope to keep me long a prisoner; and—in short, give me your opinion, Crèvecœur."

"My Lord and Sire," said the Count, "how the Duke of Burgundy must resent this horrible cruelty on the person of his near relative and

ally, is for your Majesty to judge; and what right he may have to consider it as instigated by your Majesty's emissaries, you only can know.
But my master is noble in his disposition, and made incapable, even
by the very strength of his passions, of any underhand practices. Whatever he does, will be done in the face of day, and of the two nations.
And I can but add, that it will be the wish of every counsellor around
him—excepting perhaps one—that he should behave in this matter with
mildness and generosity, as well as justice."

"Ah! Crèvecœur," said Louis, taking his hand as if affected by some
painful recollections, " how happy is the Prince who has counsellors
near him, who can guard him against the effects of his own angry passions! Their names will be read in golden letters, when the history of
his reign is perused.—Noble Crèvecœur, had it been my lot to have such
as thou art about *my* person!"

"It had in that case been your Majesty's study to have got rid of
them as fast as you could," said Le Glorieux.

"Aha! Sir Wisdom, art thou there?" said Louis, turning round, and
instantly changing the pathetic tone in which he had addressed Crèvecœur, and adopting with facility one which had a turn of gaiety in it—
"Hast *thou* followed us hither?"

"Ay, sir," answered Le Glorieux, "Wisdom must follow in motley,
where Folly leads the way in purple."

"How shall I construe that, Sir Solomon?" answered Louis—"Wouldst
thou change conditions with me?"

"Not I, by my halidome," quoth Le Glorieux, "if you would give me
fifty crowns to boot."

"Why, wherefore so?—Methinks I could be well enough contented,
as princes go, to have thee for my king."

"Ay, Sire," replied Le Glorieux; "but the question is, whether, judging of your Majesty's wit from its having lodged you here, I should not
have cause to be ashamed of having so dull a fool."

"Peace, sirrah!" said the Count of Crèvecœur; "your tongue runs
too fast."

"Let it take its course," said the King; "I know of no such fair
subject of raillery, as the follies of those who should know better.—
Here, my sagacious friend, take this purse of gold, and with it the advice,
never to be so great a fool as to deem yourself wiser than other people.
Prithee, do me so much favour as to inquire after my astrologer, Martius Galeotti, and send him hither to me presently."

"I will, without fail, my Liege," answered the jester; "and I wot well
I shall find him at Jan Dopplethur's; for philosophers, as well as fools,
know where the best wine is sold."

"Let me pray for free entrance for this learned person through your
guards, Seignior de Crèvecœur," said Louis.

"For his entrance, unquestionably," answered the Count; "but it
grieves me to add, that my instructions do not authorise me to permit

any one to quit your Majesty's apartments.—I wish your Majesty a good night," he subjoined, "and will presently make such arrangements in the outer hall, as may put the gentlemen who are to inhabit it more at their ease."

"Give yourself no trouble for them, Sir Count," replied the King, "they are men accustomed to set hardships at defiance; and, to speak truth, excepting that I wish to see Galeotti, I would desire as little further communications from without this night as may be consistent with your instructions."

"These are, to leave your Majesty," replied Crèvecœur, "undisputed possession of your own apartments. Such are my master's orders."

"Your master, Count Crèvecœur," answered Louis, "whom I may also term mine, is a right gracious master.—My dominions," he added, "are somewhat shrunk in compass, now that they have dwindled to an old hall and a bedchamber; but they are still wide enough for all the subjects which I can at present boast of."

The Count of Crèvecœur took his leave; and shortly after, they could hear the noise of the sentinels moving to their posts, accompanied with the word of command from the officers, and the hasty tread of the guard who were relieved. At length all became still, and the only sound which filled the air, was the sluggish murmur of the river Somme, as it glided, deep and muddy, under the walls of the castle.

"Go into the hall, my mates," said Louis to his train; "but do not lie down to sleep. Hold yourselves in readiness, for there is still something to be done to-night, and that of moment."

Oliver and Tristan retired to the hall accordingly, in which Le Balafré and the Provost-Marshal's two officers had remained, when the others entered the bedchamber. They found that those without had thrown fagots enough upon the fire, to serve the purpose of light and heat at the same time, and, wrapping themselves in their cloaks, had sat down on the floor, in postures which variously expressed the discomposure and dejection of their minds. Oliver and Tristan saw nothing better to be done, than to follow their example; and, never very good friends in the days of their court-prosperity, they were both equally reluctant to repose confidence in each other upon this strange and sudden reverse of fortune. So that the whole party sat in silent dejection.

Meanwhile, their master underwent, in the retirement of his secret chamber, agonies that might have atoned for some of those which had been imposed by his command. He paced the room with short and unequal steps, often stood still and clasped his hands together, and gave loose, in short, to agitation, which, in public, he had found himself able to suppress so successfully. At length, pausing, and wringing his hands, he planted himself opposite to the wicket-door, which had been pointed out by old Mornay as leading to the scene of the murder of one of his predecessors, and gradually gave voice to his feelings in a broken soliloquy.

"Charles the Simple—Charles the Simple!—what will posterity call the Eleventh Louis, whose blood will probably soon refresh the stains of thine? Louis the Fool—Louis the Driveller—Louis the Infatuated—are all terms too slight to mark the extremity of my idiocy! To think these hot-headed Liegeois, to whom rebellion is as natural as their food, would remain quiet—to dream that the Wild Beast of Ardennes would, for a moment, be interrupted in his career of force and bloodthirsty brutality —to suppose that I could use reason and arguments to any good purpose with Charles of Burgundy, until I had tried the force of such exhortations with success upon a wild bull—Fool, and double idiot that I was! But the villain Martius shall not escape—He has been at the bottom of this, he and the vile priest, the detestable Balue.[1] If I ever get out of this danger, I will tear from his head the Cardinal's cap, though I pull the scalp along with it! But the other traitor is in my hands—I am yet king enough—have yet an empire roomy enough—for the punishment of the quack-salving, word-mongering, star-gazing, lie-coining impostor, who has at once made a prisoner and a dupe of me!—The conjunction of the constellations—ay, the conjunction—He must talk nonsense which would scarce gull a thrice-sodden sheep's head, and I must be idiot enough to think I understood him! But we shall see presently what the conjunction has really boded. But first let me to my devotions."

Above the little door, in memory perhaps of the deed which had been done within, was a rude niche, containing a crucifix cut in stone. Upon this emblem the King fixed his eyes, as if about to kneel, but stopped short, as if he applied to the blessed image the principles of worldly policy, and deemed it rash to approach its presence without having secured the private intercession of some supposed favourite. He therefore turned from the crucifix as unworthy to look upon it, and selecting from the images with which, as often mentioned, his hat was completely garnished, a representation of the Lady of Clery, knelt down before it and made the following extraordinary prayer; in which, it is to be observed, the grossness of his superstition induced him, in some degree, to consider the virgin of Clery as a different person from the Madonna of Embrun, a favourite idol, to whom he often paid his vows.

"Sweet Lady of Clery," he exclaimed, clasping his hands and beating his breast while he spoke—"blessed Mother of Mercy! thou who art omnipotent with Omnipotence, have compassion with me a sinner! It is true that I have something neglected thee for thy blessed sister of Embrun; but I am a King, my power is great, my wealth boundless; and, were it otherwise, I would double the *gabelle* on my subjects, rather

---

[1] Louis kept his promise of vengeance against Cardinal La Balue, whom he always blamed as having betrayed him to Burgundy. After he had returned to his own kingdom, he caused his late favourite to be immured in one of the iron cages at Loches. These were constructed with horrible ingenuity, so that a person of ordinary size could neither stand up at his full height nor lie lengthwise in them. Some ascribe this horrid device to Balue himself. At any rate, he was confined in one of these dens for eleven years, nor did Louis permit him to be liberated till his last illness.

than not pay my debts to you both. Undo these iron doors—fill up these tremendous moats—lead me, as a mother leads a child, out of this present and pressing danger! If I have given thy sister the county of Boulogne, to be held of her for ever, have I no means of showing devotion to thee also? Thou shalt have the broad and rich province of Champagne; and its vineyards shall pour their abundance into thy convent. I had promised the province to my brother Charles; but he, thou knowest, is dead —poisoned by that wicked Abbé of Saint John d'Angely, whom, if I live, I will punish!—I promised this once before, but this time I will keep my word.—If I had any knowledge of the crime, believe, dearest patroness, it was because I knew no better method of quieting the discontents of my kingdom. Oh, do not reckon that old debt to my account to-day; but be, as thou hast ever been, kind, benignant, and easy to be entreated! Sweetest Lady, work with thy child, that he will pardon all past sins, and one—one little deed which I must do this night—nay, it is no *sin,* dearest Lady of Clery—no sin, but an act of justice privately administered; for the villain is the greatest impostor that ever poured falsehood into a Prince's ear, and leans besides to the filthy heresy of the Greeks. He is not deserving of thy protection; leave him to my care; and hold it as good service that I rid the world of him, for the man is a necromancer and wizard, that is not worth thy thought and care—a dog, the extinction of whose life ought to be of as little consequence in thine eyes, as the treading out a spark that drops from a lamp, or springs from a fire. Think not of this little matter, gentlest, kindest Lady, but only consider how thou canst best aid me in my troubles! and I here bind my royal signet to thy effigy, in token that I will keep my word concerning the county of Champagne, and that this shall be the last time I will trouble thee in affairs of blood, knowing thou art so kind, so gentle, and so tender-hearted."

After this extraordinary contract with the object of his adoration, Louis recited, apparently with deep devotion, the seven penitential psalms in Latin, and several aves and prayers especially belonging to the service of the Virgin. He then arose, satisfied that he had secured the intercession of the Saint to whom he had prayed, the rather, as he craftily reflected, that most of the sins for which he had requested her mediation on former occasions had been of a different character, and that, therefore, the Lady of Clery was less likely to consider him as a hardened and habitual shedder of blood, than the other saints whom he had more frequently made confidants of his crimes in that respect.[1]

When he had thus cleared his conscience, or rather whited it over like a sepulchre, the King thrust his head out at the door of the hall, and summoned Le Balafré into his apartment. "My good soldier," he said, "thou hast served me long, and hast had little promotion. We are here in a case where I may either live or die; but I would not willingly die

[1] Note IX.—Prayer of Louis XI.

an ungrateful man, or leave, so far as the saints may place it in my
power, either a friend or an enemy unrecompensed. Now, I have a friend
to be rewarded, that is thyself—an enemy to be punished according to
his deserts, and that is the base, treacherous villain, Martius Galeotti,
who, by his impostures and specious falsehoods, has trained me hither
into the power of my mortal enemy, with as firm a purpose of my destruction, as ever butcher had of slaying the beast which he drove to
the shambles."

"I will challenge him on that quarrel, since they say he is a fighting
blade, though he looks somewhat unwieldy," said Le Balafré. "I doubt
not but the Duke of Burgundy is so much a friend to men of the sword,
that he will allow us a fair field within some reasonable space; and if
your Majesty live so long, and enjoy so much freedom, you shall behold
me do battle in your right, and take as proper a vengeance on this philosopher as your heart could desire."

"I commend your bravery and your devotion to my service," said
the King. "But this treacherous villain is a stout man-at-arms, and I
would not willingly risk thy life, my brave soldier."

"I were no brave soldier, if it please your Majesty," said Balafré, "if
I dared not face a better man than he. A fine thing it would be for me,
who can neither read nor write, to be afraid of a fat lurdane, who has
done little else all his life!"

"Nevertheless," said the King, "it is not our pleasure so to put thee
in venture, Balafré. This traitor comes hither, summoned by our command. We would have thee, so soon as thou canst find occasion, close up
with him, and smite him under the fifth rib—Dost thou understand
me?"

"Truly I do," answered Le Balafré; "but, if it please your Majesty,
this is a matter entirely out of my course of practice. I could not kill
you a dog, unless it were in hot assault, or pursuit, or upon defiance
given, or such like."

"Why sure, *thou* dost not pretend to tenderness of heart!" said the
King; "thou who hast been first in storm and siege, and most eager,
as men tell me, on the pleasures and advantages which are gained
on such occasions by the rough heart and the bloody hand?"

"My lord," answered Le Balafré, "I have neither feared nor spared
your enemies, sword in hand. And an assault is a desperate matter, under
risks which raise a man's blood so, that, by Saint Andrew, it will not
settle for an hour or two,—which I call a fair licence for plundering after
a storm. And God pity us poor soldiers, who are first driven mad with
danger, and then madder with victory. I have heard of a legion consisting
entirely of saints; and methinks it would take them all to pray and
intercede for the rest of the army, and for all who wear plumes and
corselets, buff coats and broadswords. But what your Majesty proposes
is out of my course of practice, though I will never deny that it has
been wide enough. As for the astrologer, if he be a traitor, let him e'en

die a traitor's death—I will neither meddle nor make with it. Your Majesty has your Provost, and two of his Marshal's men without, who are more fit for dealing with him than a Scottish gentleman of my family and standing in the service."

"You say well," said the King; "but, at least, it belongs to thy duty to prevent interruption, and to guard the execution of my most just sentence."

"I will do so against all Peronne," said Le Balafré. "Your Majesty need not doubt my fealty in that which I can reconcile to my conscience which, for mine own convenience and the service of your royal Majesty, I can vouch to be a pretty large one—at least, I know I have done some deeds for your Majesty, which I would rather have eaten a handful of my own dagger than I would have done for any else."

"Let that rest," said the King; "and hear you—when Galeotti is admitted, and the door shut on him, do you stand to your weapon, and guard the entrance on the inside of the apartment. Let no one intrude —that is all I require of you. Go hence, and send the Provost-Marshal to me."

Balafré left the apartment accordingly, and in a minute afterwards Tristan l'Hermite entered from the hall.

"Welcome, gossip," said the King; "what thinkest thou of our situation?"

"As of men sentenced to death," said the Provost-Marshal, "unless there come a reprieve from the Duke."

"Reprieved or not, he that decoyed us into this snare shall go our *fourrier* to the next world, to take up lodgings for us," said the King, with a grisly and ferocious smile. "Tristan, thou hast done many an act of brave justice—*finis*—I should have said *funis coronat opus*. Thou must stand by me to the end."

"I will, my liege," said Tristan; "I am but a plain fellow, but I am grateful. I will do my duty within these walls, or elsewhere; and while I live, your Majesty's breath shall pour as potential a note of condemnation, and your sentence be as literally executed, as when you sat on your own throne. They may deal with me the next hour for it if they will—I care not."

"It is even what I expected of thee, my loving gossip," said Louis; "but hast thou good assistance?—the traitor is strong and able-bodied, and will doubtless be clamorous for aid. The Scot will do nought but keep the door; and well that he can be brought to that, by flattery and humouring. Then Oliver is good for nothing but lying, flattering, and suggesting dangerous counsels; and, *Ventre Saint-dieu!* I think is more like one day to deserve the halter himself, than to use it to another. Have you men, think you, and means, to make sharp and sure work?"

"I have Trois-Eschelles and Petit-André with me," said he—"men so expert in their office, that out of three men, they would hang up one ere his two companions were aware. And we have all resolved to live or die with your Majesty, knowing we shall have as short breath to draw when you are gone, as ever fell to the lot of any of our patients.—But what is to be our present subject, an it please your Majesty? I love to be sure of my man; for, as your Majesty is pleased sometimes to remind me, I have now and then mistaken the criminal, and strung up in his place an honest labourer, who had given your Majesty no offence."

"Most true," said the other. "Know then, Tristan, that the condemned person is Martius Galeotti.—You start, but it is even as I say. The villain hath trained us all hither by false and treacherous representations, that he might put us into the hands of the Duke of Burgundy without defence."

"But not without vengeance!" said Tristan; "were it the last act of my life, I would sting him home like an expiring wasp, should I be crushed to pieces on the next instant!"

"I know thy trusty spirit," said the King, "and the pleasure which, like other good men, thou dost find in the discharge of thy duty, since virtue, as the schoolmen say, is its own reward. But away, and prepare the priests, for the victim approaches."

"Would you have it done in your own presence, my gracious liege?" said Tristan.

Louis declined this offer; but charged the Provost-Marshal to have everything ready for the punctual execution of his commands the moment the Astrologer left his apartment; "for," said the King, "I will see the villain once more, just to observe how he bears himself towards the master whom he has led into the toils. I shall love to see the sense of approaching death strike the colour from that ruddy cheek, and dim that eye which laughed as it lied.—Oh, that there were but another with him, whose counsels aided his prognostications! But if I survive this—look to your scarlet, my Lord Cardinal! for Rome shall scarce protect you—be it spoken under favour of Saint Peter and the blessed Lady of Clery, who is all over mercy.—Why do you tarry? Go get your grooms ready. I expect the villain instantly. I pray to Heaven he take not fear and come not!—that were indeed a baulk. Begone, Tristan—thou wert not wont to be so slow when business was to be done."

"On the contrary, an it like your Majesty, you were ever wont to say that I was too fast, and mistook your purpose, and did the job on the wrong subject. Now, please your Majesty to give me a sign, just when you part with Galeotti for the night, whether the business goes on or no. I have known your Majesty once or twice change your mind, and blame me for over despatch." [1]

"Thou suspicious creature," answered King Louis, "I tell thee I will

---

[1] Varillas, in a history of Louis XI., observes, that his Provost-Marshal was often so precipitate in execution as to slay another person instead of him whom the King had indicated. This always occasioned a double execution, for the wrath or revenge of Louis was never satisfied with a vicarious punishment.

not change my mind;—but to silence thy remonstrances, observe, if I say to the knave at parting, 'There is a Heaven above us!' then let the business go on; but if I say, 'Go in peace,' you will understand that my purpose is altered."

"My head is somewhat of the dullest out of my own department," said Tristan l'Hermite. "Stay, let me rehearse—If you bid him depart in peace, I am to have him dealt upon?"

"No, no—idiot, no!" said the King; "in that case you let him pass free. But if I say, *'There is a Heaven above us!'* up with him a yard or two nearer the planets he is so conversant with."

"I wish we may have the means here," said the Provost.

"Then *up* with him or *down* with him, it matters not which," answered the King, grimly smiling.

"And the body," said the Provost, "how shall we dispose of it?"

"Let me see an instant," said the King—"the windows of the hall are too narrow; but that projecting oriel is wide enough. We will over with him into the Somme, and put a paper on his breast, with the legend, 'Let the justice of the King pass toll-free.' The Duke's officers may seize it for duties if they dare."

The Provost-Marshal left the apartment of Louis, and summoned his two assistants to council in an embrasure in the great hall, where Trois-Eschelles stuck a torch against the wall to give them light. They discoursed in whispers, little noticed by Oliver le Dain, who seemed sunk in dejection, and Le Balafré who was fast asleep.

"Comrades," said the Provost to his executioners, "perhaps you have thought that our vocation was over, or that, at least, we were more likely to be the subjects of the duty of others, than to have any more to discharge on our own parts. But courage, my mates! our gracious master has reserved for us one noble cast of our office, and it must be gallantly executed, as by men who would live in history."

"Ay, I guess how it is," said Trois-Eschelles; "our patron is like the old Kaisars of Rome, who, when things came to an extremity, or, as we would say, to the ladder foot with them, were wont to select from their own ministers of justice some experienced person, who might spare their sacred persons from the awkward attempts of a novice or blunderer in our mystery. It was a pretty custom for Ethnics; but, as a good Catholic, I should make some scruple at laying hands on the Most Christian King."

"Nay, but, brother, you are ever too scrupulous," said Petit-André. "If he issues word and warrant for his own execution, I see not how we can in duty dispute it. He that dwells at Rome must obey the Pope—the Marshal's men must do their master's bidding, and he the King's."

"Hush, you knaves!" said the Provost-Marshal, "there is here no purpose concerning the King's person, but only that of the Greek heretic pagan and Mahomedan wizard, Martius Galeotti."

"Galeotti!" answered Petit-André; "that comes quite natural. I never knew one of these legerdemain fellows, who pass their life, as one may say, in dancing upon a tight-rope, but what they came at length to caper at the end of one—*tchick!*"

"My only concern is," said Trois-Eschelles, looking upwards, "that the poor creature must die without confession."

"Tush! tush!" said the Provost-Marshal, in reply, "he is a rank heretic and necromancer—a whole college of priests could not absolve him from the doom he has deserved. Besides, if he hath a fancy that way, thou hast a gift, Trois-Eschelles, to serve him for ghostly father thyself. But, what is more material, I fear you must use your poniards, my mates; for you have not here the fitting conveniences for the exercise of your profession."

"Now, our Lady of the Isle of Paris forbid," said Trois-Eschelles, "that the King's command should find me destitute of my tools! I always wear around my body Saint Francis's cord, doubled four times, with a handsome loop at the farther end of it; for I am of the company of Saint Francis, and may wear his cowl when I am *in extremis*—I thank God and the good fathers of Saumur."

"And for me," said Petit-André, "I have always in my budget a handy block and sheaf, or a pulley as they call it, with a strong screw for securing it where I list, in case we should travel where trees are scarce, or high-branched from the ground. I have found it a great convenience."

"That will suit as well," said the Provost-Marshal; "you have but to screw your pulley into yonder beam above the door, and pass the rope over it. I will keep the fellow in some conversation near the spot until you adjust the noose under his chin, and then——"

"And then we run up the rope," said Petit-André, "and, *tchick!* our Astrologer is so far in Heaven, that he hath not a foot on earth."

"But these gentlemen," said Trois-Eschelles, looking towards the chimney, "do not these help, and so take a handsel of our vocation?"

"Hem! no," answered the Provost; "the barber only contrives mischief, which he leaves other men to execute; and for the Scot, he keeps the door when the deed is a-doing, which he hath not spirit or quickness sufficient to partake in more actively—every one to his trade."

With infinite dexterity, and even a sort of professional delight which sweetened the sense of their own precarious situation, the worthy executioners of the Provost's mandates adapted their rope and pulley for putting in force the sentence which had been uttered against Galeotti by the captive Monarch—seeming to rejoice that that last action was to be one so consistent with their past life. Tristan l'Hermite sat eyeing their proceedings with a species of satisfaction; while Oliver paid no attention to them whatever; and Ludovic Lesly, if, awakened by the bustle, he looked upon them at all, considered them as engaged in matters entirely unconnected with his own duty, and for which he was not to be regarded as responsible in one way or other.[1]

CHAPTER XXIX

RECRIMINATION

Thy time is not yet out—the devil thou servest
Has not as yet deserted thee. He aids
The friends who drudge for him, as the blind man
Was aided by the guide, who lent his shoulder
O'er rough and smooth, until he reach'd the brink
Of the fell precipice—then hurl'd him downward.
                                    Old Play.

WHEN obeying the command, or rather the request, of Louis,—for he was in circumstances in which, though a monarch, he could only *request* Le Glorieux to go in search of Martius Galeotti,—the jester had no trouble in executing his commission, betaking himself at once to the best tavern in Peronne, of which he himself was rather more than an occasional frequenter, being a great admirer of that species of liquor which reduced all other men's brains to a level with his own.

He found, or rather observed, the Astrologer in the corner of the public drinking-room—stove, as it is called in German and Flemish, from its principal furniture—sitting in close colloquy with a female in a singular, and something like a Moorish or Asiatic garb, who, as Le Glorieux approached Martius, rose as in the act to depart.

"These," said the stranger, "are news on which you may rely with absolute certainty;" and with that disappeared among the crowd of guests who sat grouped at different tables in the apartment.

"Cousin Philosopher," said the jester, presenting himself, "Heaven no sooner relieves one sentinel than it sends another to supply the place. One fool being gone, here I come another, to guide you to the apartments of Louis of France."

"And art thou the messenger?" said Martius, gazing on him with prompt apprehension, and discovering at once the jester's quality, though less intimated, as we have before noticed, than was usual, by his external appearance.

"Ay, sir, and like your learning," answered Le Glorieux; "when Power sends Folly to entreat the approach of Wisdom, 'tis a sure sign what foot the patient halts upon."

---

[1] The author has endeavoured to give to the odious Tristan l'Hermite a species of dogged and brutal fidelity to Louis, similar to the attachment of a bull-dog to his master. With all the atrocity of his execrable character, he was certainly a man of courage, and was, in his youth, made knight on the breach of Fronsac, with a great number of other young nobles, by the honour-giving hand of the elder Dunois, the celebrated hero of Charles the Fifth's reign.

"How if I refuse to come, when summoned at so late an hour by such a messenger?" said Galeotti.

"In that case we will consult your ease, and carry you," said Le Glorieux. "Here are half a score of stout Burgundian yeomen at the door, with whom He of Crèvecœur has furnished me to that effect. For know, that my friend Charles of Burgundy and I have not taken away our kinsman Louis's crown, which he was ass enough to put into our power, but have only filed and clipt it a little; and, though reduced to the size of a spangle, it is still pure gold. In plain terms, he is still paramount over his own people, yourself included, and Most Christian King of the old dining-hall in the Castle of Peronne, to which you, as his liege subject, are presently obliged to repair."

"I attend you, sir," said Martius Galeotti, and accompanied Le Glorieux accordingly—seeing, perhaps, that no evasion was possible.

"Ay, sir," said the Fool, as they went towards the Castle, "you do well; for we treat our kinsman as men use an old famished lion in his cage, and thrust him now and then a calf to mumble, to keep his old jaws in exercise."

"Do you mean," said Martius, "that the King intends me bodily injury?"

"Nay, that you can guess better than I," said the jester; "for, though the night be cloudy, I warrant you can see the stars through the mist. I know nothing of the matter, not I—only my mother always told me to go warily near an old rat in a trap, for he was never so much disposed to bite."

The Astrologer asked no more questions, and Le Glorieux, according to the custom of those of his class, continued to run on in a wild and disordered strain of sarcasm and folly mingled together, until he delivered the philosopher to the guard at the castle-gate of Peronne; where he was passed from warder to warder, and at length admitted within Herbert's Tower.

The hints of the jester had not been lost on Martius Galeotti, and he saw something which seemed to confirm them in the look and manner of Tristan, whose mode of addressing him, as he marshalled him to the King's bedchamber, was lowering, sullen, and ominous. A close observer of what passed on earth, as well as among the heavenly bodies, the pulley and the rope also caught the Astrologer's eye; and as the latter was in a state of vibration, he concluded that some one who had been busy adjusting it had been interrupted in the work by his sudden arrival. All this he saw, and summoned together his subtilty to evade the impending danger, resolved, should he find that impossible, to defend himself to the last against whomsoever should assail him.

Thus resolved, and with a step and look corresponding to the determination he had taken, Martius presented himself before Louis, alike unabashed at the miscarriage of his predictions, and undismayed at the Monarch's anger, and its probable consequences.

"Every good planet be gracious to your Majesty!" said Galeotti, with an inclination almost Oriental in manner—"Every evil constellation withhold their influences from my royal master!"

"Methinks," replied the King, "that when you look around this apartment, when you think where it is situated, and how guarded, your wisdom might consider that my propitious stars had proved faithless, and that each evil conjunction had already done its worst. Art thou not ashamed, Martius Galeotti, to see me here, and a prisoner, when you recollect by what assurances I was lured hither?"

"And art *thou* not ashamed, my royal Sire?" replied the philosopher; "thou, whose step in science was so forward, thy apprehension so quick, thy perseverance so unceasing,—art thou not ashamed to turn from the first frown of fortune, like a craven from the first clash of arms? Didst thou propose to become participant of those mysteries which raise men above the passions, the mischances, the pains, the sorrows of life, a state only to be attained by rivalling the firmness of the ancient Stoic, and dost thou shrink from the first pressure of adversity, and forfeit the glorious prize for which thou didst start as a competitor, frightened out of the course, like a scared racer, by shadowy and unreal evils?"

"Shadowy and unreal! frontless as thou art!" exclaimed the King, "is this dungeon unreal?—the weapons of the guards of my detested enemy Burgundy, which you may hear clash at the gate, are those shadows?—What, traitor, *are* real evils, if imprisonment, dethronement, and danger of life, are not so?"

"Ignorance—ignorance, my brother, and prejudice," answered the sage, with great firmness, "are the only real evils. Believe me, that Kings in the plenitude of power, if immersed in ignorance and prejudice, are less free than sages in a dungeon, and loaded with material chains. Towards this true happiness it is mine to guide you—be it yours to attend to my instructions."

"And it is to such philosophical freedom that your lessons would have guided me?" said the King, very bitterly. "I would you had told me at Plessis, that the dominion promised me so liberally was an empire over my own passions; that the success of which I was assured, related to my progress in philosophy; and that I might become as wise and as learned as a strolling mountebank of Italy! I might surely have attained this mental ascendency at a more moderate price than that of forfeiting the fairest crown in Christendom, and becoming tenant of a dungeon in Peronne! Go, sir, and think not to escape condign punishment—*There is a Heaven above us!*"

"I leave you not to your fate," replied Martius, "until I have vindicated, even in your eyes, darkened as they are, that reputation, a brighter gem than the brightest in thy crown, and at which the world shall wonder, ages after all the race of Capet are mouldered into oblivion in the charnels of Saint Denis."

"Speak on," said Louis; "thine impudence cannot make me change my purposes or my opinion—Yet as I may never again pass judgment as a King, I will not censure thee unheard. Speak, then—though the best thou canst say will be to speak the truth. Confess that I am a dupe, thou an impostor, thy pretended science a dream, and the planets which shine above us as little influential of our destiny, as their shadows, when reflected in the river, are capable of altering its course."

"And how know'st thou," answered the Astrologer boldly, "the secret influence of yonder blessed lights? Speak'st thou of their inability to influence waters, when yet thou know'st that even the weakest, the moon herself,—weakest because nearest to this wretched earth of ours,—holds under her domination, not such poor streams as the Somme, but the tides of the mighty ocean itself, which ebb and increase as her disc waxes and wanes, and watch her influence as a slave waits the nod of a Sultana? And now, Louis of Valois, answer my parable in turn—Confess, art thou not like the foolish passenger, who becomes wroth with his pilot because he cannot bring the vessel into harbour without experiencing occasionally the adverse force of winds and currents? I could indeed point to thee the probable issue of thine enterprise as prosperous, but it was in the power of Heaven alone to conduct thee thither; and if the path be rough and dangerous, was it in my power to smooth or render it more safe? Where is thy wisdom of yesterday, which taught thee so truly to discern that the ways of destiny are often ruled to our advantage, though in opposition to our wishes?"

"You remind me—you remind me," said the King hastily, "of one specific falsehood. You foretold, yonder Scot should accomplish his enterprise fortunately for my interest and honour; and thou knowest it has so terminated, that no more mortal injury could I have received, than from the impression which the issue of that affair is like to make on the excited brain of the Mad Bull of Burgundy. This is a direct falsehood—thou canst plead no evasion here—canst refer to no remote favourable turn of the tide, for which, like an idiot sitting on the bank until the river shall pass away, thou wouldst have me wait contentedly. —Here thy craft deceived thee—Thou wert weak enough to make a specific prediction, which has proved directly false."

"Which will prove most firm and true," answered the Astrologer boldly. "I would desire no greater triumph of art over ignorance, than that prediction and its accomplishment will afford. I told thee he would be faithful in any honourable commission—Hath he not been so?—I told thee he would be scrupulous in aiding any evil enterprise—Hath he not proved so? If you doubt it, go ask the Bohemian, Hayraddin Maugrabin."

The King here coloured deeply with shame and anger.

"I told thee," continued the Astrologer, "that the conjunction of planets under which he set forth, augured danger to the person—and hath not his path been beset by danger?—I told thee that it augured an advantage to the sender—and of that thou wilt soon have the benefit."

"Soon have the benefit!" exclaimed the King; "Have I not the result already, in disgrace and imprisonment?"

"No," answered the Astrologer, "the End is not as yet—thine own tongue shall ere long confess the benefit which thou hast received, from the manner in which the messenger bore himself in discharging thy commission."

"This is too—too insolent," said the King, "at once to deceive and to insult—But hence!—think not my wrongs shall be unavenged.—*There is a Heaven above us!*"

Galeotti turned to depart. "Yet stop," said Louis—"thou bearest thine imposture bravely out—Let me hear your answer to one question, and think ere you speak.—Can thy pretended skill ascertain the hour of thine own death?"

"Only by referring to the fate of another," said Galeotti.

"I understand not thine answer," said Louis.

"Know then, O King," said Martius, "that this only I can tell with certainty concerning mine own death, that it shall take place exactly twenty-four hours before that of your Majesty." [1]

"Ha! say'st thou?" said Louis, his countenance again altering.—"Hold—hold—go not—wait one moment.—Saidst thou, *my* death should follow *thine* so closely?"

"Within the space of twenty-four hours," repeated Galeotti firmly, "if there be one sparkle of true divination in those bright and mysterious intelligences, which speak, each on their courses, though without a tongue,—I wish your Majesty good rest."

"Hold—hold—go not," said the King, taking him by the arm, and leading him from the door. "Martius Galeotti, I have been a kind master to thee—enriched thee—made thee my friend—my companion—the instructor of my studies.—Be open with me, I entreat you.—Is there aught in this art of yours in very deed?—Shall this Scot's mission be, in fact, propitious to me?—And is the measure of our lives so very—*very* nearly matched? Confess, my good Martius, you speak after the trick of your trade—Confess, I pray you, and you shall have no displeasure at my hand. I am in years—a prisoner—likely to be deprived of a kingdom—to one in my condition truth is worth kingdoms, and it is from thee, dearest Martius, that I must look for this inestimable jewel."

"And I have laid it before your Majesty," said Galeotti, "at the risk that, in brutal passion, you might turn upon me and rend me."

"Who, I, Galeotti?" replied Louis mildly; "Alas! thou mistakest me!—Am I not captive,—and should not I be patient, especially since my anger can only show my impotence?—Tell me then in sincerity— Have you fooled me?—Or is your science true, and do you truly report it?"

"Your Majesty will forgive me if I reply to you," said Martius Galeotti,

[1] Note X.—Martius Galeotti.

"that time only—time and the event, will convince incredulity. It suits ill the place of confidence which I have held at the council-table of the renowned conqueror, Matthias Corvinus of Hungary—nay, in the cabinet of the Emperor himself—to reiterate assurances of that which I have advanced as true. If you will not believe me, I can but refer to the course of events. A day, or two days' patience, will prove or disprove what I have averred concerning the young Scot; and I will be contented to die on the wheel, and have my limbs broken joint by joint, if your Majesty have not advantage, and that in a most important degree, from the dauntless conduct of that Quentin Durward. But if I were to die under such tortures, it would be well your Majesty should seek a ghostly father; for, from the moment my last groan is drawn, only twenty-four hours will remain to you for confession and penitence."

Louis continued to keep hold of Galeotti's robe as he led him towards the door, and pronounced as he opened it, in a loud voice, "To-morrow we'll talk more of this. Go in peace, my learned father—*Go in peace—Go in peace!*"

He repeated these words three times; and, still afraid that the Provost-Marshal might mistake his purpose, he led the Astrologer into the hall, holding fast his robe, as if afraid that he should be torn from him, and put to death before his eyes. He did not unloose his grasp until he had not only repeated again and again the gracious phrase, "Go in peace," but even made a private signal to the Provost-Marshal, to enjoin a suspension of all proceedings against the person of the Astrologer.

Thus did the possession of some secret information, joined to audacious courage and readiness of wit, save Galeotti from the most imminent danger; and thus was Louis, the most sagacious as well as the most vindictive, amongst the monarchs of the period, cheated of his revenge by the influence of superstition upon a selfish temper, and a mind to which, from the consciousness of many crimes, the fear of death was peculiarly terrible.

He felt, however, considerable mortification at being obliged to relinquish his purposed vengeance; and the disappointment seemed to be shared by his satellites, to whom the execution was to have been committed. Le Balafré alone, perfectly indifferent on the subject, so soon as the countermanding signal was given, left the door at which he had posted himself, and in a few minutes was fast asleep.

The Provost-Marshal, as the group reclined themselves to repose in the hall after the King retired to his bedchamber, continued to eye the goodly form of the Astrologer, with the look of the mastiff watching a joint of meat which the cook had retrieved from his jaws, while his attendants communicated to each other in brief sentences their characteristic sentiments.

"The poor blinded necromancer," whispered Trois-Eschelles, with an air of spiritual unction and commiseration, to his comrade, Petit-André, "hath lost the fairest chance of expiating some of his vile sorceries, by dying through means of the cord of the blessed Saint Francis! and I had purpose, indeed, to leave the comfortable noose around his neck, to scare the foul fiend from his unhappy carcass."

"And I," said Petit-André, "have missed the rarest opportunity of knowing how far a weight of seventeen stone will stretch a three-plied cord!—It would have been a glorious experiment in our line,—and the jolly old boy would have died so easily!"

While this whispered dialogue was going forward, Martius, who had taken the opposite side of the huge stone fire-place, round which the whole group was assembled, regarded them askance, and with a look of suspicion. He first put his hand into his vest, and satisfied himself that the handle of a very sharp double-edged poniard, which he always carried about him, was disposed conveniently for his grasp; for, as we have already noticed, he was, though now somewhat unwieldy, a powerful, athletic man, and prompt and active at the use of his weapon. Satisfied that this trusty instrument was in readiness, he next took from his bosom a scroll of parchment, inscribed with Greek characters, and marked with cabalistic signs, drew together the wood in the fire-place, and made a blaze by which he could distinguish the features and attitude of all who sat or lay around—the heavy and deep slumbers of the Scottish soldier, who lay motionless, with his rough countenance as immovable as if it were cast in bronze—the pale and anxious face of Oliver, who at one time assumed the appearance of slumber, and again opened his eyes and raised his head hastily, as if stung by some internal throe, or awakened by some distant sound—the discontented, savage, bull-dog aspect of the Provost, who looked

> ——"frustrate of his will
> Not half sufficed, and greedy yet to kill"—

while the background was filled up by the ghastly hypocritical countenance of Trois-Eschelles, whose eyes were cast up towards Heaven, as if he was internally saying his devotions; and the grim drollery of Petit-André, who amused himself with mimicking the gestures and wry faces of his comrade before he betook himself to sleep.

Amidst these vulgar and ignoble countenances, nothing could show to greater advantage than the stately form, handsome mien, and commanding features of the Astrologer, who might have passed for one of the ancient magi, imprisoned in a den of robbers, and about to invoke a spirit to accomplish his liberation. And, indeed, had he been distinguished by nothing else than the beauty of the graceful and flowing beard which descended over the mysterious roll which he held in his hand, one might have been pardoned for regretting that so noble an appendage had been bestowed on one, who put both talents, learning, and the advantages of eloquence, and a majestic person, to the mean purposes of a cheat and an impostor.

Thus passed the night in Count Herbert's Tower, in the Castle of Peronne. When the first light of dawn penetrated the ancient Gothic chamber, the King summoned Oliver to his presence, who found the Monarch sitting in his night-gown, and was astonished at the alteration which one night of mortal anxiety had made in his looks. He would have expressed some anxiety on the subject, but the King silenced him by entering into a statement of the various modes by which he had previously endeavoured to form friends at the Court of Burgundy, and which Oliver was charged to prosecute so soon as he should be permitted to stir abroad. And never was that wily minister more struck with the clearness of the King's intellect, and his intimate knowledge of all the springs which influence human actions, than he was during that memorable consultation.

About two hours afterwards, Oliver accordingly obtained permission from the Count of Crèvecœur to go out and execute the commissions which his master had entrusted him with; and Louis, sending for the Astrologer, in whom he seemed to have renewed his faith, held with him, in like manner, a long consultation, the issue of which appeared to give him more spirits and confidence than he had at first exhibited; so that he dressed himself, and received the morning compliments of Crèvecœur with a calmness, at which the Burgundian Lord could not help wondering, the rather that he had already heard that the Duke had passed several hours in a state of mind which seemed to render the King's safety very precarious.

CHAPTER XXX

UNCERTAINTY

Our counsels waver like the unsteady bark,
That reels amid the strife of meeting currents.
Old Play.

IF the night passed by Louis was carefully anxious and agitated, that spent by the Duke of Burgundy, who had at no time the same mastery over his passions, and, indeed, who permitted them almost a free and uncontrolled dominion over his actions, was still more disturbed.

According to the custom of the period, two of his principal and most favoured counsellors, D'Hymbercourt and Des Comines, shared his bedchamber, couches being prepared for them near the bed of the prince. Their attendance was never more necessary than upon this night, when, distracted by sorrow, by passion, by the desire of revenge, and by the sense of honour, which forbade him to exercise it upon Louis in his present condition, the Duke's mind resembled a volcano in eruption, which throws forth all the different contents of the mountain, mingled and molten into one burning mass.

He refused to throw off his clothes, or to make any preparation for sleep; but spent the night in a succession of the most violent bursts of passion. In some paroxysms he talked incessantly to his attendants so thick and so rapidly, that they were really afraid his senses would give way; choosing for his theme, the merits and the kindness of heart of the murdered Bishop of Liege, and recalling all the instances of mutual kindness, affection, and confidence, which had passed between them, until he had worked himself into such a transport of grief, that he threw himself upon his face in the bed, and seemed ready to choke with the sobs and tears which he endeavoured to stifle. Then starting from the couch, he gave vent at once to another and more furious mood, and traversed the room hastily, uttering incoherent threats, and still more incoherent oaths of vengeance, while, stamping with his foot, according to his customary action, he invoked Saint George, Saint Andrew, and whomsoever else he held most holy, to bear witness, that he would take bloody vengeance on De la Marck, on the people of Liege, and on *him* who was the author of the whole.—These last threats, uttered more obscurely than the others, obviously concerned the person of the King; and at one time the Duke expressed his determination to send for the Duke of Normandy, the brother of the King, and with whom Louis was on the worst terms, in order to compel the captive monarch to surrender either the Crown itself, or some of its most valuable rights and appanages.

Another day and night passed in the same stormy and fitful deliberations, or rather rapid transitions of passion; for the Duke scarcely ate or drank, never changed his dress, and, altogether, demeaned himself like one in whom rage might terminate in utter insanity. By degrees he became more composed, and began to hold, from time to time, consultations with his ministers, in which much was proposed, but nothing resolved on. Comines assures us, that at one time a courier was mounted in readiness to depart for the purpose of summoning the Duke of Normandy; and in that event, the prison of the French monarch would probably have been found, as in similar cases, a brief road to his grave.

At other times, when Charles had exhausted his fury, he sat with his features fixed in stern and rigid immobility, like one who broods over some desperate deed to which he is as yet unable to work up his resolution. And unquestionably it would have needed little more than an insidious hint from any of the counsellors who attended his person, to have pushed the Duke to some very desperate action. But the nobles of Burgundy, from the sacred character attached to the person of a King, and a Lord Paramount, and from a regard to the public faith, as well as that of their Duke, which had been pledged when Louis threw himself into their power, were almost unanimously inclined to recommend moderate measures; and the arguments which D'Hymbercourt and Des Comines had now and then ventured to insinuate during the night, were, in the cooler hours of the next morning, advanced and urged by Crèvecœur and others. Possibly their zeal in behalf of the King might not be entirely disinterested. Many, as we have mentioned, had already experienced the bounty of the King; others had either estates or pretensions in France, which placed them a little under his influence; and it is certain that the treasure, which had loaded four mules when the King entered Peronne, became much lighter in the course of these negotiations.

In the course of the third day, the Count of Campo-basso brought his Italian wit to assist the counsels of Charles; and well was it for Louis, that he had not arrived when the Duke was in his first fury. Immediately on his arrival, a regular meeting of the Duke's counsellors was convened, for considering the measures to be adopted in this singular crisis.

On this occasion, Campo-basso gave his opinion, couched in the apologue of the Traveller, the Adder, and the Fox; and reminded the Duke of the advice which Reynard gave to the man, that he should crush his mortal enemy, now that chance had placed his fate at his disposal. Des Comines, who saw the Duke's eye sparkle at a proposal which his own violence of temper had already repeatedly suggested, hastened to state the possibility, that Louis might not be, in fact, so directly accessory to the sanguinary action which had been committed at Schonwaldt; that he might be able to clear himself of the imputation laid to his charge, and perhaps to make other atonement for the distractions which his intrigues had occasioned in the Duke's dominions, and those of his allies; and that an act of violence perpetrated on the King, was sure to bring both on France and Burgundy a train of the most unhappy consequences, among which not the least to be feared was, that the English might avail themselves of the commotions and civil discord which must needs ensue, to repossess themselves of Normandy and Guyenne, and renew those dreadful wars, which had only, and with difficulty, been terminated by the union of both France and Burgundy against the common enemy. Finally, he confessed, that he did not mean to urge the absolute and free dismissal of Louis; but only, that the Duke should avail himself no farther of his present condition, than merely to establish a fair and equitable treaty between the countries, with such security on the King's part, as should make it difficult for him to break his faith, or disturb the internal peace of Burgundy in future. D'Hymbercourt, Crèvecœur, and others, signified their reprobation of the violent meas, ures proposed by Campo-basso, and their opinion, that in the way of treaty more permanent advantages could be obtained, and in a manner more honourable for Burgundy, than by an action which would stain her with a breach of faith and hospitality.

The Duke listened to these arguments with his looks fixed on the ground, and his brows so knitted together as to bring his bushy eyebrows into one mass. But when Crèvecœur proceeded to say, that he did not believe Louis either knew of, or was accessory to, the atrocious act of violence committed at Schonwaldt, Charles raised his head, and darting a fierce look at his counsellor, exclaimed. "Have you too, Crève-

cœur, heard the gold of France clink?—Methinks it rings in my councils as merrily as ever the bells of Saint Dennis—Dare any one say
that Louis is not the fomenter of these feuds in Flanders?"

"My gracious lord," said Crèvecœur, "my hand has ever been more
conversant with steel than with gold; and so far am I from holding that
Louis is free from the charge of having caused the disturbances in
Flanders, that it is not long since, in the face of his whole Court, I
charged him with that breach of faith, and offered him defiance in your
name. But although his intrigues have been doubtless the original cause
of these commotions, I am so far from believing that he authorised the
death of the Archbishop, that I believe one of his emissaries publicly
protested against it; and I could produce the man were it your Grace's
pleasure to see him."

"It *is* our pleasure," said the Duke. "Saint George! can you doubt that
we desire to act justly? Even in the highest flight of our passion, we
are known for an upright and a just judge. We will see France ourself
—we will ourself charge him with our wrongs, and ourself state to him
the reparation which we expect and demand. If he shall be found guiltless of this murder, the atonement for other crimes may be more easy—
If he hath been guilty, who shall say that a life of penitence in some
retired monastery were not a most deserved and a most merciful doom?
—Who," he added, kindling as he spoke, "who shall dare to blame a
revenge yet more direct and more speedy? Let your witness attend—We
will to the Castle at the hour before noon. Some articles we will minute down with which he shall comply, or woe on his head! others shall
depend upon the proof. Break up the council, and dismiss yourselves. I
will but change my dress, as this is scarce a fitting trim in which to
wait on *my most gracious Sovereign.*"

With a deep and bitter emphasis on the last expression, the Duke
arose, and strode out of the room.

"Louis's safety, and, what is worse, the honour of Burgundy, depend
on the cast of the dice," said D'Hymbercourt to Crèvecœur and to Des
Comines—"Haste thee to the Castle, Des Comines—thou hast a better
filed tongue than either Crèvecœur or I. Explain to Louis what storm is
approaching—he will best know how to pilot himself. I trust this life-
guardsman will say nothing which can aggravate; for who knows what
may have been the secret commission with which he was charged?"

"The young man," said Crèvecœur, "seems bold, yet prudent and wary
far beyond his years. In all which he said to me he was tender of the
King's character, as of that of the Prince whom he serves. I trust he
will be equally so in the Duke's presence. I must go seek him, and also
the young Countess of Croye."

"The Countess!—you told us you had left her at Saint Bridget's
Nunnery?"

"Ay, but I was obliged," said the Count, "to send for her express, by
the Duke's orders; and she has been brought hither on a litter, as being

unable to travel otherwise. She was in a state of the deepest distress, both on account of the uncertainty of the fate of her kinswoman, the Lady Hameline, and the gloom which overhangs her own; guilty as she has been of feudal delinquency, in withdrawing herself from the protection of her liege lord, Duke Charles, who is not the person in the world most likely to view with indifference what trenches on his seigniorial rights."

The information that the young Countess was in the hands of Charles, added fresh and more pointed thorns to Louis's reflections. He was conscious that, by explaining the intrigues by which he had induced the Lady Hameline and her to resort to Peronne [Plessis], she might supply that evidence which he had removed by the execution of Zamet Maugrabin; and he knew well how much such proof of his having interfered with the rights of the Duke of Burgundy, would furnish both motive and pretext for Charles's availing himself to the uttermost of his present predicament.

Louis discoursed on these matters with great anxiety to the Sieur Des Comines, whose acute and political talents better suited the King's temper than the blunt martial character of Crèvecœur, or the feudal haughtiness of D'Hymbercourt.

"These iron-handed soldiers, my good friend Comines," he said to his future historian, "should never enter a King's cabinet, but be left with the halberds and partisans in the antechamber. Their hands are indeed made for our use, but the monarch who puts their heads to any better occupation than that of anvils for his enemies' swords and maces, ranks with the fool who presented his mistress with a dog-leash for a carcanet. It is with such as thou, Philip, whose eyes are gifted with the quick and keen sense that sees beyond the exterior surface of affairs, that Princes should share their council-table, their cabinet—what do I say?—the most secret recesses of their soul."

Des Comines, himself so keen a spirit, was naturally gratified with the approbation of the most sagacious Prince in Europe; and he could not so far disguise his internal satisfaction, but that Louis was aware he had made some impression on him.

"I would," continued he, "that I had such a servant, or rather that I were worthy to have such a one! I had not then been in this unfortunate situation; which, nevertheless, I should hardly regret, could I but discover any means of securing the services of so experienced a statist."

Des Comines said, that all his faculties, such as they were, were at the service of his Most Christian Majesty, saving always his allegiance to his rightful lord, Duke Charles of Burgundy.

"And am I one who would seduce you from that allegiance?" said Louis pathetically. "Alas! am I not now endangered by having reposed too much confidence in my vassal? and can the cause of feudal good faith be more sacred with any than with me, whose safety depends on an appeal to it?—No, Philip Des Comines—continue to serve Charles of Burgundy; and you will best serve him, by bringing round a fair accommodation with Louis of France. In doing thus, you will serve us both, and one, at least, will be grateful. I am told your appointments in his Court hardly match those of the Grand Falconer; and thus the services of the wisest counsellor in Europe are put on a level, or rather ranked below, those of a fellow who feeds and physics kites! France has wide lands—her King has much gold. Allow me, my friend, to rectify this scandalous inequality. The means are not distant—Permit me to use them."

The King produced a weighty bag of money; but Des Comines, more delicate in his sentiments than most courtiers of that time, declined the proffer, declaring himself perfectly satisfied with the liberality of his native Prince, and assuring Louis that his desire to serve him could not be increased by the acceptance of any such gratuity as he had proposed.

"Singular man!" exclaimed the King; "let me embrace the only courtier of his time, at once capable and incorruptible. Wisdom is to be desired more than fine gold; and believe me, I trust in thy kindness, Philip, at this pinch, more than I do in the purchased assistance of many who have received my gifts. I know you will not counsel your master to abuse such an opportunity, as fortune, and, to speak plain, Des Comines, as my own folly, has afforded him."

"To *abuse* it, by no means," answered the historian; "but most certainly to *use* it."

"How, and in what degree?" said Louis. "I am not ass enough to expect that I shall escape without some ransom—but let it be a reasonable one—reason I am ever willing to listen to—at Paris or at Plessis, equally as at Peronne."

"Ah, but if it like your Majesty," replied Des Comines, "Reason at Paris or Plessis was used to speak in so low and soft a tone of voice, that she could not always gain an audience of your Majesty—at Peronne, she borrows the speaking-trumpet of Necessity, and her voice becomes lordly and imperative."

"You are figurative," said Louis, unable to restrain an emotion of peevishness; "I am a dull, blunt man, Sir of Comines. I pray you leave your tropes, and come to plain ground. What does your Duke expect of me?"

"I am the bearer of no propositions, my lord," said Des Comines; "the Duke will soon explain his own pleasure; but some things occur to me as proposals, for which your Majesty ought to hold yourself prepared. As, for example, the final cession of these towns here upon the Somme."

"I expected so much," said Louis.

"That you should disown the Liegeois, and William de la Marck."

"As willingly as I disclaim Hell and Satan," said Louis.

"Ample security will be required, by hostages, or occupation of fortresses, or otherwise, that France shall in future abstain from stirring up rebellion among the Flemings."

"It is something new," answered the King, "that a vassal should demand pledges from his Sovereign: but let that pass too."

"A suitable and independent appanage for your illustrious brother, the ally and friend of my master—Normandy or Champagne. The Duke loves your father's house, my Liege."

"So well," answered Louis, "that, *mort Dieu!* he's about to make them all kings.—Is your budget of hints yet emptied!"

"Not entirely," answered the counsellor: "it will certainly be required that your Majesty shall forbear molesting, as you have done of late, the Duke de Bretagne, and that you will no longer contest the right, which he and other grand feudatories have, to strike money, to term themselves dukes and princes by the grace of God——"

"In a word, to make so many kings of my vassals. Sir Philip, would you make a fratricide of me?—You remember well my brother Charles— he was no sooner Duke of Guyenne than he died.—And what will be left to the descendant and representative of Charlemagne, after giving away these rich provinces, save to be smeared with oil at Rheims, and to eat his dinner under a high canopy?"

"We will diminish your Majesty's concern on that score, by giving you a companion in that solitary exaltation," said Philip des Comines.— "The Duke of Burgundy, though he claims not at present the title of an independent king, desires nevertheless to be freed in future from the abject marks of subjection required of him to the crown of France;—it is his purpose to close his ducal coronet with an imperial arch, and surmount it with a globe, in emblem that his dominions are independent."

"And how dares the Duke of Burgundy, the sworn vassal of France," exclaimed Louis, starting up, and showing an unwonted degree of emotion—"how dares he propose such terms to his Sovereign, as, by every law of Europe, should infer a forfeiture of his fief?"

"The doom of forfeiture it would in this case be difficult to enforce," answered Des Comines calmly.—"Your Majesty is aware, that the strict interpretation of the feudal law is becoming obsolete even in the Empire, and that superior and vassal endeavour to mend their situation in regard to each other, as they have power and opportunity.—Your Majesty's interferences with the Duke's vassals in Flanders will prove an exculpation of my master's conduct, supposing him to insist that, by enlarging his independence, France should in future be debarred from any pretext of doing so."

"Comines, Comines!" said Louis, arising again, and pacing the room in a pensive manner, "this is a dreadful lesson on the text *Væ victis!*—You cannot mean that the Duke will insist on all these hard conditions?"

"At least I would have your Majesty be in a condition to discuss them all."

"Yet moderation, Des Comines, moderation in success, is—no one knows better than you—necessary to its ultimate advantage."

"So please your Majesty, the merit of moderation is, I have observed, most apt to be extolled by the losing party. The winner holds in more esteem the prudence which calls on him not to leave an opportunity unimproved."

"Well, we will consider"—replied the King; "but at least thou hast reached the extremity of your Duke's unreasonable exaction? there can remain nothing—or if there does, for so thy brow intimates—what is it— what indeed can it be—unless it be my crown? which these previous demands, if granted, will deprive of all its lustre!"

"My lord," said Des Comines, "what remains to be mentioned, is a thing partly—indeed in a great measure—within the Duke's own power, though he means to invite your Majesty's accession to it, for in truth it touches you nearly."

"*Pasques-dieu!*" exclaimed the King impatiently, "what is it?—Speak on, Sir Philip—am I to send him my daughter for a concubine, or what other dishonour is he to put on me?"

"No dishonour, my liege; but your Majesty's cousin, the illustrious Duke of Orleans——"

"Ha!" exclaimed the King; but Des Comines proceeded without heeding the interruption.

"—Having conferred his affections on the young Countess Isabelle De Croye, the Duke expects your Majesty will, on your part, as he on his, yield your assent to the marriage, and unite with him in endowing the right noble couple with such an appanage, as, joined to the Countess's estates, may form a fit establishment for a child of France."

"Never, never!" said the King, bursting out into that emotion which he had of late suppressed with much difficulty, and striding about in a disordered haste, which formed the strongest contrast to the self-command which he usually exhibited,—"Never, never!—let them bring scissors, and shear my hair like that of the parish-fool, whom I have so richly resembled! let them bid the monastery or the grave yawn for me— let them bring red-hot basins to sear my eyes—axe or aconite—whatever they will—but Orleans shall not break his plighted faith to my daughter, or marry another while she lives!"

"Your Majesty," said Des Comines, "ere you set your mind so keenly against what is proposed, will consider your own want of power to prevent it. Every wise man, when he sees a rock giving way, withdraws from the bootless attempt of preventing the fall."

"But a brave man," said Louis, "will at least find his grave beneath it. Des Comines, consider the great loss—the utter destruction, such a marriage will bring upon my kingdom. Recollect, I have but one feeble boy, and this Orleans is the next heir—consider that the Church hath consented to his union with Joan, which unites so happily the interests of both branches of my family,—think on all this, and think too that this union has been the favourite scheme of my whole life—that I have schemed for it, fought for it, watched for it, prayed for it,—and sinned for it. Philip des Comines, I will not forego it! Think, man, think!—

pity me in this extremity—thy quick brain can speedily find some sub-stitute for this sacrifice—some ram to be offered up instead of that project which is dear to me as the Patriarch's only son was to him. Philip, pity me!—you, at least, should know, that to men of judgment and foresight, the destruction of the scheme on which they have long dwelt, and for which they have long toiled, is more inexpressibly bitter than the transient grief of ordinary men, whose pursuits are but the gratification of some temporary passion—you, who know how to sym-pathise with the deeper, the more genuine distress of baffled prudence and disappointed sagacity,—will you not feel for me?"

"My Lord and King!" replied Des Comines, "I do sympathise with your distress, in so far as duty to my master——"

"Do not mention him!" said Louis, acting, or at least appearing to act, under an irresistible and headlong impulse, which withdrew the usual guard which he maintained over his language—"Charles of Burgundy is unworthy of your attachment. He who can insult and strike his coun-sellors—he who can distinguish the wisest and most faithful among them, by the opprobrious name of Booted Head!——"

The wisdom of Philip des Comines did not prevent his having a high sense of personal consequence; and he was so much struck with the words which the King uttered, as it were, in the career of a passion which overleaped ceremony, that he could only reply by repetition of the words "Booted Head! It is impossible that my master the Duke could have so termed the servant who has been at his side since he could mount a palfrey—and that too before a foreign monarch?—it is impossible!"

Louis instantly saw the impression he had made, and avoiding alike a tone of condolence, which might have seemed insulting, and one of sympathy, which might have savoured of affectation, he said, with sim-plicity, and at the same time with dignity, "My misfortunes make me forget my courtesy, else I had not spoken to you of what it must be unpleasant for you to hear. But you have in reply taxed me with having uttered impossibilities—this touches my honour; yet I must submit to the charge, if I tell you not the circumstances which the Duke, laughing until his eyes ran over, assigned for the origin of that opprobrious name, which I will not offend your ears by repeating. Thus, then, it chanced. You, Sir Philip des Comines, were at a hunting-match with the Duke of Burgundy, your master; and when he alighted after the chase, he required your services in drawing off his boots. Reading in your looks, perhaps, some natural resentment of his disparaging treatment, he ordered you to sit down in turn, and rendered you the same office he had just received from you. But offended at your understanding him literally, he no sooner plucked one of your boots off, than he brutally beat it about your head till the blood flowed, exclaiming against the insolence of a subject, who had the presumption to accept of such a service at the hand of his Sovereign; and hence he, or his privileged fool Le Glorieux, is in the current habit of distinguishing you by the absurd and ridiculous name of *Tête-botté,* which makes one of the Duke's most ordinary subjects of pleasantry." [1]

While Louis thus spoke, he had the double pleasure of galling to the quick the person whom he addressed—an exercise which it was in his nature to enjoy, even where he had not, as in the present case, the apology, that he did so in pure retaliation—and that of observing that he had at length been able to find a point in Des Comines' character which might lead him gradually from the interests of Burgundy to those of France. But although the deep resentment which the offended courtier entertained against his master induced him at a future period to exchange the service of Charles for that of Louis, yet, at the present moment, he was contented to throw out only some general hints of his friendly inclination towards France, which he well knew the King would understand how to interpret. And indeed it would be unjust to stigmatise the memory of the excellent historian with the desertion of his master on this occasion, although he was certainly now possessed with sentiments much more favourable to Louis than when he entered the apartment.

He constrained himself to laugh at the anecdote which Louis had detailed, and then added, "I did not think so trifling a frolic would have dwelt on the mind of the Duke so long as to make it worth telling again. Some such passage there was of drawing off boots and the like, as your Majesty knows that the Duke is fond of rude play; but it has been much exaggerated in his recollection. Let it pass on."

"Ay, *let* it pass on," said the King; "it is indeed shame it should have detained us a minute.—And now, Sir Philip, I hope you are French so far as to afford me your best counsel in these difficult affairs. You have, I am well aware, the clew to the labyrinth, if you would but impart it."

"Your Majesty may command my best advice and service," replied Des Comines, "under reservation always of my duty to my own master."

This was nearly what the courtier had before stated; but he now repeated it in a tone so different, that whereas Louis understood from the former declaration, that the reserved duty to Burgundy was the prime thing to be considered, so he now saw clearly that the emphasis was reversed, and that more weight was now given by the speaker to his promise of counsel, than to a restriction which seemed interposed for the sake of form and consistency. The King resumed his own seat, and compelled Des Comines to sit by him, listening at the same time to that statesman, as if the words of an oracle sounded in his ears. Des Comines spoke in that low and impressive tone, which implies at once great sincerity and some caution, and at the same time so slowly, as if he was

[1] The story is told more bluntly, and less probably, in the French memoirs of the period, which affirm that Comines, out of a presumption inconsistent with his excellent good sense, had asked of Charles of Burgundy to draw off his boots, without having been treated with any previous familiarity to lead to such a freedom. I have endeavoured to give the anecdote a turn more consistent with the sense and prudence of the great author concerned.

desirous that the King should weigh and consider each individual word as having its own peculiar and determined meaning. "The things," he said, "which I have suggested for your Majesty's consideration, harsh as they sound in your ear, are but substitutes for still more violent proposals brought forward in the Duke's councils, by such as are more hostile to your Majesty. And I need scarce remind your Majesty, that the more direct and more violent suggestions find readiest acceptance with our master, who loves brief and dangerous measures better than those that are safe, but at the same time circuitous."

"I remember"—said the King, "I have seen him swim a river at the risk of drowning, though there was a bridge to be found for riding two hundred yards round."

"True, Sire; and he that weighs not his life against the gratification of a moment of impetuous passion, will, on the same impulse, prefer the gratification of his will to the increase of his substantial power."

"Most true," replied the King; "a fool will ever grasp rather at the appearance than the reality of authority. All this I know to be true of Charles of Burgundy. But, my dear friend Des Comines, what do you infer from these premises?"

"Simply this, my lord," answered the Burgundian, "that as your Majesty has seen a skilful angler control a large and heavy fish, and finally draw him to land by a single hair, which fish had broke through a tackle tenfold stronger, had the fisher presumed to strain the line on him, instead of giving him head enough for all his wild flourishes; even so your Majesty, by gratifying the Duke in these particulars on which he has pitched his ideas of honour, and the gratification of his revenge, may evade many of the other unpalatable propositions at which I have hinted; and which—including, I must state openly to your Majesty, some of those through which France would be most especially weakened—will slide out of his remembrance and attention, and, being referred to subsequent conferences and future discussion, may be altogether eluded."

"I understand you, my good Sir Philip; but to the matter," said the King. "To which of those happy propositions is your Duke so much wedded, that contradiction will make him unreasonable and untractable?"

"To any or to all of them, if it please your Majesty, on which you may happen to contradict him. This is precisely what your Majesty must avoid; and to take up my former parable, you must needs remain on the watch, ready to give the Duke line enough whenever he shoots away under the impulse of his rage. His fury, already considerably abated, will waste itself if he be unopposed, and you will presently find him become more friendly and more tractable."

"Still," said the King, musing, "there must be some particular demands which lie deeper at my cousin's heart than the other proposals. Were I but aware of these, Sir Philip——"

"Your Majesty may make the lightest of his demands the most important, simply by opposing it," said Des Comines; "nevertheless, my lord, thus far I can say, that every shadow of treaty will be broken off, if your Majesty renounce not William de la Marck and the Liegeois."

"I have already said that I will disown them," said the King, "and well they deserve it at my hand; the villains have commenced their uproar at a moment that might have cost me my life."

"He that fires a train of powder," replied the historian, "must expect a speedy explosion of the mine.—But more than mere disavowal of their cause will be expected of your Majesty by Duke Charles; for know, that he will demand your Majesty's assistance to put the insurrection down, and your royal presence to witness the punishment which he destines for the rebels."

"That may scarce consist with our honour, Des Comines," said the King.

"To refuse it will scarcely consist with your Majesty's safety," replied Des Comines. "Charles is determined to show the people of Flanders, that no hope, nay no promise, of assistance from France, will save them in their mutinies from the wrath and vengeance of Burgundy."

"But, Sir Philip, I will speak plainly," answered the King—"Could we but procrastinate the matter, might not these rogues of Liege make their own part good against Duke Charles? The knaves are numerous and steady—Can they not hold out their town against him?"

"With the help of the thousand archers of France whom your Majesty promised them, they might have done something; but——"

"Whom I promised them!" said the King—"Alas! good Sir Philip! you much wrong me in saying so."

"——But without whom," continued Des Comines, not heeding the interruption,—"as your Majesty will not *now* likely find it convenient to supply them,—what chance will the burghers have of making good their town, in whose walls the large breaches made by Charles after the battle of St. Tron are still unrepaired; so that the lances of Hainault, Brabant, and Burgundy, may advance to the attack twenty men in front?"

"The improvident idiots!" said the King—"If they have thus neglected their own safety, they deserve not my protection.—Pass on—I will make no quarrel for their sake."

"The next point, I fear, will sit closer to your Majesty's heart," said Des Comines.

"Ah!" replied the King, " you mean that infernal marriage! I will not consent to the breach of the contract betwixt my daughter Joan and my cousin of Orleans—it would be wresting the sceptre of France from me and my posterity; for that feeble boy the Dauphin is a blighted blossom, which will wither without fruit. This match between Joan and Orleans has been my thought by day, my dream by night—I tell thee, Sir Philip, I cannot give it up!—Besides, it is inhuman to require me, with my own hand, to destroy at once my own scheme of policy, and the happiness of a pair brought up for each other."

"Are they then so much attached?" said Des Comines.

"One of them at least is," said the King, "and the one for whom I am bound to be most anxious. But you smile, Sir Philip,—you are no believer in the force of love."

"Nay," said Des Comines, "if it please you, Sire, I am so little an infidel in that particular, that I was about to ask whether it would reconcile you in any degree to your acquiescing in the proposed marriage betwixt the Duke of Orleans and Isabelle de Croye, were I to satisfy you that the Countess's inclinations are so much fixed on another, that it is likely it will never be a match?"

King Louis sighed.—"Alas!" he said, "my good and dear friend, from what sepulchre have you drawn such dead man's comfort? *Her* inclination, indeed!—Why, to speak truth, supposing that Orleans detested my daughter Joan, yet, but for this ill-ravelled web of mischance, he must needs have married her; so you may conjecture how little chance there is of this damsel being able to refuse him under a similar compulsion, and he a Child of France besides.—Ah, no, Philip!—little fear of her standing obstinate against the suit of such a lover.—*Varium et mutabile,* Philip."

"Your Majesty may, in the present instance, undervalue the obstinate courage of this young lady. She comes of a race determinately wilful; and I have picked out of Crèvecœur that she has formed a romantic attachment to a young squire, who, to say truth, rendered her many services on the road."

"Ha!" said the King,—"an archer of my Guards, by name Quentin Durward?"

"The same, as I think," said Des Comines; "he was made prisoner along with the Countess, travelling almost alone together."

"Now, our Lord and our Lady, and Monseigneur Saint Martin, and Monseigneur Saint Julian, be praised every one of them!" said the King, "and all laud and honour to the learned Galeotti, who read in the stars that this youth's destiny was connected with mine! If the maiden be so attached to him as to make her refractory to the will of Burgundy, this Quentin hath indeed been rarely useful to me."

"I believe, my lord," answered the Burgundian, "according to Crèvecœur's report, that there is some chance of her being sufficiently obstinate; besides, doubtless, the noble Duke himself, notwithstanding what your Majesty was pleased to hint in way of supposition, will not willingly renounce his fair cousin, to whom he has been long engaged."

"Umph!" answered the King—"But you have never seen my daughter Joan.—A howlet, man!—an absolute owl, whom I am ashamed of! But let him be only a wise man, and marry her, I will give him leave to be mad *par amours* for the fairest lady in France.—And now, Philip, have you given me the full map of your master's mind?"

"I have possessed you, Sire, of those particulars on which he is at present most disposed to insist. But your Majesty well knows that the

Duke's disposition is like a sweeping torrent, which only passes smoothly forward when its waves encounter no opposition; and what may be presented to chafe him into fury, it is impossible even to guess. Were more distinct evidence of your Majesty's practices (pardon the phrase, where there is no little time for selection) with the Liegeois and William de la Marck to occur unexpectedly, the issue might be terrible.—There are strange news from that country—they say La Marck hath married Hameline the elder Countess of Croye."

"That old fool was so mad on marriage, that she would have accepted the hand of Satan," said the King; "but that La Marck, beast as he is, should have married her, rather more surprises me."

"There is a report also," continued Des Comines, "that an envoy, or herald, on La Marck's part, is approaching Peronne;—this is like to drive the Duke frantic with rage—I trust that he has no letters, or the like, to show on your Majesty's part?"

"Letters to a Wild Boar!" answered the King,—"No, no, Sir Philip, I was no such fool as to cast pearls before swine—What little intercourse I had with the brute animal was by message, in which I always employed such low-bred slaves and vagabonds, that their evidence would not be received in a trial for robbing a hen-roost."

"I can then only further recommend," said Des Comines, taking his leave, "that your Majesty should remain on your guard, be guided by events, and, above all, avoid using any language or argument with the Duke which may better become your dignity than your present condition."

"If my dignity," said the King, "grow troublesome to me,—which it seldom doth while there are deeper interests to think of,—I have a special remedy for that swelling of the heart—It is but looking into a certain ruinous closet, Sir Philip, and thinking of the death of Charles the Simple; and it cures me as effectually as the cold bath would cool a fever.— And now, my friend and monitor, must thou be gone? Well, Sir Philip, the time must come when thou wilt tire reading lessons of state policy to the Bull of Burgundy, who is incapable of comprehending your most simple argument—If Louis of Valois then lives, thou hast a friend in the Court of France. I tell thee, my Philip, it would be a blessing to my kingdom should I ever acquire thee; who, with a profound view of subjects of state, hast also a conscience, capable of feeling and discerning between right and wrong. So help me, our Lord and Lady, and Monseigneur Saint Martin, Oliver and Balue have hearts as hardened as the nether millstone; and my life is embittered by remorse and penances for the crimes they make me commit. Thou, Sir Philip, possessed of the wisdom of present and past times, canst teach how to become great without ceasing to be virtuous."

"A hard task, and which few have attained," said the historian; "but which is yet within the reach of princes, who will strive for it. Meantime, Sire, be prepared, for the Duke will presently confer with you."

Louis looked long after Philip when he left the apartment, and at length
burst into a bitter laugh. "He spoke of fishing—I have sent him home,
a trout properly tickled!—And he thinks himself virtuous because he
took no bribe, but contented himself with flattery and promises, and the
pleasure of avenging an affront to his vanity!—Why, he is but so much
the poorer for the refusal of the money—not a jot the more honest. He
must be mine, though, for he hath the shrewdest head among them.—
Well, now for nobler game! I am to face this leviathan Charles, who
will presently swim hitherward, cleaving the deep before him. I must,
like a trembling sailor, throw a tub overboard to amuse him. But I may
one day find the chance—of driving a harpoon into his entrails!" [1]

CHAPTER XXXI

THE INTERVIEW

> Hold fast thy truth, young soldier.—Gentle maiden,
> Keep you your promise plight—leave age its subtleties,
> And grey-hair'd policy its maze of falsehood;
> But be you candid as the morning sky,
> Ere the high sun sucks vapours up to stain it.
>
> *The Trial.*

On the perilous and important morning which preceded the meeting of
the two Princes in the Castle of Peronne, Oliver le Dain did his master
the service of an active and skilful agent, making interest for Louis in
every quarter, both with presents and promises; so that when the Duke's
anger should blaze forth, all around should be interested to smother, and
not to increase, the conflagration. He glided, like night, from tent to tent,
from house to house, making himself friends, but not, in the Apostle's
sense, with the Mammon of unrighteousness. As was said of another active
political agent, "his finger was in every man's palm, his mouth was in
every man's ear;" and for various reasons, some of which we have
formerly hinted at, he secured the favour of many Burgundian nobles,
who either had something to hope or fear from France, or who thought
that, were the power of Louis too much reduced, their own Duke would
be likely to pursue the road to despotic authority, to which his heart
naturally inclined him, with a daring and unopposed pace.

Where Oliver suspected his own presence or arguments might be less
acceptable, he employed that of other servants of the King; and it was
in this manner that he obtained, by the favour of the Count de Crèvecœur,
an interview betwixt Lord Crawford, accompanied by Le Balafré, and
Quentin Durward, who, since he had arrived at Peronne, had been detained in a sort of honourable confinement. Private affairs were assigned
as the cause of requesting this meeting; but it is probable that Crèvecœur,
who was afraid that his master might be stirred up in passion to do

[1] Note XI.—Philip des Comines.

something dishonourably violent towards Louis, was not sorry to afford an opportunity to Crawford to give some hints to the young archer, which might prove useful to his master.

The meeting between the countrymen was cordial, and even affecting.

"Thou art a singular youth," said Crawford, stroking the head of young Durward, as a grandsire might do that of his descendant; "Certes, you have had as meikle good fortune as if you had been born with a lucky hood on your head."

"All comes of his gaining an archer's place at such early years," said Le Balafré; "I never was so much talked of, fair nephew, because I was five-and-twenty years old before I was *hors de page.*"

"And an ill-looking mountainous monster of a page thou wert, Ludovic," said the old commander, "with a beard like a baker's shool and a back like old Wallace Wight."

"I fear," said Quentin, with downcast eyes, "I shall enjoy that title to distinction but a short time—since it is my purpose to resign the service of the Archer-guard."

Le Balafré was struck almost mute with astonishment, and Crawford's ancient features gleamed with displeasure. The former at length mustered words enough to say, "Resign!—leave your place in the Scottish Archers!—Such a thing was never dreamt of. I would not give up my situation, to be made Constable of France."

"Hush! Ludovic," said Crawford; "this youngster knows better how to shape his course with the wind than we of the old world do. His journey hath given him some pretty tales to tell about King Louis; and he is turning Burgundian, that he may make his own little profit by telling them to Duke Charles."

"If I thought so," said Le Balafré, "I would cut his throat with my own hand, were he fifty times my sister's son!"

"But you would first inquire, whether I deserved to be so treated, fair kinsman?" answered Quentin;—"and you, my lord, know that I am no tale-bearer; nor shall either question or torture draw out of me a word to King Louis's prejudice, which may have come to my knowledge while I was in his service.—So far my oath of duty keeps me silent. But I will not remain in that service, in which, besides the peril of fair battle with mine enemies, I am to be exposed to the dangers of ambuscade on the part of my friends."

"Nay, if he objects to lying in ambuscade," said the slow-witted Le Balafré, looking sorrowfully at Lord Crawford, "I am afraid, my lord, that all is over with him! I myself have had thirty bushments break upon me, and truly I think I have laid in ambuscade twice as often myself, it being a favourite practice in our King's mode of making war."

"It is so, indeed, Ludovic," answered Lord Crawford; "nevertheless, hold your peace, for I believe I understand this fear better than you do."

"I wish to our Lady, you may, my lord," answered Ludovic; "but it wounds me to the very midriff to think my sister's son should fear an ambushment."

"Young man," said Crawford, "I partly guess your meaning. You have met foul play on the road where you travelled by the King's command, and you think you have reason to charge him with being the author of it?"

"I have been threatened with foul play in the execution of the King's commission," answered Quentin; "but I have had the good fortune to elude it—whether his Majesty be innocent or guilty in the matter, I leave to God and his own conscience. He fed me when I was a-hungered —received me when I was a wandering stranger. I will never load him in his adversity with accusations which may indeed be unjust, since I heard them only from the vilest mouths."

"My dear boy—my own lad!" said Crawford, taking him in his arms— "Ye think like a Scot, every joint of you! Like one that will forget a cause of quarrel with a friend whose back is already at the wall, and remember nothing of him but his kindness."

"Since my Lord Crawford has embraced my nephew," said Ludovic Lesly, "I will embrace him also—though I would have you to know, that to understand the service of an ambushment is as necessary to a soldier, as it is to a priest to be able to read his breviary."

"Be hushed, Ludovic," said Crawford; "ye are an ass, my friend, and ken not the blessing Heaven has sent you in this braw callant.—And now tell me, Quentin, my man, hath the King any advice of this brave, Christian, and manly resolution of yours? for, poor man, he had need, in his strait, to ken what he has to reckon upon. Had he but brought the whole brigade of Guards with him!—But God's will be done—Kens he of your purpose, think you?"

"I really can hardly tell," answered Quentin; "but I assured his learned astrologer, Martius Galeotti, of my resolution to be silent on all that could injure the King with the Duke of Burgundy. The particulars which I suspect, I will not (under your favour) communicate even to your lordship; and to the philosopher I was, of course, far less willing to unfold myself."

"Ha!—aye!"—answered Lord Crawford—"Oliver did indeed tell me that Galeotti prophesied most stoutly concerning the line of conduct you were to hold; and I am truly glad to find he did so on better authority than the stars."

"*He* prophesy!" said Le Balafré, laughing; "the stars never told him that honest Ludovic Lesly used to help yonder wench of his to spend the fair ducats he flings into her lap."

"Hush! Ludovic," said his captain, "hush! thou beast, man!—If thou dost not respect my grey hairs, because I have been e'en too much of a *routier* myself, respect the boy's youth and innocence, and let us have no more of such unbecoming daffing."

"Your honour may say your pleasure," answered Ludovic Lesly; "but,

by my faith, second-sighted Saunders Souplejaw, the town-souter of
Glen-houlakin, was worth Gallotti, or Gallipotty, or whatever ye call him,
twice told, for a prophet. He foretold that all my sister's children would
die some day; and he foretold it in the very hour that the youngest was
born, and that is this lad Quentin—who, no doubt, will one day die, to
make up the prophecy—the more's the pity—the whole curney of them
is gone but himself. And Saunders foretold to myself one day, that I
should be made by marriage, which doubtless will also happen in due
time, though it hath not yet come to pass—though how or when, I can
hardly guess, as I care not myself for the wedded state, and Quentin is
but a lad. Also, Saunders predicted——"

"Nay," said Lord Crawford, "unless the prediction be singularly to
the purpose, I must cut you short, my good Ludovic; for both you and
I must now leave your nephew, with prayers to Our Lady to strengthen
him in the good mind he is in; for this is a case in which a light word
might do more mischief than all the Parliament of Paris could mend.—
My blessing with you, my lad; and be in no hurry to think of leaving
our body; for there will be good blows going presently in the eye of
day, and no ambuscade."

"And my blessing too, nephew," said Ludovic Lesly; "for, since you
have satisfied our most noble captain, I also am satisfied, as in duty
bound."

"Stay, my lord," said Quentin, and led Lord Crawford a little apart
from his uncle. "I must not forget to mention, that there is a person besides in the world, who, having learned from me these circumstances, which it is essential to King Louis's safety should at present
remain concealed, may not think that the same obligation of secrecy,
which attaches to me as the King's soldier, and as having been relieved
by his bounty, is at all binding on her."

"On *her!*" replied Crawford; "nay, if there be a woman in the secret,
the Lord ha' mercy, for we are all on the rocks again!"

"Do not suppose so, my lord," replied Durward, "but use your inter-
est with the Count of Crèvecœur to permit me an interview with the
Countess Isabelle of Croye, who is the party possessed of my secret, and
I doubt not that I can persuade her to be as silent as I shall unquestion-
ably myself remain, concerning whatever may incense the Duke against
King Louis."

The old soldier mused for a long time—looked up to the ceiling, then
down again upon the floor—then shook his head,—and at length said:
"There is something in all this, which, by my honour, I do not understand. The Countess Isabelle of Croye—an interview with a lady of her
birth, blood, and possessions!—and thou, a raw Scottish lad, so certain
of carrying thy point with her? Thou art either strangely confident, my
young friend, or else you have used your time well upon the journey.
But, by the Cross of Saint Andrew! I will move Crèvecœur in thy behalf;
and, as he truly fears that the Duke Charles may be provoked against

the King to the extremity of falling foul, I think it likely he may grant thy request, though by my honour it is a comical one!"

So saying, and shrugging up his shoulders, the old Lord left the apartment, followed by Ludovic Lesly, who, forming his looks on those of his principal, endeavoured, though knowing nothing of the cause of his wonder, to look as mysterious and important as Crawford himself.

In a few minutes Crawford returned, but without his attendant Le Balafré. The old man seemed in singular humour, laughing and chuckling to himself in a manner which strangely distorted his stern and rigid features, and at the same time shaking his head, as at something which he could not help condemning, while he found it irresistibly ludicrous. "My certes, countryman," said he, "but you are not blate—you will never lose fair lady for faint heart! Crèvecœur swallowed your proposal as he would have done a cup of vinegar, and swore to me roundly, by all the saints in Burgundy, that were less than the honour of princes and the peace of kingdoms at stake, you should never see even so much as the print of the Countess Isabelle's foot on the clay. Were it not that he had a dame, and a fair one, I would have thought that he meant to break a lance for the prize himself. Perhaps he thinks of his nephew, the County Stephen. A Countess!—would no less serve you to be minting at?—But come along—your interview with her must be brief—But I fancy you know how to make the most of little time—ho! ho! ho!—By my faith, I can hardly chide thee for the presumption, I have such a good will to laugh at it!"

With a brow like scarlet, at once offended and disconcerted by the blunt inferences of the old soldier, and vexed at beholding in what an absurd light his passion was viewed by every person of experience, Durward followed Lord Crawford in silence to the Ursuline Convent, in which the Countess was lodged, and in the parlour of which he found the Count de Crèvecœur.

"So, young gallant," said the latter sternly, "you must see the fair companion of your romantic expedition once more, it seems?"

"Yes, my Lord Count," answered Quentin firmly; "and what is more, I must see her alone."

"That shall never be," said the Count de Crèvecœur.—"Lord Crawford, I make you judge. This young lady, the daughter of my old friend and companion in arms, the richest heiress in Burgundy, has confessed a sort of a—what was I going to say?—in short, she is a fool, and your man-at-arms here a presumptuous coxcomb—In a word, they shall not meet alone."

"Then will I not speak a single word to the Countess in your presence," said Quentin, much delighted. "You have told me much that I did not dare, presumptuous as I may be, even to hope."

"Ay, truly said, my friend," said Crawford, "you have been imprudent in your communications; and, since you refer to me, and there is a good stout grating across the parlour, I would advise you to trust to it, and let them do the worst with their tongues. What, man! the life of a King, and many thousands besides. is not to be weighed with the chance of two young things whilly-whawing in ilk other's ears for a minute!"

So saying, he dragged off Crèvecœur, who followed very reluctantly, and cast many angry glances at the young Archer as he left the room.

In a moment after, the Countess Isabelle entered on the other side of the grate, and no sooner saw Quentin alone in the parlour, than she stopped short, and cast her eyes on the ground for the space of half a minute. "Yet why should I be ungrateful," she said, "because others are unjustly suspicious?—My friend—my preserver, I may almost say, so much have I been beset by treachery—my only faithful and constant friend!"

As she spoke thus, she extended her hand to him through the grate, nay, suffered him to retain it, until he had covered it with kisses, not unmingled with tears. She only said, "Durward, were we ever to meet again, I would not permit this folly."

If it be considered that Quentin had guarded her through so many perils—that he had been, in truth, her only faithful and zealous protector, perhaps my fair readers, even if countesses and heiresses should be of the number, will pardon the derogation.

But the Countess extricated her hand at length, and stepping a pace back from the grate, asked Durward, in a very embarrassed tone, what boon he had to ask of her?—"for that you have a request to make, I have learned from the old Scottish Lord, who came here but now with my cousin of Crèvecœur. Let it be but reasonable," she said, "but such as poor Isabelle can grant with duty and honour uninfringed, and you cannot tax my slender powers too highly. But, oh! do not speak hastily—do not say," she added, looking around with timidity, "aught that might, if overheard, do prejudice to us both!"

"Fear not, noble lady," said Quentin sorrowfully; "it is not *here* that I can forget the distance which fate has placed between us, or expose you to the censure of your proud kindred, as the object of the most devoted love to one, poorer and less powerful—not perhaps less noble than themselves. Let that pass like a dream of the night to all but one bosom, where, dream as it is, it will fill up the room of all existing realities."

"Hush! hush!" said Isabelle; "for your own sake,—for mine,—be silent on such a theme. Tell me rather what it is you have to ask me."

"Forgiveness to one," replied Quentin, "who, for his own selfish views, hath conducted himself as your enemy."

"I trust I forgive all my enemies," answered Isabelle; "but oh, Durward! through what scenes have your courage and presence of mind protected me!—Yonder bloody hall—the good Bishop—I knew not till yesterday half the horrors I had unconsciously witnessed!"

"Do not think on them," said Quentin, who saw the transient colour which had come to her cheek during their conference, fast fading into the most deadly paleness—"Do not look back, but look steadily forward, as they needs must who walk in a perilous road. Hearken to me. King Louis deserves nothing better at your hand, of all others, than to be proclaimed the wily and insidious politician, which he really is. But to tax him as the encourager of your flight—still more as the author of a plan to throw you into the hands of De la Marck—will at this moment produce perhaps the King's death or dethronement; and, at all events, the most bloody war between France and Burgundy which the two countries have ever been engaged in."

"These evils shall not arrive for my sake, if they can be prevented," said the Countess Isabelle; "and indeed your slightest request were enough to make me forego my revenge, were that at any time a passion which I deeply cherish. Is it possible I would rather remember King Louis's injuries, than your invaluable services?—Yet how is this to be?—When I am called before my Sovereign, the Duke of Burgundy, I must either stand silent, or speak the truth. The former would be contumacy; and to a false tale you will not desire me to train my tongue."

"Surely not," said Durward; "but let your evidence concerning Louis be confined to what you yourself positively know to be truth; and when you mention what others have reported, no matter how credibly, let it be as reports only, and beware of pledging your own personal evidence to that, which, though you may fully believe, you cannot personally know to be true. The assembled Council of Burgundy cannot refuse to a Monarch the justice, which in my country is rendered to the meanest person under accusation. They must esteem him innocent, until direct and sufficient proof shall demonstrate his guilt. Now, what does not consist with your own certain knowledge, should be proved by other evidence than your report from hearsay."

"I think I understand you," said the Countess Isabelle.

"I will make my meaning plainer," said Quentin; and was illustrating it accordingly by more than one instance, when the convent-bell tolled.

"That," said the Countess, "is a signal that we must part—part for ever!—But do not forget me, Durward; I will never forget you—your faithful services——"

She could not speak more, but again extended her hand, which was again pressed to his lips; and I know not how it was, that, in endeavouring to withdraw her hand, the Countess came so close to the grating, that Quentin was encouraged to press the adieu on her lips. The young lady did not chide him—perhaps there was no time; for Crèvecœur and Crawford, who had been from some loop-hole eye-witnesses, if not ear-witnesses also, of what was passing, rushed into the apartment, the first in a towering passion, the latter laughing, and holding the Count back.

"To your chamber, young mistress—to your chamber!" exclaimed the Count to Isabelle, who, flinging down her veil, retired in all haste,—"which should be exchanged for a cell, and bread and water.—And you, gentle sir, who are so malapert, the time will come when the interests of kings and kingdoms may not be connected with such as you are; and you shall then learn the penalty of your audacity in raising your beggarly eyes——"

"Hush! hush!—enough said—rein up—rein up," said the old Lord;—"and you, Quentin, I command you, be silent, and begone to your quarters.—There is no such room for so much scorn neither, Sir Count of Crèvecœur, that I must say now he is out of hearing—Quentin Durward is as much a gentleman as the King, only, as the Spaniard says, not so rich. He is as noble as myself, and I am chief of my name. Tush, tush! man, you must not speak to us of penalties."

"My lord, my lord," said Crèvecœur impatiently, "the insolence of these foreign mercenaries is proverbial, and should receive rather rebuke than encouragement from you, who are their leader."

"My Lord Count," answered Crawford, "I have ordered my command for these fifty years, without advice either from Frenchman or Burgundian; and I intend to do so, under your favour, so long as I shall continue to hold it."

"Well, well, my lord," said Crèvecœur, "I meant you no disrespect; your nobleness, as well as your age, entitle you to be privileged in your impatience; and for these young people, I am satisfied to overlook the past, since I will take care that they never meet again."

"Do not take that upon your salvation, Crèvecœur," said the old Lord, laughing; "mountains, it is said, may meet, and why not mortal creatures that have legs, and life and love to put those legs in motion? Yon kiss, Crèvecœur, came tenderly off—methinks it was ominous."

"You are striving again to disturb my patience," said Crèvecœur, "but I will not give you that advantage over me.—Hark! they toll the summons to the Castle—an awful meeting, of which God only can foretell the issue."

"This issue I can foretell," said the old Scottish Lord, "that if violence is to be offered to the person of the King, few as his friends are, and surrounded by his enemies, he shall neither fall alone nor unavenged; and grieved I am, that his own positive orders have prevented my taking measures to prepare for such an issue."

"My Lord of Crawford," said the Burgundian, "to anticipate such evil is the sure way to give occasion to it. Obey the orders of your royal master, and give no pretext for violence by taking hasty offence, and you will find that the day will pass over more smoothly than you now conjecture."

CHAPTER XXXII

THE INVESTIGATION

Me rather had, my heart might feel your love,
Than my displeased eye to see your courtesy.
Up, cousin, up—your heart is up, I know,
Thus high at least—although your knee—
King Richard II.

AT the first toll of the bell, which was to summon the great nobles of Burgundy together in council, with the very few French peers who could be present on the occasion, Duke Charles, followed by a part of his train, armed with partisans and battle-axes, entered the Hall of Herbert's Tower, in the Castle of Peronne. King Louis, who had expected the visit, arose and made two steps towards the Duke, and then remained standing with an air of dignity, which, in spite of the meanness of his dress, and the familiarity of his ordinary manners, he knew very well how to assume when he judged it necessary. Upon the present important crisis, the composure of his demeanour had an evident effect upon his rival, who changed the abrupt and hasty step with which he entered the apartment, into one more becoming a great vassal entering the presence of his Lord Paramount. Apparently the Duke had formed the internal resolution to treat Louis, in the outset at least, with the formalities due to his high station; but at the same time it was evident, that, in doing so, he put no small constraint upon the fiery impatience of his own disposition, and was scarce able to control the feelings of resentment, and the thirst of revenge, which boiled in his bosom. Hence, though he compelled himself to use the outward acts, and in some degree the language, of courtesy and reverence, his colour came and went rapidly— his voice was abrupt, hoarse, and broken—his limbs shook, as if impatient of the curb imposed on his motions—he frowned and bit his lip until the blood came—and every look and movement showed that the most passionate prince who ever lived, was under the dominion of one of his most violent paroxysms of fury.

The King marked this war of passion with a calm and untroubled eye; for, though he gathered from the Duke's looks a foretaste of the bitterness of death, which he dreaded alike as a mortal and a sinful man, yet he was resolved, like a wary and skilful pilot, neither to suffer himself to be disconcerted by his own fears, nor to abandon the helm, while there was a chance of saving the vessel by adroit pilotage. Therefore, when the Duke, in a hoarse and broken tone, said something of the scarcity of his accommodations, he answered with a smile, that he could not complain, since he had as yet found Herbert's Tower a better residence than it had proved to one of his ancestors.

"They told you the tradition, then?" said Charles—"Yes—here he was slain—but it was because he refused to take the cowl, and finish his days in a monastery."

"The more fool he," said Louis, affecting unconcern, "since he gained the torment of being a martyr, without the merit of being a saint."

"I come," said the Duke, "to pray your Majesty to attend a high council, at which things of weight are to be deliberated upon concerning the welfare of France and Burgundy. You will presently meet them—that is, if such be your pleasure——"

"Nay, my fair cousin," said the King, "never strain courtesy so far, as to entreat what you may so boldly command—To council, since such is your Grace's pleasure. We are somewhat shorn of our train," he added, looking upon the small suite that arranged themselves to attend him—"but you, cousin, must shine out for us both."

Marshalled by Toison d'Or, chief of the heralds of Burgundy, the Princes left the Earl Herbert's Tower, and entered the castle-yard, which Louis observed was filled with the Duke's body-guard and men-at-arms, splendidly accoutred, and drawn up in martial array. Crossing the court, they entered the Council-hall, which was in a much more modern part of the building than that of which Louis had been the tenant, and, though in disrepair, had been hastily arranged for the solemnity of a public council. Two chairs of state were erected under the same canopy, that for the King being raised two steps higher than the one which the Duke was to occupy; about twenty of the chief nobility sat, arranged in due order, on either hand of the chair of state; and thus, when both the Princes were seated, the person for whose trial, as it might be called, the council was summoned, held the highest place, and appeared to preside in it.

It was perhaps to get rid of this inconsistency, and the scruples which might have been inspired by it, that Duke Charles, having bowed slightly to the royal chair, bluntly opened the sitting with the following words:—

"My good vassals and councillors, it is not unknown to you what disturbances have arisen in our territories, both in our father's time and in our own, from the rebellion of vassals against superiors, and subjects against their princes. And lately, we have had the most dreadful proof of the height to which these evils have arrived in our case, by the scandalous flight of the Countess Isabelle of Croye, and her aunt the Lady Hameline, to take refuge with a foreign power, thereby renouncing their fealty to us, and inferring the forfeiture of their fiefs; and in another more dreadful and deplorable instance, by the sacrilegious and bloody murder of our beloved brother and ally the Bishop of Liege, and the rebellion of that treacherous city, which was but too mildly punished for the last insurrection. We have been informed that these said events may be traced, not merely to the inconstancy and folly of women, and the presumption of pampered citizens, but to the agency of foreign power, and the interference of a mighty neighbour, from whom, if good deeds could merit any return in kind, Burgundy could have expected nothing but the most sincere and devoted friendship. If this should prove truth," said the Duke, setting his teeth, and pressing his heel against the ground, "what consideration shall withhold us—the means being in our power— from taking such measures, as shall effectually, at the very source, close up the main spring, from which these evils have yearly flowed on us?"

The Duke had begun his speech with some calmness, but he elevated his voice at the conclusion: and the last sentence was spoken in a tone which made all the councillors tremble, and brought a transient fit of paleness across the King's cheek. He instantly recalled his courage, however, and addressed the council in his turn, in a tone evincing so much ease and composure, that the Duke, though he seemed desirous to interrupt or stop him, found no decent opportunity to do so.

"Nobles of France and of Burgundy," he said, "Knights of the Holy Spirit and of the Golden Fleece! since a King must plead his cause as an accused person, he cannot desire more distinguished judges, than the flower of nobleness, and muster and pride of chivalry. Our fair cousin of Burgundy hath but darkened the dispute between us, in so far as his courtesy has declined to state it in precise terms. I, who have no cause for observing such delicacy, nay, whose condition permits me not to do so, crave leave to speak more precisely. It is to Us, my lords,— to Us, his liege Lord, his kinsman, his ally,—that unhappy circumstances, perverting our cousin's clear judgment and better nature, have induced him to apply the hateful charges of seducing his vassals from their allegiance, stirring up the people of Liege to revolt, and stimulating the outlawed William de la Marck to commit a most cruel and sacrilegious murder. Nobles of France and Burgundy, I might truly appeal to the circumstances in which I now stand, as being in themselves a complete contradiction of such an accusation; for is it to be supposed, that, having the sense of a rational being left me, I should have thrown myself unreservedly into the power of the Duke of Burgundy, while I was practising treachery against him, such as could not fail to be discovered, and which, being discovered, must place me, as I now stand, in the power of a justly exasperated prince? The folly of one who should seat himself quietly down to repose on a mine, after he had lighted the match which was to cause instant explosion, would have been wisdom compared to mine. I have no doubt, that, amongst the perpetrators of those horrible treasons at Schonwaldt, villains have been busy with my name—but am I to be answerable, who have given them no right to use it?—If two silly women, disgusted on account of some romantic cause of displeasure, sought refuge at my Court, does it follow that they did so by my direction?—It will be found, when inquired into, that, since honour and chivalry forbade my sending them back prisoners to the Court of Burgundy,—which I think, gentlemen, no one who wears the collar of these Orders would suggest,—that I came as nearly as possible to the same point, by placing them in the hands of the venerable father in God, who is now a saint in heaven."—Here Louis seemed much affected, and pressed his kerchief to his eyes—"In the hands, I say, of a member of my own family, and still more closely united with that of Burgundy, whose situation, exalted condition in the Church, and alas! whose numerous virtues, qualified him to be the protector of these unhappy wanderers for a little while, and the mediator betwixt them and their liege lord. I say, therefore, the only circumstances which seem in my brother of Burgundy's hasty view of this subject, to argue unworthy suspicions against me, are such as can be explained on the fairest and most honourable motives; and I say, moreover, that no one particle of credible evidence can be brought to support the injurious charges which have induced my brother to alter his friendly looks towards one who came to him in full confidence of friendship—have caused him to turn his festive hall into a court of justice, and his hospitable apartments into a prison."

"My lord, my lord," said Charles, breaking in so soon as the King paused, "for your being here at a time so unluckily coinciding with the execution of your projects, I can only account by supposing, that those who make it their trade to impose on others, do sometimes egregiously delude themselves. The engineer is sometimes killed by the springing of his own petard.—For what is to follow, let it depend on the event of this solemn inquiry.—Bring hither the Countess Isabelle of Croye!"

As the young lady was introduced, supported on the one side by the Countess of Crèvecœur, who had her husband's commands to that effect, and on the other by the Abbess of the Ursuline convent, Charles exclaimed, with his usual harshness of voice and manner,—"Soh! sweet Princess—you, who could scarce find breath to answer us when we last laid our just and reasonable commands on you, yet have had wind enough to run as long a course as ever did hunted doe—what think you of the fair work you have made between two great Princes, and two mighty countries, that have been like to go to war for your baby face?"

The publicity of the scene, and the violence of Charles's manner, totally overcame the resolution which Isabelle had formed, of throwing herself at the Duke's feet, and imploring him to take possession of her estates, and permit her to retire into a cloister. She stood motionless, like a terrified female in a storm, who hears the thunder roll on every side of her, and apprehends, in every fresh peal, the bolt which is to strike her dead. The Countess of Crèvecœur, a woman of spirit equal to her birth, and to the beauty which she preserved even in her matronly years, judged it necessary to interfere. "My Lord Duke," she said, "my fair cousin is under my protection. I know better than your Grace how women should be treated, and we will leave this presence instantly, unless you use a tone and language more suitable to our rank and sex."

The Duke burst out into a laugh. "Crèvecœur," he said, "thy tameness hath made a lordly dame of thy Countess; but that is no affair of mine. Give a seat to yonder simple girl, to whom, so far from feeling enmity, I design the highest grace and honour.—Sit down, mistress, and tell us at your leisure what fiend possessed you to fly from your native country, and embrace the trade of a damsel adventurous."

With much pain, and not without several interruptions, Isabelle confessed, that, being absolutely determined against a match proposed to her by the Duke of Burgundy, she had indulged the hope of obtaining protection of the Court of France.

"And under protection of the French Monarch," said Charles—"Of that, doubtless, you were well assured?"

"I did indeed so think myself assured," said the Countess Isabelle, "otherwise I had not taken a step so decided."—Here Charles looked upon Louis with a smile of inexpressible bitterness, which the King supported with the utmost firmness, except that his lip grew something whiter than it was wont to be.—"But my information concerning King Louis's intentions towards us," continued the Countess, after a short pause, "was almost entirely derived from my unhappy aunt, the Lady Hameline, and her opinions were formed upon the assertions and insinuations of persons whom I have since discovered to be the vilest traitors, and most faithless wretches in the world." She then stated, in brief terms, what she had since come to learn of the treachery of Marthon, and of Hayraddin Maugrabin, and added, that she "entertained no doubt that the elder Maugrabin, called Zamet, the original adviser of their flight, was capable of every species of treachery, as well as of assuming the character of an agent of Louis without authority."

There was a pause while the Countess had continued her story, which she prosecuted, though very briefly, from the time she left the territories of Burgundy, in company with her aunt, until the storming of Schonwaldt, and her final surrender to the Count of Crèvecœur. All remained mute after she had finished her brief and broken narrative, and the Duke of Burgundy bent his fierce dark eyes on the ground, like one who seeks for a pretext to indulge his passion, but finds none sufficiently plausible to justify himself in his own eyes. "The mole," he said at length, looking upwards, "winds not his dark subterranean path beneath our feet the less certainly, that we, though conscious of his motions, cannot absolutely trace them. Yet I would know of King Louis, wherefore he maintained these ladies at his Court, had they not gone thither by his own invitation."

"I did not so entertain them, fair cousin," answered the King. "Out of compassion, indeed, I received them in privacy, but took an early opportunity of placing them under the protection of the late excellent Bishop, your own ally, and who was (may God assoil him!) a better judge than I, or any secular prince, how to reconcile the protection due to fugitives, with the duty which a king owes to his ally from whose dominions they have fled. I boldly ask this young lady, whether my reception of them was cordial, or whether it was not, on the contrary, such as made them express regret that they had made my Court their place of refuge?"

"So much was it otherwise than cordial," answered the Countess, "that it induced me, at least, to doubt how far it was possible that your Majesty should have actually given the invitation of which we had been assured, by those who called themselves your agents; since, supposing them to have proceeded only as they were duly authorised, it would have been hard to reconcile your Majesty's conduct with that to be expected from a king, a knight, and a gentleman."

The Countess turned her eyes to the King as she spoke, with a look which was probably intended as a reproach, but the breast of Louis was armed against all such artillery. On the contrary, waving slowly his expanded hands, and looking around the circle, he seemed to make a triumphant appeal to all present, upon the testimony borne to his innocence in the Countess's reply.

Burgundy, meanwhile, cast on him a look which seemed to say, that if in some degree silenced, he was as far as ever from being satisfied, and then said abruptly to the Countess,—"Methinks, fair mistress, in this account of your wanderings, you have forgot all mention of certain love-passages—So, ho! blushing already?—Certain knights of the forest, by whom your quiet was for a time interrupted. Well, that incident hath come to our ear, and something we may presently form out of it.—Tell me, King Louis, were it not well before this vagrant Helen of Troy, or of Croye, set more kings by the ears,—were it not well to carve out a fitting match for her?"

King Louis, though conscious what ungrateful proposal was likely to be made next, gave a calm and silent assent to what Charles said; but the Countess herself was restored to courage by the very extremity of her situation. She quitted the arm of the Countess of Crèvecœur, or which she had hitherto leaned, came forward timidly, yet with an air of dignity, and kneeling before the Duke's throne, thus addressed him:—
"Noble Duke of Burgundy, and my liege Lord; I acknowledge my fault in having withdrawn myself from your dominions without your gracious permission, and will most humbly acquiesce in any penalty you are pleased to impose. I place my lands and castles at your rightful disposal, and pray you only of your own bounty, and for the sake of my father's memory, to allow the last of the line of Croye, out of her large estate, such a moderate maintenance as may find her admission into a convent for the remainder of her life."

"What think you, Sire, of the young person's petition to us?" said the Duke, addressing Louis.

"As of a holy and humble motion," said the King, "which doubtless comes from that grace which ought not to be resisted or withstood."

"The humble and lowly shall be exalted," said Charles. "Arise, Countess Isabelle—we mean better for you than you have devised for yourself. We mean neither to sequestrate your estates, nor to abase your honours, but, on the contrary, will add largely to both."

"Alas! my lord," said the Countess, continuing on her knees, "it is even that well-meant goodness which I fear still more than your Grace's displeasure, since it compels me——"

"Saint George of Burgundy!" said Duke Charles, "is our will to be thwarted, and our commands disputed, at every turn? Up, I say, minion, and withdraw for the present—when we have time to think of thee we will so order matters, that, *Teste-Saint-Griz!* you shall either obey us, or do worse."

Notwithstanding this stern answer, the Countess Isabelle remained at his feet, and would probably, by her pertinacity, have driven him to say upon the spot something yet more severe, had not the Countess of Crèvecœur, who better knew that Prince's humour, interfered to raise her young friend, and to conduct her from the hall.

Quentin Durward was now summoned to appear, and presented himself before the King and Duke with that freedom, distant alike from bashful reserve and intrusive boldness, which becomes a youth at once well-born and well-nurtured, who gives honour where it is due, but without permitting himself to be dazzled or confused by the presence of those to whom it is to be rendered. His uncle had furnished him with the means of again equipping himself in the arms and dress of an Archer of the Scottish Guard, and his complexion, mien, and air, suited in an uncommon degree his splendid appearance. His extreme youth, too, prepossessed the councillors in his favour, the rather that no one could easily believe that the sagacious Louis would have chosen so very young a person to become the confidant of political intrigues; and thus the King enjoyed, in this as in other cases, considerable advantage from his singular choice of agents, both as to age and rank, where such election seemed least likely to be made. At the command of the Duke, sanctioned by that of Louis, Quentin commenced an account of his journey with the Ladies of Croye to the neighbourhood of Liege, premising a statement of King Louis's instructions, which were, that he should escort them safely to the castle of the Bishop.

"And you obeyed my orders accordingly?" said the King.

"I did, Sire," replied the Scot.

"You omit a circumstance," said the Duke. "You were set upon in the forest by two wandering knights."

"It does not become me to remember or to proclaim such an incident," said the youth, blushing ingenuously.

"But it doth not become *me* to forget it," said the Duke of Orleans. "This youth discharged his commission manfully, and maintained his trust in a manner that I shall long remember.—Come to my apartment, Archer, when this matter is over, and thou shalt find I have not forgot thy brave bearing, while I am glad to see it is equalled by thy modesty."

"And come to mine," said Dunois. "I have a helmet for thee, since I think I owe thee one." Quentin bowed low to both, and the examination was resumed. At the command of Duke Charles, he produced the written instructions which he had received for the direction of his journey.

"Did you follow these instructions literally, soldier?" said the Duke.

"No, if it please your Grace," replied Quentin. "They directed me, as you may be pleased to observe, to cross the Maes near Namur; whereas I kept the left bank, as being both the nigher and the safer road to Liege."

"And wherefore that alteration?" said the Duke.

"Because I began to suspect the fidelity of my guide," answered Quentin.

"Now mark the questions I have next to ask thee," said the Duke. "Reply truly to them, and fear nothing from the resentment of any one. But if you palter or double in your answers, I will have thee hung alive in an iron chain from the steeple of the market-house, where thou shalt wish for death for many an hour ere he come to relieve you!"

There was a deep silence ensued. At length, having given the youth time, as he thought, to consider the circumstances in which he was placed, the Duke demanded to know of Durward, who his guide was, by whom supplied, and wherefore he had been led to entertain suspicion of him? To the first of these questions, Quentin Durward answered, by naming Hayraddin Maugrabin, the Bohemian; to the second, that the guide had been recommended by Tristan l'Hermite; and in reply to the third point, he mentioned what had happened in the Franciscan convent, near Namur; how the Bohemian had been expelled from the holy house; and how, jealous of his behaviour, he had dogged him to a rendezvous with one of William de la Marck's lanzknechts, where he overheard them arrange a plan for surprising the ladies who were under his protection.

"Now, hark thee," said the Duke, "and once more remember thy life depends on thy veracity, did these villains mention their having this King's—I mean this very King Louis of France's authority, for their scheme of surprising the escort, and carrying away the ladies?"

"If such infamous fellows had said so," replied Quentin, "I know not how I should have believed them, having the word of the King himself to place in opposition to theirs."

Louis, who had listened hitherto with most earnest attention, could not help drawing his breath deeply, when he heard Durward's answer, in the manner of one from whose bosom a heavy weight has been at once removed. The Duke again looked disconcerted and moody; and, returning to the charge, questioned Quentin still more closely, whether he did not understand, from these men's private conversation, that the plots which they meditated had King Louis's sanction?

"I repeat, that I heard nothing which could authorise me to say so," answered the young man, who, though internally convinced of the King's accession to the treachery of Hayraddin, yet held it contrary to his allegiance to bring forward his own suspicions on the subject; "and if I *had* heard such men make such an assertion, I again say, that I would not have given their testimony weight against the instructions of the King himself."

"Thou art a faithful messenger," said the Duke, with a sneer; "and I venture to say, that in obeying the King's instructions, thou hast disappointed his expectations in a manner that thou mightest have smarted for, but that subsequent events have made thy bull-headed fidelity seem like good service."

"I understand you not, my lord," said Quentin Durward; "all I know is, that my master King Louis sent me to protect these ladies, and that I did so accordingly, to the extent of my ability, both in the journey to Schonwaldt, and through the subsequent scenes which took place. I understood the instructions of the King to be honourable, and I executed them honourably; had they been of a different tenor, they would not have suited one of my name or nation."

"Fier comme un Ecossois," said Charles, who, however disappointed at the tenor of Durward's reply, was not unjust enough to blame him for his boldness. "But hark thee, Archer, what instructions were those which made thee, as some sad fugitives from Schonwaldt have informed us, parade the streets of Liege, at the head of those mutineers, who afterwards cruelly murdered their temporal Prince and spiritual Father? And what harangue was it which thou didst make after that murder was committed, in which you took upon you, as agent for Louis, to assume authority among the villains who had just perpetrated so great a crime?"

"My lord," said Quentin, "there are many who could testify, that I assumed not the character of an envoy of France in the town of Liege, but had it fixed upon me by the obstinate clamours of the people themselves, who refused to give credit to any disclamation which I could make. This I told to those in the service of the Bishop when I had made my escape from the city, and recommended their attention to the security of the Castle, which might have prevented the calamity and horror of the succeeding night. It is, no doubt, true, that I did, in the extremity of danger, avail myself of the influence which my imputed character gave me, to save the Countess Isabelle, to protect my own life, and, so far as I could, to rein in the humour for slaughter, which had already broke out in so dreadful an instance. I repeat, and will maintain it with my body, that I had no commission of any kind from the King of France, respecting the people of Liege, far less instructions to instigate them to mutiny; and that, finally, when I did avail myself of that imputed character, it was as if I had snatched up a shield to protect myself in a moment of emergency, and used it, as I should surely have done, for the defence of myself and others, without inquiring whether I had a right to the heraldic emblazonments which it displayed."

"And therein my young companion and prisoner," said Crèvecœur, unable any more to remain silent, "acted with equal spirit and good sense; and his doing so cannot be justly imputed as blame to King Louis."

There was a murmur of assent among the surrounding nobility which sounded joyfully in the ears of King Louis, whilst it gave no little offence to Charles. He rolled his eyes angrily around; and the sentiments, so generally expressed by so many of his highest vassals and wisest councillors, would not perhaps have prevented his giving way to his violent and despotic temper, had not Des Comines, who foresaw the danger, prevented it, by suddenly announcing a herald from the city of Liege.

"A herald from weavers and nailers?" exclaimed the Duke—"but admit him instantly. By Our Lady, I will learn from this same herald something further of his employer's hopes and projects, than this young French-Scottish man-at-arms seems desirous to tell me!"

CHAPTER XXXIII

THE HERALD

Ariel.——Hark! they roar.
Prospero. Let them be hunted soundly.
                              The Tempest.

THERE was room made in the assembly, and no small curiosity evinced by those present to see the herald whom the insurgent Liegeois had ventured to send to so haughty a Prince as the Duke of Burgundy, while in such high indignation against them. For it must be remembered, that at this period heralds were only despatched from sovereign princes to each other upon solemn occasions; and that the inferior nobility employed pursuivants, a lower rank of officers-at-arms. It may be also noticed in passing, that Louis XI., an habitual derider of whatever did not promise real power or substantial advantage, was in especial a professed contemner of heralds and heraldry, "red, blue, and green, with all their trumpery," [1] to which the pride of his rival Charles, which was of a very different kind, attached no small degree of ceremonious importance.

The herald, who was now introduced into the presence of the monarchs, was dressed in a tabard, or coat, embroidered with the arms of his master, in which the Boar's-head made a distinguished appearance, in blazonry, which, in the opinion of the skilful, was more showy than accurate. The rest of his dress—a dress always sufficiently tawdry— was overcharged with lace, embroidery, and ornament of every kind; and the plume of feathers which he wore was so high, as if intended to sweep the roof of the hall. In short, the usual gaudy splendour of the heraldic attire was caricatured and overdone. The Boar's-head was not only repeated on every part of his dress, but even his bonnet was formed into that shape, and it was represented with gory tongue and bloody tusks, or, in proper language, *langed and dentated gules;* and there was something in the man's appearance which seemed to imply a mixture of boldness and apprehension, like one who has undertaken a

[1] For a remarkable instance of this, see Note XII.

dangerous commission, and is sensible that audacity alone can carry him through it with safety. Something of the same mixture of fear and effrontery was visible in the manner in which he paid his respects, and he showed also a grotesque awkwardness, not usual among those who were accustomed to be received in the presence of princes.

"Who art thou, in the devil's name?" was the greeting with which Charles the Bold received this singular envoy.

"I am Rouge Sanglier," answered the herald, "the officer-at-arms of William de la Marck, by the grace of God, and the election of the Chapter, Prince Bishop of Liege."

"Ha!" exclaimed Charles; but, as if subduing his own passion, he made a sign to him to proceed.

"And, in right of his wife, the Honourable Countess Hameline of Croye, Count of Croye, and Lord of Bracquemont."

The utter astonishment of Duke Charles at the extremity of boldness with which these titles were announced in his presence, seemed to strike him dumb; and the herald, conceiving, doubtless, that he had made a suitable impression by the annunciation of his character, proceeded to state his errand.

"*Annuncio vobis gaudium magnum,*" he said; "I let you, Charles of Burgundy and Earl of Flanders, to know, in my master's name, that under favour of a dispensation of our Holy Father of Rome, presently expected, and appointing a fitting substitute *ad sacra*, he proposes to exercise at once the office of Prince Bishop, and maintain the rights of Count of Croye."

The Duke of Burgundy, at this and other pauses in the herald's speech, only ejaculated "Ha!" or some similar interjection, without making any answer; and the tone of exclamation was that of one who, though surprised and moved, is willing to hear all that is to be said ere he commits himself by making an answer. To the further astonishment of all who were present, he forebore from his usual abrupt and violent gesticulations, remaining with the nail of his thumb pressed against his teeth, which was his favourite attitude when giving attention, and keeping his eyes bent on the ground, as if unwilling to betray the passion which might gleam in them.

The envoy, therefore, proceeded boldly and unabashed in the delivery of his message. "In the name, therefore, of the Prince Bishop of Liege, and Count of Croye, I am to require of you, Duke Charles, to desist from those pretensions and encroachments which you have made on the free and imperial city of Liege, by connivance with the late Louis of Bourbon, unworthy Bishop thereof."—

"Ha!" again exclaimed the Duke.

"Also to restore the banners of the community, which you took violently from the town, to the number of six-and-thirty;—to rebuild the breaches in their walls, and restore the fortifications which you tyran- nically dismantled,—and to acknowledge my master, William de la

Marck, as Prince Bishop, lawfully elected in a free Chapter of Canons, of which behold the procès-verbal."

"Have you finished?" said the Duke.

"Not yet," replied the envoy: "I am further to require your Grace, on the part of the said right noble and venerable Prince, Bishop, and Count, that you do presently withdraw the garrison from the Castle of Bracquemont, and other places of strength, belonging to the Earldom of Croye, which have been placed there, whether in your own most gracious name, or in that of Isabelle, calling herself Countess of Croye; or any other until it shall be decided by the Imperial Diet, whether the fiefs in the question shall not pertain to the sister of the late Count, my most gracious Lady Hameline, rather than to his daughter, in respect of the *jus emphyteusis*."

"Your master is most learned," replied the Duke.

"Yet," continued the herald, "the noble and venerable Prince and Count will be disposed, all other disputes betwixt Burgundy and Liege being settled, to fix upon the Lady Isabelle such an appanage as may become her quality."

"He is generous and considerate," said the Duke, in the same tone.

"Now, by a poor fool's conscience," said Le Glorieux apart, to the Count of Crèvecœur, "I would rather be in the worst cow's hide that ever died of the murrain, than in that fellow's painted coat! The poor man goes on like drunkards who only look to the other pot, and not to the score which mine host chalks up behind the lattice."

"Have you yet done?" said the Duke to the herald.

"One word more," answered Rouge Sanglier, "from my noble and venerable lord aforesaid, respecting his worthy and trusty ally, the Most Christian King—"

"Ha!" exclaimed the Duke, starting, and in a fiercer tone than he had yet used; but checking himself, he instantly composed himself again to attention.

"Which most Christian King's royal person it is rumoured that you, Charles of Burgundy, have placed under restraint, contrary to your duty as a vassal of the Crown of France, and to the faith observed among Christian Sovereigns. For which reason, my said noble and venerable master, by my mouth, charges you to put his Royal and Most Christian ally forthwith at freedom, or to receive the defiance which I am authorised to pronounce to you."

"Have you yet done?" said the Duke.

"I have," answered the herald, "and await your Grace's answer, trusting it may be such as will save the effusion of Christian blood."

"Now, by Saint George of Burgundy"—said the Duke;—but ere he could proceed further, Louis arose, and struck in with a tone of so much dignity and authority, that Charles could not interrupt him.

"Under your favour, fair cousin of Burgundy," said the King; "we ourselves crave priority of voice in replying to this insolent fellow.—

Sirrah herald, or whatever thou art, carry back notice to the perjured outlaw and murderer, William de la Marck, that the King of France will be presently before Liege, for the purpose of punishing the sacrilegious murderer of his late beloved kinsman, Louis of Bourbon; and that he proposes to gibbet De la Marck alive, for the insolence of terming himself his ally, and putting his royal name into the mouth of one of his own base messengers."

"Add whatever else on my part," said Charles, "which it may not misbecome a prince to send to a common thief, and murderer.—And begone!—Yet stay.—Never herald went from the Court of Burgundy without having cause to cry, Largesse!—Let him be scourged till the bones are laid bare!"

"Nay, but if it please your Grace," said Crèvecœur and D'Hymbercourt together, "he is a herald, and so far privileged."

"It is you, Messires," replied the Duke, "who are such owls, as to think that the tabard makes the herald. I see by that fellow's blazoning he is a mere impostor. Let Toison d'Or step forward, and question him in your presence."

In spite of his natural effrontery, the envoy of the Wild Boar of Ardennes now became pale; and that notwithstanding some touches of paint with which he had adorned his countenance. Toison d'Or, the chief herald, as we have elsewhere said, of the Duke, and King-at-arms within his dominions, stepped forward with the solemnity of one who knew what was due to his office, and asked his supposed brother, in what College he had studied the science which he professed.

"I was bred a pursuivant at the Heraldic College of Ratisbon," answered Rouge Sanglier, "and received the diploma of Ehrenhold from that same learned fraternity."

"You could not derive it from a source more worthy," answered Toison d'Or, bowing still lower than he had done before; "and if I presume to confer with you on the mysteries of our sublime science, in obedience to the orders of the most gracious Duke, it is not in hopes of giving, but of receiving knowledge."

"Go to," said the Duke impatiently. "Leave off ceremony, and ask him some question that may try his skill."

"It were injustice to ask a disciple of the worthy College of Arms at Ratisbon, if he comprehendeth the common terms of blazonry," said Toison d'Or; "but I may, without offence, crave of Rouge Sanglier to say, if he is instructed in the more mysterious and secret terms of the science, by which the more learned do emblematically, and as it were parabolically, express to each other what is conveyed to others in the ordinary language, taught in the very accidence as it were of Heraldry?"

"I understand one sort of blazonry as well as another," answered Rouge Sanglier boldly; "but it may be we have not the same terms in Germany which you have here in Flanders."

"Alas, that you will say so!" replied Toison d'Or; "our noble science, which is indeed the very banner of nobleness, and glory of generosity, being the same in all Christian countries, nay, known and acknowledged even by the Saracens and Moors. I would, therefore, pray of you to describe what coat you will after the celestial fashion, that is, by the planets."

"Blazon it yourself as you will," said Rouge Sanglier; "I will do no such apish tricks upon commandment, as an ape is made to come aloft."

"Show him a coat, and let him blazon it in his own way," said the Duke; "and if he fails, I promise him that his back shall be gules, azure, and sable."

"Here," said the herald of Burgundy, taking from his pouch a piece of parchment, "is a scroll, in which certain considerations led me to prick down, after my own poor fashion, an ancient coat. I will pray my brother, if indeed he belong to the honourable College of Arms at Ratisbon, to decipher it in fitting language."

Le Glorieux, who seemed to take great pleasure in this discussion, had by this time bustled himself close up to the two heralds. "I will help thee, good fellow," said he to Rouge Sanglier, as he looked hopelessly upon the scroll. "This, my lords and masters, represents the cat looking out at the dairy-window."

This sally occasioned a laugh, which was something to the advantage of Rouge Sanglier, as it led Toison d'Or, indignant at the misconstruction of his drawing, to explain it as the coat-of-arms assumed by Childebert, King of France, after he had taken prisoner Gandemar, King of Burgundy; representing an ounce, or tiger-cat, the emblem of the captive prince, behind a grating, or, as Toison d'Or technically defined it, "Sable, a musion passant Or, oppressed with a trellis gules, cloué of the second."

"By my bauble," said Le Glorieux, "if the cat resemble Burgundy, she has the right side of the grating nowadays."

"True, good fellow," said Louis, laughing, while the rest of the presence, and even Charles himself, seemed disconcerted at so broad a jest,—"I owe thee a piece of gold for turning something that looked like sad earnest, into the merry game which I trust it will end in."

"Silence, Le Glorieux," said the Duke; "and you, Toison d'Or, who are too learned to be intelligible, stand back,—and bring that rascal forward, some of you.—Hark ye, villain," he said in his harshest tone, "do you know the difference between argent and or, except in the shape of coined money?"

"For pity's sake, your Grace, be good unto me!—Noble King Louis, speak for me!"

"Speak for thyself," said the Duke—"In a word, art thou herald or not?"

"Only for this occasion!" acknowledged the detected official.

"Now, by St. George!" said the Duke, eyeing Louis askance, "we know no king—no gentleman—save one, who would have so prostituted the noble science on which royalty and gentry rest! save that King, who sent to Edward of England a serving man disguised as a herald." [1]

"Such a stratagem," said Louis, laughing, or affecting to laugh, "could only be justified at a Court where no heralds were at the time, and when the emergency was urgent. But though it might have passed on the blunt and thick-witted islander, no one with brains a whit better than those of a wild boar would have thought of passing such a trick upon the accomplished Court of Burgundy."

"Send him who will," said the Duke fiercely, "he shall return on their hands in poor case.—Here!—drag him to the market-place!—slash him with bridle-reins and dog-whips until the tabard hang about him in tatters!—upon the Rouge Sanglier!—ça, ça!—Haloo, haloo!"

Four or five large hounds, such as are painted in the hunting-pieces upon which Rubens and Schneiders laboured in conjunction, caught the well-known notes with which the Duke concluded, and began to yell and bay as if the boar were just roused from his lair.

"By the rood!" said King Louis, observant to catch the vein of his dangerous cousin, "since the ass has put on the boar's hide, I would set the dogs on him to bait him out of it!"

"Right, right!" exclaimed Duke Charles, the fancy exactly chiming in with his humour at the moment—"it shall be done!—uncouple the hounds!—Hyke a Talbot! hyke a Beaumont!—We will course him from the door of the Castle to the east gate."

"I trust your Grace will treat me as a beast of chase," said the fellow, putting the best face he could upon the matter, "and allow me fair law?"

"Thou art but vermin," said the Duke, "and entitled to no law, by the letter of the book of hunting, nevertheless thou shalt have sixty yards in advance, were it but for the sake of thy unparalleled impudence. —Away, away, sirs!—we will see this sport."—And the council breaking up tumultuously, all hurried, none faster than the two Princes, to enjoy the humane pastime which King Louis had suggested.

The Rouge Sanglier showed excellent sport; for, winged with terror, and having half a score of fierce boar-hounds hard at his haunches, encouraged by the blowing of horns and the woodland cheer of the hunters, he flew like the very wind, and had he not been encumbered with his herald's coat (the worst possible habit for a runner), he might fairly have escaped dog-free; he also doubled once or twice, in a manner much approved of by the spectators. None of these, nay, not even Charles himself, was so delighted with the sport as King Louis, who, partly from political considerations, and partly as being naturally pleased with the sight of human suffering when ludicrously exhibited, laughed till the tears ran from his eyes, and in his ecstasies of rapture, caught hold of the Duke's ermine cloak, as if to support himself; whilst the Duke, no less

[1] Note XII.—Disguised Herald.

delighted, flung his arm around the King's shoulder, making thus an exhibition of confidential sympathy and familiarity very much at variance with the terms on which they had so lately stood together.

At length the speed of the pseudo-herald could save him no longer from the fangs of his pursuers; they seized him, pulled him down, and would probably soon have throttled him, had not the Duke called out —"Stave and tail! stave and tail!—Take them off him!—He hath shown so good a course, that, though he has made no sport at bay, we will not have him despatched."

Several officers accordingly busied themselves in taking off the dogs; and they were soon seen coupling some up, and pursuing others which ran through the streets, shaking in sport and triumph the tattered fragments of painted cloth and embroidery rent from the tabard, which the unfortunate wearer had put on in an unlucky hour.

At this moment, and while the Duke was too much engaged with what passed before him to mind what was said behind him, Oliver le Dain, gliding behind King Louis, whispered into his ear—"It is the Bohemian, Hayraddin Maugrabin—It were not well he should come to speech of the Duke."

"He must die," answered Louis, in the same tone—"dead men tell no tales."

One instant afterwards, Tristan l'Hermite, to whom Oliver had given the hint, stepped forward before the King and the Duke, and said, in his blunt manner, "So please your Majesty and your Grace, this piece of game is mine, and I claim him—he is marked with my stamp—the fleur-de-lis is branded on his shoulder, as all men may see.—He is a known villain, and hath slain the King's subjects, robbed churches, deflowered virgins, slain deer in the royal parks——"

"Enough, enough," said Duke Charles, "he is my royal cousin's property by many a good title. What will your Majesty do with him?"

"If he is left to my disposal," said the King, "I will at least give him one lesson in the science of heraldry, in which he is so ignorant—only explain to him practically, the meaning of a cross *potence*, with a noose dangling proper."

"Not as to be by him borne, but as to bear him.—Let him take the degrees under your gossip Tristan—he is a deep professor in such mysteries."

Thus answered the Duke, with a burst of discordant laughter at his own wit, which was so cordially chorussed by Louis, that his rival could not help looking kindly at him, while he said—

"Ah, Louis, Louis! would to God thou wert as faithful a monarch as thou art a merry companion! I cannot but think often on the jovial time we used to spend together."

"You may bring it back when you will," said Louis; "I will grant you as fair terms as for very shame's sake you ought to ask in my present condition, without making yourself the fable of Christendom; and I will swear to observe them upon the holy relique which I have ever the grace to bear about my person, being a fragment of the true cross."

Here he took a small golden reliquary, which was suspended from his neck next to his shirt by a chain of the same metal, and having kissed it devoutly, continued—

"Never was false oath sworn on this most sacred relique, but it was avenged within the year."

"Yet," said the Duke, "it was the same on which you swore amity to me when you left Burgundy, and shortly after sent the Bastard of Rubempré to murder or kidnap me."

"Nay, gracious cousin, now you are ripping up ancient grievances," said the King; "I promise you that you were deceived in that matter.— Moreover, it was not upon *this* relique which I then swore, but upon another fragment of the true cross which I got from the Grand Seigneur, weakened in virtue, doubtless, by sojourning with infidels. Besides, did not the war of the Public Good break out within the year; and was not a Burgundian army encamped at Saint Dennis, backed by all the great feudatories of France; and was I not obliged to yield up Normandy to my brother?—O God, shield us from perjury on such a warrant as this!"

"Well, cousin," answered the Duke; "I do believe thou hadst a lesson to keep faith another time.—And now for once, without finesse and doubling, will you make good your promise, and go with me to punish this murdering La Marck and the Liegeois?"

"I will march against them," said Louis, "with the Ban, and Arrière-Ban of France, and the Oriflamme displayed."

"Nay, nay," said the Duke, "that is more than is needful, or maybe advisable. The presence of your Scottish Guard, and two hundred choice lances, will serve to show that you are a free agent. A large army might—"

"Make me so in effect, you would say, my fair cousin?" said the King. "Well, you shall dictate the numbers of my attendants."

"And to put this fair cause of mischief out of the way, you will agree to the Countess Isabelle of Croye wedding with the Duke of Orleans?"

"Fair cousin," said the King, "you drive my courtesy to extremity. The Duke is the betrothed bridegroom of my daughter Joan. Be generous—yield up this matter, and let us speak rather of the towns on the Somme."

"My council will talk to your Majesty of these," said Charles; "I myself have less at heart the acquisition of territory, than the redress of injuries. You have tampered with my vassals, and your royal pleasure must needs dispose of the hand of a Ward of Burgundy. Your Majesty must bestow it within the pale of your own royal family, since you have meddled with it—otherwise, our conference breaks off."

"Were I to say I did this willingly," said the King, "no one would believe me; therefore do you, my fair cousin, judge of the extent of my wish to oblige you, when I say, most reluctantly, that the parties consenting, and a dispensation from the Pope being obtained, my own objections shall be no bar to this match which you propose."

"All besides can be easily settled by our ministers," said the Duke, "and we are once more cousins and friends."

"May Heaven be praised!" said Louis, "who holding in his hand the hearts of princes, doth mercifully incline them to peace and clemency, and prevent the effusion of human blood.—Oliver," he added apart to that favourite, who ever waited around him like the familiar beside a sorcerer, "Hark thee—tell Tristan to be speedy in dealing with yonder runagate Bohemian."

CHAPTER XXXIV

THE EXECUTION

I'll take thee to the good green wood,
And make thine own hand choose the tree.
Old Ballad.

"Now God be praised, that gave us the power of laughing, and making others laugh, and shame to the dull cur who scorns the office of a jester! Here is a joke, and that none of the brightest (though it may pass, since it has amused two princes), which hath gone farther than a thousand reasons of state to prevent a war between France and Burgundy."

Such was the inference of Le Glorieux, when, in consequence of the reconciliation of which we gave the particulars in the last chapter, the Burgundian guards were withdrawn from the Castle of Peronne, the abode of the King removed from the ominous Tower of Count Herbert, and, to the great joy of both French and Burgundians, an outward show at least of confidence and friendship seemed so established between Duke Charles and his liege lord. Yet still the latter, though treated with ceremonial observance, was sufficiently aware that he continued to be the object of suspicion, though he prudently affected to overlook it, and appeared to consider himself as entirely at his ease.

Meanwhile, as frequently happens in such cases, whilst the principal parties concerned had so far made up their differences, one of the subaltern agents concerned in their intrigues was bitterly experiencing the truth of the political maxim, that if the great have frequent need of base tools, they make amends to society by abandoning them to their fate, so soon as they find them no longer useful.

This was Hayraddin Maugrabin, who, surrendered by the Duke's officers to the King's Provost-Marshal, was by him placed in the hands of his two trusty aides-de-camp, Trois-Eschelles and Petit-André, to be despatched without loss of time. One on either side of him, and followed by a few guards and a multitude of rabble,—this playing the Allegro, that the Penseroso,—he was marched off (to use a modern comparison, like Garrick between Tragedy and Comedy) to the neighbouring forest; where, to save all further trouble and ceremonial of a gibbet, and so forth, the disposers of his fate proposed to knit him up to the first sufficient tree.

They were not long in finding an oak, as Petit-André facetiously expressed it, fit to bear such an acorn; and placing the wretched criminal on a bank under a sufficient guard, they began their extemporaneous preparations for the final catastrophe. At that moment, Hayraddin, gazing on the crowd, encountered the eyes of Quentin Durward, who, thinking he recognised the countenance of his faithless guide in that of the detected impostor, had followed with the crowd to witness the execution, and assure himself of the identity.

When the executioners informed him that all was ready, Hayraddin, with much calmness, asked a single boon at their hands.

"Anything, my son, consistent with our office," said Trois-Eschelles.

"That is," said Hayraddin, "anything but my life."

"Even so," said Trois-Eschelles, "and something more; for as you seem resolved to do credit to our mystery, and die like a man, without making wry mouths—why, though our orders are to be prompt, I care not if I indulge you ten minutes longer."

"You are even too generous," said Hayraddin.

"Truly we may be blamed for it," said Petit-André; "but what of that?—I could consent almost to give my life for such a jerry-come-tumble, such a smart, tight, firm lad, who proposes to come from aloft with a grace, as an honest fellow should do."

"So that if you want a confessor," said Trois-Eschelles—

"Or a *lire* of wine," said his facetious companion—

"Or a psalm," said Tragedy—

"Or a song," said Comedy—

"Neither, my good, kind, and most expeditious friends," said the Bohemian—"I only pray to speak a few minutes with yonder Archer of the Scottish Guard."

The executioners hesitated a moment; but Trois-Eschelles recollecting that Quentin Durward was believed, from various circumstances, to stand high in the favour of their master, King Louis, they resolved to permit the interview.

When Quentin, at their summons, approached the condemned criminal, he could not but be shocked at his appearance, however justly his doom might have been deserved. The remnants of his heraldic finery, rent to tatters by the fangs of the dogs, and the clutches of the bipeds who had rescued him from their fury to lead him to the gallows, gave him at once a ludicrous and a wretched appearance. His face was discoloured with paint, and with some remnants of a fictitious beard, assumed for the purpose of disguise, and there was the paleness of death upon his cheek and upon his lips; yet, strong in passive courage, like most of his tribe, his eye, while it glistened and wandered, as well as the contorted smile of his mouth, seemed to bid defiance to the death he was about to die.

Quentin was struck partly with horror, partly with compassion, as he approached the miserable man, and these feelings probably betrayed themselves in his manner, for Petit-André called out, "Trip it more smartly, jolly Archer—This gentleman's leisure cannot wait for you, if you walk as if the pebbles were eggs, and you afraid of breaking them."

"I must speak with him in privacy," said the criminal, despair seeming to croak in his accent as he uttered the words.

"That may hardly consist with our office, my merry Leap-the-ladder," said Petit-André; "we know you for a slippery eel of old."

"I am tied with your horse-girths, hand and foot," said the criminal —"You may keep guard around me, though out of ear-shot—the Archer is your own King's servant—And if I give you ten guilders—"

"Laid out in masses, the sum may profit his poor soul," said Trois-Eschelles.

"Laid out in wine or brantwein, it will comfort my poor body," responded Petit-André. "So let them be forthcoming, my little crack-rope."

"Pay the blood-hounds their fee," said Hayraddin to Durward; "I was plundered of every stiver when they took me—it shall avail thee much."

Quentin paid the executioners their guerdon, and, like men of promise, they retreated out of hearing—keeping, however, a careful eye on the criminal's motions. After waiting an instant till the unhappy man should speak, as he still remained silent, Quentin at length addressed him, "And to this conclusion thou hast at length arrived?"

"Ay," answered Hayraddin, "it required neither astrologer, nor physiognomist, nor chiromantist, to foretell that I should follow the destiny of my family."

"Brought to this early end by thy long course of crime and treachery!" said the Scot.

"No, by the bright Aldeboran and all his brother twinklers!" answered the Bohemian. "I am brought hither by my folly, in believing that the bloodthirsty cruelty of a Frank could be restrained even by what they themselves profess to hold most sacred. A priest's vestment would have been no safer garb for me than a herald's tabard, however sanctimonious are your professions of devotion and chivalry."

"A detected impostor has no right to claim the immunities of the disguise he had usurped," said Durward.

"Detected!" said the Bohemian. "My jargon was as good as yonder old fool of a herald's;—but let it pass. As well now as hereafter."

"You abuse time," said Quentin. "If you have aught to tell me, say it quickly, and then take some care of your soul."

"Of my soul?" said the Bohemian, with a hideous laugh. "Think ye a leprosy of twenty years can be cured in an instant?—If I have a soul, it hath been in such a course since I was ten years old and more, that it would take me one month to recall all my crimes, and another to tell them to the priest;—and were such space granted me, it is five to one I would employ it otherwise."

"Hardened wretch, blaspheme not! Tell me what thou hast to say, and I leave thee to thy fate," said Durward, with mingled pity and horror.

"I have a boon to ask," said Hayraddin,—"but first I will buy it of you; for your tribe, with all their professions of charity, give nought for nought."

"I could well nigh say thy gifts perish with thee," answered Quentin, "but that thou art on the very verge of eternity.—Ask thy boon— reserve thy bounty—it can do me no good—I remember enough of your good offices of old."

"Why, I loved you," said Hayraddin, "for the matter that chanced on the banks of the Cher; and I would have helped you to a wealthy dame. You wore her scarf, which partly misled me; and indeed I thought that Hameline, with her portable wealth, was more for your market-penny than the other hen-sparrow, with her old roost at Bracquemont, which Charles has clutched, and is likely to keep his claws upon."

"Talk not so idly, unhappy man," said Quentin; "yonder officers become impatient."

"Give them ten guilders for ten minutes more," said the culprit,— who, like most in his situation, mixed with his hardihood a desire of procrastinating his fate,—"I tell thee it shall avail thee much."

"Use then well the minutes so purchased," said Durward, and easily made a new bargain with the Marshal's men.

This done, Hayraddin continued.—"Yes, I assure you I meant you well; and Hameline would have proved an easy and convenient spouse Why, she has reconciled herself even with the Boar of Ardennes, though his mode of wooing was somewhat of the roughest, and lords it yonder in his sty, as if she had fed on mast-husks and acorns all her life."

"Cease this brutal and untimely jesting," said Quentin, "or, once more I tell you, I will leave you to your fate."

"You are right," said Hayraddin, after a moment's pause; "what cannot be postponed must be faced!—Well, know then, I came hither in this accursed disguise, moved by a great reward from De la Marck, and hoping a yet mightier one from King Louis, not merely to bear the message of defiance which you may have heard of, but to tell the King an important secret."

"It was a fearful risk," said Durward.

"It was paid for as such, and such it hath proved," answered the Bohemian. "De la Marck attempted before to communicate with Louis by means of Marthon; but she could not, it seems, approach nearer to him than the astrologer, to whom she told all the passages of the journey, and of Schonwaldt; but it is a chance if her tidings ever reach Louis, except in the shape of a prophecy. But hear my secret, which is more important than aught she could tell. William de la Marck has assembled a numerous and strong force within the city of Liege, and augments it daily by means of the old priest's treasures. But he proposes not to hazard a battle with the chivalry of Burgundy, and still less to stand a siege in the dismantled town. This he will do—he will suffer the hot-brained Charles to sit down before the place without opposition; and in the night, make an outfall or sally upon the leaguer with his whole force. Many he will have in French armour, who will cry France, Saint Louis, and Denis Montjoye, as if there were a strong body of French auxiliaries in the city. This cannot choose but strike utter confusion among the Burgundians; and if King Louis, with his guards, attendants, and such soldiers as he may have with him, shall second his efforts, the Boar of Ardennes nothing doubts the discomfiture of the whole Burgundian army.—There is my secret, and I bequeath it to you. Forward, or prevent the enterprise—sell the intelligence to King Louis, or to Duke Charles, I care not—save or destroy whom thou wilt; for my part, I only grieve that I cannot spring it like a mine, to the destruction of them all!"

"It is indeed an important secret," said Quentin, instantly compre-hending how easily the national jealousy might be awakened in a camp consisting partly of French, partly of Burgundians.

"Ay, so it is," answered Hayraddin; "and now you have it, you would fain begone, and leave me without granting the boon for which I have paid beforehand."

"Tell me thy request," said Quentin—"I will grant it if it be in my power."

"Nay, it is no mighty demand—it is only in behalf of poor Klepper, my palfrey, the only living thing that may miss me.—A due mile south, you will find him feeding by a deserted collier's hut; whistle to him thus" —(he whistled a peculiar note), "and call him by his name, Klepper, he will come to you; here is his bridle under my gaberdine—it is lucky the hounds got it not, for he obeys no other. Take him, and make much of him—I do not say for his master's sake,—but because I have placed at your disposal the event of a mighty war. He will never fail you at need —night and day, rough and smooth, fair and foul, warm stables and the winter sky, are the same to Klepper; had I cleared the gates of Peronne, and got as far as where I left him, I had not been in this case.—Will you be kind to Klepper?"

"I swear to you that I will," answered Quentin, affected by what seemed a trait of tenderness in a character so hardened.

"Then fare thee well!" said the criminal—"Yet stay—stay—I would not willingly die in discourtesy, forgetting a lady's commission.—This billet is from the very gracious and extremely silly Lady of the Wild Boar of Ardennes, to her black-eyed niece—I see by your look I have chosen a willing messenger.—And one word more—I forgot to say, that in the stuffing of my saddle you will find a rich purse of gold pieces, for the sake of which I put my life on the venture which has cost me so dear. Take them, and replace a hundredfold the guilders you have bestowed on these bloody slaves—I make you mine heir."

"I will bestow them in good works, and masses for the benefit of thy soul," said Quentin.

"Name not that word again," said Hayraddin, his countenance assuming a dreadful expression; "there is—there can be—there shall be—no such thing!—it is a dream of priestcraft!"

"Unhappy—most unhappy being! Think better!—let me speed for a priest—these men will delay yet a little longer—I will bribe them to it," said Quentin—"What canst thou expect, dying in such opinions, and impenitent?"

"To be resolved into the elements," said the hardened atheist, pressing his fettered arms against his bosom; "my hope, trust, and expectation is, that the mysterious frame of humanity shall melt into the general mass of nature, to be recompounded in the other forms with which she daily supplies those which daily disappear, and return under different forms,—the watery particles to streams and showers, the earthly parts to enrich their mother earth, the airy portions to wanton in the breeze, and those of fire to supply the blaze of Aldeboran and his brethren.—In this faith have I lived, and I will die in it!—Hence! begone!—disturb me no farther!—I have spoken the last words that mortal ears shall listen to!"

Deeply impressed with the horrors of his condition, Quentin Durward yet saw that it was vain to hope to awaken him to a sense of his fearful state. He bid him, therefore, farewell; to which the criminal only replied by a short and sullen nod, as one who, plunged in reverie, bids adieu to company which distracts his thoughts. He bent his course towards the forest, and easily found where Klepper was feeding. The creature came at his call, but was for some time unwilling to be caught, snuffing and starting when the stranger approached him. At length, however, Quentin's general acquaintance with the habits of the animal, and perhaps some particular knowledge of those of Klepper, which he had often admired while Hayraddin and he travelled together, enabled him to take possession of the Bohemian's dying bequest. Long ere he returned to Peronne, the Bohemian had gone where the vanity of his dreadful creed was to be put to the final issue—a fearful experience for one who had neither expressed remorse for the past, nor apprehension for the future.

CHAPTER XXXV

A PRIZE FOR HONOUR

'Tis brave for Beauty when the best blade wins her.
The Count Palatine.

WHEN Quentin Durward reached Peronne, a council was sitting, in the issue of which he was interested more deeply than he could have apprehended, and which, though held by persons of a rank with whom one of his could scarce be supposed to have community of interest, had nevertheless the most extraordinary influence on his fortunes.

King Louis, who, after the interlude of De la Marck's envoy, had omitted no opportunity to cultivate the returning interest which that circumstance had given him in the Duke's opinion, had been engaged in consulting him, or, it might be almost said, receiving his opinion, upon the number and quality of the troops, by whom, as auxiliary to the Duke of Burgundy, he was to be attended in their joint expedition against Liege. He plainly saw the wish of Charles was to call into his camp such Frenchmen as, from their small number and high quality, might be considered rather as hostages than as auxiliaries; but, observant of Crèvecœur's advice, he assented as readily to whatever the Duke proposed, as if it had arisen from the free impulse of his own mind.

The King failed not, however, to indemnify himself for his complaisance, by the indulgence of his vindictive temper against Balue, whose counsels had led him to repose such exuberant trust in the Duke of Burgundy. Tristan, who bore the summons for moving up his auxiliary forces, had the farther commission to carry the Cardinal to the Castle of Loches and there shut him up in one of those iron cages, which he himself is said to have invented.

"Let him make proof of his own devices," said the King; "he is a man of holy Church—we may not shed his blood; but *Pasques-dieu!* his bishopric, for ten years to come, shall have an impregnable frontier to make up for its small extent!—And see the troops are brought up instantly."

Perhaps, by this prompt acquiescence, Louis hoped to evade the more unpleasing condition with which the Duke had clogged their reconciliation. But if he so hoped, he greatly mistook the temper of his cousin; for never man lived more tenacious of his purpose than Charles of Burgundy, and least of all was he willing to relax any stipulation which he had made in resentment, or revenge, of a supposed injury.

No sooner were the necessary expresses despatched to summon up the forces who were selected to act as auxiliaries, than Louis was called upon by his host to give public consent to the espousals of the Duke of Orleans and Isabelle of Croye. The King complied with a heavy sigh, and presently after urged a slight expostulation, founded upon the necessity of observing the wishes of the Duke himself.

"These have not been neglected," said the Duke of Burgundy; "Crèvecœur hath communicated with Monsieur d'Orleans, and finds him (strange to say) so dead to the honour of wedding a royal bride, that he acceded to the proposal of marrying the Countess of Croye, as the kindest proposal which father could have made to him."

"He is more ungracious and thankless," said Louis; "but the whole shall be as you, my cousin, will; if you can bring it about with consent of the parties themselves."

"Fear not that," said the Duke; and accordingly, not many minutes after the affair had been proposed, the Duke of Orleans and the Countess of Croye, the latter attended, as on the preceding occasion, by the Countess of Crèvecœur, and the Abbess of the Ursulines, were summoned to the presence of the Princes, and heard from the mouth of Charles of Burgundy, unobjected to by that of Louis, who sat in silent and moody consciousness of diminished consequence, that the union of their hands was designed by the wisdom of both Princes, to confirm the perpetual alliance which in future should take place betwixt France and Burgundy.

The Duke of Orleans had much difficulty in suppressing the joy which he felt upon the proposal, and which delicacy rendered improper in the presence of Louis; and it required his habitual awe of that monarch, to enable him to rein in his delight, so much as merely to reply, "that his duty compelled him to place his choice at the disposal of his Sovereign."

"Fair cousin of Orleans," said Louis, with sullen gravity, "since I must speak on so unpleasant an occasion, it is needless for me to remind you, that my sense of your merits had let me to propose for you a match into my own family. But, since my cousin of Burgundy thinks, that the disposing of your hand otherwise is the surest pledge of amity between his dominions and mine, I love both too well not to sacrifice to them my own hopes and wishes."

The Duke of Orleans threw himself on his knees, and kissed,—and, for once, with sincerity of attachment,—the hand which the King, with averted countenance, extended to him. In fact, he, as well as most present, saw, in the unwilling acquiescence of this accomplished dissembler, who, even with that very purpose, had suffered his reluctance to be visible, a King relinquishing his favourite project, and subjugating his paternal feelings to the necessities of state, and interest of his country. Even Burgundy was moved, and Orleans' heart smote him for the joy which he involuntarily felt on being freed from his engagement with the Princess Joan. If he had known how deeply the King was cursing him in his soul, and what thoughts of future revenge he was agitating, it is probable his own delicacy on the occasion would not have been so much hurt.

Charles next turned to the young Countess, and bluntly announced the proposed match to her, as a matter which neither admitted delay nor hesitation; adding, at the same time, that it was but a too favourable consequence of her intractability on a former occasion.

"My Lord Duke and Sovereign," said Isabelle, summoning up all her courage, "I observe your Grace's commands, and submit to them."

"Enough, enough," said the Duke, interrupting her, "we will arrange the rest.—Your Majesty," he continued, addressing King Louis, "hath had a boar's hunt in the morning, what say you to rousing a wolf in the afternoon?"

The young Countess saw the necessity of decision.—"Your Grace

mistakes my meaning," she said, speaking, though timidly, yet loudly
and decidedly enough to compel the Duke's attention, which, from some
consciousness, he would otherwise have willingly denied to her.—"My
submission," she said, "only respected those lands and estates which
your Grace's ancestors gave to mine, and which I resign to the House of
Burgundy, if my Sovereign thinks my disobedience in this matter renders
me unworthy to hold them."

"Ha! Saint George!" said the Duke, stamping furiously on the
ground, "does the fool know in what presence she is—And to whom she
speaks?"

"My lord," she replied, still undismayed, "I am before my Suzerain,
and, I trust, a just one. If you deprive me of my lands, you take away
all that your ancestors' generosity gave, and you break the only bonds
which attach us together. You gave not this poor and persecuted form,
still less the spirit which animates me—And these it is my purpose to
dedicate to Heaven in the convent of the Ursulines, under the guidance
of this Holy Mother Abbess."

The rage and astonishment of the Duke can hardly be conceived,
unless we could estimate the surprise of a falcon, against whom a dove
should ruffle its pinions in defiance.—"Will the Holy Mother receive
you without an appanage?" he said, in a voice of scorn.

"If she doth her convent, in the first instance, so much wrong," said
the Lady Isabelle, "I trust there is charity enough among the noble
friends of my house, to make up some suppport for the orphan of Croye."

"It is false!" said the Duke; "it is a base pretext to cover some secret
and unworthy passion.—My Lord of Orleans, she shall be yours, if I
drag her to the altar with my own hands!"

The Countess of Crèvecœur, a high-spirited woman, and confident in
her husband's merits and his favour with the Duke, could keep silent
no longer.—"My lord," she said, "your passions transport you into language utterly unworthy—The hand of no gentlewoman can be disposed
of by force."

"And it is no part of the duty of a Christian Prince," added the
Abbess, "to thwart the wishes of a pious soul, who, broken with the
cares and the persecutions of the world, is desirous to become the bride
of Heaven."

"Neither can my cousin of Orleans," said Dunois, "with honour accept a proposal, to which the lady has thus publicly stated her objections."

"If I were permitted," said Orleans, on whose facile mind Isabelle's
beauty had made a deep impression, "some time to endeavour to place
my pretensions before the Countess in a more favourable light——"

"My lord," said Isabelle, whose firmness was now fully supported by
the encouragement which she received from all around, "it were to no
purpose—my mind is made up to decline this alliance, though far above
my deserts."

"Nor have I time," said the Duke, "to wait till these whimsies are changed with the next change of the moon.—Monseigneur d'Orleans, she shall learn within this hour, that obedience becomes matter of necessity."

"Not in my behalf, Sire," answered the Prince, who felt that he could not, with any show of honour, avail himself of the Duke's obstinate disposition;—"to have been once openly and positively refused, is enough for a son of France. He cannot prosecute his addresses farther."

The Duke darted one furious glance at Orleans, another at Louis; and reading in the countenance of the latter, in spite of his utmost efforts to suppress his feelings, a look of secret triumph, he became outrageous.

"Write," he said to the Secretary, "our doom of forfeiture and imprisonment against this disobedient and insolent minion! She shall to the Zuchthaus, to the penitentiary, to herd with those whose lives have rendered them her rivals in effrontery!"

There was a general murmur.

"My Lord Duke," said the Count of Crèvecœur, taking the word for the rest, "this must be better thought on. We, your faithful vassals, cannot suffer such a dishonour to the nobility and chivalry of Burgundy. If the Countess hath done amiss, let her be punished—but in the manner that becomes her rank, and ours, who stand connected with her house by blood and alliance."

The Duke paused a moment, and looked full at his councillor with the stare of a bull, which, when compelled by the neat-herd from the road which he wishes to go, deliberates with himself whether to obey, or to rush on his driver, and toss him into the air.

Prudence, however, prevailed over fury—he saw the sentiment was general in his council—was afraid of the advantages which Louis might derive from seeing dissension among his vassals; and probably—for he was rather of a coarse and violent, than of a malignant temper—felt ashamed of his own dishonourable proposal.

"You are right," he said, "Crèvecœur, and I spoke hastily. Her fate shall be determined according to the rules of chivalry. Her flight to Liege hath given the signal for the Bishop's murder. He that best avenges that deed, and brings us the head of the Wild Boar of Ardennes, shall claim her hand of us; and if she denies his right, we can at least grant him her fiefs, leaving it to his generosity to allow her what means he will to retire into a convent."

"Nay!" said the Countess, "think I am the daughter of Count Reinold —of your father's old, valiant, and faithful servant. Would you hold me out as a prize to the best sword-player?"

"Your ancestress," said the Duke, "was won at a tourney—you shall be fought for in real *mêlée*. Only thus far, for Count Reinold's sake, the successful prizer shall be a gentleman, of unimpeached birth, and unstained bearings; but, be he such, and the poorest who ever drew the strap of a sword-belt through the tongue of a buckle, he shall have at least the proffer of your hand. I swear it, by Saint George, by my ducal crown, and by the Order that I wear!—Ha! Messires," he added, turning to the nobles present, "this at least is, I think, in conformity with the rules of chivalry?"

Isabelle's remonstrances were drowned in a general and jubilant assent, above which was heard the voice of old Lord Crawford, regretting the weight of years that prevented his striking for so fair a prize. The Duke was gratified by the general applause, and his temper began to flow more smoothly, like that of a swollen river when it hath subsided within its natural boundaries.

"Are we, to whom fate has given dames already," said Crèvecœur, "to be bystanders at this fair game? It does not consist with my honour to be so, for I have myself a vow to be paid at the expense of that tusked and bristled brute, De la Marck."

"Strike boldly in, Crèvecœur," said the Duke; "win her, and since thou canst not wear her thyself, bestow her where thou wilt—on Count Stephen, your nephew, if you list."

"Gramercy, my lord!" said Crèvecœur, "I will do my best in the battle; and, should I be fortunate enough to be foremost, Stephen shall try his eloquence against that of the Lady Abbess."

"I trust," said Dunois, "that the chivalry of France are not excluded from this fair contest?"

"Heaven forbid! brave Dunois," answered the Duke, "were it but for the sake of seeing you do your uttermost. But," he added, "though there be no fault in the Lady Isabelle wedding a Frenchman, it will be necessary that the Count of Croye must become a subject of Burgundy."

"Enough, enough," said Dunois, "my bar sinister may never be surmounted by the coronet of Croye—I will live and die French. But yet, though I should lose the lands, I will strike a blow for the lady."

Le Balafré dared not speak aloud in such a presence, but he muttered to himself—

"Now, Saunders Souplejaw, hold thine own!—thou always saidst the fortune of our house was to be won by marriage, and never had you such a chance to keep your word with us."

"No one thinks of me," said Le Glorieux, "who am sure to carry off the prize from all of you."

"Right, my sapient friend," said Louis; "when a woman is in the case, the greatest fool is ever the first in favour."

While the princes and their nobles thus jested over her fate, the Abbess and the Countess of Crèvecœur endeavoured in vain to console Isabelle, who had withdrawn with them from the council-presence. The former assured her that the Holy Virgin would frown on every attempt to withdraw a true votaress from the shrine of Saint Ursula; while the Countess of Crèvecœur whispered more temporal consolation, that no true knight, who might succeed in the emprise proposed, would avail himself, against her inclinations, of the Duke's award; and that perhaps the successful competitor might prove one who should find such favour in her eyes as to reconcile her to obedience. Love, like despair, catches at straws; and, faint and vague as was the hope which this insinuation conveyed, the tears of the Countess Isabelle flowed more placidly while she dwelt upon it.[1]

CHAPTER XXXVI

THE SALLY

The wretch condemn'd with life to part,
    Still, still on hope relies,
And every pang that rends the heart
    Bids expectation rise.

Hope, like a glimmering taper's light,
    Adorns and cheers the way;
And still the darker grows the night,
    Emits a brighter ray.

                                    GOLDSMITH.

FEW days had passed ere Louis had received, with a smile of gratified vengeance, the intelligence, that his favourite and his counsellor, the Cardinal Balue, was groaning within a cage of iron, so disposed as scarce to permit him to enjoy repose in any posture except when recumbent; and of which, be it said in passing, he remained the unpitied tenant for nearly twelve years. The auxiliary forces which the Duke had required Louis to bring up had also appeared; and he comforted himself that their numbers were sufficient to protect his person against violence, although too limited to cope, had such been his purpose, with the large army of Burgundy. He saw himself also at liberty, when time should suit, to resume his project of marriage between his daughter and the Duke of Orleans; and, although he was sensible to the indignity of serving with his noblest peers under the banners of his own vassal, and against the people whose cause he had abetted, he did not allow these circumstances to embarrass him in the meantime, trusting that a future day would bring him amends.—"For chance," said he to his trusty Oliver, "may indeed gain one hit, but it is patience and wisdom which win the game at last."

With such sentiments, upon a beautiful day in the latter end of harvest, the King mounted his horse; and, indifferent that he was looked upon rather as a part of the pageant of a victor, than in the light of an independent Sovereign surrounded by his guards and his chivalry, King Louis sallied from under the Gothic gateway of Peronne, to join the

---

[1] The perilling the hand of an heiress upon the event of a battle, was not so likely to take place in the fourteenth century as when the laws of chivalry were in more general observance. Yet it was not unlikely to occur to so absolute a Prince as Duke Charles, in circumstances like those supposed.

Burgundian army, which commenced at the same time its march against Liege.

Most of the ladies of distinction who were in the place, attended, dressed in their best array, upon the battlements and defences of the gate, to see the gallant show of the warriors setting forth on the expedition. Thither had the Countess Crèvecœur brought the Countess Isabelle. The latter attended very reluctantly; but the peremptory order of Charles had been, that she who was to bestow the palm in the tourney, should be visible to the knights who were about to enter the lists.

As they thronged out from under the arch, many a pennon and shield was to be seen, graced with fresh devices, expressive of the bearer's devoted resolution to become a competitor for a prize so fair. Here a charger was painted starting for the goal,—there an arrow aimed at a mark,—one knight bore a bleeding heart, indicative of his passion,—another a skull, and a coronet of laurels, showing his determination to win or die. Many others there were; and some so cunningly intricate and obscure, that they might have defied the most ingenious interpreter. Each knight, too, it may be presumed, put his courser to his mettle, and assumed his most gallant seat in the saddle, as he passed for a moment under the view of the fair bevy of dames and damsels, who encouraged their valour by their smiles, and the waving of kerchiefs and of veils. The Archer-Guard, selected almost at will from the flower of the Scottish nation, drew general applause, from the gallantry and splendour of their appearance.

And there was one among these strangers, who ventured on a demonstration of acquaintance with the Lady Isabelle, which had not been attempted even by the most noble of the French nobility. It was Quentin Durward, who, as he passed the ladies in his rank, presented to the Countess of Croye, on the point of his lance, the letter of her aunt.

"Now, by my honour," said the Count of Crèvecœur, "that is over insolent in an unworthy adventurer!"

"Do not call him so, Crèvecœur," said Dunois; "I have good reason to bear testimony to his gallantry—and in behalf of that lady, too."

"You make words of nothing," said Isabelle, blushing with shame, and partly with resentment; "it is a letter from my unfortunate aunt—She writes cheerfully, though her situation must be dreadful."

"Let us hear, let us hear what says the Boar's bride," said Crèvecœur.

The Countess Isabelle read the letter, in which her aunt seemed determined to make the best of a bad bargain, and to console herself for the haste and indecorum of her nuptials, by the happiness of being wedded to one of the bravest men of the age, who had just acquired a princedom by his valour. She implored her niece not to judge of her William (as she called him) by the report of others, but to wait till she knew him personally. He had his faults, perhaps, but they were such as belonged to characters whom she had ever venerated. William was rather addicted to wine, but so was the gallant Sir Godfrey, her grandsire;—he was something hasty and sanguinary in his temper, such had been her brother,

Reinold of blessed memory;—he was blunt in speech, few Germans were otherwise; and a little wilful and peremptory, but she believed all men loved to rule. More there was to the same purpose; and the whole concluded with the hope and request, that Isabelle would, by means of the bearer, endeavour her escape from the tyrant of Burgundy, and come to her loving kinswoman's Court of Liege, where any little differences concerning their mutual rights of succession to the Earldom might be adjusted by Isabelle's marrying Earl Eberson—a bridegroom younger indeed than his bride, but that, as she (the Lady Hameline) might perhaps say from experience, was an inequality more easy to be endured than Isabelle could be aware of.[1]

Here the Countess Isabelle stopped; the Abbess observing, with a prim aspect, that she had read quite enough concerning such worldly vanities, and the Count of Crèvecœur breaking out, "Aroint thee, deceitful witch!—Why, this device smells rank as the toasted cheese in a rat-trap—Now fie, and double fie, upon the old decoy-duck!"

The Countess of Crèvecœur gravely rebuked her husband for his violence—"The Lady Hameline," she said, "must have been deceived by De la Marck with a show of courtesy."

"He show courtesy!" said the Count—"I acquit him of all such dissimulation. You may as well expect courtesy from a literal wild boar—you may as well try to lay leaf-gold on old rusty gibbet-irons. No—idiot as she is, she is not quite goose enough to fall in love with the fox who has snapped her, and that in his very den. But you women are all alike—fair words carry it—and, I dare say, here is my pretty cousin impatient to join her aunt in this fool's paradise, and marry the Boar-Pig."

"So far from being capable of such folly," said Isabelle, "I am doubly desirous of vengeance on the murderers of the excellent Bishop, because it will, at the same time, free my aunt from the villain's power."

"Ah! there indeed spoke the voice of Croye!" exclaimed the Count; and no more was said concerning the letter.

But while Isabelle read her aunt's epistle to her friends, it must be observed that she did not think it necessary to recite a certain *postscript*, in which the Countess Hameline, lady-like, gave an account of her occupations, and informed her niece, that she had laid aside for the present a surcoat which she was working for her husband, bearing the arms of Croye and La Marck in conjugal fashion, parted per pale, because her William had determined, for purposes of policy, in the first action to have others dressed in his coat-armour, and himself to assume the arms of Orleans, with a bar sinister—in other words, those of Dunois. There was also a slip of paper in another hand, the contents of which the Countess did not think it necessary to mention, being simply these words—

[1] It is almost unnecessary to add, that the marriage of William de la Marck with the Lady Hameline, is as apocryphal as the lady herself. The real bride of the Wild Boar of Ardennes was Joan D'Arschel, Baroness of Scoonhoven.

"If you hear not of me soon, and that by the trumpet of Fame, conclude me dead, but not unworthy."

A thought, hitherto repelled as wildly incredible, now glanced with double keenness through Isabelle's soul. As female wit seldom fails in the contrivance of means, she so ordered it, that ere the troops were fully on march, Quentin Durward received from an unknown hand the billet of Lady Hameline, marked with three crosses opposite to the post-script, and having these words subjoined:—"He who feared not the arms of Orleans when on the breast of their gallant owner, cannot dread them when displayed on that of a tyrant and murderer." A thousand thousand times was this intimation kissed and pressed to the bosom of the young Scot! for it marshalled him on the path where both Honour and Love held out the reward, and possessed him with a secret unknown to others, by which to distinguish him whose death could alone give life to his hopes, and which he prudently resolved to lock up in his own bosom.

But Durward saw the necessity of acting otherwise respecting the information communicated by Hayraddin, since the proposed sally of De la Marck, unless heedfully guarded against, might prove the destruction of the besieging army; so difficult was it, in the tumultuous warfare of those days, to recover from a nocturnal surprise. After pondering on the matter, he formed the additional resolution, that he would not communicate the intelligence save personally, and to both the Princes while together; perhaps, because he felt that to mention so well-contrived and hopeful a scheme to Louis whilst in private, might be too strong a temptation to the wavering probity of that Monarch, and lead him to assist, rather than repel the intended sally. He determined, therefore, to watch for an opportunity of revealing the secret whilst Louis and Charles were met, which, as they were not particularly fond of the constraint imposed by each other's society, was not likely soon to occur.

Meanwhile the march continued, and the confederates soon entered the territories of Liege. Here the Burgundian soldiers, at least a part of them, composed of those bands who had acquired the title of *Ecorcheurs*, or flayers, showed by the usage which they gave the inhabitants, under pretext of avenging the Bishop's death, that they well deserved that honourable title; while their conduct greatly prejudiced the cause of Charles, the aggrieved inhabitants, who might otherwise have been passive in the quarrel, assuming arms in self-defence, harassing his march, by cutting off small parties, and falling back before the main body upon the city itself, thus augmenting the numbers and desperation of those who had resolved to defend it. The French, few in number, and those the choice soldiers of the country, kept, according to the King's orders, close by their respective standards, and observed the strictest discipline; a contrast which increased the suspicions of Charles, who could not help remarking that the troops of Louis demeaned themselves as if they were rather friends to the Liegeois, than allies of Burgundy.

At length, without experiencing any serious opposition, the army arrived in the rich valley of the Maes, and before the large and populous city of Liege. The Castle of Schonwaldt they found had been totally destroyed, and learned that William de la Marck, whose only talents were of a military cast, had withdrawn his whole forces into the city, and was determined to avoid the encounter of the chivalry of France and Burgundy in the open field. But the invaders were not long of experiencing the danger which must always exist in attacking a large town, however open, if the inhabitants are disposed to defend it desperately.

A part of the Burgundian vanguard, conceiving that, from the dismantled and breached state of the walls, they had nothing to do but to march into Liege at their ease, entered one of the suburbs with the shouts of "Burgundy, Burgundy! Kill, kill—all is ours—Remember Louis of Bourbon!" But as they marched in disorder through the narrow streets, and were partly dispersed for the purpose of pillage, a large body of the inhabitants issued suddenly from the town, fell furiously upon them, and made considerable slaughter. De la Marck even availed himself of the breaches in the walls, which permitted the defenders to issue out of different points, and, by taking separate routes into the contested suburb, to attack, in the front, flank, and rear, at once, the assailants, who, stunned by the furious, unexpected, and multiplied nature of the resistance offered, could hardly stand to their arms. The evening, which began to close, added to their confusion.

When this news was brought to Duke Charles, he was furious with rage, which was not much appeased by the offer of King Louis, to send the French men-at-arms into the suburbs, to rescue and bring off the Burgundian vanguard. Rejecting this offer briefly, he would have put himself at the head of his own Guards, to extricate those engaged in the incautious advance; but D'Hymbercourt and Crèvecœur entreated him to leave the service to them, and, marching into the scene of action at two points, with more order and proper arrangement for mutual support, these two celebrated captains succeeded in repulsing the Liegeois, and in extricating the vanguard, who lost, besides prisoners, no fewer than eight hundred men, of whom about a hundred were men-at-arms. The prisoners, however, were not numerous, most of them having been rescued by D'Hymbercourt, who now proceeded to occupy the contested suburb, and to place guards opposite to the town, from which it was divided by an open space, or esplanade, of five or six hundred yards, left free of buildings for the purposes of defence. There was no moat betwixt the suburb and town, the ground being rocky in that place. A gate fronted the suburb, from which sallies might be easily made, and the wall was pierced by two or three of those breaches which Duke Charles had caused to be made after the battle of Saint Tron, and which had been hastily repaired with mere barricades of timber. D'Hymbercourt turned two culverins on the gate, and placed two others opposite to the principal breach, to repel any sally from the city, and then returned to the Burgundian army, which he found in great disorder.

In fact, the main body and rear of the numerous army of the Duke had continued to advance, while the broken and repulsed vanguard was in the act of retreating; and they had come into collision with each other, to the great confusion of both. The necessary absence of D'Hymbercourt, who discharged all the duties of Maréchal du Camp, or, as we should now say, of Quarter-master-general, augmented the disorder; and to complete the whole, the night sunk down dark as a wolf's mouth: there fell a thick and heavy rain, and the ground, on which the beleaguering army must needs take up their position, was muddy, and intersected with many canals. It is scarce possible to form an idea of the confusion which prevailed in the Burgundian army, where leaders were separated from their soldiers, and soldiers from their standards and officers. Every one, from the highest to the lowest, was seeking shelter and accommodation where he could individually find it; while the wearied and wounded, who had been engaged in the battle, were calling in vain for shelter and refreshment; and while those who knew nothing of the disaster, were pressing on to have their share in the sack of the place, which they had no doubt was proceeding merrily.

When D'Hymbercourt returned, he had a task to perform of incredible difficulty, and embittered by the reproaches of his master, who made no allowance for the still more necessary duty in which he had been engaged, until the temper of the gallant soldier began to give way under the Duke's unreasonable reproaches.—"I went hence to restore some order in the van," he said, "and left the main body under your Grace's own guidance; and now, on my return, I can neither find that we have front, flank, nor rear, so utter is the confusion."

"We are the more like a barrel of herrings," answered Le Glorieux, "which is the most natural resemblance for a Flemish army."

The jester's speech made the Duke laugh, and perhaps prevented a farther prosecution of the altercation betwixt him and his general.

By dint of great exertion, a small lust-haus, or country villa of some wealthy citizen of Liege, was secured and cleared of other occupants, for the accommodation of the Duke and his immediate attendants; and the authority of D'Hymbercourt and Crèvecœur at length established a guard in the vicinity, of about forty men-at-arms, who lighted a very large fire, made with the timber of the outhouses, which they pulled down for the purpose.

A little to the left of this villa, and betwixt it and the suburb, which, as we have said, was opposite to the city-gate, and occupied by the Burgundian vanguard, lay another pleasure-house, surrounded by a garden and courtyard, and having two or three small enclosures or fields in the rear of it. In this the King of France established his own headquarters. He did not himself pretend to be a soldier, further than a natural indifference to danger and much sagacity qualified him to be called such; but he was always careful to employ the most skilful in that profession, and reposed in them the confidence they merited. Louis and his immediate attendants occupied this second villa; a part of his Scottish Guard were placed in the court, where there were outhouses and sheds to shelter them from the weather; the rest were stationed in the garden. The remainder of the French men-at-arms were quartered closely together and in good order, with alarm-posts stationed, in case of their having to sustain an attack.

Dunois and Crawford, assisted by several old officers and soldiers, amongst whom Le Balafré was conspicuous for his diligence, contrived, by breaking down walls, making openings through hedges, filling up ditches, and the like, to facilitate the communication of the troops with each other, and the orderly combination of the whole in case of necessity.

Meanwhile, the King judged it proper to go without farther ceremony to the quarters of the Duke of Burgundy, to ascertain what was to be the order of proceeding, and what co-operation was expected from him. His presence occasioned a sort of council of war to be held, of which Charles might not otherwise have dreamed.

It was then that Quentin Durward prayed earnestly to be admitted, as having something of importance to deliver to the two Princes. This was obtained without much difficulty, and great was the astonishment of Louis, when he heard him calmly and distinctly relate the purpose of William de la Marck, to make a sally upon the camp of the besiegers, under the dress and banners of the French. Louis would probably have been much better pleased to have had such important news communicated in private; but as the whole story had been publicly told in the presence of the Duke of Burgundy, he only observed, "that, whether true or false, such a report concerned them most materially."

"Not a whit!—not a whit!" said the Duke carelessly. "Had there been such a purpose as this young man announces, it had not been communicated to me by an Archer of the Scottish Guard."

"However that may be," answered Louis, "I pray you, fair cousin, you and your captains, to attend, that to prevent the unpleasing consequences of such an attack, should it be made unexpectedly, I will cause my soldiers to wear white scarfs over their armour—Dunois, see it given out on the instant—that is," he added, "if our brother and general approves of it."

"I see no objection," replied the Duke, "if the chivalry of France are willing to run the risk of having the name of Knights of the Smock-sleeve bestowed on them in future."

"It would be a right well adapted title, friend Charles," said Le Glorieux, "considering that a woman is the reward of the most valiant."

"Well spoken, Sagacity," said Louis—"Cousin, good-night, I will go arm me.—By the way, what if I win the Countess with mine own hand?"

"Your Majesty," said the Duke, in an altered tone of voice, "must then become a true Fleming."

"I cannot," answered Louis, in a tone of the most sincere confidence, "be more so than I am already, could I but bring you, my dear cousin, to believe it."

The Duke only replied by wishing the King good-night, in a tone resembling the snort of a shy horse, starting from the caress of the rider when he is about to mount, and is soothing him to stand still.

"I could pardon all his duplicity," said the Duke to Crèvecœur, "but cannot forgive his supposing me capable of the gross folly of being duped by his professions."

Louis, too, had his confidences with Oliver le Dain when he returned to his own quarters.—"This Scot," he said, "is such a mixture of shrewdness and simplicity, that I know not what to make of him. *Pasques-dieu!* think of his unpardonable folly in bringing out honest De la Marck's plan of a sally before the face of Burgundy, Crèvecœur, and all of them, instead of rounding it in my ear, and giving me at least the choice of abetting or defeating it!"

"It is better as it is, Sire," said Oliver; "there are many in your present train who would scruple to assail Burgundy undefied, or to ally themselves with De la Marck."

"Thou art right, Oliver. Such fools there are in the world, and we have no time to reconcile their scruples by a little dose of self-interest. We must be true men, Oliver, and good allies of Burgundy, for this night at least,—time may give us a chance of a better game. Go, tell no man to unarm himself; and let them shoot, in case of necessity, as sharply on those who cry *France* and *St. Denis*! as if they cried Hell and Satan! I will myself sleep in my armour. Let Crawford place Quentin Durward on the extreme point of our line of sentinels, next to the city. Let him e'en have the first benefit of the sally which he has announced to us—if his luck bear him out, it is the better for him. But take an especial care of Martius Galeotti, and see he remain in the rear, in a place of the most absolute safety—he is even but too venturous; and, like a fool, would be both swordsman and philosopher. See to these things, Oliver, and good-night—Our Lady of Clery and Monseigneur Saint Martin of Tours, be gracious to my slumbers!" [1]

CHAPTER XXXVII

THE SALLY

He look'd, and saw what numbers numberless
The city-gates out-pour'd.

Paradise Regained.

A DEAD silence soon reigned over that great host which lay in leaguer before Liege. For a long time the cries of the soldiers repeating their signals, and seeking to join their several banners, sounded like the

---

[1] Note XIII.—Attack upon Liege.

howling of bewildered dogs seeking their masters. But at length overcome with weariness by the fatigues of the day, the dispersed soldiers crowded under such shelter as they could meet with, and those who could find none, sunk down through very fatigue, under walls, hedges, and such temporary protection, there to wait for morning,—a morning which some of them were never to behold. A dead sleep fell on almost all, excepting those who kept a faint and weary watch by the lodgings of the King and the Duke. The dangers and hopes of the morrow—even the schemes of glory which many of the young nobility had founded upon the splendid prize held out to him who should avenge the murdered Bishop of Liege—glided from their recollection as they lay stupefied with fatigue and sleep. But not so with Quentin Durward. The knowledge that he alone was possessed of the means of distinguishing La Marck in the contest—the recollection by whom that information had been communicated and the fair augury which might be drawn from her conveying it to him—the thought that his fortune had brought him to a most perilous and doubtful crisis indeed, but one where there was still, at least, a chance of his coming off triumphant, banished every desire to sleep, and strung his nerves with vigour, which defied fatigue.

Posted, by the King's express order, on the extreme point between the French quarters and the town, a good way to the right of the suburb which we have mentioned, he sharpened his eye to penetrate the mass which lay before him, and excited his ears, to catch the slightest sound which might announce any commotion in the beleaguered city. But its huge clocks had successively knelled three hours after midnight, and all continued still and silent as the grave.

At length, and just when Quentin began to think the attack would be deferred till daybreak, and joyfully recollected that there would be then light enough to descry the Bar Sinister across the Fleur-de-lis of Orleans, he thought he heard in the city a humming murmur, like that of disturbed bees mustering for the defence of their hives. He listened—the noise continued; but it was of a character so undistinguished by any peculiar or precise sound, that it might be the murmur of a wind rising among the boughs of a distant grove, or perhaps some stream swollen by the late rain, which was discharging itself into the sluggish Maes with more than usual clamour. Quentin was prevented by these considerations from instantly giving the alarm, which, if done carelessly, would have been a heavy offence.

But when the noise rose louder, and seemed pouring at the same time towards his own post, and towards the suburb, he deemed it his duty to fall back as silently as possible, and call his uncle, who commanded the small body of Archers destined to his support. All were on their feet in a moment and with as little noise as possible. In less than a second, Lord Crawford was at their head, and, despatching an archer to alarm the King and his household, drew back his little party to some distance behind their watchfire, that they might not be seen by its light. The rushing sound, which had approached them more nearly, seemed suddenly to have ceased; but they still heard distinctly the more distant heavy tread of a large body of men approaching the suburb.

"The lazy Burgundians are asleep on their post," whispered Crawford; "make for the suburb, Cunningham, and awaken the stupid oxen."

"Keep well to the rear as you go," said Durward; "if ever I heard the tread of mortal men, there is a strong body interposed between us and the suburb."

"Well said, Quentin, my dainty callant," said Crawford; "thou art a soldier beyond thy years. They only make halt till the others come forward.—I would I had some knowledge where they are!"

"I will creep forward, my lord," said Quentin, "and endeavour to bring you information."

"Do so, my bonny chield; thou hast sharp ears and eyes, and goodwill —but take heed—I would not lose thee for two and a plack."

Quentin, with his harquebuss ready prepared, stole forward, through ground which he had reconnoitred carefully in the twilight of the preceding evening, until he was not only certain that he was in the neighbourhood of a very large body of men, who were standing fast betwixt the King's quarters and the suburbs, but also that there was a detached party of smaller number in advance, and very close to him. They seemed to whisper together, as if uncertain what to do next. At last, the steps of two or three *Enfans perdus*, detached from that smaller party, approached him so near as twice a pike's length. Seeing it impossible to retreat undiscovered, Quentin called out aloud, *"Qui vive?"* and was answered by *"Vive Li—Li—ege—c'est-à-dire"* (added he who spoke, correcting himself), *"Vive la France!"*—Quentin instantly fired his harquebuss—a man groaned and fell, and he himself, under the instant but vague discharge of a number of pieces, the fire of which ran in a disorderly manner along the column, and showed it to be very numerous, hastened back to the main guard.

"Admirably done, my brave boy!" said Crawford—"Now, callants, draw in within the courtyard—they are too many to mell with in the open field."

They drew within the courtyard and garden accordingly, where they found all in great order, and the King prepared to mount his horse.

"Whither away, Sire?" said Crawford; "you are safest here with your own people."

"Not so," said Louis; "I must instantly to the Duke. He must be convinced of our good faith at this critical moment, or we shall have both Liegeois and Burgundians upon us at once." And springing on his horse, he bade Dunois command the French troops without the house, and Crawford the Archer-Guard and other household troops to defend the lust-haus and its enclosures. He commanded them to bring up two sakers, and as many falconets (pieces of cannon for the field), which had been left about half a mile in the rear; and, in the meantime, to make good their posts, but by no means to advance, whatever success they might obtain; and having given these orders, he rode off, with a small escort, to the Duke's quarters.

The delay which permitted these arrangements to be carried fully into effect, was owing to Quentin's having fortunately shot the proprietor of the house, who acted as guide to the column which was designed to attack it, and whose attack, had it been made instantly, might have had a chance of being successful.

Durward, who, by the King's order, attended him to the Duke's, found the latter in a state of choleric distemperature, which almost prevented his discharging the duties of a general, which were never more necessary; for, besides the noise of a close and furious combat which had now taken place in the suburb upon the left of their whole army,—besides the attack upon the King's quarters, which was fiercely maintained in the centre,—a third column of Liegeois, of even superior numbers, had filed out from a more distant breach, and, marching by lanes, vineyards, and passes, known to themselves, had fallen upon the right flank of the Burgundian army, who, alarmed at their war-cries of *Vive la France!* and *Dennis Montjoie!* which mingled with those of *Liege* and *Rouge Sanglier,* and at the idea thus inspired, of treachery on the part of the French confederates, made a very desultory and imperfect resistance; while the Duke, foaming and swearing, and cursing his liege Lord and all that belonged to him, called out to shoot with bow and gun on all that was French, whether black or white,—alluding to the sleeves with which Louis's soldiers had designated themselves.

The arrival of the King, attended only by Le Balafré and Quentin, and half a score of Archers, restored confidence between France and Burgundy. D'Hymbercourt, Crévecœur, and others of the Burgundian leaders, whose names were then the praise and dread of war, rushed devotedly into the conflict; and, while some commanders hastened to bring up more distant troops, to whom the panic had not extended, others threw themselves into the tumult, reanimated the instinct of discipline, and while the Duke toiled in the front, shouting, hacking, and hewing, like an ordinary man-at-arms, brought their men by degrees into array, and dismayed the assailants by the use of their artillery. The conduct of Louis on the other hand, was that of a calm, collected, sagacious leader, who neither sought nor avoided danger, but showed so much self-possession and sagacity, that the Burgundian leaders readily obeyed the orders which he issued.

The scene was now become in the utmost degree animated and horrible. On the left the suburb, after a fierce contest, had been set on fire, and a wide and dreadful conflagration did not prevent the burning ruins from being still disputed. On the centre, the French troops, though pressed by immense odds, kept up so close and and constant a fire, that the little pleasure-house shone bright with the glancing flashes, as if surrounded with a martyr's crown of flames. On the left, the battle swayed backwards and forwards with varied success, as fresh reinforce-ments poured out of the town, or were brought forward from the rear of the Burgundian host; and the strife continued with unremitting fury for three mortal hours, which at length brought the dawn, so much de-sired by the besiegers. The enemy, at this period, seemed to be slacken-ing their efforts upon the right and in the centre, and several discharges of cannon were heard from the lust-haus.

"Go," said the King, to Le Balafré and Quentin, the instant his ear had caught the sound; "they have got up the sakers and falconets—the pleasure-house is safe, blessed be the Holy Virgin!—Tell Dunois to move this way, but rather nearer the walls of Liege, with all our men-at-arms, excepting what he may leave for the defence of the house, and cut in between those thick-headed Liegeois on the right and the city, from which they are supplied with recruits."

The uncle and nephew galloped off to Dunois and Crawford, who, tired of their defensive war, joyfully obeyed the summons, and, filing out at the head of a gallant body of about two hundred French gentle-men, besides squires, and the greater part of the Archers and their fol-lowers, marched across the field, trampling down the wounded, till they gained the flank of the large body of Liegeois, by whom the right of the Burgundians had been so fiercely assailed. The increasing daylight dis-covered that the enemy were continuing to pour out from the city, either for the purpose of continuing the battle on that point, or of bringing safely off the forces who were already engaged.

"By Heaven!" said Old Crawford to Dunois, "were I not certain it is *thou* that art riding by my side, I would say I saw thee among yonder banditti and burghers, marshalling and arraying them with thy mace—only, if yon be thou, thou art bigger than thou art wont to be. Art thou sure yonder armed leader is not thy wraith, thy double-man, as these Flemings call it?"

"My wraith!" said Dunois; "I know not what you mean. But yonder is a caitiff with my bearings displayed on crest and shield, whom I will presently punish for his insolence."

"In the name of all that is noble, my lord, leave the vengeance to me!" said Quentin.

"To *thee* indeed, young man?" said Dunois; "that is a modest request. —No—these things brook no substitution."—Then turning on his saddle, he called out to those around him, "Gentlemen of France, form your line, level your lances! Let the rising sunbeams shine through the bat-talions of yonder swine of Liege and hogs of Ardennes, that masquerade in our ancient coats."

The men-at-arms answered with a loud shout of "A Dunois! a Dunois! —Long live the bold Bastard!—Orleans to the rescue!"—And, with their leader in the centre, they charged at full gallop. They encountered no timid enemy. The large body which they charged, consisted (excepting some mounted officers) entirely of infantry, who, setting the butt of their lances against their feet, the front rank kneeling, the second stooping, and those behind presenting their spears over their heads, offering such resistance to the rapid charge of the men-at-arms as the hedgehog presents to his enemy. Few were able to make way through that iron wall; but of those few was Dunois, who, giving spur to his horse, and making the noble animal leap more than twelve feet at a bound, fairly broke his way into the middle of the phalanx, and made towards the object of his animosity. What was his surprise to find Quentin still by his side, and fighting in the same front with himself—youth, desperate courage, and the determination to do or die, having still kept the youth abreast with the best knight in Europe; for such was Dunois reported, and truly reported, at the period.

Their spears were soon broken; but the lanzknechts were unable to withstand the blows of their long heavy swords; while the horses and riders, armed in complete steel, sustained little injury from their lances. Still Dunois and Durward were contending with rival efforts to burst forward to the spot where he who had usurped the armorial bearings of Dunois was doing the duty of a good and valiant leader, when Dunois, observing the boar's-head and tusks—the usual bearing of William de la Marck—in another part of the conflict, called out to Quentin, "Thou art worthy to avenge the arms of Orleans! I leave thee the task.—Balafré, support your nephew; but let none dare to interfere with Dunois' boar-hunt!"

That Quentin Durward joyfully acquiesced in this division of labour cannot be doubted, and each pressed forward upon his separate object, followed, and defended from behind, by such men-at-arms as were able to keep up with them.

But at this moment the column which De la Marck had proposed to support, when his own course was arrested by the charge of Dunois, had lost all the advantages they had gained during the night; while the Burgundians, with returning day, had begun to show the qualities which belong to superior discipline. The great mass of Liegeois were compelled to retreat, and at length to fly; and, falling back on those who were engaged with the French men-at-arms, the whole became a confused tide of fighters, fliers, and pursuers, which rolled itself towards the city-walls, and at last was poured into the ample and undefended breach through which the Liegeois had sallied.

Quentin made more than human exertions to overtake the special object of his pursuit, who was still in his sight, striving, by voice and example, to renew the battle, and bravely supported by a chosen party of lanzknechts. Le Balafré, and several of his comrades, attached themselves to Quentin, much marvelling at the extraordinary gallantry displayed by so young a soldier. On the very brink of the breach, De la Marck—for it was himself—succeeded in effecting a momentary stand, and repelling some of the most forward of the pursuers. He had a mace of iron in his hand, before which everything seemed to go down, and was so much covered with blood, that it was almost impossible to discern those bearings on his shield which had so much incensed Dunois.

Quentin now found little difficuly in singling him out; for the commanding situation of which he had possessed himself, and the use he made of his terrible mace, caused many of the assailants to seek safer points of attack than that where so desperate a defender presented himself. But Quentin, to whom the importance attached to victory over this formidable antagonist was better known, sprung from his horse at the bottom of the breach, and, letting the noble animal, the gift of the Duke of Orleans, run loose through the tumult, ascended the ruins to measure swords with the Boar of Ardennes. The latter, as if he had seen his intention, turned towards Durward with mace uplifted; and they were on the point of encounter, when a dreadful shout of triumph, of tumult, and of despair, announced that the besiegers were entering the city at another point, and in the rear of those who defended the breach. Assembling around him, by voice and bugle, the desperate partners of his desperate fortune, De la Marck, at those appalling sounds, abandoned the breach, and endeavoured to effect his retreat towards a part of the city from which he might escape to the other side of the Maes. His immediate followers formed a deep body of well-disciplined men, who, never having given quarter, were resolved now not to ask it, and who, in that hour of despair, threw themselves into such firm order, that their front occupied the whole breadth of the street, through which they slowly retired, making head from time to time, and checking the pursuers, many of whom began to seek a safer occupation, by breaking into the houses for plunder. It is therefore probable that De la Marck might have effected his escape, his disguise concealing him from those who promised themselves to win honour and grandeur upon his head, but for the stanch pursuit of Quentin, his uncle Le Balafré, and some of his comrades. At every pause which was made by the lanzknechts, a furious combat took place betwixt them and the Archers, and in every *mêlée* Quentin sought De la Marck; but the latter, whose present object was to retreat, seemed to evade the young Scot's purpose of bringing him to single combat. The confusion was general in every direction. The shrieks and cries of women, the yelling of the terrified inhabitants, now subjected to the extremity of military licence, sounded horribly shrill amid the shouts of battle,— like the voice of misery and despair contending with that of fury and violence, which should be heard farthest and loudest.

It was just when De la Marck, retiring through this infernal scene, had passed the door of a small chapel of peculiar sanctity, that the shouts of "France! France!—Burgundy! Burgundy!" apprised him that a part of the besiegers were entering the farther end of the street, which was a narrow one, and that his retreat was cut off.—"Conrade," he said, "take all the men with you—Charge yonder fellows roundly and break through if you can—with me it is over. I am man enough, now that I am brought to bay, to send some of these vagabond Scots to hell before me."

His lieutenant obeyed, and, with most of the few lanzknechts who remained alive, hurried to the farther end of the street, for the purpose of charging those Burgundians who were advancing, and so forcing their way, so as to escape. About six of De la Marck's best men remained to perish with their master, and fronted the Archers, who were not many more in number,—"Sanglier! Sanglier! Hola! gentlemen of Scotland," said the ruffian but undaunted chief, waving his mace, "who longs to gain a coronet,—who strikes at the Boar of Ardennes?—You, young man, have, methinks, a hankering; but you must win ere you wear it."

Quentin heard but imperfectly the words, which were partly lost in the hollow helmet; but the action could not be mistaken, and he had but time to bid his uncle and comrades, as they were gentlemen, to stand back, when De la Marck sprung upon him with a bound like a tiger, aiming at the same time a blow with his mace, so as to make his hand and foot keep time together, and giving his stroke full advantage of the descent of his leap; but, light of foot and quick of eye, Quentin leaped aside, and disappointed an aim which would have been fatal had it taken effect.

They then closed, like the wolf and the wolf-dog, their comrades on either side remaining inactive spectators, for Le Balafré roared out for fair play, adding, "that he would venture his nephew on him, were he as wight as Wallace."

Neither was the experienced soldier's confidence unjustified; for, although the blows of the despairing robber fell like those of the hammer on the anvil, yet the quick motions, the dexterous swordsmanship, of the young Archer, enabled him to escape, and to requite them with the point of his less noisy, though more fatal weapon; and that so often and so effectually, that the huge strength of his antagonist began to give way to fatigue, while the ground on which he stood became a puddle of blood. Yet, still unabated in courage and ire, the Wild Boar of Ardennes fought on with as much mental energy as at first, and Quentin's victory seemed dubious and distant, when a female voice behind him called him by his name, ejaculating, "Help! help! for the sake of the blessed Virgin!"

He turned his head, and with a single glance beheld Gertrude Pavillon, her mantle stripped from her shoulders, dragged forcibly along by a French soldier; one of several, who, breaking into the chapel close by, had seized, as their prey, on the terrified females who had taken refuge there.

"Wait for me but one moment," exclaimed Quentin to De la Marck, and sprung to extricate his benefactress from a situation of which he conjectured all the dangers.

"I wait no man's pleasure," said De la Marck, flourishing his mace, and beginning to retreat—glad, no doubt, of being free of so formidable an assailant.

"You shall wait mine, though, by your leave," said Balafré; "I will not have my nephew baulked."—So saying, he instantly assaulted De la Marck with his two-handed sword.

Quentin found, in the meanwhile, that the rescue of Gertrude was a task more difficult than could be finished in one moment. Her captor, supported by his comrades, refused to relinquish his prize; and whilst Durward, aided by one or two of his countrymen, endeavoured to compel him to do so, the former beheld the chance which Fortune had so kindly afforded him for fortune and happiness, glide out of his reach; so that when he stood at length in the street with the liberated Gertrude, there was no one near them. Totally forgetting the defenceless situation of his companion, he was about to spring away in pursuit of the Boar of Ardennes, as the greyhound tracks the deer, when, clinging to him in her despair, she exclaimed, "For the sake of your mother's honour, leave me not here!—As you are a gentleman, protect me to my father's house, which once sheltered you and the Lady Isabelle!—For her sake leave me not!"

Her call was agonising, but it was irresistible; and bidding a mental adieu, with unutterable bitterness of feeling, to all the gay hopes which had stimulated his exertion, carried him through that bloody day, and which at one moment seemed to approach consummation, Quentin, like an unwilling spirit, who obeys a talisman which he cannot resist, protected Gertrude to Pavillon's house, and arrived in time to defend that and the Syndic himself against the fury of the licentious soldiery.

Meantime, the King and the Duke of Burgundy entered the city on horseback, and through one of the breaches. They were both in complete armour, but the latter, covered with blood from the plume to the spur, drove his steed furiously up the breach, which Louis surmounted with the stately pace of one who leads a procession. They despatched orders to stop the sack of the city, which had already commenced, and to assemble their scattered troops. The princes themselves proceeded towards the great church, both for the protection of many of the distinguished inhabitants, who had taken refuge there, and in order to hold a sort of military council after they had heard High Mass.

Busied like other officers of his rank in collecting those under his command, Lord Crawford, at the turning of one of the streets which leads to the Maes, met Le Balafré sauntering composedly towards the river, holding in his hand, by the gory locks, a human head, with as much indifference as a fowler carries a game-pouch.

"How now, Ludovic!" said his commander; "what are you doing with that carrion?"

"It is all that is left of a bit of work which my nephew shaped out, and nearly finished, and I put the last hand to," said Le Balafré—"a good fellow that I despatched yonder, and who prayed me to throw his head into the Maes.—Men have queer fancies when old Small-Back [1]

---

[1] A cant expression in Scotland for death, usually delineated as a skeleton.

is gripping them; but Small-Back must lead down the dance with us all in our time."

"And are you going to throw that head into the Maes?" said Crawford, looking more attentively on the ghastly memorial of mortality.

"Ay, truly am I," said Ludovic Lesly. "If you refuse a dying man his boon, you are likely to be haunted by his ghost, and I love to sleep sound at nights."

"You must take your chance of the ghaist, man," said Crawford; "for, by my soul, there is more lies on that dead pow than you think for. Come along with me—not a word more—Come along with me."

"Nay, for that matter," said Le Balafré, "I made him no promise; for, in truth, I had off his head before the tongue had well done wagging; and as I feared him not living, by Saint Martin of Tours, I fear him as little when he is dead. Besides, my little gossip, the merry Friar of St. Martin's, will lend me a pot of holy water."

When High Mass had been said in the Cathedral Church of Liege, and the terrified town was restored to some moderate degree of order, Louis and Charles, with their peers around, proceeded to hear the claims of those who had any to make for services performed during the battle. Those which respected the County of Croye and its fair mistress were first received, and, to the disappointment of sundry claimants who had thought themselves sure of the rich prize, there seemed doubt and mystery to involve their several pretensions. Crèvecœur showed a boar's hide such as De la Marck usually wore; Dunois produced a cloven shield, with his armorial bearings; and there were others, who claimed the merit of having despatched the murderer of the Bishop, producing similar tokens—the rich reward fixed on De la Marck's head having brought death to all who were armed in his resemblance.

There was much noise and contest among the competitors, and Charles, internally regretting the rash promise which had placed the hand and wealth of his fair vassal on such a hazard, was in hopes he might find means of evading all these conflicting claims, when Crawford pressed forward into the circle, dragging Le Balafré after him, who, awkward and bashful, followed like an unwilling mastiff towed on in a leash, as his leader exclaimed,—"Away with your hoofs and hides, and painted iron!— No one, save he who slew the Boar, can show the tusks!"

So saying, he flung on the floor the bloody head, easily known as that of De la Marck, by the singular conformation of the jaws, which in reality had a certain resemblance to those of the animal whose name he bore, and which was instantly recognised by all who had seen him.[1]

---

[1] We have already noticed the anachronism respecting the crimes of this atrocious baron; and it is scarce necessary to repeat, that if he in reality murdered the Bishop of Liege in 1482, the Count of La Marck could not be slain in the defence of Liege four years earlier. In fact, the Wild Boar of Ardennes, as he was usually termed, was of high birth, being the third son of John I., Count of La Marck and Aremberg, and ancestor of the branch called Barons of Lumain. He did not escape

"Crawford," said Louis, while Charles sat silent, in gloomy and displeased surprise, "I trust it is one of my faithful Scots who has won this prize?"

"It is Ludovic Lesly, Sire, whom we call Le Balafré," replied the old soldier.

"But is he noble?" said the Duke; "is he of gentle blood?—otherwise our promise is void."

"He is a cross ungainly piece of wood enough," said Crawford, looking at the tall, awkward, embarrassed figure of the Archer; "but I will warrant him a branch of the tree of Rothes for all that—and they have been as noble as any house in France or Burgundy, ever since it is told of their founder, that

> 'Between the less-lee [1] and the mair,
> He slew the Knight, and left him there.' "

"There is then no help for it," said the Duke, "and the fairest and richest heiress in Burgundy must be the wife of a rude mercenary soldier like this, or die secluded in a convent—and she the only child of our faithful Reginald de Croye!—I have been too rash."

And a cloud settled on his brow, to the surprise of his peers, who seldom saw him evince the slightest token of regret for the necessary consequences of an adopted resolution.

"Hold but an instant," said the Lord Crawford, "it may be better than your Grace conjectures. Hear but what this cavalier has to say.—Speak out, man, and a murrain to thee," he added, apart to Le Balafré.

But that blunt soldier, though he could make a shift to express himself intelligibly enough to King Louis, to whose familiarity he was habituated, yet found himself incapable of enunciating his resolution before so splendid an assembly as that in presence of which he then stood; and after having turned his shoulder to the princes, and preluded with a hoarse chuckling laugh, and two or three tremendous contortions of countenance, he was only able to pronounce the words "Saunders Souplejaw"—and then stuck fast.

"May it please your Majesty, and your Grace," said Crawford, "I must speak for my countryman and old comrade. You shall understand, that he has had it prophesied to him by a Seer in his own land, that the fortune of his house is to be made by marriage; but as he is, like myself, something the worse for the wear,—loves the wine-house better than a

the punishment due to his atrocity, though it did not take place at the time, or in the manner, narrated in the text. Maximilian, Emperor of Austria, caused him to be arrested at Utrecht, where he was beheaded in the year 1485, three years after the Bishop of Liege's death.

[1] An old rhyme, by which the Leslies vindicate their descent from an ancient knight, who is said to have slain a gigantic Hungarian champion, and to have formed a proper name for himself by a play of words upon the place where he fought his adversary.

lady's summer-parlour, and, in short, having some barrack tastes and likings, which would make greatness in his own person rather an encumbrance to him, he hath acted by my advice, and resigns the pretensions acquired by the fate of slaying William de la Marck, to him by whom the Wild Boar was actually brought to bay, who is his maternal nephew."

"I will vouch for that youth's services and prudence," said King Louis, overjoyed to see that fate had thrown so gallant a prize to one over whom he had some influence. "Without his prudence and vigilance, we had been ruined—It was he who made us aware of the night-sally."

"I then," said Charles, "owe him some reparation for doubting his veracity."

"And I can attest his gallantry as a man-at-arms," said Dunois.

"But," interrupted Crèvecœur, "though the uncle be a Scottish *gentillâtre,* that makes not the nephew necessarily so."

"He is of the House of Durward," said Crawford; "descended from that Allan Durward, who was High Steward of Scotland."

"Nay, if it be young Durward," said Crèvecœur, "I say no more. Fortune has declared herself on his side too plainly, for me to struggle farther with her humoursome ladyship; but it is strange, from lord to horse-boy, how wonderfully these Scots stick by each other."

"Highlanders, shoulder to shoulder!" answered Lord Crawford, laughing at the mortification of the proud Burgundian.

"We have yet to inquire," said Charles thoughtfully, "what the fair lady's sentiments may be towards this fortunate adventurer."

"By the mass!" said Crèvecœur, "I have but too much reason to believe your Grace will find her more amenable to authority than on former occasions.—But why should I grudge this youth his preferment? since, after all, it is sense, firmness, and gallantry, which have put him in possession of WEALTH, RANK, and BEAUTY!"

I HAD already sent these sheets to the press, concluding, as I thought, with a moral of excellent tendency for the encouragement of all fair-haired, blue-eyed, long-legged, stout-hearted emigrants from my native country, who might be willing in stirring times to take up the gallant profession of Cavalieros of Fortune. But a friendly monitor, one of those who like the lump of sugar which is found at the bottom of a tea-cup, as well as the flavour of the souchong itself, has entered a bitter remonstrance, and insists that I should give a precise and particular account of the espousals of the young heir of Glen-houlakin and the lovely Flemish Countess, and tell what tournaments were held, and how many lances were broken, upon so interesting an occasion; nor withhold from the curious reader the number of sturdy boys, who inherited the valour of Quentin Durward, and of bright damsels, in whom were renewed the charms of Isabelle de Croye. I replied in course of post, that times were changed, and public weddings were entirely out of fashion. In days, traces of which I myself can remember, not only were the "fifteen friends" of the hapy pair invited to witness their union, but the bridal minstrelsy still continued, as in the "Ancient Mariner," to "nod their heads" till morning shone on them. The sack-posset was eaten in the nuptial chamber —the stocking was thrown—and the bride's garter was struggled for in the presence of the happy couple whom Hymen had made one flesh. The authors of the period were laudably accurate in following its fashions. They spared you not a blush of the bride, not a rapturous glance of the bridegroom, not a diamond in her hair, nor a button on his embroidered waistcoat; until at length, with Astræa, "they fairly put their characters to bed." But how little does this agree with the modest privacy which induces our modern brides—sweet bashful darlings! to steal from pomp and plate, and admiration and flattery, and, like honest Shenstone,

> "Seek for freedom at an inn!"

To these, unquestionably, an exposure of the circumstances of publicity with which a bridal in the fifteenth century was always celebrated, must appear in the highest degree disgusting. Isabelle de Croye would be ranked in their estimation far below the maid who milks, and does the meanest chares; for even she, were it in the church-porch, would reject the hand of her journeyman shoemaker, should he propose *"faire des noces,"* as it is called on Parisian signs, instead of going down on the top of the long coach to spend the honeymoon *incognito* at Deptford or Greenwich. I will not, therefore, tell more of this matter, but will steal away from the wedding as Ariosto from that of Angelica, leaving it to whom it may please to add farther particulars after the fashion of their own imagination.

> Some better bard shall sing, in feudal state
> How Braquemont's Castle op'd its Gothic gate,
> When on the wand'ring Scot, its lovely heir
> Bestow'd her beauty and an earldom fair." [1]

[1] "E come a ritornare in sua contrada
Trovasse e buon naviglio e miglior tempo
E dell' India a Medor desse lo scettro
Forse altri cantera con miglior plettro."
ORLANDO FURIOSO, *Canto XXX, Stanza* 16.

AUTHOR'S NOTES

Note I. p. 86.—Gipsies or Bohemians

In another volume of the Waverley Novels (Guy Mannering), the reader will find some remarks on the gipsies as they are found in Scotland. But it is well known that this extraordinary variety of the human race exists in nearly the same primitive state, speaking the same language, in almost all the kingdoms of Europe, and conforming in certain respects to the manners of the people around them, but yet remaining separated from them by certain material distinctions, in which they correspond with each other, and thus maintain their pretensions to be considered as a distinct race. Their first appearance in Europe took place in the beginning of the fifteenth century, when various bands of this singular people appeared in the different countries of Europe. They claimed an Egyptian descent, and their features attested that they were of Eastern origin. The account given by these singular people was, that it was appointed to them, as a penance, to travel for a certain number of years. This apology was probably selected as being most congenial to the superstitions of the countries which they visited. Their appearance, however, and manners, strongly contradicted the allegation that they travelled from any religious motive.

Their dress and accoutrements were at once showy and squalid; those who acted as captains and leaders of any horde, and such always appeared as their commanders, were arrayed in dresses of the most showy colours, such as scarlet or light green; were well mounted; assumed the title of dukes and counts, and affected considerable consequence. The rest of the tribe were most miserable in their diet and apparel, fed without hesitation on animals which had died of disease, and were clad in filthy and scanty rags, which hardly sufficed for the ordinary purposes of common decency. Their complexion was positively Eastern, approaching to that of the Hindoos.

Their manners were as depraved as their appearance was poor and beggarly. The men were in general thieves, and the women of the most abandoned character. The few arts which they studied with success, were of a slight and idle, though ingenious description. They practised working in iron, but never upon any great scale. Many were good sportsmen, good musicians, and masters, in a word, of all those trivial arts, the practice of which is little better than mere idleness. But their ingenuity never ascended into industry. Two or three other peculiarities seem to have distinguished them in all countries. Their pretensions to read fortunes, by palmistry and by astrology, acquired them sometimes respect, but oftener drew them under suspicion as sorcerers; and lastly, the universal accusation that they augmented their horde by stealing children, subjected them to doubt and execration. From this it happened, that the pretension set up by these wanderers, of being pilgrims in the act of penance, although it was at first admitted, and in many instances obtained them protection from the governments of the countries through which they travelled, was afterwards totally disbelieved, and they were considered as incorrigible rogues and vagrants; they incurred almost everywhere sentence of banishment, and, where suffered to remain, were rather objects of persecution than of protection from the law.

There is a curious and accurate account of their arrival in France in the Journal of a Doctor of Theology, which is preserved and published by the learned Pasquier. The following is an extract: "On August 27th, 1427, came to Paris twelve penitents,

Penanciers (penance doers), as they called themselves, viz. a duke, an earl, and ten men, all on horseback, and calling themselves good Christians. They were of Lower Egypt, and gave out that, not long before, the Christians had subdued their country, and obliged them to embrace Christianity on pain of being put to death. Those who were baptized were great lords in their own country, and had a king and queen there. Soon after their conversion, the Saracens overran the country, and obliged them to renounce Christianity. When the Emperor of Germany, the King of Poland, and other Christian princes, heard of this, they fell upon them, and obliged the whole of them, both great and small, to quit the country, and go to the Pope at Rome, who enjoined them seven years' penance to wander over the world, without lying in a bed.

"They had been wandering five years when they came to Paris first; the principal people, and soon after the commonalty, about 100 or 120, reduced (according to their own account) from 1000 or 1200, when they went from home, the rest being dead, with their king and queen. They were lodged by the police at some distance from the city, at Chapel St. Denis.

"Nearly all of them had their ears bored, and wore two silver rings in each, which they said were esteemed ornaments in their country. The men were black, their hair curled; the women remarkably black, their only clothes a large old duffle garment, tied over the shoulders with a cloth or cord, and under it a miserable rocket. In short, they were the most miserable creatures that had ever been seen in France; and, notwithstanding their poverty, there were among them women who, by looking into people's hands, told their fortunes, and what was worse, they picked people's pockets of their money, and got it into their own, by telling these things through airy magic, et cætera."

Notwithstanding the ingenious account of themselves rendered by these gipsies, the Bishop of Paris ordered a friar, called Le Petit Jacobin, to preach a sermon, excommunicating all the men and women who had had recourse to these Bohemians on the subject of the future, and shown their hands for that purpose. They departed from Paris for Pontoise in the month of September.

Pasquier remarks upon this singular journal, that however the story of penance savours of a trick, these people wandered up and down France, under the eye, and with the knowledge of the magistrates, for more than a hundred years; and it was not till 1561, that a sentence of banishment was passed against them in that kingdom.

The arrival of the Egyptians (as these singular people were called) in various parts of Europe, corresponds with the period in which Timur or Tamerlane invaded Hindostan, affording its natives the choice between the Koran and death. There can be little doubt that these wanderers consisted originally of the Hindostanee tribes, who, displaced, and flying from the sabres of the Mahommedans, undertook this species of wandering life, without well knowing whither they were going. It is natural to suppose the band, as it now exists, is much mingled with Europeans; but most of these have been brought up from childhood among them, and learned all their practices.

It is strong evidence of this, that when they are in closest contact with the ordinary peasants around them, they still keep their language a mystery. There is little doubt, however, that it is a dialect of the Hindostanee, from the specimens produced by Grellman, Hoyland, and others, who have written on the subject. But the author has, besides their authority, personal occasion to know that an individual, out of mere curiosity, and availing himself with patience and assiduity of such opportunities as offered, has made himself capable of conversing with any gipsy whom he meets, or can, like the royal Hal, drink with any tinker in his own language. The astonishment excited among these vagrants in finding a stranger participant of their mystery, occasions very ludicrous scenes. It is to be hoped this gentleman will publish the knowledge he possesses on so singular a topic.

There are prudential reasons for postponing this disclosure at present; for although much more reconciled to society since they have been less the object of legal persecution, the gipsies are still a ferocious and vindictive people.

But notwithstanding this is certainly the case, I cannot but add, from my own observation of nearly fifty years, that the manners of these vagrant tribes are much ameliorated;—that I have known individuals amongst them who have united themselves to civilised society, and maintain respectable characters, and that great alteration has been wrought in their cleanliness and general mode of life.

Note II. p. 155.—GALEOTTI

Martius Galeotti was a native of Narni, in Umbria. He was secretary to Matthias Corvinus, King of Hungary, and tutor to his son, John Corvinus. While at his court, he composed a work, *De jocose dictis et factis Regis Matthiæ Corvini.* He left Hungary in 1477, and was made prisoner at Venice on a charge of having propagated heterodox opinions in a treatise entitled, *De homine interiore et corpore ejus.* He was obliged to recant some of these doctrines, and might have suffered seriously but for the protection of Sextus IV., then Pope, who had been one of his scholars. He went to France, attached himself to Louis XI., and died in his service.

Note III. p. 172.—RELIGION OF THE BOHEMIANS

It was a remarkable feature of the character of these wanderers, that they did not, like the Jews, whom they otherwise resembled in some particulars, possess or profess any particular religion, whether in form or principle. They readily conformed, as far as might be required, with the religion of any country in which they happened to sojourn, nor did they ever practise it more than was demanded of them. It is certain that in India they embraced neither the tenets of the religion of Bramah nor of Mahomet. They have hence been considered as belonging to the outcast East Indian tribes of Nuts or Parias. Their want of religion is supplied by a good deal of superstition. Such of their ritual as can be discovered, for example that belonging to marriage, is savage in the extreme, and resembles the customs of the Hottentots more than any civilised people. They adopt various observances, picked up from the religion of the country in which they live. It is, or rather was, the custom of the tribes on the Borders of England and Scotland, to attribute success to those journeys which are commenced by passing through the parish church: and they usually try to obtain permission from the beadle to do so when the church is empty, for the performance of divine service is not considered as essential to the omen. They are, therefore, totally devoid of any effectual sense of religion; and the higher, or more instructed class, may be considered as acknowledging no deity save those of Epicurus, and such is described as being the faith, or no faith, of Hayraddin Maugrabin.

I may here take notice, that nothing is more disagreeable to this indolent and voluptuous people, than being forced to follow any regular profession. When Paris was garrisoned by the Allied troops in the year 1815, the author was walking with a British officer, near a post held by the Prussian troops. He happened at the time to smoke a cigar, and was about, while passing the sentinel, to take it out of his mouth, in compliance with a general regulation to that effect, when, greatly to the astonishment of the passengers, the soldier addressed them in these words; *"Rauchen sic immerfort; verdamt sey der Preussiche dienst!"* that is, "Smoke away; may the Prussian service be d—d!" Upon looking closely at the man, he seemed plainly to be a *Zigeuner,* or gipsy, who took this method of expressing his detestation of the duty imposed on him. When the risk he ran by doing so is considered, it will be found to argue a deep degree of dislike which could make him commit himself so unwarily. If he had been overheard by a sergeant or corporal, the *prugel* would have been the slightest instrument of punishment employed.

Note IV. p. 231.—Murder of the Bishop of Liege

In assigning the present date to the murder of the Bishop of Liege, Louis de Bourbon, history has been violated. It is true that the Bishop was made prisoner by the insurgents of that city. It is also true that the report of the insurrection came to Charles with a rumour that the Bishop was slain, which excited his indignation against Louis, who was then in his power. But these things happened in 1468, and the Bishop's murder did not take place till 1482. In the months of August and September of that year, William de la Marck, called the Wild Boar of Ardennes, entered into a conspiracy with the discontented citizens of Liege against their Bishop, Louis of Bourbon, being aided with considerable sums of money by the King of France. By this means, and the assistance of many murderers and banditti, who thronged to him as to a leader befitting them, De la Marck assembled a body of troops, whom he dressed in scarlet as a uniform, with a boar's head on the left sleeve. With this little army he approached the city of Liege. Upon this the citizens, who were engaged in the conspiracy, came to their Bishop, and, offering to stand by him to the death, exhorted him to march out against these robbers. The Bishop, therefore, put himself at the head of a few troops of his own, trusting to the assistance of the people of Liege. But as soon as they came in sight of the enemy, the citizens, as before agreed, fled from the Bishop's banner, and he was left with his own handful of adherents. At this moment De la Marck charged at the head of his banditti with the expected success. The Bishop was brought before the profligate Knight, who first cut him over the face, then murdered him with his own hand, and caused his body to be exposed naked in the great square of Liege before Saint Lambert's Cathedral.

Such is the actual narrative of a tragedy which struck with horror the people of the time. The murder of the Bishop has been fifteen years antedated in the text, for reasons which the reader of romances will easily appreciate.

Note V. p. 245.—Schwarz-reiters

Fynes Morrison describes this species of soldiery as follows:—"He that at this day looks upon their *Schwarz-reiters* (that is, black horsemen), must confess, that, to make their horses 'and boots shine, they make themselves as black as colliers. These horsemen wear black clothes, and poor though they be, spend no small time in brushing them. The most of them have black horses, which, while they painfully dress, and (as I have said) delight to have their boots and shoes shine with blacking-stuff, their hands and faces become black, and thereof they have their foresaid name. Yet I have heard Germans say, that they do thus make themselves black to seem more terrible to their enemies."—Fynes Morrison's *Itinerary*. Edition 1617, p. 165.

Note VI. p. 258.—Philip des Comines

Philip des Comines was described in the former editions of this work as a little man, fitted rather for counsel than action. This was a description made at a venture, to vary the military portraits with which the age and work abound. Sleidan the historian, upon the authority of Matthieu d'A·ves, who knew Philip des Comines, and had served in his household, says he was a man of tall stature, and a noble presence. The learned Monsieur Petitot, editor of the edition of Memoirs relative to the History of France, a work of great value, intimates that Philip des Comines made a figure at the games of chivalry and pageants exhibited on the wedding of Charles of Burgundy with Margaret of England in 1468.—See the Chronicle of Jean de Troyes, in Petitot's edition of the *Memoirs Relatifs à l'Histoire de France,* vol. xiii. p. 375, note. I have looked into Oliver de la Marcke, who, in lib. ii., chapter iv., of his Memoirs, gives an ample account of these "fierce vanities," containing as many miscellaneous articles as the reticule of the old merchant of Peter Schleml, who bought shadows, and carried with him in his bag whatever any one could wish or demand in return. There are in that splendid description, knights, dames, pages, and archers, good store besides of castles, fiery dragons, and drome-daries; there are leopards riding upon lions; there are rocks, orchards, fountains, spears broken and whole, and the twelve labours of Hercules. In such a brilliant medley I had some trouble in finding Philip des Comines. He is the first named, however, of a gallant band of assailants, knights and noblemen, to the number of twenty, who, with the Prince of Orange as their leader, encountered, in a general tourney, with a party of the same number under the profligate Adolf of Cleves, who acted as challenger, by the romantic title of *Arbre d'or*. The encounter, though with arms of courtesy, was very fierce, and separated by main force, not without difficulty. Philip des Comines has, therefore, a title to be accounted *tam Marte, quam Mercurio,* though, when we consider the obscurity which has settled on the rest of this *troupe dorée*, we are at no loss to estimate the most valuable of his qualifications.

Note VII. p. 260.—Meeting of Louis and Charles after the Battle of Montl'hery

After the battle of Montl'hery, in 1465, Charles, then Compte de Charalois, had an interview with Louis under the walls of Paris, each at the head of a small party. The two princes dismounted, and walked together so deeply engaged in discussing the business of their meeting, that Charles forgot the peculiarity of his situation; and when Louis turned back towards the town of Paris, from which he came, the Count of Charalois kept him company so far as to pass the line of outworks with which Paris was surrounded, and enter a field-work which com-municated with the town by a trench. At this period he had only five or six persons in company with him. His escort caught an alarm for his safety, and his principal followers rode forward from where he had left them, remembering that his grand-father had been assassinated at Montereau in a similar parley, on 10th September 1419. To their great joy the Count returned uninjured, accompanied with a guard belonging to Louis. The Burgundians taxed him with rashness in no measured terms. "Say no more of it," said Charles; "I acknowledge the extent of my folly, but I was not aware what I was doing till I entered the redoubt."—*Memoires de* Philippe des Comines, chap. xiii.

Louis was much praised for his good faith on this occasion; and it was natural that the Duke should call it to recollection when his enemy so unexpectedly put himself in his power by his visit to Peronne.

Note VIII. p. 286

The historical facts attending this celebrated interview are expounded and enlarged upon in the foregoing chapter. Agents sent by Louis had tempted the people of Liege to rebel against their superior, Duke Charles, and persecute and murder their Bishop. But Louis was not prepared for their acting with such promptitude. They flew to arms with the temerity of a fickle rabble, took the Bishop prisoner, menaced and insulted him, and tore to pieces one or two of his canons. This news was sent to the Duke of Burgundy at the moment when Louis had so unguardedly placed himself in his power; and the consequence was, that Charles placed guards on the Castle of Peronne, and, deeply resenting the treachery of the King of France in exciting sedition in his dominions, while he pretended the most intimate friendship, he deliberated whether he should not put Louis to death.

Three days Louis was detained in this very precarious situation; and it was only his profuse liberality amongst Charles's favourites and courtiers which finally ensured him from death or deposition. Comines, who was the Duke of Burgundy's chamber-lain at the time, and slept in his apartment, says, Charles neither undressed nor slept, but flung himself from time to time on the bed, and at other times, wildly traversed the apartment. It was long before his violent temper became in any degree tractable. At length he only agreed to give Louis his liberty, on condition of his accompanying him in person against, and employing his troops in subduing, the mutineers whom his intrigues had instigated to arms.

This was a bitter and degrading alternative. But Louis, seeing no other mode of compounding for the effects of his rashness, not only submitted to this discreditable condition, but swore to it upon a crucifix said to have belonged to Charlemagne. These particulars are from Comines. There is a succinct epitome of them in Sir Nathaniel Wraxall's History of France, vol. i.

Note IX. p. 292.—Prayer of Louis XI

While I perused these passages in the old manuscript chronicle, I could not help feeling astonished that an intellect acute as that of Louis XI. certainly was, could so delude itself by a sort of superstition, of which one would think the stupidest savages incapable; but the terms of the King's prayer, on a similar occasion, as preserved by Brantome, are of a tenor fully as extraordinary. It is that which, being overheard by a fool or jester, was by him made public, and let in light on an act of fratricide, which might never have been suspected. The way in which the story is narrated by the corrupted courtier, who could jest with all that is criminal as well as with all that is profligate, is worthy the reader's notice; for such actions are seldom done where there are not men with hearts of the nether millstone, capable and willing to make them matters of laughter.

"Among the numerous good tricks of dissimulation, feints, and finesses of gallantry, which the good King (Louis XI.) did in his time, he put to death his brother, the Duke de Guyenne, at the moment when the Duke least thought of such a thing, and while the King was making the greatest show of love to him during his life, and of affection for him at his death, managing the whole concern with so much art, that it would never have been known had not the King taken into his own service a fool who had belonged to his deceased brother. But it chanced that Louis, being engaged in his devout prayers and orisons at the high altar of our Lady of Clery, whom he called his good patroness, and no person nigh except this fool, who, without his knowledge, was within earshot, he thus gave vent to his pious homilies:—

" 'Ah, my good Lady, my gentle mistress, my only friend, in whom alone I have resource, I pray you to supplicate God in my behalf, and to be my advocate with him that he may pardon me the death of my brother whom I caused to be poisoned by that wicked Abbot of Saint John. I confess my guilt to thee as to my good patroness and mistress. But then what could I do? he was perpetually causing disorder in my kingdom. Cause me then to be pardoned, my good Lady, and I know what a reward I will give thee.' "

This singular confession did not escape the jester, who upbraided the King with the fratricide in the face of the whole company at dinner, which Louis was fain to let pass without observation, in case of increasing the slander.

Note X. p. 302.—Martius Galeotti

The death of Martius Galeotti was in some degree connected with Louis XI. The astrologer was at Lyons, and hearing that the King was approaching the city, got on horseback in order to meet him. As he threw himself hastily from his horse to pay his respects to the King, he fell with a violence which, joined to his extreme corpulence, was the cause of his death in 1478.

But the acute and ready-witted expedient to escape instant death, had no reference to the history of this philosopher. The same, or nearly the same story, is told of Tiberius, who demanded of a soothsayer, Thrasullus, if he knew the day of his own death, and received for answer, it would take place just three days before that of the Emperor. On this reply, instead of being thrown over the rocks into the sea, as had been the tyrant's first intention, he was taken great care of for the rest of his life.—*Taciti Annal.* lib. vi. cap. 22.

The circumstances in which Louis XI. received a similar reply from an astrologer are as follows:—The soothsayer in question had presaged that a female favourite, to whom the King was very much attached, should die in a week. As he proved a true prophet, the King was as much incensed as if the astrologer could have prevented the evil he predicted. He sent for the philosopher, and had a party stationed to assassinate him as he retired from the royal presence. Being asked by the King concerning his own fortunes, he confessed that he perceived signs of some imminent danger. Being farther questioned concerning the day of his own death, he was shrewd enough to answer with composure, that it would be exactly three days before that of his Majesty. There was, of course, care taken that he should escape his destined fate; and he was ever after much protected by the King, as a man of real science, and intimately connected with the royal destinies.

Although almost all the historians of Louis represent him as a dupe to the common but splendid imposture of judicial astrology, yet his credulity could not be deep-rooted, if the following anecdote, reported by Bayle, be correct.

Upon one occasion, Louis intending to hunt, and doubtful of the weather, inquired of an astrologer near his person whether it would be fair. The sage, having recourse to the astrolabe, answered with confidence in the affirmative. At the entrance of the forest the royal cortège was met by a charcoal-man, who expressed to some menials of the train his surprise that the King should have thought of hunting in a day which threatened tempest. The collier's prediction proved true. The King and his court were driven from their sport well drenched; and Louis, having heard what the collier had said, ordered the man before him. "How were you more accurate in foretelling the weather, my friend," said he, "than this learned man?"— "I am an ignorant man, Sire," answered the collier, "was never at school, and cannot read or write. But I have an astrologer of my own, who shall foretell weather with any of them. It is, with reverence, the ass who carries my charcoal, who always, when bad weather is approaching, points forward his ears, walks more slowly than usual, and tries to rub himself against walls; and it was from these signs that I foretold yesterday's storm." The King burst into a fit of laughing, dismissed the astrological biped, and assigned the collier a small pension to maintain the quadruped, swearing he would never in future trust to any other astrologer than the charcoal-man's ass.

But if there is any truth in this story, the credulity of Louis was not of a nature to be removed by the failure there mentioned. He is said to have believed in the prediction of Angelo Cattho, his physician, and the friend of Comines, who foretold the death of Charles of Burgundy in the very time and hour when it took place at the battle of Morat. Upon this assurance, Louis vowed a silver screen to the shrine of Saint Martin, which he afterwards fulfilled at the expense of one hundred thousand francs. It is well known, besides, that he was the abject and devoted slave of his physicians. Coctier, or Cottier, one of their number, besides the retaining fee of ten thousand crowns, extorted from his royal patient great sums in lands and money, and, in addition to all, the Bishopric of Amiens for his nephew. He maintained over Louis unbounded influence, by using to him the most disrespectful harshness and insolence. "I know," he said to the suffering King, "that one morning you will turn me adrift like so many others. But, by Heaven, you had better beware, for you will not live eight days after you have done so!" It is unnecessary to dwell longer on the fears and superstitions of a prince, whom the wretched love of life induced to submit to such indignities.

Note XI. p. 319.—PHILIP DES COMINES

There is little doubt that, during the interesting scene at Peronne, Philip des Comines first learned intimately to know the great powers of mind of Louis XI., by which he was so much dazzled that it is impossible, in reading his Memoirs, not to be sensible that he was blinded by them to the more odious shades of his character. He entertained from this time forward a partiality to France. The historian passed into France about 1472, and rose high in the good graces of Louis XI. He afterwards became the proprietor of the Lordship of Argenton and others, a title which was given him by anticipation in the former editions of this work. He did not obtain it till he was in the French service. After the death of Louis, Philip des Comines fell under the suspicion of the daughter of Louis, called our Lady of Beaujeu, as too zealous a partisan of the rival House of Orleans. The historian himself was imprisoned for eight months in one of the iron cages he has so forcibly described. It was there that he regretted the fate of a court life. "I have ventured on the great ocean," he said, in his affliction, "and the waves have devoured me." He was subjected to a trial, and exiled from court for some years by the Parliament of Paris, being found guilty of holding intercourse with disaffected persons. He survived this cloud, however, and was afterwards employed by Charles VIII. in one or two important missions, where talents were required. Louis XII. also transferred his favour to the historian, but did not employ him. He died at his Castle of Argenton, in 1509, and was regretted as one of the most profound statesmen, and certainly the best historian of his age. In a poem to his memory by the poet Ronsard, he received the distinguished praise that he was the first to show the lustre which valour and noble blood derived from being united with learning.

Note XII. p. 341.—DISGUISED HERALD

The heralds of the middle ages, like the *feciales* of the Romans, were invested with a character which was held almost sacred. To strike a herald was a crime which inferred a capital punishment: and to counterfeit the character of such an august official was a degree of treason towards those men who were accounted the depositaries of the secrets of monarchs and the honour of nobles. Yet a prince so unscrupulous as Louis XI. did not hesitate to practise such an imposition, when he wished to enter into communication with Edward IV. of England.

Exercising that knowledge of mankind for which he was so eminent, he selected, as an agent fit for his purpose, a simple valet. This man, whose address had been known to him, he disguised as a herald, with all the insignia of his office, and sent him in that capacity to open a communication with the English army. Two things are remarkable in this transaction. First, that the stratagem, though of so fraudulent a nature, does not seem to have been necessarily called for, since all that King Louis could gain by it would be, that he did not commit himself by sending a more responsible messenger. The other circumstance worthy of notice, is, that Comines, though he mentioned the affair at great length, is so pleased with the King's shrewdness in selecting, and dexterity at indoctrinating, his pseudo-herald, that he forgets all remark on the impudence and fraud of the imposition, as well as the great risk of discovery. From both which circumstances, we are led to the conclusion, that the solemn character which the heralds endeavoured to arrogate to themselves, had already begun to lose regard among statesmen and men of the great world.

Even Ferne, zealous enough for the dignity of the herald, seems to impute this intrusion on their rights in some degree to necessity. "I have heard some," he says, "but with shame enough, allow of the action of Louis XI. of the kingdom of France, who had so unknightly a regard both of his own honour, and also of armes, that he seldom had about his court any officer-at-arms. And therefore, at such time as Edward IV., King of England, had entered France with a hostile power, and lay before the town of Saint Quentin, the same French King, for want of a herald to carry his mind to the English King, was constrained to suborn a vadelict, or common serving-man, with a trumpet-banner, having a hole made through the middest for this preposterous herauld to put his head through, and to cast it over his shoulders instead of a better coat-armour of France. And thus came this hastily-arrayed courier as a counterfeit officer-at-arms, with instructions from his sovereign's mouth to offer peace to our King. 'Well,' replies Torquatus, the other interlocutor in the dialogue, 'that fault was never yet to be seen in any of our

English Kings, nor ever shall be, I hope.' "—FERNE's *Blazen of Gentry*, 1586, p. 161.

In this curious book, the author, besides some assertions in favour of coat-armour, too nearly approaching blasphemy to be quoted, informs us, that the Apostles were gentlemen of blood, and many of them descended from that worthy conqueror, Judas Maccabæus; but through the course of time and persecution of wars, poverty oppressed the kindred, and they were constrained to servile works. So were the four doctors and fathers of the Church (Ambrose, Augustine, Hierome, and Gregorie) gentlemen both of blood and arms, p. 98. The author's copy of this rare tract (memorial of a hopeful young friend, now no more) exhibits a curious sally of the national and professional irritability of a Scottish herald.

This person appears to have been named Thomas Drysdale, Islay Herald, who purchased the volume in 1619, and seems to have perused it with patience and profit till he came to the following passage in Ferne, which enters into the distinction between sovereign and feudatory crowns. "There is also a King, and he a homager, or fœdatorie to the estate and majestie of another King, as to his superior lord, as that of Scotland to our English Empire." This assertion set on fire the Scottish blood of Islay Herald, who, forgetting the book had been printed nearly forty years before, and that the author was probably dead, writes on the margin in great wrath, and in a half text hand, *"He is a traitor and lyar in his throat, and I offer him the combat, that says Scotland's Kings were ever feudatorie to England."*

Note XIII. p. 362.—ATTACK UPON LIEGE

The Duke of Burgundy, full of resentment for the usage which the Bishop had received from the people of Liege (whose death, as already noticed, did not take place for some years after), and knowing that the walls of the town had not been repaired since they were breached by himself after the battle of Saint Tron, advanced recklessly to their chastisement. His commanders shared his presumptuous confidence; for the advanced guard of his army, under the Maréchal of Burgundy and Seigneur D'Hymbercourt, rushed upon one of the suburbs, without waiting for the rest of their army, which, commanded by the Duke in person, remained about seven or eight leagues in the rear. The night was closing, and, as the Burgundian troops observed no discipline, they were exposed to a sudden attack from a party of the citizens commanded by Jean de Vilde, who assaulting them in front and rear, threw them into great disorder, and killed more than eight hundred men, of whom one hundred were men-at-arms.

When Charles and the King of France came up, they took up their quarters in two villas situated near to the wall of the city. In the two or three days which followed, Louis was distinguished for the quiet and regulated composure with which he pressed the siege, and provided for defence in case of sallies; while the Duke of Burgundy, no way deficient in courage and who showed the rashness and want of order which was his principal characteristic, seemed also extremely suspicious that the King would desert him and join with the Liegeois.

They lay before the town for five or six days, and at length fixed the 30th of October 1468 for a general storm. The citizens, who had probably information of their intent, resolved to prevent their purpose, and determined on anticipating it by a desperate sally through the breaches in their walls. They placed at their head six hundred of the men of the little territory of Franchemont, belonging to the Bishopric of Liege, and reckoned the most valiant of their troops. They burst out of the town on a sudden, surprised the Duke of Burgundy's quarters ere his guards could put on their armour, which they had laid off to enjoy some repose before the assault. The King of France's lodgings were also attacked and endangered. A great confusion ensued, augmented incalculably by the mutual jealousy and suspicions of the French and Burgundians. The people of Liege were, however, unable to maintain their hardy enterprise, when the men-at-arms of the King and the Duke began to recover from their confusion, and were finally forced to retire within their walls, after narrowly missing the chance of surprising both King Louis and the

Duke of Burgundy, the most powerful Princes of their time. At daybreak the storm took place, as had been originally intended, and the citizens, disheartened and fatigued by the nocturnal sally, did not make so much resistance as was expected. Liege was taken, and miserably pillaged, without regard to sex or age, things sacred or things profane. These particulars are fully related by Comines in his Memoirs, liv. ii. chap. 11, 12, 13, and do not differ much from the account of the same events given in the text.

GLOSSARY

AROINT, *begone!*

ARRAS, *tapestry.*

AUBERGE, *inn.*

AUGHT POSSESSION, *article of value.*

BAIRN, *child.*

BALDRIC, *girdle.*

BARGAIN, *quarrel.*

BILBOA, *rapier.*

BLACK-JACK, *leathern drinking-vessel.*

BLATE, *bashful.*

BONNY CHIELD, *handsome fellow.*

BOORD, *joke.*

BOUILLI, *meat stewed with vegetables.*

BRANTWEIN, *brandy.*

BRAW-WARLD, *finest in the world.*

BROWST, *as much as is brewed at one time.*

CALLANT, *lad.*

CARCANET, *necklace.*

CATHAY, *China.*

CERTES, *certainly, in truth.*

CHIELD, *fellow.*

CONNED WOODCRAFT, *studied forestry.*

CORBIES, *ravens.*

COVIN-TREE, *the large tree in front of a Scottish castle.*

CRAIG, *throat.*

CULLION, *despicable fellow.*

DAFFING, *folly.*

DHU, *black.*

DODDERED, *decayed.*

DONNER AND HAGEL, *thunder and hailstones.*

DOTATIONS, *endowments.*

DRIVE A SPREAGH, *make a raid on cattle.*

DYES, *gew-gaws.*

ECORCHEURS, *flayers.*

ELF-LOCKS, *hair twisted in locks, supposed to be the work of fairies.*

ENOW, *just now.*

FALCONETS, *pieces of cannon for the field.*

FICO, *fig.*

FOR TWO AND A PLACK, *for something you value.*

FRAU, *wife, dame.*

FREMIT, *stranger, one estranged.*

GABARDINE, *a loose felt cloak.*

GABELLE, *excise duty on salt.*

GAED, *went.*

GAGE, *glove, gauntlet.*

GEAR, *possession. also matter.*

GEISTER-SEERS, *ghost-seers.*

GILLIE, *Highland footman.*

GLORIE, *glory.*

GORGET, *piece of armour for defending the throat.*

GUERDON, *reward.*

GUILDRY, *trade, guild.*

HAGEL, *hailstones.*

HANAPS, *vases.*

HARQUEBUSSES, *primitive hand-guns.*

HARRIED, *plundered.*

HEAD-TIRE, *head-dress.*

HENKER, *hangman.*

HERZOGS, *dukes.*

HONGARIE, *Hungary.*
HOWLETS, *small owls.*

JACKMAN, *retainer.*

KERCHIEF, *linen covering for the head.*
KURSCHENSCHAFT, *currier's trade.*

LANDES, *district of the deserts of loose sand in France.*
LANZKNECHTS, *spearmen, lancers.*
LEECH-CRAFT, *the study of medicine.*
LIEGES, *subjects.*
LOOM, *pot.*
LOON, *rascal.*

MAIR, *more.*
MEIKLE, *much.*
MELL, *join in battle.*
MERCY OF GOD, *broad strong poniard.*
MINTING, *aiming.*

ORIFLAMME, *sacred banner of France.*

PARTISAN, *a kind of halberd.*
PENANCIERS, *penance doers.*
PIRNS, *bobbins, reels.*
PLACK, *a copper coin, value the third part of an English penny.*
POLL, *tax, inflict the poll-tax.*
POW, *head.*

QUACK-SALVING, *administering quack remedies.*

RAKE-HELLY, *wild, debauched, vicious.*
RAVEL OUT, *set difficult matters right.*
REBEC, *a species of fiddle.*
ROUSE, *carousal.*

SACK-POSSET, *a posset made of sack, or spiced wine, milk and sugar.*
SAE, *so.*
SCHOPPEN, *magistrates.*
SCHWARZ-BIER, *black beer.*
SCHWARZ-REITERS, *black horsemen.*
SHOOL, *shovel.*
SIC, *such.*
SKAITH, *harm.*
SKENE DHU, *black knife.*
SMALL-BACK, *Death.*
SNATCH, *look.*
SOOTH BOORD, *true joke.*
SOUNDER, *a two-year-old boar.*
SPREAGH, *cattle-stealing raid.*
STERNEN-DEUTER, *star-gazers.*
STRAICK, *bushel.*
SWALLOWS' NESTS, *iron cradles whence sentinels took aim at strangers approaching the castle-walls.*
SYNDICS, *magistrates.*

TEUFEL, *devil.*
TIPPET, *halter.*
TOLEDO, *Spanish sword.*
TO-NAME, *assumed name, nom de guerre.*
TOWN-SOUTER, *shoemaker.*
TWO AND A PLACK, *something you value.*

WAUR, *worse.*
WEIN-KELLAR, *wine cellar.*
WHILLY-WHAWING, *talking in a loving fashion.*
WOODCRAFT, *acquaintance with the rules of the chase.*
WOT, *know.*

ZIGEUNER, *gipsy.*

IVANHOE

A ROMANCE

Now fitted the halter, now traversed the cart,
And often took leave,—but seemed loath to depart!

PRIOR.

INTRODUCTION

THE author of the Waverley Novels had hitherto proceeded in an unabated course of popularity, and might, in his peculiar district of literature, have been termed *L'Enfant Gâté* of success. It was plain, however,
that frequent publication must finally wear out the public favour, unless some mode could be devised to give an appearance of novelty to subsequent productions. Scottish manners, Scottish dialect, and Scottish characters of note, being those with which the author was most intimately
and familiarly acquainted, were the groundwork upon which he had
hitherto relied for giving effect to his narrative. It was, however, obvious,
that this kind of interest must in the end occasion a degree of sameness and
repetition, if exclusively resorted to, and that the reader was likely at
length to adopt the language of Edwin, in Parnell's tale:—

> ———" 'Reverse the spell,' he cries,
> 'And let it fairly now suffice,
> The gambol has been shown.' "

Nothing can be more dangerous for the fame of a professor of the fine
arts, than to permit (if he can possibly prevent it) the character of a
mannerist to be attached to him, or that he supposed capable of success
only in a particular and limited style. The public are, in general, very
ready to adopt the opinion, that he who has pleased them in one peculiar mode of composition, is, by means of that very talent, rendered
incapable of venturing upon other subjects. The effect of this disinclination, on the part of the public, towards the artificers of their pleasures,
when they attempt to enlarge their means of amusing, may be seen in
the censures usually passed by vulgar criticism upon actors or artists
who venture to change the character of their efforts, that, in so doing,
they may enlarge the scale of their art.

There is some justice in this opinion, as there always is in such as
attain general currency. It may often happen on the stage, that an actor,
by possessing in a pre-eminent degree the external qualities necessary to
give effect to comedy, may be deprived of the right to aspire to tragic
excellence; and in painting or literary composition, an artist or poet may
be master exclusively of modes of thought, and powers of expression,
which confine him to a single course of subjects. But much more frequently the same capacity which carries a man to popularity in one department will obtain for him success in another, and that must be more
particularly the case in literary composition, than either in acting or paint-

ing, because the adventurer in that department is not impeded in his exertions by any peculiarity of features, or conformation of person, proper for particular parts, or, by any peculiar mechanical habits of using the pencil, limited to a particular class of subjects.

Whether this reasoning be correct or otherwise, the present author felt that, in confining himself to subjects purely Scottish, he was not only likely to weary out the indulgence of his readers, but also greatly to limit his own power of affording them pleasure. In a highly polished country, where so much genius is monthly employed in catering for public amusement, a fresh topic, such as he had himself had the happiness to light upon, is the untasted spring of the desert:—

"Men bless their stars and call it luxury."

But when men and horses, cattle, camels, and dromedaries, have poached the spring into mud, it becomes loathsome to those who at first drank of it with rapture; and he who had the merit of discovering it, if he would preserve his reputation with the tribe, must display his talent by a fresh discovery of untasted fountains.

If the author, who finds himself limited to a particular class of subjects, endeavours to sustain his reputation by striving to add a novelty of attraction to themes of the same character which have been formerly successful under his management, there are manifest reasons why, after a certain point, he is likely to fail. If the mine be not wrought out, the strength and capacity of the miner become necessarily exhausted. If he closely imitates the narratives which he has before rendered successful, he is doomed to "wonder that they please no more." If he struggles to take a different view of the same class of subjects, he speedily discovers that what is obvious, graceful, and natural, has been exhausted; and, in order to obtain the indispensable charm of novelty, he is forced upon caricature, and, to avoid being trite, must become extravagant.

It is not, perhaps, necessary to enumerate so many reasons why the author of the Scottish Novels, as they were then exclusively termed, should be desirous to make an experiment on a subject purely English. It was his purpose, at the same time, to have rendered the experiment as complete as possible, by bringing the intended work before the public as the effort of a new candidate for their favour, in order that no degree of prejudice, whether favourable or the reverse, might attach to it, as a new production of the author of *Waverley;* but this intention was afterwards departed from, for reasons to be hereafter mentioned.

The period of the narrative adopted was the reign of Richard I., not only as abounding with characters whose very names were sure to attract general attention, but as affording a striking contrast betwixt the Saxons, by whom the soil was cultivated, and the Normans, who still reigned in it as conquerors, reluctant to mix with the vanquished, or acknowledge themselves of the same stock. The idea of this contrast was taken from the ingenious and unfortunate Logan's tragedy of "Runna-mede," in which, about the same period of history, the author had seen the Saxon and Norman barons opposed to each other on different sides of the stage. He does not recollect that there was any attempt to contrast the two races in their habits and sentiments; and indeed it was obvious, that history was violated by introducing the Saxons still existing as a high-minded and martial race of nobles.

They did, however, survive as a people, and some of the ancient Saxon families possessed wealth and power, although they were exceptions to the humble condition of the race in general. It seemed to the author, that the existence of the two races in the same country, the vanquished distinguished by their plain, homely, blunt manners, and the free spirit infused by their ancient institutions and laws; the victors, by the high spirit of military fame, personal adventure, and whatever could distinguish them as the Flower of Chivalry, might, intermixed with other characters belonging to the same time and country, interest the reader by the contrast, if the author should not fail on his part.

Scotland, however, had been of late used so exclusively as the scene of what is called Historical Romance, that the preliminary letter of Mr. Laurence Templeton became in some measure necessary. To this, as to an Introduction, the reader is referred, as expressing the author's purpose and opinions in undertaking this species of composition, under the necessary reservation, that he is far from thinking he has attained the point at which he aimed.

It is scarcely necessary to add, that there was no idea or wish to pass off the supposed Mr. Templeton as a real person. But a kind of continuation of the *Tales of my Landlord* had been recently attempted by a stranger, and it was supposed this Dedicatory Epistle might pass for some imitation of the same kind, and thus putting enquirers upon a false scent, induce them to believe they had before them the work of some new candidate for their favour.

After a considerable part of the work had been finished and printed, the publishers, who pretended to discern in it a germ of popularity, remonstrated strenuously against its appearing as an absolutely anonymous production, and contended that it should have the advantage of being announced as by the author of *Waverley*. The author did not make any obstinate opposition, for he began to be of opinion with Dr. Wheeler, in Miss Edgeworth's excellent tale of *Manœuvring*, that "Trick upon Trick" might be too much for the patience of an indulgent public, and might be reasonably considered as trifling with their favour.

The book, therefore, appeared as an avowed continuation of the Waverley Novels; and it would be ungrateful not to acknowledge, that it met with the same favourable reception as its predecessors.

Such annotations as may be useful to assist the reader in comprehending the characters of the Jew, the Templar, the Captain of the mercenaries, or Free Companions, as they were called, and others proper to the period, are added, but with a sparing hand, since sufficient information on these subjects is to be found in general history.

An incident in the tale, which had the good fortune to find favour in the eyes of many readers, is more directly borrowed from the stories of old romance. I mean the meeting of the King with Friar Tuck at the cell of the buxom hermit. The general tone of the story belongs to all ranks and all countries, which emulate each other in describing the rambles of a disguised sovereign, who, going in search of information or amusement, into the lower ranks of life, meets with adventures diverting to the reader or hearer, from the contrast betwixt the monarch's outward appearance, and his real character. The Eastern tale-teller has for his theme the disguised expeditions of Haroun Alraschid with his faithful attendants, Mesrour and Giafar, through the midnight streets of Bagdad; and Scottish tradition dwells upon the similar exploits of James V., distinguished during such excursions by the travelling name of the Goodman of Ballengeigh, as the Commander of the Faithful, when he desired to be incognito, was known by that of Il Bondocani. The French minstrels are not silent on so popular a theme. There must have been a Norman original of the Scottish metrical romance of "Rauf Colziar," in which Charlemagne is introduced as the unknown guest of a charcoalman.[1] It seems to have been the original of other poems of the kind.

In merry England there is no end of popular ballads on this theme. The poem of John the Reeve, or Steward, mentioned by Bishop Percy, in the *Reliques of English Poetry*,[2] is said to have turned on such an incident; and we have besides, the King and the Tanner of Tamworth, the King and the Miller of Mansfield, and others on the same topic. But the peculiar tale of this nature to which the author of *Ivanhoe* has to acknowledge an obligation, is more ancient by two centuries than any of these last mentioned.

It was first communicated to the public in that curious record of ancient literature, which has been accumulated by the combined exertions of Sir Egerton Brydges and Mr. Hazelwood, in the periodical work entitled the *British Bibliographer*. From thence it has been transferred by the Reverend Charles Henry Hartshorne, M.A., editor of a very curious volume, entitled *Ancient Metrical Tales, printed chiefly from original sources*, 1829. Mr. Hartshorne gives no other authority for the present fragment, except the article in the *Bibliographer*, where it is entitled "The Kyng and the Hermite." A short abstract of its contents will show its similarity to the meeting of King Richard and Friar Tuck.

King Edward (we are not told which among the monarchs of that name, but, from his temper and habits, we may suppose Edward IV.) sets forth with his court to a gallant hunting-match in Sherwood Forest,

---

[1] This very curious poem, long a *desideratum* in Scottish literature, and given up as irrecoverably lost, was lately brought to light by the researches of Dr. Irvine of the Advocates' Library, and has been reprinted by Mr. David Laing, Edinburgh.

[2] Vol. ii. p. 167.

in which, as is not unusual for princes in romance, he falls in with a deer of extraordinary size and swiftness, and pursues it closely, till he has outstripped his whole retinue, tired out hounds and horse, and finds himself alone under the gloom of an extensive forest, upon which night is descending. Under the apprehensions natural to a situation so uncomfortable, the King recollects that he has heard how poor men, when apprehensive of a bad night's lodging, pray to Saint Julian, who, in the Romish calendar, stands Quarter-Master-General to all forlorn travellers that render him due homage. Edward puts up his orisons accordingly, and by the guidance, doubtless, of the good Saint, reaches a small path, conducting him to a chapel in the forest, having a hermit's cell in its close vicinity. The King hears the reverend man, with a companion of his solitude, telling his beads within, and meekly requests of him quarters for the night. "I have no accommodations for such a lord as ye be," said the Hermit. "I live here in the wilderness upon roots and rinds, and may not receive into my dwelling even the poorest wretch that lives, unless it were to save his life." The King enquires the way to the next town, and, understanding it is by a road which he cannot find without difficulty, even if he had daylight to befriend him, he declares, that with or without the Hermit's consent, he is determined to be his guest that night. He is admitted accordingly, not without a hint from the recluse, that were he himself out of his priestly weeds, he would care little for his threats of using violence, and that he gives way to him not out of intimidation, but simply to avoid scandal.

The King is admitted into the cell—two bundles of straw are shaken down for his accommodation, but he comforts himself that he is now under shelter, and that

> "A night will soon be gone."

Other wants, however, arise. The guest becomes clamorous for supper, observing,

> "For certainly, as I you say,
> I ne had never so sorry a day,
> That I ne had a merry night."

But this indication of his taste for good cheer, joined to the annunciation of his being a follower of the Court, who had lost himself at the great hunting-match, cannot induce the niggard Hermit to produce better fare than bread and cheese, for which his guest showed little appetite; and "thin drink," which was even less acceptable. At length the King presses his host on a point to which he had more than once alluded, without obtaining a satisfactory reply:

> "Then said the King, 'by Godys grace,
> Thou wert in a merry place,
> To shoot should thou lere;
> When the foresters go to rest,

Sometyme thou might have of the best,
All of the wild deer;
I wold hold it for no scathe,
Though thou hadst bow and arrows baith,
Althoff thou best a Frere.' "

The Hermit, in return, expresses his apprehension that his guest means to drag him into some confession of offence against the forest laws, which, being betrayed to the King, might cost him his life. Edward answers by fresh assurances of secrecy, and again urges on him the necessity of procuring some venison. The Hermit replies, by once more insisting on the duties incumbent upon him as a churchman, and continues to affirm himself free from all such breaches of order:—

"Many day I have here been,
And flesh-meat I eat never,
But milk of the kye;
Warm thee well, and go to sleep,
And I will lap thee with my cope,
Softly to lye."

It would seem that the manuscript is here imperfect, for we do not find the reasons which finally induce the curtal Friar to amend the King's cheer. But acknowledging his guest to be such a "good fellow" as has seldom graced his board, the holy man at length produces the best his cell affords. Two candles are placed on a table, white bread and baked pasties are displayed by the light, besides choice of venison, both salt and fresh, from which they select collops. "I might have eaten my bread dry," said the King, "had I not pressed thee on the score of archery, but now have I dined like a prince—if we had but drink enow."

This too is afforded by the hospitable anchorite, who dispatches an assistant to fetch a pot of four gallons from a secret corner near his bed, and the whole three set in to serious drinking. This amusement is superintended by the Friar, according to the recurrence of certain fustian words, to be repeated by every compotator in turn before he drank—a species of High Jinks, as it were, by which they regulated their potations, as toasts were given in latter times. The one toper says *fusty bandias,* to which the other is obliged to reply, *strike pantnere,* and the Friar passes many jests on the King's want of memory, who sometimes forgets the words of action. The night is spent in this jolly pastime. Before his departure in the morning, the King invites his reverend host to Court, promises, at least, to requite his hospitality, and expresses himself much pleased with his entertainment. The jolly Hermit at length agrees to venture thither, and to enquire for Jack Fletcher, which is the name assumed by the King. After the Hermit has shown Edward some feats of archery, the joyous pair separate. The King rides home, and rejoins his retinue. As the romance is imperfect, we are not acquainted how the discovery takes place; but it is probably much in the same manner as in other narratives turning on the same subject, where the host, apprehensive of death for having trespassed on the respect due to his Sovereign, while incognito, is agreeably surprised by receiving honours and reward.

In Mr. Hartshorne's collection, there is a romance on the same foundation, called "King Edward and the Shepherd," [1] which, considered as illustrating manners, is still more curious than the "King and the Hermit;" but it is foreign to the present purpose. The reader has here the original legend from which the incident in the romance is derived; and the identifying the irregular Eremite with the Friar Tuck of Robin Hood's story, was an obvious expedient.

The name of Ivanhoe was suggested by an old rhyme. All novelists have had occasion at some time or other to wish with Falstaff, that they knew where a commodity of good names was to be had. On such an occasion the author chanced to call to memory a rhyme recording three names of the manors forfeited by the ancestor of the celebrated Hampden, for striking the Black Prince a blow with his racket, when they quarrelled at tennis:—

"Tring, Wing, and Ivanhoe,
For striking of a blow,
Hampden did forego,
And glad he could escape so."

The word suited the author's purpose in two material respects,—for, first, it had an ancient English sound; and secondly, it conveyed no indication whatever of the nature of the story. He presumes to hold this last quality to be of no small importance. What is called a taking title, serves the direct interest of the bookseller or publisher, who by this means sometimes sells an edition while it is yet passing the press. But if the author permits an over degree of attention to be drawn to his work ere it has appeared, he places himself in the embarrassing condition of having excited a degree of expectation which, if he proves unable to satisfy, is an error fatal to his literary reputation. Besides, when we meet such a title as the Gunpowder Plot, or any other connected with general history, each reader, before he has seen the book, has formed to himself some particular idea of the sort of manner in which the story is to be conducted, and the nature of the amusement which he is to derive from it. In this he is probably disappointed, and in that case may be naturally disposed to visit upon the author or the work, the unpleasant feelings thus excited. In such a case the literary adventurer is censured,

---

[1] Like the Hermit, the Shepherd makes havock amongst the King's game; but by means of a sling, not of a bow; like the Hermit, too, he has his peculiar phrases of compotation, the sign and countersign being Passelodion and Berafriend. One can scarce conceive what humour our ancestors found in this species of gibberish; but

"I warrant it proved an excuse for the glass."

not for having missed the work at which he himself aimed, but for not having shot off his shaft in a direction he never thought of.

On the footing of unreserved communication which the author has established with the reader, he may here add the trifling circumstance, that a roll of Norman warriors, occurring in the Auchinleck Manuscript, gave him the formidable name of Front-de-Bœuf.

Ivanhoe was highly successful upon its appearance, and may be said to have procured for its author the freedom of the Rules, since he has ever since been permitted to exercise his powers of fictitious composition in England, as well as Scotland.

The character of the fair Jewess found so much favour in the eyes of some fair readers, that the writer was censured, because, when arranging the fates of the characters of the drama, he had not assigned the hand of Wilfred to Rebecca, rather than the less interesting Rowena. But, not to mention that the prejudices of the age rendered such an union almost impossible, the author may, in passing, observe, that he thinks a character of a highly virtuous and lofty stamp, is degraded rather than exalted by an attempt to reward virtue with temporal prosperity. Such is not the recompense which Providence has deemed worthy of suffering merit, and it is a dangerous and fatal doctrine to teach young persons, the most common readers of romance, that rectitude of conduct and of principle are either naturally allied with, or adequately rewarded by, the gratification of our passions, or attainment of our wishes. In a word, if a virtuous and self-denied character is dismissed with temporal wealth, greatness, rank, or the indulgence of such a rashly formed or ill-assorted passion as that of Rebecca for Ivanhoe, the reader will be apt to say, verily Virtue has had its reward. But a glance on the great picture of life will show, that the duties of self-denial, and the sacrifice of passion to principle, are seldom thus remunerated; and that the internal consciousness of their high-minded discharge of duty, produces on their own reflections a more adequate recompense, in the form of that peace which the world cannot give or take away.

ABBOTSFORD, 1st *September,* 1830.

DEDICATORY EPISTLE

To the Rev. Dr. Dryasdust, F.A.S.

Residing in the Castle-Gate, York

Much esteemed and dear Sir,

It is scarcely necessary to mention the various and concurring reasons which induce me to place your name at the head of the following work. Yet the chief of these reasons may perhaps be refuted by the imperfections of the performance. Could I have hoped to render it worthy of your patronage, the public would at once have seen the propriety of inscribing a work designed to illustrate the domestic antiquities of England and particularly of our Saxon forefathers, to the learned author of the Essays upon the Horn of King Ulphus, and on the Lands bestowed by him upon the patrimony of St. Peter. I am conscious, however, that the slight, unsatisfactory, and trivial manner in which the result of my antiquarian researches has been recorded in the following pages, takes the work from under that class which bears the proud motto, *Detur digniori*. On the contrary, I fear I shall incur the censure of presumption in placing the venerable name of Dr. Jonas Dryasdust at the head of a publication, which the more grave antiquary will perhaps class with the idle novels and romances of the day. I am anxious to vindicate myself from such a charge; for although I might trust to your friendship for an apology in your eyes, yet I would not willingly stand convicted in those of the public of so grave a crime, as my fears led me to anticipate my being charged with.

I must therefore remind you, that when we first talked over together that class of productions, in one of which the private and family affairs of your learned northern friend, Mr. Oldbuck of Monkbarns, were so unjustifiably exposed to the public, some discussion occurred between us concerning the cause of the popularity these works have attained in this idle age, which, whatever other merit they possess, must be admitted to be hastily written, and in violation of every rule assigned to the epopeia. It seemed then to be your opinion, that the charm lay entirely in the art with which the unknown author had availed himself, like a second M'Pherson, of the antiquarian stores which lay scattered around him, supplying his own indolence or poverty of invention, by the incidents which had actually taken place in his country at no distant period, by introducing real characters, and scarcely suppressing real names. It was not above sixty or seventy years, you observed, since the whole north

397

of Scotland was under a state of government nearly as simple and as patriarchal as those of our good allies the Mohawks and Iroquois. Admitting that the author cannot himself be supposed to have witnessed those times, he must have lived, you observed, among persons who had acted and suffered in them; and even within these thirty years, such an infinite change has taken place in the manners of Scotland, that men look back upon the habits of society proper to their immediate ancestors, as we do on those of the reign of Queen Anne, or even the period of the Revolution. Having thus materials of every kind lying strewed around him, there was little, you observed, to embarrass the author, but the difficulty of choice. It was no wonder, therefore, that, having begun to work a mine so plentiful, he should have derived from his works fully more credit and profit than the facility of his labours merited.

Admitting (as I could not deny) the general truth of these conclusions, I cannot but think it strange that no attempt has been made to excite an interest for the traditions and manners of old England, similar to that which has been obtained in behalf of those of our poorer and less celebrated neighbours. The Kendal green, though its date is more ancient, ought surely to be as dear to our feelings, as the variegated tartans of the north. The name of Robin Hood, if duly conjured with, should raise a spirit as soon as that of Rob Roy; and the patriots of England deserve no less their renown in our modern circles, than the Bruces and Wallaces of Caledonia. If the scenery of the south be less romantic and sublime than that of the northern mountains, it must be allowed to possess in the same proportion superior softness and beauty; and upon the whole, we feel ourselves entitled to exclaim with the patriotic Syrian—"Are not Pharphar and Abana, rivers of Damascus, better than all the rivers of Israel?"

Your objections to such an attempt, my dear Doctor, were, you may remember, two-fold. You insisted upon the advantages which the Scotsman possessed, from the very recent existence of that state of society in which his scene was to be laid. Many now alive, you remarked, well remembered persons who had not only seen the celebrated Roy M'Gregor, but had feasted, and even fought with him. All those minute circumstances belonging to private life and domestic character, all that gives verisimilitude to a narrative, and individuality to the persons introduced, is still known and remembered in Scotland; whereas in England, civilisation has been so long complete, that our ideas of our ancestors are only to be gleaned from musty records and chronicles, the authors of which seem perversely to have conspired to suppress in their narratives all interesting details, in order to find room for flowers of monkish eloquence, or trite reflections upon morals. To match an English and a Scottish author in the rival task of embodying and reviving the traditions of their respective countries, would be, you alleged, in the highest degree unequal and unjust. The Scottish magician, you said, was, like Lucan's witch, at liberty to walk over the recent field of battle, and

to select for the subject of resuscitation by his sorceries, a body whose
limbs had recently quivered with existence, and whose throat had but
just uttered the last note of agony. Such a subject even the powerful
Erictho was compelled to select, as alone capable of being reanimated
even by *her* potent magic—

> ————gelidas leto scrutata medullas,
> Pulmonis rigidi stantes sine vulnere fibras
> Invenit, et vocem defuncto in corpore quærit.

The English author, on the other hand, without supposing him less of a
conjuror than the Northern Warlock, can, you observed, only have the
liberty of selecting his subject amidst the dust of antiquity, where nothing was to be found but dry, sapless, mouldering, and disjointed bones,
such as those which filled the valley of Jehoshaphat. You expressed, besides, your apprehension, that the unpatriotic prejudices of my countrymen would not allow fair play to such a work as that of which I endeavoured to demonstrate the probable success. And this, you said, was
not entirely owing to the more general prejudice in favour of that which
is foreign, but that it rested partly upon improbabilities, arising out of
the circumstances in which the English reader is placed. If you describe
to him a set of wild manners, and a state of primitive society existing in
the Highlands of Scotland, he is much disposed to acquiesce in the truth
of what is asserted. And reason good. If he be of the ordinary class of
readers, he has either never seen those remote districts at all, or he has
wandered through those desolate regions in the course of a summer tour,
eating bad dinners, sleeping on truckle beds, stalking from desolation
to desolation, and fully prepared to believe the strangest things that
could be told him of a people, wild and extravagant enough to be attached to scenery so extraordinary. But the same worthy person, when
placed in his own snug parlour, and surrounded by all the comforts of an
Englishman's fireside, is not half so much disposed to believe that his
own ancestors led a very different life from himself; that the shattered
tower, which now forms a vista from his window, once held a baron
who would have hung him up at his own door without any form of
trial; that the hinds, by whom his little pet-farm is managed, a few
centuries ago would have been his slaves; and that the complete influence of feudal tyranny once extended over the neighbouring village,
where the attorney is now a man of more importance than the lord of
the manor.

While I own the force of these objections, I must confess, at the same
time, that they do not appear to me to be altogether insurmountable.
The scantiness of materials is indeed a formidable difficulty; but no one
knows better than Dr. Dryasdust, that to those deeply read in antiquity,
hints concerning the private life of our ancestors lie scattered through
the pages of our various historians. bearing, indeed, a slender proportion

to the other matters of which they treat, but still, when collected to-gether, sufficient to throw considerable light upon the *vie privée* of our forefathers; indeed, I am convinced, that however I myself may fail in the ensuing attempt, yet, with more labour in collecting, or more skill in using, the materials within his reach, illustrated as they have been by the labours of Dr. Henry, of the late Mr. Strutt, and, above all, of Mr. Sharon Turner, an abler hand would have been successful; and there-fore I protest, beforehand, against any argument which may be founded on the failure of the present experiment.

On the other hand, I have already said, that if anything like a true picture of old English manners could be drawn, I would trust to the good-nature and good sense of my countrymen for insuring its favourable reception.

Having thus replied, to the best of my power, to the first class of your objections, or at least having shown my resolution to overleap the barriers which your prudence has raised, I will be brief in noticing that which is more peculiar to myself. It seemed to be your opinion, that the very office of an antiquary, employed in grave, and, as the vulgar will sometimes allege, in toilsome and minute research, must be considered as incapacitating him from successfully compounding a tale of this sort. But permit me to say, my dear Doctor, that this objection is rather for-mal than substantial. It is true, that such slight compositions might not suit the severer genius of our friend Mr. Oldbuck. Yet Horace Walpole wrote a goblin tale which has thrilled through many a bosom; and George Ellis could transfer all the playful fascination of a humour, as delight-ful as it was common, into his *Abridgement of the Ancient Metrical Ro-mances*. So that, however I may have occasion to rue my present au-dacity, I have at least the most respectable precedents in my favour.

Still the severer antiquary may think, that, by thus intermingling fiction with truth, I am polluting the well of history with modern inven-tions, and impressing upon the rising generation false ideas of the age which I describe. I cannot but in some sense admit the force of this reasoning, which I yet hope to traverse by the following considerations.

It is true, that I neither can, nor do, pretend to the observation of complete accuracy, even in matters of outward costume, much less in the more important points of language and manners. But the same motive which prevents my writing the dialogue of the piece in Anglo-Saxon or in Norman-French, and which prohibits my sending forth to the public this essay printed with the types of Caxton or Wynken de Worde, pre-vents my attempting to confine myself within the limits of the period in which my story is laid. It is necessary, for exciting interest of any kind, that the subject assumed should be, as it were, translated into the man-ners, as well as the language, of the age we live in. No fascination has ever been attached to Oriental literature, equal to that produced by Mr. Galland's first translation of the *Arabian Tales;* in which, retaining on the one hand the splendour of Eastern costume, and on the other the

wildness of Eastern fiction, he mixed these with just so much ordinary
feeling and expression, as rendered them interesting and intelligible, while
he abridged the long-winded narratives, curtailed the monotonous reflections, and rejected the endless repetitions of the Arabian original.
The tales, therefore, though less purely Oriental than in their first con-
coction, were eminently better fitted for the European market, and
obtained an unrivalled degree of public favour, which they certainly
would never have gained had not the manners and style been in some
degree familiarised to the feelings and habits of the western reader.

In point of justice, therefore, to the multitudes who will, I trust, devour this book with avidity, I have so far explained our ancient manners in modern language, and so far detailed the characters and sentiments of my persons, that the modern reader will not find himself, I
should hope, much trammelled by the repulsive dryness of mere antiquity. In this, I respectfully contend, I have in no respect exceeded
the fair license due to the author of a fictitious composition. The late
ingenious Mr. Strutt, in his romance of *Queen-Hoo Hall*, acted upon
another principle; and in distinguishing between what was ancient and
modern, forgot, as it appears to me, that extensive neutral ground, the
large proportion, that is, of manners and sentiments which are common
to us and to our ancestors, having been handed down unaltered from
them to us, or which, arising out of the principles of our common nature,
must have existed alike in either state of society. In this manner, a man
of talent, and of great antiquarian erudition, limited the popularity of his
work, by excluding from it every thing which was not sufficiently obsolete to be altogether forgotten and unintelligible.

The license which I would here vindicate, is so necessary to the execution of my plan, that I will crave your patience while I illustrate my
argument a little farther.

He who first opens Chaucer, or any other ancient poet, is so much
struck with the obsolete spelling, multiplied consonants, and antiquated
appearance of the language, that he is apt to lay the work down in
despair, as encrusted too deep with the rust of antiquity, to permit his
judging of its merits or tasting its beauties. But if some intelligent and
accomplished friend points out to him, that the difficulties by which he
is startled are more in appearance than reality, if, by reading aloud to
him, or by reducing the ordinary words to the modern orthography, he
satisfies his proselyte that only about one-tenth part of the words employed are in fact obsolete, the novice may be easily persuaded to approach the "well of English undefiled," with the certainty that a slender
degree of patience will enable him to enjoy both the humour and the
pathos with which old Geoffrey delighted the age of Cressy and of
Poictiers.

To pursue this a little farther. If our neophyte, strong in the new-
born love of antiquity, were to undertake to imitate what he had learnt
to admire, it must be allowed he would act very injudiciously if he were

to select from the Glossary the obsolete words which it contains, and
employ those exclusively of all phrases and vocables retained in modern
days. This was the error of the unfortunate Chatterton. In order to give
his language the appearance of antiquity, he rejected every word that
was modern, and produced a dialect entirely different from any that
had ever been spoken in Great Britain. He who would imitate an ancient
language with success, must attend rather to its grammatical character,
turn of expression, and mode of arrangement, than labour to collect extraordinary and antiquated terms, which, as I have already averred,
do not in ancient authors approach the number of words still in use,
though perhaps somewhat altered in sense and spelling, in the proportion of one to ten.

What I have applied to language, is still more justly applicable to
sentiments and manners. The passions, the sources from which these
must spring in all their modifications, are generally the same in all ranks
and conditions, all countries and ages; and it follows, as a matter of
course, that the opinions, habits of thinking, and actions, however influenced by the peculiar state of society, must still, upon the whole,
bear a strong resemblance to each other. Our ancestors were not more
distinct from us, surely, than Jews are from Christians; they had "eyes,
hands, organs, dimensions, senses, affections, and passions;" were "fed
with the same food, hurt with the same weapons, subject to the same
diseases, warmed and cooled by the same winter and summer," as ourselves. The tenor, therefore, of their affections and feelings, must have
borne the same general proportion to our own.

It follows, therefore, that of the materials which an author has to
use in a romance, or fictitious composition, such as I have ventured to
attempt, he will find that a great proportion, both in language and
manners, is as proper to the present time as to those of which he has laid
his time of action. The freedom of choice which this allows him, is therefore much greater, and the difficulty of his task much more diminished,
than at first appears. To take an illustration from a sister art, the anti
quarian details may be said to represent the peculiar features of a landscape under delineation of the pencil. His feudal tower must arise in
due majesty; the figures which he introduces must have the costume and
the character of their age; the piece must represent the peculiar features of the scene which he has chosen for his subject, with all its appropriate elevation of rock, or precipitate descent of cataract. His general colouring, too, must be copied from Nature: The sky must be
clouded or serene, according to the climate, and the general tints must
be those which prevail in a natural landscape. So far the painter is
bound down by the rules of his art, to a precise imitation of the features
of Nature; but it is not required that he should descend to copy all her
more minute features, or represent with absolute exactness the very
herbs, flowers, and trees, with which the spot is decorated. These, as
well as all the more minute points of light and shadow, are attributes

proper to scenery in general, natural to each situation, and subject to the artist's disposal, as his taste or pleasure may dictate.

It is true, that this license is confined in either case within legitimate bounds. The painter must introduce no ornament inconsistent with the climate or country of his landscape; he must not plant cypress trees upon Inch-Merrin, or Scottish firs among the ruins of Persepolis; and the author lies under a corresponding restraint. However far he may venture in a more full detail of passions and feelings, than is to be found in the ancient compositions which he imitates, he must introduce nothing inconsistent with the manners of the age; his knights, squires, grooms, and yeomen, may be more fully drawn than in the hard, dry delineations of an ancient illuminated manuscript, but the character and costume of the age must remain inviolate; they must be the same figures, drawn by a better pencil, or, to speak more modestly, executed in an age when the principles of art were better understood. His language must not be exclusively obsolete and unintelligible; but he should admit, if possible, no word or turn of phraseology betraying an origin directly modern. It is one thing to make use of the language and sentiments which are common to ourselves and our forefathers, and it is another to invest them with the sentiments and dialect exclusively proper to their descendants.

This, my dear friend, I have found the most difficult part of my task; and, to speak frankly, I hardly expect to satisfy your less partial judgment, and more extensive knowledge of such subjects, since I have hardly been able to please my own.

I am conscious that I shall be found still more faulty in the tone of keeping and costume, by those who may be disposed rigidly to examine my tale, with reference to the manners of the exact period in which my actors flourished: It may be, that I have introduced little which can positively be termed modern; but, on the other hand, it is extremely probable that I may have confused the manners of two or three centuries, and introduced, during the reign of Richard the First, circumstances appropriate to a period either considerably earlier or a good deal later than that era. It is my comfort, that errors of this kind will escape the general class of readers, and that I may share in the ill-deserved applause of those architects, who, in their modern Gothic, do not hesitate to introduce, without rule or method, ornaments proper to different styles and to different periods of the art. Those whose extensive researches have given them the means of judging my back-slidings with more severity, will probably be lenient in proportion to their knowledge of the difficulty of my task. My honest and neglected friend Ingulphus, has furnished me with many a valuable hint; but the light afforded by the Monk of Croydon, and Geoffrey de Vinsauff, is dimmed by such a conglomeration of uninteresting and unintelligible matter, that we gladly fly for relief to the delightful pages of the gallant Froissart, although he flourished at a period so much more remote from the date of my history. If, therefore, my dear friend, you have generosity enough to pardon the presumptuous attempt, to frame for myself a minstrel coronet, partly out of the pearls of pure antiquity, and partly from the Bristol stones and paste, with which I have endeavoured to imitate them, I am convinced your opinion of the difficulty of the task will reconcile you to the imperfect manner of its execution.

Of my materials I have but little to say: They may be chiefly found in the singular Anglo-Norman MS., which Sir Arthur Wardour preserves with such jealous care in the third drawer of his oaken cabinet, scarcely allowing any one to touch it, and being himself not able to read one syllable of its contents. I should never have got his consent, on my visit to Scotland, to read in those precious pages for so many hours, had I not promised to designate it by some emphatic mode of printing, as 𝕿𝖍𝖊 𝖂𝖆𝖗𝖉𝖔𝖚𝖗 𝕸𝖆𝖓𝖚𝖘𝖈𝖗𝖎𝖕𝖙; giving it, thereby, an individuality as important as the Bannatyne MS., the Auchinleck MS., and any other monument of the patience of a Gothic scrivener. I have sent, for your private consideration, a list of the contents of this curious piece, which I shall perhaps subjoin, with your approbation, to the third volume of my tale, in case the printer's devil should continue impatient for copy when the whole of my narrative has been imposed.

Adieu, my dear friend; I have said enough to explain, if not to vindicate, the attempt which I have made, and which, in spite of your doubts, and my own incapacity, I am still willing to believe has not been altogether made in vain.

I hope you are now well recovered from your spring fit of the gout, and shall be happy if the advice of your learned physician should recommend a tour to these parts. Several curiosities have been lately dug up near the wall, as well as at the ancient station of Habitancum. Talking of the latter, I suppose you have long since heard the news, that a sulky churlish boor has destroyed the ancient statue, or rather bas-relief, popularly called Robin of Redesdale. It seems Robin's fame attracted more visitants than was consistent with the growth of the heather, upon a moor worth a shilling an acre. Reverend as you write yourself, be revengeful for once, and pray with me that he may be visited with such a fit of the stone, as if he had all the fragments of poor Robin in that region of his viscera where the disease holds its seat. Tell this not in Gath, lest the Scots rejoice that they have at length found a parallel instance among their neighbours, to that barbarous deed which demolished Arthur's Oven. But there is no end to lamentation, when we betake ourselves to such subjects. My respectful compliments attend Miss Dryasdust; I endeavoured to match the spectacles agreeable to her commission, during my late journey to London, and hope she has received them safe, and found them satisfactory. I send this by the blind carrier, so that probably it may be some time upon its journey.[1] The last news which I hear from Edinburgh is, that the gentleman who fills the situation of Secretary to the Society of Antiquaries of Scotland,[2] is the best amateur draftsman in that kingdom, and that much is expected from his skill and zeal in delineating those specimens of national antiquity, which are either mouldering under the slow touch of time, or swept away by modern taste, with the same besom of destruction which John Knox used at the Reformation. Once more adieu; *vale tandem, non immemor mei.* Believe me to be,

Reverend, and very dear Sir

Your most faithful humble Servant,

LAURENCE TEMPLETON.

TOPPINGWOLD, NEAR EGREMONT,
CUMBERLAND, *Nov.* 17, 1817.

[1] This anticipation proved but too true, as my learned correspondent did not receive my letter until a twelvemonth after it was written. I mention this circumstance, that a gentleman attached to the cause of learning, who now holds the principal control of the post-office, may consider whether by some mitigation of the present enormous rates, some favour might not be shown to the correspondents of the principal Literary and Antiquarian Societies. I understand, indeed, that this experiment was once tried, but that the mail-coach having broke down under the weight of packages addressed to members of the Society of Antiquaries, it was relinquished as a hazardous experiment. Surely, however, it would be possible to build these vehicles in a form more substantial, stronger in the perch, and broader in the wheels, so as to support the weight of Antiquarian learning; when, if they should be found to travel more slowly, they would be not the less agreeable to quiet travellers like myself.—L. T.

[2] Mr. Skene of Rubislaw is here intimated, to whose taste and skill the author is indebted for a series of etchings, exhibiting the various localities alluded to in these novels.

IVANHOE

CHAPTER I

Thus communed these; while to their lowly dome,
The full-fed swine return'd with evening home;
Compell'd, reluctant, to the several sties,
With din obstreperous, and ungrateful cries.
                              POPE'S *Odyssey.*

IN that pleasant district of merry England which is watered by the river
Don, there extended in ancient times a large forest, covering the greater
part of the beautiful hills and valleys which lie between Sheffield and
the pleasant town of Doncaster. The remains of this extensive wood are
still to be seen at the noble seats of Wentworth, of Warncliffe Park, and
around Rotherham. Here haunted of yore the fabulous Dragon of Want-
ley; here were fought many of the most desperate battles during the
Civil Wars of the Roses! and here also flourished in ancient times those
bands of gallant outlaws, whose deeds have been rendered so popular
in English song.

Such being our chief scene, the date of our story refers to a period
towards the end of the reign of Richard I., when his return from his
long captivity had become an event rather wished than hoped for by
his despairing subjects, who were in the meantime subjected to every
species of subordinate oppression. The nobles, whose power had become
exorbitant during the reign of Stephen, and whom the prudence of
Henry the Second had scarce reduced into some degree of subjection
to the crown, had now resumed their ancient license in its utmost extent;
despising the feeble interference of the English Council of State, fortifying their castles, increasing the number of their dependants, reducing all
around them to a state of vassalage, and striving by every means in their
power, to place themselves each at the head of such forces as might enable him to make a figure in the national convulsions which appeared to
be impending.

The situation of the inferior gentry, or Franklins, as they were called,
who, by the law and spirit of the English constitution, were entitled to
hold themselves independent of feudal tyranny, became now unusually
precarious. If, as was most generally the case, they placed themselves
under the protection of any of the petty kings in their vicinity, accepted
of feudal offices in his household, or bound themselves, by mutual treaties
of alliance and protection, to support him in his enterprises, they might
indeed purchase temporary repose; but it must be with the sacrifice of

that independence which was so dear to every English bosom, and at
the certain hazard of being involved as a party in whatever rash expedition the ambition of their protector might lead him to undertake.
On the other hand, such and so multiplied were the means of vexation
and oppression possessed by the great Barons, that they never wanted
the pretext, and seldom the will, to harass and pursue, even to the very
edge of destruction, any of their less powerful neighbours, who attempted
to separate themselves from their authority, and, to trust for their protection, during the dangers of the times, to their own inoffensive conduct, and to the laws of the land.

A circumstance which greatly tended to enhance the tyranny of the
nobility, and the sufferings of the inferior classes, arose from the consequences of the Conquest by Duke William of Normandy. Four generations had not sufficed to blend the hostile blood of the Normans and
Anglo-Saxons, or to unite, by common language and mutual interests,
two hostile races, one of which still felt the elation of triumph, while
the other groaned under all the consequences of defeat. The power had
been completely placed in the hands of the Norman nobility, by the
event of the battle of Hastings, and it had been used, as our histories
assure us, with no moderate hand. The whole race of Saxon princes and
nobles had been extirpated or disinherited, with few or no exceptions;
nor were the numbers great who possessed land in the country of their
fathers, even as proprietors of the second, or of yet inferior classes. The
royal policy had long been to weaken, by every means, legal or illegal,
the strength of a part of the population which was justly considered as
nourishing the most inveterate antipathy to their victor. All the monarchs of the Norman race had shown the most marked predilection for
their Norman subjects; the laws of the chase, and many others, equally
unknown to the milder and more free spirit of the Saxon constitution,
had been fixed upon the necks of the subjugated inhabitants, to add
weight, as it were, to the feudal chains with which they were loaded.
At court, and in the castles of the great nobles, where the pomp and state
of a court was emulated, Norman-French was the only language employed; in courts of law, the pleadings and judgments were delivered in
the same tongue. In short, French was the language of honour, of chivalry,
and even of justice, while the far more manly and expressive Anglo-
Saxon was abandoned to the use of rustics and hinds, who knew no other.
Still, however, the necessary intercourse between the lords of the soil,
and those oppressed inferior beings by whom that soil was cultivated,
occasioned the gradual formation of a dialect, compounded betwixt the
French and the Anglo-Saxon, in which they could render themselves
mutually intelligible to each other; and from this necessity arose by
degrees the structure of our present English language, in which the
speech of the victors and the vanquished have been so happily blended
together; and which has since been so richly improved by importations

from the classical languages, and from those spoken by the southern nations of Europe.

This state of things I have thought it necessary to premise for the information of the general reader, who might be apt to forget, that, although no great historical events, such as war, or insurrection, mark the existence of the Anglo-Saxons as a separate people subsequent to the reign of William the Second, yet the great national distinctions betwixt them and their conquerors, the recollection of what they had formerly been, and to what they were now reduced, continued, down to the reign of Edward the Third, to keep open the wounds which the Conquest had inflicted, and to maintain a line of separation betwixt the descendants of the victor Normans and the vanquished Saxons.

The sun was setting upon one of the rich grassy glades of that forest, which we have mentioned in the beginning of the chapter. Hundreds of broad-headed, short-stemmed, wide-branched oaks, which had witnessed perhaps the stately march of the Roman soldiery, flung their gnarled arms over a thick carpet of the most delicious green sward; in some places they were intermingled with beeches, hollies, and copsewood of various descriptions, so closely as totally to intercept the level beams of the sinking sun; in others they receded from each other, forming those long sweeping vistas, in the intricacy of which the eye delights to lose itself, while imagination considers them as the paths to yet wilder scenes of silvan solitude. Here the red rays of the sun shot a broken and discoloured light, that partially hung upon the shattered boughs and mossy trunks of the trees, and there they illuminated in brilliant patches the portions of turf to which they made their way. A considerable open space, in the midst of this glade, seemed formerly to have been dedicated to the rites of Druidical superstition; for, on the summit of a hillock, so regular as to seem artificial, there still remained part of a circle of rough unhewn stones, of large dimensions. Seven stood upright; the rest had been dislodged from their places, probably by the zeal of some convert to Christianity, and lay, some prostrate near their former site, and others on the side of the hill. One large stone only had found its way to the bottom, and in stopping the course of a small brook, which glided smoothly round the foot of the eminence, gave, by its opposition, a feeble voice of murmur to the placid and elsewhere silent streamlet.

The human figures which completed this landscape, were in number two, partaking, in their dress and appearance, of that wild and rustic character, which belong to the woodlands of the West-Riding of Yorkshire at that early period. The eldest of these men had a stern, savage, and wild aspect. His garment was of the simplest form imaginable, being a close jacket with sleeves, composed of the tanned skin of some animal, on which the hair had been originally left, but which had been worn off in so many places, that it would have been difficult to distinguish, from the patches that remained, to what creature the fur had belonged.

This primeval vestment reached from the throat to the knees, and served at once all the usual purposes of body-clothing; there was no wider opening at the collar than was necessary to admit the passage of the head, from which it may be inferred that it was put on by slipping it over the head and shoulders, in the manner of a modern shirt, or ancient hauberk. Sandals, bound with thongs made of boars' hide, protected the feet, and a roll of thin leather was twined artificially round the legs, and, ascending above the calf, left the knees bare, like those of a Scottish Highlander. To make the jacket sit yet more close to the body, it was gathered at the middle by a broad leathern belt, secured by a brass buckle; to one side of which was attached a sort of scrip, and to the other a ram's horn, accoutred with a mouthpiece, for the purpose of blowing. In the same belt was stuck one of those long, broad, sharp-pointed, and two-edged knives, with a buck's-horn handle, which were fabricated in the neighbourhood, and bore even at this early period the name of a Sheffield whittle. The man had no covering upon his head, which was only defended by his own thick hair, matted and twisted together, and scorched by the influence of the sun into a rusty dark-red colour, forming a contrast with the overgrown beard upon his cheeks, which was rather of a yellow or amber hue. One part of his dress only remains, but it is too remarkable to be suppressed; it was a brass ring, resembling a dog's collar, but without any opening, and soldered fast round his neck, so loose as to form no impediment to his breathing, yet so tight as to be incapable of being removed, excepting by the use of the file. On this singular gorget was engraved, in Saxon characters, an inscription of the following purport:—"Gurth, the son of Beowulph, is the born thrall of Cedric of Rotherwood."

Beside the swineherd, for such was Gurth's occupation, was seated, upon one of the fallen Druidical monuments, a person about ten years younger in appearance, and whose dress, though resembling his companion's in form, was of better materials, and of a more fantastic appearance. His jacket had been stained of a bright purple hue, upon which there had been some attempt to paint grotesque ornaments in different colours. To the jacket he added a short cloak, which scarcely reached half way down his thigh; it was of crimson cloth, though a good deal soiled, lined with bright yellow; and as he could transfer it from one shoulder to the other, or at his pleasure draw it all around him, its width, contrasted with its want of longitude, formed a fantastic piece of drapery. He had thin silver bracelets upon his arms, and on his neck a collar of the same metal, bearing the inscription, "Wamba, the son of Witless, is the thrall of Cedric of Rotherwood." This personage had the same sort of sandals with his companion, but instead of the roll of leather thong, his legs were cased in a sort of gaiters, of which one was red and the other yellow. He was provided also with a cap, having around it more than one bell, about the size of those attached to hawks, which jingled as he turned his head to one side or other; and as he

seldom remained a minute in the same posture, the sound might be
considered as incessant. Around the edge of his cap was a stiff bandeau
of leather, cut at the top into open work, resembling a coronet, while
a prolonged bag arose from within it, and fell down on one shoulder
like an old-fashioned night-cap, or a jelly-bag, or the head-gear of a
modern hussar. It was to this part of the cap that the bells were attached; which circumstance, as well as the shape of his head-dress, and
his own half-crazed, half-cunning expression of countenance, sufficiently
pointed him out as belonging to the race of domestic clowns or jesters,
maintained in the houses of the wealthy, to help away the tedium of
those lingering hours which they were obliged to spend within doors.
He bore, like his companion, a scrip attached to his belt, but had neither
horn nor knife, being probably considered as belonging to a class whom
it is esteemed dangerous to intrust with edge-tools. In place of these
he was equipped with a sword of lath, resembling that with which Harlequin operates his wonders upon the modern stage.

The outward appearance of these two men formed scarce a stronger
contrast than their look and demeanour. That of the serf, or bondsman,
was sad and sullen; his aspect was bent on the ground with an air of
deep dejection; his aspect might be almost construed into apathy, had
not the fire which occasionally sparkled in his red eye manifested that
there slumbered, under the appearance of sullen despondency, a sense
of oppression, and a disposition to resistance. The looks of Wamba, on
the other hand, indicated, as usual with his class, a sort of vacant curiosity, and fidgetty impatience of any posture of repose, together with
the utmost self-satisfaction respecting his own situation, and the appearance which he made. The dialogue which they maintained between
them, was carried on in Anglo-Saxon, which, as we said before, was
universally spoken by the inferior classes, excepting the Norman soldiers, and the immediate personal dependants of the great feudal nobles.
But to give their conversation in the original would convey but little
information to the modern reader, for whose benefit we beg to offer
the following translation:

"The curse of St. Withold upon these infernal porkers!" said the
swineherd, after blowing his horn obstreperously, to collect together the
scattered herd of swine, which, answering his call with notes equally melo-
dious, made, however, no haste to remove themselves from the luxurious
banquet of beechmast and acorns on which they had fattened, or to
forsake the marshy banks of the rivulet, where several of them, half
plunged in mud, lay stretched at their ease, altogether regardless of the
voice of their keeper. "The curse of St. Withold upon them and upon
me!" said Gurth; " if the two-legged wolf snap not up some of them
ere nightfall, I am no true man. Here, Fangs! Fangs!" he ejaculated at
the top of his voice to a ragged wolfish-looking dog, a sort of lurcher,
half mastiff, half greyhound, which ran limping about as if with the
purpose of seconding his master in collecting the refractory grunters;

but which, in fact, from misapprehension of the swineherd's signals, ignorance of his own duty, or malice prepense, only drove them hither and thither, and increased the evil which he seemed to design to remedy. "A devil draw the teeth of him," said Gurth, "and the mother of mischief confound the Ranger of the forest, that cuts the foreclaws off our dogs, and makes them unfit for their trade! [1] Wamba, up and help me an thou beest a man; take a turn round the back o' the hill to gain the wind on them; and when thou'st got the weather-gage, thou mayst drive them before thee as gently as so many innocent lambs."

"Truly," said Wamba, without stirring from the spot, "I have consulted my legs upon this matter, and they are altogether of opinion, that to carry my gay garments through these sloughs, would be an act of unfriendship to my sovereign person and royal wardrobe; wherefore, Gurth, I advise thee to call off Fangs, and leave the herd to their destiny, which, whether they meet with bands of travelling soldiers, or of outlaws, or of wandering pilgrims, can be little else than to be converted into Normans before morning, to thy no small ease and comfort."

"The swine turned Normans to my comfort!" quoth Gurth; "expound that to me, Wamba, for my brain is too dull, and my mind too vexed, to read riddles."

"Why, how call you those grunting brutes running about on their four legs?" demanded Wamba.

"Swine, fool, swine," said the herd, "every fool knows that."

"And swine is good Saxon," said the Jester; "but how call you the sow when she is flayed, and drawn, and quartered, and hung up by the heels, like a traitor?"

"Pork," answered the swineherd.

"I am very glad every fool knows that too," said Wamba, "and pork, I think, is good Norman-French; and so when the brute lives, and is in the charge of a Saxon slave, she goes by her Saxon name; but becomes a Norman, and is called pork, when she is carried to the Castle-hall to feast among the nobles; what dost thou think of this, friend Gurth, ha?"

"It is but too true doctrine, friend Wamba, however it got into thy fool's pate."

"Nay, I can tell you more," said Wamba, in the same tone; "there is old Alderman Ox continues to hold his Saxon epithet, while he is under the charge of serfs and bondsmen such as thou, but becomes Beef, a fiery French gallant, when he arrives before the worshipful jaws that are destined to consume him. Mynheer Calf, too, becomes Monsieur de Veau in the like manner; he is Saxon when he requires tendance, and takes a Norman name when he becomes matter of enjoyment."

"By St. Dunstan," answered Gurth, "thou speakest but sad truths; little is left to us but the air we breathe, and that appears to have been

---

[1] Note I.—The Ranger of the Forest, that cuts the foreclaws off our dogs.

reserved with much hesitation, solely for the purpose of enabling us to endure the tasks they lay upon our shoulders. The finest and the fattest is for their board; the loveliest is for their couch; the best and bravest supply their foreign masters with soldiers, and whiten distant lands with their bones, leaving few here who have either will or the power to protect the unfortunate Saxon. God's blessing on our Master Cedric, he hath done the work of a man in standing in the gap; but Reginald Front-de-Bœuf is coming down to this country in person, and we shall soon see how little Cedric's trouble will avail him.—Here, here," he exclaimed again, raising his voice, "So ho! so ho! well done, Fangs! thou hast them all before thee now, and bring'st them on bravely, lad."

"Gurth," said the Jester, "I know thou thinkest me a fool, or thou wouldst not be so rash in putting thy head into my mouth. One word to Reginald Front-de-Bœuf, or Philip de Malvoisin, that thou hast spoken treason against the Norman,—and thou art but a castaway swineherd,— thou wouldst waver on one of these trees as a terror to all evil speakers against dignities."

"Dog, thou wouldst not betray me," said Gurth, "after having led me on to speak so much at disadvantage?"

"Betray thee!" answered the Jester; "no, that were the trick of a wise man; a fool cannot halt so well help himself—but soft, whom have we here?" he said, listening to the trampling of several horses which became then audible.

"Never mind whom," answered Gurth, who had now got his herd before him, and, with the aid of Fangs, was driving them down one of the long dim vistas which we have endeavoured to describe.

"Nay, but I must see the riders," answered Wamba; "perhaps they are come from Fairyland with a message from King Oberon."

"A murrain take thee," rejoined the swineherd; "wilt thou talk of such things, while a terrible storm of thunder and lightning is raging within a few miles of us? Hark, how the thunder rumbles! and for summer rain, I never saw such broad downright flat drops fall out of the clouds; the oaks, too, notwithstanding the calm weather, sob and creak with their great boughs as if announcing a tempest. Thou canst play the rational if thou wilt; credit me for once, and let us home ere the storm begins to rage, for the night will be fearful."

Wamba seemed to feel the force of this appeal, and accompanied his companion, who began his journey after catching up a long quarter-staff which lay upon the grass beside him. This second Eumæus strode hastily down the forest glade, driving before him, with the assistance of Fangs, the whole herd of his inharmonious charge.

CHAPTER II

A Monk there was, a fayre for the maistrie,
An outrider that loved venerie;
A manly man, to be an Abbot able,
Full many a daintie horse had he in stable:
And whan he rode, men might his bridle hear
Gingeling in a whistling wind as clear,
And eke as loud, as doth the chapell bell,
There as this lord was keeper of the cell.
                                CHAUCER.

NOTWITHSTANDING the occasional exhortation and chiding of his companion, the noise of the horsemen's feet continuing to approach, Wamba could not be prevented from lingering occasionally on the road, upon every pretence which occurred; now catching from the hazel a cluster of half-ripe nuts, and now turning his head to leer after a cottage maiden who crossed their path. The horsemen, therefore, soon overtook them on the road.

Their numbers amounted to ten men, of whom the two who rode foremost seemed to be persons of considerable importance, and the others their attendants. It was not difficult to ascertain the condition and character of one of these personages. He was obviously an ecclesiastic of high rank; his dress was that of a Cistercian Monk, but composed of materials much finer than those which the rule of that order admitted. His mantle and hood were of the best Flanders cloth, and fell in ample, and not ungraceful folds, around a handsome though somewhat corpulent person. His countenance bore as little the marks of self-denial, as his habit indicated contempt of worldly splendour. His features might have been called good, had there not lurked under the penthouse of his eye, that sly epicurean twinkle which indicates the cautious voluptuary. In other respects, his profession and situation had taught him a ready command over his countenance, which he could contract at pleasure into solemnity, although its natural expression was that of good-humoured social indulgence. In defiance of conventional rules, and the edicts of popes and councils, the sleeves of this dignitary were lined and turned up with rich furs, his mantle secured at the throat with a golden clasp, and the whole dress proper to his order as much refined upon and ornamented, as that of a quaker beauty of the present day, who, while she retains the garb and costume of her sect, continues to give to its simplicity, by the choice of materials and the mode of disposing them, a certain air of coquettish attraction, savouring but too much of the vanities of the world.

This worthy churchman rode upon a well-fed ambling mule, whose furniture was highly decorated, and whose bridle, according to the fashion of the day, was ornamented with silver bells. In his seat he had nothing of the awkwardness of the convent, but displayed the easy and habitual grace of a well-trained horseman. Indeed, it seemed that

so humble a conveyance as a mule, in however good case, and however
well broken to a pleasant and accommodating amble, was only used by
the gallant monk for travelling on the road. A lay brother, one of those
who followed in the train, had, for his use on other occasions, one of
the most handsome Spanish jennets ever bred at Andalusia, which
merchants used at that time to import, with great trouble and risk,
for the use of persons of wealth and distinction. The saddle and hous-
ings of this superb palfrey were covered by a long foot-cloth, which
reached nearly to the ground, and on which were richly embroidered,
mitres, crosses and other ecclesiastical emblems. Another lay brother
led a sumpter mule, loaded probably with his superior's baggage; and
two monks of his own order, of inferior station, rode together in the rear,
laughing and conversing with each other, without taking much notice of
the other members of the cavalcade.

The companion of the church dignitary was a man past forty, thin,
strong, tall, and muscular; an athletic figure, which long fatigue and
constant exercise seemed to have left none of the softer part of the
human form, having reduced the whole to brawn, bones, and sinews,
which had sustained a thousand toils, and were ready to dare a thousand more. His head was covered with a scarlet cap, faced with fur—
of that kind which the French call *mortier,* from its resemblance to the
shape of an inverted mortar. His countenance was therefore fully displayed, and its expression was calculated to impress a degree of awe,
if not of fear, upon strangers. High features, naturally strong and powerfully expressive, had been burnt almost into Negro blackness by constant exposure to the tropical sun, and might, in their ordinary state, be
said to slumber after the storm of passion had passed away; but the
projection of the veins of the forehead, the readiness with which the
upper lip and its thick black moustaches quivered upon the slightest
emotion, plainly intimated that the tempest might be again and easily
awakened. His keen, piercing, dark eyes, told in every glance a history of
difficulties subdued, and dangers dared, and seemed to challenge opposition to his wishes, for the pleasure of sweeping it from his road by a
determined exertion of courage and of will; a deep scar on his brow
gave additional sternness to his countenance, and a sinister expression
to one of his eyes, which had been slightly injured on the same occasion,
and of which the vision, though perfect, was in a slight and partial
degree distorted.

The upper dress of this personage resembled that of his companion
in shape, being a long monastic mantle; but the colour, being scarlet,
showed that he did not belong to any of the four regular orders of monks.
On the right shoulder of the mantle there was cut, in white cloth, a cross
of a peculiar form. This upper robe concealed what at first view seemed
rather inconsistent with its form, a shirt, namely, of linked mail, with
sleeves and gloves of the same, curiously plaited and interwoven, as
flexible to the body as those which are now wrought in the stocking-loom,

out of less obdurate materials. The forepart of his thighs, where the folds of his mantle permitted them to be seen, were also covered with linked mail; the knees and feet were defended by splints, or thin plates of steel, ingeniously jointed upon each other; and mail hose, reaching from the ankle to the knee, effectually protected the legs, and completed the rider's defensive armour. In his girdle he wore a long and double-edged dagger, which was the only offensive weapon about his person.

He rode, not a mule, like his companion, but a strong hackney for the road, to save his gallant war-horse, which a squire led behind, fully accoutred for battle, with a chamfron or plaited head-piece upon his head, having a short spike projecting from the front. On one side of the saddle hung a short battle-axe, richly inlaid with Damascene carving; on the other the rider's plumed head-piece and hood of mail, with a long two-handed sword, used by the chivalry of the period. A second squire held aloft his master's lance, from the extremity of which fluttered a small banderole, or streamer, bearing a cross of the same form with that embroidered upon his cloak. He also carried his small triangular shield, broad enough at the top to protect the breast, and from thence diminishing to a point. It was covered with a scarlet cloth, which prevented the device from being seen.

These two squires were followed by two attendants, whose dark visages, white turbans, and the Oriental form of their garments, showed them to be natives of some distant Eastern country.[1] The whole appearance of this warrior and his retinue was wild and outlandish; the dress of his squires was gorgeous, and his Eastern attendants wore silver collars round their throats, and bracelets of the same metal upon their swarthy arms and legs, of which the former were naked from the elbow, and the latter from mid-leg to ankle. Silk and embroidery distinguished their dresses, and marked the wealth and importance of their master; forming, at the same time, a striking contrast with the martial simplicity of his own attire. They were armed with crooked sabres, having the hilt and baldric inlaid with gold, and matched with Turkish daggers of yet more costly workmanship. Each of them bore at his saddle-bow, a bundle of darts and javelins, about four feet in length, having sharp steel heads, a weapon much in use among the Saracens, and of which the memory is yet preserved in the martial exercise called *El Jerrid*, still practised in the Eastern countries.

The steeds of these attendants were in appearance as foreign as their riders. They were of Saracen origin, and consequently of Arabian descent; and their fine slender limbs, small fetlocks, thin manes, and easy springy motion, formed a marked contrast with the large-jointed heavy horses, of which the race was cultivated in Flanders and in Normandy, for mounting the men-at-arms of the period in all the panoply of plate and mail; and which, placed by the side of those Eastern coursers, might have passed for a personification of substance and of shadow.

[1] Note II.—Negro Slaves.

The singular appearance of this cavalcade not only attracted the curiosity of Wamba, but excited even that of his less volatile companion. The monk he instantly knew to be the Prior of Jorvaulx Abbey, well known for many miles around as a lover of the chase, of the banquet, and, if fame did him not wrong, of other worldly pleasures still more inconsistent with his monastic vows.

Yet so loose were the ideas of the times respecting the conduct of the clergy, whether secular or regular, that the Prior Aymer maintained a fair character in the neighbourhood of his abbey. His free and jovial temper, and the readiness with which he granted absolution from all ordinary delinquencies, rendered him a favourite among the nobility and principal gentry, to several of whom he was allied by birth, being of a distinguished Norman family. The ladies, in particular, were not disposed to scan too nicely the morals of a man who was a professed admirer of their sex, and who possessed many means of dispelling the ennui which was too apt to intrude upon the halls and bowers of an ancient feudal castle. The Prior mingled in the sports of the field with more than due eagerness, and was allowed to possess the best-trained hawks, and the fleetest grey-hounds in the North Riding; circumstances which strongly recommended him to the youthful gentry. With the old, he had another part to play, which, when needful, he could sustain with great decorum. His knowledge of books, however superficial, was sufficient to impress upon their ignorance respect for his supposed learning; and the gravity of his deportment and language, with the high tone which he exerted in setting forth the authority of the church and of the priesthood, impressed them no less with an opinion of his sanctity. Even the common people, the severest critics of the conduct of their betters, had commiseration with the follies of Prior Aymer. He was generous; and charity, as it is well known, covereth a multitude of sins, in another sense than that in which it is said to do so in Scripture. The revenues of the monastery, of which a large part was at his disposal, while they gave him the means of supplying his own very considerable expenses, afforded also those largesses which he bestowed among the peasantry and with which he frequently relieved the distresses of the oppressed. If Prior Aymer rode hard in the chase, or remained long at the banquet,— if Prior Aymer was seen, at the early peep of dawn, to enter the postern of the abbey, as he glided home from some rendezvous which had occupied the hours of darkness, men only shrugged up their shoulders, and reconciled themselves to his irregularities, by recollecting that the same were practised by many of his brethren who had no redeeming qualities whatsoever to atone for them. Prior Aymer, therefore, and his character, were well known to our Saxon serfs, who made their rude obeisance, and received his *"benedicite mes filz,"* in return.

But the singular appearance of his companion and his attendants, arrested their attention and excited their wonder, and they could scarcely attend to the Prior of Jorvaulx' question, when he demanded if they knew of any place of harbourage in the vicinity; so much were they surprised at the half monastic, half military appearance of the swarthy stranger, and at the uncouth dress and arms of his Eastern attendants. It is probable, too, that the language in which the benediction was conferred, and the information asked, sounded ungracious, though not probably unintelligible, in the ears of the Saxon peasants.

"I asked you, my children," said the Prior, raising his voice, and using the lingua Franca, or mixed language, in which the Norman and Saxon races conversed with each other, "if there be in this neighbourhood any good man, who, for the love of God, and devotion to Mother Church, will give two of her humblest servants, with their train, a night's hospitality and refreshment?"

This he spoke with a tone of conscious importance, which formed a strong contrast to the modest terms which he thought it proper to employ.

"Two of the humblest servants of Mother Church!" repeated Wamba to himself,—but, fool as he was, taking care not to make his observation audible; "I should like to see her seneschals, her chief butlers, and her other principal domestics!"

After this internal commentary on the Prior's speech, he raised his eyes, and replied to the question which had been put.

"If the reverend fathers," he said, "loved good cheer and soft lodging, few miles of riding would carry them to the Priory of Brinxworth, where their quality could not but secure them the most honourable reception; or if they preferred spending a penitential evening, they might turn down yonder wild glade, which would bring them to the hermitage of Copmanhurst, where a pious anchoret would make them sharers for the night of the shelter of his roof and the benefit of his prayers."

The Prior shook his head at both proposals.

"Mine honest friend," said he, "if the jangling of thy bells had not dizzied thine understanding, thou mightest know *Clericus clericum non decimat;* that is to say, we churchmen do not exhaust each other's hospitality, but rather require that of the laity; giving them thus an opportunity to serve God in honouring and relieving his appointed servants."

"It is true," replied Wamba, "that I, being but an ass, am, nevertheless, honoured to bear the bells as well as your reverence's mule; notwithstanding, I did conceive that the charity of Mother Church and her servants might be said, with other charity, to begin at home."

"A truce to thine insolence, fellow," said the armed rider, breaking in on his prattle with a high and stern voice, "and tell us, if thou canst, the road to—— How call'd you your Franklin, Prior Aymer?"

"Cedric," answered the Prior; "Cedric the Saxon.—Tell me, good fellow, are we near his dwelling, and can you show us the road?"

"The road will be uneasy to find," answered Gurth, who broke silence for the first time, "and the family of Cedric retire early to rest."

"Tush, tell not me, fellow!" said the military rider; " 'tis easy for them to arise and supply the wants of travellers such as we are, who will not stoop to beg the hospitality which we have a right to command."

"I know not," said Gurth, sullenly, "if I should show the way to my master's house, to those who demand as a right, the shelter which most are fain to ask as a favour."

"Do you dispute with me, slave!" said the soldier; and, setting spurs to his horse, he caused him make a demivolte across the path, raising at the same time the riding rod which he held in his hand, with a purpose of chastising what he considered as the insolence of the peasant.

Gurth darted at him a savage and revengeful scowl, and with a fierce, yet hesitating motion, laid his hand on the haft of his knife; but the interference of Prior Aymer, who pushed his mule betwixt his companion and the swineherd, prevented the meditated violence.

"Nay, by St. Mary, brother Brian, you must not think you are now in Palestine, predominating over heathen Turks and infidel Saracens; we islanders love not blows, save those of holy Church, who chasteneth whom she loveth.—Tell me, good fellow," said he to Wamba, and seconded his speech by a small piece of silver coin, "the way to Cedric the Saxon's; you cannot be ignorant of it, and it is your duty to direct the wanderer even when his character is less sanctified than ours."

"In truth, venerable father," answered the Jester, "the Saracen head of your right reverend companion has frightened out of mine the way home—I am not sure I shall get there to-night myself."

"Tush," said the Abbot, "thou canst tell us if thou wilt. This reverend brother has been all his life engaged in fighting among the Saracens for the recovery of the Holy Sepulchre; he is of the order of Knights Templars, whom you may have heard of; he is half a monk, half a soldier."

"If he is but half a monk," said the Jester, "he should not be wholly unreasonable with those whom he meets upon the road, even if they should be in no hurry to answer questions that no way concern them."

"I forgive thy wit," replied the Abbot, "on condition thou wilt show me the way to Cedric's mansion."

"Well, then," answered Wamba, "your reverences must hold on this path till you come to a sunken cross, of which scarce a cubit's length remains above ground; then take the path to the left, for there are four which meet at Sunken Cross, and I trust your reverences will obtain shelter before the storm comes on."

The Abbot thanked his sage adviser; and the cavalcade, setting spurs to their horses, rode on as men do who wish to reach their inn before the bursting of a night-storm. As their horses' hoofs died away, Gurth said to his companion, "If they follow thy wise direction, the reverend fathers will hardly reach Rotherwood this night."

"No," said the Jester, grinning, "but they may reach Sheffield if they have good luck, and that is as fit a place for them. I am not so bad a woodsman as to show the dog where the deer lies, if I have no mind he should chase him."

"Thou art right," said Gurth; "it were ill that Aymer saw the Lady Rowena; and it were worse, it may be, for Cedric to quarrel, as is most likely he would, with this military monk. But, like good servants, let us hear and see, and say nothing."

We return to the riders, who had soon left the bondsmen far behind them, and who maintained the following conversation in the Norman-French language, usually employed by the superior classes, with the exception of the few who were still inclined to boast their Saxon descent.

"What mean these fellows by their capricious insolence?" said the Templar to the Cistercian, "and why did you prevent me from chastising it?"

"Marry, brother Brian," replied the Prior, "touching the one of them, it were hard for me to render a reason for a fool speaking according to his folly; and the other churl is of that savage, fierce, intractable race, some of whom, as I have often told you, are still to be found among the descendants of the conquered Saxons, and whose supreme pleasure it is to testify, by all means in their power, their aversion to their conquerors."

"I would soon have beat him into courtesy," observed Brian; "I am accustomed to deal with such spirits: Our Turkish captives are as fierce and intractable as Odin himself could have been; yet two months in my household, under the management of my master of the slaves, has made them humble, submissive, serviceable, and observant of your will. Marry, sir, you must beware of the poison and the dagger; for they use either with free will when you give them the slightest opportunity."

"Ay, but," answered Prior Aymer, "every land has its own manners and fashions; and, besides that, beating this fellow could procure us no information respecting the road to Cedric's house, it would have been sure to have established a quarrel betwixt you and him had we found our way thither. Remember what I told you; this wealthy Franklin is proud, fierce, jealous, and irritable; a withstander of the nobility, and even of his neighbours, Reginald Front-de-Bœuf, and Philip Malvoisin, who are no babes to strive with. He stands up so sternly for the privileges of his race, and is so proud of his uninterrupted descent from Hereward, a renowned champion of the Heptarchy, that he is universally called Cedric the Saxon; and makes a boast of his belonging to a people from whom many others endeavour to hide their descent, lest they should encounter a share of the *vae victis*, or severities imposed upon the vanquished."

"Prior Aymer," said the Templar, "you are a man of gallantry, learned in the study of beauty, and as expert as a troubadour in all matters concerning the arrets of love; but I shall expect much beauty in this cele-brated Rowena, to counterbalance the self-denial and forbearance which

I must exert, if I am to court the favour of such a seditious churl as you have described her father Cedric."

"Cedric is not her father," replied the Prior, "and is but of remote relation; she is descended from higher blood than even he pretends to, and is but distantly connected with him by birth. Her guardian, however, he is, self-constituted as I believe; but his ward is as dear to him as if she were his own child. Of her beauty you shall soon be judge; and if the purity of her complexion, and the majestic, yet soft expression of a mild blue eye, do not chase from your memory the black-tressed girls of Palestine, ay, or the houris of old Mahound's paradise, I am an infidel, and no true son of the church."

"Should your boasted beauty," said the Templar, "be weighed in the balance and found wanting, you know our wager?"

"My gold collar," answered the Prior, "against ten butts of Chian wine;—they are mine as securely as if they were already in the convent vaults, under the key of old Denis the cellarer."

"And I am myself to be judge," said the Templar, "and I am only to be convicted on my own admission, that I have seen no maiden so beautiful since Pentecost was a twelve-month. Ran it not so?—Prior, your collar is in danger; I will wear it over my gorget in the lists of Ashby-de-la-Zouche."

"Win it fairly," said the Prior, "and wear it as ye will; I will trust your giving true response, on your word as a knight and as a churchman. Yet, brother, take my advice, and file your tongue to a little more courtesy than your habits of predominating over infidel captives and Eastern bondsmen have accustomed you. Cedric the Saxon, if offended, and he is noway slack in taking offence,—is a man who, without respect to your knighthood, my high office, or the sanctity of either, would clear his house of us, and send us to lodge with the larks, though the hour were midnight. And be careful how you look on Rowena, whom he cherishes with the most jealous care; an he take the least alarm in that quarter we are but lost men. It is said he banished his only son from his family for lifting his eyes in the way of affection towards this beauty, who may be worshipped, it seems, at a distance, but is not to be approached with other thoughts than such as we bring to the shrine of the Blessed Virgin."

"Well, you have said enough," answered the Templar; "I will for a night put on the needful restraint, and deport me as meekly as a maiden; but as for the fear of his expelling us by violence, myself and squires, with Hamlet and Abdalla, I will warrant you against that disgrace. Doubt not that we shall be strong enough to make good our quarters."

"We must not let it come so far," answered the Prior; "but here is the clown's sunken cross, and the night is so dark that we can hardly see which of the roads we are to follow. He bid us turn, I think, to the left."

"To the right," said Brian, "to the best of my remembrance."

"To the left, certainly, the left; I remember his pointing with his wooden sword."

"Ay, but he held his sword in his left hand, and so pointed across his body with it," said the Templar.

Each maintained his opinion with sufficient obstinacy, as is usual in all such cases; the attendants were appealed to, but they had not been near enough to hear Wamba's directions. At length Brian remarked, what had at first escaped him in the twilight; "Here is some one either asleep, or lying dead at the foot of this cross—Hugo, stir him with the butt-end of thy lance."

This was no sooner done than the figure arose, exclaiming in good French, "Whosoever thou art, it is discourteous in you to disturb my thoughts."

"We did but wish to ask you," said the Prior, "the road to Rotherwood, the abode of Cedric the Saxon."

"I myself am bound thither," replied the stranger; "and if I had a horse, I would be your guide, for the way is somewhat intricate, though perfectly well known to me."

"Thou shalt have both thanks and reward, my friend," said the Prior, "if thou wilt bring us to Cedric's in safety."

And he caused one of his attendants to mount his own led horse, and give that upon which he had hitherto ridden to the stranger, who was to serve for a guide.

Their conductor pursued an opposite road from that which Wamba had recommended, for the purpose of misleading them. The path soon led deeper into the woodland, and crossed more than one brook, the approach to which was rendered perilous by the marches through which it flowed; but the stranger seemed to know, as if by instinct, the soundest ground and the safest points of passage; and by dint of caution and attention, brought the party safely into a wider avenue than any they had yet seen; and, pointing to a large low irregular building at the upper extremity, he said to the Prior, "Yonder is Rotherwood, the dwelling of Cedric the Saxon."

This was a joyful intimation to Aymer, whose nerves were none of the strongest, and who had suffered such agitation and alarm in the course of passing through the dangerous bogs, that he had not yet had the curiosity to ask his guide a single question. Finding himself now at his ease and near shelter, his curiosity began to awake, and he demanded of the guide who and what he was.

"A Palmer, just returned from the Holy Land," was the answer.

"You had better have tarried there to fight for the recovery of the Holy Sepulchre," said the Templar.

"True, Reverend Sir Knight," answered the Palmer, to whom the appearance of the Templar seemed perfectly familiar; "but when those who are under oath to recover the holy city, are found travelling at such a distance from the scene of their duties, can you wonder that a peaceful peasant like me should decline the task which they have abandoned?"

The Templar would have made an angry reply, but was interrupted by the Prior, who again expressed his astonishment, that their guide, after such long absence, should be so perfectly acquainted with the passes of the forest.

"I was born a native of these parts," answered their guide, and as he made the reply they stood before the mansion of Cedric;—a low irregular building, containing several courtyards or enclosures, extending over a considerable space of ground, and which, though its size argued the inhabitant to be a person of wealth, differed entirely from the tall, turretted, and castellated buildings in which the Norman nobility resided, and which had become the universal style of architecture throughout England.

Rotherwood was not, however, without defences; no habitation, in that disturbed period, could have been so, without the risk of being plundered and burnt before the next morning. A deep fosse, or ditch, was drawn round the whole building, and filled with water from a neighbouring stream. A double stockade, or palisade, composed of pointed beams, which the adjacent forest supplied, defended the outer and inner bank of the trench. There was an entrance from the west through the outer stockade, which communicated by a drawbridge, with a similar opening in the interior defences. Some precautions had been taken to place those entrances under the protection of projecting angles, by which they might be flanked in case of need by archers or slingers.

Before this entrance the Templar wound his horn loudly; for the rain, which had long threatened, began now to descend with great violence.

CHAPTER III

Then (sad relief!) from the bleak coast that hears
The German Ocean roar, deep-blooming, strong,
And yellow-hair'd, the blue-eyed Saxon came.
THOMSON's *Liberty*.

In a hall, the height of which was greatly disproportioned to its extreme length and width, a long oaken table, formed of planks rough-hewn from the forest, and which had scarcely received any polish, stood ready prepared for the evening meal of Cedric the Saxon. The roof, composed of beams and rafters, had nothing to divide the apartment from the sky excepting the planking and thatch; there was a huge fireplace at either end of the hall, but as the chimneys were constructed in a very clumsy manner, at least as much of the smoke found its way into the apartment as escaped by the proper vent. The constant vapour which this occasioned, had polished the rafters and beams of the low-browed hall, by encrusting them with a black varnish of soot. On the sides of the apartment hung implements of war and of the chase, and there were at each corner folding doors, which gave access to other parts of the extensive building.

The other appointments of the mansion partook of the rude simplicity of the Saxon period, which Cedric piqued himself upon maintaining. The floor was composed of earth mixed with lime, trodden into a hard substance, such as is often employed in flooring our modern barns. For about one quarter of the length of the apartment, the floor was raised by a step, and this space, which was called a dais, was occupied only by the principal members of the family, and visitors of distinction. For this purpose, a table richly covered with scarlet cloth was placed transversely across the platform, from the middle of which ran the longer and lower board, at which the domestics and inferior persons fed, down towards the bottom of the hall. The whole resembled the form of the letter T, or some of those ancient dinner-tables, which, arranged on the same principles, may be still seen in the antique colleges of Oxford or Cambridge. Massive chairs and settles of carved oak were placed upon the dais, and over these seats and the more elevated table was fastened a canopy of cloth, which served in some degree to protect the dignitaries who occupied that distinguished station from the weather, and especially from the rain, which in some places found its way through the ill-constructed roof.

The walls of this upper end of the hall, as far as the dais extended, were covered with hangings or curtains, and upon the floor there was a carpet, both of which were adorned with some attempts at tapestry, or embroidery, executed with brilliant or rather gaudy colouring. Over the lower range of table, the roof, as we have noticed, had no covering; the rough plastered walls were left bare, and the rude earthen floor was uncarpeted; the board was uncovered by a cloth, and rude massive benches supplied the place of chairs.

In the centre of the upper table, were placed two chairs more elevated than the rest, for the master and mistress of the family, who presided over the scene of hospitality, and from doing so derived their Saxon title of honour, which signifies "the Dividers of Bread."

To each of these chairs was added a footstool, curiously carved and inlaid with ivory, which mark of distinction was peculiar to them. One of these seats was at present occupied by Cedric the Saxon, who, though but in rank a thane, or, as the Normans called him, a Franklin, felt, at the delay of his evening meal, an irritable impatience, which might have become an alderman, whether of ancient or modern times.

It appeared, indeed, from the countenance of this proprietor, that he was of a frank, but hasty and choleric temper. He was not above the middle stature, but broad-shouldered, long-armed, and powerfully made, like one accustomed to endure the fatigue of war or of the chase; his face was broad, with large blue eyes, open and frank features, fine teeth, and a well-formed head, altogether expressive of that sort of good-humour which often lodges with a sudden and hasty temper. Pride and jealousy there was in his eye, for his life had been spent in asserting rights which were constantly liable to invasion; and the prompt, fiery, and resolute disposition of the man, had been kept constantly upon the alert by the circumstances of his situation. His long yellow hair was equally divided on the top of his head and upon his brow, and combed down on each side to the length of his shoulders; it had but little tendency to grey, although Cedric was approaching to his sixtieth year.

His dress was a tunic of forest green, furred at the throat and cuffs with what was called minever; a kind of fur inferior in quality to ermine, and formed, it is believed, of the skin of the grey squirrel. This doublet hung unbuttoned over a close dress of scarlet which sate tight to his body; he had breeches of the same, but they did not reach below the lower part of the thigh, leaving the knee exposed. His feet had sandals of the same fashion with the peasants, but of finer materials, and secured in the front with golden clasps. He had bracelets of gold upon his arms, and a broad collar of the same precious metal around his neck. About his waist he wore a richly-studded belt, in which was stuck a short straight two-edged sword, with a sharp point, so disposed as to hang almost perpendicularly by his side. Behind his seat was hung a scarlet cloth cloak lined with fur, and a cap of the same materials richly embroidered, which completed the dress of the opulent landholder when he chose to go forth. A short boar-spear, with a broad and bright steel head, also reclined against the back of his chair, which served him, when he walked abroad, for the purposes of a staff or of a weapon, as chance might require.

Several domestics, whose dress held various proportions betwixt the richness of their master's and the coarse and simple attire of Gurth the swineherd, watched the looks and waited the commands of the Saxon dignitary. Two or three servants of a superior order stood behind their master upon the dais; the rest occupied the lower part of the hall. Other attendants there were of a different description; two or three large and shaggy greyhounds, such as were then employed in hunting the stag and wolf; as many slow-hounds of a large bony breed, with thick necks, large heads, and long ears; and one or two of the smaller dogs, now called terriers, which waited with impatience the arrival of the supper; but, with the sagacious knowledge of physiognomy peculiar to their race, forbore to intrude upon the moody silence of their master, apprehensive probably of a small white truncheon which lay by Cedric's trencher, for the purpose of repelling the advances of his four-legged dependants. One grisly old wolf-dog alone, with the liberty of an indulged favourite, had planted himself close by the chair of state, and occasionally ventured to solicit notice by putting his large hairy head upon his master's knee, or pushing his nose into his hand. Even he was repelled by the stern command, "Down, Balder, down! I am not in the humour for foolery."

In fact, Cedric, as we have observed, was in no very placid state of mind. The Lady Rowena, who had been absent to attend an evening mass at a distant church, had but just returned, and was changing her garments, which had been wetted by the storm. There was as yet no tidings of Gurth and his charge, which should long since have been driven home from the forest; and such was the insecurity of the period, as to render it probable that the delay might be explained by some depredation of the outlaws, with whom the adjacent forest abounded, or by the violence of some neighbouring baron, whose consciousness of strength made him equally negligent of the laws of property. The matter was of consequence, for great part of the domestic wealth of the Saxon proprietors consisted in numerous herds of swine, especially in forest land, where those animals easily found their food.

Besides these subjects of anxiety, the Saxon thane was impatient for the presence of his favourite clown Wamba, whose jests, such as they were, served for a sort of seasoning to his evening meal, and to the deep draughts of ale and wine with which he was in the habit of accompanying it. Add to all this, Cedric had fasted since noon, and his usual supper hour was long past, a cause of irritation common to country squires, both in ancient and modern times. His displeasure was expressed in broken sentences, partly muttered to himself, partly addressed to the domestics who stood around; and particularly to his cupbearer, who offered him from time to time, as a sedative, a silver goblet filled with wine— "Why tarries the Lady Rowena?"

"She is but changing her head-gear," replied the female attendant, with as much confidence as the favourite lady's maid usually answers the master of a modern family; "you would not wish her to sit down to the banquet in her hood and kirtle? and no lady within the shire can be quicker in arraying herself than my mistress."

This undeniable argument produced a sort of acquiescent umph! on the part of the Saxon, with the addition, "I wish her devotion may choose fair weather for the next visit to St. John's Kirk;—but what, in the name of ten devils," continued he, turning to the cupbearer, and raising his voice, as if happy to have found a channel into which he might divert his indignation without fear or control—"what, in the name of ten devils, keeps Gurth so long a-field? I suppose we shall have an evil account of the herd; he was wont to be a faithful and cautious drudge, and I had destined him for something better; perchance I might even have made him one of my warders." [1]

Oswald the cupbearer modestly suggested, "that it was scarce an hour since the tolling of the curfew;" an ill-chosen apology, since it turned upon a topic so harsh to Saxon ears.

"The foul fiend," exclaimed Cedric, "take the curfew-bell, and the tyrannical bastard by whom it was devised, and the heartless slave who

---

[1] The original has *Cnichts*, by which the Saxons seem to have designated a class of military attendants, sometimes free, sometimes bondsmen, but always ranking above an ordinary domestic, whether in the royal household or in those of the aldermen and thanes. But the term cnicht, now spelt knight, having been received into the English language as equivalent to the Norman word chevalier, I have avoided using it in its more ancient sense, to prevent confusion.   L. T.

names it with a Saxon tongue to a Saxon ear! The curfew!" he added, pausing, "ay, the curfew; which compels true men to extinguish their lights, that thieves and robbers may work their deeds in darkness!—Ay, the curfew;—Reginald Front-de-Bœuf and Philip de Malvoisin know the use of the curfew as well as William the Bastard himself, or e'er a Norman adventurer that fought at Hastings. I shall hear, I guess, that my property has been swept off to save from starving the hungry banditti, whom they cannot support but by theft and robbery. My faithful slave is murdered, and my goods are taken for a prey—and Wamba—where is Wamba? Said not some one he had gone forth with Gurth?"

Oswald replied in the affirmative.

"Ay? why this is better and better! he is carried off too, the Saxon fool, to serve the Norman lord. Fools are we all indeed that serve them, and fitter subjects for their scorn and laughter, than if we were born with but half our wits. But I will be avenged," he added, starting from his chair in impatience at the supposed injury, and catching hold of his boar-spear; "I will go with my complaint to the great council; I have friends, I have followers—man to man will I appeal the Norman to the lists; let him come in his plate and his mail, and all that can render cowardice bold; I have sent such a javelin as this through a stronger fence than three of their war shields!—Haply they think me old; but they shall find, alone and childless as I am, the blood of Hereward is in the veins of Cedric.—Ah, Wilfred, Wilfred!" he exclaimed in a lower tone, "couldst thou have ruled thine unreasonable passion, thy father had not been left in his age like the solitary oak, that throws out its shattered and unprotected branches against the full sweep of the tempest!" The reflection seemed to conjure into sadness his irritated feelings. Replacing his javelin, he resumed his seat, bent his looks downward, and appeared to be absorbed in melancholy reflection.

From his musing, Cedric was suddenly awakened by the blast of a horn, which was replied to by the clamorous yells and barking of all the dogs in the hall, and some twenty or thirty which were quartered in other parts of the building. It cost some exercise of the white truncheon well seconded by the exertions of the domestics, to silence this canine clamour.

"To the gate, knaves!" said the Saxon, hastily, as soon as the tumult was so much appeased that the dependants could hear his voice. "See what tidings that horn tells us of—to announce I ween, some hership and robbery which has been done upon my lands."

Returning in less than three minutes, a warder announced, "that the Prior Aymer of Jorvaulx, and the good knight Brian de Bois-Guilbert, commander of the valiant and venerable order of Knights Templars, with a small retinue, requested hospitality and lodging for the night, being on their way to a tournament which was to be held not far from Ashby-de-la-Zouche, on the second day from the present."

"Aymer, the Prior Aymer? Brian de Bois-Guilbert?"—muttered Ced-

ric; "Normans both;—but Norman or Saxon, the hospitality of Rotherwood must not be impeached; they are welcome, since they have chosen
to halt—more welcome would they have been to have ridden further
on their way—But it were unworthy to murmur for a night's lodging and
a night's food; in the quality of guests, at least, even Normans must suppress their insolence.—Go, Hundebert," he added, to a sort of major-
domo who stood behind him with a white wand; "take six of the
attendants, and introduce the strangers to the guests' lodging. Look after
their horses and mules, and see their train lack nothing. Let them have
change of vestments if they require it, and fire, and water to wash, and
wine and ale; and bid the cooks add what they hastily can to our evening
meal; and let it be put on the board when those strangers are ready to
share it. Say to them, Hundebert, that Cedric would himself bid them
welcome, but he is under a vow never to step more than three steps from
the dais of his own hall to meet any who shares not the blood of Saxon
royalty. Begone! see them carefully tended; let them not say in their
pride, the Saxon churl has shown at once his poverty and his avarice."

The major-domo departed with several attendants, to execute his
master's commands. "The Prior Aymer!" repeated Cedric, looking to
Oswald, "the brother, if I mistake not, of Giles de Mauleverer, now lord
of Middleham?"

Oswald made a respectful sign of assent. "His brother sits in the seat,
and usurps the patrimony, of a better race, the race of Ulfgar of Middleham! but what Norman lord doth not the same? This Prior is, they
say, a free and jovial priest, who loves the wine-cup and the bugle-horn
better than bell and book: Good; let him come, he shall be welcome.
How named ye the Templar?"

"Brian de Bois-Guilbert."

"Bois-Guilbert," said Cedric, still in the musing, half-arguing tone,
which the habit of living among dependants had accustomed him to employ, and which resembled a man who talks to himself rather than to those
around him—"Bois-Guilbert? that name has been spread wide both for
good and evil. They say he is valiant as the bravest of his order; but
stained with their usual vices, pride, arrogance, cruelty, and voluptuous-
ness; a hard-hearted man, who knows neither fear of earth, nor awe of
heaven. So say the few warriors who have returned from Palestine.—
Well; it is but for one night; he shall be welcome too.—Oswald, broach
the oldest wine-cask; place the best mead, the mightiest ale, the richest
morat, the most sparkling cider, the most odoriferous pigments,[1] upon
the board; fill the largest horns—Templars and Abbots love good wines
and good measure.—Elgitha, let thy Lady Rowena know we shall not
this night expect her in the hall, unless such be her especial pleasure."

---

[1] These were drinks used by the Saxons, as we are informed by Mr. Turner:
Morat was made of honey flavoured with the juice of mulberries; Pigment was a
sweet and rich liquor, composed of wine highly spiced, and sweetened also with
honey; the other liquors need no explanation.—L. T.

"But it will be her especial pleasure," answered Elgitha, with great readiness, "for she is ever desirous to hear the latest news from Palestine."

Cedric darted at the forward damsel a glance of hasty resentment; but Rowena, and whatever belonged to her, were privileged and secure from his anger. He only replied, "Silence, maiden; thy tongue outruns thy discretion. Say my message to thy mistress, and let her do her pleasure. Here, at least, the descendant of Alfred still reigns a princess." Elgitha left the apartment.

"Palestine!" repeated the Saxon; "Palestine! how many ears are turned to the tales which dissolute crusaders, or hypocritical pilgrims, bring from that fatal land! I too might ask—I too might enquire—I too might listen with a beating heart to fables which the wily strollers devise to cheat us into hospitality—but no—The son who has disobeyed me is no longer mine; nor will I concern myself more for his fate than for that of the most worthless among the millions that ever shaped the cross on their shoulder, rushed into excess and blood-guiltiness, and called it an accomplishment of the will of God."

He knit his brows, and fixed his eyes for an instant on the ground; as he raised them, the folding doors at the bottom of the hall were cast wide, and, preceded by the major-domo with his wand, and four domestics bearing blazing torches, the guests of the evening entered the apartment.

CHAPTER IV

With sheep and shaggy goats the porkers bled,
And the proud steer was on the marble spread;
With fire prepared, they deal the morsels round,
Wine rosy bright the brimming goblets crown'd.
.   .   .   .   .   .
Disposed apart, Ulysses shares the treat;
A trivet table and ignobler seat,
The Prince assigns——
Odyssey, Book 21.

THE Prior Aymer had taken the opportunity afforded him, of changing his riding robe for one of yet more costly materials over which he wore a cope curiously embroidered. Besides the massive golden signet ring, which marked his ecclesiastical dignity, his fingers, though contrary to the canon, were loaded with precious gems; his sandals were of the finest leather which was imported from Spain; his beard trimmed to as small dimensions as his order would possibly permit, and his shaven crown concealed by a scarlet cap richly embroidered.

The appearance of the Knight Templar was also changed; and, though less studiously bedecked with ornament, his dress was as rich, and his appearance far more commanding, than that of his companion. He had exchanged his shirt of mail for an under tunic of dark purple silk, garnished with furs, over which flowed his long robe of spotless white, in ample folds. The eight-pointed cross of his order was cut on the shoulder of his mantle in black velvet. The high cap no longer invested his brows, which were only shaded by short and thick curled hair of a raven blackness, corresponding to his unusually swart complexion. Nothing could be more gracefully majestic than his step and manner, had they not been marked by a predominant air of haughtiness, easily acquired by the exercise of unresisted authority.

These two dignified persons were followed by their respective attendants, and at a more humble distance by their guide, whose figure had nothing more remarkable than it derived from the usual weeds of a pilgrim. A cloak or mantle, of coarse black serge enveloped his whole body. It was in shape something like the cloak of a modern hussar, having similar flaps for covering the arms, and was called a *Sclaveyn*, or *Sclavonian*. Coarse sandals, bound with thongs, on his bare feet; a broad and shadowy hat, with cockle-shells stitched on its brim, and a long staff shod with iron, to the upper end of which was attached a branch of palm, completed the palmer's attire. He followed modestly the last of the train which entered the hall, and, observing that the lower table scarce afforded room sufficient for the domestics of Cedric and the retinue of his guests, he withdrew to a settle placed beside and almost under one of the large chimneys, and seemed to employ himself in drying his garments, until the retreat of some one should make room at the board, or the hospitality of the steward should supply him with refreshments in the place he had chosen apart.

Cedric rose to receive his guests with an air of dignified hospitality, and, descending from the dais, or elevated part of his hall, made three steps towards them, and then awaited their approach.

"I grieve," he said, "reverend Prior, that my vow binds me to advance no farther upon this floor of my fathers, even to receive such guests as you, and this valiant Knight of the Holy Temple. But my steward has expounded to you the cause of my seeming discourtesy. Let me also pray, that you will excuse my speaking to you in my native language, and that you will reply in the same if your knowledge of it permits; if not, I sufficiently understand Norman to follow your meaning."

"Vows," said the Abbot, "must be unloosed, worthy Franklin, or permit me rather to say, worthy Thane, though the title is antiquated. Vows are the knots which tie us to Heaven—they are the cords which bind the sacrifice to the horns of the altar,—and are therefore—as I said before—to be unloosened and discharged, unless our Holy Mother Church shall pronounce the contrary. And respecting language, I willingly hold communication in that spoken by my respected grandmother, Hilda of Middleham, who died in odour of sanctity, little short, if we may presume to say so, of her glorious namesake, the blessed Saint Hilda of Whitby, God be gracious to her soul!"

When the Prior had ceased what he meant as a conciliatory harangue, his companion said briefly and emphatically, "I speak ever French, the language of King Richard and his nobles; but I understand English sufficiently to communicate with the natives of that country."

Cedric darted at the speaker one of those hasty and impatient glances, which comparisons between the two rival nations seldom failed to call forth; but, recollecting the duties of hospitality, he suppressed further show of resentment, and, motioning with his hand, caused his guests to assume two seats a little lower than his own, but placed close beside him, and gave a signal that the evening meal should be placed upon the board.

While the attendants hastened to obey Cedric's commands, his eye distinguished Gurth the swineherd, who, with his companion Wamba, had just entered the hall. "Send these loitering knaves up hither," said the Saxon, impatiently. And when the culprits came before the dais,—"How comes it, villains! that you have loitered abroad so late as this! Hast thou brought home thy charge, sirrah Gurth, or hast thou left them to robbers and marauders?"

"The herd is safe, so please ye," said Gurth.

"But it does not please me, thou knave," said Cedric, "that I should be made to suppose otherwise for two hours, and sit here devising vengeance against my neighbours for wrongs they have not done me. I tell thee, shackles and the prison-house shall punish the next offence of this kind."

Gurth, knowing his master's irritable temper, attempted no exculpation; but the Jester, who could presume upon Cedric's tolerance, by virtue of his privileges as a fool, replied for them both; "In troth, uncle Cedric, you are neither wise nor reasonable to-night."

"How, sir?" said his master; "you shall to the porter's lodge, and taste of the discipline there, if you give your foolery such license."

"First let your wisdom tell me," said Wamba, "is it just and reasonable to punish one person for the fault of another?"

"Certainly not, fool," answered Cedric.

"Then why should you shackle poor Gurth, uncle, for the fault of his dog Fangs? for I dare be sworn we lost not a minute by the way, when we had got our herd together, which Fangs did not manage until we heard the vesper-bell."

"Then hang up Fangs," said Cedric, turning hastily towards the swine-herd, "if the fault is his, and get thee another dog."

"Under favour, uncle," said the Jester, "that were still somewhat on the bow-hand of fair justice; for it was no fault of Fangs that he was lame and could not gather the herd, but the fault of those that struck off two of his fore-claws, an operation for which, if the poor fellow had been consulted, he would scarce have given his voice."

"And who dared to lame an animal which belonged to my bondsman?" said the Saxon, kindling in wrath.

"Marry, that did old Hubert," said Wamba, "Sir Philip de Malvoisin's keeper of the chase. He caught Fangs strolling in the forest, and said he chased the deer contrary to his master's right, as warden of the walk."

"The foul fiend take Malvoisin," answered the Saxon, "and his keeper both! I will teach them that the wood was disforested in terms of the great Forest Charter. But enough of this. Go to, knave, go to thy place—and thou, Gurth, get thee another dog, and should the keeper dare to touch it, I will mar his archery; the curse of a coward on my head, if I strike not off the forefinger of his right hand!—he shall draw bowstring no more.—I crave your pardon, my worthy guests. I am beset here with neighbours that match your infidels, Sir Knight, in Holy Land. But your homely fare is before you; feed, and let welcome make amends for hard fare."

The feast, however, which was spread upon the board, needed no apologies from the lord of the mansion. Swine's flesh, dressed in several modes, appeared on the lower part of the board, as also that of fowls, deer, goats, and hares, and various kinds of fish, together with huge loaves and cakes of bread, and sundry confections made of fruits and honey. The smaller sorts of wild-fowl, of which there was abundance, were not served up in platters, but brought in upon small wooden spits or broaches, and offered by the pages and domestics who bore them, to each guest in succession, who cut from them such a portion as he pleased. Beside each person of rank was placed a goblet of silver; the lower board was accommodated with large drinking horns.

When the repast was about to commence, the major-domo, or steward, suddenly raising his wand, said aloud,—"Forbear!—Place for the Lady Rowena." A side-door at the upper end of the hall now opened behind the banquet table, and Rowena, followed by four female attendants, entered the apartment. Cedric, though surprised, and perhaps not altogether agreeably so, at his ward appearing in public on this occasion, hastened to meet her, and to conduct her, with respectful ceremony, to the elevated seat at his own right hand, appropriated to the lady of the mansion. All stood up to receive her; and, replying to their courtesy by a mute gesture of salutation, she moved gracefully forward to assume her place at the board. Ere she had time to do so, the Templar whispered to the Prior, "I shall wear no collar of gold of yours at the tournament. the Chian wine is your own."

"Said I not so?" answered the Prior; "but check your raptures, the Franklin observes you."

Unheeding this remonstrance, and accustomed only to act upon the immediate impulse of his own wishes, Brian de Bois-Guilbert kept his eyes riveted on the Saxon beauty, more striking perhaps to his imagination, because differing widely from those of the Eastern sultanas.

Formed in the best proportions of her sex, Rowena was tall in stature, yet not so much as to attract observation on account of superior height. Her complexion was exquisitely fair, but the noble cast of her head and features prevented the insipidity which sometimes attaches to fair beauties. Her clear blue eye, which sate enshrined beneath a graceful eyebrow of brown sufficiently marked to give expression to the forehead, seemed capable to kindle as well as melt, to command as well as to beseech. If mildness were the more natural expression of such a combination of features, it was plain, that in the present instance, the exercise of habitual superiority, and the reception of general homage, had given to the Saxon lady a loftier character, which mingled with and qualified that bestowed by nature. Her profuse hair, of a colour betwixt brown and flaxen, was arranged in a fanciful and graceful manner in numerous ringlets, to form which art had probably aided nature. These locks were braided with gems, and being worn at full length, intimated the noble birth and free-born condition of the maiden. A golden chain, to which was attached a small reliquary of the same metal, hung round her neck. She wore bracelets on her arms, which were bare. Her dress was an undergown and kirtle of pale sea-green silk, over which hung a long loose robe, which reached to the ground, having very wide sleeves, which came down, however, very little below the elbow. This robe was crimson, and manufactured out of the very finest wool. A veil of silk, interwoven with gold, was attached to the upper part of it, which could be, at the wearer's pleasure, either drawn over the face and bosom after the Spanish fashion, or disposed as a sort of drapery round the shoulders.

When Rowena perceived the Knight Templar's eyes bent on her with an ardour that, compared with the dark caverns under which they moved, gave them the effect of lighted charcoal, she drew with dignity the veil around her face, as an intimation that the determined freedom of his glance was disagreeable. Cedric saw the motion and its cause. "Sir Templar," said he, "the cheeks of our Saxon maidens have seen too little of the sun to enable them to bear the fixed glance of a crusader."

"If I have offended," replied Sir Brian, "I crave your pardon—that is, I crave the Lady Rowena's pardon—for my humility will carry me no lower."

"The Lady Rowena," said the Prior, "has punished us all, in chastising the boldness of my friend. Let me hope she will be less cruel to the splendid train which are to meet at the tournament."

"Our going thither," said Cedric, "is uncertain. I love not these vanities, which were unknown to my fathers when England was free."

"Let us hope, nevertheless," said the Prior, "our company may determine you to travel thitherward; when the roads are so unsafe, the escort of Sir Brian de Bois-Guilbert is not to be despised."

"Sir Prior," answered the Saxon, "wheresoever I have travelled in this land, I have hitherto found myself, with the assistance of my good sword and faithful followers, in no respect needful of other aid. At present, if we indeed journey to Ashby-de-la-Zouche, we do so with my noble neighbour and countryman, Athelstane of Coningsburgh, and with such a train as would set outlaws and feudal enemies at defiance.——I drink to you, Sir Prior, in this cup of wine, which I trust your taste will approve, and I thank you for your courtesy. Should you be so rigid in adhering to monastic rule," he added, "as to prefer your acid preparation of milk, I hope you will not strain courtesy to do me reason."

"Nay," said the Priest, laughing, "it is only in our abbey that we con-fine ourselves to the *lac dulce* or the *lac acidum* either. Conversing with the world, we use the world's fashion, and therefore I answer your pledge in this honest wine, and leave the weaker liquor to my lay-brother."

"And I," said the Templar, filling his goblet, "drink wassail to the fair Rowena; for since her namesake introduced the word into England, has never been one more worthy of such a tribute. By my faith, I could pardon the unhappy Vortigorn, had he half the cause that we now wit-ness, for making shipwreck of his honour and his kingdom."

"I will spare your courtesy, Sir Knight," said Rowena with dignity, and without unveiling herself; "or rather I will tax it so far as to require of you the latest news from Palestine, a theme more agreeable to our English ears, than the compliments which your French breeding teaches."

"I have little of importance to say, lady," answered Sir Brian de Bois-Guilbert, "excepting the confirmed tidings of a truce with Saladin."

He was interrupted by Wamba, who had taken his appropriated seat upon a chair, the back of which was decorated with two ass's ears, and which was placed about two steps behind that of his master, who, from time to time, supplied him with victuals from his own trencher; a favour, however, which the Jester shared with the favourite dogs, of whom, as we have already noticed, there were several in attendance. Here sat Wamba, with a small table before him, his heels tucked up against the bar of the chair, his cheeks sucked up so as to make his jaws resemble a pair of nut-crackers, and his eyes half shut, yet watching with alert-ness every opportunity to exercise his licensed foolery.

"These truces with the infidels," he exclaimed, without caring how suddenly he interrupted the stately Templar, "make an old man of me!"

"Go to, knave, how so?" said Cedric, his features prepared to receive favourably the expected jest.

"Because," answered Wamba, "I remember three of them in my day, each of which was to endure for the course of fifty years; so that, by computation, I must be at least a hundred and fifty years old."

"I will warrant you against dying of old age, however," said the Templar, who now recognised his friend of the forest; "I will assure you from all deaths but a violent one, if you give such directions to way-farers as you did this night to the Prior and me."

"How, sirrah!" said Cedric, "misdirect travellers? We must have you whipt; you are at least as much rogue as fool."

"I pray thee, uncle," answered the Jester, "let my folly for once pro-tect my roguery. I did but make a mistake between my right hand and my left; and he might have pardoned a greater, who took a fool for his counsellor and guide."

Conversation was here interrupted by the entrance of the porter's page, who announced that there was a stranger at the gate, imploring admittance and hospitality.

"Admit him," said Cedric, "be he who or what he may;—a night like that which roars without, compels even wild animals to herd with tame, and to seek the protection of man, their mortal foe, rather than perish by the elements. Let his wants be ministered to with all care—look to it, Oswald."

And the steward left the banqueting hall to see the commands of his patron obeyed.

CHAPTER V

Hath not a Jew eyes? Hath not a Jew hands, organs, dimensions, senses, affections, passions? Fed with the same food, hurt with the same weapons, subject to the same diseases, healed by the same means, warmed and cooled by the same winter and summer, as a Christian is?

Merchant of Venice.

OSWALD, returning, whispered into the ear of his master, "It is a Jew, who calls himself Isaac of York; is it fit I should marshal him into the hall?"

"Let Gurth do thine office, Oswald," said Wamba with his usual effrontery; "the swineherd will be a fit usher to the Jew."

"St. Mary," said the Abbot, crossing himself, "an unbelieving Jew, and admitted into this presence!"

"A dog Jew," echoed the Templar, "to approach a defender of the Holy Sepulchre?"

"By my faith," said Wamba, "it would seem the Templars love the Jews' inheritance better than they do their company."

"Peace, my worthy guests," said Cedric; "my hospitality must not be bounded by your dislikes. If Heaven bore with the whole nation of stiff-necked unbelievers for more years than a layman can number, we may endure the presence of one Jew for a few hours. But I constrain no man to converse or to feed with him.—Let him have a board and a morsel apart,—unless," he said smiling, "these turban'd strangers will admit his society."

"Sir Franklin," answered the Templar, "my Saracen slaves are true Moslems, and scorn as much as any Christian to hold intercourse with a Jew."

"Now, in faith," said Wamba, "I cannot see that the worshippers of Mahound and Termagaunt have so greatly the advantage over the people once chosen by Heaven."

"He shall sit with thee, Wamba," said Cedric; "the fool and the knave will be well met."

"The fool," answered Wamba, raising the relics of a gammon of bacon, "will take care to erect a bulwark against the knave."

"Hush," said Cedric, "for here he comes."

Introduced with little ceremony, and advancing with fear and hesitation, and many a bow of deep humility, a tall thin old man, who, however, had lost by the habit of stooping much of his actual height, approached the lower end of the board. His features, keen and regular, with an aquiline nose, and piercing black eyes; his high and wrinkled forehead, and long grey hair and beard, would have been considered as handsome, had they not been the marks of a physiognomy peculiar to a race which, during those dark ages, was alike detested by the credulous and prejudiced vulgar, and persecuted by the greedy and rapacious nobility, and who, perhaps, owing to that very hatred and persecution, had adopted a national character, in which there was much, to say the least, mean and unamiable.

The Jew's dress, which appeared to have suffered considerably from the storm, was a plain russet cloak of many folds, covering a dark purple tunic. He had large boots lined with fur, and a belt around his waist, which sustained a small knife, together with a case for writing materials, but no weapon. He wore a high square yellow cap of a peculiar fashion, assigned to his nation to distinguish them from Christians, and which he doffed with great humility at the door of the hall.

The reception of this person in the hall of Cedric the Saxon, was such as might have satisfied the most prejudiced enemy of the tribes of Israel. Cedric himself coldly nodded in answer to the Jew's repeated salutations, and signed to him to take place at the lower end of the table, where, however, no one offered to make room for him. On the contrary, as he passed along the file, casting a timid supplicating glance, and turning towards each of those who occupied the lower end of the board, the Saxon domestics squared their shoulders, and continued to devour their supper with great perseverance, paying not the least attention to the wants of the new guest. The attendants of the Abbot crossed themselves, with looks of pious horror, and the very heathen Saracens, as Isaac drew near them, curled up their whiskers with indignation, and laid their hands on their poniards, as if ready to rid themselves by the most desperate means from the apprehended contamination of his nearer approach.

Probably the same motives which induced Cedric to open his hall to this son of a rejected people, would have made him insist on his attendants receiving Isaac with more courtesy. But the Abbot had, at this moment, engaged him in a most interesting discussion on the breed and character of his favourite hounds, which he would not have interrupted for matters of much greater importance than that of a Jew going to bed supperless. While Isaac thus stood an outcast in the present society, like his people among the nations, looking in vain for welcome or resting place, the pilgrim who sat by the chimney took compassion upon him, and resigned his seat, saying briefly, "Old man, my garments are dried, my hunger is appeased, thou art both wet and fasting." So saying, he gathered together, and brought to a flame, the decaying brands which lay scattered on the ample hearth; took from the larger board a mess of pottage and seethed kid, placed it upon the small table at which he had himself supped, and, without waiting the Jew's thanks, went to the other side of the hall;—whether from unwillingness to hold more close communication with the object of his benevolence, or from a wish to draw near to the upper end of the table, seemed uncertain.

Had there been painters in those days capable to execute such a subject, the Jew, as he bent his withered form, and expanded his chilled and trembling hands over the fire, would have formed no bad emblematical personification of the Winter season. Having dispelled the cold, he turned eagerly to the smoking mess which was placed before him, and ate with a haste and an apparent relish, that seemed to betoken long abstinence from food.

Meanwhile the Abbot and Cedric continued their discourse upon hunting; the Lady Rowena seemed engaged in conversation with one of her attendant females; and the haughty Templar, whose eye seemed to wander from the Jew to the Saxon beauty, revolved in his mind thoughts which appeared deeply to interest him.

"I marvel, worthy Cedric," said the Abbot, as their discourse proceeded, "that, great as your predilection is for your own manly language, you do not receive the Norman-French into your favour, so far at least as the mystery of wood-craft and hunting is concerned. Surely no tongue is so rich in the various phrases which the field-sports demand, or furnishes means to the experienced woodman so well to express his jovial art."

"Good Father Aymer," said the Saxon, "be it known to you, I care not for those over-sea refinements, without which I can well enough take my pleasure in the woods. I can wind my horn, though I call not the blast either a *recheate* or a *morte*—I can cheer my dogs on the prey, and I can flay and quarter the animal when it is brought down, without using the new-fangled jargon of *curee, arbor, nombles,* and all the babble of the fabulous Sir Tristrem." [1]

"The French," said the Templar, raising his voice with the presumptuous and authoritative tone which he used upon all occasions, "is not only the natural language of the chase, but that of love and of war, in which ladies should be won and enemies defied."

"Pledge me in a cup of wine, Sir Templar," said Cedric, "and fill an-

---

[1] There was no language which the Normans more formally separated from that of common life than the terms of the chase. The objects of their pursuit, whether bird or animal, changed their name each year, and there were a hundred conventional terms, to be ignorant of which was to be without one of the distinguishing marks of a gentleman. The reader may consult Dame Juliana Berners' book on the subject. The origin of this science was imputed to the celebrated Sir Tristrem, famous for his tragic intrigue with the beautiful Ysolte. As the Normans reserved the amusement of hunting strictly to themselves, the terms of this formal jargon were all taken from the French language.

other to the Abbot, while I look back some thirty years to tell you another tale. As Cedric the Saxon then was, his plain English tale needed no garnish from French troubadours, when it was told in the ear of beauty; and the field of Northallerton, upon the day of the Holy Standard, could tell whether the Saxon war-cry was not heard as far within the ranks of the Scottish host as the *cri de guerre* of the boldest Norman baron. To the memory of the brave who fought there!—Pledge me, my guests." He drank deep, and went on with increasing warmth. "Ay, that was a day of cleaving of shields, when a hundred banners were bent forward over the heads of the valiant, and blood flowed round like water, and death was held better than flight. A Saxon bard had called it a feast of the swords—a gathering of the eagles to the prey—the clashing of bills upon shield and helmet, the shouting of battle more joyful than the clamour of a bridal. But our bards are no more," he said; "our deeds are lost in those of another race—our language—our very name—is hastening to decay, and none mourns for it save one solitary old man— Cupbearer! knave, fill the goblets—To the strong in arms, Sir Temple, be their race or language what it will, who now bear them best in Palestine among the champions of the Cross!"

"It becomes one not wearing this badge to answer," said Sir Brian de Bois-Guilbert; "yet to whom, besides the sworn Champions of the Holy Sepulchre, can the palm be assigned among the champions of the Cross?"

"To the Knights Hospitallers," said the Abbot; "I have a brother of their order."

"I impeach not their fame," said the Templar; "nevertheless"——

"I think, friend Cedric," said Wamba, interfering, "that had Richard of the Lion's Heart been wise enough to have taken a fool's advice, he might have staid at home with his merry Englishmen, and left the recovery of Jerusalem to those same Knights who had most to do with the loss of it."

"Were there, then, none in the English army," said the Lady Rowena, "whose names are worthy to be mentioned with the Knights of the Temple, and of St. John?"

"Forgive me, lady," replied de Bois-Guilbert; "the English monarch did, indeed, bring to Palestine a host of gallant warriors, second only to those whose breasts have been the unceasing bulwark of that blessed land."

"Second to NONE," said the Pilgrim, who had stood near enough to hear, and had listened to this conversation with marked impatience. All turned towards the spot from whence this unexpected asseveration was heard. "I say," repeated the Pilgrim in a firm and strong voice, "that the English chivalry were second to NONE who ever drew sword in defence of the Holy Land. I say besides, for I saw it, that King Richard himself, and five of his knights, held a tournament after the taking of St. John-de-Acre, as challengers against all comers. I say that, on that day, each knight ran three courses, and cast to the ground three antagonists. I add, that seven of these assailants were Knights of the Temple—and Sir Brian de Bois-Guilbert well knows the truth of what I tell you."

It is impossible for language to describe the bitter scowl of rage which rendered yet darker the swarthy countenance of the Templar. In the extremity of his resentment and confusion, his quivering fingers griped towards the handle of his sword, and perhaps only withdrew, from the consciousness that no act of violence could be safely executed in that place and presence. Cedric, whose feelings were all of a right onward and simple kind, and were seldom occupied by more than one object at once, omitted, in the joyous glee with which he heard of the glory of his countrymen, to remark the angry confusion of his guest; "I would give thee this golden bracelet, Pilgrim," he said, "couldst thou tell me the names of those knights who upheld so gallantly the renown of merry England."

"That will I do blithely," replied the Pilgrim, "and without guerdon; my oath, for a time, prohibits me from touching gold."

"I will wear the bracelet for you, if you will, friend Palmer," said Wamba.

"The first in honour as in arms, in renown as in place," said the Pilgrim, "was the brave Richard, King of England."

"I forgive him," said Cedric; "I forgive him his descent from the tyrant Duke William."

"The Earl of Leicester was the second," continued the Pilgrim; "Sir Thomas Multon of Gilsland was the third."

"Of Saxon descent, he at least," said Cedric, with exultation.

"Sir Foulk Doilly the fourth," proceeded the Pilgrim.

"Saxon also, at least by the mother's side," continued Cedric, who listened with the utmost eagerness, and forgot, in part at least, his hatred to the Normans, in the common triumph of the King of England and his islanders. "And who was the fifth?" he demanded.

"The fifth was Sir Edwin Turneham."

"Genuine Saxon, by the soul of Hengist!" shouted Cedric—"And the sixth?" he continued with eagerness—"how name you the sixth?"

"The sixth," said the Palmer, after a pause, in which he seemed to recollect himself, "was a young knight of lesser renown and lower rank, assumed into that honourable company, less to aid their enterprise than to make up their number—his name dwells not in my memory."

"Sir Palmer," said Sir Brian de Bois-Guilbert scornfully, "this assumed forgetfulness, after so much has been remembered, comes too late to serve your purpose. I will myself tell the name of the knight before whose lance fortune and my horse's fault occasioned my falling—it was the Knight of Ivanhoe; nor was there one of the six that, for his years, had more renown in arms.—Yet this will I say, and loudly—that were he in England, and durst repeat, in this week's tournament, the challenge of St. John-de-Acre, I, mounted and armed as I now am, would give him every advantage of weapons, and abide the result."

"Your challenge would be soon answered," replied the Palmer, "were your antagonist near you. As the matter is, disturb not the peaceful hall with vaunts of the issue of the conflict, which you well know cannot take place. If Ivanhoe ever returns from Palestine, I will be his surety that he meets you."

"A goodly security!" said the Knight Templar; "and what do you proffer as a pledge?"

"This reliquary," said the Palmer, taking a small ivory box from his bosom, and crossing himself, "containing a portion of the true cross, brought from the Monastery of Mount Carmel."

The Prior of Jorvaulx crossed himself and repeated a paternoster, in which all devoutly joined, excepting the Jew, the Mahomedans, and the Templar; the latter of whom, without vailing his bonnet, or testifying any reverence for the alleged sanctity of the relic, took from his neck a gold chain, which he flung on the board, saying—"Let Prior Aymer hold my pledge and that of this nameless vagrant, in token that when the Knight of Ivanhoe comes within the four seas of Britain, he underlies the challenge of Brian de Bois-Guilbert, which, if he answer not, I will proclaim him as a coward on the walls of every Temple Court in Europe."

"It will not need," said the Lady Rowena, breaking silence; "My voice shall be heard, if no other in this hall is raised in behalf of the absent Ivanhoe. I affirm he will meet fairly every honourable challenge. Could my weak warrant add security to the inestimable pledge of this holy pilgrim, I would pledge name and fame that Ivanhoe gives this proud knight the meeting he desires."

A crowd of conflicting emotions seemed to have occupied Cedric, and kept him silent during this discussion. Gratified pride, resentment, embarrassment, chased each other over his broad and open brow, like the shadow of clouds drifting over a harvest-field; while his attendants, on whom the name of the sixth knight seemed to produce an effect almost electrical, hung in suspense upon their master's looks. But when Rowena spoke, the sound of her voice seemed to startle him from his silence.

"Lady," said Cedric, "this beseems not; were further pledge necessary, I myself, offended, and justly offended, as I am, would yet gage my honour for the honour of Ivanhoe. But the wager of battle is complete, even according to the fantastic fashions of Norman chivalry—Is it not, Father Aymer?"

"It is," replied the Prior; "and the blessed relic and rich chain will I bestow safely in the treasury of our convent, until the decision of this warlike challenge."

Having thus spoken, he crossed himself again and again, and after many genuflections and muttered prayers, he delivered the reliquary to Brother Ambrose, his attendant monk, while he himself swept up with less ceremony, but perhaps with no less internal satisfaction, the golden chain, and bestowed it in a pouch lined with perfumed leather, which opened under his arm. "And now, Sir Cedric," he said, "my ears are chiming vespers with the strength of your good wine—permit us another pledge to the welfare of the Lady Rowena, and indulge us with liberty to pass to our repose."

"By the Rood of Bromholme," said the Saxon, "you do but small credit to your fame, Sir Prior! Report speaks you a bonny monk, that would hear the matin chime ere he quitted his bowl; and, old as I am, I feared to have shame in encountering you. But, by my faith, a Saxon boy of twelve, in my time, would not so soon have relinquished his goblet."

The Prior had his own reasons, however, for persevering in the course of temperance which he had adopted. He was not only a professional peacemaker, but from practice a hater of all feuds and brawls. It was not altogether from a love to his neighbour, or to himself, or from a mixture of both. On the present occasion, he had an instinctive apprehension of the fiery temper of the Saxon, and saw the danger that the reckless and presumptuous spirit, of which his companion had already given so many proofs, might at length produce some disagreeable explosion. He therefore gently insinuated the incapacity of the native of any other country to engage in the genial conflict of the bowl with the hardy and strong-headed Saxons; something he mentioned, but slightly, about his own holy character, and ended by pressing his proposal to depart to repose.

The grace-cup was accordingly served round, and the guests, after making deep obeisance to their landlord and to the Lady Rowena, arose and mingled in the hall, while the heads of the family, by separate doors, retired with their attendants.

"Unbelieving dog," said the Templar to Isaac the Jew, as he passed him in the throng, "dost thou bend thy course to the tournament?"

"I do so propose," replied Isaac, bowing in all humility, "if it please your reverend valour."

"Ay," said the Knight, "to gnaw the bowels of our nobles with usury, and to gull women and boys with gauds and toys—I warrant thee store of shekels in thy Jewish scrip."

"Not a shekel, not a silver penny, not a halfling—so help me the God of Abraham!" said the Jew, clasping his hands; "I go but to seek the assistance of some brethren of my tribe to aid me to pay the fine which the Exchequer of the Jews [1] have imposed upon me—Father Jacob be my speed! I am an impoverished wretch—the very gaberdine I wear is borrowed from Reuben of Tadcaster."

The Templar smiled sourly as he replied, "Beshrew thee for a false-hearted liar!" and passing onward, as if disdaining farther conference, he communed with his Moslem slaves in a language unknown to the by-

[1] In those days the Jews were subjected to an Exchequer, specially dedicated to that purpose, and which laid them under the most exorbitant impositions.—L. T.

standers. The poor Israelite seemed so staggered by the address of the military monk, that the Templar had passed on to the extremity of the hall ere he raised his head from the humble posture which he had assumed, so far as to be sensible of his departure. And when he did look around, it was with the astonished air of one at whose feet a thunderbolt had just burst, and who hears still the astounding report ringing in his ears.

The Templar and Prior were shortly after marshalled to their sleeping apartments by the steward and the cupbearer, each attended by two torch-bearers and two servants carrying refreshments, while servants of inferior condition indicated to their retinue and to the other guests their respective places of repose.

CHAPTER VI

To buy his favour, I extend this friendship:
If he will take it, so; if not, adieu;
And, for my love, I pray you wrong me not.
                        Merchant of Venice.

As the Palmer, lighted by a domestic with a torch, past through the intricate combination of apartments of this large and irregular mansion, the cupbearer coming behind him whispered in his ear, that if he had no objection to a cup of good mead in his apartment, there were many domestics in that family who would gladly hear the news he had brought from the Holy Land, and particularly that which concerned the Knight of Ivanhoe. Wamba presently appeared to urge the same request, observing that a cup after midnight was worth three after curfew. Without disputing a maxim urged by such grave authority, the Palmer thanked them for their courtesy, but observed that he had included in his religious vow, an obligation never to speak in the kitchen on matters which were prohibited in the hall. "That vow," said Wamba to the cupbearer, "would scarce suit a serving man."

The cupbearer shrugged up his shoulders in displeasure. "I thought to have lodged him in the solere chamber," said he; "but since he is so unsocial to Christians, e'en let him take the next stall to Isaac the Jew's. —Anwold," said he to the torch-bearer, "carry the Pilgrim to the southern cell.—I give you good-night," he added, "Sir Palmer, with small thanks for short courtesy."

"Good-night, and Our Lady's benison!" said the Palmer, with composure; and his guide moved forward.

In a small antechamber, into which several doors opened, and which was lighted by a small iron lamp, they met a second interruption from the waiting-maid of Rowena, who, saying in a tone of authority, that her mistress desired to speak with the Palmer, took the torch from the hand of Anwold, and, bidding him await her return, made a sign to the Palmer to follow. Apparently he did not think it proper to decline this invitation as he had done the former; for, though his gesture indicated some surprise at the summons, he obeyed it without answer or remonstrance.

A short passage, and an ascent of seven steps, each of which was composed of a solid beam of oak, led him to the apartment of the Lady Rowena, the rude magnificence of which corresponded to the respect which was paid to her by the lord of the mansion. The walls were covered with embroidered hangings, on which different-coloured silks, interwoven with gold and silver threads, had been employed with all the art of which the age was capable, to represent the sports of hunting and hawking. The bed was adorned with the same rich tapestry, and surrounded with curtains dyed with purple. The seats had also their stained coverings, and one, which was higher than the rest, was accommodated with a footstool of ivory, curiously carved.

No fewer than four silver candelabra, holding great waxen torches, served to illuminate this apartment. Yet let not modern beauty envy the magnificence of a Saxon princess. The walls of the apartment were so ill-finished and so full of crevices, that the rich hangings shook to the night blast, and, in despite of a sort of screen intended to protect them from the wind, the flame of the torches streamed sideways into the air, like the unfurled pennon of a chieftain. Magnificence there was, with some rude attempt at taste; but of comfort there was little, and, being unknown, it was unmissed.

The Lady Rowena, with three of her attendants standing at her back, and arranging her hair ere she lay down to rest, was seated in the sort of throne already mentioned, and looked as if born to exact general homage. The Pilgrim acknowledged her claim to it by a low genuflection.

"Rise, Palmer," said she graciously. "The defender of the absent has a right to favourable reception from all who value truth, and honour manhood." She then said to her train, "Retire, excepting only Elgitha; I would speak with this holy Pilgrim."

The maidens, without leaving the apartment, retired to its further extremity, and sat down on a small bench against the wall, where they remained mute as statues, though at such a distance that their whispers could not have interrupted the conversation of their mistress.

"Pilgrim," said the lady, after a moment's pause, during which she seemed uncertain how to address him, "you this night mentioned a name—I mean," she said, with a degree of effort, "the name of Ivanhoe, in the halls where by nature and kindred it should have sounded most acceptably; and yet, such is the perverse course of fate, that of many whose hearts must have throbbed at the sound, I, only, dare ask you where, and in what condition, you left him of whom you spoke?—We heard, that, having remained in Palestine, on account of his impaired health, after the departure of the English army, he had experienced the persecution of the French faction, to whom the Templars are known to be attached."

"I know little of the Knight of Ivanhoe," answered the Palmer, with a troubled voice. "I would I knew him better, since you, lady, are interested in his fate. He hath, I believe, surmounted the persecution of his enemies in Palestine, and is on the eve of returning to England, where you, lady, must know better than I, what is his chance of happiness."

The Lady Rowena sighed deeply, and asked more particularly when the Knight of Ivanhoe might be expected in his native country, and whether he would not be exposed to great dangers by the road. On the first point, the Palmer professed ignorance; on the second, he said that the voyage might be safely made by the way of Venice and Genoa, an l from thence through France to England. "Ivanhoe," he said, "was so well acquainted with the language and manners of the French, that there was no fear of his incurring any hazard during that part of his travels."

"Would to God," said the Lady Rowena, "he were here safely arrived, and able to bear arms in the approaching tourney, in which the chivalry of this land are expected to display their address and valour. Should Athelstane of Coningsburgh obtain the prize, Ivanhoe is like to hear evil tidings when he reaches England.—How looked he, stranger, when you last saw him? Had disease laid her hand heavy upon his strength and comeliness?"

"He was darker," said the Palmer, "and thinner, than when he came from Cyprus in the train of Cœur-de-Lion, and care seemed to sit heavy on his brow; but I approached not his presence, because he is unknown to me."

"He will," said the lady, "I fear, find little in his native land to clear those clouds from his countenance. Thanks, good Pilgrim, for your information concerning the companion of my childhood.—Maidens," she said, "draw near—offer the sleeping cup to this holy man, whom I will no longer detain from repose."

One of the maidens presented a silver cup, containing a rich mixture of wine and spice, which Rowena barely put to her lips. It was then offered to the Palmer, who, after a low obeisance, tasted a few drops.

"Accept this alms, friend," continued the lady, offering a piece of gold, "in acknowledgment of thy painful travail, and of the shrines thou hast visited."

The Palmer received the boon with another low reverence, and followed Elgitha out of the apartment.

In the anteroom he found his attendant Anwold, who, taking the torch from the hand of the waiting-maid, conducted him with more haste than ceremony to an exterior and ignoble part of the building, where a number of small apartments, or rather cells, served for sleeping places to the lower order of domestics, and to strangers of mean degree.

"In which of these sleeps the Jew?" said the Pilgrim.

"The unbelieving dog," answered Anwold, "kennels in the cell next your holiness.—St. Dunstan, how it must be scraped and cleansed ere it be again fit for a Christian!"

"And where sleeps Gurth the swineherd?" said the stranger.

"Gurth," replied the bondsman, "sleeps in the cell on your right, as the Jew on that to your left; you serve to keep the child of circumcision separate from the abomination of his tribe. You might have occupied a more honourable place had you accepted of Oswald's invitation."

"It is as well as it is," said the Palmer; "the company, even of a Jew, can hardly spread contamination through an oaken partition."

So saying, he entered the cabin allotted to him, and taking the torch from the domestic's hand, thanked him, and wished him good-night. Having shut the door of his cell, he placed the torch in a candlestick made of wood, and looked around his sleeping apartment, the furniture of which was of the most simple kind. It consisted of a rude wooden stool, and still ruder hutch or bed-frame, stuffed with clean straw, and accommodated with two or three sheepskins by way of bed-clothes.

The Palmer, having extinguished his torch, threw himself, without taking off any part of his clothes, on this rude couch, and slept, or at least retained his recumbent posture, till the earliest sunbeams found their way through the little grated window, which served at once to admit both air and light to his uncomfortable cell. He then started up, and after repeating his matins, and adjusting his dress, he left it, and entered that of Isaac the Jew, lifting the latch as gently as he could.

The inmate was lying in troubled slumber upon a couch similar to that on which the Palmer himself had passed the night. Such parts of his dress as the Jew had laid aside on the preceding evening, were disposed carefully around his person, as if to prevent the hazard of their being carried off during his slumbers. There was a trouble on his brow amounting almost to agony. His hands and arms moved convulsively, as if struggling with the nightmare; and besides several ejaculations in Hebrew, the following were distinctly heard in the Norman-English, or mixed language of the country: "For the sake of the God of Abraham, spare an unhappy old man! I am poor, I am penniless—should your irons wrench my limbs asunder, I could not gratify you!"

The Palmer awaited not the end of the Jew's vision, but stirred him with his pilgrim's staff. The touch probably associated, as is usual, with some of the apprehensions excited by his dream; for the old man started up, his grey hair standing almost erect upon his head, and huddling some part of his garments about him, while he held the detached pieces with the tenacious grasp of a falcon, he fixed upon the Palmer his keen black eyes, expressive of wild surprise, and of bodily apprehension.

"Fear nothing from me, Isaac," said the Palmer, "I come as your friend."

"The God of Israel requite you," said the Jew, greatly relieved; "I dreamed—But Father Abraham be praised, it was but a dream." Then, collecting himself, he added in his usual tone, "And what may it be your pleasure to want at so early an hour with the poor Jew?"

"It is to tell you," said the Palmer, "that if you leave not this mansion instantly, and travel not with some haste, your journey may prove a dangerous one."

"Holy father!" said the Jew, "whom could it interest to endanger so poor a wretch as I am?"

"The purpose you can best guess," said the Pilgrim; "but rely on this, that when the Templar crossed the hall yesternight he spoke to his Mussulman slaves in the Saracen language, which I well understand, and charged them this morning to watch the journey of the Jew, to seize upon him when at a convenient distance from the mansion, and to conduct him to the castle of Philip de Malvoisin, or to that of Reginald Front-de-Bœuf."

It is impossible to describe the extremity of terror which seized upon the Jew at this information, and seemed at once to overpower his whole faculties. His arms fell down to his sides, and his head drooped on his breast, his knees bent under his weight, every nerve and muscle of his frame seemed to collapse and lose its energy, and he sunk at the foot of the Palmer, not in the fashion of one who intentionally stoops, kneels, or prostrates himself to excite compassion, but like a man borne down on all sides by the pressure of some invisible force, which crushes him to the earth without the power of resistance.

"Holy God of Abraham!" was his first exclamation, folding and elevating his wrinkled hands, but without raising his grey head from the pavement; "O holy Moses! O blessed Aaron! the dream is not dreamed for nought, and the vision cometh not in vain! I feel their irons already tear my sinews! I feel the rack pass over my body like the saws, and harrows, and axes of iron over the men of Rabbah, and of the cities of the children of Ammon!"

"Stand up, Isaac, and hearken to me," said the Palmer, who viewed the extremity of his distress with a compassion in which contempt was largely mingled; "you have cause for your terror, considering how your brethren have been used, in order to extort from them their hoards, both by princes and nobles; but stand up, I say, and I will point out to you the means of escape. Leave this mansion instantly, while its inmates sleep sound after the last night's revel. I will guide you by the secret paths of the forest, known as well to me as to any forester that ranges it, and I will not leave you till you are under safe conduct of some chief or baron going to the tournament, whose good-will you have probably the means of securing."

As the ears of Isaac received the hopes of escape which this speech intimated, he began gradually, and inch by inch, as it were, to raise himself up from the ground, until he fairly rested upon his knees, throwing back his long grey hair and beard, and fixing his keen black eyes upon the Palmer's face, with a look expressive at once of hope and fear, not unmingled with suspicion. But when he heard the concluding part of the sentence, his original terror appeared to revive in full force, and he dropt once more on his face, exclaiming, "*I* possess the means of securing good-will! alas! there is but one road to the favour of a Christian, and how can the poor Jew find it, whom extortions have already reduced to the misery of Lazarus?" Then, as if suspicion had overpowered his other feelings, he suddenly exclaimed, "For the love of God, young man, betray me not—for the sake of the Great Father who made us all, Jew as well as Gentile, Israelite and Ishmaelite—do me no treason! I have not means to secure the good-will of a Christian beggar, were he rating it at a single penny." As he spoke these last words, he raised himself, and grasped the Palmer's mantle with a look of the most earnest entreaty. The Pilgrim extricated himself, as if there were contamination in the touch.

"Wert thou loaded with all the wealth of thy tribe," he said, "what interest have I to injure thee?—In this dress I am vowed to poverty, nor do I change it for aught save a horse and a coat of mail. Yet think not that I care for thy company, or propose myself advantage by it; remain here if thou wilt—Cedric the Saxon may protect thee."

"Alas!" said the Jew, "he will not let me travel in his train—Saxon or Norman will be equally ashamed of the poor Israelite; and to travel by myself through the domains of Philip de Malvoisin and Reginald Front-de-Bœuf—Good youth, I will go with you! Let us haste—let us gird up our loins—let us flee!—Here is thy staff, why wilt thou tarry?"

"I tarry not," said the Pilgrim, giving way to the urgency of his companion; "but I must secure the means of leaving this place—follow me."

He led the way to the adjoining cell, which, as the reader is apprised, was occupied by Gurth the swineherd.—"Arise, Gurth," said the Pilgrim, "arise quickly. Undo the postern gate, and let out the Jew and me."

Gurth, whose occupation, though now held so mean, gave him as much consequence in Saxon England as that of Eumæus in Ithaca, was offended at the familiar and commanding tone assumed by the Palmer. "The Jew leaving Rotherwood," said he, raising himself on his elbow, and looking superciliously at him without quitting his pallet, "and travelling in company with the Palmer to boot"——

"I should as soon have dreamt," said Wamba, who entered the apartment at the instant, "of his stealing away with a gammon of bacon."

"Nevertheless," said Gurth, again laying down his head on the wooden log which served him for a pillow, "both Jew and Gentile must be content to abide the opening of the great gate—we suffer no visitors to depart by stealth at these unseasonable hours."

"Nevertheless," said the Pilgrim, in a commanding tone, "you will not, I think, refuse me that favour."

So saying, he stooped over the bed of the recumbent swineherd, and whispered something in his ear in Saxon. Gurth started up as if electrified. The Pilgrim, raising his finger in an attitude as if to express caution, added, "Gurth, beware—thou art wont to be prudent. I say, undo the postern—thou shalt know more anon."

With hasty alacrity Gurth obeyed him, while Wamba and the Jew followed, both wondering at the sudden change in the swineherd's demeanour.

"My mule, my mule!" said the Jew, as soon as they stood without the postern.

"Fetch him his mule," said the Pilgrim; "and, hearest thou,—let me have another, that I may bear him company till he is beyond these parts —I will return it safely to some of Cedric's train at Ashby. And do thou"—he whispered the rest in Gurth's ear.

"Willingly, most willingly shall it be done," said Gurth, and instantly departed to execute the commission.

"I wish I knew," said Wamba, when his comrade's back was turned, "what you Palmers learn in the Holy Land."

"To say our orisons, fool," answered the Pilgrim, "to repent our sins, and to mortify ourselves with fastings, vigils, and long prayers."

"Something more potent than that," answered the Jester; "for when would repentance or prayer make Gurth do a courtesy or fasting or vigil persuade him to lend you a mule?—I trow you might as well have told his favourite black boar of thy vigils and penance, and wouldst have gotten as civil an answer."

"Go to," said the Pilgrim, "thou art but a Saxon fool."

"Thou sayst well," said the Jester; "had I been born a Norman, as I think thou art, I would have had luck on my side, and been next door to a wise man."

At this moment Gurth appeared on the opposite side of the moat with the mules. The travellers crossed the ditch upon a drawbridge of only two planks breadth, the narrowness of which was matched with the straitness of the postern, and with a little wicket in the exterior palisade, which gave access to the forest. No sooner had they reached the mules, than the Jew, with hasty and trembling hands, secured behind the saddle a small bag of blue buckram, which he took from under his cloak, containing, as he muttered, "a change of raiment—only a change of raiment." Then getting upon the animal with more alacrity and haste than could have been anticipated from his years, he lost no time in so disposing of the skirts of his gaberdine as to conceal completely from observation the burden which he had thus deposited *en croupe*.

The Pilgrim mounted with more deliberation, reaching, as he departed, his hand to Gurth, who kissed it with the utmost possible veneration. The swineherd stood gazing after the travellers until they were lost under the boughs of the forest path, when he was disturbed from his reverie by the voice of Wamba.

"Knowest thou," said the Jester, "my good friend, Gurth, that thou art strangely courteous and most unwontedly pious on this summer morning? I would I were a black Prior or a barefoot Palmer, to avail

myself of thy unwonted zeal and courtesy—certes, I would make more
out of it than a kiss of the hand."

"Thou art no fool thus far, Wamba," answered Gurth, "though thou
arguest from appearances, and the wisest of us can do no more—But it
is time to look after my charge."

So saying, he turned back to the mansion, attended by the Jester.

Meanwhile the travellers continued to press on their journey with
a dispatch which argued the extremity of the Jew's fears, since persons
at his age are seldom fond of rapid motion. The Palmer, to whom every
path and outlet in the wood appeared to be familiar, led the way through
the most devious paths, and more than once excited anew the suspicion
of the Israelite, that he intended to betray him into some ambuscade of
his enemies.

His doubts might have been indeed pardoned; for, except perhaps the
flying fish, there was no race existing on the earth, in the air, or the
waters, who were the object of such an unintermitting, general, and
relentless persecution as the Jews of this period. Upon the slightest and
most unreasonable pretences, as well as upon accusations the most absurd
and groundless, their persons and property were exposed to every turn
of popular fury; for Norman, Saxon, Dane, and Briton, however adverse
these races were to each other, contended which should look with greatest
detestation upon a people, whom it was accounted a point of religion to
hate, to revile, to despise, to plunder, and to persecute. The kings of
the Norman race, and their independent nobles, who followed their example in all acts of tyranny maintained against this devoted people a persecution of a more regular, calculated, and self-interested kind. It is a
well-known story of King John, that he confined a wealthy Jew in one
of the royal castles, and daily caused one of his teeth to be torn out,
until, when the jaw of the unhappy Israelite was half disfurnished he
consented to pay a large sum, which it was the tyrant's object to extort
from him. The little ready money which was in the country was chiefly in
possession of this persecuted people, and the nobility hesitated not to
follow the example of their sovereign in wringing it from them by every
species of oppression, and even personal torture. Yet the passive courage
inspired by the love of gain, induced the Jews to dare the various evils
to which they were subjected, in consideration of the immense profits
which they were enabled to realise in a country naturally so wealthy as
England. In spite of every kind of discouragement, and even of the
special court of taxations already mentioned, called the Jews' Exchequer,
erected for the very purpose of despoiling and distressing them, the Jews
increased, multiplied, and accumulated huge sums, which they transferred from one hand to another by means of bills of exchange—an
invention for which commerce is said to be indebted to them, and which
enabled them to transfer their wealth from land to land, that, when
threatened with oppression in one country, their treasure might be secured in another.

The obstinacy and avarice of the Jews being thus in a measure placed in opposition to the fanaticism and tyranny of those under whom they lived, seemed to increase in proportion to the persecution with which they were visited; and the immense wealth they usually acquired in commerce, while it frequently placed them in danger, was at other times used to extend their influence, and to secure to them a certain degree of protection. On these terms they lived; and their character, influenced accordingly, was watchful, suspicious, and timid—yet obstinate, uncomplying, and skilful in evading the dangers to which they were exposed.

When the travellers had pushed on at a rapid rate through many devious paths, the Palmer at length broke silence.

"That large decayed oak," he said, "marks the boundaries over which Front-de-Bœuf claims authority—we are long since far from those of Malvoisin. There is now no fear of pursuit."

"May the wheels of their chariots be taken off," said the Jew, "like those of the host of Pharaoh, that they may drive heavily!—But leave me not, good Pilgrim—Think but of that fierce and savage Templar, with his Saracen slaves—they will regard neither territory, nor manor, nor lordship."

"Our road," said the Palmer, "should here separate; for it beseems not men of my character and thine to travel together longer than needs must be. Besides, what succour couldst thou have from me, a peaceful Pilgrim, against two armed heathens?"

"O good youth," answered the Jew, "thou canst defend me, and I know thou wouldst. Poor as I am, I will requite it—not with money, for money, so help me my Father Abraham, I have none—but"——

"Money and recompense," said the Palmer, interrupting him, "I have already said I require not of thee. Guide thee I can; and, it may be, even in some sort defend thee; since to protect a Jew against a Saracen, can scarce be accounted unworthy of a Christian. Therefore, Jew, I will see thee safe under some fitting escort. We are now not far from the town of Sheffield, where thou mayest easily find many of thy tribe with whom to take refuge."

"The blessing of Jacob be upon thee, good youth!" said the Jew; "in Sheffield I can harbour with my kinsman Zareth, and find some means of travelling forth with safety."

"Be it so," said the Palmer; "at Sheffield then we part, and half-an-hour's riding will bring us in sight of that town."

The half hour was spent in perfect silence on both parts; the Pilgrim perhaps disdaining to address the Jew, except in case of absolute necessity, and the Jew not presuming to force a conversation with a person whose journey to the Holy Sepulchre gave a sort of sanctity to his character. They paused on the top of a gently rising bank, and the Pilgrim, pointing to the town of Sheffield, which lay beneath them, repeated the words, "Here, then, we part."

"Not till you have had the poor Jew's thanks," said Isaac; "for I

presume not to ask you to go with me to my kinsman Zareth's, who
might aid me with some means of repaying your good offices."

"I have already said," answered the Pilgrim, "that I desire no recompense. If, among the huge list of thy debtors, thou wilt, for my sake
spare the gyves and the dungeon to some unhappy Christian who stands
in thy danger, I shall hold this morning's service to thee well bestowed."

"Stay, stay," said the Jew, laying hold of his garment; "something
would I do more than this, something for thyself.—God knows the Jew
is poor—yes, Isaac is the beggar of his tribe—but forgive me should I
guess what thou most lackest at this moment."

"If thou wert to guess truly," said the Palmer, "it is what thou canst
not supply, wert thou as wealthy as thou sayst thou art poor."

"As I say?" echoed the Jew; "O! believe it, I say but the truth; I
am a plundered, indebted, distressed man. Hard hands have wrung from
me my goods, my money, my ships, and all that I possessed—Yet I can
tell thee what thou lackest, and, it may be, supply it too. Thy wish even
now is for a horse and armour."

The Palmer started, and turned suddenly towards the Jew:—"What
fiend prompted that guess?" said he, hastily.

"No matter," said the Jew, smiling, "so that it be a true one—and, as
I can guess thy want, so I can supply it."

"But consider," said the Palmer, "my character, my dress, my vow."

"I know you Christians," replied the Jew, "and that the noblest of
you will take the staff and sandal in superstitious penance, and walk
afoot to visit the graves of dead men."

"Blaspheme not, Jew," said the Pilgrim, sternly.

"Forgive me," said the Jew; "I spoke rashly. But there dropt words
from you last night and this morning, that, like sparks from flint, showed
the metal within; and in the bosom of that Palmer's gown is hidden a
knight's chain and spurs of gold. They glanced as you stooped over my
bed in the morning."

The Pilgrim could not forbear smiling. "Were thy garments searched
by as curious an eye, Isaac," said he, "what discoveries might not be
made?"

"No more of that," said the Jew, changing colour; and drawing forth
his writing materials in haste, as if to stop the conversation, he began
to write upon a piece of paper which he supported on the top of his
yellow cap, without dismounting from his mule. When he had finished,
he delivered the scroll, which was in the Hebrew character, to the Pilgrim, saying, "In the town of Leicester all men know the rich Jew,
Kirjath Jairam of Lombardy; give him this scroll—he hath on sale six
Milan harnesses, the worst would suit a crowned head—ten goodly
steeds, the worst might mount a king, were he to do battle for his throne.
Of these he will give thee thy choice, with everything else that can
furnish thee forth for the tournament: when it is over, thou wilt return

them safely—unless thou shouldst have wherewith to pay their value to the owner."

"But, Isaac," said the Pilgrim, smiling, "dost thou know that in these sports, the arms and steed of the knight who is unhorsed are forfeit to his victor? Now I may be unfortunate, and so lose what I cannot replace or repay."

The Jew looked somewhat astounded at this possibility; but collecting his courage, he replied hastily. "No—no—no—It is impossible—I will not think so. The blessing of Our Father will be upon thee. Thy lance will be powerful as the rod of Moses."

So saying, he was turning his mule's head away, when the Palmer, in his turn, took hold of his gaberdine. "Nay, but Isaac, thou knowest not all the risk. The steed may be slain, the armour injured—for I will spare neither horse nor man. Besides, those of thy tribe give nothing for nothing; something there must be paid for their use."

The Jew twisted himself in the saddle, like a man in a fit of the colic; but his better feelings predominated over those which were most familiar to him. "I care not," he said, "I care not—let me go. If there is damage, it will cost you nothing—if there is usage money, Kirjath Jairam will forgive it for the sake of his kinsman Isaac. Fare thee well!—Yet hark thee, good youth," said he, turning about, "thrust thyself not too forward into this vain hurly-burly—I speak not for endangering the steed, and coat of armour, but for the sake of thine own life and limbs."

"Gramercy for thy caution," said the Palmer, again smiling; "I will use thy courtesy frankly, and it will go hard with me but I will requite it."

They parted and took different roads for the town of Sheffield.

CHAPTER VII

> Knights, with a long retinue of their squires,
> In gaudy liveries march and quaint attires;
> One laced the helm, another held the lance,
> A third the shining buckler did advance.
> The courser paw'd the ground with restless feet,
> And snorting foam'd and champ'd the golden bit.
> The smiths and armourers on palfreys ride,
> Files in their hands, and hammers at their side;
> And nails for loosen'd spears, and thongs for shields **provide**.
> The yeomen guard the streets in seemly bands;
> And clowns come crowding on, with cudgels in their hands.
>   *Palamon and Arcite.*

THE condition of the English nation was at this time sufficiently miserable. King Richard was absent a prisoner, and in the power of the perfidious and cruel Duke of Austria. Even the very place of his captivity was uncertain, and his fate but very imperfectly known to the generality of his subjects, who were, in the meantime, a prey to every species of subaltern oppression.

Prince John, in league with Philip of France, Cœur-de-Lion's mortal enemy, was using every species of influence with the Duke of Austria to prolong the captivity of his brother Richard, to whom he stood indebted for so many favours. In the meantime, he was strengthening his own faction in the kingdom, of which he proposed to dispute the succession, in case of the king's death, with the legitimate heir, Arthur Duke of Brittany, son of Geoffrey Plantagenet, the elder brother of John. This usurpation, it is well known, he afterwards effected. His own character, being light, profligate, and perfidious, John easily attached to his person and faction, not only all who had reason to dread the resentment of Richard for criminal proceedings during his absence, but also the numerous class of "lawless resolutes," whom the crusades had turned back on their country, accomplished in the vices of the East, impoverished in substance, and hardened in character, and who placed their hopes of harvest in civil commotion.

To these causes of public distress and apprehension must be added, the multitude of outlaws, who, driven to despair by the oppression of the feudal nobility, and the severe exercise of the forest laws, banded together in large gangs, and, keeping possession of the forests and the wastes, set at defiance the justice and magistracy of the country. The nobles themselves, each fortified within his own castle, and playing the petty sovereign over his own dominions, were the leaders of bands scarce less lawless and oppressive than those of the avowed depredators. To maintain these retainers, and to support the extravagance and magnificence which their pride induced them to affect, the nobility borrowed sums of money from the Jews at the most usurious interest, which gnawed into their estates like consuming cankers, scarce to be cured unless when circumstances gave them an opportunity of getting free, by exercising upon their creditors some act of unprincipled violence.

Under the various burdens imposed by this unhappy state of affairs, the people of England suffered deeply for the present, and had yet more dreadful cause to fear for the future. To augment their misery, a contagious disorder of a dangerous nature spread through the land; and, rendered more virulent by the uncleanness, the indifferent food, and the wretched lodging of the lower classes, swept off many whose fate the survivors were tempted to envy, as exempting them from the evils which were to come.

Yet amid these accumulated distresses, the poor as well as the rich, the vulgar as well as the noble, in the event of a tournament, which was the grand spectacle of that age, felt as much interested as the half-starved citizen of Madrid, who has not a real left to buy provisions for his family, feels in the issue of a bull-feast. Neither duty nor infirmity could keep youth or age from such exhibitions. The Passage of Arms, as it was called, which was to take place at Ashby, in the county of Leicester, as champions of the first renown were to take the field in the presence of Prince John himself, who was expected to grace the lists, had attracted universal attention, and an immense confluence of persons of all ranks hastened upon the appointed morning to the place of combat.

The scene was singularly romantic. On the verge of a wood, which approached to within a mile of the town of Ashby, was an extensive meadow, of the finest and most beautiful green turf, surrounded on one side by the forest, and fringed on the other by straggling oak-trees, some of which had grown to an immense size. The ground, as if fashioned on purpose for the martial display which was intended, sloped gradually down on all sides to a level bottom, which was enclosed for the lists with strong palisades, forming a space of a quarter of a mile in length, and about half as broad. The form of the enclosure was an oblong square, save that the corners were considerably rounded off, in order to afford more convenience for the spectators. The openings for the entry of the combatants were at the northern and southern extremities of the lists, accessible by strong wooden gates, each wide enough to admit two horsemen riding abreast. At each of these portals were stationed two heralds, attended by six trumpets, as many pursuivants, and a strong body of men-at-arms for maintaining order, and ascertaining the quality of the knights who proposed to engage in this martial game.

On a platform beyond the southern entrance, formed by a natural elevation of the ground, were pitched five magnificent pavilions, adorned with pennons of russet and black, the chosen colours of the five knights challengers. The cords of the tents were of the same colour. Before each pavilion was suspended the shield of the knight by whom it was occupied, and beside it stood his squire, quaintly disguised as a salvage or silvan man, or in some other fantastic dress, according to the taste of his master, and the character he was pleased to assume during the game.[1] The central pavilion, as the place of honour, had been assigned to Brian de Bois-Guilbert, whose renown in all games of chivalry, no less than his connexion with the knights who had undertaken this Passage of Arms, had occasioned him to be eagerly received into the company of the challengers, and even adopted as their chief and leader, though he had so recently joined them. On one side of his tent were pitched those of Reginald Front-de-Bœuf and Richard de Malvoisin, and on the other was the pavilion of Hugh de Grantmesnil, a noble baron in the vicinity, whose ancestor had been Lord High Steward of England in the time of the Conqueror, and his son William Rufus. Ralph de Vipont, a knight of St. John of Jerusalem, who had some ancient possessions at a place called Heather, near Ashby-de-la-Zouche, occupied the fifth pavilion. From the entrance into the lists, a gently sloping passage, ten yards in breadth, led up to the platform on which the tents were pitched. It was strongly secured by a palisade on each side, as was the esplanade in front of the pavilions, and the whole was guarded by men-at-arms.

The northern access to the lists terminated in a similar entrance of

---

[1] This sort of masquerade is supposed to have occasioned the introduction of supporters into the science of heraldry.

thirty feet in breadth, at the extremity of which was a large enclosed
space for such knights as might be disposed to enter the lists with the
challengers, behind which were placed tents containing refreshments of
every kind for their accommodation, with armourers, farriers, and other
attendants, in readiness to give their services wherever they might be
necessary.

The exterior of the lists was in part occupied by temporary galleries,
spread with tapestry and carpets, and accommodated with cushions for
the convenience of those ladies and nobles who were expected to attend
the tournament. A narrow space, betwixt these galleries and the lists,
gave accommodation for yeomanry and spectators of a better degree than
the mere vulgar, and might be compared to the pit of a theatre. The
promiscuous multitude arranged themselves upon large banks of turf
prepared for the purpose, which, aided by the natural elevation of the
ground, enabled them to overlook the galleries, and obtain a fair view
into the lists. Besides the accommodation which these stations afforded,
many hundreds had perched themselves on the branches of the trees
which surrounded the meadow; and even the steeple of a country church,
at some distance, was crowded with spectators.

It only remains to notice respecting the general arrangement, that one
gallery in the very centre of the eastern side of the lists, and consequently
exactly opposite to the spot where the shock of the combat was to take
place, was raised higher than the others, more richly decorated, and
graced by a sort of throne and canopy, on which the royal arms were
emblazoned. Squires, pages, and yeomen in rich liveries, waited around
this place of honour, which was designed for Prince John and his attendants. Opposite to this royal gallery was another, elevated to the
same height, on the western side of the lists; and more gaily, if less
sumptuously, decorated than that destined for the Prince himself. A
train of pages and of young maidens, the most beautiful who could be
selected, gaily dressed in fancy habits of green and pink, surrounded a
throne decorated in the same colours. Among pennons and flags bearing
wounded hearts, burning hearts, bleeding hearts, bows and quivers, and
all the commonplace emblems of the triumphs of Cupid, a blazoned inscription informed the spectators, that this seat of honour was designed
for *La Royen de la Beauté et des Amours*. But who was to represent the
Queen of Beauty and of Love on the present occasion, no one was prepared to guess.

Meanwhile, spectators of every description thronged forward to occupy
their respective stations, and not without many quarrels concerning those
which they were entitled to hold. Some of these were settled by the men-
at-arms with brief ceremony; the shafts of their battle-axes, and pum-
mels of their swords, being readily employed as arguments to convince
the more refractory. Others, which involved the rival claims of more
elevated persons, were determined by the heralds, or by the two marshals
of the field, William de Wyvil and Stephen de Martival, who, armed at

all points, rode up and down the lists to enforce and preserve good order among the spectators.

Gradually the galleries became filled with knights and nobles, in their robes of peace, whose long and rich-tinted mantles were contrasted with the gayer and more splendid habits of the ladies, who, in a greater proportion than even the men themselves, thronged to witness a sport, which one would have thought too bloody and dangerous to afford their sex much pleasure. The lower and interior space was soon filled by substantial yeomen and burghers, and such of the lesser gentry, as, from modesty, poverty, or dubious title, durst not assume any higher place. It was of course amongst these that the most frequent disputes for precedence occurred.

"Dog of an unbeliever," said an old man, whose threadbare tunic bore witness to his poverty, as his sword, and dagger, and golden chain intimated his pretensions to rank,—"whelp of a she-wolf! darest thou press upon a Christian, and a Norman gentleman of the blood of Montdidier?"

This rough expostulation was addressed to no other than our acquaintance Isaac, who, richly and even magnificently dressed in a gaberdine ornamented with lace and lined with fur, was endeavouring to make place in the foremost row beneath the gallery for his daughter, the beautiful Rebecca, who had joined him at Ashby, and who was now hanging on her father's arm, not a little terrified by the popular displeasure which seemed generally excited by her parent's presumption. But Isaac, though we have seen him sufficiently timid on other occasions, knew well that at present he had nothing to fear. It was not in places of general resort, or where their equals were assembled, that any avaricious or malevolent noble durst offer him injury. At such meetings the Jews were under the protection of the general law; and if that proved a weak assurance, it usually happened that there were among the persons assembled some barons, who, for their own interested motives, were ready to act as their protectors. On the present occasion, Isaac felt more than usually confident, being aware that Prince John was even then in the very act of negotiating a large loan from the Jews of York, to be secured upon certain jewels and lands. Isaac's own share in this transaction was considerable, and he well knew that the Prince's eager desire to bring it to a conclusion would ensure him his protection in the dilemma in which he stood.

Emboldened by these considerations, the Jew pursued his point, and jostled the Norman Christian, without respect either to his descent, quality, or religion. The complaints of the old man, however, excited the indignation of the bystanders. One of these, a stout well-set yeoman, arrayed in Lincoln-green, having twelve arrows stuck in his belt, with a baldric and badge of silver, and a bow of six feet length in his hand, turned short round, and while his countenance, which his constant exposure to weather had rendered brown as a hazel nut, grew darker with anger, he advised the Jew to remember that all the wealth he had acquired by

sucking the blood of his miserable victims had but swelled him like a
bloated spider, which might be overlooked while it kept in a corner, but
would be crushed if it ventured into the light. This intimation, delivered
in Norman-English with a firm voice and a stern aspect, made the Jew
shrink back; and he would have probably withdrawn himself altogether
from a vicinity so dangerous, had not the attention of every one been
called to the sudden entrance of Prince John, who at that moment entered the lists, attended by a numerous and gay train, consisting partly
of laymen, partly of churchmen, as light in their dress, and as gay in
their demeanour, as their companions. Among the latter was the Prior
of Jorvaulx, in the most gallant trim which a dignitary of the church
could venture to exhibit. Fur and gold were not spared in his garments;
and the point of his boots, outheroding the preposterous fashion of the
time, turned up so very far, as to be attached, not to his knees merely
but to his very girdle, and effectually prevented him from putting his foot
into the stirrup. This, however, was a slight inconvenience to the gallant
Abbot, who, perhaps, even rejoicing in the opportunity to display his
accomplished horsemanship before so many spectators, especially of the
fair sex, dispensed with the use of these supports to a timid-rider. The
rest of Prince John's retinue consisted of the favourite leaders of his
mercenary troops, some marauding barons and profligate attendants upon
the court, with several Knights Templars and Knights of St. John.

It may be here remarked that the knights of these two orders were
accounted hostile to King Richard, having adopted the side of Philip of
France in the long train of disputes which took place in Palestine betwixt
that monarch and the lion-hearted King of England. It was the well-
known consequence of this discord that Richard's repeated victories had
been rendered fruitless, his romantic attempts to besiege Jerusalem disappointed, and the fruit of all the glory which he had acquired had
dwindled into an uncertain truce with the Sultan Saladin. With the same
policy which had dictated the conduct of their brethren in the Holy
Land, the Templars and Hospitallers in England and Normandy attached themselves to the faction of Prince John, having little reason to
desire the return of Richard to England, or the succession of Arthur, his
legitimate heir. For the opposite reason, Prince John hated and contemned the few Saxon families of consequence which subsisted in England, and omitted no opportunity of mortifying and affronting them;
being conscious that his person and pretensions were disliked by them,
as well as by the greater part of the English commons, who feared farther
innovation upon their rights and liberties, from a sovereign of John's
licentious and tyrannical disposition.

Attended by this gallant equipage, himself well mounted and splendidly dressed in crimson and in gold, bearing upon his hand a falcon,
and having his head covered by a rich fur bonnet, adorned with a circle
of precious stones, from which his long curled hair escaped and overspread
his shoulders, Prince John, upon a grey and high-mettled palfrey, cara-

coled within the lists at the head of his jovial party, laughing loud with
his train, and eyeing with all the boldness of royal criticism the beauties
who adorned the lofty galleries.

Those who remarked in the physiognomy of the Prince a dissolute
audacity, mingled with extreme haughtiness and indifference to the feelings of others, could not yet deny to his countenance that sort of comeliness which belongs to an open set of features, well formed by nature,
modelled by art to the usual rules of courtesy, yet so far frank and
honest, that they seemed as if they disclaimed to conceal the natural
workings of the soul. Such an expression is often mistaken for manly
frankness, when in truth it arises from the reckless indifference of a
libertine disposition, conscious of superiority of birth, of wealth, or of
some other adventitious advantage, totally unconnected with personal
merit. To those who did not think so deeply, and they were the greater
number by a hundred to one, the splendour of Prince John's *rheno* (*i.e.*
fur tippet), the richness of his cloak, lined with the most costly sables,
his maroquin boots and golden spurs, together with the grace with which
he managed his palfrey, were sufficient to merit clamorous applause.

In his joyous caracole round the lists, the attention of the Prince was
called by the commotion, not yet subsided, which had attended the ambitious movement of Isaac towards the higher places of the assembly.
The quick eye of Prince John instantly recognised the Jew, but was much
more agreeably attracted by the beautiful daughter of Zion, who, terrified
by the tumult, clung close to the arm of her aged father.

The figure of Rebecca might indeed have compared with the proudest
beauties of England, even though it had been judged by as shrewd a
connoisseur as Prince John. Her form was exquisitely symmetrical, and
was shown to advantage by a sort of Eastern dress, which she wore according to the fashion of the females of her nation. Her turban of yellow
silk suited well with the darkness of her complexion. The brilliancy of
her eyes, the superb arch of her eyebrows, her well-formed aquiline nose,
her teeth as white as pearl, and the profusion of her sable tresses, which,
each arranged in its own little spiral of twisted curls, fell down upon
as much of a lovely neck and bosom as a simarre of the richest Persian
silk, exhibiting flowers in their natural colours embossed upon a purple
ground, permitted to be visible—all these constituted a combination of
loveliness, which yielded not to the most beautiful of the maidens who
surrounded her. It is true, that of the golden and pearl-studded clasps,
which closed her vest from the throat to the waist, the three uppermost
were left unfastened on account of the heat, which something enlarged
the prospect to which we allude. A diamond necklace, with pendants of
inestimable value, were by this means also made more conspicuous. The
feather of an ostrich, fastened in her turban by an agraffe set with brilliants, was another distinction of the beautiful Jewess, scoffed and sneered
at by the proud dames who sat above her, but secretly envied by those
who affected to deride them.

"By the bald scalp of Abraham," said Prince John, "yonder Jewess must be the very model of that perfection whose charms drove frantic the wisest king that ever lived! What sayest thou, Prior Aymer?—By the Temple of that wise king, which our wiser Brother Richard proved unable to recover, she is the very Bride of the Canticles!"

"The Rose of Sharon and the Lily of the Valley,"—answered the Prior, in a sort of snuffling tone; "but your Grace must remember she is still but a Jewess."

"Aye!" added Prince John, without heeding him, "and there is my Mammon of unrighteousness too—the Marquis of Marks, the Baron of Byzants, contesting for place with penniless dogs, whose threadbare cloaks have not a single cross in their pouches to keep the devil from dancing there. By the body of St. Mark, my prince of supplies, with his lovely Jewess, shall have a place in the gallery!—What is she, Isaac? Thy wife or thy daughter, that eastern houri that thou lockest under thy arm as thou wouldst thy treasure-casket?"

"My daughter Rebecca, so please your Grace," answered Isaac, with a low congee, nothing embarrassed by the Prince's salutation, in which, however, there was at least as much mockery as courtesy.

"The wiser man thou," said John, with a peal of laughter, in which his gay followers obsequiously joined. "But, daughter or wife, she should be preferred according to her beauty and thy merits.—Who sits above there?" he continued, bending his eye on the gallery. "Saxon churls, lolling at their lazy length!—out upon them!—let them sit close, and make room for my prince of usurers and his lovely daughter. I'll make the hinds know they must share the high places of the synagogue with those whom the synagogue properly belongs to."

Those who occupied the gallery to whom this injurious and unpolite speech was addressed, were the family of Cedric the Saxon, with that of his ally and kinsman, Athelstane of Coningsburgh, a personage who, on account of his descent from the last Saxon monarchs of England, was held in the highest respect by all the Saxon natives of the north of England. But with the blood of this ancient royal race, many of their infirmities had descended to Athelstane. He was comely in countenance, bulky and strong in person, and in the flower of his age—yet inanimate in expression, dull-eyed, heavy-browed, inactive and sluggish in all his motions, and so slow in resolution, that the soubriquet of one of his ancestors was conferred upon him, and he was very generally called Athelstane the Unready. His friends, and he had many, who, as well as Cedric, were passionately attached to him, contended that this sluggish temper arose not from want of courage, but from mere want of decision; others alleged that his hereditary vice of drunkenness had obscured his faculties, never of a very acute order, and that the passive courage and meek good-nature which remained behind, were merely the dregs of a character that might have been deserving of praise, but of which all the valuable parts had flown off in the progress of a long course of brutal debauchery.

It was to this person, such as we have described him, that the Prince addressed his imperious command to make place for Isaac and Rebecca. Athelstane, utterly confounded at an order which the manners and feelings of the times rendered so injuriously insulting, unwilling to obey, yet undetermined how to resist, opposed only the *vis inertiæ* to the will of John; and, without stirring or making any motion whatever of obedience, opened his large grey eyes, and stared at the Prince with an astonishment which had in it something extremely ludicrous. But the impatient John regarded it in no such light.

"The Saxon porker," he said, "is either asleep or minds me not—Prick him with your lance, De Bracy," speaking to a knight who rode near him, the leader of a band of Free Companions, or Condottieri; that is, of mercenaries belonging to no particular nation, but attached for the time to any prince by whom they were paid. There was a murmur even among the attendants of Prince John; but De Bracy, whose profession freed him from all scruples, extended his long lance over the space which separated the gallery from the lists, and would have executed the commands of the Prince before Athelstane the Unready had recovered presence of mind sufficient even to draw back his person from the weapon, had not Cedric, as prompt as his companion was tardy, unsheathed, with the speed of lightning, the short sword which he wore, and at a single blow severed the point of the lance from the handle. The blood rushed into the countenance of Prince John. He swore one of his deepest oaths, and was about to utter some threat corresponding in violence, when he was diverted from his purpose, partly by his own attendants, who gathered around him conjuring him to be patient, partly by a general exclamation of the crowd, uttered in loud applause of the spirited conduct of Cedric. The Prince rolled his eyes in indignation, as if to collect some safe and easy victim; and chancing to encounter the firm glance of the same archer whom we have already noticed, and who seemed to persist in his gesture of applause in spite of the frowning aspect which the Prince bent upon him, he demanded his reason for clamouring thus.

"I always add my hollo," said the yeoman, "when I see a good shot, or a gallant blow."

"Sayst thou?" answered the Prince; "then thou canst hit the white thyself, I'll warrant."

"A woodman's mark, and at woodman's distance, I can hit," answered the yeoman.

"And Wat Tyrrel's mark, at a hundred yards," said a voice from behind, but by whom uttered could not be discerned.

This allusion to the fate of William Rufus, his grandfather, at once incensed and alarmed Prince John. He satisfied himself, however, with commanding the men-at-arms, who surrounded the lists, to keep an eye on the braggart, pointing to the yeoman.

"By St. Grizzel," he added, "we will try his own skill, who is so ready to give his voice to the feats of others!"

"I shall not fly the trial," said the yeoman with the composure which marked his whole deportment.

"Meanwhile, stand up, ye Saxon churls," said the fiery Prince; "for by the light of Heaven, since I have said it, the Jew shall have his seat amongst ye!"

"By no means, an it please your Grace!—it is not fit for such as we to sit with the rulers of the land," said the Jew; whose ambition for precedence, though it had led him to dispute place with the extenuated and impoverished descendant of the line of Montdidier, by no means stimulated him to an intrusion upon the privileges of the wealthy Saxons.

"Up, infidel dog, when I command you," said Prince John, "or I will have thy swarthy hide stript off, and tanned for horse-furniture!"

Thus urged, the Jew began to ascend the steep and narrow steps which led up to the gallery.

"Let me see," said the Prince, "who dare stop him!" fixing his eye on Cedric, whose attitude intimated his intention to hurl the Jew down headlong.

The catastrophe was prevented by the clown Wamba, who, springing betwixt his master and Isaac, and exclaiming, in answer to the Prince's defiance, "Marry, that will I!" opposed to the beard of the Jew a shield of brawn, which he plucked from beneath his cloak, and with which, doubtless, he had furnished himself, lest the tournament should have proved longer than his appetite could endure abstinence. Finding the abomination of his tribe opposed to his very nose, while the Jester, at the same time, flourished his wooden sword above his head, the Jew recoiled, missed his footing, and rolled down the steps,—an excellent jest to the spectators, who set up a loud laughter, in which Prince John and his attendants heartily joined.

"Deal me the prize, cousin Prince," said Wamba; "I have vanquished my foe in fair fight with sword and shield," he added, brandishing the brawn in one hand and the wooden sword in the other.

"Who, and what art thou, noble champion?" said Prince John, still laughing.

"A fool by right of descent," answered the Jester; "I am Wamba, the son of Witless, who was the son of Weatherbrain, who was the son of an Alderman."

"Make room for the Jew in front of the lower ring," said Prince John, not unwilling perhaps to seize an apology to desist from his original purpose; "to place the vanquished beside the victor were false heraldry."

"Knave upon fool were worse," answered the Jester, "and Jew upon bacon worst of all."

"Gramercy! good fellow," cried Prince John, "thou pleasest me— Here, Isaac, lend me a handful of byzants."

As the Jew, stunned by the request, afraid to refuse, and unwilling to comply, fumbled in the furred bag which hung by his girdle, and was perhaps endeavouring to ascertain how few coins might pass for a handful, the Prince stooped from his jennet and settled Isaac's doubts by snatching the pouch itself from his side; and flinging to Wamba a couple of the gold pieces which it contained, he pursued his career round the lists, leaving the Jew to the derision of those around him, and himself receiving as much applause from the spectators as if he had done some honest and honourable action.

CHAPTER VIII

At this the challenger with fierce defy
His trumpet sounds; the challenged makes reply:
With clangour rings the field, resounds the vaulted sky.
Their visors closed, their lances in the rest,
Or at the helmet pointed or the crest,
They vanish from the barrier, speed the race,
And spurring see decrease the middle space.
Palamon and Arcite.

In the midst of Prince John's cavalcade, he suddenly stopt, and appealing to the Prior of Jorvaulx, declared the principal business of the day had been forgotten.

"By my halidom," said he, "we have neglected, Sir Prior, to name the fair Sovereign of Love and of Beauty, by whose white hand the palm is to be distributed. For my part, I am liberal in my ideas, and I care not if I give my vote for the black-eyed Rebecca."

"Holy Virgin," answered the Prior, turning up his eyes in horror, "a Jewess!—We should deserve to be stoned out of the lists; and I am not yet old enough to be a martyr. Besides, I swear by my patron saint, that she is far inferior to the lovely Saxon, Rowena."

"Saxon or Jew," answered the Prince, "Saxon or Jew, dog or hog, what matters it! I say, name Rebecca, were it only to mortify the Saxon churls."

A murmur arose even among his own immediate attendants.

"This passes a jest, my lord," said De Bracy; "no knight here will lay lance in rest if such an insult is attempted."

"It is the mere wantonness of insult," said one of the oldest and most important of Prince John's followers, Waldemar Fitzurse, "and if your Grace attempt it, cannot but prove ruinous to your projects."

"I entertained you, sir," said John, reining up his palfrey haughtily, "for my follower, but not for my counsellor."

"Those who follow your Grace in the paths which you tread," said Waldemar, but speaking in a low voice, "acquire the right of counsellors; for your interest and safety are not more deeply gaged than their own."

From the tone in which this was spoken, John saw the necessity of acquiescence. "I did but jest," he said; "and you turn upon me like so many adders! Name whom you will, in the fiend's name, and please yourselves."

"Nay, nay," said De Bracy, "let the fair sovereign's throne remain unoccupied until the conqueror shall be named, and then let him choose the lady by whom it shall be filled. It will add another grace to his triumph, and teach fair ladies to prize the love of valiant knights, who can exalt them to such distinction."

"If Brian de Bois-Guilbert gain the prize," said the Prior, "I will gage my rosary that I name the Sovereign of Love and Beauty."

"Bois-Guilbert," answered De Bracy, "is a good lance; but there are others around these lists, Sir Prior, who will not fear to encounter him."

"Silence, sirs," said Waldemar, "and let the Prince assume his seat. The knights and spectators are alike impatient, the time advances, and highly fit it is that the sports should commence."

Prince John, though not yet a monarch, had in Waldemar Fitzurse all the inconveniences of a favourite minister, who, in serving his sovereign, must always do so in his own way. The Prince acquiesced, however, although his disposition was precisely of that kind which is apt to be obstinate upon trifles, and, assuming his throne, and being surrounded by his followers, gave signal to the heralds to proclaim the laws of the tournament, which were briefly as follows:

First, the five challengers were to undertake all comers.

Secondly, any knight proposing to combat, might, if he pleased, select a special antagonist from among the challengers, by touching his shield. If he did so with the reverse of his lance, the trial of skill was made with what were called the arms of courtesy, that is, with lances at whose extremity a piece of round flat board was fixed, so that no danger was encountered, save from the shock of the horses and riders. But if the shield was touched with the sharp end of the lance, the combat was understood to be at *outrance*, that is, the knights were to fight with sharp weapons, as in actual battle.

Thirdly, when the knights present had accomplished their vow, by each of them breaking five lances, the Prince was to declare the victor in the first day's tourney, who should receive as prize a war-horse of exquisite beauty and matchless strength; and in addition to this reward of valour, it was now declared, he should have the peculiar honour of naming the Queen of Love and Beauty, by whom the prize should be given on the ensuing day.

Fourthly, it was announced, that, on the second day, there should be a general tournament, in which all the knights present who were desirous to win praise, might take part; and being divided into two bands, of equal numbers, might fight it out manfully, until the signal was given by Prince John to cease the combat. The elected Queen of Love and

Beauty was then to crown the knight whom the Prince should adjudge to have borne himself best in this second day, with a coronet composed of thin gold plate, cut into the shape of a laurel crown. On this second day the knightly games ceased. But on that which was to follow, feats of archery, of bull-baiting, and other popular amusements, were to be practised, for the more immediate amusement of the populace. In this manner did Prince John endeavour to lay the foundation of a popularity, which he was perpetually throwing down by some inconsiderate act of wanton aggression upon the feelings and prejudices of the people.

The lists now presented a most splendid spectacle. The sloping galleries were crowded with all that was noble, great, wealthy, and beautiful, in the northern and midland parts of England; and the contrast of the various dresses of these dignified spectators, rendered the view as gay as it was rich, while the interior and lower space, filled with the substantial burgesses and yeomen of merry England, formed, in their more plain attire, a dark fringe, or border, around this circle of brilliant embroidery, relieving, and, at the same time, setting off its splendour.

The heralds finished their proclamation with their usual cry of "Largesse, largesse, gallant knights!" and gold and silver pieces were showered on them from the galleries, it being a high point of chivalry to exhibit liberality towards those whom the age accounted at once the secretaries and the historians of honour. The bounty of the spectators was acknowledged by the customary shouts of "Love of Ladies—Death of Champions—Honour to the Generous—Glory to the Brave!" To which the more humble spectators added their acclamations, and a numerous band of trumpeters the flourish of their martial instruments. When these sounds had ceased, the heralds withdrew from the lists in gay and glittering procession, and none remained within them save the marshals of the field, who, armed cap-a-pie, sat on horseback, motionless as statues, at the opposite end of the lists. Meantime, the enclosed space at the northern extremity of the lists, large as it was, was now completely crowded with knights desirous to prove their skill against the challengers, and, when viewed from the galleries, presented the appearance of a sea of waving plumage, intermixed with glistening helmets, and tall lances, to the extremities of which were, in many cases, attached small pennons of about a span's breadth, which, fluttering in the air as the breeze caught them, joined with the restless motion of the feathers to add liveliness to the scene.

At length the barriers were opened, and five knights, chosen by lot, advanced slowly into the area; a single champion riding in front, and the other four following in pairs. All were splendidly armed, and my Saxon authority (in the Wardour Manuscript) records at great length their devices, their colours, and the embroidery of their horse trappings. It is unnecessary to be particular on these subjects. To borrow lines from a contemporary poet, who has written but too little

"The knights are dust,
And their good swords are rust,
Their souls are with the saints, we trust." [1]

Their escutcheons have long mouldered from the walls of their castles.
Their castles themselves are but green mounds and shattered ruins—
the place that once knew them knows them no more—nay, many a race
since theirs has died out and been forgotten in the very land which they
occupied, with all the authority of feudal proprietors and feudal lords.
What, then, would it avail the reader to know their names, or the eva-
nescent symbols of their martial rank!

Now, however, no whit anticipating the oblivion which awaited their
names and feats, the champions advanced through the lists, restraining
their fiery steeds, and compelling them to move slowly, while, at the same
time, they exhibited their paces, together with the grace and dexterity
of the riders. As the procession entered the lists, the sound of a wild
Barbaric music was heard from behind the tents of the challengers where
the performers were concealed. It was of eastern origin, having been
brought from the Holy Land; and the mixture of the cymbals and bells
seemed to bid welcome at once, and defiance, to the knights as they
advanced. With the eyes of an immense concourse of spectators fixed
upon them, the five knights advanced up the platform upon which the
tents of the challengers stood, and there separating themselves, each
touched slightly, and with the reverse of his lance, the shield of the
antagonist to whom he wished to oppose himself. The lower order of
spectators in general—nay, many of the higher class, and it is even said
several of the ladies, were rather disappointed at the champions choosing
the arms of courtesy. For the same sort of persons, who, in the present
day, applaud most highly the deepest tragedies, were then interested in
a tournament exactly in proportion to the danger incurred by the
champions engaged.

Having intimated their more pacific purpose, the champions retreated
to the extremity of the lists, where they remained drawn up in a line;
while the challengers, sallying each from his pavilion, mounted their
horses, and, headed by Brian de Bois-Guilbert, descended from the platform, and opposed themselves individually to the knights who had
touched their respective shields.

At the flourish of clarions and trumpets, they started out against each
other at full gallop; and such was the superior dexterity or good fortune
of the challengers, that those opposed to Bois-Guilbert, Malvoisin, and
Front-de-Bœuf, rolled on the ground. The antagonist of Grantmesnil,
instead of bearing his lance-point fair against the crest or the shield

[1] These lines are part of an unpublished poem by Coleridge, whose muse so often
tantalises with fragments which indicate her powers, while the manner in which she
flings them from her betrays her caprice, yet whose unfinished sketches display
more talent than the laboured masterpieces of others.

of his enemy swerved so much from the direct line as to break the weapon athwart the person of his opponent—a circumstance which was accounted more disgraceful than that of being actually unhorsed; because the latter might happen from accident, whereas the former evinced awkwardness and want of management of the weapon and of the horse. The fifth knight alone maintained the honour of his party, and parted fairly with the Knight of St. John, both splintering their lances without advantage on either side.

The shouts of the multitude, together with the acclamations of the heralds, and the clangour of the trumpets, announced the triumph of the victors and the defeat of the vanquished. The former retreated to their pavilions, and the latter, gathering themselves up as they could, withdrew from the lists in disgrace and dejection, to agree with their victors concerning the redemption of their arms and their horses, which, according to the laws of the tournament, they had forfeited. The fifth of their number alone tarried in the lists long enough to be greeted by the applause of the spectators, amongst whom he retreated, to the aggravation, doubtless, of his companions' mortification.

A second and a third party of knights took the field; and although they had various success, yet, upon the whole, the advantage decidedly remained with the challengers, not one of whom lost his seat or swerved from his charge—misfortunes which befell one or two of their antagonists in each encounter. The spirits, therefore, of those opposed to them, seemed to be considerably damped by their continued success. Three knights only appeared on the fourth entry, who, avoiding the shields of Bois-Guilbert and Front-de-Bœuf, contented themselves with touching those of the three other knights, who had not altogether manifested the same strength and dexterity. This politic selection did not alter the fortune of the field, the challengers were still successful; one of their antagonists was overthrown, and both the others failed in the *attaint*,[1] that is, in striking the helmet and shield of their antagonist firmly and strongly, with the lance held in a direct line, so that the weapon might break unless the champion was overthrown.

After this fourth encounter, there was a considerable pause; nor did it appear that any one was very desirous of renewing the contest. The spectators murmured among themselves; for, among the challengers, Malvoisin and Front-de-Bœuf were unpopular from their characters, and the others, except Grantmesnil, were disliked as strangers and foreigners.

But none shared the general feeling of dissatisfaction so keenly as Cedric the Saxon, who saw, in each advantage gained by the Norman challengers, a repeated triumph over the honour of England. His own education had taught him no skill in the games of chivalry, although, with the arms of his Saxon ancestors he had manifested himself, on

---

[1] This term of chivalry, transferred to the law, gives the phrase of being attainted with treason.

many occasions, a brave and determined soldier. He looked anxiously to Athelstane, who had learned the accomplishments of the age, as if desiring that he should make some personal effort to recover the victory which was passing into the hands of the Templar and his associates. But, though both stout of heart and strong of person, Athelstane had a disposition too inert and unambitious to make the exertions which Cedric seemed to expect from him.

"The day is against England, my lord," said Cedric, in a marked tone; "are you not tempted to take the lance?"

"I shall tilt to-morrow," answered Athelstane, "in the *mêlée;* it is not worth while for me to arm myself to-day."

Two things displeased Cedric in this speech. It contained the Norman word *mêlée* (to express the general conflict), and it evinced some indifference to the honour of the country; but it was spoken by Athelstane, whom he held in such profound respect, that he would not trust himself to canvass his motives or his foibles. Moreover, he had no time to make any remark, for Wamba thrust in his word, observing, "It was better, though scarce easier, to be the best man among a hundred, than the best man of two."

Athelstane took the observation as a serious compliment; but Cedric, who better understood the Jester's meaning, darted at him a severe and menacing look; and lucky it was for Wamba, perhaps, that the time and place prevented his receiving, notwithstanding his place and service, more sensible marks of his master's resentment.

The pause in the tournament was still uninterrupted, excepting by the voices of the heralds exclaiming—"Love of ladies, splintering of lances! stand forth, gallant knights, fair eyes look upon your deeds!"

The music also of the challengers breathed from time to time wild bursts expressive of triumph or defiance, while the clowns grudged a holiday which seemed to pass away in inactivity; and old knights and nobles lamented in whispers the decay of martial spirit, spoke of the triumphs of their younger days, but agreed that the land did not now supply dames of such transcendent beauty as had animated the jousts of former times. Prince John began to talk to his attendants about making ready the banquet, and the necessity of adjudging the prize to Brian de Bois-Guilbert, who had, with a single spear, overthrown two knights, and foiled a third.

At length, as the Saracenic music of the challengers concluded one of those long and high flourishes with which they had broken the silence of the lists, it was answered by a solitary trumpet, which breathed a note of defiance from the northern extremity. All eyes were turned to see the new champion which these sounds announced, and no sooner were the barriers opened than he paced into the lists. As far as could be judged of a man sheathed in armour, the new adventurer did not greatly exceed the middle size, and seemed to be rather slender than strongly made. His suit of armour was formed of steel, richly inlaid with gold, and the device on his shield was a young oak-tree pulled up by the roots, with the Spanish word *Desdichado,* signifying Disinherited. He was mounted on a gallant black horse, and as he passed through the lists he gracefully saluted the Prince and the ladies by lowering his lance. The dexterity with which he managed his steed, and something of youthful grace which he displayed in his manner, won him the favour of the multitude, which some of the lower classes expressed by calling out, "Touch Ralph de Vipont's shield—touch the Hospitaller's shield; he has the least sure seat, he is your cheapest bargain."

The champion, moving onward amid these well-meant hints, ascended the platform by the sloping alley which led to it from the lists, and, to the astonishment of all present, riding straight up to the central pavilion, struck with the sharp end of his spear the shield of Brian de Bois-Guilbert until it rung again. All stood astonished at his presumption, but none more than the redoubted Knight whom he had thus defied to mortal combat, and who, little expecting so rude a challenge, was standing carelessly at the door of the pavilion.

"Have you confessed yourself, brother," said the Templar, "and have you heard mass this morning, that you peril your life so frankly?"

"I am fitter to meet death than thou art," answered the Disinherited Knight; for by this name the stranger had recorded himself in the books of the tourney.

"Then take your place in the lists," said Bois-Guilbert, "and look your last upon the sun; for this night thou shalt sleep in paradise."

"Gramercy for thy courtesy," replied the Disinherited Knight, "and to requite it, I advise thee to take a fresh horse and a new lance, for by my honour you will need both."

Having expressed himself thus confidently, he reined his horse backward down the slope which he had ascended, and compelled him in the same manner to move backward through the lists, till he reached the northern extremity, where he remained stationary, in expectation of his antagonist. This feat of horsemanship again attracted the applause of the multitude.

However incensed at his adversary for the precautions which he recommended, Brian de Bois-Guilbert did not neglect his advice; for his honour was too nearly concerned, to permit his neglecting any means which might ensure victory over his presumptuous opponent. He changed his horse for a proved and fresh one of great strength and spirit. He chose a new and tough spear, lest the wood of the former might have been strained in the previous encounters he had sustained. Lastly, he laid aside his shield, which had received some little damage, and received another from his squires. His first had only borne the general device of his rider, representing two knights riding upon one horse, an emblem expressive of the original humility and poverty of the Templars, qualities which they had since exchanged for the arrogance and wealth that finally occasioned their suppression. Bois-Guilbert's new shield bore a raven in full flight, holding in its claws a skull, and bearing the motto, *Gare le Corbeau.*

When the two champions stood opposed to each other at the two extremities of the lists, the public expectation was strained to the highest pitch. Few augured the possibility that the encounter could terminate well for the Disinherited Knight, yet his courage and gallantry secured the general good wishes of the spectators.

The trumpets had no sooner given the signal, than the champions vanished from their posts with the speed of lightning, and closed in the centre of the lists with the shock of a thunderbolt. The lances burst into shivers up to the very grasp, and it seemed at the moment that both knights had fallen, for the shock had made each horse recoil backwards upon its haunches. The address of the riders recovered their steeds by use of the bridle and spur, and having glared on each other for an instant with eyes which seemed to flash fire through the bars of their visors, each made a demi-volte, and, retiring to the extremity of the lists, received a fresh lance from the attendants.

A loud shout from the spectators, waving of scarfs and handkerchiefs, and general acclamations, attested the interest taken by the spectators in this encounter; the most equal, as well as the best performed, which had graced the day. But no sooner had the knights resumed their station, than the clamour of applause was hushed into a silence, so deep and so dead, that it seemed the multitude were afraid even to breathe.

A few minutes' pause having been allowed, that the combatants and their horses might recover breath, Prince John with his truncheon signed to the trumpets to sound the onset. The champions a second time sprung from their stations, and closed in the centre of the lists, with the same speed, the same dexterity, the same violence, but not the same equal fortune as before.

In this second encounter, the Templar aimed at the centre of his antagonist's shield, and struck it so fair and forcibly, that his spear went to shivers, and the Disinherited Knight reeled in his saddle. On the other hand, that champion had, in the beginning of his career, directed the point of his lance towards Bois-Guilbert's shield, but, changing his aim almost in the moment of encounter, he addressed it to the helmet, a mark more difficult to hit, but which, if attained, rendered the shock more irresistible. Fair and true he hit the Norman on the visor, where his lance's point kept hold of the bars. Yet, even at this disadvantage, the Templar sustained his high reputation; and had not the girths of his saddle burst, he might not have been unhorsed. As it chanced, however, saddle, horse, and man, rolled on the ground under a cloud of dust.

To extricate himself from the stirrups and fallen steed, was to the Templar scarce the work of a moment; and, stung with madness, both at his disgrace and at the acclamations with which it was hailed by the spectators, he drew his sword and waved it in defiance of his conqueror. The Disinherited Knight sprung from his steed, and also unsheathed his sword. The marshals of the field, however, spurred their horses between them, and reminded them that the laws of the tournament did not, on the present occasion, permit this species of encounter.

"We shall meet again, I trust," said the Templar, casting a resentful glance at his antagonist; "and where there are none to separate us."

"If we do not," said the Disinherited Knight, "the fault shall not be mine. On foot or horseback, with spear, with axe, or with sword, I am alike ready to encounter thee."

More and angrier words would have been exchanged, but the marshals, crossing their lances betwixt them, compelled them to separate. The Disinherited Knight returned to his first station, and Bois-Guilbert to his tent, where he remained for the rest of the day in an agony of despair.

Without alighting from horse, the conqueror called for a bowl of wine, and opening the beaver, or lower part of his helmet, announced that he quaffed it, "To all true English hearts, and to the confusion of foreign tyrants." He then commanded his trumpet to sound a defiance to the challengers, and desired a herald to announce to them, that he should make no election, but was willing to encounter them in the order in which they pleased to advance against him.

The gigantic Front-de-Bœuf, armed in sable armour, was the first who took the field. He bore on a white shield a black bull's head, half defaced by the numerous encounters which he had undergone, and bearing the arrogant motto, *Cave Adsum*. Over this champion the Disinherited Knight obtained a slight but decisive advantage. Both Knights broke their lances fairly, but Front-de-Bœuf, who lost a stirrup in the encounter, was adjudged to have the disadvantage.

In the stranger's third encounter with Sir Philip Malvoisin, he was equally successful; striking that baron so forcibly on the casque, that the laces of the helmet broke, and Malvoisin, only saved from falling by being unhelmeted, was declared vanquished like his companions.

In his fourth combat with De Grantmesnil, the Disinherited Knight showed as much courtesy as he had hitherto evinced courage and dexterity. De Grantmesnil's horse, which was young and violent, reared and plunged in the course of the career so as to disturb the rider's aim, declining to take the advantage which this accident afforded him, raised his lance, and passing his antagonist without touching him, wheeled his horse and rode back again to his own end of the lists, offering his antagonist, by a herald, the chance of a second encounter. This De Grantmesnil declined, avowing himself vanquished as much by the courtesy as by the address of his opponent.

Ralph de Vipont summed up the list of the stranger's triumphs, being hurled to the ground with such force that the blood gushed from his nose and his mouth, and he was borne senseless from the lists.

The acclamations of thousands applauded the unanimous award of the Prince and marshals, announcing that day's honours to the Disinherited Knight.

CHAPTER IX

———In the midst was seen
A lady of a more majestic mien,
By stature and by beauty mark'd their sovereign Queen.

.   .   .   .

And as in beauty she surpass'd the choir,
So nobler than the rest was her attire;
A crown of ruddy gold enclosed her brow,
Plain without pomp, and rich without a chow;
A branch of Agnus Castus in her hand,
She bore aloft her symbol of command.
                              The Flower and the Leaf.

WILLIAM DE WYVIL and Stephen de Martival, the marshals of the field, were the first to offer their congratulations to the victor, praying him at the same time, to suffer his helmet to be unlaced, or, at least, that he would raise his visor ere they conducted him to receive the prize of the day's tourney from the hands of Prince John. The Disinherited Knight, with all knightly courtesy, declined their request, alleging, that he could not at this time suffer his face to be seen, for reasons which he had assigned to the heralds when he entered the lists. The marshals were perfectly satisfied by this reply; for amidst the frequent and capricious vows by which knights were accustomed to bind themselves in the days of chivalry, there were none more common than those by which they engaged to remain incognito for a certain space, or until some particular adventure was achieved. The marshals, therefore, pressed no farther into the mystery of the Disinherited Knight, but, announcing to Prince John the conqueror's desire to remain unknown, they requested permission to bring him before his Grace, in order that he might receive the reward of his valour.

John's curiosity was excited by the mystery observed by the stranger; and, being already displeased with the issue of the tournament, in which the challengers whom he favoured had been successively defeated by one knight, he answered haughtily to the marshals, "By the light of Our Lady's brow, this same knight hath been disinherited as well of his courtesy as of his lands, since he desires to appear before us without uncovering his face.—Wot ye, my lords," he said, turning round to his train, "who this gallant can be, that bears himself thus proudly?"

"I cannot guess," answered De Bracy, "nor did I think there had been within the four seas that girth Britain a champion that could bear down these five knights in one day's jousting. By my faith, I shall never forget the force with which he shocked De Vipont. The poor Hospitaller was hurled from his saddle like a stone from a sling."

"Boast not of that," said a Knight of St. John, who was present; "your Temple champion had no better luck. I saw your brave lance, Bois-Guilbert, roll thrice over, grasping his hands full of sand at every turn."

De Bracy, being attached to the Templars, would have replied, but was prevented by Prince John. "Silence, sirs!" he said; "what unprofitable debate have we here?"

"The victor," said De Wyvil, "still waits the pleasure of your highness."

"It is our pleasure," answered John, "that he do so wait until we learn whether there is not some one who can at least guess at his name and quality. Should he remain there till nightfall, he has had work enough to keep him warm."

"Your Grace," said Waldemar Fitzurse, "will do less than due honour to the victor, if you compel him to wait till we tell your highness that which we cannot know; at least I can form no guess—unless he be one of the good lances who accompanied King Richard to Palestine, and who are now straggling homeward from the Holy Land."

"It may be the Earl of Salisbury," said De Bracy; "he is about the same pitch."

"Sir Thomas de Multon, the Knight of Gilsland, rather," said Fitzurse; "Salisbury is bigger in the bones." A whisper arose among the train, but by whom first suggested could not be ascertained. "It might be the King —it might be Richard Cœur-de-Lion himself!"

"Over God's forbode!" said Prince John, involuntarily turning at the same time as pale as death, and shrinking as if blighted by a flash of lightning; "Waldemar!—De Bracy! brave knights and gentlemen, remember your promises, and stand truly by me!"

"Here is no danger impending," said Waldemar Fitzurse; "are you so little acquainted with the gigantic limbs of your father's son, as to think they can be held within the circumference of yonder suit of armour? —De Wyvil and Martival, you will best serve the Prince by bringing forward the victor to the throne, and ending an error that has conjured all the blood from his cheeks.—Look at him more closely," he continued, "your highness will see that he wants three inches of King Richard's height, and twice as much of his shoulder-breadth. The very horse he backs could not have carried the ponderous weight of King Richard through a single course."

While he was yet speaking, the marshals brought forward the Disinherited Knight to the foot of a wooden flight of steps, which formed the ascent from the lists to Prince John's throne. Still discomposed with the idea that his brother, so much injured, and to whom he was so much indebted, had suddenly arrived in his native kingdom, even the distinctions pointed out by Fitzurse did not altogether remove the Prince's apprehensions; and while, with a short and embarrassed eulogy upon his valour, he caused to be delivered to him the warhorse assigned as the prize, he trembled lest from the barred visor of the mailed form before him, an answer might be returned, in the deep and awful accents of Richard the Lion-hearted.

But the Disinherited Knight spoke not a word in reply to the compliment of the Prince, which he only acknowledged with a profound obeisance.

The horse was led into the lists by two grooms richly dressed, the animal itself being fully accoutred with the richest war-furniture; which, however, scarcely added to the value of the noble creature in the eyes of those who were judges. Laying one hand upon the pommel of the saddle, the Disinherited Knight vaulted at once upon the back of the steed without making use of the stirrup, and, brandishing aloft his lance, rode twice around the lists, exhibiting the points and paces of the horse with the skill of a perfect horseman.

The appearance of vanity, which might otherwise have been attributed to this display, was removed by the propriety shown in exhibiting to the best advantage the princely reward with which he had been just honoured, and the Knight was again greeted by the acclamations of all present.

In the meanwhile, the bustling Prior of Jorvaulx had reminded Prince John, in a whisper, that the victor must now display his good judgment, instead of his valour, by selecting from among the beauties who graced the galleries a lady, who should fill the throne of the Queen of Beauty and of Love, and deliver the prize of the tourney upon the ensuing day. The Prince accordingly made a sign with his truncheon, as the knight passed him in his second career around the lists. The Knight turned towards the throne, and, sinking his lance, until the point was within a foot of the ground, remained motionless, as if expecting John's command; while all admired the sudden dexterity with which he instantly reduced his fiery steed from a state of violent emotion and high excitation to the stillness of an equestrian statue.

"Sir Disinherited Knight," said Prince John, "since that is the only title by which we can address you, it is now your duty, as well as privilege, to name the fair lady, who, as Queen of Honour and of Love, is to preside over next day's festival. If, as a stranger in our land, you should require the aid of other judgment to guide your own, we can only say .that Alicia, the daughter of our gallant knight Waldemar Fitzurse, has at our court been long held the first in beauty as in place. Nevertheless, it is your undoubted prerogative to confer on whom you please this crown, by the delivery of which to the lady of your choice, the election of to-morrow's Queen will be formal and complete.—Raise your lance."

The Knight obeyed; and Prince John placed upon its point a coronet of green satin, having around its edge a circlet of gold, the upper edge of which was relieved by arrow-points and hearts placed interchangeably, like the strawberry leaves and balls upon a ducal crown.

In the broad hint which he dropped respecting the daughter of Waldemar Fitzurse, John had more than one motive, each the offspring of a mind which was a strange mixture of carelessness and presumption with low artifice and cunning. He wished to banish from the minds of the chivalry around him his own indecent and unacceptable jest respecting

the Jewess Rebecca; he was desirous of conciliating Alicia's father Waldemar, of whom he stood in awe, and who had more than once shown himself
dissatisfied during the course of the day's proceedings. He had also a wish
to establish himself in the good graces of the lady; for John was at least
as licentious in his pleasures as profligate in his ambition. But besides all
these reasons, he was desirous to raise up against the Disinherited Knight
(towards whom he already entertained a strong dislike) a powerful
enemy in the person of Waldemar Fitzurse, who was likely, he thought,
highly to resent the injury done to his daughter, in case, as was not
unlikely, the victor should make another choice.

And so indeed it proved. For the Disinherited Knight passed the
gallery close to that of the Prince, in which the Lady Alicia was seated
in the full pride of triumphant beauty, and, pacing forward as slowly
as he had hitherto rode swiftly around the lists, he seemed to exercise his
right of examining the numerous fair faces which adorned that splendid
circle.

It was worth while to see the different conduct of the beauties who
underwent this examination, during the time it was proceeding. Some
blushed, some assumed an air of pride and dignity, some looked straight
forward, and essayed to seem utterly unconscious of what was going on,
some drew back in alarm, which was perhaps affected, some endeavoured
to forbear smiling, and there were two or three who laughed outright.
There were also some who dropped their veils over their charms; but
as the Wardour Manuscript says these were fair ones of ten years standing, it may be supposed that, having had their full share of such vanities,
they were willing to withdraw their claim, in order to give a fair chance
to the rising beauties of the age.

At length the champion paused beneath the balcony in which the Lady
Rowena was placed, and the expectation of the spectators was excited
to the utmost.

It must be owned, that if an interest displayed in his success could
have bribed the Disinherited Knight, the part of the lists before which
he paused had merited his predilection. Cedric the Saxon, overjoyed at
the discomfiture of the Templar, and still more so at the miscarriage
of his two malevolent neighbours, Front-de-Bœuf and Malvoisin, had,
with his body half stretched over the balcony, accompanied the victor
in each course, not with his eyes only, but with his whole heart and
soul. The Lady Rowena had watched the progress of the day with equal
attention, though without openly betraying the same intense interest.
Even the unmoved Athelstane had shown symptoms of shaking off his
apathy, when, calling for a huge goblet of muscadine, he quaffed it to
the health of the Disinherited Knight.

Another group, stationed under the gallery occupied by the Saxons,
had shown no less interest in the fate of the day.

"Father Abraham!" said Isaac of York, when the first course was run
betwixt the Templar and the Disinherited Knight, "how fiercely that

Gentile rides! Ah, the good horse that was brought all the long way from Barbary, he takes no more care of him than if he were a wild ass's colt—and the noble armour, that was worth so many zecchins to Joseph Pareira, the armourer of Milan, besides seventy in the hundred of profits, he cares for it as little as if he had found it in the highways!"

"If he risks his own person and limbs, father," said Rebecca, "in doing such a dreadful battle, he can scarce be expected to spare his horse and armour."

"Child!" replied Isaac, somewhat heated, "thou knowest not what thou speakest—His neck and limbs are his own, but his horse and armour belong to——Holy Jacob! what was I about to say!—Nevertheless, it is a good youth—See, Rebecca! see, he is again about to go up to battle against the Philistine—Pray, child—pray for the safety of the good youth,—and of the speedy horse, and the rich armour.—God of my fathers!" he again exclaimed, "he hath conquered, and the uncircumcised Philistine hath fallen before his lance,—even as Og the King of Bashan, and Sihon, King of the Amorites, fell before the sword of our fathers!—Surely he shall take their gold and their silver, and their warhorses, and their armour of brass and of steel, for a prey and for a spoil."

The same anxiety did the worthy Jew display during every course that was run, seldom failing to hazard a hasty calculation concerning the value of the horse and armour which were forfeited to the champion upon each new success. There had been therefore no small interest taken in the success of the Disinherited Knight, by those who occupied the part of the lists before which he now paused.

Whether from indecision or some other motive of hesitation, the champion of the day remained stationary for more than a minute, while the eyes of the silent audience were riveted upon his motions; and then, gradually and gracefully sinking the point of his lance, he deposited the coronet which it supported at the feet of the fair Rowena. The trumpets instantly sounded, while the heralds proclaimed the Lady Rowena the Queen of Beauty and of Love for the ensuing day, menacing with suitable penalties those who should be disobedient to her authority. They then repeated their cry of Largesse, to which Cedric, in the height of his joy, replied by an ample donative, and to which Athelstane, though less promptly, added one equally large.

There was some murmuring among the damsels of Norman descent, who were as much unused to see the preference given to a Saxon beauty, as the Norman nobles were to sustain defeat in the games of chivalry which they themselves had introduced. But these sounds of disaffection were drowned by the popular shout of "Long live the Lady Rowena, the chosen and lawful Queen of Love and of Beauty!" To which many in the lower area added, "Long live the Saxon Princess! long live the race of the immortal Alfred!"

However unacceptable these sounds might be to Prince John, and to those around him, he saw himself nevertheless obliged to confirm the nomination of the victor, and accordingly calling to horse, he left his throne; and mounting his jennet, accompanied by his train, he again entered the lists. The Prince paused a moment beneath the gallery of the Lady Alicia, to whom he paid his compliments, observing, at the same time, to those around him—"By my halidome, sirs! if the Knight's feats in arms have shown that he hath limbs and sinews, his choice hath no less proved that his eyes are none of the clearest."

It was on this occasion, as during his whole life, John's misfortune, not perfectly to understand the characters of those whom he wished to conciliate. Waldemar Fitzurse was rather offended than pleased at the Prince stating thus broadly an opinion, that his daughter had been slighted.

"I know no right of chivalry," he said, "more precious or inalienable than that of each free knight to choose his lady-love by his own judgment. My daughter courts distinction from no one; and in her own character, and in her own sphere, will never fail to receive the full proportion of that which is her due."

Prince John replied not; but, spurring his horse, as if to give vent to his vexation, he made the animal bound forward to the gallery where Rowena was seated, with the crown still at her feet.

"Assume," he said, "fair lady, the mark of your sovereignty, to which none vows homage more sincerely than ourself, John of Anjou; and if it please you to-day, with your noble sire and friends, to grace our banquet in the Castle of Ashby, we shall learn to know the empress to whose service we devote to-morrow."

Rowena remained silent, and Cedric answered for her in his native Saxon.

"The Lady Rowena," he said, "possesses not the language in which to reply to your courtesy, or to sustain her part in your festival. I also, and the noble Athelstane of Coningsburgh, speak only the language, and practise only the manners, of our fathers. We therefore decline with thanks your Highness's courteous invitation to the banquet. To-morrow, the Lady Rowena will take upon her the state to which she has been called by the free election of the victor Knight, confirmed by the acclamations of the people."

So saying, he lifted the coronet, and placed it upon Rowena's head, in token of her acceptance of the temporary authority assigned to her.

"What says he?" said Prince John, affecting not to understand the Saxon language, in which, however, he was well skilled. The purport of Cedric's speech was repeated to him in French. "It is well," he said; "to-morrow we will ourself conduct this mute sovereign to her seat of dignity.—You, at least, Sir Knight," he added, turning to the victor, who had remained near the gallery, "will this day share our banquet?"

The Knight, speaking for the first time, in a low and hurried voice, excused himself by pleading fatigue, and the necessity of preparing for to-morrow's encounter.

"It is well," said Prince John, haughtily; "although unused to such refusals, we will endeavour to digest our banquet as we may, though ungraced by the most successful in arms, and his elected Queen of Beauty."

So saying, he prepared to leave the lists with his glittering train, and his turning his steed for that purpose was the signal for the breaking up and dispersion of the spectators.

Yet, with the vindictive memory proper to offended pride, especially when combined with conscious want of desert, John had hardly proceeded three paces, ere again, turning around, he fixed an eye of stern resentment upon the yeoman who had displeased him in the early part of the day, and issued his commands to the men-at-arms who stood near —"On your life, suffer not that fellow to escape."

The yeoman stood the angry glance of the Prince with the same unvaried steadiness which had marked his former deportment, saying, with a smile, "I have no intention to leave Ashby until the day after to-morrow—I must see how Staffordshire and Leicestershire can draw their bows—the forests of Needwood and Charnwood must rear good archers."

"I," said Prince John to his attendants, but not in direct reply,—"I will see how he can draw his own; and woe betide him unless his skill should prove some apology for his insolence!"

"It is full time," said De Bracy, "that the *outrecuidance* of these peasants should be restrained by some striking example."

Waldemar Fitzurse, who probably thought his patron was not taking the readiest road to popularity, shrugged up his shoulders and was silent. Prince John resumed his retreat from the lists, and the dispersion of the multitude became general.

In various routes, according to the different quarters from which they came, and in groups of various numbers, the spectators were seen retiring over the plain. By far the most numerous part streamed towards the town of Ashby, where many of the distinguished persons were lodged in the castle, and where others found accommodation in the town itself. Among these were most of the knights who had already appeared in the tournament, or who proposed to fight there the ensuing day, and who, as they rode slowly along, talking over the events of the day, were greeted with loud shouts by the populace. The same acclamations were bestowed upon Prince John, although he was indebted for them rather to the splendour of his appearance and train, than to the popularity of his character.

A more sincere and more general, as well as a better-merited acclamation, attended the victor of the day, until, anxious to withdraw himself from popular notice, he accepted the accommodation of one of those pavilions pitched at the extremities of the lists, the use of which was courteously tendered him by the marshals of the field. On his retiring to his tent, many who had lingered in the lists, to look upon and form conjectures concerning him, also dispersed.

The signs and sounds of a tumultous concourse of men lately crowded together in one place, and agitated by the same passing events, were now exchanged for the distant hum of voices of different groups retreating in all directions, and these speedily died away in silence. No other sounds were heard save the voices of the menials who stripped the galleries of their cushions and tapestry, in order to put them in safety for the night, and wrangled among themselves for the half-used bottles of wine and relics of the refreshment which had been served round to the spectators.

Beyond the precincts of the lists more than one forge was erected; and these now began to glimmer through the twilight, announcing the toil of the armourers, which was to continue through the whole night, in order to repair or alter the suits of armour to be used again on the morrow.

A strong guard of men-at-arms, renewed at intervals, from two hours to two hours, surrounded the lists, and kept watch during the night.

CHAPTER X

Thus, like the sad presaging raven, that tolls
The sick man's passport in her hollow beak,
And in the shadow of the silent night
Doth shake contagion from her sable wings;
Vex'd and tormented, runs poor Barrabas,
With fatal curses towards these Christians.
Jew of Malta.

THE Disinherited Knight had no sooner reached his pavilion, than squires and pages in abundance tendered their services to disarm him, to bring fresh attire, and to offer him the refreshment of the bath. Their zeal on this occasion was perhaps sharpened by curiosity, since every one desired to know who the knight was that had gained so many laurels, yet had refused, even at the command of Prince John, to lift his visor or to name his name. But their officious inquisitiveness was not gratified. The Disinherited Knight refused all other assistance save that of his own squire, or rather yeoman—a clownish-looking man, who, wrapt in a cloak of dark-coloured felt, and having his head and face half buried in a Norman bonnet made of black fur, seemed to affect the incognito as much as his master. All others being excluded from the tent, this attendant relieved his master from the more burdensome parts of his armour, and placed food and wine before him, which the exertions of the day rendered very acceptable.

The Knight had scarcely finished a hasty meal, ere his menial announced to him that five men, each leading a barbed steed, desired to speak with him. The Disinherited Knight had exchanged his armour for the long robe usually worn by those of his condition, which, being furnished with a hood, concealed the features, when such was the pleasure of the wearer, almost as completely as the visor of the helmet itself, but the twilight, which was now fast darkening, would of itself have rendered a disguise unnecessary, unless to persons to whom the face of an individual chanced to be particularly well known.

The Disinherited Knight, therefore, stept boldly forth to the front of his tent, and found in attendance the squires of the challengers, whom he easily knew by their russet and black dresses, each of whom led his master's charger, loaded with the armour in which he had that day fought.

"According to the laws of chivalry," said the foremost of these men, "I, Baldwin de Oyley, squire to the redoubted Knight Brian de Bois-Guilbert, make offer to you, styling yourself, for the present, the Disinherited Knight, of the horse and armour used by the said Brian de Bois-Guilbert in this day's Passage of Arms, leaving it with your nobleness to retain or to ransom the same, according to your pleasure; for such is the law of arms."

The other squires repeated nearly the same formula, and then stood to await the decision of the Disinherited Knight.

"To you four, sirs," replied the Knight, addressing those who had last spoken, "and to your honourable and valiant masters, I have one common reply. Commend me to the noble knights, your masters, and say, I should do ill to deprive them of steeds and arms which can never be used by braver cavaliers.—I would I could here end my message to these gallant knights; but being, as I term myself, in truth and earnest, the Disinherited, I must be thus far bound to your masters, that they will, of their courtesy, be pleased to ransom their steeds and armour, since that which I wear I can hardly term mine own."

"We stand commissioned, each of us," answered the squire of Reginald Front-de-Bœuf, "to offer a hundred zecchins in ransom of these horses and suits of armour."

"It is sufficient," said the Disinherited Knight. "Half the sum my present necessities compel me to accept; of the remaining half, distribute one moiety among yourselves, sir squires, and divide the other half betwixt the heralds and the pursuivants, and minstrels, and attendants."

The squires, with cap in hand, and low reverences, expressed their deep sense of a courtesy and generosity not often practised, at least upon a scale so extensive. The Disinherited Knight then addressed his discourse to Baldwin, the squire of Brian de Bois-Guilbert. "From your master," said he, "I will accept neither arms nor ransom. Say to him in my name, that our strife is not ended—no, not till we have fought as well with swords as with lances—as well on foot as on horseback. To this mortal quarrel he has himself defied me, and I shall not forget the challenge. —Meantime, let him be assured, that I hold him not as one of his companions, with whom I can with pleasure exchange courtesies; but rather as one with whom I stand upon terms of mortal defiance."

"My master," answered Baldwin, "knows how to requite scorn with scorn, and blows with blows, as well as courtesy with courtesy. Since you

disdain to accept from him any share of the ransom at which you have
rated the arms of the other knights, I must leave his armour and his
horse here, being well assured that he will never deign to mount the
one nor wear the other."

"You have spoken well, good Squire," said the Disinherited Knight,
"well and boldly, as it beseemeth him to speak who answers for an
absent master. Leave not, however, the horse and armour here. Restore
them to thy master; or, if he scorns to accept them, retain them, good
friend, for thine own use. So far as they are mine, I bestow them upon
you freely."

Baldwin made a deep obeisance, and retired with his companions; and
the Disinherited Knight entered the pavilion.

"Thus far, Gurth," said he, addressing his attendant, "the reputation
of English chivalry hath not suffered in my hands."

"And I," said Gurth, "for a Saxon swineherd, have not ill played the
personage of a Norman squire-at-arms."

"Yea, but," answered the Disinherited Knight, "thou hast ever kept
me in anxiety lest thy clownish bearing should discover thee."

"Tush!" said Gurth, "I fear discovery from none, saving my playfellow, Wamba the Jester, of whom I could never discover whether he
were most knave or fool. Yet I could scarce choose but laugh, when my
old master passed so near to me, dreaming all the while that Gurth
was keeping his porkers many a mile off, in the thickets and swamps
of Rotherwood. If I am discovered"——

"Enough," said the Disinherited Knight, "thou knowest my promise."

"Nay, for that matter," said Gurth, "I will never fail my friend for
fear of my skin-cutting. I have a tough hide, that will bear knife or
scourge as well as any boar's hide in my herd."

"Trust me, I will requite the risk you run for my love, Gurth," said
the Knight. "Meanwhile, I pray you to accept these ten pieces of gold."

"I am richer," said Gurth, putting them into his pouch, "than ever
was swineherd or bondsman."

"Take this bag of gold to Ashby," continued his master, "and find out
Isaac the Jew of York, and let him pay himself for the horse and arms
with which his credit supplied me."

"Nay, by St. Dunstan," replied Gurth, "that I will not do."

"How, knave," replied his master, "wilt thou not obey my commands?"

"So they be honest, reasonable, and Christian commands," replied
Gurth; "but this is none of these. To suffer the Jew to pay himself
would be dishonest, for it would be cheating my master; and unreasonable, for it were the part of a fool; and unchristian, since it would be
plundering a believer to enrich an infidel."

"See him contented, however, thou stubborn varlet," said the Disinherited Knight.

"I will do so," said Gurth, taking the bag under his cloak and leaving

the apartment; "and it will go hard," he muttered, "but I content him
with one-half of his own asking." So saying he departed, and left the
Disinherited Knight to his own perplexed ruminations; which, upon
more accounts than it is now possible to communicate to the reader,
were of a nature peculiarly agitating and painful.

We must now change the scene to the village of Ashby, or rather to
a country house in its vicinity belonging to a wealthy Israelite, with
whom Isaac, his daughter, and retinue, had taken up their quarters; the
Jews, it is well known, being as liberal in exercising the duties of hospitality and charity among their own people, as they were alleged to be
reluctant and churlish in extending them to those whom they termed
Gentiles, and whose treatment of them certainly merited little hospitality
at their hand.

In an apartment, small indeed, but richly furnished with decorations
of an Oriental taste, Rebecca was seated on a heap of embroidered
cushions, which, piled along a low platform that surrounded the chamber, served, like the estrada of the Spaniards, instead of chairs and
stools. She was watching the motions of her father with a look of anxious
and filial affection, while he paced the apartment with a dejected mien
and disordered step; sometimes clasping his hands together—sometimes
casting his eyes to the roof of the apartment, as one who laboured under
great mental tribulation. "Oh, Jacob!" he exclaimed—"Oh, all ye twelve
Holy Fathers of our tribe! what a losing venture is this for one who
hath duly kept every jot and tittle of the law of Moses—Fifty zecchins
wrenched from me at one clutch, and by the talons of a tyrant!"

"But, father," said Rebecca, "you seemed to give the gold to Prince
John willingly."

"Willingly? the blotch of Egypt upon him!—Willingly, saidst thou?
—Ay, as willingly as when, in the Gulf of Lyons, I flung over my mer-
chandise to lighten the ship, while she laboured in the tempest—robed
the seething billows in my choice silks—perfumed their briny foam with
myrrh and aloes—enriched their caverns with gold and silver work! And
was not that an hour of unutterable misery, though my own hands made
the sacrifice?"

"But it was a sacrifice which Heaven exacted to save our lives," answered Rebecca, "and the God of our fathers has since blessed your
store and your gettings."

"Ay," answered Isaac, "but if the tyrant lays hold on them as he did
to-day, and compels me to smile while he is robbing me?—O, daughter,
disinherited and wandering as we are, the worst evil which befalls our
race is, that when we are wronged and plundered, all the world laughs
around, and we are compelled to suppress our sense of injury, and to
smile tamely, when we would revenge bravely."

"Think not thus of it, my father," said Rebecca; "we also have advantages. These Gentiles, cruel and oppressive as they are, are in some
sort dependent on the dispersed children of Zion, whom they despise

and persecute. Without the aid of our wealth, they could neither furnish forth their hosts in war, nor their triumphs in peace; and the gold which we lend them returns with increase to our coffers. We are like the herb which flourisheth most when it is most trampled on. Even this day's pageant had not proceeded without the consent of the despised Jew, who furnished the means."

"Daughter," said Isaac, "thou hast harped upon another string of sorrow. The goodly steed and the rich armour, equal to the full profit of my adventure with our Kirjath Jairam of Leicester—there is a dead loss too—ay, a loss which swallows up the gains of a week; ay, of the space between two Sabaoths—and yet it may end better than I now think, for 'tis a good youth."

"Assuredly," said Rebecca, "you shall not repent you of requiting the good deed received of the stranger knight."

"I trust so, daughter," said Isaac, "and I trust too in the rebuilding of Zion; but as well do I hope with my own bodily eyes to see the walls and battlements of the new Temple, as to see a Christian, yea, the very best of Christians, repay a debt to a Jew, unless under the awe of the judge and jailor."

So saying, he resumed his discontented walk through the apartment; and Rebecca, perceiving that her attempts at consolation only served to awaken new subjects of complaint, wisely desisted from her unavailing efforts—a prudential line of conduct, and we recommend to all who set up for comforters and advisers to follow it in the like circumstances.

The evening was now becoming dark, when a Jewish servant entered the apartment, and placed upon the table two silver lamps, fed with perfumed oil; the richest wines, and the most delicate refreshments, were at the same time displayed by another Israelitish domestic on a small ebony table, inlaid with silver; for, in the interior of their houses, the Jews refused themselves no expensive indulgences. At the same time the servant informed Isaac that a Nazarene (so they termed Christians, while conversing among themselves) desired to speak with him. He that would live by traffic must hold himself at the disposal of every one claiming business with him. Isaac at once replaced on the table the untasted glass of Greek wine which he had just raised to his lips, and saying hastily to his daughter, "Rebecca, veil thyself," commanded the stranger to be admitted.

Just as Rebecca had dropped over her fine features a screen of silver gauze which reached to her feet, the door opened, and Gurth entered, wrapt in the ample folds of his Norman mantle. His appearance was rather suspicious than prepossessing, especially as, instead of doffing his bonnet, he pulled it still deeper over his rugged brow.

"Art thou Isaac the Jew of York?" said Gurth, in Saxon.

"I am," replied Isaac, in the same language (for his traffic had rendered every tongue spoken in Britain familiar to him)—"and who art thou?"

"That is not to the purpose," answered Gurth.

"As much as my name is to thee," replied Isaac; "for without knowing thine, how can I hold intercourse with thee?"

"Easily," answered Gurth; "I, being to pay money, must know that I deliver it to the right person; thou, who are to receive it, will not, I think, care very greatly by whose hands it is delivered."

"O," said the Jew, "you are come to pay moneys? Holy Father Abraham! that altereth our relation to each other. And from whom dost thou bring it?"

"From the Disinherited Knight," said Gurth, "victor in this day's tournament. It is the price of the armour supplied to him by Kirjath Jairam of Leicester, on thy recommendation. The steed is restored to thy stable. I desire to know the amount of the sum which I am to pay for the armour."

"I said he was a good youth!" exclaimed Isaac, with joyful exultation. "A cup of wine will do thee no harm," he added, filling and handing to the swineherd a richer draught than Gurth had ever before tasted. "And how much money," continued Isaac, "hast thou brought with thee?"

"Holy Virgin!" said Gurth, setting down the cup, "what nectar these unbelieving dogs drink, while true Christians are fain to quaff ale as muddy and thick as the draff we give to hogs!—What money have I brought with me?" continued the Saxon, when he had finished this uncivil ejaculation, "even but a small sum; something in hand the whilst. What, Isaac! thou must bear a conscience, though it be a Jewish one."

"Nay, but," said Isaac, "thy master has won goodly steeds and rich armours with the strength of his lance, and of his right hand—but 'tis a good youth—the Jew will take these in present payment, and render him back the surplus."

"My master has disposed of them already," said Gurth.

"Ah! that was wrong," said the Jew, "that was the part of a fool. No Christian here could buy so many horses and armour—no Jew except myself would give him half the values. But thou hast a hundred zecchins with thee in that bag," said Isaac, prying under Gurth's cloak, "it is a heavy one."

"I have heads for cross-bow bolts in it," said Gurth, readily.

"Well, then,"—said Isaac, panting and hesitating between habitual love of gain and a new-born desire to be liberal in the present instance, "If I should say that I would take eighty zecchins for the good steed and the rich armour, which leaves me not a gilder's profit, have you money to pay me?"

"Barely," said Gurth, though the sum demanded was more reasonable than he expected, "and it will leave my master nigh penniless. Nevertheless, if such be your least offer, I must be content."

"Fill thyself another goblet of wine," said the Jew. "Ah! eighty zecchins is too little. It leaveth no profit for the usages of the moneys;

and, besides, the good horse may have suffered wrong in this day's encounter. O, it was a hard and a dangerous meeting! man and steed rushing on each other like wild bulls of Bashan! The horse cannot but have had wrong."

"And I say," replied Gurth, "he is sound, wind and limb; and you may see him now in your stable. And I say, over and above, that seventy zecchins is enough for the armour, and I hope a Christian's word is as good as a Jew's. If you will not take seventy, I will carry this bag" (and he shook it till the contents jingled) "back to my master."

"Nay, nay!" said Isaac; "lay down the talents—the shekels—the eighty zecchins, and thou shalt see I will consider thee liberally."

Gurth at length complied; and telling out eighty zecchins upon the table, the Jew delivered out to him an acquittance for the horse and suit of armour. The Jew's hand trembled for joy as he wrapped up the first seventy pieces of gold. The last ten he told over with much deliberation, pausing, and saying something as he took each piece from the table, and dropt it into his purse. It seemed as if his avarice were struggling with his better nature, and compelling him to pouch zecchin after zecchin, while his generosity urged him to restore some part at least to his benefactor, or as a donation to his agent. His whole speech ran nearly thus:

"Seventy-one—seventy-two; thy master is a good youth—seventy-three, an excellent youth—seventy-four—that piece hath been clipt within the ring—seventy-five—and that looketh light of weight—seventy-six—when thy master wants money, let him come to Isaac of York—seventy-seven—that is, with reasonable security." Here he made a considerable pause, and Gurth had good hope that the last three pieces might escape the fate of their comrades; but the enumeration proceeded.—"Seventy-eight—thou art a good fellow—seventy-nine—and deservest something for thyself"——

Here the Jew paused again, and looked at the last zecchin, intending, doubtless, to bestow it upon Gurth. He weighed it upon the tip of his finger, and made it ring by dropping it upon the table. Had it rung too flat, or had it felt a hair's breadth too light, generosity had carried the day; but, unhappily for Gurth, the chime was full and true, the zecchin plump, newly coined, and a grain above weight. Isaac could not find in his heart to part with it, so dropt it into his purse as if in absence of mind, with the words, "Eighty completes the tale, and I trust thy master will reward thee handsomely.—Surely," he added, looking earnestly at the bag, "thou hast more coins in that pouch?"

Gurth grinned, which was his nearest approach to a laugh, as he replied, "About the same quantity which thou hast just told over so carefully." He then folded the quittance, and put it under his cap, adding,—"Peril of thy beard, Jew, see that this be full and ample!" He filled himself, unbidden, a third goblet of wine, and left the apartment without ceremony.

"Rebecca," said the Jew, "that Ishmaelite hath gone somewhat beyond me. Nevertheless his master is a good youth—ay, and I am well pleased that he hath gained shekels of gold and shekels of silver, even by the speed of his horse and by the strength of his lance, which, like that of Goliath the Philistine, might vie with a weaver's beam."

As he turned to receive Rebecca's answer, he observed, that during his chaffering with Gurth, she had left the apartment unperceived.

In the meanwhile, Gurth had descended the stair, and, having reached the dark antechamber or hall, was puzzling about to discover the entrance, when a figure in white, shown by a small silver lamp which she held in her hand, beckoned him into a side apartment. Gurth had some reluctance to obey the summons. Rough and impetuous as a wild boar, where only earthly force was to be apprehended, he had all the characteristic terrors of a Saxon respecting fawns, forest-fiends, white women, and the whole of the superstitions which his ancestors had brought with them from the wilds of Germany. He remembered, moreover, that he was in the house of a Jew, a people who, besides the other unamiable qualities which popular report ascribed to them, were supposed to be profound necromancers and cabalists. Nevertheless, after a moment's pause, he obeyed the beckoning summons of the apparition, and followed her into the apartment which she indicated, where he found to his joyful surprise that his fair guide was the beautiful Jewess whom he had seen at the tournament, and a short time in her father's apartment.

She asked him the particulars of his transaction with Isaac, which he detailed accurately.

"My father did but jest with thee, good fellow," said Rebecca; "he owes thy master deeper kindness than these arms and steed could pay, were their value tenfold. What sum didst thou pay my father even now?"

"Eighty zecchins," said Gurth, surprised at the question.

"In this purse," said Rebecca, "thou wilt find a hundred. Restore to thy master that which is his due, and enrich thyself with the remainder. Haste—begone—stay not to render thanks! and beware how you pass through this crowded town, where thou mayest easily lose both thy burden and thy life.—Reuben," she added, clapping her hands together, "light forth this stranger, and fail not to draw lock and bar behind him."

Reuben, a dark-brow'd and black-bearded Israelite, obeyed her summons, with a torch in his hand; undid the outward door of the house, and conducting Gurth across a paved court, let him out through a wicket in the entrance-gate, which he closed behind him with such bolts and chains as would well have become that of a prison.

"By St. Dunstan," said Gurth, as he stumbled up the dark avenue, "this is no Jewess, but an angel from heaven! Ten zecchins from my brave young master—twenty from this pearl of Zion—Oh, happy day! —Such another, Gurth, will redeem thy bondage, and make thee a

brother as free of thy guild as the best. And then do I lay down my
swineherd's horn and staff, and take the freeman's sword and buckler,
and follow my young master to the death, without hiding either my face
or my name."

CHAPTER XI

> *1st Outlaw.* Stand, sir, and throw us that you
>   have about you;
> If not, we'll make you sit, and rifle you.
>   *Speed.* Sit, we are undone! these are the villains
> That all travellers do fear so much.
>   *Val.* My friends,——
>   *1st Out.* That's not so, sir, we are your enemies.
>   *2d Out.* Peace! we'll hear him.
>   *3d Out.* Ay, by my beard, will we;
> For he's a proper man.
> *Two Gentlemen of Verona.*

THE nocturnal adventures of Gurth were not yet concluded; indeed he
himself became partly of that mind, when, after passing one or two straggling houses which stood in the outskirts of the village, he found himself
in a deep lane, running between two banks overgrown with hazel and
holly, while here and there a dwarf oak flung its arms altogether across
the path. The lane was moreover much rutted and broken up by the
carriages which had recently transported articles of various kinds to
the tournament; and it was dark, for the banks and bushes intercepted
the light of the harvest moon.

From the village were heard the distant sounds of revelry, mixed occasionally with loud laughter, sometimes broken by screams, and sometimes by wild strains of distant music. All these sounds, intimating the
disorderly state of the town, crowded with military nobles and their
dissolute attendants, gave Gurth some uneasiness. "The Jewess was right,"
he said to himself. "By heaven and St. Dunstan, I would I were safe
at my journey's end with all this treasure! Here are such numbers, I
will not say of arrant thieves, but of errant knights and errant squires,
errant monks and errant minstrels, errant jugglers and errant jesters, that
a man with a single merk would be in danger, much more a poor swineherd with a whole bagful of zecchins. Would I were out of the shade of
these infernal bushes, that I might at least see any of St. Nicholas's
clerks before they spring on my shoulders."

Gurth accordingly hastened his pace, in order to gain the open common to which the lane led, but was not so fortunate as to accomplish his
object. Just as he had attained the upper end of the lane, where the underwood was thickest, four men sprung upon him, even as his fears anticipated, two from each side of the road, and seized him so fast, that
resistance, if at first practicable, would have been now too late.—

"Surrender your charge," said one of them; "we are the deliverers of the commonwealth, who ease every man of his burden."

"You should not ease me of mine so lightly," muttered Gurth, whose surly honesty could not be tamed even by the pressure of immediate violence,—"had I but in my power to give three strokes in its defense."

"We shall see that presently," said the robber; and, speaking to his companion, he added, "bring along the knave. I see he would have his head broken, as well as his purse cut, and so be let blood in two veins at once."

Gurth was hurried along agreeably to this mandate, and having been dragged somewhat roughly over the bank, on the left-hand side of the lane, found himself in a straggling thicket, which lay betwixt it and the open common. He was compelled to follow his rough conductors into the very depth of this cover, where they stopt unexpectedly in an irregular open space, free in a great measure from trees, and on which, therefore, the beams of the moon fell without much interruption from boughs and leaves. Here his captors were joined by two other persons, apparently belonging to the gang. They had short swords by their sides, and quarter-staves in their hands, and Gurth could now observe that all six wore visors, which rendered their occupation a matter of no question, even had their former proceedings left it in doubt.

"What money hast thou, churl?" said one of the thieves.

"Thirty zecchins of my own property," answered Gurth, doggedly.

"A forfeit—a forfeit," shouted the robbers; "a Saxon hath thirty zecchins, and returns sober from a village. An undeniable and unredeemable forfeit of all he hath about him."

"I hoarded it to purchase my freedom," said Gurth.

"Thou art an ass," replied one of the thieves; "three quarts of double ale had rendered thee as free as thy master, ay, and freer too, if he be a Saxon like thyself."

"A sad truth," replied Gurth; "but if these same thirty zecchins will buy my freedom from you, unloose my hands, and I will pay them to you."

"Hold," said one who seemed to exercise some authority over the others; "this bag which thou bearest, as I can feel through thy cloak, contains more coin than thou hast told us of."

"It is the good knight my master's," answered Gurth, "of which, assuredly, I would not have spoken a word, had you been satisfied with working your will upon mine own property."

"Thou art an honest fellow," replied the robber, "I warrant thee; and we worship not St. Nicholas so devoutly but what thy thirty zecchins may yet escape, if thou deal uprightly with us. Meantime render up thy trust for the time." So saying, he took from Gurth's breast the large leathern pouch, in which the purse given him by Rebecca was enclosed, as well as the rest of the zecchins, and then continued his interrogation. —"Who is thy master?"

"The Disinherited Knight," said Gurth.

"Whose good lance," replied the robber, "won the prize in to-day's tourney? What is his name and lineage?"

"It is his pleasure," answered Gurth, "that they be concealed; and from me, assuredly, you will learn nought of them."

"What is thine own name and lineage?"

"To tell that," said Gurth, "might reveal my master's."

"Thou art a saucy groom," said the robber, "but of that anon. How comes thy master by this gold? is it of his inheritance, or by what means hath it accrued to him?"

"By his good lance," answered Gurth.—"These bags contain the ransom of four good horses, and four good suits of armour."

"How much is there?" demanded the robber.

"Two hundred zecchins."

"Only two hundred zecchins!" said the bandit; "your master hath dealt liberally by the vanquished, and put them to a cheap ransom. Name those who paid the gold."

Gurth did so.

"The armour and horse of the Templar Brian de Bois-Guilbert, at what ransom were they held?—Thou seest thou canst not deceive me."

"My master," replied Gurth, "will take nought from the Templar save his life's-blood. They are on terms of mortal defiance, and cannot hold courteous intercourse together."

"Indeed!"—repeated the robber, and paused after he had said the word. "And what wert thou now doing at Ashby with such a charge in thy custody?"

"I went thither to render to Isaac the Jew of York," replied Gurth, "the price of a suit of armour with which he fitted my master for this tournament."

"And how much didst thou pay to Isaac?—Methinks, to judge by weight, there is still two hundred zecchins in this pouch."

"I paid to Isaac," said the Saxon, "eighty zecchins, and he restored me a hundred in lieu thereof."

"How! what!" exclaimed all the robbers at once; "darest thou trifle with us, that thou tellest such improbable lies?"

"What I tell you," said Gurth, "is as true as the moon is in heaven. You will find the just sum in a silken purse within the leathern pouch, and separate from the rest of the gold."

"Bethink thee, man," said the Captain, "thou speakest of a Jew,— of an Israelite,—as unapt to restore gold, as the dry sand of his deserts to return the cup of water which the pilgrim spills upon them."

"There is no more mercy in them," said another of the banditti, "than in an unbribed sheriff's officer."

"It is, however, as I say," said Gurth.

"Strike a light instantly," said the Captain; "I will examine this said purse; and if it be as this fellow says, the Jew's bounty is little less miraculous than the stream which relieved his fathers in the wilderness."

A light was procured accordingly, and the robber proceeded to examine the purse. The others crowded around him, and even two who had hold of Gurth relaxed their grasp while they stretched their necks to see the issue of the search. Availing himself of their negligence, by a sudden exertion of strength and activity, Gurth shook himself free of their hold, and might have escaped, could he have resolved to leave his master's property behind him. But such was no part of his intention. He wrenched a quarter-staff from one of the fellows, struck down the Captain, who was altogether unaware of his purpose, and had wellnigh repossessed himself of the pouch and treasure. The thieves, however, were too nimble for him, and again secured both the bag and the trusty Gurth.

"Knave!" said the Captain, getting up, "thou hast broken my head; and with other men of our sort thou wouldst fare the worse for thy insolence. But thou shalt know thy fate instantly. First let us speak of thy master; the knight's matters must go before the squire's, according to due order of chivalry. Stand thou fast in the meantime—if thou stir again, thou shalt have that will make thee quiet for life—Comrades!" he then said, addressing his gang, "this purse is embroidered with Hebrew characters, and I well believe the yeoman's tale is true. The errant knight, his master, must needs pass us toll-free. He is too like ourselves for us to make booty of him, since dogs should not worry dogs where wolves and foxes are to be found in abundance."

"Like us?" answered one of the gang; "I should like to hear how that is made good."

"Why, thou fool," answered the Captain, "is he not poor and disinherited as we are?—Doth he not win his substance at the sword's point as we do?—Hath he not beaten Front-de-Bœuf and Malvoisin, even as we would beat them if we could? Is he not the enemy to life and death of Brian de Bois-Guilbert, whom we have so much reason to fear? And were all this otherwise, wouldst thou have us show a worse conscienc⌐ than an unbeliever, a Hebrew Jew?"

"Nay, that were a shame," muttered the other fellow; "and yet, when I served in the band of stout old Gandelyn, we had no such scruples of conscience. And this insolent peasant,—he too, I warrant me, is to be dismissed scatheless?"

"Not if thou canst scathe him," replied the Captain.—"Here, fellow," continued he, addressing Gurth, "canst thou use the staff, that thou starts to it so readily?"

"I think," said Gurth, "thou shouldst be best able to reply to that question."

"Nay, by my troth, thou gavest me a round knock," replied the Captain; "do as much for this fellow, and thou shalt pass scot-free; and if thou dost not—why, by my faith, as thou art such a sturdy knave, I think I must pay thy ransom myself.—Take thy staff, Miller," he added.

"and keep thy head; and do you others let the fellow go, and give him a staff—there is light enough to lay on load by."

The two champions being alike armed with quarter-staves, stepped forward into the centre of the open space, in order to have the full benefit of the moonlight; the thieves in the meantime laughing, and crying to their comrade, "Miller! beware thy toll-dish." The Miller, on the other hand, holding his quarter-staff by the middle, and making it flourish round his head after the fashion which the French call *faire le moulinet*, exclaimed boastfully, "Come on, churl, an thou darest: thou shalt feel the strength of a miller's thumb!"

"If thou be'st a miller," answered Gurth, undauntedly, making his weapon play around his head with equal dexterity, "thou art doubly a thief, and I, as a true man, bid thee defiance."

So saying, the two champions closed together, and for a few minutes they displayed great equality in strength, courage, and skill, intercepting and returning the blows of their adversary with the most rapid dexterity, while, from the continued clatter of their weapons, a person at a distance might have supposed that there were at least six persons engaged on each side. Less obstinate, and even less dangerous combats, have been described in good heroic verse; but that of Gurth and the Miller must remain unsung, for want of a sacred poet to do justice to its eventful progress. Yet, though quarter-staff play be out of date, what we can in prose we will do for these bold champions.

Long they fought equally, until the Miller began to lose temper at finding himself so stoutly opposed, and at hearing the laughter of his companions, who, as usual in such cases, enjoyed his vexation. This was not a state of mind favourable to the noble game of quarter-staff, in which, as in ordinary cudgel-playing, the utmost coolness is requisite; and it gave Gurth, whose temper was steady, though surly, the opportunity of acquiring a decided advantage, in availing himself of which he displayed great mastery.

The Miller pressed furiously forward, dealing blows with either end of his weapon alternately, and striving to come to half-staff distance, while Gurth defended himself against the attack, keeping his hands about a yard asunder, and covering himself by shifting his weapon with great celerity, so as to protect his head and body. Thus did he maintain the defensive, making his eye, foot, and hand keep true time, until, observing his antagonist to lose wind, he darted the staff at his face with his left hand; and, as the Miller endeavoured to parry the thrust, he slid his right hand down to his left, and with the full swing of the weapon struck his opponent on the left side of the head, who instantly measured his length upon the green sward.

"Well and yeomanly done!" shouted the robbers; "fair play and old England for ever! The Saxon hath saved both his purse and his hide, and the Miller has met his match."

"Thou mayst go thy ways, my friend," said the Captain, addressing

Gurth, in special confirmation of the general voice, "and I will cause
two of my comrades to guide thee by the best way to thy master's
pavilion, and to guard thee from night-walkers that might have less tender consciences than ours; for there is many one of them upon the
amble in such a night as this. Take heed, however," he added sternly;
"remember thou hast refused to tell thy name—ask not after ours, nor
endeavour to discover who or what we are; for, if thou makest such an
attempt, thou wilt come by worse fortune than has yet befallen thee."

Gurth thanked the Captain for his courtesy, and promised to attend
to his recommendation. Two of the outlaws, taking up their quarter-
staves, and desiring Gurth to follow close in the rear, walked roundly
forward along a by-path, which traversed the thicket and the broken
ground adjacent to it. On the very verge of the thicket two men spoke
to his conductors, and receiving an answer in a whisper, withdrew into
the wood, and suffered them to pass unmolested. This circumstance induced Gurth to believe both that the gang was strong in numbers, and
that they kept regular guards around their place of rendezvous.

When they arrived on the open heath, where Gurth might have had
some trouble in finding his road, the thieves guided him straight for ·
ward to the top of a little eminence, whence he could see, spread beneath
him in the moonlight, the palisades of the lists, the glimmering pavilions
pitched at either end, with the pennons which adorned them fluttering
in the moonbeams, and from which could be heard the hum of the song
with which the sentinels were beguiling their night-watch.

Here the thieves stopt.

"We go with you no farther," said they; "it were not safe that we
should do so.—Remember the warning you have received—keep secret
what has this night befallen you, and you will have no room to repent
it—neglect what is now told you, and the Tower of London shall not
protect you against our revenge."

"Good night to you, kind sirs," said Gurth; "I shall remember your
orders, and trust that there is no offence in wishing you a safer and an
honester trade."

Thus they parted, the outlaws returning in the direction from whence
they had come, and Gurth proceeding to the tent of his master, to whom,
notwithstanding the injunction he had received, he communicated the
whole adventures of the evening.

The Disinherited Knight was filled with astonishment, no less at the
generosity of Rebecca, by which, however, he resolved he would not
profit, than that of the robbers, to whose profession such a quality
seemed totally foreign. His course of reflections upon these singular circumstances was, however, interrupted by the necessity for taking repose,
which the fatigue of the preceding day, and the propriety of refreshing
himself for the morrow's encounter, rendered alike indispensable.

The knight, therefore, stretched himself for repose upon a rich couch
with which the tent was provided; and the faithful Gurth, extending his

hardy limbs upon a bear-skin which formed a sort of carpet to the pavilion, laid himself across the opening of the tent, so that no one could enter without awakening him.

CHAPTER XII

The heralds left their pricking up and down,
Now ringen trumpets loud and clarion.
There is no more to say, but east and west,
In go the speares sadly in the rest,
In goth the sharp spur into the side,
There see men who can just and who can ride;
There shiver shaftes upon shieldes thick,
He feeleth through the heart-spone the prick;
Up springen speares, twenty feet in height,
Out go the swordes to the silver bright;
The helms they to-hewn and to-shred;
Out bursts the blood with stern streames red.
                                        CHAUCER.

MORNING arose in unclouded splendour, and ere the sun was much above the horizon, the idlest or the most eager of the spectators appeared on the common, moving to the lists as to a general centre, in order to secure a favourable situation for viewing the continuation of the expected games.

The marshals and their attendants appeared next on the field, together with the heralds, for the purpose of receiving the names of the knights who intended to joust, with the side which each chose to espouse. This was a necessary precaution, in order to secure equality betwixt the two bodies who should be opposed to each other.

According to due formality, the Disinherited Knight was to be considered as leader of the one body, while Brian de Bois-Guilbert, who had been rated as having done second-best in the preceding day, was named first champion of the other band. Those who had concurred in the challenge adhered to his party of course, excepting only Ralph de Vipont, whom his fall had rendered unfit so soon to put on his armour. There was no want of distinguished and noble candidates to fill up the ranks on either side.

In fact, although the general tournament, in which all knights fought at once, was more dangerous than single encounters, they were, nevertheless, more frequented and practised by the chivalry of the age. Many knights, who had not sufficient confidence in their own skill to defy a single adversary of high reputation, were, nevertheless, desirous of displaying their valour in the general combat, where they might meet others with whom they were more upon an equality. On the present occasion, about fifty knights were inscribed as desirous of combating upon each side, when the marshals declared that no more could be admitted, to the disappointment of several who were too late in preferring their claim to be included.

About the hour of ten o'clock, the whole plain was crowded with horsemen, horsewomen, and foot-passengers, hastening to the tournament; and shortly after, a grand flourish of trumpets announced Prince John and his retinue, attended by many of those knights who meant to take share in the game, as well as others who had no such intention.

About the same time arrived Cedric the Saxon, with the Lady Rowena, unattended, however, by Athelstane. This Saxon lord had arrayed his tall and strong person in armour, in order to take his place among the combatants; and, considerably to the surprise of Cedric, had chosen to enlist himself on the part of the Knight Templar. The Saxon, indeed, had remonstrated strongly with his friend upon the injudicious choice he had made of his party; but he had only received that sort of answer usually given by those who are more obstinate in following their own course, than strong in justifying it.

His best, if not his only reason, for adhering to the party of Brian de Bois-Guilbert, Athelstane had the prudence to keep to himself. Though his apathy of disposition prevented his taking any means to recommend himself to the Lady Rowena, he was, nevertheless, by no means insensible to her charms, and considered his union with her as a matter already fixed beyond doubt, by the assent of Cedric and her other friends. It had therefore been with smothered displeasure that the proud though indolent Lord Coningsburgh beheld the victor of the preceding day select Rowena as the object of that honour which it became his privilege to confer. In order to punish him for a preference which seemed to interfere with his own suit, Athelstane, confident of his strength, and to whom his flatterers, at least, ascribed great skill in arms, had determined not only to deprive the Disinherited Knight of his powerful succour, but, if an opportunity should occur, to make him feel the weight of his battle-axe.

De Bracy, and other knights attached to Prince John, in obedience to a hint from him, had joined the party of the challengers, John being desirous to secure, if possible, the victory to that side. On the other hand, many other knights, both English and Norman, natives and strangers, took part against the challengers, the more readily that the opposite band was to be led by so distinguished a champion as the Disinherited Knight had approved himself.

As soon as Prince John observed that the destined Queen of the day had arrived upon the field, assuming that air of courtesy which sat well upon him when he was pleased to exhibit it, he rode forward to meet her, doffed his bonnet, and, alighting from his horse, assisted the Lady Rowena from her saddle, while his followers uncovered at the same time, and one of the most distinguished dismounted to hold her palfrey.

"It is thus," said Prince John, "that we set the dutiful example of loyalty to the Queen of Love and Beauty, and are ourselves her guide to the throne which she must this day occupy.—Ladies," he said, "attend your Queen, as you wish in your turn to be distinguished by like honours."

So saying, the Prince marshalled Rowena to the seat of honour opposite his own, while the fairest and most distinguished ladies present crowded after her to obtain places as near as possible to their temporary sovereign.

No sooner was Rowena seated, than a burst of music, half drowned by the shouts of the multitude, greeted her new dignity. Meantime, the sun shone fierce and bright upon the polished arms of the knights of either side, who crowded the opposite extremities of the lists, and held eager conference together concerning the best mode of arranging their line of battle, and supporting the conflict.

The heralds then proclaimed silence until the laws of the tourney should be rehearsed. These were calculated in some degree to abate the dangers of the day; a precaution the more necessary, as the conflict was to be maintained with sharp swords and pointed lances.

The champions were therefore prohibited to thrust with the sword, and were confined to striking. A knight, it was announced, might use a mace or battle-axe at pleasure, but the dagger was a prohibited weapon. A knight unhorsed might renew the fight on foot with any other on the opposite side in the same predicament; but mounted horsemen were in that case forbidden to assail him. When any knight could force his antagonist to the extremity of the lists, so as to touch the palisade with his person or arms, such opponent was obliged to yield himself vanquished, and his armour and horse were placed at the disposal of the conqueror. A knight thus overcome was not permitted to take further share in the combat. If any combatant was struck down, and unable to recover his feet, his squire or page might enter the lists, and drag his master out of the press; but in that case the knight was adjudged vanquished, and his arms and horse declared forfeited. The combat was to cease as soon as Prince John should throw down his leading staff, or truncheon; another precaution usually taken to prevent the unnecessary effusion of blood by the too long endurance of a sport so desperate. Any knight breaking the rules of the tournament, or otherwise transgressing the rules of honourable chivalry, was liable to be stript of his arms, and, having his shield reversed, to be placed in that posture astride upon the bars of the palisade, and exposed to public derision, in punishment of his unknightly conduct. Having announced these precautions, the heralds concluded with an exhortation to each good knight to do his duty, and to merit favour from the Queen of Beauty and Love.

This proclamation having been made, the heralds withdrew to their stations. The knights, entering at either end of the lists in long procession, arranged themselves in a double file, precisely opposite to each other, the leader of each party being in the centre of the foremost rank, a post which he did not occupy until each had carefully arranged the ranks of his party, and stationed every one in his place.

It was a goodly, and at the same time an anxious, sight, to behold so many gallant champions, mounted bravely, and armed richly, stand ready prepared for an encounter so formidable, seated on their war-saddles like so many pillars of iron, and awaiting the signal of encounter with the same ardour as their generous steeds, which, by neighing and pawing the ground, gave signal of their impatience.

As yet the knights held their long lances upright, their bright points glancing to the sun, and the streamers with which they were decorated fluttering over the plumage of the helmets. Thus they remained while the marshals of the field surveyed their ranks with the utmost exactness, lest either party had more or fewer than the appointed number. The tale was found exactly complete. The marshals then withdrew from the lists, and William de Wyvil, with a voice of thunder, pronounced the signal words—*Laissez aller!* The trumpets sounded as he spoke—the spears of the champions were at once lowered and placed in the rests— the spurs were dashed into the flanks of the horses, and the two fore- most ranks of either party rushed upon each other in full gallop, and met in the middle of the lists with a shock, the sound of which was heard at a mile's distance. The rear rank of each party advanced at a slower pace to sustain the defeated, and follow up the success of the victors of their party.

The consequences of the encounter were not instantly seen, for the dust raised by the trampling of so many steeds darkened the air, and it was a minute ere the anxious spectators could see the fate of the encounter. When the fight became visible, half the knights on each side were dismounted, some by the dexterity of their adversary's lance,—some by the superior weight and strength of opponents, which had borne down both horse and man,—some lay stretched on earth as if never more to rise,—some had already gained their feet, and were closing hand to hand with those of their antagonists who were in the same predicament,— and several on both sides, who had received wounds by which they were disabled, were stopping their blood by their scarfs, and endeavouring to extricate themselves from the tumult. The mounted knights, whose lances had been almost all broken by the fury of the encounter, were now closely engaged with their swords, shouting their war-cries, and ex- changing buffets, as if honour and life depended on the issue of the combat.

The tumult was presently increased by the advance of the second rank on either side, which, acting as a reserve, now rushed on to aid their companions. The followers of Brian de Bois-Guilbert shouted—*"Ha! Beau-seant! Beau-seant!"* [1]—For the Temple—For the Temple!" The opposite party shouted in answer—*Desdichado! Desdichado!"*—which watchword they took from the motto upon their leader's shield.

The champions thus encountering each other with the utmost fury, and with alternate success, the tide of battle seemed to flow now toward the southern, now toward the northern extremity of the lists, as the one

---

[1] *Beau-seant* was the name of the Templars' banner, which was half black, half white, to intimate, it is said, that they were candid and fair towards Christians, but black and terrible towards infidels.

or the other party prevailed. Meantime the clang of the blows, and the shouts of the combatants, mixed fearfully with the sound of the trumpets, and drowned the groans of those who fell, and lay rolling defenceless beneath the feet of the horses. The splendid armour of the combatants was now defaced with dust and blood, and gave way at every stroke of the sword and battle-axe. The gay plumage, shorn from the crests, drifted upon the breeze like snow-flakes. All that was beautiful and graceful in the martial array had disappeared, and what was now visible was only calculated to awake terror or compassion.

Yet such is the force of habit, that not only the vulgar spectators, who are naturally attracted by sights of horror, but even the ladies of distinction, who crowded the galleries, saw the conflict with a thrilling interest certainly, but without a wish to withdraw their eyes from a sight so terrible. Here and there, indeed, a fair cheek might turn pale, or a faint scream might be heard, as a lover, a brother, or a husband, was struck from his horse. But, in general, the ladies around encouraged the combatants, not only by clapping their hands and waving their veils and kerchiefs, but even by exclaiming, "Brave lance! Good sword!" when any successful thrust or blow took place under their observation.

Such being the interest taken by the fair sex in this bloody game, that of the men is the more easily understood. It showed itself in loud acclamations upon every change of fortune, while all eyes were so riveted on the lists, that the spectators seemed as if they themselves had dealt and received the blows which were there so freely bestowed. And between every pause was heard the voice of the heralds, exclaiming, "Fight on, brave knights! Man dies, but glory lives!—Fight on—death is better than defeat!—Fight on, brave knights!—for bright eyes behold your deeds!"

Amid the varied fortunes of the combat, the eyes of all endeavoured to discover the leaders of each band, who, mingling in the thick of the fight, encouraged their companions both by voice and example. Both displayed great feats of gallantry, nor did either Bois-Guilbert or the Disinherited Knight find in the ranks opposed to them a champion who could be termed their unquestioned match. They repeatedly endeavoured to single out each other, spurred by mutual animosity, and aware that the fall of either leader might be considered as decisive of victory. Such, however, was the crowd and confusion, that, during the earlier part of the conflict, their efforts to meet were unavailing, and they were repeatedly separated by the eagerness of their followers, each of whom was anxious to win honour, by measuring his strength against the leader of the opposite party.

But when the field became thin by the numbers on either side who had yielded themselves vanquished, had been compelled to the extremity of the lists, or been otherwise rendered incapable of continuing the strife, the Templar and the Disinherited Knight at length encountered hand to hand, with all the fury that mortal animosity, joined to rivalry of honour, could inspire. Such was the address of each in parrying and striking, that the spectators broke forth into a unanimous and involuntary shout, expressive of their delight and admiration.

But at this moment the party of the Disinherited Knight had the worst; the gigantic arm of Front-de-Bœuf on the one flank, and the ponderous strength of Athelstane on the other, bearing down and dispersing those immediately exposed to them. Finding themselves freed from their immediate antagonists, it seems to have occurred to both these knights at the same instant, that they would render the most decisive advantage to their party, by aiding the Templar in his contest with his rival. Turning their horses, therefore, at the same moment, the Norman spurred against the Disinherited Knight on the one side, and the Saxon on the other. It was utterly impossible that the object of this unequal and unexpected assault could have sustained it, had he not been warned by a general cry from the spectators, who could not but take interest in one exposed to such disadvantage.

"Beware! beware! Sir Disinherited!" was shouted so universally, that the knight became aware of his danger; and, striking a full blow at the Templar, he reined back his steed in the same moment, so as to escape the charge of Athelstane and Front-de-Bœuf. These knights, therefore, their aim being thus eluded, rushed from opposite sides betwixt the object of their attack and the Templar, almost running their horses against each other ere they could stop their career. Recovering their horses, however, and wheeling them round, the whole three pursued their united purpose of bearing to the earth the Disinherited Knight.

Nothing could have saved him, except the remarkable strength and activity of the noble horse which he had won on the preceding day.

This stood him in the more stead, as the horse of Bois-Guilbert was wounded, and those of Front-de-Bœuf and Athelstane were both tired with the weight of their gigantic masters, clad in complete armour, and with the preceding exertions of the day. The masterly horsemanship of the Disinherited Knight, and the activity of the noble animal which he mounted, enabled him for a few minutes to keep at sword's point his three antagonists, turning and wheeling with the agility of a hawk on the wing, keeping his enemies as far separate as he could, and rushing now against the one, now against the other, dealing sweeping blows with his sword, without waiting to receive those which were aimed at him in return.

But although the lists rang with the applauses of his dexterity, it was evident that he must at last be overpowered; and the nobles around Prince John implored him with one voice to throw down his warder, and to save so brave a knight from the disgrace of being overcome by odds.

"Not I, by the light of Heaven!" answered Prince John; "this same springal, who conceals his name, and despises our proffered hospitality, hath already gained one prize, and may now afford to let others have their turn." As he spoke thus, an unexpected incident changed the fortune of the day.

There was among the ranks of the Disinherited Knight a champion in black armour, mounted on a black horse, large of size, tall, and to all appearance powerful and strong, like the rider by whom he was mounted. This knight, who bore on his shield no device of any kind, had hitherto evinced very little interest in the event of the fight, beating off with seeming ease those combatants who attacked him, but neither pursuing his advantages, nor himself assailing any one. In short, he had hitherto acted the part rather of a spectator than of a party in the tournament, a circumstance which procured him among the spectators, the name of *Le Noir Faineant,* or the Black Sluggard.

At once this knight seemed to throw aside his apathy, when he discovered the leader of his party so hard bested; for, setting spurs to his horse, which was quite fresh, he came to his assistance like a thunderbolt, exclaiming, in a voice like a trumpet-call, *"Desdichado,* to the rescue!" It was high time; for, while the Disinherited Knight was pressing upon the Templar, Front-de-Bœuf had got nigh to him with his uplifted sword; but ere the blow could descend, the Sable Knight dealt a stroke on his head, which, glancing from the polished helmet, lighted with violence scarcely abated on the *chamfron* of the steed, and Front-de-Bœuf rolled on the ground, both horse and man equally stunned by the fury of the blow. *Le Noir Faineant* then turned his horse upon Athelstane of Coningsburgh; and his own sword having been broken in his encounter with Front-de-Bœuf, he wrenched from the hand of the bulky Saxon the battle-axe which he wielded, and, like one familiar with the use of the weapon, bestowed him such a blow upon the crest, that Athelstane also lay senseless on the field. Having achieved this double feat, for which he was the more highly applauded that it was totally unexpected from him, the knight seemed to resume the sluggishness of his character, returning calmly to the northern extremity of the lists, leaving his leader to cope as he best could with Brian de Bois-Guilbert. This was no longer matter of so much difficulty as formerly. The Templar's horse had bled much, and gave way under the shock of the Disinherited Knight's charge. Brian de Bois-Guilbert rolled on the field, encumbered with the stirrup from which he was unable to draw his foot. His antagonist sprung from horseback, waved his fatal sword over the head of his adversary, and commanded him to yield himself; when Prince John, more moved by the Templar's dangerous situation than he had been by that of his rival, saved him the mortification of confessing himself vanquished, by casting down his warder, and putting an end to the conflict.

It was, indeed, only the relics and embers of the fight which continued to burn; for of the few knights who still continued in the lists, the greater part had, by tacit consent, forborne the conflict for some time, leaving it to be determined by the strife of the leaders.

The squires, who had found it a matter of danger and difficulty to attend their masters during the engagement, now thronged into the lists to pay their dutiful attendance to the wounded, who were removed with the utmost care and attention to the neighbouring pavilions, or to the quarters prepared for them in the adjoining village.

Thus ended the memorable field of Ashby-de-la-Zouche, one of the most gallantly contested tournaments of that age; for although only four knights, including one who was smothered by the heat of his armour, had died upon the field, yet upwards of thirty were desperately wounded, four or five of whom never recovered. Several more were disabled for life; and those who escaped best carried the marks of the conflict to the grave with them. Hence it is always mentioned in the old records, as the Gentle and Joyous Passage of Arms of Ashby.

It being now the duty of Prince John to name the knight who had done best, he determined that the honour of the day remained with the knight whom the popular voice had termed *Le Noir Faineant*. It was pointed out to the Prince, in impeachment of this decree, that the victory had been in fact won by the Disinherited Knight, who, in the course of the day, had overcome six champions with his own hand, and who had finally unhorsed and struck down the leader of the opposite party. But Prince John adhered to his own opinion, on the ground that the Disinherited Knight and his party had lost the day but for the powerful assistance of the Knight of the Black Armour, to whom, therefore, he persisted in awarding the prize.

To the surprise of all present, however, the knight thus preferred was nowhere to be found. He had left the lists immediately when the conflict ceased, and had been observed by some spectators to move down one of the forest glades with the same slow pace and listless and indifferent manner which had procured him the epithet of the Black Sluggard. After he had been summoned twice by sound of trumpet, and proclamation of the heralds, it became necessary to name another to receive the honours which had been assigned to him. Prince John had now no further excuse for resisting the claim of the Disinherited Knight, whom, therefore, he named the champion of the day.

Through a field slippery with blood, and encumbered with broken armour and the bodies of slain and wounded horses, the marshals of the lists again conducted the victor to the foot of Prince John's throne.

"Disinherited Knight," said Prince John, "since by that title only you will consent to be known to us, we a second time award to you the honours of this tournament, and announce to you your right to claim and receive from the hands of the Queen of Love and Beauty, the Chaplet of Honour which your valour has justly deserved." The Knight bowed low and gracefully, but returned no answer.

While the trumpets sounded, while the heralds strained their voices in proclaiming honour to the brave and glory to the victor—while ladies waved their silken kerchiefs and embroidered veils, and while all ranks

joined in a clamorous shout of exultation, the marshals conducted the
Disinherited Knight across the lists to the foot of that throne of honour
which was occupied by the Lady Rowena.

On the lower step of this throne the champion was made to kneel down.
Indeed his whole action since the fight had ended, seemed rather to have
been upon the impulse of those around him than from his own free will;
and it was observed that he tottered as they guided him the second time
across the lists. Rowena, descending from her station with a graceful
and dignified step, was about to place the chaplet which she held in her
hand upon the helmet of the champion, when the marshals exclaimed
with one voice, "It must not be thus—his head must be bare." The
knight muttered faintly a few words, which were lost in the hollow of
his helmet, but their purport seemed to be a desire that his casque might
not be removed.

Whether from love of form, or from curiosity, the marshals paid no
attention to his expressions of reluctance, but unhelmed him by cutting
the laces of his casque, and undoing the fastening of his gorget. When the
helmet was removed, the well-formed, yet sun-burnt features of a young
man of twenty-five were seen, amidst a profusion of short fair hair. His
countenance was as pale as death, and marked in one or two places with
streaks of blood.

Rowena had no sooner beheld him than she uttered a faint shriek;
but at once summoning up the energy of her disposition, and compelling
herself, as it were, to proceed, while her frame yet trembled with the
violence of sudden emotion, she placed upon the drooping head of the
victor the splendid chaplet which was the destined reward of the day,
and pronounced, in a clear and distinct tone, these words: "I bestow on
thee this chaplet, Sir Knight, as the meed of valour assigned to this day's
victor:" Here she paused a moment, and then firmly added, "And
upon brows more worthy could a wreath of chivalry never be placed!"

The knight stooped his head, and kissed the hand of the lovely Sovereign by whom his valour had been rewarded; and then, sinking yet
farther forward, lay prostrate at her feet.

There was a general consternation. Cedric, who had been struck mute
by the sudden appearance of his banished son, now rushed forward, as
if to separate him from Rowena. But this had been already accomplished by the marshals of the field, who, guessing the cause of Ivanhoe's
swoon, had hastened to undo his armour, and found that the head of
a lance had penetrated his breastplate, and inflicted a wound in his side.

CHAPTER XIII

"Heroes, approach !" Atrides thus aloud,
"Stand forth distinguish'd from the circling crowd,
Ye who by skill or manly force may claim,
Your rivals to surpass and merit fame.
This cow, worth twenty oxen is decreed,
For him who farthest sends the winged reed."
Iliad.

THE name of Ivanhoe was no sooner pronounced than it flew from mouth to mouth, with all the celerity with which eagerness could convey and curiosity receive it. It was not long ere it reached the circle of the Prince, whose brow darkened as he heard the news. Looking around him, however, with an air of scorn, "My Lords," said he, "and especially you, Sir Prior, what think ye of the doctrine the learned tell us, concerning innate attractions and antipathies? Methinks that I felt the presence of my brother's minion, even when I least guessed whom yonder suit of armour enclosed."

"Front-de-Bœuf must prepare to restore his fief of Ivanhoe," said De Bracy, who, having discharged his part honourably in the tournament, had laid his shield and helmet aside, and again mingled with the Prince's retinue.

"Ay," answered Waldemar Fitzurse, "this gallant is likely to reclaim the castle and manor which Richard assigned to him, and which your Highness's generosity has since given to Front-de-Bœuf."

"Front-de-Bœuf," replied John, "is a man more willing to swallow three manors such as Ivanhoe than to disgorge one of them. For the rest, sirs, I hope none here will deny my right to confer the fiefs of the crown upon the faithful followers who are around me, and ready to perform the usual military service, in the room of those who have wandered to foreign countries, and can neither render homage nor service when called upon."

The audience were too much interested in the question not to pronounce the Prince's assumed right altogether indubitable. "A generous Prince!—a most noble Lord, who thus takes upon himself the task of rewarding his faithful followers!"

Such were the words which burst from the train, expectants all of them of similar grants at the expense of King Richard's followers and favourites, if indeed they had not as yet received such. Prior Aymer also assented to the general proposition, observing, however, "that the blessed Jerusalem could not indeed be termed a foreign country. She was *communis mater*—the mother of all Christians. But he saw not," he declared, "how the Knight of Ivanhoe could plead any advantage from this, since he" (the Prior) "was assured that the crusaders, under Richard, had never proceeded much farther than Askalon, which, as all the world knew, was a town of the Philistines, and entitled to none of the privileges of the Holy City."

Waldemar, whose curiosity had led him towards the place where Ivanhoe had fallen to the ground, now returned. "The gallant," said he, "is likely to give your Highness little disturbance, and to leave Front-de-Bœuf in the quiet possession of his gains—he is severely wounded."

"Whatever becomes of him," said Prince John, "he is victor of the day; and were he tenfold our enemy, or the devoted friend of our brother, which is perhaps the same, his wounds must be looked to—our own physician shall attend him."

A stern smile curled the Prince's lip as he spoke. Waldemar Fitzurse hastened to reply, that Ivanhoe was already removed from the lists, and in the custody of his friends.

"I was somewhat afflicted," he said, "to see the grief of the Queen of Love and Beauty, whose sovereignty of a day this event has changed into mourning. I am not a man to be moved by a woman's lament for her lover, but this same Lady Rowena suppressed her sorrow with such dignity of manner, that it could only be discovered by her folded hands, and her tearless eye, which trembled as it remained fixed on the lifeless form before her."

"Who is this Lady Rowena," said Prince John, "of whom we have heard so much?"

"A Saxon heiress of large possessions," replied the Prior Aymer; "a rose of loveliness, and a jewel of wealth; the fairest among a thousand, a bundle of myrrh, and a cluster of camphire."

"We shall cheer her sorrows," said Prince John, "and amend her blood, by wedding her to a Norman. She seems a minor and must therefore be at our royal disposal in marriage.—How sayst thou, De Bracy? What thinkst thou of gaining fair lands and livings, by wedding a Saxon, after the fashion of the followers of the Conqueror?"

"If the lands are to my liking, my lord," answered De Bracy, "it will be hard to displease me with a bride; and deeply will I hold myself bound to your highness for a good deed, which will fulfil all promises made in favour of your servant and vassal."

"We will not forget it," said Prince John; "and that we may instantly go to work, command our seneschal presently to order the attendance of the Lady Rowena and her company—that is, the rude churl her guardian, and the Saxon ox whom the Black Knight struck down in the tournament, upon this evening's banquet.—De Bigot," he added to his seneschal, "thou wilt word this our second summons so courteously, as to gratify the pride of these Saxons, and make it impossible for them again to refuse; although, by the bones of Becket, courtesy to them is casting pearls before swine."

Prince John had proceeded thus far, and was about to give the signal for retiring from the lists, when a small billet was put into his hand.

"From whence?" said Prince John, looking at the person by whom
it was delivered.

"From foreign parts, my lord, but from whence I know not," replied
his attendant. "A Frenchman brought it hither, who said he had ridden
night and day to put it into the hands of your highness."

The Prince looked narrowly at the superscription, and then at the seal,
placed so as to secure the flox-silk with which the billet was surrounded,
and which bore the impression of three fleurs-de-lis. John then opened
the billet with apparent agitation, which visibly and greatly increased
when he had perused the contents, which were expressed in these words—
"Take heed to yourself, for the Devil is unchained!"

The Prince turned as pale as death, looked first on the earth, and then
up to heaven, like a man who has received news that sentence of execution has been passed upon him. Recovering from the first effects of his
surprise, he took Waldemar Fitzurse and De Bracy aside, and put the
billet into their hands successively. "It means," he added, in a faltering
voice, "that my brother Richard has obtained his freedom."

"This may be a false alarm, or a forged letter," said De Bracy.

"It is France's own hand and seal," replied Prince John.

"It is time, then," said Fitzurse, "to draw our party to a head, either
at York, or some other centrical place. A few days later, and it will be
indeed too late. Your highness must break short this present mummery."

"The yeomen and commons," said De Bracy, "must not be dismissed
discontented, for lack of their share in the sports."

"The day," said Waldemar, "is not yet very far spent—let the archers
shoot a few rounds at the target, and the prize be adjudged. This will be
an abundant fulfilment of the Prince's promises, so far as this herd of
Saxon serfs is concerned."

"I thank thee, Waldemar," said the Prince; "thou remindest me, too,
that I have a debt to pay to that insolent peasant who yesterday insulted
our person. Our banquet also shall go forward to-night as we proposed.
Were this my last hour of power, it should be an hour sacred to revenge
and to pleasure—let new cares come with to-morrow's new day."

The sound of the trumpets soon recalled those spectators who had
already begun to leave the field; and proclamation was made that Prince
John, suddenly called by high and peremptory public duties, held himself obliged to discontinue the entertainments of to-morrow's festival:
Nevertheless, that, unwilling so many good yeomen should depart without a trial of skill, he was pleased to appoint them, before leaving the
ground, presently to execute the competition of archery intended for the
morrow. To the best archer a prize was to be awarded, being a bugle-
horn, mounted with silver, and a silver baldric richly ornamented with
a medallion of St. Hubert, the patron of silvan sport.

More than thirty yeomen at first presented themselves as competitors,
several of whom were rangers and under-keepers in the royal forests of
Needwood and Charnwood. When, however, the archers understood with

whom they were to be matched, upwards of twenty withdrew themselves from the contest, unwilling to encounter the dishonour of almost certain defeat. For in those days the skill of each celebrated marksman was as well known for many miles round him, as the qualities of a horse trained at Newmarket are familiar to those who frequent that well-known meeting.

The diminished list of competitors for silvan fame still amounted to eight. Prince John stepped from his royal seat to view more nearly the persons of these chosen yeomen, several of whom wore the royal livery. Having satisfied his curiosity by this investigation, he looked for the object of his resentment, whom he observed standing on the same spot, and with the same composed countenance which he had exhibited upon the preceding day.

"Fellow," said Prince John, "I guessed by thy insolent babble thou wert no true lover of the long-bow, and I see thou darest not adventure thy skill among such merry-men as stand yonder."

"Under favour, sir," replied the yeoman, "I have another reason for refraining to shoot, besides the fearing discomfiture and disgrace."

"And what is thy other reason?" said Prince John, who, for some cause which perhaps he could not himself have explained, felt a painful curiosity respecting this individual.

"Because," replied the woodsman, "I know not if these yeomen and I are used to shoot at the same marks; and because, moreover, I know not how your Grace might relish the winning of a third prize by one who has unwittingly fallen under your displeasure."

Prince John coloured as he put the question, "What is thy name, yeoman?"

"Locksley," answered the yeoman.

"Then, Locksley," said Prince John, "thou shalt shoot in thy turn, when these yeomen have displayed their skill. If thou carriest the prize, I will add to it twenty nobles; but if thou losest it, thou shalt be stript of thy Lincoln green, and scourged out of the lists with bowstrings, for a wordy and insolent braggart."

"And how if I refuse to shoot on such a wager?" said the yeoman.— "Your Grace's power, supported, as it is, by so many men-at-arms, may indeed easily strip and scourge me, but cannot compel me to bend or to draw my bow."

"If thou refusest my fair proffer," said the Prince, "the Provost of the lists shall cut thy bowstring, break thy bow and arrows, and expel thee from the presence as a faint-hearted craven."

"This is no fair chance you put on me, proud Prince," said the yeoman, "to compel me to peril myself against the best archers of Leicester and Staffordshire, under the penalty of infamy if they should overshoot me. Nevertheless, I will obey your pleasure."

"Look to him close, men-at-arms," said Prince John, "his heart is sinking; I am jealous lest he attempt to escape the trial.—And do you, good fellows, shoot boldly round; a buck and a butt of wine are ready for your refreshment in yonder tent, when the prize is won."

A target was placed at the upper end of the southern avenue which led to the lists. The contending archers took their station in turn, at the bottom of the southern access, the distance between that station and the mark allowing full distance for what was called a shot at rovers. The archers, having previously determined by lot their order of precedence, were to shoot each three shafts in succession. The sports were regulated by an officer of inferior rank, termed the Provost of the Games; for the high rank of the marshals of the lists would have been held degraded, had they condescended to superintend the sports of the yeomanry.

One by one the archers, stepping forward, delivered their shafts yeo-manlike and bravely. Of twenty-four arrows, shot in succession, ten were fixed in the target, and the others ranged so near it, that, considering the distance of the mark, it was accounted good archery. Of the ten shafts which hit the target, two within the inner ring were shot by Hubert, a forester in the service of Malvoisin, who was accordingly pronounced victorious.

"Now, Locksley," said Prince John to the bold yeoman, with a bitter smile, "wilt thou try conclusions with Hubert, or wilt thou yield up bow, baldric, and quiver, to the Provost of the sports?"

"Sith it be no better," said Locksley, "I am content to try my fortune; on condition that when I have shot two shafts at yonder mark of Hubert's, he shall be bound to shoot one at that which I shall propose."

"That is but fair," answered Prince John, "and it shall not be refused thee.—If thou dost beat this braggart, Hubert, I will fill the bugle with silver-pennies for thee."

"A man can do but his best," answered Hubert; "but my grandsire drew a good long bow at Hastings, and I trust not to dishonour his memory."

The former target was now removed, and a fresh one of the same size placed in its room. Hubert, who, as victor in the first trial of skill, had the right to shoot first, took his aim with great deliberation, long measur-ing the distance with his eye, while he held in his hand his bended bow, with the arrow placed on the string. At length he made a step forward, and raising the bow at the full stretch of his left arm, till the centre or grasping-place was nigh level with his face, he drew his bowstring to his ear. The arrow whistled through the air, and lighted within the inner ring of the target, but not exactly in the centre.

"You have not allowed for the wind, Hubert," said his antagonist, bending his bow, "or that had been a better shot."

So saying, and without showing the least anxiety to pause upon his aim, Locksley stept to the appointed station, and shot his arrow as carelessly in appearance as if he had not even looked at the mark. He was speaking almost at the instant that the shaft left the bowstring, yet it alighted in the target two inches nearer to the white spot which marked the centre than that of Hubert.

"By the light of heaven!" said Prince John to Hubert, "an thou suffer that runagate knave to overcome thee, thou art worthy of the gallows!"

Hubert had but one set speech for all occasions.

"An your highness were to hang me," he said, "a man can do but his best. Nevertheless, my grandsire drew a good bow"—

"The foul fiend on thy grandsire and all his generation!" interrupted John, "shoot, knave, and shoot thy best, or it shall be the worse for thee!"

Thus exhorted, Hubert resumed his place, and not neglecting the caution which he had received from his adversary, he made the necessary allowance for a very light air of wind, which had just arisen, and shot so successfully that his arrow alighted in the very centre of the target.

"A Hubert! a Hubert!" shouted the populace, more interested in a known person than in a stranger. "In the clout!—in the clout!—a Hubert for ever!"

"Thou canst not mend that shot, Locksley," said the Prince, with an insulting smile.

"I will notch his shaft for him, however," replied Locksley.

And letting fly his arrow with a little more precaution than before, it lighted right upon that of his competitor, which it split to shivers. The people who stood around were so astonished at his wonderful dexterity, that they could not even give vent to their surprise in their usual clamour. "This must be the devil, and no man of flesh and blood," whispered the yeomen to each other; "such archery was never seen since a bow was first bent in Britain."

"And now," said Locksley, "I will crave your Grace's permission to plant such a mark as is used in the North Country; and welcome every brave yeoman who shall try a shot at it to win a smile from the bonny lass he loves best."

He then turned to leave the lists. "Let your guards attend me," he said, "if you please—I go but to cut a rod from the next willow-bush."

Prince John made a signal that some attendants should follow him in case of his escape: but the cry of "Shame! shame!" which burst from the multitude, induced him to alter his ungenerous purpose.

Locksley returned almost instantly with a willow wand about six feet in length, perfectly straight, and rather thicker than a man's thumb. He began to peel this with great composure, observing at the same time, that to ask a good woodsman to shoot at a target so broad as had hitherto been used, was to put shame upon his skill. "For his own part," he said, "and in the land where he was bred, men would as soon take for their mark King Arthur's round-table, which held sixty knights around it. A child of seven years old," he said, "might hit yonder target with a headless shaft; but," added he, walking deliberately to the other end of the lists, and sticking the willow wand upright in the ground, "he that hits that rod at five-score yards, I call him an archer fit to bear both bow and quiver before a king, an it were the stout King Richard himself."

"My grandsire," said Hubert, "drew a good bow at the battle of Hastings, and never shot at such a mark in his life—and neither will I. If this yeoman can cleave that rod, I give him the bucklers—or rather, I yield to the devil that is in his jerkin, and not to any human skill; a man can but do his best, and I will not shoot where I am sure to miss. I might as well shoot at the edge of our parson's whittle, or at a wheat straw, or at a sunbeam, as at a twinkling white streak which I can hardly see."

"Cowardly dog!" said Prince John.—"Sirrah Locksley, do thou shoot; but, if thou hittest such a mark, I will say thou art the first man ever did so. Howe'er it be, thou shalt not crow over us with a mere show of superior skill."

"I will do my best, as Hubert says," answered Locksley, "no man can do more."

So saying, he again bent his bow, but on the present occasion looked with attention to his weapon, and changed the string, which he thought was no longer truly round, having been a little frayed by the two former shots. He then took his aim with some deliberation, and the multitude awaited the event in breathless silence. The archer vindicated their opinion of his skill: his arrow split the willow rod against which it was aimed. A jubilee of acclamations followed; and even Prince John, in admiration of Locksley's skill, lost for an instant his dislike to his person. "These twenty nobles," he said, "which, with the bugle, thou hast fairly won, are thine own; we will make them fifty, if thou wilt take livery and service with us as a yeoman of our body guard, and be near our person. For never did so strong a hand bend a bow, or so true an eye direct a shaft."

"Pardon me, noble Prince," said Locksley; "but I have vowed, that if ever I take service, it should be with your royal brother King Richard. These twenty nobles I leave to Hubert, who has this day drawn as brave a bow as his grandsire did at Hastings. Had his modesty not refused the trial, he would have hit the wand as well as I."

Hubert shook his head as he received with reluctance the bounty of the stranger, and Locksley, anxious to escape further observation, mixed with the crowd, and was seen no more.

The victorious archer would not perhaps have escaped John's attention so easily, had not that Prince had other subjects of anxious and more important meditation pressing upon his mind at that instant. He called upon his chamberlain as he gave the signal for retiring from the lists, and commanded him instantly to gallop to Ashby, and seek out Isaac the Jew. "Tell the dog," he said, "to send me, before sun-down, two thousand crowns. He knows the security; but thou mayst show him this ring for a token. The rest of the money must be paid at York within six days. If he neglects, I will have the unbelieving villain's head. Look that thou pass him not on the way; for the circumcised slave was displaying his stolen finery amongst us."

So saying, the Prince resumed his horse, and returned to Ashby, the whole crowd breaking up and dispersing upon his retreat.

CHAPTER XIV

> In rough magnificence array'd,
> When ancient Chivalry display'd
> The pomp of her heroic games,
> And crested chiefs and tissued dames
> Assembled, at the clarion's call,
> In some proud castle's high arch'd hall.
> WARTON.

PRINCE JOHN held his high festival in the Castle of Ashby. This was not the same building of which the stately ruins still interest the traveller, and which was erected at a later period by the Lord Hastings, High Chamberlain of England, one of the first victims of the tyranny of Richard the Third, and yet better known as one of Shakespeare's characters than by his historical fame. The castle and town of Ashby, at this time, belonged to Roger de Quincy, Earl of Winchester, who, during the period of our history, was absent in the Holy Land. Prince John, in the meanwhile, occupied his castle, and disposed of his domains without scruple; and seeking at present to dazzle men's eyes by his hospitality and magnificence, had given orders for great preparations, in order to render the banquet as splendid as possible.

The purveyors of the Prince, who exercised on this and other occasions the full authority of royalty, had swept the country of all that could be collected which was esteemed fit for their master's table. Guests also were invited in great numbers; and in the necessity in which he then found himself of courting popularity, Prince John had extended his invitation to a few distinguished Saxon and Danish families, as well as to the Norman nobility and gentry of the neighbourhood. However despised and degraded on ordinary occasions, the great numbers of the Anglo-Saxons must necessarily render them formidable in the civil commotions which seemed approaching, and it was an obvious point of policy to secure popularity with their leaders.

It was accordingly the Prince's intention, which he for some time maintained, to treat these unwonted guests with a courtesy to which they had been little accustomed. But although no man with less scruple made his ordinary habits and feelings bend to his interest, it was the misfortune of this Prince, that his levity and petulance were perpetually breaking out, and undoing all that had been gained by his previous dissimulation.

Of this fickle temper he gave a memorable example in Ireland, when sent thither by his father, Henry the Second, with the purpose of buying golden opinions of the inhabitants of that new and important acquisition to the English crown. Upon this occasion the Irish chieftains contended which should first offer to the young Prince their loyal homage and the kiss of peace. But, instead of receiving their salutations with courtesy, John and his petulant attendants could not resist the temptation of pulling the long beards of the Irish chieftains; a conduct which, as might have been expected, was highly resented by these insulted dignitaries, and produced fatal consequences to the English domination in Ireland. It is necessary to keep these inconsistencies of John's character in view, that the reader may understand his conduct during the present evening.

In execution of the resolution which he had formed during his cooler moments, Prince John received Cedric and Athelstane with distinguished courtesy, and expressed his disappointment, without resentment, when the indisposition of Rowena was alleged by the former as a reason for her not attending upon his gracious summons. Cedric and Athelstane were both dressed in the ancient Saxon garb, which, although not unhandsome in itself, and in the present instance composed of costly materials, was so remote in shape and appearance from that of the other guests, that Prince John took great credit to himself with Waldemar Fitzurse for refraining from laughter at a sight which the fashion of the day rendered ridiculous. Yet, in the eye of sober judgment, the short close tunic and long mantle of the Saxons was a more graceful, as well as a more convenient dress, than the garb of the Normans, whose under garment was a long doublet, so loose as to resemble a shirt or waggoner's frock, covered by a cloak of scanty dimensions, neither fit to defend the wearer from cold or from rain, and the only purpose of which appeared to be to display as much fur, embroidery, and jewellery work, as the ingenuity of the tailor could contrive to lay upon it. The Emperor Charlemagne, in whose reign they were first introduced, seems to have been very sensible of the inconveniences arising from the fashion of this garment. "In Heaven's name," said he, "to what purpose serve these abridged cloaks? If we are in bed they are no cover, on horseback they are no protection from the wind and rain, and when seated, they do not guard our legs from the damp or the frost."

Nevertheless, spite of this imperial objurgation, the short cloaks continued in fashion down to the time of which we treat, and particularly among the princes of the House of Anjou. They were therefore in universal use among Prince John's courtiers; and the long mantle, which formed the upper garment of the Saxons, was held in proportional derision.

The guests were seated at a table which groaned under the quantity of good cheer. The numerous cooks who attended on the Prince's progress, having exerted all their art in varying the forms in which the ordinary provisions were served up, had succeeded almost as well as the modern professors of the culinary art in rendering them perfectly unlike their natural appearance. Besides these dishes of domestic origin, there were various delicacies brought from foreign parts, and a quantity of rich pastry, as well as of the simnel-bread and wastle cakes, which were only used at the tables of the highest nobility. The banquet was crowned with the richest wines, both foreign and domestic.

But, though luxurious, the Norman nobles were not, generally speaking, an intemperate race. While indulging themselves in the pleasures of the table, they aimed at delicacy, but avoided excess, and were apt to attribute gluttony and drunkenness to the vanquished Saxons, as vices peculiar to their inferior station. Prince John, indeed, and those who courted his pleasure by imitating his foibles, were apt to indulge to excess in the pleasures of the trencher and the goblet; and indeed it is well known that his death was occasioned by a surfeit upon peaches and new ale. His conduct, however, was an exception to the general manners of his countrymen.

With sly gravity, interrupted only by private signs to each other, the Norman knights and nobles beheld the ruder demeanour of Athelstane and Cedric at a banquet, to the form and fashion of which they were unaccustomed. And while their manners were thus the subject of sarcastic observation, the untaught Saxons unwittingly transgressed several of the arbitrary rules established for the regulation of society. Now, it is well known, that a man may with more impunity be guilty of an actual breach either of real good breeding or of good morals, than appear ignorant of the most minute point of fashionable etiquette. Thus Cedric, who dried his hands with a towel, instead of suffering the moisture to exhale by waving them gracefully in the air, incurred more ridicule than his companion Athelstane, when he swallowed to his own single share the whole of a large pasty composed of the most exquisite foreign delicacies, and termed at that time a *Karum-pie*. When, however, it was discovered, by a serious cross-examination, that the Thane of Coningsburgh (or Franklin, as the Normans termed him) had no idea what he had been devouring, and that he had taken the contents of the Karum-pie for larks and pigeons, whereas they were in fact beccaficoes and nightingales, his ignorance brought him in for an ample share of the ridicule which would have been more justly bestowed on his gluttony.

The long feast had at length its end; and, while the goblet circulated freely, men talked of the feats of the preceding tournament,—of the unknown victor in the archery games, of the Black Knight, whose self-denial had induced him to withdraw from the honours he had won,—and of the gallant Ivanhoe, who had so dearly bought the honours of the day. The topics were treated with military frankness, and the jest and laugh went round the hall. The brow of Prince John alone was overclouded during these discussions; some overpowering care seemed agitating his mind, and it was only when he received occasional hints from his attendants, that he seemed to take interest in what was passing around him. On such occasions he would start up, quaff a cup of wine as if to raise his spirits, and then mingle in the conversation by some observation made abruptly or at random.

"We drink this beaker," said he, "to the health of Wilfred of Ivanhoe, champion of this Passage of Arms, and grieve that his wound renders him absent from our board. Let all fill to the pledge, and especially Cedric of Rotherwood, the worthy father of a son so promising."

"No, my lord," replied Cedric, standing up, and placing on the table his untasted cup, "I yield not the name of son to the disobedient youth, who at once despises my commands, and relinquishes the manners and customs of his fathers."

" 'Tis impossible," cried Prince John, with well-feigned astonishment, "that so gallant a knight should be an unworthy or disobedient son!"

"Yet, my lord," answered Cedric, "so it is with this Wilfred. He left my homely dwelling to mingle with the gay nobility of your brother's court, where he learned to do those tricks of horsemanship which you prize so highly. He left it contrary to my wish and command; and in the days of Alfred that would have been termed disobedience—ay, and a crime severely punishable."

"Alas!" replied Prince John, with a deep sigh of affected sympathy, "since your son was a follower of my unhappy brother, it need not be enquired where or from whom he learned the lesson of filial disobedience."

Thus spake Prince John, wilfully forgetting, that of all the sons of Henry the Second, though no one was free from the charge, he himself had been most distinguished for rebellion and ingratitude to his father.

"I think," said he, after a moment's pause, "that my brother proposed to confer upon his favourite the rich manor of Ivanhoe."

"He did endow him with it," answered Cedric; "nor is it my least quarrel with my son, that he stooped to hold, as a feudal vassal, the very domains which his fathers possessed in free and independent right."

"We shall then have your willing sanction, good Cedric," said Prince John, "to confer this fief upon a person whose dignity will not be diminished by holding land of the British crown.—Sir Reginald Front-de-Bœuf," he said, turning towards that Baron, "I trust you will so keep the goodly Barony of Ivanhoe, that Sir Wilfred shall not incur his father's farther displeasure by again entering upon that fief."

"By St. Anthony!" answered the black-brow'd giant, "I will consent that your highness shall hold me a Saxon, if either Cedric or Wilfred, or the best that ever bore English blood, shall wrench from me the gift with which your highness has graced me."

"Whoever shall call thee Saxon, Sir Baron," replied Cedric, offended at a mode of expression by which the Normans frequently expressed their habitual contempt of the English, "will do thee an honour as great as it is undeserved."

Front-de-Bœuf would have replied, but Prince John's petulance and levity got the start.

"Assuredly," said he, "my lords, the noble Cedric speaks truth; and his race may claim precedence over us as much in the length of their pedigrees as in the longitude of their cloaks."

"They go before us indeed in the field—as deer before dogs," said Malvoisin.

"And with good right may they go before us—forget not," said the Prior Aymer, "the superior decency and decorum of their manners."

"Their singular abstemiousness and temperance," said De Bracy, forgetting the plan which promised him a Saxon bride.

"Together with the courage and conduct," said Brian de Bois-Guilbert, "by which they distinguished themselves at Hastings and elsewhere."

While, with smooth and smiling cheek, the courtiers, each in turn, followed their Prince's example, and aimed a shaft of ridicule at Cedric, the face of the Saxon became inflamed with passion, and he glanced his eyes fiercely from one to another, as if the quick succession of so many injuries had prevented his replying to them in turn; or, like a baited bull, who, surrounded by his tormenters, is at a loss to choose from among them the immediate object of his revenge. At length he spoke, in a voice half choked with passion; and, addressing himself to Prince John as the head and front of the offence which he had received, "Whatever," he said, "have been the follies and vices of our race, a Saxon would have been held *nidering*" [1] (the most emphatic term for abject worthlessness), "who should in his own hall, and while his own wine-cup passed, have treated, or suffered to be treated, an unoffending guest as your highness has this day beheld me used; and whatever was the misfortune of our fathers on the field of Hastings, those may at least be silent," here he looked at Front-de-Bœuf and the Templar, "who have within these few hours once and again lost saddle and stirrup before the lance of a Saxon."

"By my faith, a biting jest!" said Prince John. "How like you it, sirs?— Our Saxon subjects rise in spirit and courage; become shrewd in wit, and bold in bearing, in these unsettled times—What say ye, my lords?— By this good light, I hold it best to take our galleys, and return to Normandy in time."

"For fear of the Saxons?" said De Bracy, laughing; "we should need no weapon but our hunting spears to bring these boars to bay."

"A truce with your raillery, Sir Knights," said Fitzurse;—"and it were well," he added, addressing the Prince, "that your highness should assure the worthy Cedric there is no insult intended him by jest, which must sound but harshly in the ear of a stranger."

"Insult?" answered Prince John, resuming his courtesy of demeanour; "I trust it will not be thought that I could mean, or permit any, to be

---

[1] There was nothing accounted so ignominious among the Saxons as to merit this disgraceful epithet. Even William the Conqueror, hated as he was by them, continued to draw a considerable army of Anglo-Saxons to his standard, by threatening to stigmatise those who staid at home, as *nidering*. Bartholinus, I think, mentions a similar phrase which had like influence on the Danes.—L. T.

offered in my presence. Here! I fill my cup to Cedric himself, since he refuses to pledge his son's health."

The cup went round amid the well-dissembled applause of the courtiers, which, however, failed to make the impression on the mind of the Saxon that had been designed. He was not naturally acute of perception, but those too much undervalued his understanding who deemed that this flattering compliment would obliterate the sense of the prior insult. He was silent, however, when the royal pledge again passed round, "To Sir Athelstane of Coningsburgh."

The Knight made his obeisance, and showed his sense of the honour by draining a huge goblet in answer to it.

"And now, sirs," said Prince John, who began to be warmed with the wine which he had drank, "having done justice to our Saxon guests, we will pray of them some requital to our courtesy.—Worthy Thane," he continued, addressing Cedric, "may we pray you to name to us some Norman whose mention may least sully your mouth, and to wash down with a goblet of wine all bitterness which the sound may leave behind it?"

Fitzurse arose while Prince John spoke, and gliding behind the seat of the Saxon, whispered to him not to omit the opportunity of putting an end to unkindness betwixt the two races, by naming Prince John. The Saxon replied not to this politic insinuation, but, rising up, and filling his cup to the brim, he addressed Prince John in these words: "Your highness has required that I should name a Norman deserving to be remembered at our banquet. This, perchance, is a hard task, since it calls on the slave to sing the praises of the master—upon the vanquished, while pressed by all the evils of conquest, to sing the praises of the conqueror. Yet I *will* name a Norman—the first in arms and in place—the best and the noblest of his race. And the lips that shall refuse to pledge me to his well-earned fame, I term false and dishonoured, and will so maintain them with my life.—I quaff this goblet to the health of Richard the Lion-hearted!"

Prince John, who had expected that his own name would have closed the Saxon's speech, started when that of his injured brother was so unexpectedly introduced. He raised mechanically the wine-cup to his lips, then instantly set it down, to view the demeanour of the company at this unexpected proposal, which many of them felt it as unsafe to oppose as to comply with. Some of them, ancient and experienced courtiers, closely imitated the example of the Prince himself, raising the goblet to their lips, and again replacing it before them. There were many who, with a more generous feeling, exclaimed, "Long live King Richard; and may he be speedily restored to us!" And some few, among whom were Front-de-Bœuf and the Templar, in sullen disdain suffered their goblets to stand untasted before them. But no man ventured directly to gainsay a pledge filled to the health of the reigning monarch.

Having enjoyed his triumph for about a minute, Cedric said to his companion, "Up, noble Athelstane! we have remained here long enough, since we have requited the hospitable courtesy of Prince John's banquet. Those who wish to know further of our rude Saxon manners must henceforth seek us in the homes of our fathers, since we have seen enough of royal banquets, and enough of Norman courtesy."

So saying, he arose and left the banqueting room, followed by Athelstane, and by several other guests, who, partaking of the Saxon lineage, held themselves insulted by the sarcasms of Prince John and his courtiers.

"By the bones of St. Thomas," said Prince John, as they retreated, "the Saxon churls have borne off the best of the day, and have retreated with triumph!"

"*Conclamatum est, poculatum est,*" said Prior Aymer; "we have drunk and we have shouted,—it were time we left our wine flagons."

"The monk hath some fair penitent to shrive to-night, that he is in such a hurry to depart," said De Bracy.

"Not so, Sir Knight," replied the Abbot; "but I must move several miles forward this evening upon my homeward journey."

"They are breaking up," said the Prince in a whisper to Fitzurse; "their fears anticipate the event, and this coward Prior is the first to shrink from me."

"Fear not, my lord," said Waldemar; "I will show him such reasons as shall induce him to join us when we hold our meeting at York.—Sir Prior," he said, "I must speak with you in private, before you mount your palfrey."

The other guests were now fast dispersing, with the exception of those immediately attached to Prince John's faction, and his retinue.

"This, then, is the result of your advice," said the Prince, turning an angry countenance upon Fitzurse; "that I should be bearded at my own board by a drunken Saxon churl, and that, on the mere sound of my brother's name, men should fall off from me as if I had the leprosy?"

"Have patience, sir," replied his counsellor; "I might retort your accusation, and blame the inconsiderate levity which foiled my design, and misled your own better judgment. But this is no time for recrimination. De Bracy and I will instantly go among these shuffling cowards, and convince them they have gone too far to recede."

"It will be in vain," said Prince John, pacing the apartment with disordered steps, and expressing himself with an agitation to which the wine he had drank partly contributed—"It will be in vain—they have seen the handwriting on the wall—they have marked the paw of the lion in the sand—they have heard his approaching roar shake the wood—nothing will reanimate their courage."

"Would to God," said Fitzurse to De Bracy, "that aught could reanimate his own! His brother's very name is an ague to him. Unhappy are the counsellors of a Prince who wants fortitude and perseverance alike in good and in evil!"

CHAPTER XV

And yet he thinks,—ha, ha, ha, ha,—he thinks
I am the tool and servant of his will.
Well, let it be; through all the maze of trouble
His plots and base oppression must create,
I'll shape myself a way to higher things,
And who will say 'tis wrong?

Basil, a Tragedy.

No spider ever took more pains to repair the shattered meshes of his web, than did Waldemar Fitzurse to reunite and combine the scattered members of Prince John's cabal. Few of these were attached to him from inclination, and none from personal regard. It was therefore necessary, that Fitzurse should open to them new prospects of advantage, and remind them of those which they at present enjoyed. To the young and wild nobles, he held out the prospect of unpunished license and uncontrolled revelry; to the ambitious, that of power, and to the covetous, that of increased wealth and extended domains. The leaders of the mercenaries received a donation in gold; an argument of the most persuasive to their minds, and without which all others would have proved in vain. Promises were still more liberally distributed than money by this active agent; and, in fine, nothing was left undone that could determine the wavering, or animate the disheartened. The return of King Richard he spoke of as an event altogether beyond the reach of probability; yet, when he observed, from the doubtful looks and uncertain answers which he received, that this was the apprehension by which the minds of his accomplices were most haunted, he boldly treated that event, should it really take place, as one which ought not to alter their political calculations.

"If Richard returns," said Fitzurse, "he returns to enrich his needy and impoverished crusaders at the expense of those who did not follow him to the Holy Land. He returns to call to a fearful reckoning those who, during his absence, have done aught that can be construed offence or encroachment upon either the laws of the land or the privileges of the crown. He returns to avenge upon the Orders of the Temple and the Hospital, the preference which they showed to Philip of France during the wars in the Holy Land. He returns, in fine, to punish as a rebel every adherent of his brother Prince John. Are ye afraid of his power?" continued the artful confidant of that Prince, "we acknowledge him a strong and valiant knight; but these are not the days of King Arthur, when a champion could encounter an army. If Richard indeed comes back, it must be alone,—unfollowed—unfriended. The bones of his gallant army have whitened the sands of Palestine. The few of his followers who have returned have straggled hither like this Wilfred of Ivanhoe, beggared and broken men.—And what talk ye of Richard's right of birth?" he proceeded, in answer to those who objected scruples on that head. "Is Richard's title of primogeniture more decidedly certain than that of Duke

Robert of Normandy, the Conqueror's eldest son? And yet William the Red, and Henry, his second and third brothers, were successively preferred to him by the voice of the nation. Robert had every merit which can be pleaded for Richard; he was a bold knight, a good leader, generous to his friends and to the church, and, to crown the whole, a crusader and a conqueror of the Holy Sepulchre; and yet he died a blind and miserable prisoner in the Castle of Cardiff, because he opposed himself to the will of the people, who chose that he should not rule over them. It is our right," he said, "to choose from the blood royal the prince who is best qualified to hold the supreme power—that is," said he, correcting himself, "him whose election will best promote the interests of the nobility. In personal qualifications," he added, "it was possible that Prince John might be inferior to his brother Richard, but when it was considered that the latter returned with the sword of vengeance in his hand, while the former held out rewards, immunities, privileges, wealth, and honours, it could not be doubted which was the king whom in wisdom the nobility were called on to support."

These, and many more arguments, some adapted to the peculiar circumstances of those whom he addressed, had the expected weight with the nobles of Prince John's faction. Most of them consented to attend the proposed meeting at York, for the purpose of making general arrangements for placing the crown upon the head of Prince John.

It was late at night, when, worn out and exhausted with his various exertions, however gratified with the result, Fitzurse, returning to the Castle of Ashby, met with De Bracy, who had exchanged his banqueting garments for a short green kirtle, with hose of the same cloth and colour, a leathern cap or headpiece, a short sword, a horn slung over his shoulder, a long bow in his hand, and a bundle of arrows stuck in his belt. Had Fitzurse met this figure in an outer apartment, he would have passed him without notice, as one of the yeomen of the guard; but finding him in the inner hall, he looked at him with more attention, and recognized the Norman knight in the dress of an English yeoman.

"What mummery is this, De Bracy?" said Fitzurse, somewhat angrily; "is this a time for Christmas gambols and quaint maskings, when the fate of our master, Prince John, is on the very verge of decision? Why hast thou not been, like me, among these heartless cravens, whom the very name of King Richard terrifies, as it is said to do the children of the Saracens?"

"I have been attending to mine own business," answered De Bracy calmly, "as you, Fitzurse, have been minding yours."

"I minding mine own business!" echoed Waldemar; "I have been engaged in that of Prince John, our joint patron."

"As if thou hadst any other reason for that, Waldemar," said De Bracy, "than the promotion of thine own individual interest? Come, Fitzurse, we know each other—ambition is thy pursuit, pleasure is mine, and they become our different ages. Of Prince John thou thinkest as I do; that he is too weak to be a determined monarch, too tyrannical to be an easy monarch, too insolent and presumptuous to be a popular monarch, and too fickle and timid to be long a monarch of any kind. But he is a monarch by whom Fitzurse and De Bracy hope to rise and thrive; and therefore you aid him with your policy, and I with the lances of my Free Companions."

"A hopeful auxiliary," said Fitzurse impatiently; "playing the fool in the very moment of utter necessity.—What on earth dost thou purpose by this absurd disguise at a moment so urgent?"

"To get me a wife," answered De Bracy coolly, "after the manner of the tribe of Benjamin."

"The tribe of Benjamin?" said Fitzurse; "I comprehend thee not."

"Wert thou not in presence yester-even," said De Bracy, "when we heard the Prior Aymer tell us a tale in reply to the romance which was sung by the Minstrel?—He told how, long since in Palestine, a deadly feud arose between the tribe of Benjamin and the rest of the Israelitish nation; and how they cut to pieces wellnigh all the chivalry of that tribe; and how they swore by our blessed Lady, that they would not permit those who remained to marry in their lineage; and how they became grieved for their vow, and sent to consult his holiness the Pope how they might be absolved from it; and how, by the advice of the Holy Father, the youth of the tribe of Benjamin carried off from a superb tournament all the ladies who were there present, and thus won them wives without the consent either of their brides or their brides' families."

"I have heard the story," said Fitzurse, "though either the Prior or thou has made some singular alterations in date and circumstances."

"I tell thee," said De Bracy, "that I mean to purvey me a wife after the fashion of the tribe of Benjamin; which is as much as to say, that in this same equipment I will fall upon that herd of Saxon bullocks, who have this night left the castle, and carry off from them the lovely Rowena."

"Art thou mad, De Bracy?" said Fitzurse. "Bethink thee that, though the men be Saxons, they are rich and powerful and regarded with the more respect by their countrymen, that wealth and honour are but the lot of few of Saxon descent."

"And should belong to none," said De Bracy; "the work of the Conquest should be completed."

"This is no time for it at least," said Fitzurse; "the approaching crisis renders the favour of the multitude indispensable, and Prince John cannot refuse justice to any one who injures their favourites."

"Let him grant it, if he dare," said De Bracy; "he will soon see the difference betwixt the support of such a lusty lot of spears as mine, and that of a heartless mob of Saxon churls. Yet I mean no immediate discovery of myself. Seem I not in this garb as bold a forester as ever blew horn? The blame of the violence shall rest with the outlaws of the Yorkshire forests. I have sure spies on the Saxon's motions—To-night they sleep in the convent of Saint Wittol, or Withold, or whatever they

call that churl of a Saxon Saint at Burton-on-Trent. Next day's march
brings them within our reach, and, falcon-ways, we swoop on them at
once. Presently after I will appear in mine own shape, play the courteous
knight, rescue the unfortunate and afflicted fair one from the hands
of the rude ravishers, conduct her to Front-de-Bœuf's Castle, or to Normandy, if it should be necessary, and produce her not again to her kindred until she be the bride and dame of Maurice de Bracy."

"A marvellously sage plan," said Fitzurse, "and, as I think, not entirely of thine own device.—Come, be frank, De Bracy, who aided thee
in the invention? and who is to assist in the execution? for, as I think,
thine own band lies as far off as York."

"Marry, if thou must needs know," said De Bracy, "it was the Templar
Brian de Bois-Guilbert that shaped out the enterprise which the adventure of the men of Benjamin suggested to me. He is to aid me in the onslaught, and he and his followers will impersonate the outlaws, from whom
my valorous arm is, after changing my garb, to rescue the lady."

"By my halidome," said Fitzurse, "the plan was worthy of your united
wisdom! and thy prudence, De Bracy, is most especially manifested in
the project of leaving the lady in the hands of thy worthy confederate.
Thou mayst, I think, succeed in taking her from her Saxon friends, but
how thou wilt rescue her afterwards from the clutches of Bois-Guilbert
seems considerably more doubtful—He is a falcon well accustomed to
pounce on a partridge, and to hold his prey fast."

"He is a Templar," said De Bracy, "and cannot therefore rival me
in my plan of wedding this heiress;—and to attempt aught dishonourable
against the intended bride of De Bracy—By Heaven! were he a whole
Chapter of his Order in his single person, he dared not do me such an
injury!"

"Then since nought that I can say," said Fitzurse, "will put this folly
from thy imagination (for well I know the obstinacy of thy disposition),
at least waste as little time as possible—let not thy folly be lasting as
well as untimely."

"I tell thee," answered De Bracy, "that it will be the work of a few
hours, and I shall be at York at the head of my daring and valorous
fellows, as ready to support any bold design as thy policy can be to
form one.—But I hear my comrades assembling, and the steeds stamping and neighing in the outer court.—Farewell.—I go, like a true knight,
to win the smiles of beauty."

"Like a true knight?" repeated Fitzurse, looking after him; "like a
fool, I should say, or like a child, who will leave the most serious and
needful occupation, to chase the down of the thistle that drives past him.
—But it is with such tools that I must work; and for whose advantage?
—For that of a Prince as unwise as he is profligate, and as likely to be
an ungrateful master as he has already proved a rebellious son and an
unnatural brother.—But he—he, too, is but one of the tools with which

I labour; and, proud as he is, should he presume to separate his interest from mine, this is a secret which he shall soon learn."

The meditations of the statesman were here interrupted by the voice of the Prince from an interior apartment, calling out, "Noble Waldemar Fitzurse!" and, with bonnet doffed, the future Chancellor (for to such high preferment did the wily Norman aspire) hastened to receive the orders of the future sovereign.

CHAPTER XVI

Far in a wild, unknown to public view,
From youth to age a reverend hermit grew;
The moss his bed, the cave his humble cell,
His food the fruits, his drink the crystal well;
Remote from man, with God he pass'd his days,
Prayer all his business—all his pleasure praise.

PARNELL.

THE reader cannot have forgotten that the event of the tournament was decided by the exertions of an unknown knight whom, on account of the passive and indifferent conduct which he had manifested on the former part of the day, the spectators had entitled, *Le Noir Faineant*. This knight had left the field abruptly when the victory was achieved; and when he was called upon to receive the reward of his valour, he was nowhere to be found. In the meantime, while summoned by heralds and by trumpets, the knight was holding his course northward, avoiding all frequented paths, and taking the shortest road through the woodlands. He paused for the night at a small hostelry lying out of the ordinary route, where, however, he obtained from a wandering minstrel news of the event of the tourney.

On the next morning the knight departed early, with the intention of making a long journey; the condition of his horse, which he had carefully spared during the preceding morning, being such as enabled him to travel far without the necessity of much repose. Yet his purpose was baffled by the devious paths through which he rode, so that when evening closed upon him, he only found himself on the frontiers of the West Riding of Yorkshire. By this time both horse and man required refreshment, and it became necessary, moreover, to look out for some place in which they might spend the night, which was now fast approaching.

The place where the traveller found himself seemed unpropitious for obtaining either shelter or refreshment, and he was likely to be reduced to the usual expedient of knights-errant, who, on such occasions, turned their horses to graze, and laid themselves down to meditate on their lady-mistress, with an oak-tree for a canopy. But the Black Knight either had no mistress to meditate upon, or, being as indifferent in love as he seemed to be in war, was not sufficiently occupied by passionate reflections upon her beauty and cruelty, to be able to parry the effects of fatigue and hunger, and suffer love to act as a substitute for the solid comforts of a bed and supper. He felt dissatisfied, therefore, when looking around, he found himself deeply involved in woods, through which indeed there were many open glades, and some paths, but such as seemed only formed by the numerous herds of cattle which grazed in the forest, or by the animals of chase, and the hunters who made prey of them.

The sun, by which the knight had chiefly directed his course, had now sunk behind the Derbyshire hills on his left, and every effort which he might make to pursue his journey was as likely to lead him out of his road as to advance him on his route. After having in vain endeavoured to select the most beaten path, in hopes it might lead to the cottage of some herdsman, or the silvan lodge of a forester, and having repeatedly found himself totally unable to determine on a choice, the knight resolved to trust to the sagacity of his horse; experience having, on former occasions, made him acquainted with the wonderful talent possessed by these animals for extricating themselves and their riders on such emergencies.

The good steed, grievously fatigued with so long a day's journey under a rider cased in mail, had no sooner found, by the slackened reins, that he was abandoned to his own guidance, than he seemed to assume new strength and spirit; and whereas formerly he had scarce replied to the spur, otherwise than by a groan, he now, as if proud of the confidence reposed in him, pricked up his ears, and assumed, of his own accord, a more lively motion. The path which the animal adopted rather turned off from the course pursued by the knight during the day; but as the horse seemed confident in his choice, the rider abandoned himself to his discretion.

He was justified by the event; for the footpath soon after appeared a little wider and more worn, and the tinkle of a small bell gave the knight to understand that he was in the vicinity of some chapel or hermitage.

Accordingly, he soon reached an open plat of turf, on the opposite side of which a rock, rising abruptly from a gently sloping plain, offered its grey and weatherbeaten front to the traveller. Ivy mantled its sides in some places, and in others oaks and holly bushes, whose roots found nourishment in the cliffs of the crag, waved over the precipices below, like the plumage of the warrior over his steel helmet, giving grace to that whose chief expression was terror. At the bottom of the rock, and leaning, as it were, against it, was constructed a rude hut, built chiefly of the trunks of trees felled in the neighbouring forest, and secured against the weather by having its crevices stuffed with moss mingled with clay. The stem of a young fir-tree lopped of its branches, with a piece of wood tied across near the top, was planted upright by the door, as a rude emblem of the holy cross. At a little distance on the right hand, a fountain of the purest water trickled out of the rock, and was received in a hollow stone, which labour had formed into a rustic basin. Escaping from thence, the stream murmured down the descent by a channel which its course had long worn, and so wandered through the little plain to lose itself in the neighbouring wood.

Beside this fountain were the ruins of a very small chapel, of which the roof had partly fallen in. The building, when entire, had never been above sixteen feet long by twelve feet in breadth, and the roof, low in proportion, rested upon four concentric arches which sprung from the four corners of the building, each supported upon a short and heavy pillar. The ribs of two of these arches remained, though the roof had fallen down betwixt them; over the others it remained entire. The entrance to this ancient place of devotion was under a very low round arch, ornamented by several courses of that zig-zag moulding, resembling shark's teeth, which appears so often in the more ancient Saxon architecture. A belfry rose above the porch on four small pillars, within which hung the green and weatherbeaten bell, the feeble sounds of which had been some time before heard by the Black Knight.

The whole peaceful and quiet scene lay glimmering in twilight before the eyes of the traveller, giving him good assurance of lodging for the night; since it was a special duty of those hermits who dwelt in the woods, to exercise hospitality towards benighted or bewildered passengers.

Accordingly, the knight took no time to consider minutely the particulars which we have detailed, but thanking Saint Julian (the patron of travellers) who had sent him good harbourage, he leaped from his horse and assailed the door of the hermitage with the butt of his lance, in order to arouse attention and gain admittance.

It was some time before he obtained any answer, and the reply, when made, was unpropitious.

"Pass on, whosoever thou art," was the answer given by a deep hoarse voice from within the hut, "and disturb not the servant of God and St. Dunstan in his evening devotions."

"Worthy father," answered the knight, "here is a poor wanderer bewildered in these woods, who gives thee the opportunity of exercising thy charity and hospitality."

"Good brother," replied the inhabitant of the hermitage, "it has pleased Our Lady and St. Dunstan to destine me for the object of those virtues, instead of the exercise thereof. I have no provisions here which even a dog would share with me, and a horse of any tenderness of nurture would despise my couch—pass therefore on thy way, and God speed thee."

"But how," replied the knight, "is it possible for me to find my way through such a wood as this, when darkness is coming on? I pray you, reverend father, as you are a Christian, to undo your door, and at least point out to me my road."

"And I pray you, good Christian brother," replied the anchorite, "to disturb me no more. You have already interrupted one *pater*, two *aves*, and a *credo,* which I, miserable sinner that I am, should, according to my vow, have said before moonrise."

"The road—the road!" vociferated the knight, "give me directions for the road, if I am to expect no more from thee."

"The road," replied the hermit, "is easy to hit. The path from the wood leads to a morass, and from thence to a ford, which, as the rains have abated, may now be passable. When thou hast crossed the ford, thou wilt take care of thy footing up the left bank, as it is somewhat precipitous; and the path, which hangs over the river, has lately, as I learn (for I seldom leave the duties of my chapel), given way in sundry places. Thou wilt then keep straight forward"——

"A broken path—a precipice—a ford, and a morass!" said the knight, interrupting him.—"Sir Hermit, if you were the holiest that ever wore beard or told bead, you shall scarce prevail on me to hold this road to-night. I tell thee, that thou, who livest by the charity of the country —ill-deserved, as I doubt it is—hast no right to refuse shelter to the wayfarer when in distress. Either open the door quickly, or, by the rood, I will beat it down and make entry for myself."

"Friend wayfarer," replied the hermit, "be not importunate; if thou puttest me to use the carnal weapon in mine own defence, it will be e'en the worse for you."

At this moment a distant noise of barking and growling, which the traveller had for some time heard, became extremely loud and furious, and made the knight suppose that the hermit, alarmed by his threat of making forcible entry, had called the dogs who made this clamour to aid him in his defence, out of some inner recess in which they had been kennelled. Incensed at this preparation on the hermit's part for making good his inhospitable purpose, the knight struck the door so furiously with his foot, that posts as well as staples shook with violence.

The anchorite, not caring again to expose his door to a similar shock, now called out aloud, "Patience, patience—spare thy strength, good traveller, and I will presently undo the door, though, it may be, my doing so will be little to thy pleasure."

The door accordingly was opened; and the hermit, a large, strong-built man, in his sackcloth gown and hood, girt with a rope of rushes, stood before the knight. He had in one hand a lighted torch, or link, and in the other a baton of crab-tree, so thick and heavy, that it might well be termed a club. Two large shaggy dogs, half greyhound half mastiff, stood ready to rush upon the traveller as soon as the door should be opened. But when the torch glanced upon the lofty crest and golden spurs of the knight, who stood without, the hermit, altering probably his original intentions, repressed the rage of his auxiliaries, and, changing his tone to a sort of churlish courtesy, invited the knight to enter his hut, making excuse for his unwillingness to open his lodge after sunset, by alleging the multitude of robbers and outlaws who were abroad, and who gave no honour to Our Lady or St. Dunstan, nor to those holy men who spent life in their service.

"The poverty of your cell, good father," said the knight, looking around him, and seeing nothing but a bed of leaves, a crucifix rudely carved in oak, a missal, with a rough-hewn table and two stools, and one or two clumsy articles of furniture—"the poverty of your cell should seem a sufficient defence against any risk of thieves, not to mention the aid of two trusty dogs, large and strong enough, I think, to pull down a stag, and of course, to match with most men."

"The good keeper of the forest," said the hermit, "hath allowed me the use of these animals, to protect my solitude until the times shall mend."

Having said this, he fixed his torch in a twisted branch of iron which served for a candlestick; and, placing the oaken trivet before the embers of the fire, which he refreshed with some dry wood, he placed a stool upon one side of the table, and beckoned to the knight to do the same upon the other.

They sat down, and gazed with great gravity at each other, each thinking in his heart that he had seldom seen a stronger or more athletic figure than was placed opposite to him.

"Reverend hermit," said the knight, after looking long and fixedly at his host, "were it not to interrupt your devout meditations, I would pray to know three things of your holiness; first, where I am to put my horse?—secondly, what I can have for supper?—thirdly, where I am to take up my couch for the night?"

"I will reply to you," said the hermit, "with my finger, it being against my rule to speak by words where signs can answer the purpose." So saying, he pointed successively to two corners of the hut. "Your stable," said he, "is there—your bed there; and," reaching down a platter with two handfuls of parched peas upon it from the neighbouring shelf, and placing it upon the table, he added, "your supper is here."

The knight shrugged his shoulders, and leaving the hut, brought in his horse (which in the interim he had fastened to a tree), unsaddled him with much attention, and spread upon the steed's weary back his own mantle.

The hermit was apparently somewhat moved to compassion by the anxiety as well as address which the stranger displayed in tending his horse; for, muttering something about provender left for the keeper's palfrey, he dragged out of a recess a bundle of forage, which he spread before the knight's charger, and immediately afterwards shook down a quantity of dried fern in the corner which he had assigned for the rider's couch. The knight returned him thanks for his courtesy; and, this duty done, both resumed their seats by the table, whereon stood the trencher of pease placed between them. The hermit, after a long grace, which had once been Latin, but of which original language few traces remained, excepting here and there the long rolling termination of some word or phrase, set example to his guest, by modestly putting into a very large mouth, furnished with teeth which might have ranked with those of a boar both in sharpness and whiteness, some three or four dried pease, a miserable grist as it seemed for so large and able a mill.

The knight, in order to follow so laudable an example, laid aside his helmet, his corslet, and the greater part of his armour, and showed to the hermit a head thick-curled with yellow hair, high features, blue eyes, remarkably bright and sparkling, a mouth well formed, having an upper lip clothed with mustachoes darker than his hair, and bearing altogether the look of a bold, daring, and enterprising man, with which his strong form well corresponded.

The hermit, as if wishing to answer to the confidence of his guest, threw back his cowl, and showed a round bullet head belonging to a man in the prime of life. His close-shaven crown, surrounded by a circle of stiff curled black hair, had something the appearance of a parish pinfold begirt by its high hedge. The features expressed nothing of monastic austerity, or of ascetic privations; on the contrary, it was a bold bluff countenance, with broad black eyebrows, a well-turned forehead, and cheeks as round and vermilion as those of a trumpeter, from which descended a long and curly black beard. Such a visage, joined to the brawny form of the holy man, spoke rather of sirloins and haunches, than of pease and pulse. This incongruity did not escape the guest. After he had with great difficulty accomplished the mastication of a mouthful of the dried pease, he found it absolutely necessary to request his pious entertainer to furnish him with some liquor; who replied to his request by placing before him a large can of the purest water from the fountain.

"It is from the well of St. Dunstan," said he, "in which, betwixt sun and sun, he baptized five hundred heathen Danes and Britons—blessed be his name!" And applying his black beard to the pitcher, he took a draught much more moderate in quantity than his encomium seemed to warrant.

"It seems to me, reverend father," said the knight, "that the small morsels which you eat, together with this holy, but somewhat thin beverage, have thriven with you marvellously. You appear a man more fit to win the ram at a wrestling match, or the ring at a bout at quarter-staff, or the bucklers at a sword-play, than to linger out your time in this desolate wilderness, saying masses, and living upon parched pease and cold water."

"Sir Knight," answered the hermit, "your thoughts, like those of the ignorant laity, are according to the flesh. It has pleased Our Lady and my patron saint to bless the pittance to which I restrain myself, even as the pulse and water was blessed to the children Shadrach, Meshech, and Abednego, who drank the same rather than defile themselves with the wine and meats which were appointed them by the King of the Saracens."

"Holy father," said the knight, "upon whose countenance it hath pleased Heaven to work such a miracle, permit a sinful layman to crave thy name?"

"Thou mayst call me," answered the hermit, "the Clerk of Copmanhurst, for so I am termed in these parts—They add, it is true, the epithet holy, but I stand not upon that, as being unworthy of such addition.—And now, valiant knight, may I pray ye for the name of my honourable guest?"

"Truly," said the knight, "Holy Clerk of Copmanhurst, men call me in these parts the Black Knight,—many, sir, add to it the epithet of Sluggard, whereby I am no way ambitious to be distinguished."

The hermit could scarcely forbear from smiling at his guest's reply.

"I see," said he, "Sir Sluggish Knight, that thou art a man of prudence and of counsel; and moreover, I see that my poor monastic fare likes thee not, accustomed, perhaps, as thou hast been, to the licence of courts and of camps, and the luxuries of cities; and now I bethink me, Sir Sluggard, that when the charitable keeper of this forest-walk left these dogs for my protection, and also those bundles of forage, he left me also some food, which, being unfit for my use, the very recollection of it had escaped me amid my more weighty meditations."

"I dare be sworn he did so," said the knight; "I was convinced that there was better food in the cell, Holy Clerk, since you first doffed your cowl.—Your keeper is ever a jovial fellow; and none who beheld thy grinders contending with these pease, and thy throat flooded with this ungenial element, could see thee doomed to such horse-provender and horse-beverage" (pointing to the provisions upon the table), "and refrain from mending thy cheer. Let us see the keeper's bounty, therefore, without delay."

The hermit cast a wistful look upon the knight, in which there was a sort of comic expression of hesitation, as if uncertain how far he should act prudently in trusting his guest. There was, however, as much of bold frankness in the knight's countenance as was possible to be expressed by features. His smile, too, had something in it irresistibly comic, and gave an assurance of faith and loyalty, with which his host could not refrain from sympathising.

After exchanging a mute glance or two, the hermit went to the farther side of the hut, and opened a hutch, which was concealed with great care and some ingenuity. Out of the recesses of a dark closet, into which this aperture gave admittance, he brought a large pasty, baked in a pewter platter of unusual dimensions. This mighty dish he placed before his guest, who, using his poniard to cut it open, lost no time in making himself acquainted with its contents.

"How long is it since the good keeper has been here?" said the knight to his host, after having swallowed several hasty morsels of this reinforcement to the hermit's good cheer.

"About two months," answered the father hastily.

"By the true Lord," answered the knight, "everything in your hermitage is miraculous, Holy Clerk! for I would have been sworn that the fat buck which furnished this venison had been running on foot within the week."

The hermit was somewhat discountenanced by this observation; and, moreover, he made but a poor figure while gazing on the diminution of the pasty, on which his guest was making desperate inroads; a warfare in which his previous profession of abstinence left him no pretext for joining.

"I have been in Palestine, Sir Clerk," said the knight, stopping short of a sudden, "and I bethink me it is a custom there that every host who entertains a guest shall assure him of the wholesomeness of his food, by partaking of it along with him. Far be it from me to suspect so holy a man of aught inhospitable; nevertheless I will be highly bound to you would you comply with this Eastern custom."

"To ease your unnecessary scruples, Sir Knight, I will for once depart from my rules," replied the hermit. And as there were no forks in those days, his clutches were instantly in the bowels of the pasty.

The ice of ceremony being once broken, it seemed matter of rivalry between the guest and the entertainer which should display the best appetite; and although the former had probably fasted longest, yet the hermit fairly surpassed him.

"Holy Clerk," said the knight, when his hunger was appeased, "I would gage my good horse yonder against a zecchin, that that same honest keeper to whom we are obliged for the venison has left thee a stoup of wine, or a runlet of canary, or some such trifle, by way of ally to this noble pasty. This would be a circumstance, doubtless, totally unworthy to dwell in the memory of so rigid an anchorite; yet, I think, were you to search yonder crypt once more, you would find that I am right in my conjecture."

The hermit only replied by a grin; and returning to the hutch, he produced a leathern bottle, which might contain about four quarts. He also brought forth two large drinking cups, made out of the horn of the urus, and hooped with silver. Having made this goodly provision for washing down the supper, he seemed to think no farther ceremonious scruple necessary on his part; but filling both cups, and saying, in the Saxon fashion, *"Waes hael,* Sir Sluggish Knight!" he emptied his own at a draught.

"Drink hael, Holy Clerk of Copmanhurst!" answered the warrior, and did his host reason in a similar brimmer.

"Holy Clerk," said the stranger, after the first cup was thus swallowed, "I cannot but marvel that a man possessed of such thews and sinews as thine, and who therewithal shows the talent of so goodly a trencher-man, should think of abiding by himself in this wilderness. In my judgment, you are fitter to keep a castle, or a fort, eating of the fat and drinking of the strong, than to live here upon pulse and water, or even upon the charity of the keeper. At least, were I as thou, I should

find myself both disport and plenty out of the king's deer. There is many
a goodly herd in these forests, and a buck will never be missed that goes
to the use of Saint Dunstan's chaplain."

"Sir Sluggish Knight," replied the Clerk, "these are dangerous words,
and I pray you to forbear them. I am true hermit to the king and law,
and were I to spoil my liege's game, I should be sure of the prison, and,
an my gown saved me not, were in some peril of hanging."

"Nevertheless, were I as thou," said the knight, "I would take my
walk by moonlight, when foresters and keepers were warm in bed, and
ever and anon,—as I pattered my prayers,—I would let fly a shaft among
the herds of dun deer that feed in the glades—Resolve me, Holy Clerk,
hast thou never practised such a pastime?"

"Friend Sluggard," answered the hermit, "thou hast seen all that can
concern thee of my housekeeping, and something more than he deserves
who takes up his quarters by violence. Credit me, it is better to enjoy
the good which God sends thee, than to be impertinently curious how it
comes. Fill thy cup, and welcome; and do not, I pray thee, by further
impertinent enquiries, put me to show that thou couldst hardly have
made good thy lodging had I been earnest to oppose thee."

"By my faith," said the knight, "thou makest me more curious than
ever! Thou art the most mysterious hermit I ever met; and I will know
more of thee ere we part. As for thy threats, know, holy man, thou
speakest to one whose trade it is to find out danger wherever it is to
be met with."

"Sir Sluggish Knight, I drink to thee," said the hermit; "respecting
thy valour much, but deeming wondrous slightly of thy discretion. If
thou will take equal arms with me, I will give thee, in all friendship and
brotherly love, such sufficing penance and complete absolution, that thou
shalt not for the next twelve months sin the sin of excess of curiosity."

The knight pledged him, and desired him to name his weapons.

"There is none," replied the hermit, "from the scissors of Delilah, and
the tenpenny nail of Jael, to the scimitar of Goliath, at which I am
not a match for thee—But, if I am to make the election, what sayest
thou, good friend, to these trinkets?"

Thus speaking, he opened another hutch, and took out from it a
couple of broadswords and bucklers, such as were used by the yeomanry
of the period. The knight, who watched his motions, observed that this
second place of concealment was furnished with two or three good long-
bows, a cross-bow, a bundle of bolts for the latter, and half-a-dozen
sheaves of arrows for the former. A harp, and other matters of a very
uncanonical appearance, were also visible when this dark recess was
opened.

"I promise thee, brother Clerk," said he, "I will ask thee no more
offensive questions. The contents of that cupboard are an answer to all
my enquiries; and I see a weapon there" (here he stooped and took out

the harp) "on which I would more gladly prove my skill with thee, than at the sword and buckler."

"I hope, Sir Knight," said the hermit, "thou hast given no good reason for thy surname of the Sluggard. I do promise thee I suspect thee grievously. Nevertheless, thou art my guest, and I will not put thy manhood to the proof without thine own free will. Sit thee down, then, and fill thy cup; let us drink, sing and be merry. If thou knowest ever a good lay, thou shalt be welcome to a nook of pasty at Copmanhurst so long as I serve the chapel of St. Dunstan, which, please God, shall be till I change my grey covering for one of green turf. But come, fill a flagon, for it will crave some time to tune the harp; and nought pitches the voice and sharpens the ear like a cup of wine. For my part, I love to feel the grape at my very finger-ends before they make the harp-strings tinkle." [1]

CHAPTER XVII

At eve, within yon studious nook,
I ope my brass-embossed book,
Portray'd with many a holy deed
Of martyrs crown'd with heavenly meed;
Then, as my taper waxes dim,
Chant, ere I sleep, my measured hymn.

.   .   .   .

Who but would cast his pomp away,
To take my staff and amice grey,
And to the world's tumultuous stage,
Prefer the peaceful HERMITAGE?

WARTON.

NOTWITHSTANDING the prescription of the genial hermit, with which his guest willingly complied, he found it no easy matter to bring the harp to harmony.

"Methinks, holy father," said he, "the instrument wants one string, and the rest have been somewhat misused."

"Ay, mark'st thou that?" replied the hermit; "that shows thee a master of the craft. Wine and wassail," he added, gravely casting up his eyes— "all the fault of wine and wassail!—I told Alan-a-Dale, the northern minstrel, that he would damage the harp if he touched it after the seventh cup, but he would not be controlled—Friend, I drink to thy successful performance."

So saying he took off his cup with much gravity, at the same time shaking his head at the intemperance of the Scottish harper.

The knight, in the meantime, had brought the strings into some order, and after a short prelude, asked his host whether he would choose a

---

[1] THE JOLLY HERMIT.—All readers, however slightly acquainted with black letter, must recognise in the Clerk of Copmanhurst, Friar Tuck, the buxom Confessor of Robin Hood's gang, the Curtal Friar of Fountain's Abbey.

sirvente in the language of *oc,* or a *lai* in the language of *oui,* or a *virelai,* or a ballad in the vulgar English.[1]

"A ballad, a ballad," said the hermit, "against all the *ocs* and *ouis* of France. Downright English am I, Sir Knight, and downright English was my patron St. Dunstan, and scorned *oc* and *oui,* as he would have scorned the parings of the devil's hoof—downright English alone shall be sung in this cell."

"I will assay, then," said the knight, "a ballad composed by a Saxon glee-man, whom I knew in Holy Land."

It speedily appeared, that if the knight was not a complete master of the minstrel art, his taste for it had at least been cultivated under the best instructors. Art had taught him to soften the faults of a voice which had little compass, and was naturally rough rather than mellow, and, in short, had done all that culture can do in supplying natural deficiencies. His performance, therefore, might have been termed very respectable by abler judges than the hermit, especially as the knight threw into the notes now a degree of spirit, and now of plaintive enthusiasm, which gave force and energy to the verses which he sung.

THE CRUSADER'S RETURN

I

> High deeds achieved of knightly fame,
> From Palestine the champion came;
> The cross upon his shoulders borne,
> Battle and blast had dimm'd and torn.
> Each dint upon his batter'd shield
> Was token of a foughten field;
> And thus, beneath his lady's bower,
> He sung, as fell the twilight hour:—

2

> "Joy to the fair!—thy knight behold,
> Return'd from yonder land of gold;
> No wealth he brings, nor wealth can need,
> Save his good arms, and battle-steed;
> His spurs, to dash against a foe,
> His lance and sword to lay him low;
> Such all the trophies of his toil,
> Such—and the hope of Tekla's smile!

3

> "Joy to the fair! whose constant knight
> Her favour fired to feats of might;

[1] Note III.—Minstrelsy.

Unnoted shall she not remain,
Where meet the bright and noble train;
Minstrel shall sing and herald tell—
'Mark yonder maid of beauty well,
'Tis she for whose bright eyes was won
The listed field at Askalon!

4

" 'Note well her smile!—it edged the blade
Which fifty wives to widows made,
When, vain his strength and Mahound's spell,
Iconium's turban'd Soldan fell.
Seest thou her locks, whose sunny glow
Half shows, half shades, her neck of snow?
Twines not of them one golden thread,
But for its sake a Paynim bled.'

5

"Joy to the fair!—my name unknown,
Each deed, and all its praise thine own;
Then, oh! unbar this churlish gate,
The night dew falls, the hour is late.
Inured to Syria's glowing breath,
I feel the north breeze chill as death;
Let grateful love quell maiden shame,
And grant him bliss who brings thee fame."

During this performance, the hermit demeaned himself much like a first-rate critic of the present day at a new opera. He reclined back upon his seat, with his eyes half shut; now, folding his hands and twisting his thumbs, he seemed absorbed in attention, and anon, balancing his expanded palms, he gently flourished them in time to the music. At one or two favourite cadences, he threw in a little assistance of his own, where the knight's voice seemed unable to carry the air so high as his worshipful taste approved. When the song was ended, the anchorite emphatically declared it a good one, and well sung.

"And yet," said he, "I think my Saxon countrymen had herded long enough with the Normans to fall into the tone of their melancholy ditties. What took the honest knight from home? or what could he expect but to find his mistress agreeably engaged with a rival on his return, and his serenade, as they call it, as little regarded as the cater-wauling of a cat in the gutter? Nevertheless, Sir Knight, I drink this cup to thee, to the success of all true lovers—I fear you are none," he added, on observing that the knight (whose brain began to be heated with these repeated draughts) qualified his flagon from the water pitcher.

"Why," said the knight, "did you not tell me that this water was from the well of your blessed patron, St. Dunstan?"

"Ay, truly," said the hermit, "and many a hundred of pagans did he baptize there, but I never heard that he drank any of it. Everything should be put to its proper use in this world. St. Dunstan knew, as well as any one, the prerogatives of a jovial friar."

And so saying, he reached the harp, and entertained his guest with the following characteristic song, to a sort of derry-down chorus, appropriate to an old English ditty.[1]

THE BAREFOOTED FRIAR

1

I'll give thee, good fellow, a twelvemonth or twain,
To search Europe through, from Byzantium to Spain;
But ne'er shall you find, should you search till you tire,
So happy a man as the Barefooted Friar.

2

Your knight for his lady pricks forth in career,
And is brought home at even-song prick'd through with a spear;
I confess him in haste—for his lady desires
No comfort on earth save the Barefooted Friar's.

3

Your monarch?—Pshaw! many a prince has been known
To barter his robes for our cowl and our gown,
But which of us e'er felt the idle desire
To exchange for a crown the grey hood of a Friar!

4

The Friar has walk'd out, and where'er he has gone,
The land and its fatness is mark'd for his own;
He can roam where he lists, he can stop when he tires,
For every man's house is the Barefooted Friar's.

5

He's expected at noon, and no wight till he comes
May profane the great chair, or the porridge of plums;
For the best of the cheer, and the seat by the fire,
Is the undenied right of the Barefooted Friar.

[1] It may be proper to remind the reader, that the chorus of "derry down" is supposed to be as ancient, not only as the times of the Heptarchy, but as those of the Druids, and to have furnished the chorus to the hymns of those venerable persons when they went to the wood to gather mistletoe.

6

He's expected at night, and the pasty's made hot,
They broach the brown ale, and they fill the black pot,
And the goodwife would wish the goodman in the mire,
Ere he lack'd a soft pillow, the Barefooted Friar.

7

Long flourish the sandal, the cord, and the cope,
The dread of the devil and trust of the Pope;
For to gather life's roses, unscathed by the briar,
Is granted alone to the Barefooted Friar.

"By my troth," said the knight, "thou hast sung well and lustily, and in high praise of thine order. And, talking of the devil, Holy Clerk, are you not afraid that he may pay you a visit during some of your uncanonical pastimes?"

"I uncanonical!" answered the hermit; "I scorn the charge—I scorn it with my heels!—I serve the duty of my chapel duly and truly—Two masses daily, morning and evening, primes, noons, and vespers, *aves, credos, paters*"——

"Excepting moonlight nights, when the venison is in season," said his guest.

"*Exceptis excipiendis,*" replied the hermit, "as our old abbot taught me to say, when impertinent laymen should ask me if I kept every punctilio of mine order."

"True, holy father," said the knight, "but the devil is apt to keep an eye on such exceptions; he goes about, thou knowest, like a roaring lion."

"Let him roar here if he dares," said the friar; "a touch of my cord will make him roar as loud as the tongs of St. Dunstan himself did. I never feared man, and I as little fear the devil and his imps. Saint Dunstan, Saint Dubric, Saint Winibald, Saint Winifred, Saint Swibert, Saint Willick, not forgetting Saint Thomas a Kent, and my own poor merits to speed, I defy every devil of them, come cut and long tail.— But to let you into a secret, I never speak upon such subjects, my friend, until after morning vespers."

He changed the conversation; fast and furious grew the mirth of the parties, and many a song was exchanged betwixt them, when their revels were interrupted by a loud knocking at the door of the hermitage.

The occasion of this interruption we can only explain by resuming the adventures of another set of our characters; for, like old Ariosto, we do not pique ourselves upon continuing uniformly to keep company with any one personage of our drama.

CHAPTER XVIII

Away! Our journey lies through dell and dingle,
Where the blithe fawn trips by its timid mother,
Where the broad oak, with intercepting boughs,
Chequers the sunbeam in the green-sward alley—
Up and away!—for lovely paths are these
To tread, when the glad Sun is on his throne;
Less pleasant, and less safe, when Cynthia's lamp
With doubtful glimmer lights the dreary forest.
Ettrick Forest.

WHEN Cedric the Saxon saw his son drop down senseless in the lists at Ashby, his first impulse was to order him into the custody and care of his own attendants, but the words choked in his throat. He could not bring himself to acknowledge, in presence of such an assembly, the son whom he had renounced and disinherited. He ordered, however, Oswald to keep an eye upon him; and directed that officer, with two of his serfs, to convey Ivanhoe to Ashby as soon as the crowd had dispersed. Oswald, however, was anticipated in this good office. The crowd dispersed, indeed, but the knight was nowhere to be seen.

It was in vain that Cedric's cupbearer looked around for his young master—he saw the bloody spot on which he had lately sunk down, but himself he saw no longer; it seemed as if the fairies had conveyed him from the spot. Perhaps Oswald (for the Saxons were very superstitious) might have adopted some such hypothesis, to account for Ivanhoe's disappearance, had he not suddenly cast his eye upon a person attired like a squire, in whom he recognised the features of his fellow-servant Gurth. Anxious concerning his master's fate, and in despair at his sudden disappearance, the translated swineherd was searching for him everywhere, and had neglected, in doing so, the concealment on which his own safety depended. Oswald deemed it his duty to secure Gurth, as a fugitive of whose fate his master was to judge.

Renewing his enquiries concerning the fate of Ivanhoe, the only information which the cupbearer could collect from the bystanders was, that the knight had been raised with care by certain well-attired grooms, and placed in a litter belonging to a lady among the spectators, which had immediately transported him out of the press. Oswald, on receiving this intelligence, resolved to return to his master for farther instructions, carrying along with him Gurth, whom he considered in some sort as a deserter from the service of Cedric.

The Saxon had been under very intense and agonising apprehensions concerning his son; for Nature had asserted her rights, in spite of the patriotic stoicism which laboured to disown her. But no sooner was he informed that Ivanhoe was in careful, and probably in friendly hands, than the paternal anxiety which had been excited by the dubiety of his fate, gave way anew to the feeling of injured pride and resentment, at what he termed Wilfred's filial disobedience. "Let him wander his way," said he—"Let those leech his wounds for whose sake he encountered them. He is fitter to do the juggling tricks of the Norman chivalry than to maintain the fame and honour of his English ancestry with the glaive and brown-bill, the good old weapons of his country."

"If to maintain the honour of ancestry," said Rowena, who was present, "it is sufficient to be wise in council and brave in execution— to be boldest among the bold, and gentlest among the gentle, I know no voice, save his father's"——

"Be silent, Lady Rowena!—on this subject only I hear you not. Prepare yourself for the Prince's festival: we have been summoned thither with unwonted circumstance of honour and of courtesy, such as the haughty Normans have rarely used to our race since the fatal day of Hastings. Thither will I go, were it only to show these proud Normans how little the fate of a son, who could defeat their bravest, can affect a Saxon."

"Thither," said Rowena, "do I NOT go; and I pray you to beware, lest what you mean for courage and constancy, shall be accounted hardness of heart."

"Remain at home then, ungrateful lady," answered Cedric; "thine is the hard heart, which can sacrifice the weal of an oppressed people to an idle and unauthorised attachment. I seek the noble Athelstane, and with him attend the banquet of John of Anjou."

He went accordingly to the banquet, of which we have already mentioned the principal events. Immediately upon retiring from the castle, the Saxon thanes, with their attendants, took horse; and it was during the bustle which attended their doing so, that Cedric, for the first time, cast his eyes upon the deserter Gurth. The noble Saxon had returned from the banquet, as we have seen, in no very placid humour, and wanted but a pretext for wreaking his anger upon some one. "The gyves!" he said, "the gyves!—Oswald—Hundibert!—Dogs and villains!—why leave you the knave unfettered?"

Without daring to remonstrate, the companions of Gurth bound him with a halter, as the readiest cord which occurred. He submitted to the operation without remonstrance, except that, darting a reproachful look at his master, he said, "This comes of loving your flesh and blood better than mine own."

"To horse, and forward!" said Cedric.

"It is indeed full time," said the noble Athelstane; "for, if we ride not the faster, the worthy Abbot Waltheoff's preparations for a rere-supper [1] will be altogether spoiled."

The travellers, however, used such speed as to reach the convent of St. Withold's before the apprehended evil took place. The Abbot, himself of ancient Saxon descent, received the noble Saxons with the profuse

---

[1] A rere-supper was a night-meal, and sometimes signified a collation, which was given at a late hour, after the regular supper had made its appearance.—L. T.

and exuberant hospitality of their nation, wherein they indulged to a
late, or rather an early hour; nor did they take leave of their reverend
host the next morning until they had shared with him a sumptuous
refection.

As the cavalcade left the court of the monastery, an incident happened
somewhat alarming to the Saxons, who, of all people of Europe, were
most addicted to a superstitious observance of omens, and to whose
opinions can be traced most of those notions upon such subjects, still
to be found among our popular antiquities. For the Normans being a
mixed race, and better informed according to the information of the
times, had lost most of the superstitious prejudices which their ancestors
had brought from Scandinavia, and piqued themselves upon thinking
freely on such topics.

In the present instance, the apprehension of impending evil was inspired by no less respectable a prophet than a large lean black dog,
which, sitting upright, howled most piteously as the foremost riders
left the gate, and presently afterwards, barking wildly, and jumping
to and fro, seemed bent upon attaching itself to the party.

"I like not that music, father Cedric," said Athelstane; for by this
title of respect he was accustomed to address him.

"Nor I either, uncle," said Wamba; "I greatly fear we shall have to
pay the piper."

"In my mind," said Athelstane, upon whose memory the Abbot's good
ale (for Burton was already famous for that genial liquor) had made a
favourable impression,—"in my mind we had better turn back, and
abide with the Abbot until the afternoon. It is unlucky to travel where
your path is crossed by a monk, a hare, or a howling dog, until you
have eaten your next meal."

"Away!" said Cedric, impatiently; "the day is already too short for
our journey. For the dog, I know it to be the cur of the runaway slave
Gurth, a useless fugitive like its master."

So saying, and rising at the same time in his stirrups, impatient at
the interruption of his journey, he launched his javelin at poor Fangs—
for Fangs it was, who, having traced his master thus far upon his stolen
expedition, had here lost him, and was now, in his uncouth way, rejoicing
at his reappearance. The javelin inflicted a wound upon the animal's
shoulder, and narrowly missed pinning him to the earth; and Fangs fled
howling from the presence of the enraged thane. Gurth's heart swelled
within him; for he felt this meditated slaughter of his faithful adherent
in a degree much deeper than the harsh treatment he had himself
received. Having in vain attempted to raise his hand to his eyes, he
said to Wamba, who, seeing his master's ill humour had prudently retreated to the rear, "I pray thee, do me the kindness to wipe my eyes with
the skirt of thy mantle; the dust offends me, and these bonds will not
let me help myself one way or another."

Wamba did him the service he required, and they rode side by side for some time, during which Gurth maintained a moody silence. At length he could repress his feelings no longer.

"Friend Wamba," said he, "of all those who are fools enough to serve Cedric, thou alone hast dexterity enough to make thy folly acceptable to him. Go to him, therefore, and tell him that neither for love nor fear will Gurth serve him longer. He may strike the head from me—he may scourge me—he may load me with irons—but henceforth he shall never compel me either to love or to obey him. Go to him, then, and tell him that Gurth the son of Beowulph renounces his service."

"Assuredly," said Wamba, "fool as I am, I shall not do your fool's errand. Cedric hath another javelin stuck into his girdle, and thou knowest he does not always miss his mark."

"I care not," replied Gurth, "how soon he makes a mark of me. Yesterday he left Wilfred, my young master, in his blood. To-day he has striven to kill before my face the only other living creature that ever showed me kindness. By St. Edmund, St. Dunstan, St. Withold, St. Edward the Confessor, and every other Saxon saint in the calendar" (for Cedric never swore by any that was not of Saxon lineage, and all his household had the same limited devotion), "I will never forgive him!"

"To my thinking now," said the Jester, who was frequently wont to act as peace-maker in the family, "our master did not propose to hurt Fangs, but only to affright him. For, if you observed, he rose in his stirrups, as thereby meaning to overcast the mark; and so he would have done, but Fangs happening to bound up at the very moment, received a scratch, which I will be bound to heal with a penny's breadth of tar."

"If I thought so," said Gurth—"if I could but think so—but no—I saw the javelin was well aimed—I heard it whiz through the air with all the wrathful malevolence of him who cast it, and it quivered after it had pitched in the ground, as if with regret for having missed its mark. By the hog dear to St. Anthony, I renounce him!"

And the indignant swineherd resumed his sullen silence, which no efforts of the Jester could again induce him to break.

Meanwhile Cedric and Athelstane, the leaders of the troop, conversed together on the state of the land, on the dissensions of the royal family, on the feuds and quarrels among the Norman nobles, and on the chance which there was that the oppressed Saxons might be able to free themselves from the yoke of the Normans, or at least to elevate themselves into national consequence and independence, during the civil convulsions which were likely to ensue. On this subject Cedric was all animation. The restoration of the independence of his race was the idol of his heart, to which he had willingly sacrificed domestic happiness and the interests of his own son. But, in order to achieve this great revolution in favour of the native English, it was necessary that they should be united among themselves, and act under an acknowledged head. The necessity of choosing their chief from the Saxon blood-royal was not only evident in itself, but had been made a solemn condition by those whom Cedric had intrusted with his secret p'ans and hopes. Athelstane had this quality at least; and though he had few mental accomplishments or talents to recommend him as a leader, he had still a goodly person, was no coward, had been accustomed to martial exercises, and seemed willing to defer to the advice of counsellors more wise than himself. Above all, he was known to be liberal and hospitable, and believed to be good-natured. But whatever pretensions Athelstane had to be considered as head of the Saxon confederacy, many of that nation were disposed to prefer to his the title of the Lady Rowena, who drew her descent from Alfred, and whose father having been a chief renowned for wisdom, courage, and generosity, his memory was highly honoured by his oppressed countrymen.

It would have been no difficult thing for Cedric, had he been so disposed, to have placed himself at the head of a third party, as formidable at least as any of the others. To counterbalance their royal descent, he had courage, activity, energy, and, above all, that devoted attachment to the cause which had procured him the epithet of THE SAXON, and his birth was inferior to none, excepting only that of Athelstane and his ward. These qualities, however, were unalloyed by the slightest shade of selfishness; and, instead of dividing yet farther his weakened nation by forming a faction of his own, it was a leading part of Cedric's plan to extinguish that which already existed, by promoting a marriage betwixt Rowena and Athelstane. An obstacle occurred to this his favourite project, in the mutual attachment of his ward and his son; and hence the original cause of the banishment of Wilfred from the house of his father.

This stern measure Cedric had adopted, in hopes that, during Wilfred's absence, Rowena might relinquish her preference, but in this hope he was disappointed; a disappointment which might be attributed in part to the mode in which his ward had been educated. Cedric, to whom the name of Alfred was as that of a deity, had treated the sole remaining scion of that great monarch with a degree of observance, such as, perhaps, was in those days scarce paid to an acknowledged princess. Rowena's will had been in almost all cases a law to his household; and Cedric himself, as if determined that her sovereignty should be fully acknowledged within that little circle at least, seemed to take a pride in acting as the first of her subjects. Thus trained in the exercise not only of free will, but despotic authority, Rowena was, by her previous education, disposed both to resist and to resent any attempt to control her affections, or dispose of her hand contrary to her inclinations, and to assert her independence in a case in which even those females who had been trained up to obedience and subjection, are not infrequently apt to dispute the authority of guardians and parents. The opinions which she felt strongly, she avowed boldly; and Cedric, who could not free himself from his habitual deference to her opinions, felt totally at a loss how to enforce his authority of guardian.

It was in vain that he attempted to dazzle her with the prospect of a visionary throne. Rowena, who possessed strong sense, neither considered his plan as practicable, nor as desirable, so far as she was concerned, could it have been achieved. Without attempting to conceal her avowed preference of Wilfred of Ivanhoe, she declared that, were that favoured knight out of question, she would rather take refuge in a convent than share a throne with Athelstane, whom, having always despised, she now began, on account of the trouble she received on his account, thoroughly to detest.

Nevertheless, Cedric, whose opinion of women's constancy was far from strong, persisted in using every means in his power to bring about the proposed match, in which he conceived he was rendering an important service to the Saxon cause. The sudden and romantic appearance of his son in the lists at Ashby, he had justly regarded as almost a death's blow to his hopes. His paternal affection, it is true, had for an instant gained the victory over pride and patriotism; but both had returned in full force, and under their joint operation, he was now bent upon making a determined effort for the union of Athelstane and Rowena, together with expediting those other measures which seemed necessary to forward the restoration of Saxon independence.

On this last subject, he was now labouring with Athelstane, not without having reason, every now and then, to lament, like Hotspur, that he should have moved such a dish of skimmed milk to so honourable an action. Athelstane, it is true, was vain enough, and loved to have his ears tickled with tales of his high descent, and of his right by inheritance to homage and sovereignty. But his pretty vanity was sufficiently gratified by receiving this homage at the hands of his immediate attendants, and of the Saxons who approached him. If he had the courage to encounter danger, he at least hated the trouble of going to seek it; and while he agreed in the general principles laid down by Cedric concerning the claim of the Saxons to independence, and was still more easily convinced of his own title to reign over them when that independence should be attained, yet when the means of asserting these rights came to be discussed, he was still "Athelstane the Unready," slow, irresolute, procrastinating, and unenterprising. The warm and impassioned exhortations of Cedric had as little effect upon his impassive temper as red-hot balls alighting in the water, which produce a little sound and smoke, and are instantly extinguished.

If, leaving this task, which might be compared to spurring a tired jade, or to hammering upon cold iron, Cedric fell back to his ward Rowena, he received little more satisfaction from conferring with her. For, as his presence interrupted the discourse between the lady and her favourite attendant upon the gallantry and fate of Wilfred, Elgitha failed not to revenge both her mistress and herself, by recurring to the overthrow of

Athelstane in the lists, the most disagreeable subject which could greet the ears of Cedric. To this sturdy Saxon, therefore, the day's journey was fraught with all manner of displeasure and discomfort; so that he more than once internally cursed the tournament, and him who had proclaimed it, together with his own folly in ever thinking of going thither.

At noon, upon the motion of Athelstane, the travellers paused in a woodland shade by a fountain, to repose their horses and partake of some provisions, with which the hospitable Abbot had loaded a sumpter mule. Their repast was a pretty long one; and these several interruptions rendered it impossible for them to hope to reach Rotherwood without travelling all night, a conviction which induced them to proceed on their way at a more hasty pace than they had hitherto used.

CHAPTER XIX

A train of armed men, some noble dame
Escorting (so their scatter'd words discover'd,
As unperceived I hung upon their rear),
Are close at hand, and mean to pass the night
Within the castle.
                                    Orra, a Tragedy.

THE travellers had now reached the verge of the wooded country, and were about to plunge into its recesses, held dangerous at that time from the number of outlaws whom oppression and poverty had driven to despair, and who occupied the forests in such large bands as could easily bid defiance to the feeble police of the period. From these rovers, however, notwithstanding the lateness of the hour, Cedric and Athelstane accounted themselves secure, as they had in attendance ten servants, besides Wamba and Gurth, whose aid could not be counted upon, the one being a jester and the other a captive. It may be added, that in travelling thus late through the forest, Cedric and Athelstane relied on their descent and character, as well as their courage. The outlaws, whom the severity of the forest laws had reduced to this roving and desperate mode of life, were chiefly peasants and yeomen of Saxon descent, and were generally supposed to respect the persons and property of their countrymen.

As the travellers journeyed on their way, they were alarmed by repeated cries for assistance; and when they rode up to the place from whence they came, they were surprised to find a horse-litter placed upon the ground, beside which sat a young woman, richly dressed in the Jewish fashion, while an old man whose yellow cap proclaimed him to belong to the same nation, walked up and down with gestures expressive of the deepest despair, and wrung his hands, as if affected by some strange disaster.

To the enquiries of Athelstane and Cedric, the old Jew could for some time only answer by invoking the protection of all the patriarchs of the Old Testament successively against the sons of Ishmael, who were coming to smite them, hip and thigh, with the edge of the sword. When he began to come to himself out of this agony of terror, Isaac of York (for it was our old friend) was at length able to explain, that he had hired a body-guard of six men at Ashby, together with mules for carrying the litter of a sick friend. This party had undertaken to escort him as far as Doncaster. They had come thus far in safety; but having received information from a wood-cutter that there was a strong band of outlaws lying in wait in the woods before them, Isaac's mercenaries had not only taken flight, but had carried off with them the horses which bore the litter, and left the Jew and his daughter without the means either of defence or of retreat, to be plundered, and probably murdered, by the banditti, who they expected every moment would bring down upon them. "Would it but please your valours," added Isaac, in a tone of deep humiliation, "to permit the poor Jews to travel under your safeguard, I swear by the tables of our law, that never has favour been conferred upon a child of Israel since the days of our captivity, which shall be more gratefully acknowledged."

"Dog of a Jew!" said Athelstane, whose memory was of that petty kind which stores up trifles of all kinds, but particularly trifling offences, "dost not remember how thou didst beard us in the gallery at the tilt-yard? Fight or flee, or compound with the outlaws as thou dost list, ask neither aid nor company from us; and if they rob only such as thee, who rob all the world, I, for mine own share, shall hold them right honest folk."

Cedric did not assent to the severe proposal of his companion.

"We shall do better," said he, "to leave them two of our attendants and two horses to convey them back to the next village. It will diminish our strength but little; and with your good sword, noble Athelstane, and the aid of those who remain, it will be light work for us to face twenty of those runagates."

Rowena, somewhat alarmed by the mention of outlaws in force, and so near them, strongly seconded the proposal of her guardian. But Rebecca, suddenly quitting her dejected posture, and making her way through the attendants to the palfrey of the Saxon lady, knelt down, and, after the Oriental fashion in addressing superiors, kissed the hem of Rowena's garment. Then rising, and throwing back her veil, she implored her in the great name of the God whom they both worshipped, and by that revelation of the Law upon Mount Sinai, in which they both believed, that she would have compassion upon them, and suffer them to go forward under their safeguard. "It is not for myself that I pray this favour," said Rebecca; "nor is it even for that poor old man. I know, that to wrong and to spoil our nation is a light fault, if not a merit, with the Christians; and what is it to us whether it be done in the city, in the desert, or in the field? But it is in the name of one dear to many, and dear even to you, that I beseech you to let this sick person be transported with care and tenderness under your protection. For, if evil chance him, the last moment of your life would be embittered with regret for denying that which I ask of you."

The noble and solemn air with which Rebecca made this appeal, gave it double weight with the fair Saxon.

"The man is old and feeble," she said to her guardian, "the maiden young and beautiful, their friend sick and in peril of his life—Jews though they be, we cannot as Christians leave them in this extremity. Let them unload two of the sumpter-mules, and put the baggage behind two of the serfs. The mules may transport the litter, and we have led horses for the old man and his daughter."

Cedric readily assented to what she proposed, and Athelstane only added the condition, "that they should travel in the rear of the whole party, where Wamba," he said, "might attend them with his shield of boar's brawn."

"I have left my shield in the tilt-yard," answered the Jester, "as has been the fate of many a better knight than myself."

Athelstane coloured deeply, for such had been his own fate on the last day of the tournament; while Rowena, who was pleased in the same proportion, as if to make amends for the brutal jest of her unfeeling suitor, requested Rebecca to ride by her side.

"It were not fit I should do so," answered Rebecca, with proud humility, "where my society might be held a disgrace to my protectress."

By this time the change of baggage was hastily achieved; for the single word "outlaws" rendered every one sufficiently alert, and the approach of twilight made the sound yet more impressive. Amid the bustle, Gurth was taken from horseback, in the course of which removal he prevailed upon the Jester to slack the cord with which his arms were bound. It was so negligently refastened, perhaps intentionally, on the part of Wamba, that Gurth found no difficulty in freeing his arms altogether from bondage, and then, gliding into the thicket, he made his escape from the party.

The bustle had been considerable, and it was some time before Gurth was missed; for, as he was to be placed for the rest of the journey behind a servant, every one supposed that some other of his companions had him under his custody, and when it began to be whispered among them that Gurth had actually disappeared, they were under such immediate expectation of an attack from the outlaws, that it was not held convenient to pay much attention to the circumstance.

The path upon which the party travelled was now so narrow, as not to admit, with any sort of convenience, above two riders abreast, and began to descend into a dingle, traversed by a brook whose banks were broken, swampy, and overgrown with dwarf willows. Cedric and Athelstane, who were at the head of their retinue, saw the risk of being attacked at this pass; but neither of them having had much practice in war, no better mode of preventing the danger occurred to them than that they should hasten through the defile as fast as possible. Advancing, therefore, without much order, they had just crossed the brook with a part of their followers, when they were assailed in front, flank, and rear at once, with an impetuosity to which, in their confused and ill-prepared condition, it was impossible to offer effectual resistance. The shout of "A white dragon!—a white dragon!—Saint George for merry England!" war-cries adopted by the assailants, as belonging to their assumed character of Saxon outlaws, was heard on every side, and on every side enemies appeared with a rapidity of advance and attack which seemed to multiply their numbers.

Both the Saxon chiefs were made prisoners at the same moment, and each under circumstances expressive of his character. Cedric, the instant that an enemy appeared, launched at him his remaining javelin, which, taking better effect than that which he had hurled at Fangs, nailed the man against an oak-tree that happened to be close behind him. Thus far successful, Cedric spurred his horse against a second, drawing his sword at the same time, and striking with such inconsiderate fury, that his weapon encountered a thick branch which hung over him, and he was disarmed by the violence of his own blow. He was instantly made prisoner, and pulled from his horse by two or three of the banditti who crowded around him. Athelstane shared his captivity, his bridle having been seized, and he himself forcibly dismounted, long before he could draw his weapon, or assume any posture of effectual defence.

The attendants, embarrassed with baggage, surprised and terrified at the fate of their masters, fell an easy prey to the assailants; while the Lady Rowena, in the centre of the cavalcade, and the Jew and his daughter in the rear, experienced the same misfortune.

Of all the train none escaped except Wamba, who showed upon the occasion much more courage than those who pretended to greater sense. He possessed himself of a sword belonging to one of the domestics, who was just drawing it with a tardy and irresolute hand, laid it about him like a lion, drove back several who approached him, and made a brave though ineffectual attempt to succour his master. Finding himself overpowered, the Jester at length threw himself from his horse, plunged into the thicket, and, favoured by the general confusion, escaped from the scene of action.

Yet the valiant Jester, as soon as he found himself safe, hesitated more than once whether he should not turn back and share the captivity of a master to whom he was sincerely attached.

"I have heard men talk of the blessings of freedom," he said to himself, "but I wish any wise man would teach me what use to make of it now that I have it."

As he pronounced these words aloud, a voice very near him called out in a low and cautious tone, "Wamba!" and, at the same time, a dog which he recognised to be Fangs, jumped up and fawned upon him.

"Gurth!" answered Wamba, with the same caution, and the swineherd immediately stood before him.

"What is the matter?" said he eagerly; "what mean these cries, and that clashing of swords?"

"Only a trick of the times," said Wamba; "they are all prisoners."

"Who are prisoners?" exclaimed Gurth, impatiently.

"My lord, and my lady, and Athelstane, and Hundibert, and Oswald."

"In the name of God!" said Gurth, "how came they prisoners?—and to whom?"

"Our master was too ready to fight," said the Jester; "and Athelstane was not ready enough, and no other person was ready at all. And they are prisoners to green cassocks, and black visors. And they lie all tumbled about on the green like the crab-apples that you shake down to your swine. And I would laugh at it," said the honest Jester, "if I could for weeping." And he shed tears of unfeigned sorrow.

Gurth's countenance kindled—"Wamba," he said, "thou hast a weapon, and thy heart was ever stronger than thy brain—we are only two—but a sudden attack from men of resolution will do much—follow me!"

"Whither?—and for what purpose?" said the Jester.

"To rescue Cedric."

"But you have renounced his service but now," said Wamba.

"That," said Gurth, "was but while he was fortunate—follow me!"

As the Jester was about to obey, a third person suddenly made his appearance, and commanded them both to halt. From his dress and arms, Wamba would have conjectured him to be one of those outlaws who had just assailed his master; but, besides that he wore no mask, the glittering baldric across his shoulder, with the rich bugle-horn which it supported, as well as the calm and commanding expression of his voice and manner, made him, notwithstanding the twilight recognise Locksley the yeoman, who had been victorious, under such disadvantageous circumstances, in the contest for the prize of archery.

"What is the meaning of all this," said he, "or who is it that rifle, and ransom, and make prisoners, in these forests?"

"You may look at their cassocks close by," said Wamba, "and see whether they be thy children's coats or no—for they are as like thine own as one green pea-cod is to another."

"I will learn that presently," answered Locksley; "and I charge ye, on peril of your lives, not to stir from the place where ye stand, until I have returned. Obey me, and it shall be the better for you and your masters.—Yet stay, I must render myself as like these men as possible."

So saying he unbuckled his baldric with the bugle, took a feather from his cap, and gave them to Wamba; then drew a vizard from his pouch, and, repeating his charges to them to stand fast, went to execute his purposes of reconnoitring.

"Shall we stand fast, Gurth?" said Wamba; "or shall we e'en give him leg-bail? In my foolish mind, he had all the equipage of a thief too much in readiness, to be himself a true man."

"Let him be the devil," said Gurth, "an he will. We can be no worse of waiting his return. If he belong to that party, he must already have given them the alarm, and it will avail nothing either to fight or fly. Besides, I have late experience, that arrant thieves are not the worst men in the world to have to deal with."

The yeoman returned in the course of a few minutes.

"Friend Gurth," he said, "I have mingled among yon men, and have learnt to whom they belong, and whither they are bound. There is, I think, no chance that they will proceed to any actual violence against their prisoners. For three men to attempt them at this moment were little else than madness; for they are good men of war, and have, as such, placed sentinels to give the alarm when any one approaches. But I trust soon to gather such a force as may act in defiance of all their precautions; you are both servants, and, as I think, faithful servants, of Cedric the Saxon, the friend of the rights of Englishmen. He shall not want English hands to help him in this extremity. Come then with me, until I gather more aid."

So saying, he walked through the wood at a great pace, followed by the jester and the swine-herd. It was not consistent with Wamba's humor to travel long in silence.

"I think," said he, looking at the baldric and bugle which he still carried, "that I saw the arrow shot which won this gay prize, and that not so long since as Christmas."

"And I," said Gurth, "could take it on my halidome, that I have heard the voice of the good yeoman who won it, by night as well as by day, and that the moon is not three days older since I did so."

"Mine honest friends," replied the yeoman, "who, or what I am, is little to the present purpose; should I free your master, you will have reason to think me the best friend you have ever had in your lives. And whether I am known by one name or another—or whether I can draw a bow as well or better than a cow-keeper, or whether it is my pleasure to walk in sunshine or by moonlight, are matters, which, as they do not concern you, so neither need ye busy yourselves respecting them."

"Our heads are in the lion's mouth," said Wamba, in a whisper to Gurth, "get them out how we can."

"Hush—be silent," said Gurth. "Offend him not by thy folly, and I trust sincerely that all will go well."

CHAPTER XX

When autumn nights were long and drear,
 And forest walks were dark and dim,
How sweetly on the pilgrim's ear
 Was wont to steal the hermit's hymn!

Devotion borrows Music's tone,
 And Music took Devotion's wing;
And, like the bird that hails the sun,
 They soar to heaven, and soaring sing.
The Hermit of St. Clement's Well.

I T was after three hours' good walking that the servants of Cedric, with their mysterious guide, arrived at a small opening in the forest, in the centre of which grew an oak tree of enormous magnitude, throwing its twisted branches in every direction. Beneath this tree four or five yeomen lay stretched on the ground, while another, as sentinel, walked to and fro in the moonlight shade.

Upon hearing the sound of feet approaching, the watch instantly gave the alarm, and the sleepers as suddenly started up and bent their bows. Six arrows placed on the string were pointed towards the quarter from which the travellers approached when their guide, being recognised, was welcomed with every token of respect and attachment, and all signs and fears of a rough reception at once subsided.

"Where is the Miller?" was his first question.

"On the road towards Rotherham."

"With how many?" demanded the leader, for such he seemed to be.

"With six men and good hope of booty, if it please St. Nicholas."

"Devoutly spoken," said Locksley; "and where is Allan-a-dale?"

"Walked up towards the Watling-street, to watch for the Prior of Jorvaulx."

"That is well thought on also," replied the Captain;—"and where is the Friar?"

"In his cell."

"Thither will I go," said Locksley. "Disperse and seek your companions. Collect what force you can, for there's game afoot that must be hunted hard, and will turn to bay. Meet me here by daybreak.—And, stay," he added, "I have forgotten what is most necessary of the whole— Two of you take the road quickly towards Torquilstone, the Castle of Front-de-Bœuf. A set of gallants, who have been masquerading in such guise as our own, are carrying a band of prisoners thither—Watch them closely, for even if they reach the castle before we collect our force, our honour is concerned to punish them, and we will find means to do so. Keep a close watch on them therefore; and dispatch one of your comrades, the lightest of foot, to bring the news of the yeomen thereabout."

They promised implicit obedience, and departed with alacrity on their different errands. In the meanwhile, their leader and his two companions, who now looked upon him with great respect, as well as some fear, pursued their way to the Chapel of Copmanhurst.

When they had reached the little moonlight glade, having in front the reverend, though ruinous chapel, and the rude hermitage, so well suited to ascetic devotion, Wamba whispered to Gurth, "If this be the habitation of a thief, it makes good the old proverb, The nearer the church the farther from God.—And by my cockscomb," he added, "I think it be even so—Hearken but to the black sanctus which they are singing in the hermitage!"

In fact the anchorite and his guest were performing, at the full extent of their very powerful lungs, an old drinking song, of which this was the burden:—

> "Come, trowl the brown bowl to me,
>   Bully boy, bully boy,
>   Come, trowl the brown bowl to me:
>   Ho! jolly Jenkin, I spy a knave in drinking,
>   Come, trowl the brown bowl to me."

"Now, that is not ill sung," said Wamba, who had thrown in a few of his own flourishes to help out the chorus. "But who, in the saint's name, ever expected to have heard such a jolly chant come from out a hermit's cell at midnight!"

"Mary, that should I," said Gurth, "for the jolly Clerk of Copmanhurst is a known man, and kills half the deer that are stolen in this walk. Men say that the keeper has complained to his official, and that he will be stripped of his cowl and cope altogether, if he keep not better order."

While they were thus speaking, Locksley's loud and repeated knocks had at length disturbed the anchorite and his guest. "By my beads," said the hermit, stopping short in a grand flourish, "here come more benighted guests. I would not for my cowl that they found us in this goodly exercise. All men have their enemies, good Sir Sluggard; and there be those malignant enough to construe the hospitable refreshment which I have been offering to you, a weary traveller, for the matter of three short hours, into sheer drunkenness and debauchery, vices alike alien to my profession and my disposition."

"Base calumniators!" replied the knight; "I would I had the chastising of them. Nevertheless, Holy Clerk, it is true that all have their enemies; and there be those in this very land whom I would rather speak to through the bars of my helmet than barefaced."

"Get thine iron pot on thy head then, friend Sluggard, as quickly as thy nature will permit," said the hermit, "while I remove these pewter flagons, whose late contents run strangely in mine own pate; and to drown the clatter—for, in faith, I feel somewhat unsteady—strike into the tune which thou hearest me sing; it is no matter for the words—I scarce know them myself."

So saying, he struck up a thundering *De profundis clamavi,* under cover of which he removed the apparatus of their banquet: while the knight, laughing heartily, and arming himself all the while, assisted his host with his voice from time to time as his mirth permitted.

"What devil's matins are you after at this hour?" said a voice from without.

"Heaven forgive you, Sir Traveller!" said the hermit, whose own noise, and perhaps his nocturnal potations, prevented from recognising accents which were tolerably familiar to him—"Wend on your way, in the name of God and St. Dunstan, and disturb not the devotions of me and my holy brother."

"Mad priest," answered the voice from without, "open to Locksley!"

"All's safe—all's right," said the hermit to his companion.

"But who is he?" said the Black Knight; "it imports me much to know."

"Who is he?" answered the hermit; "I tell thee he is a friend."

"But what friend?" answered the knight; "for he may be friend to thee and none of mine?"

"What friend?" replied the hermit; "that, now, is one of the questions that is more easily asked than answered. What friend?—why, he is, now that I bethink me a little, the very same honest keeper I told thee of a while since."

"Ay, as honest a keeper as thou art a pious hermit," replied the knight, "I doubt it not. But undo the door to him before he beat it from its hinges."

The dogs, in the meantime, which had made a dreadful baying at the commencement of the disturbance, seemed now to recognise the voice of him who stood without; for, totally changing their manner, they scratched and whined at the door, as if interceding for his admission. The hermit speedily unbolted his portal, and admitted Locksley, with his two companions.

"Why, hermit," was the yeoman's first question as soon as he beheld the knight, "what boon companion hast thou here?"

"A brother of our order," replied the friar, shaking his head; "we have been at our orisons all night."

"He is a monk of the church militant, I think," answered Locksley; "and there be more of them abroad. I tell thee, friar, thou must lay down the rosary and take up the quarter-staff; we shall need every one of our merry men, whether clerk or layman.—But," he added, taking him a step aside, "art thou mad? to give admittance to a knight thou dost not know? Hast thou forgot our articles?"

"Not know him!" replied the friar, boldly, "I know him as well as the beggar knows his dish."

"And what is his name, then?" demanded Locksley.

"His name," said the hermit—"his name is Sir Anthony of Scrabelstone—as if I would drink with a man, and did not know his name!"

"Thou hast been drinking more than enough, friar," said the wood-man, "and, I fear, prating more than enough too."

"Good yeoman," said the knight, coming forward, "be not wroth with my merry host. He did but afford me the hospitality which I would have compelled from him if he had refused it."

"Thou compel!" said the friar; "wait but till I have changed this grey gown for a green cassock, and if I make not quarter-staff ring twelve upon thy pate, I am neither true clerk nor good woodsman."

While he spoke thus, he stript off his gown, and appeared in a close black buckram doublet and drawers, over which he speedily did on a cassock of green, and hose of the same colour. "I pray thee truss my points," said he to Wamba, "and thou shalt have a cup of sack for thy labour."

"Gramercy for thy sack," said Wamba; "but think'st thou it is lawful for me to aid you to transmew thyself from a holy hermit into a sinful forester?"

"Never fear," said the hermit; "I will but confess the sins of my green cloak to my greyfriar's frock, and all shall be well again."

"Amen!" answered the Jester; "a broadcloth penitent should have a sackcloth confessor, and your frock may absolve my motley doublet into the bargain."

So saying, he accommodated the friar with his assistance in tying the endless number of points, as the laces which attached the hose to the doublet were then termed.

While they were thus employed, Locksley led the knight a little apart, and addressed him thus:—"Deny it not, Sir Knight—you are he who decided the victory to the advantage of the English against the strangers on the second day of the tournament of Ashby."

"And what follows if you guess truly, good yeoman?" replied the knight.

"I should in that case hold you," replied the yeoman, "a friend to the weaker party."

"Such is the duty of a true knight at least," replied the Black Champion; "and I would not willingly that there were reason to think otherwise of me."

"But for my purpose," said the yeoman, "thou shouldst be as well a good Englishman as a good knight; for that which I have to speak of concerns, indeed, the duty of every honest man, but is more especially that of a true-born native of England."

"You can speak to no one," replied the knight, "to whom England, and the life of every Englishman, can be dearer than to me."

"I would willingly believe so," said the woodsman, "for never had this country such need to be supported by those who love her. Hear me, and I will tell thee of an enterprise, in which, if thou be'st really that which thou seemest, thou mayst take an honourable part. A band of villains, in the disguise of better men than themselves, have made themselves master of the person of a noble Englishman, called Cedric the Saxon, together with his ward, and his friend Athelstane of Conings-burgh, and have transported them to a castle in this forest, called Tor-quilstone. I ask of thee, as a good knight and a good Englishman, wilt thou aid in their rescue?"

"I am bound by my vow to do so," replied the knight; "but I would willingly know who you are who request my assistance in their behalf?"

"I am," said the forester, "a nameless man; but I am the friend of my country, and of my country's friends—With this account of me you must for the present remain satisfied, the more especially since you your-self desire to continue unknown. Believe, however, that my word, when pledged, is as inviolate as if I wore golden spurs."

"I willingly believe it," said the knight; "I have been accustomed to study men's countenances, and I can read in thine honesty and resolu-tion. I will, therefore, ask thee no farther questions, but aid thee in setting at freedom these oppressed captives; which done, I trust we shall part better acquainted, and well satisfied with each other."

"So," said Wamba to Gurth,—for the friar being now fully equipped, the Jester, having approached to the other side of the hut, had heard the conclusion of the conversation,—"So we have got a new ally?—I trust the valour of the knight will be truer metal than the religion of the hermit, or the honesty of the yeoman; for this Locksley looks like a born deer-stealer, and the priest like a lusty hypocrite."

"Hold thy peace, Wamba," said Gurth; "it may all be as thou dost guess; but were the horned devil to rise and proffer me his assistance to set at liberty Cedric and the Lady Rowena, I fear I should hardly have religion enough to refuse the foul fiend's offer, and bid him get be-hind me."

The friar was now completely accoutred as a yeoman, with sword and buckler, bow, and quiver, and a strong partisan over his shoulder. He left his cell at the head of the party, and, having carefully locked the door, deposited the key under the threshold.

"Art thou in condition to do good service, friar," said Locksley, "or does the brown bowl still run in thy head?"

"Not more than a draught of St. Dunstan's fountain will allay," an-swered the priest; "something there is of a whizzing in my brain, and of instability in my legs, but you shall presently see both pass away."

So saying, he stepped to the stone basin, in which the waters of the fountain as they fell formed bubbles which danced in the white moon-light, and took so long a draught as if he had meant to exhaust the spring.

"When didst thou drink as deep a draught of water before, Holy Clerk of Copmanhurst?" said the Black Knight.

"Never since my wine-butt leaked, and let out its liquor by an illegal vent," replied the friar, "and so left me nothing to drink but my patron's bounty here."

Then plunging his hands and head into the fountain, he washed from them all marks of the midnight revel.

Thus refreshed and sobered, the jolly priest twirled his heavy partisan round his head with three fingers, as if he had been balancing a reed, exclaiming at the same time, "Where be those false ravishers, who carry off wenches against their will? May the foul fiend fly off with me, if I am not man enough for a dozen of them."

"Swearest thou, Holy Clerk?" said the Black Knight.

"Clerk me no Clerks," replied the transformed priest; "by Saint George and the Dragon, I am no longer a shaveling than while my frock is on my back—When I am cased in my green cassock, I will drink, swear, and woo a lass, with any blithe forester in the West Riding."

"Come on, Jack Priest," said Locksley, "and be silent; thou art as noisy as a whole convent on a holy eve, when the Father Abbot has gone to bed.—Come on you, too, my masters, tarry not to talk of it— I say, come on, we must collect all our forces, and few enough we shall have, if we are to storm the Castle of Reginald Front-de-Bœuf."

"What! is it Front-de-Bœuf," said the Black Knight, "who has stopt on the king's highway the king's liege subjects?—Is he turned thief and oppressor?"

"Oppressor he ever was," said Locksley.

"And for thief," said the priest, "I doubt if ever he were even half so honest a man as many a thief of my acquaintance."

"Move on, priest, and be silent," said the yeoman; "it were better you led the way to the place of rendezvous, than say what should be left unsaid, both in decency and prudence."

CHAPTER XXI

> Alas, how many hours and years have past,
> Since human forms have round this table sate
> Or lamp, or taper, on its surface gleam'd!
> Methinks, I hear the sound of time long pass'd
> Still murmuring o'er us, in the lofty void
> Of these dark arches, like the ling'ring voices
> Of those who long within their graves have slept.
>   *Orra, a Tragedy.*

WHILE these measures were taking in behalf of Cedric and his companions, the armed men by whom the latter had been seized, hurried their captives along towards the place of security, where they intended to imprison them. But darkness came on fast and the paths of the wood seemed but imperfectly known to the marauders. They were compelled to make several long halts, and once or twice to return on their road to resume the direction which they wished to pursue. The summer morn had dawned upon them ere they could travel in full assurance that they held the right path. But confidence returned with light, and the cavalcade now moved rapidly forward. Meanwhile, the following dialogue took place between the two leaders of the banditti.

"It is time thou shouldst leave us, Sir Maurice," said the Templar to De Bracy, "in order to prepare the second part of thy mystery. Thou art next, thou knowest, to act the Knight Deliverer."

"I have thought better of it," said De Bracy; "I will not leave thee till the prize is fairly deposited in Front-de-Bœuf's castle. There will I appear before the Lady Rowena in mine own shape, and trust that she will set down to the vehemence of my passion the violence of which I have been guilty."

"And what has made thee change thy plan, De Bracy?" replied the Knight Templar.

"That concerns thee nothing," answered the companion.

"I would hope, however, Sir Knight," said the Templar, "that this alteration of measures arises from no suspicion of my honourable meaning, such as Fitzurse endeavoured to instil into thee?"

"My thoughts are my own," answered De Bracy; "the fiend laughs, they say, when one thief robs another; and we know, that were he to spit fire and brimstone instead, it would never prevent a Templar from following his bent."

"Or the leader of a Free Company," answered the Templar, "from dreading at the hands of a comrade and friend, the injustice he does to all mankind."

"This is unprofitable and perilous recrimination," answered De Bracy; "suffice it to say, I know the morals of the Temple-Order, and I will not give thee the power of cheating me out of the fair prey for which I have run such risks."

"Psha," replied the Templar, "what hast thou to fear?—Thou knowest the vows of our order."

"Right well," said De Bracy, "and also how they are kept. Come, Sir Templar, the laws of gallantry have a liberal interpretation in Palestine, and this is a case in which I will trust nothing to your conscience."

"Hear the truth, then," said the Templar; "I care not for your blue-eyed beauty. There is in that train one who will make me a better mate."

"What! wouldst thou stoop to the waiting damsel?" said De Bracy.

"No, Sir Knight," said the Templar, haughtily. "To the waiting-woman will I not stoop. I have a prize among the captives as lovely as thine own."

"By the mass, thou meanest the fair Jewess!" said De Bracy.

"And if I do," said Bois-Guilbert, "who shall gainsay me?"

"No one that I know," said De Bracy, "unless it be your vow of celibacy, or a check of conscience for an intrigue with a Jewess."

"For my vow," said the Templar, "our Grand Master hath granted me a dispensation. And for my conscience, a man that has slain three hundred Saracens, need not reckon up every little failing, like a village girl at her first confession upon Good Friday eve."

"Thou knowest best thine own privileges," said De Bracy. "Yet I would have sworn thy thought had been more on the old usurer's money bags, than on the black eyes of the daughter."

"I can admire both," answered the Templar; "besides the old Jew is but half-prize. I must share his spoils with Front-de-Bœuf, who will not lend us the use of his castle for nothing. I must have something that I can term exclusively my own by this foray of ours, and I have fixed on the lovely Jewess as my peculiar prize. But, now thou knowest my drift, thou wilt resume thine own original plan, wilt thou not?—Thou hast nothing, thou seest, to fear from my interference."

"No," replied De Bracy, "I will remain beside my prize. What thou sayest is passing true, but I like not the privileges acquired by the dispensation of the Grand Master, and the merit acquired by the slaughter of three hundred Saracens. You have too good a right to a free pardon, to render you very scrupulous about peccadilloes."

While this dialogue was proceeding, Cedric was endeavouring to wring out of those who guarded him an avowal of their character and purpose. "You should be Englishmen," said he; "and yet, sacred Heaven! you prey upon your countrymen as if you were very Normans. You should be my neighbours, and, if so, my friends; for which of my English neighbours have reason to be otherwise? I tell ye, yeomen, that even those among ye who have been branded with outlawry have had from me protection; for I have pitied their miseries, and curst the oppression of their tyrannic nobles. What, then, would you have of me? or in what can this violence serve ye?—Ye are worse than brute beasts in your actions, and will you imitate them in their very dumbness?"

It was in vain that Cedric expostulated with his guards, who had too many good reasons for their silence to be induced to break it either by his wrath or his expostulations. They continued to hurry him along, travelling at a very rapid rate, until, at the end of an avenue of huge trees, arose Torquilstone, now the hoary and ancient castle of Reginald Front-de-Bœuf. It was a fortress of no great size, consisting of a donjon, or large and high square tower, surrounded by buildings of inferior height, which were encircled by an inner court-yard. Around the exterior wall was a deep moat, supplied with water from a neighbouring rivulet. Front-de-Bœuf, whose character placed him often at feud with his enemies, had made considerable additions to the strength of his castle, by building towers upon the outward wall, so as to flank it at every angle. The access, as usual in castles of the period, lay through an arched barbican, or outwork, which was terminated and defended by a small turret at each corner.

Cedric no sooner saw the turrets of Front-de-Bœuf's castle raise their grey and moss-grown battlements, glimmering in the morning sun above the wood by which they were surrounded, than he instantly augured more truly concerning the cause of his misfortune.

"I did injustice," he said, "to the thieves and outlaws of these woods, when I supposed such banditti to belong to their bands; I might as justly have confounded the foxes of these brakes with the ravening wolves of France. Tell me, dogs—is it my life or my wealth that your master aims at? Is it too much that two Saxons, myself and the noble Athelstane, should hold land in the country which was once the patrimony of our race?—Put us then to death, and complete your tyranny by taking our lives, as you began with our liberties. If the Saxon Cedric cannot rescue England, he is willing to die for her. Tell your tyrannical master, I do only beseech him to dismiss the Lady Rowena in honour and safety. She is a woman, and he need not dread her; and with us will die all who dare fight in her cause."

The attendants remained as mute to this address as to the former, and they now stood before the gate of the castle. De Bracy winded his horn three times, and the archers and cross-bow men, who had manned the wall upon seeing their approach, hastened to lower the drawbridge, and admit them. The prisoners were compelled by their guards to alight, and were conducted to an apartment where a hasty repast was offered them, of which none but Athelstane felt any inclination to partake. Neither had the descendant of the Confessor much time to do justice to the good cheer placed before them, for their guards gave him and Cedric to understand that they were to be imprisoned in a chamber apart from Rowena. Resistance was vain; and they were compelled to follow to a large room, which, rising on clumsy Saxon pillars, resembled those refectories and chapter-houses which may be still seen in the most ancient parts of our most ancient monasteries.

The Lady Rowena was next separated from her train, and conducted, with courtesy, indeed, but still without consulting her inclination, to a distant apartment. The same alarming distinction was conferred on Rebecca, in spite of her father's entreaties, who offered even money, in this extremity of distress, that she might be permitted to abide with him. "Base unbeliever," answered one of his guards, "when thou hast seen thy lair, thou wilt not wish thy daughter to partake it." And, without further discussion, the old Jew was forcibly dragged off in a different direction from the other prisoners. The domestics, after being carefully searched and disarmed, were confined in another part of the castle; and Rowena was refused even the comfort she might have derived from the attendance of her handmaiden Elgitha.

The apartment in which the Saxon chiefs were confined, for to them we turn our first attention, although at present used as a sort of guard-room, had formerly been the great hall of the castle. It was now abandoned to meaner purposes, because the present lord, among other additions to the convenience, security, and beauty of his baronial residence, had erected a new and noble hall, whose vaulted roof was supported by lighter and more elegant pillars, and fitted up with that higher degree of ornament, which the Normans had already introduced into architecture.

Cedric paced the apartment, filled with indignant reflections on the past and on the present, while the apathy of his companion served, instead of patience and philosophy, to defend him against everything save the inconvenience of the present moment; and so little did he feel even this last, that he was only from time to time roused to a reply by Cedric's animated and impassioned appeal to him.

"Yes," said Cedric, half speaking to himself and half addressing himself to Athelstane, "it was in this very hall that my father feasted with Torquil Wolfganger, when he entertained the valiant and unfortunate Harold, then advancing against the Norwegians, who had united themselves to the rebel Tosti. It was in this hall that Harold returned the magnanimous answer to the ambassador of his rebel brother. Oft have I heard my father kindle as he told the tale. The envoy of Tosti was admitted, when this ample room could scarce contain the crowd of noble Saxon leaders who were quaffing the blood-red wine around their monarch."

"I hope," said Athelstane, somewhat moved by this part of his friend's discourse, "they will not forget to send us some wine and refections at noon—we had scarce a breathing-space allowed to break our fast, and I never have the benefit of my food when I eat immediately after dismounting from horseback, though the leeches recommend that practice."

Cedric went on with his story without noticing this interjectional observation of his friend.

"The envoy of Tosti," he said, "moved up the hall, undismayed by the frowning countenances of all around him, until he made his obeisance before the throne of King Harold.

" 'What terms,' he said, 'Lord King, hath thy brother Tosti to hope, if he should lay down his arms, and crave peace at thy hands?'

" 'A brother's love,' cried the generous Harold, 'and the fair earldom of Northumberland.'

" 'But should Tosti accept these terms,' continued the envoy, 'what lands shall be assigned to his faithful ally, Hardrada, King of Norway?'

" 'Seven feet of English ground,' answered Harold, fiercely, 'or, as Hardrada is said to be a giant, perhaps we may allow him twelve inches more.'

"The hall rung with acclamations, and cup and horn was filled to the Norwegian, who should be speedily in possession of his English territory."

"I could have pledged him with all my soul," said Athelstane, "for my tongue cleaves to my palate."

"The baffled envoy," continued Cedric, pursuing with animation his tale, though it interested not the listener, "retreated, to carry to Tosti and his ally the ominous answer of his injured brother. It was then that the distant towers of York, and the bloody streams of the Derwent,[1]

---

[1] Note IV.—Battle of Stamford.

beheld that direful conflict, in which, after displaying the most undaunted valour, the King of Norway, and Tosti, both fell, with ten
thousand of their bravest followers. Who would have thought that upon
the proud day when this battle was won, the very gale which waved the
Saxon banners in triumph, was filling the Norman sails, and impelling
them to the fatal shores of Sussex?—Who would have thought that
Harold, within a few brief days, would himself possess no more of his
kingdom than the share which he allotted in his wrath to the Norwegian
invader?—Who would have thought that you, noble Athelstane—that
you, descended of Harold's blood, and that I, whose father was not the
worst defender of the Saxon crown, should be prisoners to a vile Norman,
in the very hall in which our ancestors held such high festival?"

"It is sad enough," replied Athelstane; "but I trust they will hold us
to a moderate ransom—At any rate it cannot be their purpose to starve
us outright; and yet, although it is high noon, I see no preparations for
serving dinner. Look up at the window, noble Cedric, and judge by the
sunbeams if it is not on the verge of noon."

"It may be so," answered Cedric; "but I cannot look on that stained
lattice without its awakening other reflections than those which concern the passing moment, or its privations. When that window was
wrought, my noble friend, our hardy fathers knew not the art of making
glass, or of staining it—The pride of Wolfganger's father brought an
artist from Normandy to adorn his hall with this new species of em-
blazonment, that breaks the golden light of God's blessed day into so
many fantastic hues. The foreigner came here poor, beggarly, cringing,
and subservient, ready to doff his cap to the meanest native of the household. He returned pampered and proud, to tell his rapacious countrymen
of the wealth and the simplicity of the Saxon nobles—a folly, oh, Athelstane, foreboded of old, as well as foreseen by those descendants of
Hengist and his hardy tribes, who retained the simplicity of their manners.
We made these strangers our bosom friends, our confidential servants;
we borrowed their artists and their arts, and depised the honest simplicity and hardihood with which our brave ancestors supported themselves, and we became enervated by Norman arts long ere we fell under
Norman arms. Far better was our homely diet, eaten in peace and liberty,
than the luxurious dainties, the love of which hath delivered us as bondsmen to the foreign conqueror!"

"I should," replied Athelstane, "hold very humble diet a luxury at
present; and it astonishes me, noble Cedric, that you can bear so truly
in mind the memory of past deeds, when it appeareth you forget the very
hour of dinner."

"It is time lost," muttered Cedric apart and impatiently, "to speak
to him of aught else but that which concerns his appetite! The soul of
Hardicanute hath taken possession of him, and he hath no pleasure save
to fill, to swill, and to call for more.—Alas!" said he, looking at Athelstane with compassion, "that so dull a spirit should be lodged in so

goodly a form! Alas! that such an enterprise as the regeneration of England should turn on a hinge so imperfect! Wedded to Rowena, indeed, her nobler and more generous soul may yet awake the better nature which is torpid within him. Yet how should this be, while Rowena, Athelstane, and I myself, remain the prisoners of this brutal marauder, and have been made so perhaps from a sense of the dangers which our liberty might bring to the usurped power of his nation?"

While the Saxon was plunged in these painful reflections, the door of their prison opened, and gave entrance to a sewer, holding his white rod of office. This important person advanced into the chamber with a grave pace, followed by four attendants, bearing in a table covered with dishes, the sight and smell of which seemed to be an instant compensation to Athelstane for all the inconvenience he had undergone. The persons who attended on the feast were masked and cloaked.

"What mummery is this?" said Cedric; "think you that we are ignorant whose prisoners we are, when we are in the castle of your master? Tell him," he continued, willing to use this opportunity to open a negotiation for his freedom,—"Tell your master, Reginald Front-de-Bœuf, that we know no reason he can have for withholding our liberty, excepting his unlawful desire to enrich himself at our expense. Tell him that we yield to his rapacity, as in similar circumstances we should do to that of a literal robber. Let him name the ransom at which he rates our liberty, and it shall be paid, providing the exaction is suited to our means."

The sewer made no answer, but bowed his head.

"And tell Sir Reginald Front-de-Bœuf," said Athelstane, "that I send him my mortal defiance, and challenge him to combat with me, on foot or horseback, at any secure place, within eight days after our liberation; which, if he be a true knight, he will not, under these circumstances, venture to refuse or to delay."

"I shall deliver to the knight your defiance," answered the sewer; "meanwhile I leave you to your food."

The challenge of Athelstane was delivered with no good grace; for a large mouthful, which required the exercise of both jaws at once, added to a natural hesitation, considerably damped the effect of the bold defiance it contained. Still, however, his speech was hailed by Cedric as an incontestable token of reviving spirit in his companion, whose previous indifference had begun, notwithstanding his respect for Athelstane's descent, to wear out his patience. But he now cordially shook hands with him in token of his approbation, and was somewhat grieved when Athelstane observed, "that he would fight a dozen such men as Front-de-Bœuf, if, by so doing, he could hasten his departure from a dungeon where they put so much garlic into their pottage." Notwithstanding this intimation of a relapse into the apathy of sensuality, Cedric placed himself opposite to Athelstane, and soon showed, that if the distresses of his country could banish the recollection of food while the table was uncovered, yet no sooner were the victuals put there, than he proved that the appetite of his Saxon ancestors had descended to him along with their other qualities.

The captives had not long enjoyed their refreshment, however, ere their attention was disturbed even from this most serious occupation by the blast of a horn winded before the gate. It was repeated three times, with as much violence as if it had been blown before an enchanted castle by the destined knight, at whose summons halls and towers, barbican and battlement, were to roll off like a morning vapour. The Saxons started from the table, and hastened to the window. But their curiosity was disappointed; for these outlets only looked upon the court of the castle, and the sound came from beyond its precincts. The summons, however, seemed of importance, for a considerable degree of bustle instantly took place in the castle.

CHAPTER XXII

My daughter—O my ducats—O my daughter!
————O my Christian ducats!
Justice—the Law—my ducats, and my daughter!
Merchant of Venice.

LEAVING the Saxon chiefs to return to their banquet as soon as their ungratified curiosity should permit them to attend to the calls of their half-satiated appetite, we have to look in upon the yet more severe imprisonment of Isaac of York. The poor Jew had been hastily thrust into a dungeon-vault of the castle, the floor of which was deep beneath the level of the ground, and very damp, being lower than even the moat itself. The only light was received through one or two loop-holes far above the reach of the captive's hand. These apertures admitted, even at mid-day, only a dim and uncertain light, which was changed for utter darkness long before the rest of the castle had lost the blessing of day. Chains and shackles, which had been the portion of former captives, from whom active exertions to escape had been apprehended, hung rusted and empty on the walls of the prison, and in the rings of one of those sets of fetters there remained two mouldering bones, which seemed to have been once those of the human leg, as if some prisoner had been left not only to perish there, but to be consumed to a skeleton.

At one end of this ghastly apartment was a large fire-grate, over the top of which were stretched some transverse iron bars, half devoured with rust.

The whole appearance of the dungeon might have appalled a stouter heart than that of Isaac, who, nevertheless, was more composed under the imminent pressure of danger, than he had seemed to be while affected by terrors, of which the cause was as yet remote and contingent. The lovers of the chase say that the hare feels more agony during the pur-

suit of the greyhounds, than when she is struggling in their fangs.[1]
And thus it is probable, that the Jews, by the very frequency of their
fear on all occasions, had their minds in some degree prepared for every
effort of tyranny which could be practised upon them; so that no aggression, when it had taken place, could bring with it that surprise which
is the most disabling quality of terror. Neither was it the first time that
Isaac had been placed in circumstances so dangerous. He had therefore
experience to guide him, as well as hope, that he might again, as formerly, be delivered as a prey from the fowler. Above all, he had upon
his side the unyielding obstinacy of his nation, and that unbending resolution, with which Israelites have been frequently known to submit to
the uttermost evils which power and violence can inflict upon them,
rather than gratify their oppressors by granting their demands.

In this humour of passive resistance, and with his garment collected
beneath him to keep his limbs from the wet pavement, Isaac sat in a
corner of his dungeon, where his folded hands, his dishevelled hair and
beard, his furred cloak and high cap, seen by the wiry and broken
light, would have afforded a study for Rembrandt, had that celebrated
painter existed at the period. The Jew remained, without altering his
position, for nearly three hours, at the expiry of which steps were heard
on the dungeon stair. The bolts screamed as they were withdrawn—the
hinges creaked as the wicket opened, and Reginald Front-de-Bœuf, followed by the two Saracen slaves of the Templar, entered the prison.

Front-de-Bœuf, a tall and strong man, whose life had been spent in
public war or in private feuds and broils, and who had hesitated at no
means of extending his feudal power, had features corresponding to his
character, and which strongly expressed the fiercer and more malignant
passions of the mind. The scars with which his visage was seamed, would,
on features of a different cast, have excited the sympathy and veneration
due to the marks of honourable valour; but, in the peculiar case of
Front-de-Bœuf, they only added to the ferocity of his countenance, and
to the dread which his presence inspired. This formidable baron was clad
in a leathern doublet, fitted close to his body, which was frayed and
soiled with the stains of his armour. He had no weapon, excepting a
poniard at his belt, which served to counterbalance the weight of the
bunch of rusty keys that hung at his right side.

The black slaves who attended Front-de-Bœuf were stripped of their
gorgeous apparel, and attired in jerkins and trowsers of coarse linen,
their sleeves being tucked up above the elbow, like those of butchers
when about to exercise their function in the slaughter-house. Each had
in his hand a small pannier; and, when they entered the dungeon, they
stopt at the door until Front-de-Bœuf himself carefully locked and double-locked it. Having taken this precaution, he advanced slowly up the
apartment towards the Jew, upon whom he kept his eye fixed, as if

---

[1] *Nota Bene.*—We by no means warrant the accuracy of this piece of natural
history, which we give on the authority of the Wardour MS.—L. T.

he wished to paralyze him with his glance, as some animals are said to fascinate their prey. It seemed indeed as if the sullen and malignant eye of Front-de-Bœuf possessed some portion of that supposed power over his unfortunate prisoner. The Jew sate with his mouth a-gape, and his eyes fixed on the savage baron with such earnestness of terror, that his frame seemed literally to shrink together, and to diminish in size while encountering the fierce Norman's fixed and baleful gaze. The unhappy Isaac was deprived not only of the power of rising to make the obeisance which his terror dictated, but he could not even doff his cap, or utter any word of supplication; so strongly was he agitated by the conviction that tortures and death were impending over him.

On the other hand, the stately form of the Norman appeared to dilate in magnitude, like that of the eagle, which ruffles up its plumage when about to pounce on its defenceless prey. He paused within three steps of the corner in which the unfortunate Jew had now, as it were, coiled himself up into the smallest possible space, and made a sign for one of the slaves to approach. The black satellite came forward accordingly, and, producing from his basket a large pair of scales and several weights, he laid them at the feet of Front-de-Bœuf, and again retired to the respectful distance at which his companion had already taken his station.

The motions of these men were slow and solemn, as if there impended over their souls some preconception of horror and of cruelty. Front-de-Bœuf himself opened the scene by thus addressing his ill-fated captive.

"Most accursed dog of an accursed race," he said, awaking with his deep and sullen voice the sullen echoes of his dungeon vault, "seest thou these scales?"

The unhappy Jew returned a feeble affirmative.

"In these very scales shalt thou weigh me out," said the relentless Baron, "a thousand silver pounds, after the just measure and weight of the Tower of London."

"Holy Abraham!" returned the Jew, finding voice through the very extremity of his danger, "heard man ever such a demand?—Who ever heard, even in a minstrel's tale, of such a sum as a thousand pounds of silver?—What human sight was ever blessed with the vision of such a mass of treasure?—Not within the walls of York, ransack my house and that of all my tribe, wilt thou find the tithe of that huge sum of silver that thou speakest of."

"I am reasonable," answered Front-de-Bœuf, "and if silver be scant, I refuse not gold. At the rate of a mark of gold for each six pounds of silver, thou shalt free thy unbelieving carcass from such punishment as thy heart has never even conceived."

"Have mercy on me, noble knight!" exclaimed Isaac; "I am old, and poor, and helpless. It were unworthy to triumph over me—It is a poor deed to crush a worm."

"Old thou mayst be," replied the knight; "more shame to their folly who have suffered thee to grow grey in usury and knavery—Feeble thou mayst be, for when had a Jew either heart or hand—But rich it is well known thou art."

"I swear to you, noble knight," said the Jew, "by all which I believe, and by all which we believe in common"——

"Perjure not thyself," said the Norman, interrupting him, "and let not thine obstinacy seal thy doom, until thou hast seen and well considered the fate that awaits thee. Think not I speak to thee only to excite thy terror, and practise on the base cowardice thou hast derived from thy tribe. I swear to thee by that which thou dost NOT believe, by the gospel which our church teaches, and by the keys which are given her to bind and to loose, that my purpose is deep and peremptory. This dungeon is no place for trifling. Prisoners ten thousand times more distinguished than thou have died within these walls, and their fate hath never been known! But for thee is reserved a long and lingering death, to which theirs were luxury."

He again made a signal for the slaves to approach, and spoke to them apart, in their own language; for he also had been in Palestine, where, perhaps, he had learnt his lesson of cruelty. The Saracens produced from their baskets a quantity of charcoal, a pair of bellows, and a flask of oil. While the one struck a light with a flint and steel, the other disposed the charcoal in the large rusty grate which we have already mentioned, and exercised the bellows until the fuel came to a red glow.

"Seest thou, Isaac," said Front-de-Bœuf, "the range of iron bars above that glowing charcoal? [1]—on that warm couch thou shalt lie, stripped of thy clothes as if thou wert to rest on a bed of down. One of these slaves shall maintain the fire beneath thee, while the other shall anoint thy wretched limbs with oil, lest the roast should burn.—Now, choose betwixt such a scorching bed and the payment of a thousand pounds of silver; for, by the head of my father, thou hast no other option."

"It is impossible," exclaimed the miserable Jew—"it is impossible that your purpose can be real! The good God of nature never made a heart capable of exercising such cruelty!"

"Trust not to that, Isaac," said Front-de-Bœuf, "it were a fatal error. Dost thou think that I, who have seen a town sacked, in which thousands of my Christian countrymen perished by sword, by flood, and by fire, will blench from my purpose for the outcries or screams of one single wretched Jew?—or thinkest thou that these swarthy slaves, who have neither law, country, nor conscience, but their master's will—who use the poison, or the stake, or the poniard, or the cord, at his slightest wink—thinkest thou that *they* will have mercy, who do not even understand the language in which it is asked?—Be wise, old man; discharge thyself of a portion of thy superfluous wealth; repay to the hands of a Christian a part of what thou hast acquired by the usury thou hast practised on those of his religion. Thy cunning may soon swell out once

[1] Note V.—The range of iron bars above that glowing charcoal.

more thy shrivelled purse, but neither leech nor medicine can restore thy scorched hide and flesh wert thou once stretched on these bars. Tell down thy ransom, I say, and rejoice that at such rate thou canst redeem thee from a dungeon, the secrets of which few have returned to tell. I waste no more words with thee—choose between thy dross and thy flesh and blood, and as thou choosest, so shall it be."

"So may Abraham, Jacob, and all the fathers of our people assist me," said Isaac, "I cannot make the choice, because I have not the means of satisfying your exorbitant demand!"

"Seize him and strip him, slaves," said the knight, "and let the fathers of his race assist him if they can."

The assistants, taking their directions more from the Baron's eye and his hand than his tongue, once more stepped forward, laid hands on the unfortunate Isaac, plucked him up from the ground, and, holding him between them, waited the hardhearted Baron's farther signal. The unhappy Jew eyed their countenances and that of Front-de-Bœuf, in hope of discovering some symptoms of relenting; but that of the Baron exhibited the same cold, half-sullen, half-sarcastic smile which had been the prelude to his cruelty; and the savage eyes of the Saracens, rolling gloomily under their dark brows, acquiring a yet more sinister expression by the whiteness of the circle which surrounds the pupil, evinced rather the secret pleasure which they expected from the approaching scene, than any reluctance to be its directors or agents. The Jew then looked at the glowing furnace, over which he was presently to be stretched, and seeing no chance of his tormentor's relenting, his resolution gave way.

"I will pay," he said, "the thousand pounds of silver—That is," he added, after a moment's pause, "I will pay it with the help of my brethren; for I must beg as a mendicant at the door of our synagogue ere I make up so unheard-of a sum.—When and where must it be delivered?"

"Here," replied Front-de-Bœuf, "here it must be delivered—weighed it must be—weighed and told down on this very dungeon floor.—Thinkest thou I will part with thee until thy ransom is secure?"

"And what is to be my surety," said the Jew, "that I shall be at liberty after this ransom is paid?"

"The word of a Norman noble, thou pawn-broking slave," answered Front-de-Bœuf; "the faith of a Norman nobleman, more pure than the gold and silver of thee and all thy tribe."

"I crave pardon, noble lord," said Isaac timidly, "but wherefore should I rely wholly on the word of one who will trust nothing to mine?"

"Because thou canst not help it, Jew," said the knight, sternly. "Wert thou now in thy treasure-chamber at York, and were I craving a loan of thy shekels, it would be thine to dictate the time of payment, and the pledge of security. This is *my* treasure-chamber. Here I have thee at advantage, nor will I again deign to repeat the terms on which I grant thee liberty."

The Jew groaned deeply.—"Grant me," he said, "at least with my own liberty, that of the companions with whom I travel. They scorned me as a Jew, yet they pitied my desolation, and because they tarried to aid me by the way, a share of my evil hath come upon them; moreover, they may contribute in some sort to my ransom."

"If thou meanest yonder Saxon churls," said Front-de-Bœuf, "their ransom will depend upon other terms than thine. Mind thine own concerns, Jew, I warn thee, and meddle not with those of others."

"I am, then," said Isaac, "only to be set at liberty, together with mine wounded friend?"

"Shall I twice recommend it," said Front-de-Bœuf, "to a son of Israel, to meddle with his own concerns, and leave those of others alone?— Since thou hast made thy choice, it remains but that thou payest down thy ransom, and that at a short day."

"Yet hear me," said the Jew—"for the sake of that very wealth which thou wouldst obtain at the expense of thy"——Here he stopt short, afraid of irritating the savage Norman. But Front-de-Bœuf only laughed, and himself filled up the blank at which the Jew had hesitated. "At the expense of my conscience, thou wouldst say, Isaac; speak it out—I tell thee, I am reasonable. I can bear the reproaches of a loser, even when that loser is a Jew. Thou wert not so patient, Isaac, when thou didst invoke justice against Jacques Fitzdotterel, for calling thee a usurious blood-sucker, when thy exactions had devoured his patrimony."

"I swear by the Talmud," said the Jew, "that your valour has been misled in that matter. Fitzdotterel drew his poniard upon me in mine own chamber, because I craved him for mine own silver. The term of payment was due at the Passover."

"I care not what he did," said Front-de-Bœuf; "the question is, when shall I have mine own?—when shall I have the shekels, Isaac?"

"Let my daughter Rebecca go forth to York," answered Isaac, "with your safe conduct, noble knight, and so soon as man and horse can return, the treasure"——Here he groaned deeply, but added, after the pause of a few seconds,—"The treasure shall be told down on this very floor."

"Thy daughter!" said Front-de-Bœuf, as if surprised,—"By heavens, Isaac, I would I had known of this. I deemed that yonder black-browed girl had been thy concubine, and I gave her to be a handmaiden to Sir Brian de Bois-Guilbert, after the fashion of patriarchs and heroes of the days of old, who set us in these matters a wholesome example."

The yell which Isaac raised at this unfeeling communication made the very vault to ring, and astounded the two Saracens so much that they let go their hold of the Jew. He availed himself of his enlargement to throw himself on the pavement, and clasp the knees of Front-de-Bœuf.

"Take all that you have asked," said he, "Sir Knight—take ten times more—reduce me to ruin and to beggary, if thou wilt,—nay, pierce me with thy poniard, broil me on that furnace, but spare my daughter, deliver her in safety and honour!—As thou art born of woman spare the honour of a helpless maiden—She is the image of my deceased

Rachel, she is the last of six pledges of her love—Will you deprive a widowed husband of his sole remaining comfort?—Will you reduce a father to wish that his only living child were laid beside her dead mother, in the tomb of our fathers?"

"I would," said the Norman, somewhat relenting, "that I had known of this before. I thought your race had loved nothing save their money-bags."

"Think not so vilely of us, Jews though we be," said Isaac, eager to improve the moment of apparent sympathy; "the hunted fox, the tortured wild-cat loves its young—the despised and persecuted race of Abraham love their children!"

"Be it so," said Front-de-Bœuf; "I will believe it in future, Isaac, for thy very sake—but it aids us not now, I cannot help what has happened, or what is to follow; my word is passed to my comrade in arms, nor would I break it for ten Jews and Jewesses to boot. Besides, why shouldst thou think evil is to come to the girl, even if she became Bois-Guilbert's booty?"

"There will, there must!" exclaimed Isaac, wringing his hands in agony; "When did Templar breathe aught but cruelty to men, and dishonour to women!"

"Dog of an infidel," said Front-de-Bœuf, with sparkling eyes, and not sorry, perhaps, to seize a pretext for working himself into a passion, "blaspheme not the Holy Order of the Temple of Zion, but take thought instead to pay me the ransom thou hast promised, or woe betide thy Jewish throat!"

"Robber and villain!" said the Jew, retorting the insults of his oppressor with passion, which, however impotent, he now found it impossible to bridle, "I will pay thee nothing—not one silver penny will I pay thee, unless my daughter is delivered to me in safety and honour?"

"Art thou in thy senses, Israelite?" said the Norman, sternly—"has thy flesh and blood a charm against heated iron and scalding oil?"

"I care not!" said the Jew, rendered desperate by paternal affection; "do thy worst. My daughter is my flesh and blood, dearer to me a thousand times than those limbs which thy cruelty threatens. No silver will I give thee, unless I were to pour it molten down thy avaricious throat —no, not a silver penny will I give thee, Nazarene, were it to save thee from the deep damnation thy whole life has merited! Take my life if thou wilt, and say, the Jew, amidst his tortures, knew how to disappoint the Christian."

"We shall see that," said Front-de-Bœuf; "for by the blessed rood, which is the abomination of thy accursed tribe, thou shalt feel the extremities of fire and steel!—Strip him, slaves, and chain him down upon the bars."

In spite of the feeble struggles of the old man, the Saracens had already torn from him his upper garment, and were proceeding totally to disrobe him, when the sound of a bugle, twice winded without the castle, penetrated even to the recesses of the dungeon, and immediately after loud voices were heard calling for Sir Reginald Front-de-Bœuf. Unwilling to be found engaged in his hellish occupation, the savage Baron gave the slaves a signal to restore Isaac's garment, and, quitting the dungeon with his attendants, he left the Jew to thank God for his own deliverance, or to lament over his daughter's captivity, and probable fate, as his personal or paternal feelings might prove strongest.

CHAPTER XXIII

> Nay, if the gentle spirit of moving words
> Can no way change you to a milder form,
> I'll woo you, like a soldier, at arms' end,
> And love you 'gainst the nature of love, force you.
> *Two Gentlemen of Verona.*

THE apartment to which the Lady Rowena had been introduced was fitted up with some rude attempts at ornament and magnificence, and her being placed there might be considered as a peculiar mark of respect not offered to the other prisoners. But the wife of Front-de-Bœuf, for whom it had been originally furnished, was long dead, and decay and neglect had impaired the few ornaments with which her taste had adorned it. The tapestry hung down from the walls in many places, and in others was tarnished and faded under the effects of the sun, or tattered and decayed by age. Desolate, however, as it was, this was the apartment of the castle which had been judged most fitting for the accommodation of the Saxon heiress; and here she was left to meditate upon her fate, until the actors in this nefarious drama had arranged the several parts which each of them was to perform. This had been settled in a council held by Front-de-Bœuf, De Bracy, and the Templar, in which, after a long and warm debate concerning the several advantages which each insisted upon deriving from his peculiar share in this audacious enterprise, they had at length determined the fate of their unhappy prisoners.

It was about the hour of noon, therefore, when De Bracy, for whose advantage the expedition had been first planned, appeared to prosecute his views upon the hand and possessions of the Lady Rowena.

The interval had not entirely been bestowed in holding council with his confederates, for De Bracy had found leisure to decorate his person with all the foppery of the times. His green cossack and vizard were now flung aside. His long luxuriant hair was trained to flow in quaint tresses down his richly furred cloak. His beard was closely shaved, his doublet reached to the middle of his leg, and the girdle which secured it, and at the same time supported his ponderous sword, was embroidered and embossed with gold work. We have already noticed the extravagant fashion of the shoes at this period, and the points of Maurice de Bracy's might have challenged the prize of extravagance with the gayest, being

turned up and twisted like the horns of a ram. Such was the dress of a
gallant of the period; and, in the present instance, that effect was aided
by the handsome person and good demeanour of the wearer, whose manners partook alike of the grace of a courtier, and the frankness of a
soldier.

He saluted Rowena by doffing his velvet bonnet, garnished with a
golden brooch, representing St. Michael trampling down the Prince of
Evil. With this, he gently motioned the lady to a seat; and, as she still
retained her standing posture, the knight ungloved his right hand, and
motioned to conduct her thither. But Rowena declined, by her gesture,
the proffered compliment, and replied, "If I be in the presence of my
jailor, Sir Knight—nor will circumstances allow me to think otherwise
—it best becomes his prisoner to remain standing till she learns her
doom."

"Alas! fair Rowena," returned De Bracy, "you are in the presence of
your captive, not your jailor; and it is from your fair eyes that De Bracy
must receive that doom which you fondly expect from him."

"I know you not, sir," said the lady, drawing herself up with all the
pride of offended rank and beauty; "I know you not—and the insolent
familiarity with which you apply to me the jargon of a troubadour, forms
no apology for the violence of a robber."

"To thyself, fair maid," answered De Bracy, in his former tone—"to
thine own charms be ascribed whate'er I have done which passed the
respect due to her, whom I have chosen queen of my heart, and loadstar
of my eyes."

"I repeat to you, Sir Knight, that I know you not, and that no man
wearing chain and spurs ought thus to intrude himself upon the presence
of an unprotected lady."

"That I am unknown to you," said De Bracy, "is indeed my misfortune; yet let me hope that De Bracy's name has not been always
unspoken, when minstrels or heralds have praised deeds of chivalry,
whether in the lists or in the battlefield."

"To heralds and to minstrels, then, leave thy praise, Sir Knight," replied Rowena, "more suiting for their mouths than for thine own; and
tell me which of them shall record in song, or in book of tourney, the
memorable conquest of this night, a conquest obtained over an old man,
followed by a few timid hinds; and its booty, an unfortunate maiden,
transported against her will to the castle of a robber?"

"You are unjust, Lady Rowena," said the knight, biting his lips in some
confusion, and speaking in a tone more natural to him than that of affected gallantry, which he had at first adopted; "yourself free from
passion, you can allow no excuse for the frenzy of another, although
caused by your own beauty."

"I pray you, Sir Knight," said Rowena, "to cease a language so commonly used by strolling minstrels, that it becomes not the mouth of
knights or nobles. Certes, you constrain me to sit down, since you enter

upon such commonplace terms, of which each vile crowder hath a stock that might last from hence to Christmas."

"Proud damsel," said De Bracy, incensed at finding his gallant style procured him nothing but contempt—"proud damsel, thou shalt be as proudly encountered. Know then, that I have supported my pretensions to your hand in the way that best suited thy character. It is meeter for thy humour to be wooed with bow and bill, than in set terms, and in courtly language."

"Courtesy of tongue," said Rowena, "when it is used to veil churlishness of deed, is but a knight's girdle around the breast of a base clown. I wonder not that the restraint appears to gall you—more it were for your honour to have retained the dress and language of an outlaw, than to veil the deeds of one under an affectation of gentle language and demeanour."

"You counsel well, lady," said the Norman; "and in the bold language which best justifies bold action, I tell thee, thou shalt never leave this castle, or thou shalt leave it as Maurice de Bracy's wife. I am not wont to be baffled in my enterprises, nor needs a Norman noble scrupulously to vindicate his conduct to the Saxon maiden whom he distinguishes by the offer of his hand. Thou art proud, Rowena, and thou art the fitter to be my wife. By what other means couldst thou be raised to high honour and to princely place, saving by my alliance? How else wouldst thou escape from the mean precincts of a country grange, where Saxons herd with the swine which form their wealth, to take thy seat, honoured as thou shouldst be, and shalt be, amid all in England that is distinguished by beauty, or dignified by power?"

"Sir Knight," replied Rowena, "the grange which you contemn hath been my shelter from infancy; and, trust me, when I leave it—should that day ever arrive—it shall be with one who has not learnt to despise the dwelling and manners in which I have been brought up."

"I guess your meaning, lady," said De Bracy, "though you may think it lies too obscure from my apprehension. But dream not, that Richard Cœur de Lion will ever resume his throne, far less that Wilfred of Ivanhoe, his minion, will ever lead thee to his footstool, to be there welcomed as the bride of a favourite. Another suitor might feel jealousy while he touched this string; but my firm purpose cannot be changed by a passion so childish and so hopeless. Know, lady, that this rival is in my power, and that it rests but with me to betray the secret of his being within the castle to Front-de-Bœuf, whose jealousy will be more fatal than mine."

"Wilfred here?" said Rowena, in disdain; "that is as true as that Front-de-Bœuf is his rival."

De Bracy looked at her steadily for an instant. "Wert thou really ignorant of this?" said he; "didst thou not know that Wilfred of Ivanhoe travelled in the litter of the Jew?—a meet conveyance for the crusader, whose doughty arm was to reconquer the Holy Sepulchre!" And he laughed scornfully.

"And if he is here," said Rowena, compelling herself to a tone of indifference, though trembling with an agony of apprehension which she could not suppress, "in what is he the rival of Front-de-Bœuf? or what has he to fear beyond a short imprisonment, and an honourable ransom, according to the use of chivalry?"

"Rowena," said De Bracy, "art thou, too, deceived by the common error of thy sex, who think there can be no rivalry but that respecting their own charms? Knowest thou not there is a jealousy of ambition and of wealth, as well as of love; and that this our host, Front-de-Bœuf, will push from his road him who opposes his claim to the fair barony of Ivanhoe, as readily, eagerly, and unscrupulously, as if he were preferred to him by some blue-eyed damsel? But smile on my suit, lady, and the wounded champion shall have nothing to fear from Front-de-Bœuf, whom else thou mayst mourn for, as in the hands of one who has never shown compassion."

"Save him, for the love of Heaven!" said Rowena, her firmness giving way under terror for her lover's impending fate.

"I can—I will—it is my purpose," said De Bracy; "for, when Rowena consents to be the bride of De Bracy, who is it shall dare to put forth a violent hand upon her kinsman—the son of her guardian—the companion of her youth? But it is thy love must buy his protection. I am not romantic fool enough to further the fortune, or avert the fate, of one who is likely to be a successful obstacle between me and my wishes. Use thine influence with me in his behalf, and he is safe,—refuse to employ it, Wilfred dies, and thou thyself art not the nearer to freedom."

"Thy language," answered Rowena, "hath in its indifferent bluntness something which cannot be reconciled with the horrors it seems to express. I believe not that thy purpose is so wicked, or thy power so great."

"Flatter thyself, then, with that belief," said De Bracy, "until time shall prove it false. Thy lover lies wounded in this castle—thy preferred lover. He is a bar betwixt Front-de-Bœuf and that which Front-de-Bœuf loves better than either ambition or beauty. What will it cost beyond the blow of a poniard, or the thrust of a javelin, to silence his opposition for ever? Nay, were Front-de-Bœuf afraid to justify a deed so open, let the leech but give his patient a wrong draught—let the chamberlain, or the nurse who tends him, but pluck the pillow from his head, and Wilfred, in his present condition, is sped without the effusion of blood. Cedric also"——

"And Cedric also," said Rowena, repeating his words; "my noble—my generous guardian! I deserved the evil I have encountered, for forgetting his fate even in that of his son!"

"Cedric's fate also depends upon thy determination," said De Bracy; "and I leave thee to form it."

Hitherto, Rowena had sustained her part in this trying scene with undismayed courage, but it was because she had not considered the dan-ger as serious and imminent. Her disposition was naturally that which physiognomists consider as proper to fair complexions, mild, timid, and gentle; but it had been tempered, and, as it were, hardened, by the cir-cumstances of her education. Accustomed to see the will of all, even of Cedric himself (sufficiently arbitrary with others), give way before her wishes, she had acquired that sort of courage and self-confidence which arises from the habitual and constant deference of the circle in which we move. She could scarce conceive the possibility of her will being opposed, far less that of its being treated with total disregard.

Her haughtiness and habit of domination was, therefore, a fictitious character, induced over that which was natural to her, and it deserted her when her eyes were opened to the extent of her own danger, as well as that of her lover and her guardian; and when she found her will, the slightest expression of which was wont to command respect and attention, now placed in opposition to that of a man of a strong, fierce, and determined mind, who possessed the advantage over her, and was resolved to use it, she quailed before him.

After casting her eyes around, as if to look for the aid which was no-where to be found, and after a few broken interjections, she raised her hands to heaven, and burst into a passion of uncontrolled vexation and sorrow. It was impossible to see so beautiful a creature in such extremity without feeling for her, and De Bracy was not unmoved, though he was yet more embarrassed than touched. He had, in truth, gone too far to recede; and yet, in Rowena's present condition, she could not be acted on either by argument or threats. He paced the apartment to and fro, now vainly exhorting the terrified maiden to compose herself, now hesi-tating concerning his own line of conduct.

If, thought he, I should be moved by the tears and sorrow of this disconsolate damsel, what should I reap but the loss of those fair hopes for which I have encountered so much risk, and the ridicule of Prince John and his jovial comrades? "And yet," he said to himself, "I feel myself ill framed for the part which I am playing. I cannot look on so fair a face while it is disturbed with agony, or on those eyes when they are drowned in tears. I would she had retained her original haughtiness of disposition, or that I had a larger share of Front-de-Bœuf's thrice-tem-pered hardness of heart!"

Agitated by these thoughts, he could only bid the unfortunate Rowena be comforted, and assure her, that as yet she had no reason for the excess of despair to which she was now giving way. But in this task of con-solation De Bracy was interrupted by the horn, "hoarse-winded blowing far and keen," which had at the same time alarmed the other inmates of the castle, and interrupted their several plans of avarice and of licence. Of them all, perhaps, De Bracy least regretted the interruption; for his conference with the Lady Rowena had arrived at a point where he found it equally difficult to prosecute or to resign his enterprise.

And here we cannot but think it necessary to offer some better proof than the incidents of an idle tale, to vindicate the melancholy representation of manners which has been just laid before the reader. It is grievous to think that those valiant barons, to whose stand against the crown the liberties of England were indebted for their existence, should themselves have been such dreadful oppressors, and capable of excesses contrary not only to the laws of England, but to those of nature and humanity. But, alas! we have only to extract from the industrious Henry one of those numerous passages which he has collected from contemporary historians, to prove that fiction itself can hardly reach the dark reality of the horrors of the period.

The description given by the author of the Saxon Chronicle of the cruelties exercised in the reign of King Stephen by the great barons and lords of castles, who were all Normans, affords a strong proof of the excesses of which they were capable when their passions were inflamed. "They grievously oppressed the poor people by building castles; and when they were built, they filled them with wicked men, or rather devils, who seized both men and women who they imagined had any money, threw them into prison, and put them to more cruel tortures than the martyrs ever endured. They suffocated some in mud, and suspended others by the feet, or the head, or the thumbs, kindling fires below them. They squeezed the heads of some with knotted cords till they pierced their brains, while they threw others into dungeons swarming with serpents, snakes, and toads." But it would be cruel to put the reader to the pain of perusing the remainder of this description.[1]

As another instance of these bitter fruits of conquest, and perhaps the strongest that can be quoted, we may mention, that the Empress Matilda, though a daughter of the King of Scotland, and afterwards both Queen of England and Empress of Germany, the daughter, the wife, and the mother of monarchs, was obliged, during her early residence for education in England, to assume the veil of a nun, as the only means of escaping the licentious pursuit of the Norman nobles. This excuse she stated before a great council of the clergy of England, as the sole reason for her having taken the religious habit. The assembled clergy admitted the validity of the plea, and the notoriety of the circumstances upon which it was founded; giving thus an indubitable and most remarkable testimony to the existence of that disgraceful licence by which that age was stained. It was a matter of public knowledge, they said, that after the conquest of King William, his Norman followers, elated by so great a victory, acknowledged no law but their own wicked pleasure, and not only despoiled the conquered Saxons of their lands and their goods, but invaded the honour of their wives and of their daughters with the most unbridled licence; and hence it was then common for matrons and maidens of noble families to assume the veil, and take shelter in con-

[1] Henry's *Hist*. edit. 1805, vol. vii. p. 346.

vents, not as called thither by the vocation of God, but solely to preserve their honour from the unbridled wickedness of man.

Such and so licentious were the times, as announced by the public declaration of the assembled clergy, recorded by Eadmer; and we need add nothing more to vindicate the probability of the scenes which we have detailed, and are about to detail, upon the more apocryphal authority of the Wardour MS.

CHAPTER XXIV

I'll woo her as the lion woos his bride.

Douglas.

WHILE the scenes we have described were passing in other parts of the castle, the Jewess Rebecca awaited her fate in a distant and sequestered turret. Hither she had been led by two of her disguised ravishers, and on being thrust into the little cell, she found herself in the presence of an old sibyl, who kept murmuring to herself a Saxon rhyme, as if to beat time to the revolving dance which her spindle was performing upon the floor. The hag raised her head as Rebecca entered, and scowled at the fair Jewess with the malignant envy with which old age and ugliness, when united with evil conditions, are apt to look upon youth and beauty.

"Thou must up and away, old house-cricket," said one of the men; "our noble master commands it—Thou must e'en leave this chamber to a fairer guest."

"Aye," grumbled the hag, "even thus is service requited. I have known when my bare word would have cast the best man-at-arms among ye out of saddle and out of service; and now must I up and away at the command of every groom such as thou."

"Good Dame Urfried," said the other man, "stand not to reason on it, but up and away. Lord's hests must be listened to with a quick ear. Thou hast had thy day, old dame, but thy sun has long been set. Thou art now the very emblem of an old war-horse turned out on the barren heath—thou hast had thy paces in thy time, but now a broken amble is the best of them—Come, amble off with thee."

"Ill omens dog ye both!" said the old woman; "and a kennel be your burying-place! May the evil demon Zernebock tear me limb from limb, if I leave my own cell ere I have spun out the hemp on my distaff!"

"Answer it to our lord, then, old housefiend," said the man, and retired; leaving Rebecca in company with the old woman, upon whose presence she had been thus unwillingly forced.

"What devil's deed have they now in the wind?" said the old hag, murmuring to herself, yet from time to time casting a sidelong and malignant glance at Rebecca; "but it is easy to guess—Bright eyes, black locks, and a skin like paper, ere the priest stains it with his black unguent—Ay, it is easy to guess why they send her to this lone turret, whence a shriek could no more be heard than at the depth of five hundred fathoms beneath the earth.—Thou wilt have owls for thy neighbours, fair one; and their screams will be heard as far, and as much regarded, as thine own. Outlandish, too," she said, marking the dress and turban of Rebecca—"What country art thou of?—a Saracen? or an Egyptian?— Why dost thou not answer?—thou canst weep, canst thou not speak?"

"Be not angry, good mother," said Rebecca.

"Thou needst say no more," replied Urfried; "men know a fox by the train, and a Jewess by her tongue."

"For the sake of mercy," said Rebecca, "tell me what I am to expect as the conclusion of the violence which hath dragged me hither! Is it my life they seek, to atone for my religion? I will lay it down cheerfully."

"Thy life, minion?" answered the sibyl; "what would taking thy life pleasure them?—Trust me, thy life is in no peril. Such usage shalt thou have as was once thought good enough for a noble Saxon maiden. And shall a Jewess, like thee, repine because she hath no better? Look at me —I was as young and twice as fair as thou, when Front-de-Bœuf, father of this Reginald, and his Normans, stormed this castle. My father and his seven sons defended their inheritance from story to story, from chamber to chamber—There was not a room, not a step of the stair, that was not slippery with their blood. They died—they died every man; and ere their bodies were cold, and ere their blood was dried, I had become the prey and the scorn of the conqueror!"

"Is there no help?—Are there no means of escape?" said Rebecca— "Richly, richly would I requite thine aid."

"Think not of it," said the hag; "from hence there is no escape but through the gates of death; and it is late, late," she added, shaking her grey head, "ere these open to us—Yet it is comfort to think that we leave behind us on earth those who shall be wretched as ourselves. Fare thee well, Jewess!—Jew or Gentile, thy fate would be the same; for thou hast to do with them that have neither scruple nor pity. Fare thee well, I say. My thread is spun out—thy task is yet to begin."

"Stay! stay! for Heaven's sake!" said Rebecca; "stay, though it be to curse and to revile me—thy presence is yet some protection."

"The presence of the mother of God were no protection," answered the old woman. "There she stands," pointing to a rude image of the Virgin Mary, "see if she can avert the fate that awaits thee."

She left the room as she spoke, her features writhed into a sort of sneering laugh, which made them seem even more hideous than their habitual frown. She locked the door behind her, and Rebecca might hear her curse every step for its steepness, as slowly and with difficulty she descended the turret-stair.

Rebecca was now to expect a fate even more dreadful than that of Rowena; for what probability was there that either softness or cere- mony would be used towards one of her oppressed race, whatever shadow of these might be preserved towards a Saxon heiress? Yet had the Jewess this advantage, that she was better prepared by habits of thought, and by natural strength of mind, to encounter the dangers to which she was exposed. Of a strong and observing character, even from her earliest years, the pomp and wealth which her father displayed within his walls, or which she witnessed in the houses of other wealthy Hebrews, had not been able to blind her to the precarious circumstances under which they were enjoyed. Like Damocles at his celebrated banquet, Rebecca perpetually beheld, amid that gorgeous display, the sword which was suspended over the heads of her people by a single hair. These reflections had tamed and brought down to a pitch of sounder judgment a temper, which, under other circumstances, might have waxed haughty, supercilious, and obstinate.

From her father's example and injunctions, Rebecca had learnt to bear herself courteously towards all who approached her. She could not indeed imitate his excess of subservience, because she was a stranger to the meanness of mind, and to the constant state of timid apprehension, by which it was dictated; but she bore herself with a proud humility, as if submitting to the evil circumstances in which she was placed as the daughter of a despised race, while she felt in her mind the consciousness that she was entitled to hold a higher rank from her merit, than the arbitrary despotism of religious prejudice permitted her to aspire to.

Thus prepared to expect adverse circumstances, she had acquired the firmness necessary for acting under them. Her present situation required all her presence of mind, and she summoned it up accordingly.

Her first care was to inspect the apartment; but it afforded few hopes either of escape or protection. It contained neither secret passage nor trap-door, and unless where the door by which she had entered joined the main building, seemed to be circumscribed by the round exterior wall of the turret. The door had no inside bolt or bar. The single window opened upon an embattled space surmounting the turret, which gave Rebecca, at first sight, some hopes of escaping; but she soon found it had no communication with any other part of the battlements, being an isolated bartisan, or balcony, secured, as usual, by a parapet, with embrasures, at which a few archers might be stationed for defending the turret, and flanking with their shot the wall of the castle on that side.

There was therefore no hope but in passive fortitude, and in that strong reliance on Heaven natural to great and generous characters. Rebecca, however erroneously taught to interpret the promises of Scripture to the chosen people of Heaven, did not err in supposing the present to be their hour of trial, or in trusting that the children of Zion would be one day called in with the fulness of the Gentiles. In the meanwhile, all around her showed that their present state was that of punishment and probation, and that it was their especial duty to suffer without sinning. Thus prepared to consider herself as the victim of misfortune, Rebecca had early reflected upon her own state, and schooled her mind to meet the dangers which she had probably to encounter.

The prisoner trembled, however, and changed colour, when a step was heard on the stair, and the door of the turret-chamber slowly opened, and a tall man, dressed as one of those banditti to whom they owed their misfortune, slowly entered, and shut the door behind him; his cap, pulled down upon his brows, concealed the upper part of his face, and he held his mantle in such a manner as to muffle the rest. In this guise, as if prepared for the execution of some deed, at the thought of which he was himself ashamed, he stood before the affrighted prisoner; yet, ruffian as his dress bespoke him, he seemed at a loss to express what purpose had brought him thither, so that Rebecca, making an effort upon herself, had time to anticipate his explanation. She had already unclasped two costly bracelets and a collar, which she hastened to proffer to the supposed outlaw, concluding naturally that to gratify his avarice was to bespeak his favour.

"Take these," she said, "good friend, and for God's sake be merciful to me and my aged father! These ornaments are of value, yet are they trifling to what he would bestow to obtain our dismissal from this castle, free and uninjured."

"Fair flower of Palestine," replied the outlaw, "these pearls are orient, but they yield in whiteness to your teeth; the diamonds are brilliant, but they cannot match your eyes; and ever since I have taken up this wild trade, I have made a vow to prefer beauty to wealth."

"Do not do yourself such wrong," said Rebecca; "take ransom, and have mercy!—Gold will purchase you pleasure,—to misuse us, could only bring thee remorse. My father will willingly satiate thy utmost wishes; and if thou wilt act wisely, thou mayst purchase with our spoils thy restoration to civil society—mayst obtain pardon for past errors, and be placed beyond the necessity of committing more."

"It is well spoken," replied the outlaw in French, finding it difficult probably to sustain, in Saxon, a conversation which Rebecca had opened in that language; "but know, bright lily of the vale of Baca! that thy father is already in the hands of a powerful alchemist, who knows how to convert into gold and silver even the rusty bars of a dungeon grate. The venerable Isaac is subjected to an alembic, which will distil from him all he holds dear, without any assistance from my requests or thy entreaty. Thy ransom must be paid by love and beauty, and in no other coin will I accept it."

"Thou art no outlaw," said Rebecca, in the same language in which he addressed her; "no outlaw had refused such offers. No outlaw in this land uses the dialect in which thou hast spoken. Thou art no outlaw, but a Norman—a Norman, noble perhaps in birth—O, be so in thy actions, and cast off this fearful mask of outrage and violence!"

"And thou, who canst guess so truly," said Brian de Bois-Guilbert, dropping the mantle from his face, "art no true daughter of Israel, but in all, save youth and beauty, a very witch of Endor. I am not an outlaw, then, fair rose of Sharon. And I am one who will be more prompt to hang thy neck and arms with pearls and diamonds, which so well become them, than to deprive thee of these ornaments."

"What wouldst thou have of me," said Rebecca, "if not, my wealth?—We can have nought in common between us—you are a Christian—I am a Jewess.—Our union were contrary to the laws, alike of the church and the synagogue."

"It were so, indeed," replied the Templar, laughing; "wed with a Jewess? *Despardieux!*—Not if she were the Queen of Sheba! And know, besides, sweet daughter of Zion, that were the most Christian king to offer me his most Christian daughter, with Languedoc for a dowry, I could not wed her. It is against my vow to love any maiden, otherwise than *par amours*, as I will love thee. I am a Templar. Behold the cross of my Holy Order."

"Darest thou appeal to it," said Rebecca, "on an occasion like the present?"

"And if I do so," said the Templar, "it concerns not thee, who art no believer in the blessed sign of our salvation."

"I believe as my fathers taught," said Rebecca; "and may God forgive my belief if erroneous! But you, Sir Knight, what is *yours*, when you appeal without scruple to that which you deem most holy, even while you are about to transgress the most solemn of your vows as a knight, and as a man of religion?"

"It is gravely and well preached, O daughter of Sirach!" answered the Templar; "but, gentle Ecclesiastica, thy narrow Jewish prejudices make thee blind to our high privilege. Marriage were an enduring crime on the part of a Templar; but what lesser folly I may practise, I shall speedily be absolved from at the next Preceptory of our Order. Not the wisest of monarchs, not his father, whose examples you must needs allow are weighty, claimed wider privileges than we poor soldiers of the Temple of Zion have won by our zeal in its defence. The protectors of Solomon's Temple may claim licence by the example of Solomon."

"If thou readest the Scripture," said the Jewess, "and the lives of the saints, only to justify thine own licence and profligacy, thy crime is like that of him who extracts poison from the most healthful and necessary herbs."

The eyes of the Templar flashed fire at this reproof—"Hearken," he said, "Rebecca; I have hitherto spoken mildly to thee, but now my language shall be that of a conqueror. Thou art the captive of my bow and spear—subject to my will by the laws of all nations; nor will I abate an inch of my right, or abstain from taking by violence what thou refusest to entreaty or necessity."

"Stand back," said Rebecca—"stand back, and hear me ere thou offerest to commit a sin so deadly! My strength thou mayst indeed overpower, for God made women weak, and trusted their defence to man's generosity. But I will proclaim thy villainy, Templar, from one end of Europe to the other. I will owe to the superstition of thy brethren what their compassion might refuse me. Each Preceptory—each Chapter of thy Order, shall learn, that, like a heretic, thou hast sinned with a Jewess. Those who tremble not at thy crime, will hold thee accursed for having so far dishonoured the cross thou wearest, as to follow a daughter of my people."

"Thou art keen-witted, Jewess," replied the Templar, well aware of the truth of what she spoke, and that the rules of his Order condemned in the most positive manner, and under high penalties, such intrigues as he now prosecuted, and that, in some instances, even degradation had followed upon it—"thou art sharp-witted," he said; "but loud must be thy voice of complaint, if it is heard beyond the iron walls of this castle; within these, murmurs, laments, appeals to justice, and screams for help, die alike silent away. One thing only can save thee, Rebecca. Submit to thy fate—embrace our religion, and thou shalt go forth in such state, that many a Norman lady shall yield as well in pomp as in beauty to the favourite of the best lance among the defenders of the Temple."

"Submit to my fate!" said Rebecca—"and, sacred Heaven! to what fate?—embrace thy religion! and what religion can it be that harbours such a villain?—*thou* the best lance of the Templars!—Craven knight! —forsworn priest! I spit at thee, and I defy thee.—The God of Abraham's promise hath opened an escape to his daughter—even from this abyss of infamy!"

As she spoke, she threw open the latticed window which led to the bartisan, and in an instant after stood on the very verge of the parapet, with not the slightest screen between her and the tremendous depth below. Unprepared for such a desperate effort, for she had hitherto stood perfectly motionless, Bois-Guilbert had neither time to intercept nor to stop her. As he offered to advance, she exclaimed, "Remain where thou art, proud Templar, or at thy choice advance!—one foot nearer, and I plunge myself from the precipice; my body shall be crushed out of the very form of humanity upon the stones of that court-yard ere it becomes the victim of thy brutality!"

As she spoke this, she clasped her hands and extended them towards heaven, as if imploring mercy on her soul before she made that final plunge. The Templar hesitated, and a resolution which had never yielded to pity or distress, gave way to his admiration of her fortitude. "Come down," he said, "rash girl!—I swear by earth, and sea, and sky, I will offer thee no offence."

"I will not trust thee, Templar," said Rebecca; "thou hast taught me better how to estimate the virtues of thine Order. The next Preceptory would grant thee absolution for an oath, the keeping of which concerned nought but the honour or the dishonour of a miserable Jewish maiden."

"You do me injustice," exclaimed the Templar fervently; "I swear to you by the name which I bear—by the cross on my bosom—by the sword on my side—by the ancient crest of my fathers do I swear, I will do thee no injury whatsoever! If not for thyself, yet for thy father's sake forbear! I will be his friend, and in this castle he will need a powerful one."

"Alas!" said Rebecca, "I know it but too well—dare I trust thee?"

"May my arms be reversed, and my name dishonoured," said Brian de Bois-Guilbert, "if thou shalt have reason to complain of me! Many a law, many a commandment have I broken, but my word never."

"I will then trust thee," said Rebecca, "thus far;" and she descended from the battlement, but remained standing close by one of the embrasures, or *machicolles*, as they were then called.—"Here," she said, "I take my stand. Remain where thou art, and if thou shalt attempt to diminish by one step the distance now between us, thou shalt see that the Jewish maiden will rather trust her soul with God, than her honour to the Templar!"

While Rebecca spoke thus, her high and firm resolve, which corresponded so well with the expressive beauty of her countenance, gave to her looks, air, and manner, a dignity that seemed more than mortal. Her glance quailed not, her cheek blanched not, for the fear of a fate so instant and so horrible; on the contrary, the thought that she had her fate at her command, and could escape at will from infamy to death, gave a yet deeper colour of carnation to her complexion, and a yet more brilliant fire to her eye. Bois-Guilbert, proud himself and high-spirited, thought he had never beheld beauty so animated and so commanding.

"Let there be peace between us, Rebecca," he said.

"Peace, if thou wilt," answered Rebecca—"Peace—but with this space between."

"Thou needst no longer fear me," said Bois-Guilbert.

"I fear thee not," replied she; "thanks to him that reared this dizzy tower so high, that nought could fall from it and live—thanks to him, and to the God of Israel!—I fear thee not."

"Thou dost me injustice," said the Templar; "by earth, sea, and sky, thou dost me injustice! I am not naturally that which you have seen me, hard, selfish, and relentless. It was woman that taught me cruelty, and on woman therefore I have exercised it; but not upon such as thou. Hear me, Rebecca—Never did knight take lance in his hand with a heart more devoted to the lady of his love than Brian de Bois-Guilbert. She, the daughter of a petty baron, who boasted for all his domains but a ruinous tower, and an unproductive vineyard, and some few leagues of the barren Landes of Bordeaux, her name was known wherever deeds of arms were done, known wider than that of many a lady's that had a county for a dowry.—Yes," he continued, pacing up and down the little platform, with an animation in which he seemed to lose all consciousness of Rebecca's presence—"Yes, my deeds, my danger, my blood, made the name of Adelaide de Montemare known from the court of Castile to that of Byzantium. And how was I requited?—When I returned with my dear-bought honours, purchased by toil and blood, I found her wedded to a Gascon squire, whose name was never heard beyond the limits of his own paltry domain! Truly did I love her, and bitterly did I revenge me of her broken faith! But my vengeance has recoiled on myself. Since that day I have separated myself from life and its ties—My manhood must know no domestic home—must be soothed by no affectionate wife— My age must know no kindly hearth—My grave must be solitary, and no offspring must outlive me, to bear the ancient name of Bois-Guilbert. At the feet of my Superior I have laid down the right of self-action— the privilege of independence. The Templar, a serf in all but the name, can possess neither lands nor goods, and lives, moves, and breathes, but at the will and pleasure of another."

"Alas!" said Rebecca, "what advantages could compensate for such an absolute sacrifice?"

"The power of vengeance, Rebecca," replied the Templar, "and the prospects of ambition."

"An evil recompense," said Rebecca, "for the surrender of the rights which are dearest to humanity."

"Say not so, maiden," answered the Templar; "revenge is a feast for the gods! And if they have reserved it, as priests tell us, to themselves, it is because they hold it an enjoyment too precious for the possession of mere mortals.—And ambition? it is a temptation which could disturb even the bliss of heaven itself."—He paused a moment, and then added, "Rebecca! she who could prefer death to dishonour, must have a proud and a powerful soul. Mine thou must be!—Nay, start not," he added, "it must be with thine own consent, and on thine own terms. Thou must consent to share with me hopes more extended than can be viewed from the throne of a monarch!—Hear me ere you answer, and judge ere you refuse.—The Templar loses, as thou hast said, his social rights, his power of free agency, but he becomes a member and a limb of a mighty body, before which thrones already tremble,—even as the single drop of rain which mixes with the sea becomes an individual part of that resistless ocean, which undermines rocks and engulfs royal armadas. Such a swelling flood is that powerful league. Of this mighty Order I am no mean member, but already one of the Chief Commanders, and may well aspire one day to hold the batoon of Grand Master. The poor soldiers of the Temple will not alone place their foot upon the necks of kings— a hemp-sandall'd monk can do that. Our mailed step shall ascend their throne—our gauntlet shall wrench the sceptre from their gripe. Not the reign of your vainly-expected Messiah offers such power to your dispersed tribes as my ambition may aim at. I have sought but a kindred spirit to share it, and I have found such in thee."

"Sayest thou this to one of my people?" answered Rebecca. "Bethink thee"——

"Answer me not," said the Templar, "by urging the difference of our creeds; within our secret conclaves we hold these nursery tales in derision. Think not we long remained blind to the idiotical folly of our founders, who forswore every delight of life for the pleasure of dying martyrs by hunger, by thirst, and by pestilence, and by the swords of savages, while they vainly strove to defend a barren desert, valuable only in the eyes of superstition. Our Order soon adopted bolder and wider views, and found out a better indemnification for our sacrifices. Our immense possessions in every kingdom of Europe, our high military fame, which brings within our circle the flower of chivalry from every Christian clime—these are dedicated to ends of which our pious founders little dreamed, and which are equally concealed from such weak spirits as embrace our Order on the ancient principles, and whose superstition makes them our passive tools. But I will not farther withdraw the veil of our mysteries. That bugle-sound announces something which may require my presence. Think on what I have said.—Farewell!—I do not say forgive me the violence I have threatened, for it was necessary to the display of thy character. Gold can be only known by the application of the touchstone. I will soon return, and hold further conference with thee."

He re-entered the turret-chamber, and descended the stair, leaving Rebecca scarcely more terrified at the prospect of the death to which she had been so lately exposed, than at the furious ambition of the bold bad man in whose power she found herself so unhappily placed. When she entered the turret-chamber, her first duty was to return thanks to the God of Jacob for the protection which he had afforded her, and to implore its continuance for her and for her father. Another name glided into her petition—it was that of the wounded Christian, whom fate had placed in the hands of blood-thirsty men, his avowed enemies. Her heart indeed checked her, as if, even in communing with the Deity in prayer, she mingled in her devotions the recollection of one with whose fate hers could have no alliance—a Nazarene, and an enemy to her faith. But the petition was already breathed, nor could all the narrow prejudices of her sect induce Rebecca to wish it recalled.

CHAPTER XXV

A damn'd cramp piece of penmanship as ever
I saw in my life!

She Stoops to Conquer.

WHEN the Templar reached the hall of the castle, he found De Bracy already there. "Your love-suit," said De Bracy, "hath, I suppose, been disturbed, like mine, by this obstreperous summons. But you have come later and more reluctantly, and therefore I presume your interview has proved more agreeable than mine."

"Has your suit, then, been unsuccessfully paid to the Saxon heiress?" said the Templar.

"By the bones of Thomas à Becket," answered De Bracy, "the Lady

Rowena must have heard that I cannot endure the sight of women's tears."

"Away!" said the Templar; "thou a leader of a Free Company, and regard a woman's tears! A few drops sprinkled on the torch of love make the flame blaze the brighter."

"Gramercy for the few drops of thy sprinkling," replied De Bracy; "but this damsel hath wept enough to extinguish a beacon-light. Never was such wringing of hands and such overflowing of eyes, since the days of St. Niobe, of whom Prior Aymer told us.[1] A water-fiend hath possessed the fair Saxon."

"A legion of fiends have occupied the bosom of the Jewess," replied the Templar; "for, I think no single one, not even Apollyon himself, could have inspired such indomitable pride and resolution.—But where is Front-de-Bœuf? That horn is sounded more and more clamorously."

"He is negotiating with the Jew, I suppose," replied De Bracy, coolly; "probably the howls of Isaac have drowned the blast of the bugle. Thou mayst know, by experience, Sir Brian, that a Jew parting with his treasures on such terms as our friend Front-de-Bœuf is like to offer, will raise a clamour loud enough to be heard over twenty horns and trumpets to boot. But we will make the vassals call him."

They were soon after joined by Front-de-Bœuf, who had been disturbed in this tyrannic cruelty in the manner with which the reader is acquainted, and had only tarried to give some necessary directions.

"Let us see the cause of this cursed clamour," said Front-de-Bœuf— "here is a letter, and, if I mistake not, it is in Saxon."

He looked at it, turning it round and round as if he had had really some hopes of coming at the meaning by inverting the position of the paper, and then handed it to De Bracy.

"It may be magic spells for aught I know," said De Bracy, who possessed his full proportion of the ignorance which characterised the chivalry of the period. "Our chaplain attempted to teach me to write," he said, "but all my letters were formed like spear-heads and sword-blades, and so the old shaveling gave up the task."

"Give it me," said the Templar. "We have that of the priestly character, that we have some knowledge to enlighten our valour."

"Let us profit by your most reverend knowledge, then," said De Bracy; "what says the scroll?"

"It is a formal letter of defiance," answered the Templar; "but, by our Lady of Bethlehem, if it be not a foolish jest, it is the most extraordinary cartel that ever was sent across the drawbridge of a baronial castle."

"Jest!" said Front-de-Bœuf, "I would gladly know who dares jest with me in such a matter!—Read it, Sir Brian."

The Templar accordingly read it as follows:—

[1] I wish the Prior had also informed them when Niobe was sainted. Probably during that enlightened period when
"Pan to Moses lent his pagan horn."   L. T

"I, Wamba, the son of Witless, Jester to a noble and free-born man, Cedric of Rotherwood, called the Saxon; and I Gurth, the son of Beowulph, the swineherd"——

"Thou art mad," said Front-de-Bœuf, interrupting the reader.

"By St. Luke, it is so set down," answered the Templar. Then resuming his task, he went on—"I, Gurth, the son of Beowulph, swineherd unto the said Cedric, with the assistance of our allies and confederates, who make common cause with us in this our feud, namely, the good knight, called for the present *Le Noir Faineant*, and the stout yeoman, Robert Locksley, called Cleave-the-wand, Do you, Reginald Front-de-Bœuf, and your allies and accomplices whomsoever, to wit, that whereas you have, without cause given or feud declared, wrongfully and by mastery seized upon the person of our lord and master the said Cedric; also upon the person of a noble and freeborn damsel, the Lady Rowena of Hargottstandstede; also upon the person of a noble and freeborn man, Athelstane of Coningsburgh; also upon the persons of certain freeborn men, their *cnichts;* also upon certain serfs, their born bondsmen; also upon a certain Jew, named Isaac of York, together with his daughter, a Jewess, and certain horses and mules: Which noble persons, with their *cnichts* and slaves, and also with the horses and mules, Jew and Jewess beforesaid, were all in peace with his majesty, and travelling as liege subjects upon the king's highway; therefore we require and demand that the said noble persons, namely, Cedric of Rotherwood, Rowena of Hargottstandstede, Athelstane of Coningsburgh, with their servants, *cnichts,* and followers, also the horses and mules, Jew and Jewess aforesaid, together with all goods and chattels to them pertaining, be, within an hour after the delivery hereof, delivered to us, or to those whom we shall appoint to receive the same, and that untouched and unharmed in body and goods. Failing of which, we do pronounce to you, that we hold ye as robbers and traitors, and will wager our bodies against ye in battle, siege, or otherwise, and do our utmost to your annoyance and destruction. Wherefore may God have you in his keeping.—Signed by us upon the eve of St. Withold's day, under the great trysting oak in the Hart-hill Walk, the above being written by a holy man, Clerk to God, our Lady, and St. Dunstan, in the Chapel of Copmanhurst."

At the bottom of this document was scrawled, in the first place, a rude sketch of a cock's head and comb, with a legend expressing this hieroglyphic to be the sign-manual of Wamba, son of Witless. Under this respectable emblem stood a cross stated to be the mark of Gurth, the son of Beowulph. Then was written, in rough bold characters, the words, *Le Noir Faineant*. And, to conclude the whole, an arrow, neatly enough drawn, was described as the mark of the yeoman Locksley.

The knights heard this uncommon document read from end to end, and then gazed upon each other in silent amazement, as being utterly at a loss to know what it could portend. De Bracy was the first to break silence by an uncontrollable fit of laughter, wherein he was joined, though with more moderation, by the Templar. Front-de-Bœuf, on the contrary, seemed impatient of their ill-timed jocularity.

"I give you plain warning," he said, "fair sirs, that you had better consult how to bear yourselves under these circumstances, than give way to such misplaced merriment."

"Front-de-Bœuf has not recovered his temper since his late overthrow," said De Bracy to the Templar; "he is cowed at the very idea of a cartel, though it come but from a fool and a swineherd."

"By St. Michael," answered Front-de-Bœuf, "I would thou couldst stand the whole brunt of this adventure thyself, De Bracy. These fellows dared not have acted with such inconceivable impudence, had they not been supported by some strong bands. There are enough of outlaws in this forest to resent my protecting the deer. I did but tie one fellow, who was taken redhanded and in the act, to the horns of a wild stag, which gored him to death in five minutes, and I had as many arrows shot at me as there were launched against yonder target at Ashby.—Here, fellow," he added, to one of his attendants, "hast thou sent out to see by what force this precious challenge is to be supported?"

"There are at least two hundred men assembled in the woods," answered a squire who was in attendance.

"Here is a proper matter!" said Front-de-Bœuf; "this comes of lending you the use of my castle, that cannot manage your undertaking quietly but you must bring this nest of hornets about my ears!"

"Of hornets?" said De Bracy; "of stingless drones rather; a band of lazy knaves, who take to the wood, and destroy the venison rather than labour for their maintenance."

"Stingless!" replied Front-de-Bœuf; "fork-headed shafts of a clothyard in length, and these shot within the breadth of a French crown, are sting enough."

"For shame, Sir Knight!" said the Templar. "Let us summon our people, and sally forth upon them. One knight—ay, one man-at-arms, were enough for twenty such peasants."

"Enough, and too much," said De Bracy, "I should only be ashamed to couch lance against them."

"True," answered Front-de-Bœuf; "were they black Turks or Moors, Sir Templar, or the craven peasants of France, most valiant De Bracy; but these are English yeomen, over whom we shall have no advantage, save what we may derive from our arms and horses, which will avail us little in the glades of the forest. Sally, saidst thou? we have scarce men enough to defend the castle. The best of mine are at York, so is all your band, De Bracy; and we have scarcely twenty, besides the handful that were engaged in this mad business."

"Thou dost not fear," said the Templar, "that they can assemble in force sufficient to attempt the castle?"

"Not so, Sir Brian," answered Front-de-Bœuf. "These outlaws have indeed a daring captain; but without machines, scaling ladders, and experienced leaders, my castle may defy them."

"Send to thy neighbours," said the Templar, "let them assemble their people, and come to the rescue of three knights, besieged by a jester and a swine-herd in the baronial castle of Reginald Front-de-Bœuf!"

"You jest, Sir Knight," answered the baron; "but to whom should I send?—Malvoisin is by this time at York with his retainers, and so are my other allies; and so should I have been, but for this infernal enterprise."

"Then send to York, and recall our people," said De Bracy. "If they abide the shaking of my standard, or the sight of my Free Companions, I will give them credit for the boldest outlaws ever bent bow in greenwood."

"And who shall bear such a message?" said Front-de-Bœuf; "they will beset every path, and rip the errand out of his bosom.—I have it," he added, after pausing for a moment—"Sir Templar, thou canst write as well as read, and if we can but find the writing materials of my chaplain, who died a twelvemonth since in the midst of his Christmas carousals"——

"So please ye," said the squire, who was still in attendance, "I think old Urfried has them somewhere in keeping, for love of the confessor. He was the last man, I have heard her tell, who ever said aught to her, which man ought in courtesy to address to maid or matron."

"Go, search them out, Engelred," said Front-de-Bœuf; "and then, Sir Templar, thou shalt return an answer to this bold challenge."

"I would rather do it at the sword's point than at that of the pen," said Bois-Guilbert; "but be it as you will."

He sat down accordingly, and indited, in the French language, an epistle of the following tenor:—

"Sir Reginald Front-de-Bœuf, with his noble and knightly allies and confederates, receive no defiances at the hands of slaves, bondsmen, or fugitives. If the person calling himself the Black Knight have indeed a claim to the honours of chivalry, he ought to know that he stands degraded by his present association, and has no right to ask reckoning at the hands of good men of noble blood. Touching the prisoners we have made, we do in Christian charity require you to send a man of religion, to receive their confession, and reconcile them with God; since it is our fixed intention to execute them this morning before noon, so that their heads being placed on the battlements, shall show to all men how lightly we esteem those who have bestirred themselves in their rescue. Wherefore, as above, we require you to send a priest to reconcile them to God, in doing which you shall render them the last earthly service."

This letter being folded, was delivered to the squire, and by him to the messenger who waited without, as the answer to that which he had brought.

The yeoman having thus accomplished his mission, returned to the headquarters of the allies, which were for the present established under a venerable oak tree, about three arrow-flights distant from the castle. Here Wamba and Gurth, with their allies the Black Knight and Locksley, and the jovial hermit, awaited with impatience an answer to their summons. Around, and at a distance from them, were seen many a bold yeoman, whose silvan dress and weatherbeaten countenance showed the ordinary nature of their occupation. More than two hundred had already assembled, and others were fast coming in. Those whom they obeyed as leaders were only distinguished from the others by a feather in the cap, their dress, arms, and equipments being in all other respects the same.

Besides these bands, a less orderly and a worse armed force, consisting of the Saxon inhabitants of the neighbouring township, as well as many bondsmen and servants from Cedric's extensive estate, had already arrived, for the purpose of assisting in his rescue. Few of these were armed otherwise than with such rustic weapons as necessity sometimes converts to military purposes. Boar-spears, scythes, flails, and the like, were their chief arms; for the Normans, with the usual policy of conquerors, were jealous of permitting to the vanquished Saxons the possession or the use of swords and spears. These circumstances rendered the assistance of the Saxons far from being so formidable to the besieged, as the strength of the men themselves, their superior numbers, and the animation inspired by a just cause, might otherwise well have made them. It was to the leaders of this motley army that the letter of the Templar was now delivered.

Reference was at first made to the chaplain for an exposition of its contents.

"By the crook of St. Dunstan," said that worthy ecclesiastic, "which hath brought more sheep within the sheepfold than the crook of e'er another saint in Paradise, I swear that I cannot expound unto you this jargon, which, whether it be French or Arabic, is beyond my guess."

He then gave the letter to Gurth, who shook his head gruffly, and passed it to Wamba. The Jester looked at each of the four corners of the paper with such a grin of affected intelligence as a monkey is apt to assume upon similar occasions, then cut a caper, and gave the letters to Locksley.

"If the long letters were bows, and the short letters broad arrows, I might know something of the matter," said the brave yeoman; "but as the matter stands, the meaning is as safe, for me, as the stag that's at twelve miles distance."

"I must be clerk, then," said the Black Knight; and taking the letter from Locksley, he first read it over to himself, and then explained the meaning in Saxon to his confederates.

"Execute the noble Cedric!" exclaimed Wamba; "by the rood, thou must be mistaken, Sir Knight."

"Not I, my worthy friend," replied the knight, "I have explained the words as they are here set down."

"Then, by St. Thomas of Canterbury," replied Gurth, "we will have the castle, should we tear it down with our hands!"

"We have nothing else to tear it with," replied Wamba; "but mine are scarce fit to make mammocks of freestone and mortar."

" 'Tis but a contrivance to gain time," said Locksley; "they dare not do a deed for which I could exact a fearful penalty."

"I would," said the Black Knight, "there were some one among us who could obtain admission into the castle, and discover how the case stands with the besieged. Methinks, as they require a confessor to be sent, this holy hermit might at once exercise his pious vocation, and procure us the information we desire."

"A plague on thee, and thy advice!" said the pious hermit; "I tell thee, Sir Slothful Knight, that when I doff my friar's frock, my priesthood, my sanctity, my very Latin, are put off along with it; and when in my green jerkin, I can better kill twenty deer than confess one Christian."

"I fear," said the Black Knight, "I fear greatly, there is no one here that is qualified to take upon him, for the nonce, this same character of father confessor?"

All looked on each other, and were silent.

"I see," said Wamba, after a short pause, "that the fool must be still the fool, and put his neck in the venture which wise men shrink from. You must know, my dear cousins and countrymen, that I wore russet before I wore motley, and was bred to be a friar, until a brain-fever came upon me and left me just wit enough to be a fool. I trust, with the assistance of the good hermit's frock, together with the priesthood, sanctity, and learning which are stitched into the cowl of it, I shall be found qualified to administer both worldly and ghostly comfort to our worthy master Cedric, and his companions in adversity."

"Hath he sense enough, thinkst thou?" said the Black Knight, addressing Gurth.

"I know not," said Gurth; "but if he hath not, it will be the first time he hath wanted wit to turn his folly to account."

"On with the frock, then, good fellow," quoth the Knight, "and let thy master send us an account of their situation within the castle. Their numbers must be few, and it is five to one they may be accessible by a sudden and bold attack. Time wears—away with thee."

"And, in the meantime," said Locksley, "we will beset the place so closely, that not so much as a fly shall carry news from thence. So that, my good friend," he continued, addressing Wamba, "thou mayst assure these tyrants, that whatever violence they exercise on the persons of their prisoners, shall be most severely repaid upon their own."

"*Pax vobiscum*," said Wamba, who was now muffled in his religious disguise.

And so saying, he imitated the solemn and stately deportment of a friar, and departed to execute his mission.

CHAPTER XXVI

The hottest horse will oft be cool,
The dullest will show fire;
The friar will often play the fool,
The fool will play the friar.
Old Song.

WHEN the Jester, arrayed in the cowl and frock of the hermit, and having his knotted cord twisted round his middle, stood before the portal of the castle of Front-de-Bœuf, the warder demanded of him his name and errand.

"*Pax vobiscum,*" answered the Jester, "I am a poor brother of the Order of St. Francis, who come hither to do my office to certain unhappy prisoners now secured within this castle."

"Thou art a bold friar," said the warder, "to come hither, where, saving our own drunken confessor, a cock of thy feather hath not crowed these twenty years."

"Yet, I pray thee, do mine errand to the lord of the castle," answered the pretended friar; "trust me it will find good acceptance with him, and the cock shall crow, that the whole castle shall hear him."

"Gramercy," said the warder; "but if I come to shame for leaving my post upon thine errand, I will try whether a friar's grey gown be proof against a grey-goose shaft."

With this threat he left his turret, and carried to the hall of the castle his unwonted intelligence, that a holy friar stood before the gate and demanded instant admission. With no small wonder he received his master's commands to admit the holy man immediately; and, having previously manned the entrance to guard against surprise, he obeyed, without further scruple, the commands which he had received. The hare-brained self-conceit which had emboldened Wamba to undertake this dangerous office, was scarce sufficient to support him when he found himself in the presence of a man so dreadful and so much dreaded, as Reginald Front-de-Bœuf, and he brought out his *pax vobiscum,* to which he, in a good measure, trusted for supporting his character, with more anxiety and hesitation than had hitherto accompanied it. But Front-de-Bœuf was accustomed to see men of all ranks tremble in his presence, so that the timidity of the supposed father did not give him any cause of suspicion. "Who and whence art thou, priest?" said he.

"*Pax vobiscum,*" reiterated the Jester, "I am a poor servant of St. Francis, who, travelling through this wilderness, have fallen among thieves (as Scripture hath it)—*quidam viator incidit in latrones*—which thieves have sent me unto this castle in order to do my ghostly office on two persons condemned by your honourable justice."

"Ay, right," answered Front-de-Bœuf; "and canst thou tell me, holy father, the number of those banditti?"

"Gallant sir," answered the Jester, "*nomen illis legio,* their name is legion."

"Tell me in plain terms what numbers there are, or, priest, thy cloak and cord will ill protect thee."

"Alas!" said the supposed friar, "*cor meum eructavit,* that is to say, I was like to burst with fear! but I conceive they may be—what of yeomen—what of commons, at least five hundred men."

"What!" said the Templar, who came into the hall that moment, "muster the wasps so thick here? it is time to stifle such a mischievous brood." Then taking Front-de-Bœuf aside, "Knowest thou the priest?"

"He is a stranger from a distant convent," said Front-de-Bœuf; "I know him not."

"Then trust him not with thy purpose in words," answered the Templar. "Let him carry a written order to De Bracy's company of Free Companions, to repair instantly to their master's aid. In the meantime, and that the shaveling may suspect nothing, permit him to go freely about his task of preparing these Saxon hogs for the slaughter-house."

"It shall be so," said Front-de-Bœuf. And he forthwith appointed a domestic to conduct Wamba to the apartment where Cedric and Athelstane were confined.

The impatience of Cedric had been rather enhanced than diminished by his confinement. He walked from one end of the hall to the other, with the attitude of one who advances to charge an enemy, or to storm the breach of a beleaguered place, sometimes ejaculating to himself, sometimes addressing Athelstane, who stoutly and stoically awaited the issue of the adventure, digesting, in the meantime, with great composure, the liberal meal which he had made at noon, and not greatly interesting himself about the duration of his captivity, which, he concluded, would, like all earthly evils, find an end in Heaven's good time.

"*Pax vobiscum,*" said the Jester, entering the apartment; "the blessing of St. Dunstan, St. Dennis, St. Duthoc and all other saints whatsoever, be upon ye and about ye."

"Enter freely," answered Cedric to the supposed friar; "with what intent art thou come hither?"

"To bid you prepare yourselves for death," answered the Jester.

"It is impossible!" replied Cedric, starting. "Fearless and wicked as they are, they dare not attempt such open gratuitous cruelty!"

"Alas!" said the Jester, "to restrain them by their sense of humanity, is the same as to stop a runaway horse with a bridle of silk thread. Bethink thee, therefore, noble Cedric, and you also, gallant Athelstane, what crimes you have committed in the flesh; for this very day will ye be called to answer at a higher tribunal."

"Hearest thou this, Athelstane?" said Cedric; "we must rouse up our hearts to this last action, since better it is we should die like men, than like slaves."

"I am ready," answered Athelstane, "to stand the worst of their malice, and shall walk to my death with as much composure as ever I did to my dinner."

"Let us then unto our holy gear, father," said Cedric.

"Wait yet a moment, good uncle," said the Jester, in his natural tone; "better look long before you leap in the dark."

"By my faith," said Cedric, "I should know that voice!"

"It is that of your trusty slave and jester," answered Wamba, throwing back his cowl. "Had you taken a fool's advice formerly, you would not have been here at all. Take a fool's advice now, and you will not be here long."

"How mean'st thou, knave?" answered the Saxon.

"Even thus," replied Wamba; "take thou this frock and cord, which are all the orders I ever had, and march quietly out of the castle, leaving me your cloak and girdle to take the long leap in thy stead."

"Leave thee in my stead!" said Cedric, astonished at the proposal; "why, they would hang thee, my poor knave."

"E'en let them do as they are permitted," said Wamba; "I trust—no disparagement to your birth—that the son of Witless may hang in a chain with as much gravity as the chain hung upon his ancestor the alderman."

"Well, Wamba," answered Cedric, "for one thing will I grant thy request. And that is, if thou wilt make the exchange of garments with Lord Athelstane instead of me."

"No, by St. Dunstan," answered Wamba; "there were little reason in that. Good right there is, that the son of Witless should suffer to save the son of Hereward; but little wisdom there were in his dying for the benefit of one whose fathers were strangers to his."

"Villain," said Cedric, "the fathers of Athelstane were monarchs of England!"

"They might be whomsoever they pleased," replied Wamba; "but my neck stands too straight upon my shoulders to have it twisted for their sake. Wherefore, good my master, either take my proffer yourself, or suffer me to leave this dungeon as free as I entered."

"Let the old tree wither," continued Cedric, "so the stately hope of the forest be preserved. Save the noble Athelstane, my trusty Wamba! it is the duty of each who has Saxon blood in his veins. Thou and I will abide together the utmost rage of our injurious oppressors, while he, free and safe, shall arouse the awakened spirits of our countrymen to avenge us."

"Not so, father Cedric," said Athelstane, grasping his hand,—for, when roused to think or act, his deeds and sentiments were not unbecoming his high race—"Not so," he continued; "I would rather remain in this hall a week without food save the prisoner's stinted loaf, or drink save the prisoner's measure of water, than embrace the opportunity to escape which the slave's untaught kindness has purveyed for his master."

"You are called wise men, sirs," said the Jester, "and I a crazed fool; but, uncle Cedric, and cousin Athelstane, the fool shall decide this controversy for ye, and save ye the trouble of straining courtesies any farther. I am like John-a-Duck's mare, that will let no man mount her but John-a-Duck, I came to save my master, and if he will not consent— basta—I can but go away home again. Kind service cannot be chucked from hand to hand like a shuttlecock or stool-ball. I'll hang for no man but my own born master."

"Go, then, noble Cedric," said Athelstane, "neglect not this opportunity. Your presence without may encourage friends to our rescue— your remaining here would ruin us all."

"And is there any prospect, then, of rescue from without?" said Cedric, looking to the Jester.

"Prospect, indeed!" echoed Wamba; "let me tell you, when you fill my cloak, you are wrapped in a general's cassock. Five hundred men are there without, and I was this morning one of their chief leaders. My fool's cap was a casque, and my bauble a truncheon. Well, we shall see what good they will make by exchanging a fool for a wise man. Truly, I fear they will lose in valour what they may gain in discretion. And so farewell, master, and be kind to poor Gurth and his dog Fangs; and let my cockscomb hang in the hall at Rotherwood, in memory that I flung away my life for my master, like a faithful——fool."

The last word came out with a sort of double expression, betwixt jest and earnest. The tears stood in Cedric's eyes.

"Thy memory shall be preserved," he said, "while fidelity and affection have honour upon earth! But that I trust I shall find the means of saving Rowena, and thee, Athelstane, and thee also, my poor Wamba, thou shouldst not overbear me in this matter."

The exchange of dress was now accomplished, when a sudden doubt struck Cedric.

"I know no language," he said, "but my own, and a few words of their mincing Norman. How shall I bear myself like a reverend brother?"

"The spell lies in two words," replied Wamba—"*Pax vobiscum* will answer all queries. If you go or come, eat or drink, bless or ban, *Pax vobiscum* carries you through it all. It is as useful to a friar as a broomstick to a witch, or a wand to a conjurer. Speak it but thus, in a deep grave tone,—*Pax vobiscum!*—it is irresistible—Watch and ward, knight and squire, foot and horse, it acts as a charm upon them all. I think, if they bring me out to be hanged to-morrow, as is much to be doubted they may, I will try its weight upon the finisher of the sentence."

"If such prove the case," said his master, "my religious orders are soon taken—*Pax vobiscum*. I trust I shall remember the password.—Noble

Athelstane, farewell; and farewell, my poor boy, whose heart might make amends for a weaker head—I will save you, or return and die with you. The royal blood of our Saxon kings shall not be spilt while mine beats in my veins; nor shall one hair fall from the head of the kind knave who risked himself for his master, if Cedric's peril can prevent it.—Farewell."

"Farewell, noble Cedric," said Athelstane; "remember it is the true part of a friar to accept refreshment, if you are offered any."

"Farewell, uncle," added Wamba; "and remember *Pax vobiscum.*"

Thus exhorted, Cedric sallied forth upon his expedition; and it was not long ere he had occasion to try the force of that spell which his Jester had recommended as omnipotent. In a low-arched and dusky passage, by which he endeavoured to work his way to the hall of the castle, he was interrupted by a female form.

"Pax vobiscum!" said the psuedo friar, and was endeavouring to hurry past, when a soft voice replied, *"Et vobis—quæso, domine reverendissime, pro misericordia vestra."*

"I am somewhat deaf," replied Cedric, in good Saxon, and at the same time muttered to himself, "A curse on the fool and his *Pax vobiscum!* I have lost my javelin at the first cast."

It was, however, no unusual thing for a priest of those days to be deaf of his Latin ear, and this the person who now addressed Cedric knew full well.

"I pray you of dear love, reverend father," she replied in his own language, "that you will deign to visit with your ghostly comfort a wounded prisoner of this castle, and have such compassion upon him and us as thy holy office teaches—Never shall good deed so highly advantage thy convent."

"Daughter," answered Cedric, much embarrassed, "my time in this castle will not permit me to exercise the duties of mine office—I must presently forth—there is life and death upon my speed."

"Yet, father, let me entreat you by the vow you have taken on you," replied the suppliant, "not to leave the oppressed and endangered without counsel or succour."

"May the fiend fly away with me, and leave me in Ifrin with the souls of Odin and of Thor!" answered Cedric impatiently, and would probably have proceeded in the same tone of total departure from his spiritual character, when the colloquy was interrupted by the harsh voice of Urfried, the old crone of the turret.

"How, minion," said she to the female speaker, "is this the manner in which you requite the kindness which permitted thee to leave thy prison-cell yonder?—Puttest thou the reverend man to use ungracious language to free himself from the importunities of a Jewess?"

"A Jewess!" said Cedric, availing himself of the information to get clear of their interruption,—"Let me pass, woman! stop me not at your peril. I am fresh from my holy office, and would avoid pollution."

"Come this way, father," said the old hag, "thou art a stranger in this castle, and canst not leave it without a guide. Come hither, for I would speak with thee.—And you, daughter of an accursed race, go to the sick man's chamber, and tend him until my return; and woe betide you if you again quit it without my permission!"

Rebecca retreated. Her importunities had prevailed upon Urfried to suffer her to quit the turret, and Urfried had employed her services where she herself would most gladly have paid them, by the bedside of the wounded Ivanhoe. With an understanding awake to their dangerous situation, and prompt to avail herself of each means of safety which occurred, Rebecca had hoped something from the presence of a man of religion, who, she learned from Urfried, had penetrated into this godless castle. She watched the return of the supposed ecclesiastic, with the purpose of addressing him, and interesting him in favour of the prisoners; with what imperfect success the reader has been just acquainted.

CHAPTER XXVII

Fond wretch! and what canst thou relate,
    But deeds of sorrow, shame, and sin?
Thy deeds are proved—thou know'st thy fate;
    But come, thy tale—begin—begin.

. . . . .

But I have griefs of other kind,
    Troubles and sorrows more severe;
Give me to ease my tortured mind,
    Lend to my woes a patient ear;
And let me, if I may not find
    A friend to help—find one to hear.
                          CRABBE's *Hall of Justice.*

WHEN Urfried had with clamours and menaces driven Rebecca back to the apartment from which she had sallied, she proceeded to conduct the unwilling Cedric into a small apartment, the door of which she heedfully secured. Then fetching from a cupboard a stoup of wine and two flagons, she placed them on the table, and said in a tone rather asserting a fact than asking a question, "Thou art Saxon, father—Deny it not," she continued, observing that Cedric hastened not to reply; "the sounds of my native language are sweet to mine ears, though seldom heard save from the tongues of the wretched and degraded serfs on whom the proud Normans impose the meanest drudgery of this dwelling. Thou art a Saxon, father—a Saxon, and, save as thou art a servant of God, a freeman.—Thine accents are sweet in mine ear."

"Do not Saxon priests visit this castle, then?" replied Cedric; "it were, methinks, their duty to comfort the outcast and oppressed children of the soil."

"They come not, or if they come, they better love to revel at the boards of their conquerors," answered Urfried, "than to hear the groans of their countrymen—so, at least, report speaks of them—of myself I can say little. This castle, for ten years, has opened to no priest save the debauched Norman chaplain who partook the nightly revels of Front-de-Bœuf, and he has been long gone to render an account of his stewardship. —But thou art a Saxon—a Saxon priest, and I have one question to ask of thee."

"I am a Saxon," answered Cedric, "but unworthy, surely, of the name of priest. Let me begone on my way—I swear I will return, or send one of our fathers more worthy to hear your confession."

"Stay yet a while," said Urfried; "the accents of the voice which thou hearest now will soon be choked with the cold earth, and I would not descend to it like the beast I have lived. But wine must give me strength to tell the horrors of my tale." She poured out a cup, and drank it with a frightful avidity, which seemed desirous of draining the last drop in the goblet. "It stupefies," she said, looking upwards as she finished her draught, "but it cannot cheer—Partake it, father, if you would hear my tale without sinking down upon the pavement." Cedric would have avoided pledging her in this ominous conviviality, but the sign whi she made to him expressed impatience and despair. He complied with her request, and answered her challenge in a large wine-cup; she then proceeded with her story, as if appeased by his complaisance.

"I was not born," she said, "father, the wretch that thou now seest me. I was free, was happy, was honoured, loved and was beloved. I am now a slave, miserable and degraded—the sport of my masters' passions while I had yet beauty—the object of their contempt, scorn, and hatred, since it has passed away. Dost thou wonder, father, that I should hate mankind, and, above all, the race that has wrought this change in me? Can the wrinkled decrepit hag before thee, whose wrath must vent itself in impotent curses, forget she was once the daughter of the noble Thane of Torquilstone, before whose frown a thousand vassals trembled?"

"Thou the daughter of Torquil Wolfganger!" said Cedric, receding as he spoke, "thou—thou—the daughter of that noble Saxon, my father's friend and companion in arms!"

"Thy father's friend!" echoed Urfried; "then Cedric called the Saxon stands before me, for the noble Hereward of Rotherwood had but one son, whose name is well known among his countrymen. But if thou art Cedric of Rotherwood, why this religious dress? hast thou too despaired of saving thy country, and sought refuge from oppression in the shade of the convent?"

"It matters not who I am," said Cedric; "proceed, unhappy woman, with thy tale of horror and guilt!—Guilt there must be—there is guilt even in thy living to tell it."

"There is—there is," answered the wretched woman, "deep, black, damning guilt,—guilt, that lies like a load at my breast—guilt, that all the penitential fires of hereafter cannot cleanse.—Yes, in these halls, stained with the noble and pure blood of my father and my brethren—in these very halls, to have lived the paramour of their murderer, the slave at once and the partaker of his pleasures, was to render every breath which I drew of vital air, a crime and a curse."

"Wretched woman!" exclaimed Cedric. "And while the friends of thy father—while each true Saxon heart, as it breathed a requiem for his soul, and those of his valiant sons, forgot not in their prayers the murdered Ulrica—while all mourned and honoured the dead, thou hast lived to merit our hate and execration—lived to unite thyself with the vile tyrant who murdered thy nearest and dearest—who shed the blood of infancy, rather than a male of the noble house of Torquil Wolfganger should survive—with him hast thou lived to unite thyself, and in the bands of lawless love!"

"In lawless bands, indeed, but not in those of love!" answered the hag; "love will sooner visit the regions of eternal doom, than those unhallowed vaults.—No, with that at least I cannot reproach myself—hatred to Front-de-Bœuf and his race governed my soul most deeply, even in the hour of his guilty endearments."

"You hated him, and yet you lived," replied Cedric; "wretch! was there no poniard—no knife—no bodkin!—Well was it for thee, since thou didst prize such an existence, that the secrets of a Norman castle are like those of the grave. For had I but dreamed of the daughter of Torquil living in foul communion with the murderer of her father, the sword of a true Saxon had found thee out even in the arms of thy paramour!"

"Wouldst thou indeed have done this justice to the name of Torquil?" said Ulrica, for we may now lay aside her assumed name of Urfried; "thou art then the true Saxon report speaks thee! for even within these accursed walls, where, as thou well sayest, guilt shrouds itself in inscrutable mystery, even there has the name of Cedric been sounded—and I, wretched and degraded, have rejoiced to think that there yet breathed an avenger of our unhappy nation.—I also have had my hours of vengeance—I have fomented the quarrels of our foes, and heated drunken revelry into murderous broil—I have seen their blood flow—I have heard their dying groans!—Look on me, Cedric—are there not still left on this foul and faded face some traces of the features of Torquil?"

"Ask me not of them, Ulrica," replied Cedric, in a tone of grief mixed with abhorrence; "these traces form such a resemblance as arises from the grave of the dead, when a fiend has animated the lifeless corpse."

"Be it so," answered Ulrica; "yet wore these fiendish features the mask of a spirit of light when they were able to set at variance the elder Front-de-Bœuf and his son Reginald! The darkness of hell should hide what followed, but revenge must lift the veil, and darkly intimate what it would raise the dead to speak aloud. Long had the smouldering fire of

discord glowed between the tyrant father and his savage son—long had
I nursed, in secret, the unnatural hatred—it blazed forth in an hour of
drunken wassail, and at his own board fell my oppressor by the hand of
his own son—such are the secrets these vaults conceal!—Rend asunder,
ye accursed arches," she added, looking up towards the roof, "and bury
in your fall all who are conscious of the hideous mystery!"

"And thou, creature of guilt and misery," said Cedric, "what became
thy lot on the death of thy ravisher?"

"Guess it, but ask it not.—Here—here I dwelt, till age, premature
age, has stamped its ghastly features on my countenance—scorned and
insulted where I was once obeyed, and compelled to bound the revenge
which had once such ample scope, to the efforts of petty malice of a discontented menial, or the vain or unheeded curses of an impotent hag—
condemned to hear from my lonely turret the sounds of revelry in which
I once partook, or the shrieks and groans of new victims of oppression."

"Ulrica," said Cedric, "with a heart which still, I fear, regrets the lost
reward of thy crimes, as much as the deeds by which thou didst acquire
that meed, how didst thou dare to address thee to one who wears this
robe? Consider, unhappy woman, what could the sainted Edward himself
do for thee, were he here in bodily presence? The royal confessor was
endowed by Heaven with power to cleanse the ulcers of the body, but
only God himself can cure the leprosy of the soul."

"Yet, turn not from me, stern prophet of wrath," she exclaimed, "but
tell me, if thou canst, in what shall terminate these new and awful feelings that burst on my solitude—Why do deeds, long since done, rise
before me in new and irresistible horrors? What fate is prepared beyond
the grave for her, to whom God has assigned on earth a lot of such unspeakable wretchedness? Better had I turn to Woden, Hertha, and Zernebock—to Mista, and to Skogula, the gods of our yet unbaptized ancestors, than endure the dreadful anticipations which have of late haunted
my waking and my sleeping hours!"

"I am no priest," said Cedric, turning with disgust from this miserable
picture of guilt, wretchedness, and despair; "I am no priest, though I
wear a priest's garment."

"Priest or layman," answered Ulrica, "thou art the first I have seen
for twenty years, by whom God was feared or man regarded; and dost
thou bid me despair?"

"I bid thee repent," said Cedric. "Seek to prayer and penance, and
mayest thou find acceptance! But I cannot, I will not, longer abide with
thee."

"Stay yet a moment!" said Ulrica; "leave me not now, son of my
father's friend, lest the demon who has governed my life should tempt me
to avenge myself of thy hard-hearted scorn—Thinkest thou, if Front-de-
Bœuf found Cedric the Saxon in his castle, in such a disguise, that thy
life would be a long one?—Already his eye has been upon thee like a
falcon on his prey."

"And be it so," said Cedric; "and let him tear me with beak and talons, ere my tongue say one word which my heart doth not warrant. I will die a Saxon—true in word, open in deed—I bid thee avaunt!—touch me not, stay me not!—The sight of Front-de-Bœuf himself is less odious to me than thou, degraded and degenerate as thou art."

"Be it so," said Ulrica, no longer interrupting him; "go thy way, and forget, in the insolence of thy superiority, that the wretch before thee is the daughter of thy father's friend.—Go thy way—if I am separated from mankind by my sufferings—separated from those whose aid I might most justly expect—not less will I be separated from them in my revenge!—No man shall aid me, but the ears of all men shall tingle to hear of the deed which I shall dare to do!—Farewell!—thy scorn has burst the last tie which seemed yet to unite me to my kind—a thought that my woes might claim the compassion of my people."

"Ulrica," said Cedric, softened by this appeal, "hast thou borne up and endured to live through so much guilt and so much misery, and wilt thou now yield to despair when thine eyes are opened to thy crimes, and when repentance were thy fitter occupation?"

"Cedric," answered Ulrica, "thou little knowest the human heart. To act as I have acted, to think as I have thought, requires the maddening love of pleasure, mingled with the keen appetite of revenge, the proud consciousness of power; draughts too intoxicating for the human heart to bear, and yet retain the power to prevent. Their force has long passed away—Age has no pleasures, wrinkles have no influence, revenge itself dies away in impotent curses. Then comes remorse, with all its vipers, mixed with vain regrets for the past, and despair for the future!—Then, when all other strong impulses have ceased, we become like the fiends in hell, who may feel remorse, but never repentance.—But thy words have awakened a new soul within me—Well hast thou said, all is possible for those who dare to die!—Thou hast shown me the means of revenge, and be assured I will embrace them. It has hitherto shared this wasted bosom with other and with rival passions—henceforward it shall possess me wholly, and thou thyself shalt say that, whatever was the life of Ulrica, her death well became the daughter of the noble Torquil. There is a force without beleaguering this accursed castle—hasten to lead them to the attack, and when thou shalt see a red flag wave from the turret on the eastern angle of the donjon, press the Normans hard—they will have enough to do within, and you may win the wall in spite both of bow and mangonel.—Begone, I pray thee—follow thine own fate, and leave me to mine."

Cedric would have enquired farther into the purpose which she thus darkly announced, but the stern voice of Front-de-Bœuf was heard, exclaiming, "Where tarries this loitering priest? By the scallop-shell of Compostella, I will make a martyr of him, if he loiters here to hatch treason among my domestics!"

"What a true prophet," said Ulrica, "is an evil conscience! But heed him not—out and to thy people—Cry your Saxon onslaught, and let them sing their war-song of Rollo, if they will; vengeance shall bear a burden to it."

As she thus spoke, she vanished through a private door, and Reginald Front-de-Bœuf entered the apartment. Cedric, with some difficulty, compelled himself to make obeisance to the haughty Baron, who returned his courtesy with a slight inclination of the head.

"Thy penitents, father, have made a long shrift—it is the better for them, since it is the last they shall ever make. Hast thou prepared them for death?"

"I found them," said Cedric, in such French as he could command, "expecting the worst, from the moment they knew into whose power they had fallen."

"How now, Sir Friar," replied Front-de-Bœuf, "thy speech, methinks, smacks of a Saxon tongue?"

"I was bred in the convent of St. Withold of Burton," answered Cedric.

"Ay?" said the Baron; "it had been better for thee to have been a Norman, and better for my purpose too; but need has no choice of messengers. That St. Withold's of Burton is a howlet's nest worth the harrying. The day will soon come that the frock shall protect the Saxon as little as the mail-coat."

"God's will be done," said Cedric, in a voice tremulous with passion, which Front-de-Bœuf imputed to fear.

"I see," said he, "thou dreamest already that our men-at-arms are in thy refectory and thy ale-vaults. But do me one cast of thy holy office, and, come what list of others, thou shalt sleep as safe in thy cell as a snail within his shell of proof."

"Speak your commands," said Cedric, with suppressed emotion.

"Follow me through this passage, then, that I may dismiss thee by the postern."

And as he strode on his way before the supposed friar, Front-de-Bœuf thus schooled him in the part which he desired he should act.

"Thou seest, Sir Friar, yon herd of Saxon swine, who have dared to environ this castle of Torquilstone—Tell them whatever thou hast a mind of the weakness of this fortalice, or aught else that can detain them before it for twenty-four hours. Meantime bear thou this scroll—But soft—canst read, Sir Priest?"

"Not a jot I," answered Cedric, "save on my breviary; and then I know the characters, because I have the holy service by heart, praised be Our Lady and St. Withold!"

"The fitter messenger for my purpose.—Carry thou this scroll to the castle of Philip de Malvoisin; say it cometh from me, and is written by the Templar Brian de Bois-Guilbert, and that I pray him to send it to York with all the speed man and horse can make. Meanwhile, tell him to doubt nothing, he shall find us whole and sound behind our battlement—Shame on it, that we should be compelled to hide thus by a pack of runagates, who are wont to fly even at the flash of our pennons and the tramp of our horses! I say to thee, priest, contrive some cast of thine art to keep the knaves where they are, until our friends bring up their lances. My vengeance is awake, and she is a falcon that slumbers not till she has been gorged."

"By my patron saint," said Cedric, with deeper energy than became his character, "and by every saint who has lived and died in England, your commands shall be obeyed! Not a Saxon shall stir from before these walls, if I have art and influence to detain them there."

"Ha!" said Front-de-Bœuf, "thou changest thy tone, Sir Priest, and speakest brief and bold, as if thy heart were in the slaughter of the Saxon herd; and yet thou art thyself of kindred to the swine?"

Cedric was no ready practiser of the art of dissimulation, and would at this moment have been much the better of a hint from Wamba's more fertile brain. But necessity, according to the ancient proverb, sharpens invention, and he muttered something under his cowl concerning the men in question being excommunicated outlaws both to church and to kingdom.

"*Despardieux*," answered Front-de-Bœuf, "thou hast spoken the very truth—I forgot that the knaves can strip a fat abbot, as well as if they had been born south of yonder salt channel. Was it not he of St. Ives whom they tied to an oak tree, and compelled to sing a mass while they were rifling his mails and his wallets?—No, by our Lady—that jest was played by Gualtier of Middleton, one of our own companions-at-arms. But they were Saxons who robbed the chapel of St. Bees of cup, candlestick, and chalice, were they not?"

"They were godless men," answered Cedric.

"Ay, and they drank out all the good wine and ale that lay in store for many a secret carousal, when ye pretend ye are but busied with vigils and primes!—Priest, thou art bound to revenge such sacrilege."

"I am indeed bound to vengeance," murmured Cedric; "St. Withold knows my heart."

Front-de-Bœuf, in the meanwhile, led the way to a postern, where, passing the moat on a single plank, they reached a small barbican, or exterior defence, which communicated with the open field by a well-fortified sallyport.

"Begone, then; and if thou wilt do mine errand, and if thou return thither when it is done, thou shalt see Saxon flesh cheap as ever was hog's in the shambles of Sheffield. And, hark thee, thou seemest to be a jolly confessor—come hither after the onslaught, and thou shalt have as much Malvoisie as would drench thy whole convent."

"Assuredly we shall meet again," answered Cedric

"Something in hand the whilst," continued the Norman; and, as they parted at the postern door, he thrust into Cedric's reluctant hand a gold byzant, adding, "Remember, I will flay off both cowl and skin, if thou failest in thy purpose."

"And full leave will I give thee to do both," answered Cedric, leaving the postern, and striding forth over the free field with a joyful step, "if, when we meet next, I deserve not better at thine hand."—Turning then back towards the castle, he threw the piece of gold towards the donor, exclaiming at the same time, "False Norman, thy money perish with thee!"-

Front-de-Bœuf heard the words imperfectly, but the action was suspicious—"Archers," he called to the warders on the outward battlements, "send me an arrow through yon monk's frock!—yet stay," he said, as his retainers were bending their bows, "it avails not—we must thus far trust him since we have no better shift. I think he dares not betray me —at the worst I can but treat with these Saxon dogs whom I have safe in kennel.—Ho! Giles jailor, let them bring Cedric of Rotherwood before me, and the other churl, his companion—him I mean of Conings- burgh—Athelstane there, or what they call him? Their very names are an encumbrance to a Norman knight's mouth, and have, as it were, a flavour of bacon—Give me a stoup of wine, as jolly Prince John said, that I may wash away the relish—place it in the armoury, and thither lead the prisoners."

His commands were obeyed; and, upon entering that Gothic apart- ment, hung with many spoils won by his own valour and that of his father, he found a flagon of wine on the massive oaken table, and the two Saxon captives under the guard of four of his dependants. Front-de-Bœuf took a long draught of wine, and then addressed his prisoners;—for the manner in which Wamba drew the cap over his face, the change of dress, the gloomy and broken light, and the Baron's imperfect acquaintance with the features of Cedric (who avoided his Norman neighbours, and seldom stirred beyond his own domains), prevented him from discovering that the most important of his captives had made his escape.

"Gallants of England," said Front-de-Bœuf, "how relish ye your entertainment at Torquilstone?—Are ye yet aware what your *surquedy* and *outrecuidance* merit, for scoffing at the entertainment of a prince of the House of Anjoù?—Have ye forgotten how ye requited the un- merited hospitality of the royal John? By God and St Dennis, an ye pay not the richer ransom, I will hang ye up by the feet from the iron bars of these windows, till the kites and hooded crows have made skele- tons of you!—Speak out, ye Saxon dogs—what bid ye for your worth- less lives?—How say you, you of Rotherwood?"

"Not a doit I," answered poor Wamba—"and for hanging up by the feet, my brain has been topsy-turvy, they say, ever since the biggin was bound first round my head; so turning me upside down may peradventure restore it again."

"Saint Genevieve!" said Front-de-Bœuf, "what have we got here?" And with the back of his hand he struck Cedric's cap from the head of the Jester, and throwing open his collar, discovered the fatal badge of servitude, the silver collar around his neck.

"Giles—Clement—dogs and varlets!" exclaimed the furious Norman "what have you brought me here?"

"I think I can tell you," said De Bracy, who just entered the apartment. "This is Cedric's clown, who fought so manful a skirmish with Isaac of York about a question of precedence."

"I shall settle it for them both," replied Front-de-Bœuf; "they shall hang on the same gallows, unless his master and this boar of Coningsburgh will pay well for their lives. Their wealth is the least they can surrender; they must also carry off with them the swarms that are besetting the castle, subscribe a surrender of their pretended immunities, and live under us as serfs and vassals; too happy if, in the new world that is about to begin, we leave them the breath of their nostrils.—Go," said he to two of his attendants, "fetch me the right Cedric hither, and I pardon your error for once; the rather that you but mistook a fool for a Saxon franklin."

"Ay, but," said Wamba, "your chivalrous excellency will find there are more fools than franklins among us."

"What means the knave?" said Front-de-Bœuf, looking towards his followers, who, lingering and loath, faltered forth their belief, that if this were not Cedric who was there in presence, they knew not what was become of him.

"Saints of Heaven!" exclaimed De Bracy, "he must have escaped in the monk's garments!"

"Fiends of hell!" echoed Front-de-Bœuf, "it was then the boar of Rotherwood whom I ushered to the postern, and dismissed with my own hands! —And thou," he said to Wamba, "whose folly could overreach the wisdom of idiots yet more gross than thyself—I will give thee holy orders —I will shave thy crown for thee!—Here, let them tear the scalp from his head, and then pitch him headlong from the battlements—Thy trade is to jest, canst thou jest now?"

"You deal with me better than your word, noble knight," whimpered forth poor Wamba, whose habits of buffoonery were not to be overcome even by the immediate prospect of death; "if you give me the red cap you propose, out of a simple monk you will make a cardinal."

"The poor wretch," said De Bracy, "is resolved to die in his vocation. —Front-de-Bœuf, you shall not slay him.—Give him to me to make sport for my Free Companions.—How sayst thou, knave? Wilt thou take heart of grace, and go to the wars with me?"

"Ay, with my master's leave," said Wamba; "for, look you, I must not slip collar" (and he touched that which he wore) "without his permission."

"Oh, a Norman saw will soon cut a Saxon collar," said De Bracy.

"Ay, noble sir," said Wamba, "and thence goes the proverb—

'Norman saw on English oak,
  On English neck a Norman yoke;

Norman spoon in English dish,
And England ruled as Normans wish;
Blithe world to England never will be more,
Till England's rid of all the four.' "

"Thou dost well, De Bracy," said Front-de-Bœuf, "to stand there
listening to a fool's jargon, when destruction is gaping for us! Seest thou
not we are overreached, and that our proposed mode of communicating
with our friends without has been disconcerted by this same motley gentleman thou art so fond to brother? What views have we to expect but
instant storm?"

"To the battlements then," said De Bracy; "when didst thou ever
see me the graver for the thoughts of battle? Call the Templar yonder,
and let him fight but half so well for his life as he has done for his
Order—Make thou to the walls thyself with thy huge body—Let me do
my poor endeavour in my own way, and I tell thee the Saxon outlaws
may as well attempt to scale the clouds, as the castle of Torquilstone;
or, if you will treat with the banditti, why not employ the mediation of
this worthy franklin, who seems in such deep contemplation of the wine-
flagon?—Here, Saxon," he continued, addressing Athelstane, and handing the cup to him, "rinse thy throat with that noble liquor, and rouse
up thy soul to say what thou wilt do for thy liberty."

"What a man of mould may," answered Athelstane, "providing it be
what a man of manhood ought.—Dismiss me free, with my companions,
and I will pay a ransom of a thousand marks."

"And wilt moreover assure us the retreat of that scum of mankind
who are swarming around the castle, contrary to God's peace and the
king's?" said Front-de-Bœuf.

"In so far as I can," answered Athelstane, "I will withdraw them; and
I fear not but that my father Cedric will do his best to assist me."

"We are agreed then," said Front-de-Bœuf—"thou and they are to
be set at freedom, and peace is to be on both sides, for payment of a
thousand marks. It is a trifling ransom, Saxon, and thou wilt owe gratitude to the moderation which accepts of it in exchange of your persons.
But mark, this extends not to the Jew Isaac."

"Nor to the Jew Isaac's daughter," said the Templar, who had now
joined them.

"Neither," said Front-de-Bœuf, "belong to this Saxon's company."

"I were unworthy to be called Christian, if they did," replied Athelstane: "deal with the unbelievers as ye list."

"Neither does the ransom include the Lady Rowena," said De Bracy.
"It shall never be said I was scared out of a fair prize without striking
a blow for it."

"Neither," said Front-de-Bœuf, "does our treaty refer to this wretched
Jester, whom I retain, that I may make him an example to every knave
who turns jest into earnest."

"The Lady Rowena," answered Athelstane, with the most steady countenance, "is my affianced bride. I will be drawn by wild horses before I consent to part with her. The slave Wamba has this day saved the life of my father Cedric—I will lose mine ere a hair of his head be injured."

"Thy affianced bride?—The Lady Rowena the affianced bride of a vassal like thee?" said De Bracy; "Saxon, thou dreamest that the days of thy seven kingdoms are returned again. I tell thee, the Princes of the House of Anjoù confer not their wards on men of such lineage as thine."

"My lineage, proud Norman," replied Athelstane, "is drawn from a source more pure and ancient than that of a beggarly Frenchman, whose living is won by selling the blood of the thieves whom he assembles under his paltry standard. Kings were my ancestors, strong in war and wise in council, who every day feasted in their hall more hundreds than thou canst number individual followers; whose names have been sung by minstrels, and their laws recorded by Wittenagemotes; whose bones were interred amid the prayers of saints, and over whose tombs min-sters have been builded."

"Thou hast it, De Bracy," said Front-de-Bœuf, well pleased with the rebuff which his companion had received; "the Saxon hath hit thee fairly."

"As fairly as a captive can strike," said De Bracy, with apparent carelessness; "for he whose hands are tied should have his tongue at freedom.—But thy glibness of reply, comrade," rejoined he, speaking to Athelstane, "will not win the freedom of the Lady Rowena."

To this Athelstane, who had already made a longer speech than was his custom to do on any topic, however interesting, returned no answer. The conversation was interrupted by the arrival of a menial, who an-nounced that a monk demanded admittance at the postern gate.

"In the name of Saint Bennet, the prince of these bull-beggars," said Front-de-Bœuf, "have we a real monk this time, or another impostor? Search him, slaves—for an ye suffer a second impostor to be palmed upon you, I will have your eyes torn out, and hot coals put into the sockets."

"Let me endure the extremity of your anger, my lord," said Giles, "if this be not a real shaveling. Your squire Jocelyn knows him well, and will vouch him to be brother Ambrose, a monk in attendance upon the Prior of Jorvaulx."

"Admit him," said Front-de-Bœuf; "most likely he brings us news from his jovial master. Surely the devil keeps holiday, and the priests are relieved from duty, that they are strolling thus wildly through the country. Remove these prisoners; and, Saxon, think on what thou hast heard."

"I claim," said Athelstane, "an honourable imprisonment, with due care of my board and of my couch, as becomes my rank, and as is due to one who is in treaty for ransom. Moreover, I hold him that deems himself the best of you, bound to answer to me with his body for this aggression on my freedom. This defiance hath already been sent to thee by thy sewer; thou underliest it, and art bound to answer me—There lies my glove."

"I answer not the challenge of my prisoner," said Front-de-Bœuf; "nor shalt thou, Maurice de Bracy.—Giles," he continued, "hang the franklin's glove upon the tine of yonder branched antlers: there it shall remain until he is a freeman. Should he then presume to demand it, or to affirm he was unlawfully made my prisoner, by the belt of Saint Christopher, he will speak to one who hath never refused to meet a foe on foot or on horseback, alone or with his vassals at his back!"

The Saxon prisoners were accordingly removed, just as they introduced the monk Ambrose, who appeared to be in great perturbation.

"This is the real *Deus vobiscum*," said Wamba, as he passed the reverend brother; "the others were but counterfeits."

"Holy Mother!" said the monk, as he addressed the assembled knights, "I am at last safe and in Christian keeping!"

"Safe thou art," replied De Bracy; "and for Christianity, here is the stout Baron Reginald Front-de-Bœuf, whose utter abomination is a Jew; and the Good Knight Templar, Brian de Bois-Guilbert, whose trade is to slay Saracens—If these are not good marks of Christianity, I know no other which they bear about them."

"Ye are friends and allies of our reverend father in God, Aymer, Prior of Jorvaulx," said the monk, without noticing the tone of De Bracy's reply; "ye owe him aid both by knightly faith and holy charity; for what saith the blessed Saint Augustin, in his treatise *De Civitate Dei*"——

"What saith the devil!" interrupted Front-de-Bœuf; "or rather what dost *thou* say, Sir Priest? We have little time to hear texts from the holy fathers."

"*Sancta Maria!*" ejaculated Father Ambrose, "how prompt to ire are these unhallowed laymen!—But be it known to you, brave knights, that certain murderous caitiffs, casting behind them fear of God, and reverence of his church, and not regarding the bull of the holy see, *Si quis, suadente Diabolo*"——

"Brother priest," said the Templar, "all this we know or guess at—tell us plainly, is thy master, the Prior, made prisoner, and to whom?"

"Surely," said Ambrose, "he is in the hands of the men of Belial, infesters of these woods, and contemners of the holy text, 'Touch not mine anointed, and do my prophets nought of evil.'"

"Here is a new argument for our swords, sirs," said Front-de-Bœuf, turning to his companions; "and so, instead of reaching us any assistance, the Prior of Jorvaulx requests aid at our hands? a man is well helped of these lazy churchmen when he hath most to do!—But speak out, priest, and say at once, what doth thy master expect from us?"

"So please you," said Ambrose, "violent hands having been imposed on my reverend superior, contrary to the holy ordinance, which I did already quote, and the men of Belial having rifled his mails and budgets, and stripped him of two hundred marks of pure refined gold, they do yet demand of him a large sum beside, ere they will suffer him to depart from their uncircumcised hands. Wherefore the reverend father in God prays you, as his dear friends, to rescue him, either by paying down the ransom at which they hold him, or by force of arms, at your best discretion."

"The foul fiend quell the Prior!" said Front-de-Bœuf; "his morning's draught has been a deep one. When did thy master hear of a Norman baron unbuckling his purse to relieve a churchman, whose bags are ten times as weighty as ours?—And how can we do aught by valour to free him, that are cooped up here by ten times our number, and expect an assault every moment?"

"And that was what I was about to tell you," said the monk, "had your hastiness allowed me time. But, God help me, I am old, and these foul onslaughts distract an aged man's brain. Nevertheless, it is of verity that they assemble a camp, and raise a bank against the walls of this castle."

"To the battlements!" cried De Bracy, "and let us mark what these knaves do without;" and so saying, he opened a latticed window which led to a sort of bartisan or projecting balcony, and immediately called from thence to those in the apartment—"Saint Dennis, but the old monk hath brought true tidings!—They bring forward mantelets and pavisses,[1] and the archers muster on the skirts of the wood like a dark cloud before a hailstorm."

Reginald Front-de-Bœuf also looked out upon the field, and immediately snatched his bugle; and, after winding a long and loud blast, commanded his men to their posts on the walls.

"De Bracy, look to the eastern side, where the walls are lowest—Noble Bois-Guilbert, thy trade hath well taught thee how to attack and defend, look thou to the western side—I myself will take post at the barbican. Yet, do not confine your exertions to any one spot, noble friends!—we must this day be everywhere, and multiply ourselves, were it possible, so as to carry by our presence succour and relief wherever the attack is hottest. Our numbers are few, but activity and courage may supply that defect, since we have only to do with rascal clowns."

"But, noble knights," exclaimed Father Ambrose, amidst the bustle and confusion occasioned by the preparations for defence, "will none of ye hear the message of the reverend father in God, Aymer, Prior of Jorvaulx?—I beseech thee to hear me, noble Sir Reginald!"

"Go patter thy petitions to heaven," said the fierce Norman, "for we on earth have no time to listen to them—Ho! there, Anselm! see that seething pitch and oil are ready to pour on the heads of these audacious

---

[1] Mantelets were temporary and movable defences formed of planks, under cover of which the assailants advanced to the attack of fortified places of old. Pavisses were a species of large shields covering the whole person, employed on the same occasions.

traitors—Look that the cross-bowmen lack not bolts.[1]--Fling abroad my banner with the old bull's head—the knaves shall soon find with whom they have to do this day!"

"But, noble sir," continued the monk, persevering in his endeavours to draw attention, "consider my vow of obedience, and let me discharge myself of my Superior's errand."

"Away with this prating dotard," said Front-de-Bœuf, "lock him up in the chapel, to tell his beads till the broil be over. It will be a new thing to the saints in Torquilstone to hear aves and paters; they have not been so honoured, I trow, since they were cut out of stone."

"Blaspheme not the holy saints, Sir Reginald," said De Bracy, "we shall have need of their aid to-day before yon rascal rout disband."

"I expect little aid from their hand," said Front-de-Bœuf, "unless we were to hurl them from the battlements on the heads of the villains. There is a huge lumbering Saint Christopher yonder, sufficient to bear a whole company to the earth."

The Templar had in the meantime been looking out on the proceedings of the besiegers, with rather more attention than the brutal Front-de-Bœuf or his giddy companion.

"By the faith of mine order," he said, "these men approach with more touch of discipline than could have been judged, however they come by it. See ye how dexterously they avail themselves of every cover which a tree or bush affords, and shun exposing themselves to the shot of our cross-bows? I spy neither banner nor pennon among them, and yet will I gage my golden chain, that they are led on by some noble knight or gentleman, skilful in the practice of wars."

"I espy him," said De Bracy; "I see the waving of a knight's crest, and the gleam of his armour. See yon tall man in the black mail, who is busied marshalling the farther troop of the rascaille yeomen—by Saint Dennis, I hold him to be the same whom we called *Le Noir Faineant*, who overthrew thee, Front-de-Bœuf, in the lists at Ashby."

"So much the better," said Front-de-Bœuf, "that he comes here to give me my revenge. Some hilding fellow he must be, who dared not stay to assert his claim to the tourney prize which chance had assigned him. I should in vain have sought for him where knights and nobles seek their foes, and right glad am I he hath here shown himself among yon villain yeomanry."

The demonstrations of the enemy's immediate approach cut off all farther discourse. Each knight repaired to his post, and at the head of the few followers whom they were able to muster, and who were in numbers inadequate to defend the whole extent of the walls; they awaited with calm determination the threatened assault.

---

[1] The bolt was the arrow peculiarly fitted to the cross-bow, as that of the long-bow was called a shaft. Hence the English proverb--"I will either make a shaft or bolt of it," signifying a determination to make one use or other of the thing spoken of.

CHAPTER XXVIII

This wandering race, sever'd from other men,
Boast yet their intercourse with human arts;
The seas, the woods, the deserts, which they haunt,
Find them acquainted with their secret treasures:
And unregarded herbs, and flowers, and blossoms,
Display undreamt-of powers when gather'd by them.
The Jew.

OUR history must needs retrograde for the space of a few pages, to inform the reader of certain passages material to his understanding the
rest of this important narrative. His own intelligence may indeed have
easily anticipated that, when Ivanhoe sunk down, and seemed abandoned
by all the world, it was the importunity of Rebecca which prevailed on
her father to have the gallant young warrior transported from the lists
to the house which for the time the Jews inhabited in the suburbs of
Ashby.

It would not have been difficult to have persuaded Isaac to this step
in any other circumstances, for his disposition was kind and grateful.
But he had also the prejudices and scrupulous timidity of his persecuted
people, and those were to be conquered.

"Holy Abraham!" he exclaimed, "he is a good youth, and my heart
bleeds to see the gore trickle down his rich embroidered hacqueton, and
his corslet of goodly price—but to carry him to our house!—damsel, hast
thou well considered?—he is a Christian, and by our law we may not
deal with the stranger and Gentile, save for the advantage of our commerce."

"Speak not so, my dear father," replied Rebecca; "we may not indeed mix with them in banquet and in jollity; but in wounds and in
misery, the Gentile becometh the Jew's brother."

"I would I knew what the Rabbi Jacob Ben Tudela would opine
on it," replied Isaac;—"nevertheless, the good youth must not bleed
to death. Let Seth and Reuben bear him to Ashby."

"Nay, let them place him in my litter," said Rebecca; "I will mount
one of the palfreys."

"That were to expose thee to the gaze of those dogs of Ishmael and
of Edom," whispered Isaac, with a suspicious glance towards the crowd
of knights and squires. But Rebecca was already busied in carrying
her charitable purpose into effect, and listed not what he said, until
Isaac, seizing the sleeve of her mantle, again exclaimed, in a hurried
voice—"Beard of Aaron!—what if the youth perish!—if he die in our
custody, shall we not be held guilty of his blood, and be torn to pieces
by the multitude?"

"He will not die, my father," said Rebecca, gently extricating herself
from the grasp of Isaac—"he will not die unless we abandon him; and
if so, we are indeed answerable for his blood to God and to man."

"Nay," said Isaac, releasing his hold, "it grieveth me as much to see the drops of his blood, as if they were so many golden byzants from mine own purse; and I well know, that the lessons of Miriam, daughter of the Rabbi Manasses of Byzantium, whose soul is in Paradise, have made thee skilful in the art of healing, and that thou knowest the craft of herbs and the force of elixirs. Therefore, do as thy mind giveth thee —thou art a good damsel, a blessing, and a crown, and a song of rejoicing unto me and unto my house, and unto the people of my fathers."

The apprehensions of Isaac, however, were not ill founded; and the generous and grateful benevolence of his daughter exposed her, on her return to Ashby, to the unhallowed gaze of Brian de Bois-Guilbert. The Templar twice passed and repassed them on the road, fixing his bold and ardent look on the beautiful Jewess; and we have already seen the consequences of the admiration which her charms excited, when accident threw her into the power of that unprincipled voluptuary.

Rebecca lost no time in causing the patient to be transported to their temporary dwelling, and proceeded with her own hands to examine and to bind up his wounds. The youngest reader of romances and romantic ballads must recollect how often the females, during the dark ages, as they are called, were initiated into the mysteries of surgery, and how frequently the gallant knight submitted the wounds of his person to her cure, whose eyes had yet more deeply penetrated his heart.

But the Jews, both male and female, possessed and practised the medical science in all its branches, and the monarchs and powerful barons of the time frequently committed themselves to the charge of some experienced sage among this despised people, when wounded or in sickness. The aid of the Jewish physicians was not the less eagerly sought after, though a general belief prevailed among the Christians, that the Jewish Rabbins were deeply acquainted with the occult sciences, and particularly with the cabalistical art, which had its name and origin in the studies of the sages of Israel. Neither did the Rabbins disown such acquaintance with supernatural arts, which added nothing (for what could add aught?) to the hatred with which their nation was regarded, while it diminished the contempt with which that malevolence was mingled. A Jewish magician might be the subject of equal abhorrence with a Jewish usurer, but he could not be equally despised. It is besides probable, considering the wonderful cures they are said to have performed, that the Jews possessed some secrets of the healing art peculiar to themselves, and which, with the exclusive spirit arising out of their condition, they took great care to conceal from the Christians amongst whom they dwelt.

The beautiful Rebecca had been heedfully brought up in all the knowledge proper to her nation, which her apt and powerful mind had retained, arranged, and enlarged, in the course of a progress beyond her years, her sex, and even the age in which she lived. Her knowledge of medicine and of the healing art had been acquired under an aged Jewess, the daughter of one of their most celebrated doctors, who loved Rebecca as her own child, and was believed to have communicated to her secrets, which had been left to herself by her sage father at the same time, and under the same circumstances. The fate of Miriam had been to fall a sacrifice to the fanaticism of the times; but her secrets had survived in her apt pupil.

Rebecca, thus endowed with knowledge as with beauty, was universally revered and admired by her own tribe, who almost regarded her as one of those gifted women mentioned in sacred history. Her father himself, out of reverence for her talents, which involuntarily mingled itself with his unbounded affection, permitted the maiden a greater liberty than was usually indulged to those of her sex by the habits of her people, and was, as we have just seen, frequently guided by her opinion, even in preference to his own.

When Ivanhoe reached the habitation of Isaac, he was still in a state of unconsciousness, owing to the profuse loss of blood which had taken place during his exertions in the lists. Rebecca examined the wound, and having applied to it such vulnerary remedies as her art prescribed, informed her father that if fever could be averted, of which the great bleeding rendered her little apprehensive, and if the healing balsam of Miriam retained its virtue, there was nothing to fear for his guest's life, and that he might with safety travel to York with them on the ensuing day. Isaac looked a little blank at this annunciation. His charity would willingly have stopped short at Ashby, or at most would have left the wounded Christian to be tended in the house where he was residing at present, with an assurance to the Hebrew to whom it belonged, that all expenses should be duly discharged. To this, however, Rebecca opposed many reasons, of which we shall only mention two that had peculiar weight with Isaac. The one was, that she would on no account put the phial of precious balsam into the hands of another physician even of her own tribe, lest that valuable mystery should be discovered; the other, that this wounded knight, Wilfred of Ivanhoe, was an intimate favourite of Richard Cœur-de-Lion, and that, in case the monarch should return, Isaac, who had supplied his brother John with treasure to prosecute his rebellious purposes, would stand in no small need of a powerful protector who enjoyed Richard's favour.

"Thou art speaking but sooth, Rebecca," said Isaac, giving way to these weighty arguments—"it were an offending of Heaven to betray the secrets of the blessed Miriam; for the good which Heaven giveth is not rashly to be squandered upon others, whether it be talents of gold and shekels of silver, or whether it be the secret mysteries of a wise physician —assuredly they should be preserved to those to whom Providence hath vouchsafed them. And him whom the Nazarenes of England call the Lion's Heart, assuredly it were better for me to fall into the hands of a strong lion of Idumea than into his, if he shall have got assurance of my dealing with his brother. Wherefore I will lend ear to thy counsel, and this youth shall journey with us unto York, and our house shall be as a home to him until his wounds shall be healed. And if he of the Lion Heart shall return to the land, as is now noised abroad, then shall this Wilfred of Ivanhoe be unto me as a wall of defence, when the king's displeasure shall burn high against thy father. And if he doth not return, this Wilfred may natheless repay us our charges when he shall gain treasure by the strength of his spear and of his sword, even as he did yesterday and this day also. For the youth is a good youth, and keepeth the day which he appointeth, and restoreth that which he borroweth, and succoureth the Israelite, even the child of my father's house, when he is encompassed by strong thieves and sons of Belial."

It was not until evening was nearly closed that Ivanhoe was restored to consciousness of his situation. He awoke from a broken slumber, under the confused impressions which are naturally attendant on the recovery from a state of insensibility. He was unable for some time to recall exactly to memory the circumstances which had preceded his fall in the lists, or to make out any connected chain of the events in which he had been engaged upon yesterday. A sense of wounds and injury, joined to great weakness and exhaustion, was mingled with the recollection of blows dealt and received, of steeds rushing upon each other, overthrowing and overthrown—of shouts and clashing of arms, and all the heady tumult of a confused fight. An effort to draw aside the curtain of his couch was in some degree successful, although rendered difficult by the pain of his wound.

To his great surprise he found himself in a room magnificently furnished, but having cushions instead of chairs to rest upon, and in other respects partaking so much of Oriental costume that he began to doubt whether he had not, during his sleep, been transported back again to the land of Palestine. The impression was increased, when, the tapestry being drawn aside, a female form, dressed in a rich habit, which partook more of the Eastern taste than that of Europe, glided through the door which it concealed, and was followed by a swarthy domestic.

As the wounded knight was about to address this fair apparition, she imposed silence by placing her slender finger upon her ruby lips, while the attendant, approaching him, proceeded to uncover Ivanhoe's side, and the lovely Jewess satisfied herself that the bandage was in its place, and the wound doing well. She performed her task with a graceful and dignified simplicity and modesty which might, even in more civilised days, have served to redeem it from whatever might seem repugnant to female delicacy. The idea of so young and beautiful a person engaged in attendance on a sick-bed, or in dressing the wound of one of a different sex, was melted away and lost in that of a beneficent being contributing her effectual aid to relieve pain, and to avert the stroke of death. Rebecca's few and brief directions were given in the Hebrew language to the old domestic; and he, who had been frequently her assistant in similar cases, obeyed them without reply.

The accents of an unknown tongue, however harsh they might have sounded when uttered by another, had, coming from the beautiful Rebecca, the romantic and pleasing effect which fancy ascribes to the charms pronounced by some beneficent fairy, unintelligible, indeed, to the ear, but, from the sweetness of utterance, and benignity of aspect, which accompanied them, touching and affecting to the heart. Without making an attempt at further question, Ivanhoe suffered them in silence to take the measures they thought most proper for his recovery; and it was not until those were completed, and this kind physician about to retire, that his curiosity could no longer be suppressed.—"Gentle maiden," he began in the Arabian tongue, with which his Eastern travels had rendered him familiar, and which he thought most likely to be understood by the turban'd and caftan'd damsel who stood before him—"I pray you, gentle maiden, of your courtesy"——

But here he was interrupted by his fair physician, a smile which she could scarce suppress dimpling for an instant a face whose general expression was that of contemplative melancholy. "I am of England, Sir Knight, and speak the English tongue, although my dress and my lineage belong to another climate."

"Noble damsel,"—again the Knight of Ivanhoe began; and again Rebecca hastened to interrupt him.

"Bestow not on me, Sir Knight," she said, "the epithet of noble. It is well you should speedily know that your hand-maiden is a poor Jewess, the daughter of that Isaac of York, to whom you were so lately a good and kind lord. It well becomes him, and those of his household, to render to you such careful tendance as your present state necessarily demands."

I know not whether the fair Rowena would have been altogether satisfied with the species of emotion with which her devoted knight had hitherto gazed on the beautiful features, and fair form, and lustrous eyes of the lovely Rebecca; eyes whose brilliancy was shaded, and, as it were, mellowed, by the fringe of her long silken eye-lashes, and which a minstrel would have compared to the evening star darting its rays through a bower of jessamine. But Ivanhoe was too good a Catholic to retain the same class of feelings towards a Jewess. This Rebecca had foreseen, and for this very purpose she had hastened to mention her father's name and lineage; yet—for the fair and wise daughter of Isaac was not without a touch of female weakness—she could not but sigh internally when the glance of respectful admiration, not altogether unmixed with tenderness, with which Ivanhoe had hitherto regarded his unknown benefactress, was exchanged at once for a manner cold, composed, and collected, and fraught with no deeper feeling than that which expressed a grateful sense of courtesy received from an unexpected quarter, and from one of an inferior race. It was not that Ivanhoe's former carriage expressed more than that general devotional homage which youth always pays to beauty; yet it was mortifying that one word should operate as a spell to remove poor Rebecca, who could not be supposed altogether ignorant of her title

to such homage, into a degraded class, to whom it could not be honourably rendered.

But the gentleness and candour of Rebecca's nature imputed no fault
to Ivanhoe for sharing in the universal prejudices of his age and religion. On the contrary, the fair Jewess, though sensible her patient now
regarded her as one of a race of reprobation, with whom it was disgraceful to hold any beyond the most necessary intercourse, ceased not to
pay the same patient and devoted attention to his safety and convales-
cence. She informed him of the necessity they were under of removing
to York, and of her father's resolution to transport him thither, and
tend him in his own house until his health should be restored. Ivanhoe
expressed great repugnance to this plan, which he grounded on unwillingness to give farther trouble to his benefactors.

"Was there not," he said, "in Ashby, or near it, some Saxon franklin,
or even some wealthy peasant, who would endure the burden of a
wounded countryman's residence with him until he should be again able
to bear his armour?—Was there no convent of Saxon endowment where
he could be received?—Or could he not be transported as far as Burton, where he was sure to find hospitality with Waltheoff, the Abbot of
St. Withold's, to whom he was related?"

"Any, the worst of these harbourages," said Rebecca, with a melancholy smile, "would unquestionably be more fitting for your residence
than the abode of a despised Jew; yet, Sir Knight, unless you would dismiss your physician, you cannot change your lodging. Our nation, as
you well know, can cure wounds, though we deal not in inflicting them:
and in our own family, in particular, are secrets which have been handed
down since the days of Solomon, and of which you have already experienced the advantages. No Nazarene—I crave your forgiveness, Sir Knight
—no Christian leech within the four seas of Britain could enable you
to bear your corslet within a month."

"And how soon wilt *thou* enable me to brook it?" said Ivanhoe impatiently.

"Within eight days, if thou wilt be patient and conformable to my
directions," replied Rebecca.

"By Our Blessed Lady," said Wilfred, "if it be not a sin to name
her here, it is no time for me or any true knight to be bedridden; and
if thou accomplish thy promise, maiden, I will pay thee with my casque
full of crowns, come by them as I may."

"I will accomplish my promise," said Rebecca, "and thou shalt bear
thine armour on the eighth day from hence, if thou wilt grant me but
one boon in the stead of the silver thou dost promise me."

"If it be within my power, and such as a true Christian knight may
yield to one of thy people," replied Ivanhoe, "I will grant thy boon
blithely and thankfully."

"Nay," answered Rebecca, "I will but pray of thee to believe henceforward that a Jew may do good service to a Christian without desiring

other guerdon than the blessing of the Great Father who made both Jew and Gentile."

"It were a sin to doubt it, maiden," replied Ivanhoe; "and I repose myself on thy skill without further scruple or question, well trusting you will enable me to bear my corslet on the eighth day. And now, my kind leech, let me enquire of the news abroad. What of the noble Saxon Cedric and his household?—what of the lovely Lady"—— He stopt, as if unwilling to speak Rowena's name in the house of a Jew—"Of her, I mean, who was named Queen of the tournament?"

"And who was selected by you, Sir Knight, to hold that dignity, with judgment which was admired as much as your valour," replied Rebecca.

The blood which Ivanhoe had lost did not prevent a flush from crossing his cheek, feeling that he had incautiously betrayed his deep interest in Rowena by the awkward attempt he had made to conceal it.

"It was less of her I would speak," said he, "than of Prince John; and I would fain know somewhat of a faithful squire, and why he now attends me not?"

"Let me use my authority as a leech," answered Rebecca; "and enjoin you to keep silence, and avoid agitating reflections, whilst I apprise you of what you desire to know. Prince John hath broken off the tournament, and set forward in all haste towards York, with the nobles, knights, and churchmen of his party, after collecting such sums as they could wring, by fair means or foul, from those who are esteemed the wealthy of the land. It is said he designs to assume his brother's crown."

"Not without a blow struck in its defence," said Ivanhoe, raising himself upon the couch, "if there were but one true subject of England. I will fight for Richard's title with the best of them—ay, one or two, in his just quarrel!"

"But that you may be able to do so," said Rebecca, touching his shoulder with her hand, "you must now observe my directions, and remain quiet."

"True, maiden," said Ivanhoe, "as quiet as these disquieted times will permit—And of Cedric and his household?"

"His steward came but brief while since," said the Jewess, "panting with haste, to ask my father for certain monies, the price of wool the growth of Cedric's flocks, and from him I learned that Cedric and Athelstane of Coningsburgh had left Prince John's lodging in high displeasure, and were about to set forth on their return homeward."

"Went any lady with them to the banquet?" said Wilfred.

"The Lady Rowena," said Rebecca, answering the question with more precision than it had been asked—"The Lady Rowena went not to the Prince's feast, and, as the steward reported to us, she is now on her journey back to Rotherwood with her guardian Cedric. And touching your faithful squire Gurth"——

"Ha!" exclaimed the knight, "knowest thou his name?—But thou dost," he immediately added, "and well thou mayst, for it was from thy hand, and, as I am now convinced, from thine own generosity of spirit, that he received but yesterday a hundred zecchins."

"Speak not of that," said Rebecca, blushing deeply; "I see how easy it is for the tongue to betray what the heart would gladly conceal."

"But this sum of gold," said Ivanhoe, gravely, "my honour is concerned in repaying it to your father."

"Let it be as thou wilt," said Rebecca, "when eight days have passed away; but think not, and speak not now, of aught that may retard thy recovery."

"Be it so, kind maiden," said Ivanhoe; "I were most ungrateful to dispute thy commands. But one word of the fate of poor Gurth, and I have done with questioning thee."

"I grieve to tell thee, Sir Knight," answered the Jewess, "that he is in custody by the order of Cedric."—And then, observing the distress which her communication gave to Wilfred, she instantly added, "But the steward Oswald said, that if nothing occurred to renew his master's displeasure against him, he was sure that Cedric would pardon Gurth, a faithful serf, and one who stood high in favour, and who had but committed this error out of the love which he bore to Cedric's son. And he said, moreover, that he and his comrades, and especially Wamba the Jester, were resolved to warn Gurth to make his escape by the way, in case Cedric's ire against him could not be mitigated."

"Would to God they may keep their purpose!" said Ivanhoe; "but it seems as if I were destined to bring ruin on whomsoever hath shown kindness to me. My king, by whom I was honoured and distinguished, thou seest that the brother most indebted to him is raising his arms to grasp his crown;—my regard hath brought restraint and trouble on the fairest of her sex;—and now my father in his mood may slay this poor bondsman but for his love and loyal service to me!—Thou seest, maiden, what an ill-fated wretch thou dost labour to assist; be wise and let me go ere the misfortunes which track my footsteps like slot-hounds shall involve thee also in their pursuit."

"Nay," said Rebecca, "thy weakness and thy grief, Sir Knight, make thee miscalculate the purposes of Heaven. Thou hast been restored to thy country when it most needed the assistance of a strong hand and a true heart, and thou hast humbled the pride of thine enemies and those of thy king, when their horn was most highly exalted; and for the evil which thou hast sustained, seest thou not that Heaven has raised thee a helper and a physician, even among the most despised of the land?— Therefore, be of good courage, and trust that thou art preserved for some marvel which thine arm shall work before this people. Adieu— and having taken the medicine which I shall send thee by the hand of Reuben, compose thyself again to rest, that thou mayest be the more able to endure the journey on the succeeding day."

Ivanhoe was convinced by the reasoning, and obeyed the directions, of Rebecca. The draught which Reuben administered was of a sedative and narcotic quality, and secured the patient sound and undisturbed slumbers. In the morning his kind physician found him entirely free from feverish symptoms, and fit to undergo the fatigue of a journey.

He was deposited in the horse-litter which had brought him from the lists, and every precaution taken for his travelling with ease. In one circumstance only even the entreaties of Rebecca were unable to secure sufficient attention to the accommodation of the wounded knight. Isaac, like the enriched traveller of Juvenal's tenth satire, had ever the fear of robbery before his eyes, conscious that he would be alike accounted fair game by the marauding Norman noble and by the Saxon outlaw. He therefore journeyed at a great rate and made short halts, and shorter repasts, so that he passed by Cedric and Athelstane who had several hours the start of him, but who had been delayed by their protracted feasting at the convent of Saint Withold's. Yet such was the virtue of Miriam's balsam, or such the strength of Ivanhoe's constitution, that he did not sustain from the hurried journey that inconvenience which his kind physician had apprehended.

In another point of view, however, the Jew's haste proved somewhat more than good speed. The rapidity with which he insisted on travelling bred several disputes between him and the party whom he had hired to attend him as a guard. These men were Saxons, and not free by any means from the national love of ease and good living which the Normans stigmatised as laziness and gluttony. Reversing Shylock's position, they had accepted the employment in hopes of feeding upon the wealthy Jew, and were very much displeased when they found themselves disappointed by the rapidity with which he insisted on their proceeding. They remonstrated also upon the risk of damage to their horses by these forced marches. Finally, there arose betwixt Isaac and his satellites a deadly feud concerning the quantity of wine and ale to be allowed for consumption at each meal. And thus it happened, that when the alarm of danger approached, and that which Isaac feared was likely to come upon him, he was deserted by the discontented mercenaries on whose protection he had relied without using the means necessary to secure their attachment.

In this deplorable condition the Jew, with his daughter and his wounded patient, were found by Cedric, as has already been noticed, and soon afterwards fell into the power of De Bracy and his confederates. Little notice was at first taken of the horse-litter, and it might have remained behind but for the curiosity of De Bracy, who looked into it under the impression that it might contain the object of his enterprise, for Rowena had not unveiled herself. But De Bracy's astonishment was considerable, when he discovered that the litter contained a wounded man, who, conceiving himself to have fallen into the power of Saxon outlaws, with whom his name might be a protection for himself and his friends, frankly avowed himself to be Wilfred of Ivanhoe.

The ideas of chivalrous honour, which, amidst his wildness and levity, never utterly abandoned De Bracy, prohibited him from doing the knight any injury in his defenceless condition, and equally interdicted his be-traying him to Front-de-Bœuf, who would have had no scruples to put to death, under any circumstances, the rival claimant of the fief of Ivanhoe. On the other hand, to liberate a suitor preferred by the Lady Rowena, as the events of the tournament, and indeed Wilfred's previous banishment from his father's house, had made matter of notoriety, was a pitch far above the flight of De Bracy's generosity. A middle course betwixt good and evil was all which he found himself capable of adopt-ing, and he commanded two of his own squires to keep close by the litter, and to suffer no one to approach it. If questioned, they were directed by their master to say that the empty litter of the Lady Ro-wena was employed to transport one of their comrades who had been wounded in the scuffle. On arriving at Torquilstone, while the Knight Templar and the lord of that castle were each intent upon their own schemes, the one on the Jew's treasure, and the other on his daughter De Bracy's squires conveyed Ivanhoe, still under the name of a wounded comrade, to a distant apartment. This explanation was accordingly re-turned by these men to Front-de-Bœuf, when he questioned them why they did not make for the battlements upon the alarm.

"A wounded companion!" he replied in great wrath and astonishment. "No wonder that churls and yeomen wax so presumptuous as even to lay leaguer before castles, and that clowns and swineherds send defiances to nobles, since men-at-arms have turned sick men's nurses, and Free Companions are grown keepers of dying folk's curtains, when the castle is about to be assailed.—To the battlements, ye loitering villains!" he exclaimed, raising his stentorian voice till the arches around rung again, "to the battlements, or I will splinter your bones with this truncheon!"

The men sulkily replied, "that they desired nothing better than to go to the battlements, providing Front-de-Bœuf would bear them out with their master, who had commanded them to tend the dying man."

"The dying man, knaves!" rejoined the Baron; "I promise thee we shall all be dying men an we stand not to it the more stoutly. But I will relieve the guard upon this caitiff companion of yours.—Here, Urfried —hag—fiend of a Saxon witch—hearest me not?—tend me this bed-ridden fellow, since he must needs be tended, whilst these knaves use their weapons.—Here be two arblasts, comrades, with windlaces and quarrells [1]—to the barbican with you, and see you drive each bolt through a Saxon brain."

The men, who, like most of their description, were fond of enterprise and detested inaction, went joyfully to the scene of danger, as they were commanded, and thus the charge of Ivanhoe was transferred to Urfried, or Ulrica. But she, whose brain was burning with remembrance

---

[1] The arblast was a cross-bow, the windlace the machine used in bending that weapon, and the quarrell, so called from its square or diamond-shaped head, was the bolt adapted to it.

of injuries and hopes of vengeance, was readily induced to devolve upon Rebecca the care of her patient.

CHAPTER XXIX

Ascend the watch-tower yonder, valiant soldier,
Look on the field, and say how goes the battle.
              SCHILLER's *Maid of Orleans.*

A MOMENT of peril is often also a moment of open-hearted kindness and affection. We are thrown off our guard by the general agitation of our feelings, and betray the intensity of those, which, at more tranquil periods, our prudence at least conceals, if it cannot altogether suppress them. In finding herself once more by the side of Ivanhoe, Rebecca was astonished at the keen sensation of pleasure which she experienced, even at a time when all around them both was danger, if not despair. As she felt his pulse, and enquired after his health, there was a softness in her touch and in her accents, implying a kinder interest than she would herself have been pleased to have voluntarily expressed. Her voice faltered and her hand trembled, and it was only the cold question of Ivanhoe, "Is it you, gentle maiden?" which recalled her to herself, and reminded her the sensations which she felt were not and could not be mutual. A sigh escaped, but it was scarce audible; and the questions which she asked the knight concerning his state of health were put in the tone of calm friendship. Ivanhoe answered her hastily that he was, in point of health, as well, and better than he could have expected—"Thanks," he said, "dear Rebecca, to thy helpful skill."

"He calls me *dear* Rebecca," said the maiden to herself, "but it is in the cold and careless tone which ill suits the word. His war-horse—his hunting hound, are dearer to him than the despised Jewess!"

"My mind, gentle maiden," continued Ivanhoe, "is more disturbed by anxiety, than my body with pain. From the speeches of these men who were my warders just now, I learn that I am a prisoner, and, if I judge aright of the loud hoarse voice which even now dispatched them hence on some military duty, I am in the castle of Front-de-Bœuf—If so, how will this end, or how can I protect Rowena and my father?"

"He names not the Jew or Jewess," said Rebecca, internally; "Yet what is our portion in him, and how justly am I punished by Heaven for letting my thoughts dwell upon him!" She hastened after this brief self-accusation to give Ivanhoe what information she could; but it amounted only to this, that the Templar Bois-Guilbert, and the Baron Front-de-Bœuf, were commanders within the castle; that it was beleaguered from without, but by whom she knew not. She added that there was a Christian priest within the castle who might be possessed of more information.

"A Christian priest!" said the knight, joyfully; "fetch him hither,

Rebecca, if thou canst—say a sick man desires his ghostly counsel—say what thou wilt, but bring him—something I must do or attempt, but how can I determine until I know how matters stand without?"

Rebecca, in compliance with the wishes of Ivanhoe, made that attempt to bring Cedric into the wounded knight's chamber which was defeated as we have already seen by the interference of Urfried, who had been also on the watch to intercept the supposed monk. Rebecca retired to communicate to Ivanhoe the result of her errand.

They had not much leisure to regret the failure of this source of intelligence, or to contrive by what means it might be supplied; for the noise within the castle, occasioned by the defensive preparations which had been considerable for some time, now increased into tenfold bustle and clamour. The heavy, yet hasty step of the men-at-arms, traversed the battlements, or resounded on the narrow and winding passages and stairs which led to the various bartisans and points of defence. The voices of the knights were heard animating their followers or directing means of defence, while their commands were often drowned in the clashing of armour or the clamorous shouts of those whom they addressed. Tremendous as these sounds were, and yet more terrible from the awful event which they presaged, there was a sublimity mixed with them which Rebecca's high-toned mind could feel even in that moment of terror. Her eye kindled, although the blood fled from her cheeks; and there was a strong mixture of fear, and of a thrilling sense of the sublime, as she repeated, half whispering to herself, half speaking to her companion, the sacred text,—"The quiver rattleth—the glittering spear and the shield—the noise of the captains and the shouting!"

But Ivanhoe was like the war-horse of that sublime passage, glowing with impatience at his inactivity, and with his ardent desire to mingle in the affray of which these sounds were the introduction. "If I could but drag myself," he said, "to yonder window, that I might see how this brave game is like to go—If I had but bow to shoot a shaft, or battle-axe to strike were it but a single blow for our deliverance!—It is in vain—it is in vain—I am alike nerveless and weaponless!"

"Fret not thyself, noble knight," answered Rebecca, "that sounds have ceased of a sudden—it may be they join not battle."

"Thou knowest nought of it," said Wilfred, impatiently; "this dead pause only shows that the men are at their posts on the walls, and expecting an instant attack; what we have heard was but the instant muttering of the storm—it will burst anon in all its fury—Could I but reach yonder window!"

"Thou wilt but injure thyself by the attempt, noble knight," replied his attendant. Observing his extreme solicitude, she firmly added, "I myself will stand at the lattice, and describe to you as I can what passes without."

"You must not—you shall not!" exclaimed Ivanhoe; "each lattice, each aperture, will be soon a mark for the archers; some random shaft"——

"It shall be welcome!" murmured Rebecca, as with firm pace she ascended two or three steps, which led to the window of which they spoke.

"Rebecca, dear Rebecca!" exclaimed Ivanhoe, "this is no maiden's pastime—do not expose thyself to wounds and death, and render me for ever miserable for having given the occasion; at least, cover thyself with yonder ancient buckler, and show as little of your person at the lattice as may be."

Following with wonderful promptitude the directions of Ivanhoe, and availing herself of the protection of the large ancient shield, which she placed against the lower part of the window, Rebecca, with tolerable security to herself, could witness part of what was passing without the castle, and report to Ivanhoe the preparations which the assailants were making for the storm. Indeed the situation which she thus obtained was peculiarly favourable for this purpose, because, being placed on an angle of the main building, Rebecca could not only see what passed beyond the precincts of the castle, but also commanded a view of the outwork likely to be the first object of the meditated assault. It was an exterior fortification of no great height or strength, intended to protect the postern-gate, through which Cedric had been recently dismissed by Front-de-Bœuf. The castle moat divided this species of barbican from the rest of the fortress, so that, in case of its being taken, it was easy to cut off the communication with the main building, by withdrawing the temporary bridge. In the outwork was a sallyport corresponding to the postern of the castle, and the whole was surrounded by a strong palisade. Rebecca could observe, from the number of men placed for the defence of this post, that the besieged entertained apprehensions for its safety; and from the mustering of the assailants in a direction nearly opposite to the outwork, it seemed no less plain that it had been selected as a vulnerable point of attack.

These appearances she hastily communicated to Ivanhoe, and added, "The skirts of the wood seem lined with archers, although only a few are advanced from its dark shadow."

"Under what banner?" asked Ivanhoe.

"Under no ensign of war which I can observe," answered Rebecca.

"A singular novelty," muttered the knight, "to advance to storm such a castle without pennon or banner displayed!—Seest thou who they be that act as leaders?"

"A knight, clad in sable armour, is the most conspicuous," said the Jewess; "he alone is armed from head to heel, and seems to assume the direction of all around him."

"What device does he bear on his shield?" replied Ivanhoe.

"Something resembling a bar of iron, and a padlock painted blue on the black shield." [1]

"A fetterlock and shacklebolt azure," said Ivanhoe! "I know not who may bear the device, but well I ween it might now be mine own. Canst thou not see the motto?"

"Scarce the device itself at this distance," replied Rebecca; "but when the sun glances fair upon the shield, it shows as I tell you."

"Seem there no other leaders?" exclaimed the anxious enquirer.

"None of mark and distinction that I can behold from this station," said Rebecca; "but, doubtless, the other side of the castle is also assailed. They appear even now preparing to advance—God of Zion, protect us!—What a dreadful sight!—Those who advance first bear huge shields and defences made of plank; the others follow, bending their bows as they come on.—They raise their bows!—God of Moses, forgive the creatures thou hast made!"

Her description was here suddenly interrupted by the signal for assault, which was given by the blast of a shrill bugle, and at once answered by a flourish of the Norman trumpets from the battlements, which, mingled with the deep and hollow clang of the nakers (a species of kettle-drum), retorted in notes of defiance the challenge of the enemy. The shouts of both parties augmented the fearful din, the assailants crying, "Saint George for merry England!" and the Normans answering them with loud cries of *En avant De Bracy!—Beauseant! Beauseant!—Front-de-Bœuf à la rescourse!* according to the war-cries of their different commanders.

It was not, however, by clamour that the contest was to be decided, and the desperate efforts of the assailants were met by an equally vigorous defence on the part of the besieged. The archers, trained by their woodland pastimes to the most effective use of the long-bow, shot, to use the appropriate phrase of the time, so "wholly together," that no point at which a defender could show the least part of his person, escaped their cloth-yard shafts. By this heavy discharge, which continued as thick and sharp as hail, while, notwithstanding, every arrow had its individual aim, and flew by scores together against each embrasure and opening in the parapets, as well as at every window where a defender either occasionally had post, or might be suspected to be stationed,—by this sustained discharge, two or three of the garrison were slain, and several others wounded. But, confident in their armour of proof, and in the cover which their situation afforded, the followers of Front-de-Bœuf, and his allies, showed an obstinacy in defence proportioned to the fury of

---

[1] The author has been here upbraided with false heraldry, as having charged metal upon metal. It should be remembered, however, that heraldry had only its first rude origin during the Crusades, and that all the minutiæ of its fantastic science were the work of time, and introduced at a much later period. Those who think otherwise must suppose that the Goddess of *Armoirers,* like the Goddess of Arms, sprung into the world completely equipped in all the gaudy trappings of the department she presides over.

the attack, and replied with the discharge of their large cross-bows, as well as with their long-bows, slings, and other missile weapons, to the close and continued shower of arrows; and, as the assailants were necessarily but indifferently protected, did considerably more damage than they received at their hand. The whizzing of shafts and of missiles, on both sides, was only interrupted by the shouts which arose when either side inflicted or sustained some notable loss.

"And I must lie here like a bedridden monk," exclaimed Ivanhoe, "while the game that gives me freedom or death is played out by the hand of others!—Look from the window once again, kind maiden, but beware that you are not marked by the archers beneath—Look out once more, and tell me if they yet advance to the storm."

With patient courage, strengthened by the interval which she had employed in mental devotion, Rebecca again took post at the lattice, sheltering herself, however, so as not to be visible from beneath.

"What dost thou see, Rebecca?" again demanded the wounded knight.

"Nothing but the cloud of arrows flying so thick as to dazzle mine eyes, and to hide the bowmen who shoot them."

"That cannot endure," said Ivanhoe; "if they press not right on to carry the castle by pure force of arms, the archery may avail but little against stone walls and bulwarks. Look for the Knight of the Fetterlock, fair Rebecca, and see how he bears himself; for as the leader is, so will his followers be."

"I see him not," said Rebecca.

"Foul craven!" exclaimed Ivanhoe; "does he blench from the helm when the wind blows highest?"

"He blenches not! he blenches not!" said Rebecca, "I see him now; he leads a body of men close under the outer barrier of the barbican.[1]— They pull down the piles and palisades; they hew down the barriers with axes.—His high black plume floats abroad over the throng, like a raven over the field of the slain.—They have made a breach in the barriers— they rush in—they are thrust back!—Front-de-Bœuf heads the defenders; I see his gigantic form above the press. They throng again to the breach, and the pass is disputed hand to hand, and man to man. God of Jacob! it is the meeting of two fierce tides—the conflict of two oceans moved by adverse winds!"

She turned her head from the lattice, as if unable longer to endure a sight so terrible.

"Look forth again, Rebecca," said Ivanhoe, mistaking the cause of her retiring; "the archery must in some degree have ceased, since they are now fighting hand to hand.—Look again, there is now less danger."

---

[1] Every Gothic castle and city had, beyond the outer-walls, a fortification composed of palisades, called the barriers, which were often the scene of severe skirmishes, as these must necessarily be carried before the walls themselves could be approached. Many of those valiant feats of arms which adorn the chivalrous pages of Froissart took place at the barriers of besieged places.

Rebecca again looked forth, and almost immediately exclaimed, "Holy prophets of the law! Front-de-Bœuf and the Black Knight fight hand to hand on the breach, amid the roar of their followers, who watch the progress of the strife—Heaven strike with the cause of the oppressed and of the captive!" She then uttered a loud shriek, and exclaimed, "He is down!—he is down!"

"Who is down?" cried Ivanhoe; "for our dear Lady's sake, tell me which has fallen?"

"The Black Knight," answered Rebecca, faintly; then instantly again shouted with joyful eagerness—"But no—but no!—the name of the Lord of Hosts be blessed!—he is on foot again, and fights as if there were twenty men's strength in his single arm—His sword is broken— he snatches an axe from a yeoman—he presses Front-de-Bœuf with blow on blow—The giant stoops and totters like an oak under the steel of the woodman—he falls—he falls!"

"Front-de-Bœuf?" exclaimed Ivanhoe.

"Front-de-Bœuf!" answered the Jewess; "his men rush to the rescue, headed by the haughty Templar—their united force compels the champion to pause—They drag Front-de-Bœuf within the walls."

"The assailants have won the barriers, have they not?" said Ivanhoe.

"They have—they have!" exclaimed Rebecca—"and they press the besieged hard upon the outer wall; some plant ladders, some swarm like bees, and endeavour to ascend upon the shoulders of each other—down go stones, beams, and trunks of trees upon their heads, and as fast as they bear the wounded to the rear, fresh men supply their places in the assault—Great God! hast thou given men thine own image, that it should be thus cruelly defaced by the hands of their brethren!"

"Think not of that," said Ivanhoe; "this is no time for such thought —Who yield?—who push their way?"

"The ladders are thrown down," replied Rebecca, shuddering; "the soldiers lie grovelling under them like crushed reptiles—The besieged have the better."

"Saint George strike for us!" exclaimed the knight; "do the false yeomen give way?"

"No!" exclaimed Rebecca, "they bear themselves right yeomanly —the Black Knight approaches the postern with his huge axe—the thundering blows which he deals, you may hear above all the din and shouts of the battle—Stones and beams are hailed down on the bold champion —he regards them no more than if they were thistledown or feathers!"

"By Saint John of Acre," said Ivanhoe, raising himself joyfully on his couch, "methought there were but one man in England that might do such a deed!"

"The postern gate shakes," continued Rebecca, "it crashes—it is splintered by his blows—they rush in—the outwork is won—Oh, God! —they hurl the defenders from the battlements—they throw them into the moat—O men, if ye be indeed men, spare them that can resist no longer!"

"The bridge—the bridge which communicates with the castle—have they won that pass?" exclaimed Ivanhoe.

"No," replied Rebecca, "the Templar has destroyed the plank on which they crossed—few of the defenders escaped with him into the castle—the shrieks and cries which you hear tell the fate of the others —Alas!—I see it is still more difficult to look upon victory than upon battle."

"What do they now, maiden?" said Ivanhoe; "look forth yet again— this is no time to faint at bloodshed."

"It is over for the time," answered Rebecca; "our friends strengthen themselves within the outwork which they have mastered, and it affords them so good a shelter from the foemen's shot, that the garrison only bestow a few bolts on it from interval to interval, as if rather to disquiet than effectually to injure them."

"Our friends," said Wilfred, "will surely not abandon an enterprise so gloriously begun and so happily attained.—O no! I will put my faith in the good knight whose axe hath rent heart-of-oak and bars of iron.—Singular," he again muttered to himself, "if there be two who can do a deed of such *derring-do!*—a fetterlock, and a shacklebolt on a field sable—what may that mean?—seest thou nought else, Rebecca, by which the Black Knight may be distinguished?"

"Nothing," said the Jewess; "all about him is black as the wing of the night raven. Nothing can I spy that can mark him further—but having once seen him put forth his strength in battle, methinks I could know him again among a thousand warriors. He rushes to the fray as if he were summoned to a banquet. There is more than mere strength, there seems as if the whole soul and spirit of the champion were given to every blow which he deals upon his enemies. God assoilzie him of the sin of bloodshed!—it is fearful, yet magnificent, to behold how the arm and heart of one man can triumph over hundreds."

"Rebecca," said Ivanhoe, "thou hast painted a hero; surely they rest but to refresh their force, or to provide the means of crossing the moat—Under such a leader as thou hast spoken this knight to be, there are no craven fears, no cold-blooded delays, no yielding up a gallant emprise; since the difficulties which render it arduous render it also glorious. I swear by the honour of my house—I vow by the name of my bright lady-love, I would endure ten years' captivity to fight one day by that good knight's side in such a quarrel as this!"

"Alas," said Rebecca, leaving her station at the window, and approaching the couch of the wounded knight, "this impatient yearning after action—this struggling with and repining at your present weakness, will not fail to injure your returning health—How couldst thou hope to inflict wounds on others, ere that be healed which thou thyself hast received?"

"Rebecca," he replied, "thou knowest not how impossible it is for one trained to actions of chivalry to remain passive as a priest, or a woman, when they are acting deeds of honour around him. The love of battle is the food upon which we live—the dust of the *mêlée* is the breath of our nostrils! We live not—we wish not to live—longer than while we are victorious and renowned—Such, maiden, are the laws of chivalry to which we are sworn, and to which we offer all that we hold dear."

"Alas!" said the fair Jewess, "and what is it, valiant knight, save an offering of sacrifice to a demon of vainglory, and a passing through the fire to Moloch!—What remains to you as the prize of all the blood you have spilled—of all the travail and pain you have endured—of all the tears which your deeds have caused, when death hath broken the strong man's spear, and overtaken the speed of his war-horse?"

"What remains?" cried Ivanhoe; "Glory, maiden, glory! which gilds our sepulchre and embalms our name."

"Glory?" continued Rebecca; "alas, is the rusted mail which hangs as a hatchment over the champion's dim and mouldering tomb—is the defaced sculpture of the inscription which the ignorant monk can hardly read to the enquiring pilgrim—are these sufficient rewards for the sacrifice of every kindly affection, for a life spent miserably that ye may make others miserable? Or is there such virtue in the rude rhymes of a wandering bard, that domestic love, kindly affection, peace, and happiness are so wildly bartered, to become the hero of those ballads which vagabond minstrels sing to drunken churls over their evening ale?"

"By the soul of Hereward!" replied the knight impatiently, "thou speakest, maiden, of thou knowest not what. Thou wouldst quench the pure light of chivalry, which alone distinguishes the noble from the base, the gentle knight from the churl and the savage; which rates our life far, far beneath the pitch of our honour; raises us victorious over pain, toil, and suffering, and teaches us to fear no evil but disgrace. Thou art no Christian, Rebecca; and to thee are unknown those high feelings which swell the bosom of a noble maiden when her lover hath done some deed of emprise which sanctions his flame. Chivalry!—why, maiden, she is the nurse of pure and high affection—the stay of the oppressed, the redresser of grievances, the curb of the power of the tyrant—Nobility were but an empty name without her, and liberty finds the best protection in her lance and her sword."

"I am, indeed," said Rebecca, "sprung from a race whose courage was distinguished in the defence of their own land, but who warred not, even while yet a nation, save at the command of the Deity, or in defending their country from oppression. The sound of the trumpet wakes Judah no longer, and her despised children are now but the unresisting victims of hostile and military oppression. Well hast thou spoken, Sir Knight, —until the God of Jacob shall raise up for his chosen people a second

Gideon, or a new Maccabeus, it ill beseemeth the Jewish damsel to speak of battle or of war."

The high-minded maiden concluded the argument in a tone of sorrow, which deeply expressed her sense of the degradation of her people, embittered perhaps by the idea that Ivanhoe considered her as one not entitled to interfere in a case of honour, and incapable of entertaining or expressing sentiments of honour and generosity.

"How little he knows this bosom," she said, "to imagine that cowardice or meanness of soul must needs be its guests, because I have censured the fantastic chivalry of the Nazarenes! Would to heaven that the shedding of mine own blood, drop by drop, could redeem the captivity of Judah! Nay, would to God it could avail to set free my father, and this his benefactor, from the chains of the oppressor! The proud Christian should then see whether the daughter of God's chosen people dared not to die as bravely as the vainest Nazarene maiden, that boasts her descent from some petty chieftain of the rude and frozen north!"

She then looked towards the couch of the wounded knight.

"He sleeps," she said; "nature exhausted by sufferance and the waste of spirits, his wearied frame embraces the first moment of temporary relaxation to sink into slumber. Alas! is it a crime that I should look upon him, when it may be for the last time?—When yet but a short space, and those fair features will be no longer animated by the bold and buoyant spirit which forsakes them not even in sleep!—When the nostril shall be distended, the mouth agape, the eyes fixed and bloodshot; and when the proud and noble knight may be trodden on by the lowest caitiff of this accursed castle, yet stir not when the heel is lifted up against him!—And my father!—oh, my father! evil is it with his daughter, when his grey hairs are not remembered because of the golden locks of youth!—What know I but that these evils are the messengers of Jehovah's wrath to the unnatural child, who thinks of a stranger's captivity before a parent's? who forgets the desolation of Judah, and looks upon the comeliness of a Gentile and a stranger?—But I will tear this folly from my heart, though every fibre bleed as I rend it away!"

She wrapped herself closely in her veil, and sat down at a distance from the couch of the wounded knight, with her back turned towards it, fortifying, or endeavouring to fortify her mind, not only against the impending evils from without, but also against those treacherous feelings which assailed her from within.

ADDITION TO NOTE ATTACHED TO PAGE 617

In corroboration of what is above stated in Note at page 617 it may be observed, that the arms, which were assumed by Godfrey of Boulogne himself, after the conquest of Jerusalem, was a cross counter patent cantoned with four little crosses or, upon a field azure, displaying thus metal upon metal. The heralds have tried to explain this undeniable fact in different modes—but Ferne gallantly contends. that a prince of Godfrey's qualities should not be found by the ordinary rules. The Scottish Nisbet, and the same Ferne, insist that the chiefs of the Crusade must have assigned to Godfrey this extraordinary and unwonted coat-of-arms, in order to induce those who should behold them to make enquiries; and hence give them the name of *arma inquirenda*. But with reverence to these grave authorities, it seems unlikely that the assembled princes of Europe should have adjudged to Godfrey a coat armorial so much contrary to the general rule, if such rule had then existed; at any rate, it proves that metal upon metal, now accounted a solecism in heraldry, was admitted in other cases similar to that in the text. See Ferne's *Blazon of Gentrie,* p. 238. Edition 1586. Nisbet's *Heraldry,* vol. i. p. 113. Second Edition.

CHAPTER XXX

Approach the chamber, look upon his bed.
His is the passing of no peaceful ghost,
Which, as the lark arises to the sky,
'Mid morning's sweetest breeze and softest dew,
Is wing'd to heaven by good men's sighs and tears!—
Anselm parts otherwise.

Old Play.

DURING the interval of quiet which followed the first success of the besiegers, while the one party was preparing to pursue their advantage, and the other to strengthen their means of defence, the Templar and De Bracy held brief council together in the hall of the castle.

"Where is Front-de-Bœuf?" said the latter, who had superintended the defence of the fortress on the other side; "men say he hath been slain."

"He lives," said the Templar, coolly, "lives as yet; but had he worn the bull's head of which he bears the name, and ten plates of iron to fence it withal, he must have gone down before yonder fatal axe. Yet a few hours, and Front-de-Bœuf is with his fathers—a powerful limb lopped off Prince John's enterprise."

"And a brave addition to the kingdom of Satan," said De Bracy; "this comes of reviling saints and angels, and ordering images of holy things and holy men to be flung down on the heads of these rascaille yeomen."

"Go to—thou art a fool," said the Templar; "thy superstition is upon a level with Front-de-Bœuf's want of faith; neither of you can render a reason for your belief or unbelief."

"Benedicite, Sir Templar," replied De Bracy, "I pray you to keep better rule with your tongue when I am the theme of it. By the Mother of Heaven, I am a better Christian man than thou and thy fellowship; for the *bruit* goeth shrewdly out, that the most holy Order of the Temple of Zion nurseth not a few heretics within its bosom, and that Sir Brian de Bois-Guilbert is of the number."

"Care not thou for such reports," said the Templar; "but let us think of making good the castle.—How fought these villain yeomen on thy side?"

"Like fiends incarnate," said De Bracy. "They swarmed close up to the walls, headed, as I think, by the knave who won the prize at the archery, for I knew his horn and baldric. And this is old Fitzurse's boasted policy, encouraging these malapert knaves to rebel against us! Had I not been armed in proof, the villain had marked me down seven times with as little remorse as if I had been a buck in season. He told every rivet on my armour with a cloth-yard shaft, that rapped against my ribs with as little compunction as if my bones had been of iron— But that I wore a shirt of Spanish mail under my plate-coat, I had been fairly sped."

"But you maintained your post?" said the Templar. "We lost the outwork on our part."

"That is a shrewd loss," said De Bracy; "the knaves will find cover there to assault the castle more closely, and may, if not well watched, gain some unguarded corner of a tower, or some forgotten window, and so break in upon us. Our numbers are too few for the defence of every point, and the men complain that they can nowhere show themselves, but they are the mark for as many arrows as a parish-butt on a holyday even. Front-de-Bœuf is dying too, so we shall receive no more aid from his bull's head and brutal strength. How think you, Sir Brian, were we not better make a virtue of necessity, and compound with the rogues by delivering up our prisoners?"

"How?" exclaimed the Templar; "deliver up our prisoners, and stand an object alike of ridicule and execration, as the doughty warriors who dared by a night-attack to possess themselves of the persons of a party of defenceless travellers, yet could not make good a strong castle against a vagabond troop of outlaws, led by swineherds, jesters, and the very refuse of mankind?—Shame on thy counsel, Maurice de Bracy!—The ruins of this castle shall bury both my body and my shame, ere I consent to such base and dishonourable composition."

"Let us to the walls, then," said De Bracy, carelessly; "that man never breathed, be he Turk or Templar, who held life at lighter rate than I do. But I trust there is no dishonour in wishing I had here some two scores of my gallant troop of Free Companions?—Oh, my brave lances! If ye knew but how hard your captain were this day bested, how soon should I see my banner at the head of your clump of spears! And how short while would these rabble villains stand to endure your encounter!"

"Wish for whom thou wilt," said the Templar, "but let us make what defence we can with the soldiers who remain—They are chiefly Front-de-Bœuf's followers, hated by the English for a thousand acts of insolence and oppression."

"The better," said De Bracy; "the rugged slaves will defend themselves to the last drop of their blood, ere they encounter the revenge of the peasants without. Let us up and be doing, then, Brian de Bois-Guilbert; and, live or die, thou shalt see Maurice de Bracy bear himself this day as a gentleman of blood and lineage."

"To the walls!" answered the Templar; and they both ascended the battlements to do all that skill could dictate, and manhood accomplish, in defence of the place. They readily agreed that the point of greatest danger was that opposite to the outwork of which the assailants had possessed themselves. The castle, indeed, was divided from that barbican by the moat, and it was impossible that the besiegers could assail the postern-door, with which the outwork corresponded, without surmounting that obstacle; but it was the opinion both of the Templar and De Bracy, that the besiegers, if governed by the same policy their leader had already displayed, would endeavour by a formidable assault, to draw the chief part of the defenders' observation to this point, and take measures to avail themselves of every negligence which might take place in the defence elsewhere. To guard against such an evil, their numbers only permitted the knights to place sentinels from space to space along the walls in communication with each other, who might give the alarm whenever danger was threatened. Meanwhile, they agreed that De Bracy should command the defence at the postern, and the Templar should keep with him a score of men or thereabouts as a body of reserve, ready to hasten to any other point which might be suddenly threatened. The loss of the barbican had also this unfortunate effect, that, notwithstanding the superior height of the castle walls, the besieged could not see from them, with the same precision as before, the operations of the enemy; for some straggling underwood approached so near the sally-port of the outwork, that the assailants might introduce into it whatever force they thought proper, not only under cover, but even without the knowledge of the defenders. Utterly uncertain, therefore, upon what point the storm was to burst, De Bracy and his companion were under the necessity of pro-viding against every possible contingency, and their followers, however brave, experienced the anxious dejection of mind incident to men en-closed by enemies, who possessed the power of choosing their time and mode of attack.

Meanwhile, the lord of the beleaguered and endangered castle lay upon a bed of bodily pain and mental agony. He had not the usual resource of bigots in that superstitious period, most of whom were wont to atone for the crimes they were guilty of by liberality to the church, stupefying by this means their terrors by the idea of atonement and forgiveness; and although the refuge which success thus purchased, was no more like to the peace of mind which follows on sincere repentance, than the turbid stupefaction procured by opium resembles healthy and natural slumbers, it was still a state of mind preferable to the agonies of awak-ened remorse. But among the vices of Front-de-Bœuf, a hard and griping man, avarice was predominant; and he preferred setting church and churchmen at defiance, to purchasing from them pardon and absolution at the price of treasure and of manors. Nor did the Templar, an infidel of another stamp, justly characterise his associate, when he said Front-de-Bœuf could assign no cause for his unbelief and contempt for the estab-lished faith, for the Baron would have alleged that the Church sold her wares too dear, that the spiritual freedom which she put up to sale was only to be bought like that of the chief captain of Jerusalem, "with a great sum," and Front-de-Bœuf preferred denying the virtue of the medicine, to paying the expense of the physician.

But the moment had now arrived when earth and all his treasures were gliding from before his eyes, and when the savage Baron's heart, though hard as a nether millstone, became appalled as he gazed forward into the waste darkness of futurity. The fever of his body aided the impatience and agony of his mind, and his death-bed exhibited a mixture of the newly awakened feelings of horror, combating with the fixed and inveterate obstinacy of his disposition;—a fearful state of mind, only to be equalled in those tremendous regions, where there are complaints without hope, remorse without repentance, a dreadful sense of present agony, and a presentiment that it cannot cease or be diminished!

"Where be these dog-priests now," growled the Baron, "who set such price on their ghostly mummery?—where be all those unshod Carmelites, for whom old Front-de-Bœuf founded the convent of St. Anne, robbing his heir of many a fair rood of meadow, and many a fat field and close—where be the greedy hounds now?—Swilling, I warrant me, at the ale, or playing their juggling tricks, at the bedside of some miserly churl.—Me, the heir of their founder—me, whom their foundation binds them to pray for—me—ungrateful villains as they are!—they suffer to die like the houseless dog on yonder common, unshriven, and unhouseled!—Tell the Templar to come hither—he is a priest, and may do something—But no!—as well confess myself to the devil as to Brian de Bois-Guilbert, who recks neither of heaven nor of hell.—I have heard old men talk of prayer—prayer by their own voice—such need not to court or to bribe the false priest—But I—I dare not!"

"Lives Reginald Front-de-Bœuf," said a broken and shrill voice close by his bedside, "to say there is that which he dares not!"

The evil conscience and the shaken nerves of Front-de-Bœuf heard, in this strange interruption to his soliloquy, the voice of one of those demons, who, as the superstition of the times believed, beset the beds of dying men, to distract their thoughts, and turn them from the meditations which concerned their eternal welfare. He shuddered and drew himself together; but, instantly summoning up his wonted resolution, he exclaimed, "Who is there?—what art thou, that darest to echo my words in a tone like that of the night-raven?—Come before my couch that I may see thee."

"I am thine evil angel, Reginald Front-de-Bœuf," replied the voice.

"Let me behold thee then in thy bodily shape, if thou be'st indeed a fiend," replied the dying knight; "think not that I will blench from thee.—By the eternal dungeon, could I but grapple with these horrors that hover round me, as I have done with mortal dangers, heaven or hell should never say that I shrunk from the conflict!"

"Think on thy sins, Reginald Front-de-Bœuf," said the almost unearthly voice, "on rebellion, on rapine, on murder!—Who stirred up the licentious John to war against his grey-headed father—against his generous brother?"

"Be thou fiend, priest, or devil," replied Front-de-Bœuf, "thou liest in thy throat!—Not I stirred John to rebellion—not I alone—there were fifty knights and barons, the flower of the midland counties—better men never laid lance in rest—And must I answer for the fault done by fifty?—False fiend, I defy thee! Depart, and haunt my couch no more—let me die in peace if thou be mortal—if thou be a demon, thy time is not yet come."

"In peace thou shalt NOT die," repeated the voice; "even in death shalt thou think on thy murders—on the groans which this castle has echoed—on the blood that is engrained in its floors!"

"Thou canst not shake me by thy petty malice," answered Front-de-Bœuf, with a ghastly and constrained laugh. "The infidel Jew—it was merit with heaven to deal with him as I did, else wherefore are men canonized who dip their hands in the blood of Saracens?—The Saxon porkers, whom I have slain, they were the foes of my country, and of my lineage, and of my liege lord.—Ho! ho! thou seest there is no crevice in my coat of plate—Art thou fled?—art thou silenced?"

"No, foul parricide!" replied the voice; "think of thy father!—think of his death!—think of his banquet-room flooded with his gore, and that poured forth by the hand of a son!"

"Ha!" answered the Baron, after a long pause, "an thou knowest that, thou art indeed the author of evil, and as omniscient as the monks call thee!—That secret I deemed locked in my own breast, and in that of one besides—the temptress, the partaker of my guilt.—Go, leave me, fiend! and seek the Saxon witch Ulrica, who alone could tell thee what she and I alone witnessed.—Go, I say, to her, who washed the wounds, and straightened the corpse, and gave the slain man the outward show of one parted in time and in the course of nature—Go to her, she was my temptress, the foul provoker, the more foul rewarder, of the deed—let her as well as I, taste of the tortures which anticipate hell!"

"She already tastes them," said Ulrica, stepping before the couch of Front-de-Bœuf; "she hath long drunken of this cup, and its bitterness is now sweetened to see that thou dost partake it.—Grind not thy teeth, Front-de-Bœuf—roll not thine eyes—clench not thy hand, nor shake it at me with that gesture of menace!—the hand which, like that of thy renowned ancestor who gained thy name, could have broken with one stroke the skull of a mountain-bull, is now unnerved and powerless as mine own!"

"Vile murderous hag!" replied Front-de-Bœuf; "detestable screech-owl! it is then thou who art come to exult over the ruins thou hast assisted to lay low?"

"Ay, Reginald Front-de-Bœuf," answered she, "it is Ulrica!—it is the daughter of the murdered Torquil Wolfganger!—it is the sister of his slaughtered sons!—it is she who demands of thee, and of thy father's house, father and kindred, name and fame—all that she has lost by the name of Front-de-Bœuf!—Think of my wrongs, Front-de-Bœuf, and answer me if I speak not truth. Thou hast been my evil angel, and I will be thine—I will dog thee till the very instant of dissolution!"

"Detestable fury!" exclaimed Front-de-Bœuf, "that moment shalt thou never witness—Ho! Giles, Clement, and Eustace! Saint Maur, and Stephen! seize this damned witch, and hurl her from the battlements headlong—she has betrayed us to the Saxon!—Ho! Saint Maur! Clement! false-hearted knaves, where tarry ye?"

"Call on them again, valiant Baron," said the hag, with a smile of grisly mockery; "summon thy vassals around thee, doom them that loiter to the scourge and the dungeon—But know, mighty chief," she continued, suddenly changing her tone, "thou shalt have neither answer, nor aid, nor obedience at their hands.—Listen to these horrid sounds," for the din of the recommenced assault and defence now rung fearfully loud from the battlements of the castle; "In that war-cry is the downfall of thy house—The blood-cemented fabric of Front-de-Bœuf's power totters to the foundation, and before the foes he most despised!—The Saxon, Reginald!—the scorned Saxon assails thy walls!—Why liest thou here, like a worn-out hind, when the Saxon storms thy place of strength?"

"Gods and fiends!" exclaimed the wounded knight; "O, for one moment's strength, to drag myself to the *mêlée*, and perish as becomes my name!"

"Think not of it, valiant warrior!" replied she; "thou shalt die no soldier's death, but perish like the fox in his den, when the peasants have set fire to the cover around it."

"Hateful hag, thou liest!" exclaimed Front-de-Bœuf; "my followers bear them bravely—my walls are strong and high—my comrades in arms fear not a whole host of Saxons, were they headed by Hengist and Horsa! —The war-cry of the Templar and of the Free Companions rises high over the conflict! And by mine honour, when we kindle the blazing beacon, for joy of our defence, it shall consume thee, body and bones; and I shall live to hear thou art gone from early fires to those of that hell which never sent forth an incarnate fiend more utterly diabolical!"

"Hold thy belief," replied Ulrica, "till the proof reach thee—But, no!" she said, interrupting herself, "thou shalt know, even now, the doom which all thy power, strength, and courage is unable to avoid, though it is prepared for thee by this feeble hand. Markest thou the smouldering and suffocating vapour which already eddies in sable folds through the chamber?—Didst thou think it was but the darkening of thy bursting eyes—the difficulty of thy cumbered breathing? No! Front-de-Bœuf, there is another cause—Rememberest thou the magazine of fuel that is stored beneath these apartments?"

"Woman!" he exclaimed with fury, "thou hast not set fire to it?— By heaven, thou hast, and the castle is in flames!"

"They are fast rising at least," said Ulrica, with frightful composure; "and a signal shall soon wave to warn the besiegers to press hard upon those who would extinguish them.—Farewell, Front-de-Bœuf!—May Mista, Skogula, and Zernebock, gods of the ancient Saxons—fiends, as the priests now call them—supply the place of comforters at your dying bed, which Ulrica now relinquishes!—But know, if it will give thee comfort to know it, that Ulrica is bound to the same dark coast with thyself, the companion of thy punishment as the companion of thy guilt.—And now, parricide, farewell for ever!—May each stone of this vaulted roof fine a tongue to echo that title into thine ear!"

So saying, she left the apartment; and Front-de-Bœuf could hear the crash of the ponderous key, as she locked and double-locked the door behind her, thus cutting off the most slender chance of escape. In the extremity of agony he shouted upon his servants and allies—"Stephen and Saint Maur!—Clement and Giles!—I burn here unaided!—To the rescue—to the rescue, brave Bois-Guilbert, valiant De Bracy!—It is Front-de-Bœuf who calls!—It is your master, ye traitor squires!—Your ally—your brother in arms, ye perjured and faithless knights!—all the curses due to traitors upon your recreant heads, do you abandon me to perish thus miserably!—They hear me not—they cannot hear me—my voice is lost in the din of battle.—The smoke rolls thicker and thicker—the fire has caught upon the floor below—O, for one draught of the air of heaven, were it to be purchased by instant annihilation!" And in the mad frenzy of despair, the wretch now shouted with the shouts of the fighters, now muttered curses on himself, on mankind, and on Heaven itself.—"The red fire flashes through the thick smoke!" he exclaimed; "the demon marches against me under the banner of his own element—Foul spirit, avoid!—I go not with thee without my comrades—all, all are thine, that garrison these walls—Thinkest thou Front-de-Bœuf will be singled out to go alone?—No—the infidel Templar—the licentious De Bracy—Ulrica, the foul murdering strumpet—the men who aided my enterprises—the dog Saxons and accursed Jews, who are my prisoners—all, all shall attend me—a goodly fellowship as ever took the downward road—Ha, ha, ha!" and he laughed in his frenzy till the vaulted roof rang again. "Who laughed there?" exclaimed Front-de-Bœuf, in altered mood, for the noise of the conflict did not prevent the echoes of his own mad laughter from returning upon his ear—"who laughed there?—Ulrica, was it thou?—Speak, witch, and I forgive thee—for, only thou or the fiend of hell himself could have laughed at such a moment. Avaunt—avaunt!"——

But it were impious to trace any farther the picture of the blasphemer and parricide's deathbed.

CHAPTER XXXI

Once more unto the breach, dear friends, once more,
Or close the wall up with our English dead,
——————————And you, good yeomen,
Whose limbs were made in England, show us here
The mettle of your pasture—let us swear
That you are worth your breeding.
                                    King Henry V.

CEDRIC, although not greatly confident in Ulrica's message, omitted not to communicate her promise to the Black Knight and Locksley. They were well pleased to find they had a friend within the place, who might, in the moment of need, be able to facilitate their entrance, and readily agreed with the Saxon that a storm, under whatever disadvantages, ought to be attempted, as the only means of liberating the prisoners now in the hands of the cruel Front-de-Bœuf.

"The royal blood of Alfred is endangered," said Cedric.

"The honour of a noble lady is in peril," said the Black Knight.

"And, by the Saint Christopher at my baldric," said the good yeoman, "were there no other cause than the safety of that poor faithful knave, Wamba, I would jeopard a point ere a hair of his head were hurt."

"And so would I," said the Friar; "what, sirs! I trust well that a fool—I mean, d'ye see me, sirs, a fool that is free of his guild and master of his craft, and can give as much relish and flavour to a cup of wine as ever a flitch of bacon can—I say, brethren, such a fool shall never want a wise clerk to pray for or fight for him at a strait, while I can say a mass or flourish a partisan."

And with that he made his heavy halbert to play around his head as a shepherd boy flourishes his light crook.

"True, Holy Clerk," said the Black Knight, "true as if Saint Dunstan himself had said it.—And now, good Locksley, were it not well that noble Cedric should assume the direction of this assault?"

"Not a jot I," returned Cedric; "I have never been wont to study either how to take or how to hold out those abodes of tyrannic power, which the Normans have erected in this groaning land. I will fight among the foremost; but my honest neighbours well know I am not a trained soldier in the discipline of wars, or the attack of strongholds."

"Since it stands thus with noble Cedric," said Locksley, "I am most willing to take on me the direction of the archery; and ye shall hang me up on my own trysting-tree, an the defenders be permitted to show themselves over the walls without being struck with as many shafts as there are cloves in a gammon of bacon at Christmas."

"Well said, stout yeoman," answered the Black Knight; "and if I be thought worthy to have a charge in these matters, and can find among these brave men as many as are willing to follow a true English knight, for so I may surely call myself, I am ready, with such skill as my experience has given me, to lead them to the attack of these walls."

The parts being thus distributed to the leaders, they commenced the first assault, of which the reader has already heard the issue.

When the barbican was carried, the Sable Knight sent notice of the happy event to Locksley, requesting him at the same time to keep such a strict observation on the castle as might prevent the defenders from combining their force for a sudden sally, and recovering the outwork which they had lost. This the knight was chiefly desirous of avoiding, conscious that the men whom he led, being hasty and untrained volunteers, imperfectly armed and unaccustomed to discipline, must, upon any sudden attack, fight at great disadvantage with the veteran soldiers of the Norman knights, who were well provided with arms both defensive and offensive; and who, to match the zeal and high spirit of the besiegers, had all the confidence which arises from perfect discipline and the habitual use of weapons.

The knight employed the interval in causing to be constructed a sort of floating bridge, or long raft, by means of which he hoped to cross the moat in despite of the resistance of the enemy. This was a work of some time, which the leaders the less regretted, as it gave Ulrica leisure to execute her plan of diversion in their favour, whatever that might be.

When the raft was completed, the Black Knight addressed the besiegers:—"It avails not waiting here longer, my friends; the sun is descending to the west—and I have that upon my hands which will not permit me to tarry with you another day. Besides, it will be a marvel if the horsemen come not upon us from York, unless we speedily accomplish our purpose. Wherefore, one of ye go to Locksley, and bid him commence a discharge of arrows on the opposite side of the castle, and move forward as if about to assault it; and you, true English hearts, stand by me, and be ready to thrust the raft endlong over the moat whenever the postern on our side is thrown open. Follow me boldly across, and aid me to burst yon sallyport in the main wall of the castle. As many of you as like not this service, or are but ill armed to meet it, do you man the top of the outwork, draw your bowstrings to your ears, and mind you quell with your shot whatever shall appear to man the rampart—Noble Cedric, wilt thou take the direction of those which remain?"

"Not so, by the soul of Hereward!" said the Saxon; "lead I cannot; but may posterity curse me in my grave, if I follow not with the foremost wherever thou shalt point the way—The quarrel is mine, and well it becomes me to be in the van of the battle."

"Yet, bethink thee, noble Saxon," said the knight, "thou hast neither hauberk, nor corslet, nor aught but that light helmet, target, and sword."

"The better!" answered Cedric; "I shall be the lighter to climb these walls. And,—forgive the boast, Sir Knight,—thou shalt this day see the

naked breast of a Saxon as boldly presented to the battle as ever yet beheld the steel corslet of a Norman."

"In the name of God, then," said the knight, "fling open the door, and
launch the floating bridge."

The portal, which led from•the inner-wall of the barbican to the moat,
and which corresponded with a sallyport in the main wall of the castle,
was now suddenly opened; the temporary bridge was then thrust forward, and soon flashed in the waters, extending its length between the
castle and outwork, and forming a slippery and precarious passage for
two men abreast to cross the moat. Well aware of the importance of
taking the foe by surprise, the Black Knight, closely followed by Cedric,
threw himself upon the bridge, and reached the opposite side. Here he
began to thunder with his axe upon the gate of the castle protected in
part from the shot and stones cast by the defenders by the ruins of the
former drawbridge, which the Templar had demolished in his retreat
from the barbican, leaving the counterpoise still attached to the upper
part of the portal. The followers of the knight had no such shelter; two
were instantly shot with cross-bow bolts, and two more fell into the moat;
the others retreated back into the barbican.

The situation of Cedric and of the Black Knight was now truly dangerous, and would have been still more so, but for the constancy of the
archers in the barbican, who ceased not to shower their arrows upon the
battlements, distracting the attention of those by whom they were
manned, and thus affording a respite to their two chiefs from the storm
of missiles which must otherwise have overwhelmed them. But their situation was eminently perilous, and was becoming more so with every
moment.

"Shame on ye all!" cried De Bracy to the soldiers around him; "do
ye call yourselves cross-bowmen, and let these two dogs keep their
station under the walls of the castle?—Heave over the coping stones
from the battlement, an better may not be—Get pick-axe and levers,
and down with that huge pinnacle!" pointing to a heavy piece of stone
carved-work that projected from the parapet.

At this moment the besiegers caught sight of the red flag upon the
angle of the tower which Ulrica had described to Cedric. The stout
yeoman Locksley was the first who was aware of it, as he was hasting to
the outwork, impatient to see the progress of the assault.

"Saint George!" he cried, "Merry Saint George for England!—To
the charge, bold yeomen!—why leave ye the good knight and noble
Cedric to storm the pass alone?—make in, mad priest, show thou canst
fight for thy rosary,—make in, brave yeomen!—the castle is ours, we
have friends within—See yonder flag, it is the appointed signal—Torquilstone is ours!—Think of honour, think of spoil—One effort, and the
place is ours!"

With that he bent his good bow, and sent a shaft right through the
breast of one of the men-at-arms, who, under De Bracy's direction, was

loosening a fragment from one of the battlements to precipitate on the heads of Cedric and the Black Knight. A second soldier caught from the hands of the dying man the iron crow, with which he heaved at and had loosened the stone pinnacle, when, receiving an arrow through his head-piece, he dropped from the battlements into the moat a dead man. The men-at-arms were daunted, for no armour seemed proof against the shot of this tremendous archer.

"Do you give ground, base knaves!" said De Bracy; *"Mount joye Saint Dennis!*—Give me the lever!"

And, snatching it up, he again assailed the loosened pinnacle, which was of weight enough, if thrown down, not only to have destroyed the remnant of the drawbridge, which sheltered the two foremost assailants, but also to have sunk the rude float of planks over which they had crossed. All saw the danger, and the boldest, even the stout Friar himself avoided setting foot on the raft. Thrice did Locksley bend his shaft against De Bracy, and thrice did his arrow bound back from the knight's armour of proof.

"Curse on thy Spanish steel-coat!" said Locksley, "had English smith forged it, these arrows had gone through, an as if it had been silk or sendal." He then began to call out, "Comrades! friends! noble Cedric! bear back, and let the ruin fall."

His warning voice was unheard, for the din which the knight himself occasioned by his strokes upon the postern would have drowned twenty war-trumpets. The faithful Gurth indeed sprung forward on the planked bridge, to warn Cedric of his impending fate, or to share it with him. But his warning would have come too late; the massive pinnacle already tottered, and De Bracy, who still heaved at his task, would have accomplished it, had not the voice of the Templar sounded close in his ears:—

"All is lost, De Bracy, the castle burns."

"Thou art mad to say so!" replied the knight.

"It is all in a light flame on the western side. I have striven in vain to extinguish it."

With the stern coolness which formed the basis of his character, Brian de Bois-Guilbert communicated this hideous intelligence, which was not so calmly received by his astonished comrade.

"Saints of Paradise!" said De Bracy; "what is to be done? I vow to Saint Nicholas of Limoge a candlestick of pure gold"——

"Spare thy vow," said the Templar, "and mark me. Lead thy men down, as if to a sally; throw the postern-gate open—There are but two men who occupy the float, fling them into the moat and push across for the barbican. I will charge from the main gate, and attack the barbican on the outside; and if we can regain that post, be assured we shall defend ourselves until we are relieved, or at least till they grant us fair quarter."

"It is well thought upon," said De Bracy; "I will play my part— Templar, thou wilt not fail me?"

"Hand and glove, I will not!" said Bois-Guilbert. "But haste thee, in the name of God!"

De Bracy hastily drew his men together, and rushed down to the postern-gate, which he caused instantly to be thrown open. But scarce was this done ere the portentous strength of the Black Knight forced his way inward in spite of De Bracy and his followers. Two of the foremost instantly fell, and the rest gave way notwithstanding all their leader's efforts to stop them.

"Dogs!" said De Bracy, "will ye let *two* men win our only pass for safety?"

"He is the devil!" said a veteran man-at-arms, bearing back from the blows of their sable antagonist.

"And if he be the devil," replied De Bracy, "would you fly from him into the mouth of hell?—the castle burns behind us, villains!—let despair give you courage, or let me forward! I will cope with this champion myself."

And well and chivalrous did De Bracy that day maintain the fame he had acquired in the civil wars of that dreadful period. The vaulted passage to which the postern gave entrance, and in which these two re- doubted champions were now fighting hand to hand, rung with the furi- ous blows which they dealt each other, De Bracy with his sword, the Black Knight with his ponderous axe. At length the Norman received a blow, which, though its force was partly parried by his shield, for other- wise never more would De Bracy have again moved limb, descended yet with such violence on his crest, that he measured his length on the paved floor.

"Yield thee, De Bracy," said the Black Champion, stooping over him, and holding against the bars of his helmet the fatal poniard with which the knights dispatched their enemies (and which was called the dagger of mercy),—"yield thee, Maurice de Bracy, rescue or no rescue, or thou art but a dead man."

"I will not yield," replied De Bracy faintly, "to an unknown con- queror. Tell me thy name, or work thy pleasure on me—it shall never be said that Maurice de Bracy was prisoner to a nameless churl."

The Black Knight whispered something into the ear of the vanquished.

"I yield me to be true prisoner, rescue or no rescue," answered the Norman, exchanging his tone of stern and determined obstinacy for one of deep though sullen submission.

"Go to the barbican," said the victor, in a tone of authority, "and there wait my further orders."

"Yet first, let me say," said De Bracy, "what it imports thee to know. Wilfred of Ivanhoe is wounded and a prisoner, and will perish in the burning castle without present help."

"Wilfred of Ivanhoe!" exclaimed the Black Knight—"prisoner, and perish!—The life of every man in the castle shall answer it if a hair of his head be singed—Show me his chamber!"

"Ascend yonder winding stair," said De Bracy; "it leads to his apartment—Wilt thou not accept my guidance?" he added, in a submissive voice.

"No. To the barbican, and there wait my orders. I trust thee not, De Bracy."

During this combat and the brief conversation which ensued, Cedric at the head of a body of men, among whom the Friar was conspicuous, had pushed across the bridge as soon as they saw the postern open, and drove back the dispirited and despairing followers of De Bracy, of whom some asked quarter, some offered vain resistance, and the greater part fled towards the court-yard. De Bracy himself arose from the ground, and cast a sorrowful glance after his conqueror. "He trusts me not!" he repeated; "but have I deserved his trust?" He then lifted his sword from the floor, took off his helmet in token of submission, and, going to the barbican, gave up his sword to Locksley, whom he met by the way.

As the fire augmented, symptoms of it became soon apparent in the chamber where Ivanhoe was watched and tended by the Jewess Rebecca. He had been awakened from his brief slumber by the noise of the battle; and his attendant, who had, at his anxious desire, again placed herself at the window to watch and report to him the fate of the attack, was for some time prevented from observing either, by the increase of the smouldering and stifling vapour. At length the volumes of smoke which rolled into the apartment—the cries for water, which were heard even above the din of the battle made them sensible of the progress of this new danger.

"The castle burns," said Rebecca; "it burns!—What can we do to save ourselves?"

"Fly, Rebecca, and save thine own life," said Ivanhoe, "for no human aid can avail me."

"I will not fly," answered Rebecca; "we will be saved or perish together—And yet, great God!—my father, my father—what will be his fate!"

At this moment the door of the apartment flew open, and the Templar presented himself,—a ghastly figure, for his gilded armour was broken and bloody, and the plume was partly shorn away, partly burnt from his casque. "I have found thee," said he to Rebecca; "thou shalt prove I will keep my word to share weal and woe with thee—There is but one path to safety, I have cut my way through fifty dangers to point it to thee— up, and instantly follow me!" [1]

"Alone," answered Rebecca, "I will not follow thee. If thou wert born of woman—if thou hast but a touch of human charity in thee—if thy

---

[1] The author has some idea that this passage is imitated from the appearance of Philidaspes, before the divine Mandane, when the city of Babylon is on fire, and he proposes to carry her from the flames. But the theft, if there be one, would be rather too severely punished by the penance of searching for the original passage through the interminable volumes of the Grand Cyrus.

heart be not hard as thy breastplate—save my aged father—save this
wounded knight!"

"A knight," answered the Templar, with his characteristic calmness,
"a knight, Rebecca, must encounter his fate, whether it meet him in the
shape of sword or flame—and who recks how or where a Jew meets with
his?"

"Savage warrior," said Rebecca, "rather will I perish in the flames
than accept safety from thee!"

"Thou shalt not choose, Rebecca--once didst thou foil me, but never
mortal did so twice."

So saying, he seized on the terrified maiden, who filled the air with
her shrieks, and bore her out of the room in his arms in spite of her cries,
and without regarding the menaces and defiance which Ivanhoe thundered against him. "Hound of the Temple—stain to thine order—set free
the damsel! Traitor of Bois-Guilbert, it is Ivanhoe commands thee!—
Villain, I will have thy heart's blood!"

"I had not found thee, Wilfred," said the Black Knight, who at that
instant entered the apartment, "but for thy shouts."

"If thou be'st true knight," said Wilfred, "think not of me—pursue
yon ravisher—save the Lady Rowena—look to the noble Cedric!"

"In their turn," answered he of the fetterlock, "but thine is first."

And seizing upon Ivanhoe, he bore him off with as much ease as the
Templar had carried off Rebecca, rushed with him to the postern, and
having there delivered his burden to the care of two yeomen, he again
entered the castle to assist in the rescue of the other prisoners.

One turret was now in bright flames, which flashed out furiously from
window and shot-hole. But in other parts, the great thickness of the
walls and the vaulted roofs of the apartments, resisted the progress of the
flames, and there the rage of man still triumphed, as the scarce more dreadful element held mastery elsewhere; for the besiegers pursued the defenders of the castle from chamber to chamber, and satiated in their
blood the vengeance which had long animated them against the soldiers
of the tyrant Front-de-Bœuf. Most of the garrison resisted to the uttermost—few of them asked quarter—none received it. The air was filled
with groans and clashing of arms—the floors were slippery with the blood
of despairing and expiring wretches.

Through this scene of confusion, Cedric rushed in quest of Rowena,
while the faithful Gurth, following him closely through the *mêlée,* neglected his own safety while he strove to avert the blows that were aimed
at his master. The noble Saxon was so fortunate as to reach his ward's
apartment just as she had abandoned all hope of safety, and, with a
crucifix clasped in agony to her bosom, sat in expectation of instant
death. He committed her to the charge of Gurth, to be conducted in
safety to the barbican, the road to which was now cleared of the enemy,
and not yet interrupted by the flames. This accomplished, the loyal
Cedric hastened in quest of his friend Athelstane, determined, at every

risk to himself, to save that last scion of Saxon royalty. But ere Cedric penetrated as far as the old hall in which he had himself been a prisoner, the inventive genius of Wamba had procured liberation for himself and his companion in adversity.

When the noise of the conflict announced that it was at the hottest, the Jester began to shout, with the utmost power of his lungs, "Saint George and the dragon!—Bonny St. George for merry England!—The castle is won!" And these sounds he rendered yet more fearful, by banging against each other two or three pieces of rusty armour which lay scattered around the hall.

A guard, which had been stationed in the outer, or anteroom, and whose spirits were already in a state of alarm, took flight at Wamba's clamour, and, leaving the door open behind them, ran to tell the Templar that foemen had entered the old hall. Meantime the prisoners found no difficulty in making their escape to the anteroom, and from thence into the court of the castle, which was now the last scene of contest. Here sat the fierce Templar, mounted on horseback, surrounded by several of the garrison, both on horse and foot, who had united their strength to that of this renowned leader, in order to secure the last chance of safety and retreat which remained to them. The drawbridge had been lowered by his orders, but the passage was beset; for the archers, who had hitherto only annoyed the castle on that side by their missiles, no sooner saw the flames breaking out, and the bridge lowered, than they thronged to the entrance, as well to prevent the escape of the garrison, as to secure their own share of booty ere the castle should be burnt down. On the other hand, a party of the besiegers who had entered by the postern were now issuing out into the court-yard, and attacking with fury the remnant of the defenders who were thus assaulted on both sides at once.

Animated, however, by despair, and supported by the example of their indomitable leader, the remaining soldiers of the castle fought with the utmost valour; and, being well armed, succeeded more than once in driving back the assailants, though much inferior in numbers. Rebecca, placed on horseback before one of the Templar's Saracen slaves, was in the midst of the little party; and Bois-Guilbert, notwithstanding the confusion of the bloody fray, showed every attention to her safety. Repeatedly he was by her side, and, neglecting his own defence, held before her the fence of his triangular steel-plated shield; and anon, starting from his position by her, he cried his war-cry, dashed forward, struck to earth the most forward of the assailants, and was on the same instant once more at her bridle rein.

Athelstane, who, as the reader knows, was slothful, but not cowardly, beheld the female form whom the Templar protected thus sedulously, and doubted not that it was Rowena whom the knight was carrying off, in despite of all resistance which could be offered.

"By the soul of Saint Edward," he said, "I will rescue her from yonder over-proud knight, and he shall die by my hand!"

"Think what you do!" cried Wamba; "hasty hand catches frog for fish—by my bauble, yonder is none of my Lady Rowena—see but her long dark locks!—Nay, an ye will not know black from white, ye may be leader, but I will be no follower—no bones of mine shall be broken unless I know for whom.—And you without armour too!—Bethink you, silk bonnet never kept out steel blade.—Nay, then, if wilful will to water, wilful must drench.—*Deus vobiscum,* most doughty Athelstane!" —he concluded, loosening the hold which he had hitherto kept upon the Saxon's tunic.

To snatch a mace from the pavement, on which it lay beside one whose dying grasp had just relinquished it—to rush on the Templar's band, and to strike in quick succession to the right and left, levelling a warrior at each blow, was, for Athelstane's great strength, now animated with unusual fury, but the work of a single moment; he was soon within two yards of Bois-Guilbert, whom he defied in his loudest tone.

"Turn, false-hearted Templar! let go her whom thou art unworthy to touch—turn, limb of a band of murdering and hypocritical robbers!"

"Dog!" said the Templar, grinding his teeth, "I will teach thee to blaspheme the holy Order of the Temple of Zion;" and with these words, half-wheeling his steed, he made a demi-courbette towards the Saxon, and rising in the stirrups, so as to take full advantage of the descent of the horse, he discharged a fearful blow upon the head of Athelstane.

Well said Wamba, that silken bonnet keeps out no steel blade. So trenchant was the Templar's weapon, that it shore asunder, as it had been a willow twig, the tough and plaited handle of the mace, which the ill-fated Saxon reared to parry the blow, and, descending on his head, levelled him with the earth.

"Ha! Beau-seant!" exclaimed Bois-Guilbert, "thus be it to the maligners of the Temple-knights!" Taking advantage of the dismay which was spread by the fall of Athelstane, and calling aloud, "Those who would save themselves, follow me!" he pushed across the drawbridge, dispersing the archers who would have intercepted them. He was followed by his Saracens, and some five or six men-at-arms, who had mounted their horses. The Templar's retreat was rendered perilous by the numbers of arrows shot off at him and his party; but this did not prevent him from galloping round to the barbican, of which according to his previous plan, he supposed it possible De Bracy might have been in possession.

"De Bracy! De Bracy!" he shouted, "art thou there?"

"I am here," replied De Bracy, "but I am a prisoner."

"Can I rescue thee?" cried Bois-Guilbert.

"No," replied De Bracy; "I have rendered me, rescue or no rescue. I will be true prisoner. Save thyself—there are hawks abroad—put the seas betwixt you and England—I dare not say more."

"Well," answered the Templar, "an thou wilt tarry there, remember I have redeemed word and glove. Be the hawks where they will, methinks the walls of the Preceptory of Templestowe will be cover sufficient, and thither will I, like heron to her haunt."

Having thus spoken, he galloped off with his followers.

Those of the castle, who had not gotten to horse, still continued to fight desperately with the besiegers, after the departure of the Templar, but rather in despair of quarter than that they entertained any hope of escape. The fire was spreading rapidly through all parts of the castle, when Ulrica, who had first kindled it, appeared on a turret, in the guise of one of the ancient furies, yelling forth a war-song, such as was of yore raised on the field of battle by the scalds of the yet heathen Saxons. Her long dishevelled grey hair flew back from her uncovered head; the inebriating delight of gratified vengeance contended in her eyes with the fire of insanity; and she brandished the distaff which she held in her hand, as if she had been one of the Fatal Sisters, who spin and abridge the thread of human life. Tradition has preserved some wild strophes of the barbarous hymn which she chanted wildly amid that scene of fire and of slaughter:—

1

Whet the bright steel,
Sons of the White Dragon!
Kindle the torch,
Daughter of Hengist!
The steel glimmers not for the carving of the banquet.
It is hard, broad, and sharply pointed;
The torch goeth not to the bridal chamber,
It steams and glitters blue with sulphur.
Whet the steel, the raven croaks!
Light the torch, Zernebock is yelling!
Whet the steel, sons of the Dragon!
Kindle the torch, daughter of Hengist!

2

The black cloud is low over the thane's castle;
The eagle screams—he rides on its bosom.
Scream not, grey rider of the sable cloud,
Thy banquet is prepared!
The maidens of Valhalla look forth,
The race of Hengist will send them guests.
Shake your black tresses, maidens of Valhalla!
And strike your loud timbrels for joy!
Many a haughty step bends to your halls,
Many a helmed head.

3

Dark sits the evening upon the thane's castle,
The black clouds gather round;
Soon shall they be red as the blood of the valiant!
The destroyer of forests shall shake his red crest against them.
He, the bright consumer of palaces,
Broad waves he his blazing banner,
Red, wide, and dusky,
Over the strife of the valiant:
His joy is in the clashing swords and broken bucklers;
He loves to lick the hissing blood as it bursts warm from
    the wound!

4

All must perish!
The sword cleaveth the helmet;
The strong armour is pierced by the lance;
Fire devoureth the dwelling of princes,
Engines break down the fences of the battle.
All must perish!
The race of Hengist is gone—
The name of Horsa is no more!
Shrink not then from your doom, sons of the sword!
Let your blades drink blood like wine;
Feast ye in the banquet of slaughter,
By the light of the blazing halls!
Strong be your swords while your blood is warm,
And spare neither for pity nor fear,
For vengeance hath but an hour;
Strong hate itself shall expire!
I also must perish! [1]

The towering flames had now surmounted every obstruction, and rose
to the evening skies one huge and burning beacon, seen far and wide
through the adjacent country. Tower after tower crashed down, with
blazing roof and rafter; and the combatants were driven from the court-
yard. The vanquished, of whom very few remained, scattered and escaped into the neighbouring wood. The victors, assembling in large
bands, gazed with wonder, not unmixed with fear, upon the flames, in
which their own ranks and arms glanced dusky red. The maniac figure
of the Saxon Ulrica was for a long time visible on the lofty stand she
had chosen, tossing her arms abroad with wild exultation, as if she
reigned empress of the conflagration which she had raised. At length,
with a terrific crash, the whole turret gave way, and she perished in the

---

[1] Note VI.—Ulrica's Death Song.

flames which had consumed her tyrant. An awful pause of horror silenced each murmur of the armed spectators, who, for the space of several minutes, stirred not a finger, save to sign the cross. The voice of Locksley was then heard, "Shout, yeomen!—the den of tyrants is no more! Let each bring his spoil to our chosen place of rendezvous at the trysting-tree in the Harthill-walk; for there at break of day will we make just partition among our own bands, together with our worthy allies in this great deed of vengeance."

CHAPTER XXXII

> Trust me each state must have its policies:
> Kingdoms have edicts, cities have their charters;
> Even the wild outlaw, in his forest-walk,
> Keeps yet some touch of civil discipline;
> For not since Adam wore his verdant apron,
> Hath man with man in social union dwelt,
> But laws were made to draw that union closer.
> *Old Play.*

THE daylight had dawned upon the glades of the oak forest. The green boughs glittered with all their pearls of dew. The hind led her fawn from the covert of high fern to the more open walks of the greenwood, and no huntsman was there to watch or intercept the stately hart, as he paced at the head of the antler'd herd.

The outlaws were all assembled around the trysting-tree in the Harthill-walk, where they had spent the night in refreshing themselves after the fatigues of the siege, some with wine, some with slumber, many with hearing and recounting the events of the day, and computing the heaps of plunder which their success had placed at the disposal of their chief.

The spoils were indeed very large; for, notwithstanding that much was consumed, a great deal of plate, rich armour, and splendid clothing, had been secured by the exertions of the dauntless outlaws, who could be appalled by no danger when such rewards were in view. Yet so strict were the laws of their society, that no one ventured to appropriate any part of the booty, which was brought into one common mass, to be at the disposal of their leader.

The place of rendezvous was an aged oak; not however the same to which Locksley had conducted Gurth and Wamba in the earlier part of the story, but one which was the centre of a silvan amphitheatre, within half a mile of the demolished castle of Torquilstone. Here Locksley assumed his seat—a throne of turf erected under the twisted branches of the huge oak, and the silvan followers were gathered around him. He assigned to the Black Knight a seat at his right hand, and to Cedric a place upon his left.

"Pardon my freedom, noble sirs," he said, "but in these glades I am monarch—they are my kingdom; and these my wild subjects would reck but little of my power, were I, within my own dominions, to yield place to mortal man.—Now, sirs, who hath seen our chaplain? where is our curtal Friar? A mass amongst Christian men best begins a busy morning."—No one had seen the Clerk of Copmanhurst. "Over gods forbode!" said the outlaw chief, 'I trust the jolly priest hath but abidden by the wine-pot a thought too late. Who saw him since the castle was ta'en?"

"I," quoth the Miller, "marked him busy about the door of a cellar, swearing by each saint in the calendar he would taste the smack of Front-de-Bœuf's Gascoigne wine."

"Now, the saints, as many as there be of them," said the captain, "forefend, lest he has drunk too deep of the wine-butts, and perished by the fall of the castle!—Away, Miller!—take with you enow of men, seek the place where you last saw him—throw water from the moat on the scorching ruins—I will have them removed stone by stone ere I lose my curtal Friar."

The numbers who hastened to execute this duty, considering that an interesting division of spoil was about to take place, showed how much the troop had at heart the safety of their spiritual father.

"Meanwhile, let us proceed," said Locksley; "for when this bold deed shall be sounded abroad, the bands of De Bracy, of Malvoisin, and other allies of Front-de-Bœuf, will be in motion against us, and it were well for our safety that we retreat from the vicinity.—Noble Cedric," he said, turning to the Saxon, "that spoil is divided into two portions; do thou make choice of that which best suits thee, to recompense thy people who were partakers with us in this adventure."

"Good yeoman," said Cedric, "my heart is oppressed with sadness. The noble Athelstane of Coningsburgh is no more—the last sprout of the sainted Confessor! Hopes have perished with him which can never return!—A sparkle hath been quenched by his blood, which no human breath can again rekindle! My people, save the few who are now with me, do but tarry my presence to transport his honoured remains to their last mansion. The Lady Rowena is desirous to return to Rotherwood, and must be escorted by a sufficient force. I should, therefore, ere now, have left this place; and I waited—not to share the booty, for, so help me God and Saint Withold! as neither I nor any of mine will touch the value of a liard,—I waited but to render my thanks to thee and to thy bold yeomen, for the life and honour ye have saved."

"Nay, but," said the chief outlaw, "we did but half the work at most—take of the spoil what may reward your own neighbours and followers."

"I am rich enough to reward them from mine own wealth," answered Cedric.

"And some," said Wamba, "have been wise enough to reward themselves; they do not march off empty-handed altogether. We do not all wear motley."

"They are welcome," said Locksley, "our laws bind none but ourselves."

"But, thou, my poor knave," said Cedric, turning about and embracing his Jester, "how shall I reward thee, who feared not to give thy body to chains and death instead of mine!—All forsook me, when the poor fool was faithful!"

A tear stood in the eye of the rough Thane as he spoke—a mark of feeling which even the death of Athelstane had not extracted; but there was something in the half-instinctive attachment of his clown that waked his nature more keenly than even grief itself.

"Nay," said the Jester, extricating himself from his Master's caress, "if you pay my service with the water of your eye, the Jester must weep for company, and then what becomes of his vocation?—But, uncle, if you would indeed pleasure me, I pray you to pardon my playfellow Gurth, who stole a week from your service to bestow it on your son."

"Pardon him!" exclaimed Cedric; "I will both pardon and reward him. Kneel down, Gurth."—The swineherd was in an instant at his master's feet—"THEOW and ESNE art thou no longer," said Cedric, touching him with a wand; "FOLKFREE and SACLESS art thou in town and from town, in the forest as in the field. A hide of land I give to thee in my steads of Walbrugham, from me and mine to thee and thine aye and for ever; and God's malison on his head who this gainsays!"

No longer a serf, but a freeman and a landholder, Gurth sprung upon his feet, and twice bounded aloft to almost his own height from the ground.

"A smith and a file," he cried, "to do away the collar from the neck of a freeman!—Noble master! doubled is my strength by your gift, and doubly will I fight for you! There is a free spirit in my breast—I am a man changed to myself and all around. Ha, Fangs!" he continued,—for that faithful cur, seeing his master thus transported, began to jump upon him, to express his sympathy,—"knowest thou thy master still?"

"Ay," said Wamba, "Fangs and I still know thee, Gurth, though we must needs abide by the collar; it is only thou art likely to forget both us and thyself."

"I shall forget myself indeed ere I forget thee, true comrade," said Gurth; "and were freedom fit for thee, Wamba, the master would not let thee want it."

"Nay," said Wamba, "never think I envy thee, brother Gurth; the serf sits by the hall-fire when the freeman must forth to the field of battle. And what saith Oldhelm of Malmsbury—'Better a fool at a feast than a wise man at a fray.'"

The tramp of horses was now heard, and the Lady Rowena appeared, surrounded by several riders, and a much stronger party of footmen, who joyfully shook their pikes and clashed their brown-bills for joy of her freedom. She herself, richly attired, and mounted on a dark chestnut palfrey, had recovered all the dignity of her manner, and only an unwonted degree of paleness showed the sufferings she had undergone. Her lovely brow, though sorrowful, bore on it a cast of reviving hope for the future, as well as of grateful thankfulness for the past deliverance—

She knew that Ivanhoe was safe, and she knew that Athelstane was dead. The former assurance filled her with the most sincere delight; and if she did not absolutely rejoice at the latter, she might be pardoned for feeling the full advantage at being freed from further persecution on the only subject in which she had ever been contradicted by her guardian Cedric.

As Rowena bent her steed towards Locksley's seat, that bold yeoman, with all his followers, rose to receive her, as if by a general instinct of courtesy. The blood rose to her cheeks, as, courteously waving her hand, and bending so low that her beautiful and loose tresses were for an instant mixed with the flowing mane of her palfrey, she expressed in few but apt words her obligations and her gratitude to Locksley and her other deliverers.—"God bless you, brave men," she concluded, "God and Our Lady bless you and requite you for gallantly perilling yourselves in the cause of the oppressed!—If any of you should hunger, remember Rowena has food—if you should thirst, she has many a butt of wine and brown ale—and if the Normans drive ye from these walks, Rowena has forests of her own, where her gallant deliverers may range at full freedom, and never ranger ask whose arrow hath struck down the deer."

"Thanks, gentle lady," said Locksley; "thanks from my company and myself. But, to have saved you requites itself. We who walk the greenwood do many a wild deed, and the Lady Rowena's deliverance may be received as an atonement."

Again bowing from her palfrey, Rowena turned to depart; but pausing a moment, while Cedric, who was to attend her, was also taking his leave, she found herself unexpectedly close by the prisoner De Bracy. He stood under a tree in deep meditation, his arms crossed upon his breast, and Rowena was in hopes she might pass him unobserved. He looked up, however, and, when aware of her presence, a deep flush of shame suffused his handsome countenance. He stood a moment most irresolute; then, stepping forward, took her palfrey by the rein, and bent his knee before her.

"Will the Lady Rowena deign to cast an eye on a captive knight—on a dishonoured soldier?"

"Sir Knight," answered Rowena, "in enterprises such as yours, the real dishonour lies not in failure, but in success."

"Conquest, lady, should soften the heart," answered De Bracy; "let me but know that the Lady Rowena forgives the violence occasioned by an ill-fated passion, and she shall soon learn that De Bracy knows how to serve her in nobler ways."

"I forgive you, Sir Knight," said Rowena, "as a Christian."

"That means," said Wamba, "that she does not forgive him at all."

"But I can never forgive the misery and desolation your madness has occasioned," continued Rowena.

"Unloose your hold on the lady's rein," said Cedric, coming up. "By the bright sun above us, but it were shame, I would pin thee to the earth with my javelin—but be well assured, thou shalt smart, Maurice de Bracy, for thy share in this foul deed."

"He threatens safely who threatens a prisoner," said De Bracy; "but when had a Saxon any touch of courtesy?"

Then retiring two steps backward, he permitted the lady to move on.

Cedric, ere they departed, expressed his peculiar gratitude to the Black Champion, and earnestly entreated him to accompany him to Rotherwood.

"I know," he said, "that ye errant knights desire to carry your fortunes on the point of your lance, and reck not of land or goods; but war is a changeful mistress, and a home is sometimes desirable even to the champion, whose trade is wandering. Thou hast earned one in the halls of Rotherwood, noble knight. Cedric has wealth enough to repair the injuries of fortune, and all he has is his deliverer's. Come, therefore, to Rotherwood, not as a guest, but as a son or brother."

"Cedric has already made me rich," said the Knight,—"he has taught me the value of Saxon virtue. To Rotherwood will I come, brave Saxon, and that speedily; but, as now, pressing matters of moment detain me from your halls. Peradventure when I come hither, I will ask such a boon as will put even thy generosity to the test."

"It is granted ere spoken out," said Cedric, striking his ready hand into the gauntleted palm of the Black Knight,—"it is granted already, were it to affect half my fortune."

"Gage not thy promise so lightly," said the Knight of the Fetterlock; "yet well I hope to gain the boon I shall ask. Meanwhile, adieu."

"I have but to say," added the Saxon, "that, during the funeral rites of the noble Athelstane, I shall be an inhabitant of the halls of his castle of Coningsburgh—They will be open to all who choose to partake of the funeral banqueting; and, I speak in name of the noble Edith, mother of the fallen prince, they will never be shut against him who laboured so bravely, though unsuccessfully, to save Athelstane from Norman chains and Norman steel."

"Ay, ay," said Wamba, who had resumed his attendance on his master, "rare feeding there will be—pity that the noble Athelstane cannot banquet at his own funeral. But he," continued the Jester, lifting up his eyes gravely, "is supping in Paradise, and doubtless does honour to the cheer."

"Peace, and move on," said Cedric, his anger at this untimely jest being checked by the recollection of Wamba's recent services. Rowena waved a graceful adieu to him of the Fetterlock—the Saxon bade God speed him, and on they moved through a wide glade of the forest.

They had scarce departed, ere a sudden procession moved from under the greenwood branches, swept slowly round the silvan amphitheatre, and took the same direction with Rowena and her followers. The priests of a neighbouring convent, in expectation of the ample donation, or *soul-scat*, which Cedric had propined, attended upon the car in which the body of Athelstane was laid, and sang hymns as it was sadly and slowly borne on the shoulders of his vassals to his castle of Conings-burgh, to be there deposited in the grave of Hengist, from whom the deceased derived his long descent. Many of his vassals had assembled at the news of his death, and followed the bier with all the external marks, at least, of dejection and sorrow. Again the outlaws arose, and paid the same rude and spontaneous homage to death, which they had so lately rendered to beauty—the slow chant and mournful step of the priests brought back to their remembrance such of their comrades as had fallen in the yesterday's affray. But such recollections dwell not long with those who lead a life of danger and enterprise, and ere the sound of the death-hymn had died on the wind, the outlaws were again busied in the distribution of their spoil.

"Valiant knight," said Locksley to the Black Champion, "without whose good heart and mighty arm our enterprise must altogether have failed, will it please you to take from that mass of spoil whatever may best serve to pleasure you, and to remind you of this my trysting-tree?"

"I accept the offer," said the Knight, "as frankly as it is given; and I ask permission to dispose of Sir Maurice de Bracy at my own pleasure."

"He is thine already," said Locksley, "and, well for him! else the tyrant had graced the highest bough of this oak, with as many of his Free Companions as we could gather, hanging thick as acorns around him. —But he is thy prisoner, and he is safe, though he had slain my father."

"De Bracy," said the Knight, "thou art free—depart. He whose prisoner thou art scorns to take mean revenge for what is past. But beware of the future, lest a worse thing befall thee.—Maurice de Bracy, I say BEWARE!"

De Bracy bowed low and in silence, and was about to withdraw, when the yeomen burst at once into a shout of execration and derision. The proud knight instantly stopped, turned back, folded his arms, drew up his form to its full height, and exclaimed, "Peace, ye yelping curs! who open upon a cry which ye followed not when the stag was at bay. De Bracy scorns your censure as he would disdain your applause. To your brakes and caves, ye outlawed thieves! and be silent when aught knightly or noble is but spoken within a league of your fox-earths."

This ill-timed defiance might have procured for De Bracy a volley of arrows, but for the hasty and imperative interference of the outlaw chief. Meanwhile the knight caught a horse by the rein, for several which had been taken in the stables of Front-de-Bœuf stood accoutred around, and were a valuable part of the booty. He threw himself upon the saddle, and galloped off through the wood.

When the bustle occasioned by this incident was somewhat com-posed, the chief outlaw took from his neck the rich horn and baldric which he had recently gained at the strife of archery near Ashby.

"Noble knight," he said to him of the Fetterlock, "if you disdain not to grace by your acceptance a bugle which an English yeoman has once worn, this I will pray you to keep as a memorial of your gallant bearing —and, if ye have aught to do, and, as happeneth oft to a gallant knight, ye chance to be hard bested in any forest between Trent and Tees, wind three mots [1] upon the horn thus, *Wasa-hoa!* and it may well chance ye shall find helpers and rescue."

He then gave breath to the bugle, and winded once and again the call which he described, until the knight had caught the notes.

"Gramercy for the gift, bold yeoman," said the Knight; "and better help than thine and thy rangers would I never seek, were it at my utmost need." And then in his turn winded the call till all the greenwood rang.

"Well blown and clearly," said the yeoman; "beshrew me an thou knowest not as much of woodcraft as of war!—thou hast been a striker of deer in thy day, I warrant.—Comrades, mark these three mots—it is the call of the Knight of the Fetterlock; and he who hears it, and hastens not to serve him at his need, I will have him scourged out of our band with his own bowstring."

"Long live our leader!" shouted the yeomen, "and long live the Black Knight of the Fetterlock!—May he soon use our service, to prove how readily it will be paid."

Locksley now proceeded to the distribution of the spoil which he performed with the most laudable impartiality. A tenth part of the whole was set apart for the church, and for pious uses; a portion was next allotted to a sort of public treasury; a part was assigned to the widows and children of those who had fallen, or to be expended in masses for the soul of such as had left no surviving family. The rest was divided amongst the outlaws, according to their rank and merit; and the judgment of the chief, on all such doubtful questions as occurred, was delivered with great shrewdness, and received with absolute sub- mission. The Black Knight was not a little surprised to find that men, in a state so lawless, were nevertheless among themselves so regularly and equitably governed, and all that he observed added to his opinion of the justice and judgment of their leader.

When each had taken his own proportion of the booty, and while the treasurer, accompanied by four tall yeomen, was transporting that be- longing to the state to some place of concealment or of security, the portion devoted to the church still remained unappropriated.

"I would," said the leader, "we could hear tidings of our joyous chap- lain—he was never wont to be absent when meat was to be blessed, or spoil to be parted; and it is his duty to take care of these the tithes of our successful enterprise. It may be the office has helped to cover some of his canonical irregularities. Also, I have a holy brother of his a prisoner at no great distance, and I would fain have the Friar to help

---

[1] The notes upon the bugle were anciently called mots, and are distinguished in the old treatises on hunting, not by musical characters, but by written words.

me to deal with him in due sort—I greatly misdoubt the safety of the bluff priest."

"I were right sorry for that," said the Knight of the Fetterlock, "for I stand indebted to him for the joyous hospitality of a merry night in his cell. Let us to the ruins of the castle; it may be we shall there learn some tidings of him."

While they thus spoke, a loud shout among the yeomen announced the arrival of him for whom they feared, as they learned from the stentorian voice of the Friar himself, long before they saw his burly person.

"Make room, my merry-men!" he exclaimed; "room for your godly father and his prisoner. Cry welcome once more.—I come, noble leader, like an eagle with my prey in my clutch." And making his way through the ring, amidst the laughter of all around, he appeared in majestic triumph, his huge partisan in one hand, and in the other a halter, one end of which was fastened to the neck of the unfortunate Isaac of York, who, bent down by sorrow and terror, was dragged on by the victorious priest, who shouted aloud, "Where is Allan-a-Dale, to chronicle me in a ballad, or if it were but a lay?—By Saint Hermangild, the jingling crowder is ever out of the way where is an apt theme for exalting valour!"

"Curtal Priest," said the captain, "thou hast been at a wet mass this morning, as early as it is. In the name of Saint Nicholas, whom hast thou got here?"

"A captive to my sword and to my lance, noble captain," replied the Clerk of Copmanhurst; "to my bow and to my halberd, I should rather say; and yet I have redeemed him by my divinity from a worse captivity. Speak, Jew—have I not ransomed thee from Sathanas?—have I not taught thee thy *credo*, thy *pater*, and thine *Ave Maria?*—Did I not spend the whole night in drinking to thee, and in expounding of mysteries?"

"For the love of God!" ejaculated the poor Jew, "will no one take me out of the keeping of this mad—I mean this holy man?"

"How's this, Jew?" said the Friar, with a menacing aspect; "dost thou recant, Jew?—Bethink thee, if thou dost relapse into thine infidelity, though thou art not so tender as a suckling pig—I would I had one to break my fast upon—thou art not too tough to be roasted! Be conformable, Isaac, and repeat the words after me. *Ave Maria!*"—

"Nay, we will have no profanation, mad priest," said Locksley; "let us rather hear where you found this prisoner of thine."

"By Saint Dunstan," said the Friar, "I found him where I sought for better ware! I did step into the cellarage to see what might be rescued there; for though a cup of burnt wine, with spice, be an evening's draught for an emperor, it were waste, methought, to let so much good liquor be mulled at once; and I had caught up one runlet of sack, and was coming to call more aid among these lazy knaves, who are ever to seek when a good deed is to be done, when I was advised of a strong door. Aha! thought I, here is the choicest juice of all in this secret crypt; and the knave butler, being disturbed in his vocation, hath left the key in the door. In therefore I went, and found just nought besides a commodity of rusted chains and this dog of a Jew, who presently rendered himself my prisoner, rescue or no rescue. I did but refresh myself after the fatigue of the action, with the unbeliever, with one humming cup of sack, and was proceeding to lead forth my captive, when crash after crash, as with wild thunder-dint and levin-fire, down toppled the masonry of an outer tower (marry beshrew their hands that built it not the firmer!) and blocked up the passage. The roar of one falling tower followed another —I gave up thought of life; and deeming it a dishonour to one of my profession to pass out of this world in company with a Jew, I heaved up my halberd to beat his brains out; but I took pity on his grey hairs, and judged it better to lay down the partisan, and take up my spiritual weapon for his conversion. And truly, by the blessing of Saint Dunstan, the seed has been sown in good soil; only that, with speaking to him of mysteries through the whole night, and being in a manner fasting (for the few draughts of sack which I sharpened my wits with were not worth marking), my head is well-nigh dizzied, I trow.—But I was clean exhausted.—Gilbert and Wibbald know in what state they found me— quite and clean exhausted."

"We can bear witness," said Gilbert; "for when we had cleared away the ruin, and by Saint Dunstan's help lighted upon the dungeon stair, we found the runlet of sack half empty, the Jew half dead, and the Friar more than half—exhausted, as he calls it."

"Ye be knaves! ye lie!" retorted the offended Friar; "it was you and your gormandizing companions that drank up the sack, and called it your morning draught—I am a pagan, an I kept it not for the captain's own throat. But what recks it? The Jew is converted, and understands all I have told him, very nearly, if not altogether, as well as myself."

"Jew," said the captain, "is this true? hast thou renounced thine unbelief?"

"May I so find mercy in your eyes," said the Jew, "as I know not one word which the reverend prelate spake to me all this fearful night. Alas! I was so distraught with agony, and fear, and grief, that had our holy father Abraham come to preach to me, he had found but a deaf listener."

"Thou liest, Jew, and thou knowest thou dost," said the Friar; "I will remind thee of but one word of our conference—thou didst promise to give all thy substance to our holy Order."

"So help me the promise, fair sirs," said Isaac, even more alarmed than before, "as no such sounds ever crossed my lips! Alas! I am an aged beggar'd man—I fear me a childless—have ruth on me, and let me go!"

"Nay," said the Friar, "if thou dost retract vows made in favour of holy church, thou must do penance."

Accordingly, he raised his halberd, and would have laid the staff of it lustily on the Jew's shoulders had not the Black Knight stopped the blow, and thereby transferred the Holy Clerk's resentment to himself.

"By Saint Thomas of Kent," said he, "an I buckle to my gear, I will teach thee, sir lazy lover, to mell with thine own matters, maugre thine iron case there!"

"Nay, be not wroth with me," said the Knight; "thou knowest I am thy sworn friend and comrade."

"I know no such thing," answered the Friar; "and defy thee for a meddling coxcomb!"

"Nay, but," said the Knight, who seemed to take a pleasure in provoking his quondam host, "hast thou forgotten how, that for my sake (for I say nothing of the temptation of the flagon and the pasty) thou didst break thy vow of fast and vigil?"

"Truly, friend," said the Friar, clenching his huge fist, "I will bestow a buffet on thee."

"I accept of no such presents," said the Knight; "I am content to take thy cuff [1] as a loan, but I will repay thee with usury as deep as ever thy prisoner there exacted in his traffic."

"I will prove that presently," said the Friar.

"Hola!" cried the captain, "what art thou after, mad Friar? brawling beneath our trysting-tree?"

"No brawling," said the Knight, "it is but a friendly interchange of courtesy.—Friar, strike an thou darest—I will stand thy blow, if thou wilt stand mine."

"Thou hast the advantage with that iron pot on thy head," said the churchman; "but have at thee. Down thou goest, an thou wert Goliath of Gath in his brazen helmet."

The Friar bared his brawny arm up to the elbow, and putting his full strength to the blow, gave the Knight a buffet that might have felled an ox. But his adversary stood firm as a rock. A loud shout was uttered by all the yeomen around; for the clerk's cuff was proverbial amongst them, and there were few who, in jest or earnest, had not had occasion to know its vigour.

"Now, Priest," said the Knight, pulling off his gauntlet, "if I had vantage on my head I will have none on my hand—stand fast as a true man."

"*Genam meam dedi vapulatori*—I have given my cheek to the smiter," said the priest; "an thou canst stir me from the spot, fellow, I will freely bestow on thee the Jew's ransom."

So spoke the burly priest, assuming, on his part, high defiance. But who may resist his fate? The buffet of the Knight was given with such strength and good will, that the Friar rolled head over heels upon the plain, to the great amazement of all the spectators. But he arose neither angry nor crestfallen.

---

[1] Note VII.—Richard Cœur-de-Lion.

"Brother," said he to the Knight, "thou shouldst have used thy strength with more discretion. I had mumbled but a lame mass an thou hadst broken my jaw, for the piper plays ill that wants the nether chops Nevertheless, there is my hand in friendly witness that I will exchange no more cuffs with thee, having been a loser by the barter. End now all unkindness. Let us put the Jew to ransom, since the leopard will not change his spots, and a Jew he will continue to be."

"The priest," said Clement, "is not half so confident of the Jew's conversion since he received that buffet on the ear."

"Go to, knave, what pratest thou of conversions?—what, is there no respect?—all masters and no men?—I tell thee, fellow, I was somewhat totty when I received the good knight's blow, or I had kept my ground under it. But an thou gibest more of it, thou shalt learn I can give as well as take."

"Peace all!" said the captain. "And thou, Jew, think of thy ransom; thou needest not to be told that thy race are held to be accursed in all Christian communities, and trust me that we cannot endure thy presence among us. Think, therefore, of an offer, while I examine a prisoner of another cast."

"Were many of Front-de-Bœuf's men taken?" demanded the Black Knight.

"None of note enough to be put to ransom," answered the captain; "a set of hilding fellows there were, whom we dismissed to find them a new master—enough had been done for revenge and profit; the bunch of them were not worth a cardecu. The prisoner I speak of is better booty—a jolly monk riding to visit his leman, and I may judge by his horsegear and wearing apparel. Here cometh the worthy prelate, as pert as a pyet." And between two yeomen, was brought before the silvan throne of the outlaw chief, our old friend, Prior Aymer of Jorvaulx.

CHAPTER XXXIII

——Flower of warriors,
How is't with Titus Lartius?
Marcius. As with a man busied about decrees,
Condemning some to death and some to exile,
Ransoming him, or pitying, threatening the other.
Coriolanus.

THE captive abbot's features and manners exhibited a whimsical mixture of offended pride, and deranged foppery and bodily terror.

"Why, how now, my masters?" said he, with a voice in which all three emotions were blended. "What order is this among ye? Be ye Turks or Christians that handle a churchman?—Know ye what it is, *manus imponere in servos Domini?* Ye have plundered my mails—torn my cope of curious cut lace, which might have served a cardinal!—Another in my place would have been at his *excommunicabo vos;* but I am

placable, and if ye order forth my palfreys, release my brethren, and
restore my mails, tell down with all speed an hundred crowns to be expended in masses at the high altar of Jorvaulx Abbey, and make your
vow to eat no venison until next Pentecost, it may be you shall hear little
more of this mad frolic."

"Holy father," said the chief outlaw, "it grieves me to think that you
have met with such usage from any of my followers, as calls for your
fatherly reprehension."

"Usage!" echoed the priest, encouraged by the mild tone of the silvan
leader; "it were usage fit for no hound of good race—much less for a
Christian—far less for a priest—and least of all for the Prior of the holy
community of Jorvaulx. Here is a profane and drunken minstrel called
Allan-a-Dale—*nebulo quidam*—who has menaced me with corporal punishment—nay, with death itself, an I pay not down four hundred crowns
of ransom, to be the boot of all the treasure he hath already robbed me
of—gold chains and gymmal rings to an unknown value; besides what
is broken and spoiled among their rude hands, such as my pouncet-box
and silver crisping-tongs."

"It is impossible that Allan-a-Dale can have thus treated a man of
your reverend bearing," replied the captain.

"It is true as the gospel of Saint Nicodemus," said the Prior; "he
swore, with many a cruel north-country oath, that he would hang me
up on the highest tree in the greenwood."

"Did he so in very deed? Nay, then, reverend father, I think you had
better comply with his demands—for Allan-a-Dale is the very man to
abide by his word when he has so pledged it." [1]

"You do but jest with me," said the astounded Prior, with a forced
laugh; "and I love a good jest with all my heart. But, ha! ha! ha! when
the mirth has lasted the livelong night, it is time to be grave in the
morning."

"And I am grave as a father confessor," replied the outlaw; "you must
pay a round ransom, Sir Prior, or your convent is likely to be called
to a new election; for your place will know you no more."

"Are ye Christians," said the Prior, "and hold this language to a
churchman?"

"Christians! ay, marry, are we and have divinity among us to boot,"
answered the outlaw. "Let our buxom chaplain stand forth, and expound
to this reverend father the texts which concern this matter."

The Friar, half-drunk, half-sober, had huddled a friar's frock over
his green cassock, and now summoning together whatever scraps of learning he had acquired by rote in former days, "Holy father," said he,
"*Deus faciat salvam benignitatem vestram*—You are welcome to the
greenwood."

---

[1] A commissary is said to have received similar consolation from a certain com-
mander-in-chief, to whom he complained that a general officer had used some such
threat towards him as that in the text.

"What profane mummery is this?" said the Prior. "Friend, if thou be'st indeed of the church, it were a better deed to show me how I may escape from these men's hands, than to stand ducking and grinning here like a morris-dancer."

"Truly, reverend father," said the Friar, "I know but one mode in which thou mayst escape. This is Saint Andrew's day with us, we are taking our tithes."

"But not of the church, then, I trust, my good brother?" said the Prior.

"Of church and lay," said the Friar; "and therefore, Sir Prior, *facite vobis amicos de Mammone iniquitatis*—make yourselves friends of the mammon of unrighteousness, for no other friendship is like to serve your turn."

"I love a jolly woodsman at heart," said the Prior, softening his tone; "come, ye must not deal too hard with me—I can well of woodcraft, and can wind a horn clear and lustily, and hollo till every oak rings again. Come, ye must not deal too hard with me."

"Give him a horn," said the outlaw; "we will prove the skill he boasts of."

The Prior Aymer winded a blast accordingly. The captain shook his head.

"Sir Prior," he said, "thou blowest a merry note, but it may not ransom thee—we cannot afford, as the legend on a good knight's shield hath it, to set thee free for a blast. Moreover, I have found thee—thou art one of those who, with new French graces and Tra-li-ras, disturb the ancient English bugle notes.—Prior, that last flourish on the recheat hath added fifty crowns to thy ransom, for corrupting the true old manly blasts of venerie."

"Well, friend," said the Abbot peevishly, "thou art ill to please with thy woodcraft. I pray thee be more conformable in this matter of my ranson. At a word—since I must needs, for once, hold a candle to the devil—what ransom am I to pay for walking on Walting-street, without having fifty men at my back?"

"Were it not well," said the lieutenant of the gang apart to the captain, "that the Prior should name the Jew's ransom, and the Jew name the Prior's?"

"Thou art a mad knave," said the captain, "but thy plan transcends! —Here, Jew, step forth—Look at that holy Father Aymer, Prior of the rich Abbey of Jorvaulx, and tell us at what ransom we should hold him? Thou knowest the income of his convent, I warrant thee."

"O, assuredly," said Isaac. "I have trafficked with the good fathers, and brought wheat and barley, and fruits of the earth, and also much wood. O, it is a rich abbey-stede, and they do live upon the fat, and drink the sweet wines upon the lees, these good fathers of Jorvaulx. Ah, if an outcast like me had such a home to go to, and such incomings by the year and by the month, I would pay much gold and silver to redeem my captivity."

"Hound of a Jew!" exclaimed the Prior, "no one knows better than thy own cursed self, that our holy house of God is indebted for the finishing of our chancel"——

"And for the storing of your cellars in the last season with the due allowance of Gascon wine," interrupted the Jew; "but that—that is small matters."

"Hear the infidel dog!" said the churchman; "he jangles as if our holy community did come under debts for the wines we have a license to drink, *propter necessitatem, et ad frigus depellendum.* The circumcised villain blasphemeth the holy church, and Christian men listen and rebuke him not!"

"All this helps nothing," said the leader. "Isaac, pronounce what he may pay, without flaying both hide and hair."

"An six hundred crowns," said Isaac, "the good Prior might well pay to your valours, and never sit less soft in his stall."

"Six hundred crowns," said the leader, gravely; "I am contented— thou hast well spoken, Isaac—six hundred crowns. It is a sentence, Sir Prior."

"A sentence!—a sentence!" exclaimed the band; "Solomon had not done it better."

"Thou hearest thy doom, Prior," said the leader.

"Ye are mad, my masters," said the Prior; "where am I to find such a sum? If I sell the very pyx and candlesticks on the altar at Jorvaulx, I shall scarce raise the half; and it will be necessary for that purpose that I go to Jorvaulx myself; ye may retain as borrows [1] my two priests."

"That will be but blind trust," said the outlaw; "we will retain thee, Prior, and send them to fetch thy ransom. Thou shalt not want a cup of wine and a collop of venison the while; and if thou lovest woodcraft, thou shalt see such as your north country never witnessed."

"Or, if so please you," said Isaac, willing to curry favour with the outlaws, "I can send to York for the six hundred crowns, out of certain monies in my hands, if so be that the most reverend Prior present will grant me a quittance."

"He shall grant thee whatever thou dost list, Isaac," said the captain; "and thou shalt lay down the redemption money for Prior Aymer as well as for thyself."

"For myself! ah, courageous sirs," said the Jew, "I am a broken and impoverished man; a beggar's staff must be my portion through life, supposing I were to pay you fifty crowns."

"The Prior shall judge of that matter," replied the captain. "How say you, Father Aymer? Can the Jew afford a good ransom?"

"*Can* he afford a ransom?" answered the Prior—"Is he not Isaac of York, rich enough to redeem the captivity of the ten tribes of Israel, who were led into Assyrian bondage? I have seen but little of him

---

[1] Burghs, or borrows, signifies pledges. Hence our word to borrow, because we pledge ourselves to restore what is lent.

myself, but our cellarer and treasurer have dealt largely with him, and report says that his house at York is so full of gold and silver as is a shame in any Christian land. Marvel it is to all living Christian hearts that such gnawing adders should be suffered to eat into the bowels of the state, and even of the holy church herself, with foul usuries and extortions."

"Hold, father," said the Jew, "mitigate and assuage your choler. I pray of your reverence to remember that I force my monies upon no one. But when churchmen and laymen, prince and prior, knight and priest, come knocking to Isaac's door, they borrow not his shekels with these uncivil terms. It is then, Friend Isaac, will you pleasure us in this matter, and our day shall be truly kept, so God sa' me?—and Kind Isaac, if ever you served man, show yourself a friend in this need! And when the day comes, and I ask my own, then what hear I but Damned Jew, and The curse of Egypt on your tribe, and all that may stir up the rude and uncivil populace against poor strangers!"

"Prior," said the captain, "Jew though he be, he hath in this spoken well. Do thou, therefore, name his ransom, as he named thine, without farther rude terms."

"None but *latro famosus*—the interpretation whereof," said the Prior, "will I give at some other time and tide—would place a Christian prelate and an unbaptized Jew upon the same bench. But since ye require me to put a price upon this caitiff, I tell you openly that ye will wrong yourselves if you take from him a penny under a thousand crowns."

"A sentence!—a sentence!" exclaimed the chief outlaw.

"A sentence!—a sentence!" shouted his assessors; "the Christian has shown his good nurture, and dealt with us more generously than the Jew."

"The God of my fathers help me!" said the Jew; "will ye bear to the ground an impoverished creature? I am this day childless, and will ye deprive me of the means of livelihood?"

"Thou wilt have the less to provide for, Jew, if thou art childless," said Aymer.

"Alas! my lord," said Isaac, "your law permits you not to know how the child of our bosom is entwined with the strings of our heart—O Rebecca! daughter of my beloved Rachel! were each leaf on that tree a zecchin, and each zecchin mine own, all that mass of wealth would I give to know whether thou art alive, and escaped the hands of the Nazarene!"

"Was not thy daughter dark-haired?" said one of the outlaws; "and wore she not a veil of twisted sendal, broidered with silver?"

"She did!—she did!" said the old man, trembling with eagerness, as formerly with fear. "The blessing of Jacob be upon thee! canst thou tell me aught of her safety?"

"It was she, then," said the yeoman, "who was carried off by the proud Templar, when he broke through our ranks on yester-even. I had drawn my bow to send a shaft after him, but spared him even for the sake of the damsel, who I feared might take harm from the arrow."

"Oh!" answered the Jew, "I would to God thou hadst shot, though the arrow had pierced her bosom! Better the tomb of her fathers than the dishonourable couch of the licentious and savage Templar. Ichabod! Ichabod! the glory hath departed from my house!"

"Friends," said the chief, looking round, "the old man is but a Jew, natheless his grief touches me.—Deal uprightly with us, Isaac—will paying this ransom of a thousand crowns leave thee altogether penniless?"

Isaac, recalled to think of his worldly goods, the love of which, by dint of inveterate habit, contended even with his parental affection, grew pale, stammered, and could not deny there might be some small surplus.

"Well—gc to—what though there be," said the outlaw, "we will not reckon with thee too closely. Without treasure thou mayst as well hope to redeem thy child from the clutches of Sir Brian de Bois-Guilbert, as to shoot a stag-royal with a headless shaft. We will take thee at the same ransom with Prior Aymer, or rather at one hundred crowns lower, which hundred crowns shall be mine own peculiar loss, and not light upon this worshipful community; and so we shall avoid the heinous offence of rating a Jew merchant as high as a Christian prelate, and thou wilt have six hundred crowns remaining to treat for thy daughter's ransom. Templars love the glitter of silver shekels as well as the sparkle of black eyes. Hasten to make thy crowns chink in the ear of De Bois-Guilbert, ere worse comes of it. Thou wilt find him, as our scouts have brought notice, at the next Preceptory house of his Order. Said I well, my merry mates?"

The yeomen expressed their wonted acquiescence in their leader's opinion; and Isaac, relieved of one half of his apprehensions, by learning that his daughter lived, and might possibly be ransomed, threw himself at the feet of the generous outlaw, and, rubbing his beard against his buskins, sought to kiss the hem of his green cassock. The captain drew himself back, and extricated himself from the Jew's grasp, not without some marks of contempt.

"Nay, beshrew thee, man, up with thee! I am English born, and love no such Eastern prostrations—Kneel to God, and not to a poor sinner, like me."

"Ay, Jew," said Prior Aymer, "kneel to God, as represented in the servant of his altar, and who knows, with thy sincere repentance and due gifts to the shrine of Saint Robert, what grace thou mayst acquire for thyself and thy daughter Rebecca? I grieve for the maiden, for she is of fair and comely countenance,—I beheld her in the lists of Ashby. Also Brian de Bois-Guilbert is one with whom I may do much—bethink thee how thou mayst deserve my good word with him."

"Alas! alas!" said the Jew, "on every hand the spoilers arise against me—I am given as a prey unto the Assyrian, and a prey unto him of Egypt."

"And what else should be the lot of thy accursed race?" answered the Prior; "for what saith holy writ, *verbum Domini projecerunt, et sapientia est nulla in eis*—they have cast forth the word of the Lord, and there is no wisdom in them; *propterea dabo mulieres eorum exteris*—I will give their women to strangers, that is to the Templar, as in the present matter; *et thesauros eorum hæredibus alienis,* and their treasures to others—as in the present case to these honest gentlemen."

Isaac groaned deeply, and began to wring his hands, and to relapse into his state of desolation and despair. But the leader of the yeomen led him aside.

"Advise thee well, Isaac," said Locksley, "what thou wilt do in this matter; my counsel to thee is to make a friend of this churchman. He is vain, Isaac, and he is covetous; at least he needs money to supply his profusion. Thou canst easily gratify his greed; for think not that I am blinded by thy pretexts of poverty. I am intimately acquainted, Isaac, with the very iron chest in which thou dost keep thy money-bags. What! know I not the great stone beneath the apple tree, that leads into the vaulted chamber under thy garden at York?" The Jew grew as pale as death. "But fear nothing from me," continued the yeoman, "for we are of old acquainted. Dost thou not remember the sick yeoman whom thy fair daughter Rebecca redeemed from the gyves at York, and kept him in thy house till his health was restored, when thou didst dismiss him recovered, and with a piece of money?—Usurer as thou art, thou didst never place coin at better interest than that poor silver mark, for it has this day saved thee five hundred crowns."

"And thou art he whom we called Diccon Bend-the-Bow?" said Isaac; "I thought ever I knew the accent of thy voice."

"I am Bend-the-Bow," said the captain, "and Locksley, and have a good name besides all these."

"But thou art mistaken, good Bend-the-Bow, concerning that same vaulted apartment. So help me Heaven, as there is nought in it but some merchandises which I will gladly part with to you—one hundred yards of Lincoln green to make doublets to thy men, and a hundred staves of Spanish yew to make bows, and one hundred silken bow-strings, tough, round, and sound—these will I send thee for thy good-will, honest Diccon, and thou wilt keep silence about the vault, my good Diccon."

"Silent as a dormouse," said the outlaw; "and never trust me but I am grieved for thy daughter. But I may not help it. The Templar's lances are too strong for my archery in the open field—they would scatter us like dust. Had I but known it was Rebecca when she was borne off, something might have been done; but now thou must needs proceed by policy. Come, shall I treat for thee with the Prior?"

"In God's name, Diccon, an thou canst, aid me to recover the child of my bosom!"

"Do not thou interrupt me with thine ill-timed avarice," said the outlaw, "and I will deal with him in thy behalf."

He then turned from the Jew, who followed him, however, as closely as his shadow.

"Prior Aymer," said the captain, "come apart with me under this tree. Men say thou dost love wine, and a lady's smile, better than beseems thy Order, Sir Priest; but with that I have nought to do. I have heard, too, that thou dost love a brace of good dogs and a fleet horse, and it may well be that, loving things which are costly to come by, thou hatest not a purse of gold. But I have never heard that thou didst love oppression or cruelty. Now, here is Isaac willing to give thee the means of pleasure and pastime in a bag containing one hundred marks of silver, if thy intercession with thine ally the Templar shall avail to procure the freedom of his daughter."

"In safety and honour, as when taken from me," said the Jew, "otherwise it is no bargain."

"Peace, Isaac," said the outlaw, "or I give up thine interest—What say you to this my purpose, Prior Aymer?"

"The matter," quoth the Prior, "is of a mixed condition; for, if I do a good deed on the one hand, yet, on the other, it goeth to the vantage of a Jew, and in so much is against my conscience. Yet, if the Israelite will advantage the Church by giving me somewhat over to the building of our dortour, I will take it on my conscience to aid him in the matter of his daughter."

"For a score of marks to the dortour," said the outlaw. "Be still, I say, Isaac!—or for a brace of silver candlesticks to the altar, we will not stand with you."

"Nay, but, good Diccon Bend-the-Bow," said Isaac, endeavouring to interpose.

"Good Jew—good beast—good earthworm!" said the yeoman, losing patience; "an thou dost go on to put thy filthy lucre in the balance with thy daughter's life and honour, by Heaven, I will strip thee of every maravedi thou hast in the world, before three days are out!"

Isaac shrunk together, and was silent.

"And what pledge am I to have for all this?" said the Prior.

"When Isaac returns successful through your mediation," said the outlaw, "I swear by Saint Hubert, I will see that he pays thee the money in good silver, or I will reckon with him for it in such sort, he had better have paid twenty such sums."

"Well, then, Jew," said Aymer, "since I must needs meddle in this matter, let me have the use of thy writing-tablets—though, hold—rather than use thy pen, I would fast for twenty-four hours, and where shall I find one?"

"If your holy scruples can dispense with using the Jew's tablets, for the pen I can find a remedy," said the yeoman; and, bending his bow, he aimed his shaft at a wild-goose which was soaring over their heads, the advanced-guard of a phalanx of his tribe, which were winging their way to the distant and solitary fens of Holderness. The bird came fluttering down, transfixed with the arrow.

"There, Prior," said the captain, "are quills enow to supply all the monks of Jorvaulx for the next hundred years, an they take not to writing chronicles."

The Prior sat down, and at great leisure indited an epistle to Brian de Bois-Guilbert, and having carefully sealed up the tablets, delivered them to the Jew, saying, "This will be thy safe-conduct to the Preceptory of Templestowe, and, as I think, is most likely to accomplish the delivery of thy daughter, if it be well backed with proffers of advantage and commodity at thine own hand; for, trust me well, the good Knight Bois-Guilbert is of their confraternity that do nought for nought."

"Well, Prior," said the outlaw, "I will detain thee no longer here than to give the Jew a quittance for the six hundred crowns at which thy ransom is fixed—I accept of him for my paymaster; and if I hear that ye boggle at allowing him in his accompts the sum so paid by him, Saint Mary refuse me, an I burn not the abbey over thine head, though I hang ten years the sooner!"

With a much worse grace than that wherewith he had penned the letter to Bois-Guilbert, the Prior wrote an acquittance, discharging Isaac of York of six hundred crowns, advanced to him in his need for acquittal of his ransom, and faithfully promising to hold true compt with him for that sum.

"And now," said Prior Aymer, "I will pray you of restitution of my mules and palfreys, and the freedom of the reverend brethren attending upon me, and also of the gymmal rings, jewels, and fair vestures of which I have been despoiled, having now satisfied you for my ransom as a true prisoner."

"Touching your brethren, Sir Prior," said Locksley, "they shall have present freedom, it were unjust to detain them; touching your horses and mules, they shall also be restored, with such spending-money as may enable you to reach York, for it were cruel to deprive you of the means of journeying. But as concerning rings, jewels, chains, and what else, you must understand that we are men of tender consciences, and will not yield to a venerable man like yourself, who should be dead to the vanities of this life, the strong temptation to break the rule of his foundation, by wearing rings, chains, or other vain gauds."

"Think what you do, my masters," said the Prior, "ere you put your hand on the Church's patrimony. These things are *inter res sacres*, and I wot not what judgment might ensue were they to be handled by laical hands."

"I will take care of that, reverend Prior," said the hermit of Copmanhurst; "for I will wear them myself."

"Friend, or brother," said the Prior, in answer to this solution of his doubts, "if thou hast really taken religious orders, I pray thee to look how thou wilt answer to thine official for the share thou hast taken in this day's work."

"Friend Prior," returned the hermit, "you are to know that I belong to a little diocese, where I am my own diocesan, and care as little for the Bishop of York as I do for the Abbot of Jorvaulx, the Prior, and all the convent."

"Thou art utterly irregular," said the Prior; "one of those disorderly men, who, taking on them the sacred character without due cause, profane the holy rites, and endanger the souls of those who take counsel at their hands; *lapides pro pane condonantes iis,* giving them stones instead of bread, as the Vulgate hath it."

"Nay," said the Friar, "an my brain-pan could have been broken by Latin, it had not held so long together.—I say, that easing a world of such misproud priests as thou art of their jewels and their grimcracks is a lawful spoiling of the Egyptians."

"Thou b'est a hedge-priest," [1] said the Prior, in great wrath, *"excommunicabo vos."*

"Thou be'st thyself more like a thief and a heretic," said the Friar, equally indignant; "I will pouch up no such affront before my parishioners, as thou thinkest it not shame to put upon me, although I be a reverend brother to thee. *Ossa ejus perfringam,* I will break your bones, as the Vulgate hath it."

"Hola!" cried the captain, "come the reverend brethren to such terms? —Keep thine assurance of peace, Friar.—Prior, an thou hast not made thy peace perfect with God, provoke the Friar no further. Hermit, let the reverend father depart in peace, as a ransomed man."

The yeomen separated the incensed priests, who continued to raise their voices, vituperating each other in bad Latin, which the Prior delivered the more fluently, and the Hermit with the greater vehemence. The Prior at length recollected himself sufficiently to be aware that he was compromising his dignity, by squabbling with such a hedge-priest as the outlaw's chaplain, and being joined by his attendants, rode off with considerably less pomp, and in a much more apostolical condition, so far as worldly matters were concerned, than he had exhibited before this rencounter.

It remained that the Jew should produce some security for the ransom which he was to pay on the Prior's account, as well as upon his own. He gave, accordingly, an order sealed with his signet, to a brother of his tribe at York, requiring him to pay to the bearer the sum of a thousand crowns, and to deliver certain merchandises specified in the note.

"My brother Sheva," he said, groaning deeply, "hath the key of my warehouses."

"And of the vaulted chamber," whispered Locksley.

1 Note VIII.—Hedge-Priests.

"No, no—may heaven forfend!" said Isaac; "evil is the hour that let any one whomsoever into that secret!"

"It is safe with me," said the outlaw, "so be that this thy scroll produce the sum therein nominated and set down. But what now, Isaac? art dead? art stupefied? hath the payment of a thousand crowns put thy daughter's peril out of thy mind?"

The Jew started to his feet—"No, Diccon, no—I will presently set forth.—Farewell, thou whom I may not call good, and dare not and will not call evil."

Yet ere Isaac departed, the outlaw chief bestowed on him this parting advice:—"Be liberal of thine offers, Isaac, and spare not thy purse for thy daughter's safety. Credit me, that the gold thou shalt spare in her cause, will hereafter give thee as much agony as if it were poured molten down thy throat."

Isaac acquiesced with a deep groan, and set forth on his journey, accompanied by two tall foresters, who were to be his guides, and at the same time his guards, through the wood.

The Black Knight, who had seen with no small interest these various proceedings, now took his leave of the outlaw in turn; nor could he avoid expressing his surprise at having witnessed so much of civil policy amongst persons cast out from all the ordinary protection and influence of the laws.

"Good fruit, Sir Knight," said the yeoman, "will sometimes grow on a sorry tree; and evil times are not always productive of evil alone and unmixed. Amongst those who are drawn into this lawless state, there are, doubtless, numbers who wish to exercise its license with some moderation, and some who regret, it may be, that they are obliged to follow such a trade at all."

"And to one of those," said the Knight, "I am now, I presume, speaking?"

"Sir Knight," said the outlaw, "we have each our secret. You are welcome to form your judgment of me, and I may use my conjectures touching you, though neither of our shafts may hit the mark they are shot at. But as I do not pray to be admitted into your mystery, be not offended that I preserve my own."

"I crave pardon, brave outlaw," said the Knight, "your reproof is just. But it may be we shall meet hereafter with less of concealment on either side. Meanwhile we part friends, do we not?"

"There is my hand upon it," said Locksley; "and I will call it the hand of a true Englishman, though an outlaw for the present."

"And there is mine in return," said the Knight, "and I hold it honoured by being clasped with yours. For he that does good, having the unlimited power to do evil, deserves praise not only for the good which he performs, but for the evil which he forbears. Fare thee well, gallant outlaw!"

Thus parted that fair fellowship; and He of the Fetterlock, mounting upon his strong war-horse, rode off through the forest.

CHAPTER XXXIV

King John. I'll tell thee what, my friend,
He is a very serpent in my way;
And wheresoe'er this foot of mine doth tread,
He lies before me.—Dost thou understand me?
                              King John.

THERE was brave feasting in the Castle of York, to which Prince John had invited those nobles, prelates, and leaders, by whose assistance he hoped to carry through his ambitious projects upon his brother's throne. Waldemar Fitzurse, his able and politic agent, was at secret work among them, tempering all to that pitch of courage which was necessary in making an open declaration of their purpose. But their enterprise was delayed by the absence of more than one main limb of the confederacy. The stubborn and daring, though brutal courage of Front-de-Bœuf; the buoyant spirits and bold bearing of De Bracy; the sagacity, martial experience, and renowned valour of Brian de Bois-Guilbert, were important to the success of their conspiracy; and, while cursing in secret their unnecessary and unmeaning absence, neither John nor his adviser dared to proceed without them. Isaac the Jew also seemed to have vanished, and with him the hope of certain sums of money, making up the subsidy for which Prince John had contracted with that Israelite and his brethren. This deficiency was likely to prove perilous in an emergency so critical.

It was on the morning after the fall of Torquilstone that a confused report began to spread abroad in the city of York, that De Bracy and Bois-Guilbert, with their confederate Front-de-Bœuf, had been taken or slain. Waldemar brought the rumour to Prince John, announcing that he feared its truth the more that they had set out with a small attendance, for the purpose of committing an assault on the Saxon Cedric and his attendants. At another time the Prince would have treated this deed of violence as a good jest; but now that it interfered with and impeded his own plans, he exclaimed against the perpetrators, and spoke of the broken laws, and the infringement of public order and of private property, in a tone which might have become King Alfred.

"The unprincipled marauders," he said—"were I ever to become monarch of England, I would hang such transgressors over the drawbridges of their own castles."

"But to become monarch of England," said his Ahithophel coolly, "it is necessary not only that your Grace should endure the transgressions of these unprincipled marauders, but that you should afford them your protection, notwithstanding your laudable zeal for the laws they are in the habit of infringing. We shall be finely helped, if the churl Saxons should have realised your Grace's vision, of converting feudal drawbridges into gibbets; and yonder bold-spirited Cedric seemeth one to whom such an imagination might occur. Your Grace is well aware it will be dangerous to stir without Front-de-Bœuf, De Bracy, and the Templar; and yet we have gone too far to recede with safety."

Prince John struck his forehead with impatience, and then began to stride up and down the apartment.

"The villains," he said, "the base treacherous villains, to desert me at this pinch!"

"Nay, say rather the feather-pated giddy madmen," said Waldemar, "who must be toying with follies when such business was in hand."

"What is to be done?" said the Prince, stopping short before Waldemar.

"I know nothing which can be done," answered his counsellor, "save that which I have already taken order for. I came not to bewail this evil chance with your Grace, until I had done my best to remedy it."

"Thou art ever my better angel, Waldemar," said the Prince, "and when I have such a chancellor to advise withal, the reign of John will be renowned in our annals. What hast thou commanded?"

"I have ordered Louis Winkelbrand, De Bracy's lieutenant, to cause his trumpet sound to horse, and to display his banner, and to set presently forth towards the castle of Front-de-Bœuf, to do what yet may be done for the succour of our friends."

Prince John's face flushed with the pride of a spoilt child, who has undergone what it conceives to be an insult.

"By the face of God!" he said, "Waldemar Fitzurse, much hast thou taken upon thee! and over malapert thou wert to cause trumpet to blow, or banner to be raised, in a town where ourselves were in presence, without our express command."

"I crave your Grace's pardon," said Fitzurse, internally cursing the idle vanity of his patron; "but when time pressed, and even the loss of minutes might be fatal, I judged it best to take this much burden upon me, in a matter of such importance to your Grace's interest."

"Thou art pardoned, Fitzurse," said the Prince, gravely; "thy purpose hath atoned for thy hasty rashness. But whom have we here?—De Bracy himself, by the rood!—and in strange guise doth he come before us."

It was indeed De Bracy—"bloody with spurring, fiery red with speed." His armour bore all the marks of the late obstinate fray, being broken, defaced, and stained with blood in many places, and covered with clay and dust from the crest to the spur. Undoing his helmet, he placed it on the table, and stood a moment as if to collect himself before he told his news.

"De Bracy," said Prince John, "what means this?—Speak, I charge thee!—Are the Saxons in rebellion?"

"Speak, De Bracy," said Fitzurse, almost in the same moment with his master, "thou wert wont to be a man—Where is the Templar?—where Front-de-Bœuf?"

"The Templar is fled," said De Bracy; "Front-de-Bœuf you will never see more. He has found a red grave among the blazing rafters of his own castle, and I alone am escaped to tell you."

"Cold news," said Waldemar, "to us, though you speak of fire and conflagration."

"The worst news is not yet said," answered De Bracy; and, coming up to Prince John, he uttered in a low and emphatic tone—"Richard is in England—I have seen and spoken with him."

Prince John turned pale, tottered, and caught at the back of an oaken bench to support himself—much like to a man who receives an arrow in his bosom.

"Thou ravest, De Bracy," said Fitzurse, "it cannot be."

"It is as true as truth itself," said De Bracy; "I was his prisoner, and spoke with him."

"With Richard Plantagenet, sayest thou?" continued Fitzurse.

"With Richard Plantagenet," replied De Bracy, "with Richard Cœur-de-Lion—with Richard of England."

"And thou wert his prisoner?" said Waldemar; "he is then at the head of a power?"

"No—only a few outlawed yeomen were around him, and to these his person is unknown. I heard him say he was about to depart from them. He joined them only to assist at the storming of Torquilstone."

"Ay," said Fitzurse, "such is indeed the fashion of Richard—a true knight-errant he, and will wander in wild adventure, trusting the prowess of his single arm, like any Sir Guy or Sir Bevis, while the weighty affairs of his kingdom slumber, and his own safety is endangered. What dost thou propose to do, De Bracy?"

"I?—I offered Richard the service of my Free Lances, and he refused them—I will lead them to Hull, seize on shipping, and embark for Flanders; thanks to the bustling times, a man of action will always find employment. And thou, Waldemar, wilt thou take lance and shield, and lay down thy policies, and wend along with me, and share the fate which God sends us?"

"I am too old, Maurice, and I have a daughter," answered Waldemar.

"Give her to me, Fitzurse, and I will maintain her as fits her rank, with the help of lance and stirrup," said De Bracy.

"Not so," answered Fitzurse; "I will take sanctuary in this church of Saint Peter—the Archbishop is my sworn brother."

During this discourse, Prince John had gradually awakened from the stupor into which he had been thrown by the unexpected intelligence, and had been attentive to the conversation which passed betwixt his followers. "They fall off from me," he said to himself, "they hold no more by me than a withered leaf by the bough when a breeze blows on it! Hell and fiends! can I shape no means for myself when I am deserted by these cravens?" He paused, and there was an expression of diabolical passion in the constrained laugh with which he at length broke in on their conversation.

"Ha, ha, ha! my good lords, by the light of Our Lady's brow, I held ye sage men, bold men, ready-witted men; yet ye throw down wealth,

honour, pleasure, all that our noble game promised you, at the moment
it might be won by one bold cast!"

"I understand you not," said De Bracy. "As soon as Richard's return
is blown abroad, he will be at the head of an army, and all is then over
with us. I would counsel you, my lord, either to fly to France or take
the protection of the Queen Mother."

"I seek no safety for myself," said Prince John, haughtily; "that I
could secure by a word spoken to my brother. But although you, De
Bracy, and you, Waldemar Fitzurse, are so ready to abandon me, I
should not greatly delight to see your heads blackening on Clifford's
gate yonder. Thinkest thou, Waldemar, that the wily Archbishop will not
suffer thee to be taken from the very horns of the altar, would it make
his peace with King Richard? And forgettest thou, De Bracy, that Robert
Estoteville lies betwixt thee and Hull with all his forces, and that the
Earl of Essex is gathering his followers? If we had reason to fear these
levies even before Richard's return, trowest thou there is any doubt now
which party their leaders will take? Trust me, Estoteville alone has
strength enough to drive all thy Free Lances into the Humber."—Waldemar Fitzurse and De Bracy looked in each other's faces with blank dismay.—"There is but one road to safety," continued the Prince, and his
brow grew black as midnight; "this object of our terror journeys alone;
he must be met withal."

"Not by me," said De Bracy, hastily; "I was his prisoner, and he took
me to mercy. I will not harm a feather in his crest."

"Who spoke of harming him?" said Prince John, with a hardened
laugh; "the knave will say next that I meant he should slay him! No—a
prison were better; and whether in Britain or Austria, what matters it?
Things will be but as they were when we commenced our enterprise. It
was founded on the hope that Richard would remain a captive in Germany. Our uncle Robert lived and died in the castle of Cardiff."

"Ay, but," said Waldemar, "your sire Henry sate more firm in his
seat than your Grace can. I say the best prison is that which is made
by the sexton—no dungeon like a church vault! I have said my say."

"Prison or tomb," said De Bracy, "I wash my hands of the whole
matter."

"Villain!" said Prince John, "thou wouldst not bewray our counsel?"

"Counsel was never bewrayed by me," said De Bracy, haughtily, "nor
must the name of villain be coupled with mine!"

"Peace, Sir Knight!" said Waldemar; "and you, good my lord, forgive the scruples of valiant De Bracy; I trust I shall soon remove them."

"That passes your eloquence, Fitzurse," replied the Knight.

"Why, good Sir Maurice," rejoined the wily politician, "start not aside
like a scared steed, without, at least, considering the object of your
terror. This Richard—but a day since, and it would have been thy
dearest wish to have met him hand to hand in the ranks of battle—a
hundred times I have heard thee wish it."

"Ay," said De Bracy, "but that was as thou sayest, hand to hand, and in the ranks of battle! Thou never heardest me breathe a thought of assaulting him alone, and in a forest."

"Thou art no good knight if thou dost scruple at it," said Waldemar. "Was it in battle that Lancelot de Lac and Sir Tristram won renown? or was it not by encountering gigantic knights under the shade of deep and unknown forests?"

"Ay, but I promise you," said De Bracy, "that neither Tristram nor Lancelot would have been match, hand to hand, for Richard Plantagenet, and I think it was not their wont to take odds against a single man."

"Thou art mad, De Bracy—what is it we propose to thee, a hired and retained captain of Free Companions, whose swords are purchased for Prince John's service? Thou art apprised of our enemy, and then thou scruplest, though thy patron's fortunes, those of thy comrades, thine own, and the life and honour of every one amongst us, be at stake!"

"I tell you," said De Bracy, sullenly, "that he gave me my life. True, he sent me from his presence, and refused my homage—so far I own him neither favour nor allegiance—but I will not lift hand against him."

"It needs not—send Louis Winkelbrand and a score of thy lances."

"Ye have sufficient ruffians of your own," said De Bracy; "not one of mine shall budge on such an errand."

"Art thou so obstinate, De Bracy?" said Prince John; "and wilt thou forsake me, after so many protestations of zeal for my service?"

"I mean it not," said De Bracy; "I will abide by you in aught that becomes a knight, whether in the lists or in the camp; but this highway practice comes not within my vow."

"Come hither, Waldemar," said Prince John. "An unhappy prince am I. My father, King Henry, had faithful servants—He had but to say that he was plagued with a factious priest, and the blood of Thomas-a-Becket, saint though he was, stained the steps of his own altar.—Tracy, Morville, Brito,[1] loyal and daring subject, your names, your spirit, are extinct! and although Reginald Fitzurse hath left a son, he hath fallen off from his father's fidelity and courage."

"He has fallen off from neither," said Waldemar Fitzurse; "and since it may not better be, I will take on me the conduct of this perilous enterprise. Dearly, however, did my father purchase the praise of a zealous friend; and yet did his proof of loyalty to Henry fall far short of what I am about to afford; for rather would I assail a whole calendar of saints, than put spear in rest against Cœur-de-Lion. De Bracy, to thee I must trust to keep up the spirits of the doubtful, and to guard Prince John's person. If you receive such news as I trust to send you, our enterprise will no longer wear a doubtful aspect. Page," he said, "hie to my lodgings, and tell my armourer to be there in readiness; and bid Stephen

---

[1] Reginald Fitzurse, William de Tracy, Hugh de Morville, and Richard Brito, were the gentlemen of Henry the Second's household, who, instigated by some passionate expressions of their sovereign, slew the celebrated Thomas à Becket.

Wetheral, Broad Thoresby, and the Three Spears of Spyinghow, come to me instantly; and let the scout-master, Hugh Bardon, attend me also.—Adieu, my Prince, till better times." Thus speaking, he left the apartment.

"He goes to make my brother prisoner," said Prince John to De Bracy, "with as little touch of compunction, as if it but concerned the liberty of a Saxon franklin. I trust he will observe our orders, and use our dear Richard's person with all due respect."

De Bracy only answered by a smile.

"By the light of our Lady's brow," said Prince John, "our orders to him were most precise—though it may be you heard them not, as we stood together in the oriel window.—Most clear and positive was our charge that Richard's safety should be cared for, and woe to Waldemar's head if he transgress it!"

"I had better pass to his lodgings," said De Bracy, "and make him fully aware of your Grace's pleasure! for, as it quite escaped my ear, it may not perchance have reached that of Waldemar."

"Nay, nay," said Prince John, impatiently. "I promise thee he heard me; and, besides, I have further occupation for thee. Maurice, come hither; let me lean on thy shoulder."

They walked a turn through the hall in this familiar posture and Prince John, with an air of the most confidential intimacy, proceeded to say, "What thinkest thou of this Waldemar Fitzurse, my De Bracy?—He trusts to be our Chancellor. Surely we will pause ere we give an office so high to one who shows evidently how little he reverences our blood, by his so readily undertaking this enterprise against Richard. Thou dost think, I warrant, that thou hast lost somewhat of our regard, by thy boldly declining this unpleasing task. But no, Maurice! I rather honour thee for thy virtuous constancy. There are things most necessary to be done, the perpetrator of which we neither love nor honour; and there may be refusals to serve us, which shall rather exalt in our estimation those who deny our request. The arrest of my unfortunate brother forms no such good title to the high office of Chancellor, as thy chivalrous and courageous denial establishes in thee to the truncheon of High Marshal. Think of this, De Bracy, and begone to thy charge."

"Fickle tyrant!" muttered De Bracy, as he left the presence of the Prince; "evil luck have they who trust thee. Thy Chancellor, indeed! He who hath the keeping of thy conscience shall have an easy charge, I trow. But High Marshal of England! that," he said, extending his arm, as if to grasp the baton of office, and assuming a loftier stride along the ante-chamber, "that is indeed a prize worth playing for!"

De Bracy had no sooner left the apartment than Prince John summoned an attendant.

"Bid Hugh Bardon, our scout-master, come hither, as soon as he shall have spoken with Waldemar Fitzurse."

The scout-master arrived after a brief delay, during which John traversed the apartment with unequal and disordered steps.

"Bardon," said he, "what did Waldemar desire of thee?"

"Two resolute men, well acquainted with these northern wilds, and skilful in tracking the tread of man and horse."

"And thou hast fitted him?"

"Let your grace never trust me else," answered the master of the spies. "One is from Hexamshire; he is wont to trace the Tynedale and Teviotdale thieves, as a bloodhound follows the slot of a hurt deer. The other is Yorkshire bred, and has twanged his bowstring right oft in merry Sherwood; he knows each glade and dingle, copse and high-wood, betwixt this and Richmond."

" 'Tis well," said the Prince.—"Goes Waldemar forth with them?"

"Instantly," said Bardon.

"With what attendance?" asked John, carelessly.

"Broad Thoresby goes with him, and Wetheral, whom they call, for his cruelty, Stephen Steelheart; and three northern men-at-arms that belonged to Ralph Middleton's gang—they are called the Spears of Spyinghow."

" 'Tis well," said Prince John; then added, after a moment's pause, "Bardon, it imports our service that thou keep a strict watch on Maurice de Bracy—so that he shall not observe it, however. And let us know of his motions from time to time—with whom he converses, what he proposeth. Fail not in this, as thou wilt be answerable."

Hugh Bardon bowed, and retired.

"If Maurice betrays me," said Prince John—"if he betrays me, as his bearing leads me to fear, I will have his head, were Richard thundering at the gates of York."

CHAPTER XXXV

Arouse the tiger of Hyrcanian deserts,
Strive with the half-starved lion for his prey;
Lesser the risk, than rouse the slumbering fire
Of wild Fanaticism.

Anonymous.

OUR tale now returns to Isaac of York. Mounted upon a mule, the gift of the outlaw, with two tall yeomen to act as his guard and guides, the Jew had set out for the Preceptory of Templestowe, for the purpose of negotiating his daughter's redemption. The Preceptory was about a day's journey from the demolished castle of Torquilstone, and the Jew had hoped to reach it before nightfall; accordingly having dismissed his guides at the verge of the forest, and rewarded them with a piece of silver, he began to press on with such speed as his weariness permitted him to exert. But his strength failed him totally ere he had reached within four miles of the Temple-Court; racking pains shot along his back and through his limbs, and the excessive anguish which he felt at heart being now augmented by bodily suffering, he was rendered altogether incapable of proceeding farther than a small market-town, where dwelt a Jewish Rabbi of his tribe, eminent in the medical profession, and to whom Isaac was well known. Nathan Ben Israel received his suffering countryman with that kindness which the law prescribed, and which the Jews prac. tised to each other. He insisted on his betaking himself to repose, and used such remedies as were then in most repute to check the progress of the fever, which terror, fatigue, ill usage, and sorrow, had brought upon the poor old Jew.

On the morrow, when Isaac proposed to rise and pursue his journey, Nathan remonstrated against his purpose, both as his host and as his physician. It might cost him, he said, his life. But Isaac replied that more than life and death depended upon his going that morning to Templestowe.

"To Templestowe!" said his host with surprise; again felt his pulse, and then muttered to himself, "His fever is abated, yet seems his mind somewhat alienated and disturbed."

"And why not to Templestowe?" answered his patient. "I grant thee, Nathan, that it is a dwelling of those to whom the despised Children of the Promise are a stumbling-block and an abomination; yet thou knowest that pressing affairs of traffic sometimes carry us among these blood-thirsty Nazarene soldiers, and that we visit the Preceptories of the Templars, as well as the Commanderies of the Knights Hospitallers, as they are called." [1]

"I know it well," said Nathan; "but wottest thou that Lucas de Beaumanoir, the chief of their order, and whom they term Grand Master, is now himself at Templestowe?"

"I know it not," said Isaac; "our last letters from our brethren at Paris advised us that he was at that city, beseeching Philip for aid against the Sultan Saladine."

"He hath since come to England, unexpected by his brethren," said Ben Israel; "and he cometh among them with a strong and outstretched arm to correct and to punish. His countenance is kindled in anger against those who have departed from the vow which they have made, and great is the fear of those sons of Belial. Thou must have heard of his name?"

"It is well known unto me," said Isaac; "the Gentiles deliver this Lucas Beaumanoir as a man zealous to slaying for every point of the Nazarene law; and our brethren have termed him a fierce destroyer of the Saracens, and a cruel tyrant to the Children of the Promise."

"And truly have they termed him," said Nathan the physician. "Other Templars may be moved from the purpose of their heart by pleasure, or

---

[1] The establishments of the Knight Templars were called Preceptories, and the title of those who presided in the Order was Preceptor; as the principal Knights of Saint John were termed Commanders, and their houses Commanderies. But these terms were sometimes, it would seem, used indiscriminately.

bribed by promise of gold and silver; but Beaumanoir is of a different stamp—hating sensuality, despising treasure, and pressing forward to that which they call the crown of martyrdom—The God of Jacob speedily send it unto him, and unto them all! Specially hath this proud man extended his glove over the children of Judah, as holy David over Edom, holding the murder of a Jew to be an offering of as sweet savour as the death of a Saracen. Impious and false things has he said even of the virtues of our medicines, as if they were the devices of Satan—the Lord rebuke him!"

"Nevertheless," said Isaac, "I must present myself at Templestowe, though he hath made his face like unto a fiery furnace seven times heated."

He then explained to Nathan the pressing cause of his journey. The Rabbi listened with interest, and testified his sympathy after the fashion of his people, rending his clothes, and saying, "Ah, my daughter!—ah, my daughter!—Alas! for the beauty of Zion!—Alas! for the captivity of Israel!"

"Thou seest," said Isaac, "how it stands with me, and that I may not tarry. Peradventure, the presence of this Lucas Beaumanoir, being the chief man over them, may turn Brian de Bois-Guilbert from the ill which he doth meditate, and that he may deliver to me my beloved daughter Rebecca."

"Go thou," said Nathan Ben Israel, "and be wise, for wisdom availed Daniel in the den of lions into which he was cast; and may it go well with thee, even as thine heart wisheth. Yet, if thou canst, keep thee from the presence of the Grand Master, for to do foul scorn to our people is his morning and evening delight. It may be if thou couldst speak with Bois-Guilbert in private, thou shalt the better prevail with him; for men say that these accursed Nazarenes are not of one mind in the Preceptory—May their counsels be confounded and brought to shame! But do thou, brother, return to me as if it were to the house of thy father, and bring me word how it has sped with thee; and well do I hope thou wilt bring with thee Rebecca, even the scholar of the wise Miriam, whose cures the Gentiles slandered as if they had been wrought by necromancy."

Isaac accordingly bade his friend farewell, and about an hour's riding brought him before the Preceptory of Templestowe.

This establishment of the Templars was seated amidst fair meadows and pastures, which the devotion of the former Preceptor had bestowed upon their order. It was strong and well fortified, a point never neglected by these knights, and which the disordered state of England rendered peculiarly necessary. Two halberdiers, clad in black, guarded the draw-bridge, and others, in the same sad livery, glided to and fro upon the walls with a funereal pace, resembling spectres more than soldiers. The inferior officers of the order were thus dressed, ever since their use of white garments, similar to those of the knights and esquires, had given rise to a combination of certain false brethren in the mountains of Palestine, terming themselves Templars, and bringing great dishonour on the order. A knight was now and then seen to cross the court in his long white cloak, his head depressed on his breast, and his arms folded. They passed each other, if they chanced to meet, with a slow, solemn, and mute greeting; for such was the rule of their order, quoting thereupon the holy texts, "In many words thou shalt not avoid sin," and, "Life and death are in the power of the tongue." In a word, the stern ascetic rigour of the Temple discipline, which had been so long exchanged for prodigal and licentious indulgence, seemed at once to have revived at Templestowe under the severe eye of Lucas Beaumanoir.

Isaac paused at the gate, to consider how he might seek entrance in the manner most likely to bespeak favour; for he was well aware that to his unhappy race the reviving fanaticism of the order was not less dangerous than their unprincipled licentiousness; and that his religion would be the object of hate and persecution in the one case, as his wealth would have exposed him in the other to the extortions of unrelenting oppression.

Meantime Lucas Beaumanoir walked in a small garden belonging to the Preceptory, included within the precincts of its exterior fortification, and held sad and confidential communication with a brother of his order, who had come in his company from Palestine.

The Grand Master was a man advanced in age, as was testified by his long grey beard, and the shaggy grey eye-brows overhanging eyes, of which, however, years had been unable to quench the fire. A formidable warrior, his thin and severe features retained the soldier's fierceness of expression; an ascetic bigot, they were no less marked by the emaciation of abstinence, and the spiritual pride of the self-satisfied devotee. Yet with these severer traits of physiognomy, there was mixed somewhat striking and noble, arising, doubtless, from the great part which his high office called upon him to act among monarchs and princes, and from the habitual exercise of supreme authority over the valiant and high-born knights, who were united by the rules of the order. His stature was tall, and his gait, undepressed by age and toil, was erect and stately. His white mantle was shaped with severe regularity, according to the rule of Saint Bernard himself, being composed of what was then called Burrel cloth, exactly fitted to the size of the wearer, and bearing on the left shoulder the octangular cross peculiar to the order, formed of red cloth. No vair or ermine decked this garment; but in respect of his age, the Grand Master, as permitted by the rule, wore his doublet lined and trimmed with the softest lambskin, dressed with the wool outwards, which was the nearest approach he could regularly make to the use of fur, then the greatest luxury of dress. In his hand he bore that singular *abacus*, or staff of office, with which Templars are usually represented, having at the upper end a round plate, on which was engraved the cross of the order, inscribed within a circle or orle, as heralds term it. His companion, who attended on this great personage, had nearly the same dress in all respects, but his extreme deference towards his Superior showed that no other equality subsisted between them. The Preceptor, for such he was in rank, walked not in a line with the Grand Master, but just so far behind that Beaumanoir could speak to him without turning round his head.

"Conrade," said the Grand Master, "dear companion of my battles and my toils, to thy faithful bosom alone can I confide my sorrows. To thee alone can I tell how oft, since I came to this kingdom, I have desired to be dissolved and to be with the just. Not one object in England hath met mine eye which it could rest upon with pleasure, save the tombs of our brethren, beneath the massive roof of our Temple Church in yonder proud capital. O, valiant Robert de Ros! did I exclaim internally, as I gazed upon these good soldiers of the cross, where they lie sculptured on their sepulchres,—O, worthy William de Mareschal! open your marble cells, and take to your repose a weary brother, who would rather strive with a hundred thousand pagans than witness the decay of our Holy Order!"

"It is but true," answered Conrade Mont-Fitchet; "it is but too true; and the irregularities of our brethren in England are even more gross than those in France."

"Because they are more wealthy," answered the Grand Master. "Bear with me, brother, although I should something vaunt myself. Thou knowest the life I have led, keeping each point of my order, striving with devils embodied and disembodied, striking down the roaring lion, who goeth about seeking whom he may devour, like a good knight and devout priest, wheresoever I met with him—even as blessed Saint Bernard hath prescribed to us in the forty-fifth capital of our rule, *Ut Leo semper feriatur*.[1] But by the Holy Temple! the zeal which hath devoured my substance and my life, yea, the very nerves and marrow of my bones; by that very Holy Temple I swear to thee, that save thyself and some few that still retain the ancient severity of our order, I look upon no brethren whom I can bring my soul to embrace under that holy name. What say our statutes, and how do our brethren observe them? They should wear no vain or worldly ornament, no crest upon their helmet, no gold upon stirrup or bridle-bit; yet who now go pranked out so proudly and so gaily as the poor soldiers of the Temple? They are forbidden by our statutes to take one bird by means of another, to shoot beasts with bow or arblast, to halloo to a hunting-horn, or to spur the horse after game. But now, at hunting and hawking, and each idle sport of wood and river, who so prompt as the Templars in all these fond vanities? They are forbidden to read, save what their Superior permitted, or listen

---

[1] In the ordinances of the Knights of the Temple, this phrase is repeated in a variety of forms, and occurs in almost every chapter, as if it were the signal-word of the order; which may account for its being so frequently put in the Grand Master's mouth.

to what is read, save such holy things as may be recited aloud during the hours of reflection; but lo! their ears are at the command of idle minstrels, and their eyes study empty romaunts. They were commanded to extirpate magic and heresy. Lo! they are charged with studying the accursed cabalistical secrets of the Jews, and the magic of the Paynim Saracens. Simpleness of diet was prescribed to them, roots, pottage, gruels, eating flesh but thrice a-week, because the accustomed feeding on flesh is a dishonourable corruption of the body; and behold, their tables groan under delicate fare! Their drink was to be water, and now, to drink like a Templar is the boast of each jolly boon companion! This very garden, filled as it is with curious herbs and trees sent from the Eastern climes, better becomes the harem of an unbelieving Emir, than the plot which Christian Monks should devote to raise their homely pot-herbs. And O, Conrade! well it were that the relaxation of discipline stopped even here! Well thou knowest that we were forbidden to receive those devout women, who at the beginning were associated as sisters of our order, because, saith the forty-sixth chapter, the Ancient Enemy hath, by female society, withdrawn many from the right path to paradise. Nay, in the last capital, being, as it were, the cope-stone which our blessed founder placed on the pure and undefiled doctrine which he had enjoined, we are prohibited from offering, even to our sisters and our mothers, the kiss of affection—*ut omnium mulierum fugiantur oscula*. I shame to speak—I shame to think—of the corruptions which have rushed in upon us even like a flood. The souls of our pure founders, the spirits of Hugh de Payen and Godfrey de Saint Omer, and of the blessed Seven who first joined in dedicating their lives to the service of the Temple, are disturbed even in the enjoyment of paradise itself. I have seen them, Conrade, in the visions of the night—their sainted eyes shed tears for the sins and follies of their brethren, and for the foul and shameful luxury in which they wallow. Beaumanior, they say, thou slumberest— awake! There is a stain in the fabric of the Temple, deep and foul as that left by the streaks of leprosy on the walls of the infected houses of old.[1] The soldiers of the Cross, who should shun the glance of a woman as the eye of a basilisk, live in open sin, not with the females of their own race only, but with the daughters of the accursed heathen, and more accursed Jew. Beaumanoir, thou sleepest; up, and avenge our cause! Slay the sinners, male and female! Take to thee the brand of Phineas! The vision fled, Conrade, but as I awaked I could still hear the clank of their mail, and see the waving of their white mantles. And I will do according to their word, I WILL purify the fabric of the Temple! and the unclean stones in which the plague is, I will remove and cast out of the building."

"Yet bethink thee, reverend father," said Mont-Fitchet, "the stain

[1] See the 13th chapter of Leviticus.

hath become engrained by time and consuetude; let thy reformation be cautious, as it is just and wise."

"No, Mont-Fitchet," answered the stern old man—"it must be sharp and sudden—the order is on the crisis of its fate. The sobriety, self-devotion, and piety of our predecessors, made us powerful friends—our presumption, our wealth, our luxury, have raised up against us mighty enemies. We must cast away these riches, which are a temptation to princes—we must lay down that presumption, which is an offence to them—we must reform that license of manners, which is a scandal to the whole Christian world! Or—mark my words—the Order of the Temple will be utterly demolished—and the place thereof shall no more be known among the nations."

"Now may God avert such a calamity!" said the Preceptor.

"Amen," said the Grand Master, with solemnity, "but we must deserve his aid. I tell thee, Conrade, that neither the powers in Heaven, nor the powers on earth, will longer endure the wickedness of this generation. My intelligence is sure—the ground on which our fabric is reared is already undermined, and each addition we make to the structure of our greatness will only sink it the sooner in the abyss. We must retrace our steps, and show ourselves the faithful Champions of the Cross, sacrificing to our calling, not alone our blood and our lives—not alone our lusts and our vices—but our ease, our comforts, and our natural affections, and act as men convinced that many a pleasure which may be lawful to others, is forbidden to the avowed soldier of the Temple."

At this moment a squire, clothed in a threadbare vestment (for the aspirants after this holy order wore during their noviciate the cast-off garments of the knights), entered the garden, and, bowing profoundly before the Grand Master, stood silent, awaiting his permission ere he presumed to tell his errand.

"Is it not more seemly," said the Grand Master, "to see this Damian, clothed in the garments of Christian humility, thus appear with reverend silence before his superior, than but two days since, when the fond fool was decked in a painted coat, and jangling as pert and as proud as any popinjay? Speak, Damian, we permit thee. What is thine errand?"

"A Jew stands without the gate, noble and reverend father," said the squire, "who prays to speak with brother Brian de Bois-Guilbert."

"Thou wert right to give me knowledge of it," said the Grand Master; "in our presence a preceptor is but as a common compeer of our order, who may not walk according to his own will, but to that of his Master— even according to the text, 'In the hearing of the ear he hath obeyed me.' It imports us especially to know of this Bois-Guilbert's proceedings," said he, turning to his companion.

"Report speaks him brave and valiant," said Conrade.

"And truly is he so spoken of," said the Grand Master; "in our valour only we are not degenerated from our predecessors, the heroes of the cross. But brother Brian came into our order, a moody and disappointed man, stirred, I doubt not, to take our vows and to renounce the world, not in sincerity of soul, but as one whom some touch of light discontent had driven into penitence. Since then, he hath become an active and earnest agitator, a murmurer, and a machinator, and a leader amongst those who impugn our authority; not considering that the rule is given to the Master even by the symbol of the staff and the rod—the staff to support the infirmities of the weak—the rod to correct the faults of delinquents. Damian," he continued, "lead the Jew to our presence."

The squire departed with a profound reverence, and in a few minutes returned marshalling in Isaac of York. No naked slave, ushered into the presence of some mighty prince, could approach his judgment-seat with more profound reverence and terror than that with which the Jew drew near to the presence of the Grand Master. When he had approached within the distance of three yards, Beaumanoir made a sign with his staff that he should come no farther. The Jew kneeled down on the earth, which he kissed in token of reverence; then rising, stood before the Templars, his hands folded on his bosom, his head bowed on his breast, in all the submission of Oriental slavery.

"Damian," said the Grand Master, "retire, and have a guard ready to await our sudden call; and suffer no one to enter the garden until we shall leave it." The squire bowed and retreated. "Jew," continued the haughty old man, "mark me. It suits not our condition to hold with thee long communication, nor do we waste words or time upon any one. Wherefore be brief in thy answers to what questions I shall ask thee, and let thy words be of truth; for if thy tongue doubles with me, I will have it torn from thy misbelieving jaws."

The Jew was about to reply, but the Grand Master went on.

"Peace, unbeliever!—not a word in our presence, save in answers to our questions. What is thy business with our brother Brian de Bois-Guilbert?"

Isaac gasped with terror and uncertainty. To tell his tale might be interpreted into scandalising the order; yet, unless he told it, what hope could he have of achieving his daughter's deliverance? Beaumanoir saw his mortal apprehension, and condescended to give him some assurance.

"Fear nothing," he said, "for thy wretched person, Jew, so thou dealest uprightly in this matter. I demand again to know from thee thy business with Brian de Bois-Guilbert?"

"I am bearer of a letter," stammered out the Jew, "so please your reverend valour, to that good knight, from Prior Aymer of the Abbey of Jorvaulx."

"Said I not these were evil times, Conrade?" said the Master. "A Cistertian Prior sends a letter to a soldier of the Temple, and can find no more fitting messenger than an unbelieving Jew. Give me the letter."

The Jew, with trembling hands, undid the folds of his Armenian cap, in which he had deposited the Prior's tablets for the great security, and was about to approach, with hand extended and body crouched, to place it within the reach of his grim interrogator.

"Back, dog!" said the Grand Master; "I touch not misbelievers, save with the sword. Conrade, take thou the letter from the Jew, and give it to me."

Beaumanoir, being thus possessed of the tablets, inspected the outside carefully, and then proceeded to undo the pack-thread which secured its folds. "Reverend father," said Conrade, interposing, though with much deference, "wilt thou break the seal?"

"And will I not?" said Beaumanoir, with a frown. "Is it not written in the forty-second capital, *De Lectione Literarum,* that a Templar shall not receive a letter, no not from his father, without communicating the same to the Grand Master, and reading it in his presence?"

He then perused the letter in haste, with an expression of surprise and horror; read it over again more slowly; then holding it out to Conrade with one hand, and slightly striking it with the other, exclaimed—"Here is goodly stuff for one Christian man to write to another, and both members, and no inconsiderable members, of religious professions! When," said he solemnly, and looking upward, "wilt thou come with thy fanners to purge the thrashing-floor?"

Mont-Fitchet took the letter from his superior, and was about to peruse it. "Read it aloud, Conrade," said the Grand Master, "and do thou" (to Isaac) "attend to the purport of it, for we will question thee concerning it."

Conrade read the letter, which was in these words: "Aymer, by divine grace, Prior of the Cistertian house of Saint Mary's of Jorvaulx, to Sir Brian de Bois-Guilbert, a Knight of the holy Order of the Temple, wisheth health, with the bounties of King Bacchus and of my Lady Venus. Touching our present condition, dear Brother, we are a captive in the hands of certain lawless and godless men, who have not feared to detain our person, and put us to ransom; whereby we have also learned of Front-de Bœuf's misfortune, and that thou hast escaped with that fair Jewish sorceress, whose black eyes have bewitched thee. We are heartily rejoiced of thy safety; nevertheless, we pray thee to be on thy guard in the matter of this second Witch of Endor; for we are privately assured that your Great Master, who careth not a bean for cherry cheeks and black eyes, comes from Normandy to diminish your mirth, and amend your misdoings. Wherefore we pray you heartily to beware, and to be found watching, even as the Holy Text hath it, *Invenientur vigilantes.* And the wealthy Jew her father, Isaac of York, having prayed of me letters in his behalf, I gave him these, earnestly advising, and in a sort entreating, that you do hold the damsel to ransom, seeing he will pay you from his bags as much as may find fifty damsels upon safer terms, whereof I trust to have my part when we make merry together, as true brothers, not forgetting the wine-cup. For what saith the text,

Vinum lætificat cor hominis; and again, *Rex delectabitur pulchritudine tua.*

"Till which merry meeting, we wish you farewell. Given from this den of thieves, about the hour of matins,

"AYMER PR. S. M. JORVOLCIENCIS.

"Postscriptum. Truly your golden chain hath not long abidden with me, and will now sustain, around the neck of an outlaw deer-stealer, the whistle wherewith he calleth on his hounds."

"What sayest thou to this, Conrade?" said the Grand Master. "Den of thieves! and a fit residence is a den of thieves for such a prior. No wonder that the hand of God is upon us, and that in the Holy Land we lose place by place, foot by foot, before the infidels, when we have such churchmen as this Aymer. And what meaneth he, I trow, by this second Witch of Endor?" said he to his confidant, something apart.

Conrade was better acquainted (perhaps by practice) with the jargon of gallantry, than was his superior; and he expounded the passage which embarrassed the Grand Master to be a sort of language used by worldly men towards those whom they loved *par amours;* but the explanation did not satisfy the bigoted Beaumanoir.

"There is more in it than thou dost guess, Conrade; thy simplicity is no match for this deep abyss of wickedness. This Rebecca of York was a pupil of that Miriam of whom thou hast heard. Thou shalt hear the Jew own it even now." Then turning to Isaac, he said aloud, "Thy daughter, then, is prisoner with Brian de Bois-Guilbert?"

"Ay, reverend valorous sir," stammered poor Isaac, "and whatever ransom a poor man may pay for her deliverance"——

"Peace!" said the Grand Master. "This thy daughter hath practised the art of healing, hath she not?"

"Ay, gracious sir," answered the Jew, with more confidence; "and knight and yeoman, squire and vassal may bless the goodly gift which Heaven hath assigned to her. Many a one can testify that she hath recovered them by her art, when every other human aid hath proved vain; but the blessing of the God of Jacob was upon her."

Beaumanoir turned to Mont-Fitchet with a grim smile. "See, brother," he said, "the deceptions of the devouring enemy! Behold the baits with which he fishes for souls, giving a poor space of earthly life in exchange for eternal happiness hereafter. Well said our blessed rule, *Semper percutiatur leo vorans.* Up on the lion! Down with the destroyer!" said he, shaking aloft his mystic abacus, as if in defiance of the powers of darkness. "Thy daughter worketh the cures, I doubt not," thus he went on to address the Jew, "by words and sigils, and periapts, and other cabalistical mysteries."

"Nay, reverend and brave knight," answered Isaac, "but in chief measure by a balsam of marvellous virtue."

"Where had she that secret?" said Beaumanoir.

"It was delivered to her," answered Isaac, reluctantly, "by Miriam, a sage matron of our tribe."

"Ah, false Jew!" said the Grand Master; "was it not from that same witch Miriam, the abomination of whose enchantments have been heard of throughout every Christian land?" exclaimed the Grand Master, crossing himself. "Her body was burnt at a stake, and her ashes were scattered to the four winds; and so be it with me and mine order, if I do not as much to her pupil, and more also! I will teach her to throw spell and incantation over the soldiers of the blessed Temple. There, Damian, spurn this Jew from the gate—shoot him dead if he oppose or turn again. With his daughter we will deal as the Christian law and our own high office warrant."

Poor Isaac was hurried off accordingly, and expelled from the preceptory; all his entreaties, and even his offers, unheard and disregarded. He could do no better than return to the house of the rabbi, and endeavour, through his means, to learn how his daughter was to be disposed of. He had hitherto feared for her honour, he was now to tremble for her life. Meanwhile, the Grand Master ordered to his presence the Preceptor of Templestowe.

CHAPTER XXXVI

Say not my art is fraud—all live by seeming.
The beggar begs with it, and the gay courtier
Gains land and title, rank and rule, by seeming;
The clergy scorn it not, and the bold soldier
Will eke with it his service.—All admit it,
All practise it; and he who is content
With showing what he is, shall have small credit
In church, or camp, or state—So wags the world.
                                        Old play.

ALBERT MALVOISIN, President, or, in the language of the order, Preceptor, of the establishment of Templestowe, was brother to that Philip Malvoisin who has been already occasionally mentioned in this history, and was, like that baron, in close league with Brian de Bois-Guilbert.

Amongst dissolute and unprincipled men, of whom the Temple Order included but too many, Albert of Templestowe might be distinguished; but with this difference from the audacious Bois-Guilbert, that he knew how to throw over his vices and his ambition the veil of hypocrisy, and to assume in his exterior the fanaticism which he internally despised. Had not the arrival of the Grand Master been so unexpectedly sudden, he would have seen nothing at Templestowe which might have appeared to argue any relaxation of discipline. And, even although surprised, and, to a certain extent, detected, Albert Malvoisin listened with such respect and apparent contrition to the rebuke of his superior, and made such haste to reform the particulars he censured,—succeeded, in fine, so well in giving an air of ascetic devotion to a family which had been lately devoted to license and pleasure, that Lucas Beaumanoir began to entertain a higher opinion of the Preceptor's morals, than the first appearance of the establishment had inclined him to adopt.

But these favourable sentiments on the part of the Grand Master were greatly shaken by the intelligence that Albert had received within a house of religion the Jewish captive, and, as was to be feared, the paramour of a brother of the order; and when Albert appeared before him, he was regarded with unwonted sternness.

"There is in this mansion, dedicated to the purposes of the holy Order of the Temple," said the Grand Master, in a severe tone, "a Jewish woman, brought hither by a brother of religion, by your connivance, Sir Preceptor."

Albert Malvoisin was overwhelmed with confusion; for the unfortunate Rebecca had been confined in a remote and secret part of the building, and every precaution used to prevent her residence there from being known. He read in the looks of Beaumanoir ruin to Bois-Guilbert and to himself, unless he should be able to avert the impending storm.

"Why are you mute?" continued the Grand Master.

"Is it permitted to me to reply?" answered the Preceptor, in a tone of the deepest humility, although by the question he only meant to gain an instant's space for arranging his ideas.

"Speak, you are permitted," said the Grand Master. "Speak, and say, knowest thou the capital of our holy rule,—*De commilitonibus Templi in sancta civitate, qui cum miserrimis mulieribus versantur, propter oblectationem carnis?*" [1]

"Surely, most reverend father," answered the Preceptor, "I have not risen to this office in the order, being ignorant of one of its most important prohibitions."

"How comes it, then, I demand of thee once more, that thou hast suffered a brother to bring a paramour, and that paramour a Jewish sorceress, into this holy place, to the stain and pollution thereof?"

"A Jewish sorceress!" echoed Albert Malvoisin; "good angels guard us!"

"Ay, brother, a Jewish sorceress!" said the Grand Master, sternly. "I have said it. Darest thou deny that this Rebecca, the daughter of that wretched usurer Isaac of York, and the pupil of the foul witch Miriam, is now—shame to be thought or spoken!—lodged within this thy preceptory?"

"Your wisdom, reverend father," answered the Preceptor, "hath rolled away the darkness from my understanding. Much did I wonder that so good a knight as Brian de Bois-Guilbert seemed so fondly besotted on the charms of this female, whom I received into this house merely to place

---

[1] The edict which he quotes, is against communion with women of light character

a bar betwixt their growing intimacy, which else might have been cemented at the expense of the fall of our valiant and religious brother."

"Hath nothing, then, as yet passed betwixt them in breach of his vow?" demanded the Grand Master.

"What! under this roof?" said the Preceptor, crossing himself; "Saint Magdalene and the ten thousand virgins forbid! No! if I have sinned in receiving her here, it was in the erring thought that I might thus break off our brother's besotted devotion to this Jewess, which seemed to me so wild and unnatural, that I could not but ascribe it to some touch of insanity, more to be cured by pity than reproof. But since your reverend wisdom hath discovered this Jewish quean to be a sorceress, perchance it may account fully for his enamoured folly."

"It doth! it doth!" said Beaumanoir. "See, brother Conrade, the peril of yielding to the first devices and blandishments of Satan! We look upon woman only to gratify the lust of the eye, and to take pleasure in what men call her beauty; and the ancient enemy, the devouring lion, obtains power over us, to complete, by talisman and spell, a work which was begun by idleness and folly. It may be that our brother Bois-Guilbert does in this matter deserve rather pity than severe chastisement; rather the support of the staff, than the strokes of the rod, and that our admonitions and prayers may turn him from his folly, and restore him to his brethren."

"It were deep pity," said Conrade Mont-Fitchet, "to lose to the order one of its best lances, when the holy community most requires the aid of its sons. Three hundred Saracens hath this Brian de Bois-Guilbert slain with his own hand."

"The blood of these accursed dogs," said the Grand Master, "shall be a sweet and acceptable offering to the saints and angels whom they despise and blaspheme; and with their aid will we counteract the spells and charms with which our brother is entwined as in a net. He shall burst the bands of this Delilah, as Samson burst the two new cords with which the Philistines had bound him, and shall slaughter the infidels, even heaps upon heaps. But concerning this foul witch, who hath flung her enchantments over a brother of the Holy Temple, assuredly she shall die the death."

"But the laws of England," said the Preceptor, who, though delighted that the Grand Master's resentment, thus fortunately averted from himself and Bois-Guilbert, had taken another direction, began now to fear he was carrying it too far.

"The laws of England," interrupted Beaumanoir, "permit and enjoin each judge to execute justice within his own jurisdiction. The most petty baron may arrest, try, and condemn a witch found within his own domain. And shall that power be denied to the Grand Master of the Temple within a preceptory of his order? No!—we will judge and condemn. The witch shall be taken out of the land, and the wickedness thereof shall be forgiven. Prepare the Castle-hall for the trial of the sorceress."

Albert Malvoisin bowed and retired—not to give directions for preparing the hall, but to seek out Brian de Bois-Guilbert, and communicate to him how matters were likely to terminate. It was not long ere he found him, foaming with indignation at a repulse he had anew sustained from the fair Jewess. "The unthinking," he said, "the ungrateful, to scorn him who, amidst blood and flames, would have saved her life at the risk of his own! By Heaven, Malvoisin! I abode until roof and rafters crackled and crashed around me. I was the butt of a hundred arrows; they rattled on mine armour like hailstones against a latticed casement, and the only use I made of my shield was for her protection. This did I endure for her; and now the self-willed girl upbraids me that I did not leave her to perish, and refuses me not only the slightest proof of gratitude, but even the most distant hope that ever she will be brought to grant any. The devil that possessed her race with obstinacy has concentrated its full force in her single person!"

"The devil," said the Preceptor, "I think, possessed you both. How oft have I preached to you caution, if not continence? Did I not tell you that there were enough willing Christian damsels to be met with, who would think it sin to refuse so brave a knight *le don d'amoureux merci*, and you must needs anchor your affection on a wilful, obstinate Jewess! By the mass, I think old Lucas Beaumanoir guesses right, when he maintains she hath cast a spell over you."

"Lucas Beaumanoir!" said Bois-Guilbert, reproachfully. "Are these your precautions, Malvoisin? Hast thou suffered the dotard to learn that Rebecca is in the Preceptory?"

"How could I help it?" said the Preceptor. "I neglected nothing that could keep secret your mystery; but it is betrayed, and whether by the devil or no, the devil only can tell. But I have turned the matter as I could; you are safe if you renounce Rebecca. You are pitied—the victim of magical delusion. She is a sorceress, and must suffer as such."

"She shall not, by Heaven!" said Bois-Guilbert.

"By Heaven, she must and will!" said Malvoisin. "Neither you nor any one else can save her. Lucas Beaumanoir hath settled that the death of a Jewess will be a sin-offering sufficient to atone for all the amorous indulgences of the Knights Templars; and thou knowest he hath both the power and will to execute so reasonable and pious a purpose."

"Will future ages believe that such stupid bigotry ever existed!" said Bois-Guilbert, striding up and down the apartment.

"What they may believe, I know not," said Malvoisin, calmly; "but I know well that in this our day clergy and laymen, take ninety-nine to the hundred, will cry *amen* to the Grand Master's sentence."

"I have it," said Bois-Guilbert. "Albert, thou art my friend. Thou must connive at her escape, Malvoisin, and I will transport her to some place of greater security and secrecy."

"I cannot, if I would," replied the Preceptor; "the mansion is filled with the attendants of the Grand Master, and others who are devoted to him. And, to be frank with you, brother, I would not embark with you in this matter, even if I could hope to bring my bark to haven. I have risked enough already for your sake. I have no mind to encounter a sentence of degradation, or even to lose my preceptory, for the sake of a painted piece of Jewish flesh and blood. And you, if you will be guided by my counsel, will give up this wild-goose chase, and fly your hawk at some other game. Think, Bois-Guilbert, thy present rank, thy future honours, all depend on thy place in the order. Shouldst thou adhere perversely to thy passion for this Rebecca, thou wilt give Beaumanoir the power of expelling thee, and he will not neglect it. He is jealous of the truncheon which he holds in his trembling gripe, and he knows thou stretchest thy bold hand towards it. Doubt not he will ruin thee, if thou affordest him a pretext so fair as thy protection of a Jewish sorceress. Give him his scope in this matter, for thou canst not control him. When the staff is in thine own firm grasp, thou mayest caress the daughters of Judah, or burn them, as may best suit thine own humour."

"Malvoisin," said Bois-Guilbert, "thou art a cold-blooded"——

"Friend," said the Preceptor, hastening to fill up the blank, in which Bois-Guilbert would probably have placed a worse word,—"a cold-blooded friend I am, and therefore more fit to give thee advice. I tell thee once more, that thou canst not save Rebecca. I tell thee once more thou canst but perish with her. Go hie thee to the Grand Master —throw thyself at his feet and tell him"——

"Not at his feet, by Heaven! but to the dotard's very beard will I say"——

"Say to him, then, to his beard," continued Malvoisin, coolly, "that you love this captive Jewess to distraction; and the more thou dost enlarge on thy passion, the greater will be his haste to end it by the death of the fair enchantress; while thou, taken in flagrant delict by the avowal of a crime contrary to thine oath, canst hope no aid of thy brethren, and must exchange all thy brilliant visions of ambition and power to lift perhaps a mercenary spear in some of the petty quarrels between Flanders and Burgundy."

"Thou speakest the truth, Malvoisin," said Brian de Bois-Guilbert, after a moment's reflection. "I will give the hoary bigot no advantage over me; and for Rebecca, she hath not merited at my hand that I should expose rank and honour for her sake. I will cast her off—yes, I will leave her to her fate, unless"——

"Qualify not thy wise and necessary resolution," said Malvoisin; "women are but the toys which amuse our lighter hours—ambition is the serious business of life. Perish a thousand such frail baubles as this Jewess before thy manly step pause in the brilliant career that lies stretched before thee! For the present we part, nor must we be seen to hold close conversation—I must order the hall for his judgment-seat."

"What!" said Bois-Guilbert, "so soon?"

"Ay," replied the Preceptor, "trial moves rapidly on when the judge has determined the sentence beforehand."

"Rebecca," said Bois-Guilbert, when he was left alone, "thou art like to cost me dear. Why cannot I abandon thee to thy fate, as this calm hypocrite recommends? One effort will I make to save thee—but beware of ingratitude! for if I am again repulsed, my vengeance shall equal my love. The life and honour of Bois-Guilbert must not be hazarded where contempt and reproaches are his only reward."

The Preceptor had hardly given the necessary orders when he was joined by Conrade Mont-Fitchet, who acquainted him with the Grand Master's resolution to bring the Jewess to instant trial for sorcery.

"It is surely a dream," said the Preceptor; "we have many Jewish physicians, and we call them not wizards though they work wonderful cures."

"The Grand Master thinks otherwise," said Mont-Fitchet; "and, Albert, I will be upright with thee—wizard or not, it were better that this miserable damsel die than that Brian de Bois-Guilbert should be lost to the order, or the order divided by internal dissension. Thou knowest his high rank, his fame in arms—thou knowest the zeal with which many of our brethren regard him—but all this will not avail him with our Grand Master should he consider Brian as the accomplice, not the victim, of this Jewess. Were the souls of the twelve tribes in her single body it were better she suffered alone than that Bois-Guilbert were partner in her destruction."

"I have been working him even now to abandon her," said Malvoisin; "but still, are there grounds enough to condemn this Rebecca for sorcery? Will not the Grand Master change his mind when he sees that the proofs are so weak?"

"They must be strengthened, Albert," replied Mont-Fitchet, "they must be strengthened. Dost thou understand me?"

"I do," said the Preceptor, "nor do I scruple to do aught for advancement of the order, but there is little time to find engines fitting."

"Malvoisin, they *must* be found," said Conrade; "well will it advantage both the order and thee. This Templestowe is a poor preceptory, that of Maison-Dieu is worth double its value—thou knowest my interest with our old chief—find those who can carry this matter through, and thou art Preceptor of Maison-Dieu in the fertile Kent. How sayst thou?"

"There is," replied Malvoisin, "among those who came hither with Bois-Guilbert, two fellows whom I well know; servants they were to my brother Philip de Malvoisin, and passed from his service to that of Front-de-Bœuf. It may be they know something of the witcheries of this woman."

"Away, seek them out instantly—and hark thee, if a byzant or two will sharpen their memory, let them not be wanting."

"They would swear the mother that bore them a sorceress for a zec-chin," said the Preceptor.

"Away, then," said Mont-Fitchet; "at noon the affair will proceed. I have not seen our senior in such earnest preparation since he condemned to the stake Hamet Alfagi, a convert who relapsed to the Moslem faith."

The ponderous castle-bell had tolled the point of noon, when Rebecca heard a trampling of feet upon the private stair which led to her place of confinement. The noise announced the arrival of several persons, and the circumstance rather gave her joy; for she was more afraid of the solitary visits of the fierce and passionate Bois-Guilbert than of any evil that could befall her besides. The door of the chamber was unlocked, and Conrade and the Preceptor Malvoisin entered, attended by four warders clothed in black, and bearing halberds.

"Daughter of an accursed race!" said the Preceptor, "arise and follow us."

"Whither," said Rebecca, "and for what purpose?"

"Damsel," answered Conrade, "it is not for thee to question, but to obey. Nevertheless, be it known to thee, that thou art to be brought before the tribunal of the Grand Master of our Holy Order, there to answer for thine offences."

"May the God of Abraham be praised!" said Rebecca, folding her hands devoutly; "the name of a judge, though an enemy to my people, is to me as the name of a protector. Most willingly do I follow thee—permit me only to wrap my veil around my head."

They descended the stair with slow and solemn step, traversed a long gallery, and, by a pair of folding doors placed at the end, entered the great hall in which the Grand Master had for the time established his court of justice.

The lower part of this ample apartment was filled with squires and yeomen, who made way not without some difficulty for Rebecca, attended by the Preceptor and Mont-Fitchet, and followed by the guard of halberdiers, to move forward to the seat appointed for her. As she passed through the crowd, her arms folded and her head depressed, a scrap of paper was thrust into her hand, which she received almost unconsciously, and continued to hold without examining its contents. The assurance that she possessed some friend in this awful assembly gave her courage to look around, and to mark into whose presence she had been conducted. She gazed, accordingly, upon the scene, which we shall endeavour to describe in the next chapter.

CHAPTER XXXVII

Stern was the law which bade its vot'ries leave
At human woes with human hearts to grieve;
Stern was the law, which at the winning wile
Of frank and harmless mirth forbade to smile;
But sterner still, when high the iron-rod
Of tyrant power she shook, and call'd that power of God.
                                          The Middle Ages.

THE tribunal, erected for the trial of the innocent and unhappy Rebecca, occupied the dais or elevated part of the upper end of the great hall— a platform, which we have already described as the place of honour, destined to be occupied by the most distinguished inhabitants or guests of an ancient mansion.

On an elevated seat, directly before the accused, sat the Grand Master of the Temple, in full and ample robes of flowing white, holding in his hand the mystic staff, which bore the symbol of the order. At his feet was placed a table, occupied by two scribes, chaplains of the order, whose duty it was to reduce to formal record the proceedings of the day. The black dresses, bare scalps, and demure looks of these churchmen, formed a strong contrast to the warlike appearance of the knights who attended, either as residing in the preceptory, or as come thither to attend upon their Grand Master. The Preceptors, of whom there were four present, occupied seats lower in height, and somewhat drawn back behind that of their superior; and the knights, who enjoyed no such rank in the order, were placed on benches still lower, and preserving the same distance from the Preceptors as these from the Grand Master. Behind them, but still upon the dais or elevated portion of the hall, stood the esquires of the order, in white dresses of an inferior quality.

The whole assembly wore an aspect of the most profound gravity; and in the faces of the knights might be perceived traces of military daring, united with the solemn carriage becoming men of a religious profession, and which, in the presence of their Grand Master, failed not to sit upon every brow.

The remaining and lower part of the hall was filled with guards, holding partisans, and with other attendants whom curiosity had drawn thither, to see at once a Grand Master and a Jewess sorceress. By far the greater part of those inferior persons were, in one rank or other, connected with the order, and were accordingly distinguished by their black dresses. But peasants from the neighbouring country were not refused admittance; for it was the pride of Beaumanoir to render the edifying spectacle of the justice which he administered as public as possible. His large blue eyes seemed to expand as he gazed around the assembly, and his countenance appeared elated by the conscious dignity, and imaginary merit, of the part which he was about to perform. A psalm, which he himself accompanied with a deep mellow voice, which age had not deprived of its powers, commenced the proceedings of the day; and the solemn sounds, *Venite exultemus Domino,* so often sung by the Templars before engaging with earthly adversaries was judged by Lucas most appropriate to introduce the approaching triumph, for such he deemed it, over the powers of darkness. The deep prolonged notes, raised by a hundred masculine voices accustomed to combine in the choral chant, arose to the vaulted roof of the hall, and rolled on amongst its arches with the pleasing yet solemn sound of the rushing of mighty waters.

When the sounds ceased, the Grand Master glanced his eye slowly around the circle, and observed that the seat of one of the preceptors was vacant. Brian de Bois-Guilbert, by whom it had been occupied, had left his place, and was now standing near the extreme corner of one of the benches occupied by the Knights Companions of the Temple, one hand extending his long mantle, so as in some degree to hide his face; while the other held his cross-handled sword, with the point of which, sheathed as it was, he was slowly drawing lines upon the oaken floor.

"Unhappy man!" said the Grand Master, after favouring him with a glance of compassion. "Thou seest, Conrade, how this holy work distresses him. To this can the light look of woman, aided by the Prince of the Powers of this world, bring a valiant and worthy knight! Seest thou he cannot look upon us; he cannot look upon her; and who knows by what impulse from his tormentor his hand forms these cabalistic lines upon the floor?—It may be our life and safety are thus aimed at; but we spit at and defy the foul enemy. *Semper Leo percutiatur!*"

This was communicated apart to his confidential follower, Conrade Mont-Fitchet. The Grand Master then raised his voice, and addressed the assembly.

"Reverend and valiant men, Knights, Preceptors, and Companions of this Holy Order, my brethren and my children!—you also, well-born and pious Esquires, who aspire to wear this holy Cross!—and you, also, Christian brethren, of every degree!—Be it known to you, that it is not defect of power in us which hath occasioned the assembling of this congregation; for, however unworthy in our person, yet to us is committed, with this batoon, full power to judge and to try all that regards the weal of this our Holy Order. Holy Saint Bernard, in the rule of our knightly and religious profession, hath said, in the fifty-ninth capital,[1] that he would not that brethren be called together in council, save at the will and command of the Master; leaving it free to us, as to those more worthy fathers who have preceded us in this our office, to judge, as well of the occasion as of the time and place in which a chapter of the whole order, or of any part thereof, may be convoked. Also, in all such chapters, it is our duty to hear the advice of our brethren, and to proceed according to our own pleasure. But when the raging wolf hath made an inroad upon the flock, and carried off one member thereof, it is the

---

[1] The reader is again referred to the Rules of the Poor Military Brotherhood of the Temple, which occur in the Works of St. Bernard.—L. T.

duty of the kind shepherd to call his comrades together, that with bows and slings they may quell the invader, according to our well-known rule, that the lion is ever to be beaten down. We have therefore summoned to our presence a Jewish woman, by name Rebecca, daughter of Isaac of York—a woman infamous for sortileges and for witcheries; whereby she hath maddened the blood, and besotted the brain, not of a churl but of a Knight—not of a secular Knight, but of one devoted to the service of the Holy Temple—not of a Knight Companion, but of a Preceptor of our order, first in honour as in place. Our brother, Brian de Bois-Guilbert, is well known to ourselves, and to all degrees who now hear me, as a true and zealous champion of the cross, by whose arm many deeds of valour have been wrought in the Holy Land, and the holy places purified from pollution by the blood of those infidels who defiled them. Neither have our brother's sagacity and prudence been less in repute among his brethren than his valour and discipline; in so much that knights, both in eastern and western lands, have named De Bois-Guilbert as one who may well be put in nomination as successor to this batoon, when it shall please Heaven to release us from the toil of bearing it. If we were told that such a man, so honoured, and so honourable, suddenly casting away regard for his character, his vows, his brethren, and his prospects, had associated to himself a Jewish damsel, wandered in this lewd company, through solitary places, defended her person in preference to his own, and, finally, was so utterly blinded and besotted by his folly, as to bring her even to one of our own preceptories, what should we say but that the noble knight was possessed by some evil demon, or influenced by some wicked spell? If we could suppose it otherwise, think not rank, valour, high repute, or any earthly consideration should prevent us from visiting him with punishment, that the evil thing might be removed, even according to the text, *Auferte malum ex vobis.* For various and heinous are the acts of transgression against the rule of our blessed order in this lamentable history,—1st, He hath walked according to his proper will, contrary to capital 33, *Quod nullus juxta propriam voluntatem incedat.* 2d, He hath held communication with an excommunicated person, capital 57, *Ut fratres non participent cum excommunicatis,* and therefore hath a portion in *Anathema Maranatha.* 3d, He hath conversed with strange women, contrary to the capital, *Ut fratres non conversantur cum extraneis mulieribus.* 4th, He hath not avoided, nay, he hath, it is to be feared, solicited the kiss of woman; by which, saith the last rule of our renowned order, *Ut fugiantur oscula,* the soldiers of the cross are brought into a snare. For which heinous and multiplied guilt, Brian de Bois-Guilbert should be cut off and cast out from our congregation, were he the right hand and right eye thereof."

He paused. A low murmur went through the assembly. Some of the younger part, who had been inclined to smile at the statute *De osculis fugiendis,* became now grave enough, and anxiously waited what the Grand Master was next to propose.

"Such," he said, "and so great should indeed be the punishment of a Knight Templar, who wilfully offended against the rules of his order in such weighty points. But if, by means of charms and of spells, Satan had obtained dominion over the Knight, perchance because he cast his eyes too lightly upon a damsel's beauty, we are then rather to lament than chastise his backsliding; and, imposing on him only such penance as may purify him from his iniquity, we are to turn the full edge of our indignation upon the accursed instrument, which had so well-nigh occasioned his utter falling away. Stand forth, therefore, and bear witness, ye who have witnessed these unhappy doings, that we may judge of the sum and bearing thereof; and judge whether our justice may be satisfied with the punishment of this infidel woman, or if we must go on, with a bleeding heart, to the further proceeding against our brother."

Several witnesses were called upon to prove the risks to which Bois-Guilbert exposed himself in endeavouring to save Rebecca from the blazing castle, and his neglect of his personal defence in attending to her safety. The men gave these details with the exaggerations common to vulgar minds which have been strongly excited by any remarkable event, and their natural disposition to the marvellous was greatly increased by the satisfaction which their evidence seemed to afford to the eminent person for whose information it had been delivered. Thus the dangers which Bois-Guilbert surmounted, in themselves sufficiently great, became portentous in their narrative. The devotion of the Knight to Rebecca's defence was exaggerated beyond the bounds, not only of discretion, but even of the most frantic excess of chivalrous zeal; and his deference to what she said, even although her language was often severe and upbraiding, was painted as carried to an excess, which, in a man of his haughty temper, seemed almost preternatural.

The Preceptor of Templestowe was then called on to describe the manner in which Bois-Guilbert and the Jewess arrived at the Preceptory. The evidence of Malvoisin was skilfully guarded. But while he apparently studied to spare the feelings of Bois-Guilbert, he threw in, from time to time, such hints as seemed to infer that he laboured under some temporary alienation of mind, so deeply did he appear to be enamoured of the damsel whom he brought along with him. With sighs of penitence, the Preceptor avowed his own contrition for having admitted Rebecca and her lover within the walls of the preceptory—"But my defence," he concluded, "has been made in my confession to our most reverend father the Grand Master; he knows my motives were not evil, though my conduct may have been irregular. Joyfully will I submit to any penance he shall assign me."

"Thou hast spoken well, Brother Albert," said Beaumanoir; "thy motives were good, since thou didst judge it right to arrest thine erring brother in his career of precipitate folly. But thy conduct was wrong; as he that would stop a runaway steed, and seizing by the stirrup instead of the bridle, receiveth injury himself, instead of accomplishing his purpose. Thirteen paternosters are assigned by our pious founder for matins, and nine for vespers; be those services doubled by thee. Thrice a-week are Templars permitted the use of flesh; but do thou keep fast for all the seven days. This do for six weeks to come, and thy penance is accomplished."

With a hypocritical look of the deepest submission the Preceptor of Templestowe bowed to the ground before his superior, and resumed his seat.

"Were it not well, brethren," said the Grand Master, "that we examine something into the former life and conversation of this woman, specially that we may discover whether she be one likely to use magical charms and spells, since the truths which we have heard may well incline us to suppose, that in this unhappy course our erring brother has been acted upon by some infernal enticement and delusion?"

Herman of Goodalricke was the Fourth Preceptor present; the other three were Conrade, Malvoisin, and Bois-Guilbert himself. Herman was an ancient warrior, whose face was marked with scars inflicted by the sabre of the Moslemah, and had great rank and consideration among his brethren. He arose and bowed to the Grand Master, who instantly granted him license of speech. "I would crave to know, most Reverend Father, of our valiant brother, Brian de Bois-Guilbert, what he says to these wondrous accusations, and with what eye he himself now regards his unhappy intercourse with this Jewish maiden?"

"Brian de Bois-Guilbert," said the Grand Master, "thou hearest the question which our Brother of Goodalricke desirest thou shouldst answer. I command thee to reply to him."

Bois-Guilbert turned his head towards the Grand Master when thus addressed, and remained silent.

"He is possessed by a dumb devil," said the Grand Master. "Avoid thee, Sathanas! Speak, Brian de Bois-Guilbert, I conjure thee, by this symbol of our Holy Order."

Bois-Guilbert made an effort to suppress his rising scorn and indignation, the expression of which, he was well aware, would have little availed him. "Brian de Bois-Guilbert," he answered, "replies not, most Reverend Father, to such wild and vague charges. If his honour be impeached, he will defend it with his body, and with that sword which has often fought for Christendom."

"We forgive thee, Brother Brian," said the Grand Master; "though that thou hast boasted thy warlike achievements before us, is a glorifying of thine own deeds, and cometh of the enemy who tempteth us to exalt our own worship. But thou hast our pardon, judging thou speakest less of thine own suggestion than from the impulse of him whom, by Heaven's leave, we will quell and drive forth from our assembly." A glance of disdain flashed from the dark fierce eyes of Bois-Guilbert, but he made no reply. "And now," pursued the Grand Master, "since our brother Goodalricke's question has been thus imperfectly answered, pursue we our quest, brethren, and with our patron's assistance, we will search to the bottom this mystery of iniquity. Let those who have aught to witness of the life and conversation of this Jewish woman, stand forth before us." There was a bustle in the lower part of the hall, and when the Grand Master enquired the reason, it was replied, there was in the crowd a bedridden man, whom the prisoner had restored to the perfect use of his limbs, by a miraculous balsam.

The poor peasant, a Saxon by birth, was dragged forward to the bar, terrified at the penal consequences which he might have incurred by the guilt of having been cured of the palsy by a Jewish damsel. Perfectly cured he certainly was not, for he supported himself forward on crutches to give evidence. Most unwilling was his testimony, and given with many tears; but he admitted that two years since, when residing at York, he was suddenly afflicted with a sore disease while labouring for Isaac the rich Jew in his vocation of a joiner; that he had been unable to stir from his bed until the remedies applied by Rebecca's directions, and especially a warming and spicy-smelling balsam, had in some degree restored him to the use of his limbs. Moreover, he said, she had given him a pot of that precious ointment, and furnished him with a piece of money withal to return to the house of his father near to Templestowe. "And may it please your gracious reverence," said the man, "I cannot think the damsel meant harm by me, though she hath the ill hap to be a Jewess; for even when I used her remedy, I said the Pater and the Creed, and it never operated a whit less kindly."

"Peace, slave," said the Grand Master, "and begone! It well suits brutes like thee to be tampering and trinketing with hellish cures, and to be giving your labour to the sons of mischief. I tell thee, the fiend can impose diseases for the very purpose of removing them, in order to bring into credit some diabolical fashion of cure. Hast thou that unguent of which thou speakest?"

The peasant, fumbling in his bosom with a trembling hand, produced a small box, bearing some Hebrew characters on the lid, which was, with most of the audience, a sure proof that the devil had stood apothecary. Beaumanoir, after crossing himself, took the box into his hand, and, learned in most of the Eastern tongues, read with ease the motto on the lid,—*The Lion of the Tribe of Judah hath conquered.* "Strange powers of Sathanas," said he, "which can convert Scripture into blasphemy, mingling poison with our necessary food! Is there no leech here who can tell us the ingredients of this mystic unguent?"

Two mediciners, as they called themselves, the one a monk, the other a barber, appeared, and avouched they knew nothing of the materials, excepting that they savoured of myrrh and camphire, which they took to be Oriental herbs. But with the true professional hatred to a successful practitioner of their art, they insinuated that, since the medicine was beyond their own knowledge, it must necessarily have been compounded from an unlawful and magical pharmacopeia; since they themselves, though no conjuror, fully understood every branch of their art, so far as it might be exercised with the good faith of a Christian. When this medical research was ended, the Saxon peasant desired humbly to have back the medicine which he had found so salutary; but the Grand Master frowned severely at the request. "What is thy name, fellow?" said he to the cripple.

"Higg, the son of Snell," answered the peasant.

"Then Higg, son of Snell," said the Grand Master, "I tell thee it is better to be bedridden than to accept the benefit of unbelievers' medicine that thou mayest arise and walk; better to despoil infidels of their treasure by the strong hand than to accept of them benevolent gifts, or do them service for wages. Go thou, and do as I have said."

"Alack," said the peasant, "and it shall not displease your reverence, the lesson comes too late for me, for I am but a maimed man; but I will tell my two brethren, who serve the rich Rabbi Nathan Ben Samuel, that your mastership says it is more lawful to rob him than to render him faithful service."

"Out with the prating villain!" said Beaumanoir, who was not prepared to refute this practical application of his general maxim.

Higg, the son of Snell, withdrew into the crowd, but interested in the fate of his benefactress, lingered until he should learn her doom, even at the risk of again encountering the frown of that severe judge, the terror of which withered his very heart within him.

At this period of the trial, the Grand Master commanded Rebecca to unveil herself. Opening her lips for the first time, she replied patiently, but with dignity,—"That it was not the wont of the daughters of her people to uncover their faces when alone in an assembly of strangers." The sweet tones of her voice, and the softness of her reply, impressed on the audience a sentiment of pity and sympathy. But Beaumanoir, in whose mind the suppression of each feeling of humanity which could interfere with his imagined duty, was a virtue of itself, repeated his commands that his victim should be unveiled. The guards were about to remove her veil accordingly, when she stood up before the Grand Master and said, "Nay, but for the love of your own daughters—Alas," she said, recollecting herself, "ye have no daughters!—yet for the remembrance of your mothers, for the love of your sisters, and of female decency, let me not be thus handled in your presence; it suits not a maiden to be disrobed by such rude grooms. I will obey you," she added, with an expression of patient sorrow in her voice, which had almost melted the heart of Beaumanoir himself; "ye are elders among your people, and at your command I will show the features of an ill-fated maiden."

She withdrew her veil, and looked on them with a countenance in which bashfulness contended with dignity. Her exceeding beauty excited a murmur of surprise, and the younger knights told each other with their eyes, in silent correspondence, that Brian's best apology was in the power of her real charms, rather than of her imaginary witchcraft. But Higg, the son of Snell, felt most deeply the effect produced by the sight of the countenance of his benefactress. "Let me go forth," he said to the warders at the door of the hall,—"let me go forth! To look at her again will kill me, for I have had a share in murdering her."

"Peace, poor man," said Rebecca, when she heard his exclamation; "thou hast done me no harm by speaking the truth—thou canst not aid me by thy complaints or lamentations. Peace, I pray thee—go home and save thyself."

Higg was about to be thrust out by the compassion of the warders, who were apprehensive lest his clamorous grief should draw upon them reprehension, and upon himself punishment. But he promised to be silent, and was permitted to remain. The two men-at-arms, with whom Albert Malvoisin had not failed to communicate upon the import of their testimony, were now called forward. Though both were hardened and inflexible villains, the sight of the captive maiden, as well as her excelling beauty, at first appeared to stagger them; but an expressive glance from the Preceptor of Templestowe restored them to their dogged composure; and they delivered, with a precision which would have seemed suspicious to more impartial judges, circumstances either altogether fictitious or trivial, and natural in themselves, but rendered pregnant with suspicion by the exaggerated manner in which they were told, and the sinister commentary which the witnesses added to the facts. The circumstances of their evidence would have been, in modern days, divided into two classes—those which were immaterial, and those which were actually and physically impossible. But both were, in those ignorant and superstitious times, easily credited as proofs of guilt. The first class set forth that Rebecca was heard to mutter to herself in an unknown tongue; that the songs she sung by fits were of a strangely sweet sound, which made the ears of the hearer tingle, and his heart throb; that she spoke at times to herself, and seemed to look upward for a reply; that her garments were of a strange and mystic form, unlike those of women of good repute; that she had rings impressed with cabalistical devices, and that strange characters were broidered on her veil.

All these circumstances, so natural and so trivial, were gravely listened to as proofs, or, at least, as affording strong suspicions that Rebecca had unlawful correspondence with mystical powers.

But there was less equivocal testimony, which the credulity of the assembly, or the greater part, greedily swallowed, however incredible. One of the soldiers had seen her work a cure upon a wounded man brought with them to the castle of Torquilstone. She did, he said, make certain signs upon the wound, and repeated certain mysterious words, which he blessed God he understood not, when the iron head of a square crossbow bolt disengaged itself from the wound, the bleeding was staunched, the wound was closed, and the dying man was, within a quarter of an hour, walking upon the ramparts, and assisting the witness in managing a mangonel, or machine for hurling stones. This legend was probably founded upon the fact that Rebecca had attended on the wounded Ivanhoe when in the castle of Torquilstone. But it was the more difficult to dispute the accuracy of the witness, as, in order to produce real evidence in support of his verbal testimony, he drew from his pouch the very bolt-head, which, according to his story, had been miraculously extracted from the wound; and as the iron weighed a full ounce, it completely confirmed the tale, however marvellous.

His comrade had been a witness from a neighbouring battlement of the scene betwixt Rebecca and Bois-Guilbert, when she was upon the point of precipitating herself from the top of the tower. Not to be behind his companion, this fellow stated that he had seen Rebecca perch herself upon the parapet of the turret, and there take the form of a milk-white swan, under which appearance she flitted three times round the castle of Torquilstone; then again settle on the turret, and once more assume the female form.

Less than one half of this weighty evidence would have been sufficient to convict any old woman, poor and ugly, even though she had not been a Jewess. United with that fatal circumstance, the body of proof was too weighty for Rebecca's youth, though combined with the most exquisite beauty.

The Grand Master had collected the suffrages, and now in a solemn tone demanded of Rebecca what she had to say against the sentence of condemnation which he was about to pronounce.

"To invoke your pity," said the lovely Jewess, with a voice somewhat tremulous with emotion, "would, I am aware, be as useless as I should hold it mean. To state that to relieve the sick and wounded of another religion cannot be displeasing to the acknowledged Founder of both our faiths were also unavailing; to plead that many things which these men (whom may Heaven pardon!) have spoken against me are impossible, would avail me but little since you believe in their possibility; and still less would it advantage me to explain, that the peculiarities of my dress, language, and manners are those of my people—I had wellnigh said of my country, but alas! we have no country. Nor will I even vindicate myself at the expense of my oppressor, who stands there listening to the fictions and surmises which seem to convert the tyrant into the victim. God be judge between him and me! but rather would I submit to ten such deaths as your pleasure may denounce against me than listen to the suit which that man of Belial has urged upon me—friendless, defenceless, and his prisoner. But he is of your own faith, and his lightest affirmation would weigh down the most solemn protestations of the distressed Jewess. I will not therefore return to himself the charge brought against me—but to himself—yes, Brian de Bois-Guilbert, to thyself I appeal whether these accusations are not false? as monstrous and calumnious as they are deadly?"

There was a pause; all eyes turned to Brian de Bois-Guilbert. He was silent.

"Speak," she said, "if thou art a man, if thou art a Christian, speak! I conjure thee, by the habit which thou dost wear, by the name thou dost inherit, by the knighthood thou dost vaunt, by the honour of thy mother, by the tomb and the bones of thy father, I conjure thee to say are these things true?"

"Answer her, brother," said the Grand Master, "if the enemy with whom thou dost wrestle will give thee power."

In fact, Bois-Guilbert seemed agitated by contending passions which almost convulsed his features, and it was with a constrained voice that at last he replied, looking to Rebecca,—"The scroll!—the scroll!"

"Ay," said Beaumanoir, "this is indeed testimony! The victim of her witcheries can only name the fatal scroll, the spell inscribed on which is, doubtless, the cause of his silence."

But Rebecca put another interpretation on the words extorted as it were from Bois-Guilbert, and glancing her eye upon the slip of parchment which she continued to hold in her hand, she read written thereupon in the Arabian character, *Demand a Champion!* The murmuring commentary which ran through the assembly at the strange reply of Bois-Guilbert gave Rebecca leisure to examine and instantly to destroy the scroll unobserved. When the whisper had ceased, the Grand Master spoke.

"Rebecca, thou canst derive no benefit from the evidence of this unhappy knight, for whom, as we well perceive, the enemy is yet too powerful. Hast thou aught else to say?"

"There is yet one chance of life left to me," said Rebecca, "even by your own fierce laws. Life has been miserable—miserable, at least, of late—but I will not cast away the gift of God while he affords me the means of defending it. I deny this charge; I maintain my innocence, and I declare the falsehood of this accusation. I challenge the privilege of trial by combat, and will appear by my champion."

"And who, Rebecca," replied the Grand Master, "will lay lance in rest for a sorceress? who will be the champion of a Jewess?"

"God will raise me up a champion," said Rebecca. "It cannot be that in merry England—the hospitable, the generous, the free—where so many are ready to peril their lives for honour, there will not be found one to fight for justice. But it is enough, that I challenge the trial by combat—there lies my gage."

She took her embroidered glove from her hand, and flung it down before the Grand Master with an air of mingled simplicity and dignity which excited universal surprise and admiration.

CHAPTER XXXVIII

――――There I throw my gage,
To prove it on thee to the extremest point
Of martial daring.

Richard II.

EVEN Lucas Beaumanoir himself was affected by the mien and appearance of Rebecca. He was not originally a cruel or even a severe man; but with passions by nature cold, and with a high, though mistaken, sense of duty, his heart had been gradually hardened by the ascetic life which he pursued, the supreme power which he enjoyed, and the supposed necessity of subduing infidelity and eradicating heresy, which he conceived peculiarly incumbent on him. His features relaxed in their usual severity as he gazed upon the beautiful creature before him, alone, unfriended, and defending herself with so much spirit and courage. He crossed himself twice, as doubting whence arose the unwonted softening of a heart, which on such occasions used to resemble in hardness the steel of his sword. At length he spoke.

"Damsel," he said, "if the pity I feel for thee arise from any practice thine evil arts have made on me, great is thy guilt. But I rather judge it the kinder feelings of nature, which grieves that so goodly a form should be a vessel of perdition. Repent, my daughter, confess thy witchcrafts, turn thee from thine evil faith, embrace this holy emblem, and all shall yet be well with thee here and hereafter. In some sisterhood of the strictest order shalt thou have time for prayer and fitting penance, and that repentance not to be repented of. This do and live. What has the law of Moses done for thee that thou shouldest die for it?"

"It was the law of my fathers," said Rebecca; "it was delivered in thunders and in storms upon the mountain of Sinai, in cloud and in fire. This, if ye are Christians, ye believe—it is, you say, recalled; but so my teachers have not taught me."

"Let our chaplain," said Beaumanoir, "stand forth, and tell this obstinate infidel"――

"Forgive the interruption," said Rebecca, meekly; "I am a maiden, unskilled to dispute for my religion, but I can die for it, if it be God's will. Let me pray your answer to my demand of a champion."

"Give me her glove," said Beaumanoir. "This is indeed," he continued, as he looked at the flimsy texture and slender fingers, "a slight and frail gage for a purpose so deadly! Seest thou, Rebecca, as this thin and light glove of thine is to one of our heavy steel gauntlets, so is thy cause to that of the Temple, for it is our order which thou hast defied."

"Cast my innocence into the scale," answered Rebecca, "and the glove of silk shall outweigh the glove of iron."

"Then thou dost persist in thy refusal to confess thy guilt, and in that bold challenge which thou hast made?"

"I do persist, noble sir," answered Rebecca.

"So be it then, in the name of Heaven," said the Grand Master; "and may God show the right!"

"Amen," replied the Preceptors around him, and the word was deeply echoed by the whole assembly.

"Brethren," said Beaumanoir, "you are aware that we might well have refused to this woman the benefit of the trial by combat—but though a Jewess and an unbeliever, she is also a stranger and defence-less, and God forbid that she should ask the benefit of our mild laws, and that it should be refused to her. Moreover, we are knights and sol-diers, as well as men of religion, and shame it were to us upon any pretence, to refuse proffered combat. Thus, therefore, stands the case. Rebecca, the daughter of Isaac of York, is, by many frequent and sus-picious circumstances, defamed of sorcery practised on the person of a noble knight of our holy order, and hath challenged the combat in proof of her innocence. To whom, reverend brethren, is it your opinion that we should deliver the gage of battle, naming him, at the same time, to be our champion on the field?"

"To Brian de Bois-Guilbert, whom it chiefly concerns," said the Preceptor of Goodalricke, "and who, moreover, best knows how the truth stands in this matter."

"But if," said the Grand Master, "our Brother Brian be under the influence of a charm or a spell—we speak but for the sake of precaution, for to the arm of none of our holy order would we more willingly confide this or a more weighty cause."

"Reverend father," answered the Preceptor of Goodalricke, "no spell can effect the champion who comes forward to fight for the judgment of God."

"Thou sayest right, brother," said the Grand Master. "Albert Mal-voisin, give this gage of battle to Brian de Bois-Guilbert. It is our charge to thee, brother," he continued, addressing himself to Bois-Guilbert, "that thou do thy battle manfully, nothing doubting that the good cause shall triumph. And do thou, Rebecca, attend, that we assign thee the third day from the present to find a champion."

"That is but brief space," answered Rebecca, "for a stranger•who is also of another faith to find one who will do battle, wagering life and honour for her cause, against a knight who is called an approved soldier."

"We may not extend it," answered the Grand Master; "the field must be foughten in our own presence, and divers weighty causes call us on the fourth day from hence."

"God's will be done!" said Rebecca; "I put my trust in Him to whom an instant is as effectual to save as a whole age."

"Thou hast spoken well, damsel," said the Grand Master; "but well know we who can array himself like an angel of light. It remains but to name a fitting place of combat, and, if it so hap, also of execution. Where is the Preceptor of this house?"

Albert Malvoisin, still holding Rebecca's glove in his hand, was speaking to Bois-Guilbert very earnestly, but in a low voice.

"How!" said the Grand Master, "will he not receive the gage?"

"He will—he doth, most Reverend Father," said Malvoisin, slipping the glove under his own mantle. "And for the place of combat, I hold the fittest to be the lists of Saint George belonging to this preceptory, and used by us for military exercise."

"It is well," said the Grand Master. "Rebecca, in those lists shalt thou produce thy champion; and if thou failest to do so, or if thy champion shall be discomfited by the judgment of God, thou shalt then die the death of a sorceress, according to doom. Let this our judgment be recorded, and the record read aloud, that no one may pretend ignorance."

One of the chaplains, who acted as clerks to the chapter, immediately engrossed the order in a huge volume, which contained the proceedings of the Templar Knights when solemnly assembled on such occasions; and when he had finished writing, the other read aloud the sentence of the Grand Master, which, when translated from the Norman French in which it was couched, was expressed as follows:—

"Rebecca, a Jewess, daughter of Isaac of York, being attainted of sorcery, seduction, and other damnable practices practised on a Knight of the most Holy Order of the Temple of Zion, doth deny the same; and saith, that the testimony delivered against her this day is false, wicked, and disloyal; and that by lawful *essoine* [1] of her body as being unable to combat in her own behalf, she doth offer, by a champion instead thereof, to avouch her case, he performing his loyal *devoir* in all knightly sort, with such arms as to gage of battle do fully appertain, and that at her peril and cost. And therewith she proffered her gage. And the gage having been delivered to the noble Lord and Knight, Brian de Bois-Guilbert, of the Holy Order of the Temple of Zion, he was appointed to do this battle in behalf of his order and himself, as injured and impaired by the practices of the appellant. Wherefore the most reverend Father and puissant Lord, Lucas Marquis of Beaumanoir did allow of the said challenge, and of the said *essoine* of the appellant's body, and assigned the third day for the said combat, the place being the enclosure called the lists of Saint George, near to the Preceptory of Templestowe. And the Grand Master appoints the appellant to appear there by her champion, on pain of doom, as a person convicted of sorcery or seduction; and also the defendant so to appear, under the penalty of being held and adjudged recreant in case of default; and the noble Lord and most reverend Father aforesaid appointed the battle to be done in his own presence, and according to all that is commendable and profitable in such a case. And may God aid the just cause!"

"Amen!" said the Grand Master; and the word was echoed by all around. Rebecca spoke not, but she looked up to heaven, and, folding

---

[1] *Essoine* signifies excuse, and here relates to the appellant's privilege of appearing by her champion, in excuse of her own person on account of her sex.

hei hands, remained for a minute without change of attitude. She then modestly reminded the Grand Master, that she ought to be permitted some opportunity of free communication with her friends, for the purpose of making her condition known to them, and procuring, if possible, some champion to fight in her behalf.

"It is just and lawful," said the Grand Master; "choose what messenger thou shalt trust, and he shall have free communication with thee in thy prison-chamber."

"Is there," said Rebecca, "any one here, who, either for love of a good cause, or for ample hire, will do the errand of a distressed being?"

All were silent; for none thought it safe, in the presence of the Grand Master, to avow any interest in the calumniated prisoner, lest he should be suspected of leaning towards Judaism. Not even the prospect of reward, far less any feelings of compassion alone, could surmount this apprehension.

Rebecca stood for a few moments in indescribable anxiety, and then exclaimed, "Is it really thus? And, in English land, am I to be deprived of the poor chance of safety which remains to me, for want of an act of charity which would not be refused to the worst criminal?"

Higg, the son of Snell, at length replied, "I am but a maimed man, but that I can at all stir or move was owing to her charitable assistance. I will do thine errand," he added, addressing Rebecca, "as well as a crippled object can, and happy were my limbs fleet enough to repair the mischief done by my tongue. Alas! when I boasted of thy charity, I little thought I was leading thee into danger!"

"God," said Rebecca, "is the disposer of all. He can turn back the captivity of Judah, even by the weakest instrument. To execute his message the snail is as sure a messenger as the falcon. Seek out Isaac of York—here is that will pay for horse and man—let him have this scroll. I know not if it be of Heaven the spirit which inspires me, but most truly do I judge that I am not to die this death, and that a champion will be raised up for me. Farewell! Life and death are in thy haste."

The peasant took the scroll, which contained only a few lines in Hebrew. Many of the crowd would have dissuaded him from touching a document so suspicious; but Higg was resolute in the service of his benefactress. She had saved his body, he said, and he was confident she did not mean to peril his soul.

"I will get me," he said, "my neighbour Buthan's good capul,[1] and I will be at York within as brief space as man and beast may."

But as it fortuned, he had no occasion to go so far, for within a quarter of a mile from the gate of the preceptory he met with two riders, whom, by their dress and their huge yellow caps, he knew to be Jews; and, on approaching more nearly, discovered that one of them was his ancient employer, Isaac of York. The other was the Rabbi Ben Samuel; and

---

[1] *Capul, i.e.* horse; in a more limited sense, work-horse.

both had approached as near to the preceptory as they dared, on hearing that the Grand Master had summoned a chapter for the trial of a sorceress.

"Brother Ben Samuel," said Isaac, "my soul is disquieted, and I wot not why. This charge of necromancy is right often used for cloaking evil practices on our people."

"Be of good comfort, brother," said the physician; "thou canst deal with the Nazarenes as one possessing the mammon of unrighteousness, and canst therefore purchase immunity at their hands—it rules the savage minds of those ungodly men, even as the signet of the mighty Solomon was said to command the evil genii. But what poor wretch comes hither upon his crutches, desiring, as I think, some speech of me? Friend," continued the physician, addressing Higg, the son of Snell, "I refuse thee not the aid of mine art, but I relieve not with one asper those who beg for alms upon the highway. Out upon thee! Hast thou the palsy in thy legs? then let thy hands work for thy livelihood; for, albeit thou be'st unfit for a speedy post, or for a careful shepherd, or for the warfare, or for the service of a hasty master, yet there be occupations—How now, brother?" said he, interrupting his harangue to look towards Isaac, who had but glanced at the scroll which Higg offered, when, uttering a deep groan, he fell from his mule like a dying man, and lay for a minute insensible.

The rabbi now dismounted in great alarm, and hastily applied the remedies which his art suggested for the recovery of his companion. He had even taken from his pocket a cupping apparatus, and was about to proceed to phlebotomy, when the object of his anxious solicitude suddenly revived, but it was to dash his cap from his head, and to throw dust on his grey hairs. The physician was at first inclined to ascribe this sudden and violent emotion to the effects of insanity; and, adhering to his original purpose, began once again to handle his implements. But Isaac soon convinced him of his error.

"Child of my sorrow," he said, "well shouldst thou be called Benoni, instead of Rebecca! Why should thy death bring down my grey hairs to the grave, till, in the bitterness of my heart, I curse God and die!"

"Brother," said the rabbi, in great surprise, "art thou a father in Israel, and dost thou utter words like unto these? I trust that the child of thy house yet liveth?"

"She liveth," answered Isaac; "but it is as Daniel, who was called Beltheshazzar, even when within the den of the lions. She is captive unto those men of Belial, and they will wreak their cruelty upon her, sparing neither for her youth nor her comely favour. O! she was as a crown of green palms to my grey locks; and she must wither in a night, like the gourd of Jonah! Child of my love!—child of my old age!—oh, Rebecca, daughter of Rachel! the darkness of the shadow of death hath encompassed thee."

"Yet read the scroll," said the rabbi; "peradventure it may be that we may yet find out a way of deliverance."

"Do thou read, brother," answered Isaac, "for mine eyes are as a fountain of water."

The physician read, but in their native language, the following words:—

"To Isaac, the son of Adonikam, whom the Gentiles call Isaac of York, peace and the blessing of the promise be multiplied unto thee!—My father, I am as one doomed to die for that which my soul knoweth not—even for the crime of witchcraft. My father, if a strong man can be found to do battle for my cause with sword and spear, according to the custom of the Nazarenes, and that within the lists of Templestowe, on the third day from this time, peradventure our father's God will give him strength to defend the innocent, and her who hath none to help her. But if this may not be, let the virgins of our people mourn for me as for one cast off, and for the hart that is stricken by the hunter, and for the flower which is cut down by the scythe of the mower. Wherefore look now what thou doest, and whether there be any rescue. One Nazarene warrior might indeed bear arms in my behalf, even Wilfred, son of Cedric, whom the Gentiles call Ivanhoe. But he may not yet endure the weight of his armour. Nevertheless, send the tidings unto him, my father; for he hath favour among the strong men of his people, and as he was our companion in the house of bondage, he may find some one to do battle for my sake. And say unto him, even unto him, even unto Wilfred, the son of Cedric, that if Rebecca live, or if Rebecca die, she liveth or dieth wholly free of the guilt she is charged withal. And if it be the will of God that thou shalt be deprived of thy daughter, do not thou tarry, old man, in this land of bloodshed and cruelty; but betake thyself to Cordova, where thy brother liveth in safety, under the shadow of the throne, even of the throne of Boabdil the Saracen; for less cruel are the cruelties of the Moors unto the race of Jacob, than the cruelties of the Nazarenes of England."

Isaac listened with tolerable composure while Ben Samuel read the letter, and then again resumed the gestures and exclamations of Oriental sorrow, tearing his garments, besprinkling his head with dust, and ejaculating, "My daughter! my daughter! flesh of my flesh, and bone of my bone!"

"Yet," said the rabbi, "take courage, for this grief availeth nothing. Gird up thy loins, and seek out this Wilfred, the son of Cedric. It may be he will help thee with counsel or with strength; for the youth hath favour in the eyes of Richard, called of the Nazarenes Cœur-de-Lion, and the tidings that he hath returned are constant in the land. It may be that he may obtain his letter, and his signet, commanding these men of blood, who take their name from the Temple to the dishonour thereof that they proceed not in their purposed wickedness."

"I will seek him out," said Isaac, "for he is a good youth, and hath compassion for the exile of Jacob. But he cannot bear his armour, and what other Christian shall do battle for the oppressed of Zion?"

"Nay, but," said the rabbi, "thou speakest as one that knoweth not the Gentiles. With gold shalt thou buy their valour, even as with gold thou buyest thine own safety. Be of good courage, and do thou set forward to find out this Wilfred of Ivanhoe. I will also up and be doing, for great sin it were to leave thee in thy calamity. I will hie me to the city of York, where many warriors and strong men are assembled, and doubt not I will find among them some one who will do battle for thy daughter; for gold is their god, and for riches will they pawn their lives as well as their lands. Thou wilt fulfil, my brother, such promise as I may make unto them in thy name?"

"Assuredly, brother," said Isaac, "and Heaven be praised that raised me up a comforter in my misery. Howbeit, grant them not their full demand at once, for thou shalt find it the quality of this accursed people that they will ask pounds and peradventure accept of ounces. Nevertheless, be it as thou willest, for I am distracted in this thing, and what would my gold avail me if the child of my love should perish!"

"Farewell," said the physician, "and may it be to thee as thy heart desireth."

They embraced accordingly, and departed on their several roads. The cripple peasant remained for some time looking after them.

"These dog-Jews!" said he, "to take no more notice of a free guildbrother, than if I were a bond slave or a Turk, or a circumcised Hebrew like themselves! They might have flung me a mancus or two, however. I was not obliged to bring their unhallowed scrawls, and run the risk of being bewitched, as more folks than one told me. And what care I for the bit of gold that the wench gave me, if I am to come to harm from the priest next Easter at confession, and be obliged to give him twice as much to make it up with him, and be called the Jew's flying post all my life, as it may hap, into the bargain? I think I was bewitched in earnest when I was beside that girl? But it was always so with Jew or Gentile, whosoever came near her—none could stay when she had an errand to go—and still, whenever I think of her, I would give shop and tools to save her life."

CHAPTER XXXIX

O maid, unrelenting and cold as thou art,
My bosom is proud as thine own.
SEWARD.

IT was in the twilight of the day when her trial, if it could be called such, had taken place, that a low knock was heard at the door of Rebecca's prison-chamber. It disturbed not the inmate, who was then engaged in the evening prayer recommended by her religion, and which concluded with a hymn we have ventured thus to translate into English.

> When Israel, of the Lord beloved,
>   Out of the land of bondage came,
> Her father's God before her moved,
>   An awful guide, in smoke and flame.
> By day, along the astonish'd lands
>   The cloudy pillar glided slow;
> By night, Arabia's crimson sands
>   Returned the fiery column's glow.
>
> There rose the choral hymn of praise,
>   And trump and timbrel answer'd keen,
> And Zion's daughters poured their lays,
>   With priest's and warrior's voice between.
> No portents now our foes amaze,
>   Forsaken Israel wanders lone;
> Our fathers would not know THY ways,
>   And THOU hast left them to their own.
>
> But, present still, though now unseen;
>   When brightly shines the prosperous day,
> Be thoughts of THEE a cloudy screen
>   To temper the deceitful ray.
> And oh, when stoops on Judah's path
>   In shade and storm the frequent night,
> Be THOU, long-suffering, slow to wrath,
>   A burning, and a shining light!
>
> Our harps we left by Babel's streams,
>   The tyrant's jest, the Gentile's scorn;
> No censer round our altar beams,
>   And mute our timbrel, trump, and horn.
> But THOU hast said, the blood of goat,
>   The flesh of rams, I will not prize;
> A contrite heart, and humble thought,
>   Are mine accepted sacrifice.

When the sounds of Rebecca's devotional hymn had died away in silence, the low knock at the door was again renewed. "Enter," she said, "if thou art a friend; and if a foe, I have not the means of refusing thy entrance."

"I am," said Brian de Bois-Guilbert, entering the apartment, "friend or foe, Rebecca, as the event of this interview shall make me."

Alarmed at the sight of this man, whose licentious passion she considered as the root of her misfortunes, Rebecca drew backward with a

cautious and alarmed, yet not a timorous demeanour, into the farthest
corner of the apartment, as if determined to retreat as far as she could,
but to stand her ground when retreat became no longer possible. She
drew herself into an attitude not of defiance, but of resolution, as one
that would avoid provoking assault, yet was resolute to repel it, being
offered, to the utmost of her power.

"You have no reason to fear me, Rebecca," said the Templar; "or if I
must so qualify my speech, you have at least *now* no reason to fear me."

"I fear you not, Sir Knight," replied Rebecca, although her short-
drawn breath seemed to belie the heroism of her accents; "my trust is
strong, and I fear thee not."

"You have no cause," answered Bois-Guilbert, gravely; "my former
frantic attempts you have not now to dread. Within your call are guards,
over whom I have no authority. They are designed to conduct you to
death, Rebecca, yet would not suffer you to be insulted by any one, even
by me, were my frenzy—for frenzy it is—to urge me so far."

"May heaven be praised!" said the Jewess; "death is the least of my
apprehensions in this den of evil."

"Ay," replied the Templar, "the idea of death is easily received by
the courageous mind, when the road to it is sudden and open. A thrust with
a lance, a stroke with a sword, were to me little. To you, a spring from a
dizzy battlement, a stroke with a sharp poniard, has no terrors, compared
with what either thinks disgrace. Mark me—I say this—perhaps mine
own sentiments of honour are not less fantastic, Rebecca, than thine
are; but we know alike how to die for them."

"Unhappy man," said the Jewess; "and art thou condemned to expose thy life for principles, of which thy sober judgment does not acknowledge the solidity? Surely this is a parting with your treasure for that
which is not bread—but deem not so of me. Thy resolution may fluctuate
on the wild and changeful billows of human opinion, but mine is anchored
on the Rock of Ages."

"Silence, maiden," answered the Templar; "such discourse now avails
but little. Thou art condemned to die not a sudden and easy death, such
as misery chooses, and despair welcomes, but a slow, wretched, protracted course of torture, suited to what the diabolical bigotry of these
men calls thy crime."

"And to whom—if such my fate—to whom do I owe this?" said Rebecca; "surely only to him, who, for a most selfish and brutal cause,
dragged me hither, and who now, for some unknown purpose of his own,
strives to exaggerate the wretched fate to which he exposed me."

"Think not," said the Templar, "that I have so exposed thee; I would
have bucklered thee against such danger with my own bosom, as freely
as ever I exposed it to the shafts which had otherwise reached thy life."

"Had thy purpose been the honourable protection of the innocent,"
said Rebecca, "I had thanked thee for thy care—as it is, thou hast

claimed merit for it so often, that I tell thee life is worth nothing to me, preserved at the price which thou wouldst exact for it."

"Truce with thine upbraidings, Rebecca," said the Templar; "I have my own cause of grief, and brook not that thy reproaches should add to it."

"What is thy purpose, then, Sir Knight?" said the Jewess; "speak it briefly. If thou hast aught to do, save to witness the misery thou hast caused, let me know it; and then, if so it please you, leave me to myself— the step between time and eternity is short but terrible, and I have few moments to prepare for it."

"I perceive, Rebecca," said Bois-Guilbert, "that thou dost continue to burden me with the charge of distresses, which most fain would I have prevented."

"Sir Knight," said Rebecca, "I would avoid reproaches. But what is more certain than that I owe my death to thine unbridled passion?"

"You err—you err," said the Templar, hastily, "if you impute what I could neither foresee nor prevent to my purpose or agency. Could I guess the unexpected arrival of yon dotard, whom some flashes of frantic valour, and the praises yielded by fools to the stupid self-torments of an ascetic, have raised for the present above his own merits, above common sense, above me, and above the hundreds of our order who think and feel as men free from such silly and fantastic prejudices as are the grounds of his opinions and actions?"

"Yet," said Rebecca, "you sate a judge upon me, innocent—most innocent—as you knew me to be—you concurred in my condemnation, and, if I aright understood, are yourself to appear in arms to assert my guilt, and assure my punishment."

"Thy patience, maiden," replied the Templar. "No race knows so well as thine own tribes how to submit to the time, and so to trim their bark as to make advantage even of an adverse wind."

"Lamented be the hour," said Rebecca, "that has taught such art to the House of Israel! but adversity bends the heart as fire bends the stubborn steel, and those who are no longer their own governors, and the denizens of their own free independent state, must crouch before strangers. It is our curse, Sir Knight, deserved, doubtless, by our own misdeeds and those of our fathers; but you—you who boast your freedom as your birthright, how much deeper is your disgrace when you stoop to soothe the prejudices of others, and that against your own conviction?"

"Your words are bitter, Rebecca," said Bois-Guilbert, pacing the apartment with impatience, "but I came not hither to bandy reproaches with you. Know that Bois-Guilbert yields not to created man, although circumstances may for a time induce him to alter his plan. His will is the mountain stream, which may indeed be turned for a little space aside by the rock, but fails not to find its course to the ocean. That scroll which warned thee to demand a champion, from whom couldst thou think it came, if not from Bois-Guilbert? In whom else couldst thou have excited such interest?"

"A brief respite from instant death," said Rebecca, "which will little avail me—was this all thou couldst do for one, on whose head thou hast heaped sorrow, and whom thou hast brought near even to the verge of the tomb?"

"No, maiden," said Bois-Guilbert, "this was *not* all that I purposed. Had it not been for the accursed interference of yon fanatical dotard, and the fool of Goodalricke, who, being a Templar, affects to think the judge according to the ordinary rules of humanity, the office of the Champion Defender had devolved, not on a Preceptor, but on a Champion of the Order. Then I myself—such was my purpose—had, on the sounding of the trumpet, appeared in the lists as thy champion, disguised indeed in the fashion of a roving knight, who seeks adventures to prove his shield and spear; and then, let Beaumanoir have chosen not one, but two or three of the brethren here assembled, I had not doubted to cast them out of the saddle with my single lance. Thus, Rebecca, should thine innocence have been avouched, and to thine own gratitude would I have trusted for the reward of my victory."

"This, Sir Knight," said Rebecca, "is but idle boasting—a brag of what you would have done had you not found it convenient to do otherwise. You received my glove, and my champion, if a creature so desolate can find one, must encounter your lance in the lists—yet you would assume the air of my friend and protector!"

"Thy friend and protector," said the Templar, gravely, "I will yet be—but mark at what risk, or rather at what certainty, of dishonour; and then blame me not if I make my stipulations, before I offer up all that I have hitherto held dear, to save the life of a Jewish maiden."

"Speak," said Rebecca; "I understand thee not."

"Well, then," said Bois-Guilbert, "I will speak as freely as ever did doting penitent to his ghostly father, when placed in the tricky confessional. Rebecca, if I appear not in these lists I lose fame and rank—lose that which is the breath of my nostrils, the esteem, I mean, in which I am held by my brethren, and the hopes I have of succeeding to that mighty authority, which is now wielded by the bigoted dotard Lucas de Beaumanoir, but of which I should make a far different use. Such is my certain doom, except I appear in arms against thy cause. Accursed be he of Goodalricke, who baited this trap for me! and doubly accursed Albert de Malvoisin, who withheld me from the resolution I had formed, of hurling back the glove at the face of the superstitious and superannuated fool, who listened to a charge so absurd, and against a creature so high in mind, and so lovely in form as thou art!"

"And what now avails rant or flattery?" answered Rebecca. "Thou hast made thy choice between causing to be shed the blood of an innocent woman, or of endangering thine own earthly state and earthly hopes. What avails it to reckon together?—thy choice is made."

"No, Rebecca," said the knight, in a softer tone, and drawing nearer towards her; "my choice is NOT made—nay, mark, it is thine to make the election. If I appear in the lists, I must maintain my name in arms; and if I do so, championed or unchampioned, thou diest by the stake and faggot, for there lives not the knight who hath coped with me in arms on equal issue, or on terms of vantage, save Richard Cœur-de-Lion, and his minion of Ivanhoe. Ivanhoe, as thou well knowest, is unable to bear his corslet, and Richard is in a foreign prison. If I appear, then thou diest, even although thy charms should instigate some hot-headed youth to enter the lists in thy defence."

"And what avails repeating this so often?" said Rebecca.

"Much," replied the Templar; "for thou must learn to look at thy fate on every side."

"Well, then, turn the tapestry," said the Jewess, "and let me see the other side."

"If I appear," said Bois-Guilbert, "in the fatal lists, thou diest by a slow and cruel death, in pain such as they say is destined to the guilty hereafter. But if I appear not, then am I a degraded and dishonoured knight, accused of witchcraft and of communion with infidels—the illustrious name which has grown yet more so under my wearing, becomes a hissing and a reproach. I lose fame, I lose honour, I lose the prospect of such greatness as scarce emperors attain to—I sacrifice mighty ambition, I destroy schemes built as high as the mountains with which heathens say their heaven was once nearly scaled—and yet, Rebecca," he added, throwing himself at her feet, "this greatness will I sacrifice, this fame will I renounce, this power will I forego, even now when it is half within my grasp, if thou wilt say, Bois-Guilbert, I receive thee for my lover."

"Think not of such foolishness, Sir Knight," answered Rebecca, "but hasten to the Regent, the Queen Mother, and to Prince John—they cannot, in honour to the English crown, allow of the proceedings of your Grand Master. So shall you give me protection without sacrifice on your part, or the pretext of requiring any requital from me."

"With these I deal not," he continued, holding the train of her robe; "it is thee only I address; and what can counter-balance thy choice? Bethink thee, were I a fiend, yet death is a worse, and it is death who is my rival."

"I weigh not these evils," said Rebecca, afraid to provoke the wild knight, yet equally determined neither to endure his passion, nor even feign to endure it. "Be a man, be a Christian! If indeed thy faith recommends that mercy which rather your tongues than your actions pretend, save me from this dreadful death, without seeking a requital which would change thy magnanimity into base barter."

"No, damsel!" said the proud Templar, springing up, "thou shalt not thus impose on me—if I renounce present fame and future ambition, I renounce it for thy sake, and we will escape in company. Listen to

me, Rebecca," he said, again softening his tone; "England,—Europe,—
is not the world. There are spheres in which we may act, ample enough
even for my ambition. We will go to Palestine, where Conrade, Marquis
of Montserrat, is my friend—a friend free as myself from the doting
scruples which fetter our free-born reason—rather with Saladin will
we league ourselves, than endure the scorn of the bigots whom we contemn. I will form new paths to greatness," he continued, again traversing
the room with hasty strides—"Europe shall hear the loud step of him
she has driven from her sons! Not the millions whom her crusaders send
to slaughter, can do so much to defend Palestine—not the sabres of the
thousands and ten thousands of Saracens can hew their way so deep into
that land for which nations are striving, as the strength and policy of
me and those brethren, who, in despite of yonder old bigot, will adhere
to me in good and evil. Thou shalt be a queen, Rebecca—on Mount
Carmel shall we pitch the throne which my valour will gain for you, and
I will exchange my long-desired batoon for a sceptre!"

"A dream," said Rebecca; "an empty vision of the night, which, were
it a waking reality, affects me not. Enough, that the power which thou
mightest acquire, I will never share; nor hold I so light of country or
religious faith, as to esteem him who is willing to barter these ties, and cast
away the bonds of the order of which he is a sworn member, in order to
gratify an unruly passion for the daughter of another people. Put not a
price on my deliverance, Sir Knight—sell not a deed of generosity—protect the oppressed for the sake of charity, and not for a selfish advantage.
Go to the throne of England; Richard will listen to my appeal from these
cruel men."

"Never, Rebecca!" said the Templar, fiercely. "If I renounce my
order, for thee alone will I renounce it. Ambition shall remain mine, if
thou refuse my love; I will not be fooled on all hands. Stoop my crest
to Richard?—ask a boon of that heart of pride? Never, Rebecca, will I
place the order of the Temple at his feet in my person. I may forsake the
order, I never will degrade or betray it."

"Now God be gracious to me," said Rebecca, "for the succour of man
is wellnigh hopeless!"

"It is indeed," said the Templar; "for, proud as thou art, thou hast
in me found thy match. If I enter the lists with my spear in rest, think
not any human consideration shall prevent my putting forth my strength;
and think then upon thine own fate—to die the dreadful death of the
worst of criminals—to be consumed upon a blazing pile—dispersed to
the elements of which our strange forms are so mystically composed—
not a relic left of that graceful frame, from which we could say this lived
and moved! Rebecca, it is not in woman to sustain this prospect—thou
wilt yield to my suit."

"Bois-Guilbert," answered the Jewess, "thou knowest not the heart
of woman, or hast only conversed with those who are lost to her best
feelings. I tell thee, proud Templar, that not in thy fiercest battles hast

thou displayed more of thy vaunted courage than has been shown by woman when called upon to suffer by affection or auty. I am myself a woman, tenderly nurtured, naturally fearful of danger, and impatient of pain—yet, when we enter those fatal lists, thou to fight and I to suffer, I feel the strong assurance within me that my courage shall mount higher than thine. Farewell—I waste no more words on thee; the time that remains on earth to the daughter of Jacob must be otherwise spent—she must seek the Comforter, who may hide his face from his people, but whoever opens his ear to the cry of those who seek him in sincerity and in truth."

"We part then thus?" said the Templar, after a short pause; "would to Heaven that we had never met, or that thou hadst been noble in birth and Christian in faith! Nay, by Heaven! when I gaze on thee, and think when and how we are next to meet, I could even wish myself one of thine own degraded nation; my hand conversant with ingots and shekels, instead of spear and shield; my head bent down before each petty noble, and my look only terrible to the shivering and bankrupt debtor,—this could I wish, Rebecca, to be near to thee in life, and to escape the fearful share I must have in thy death."

"Thou hast spoken the Jew," said Rebecca, "as the persecution of such as thou art has made him. Heaven in ire has driven him from his country, but industry has opened to him the only road to power and to influence, which oppression has left unbarred. Read the ancient history of the people of God, and tell me if those, by whom Jehovah wrought such marvels among the nations, were then a people of misers and of usurers! And know, proud knight, we number names amongst us to which your boasted northern nobility is as the gourd compared with the cedar —names that ascend far back to those high times when the Divine Presence shook the mercy-seat between the cherubim, and which derive their splendour from no earthly prince, but from the awful Voice, which bade their fathers be nearest of the congregation to the Vision. Such were the princes of the house of Jacob."

Rebecca's colour rose as she boasted the ancient glories of her race, but faded as she added, with a sigh, "such *were* the princes of Judah, now such no more! They are trampled down like the shorn grass, and mixed with the mire of the ways. Yet are there those among them who shame not such high descent, and of such shall be the daughter of Isaac the son of Adonikam! Farewell! I envy not thy blood-won honours, I envy not thy barbarous descent from northern heathens, I envy thee not thy faith, which is ever in thy mouth, but never in thy heart nor in thy practice."

"There is a spell on me, by Heaven!" said Bois-Guilbert. "I almost think yon besotted skeleton spoke truth, and that the reluctance with which I part from thee hath something in it more than is natural. Fair creature!" he said, approaching near her, but with great respect, "so young, so beautiful, so fearless of death! and yet doomed to die, and

with infamy and agony. Who would not weep for thee? The tear that has
been a stranger to these eyelids for twenty years moistens them as I gaze
on thee. But it must be—nothing may now save thy life. Thou and I are
but the blind instruments of some irresistible fatality, that hurries us
along, like goodly vessels driving before the storm, which are dashed
against each other, and so perish. Forgive me, then, and let us part at
least as friends part. I have assailed thy resolution in vain, and mine own
is fixed as the adamantine decrees of fate."

"Thus," said Rebecca, "do men throw on fate the issue of their own
wild passions. But I do forgive thee, Bois-Guilbert, though the author
of my early death. There are noble things which cross over thy powerful
mind; but it is the garden of the sluggard, and the weeds have rushed
up, and conspired to choke the fair and wholesome blossom."

"Yes," said the Templar, "I am, Rebecca, as thou hast spoken me,
untaught, untamed—and proud, that, amidst a shoal of empty fools and
crafty bigots, I have retained the pre-eminent fortitude that places me
above them. I have been a child of battle from my youth upward, high
in my views, steady and inflexible in pursuing them. Such must I remain
—proud, inflexible, and unchanging; and of this the world shall have
proof. But thou forgivest me, Rebecca?"

"As freely as ever victim forgave her executioner."

"Farewell, then," said the Templar, and left the apartment.

The Preceptor Albert waited impatiently in an adjacent chamber the
return of Bois-Guilbert.

"Thou hast tarried long," he said; "I have been as if stretched on
red-hot iron with very impatience. What if the Grand Master or his spy
Conrade had come hither? I had paid dear for my complaisance. But
what ails thee, brother? Thy step totters, thy brow is as black as night.
Art thou well, Bois-Guilbert?"

"Ay," answered the Templar, "as well as the wretch who is doomed
to die within an hour. Nay, by the rood, not half so well, for there be
those in such state, who can lay down life like a cast-off garment. By
Heaven, Malvoisin, yonder girl hath wellnigh unmanned me. I am half
resolved to go to the Grand Master, abjure the order to his very teeth,
and refuse to act the brutality which his tyranny has imposed on me."

"Thou art mad," answered Malvoisin; "thou mayst thus indeed utterly
ruin thyself, but canst not even find a chance thereby to save the life
of this Jewess, which seems so precious in thine eyes. Beaumanoir will
name another of the order to defend his judgment in thy place, and the
accused will as assuredly perish as if thou hadst taken the duty imposed
on thee."

" 'Tis false—I will myself take arms in her behalf," answered the
Templar, haughtily; "and, should I do so, I think, Malvoisin, that thou
knowest not one of the order, who will keep his saddle before the point
of my lance."

"Ay, but thou forgettest," said the wily adviser, "thou wilt have neither leisure nor opportunity to execute this mad project. Go to Lucas Beaumanoir, and say thou hast renounced thy vow of obedience, and see how long the despotic old man will leave thee in personal freedom. The words shall scarce have left thy lips, ere thou wilt either be an hundred feet under ground, in the dungeon of the preceptory, to abide trial as a recreant knight; or, if his opinion holds concerning thy possession, thou wilt be enjoying straw, darkness, and chains in some distant convent cell, stunned with exorcisms, and drenched with holy water, to expel the foul fiend which hath obtained dominion over thee. Thou must to the lists, Brian, or thou art a lost and dishonoured man."

"I will break forth and fly," said Bois-Guilbert, "fly to some distant land, to which folly and fanaticism have not yet found their way. No drop of the blood of this most excellent creature shall be spilled by my sanction."

"Thou canst not fly," said the Preceptor; "thy ravings have excited suspicion, and thou wilt not be permitted to leave the preceptory. Go and make the essay—present thyself before the gate, and command the bridge to be lowered, and mark what answer thou shalt receive. Thou art surprised and offended; but is it not the better for thee? Wert thou to fly, what would ensue but the reversal of thy arms, the dishonour of thine ancestry, the degradation of thy rank? Think on it. Where shall thine old companions in arms hide their heads when Brian de Bois-Guilbert, the best lance of the Templars, is proclaimed recreant, amid the hisses of the assembled people? What grief will be at the Court of France! With what joy will the haughty Richard hear the news, that the knight that set him hard in Palestine, and wellnigh darkened his renown, has lost fame and honour for a Jewish girl, whom he could not even save by so costly a sacrifice!"

"Malvoisin," said the Knight, "I thank thee—thou hast touched the string at which my heart most readily thrills! Come of it what may, recreant shall never be added to the name of Bois-Guilbert. Would to God, Richard, or any of his vaunting minions of England, would appear in these lists! But they will be empty—no one will risk to break a lance for the innocent, the forlorn."

"The better for thee, if it prove so," said the Preceptor; "if no champion appears, it is not by thy means that this unlucky damsel shall die, but by the doom of the Grand Master, with whom rests all the blame, and who will count that blame for praise and commendation."

"True," said Bois-Guilbert; "if no champion appears, I am but a part of the pageant, sitting indeed on horseback in the lists, but having no part in what is to follow."

"None whatever," said Malvoisin; "no more than the armed image of Saint George when it makes part of a procession."

"Well, I will resume my resolution," replied the haughty Templar. "She has despised me—repulsed me—reviled me. And wherefore should

I offer up for her whatever of estimation I have in the opinion of others? Malvoisin, I will appear in the lists."

He left the apartment hastily as he uttered these words and the Preceptor followed, to watch and confirm him in his resolution; for in Bois-Guilbert's fame he had himself a strong interest, expecting much advantage from his being one day at the head of the order, not to mention the preferment of which Mont-Fitchet had given him hopes, on condition he would forward the condemnation of the unfortunate Rebecca. Yet although, in combating his friend's better feelings, he possessed all the advantage which a wily, composed, selfish disposition has over a man agitated by strong and contending passions, it required all Malvoisin's art to keep Bois-Guilbert steady to the purpose he had prevailed on him to adopt. He was obliged to watch him closely to prevent his resuming his purpose of flight, to intercept his communication with the Grand Master, lest he should come to an open rupture with his superior, and to renew, from time to time, the various arguments by which he endeavoured to show that, in appearing as champion on this occasion, Bois-Guilbert, without either accelerating or ensuing the fate of Rebecca, would follow the only course by which he could save himself from degradation and disgrace.

CHAPTER XL

Shadows avaunt!—Richard's himself again.
                                Richard III.

WHEN the Black Knight—for it becomes necessary to resume the train of his adventures—left the trysting-tree of the generous outlaw, he held his way straight to a neighbouring religious house, of small extent and revenue, called the Priory of St. Botolph, to which the wounded Ivanhoe had been removed when the castle was taken, under the guidance of the faithful Gurth and the magnanimous Wamba. It is unnecessary at present to mention what took place in the interim betwixt Wilfred and his deliverer; suffice it to say, that after long and grave communication, messengers were dispatched by the Prior in several directions, and that on the succeeding morning the Black Knight was about to set forth on his journey, accompanied by the jester Wamba, who attended as his guide.

"We will meet," he said to Ivanhoe, "at Coningsburgh, the castle of the deceased Athelstane, since there thy father Cedric holds the funeral feast for his noble relation. I would see your Saxon kindred together, Sir Wilfred, and become better acquainted with them than heretofore. Thou also wilt meet me; and it shall be my task to reconcile thee to thy father."

So saying, he took an affectionate farewell of Ivanhoe, who expressed an anxious desire to attend upon his deliverer. But the Black Knight would not listen to the proposal.

"Rest this day; thou wilt have scarce strength enough to travel on the next. I will have no guide with me but honest Wamba, who can play priest or fool as I shall be most in the humour."

"And I," said Wamba, "will attend you with all my heart. I would fain see the feasting at the funeral of Athelstane; for, if it be not full and frequent, he will rise from the dead to rebuke cook, sewer, and cup-bearer; and that were a sight worth seeing. Always, Sir Knight, I will trust your valour with making my excuse to my master Cedric, in case mine own wit should fail."

"And how should my poor valour succeed, Sir Jester, when thy light wit halts?—resolve me that."

"Wit, Sir Knight," replied the Jester, "may do much. He is a quick, apprehensive knave who sees his neighbour's blind side, and knows how to keep the lee-gage when his passions are blowing high. But valour is a sturdy fellow, that makes all split. He rows against both wind and tide, and makes way notwithstanding; and, therefore, good Sir Knight, while I take advantage of the fair weather in our noble master's temper, I will expect you to bestir yourself when it grows rough."

"Sir Knight of the Fetterlock, since it is your pleasure so to be distinguished," said Ivanhoe, "I fear me you have chosen a talkative and a troublesome fool to be your guide. But he knows every path and alley in the woods as well as e'er a hunter who frequents them; and the poor knave, as thou hast partly seen, is as faithful as steel."

"Nay," said the Knight, "an he have the gift of showing my road, I shall not grumble with him that he desires to make it pleasant. Fare thee well, kind Wilfred; I charge thee not to attempt to travel till to-morrow at earliest."

So saying, he extended his hand to Ivanhoe, who pressed it to his lips, took leave of the Prior, mounted his horse, and departed with Wamba for his companion. Ivanhoe followed them with his eyes, until they were lost in the shades of the surrounding forest, and then returned into the convent.

But shortly after matin-song, he requested to see the Prior. The old man came in haste, and enquired anxiously after the state of his health.

"It is better," he said, "than my fondest hope could have anticipated; either my wound has been slighter than the effusion of blood led me to suppose, or this balsam hath wrought a wonderful cure upon it. I feel already as if I could bear my corslet; and so much the better, for thoughts pass in my mind which render me unwilling to remain here longer in inactivity."

"Now, the saints forbid," said the Prior, "that the son of the Saxon Cedric should leave our convent ere his wounds were healed! It were shame to our profession were we to suffer it."

"Nor would I desire to leave your hospitable roof, venerable father," said Ivanhoe, "did I not feel myself able to endure the journey, and compelled to undertake it."

"And what can have urged you to so sudden a departure?" said the Prior.

"Have you never, holy father," answered the knight, "felt an apprehension of approaching evil, for which you in vain attempted to assign a cause? Have you never found your mind darkened, like the sunny landscape, by the sudden cloud, which augurs a coming tempest? And thinkest thou not that such impulses are deserving of attention, as being the hints of our guardian spirits that danger is impending?"

"I may not deny," said the Prior, crossing himself, "that such things have been, and have been of Heaven; but then such communications have had a visibly useful scope and tendency. But thou, wounded as thou art, what avails it thou shouldst follow the steps of him whom thou couldst not aid, were he to be assaulted?"

"Prior," said Ivanhoe, "thou dost mistake. I am stout enough to exchange buffets with any who will challenge me to such a traffic. But were it otherwise, may I not aid him were he in danger, by other means than by force of arms? It is but too well known that the Saxons love not the Norman race, and who knows what may be the issue, if he break in upon them when their hearts are irritated by the death of Athelstane, and their heads heated by the carousal in which they will indulge themselves? I hold his entrance among them at such a moment most perilous, and I am resolved to share or avert the danger; which, that I may the better do, I would crave of thee the use of some palfrey whose pace may be softer than that of my *destrier*."

"Surely," said the worthy churchman; "you shall have mine own ambling jennet, and I would it ambled as easy for your sake as that of the Abbot of Saint Albans. Yet this will I say for Malkin, for so I call her, that unless you were to borrow a ride on the juggler's steed that paces a horn-pipe amongst the eggs, you could not go a journey on a creature so gentle and smooth-paced. I have composed many a homily on her back, to the edification of my brethren of the convent, and many poor Christian souls."

"I pray you, reverend father," said Ivanhoe, "let Malkin be got ready instantly, and bid Gurth attend me with mine arms."

"Nay but, fair sir," said the Prior, "I pray you to remember that Malkin hath as little skill in arms as her master, and that I warrant not her enduring the sight or weight of your full panoply. O, Malkin, I promise you, is a beast of judgment, and will contend against any undue weight. I did but borrow the *Fructus Temporum* from the priest of Saint Bees, and I promise you she would not stir from the gate until I had exchanged the huge volume for my little breviary."

"Trust me, holy father," said Ivanhoe, "I will not distress her with too much weight, and if she calls a combat with me, it is odds but she has the worst."

This reply was made while Gurth was buckling on the knight's heels a pair of large gilded spurs, capable of convincing any restive horse that his best safety lay in being conformable to the will of his rider.

The deep and sharp rowels with which Ivanhoe's heels were now armed, began to make the worthy Prior repent of his courtesy, and ejaculate,— "Nay but, fair sir, now I bethink me, my Malkin abideth not the spur. Better it were that you tarry for the mare of our manciple down at the Grange, which may be had in little more than an hour, and cannot but be tractable, in respect that she draweth much of our winter fire-wood, and eateth no corn."

"I thank you, reverend father, but will abide by your first offer, as I see Malkin is already led forth to the gate. Gurth shall carry mine armour; and for the rest, rely on it, that as I will not overload Malkin's back, she shall not overcome my patience. And now, farewell!"

Ivanhoe now descended the stair more hastily and easily than his wound promised, and threw himself upon the jennet, eager to escape the importunity of the Prior, who stuck as closely to his side as his age and fatness would permit, now singing the praises of Malkin, now recommending caution to the knight in managing her.

"She is at the most dangerous period for maidens as well as mares," said the old man, laughing at his own jest, "being barely in her fifteenth year."

Ivanhoe, who had other web to weave than to stand canvassing a palfrey's paces with its owner, lent but a deaf ear to the Prior's grave advices and facetious jests, and having leapt on his mare, and commanded his squire (for such Gurth now called himself) to keep close by his side, he followed the track of the Black Knight into the forest, while the Prior stood at the gate of the convent looking after him, and ejaculating,—"Saint Mary! how prompt and fiery be these men of war! I would I had not trusted Malkin to his keeping, for, crippled as I am with the cold rheum, I am undone if aught but good befalls her. And yet," said he, recollecting himself, "as I would not spare my own old and disabled limbs in the good cause of Old England, so Malkin must e'en run her hazard on the same venture; and it may be they will think our poor house worthy of some munificent guerdon—or, it may be, they will send the old Prior a pacing nag. And if they do none of these, as great men will forget little men's service, truly I shall hold me well repaid in having done that which is right. And it is now wellnigh the fitting time to summon the brethren to breakfast in the refectory. Ah! I doubt they obey that call more cheerily than the bells for primes and matins."

So the Prior of Saint Botolph's hobbled back again into the refectory, to preside over the stock-fish and ale, which was just serving out for the friars' breakfast. Pursy and important, he sat him down at the table, and many a dark word he threw out, of benefits to be expected to the convent, and high deeds of service done by himself, which, at another season, would have attracted observation. But as the stock-fish was highly salted, and the ale reasonably powerful, the jaws of the brethren were too anxiously employed to admit of their making much use of their ears; nor do we read of any of the fraternity, who was tempted to speculate upon the mysterious hints of their superior, except Father Diggory, who was severely afflicted by the toothache, so that he could only eat on one side of his jaws.

In the meantime, the Black Champion and his guide were pacing at their leisure through the recesses of the forest; the good Knight whiles humming to himself the lay of some enamoured troubadour, sometimes encouraging by questions the prating disposition of his attendant, so that their dialogue formed a whimsical mixture of song and jest, of which we would fain give our readers some idea. You are then to imagine this Knight, such as we have already described him, strong of person, tall, broad-shouldered, and large of bone, mounted on his mighty black charger, which seemed made on purpose to bear his weight, so easily he paced forward under it, having the visor of his helmet raised, in order to admit freedom of breath, yet keeping the beaver, or under part, closed, so that his features could be but imperfectly distinguished. But his ruddy embrowned cheek-bones could be plainly seen, and the large and bright blue eyes, that flashed from under the dark shade of the raised visor; and the whole gesture and look of the champion expressed careless gaiety and fearless confidence—a mind which was unapt to apprehend danger, and prompt to defy it when most imminent—yet with whom danger was a familiar thought, as with one whose trade was war and adventure.

The jester wore his usual fantastic habit, but late accidents had led him to adopt a good cutting falchion, instead of his wooden sword, with a targe to match it; of both which weapons he had, notwithstanding his profession, shown himself a skilful master during the storming of Torquilstone. Indeed, the infirmity of Wamba's brain consisted chiefly in a kind of impatient irritability, which suffered him not long to remain quiet in any posture, or adhere to any certain train of ideas, although he was for a few minutes alert enough in performing any immediate task, or in apprehending any immediate topic. On horseback, therefore, he was perpetually swinging himself backwards and forwards, now on the horse's ears, then anon on the very rump of the animal,—now hanging both his legs on one side, and now sitting with his face to the tail, moping, mowing, and making a thousand apish gestures, until his palfrey took his freaks so much to heart as fairly to lay him at his length on the green grass—an incident which greatly amused the Knight, but compelled his companion to ride more steadily thereafter.

At the point of their journey at which we take them up, this joyous pair were engaged in singing a virelai, as it was called, in which the clown bore a mellow burden, to the better instructed Knight of the Fetterlock. And thus run the ditty:—

Anna-Marie, love, up is the sun,
Anna-Marie, love, morn is begun,
Mists are dispersing, love, birds singing free,
Up in the morning, love, Anna-Marie.
Anna-Marie, love, up in the morn,
The hunter is winding blithe sounds on his horn,
The echo rings merry from rock and from tree,
'Tis come to arouse thee, love, Anna-Marie.

WAMBA

O Tybalt, love, Tybalt, awake me not yet,
Around my soft pillow while softer dreams flit,
For what are the joys that in waking we prove,
Compared with these visions, O Tybalt, my love?
Let the birds to the rise of the mist carol shrill,
Let the hunter blow out his loud horn on the hill,
Softer sounds, softer pleasures, in slumber I prove,—
But think not I dreamt of thee, Tybalt, my love.

"A dainty song," said Wamba, when they had finished their carol, "and I swear by my bauble, a pretty moral!—I used to sing it with Gurth, once my playfellow, and now, by the grace of God and his master, no less than a freeman; and we once came by the cudgel for being so entranced by the melody, that we lay in bed two hours after sunrise, singing the ditty betwixt sleeping and waking—my bones ache at thinking of the tune ever since. Nevertheless, I have played the part of Anna-Marie, to please you, fair sir."

The Jester next struck into another carol, a sort of comic ditty, to which the Knight, catching up the tune, replied in the like manner.

KNIGHT AND WAMBA

There came three merry men from south, west, and north,
  Ever more sing the roundelay;
To win the Widow of Wycombe forth,
  And where was the widow might say them nay?

The first was a knight, and from Tynedale he came,
  Ever more sing the roundelay;
And his fathers, God save us, were men of great fame,
  And where was the widow might say him nay?

Of his father the laird, of his uncle the squire,
  He boasted in rhyme and roundelay;
She bade him go bask by his sea-coal fire,
  For she was the widow would say him nay.

WAMBA

The next that came forth, swore by blood and by nails,
  Merrily sing the roundelay;
Hur's a gentleman, God wot, and hur's lineage was of Wales,
  And where was the widow might say him nay?

Sir David ap Morgan ap Griffith ap Hugh
  Ap Tudor ap Rhice, quoth his roundelay;
She said that one widow for so many was too few,
  And she bade the Welshman wend his way.

But then next came a yeoman, a yeoman of Kent,
  Jollily singing his roundelay;
He spoke to the widow of living and rent,
  And where was the widow could say him nay?

BOTH

So the knight and the squire were both left in the mire,
  There for to sing their roundelay;
For a yeoman of Kent, with his yearly rent,
  There never was a widow could say him nay.

"I would, Wamba," said the Knight, "that our host of the trysting-tree, or the jolly Friar, his chaplain, heard this thy ditty in praise of our bluff yeoman."

"So would not I," said Wamba, "but for the horn that hangs at your baldric."

"Ay," said the Knight, "this is a pledge of Locksley's good-will, though I am not like to need it. Three mots on this bugle will, I am assured, bring round, at our need, a jolly band of yonder honest yeomen."

"I would say, Heaven forefend," said the jester, "were it not that that fair gift is a pledge they would let us pass peaceably."

"Why, what meanest thou?" said the Knight; "thinkest thou that but for this pledge of fellowship they would assault us?"

"Nay, for me I say nothing," said Wamba; "for green trees have ears as well as stone walls. But canst thou construe me this, Sir Knight—When is thy wine-pitcher and thy purse better empty than full?"

"Why, never, I think," replied the Knight.

"Thou never deservest to have a full one in thy hand, for so simple an answer! Thou hadst best empty thy pitcher ere thou pass it to a Saxon, and leave thy money at home ere thou walk in the greenwood."

"You hold our friends for robbers, then?" said the Knight of the Fetterlock.

"You hear me not say so, fair sir," said Wamba; "it may relieve a man's steed to take off his mail when he hath a long journey to make;

and, certes, it may do good to the rider's soul to ease him of that which is the root of evil; therefore will I give no hard names to those who do such services. Only I would wish my mail at home, and my purse in my chamber, when I meet with these good fellows, because it might save them some trouble."

"*We* are bound to pray for them, my friend, notwithstanding the fair character thou dost afford them."

"Pray for them with all my heart," said Wamba; "but in the town, not in the greenwood, like the Abbot of Saint Bees, whom they caused to say mass with an old hollow oak-tree for his stall."

"Say as thou list, Wamba," replied the Knight, "these yeomen did thy master Cedric yeomanly service at Torquilstone."

"Ay, truly," answered Wamba; "but that was in the fashion of their trade with Heaven."

"Their trade, Wamba! how mean you by that?" replied his companion.

"Marry, thus," said the jester. "They make up a balanced account with Heaven, as our old cellarer used to call his ciphering, as fair as Isaac the Jew keeps with his debtors, and, like him, give out a very little, and take large credit for doing so; reckoning, doubtless, on their own behalf the seven-fold usury which the blessed text hath promised to charitable loans."

"Give me an example of your meaning, Wamba,—I know nothing of ciphers or rates of usage," answered the Knight.

"Why," said Wamba, "an your valour be so dull, you will please to learn that those honest fellows balance a good deed with one not quite so laudable; as a crown given to a begging friar with an hundred byzants taken from a fat abbot, or a wench kissed in the greenwood with the relief of a poor widow."

"Which of these was the good deed, which was the felony?" interrupted the Knight.

"A good gibe! a good gibe!" said Wamba; "keeping witty company sharpeneth the apprehension. You said nothing so well, Sir Knight, I will be sworn, when you held drunken vespers with the bluff hermit. But to go on. The merry-men of the forest set off the building of a cottage with the burning of a castle, the thatching of a choir against the robbing of a church, the setting free a poor prisoner against the murder of a proud sheriff; or, to come nearer to our point, the deliverance of a Saxon franklin against the burning alive of a Norman baron. Gentle thieves they are, in short, and courteous robbers; but it is ever the luckiest to meet with them when they are at the worst."

"How so, Wamba?" said the Knight.

"Why, then they have some compunction, and are for making up matters with Heaven. But when they have struck an even balance, Heaven help them with whom they next open account! The travellers who first

met them after their good service at Torquilstone would have a woful
flaying. And yet," said Wamba, coming close up to the Knight's side,
"there be companions who are far more dangerous for travellers to meet
than yonder outlaws."

"And who may they be, for you have neither bears nor wolves, I
trow?" said the Knight.

"Marry, sir, but we have Malvoisin's men-at-arms," said Wamba; "and
let me tell you, that, in time of civil war, a halfscore of these is worth
a band of wolves at any time. They are now expecting their harvest, and
are reinforced with the soldiers that escaped from Torquilstone. So that,
should we meet with a band of them, we are like to pay for our feats
of arms. Now, I pray you, Sir Knight, what would you do if we met two
of them?"

"Pin the villains to the earth with my lance, Wamba, if they offered
us any impediment."

"But what if there were four of them?"

"They should drink of the same cup," answered the Knight.

"What if six," continued Wamba, "and we as we now are, barely two
—would you not remember Locksley's horn?"

"What!—sound for aid," exclaimed the Knight, "against a score of
such *rascaille* as these, whom one good knight could drive before him,
as the wind drives the withered leaves?"

"Nay, then," said Wamba, "I will pray you for a close sight of that
same horn that hath so powerful a breath."

The Knight undid the clasp of the baldric, and indulged his fellow-
traveller, who immediately hung the bugle round his own neck.

"Tra-lira-la," said he, whistling the notes; "nay, I know my gamut
as well as another."

"How mean you, knave?" said the Knight; "restore me the bugle."

"Content you, Sir Knight, it is in safe keeping. When Valour and
Folly travel, Folly should bear the horn, because she can blow the best."

"Nay but, rogue," said the Black Knight, "this exceedeth thy licence.
Beware ye tamper not with my patience."

"Urge me not with violence, Sir Knight," said the jester, keeping at
a distance from the impatient champion, "or Folly will show a clean
pair of heels, and leave Valour to find out his way through the wood as
best he may."

"Nay, thou hast hit me there," said the Knight; "and, sooth to say,
I have little time to jangle with thee. Keep the horn an thou wilt, but
let us proceed on our journey."

"You will not harm me, then?" said Wamba.

"I tell thee no, thou knave!"

"Ay, but pledge me your knightly word for it," continued Wamba,
as he approached with great caution.

"My knightly word I pledge; only come on with thy foolish self."

"Nay, then, Valour and Folly are once more boon companions," said the jester, coming up frankly to the Knight's side; "but, in truth, I love not such buffets as that you bestowed on the burly Friar, when his holiness rolled on the green like a king of the nine-pins. And now that Folly wears the horn, let Valour rouse himself, and shake his mane; for, if I mistake not, there are company in yonder brake that are on the lookout for us."

"What makes thee judge so?" said the Knight.

"Because I have twice or thrice noticed the glance of a morrion from amongst the green leaves. Had they been honest men, they had kept the path. But yonder thicket is a choice chapel for the Clerks of Saint Nicholas."

"By my faith," said the Knight, closing his visor, "I think thou be'st in the right on't."

And in good time did he close it, for three arrows flew at the same instant from the suspected spot against his head and breast, one of which would have penetrated to the brain, had it not been turned aside by the steel visor. The other two were averted by the gorget, and by the shield which hung around his neck.

"Thanks, trusty ramourer," said the Knight. "Wamba, let us close with them," and he rode straight to the thicket. He was met by six or seven men-at-arms, who ran against him with their lances at full career. Three of the weapons struck against him, and splintered with as little effect as if they had been driven against a tower of steel. The Black Knight's eyes seemed to flash fire even through the aperture of his visor. He raised himself in his stirrups with an air of inexpressible dignity, and exclaimed, "What means this, my masters!" The men made no other reply than by drawing their swords and attacking him on every side, crying, "Die, tyrant!"

"Ha! Saint Edward! Ha! Saint George!" said the Black Knight, striking down a man at every invocation; "have we traitors here?"

His opponents, desperate as they were, bore back from an arm which carried death in every blow, and it seemed as if the terror of his single strength was about to gain the battle against such odds, when a knight, in blue armour, who had hitherto kept himself behind the other assailants, spurred forward with his lance, and taking aim, not at the rider but at the steed, wounded the noble animal mortally.

"That was a felon stroke!" exclaimed the Black Knight, as the steed fell to the earth, bearing his rider along with him.

And at this moment, Wamba winded the bugle, for the whole had passed so speedily that he had not time to do so sooner. The sudden sound made the murderers bear back once more, and Wamba, though so imperfectly weaponed, did not hesitate to rush in and assist the Black Knight to rise.

"Shame on ye, false cowards!" exclaimed he in the blue harness, who seemed to lead the assailants, "do ye fly from the empty blast of a horn blown by a jester?"

Animated by his words, they attacked the Black Knight anew, whose best refuge was now to place his back against an oak, and defend himself with his sword. The felon knight, who had taken another spear, watching the moment when his formidable antagonist was most closely pressed, galloped against him in hopes to nail him with his lance against the tree, when his purpose was again intercepted by Wamba. The jester, making up by agility the want of strength, and little noticed by the men-at-arms, who were busied in their more important object, hovered on the skirts of the fight, and effectually checked the fatal career of the Blue Knight, by hamstringing his horse with a stroke of his sword. Horse and man went to the ground; yet the situation of the Knight of the Fetterlock continued very precarious, as he was pressed close by several men completely armed, and began to be fatigued by the violent exertions necessary to defend himself on so many points at nearly the same moment, when a grey-goose shaft suddenly stretched on the earth one of the most formidable of his assailants, and a band of yeomen broke forth from the glade, headed by Locksley and the jovial Friar, who, taking ready and effectual part in the fray, soon disposed of the ruffians, all of whom lay on the spot dead or mortally wounded. The Black Knight thanked his deliverers with a dignity they had not observed in his former bearing, which hitherto had seemed rather that of a blunt bold soldier than of a person of exalted rank.

"It concerns me much," he said, "even before I express my full gratitude to my ready friends, to discover, if I may, who have been my unprovoked enemies. Open the visor of that blue knight, Wamba, who seems the chief of these villains."

The jester instantly made up to the leader of the assassins, who, bruised by his fall, and entangled under the wounded steed, lay incapable either of flight or resistance.

"Come, valiant sir," said Wamba, "I must be your armourer as well as your equerry. I have dismounted you, and now I will unhelm you."

So saying, with no very gentle hand, he undid the helmet of the blue knight, which, rolling to a distance on the grass, displayed to the Knight of the Fetterlock grizzled locks, and a countenance he did not expect to have seen under such circumstances.

"Waldemar Fitzurse!" he said in astonishment; "what could urge one of thy rank and seeming worth to so foul an undertaking?"

"Richard," said the captive knight, looking up to him, "thou knowest little of mankind, if thou knowest not to what ambition and revenge can lead every child of Adam."

"Revenge?" answered the Black Knight; "I never wronged thee. On me thou hast nought to revenge."

"My daughter, Richard, whose alliance thou didst scorn—was that no injury to a Norman, whose blood is noble as thine own?"

"Thy daughter?" replied the Black Knight; "a proper cause of enmity, and followed up to a bloody issue! Stand back, my masters, I would speak to him alone. And now, Waldemar Fitzurse, say me the truth —confess who set thee on this traitorous deed."

"Thy father's son," answered Waldemar, "who, in so doing, did but avenge on thee thy disobedience to thy father."

Richard's eyes sparkled with indignation, but his better nature overcame it. He pressed his hand against his brow, and remained an instant gazing on the face of the humbled baron, in whose features pride was contending with shame.

"Thou dost not ask thy life, Waldemar," said the King.

"He that is in the lion's clutch," answered Fitzurse, "knows it were needless."

"Take it, then, unasked," said Richard; "the lion preys not on prostrate carcasses. Take thy life, but with this condition, that in three days thou shalt leave England, and go to hide thine infamy in thy Norman castle, and that thou wilt never mention the name of John of Anjou as connected with thy felony. If thou art found on English ground after the space I have allotted thee, thou diest—or if thou breathest aught that can attaint the honour of my house, by Saint George! not the altar itself shall be a sanctuary. I will hang thee out to feed the ravens, from the very pinnacle of thine own castle. Let this knight have a steed, Locksley, for I see your yeomen have caught those which were running loose, and let him depart unharmed."

"But that I judge I listen to a voice whose behests must not be disputed," answered the yeoman, "I would send a shaft after the skulking villain that should spare him the labour of a long journey."

"Thou bearest an English heart, Locksley," said the Black Knight, "and well dost judge thou art the more bound to obey my behest—I am Richard of England!"

At these words pronounced in a tone of majesty suited to the high rank, and no less distinguished character of Cœur-de-Lion, the yeomen at once kneeled down before him, and at the same time tendered their allegiance, and implored pardon for their offences.

"Rise, my friends," said Richard, in a gracious tone, looking on them with a countenance in which his habitual good humour had already conquered the blaze of hasty resentment, and whose features retained no mark of the late desperate conflict, excepting the flush arising from exertion,—"Arise," he said, "my friends! Your misdemeanours, whether in forest or field, have been atoned by the loyal services you rendered my distressed subjects before the walls of Torquilstone, and the rescue you have this day afforded to your sovereign. Arise, my liegemen, and be good subjects in future. And thou, brave Locksley"——

"Call me no longer Locksley, my liege, but know me under the name, which I fear, fame hath blown too widely not to have reached even your royal ears. I am Robin Hood of Sherwood Forest." [1]

"King of outlaws, and prince of good fellows!" said the King, "who hath not heard a name that has been borne as far as Palestine? But be assured, brave outlaw, that no deed done in our absence, and in the turbulent times to which it hath given rise, shall be remembeerd to thy disadvantage."

"True says the proverb," said Wamba, interposing his word, but with some abatement of his usual petulance,—

> 'When the cat is away,
> The mice will play.' "

"What, Wamba, art thou there?" said Richard; "I have been so long of hearing thy voice, I thought thou hadst taken flight."

"I take flight!" said Wamba; "when do you ever find Folly separated from Valour? There lies the trophy of my sword, that good grey gelding, whom I heartily wish upon his legs again, conditioning his master lay there houghed in his place. It is true, I gave a little ground at first, for a motley jacket does not brook lance-heads, as a steel doublet will. But if I fought not at sword's point, you will grant me that I sounded the onset."

"And to good purpose, honest Wamba," replied the King. "Thy good service shall not be forgotten."

"*Confiteor! Confiteor!*" exclaimed, in a submissive tone, a voice near the King's side—"my Latin will carry me no farther, but I confess my deadly treason, and pray leave to have absolution before I am led to execution!"

Richard looked around, and beheld the jovial Friar on his knees, telling his rosary, while his quarter-staff, which had not been idle during the skirmish, lay on the grass beside him. His countenance was gathered so as he thought might best express the most profound contrition, his eyes being turned up, and the corners of his mouth drawn down, as Wamba expressed it, like the tassels at the mouth of a purse. Yet this demure affectation of extreme penitence was whimsically belied by a ludicrous meaning which lurked in his huge features, and seemed to pronounce his fear and repentance alike hypocritical.

"For what art thou cast down, mad priest?" said Richard; "art thou afraid thy diocesan should learn how truly thou dost serve Our Lady and Saint Dunstan? Tush, man! fear it not; Richard of England betrays no secrets that pass over the flagon."

"Nay, most gracious sovereign," answered the hermit (well known to the curious in penny-histories of Robin Hood, by the name of Friar

---

[1] From the ballads of Robin Hood, we learn that this celebrated outlaw, when in disguise, sometimes assumed the name of Locksley, from a village where he was born, but where situated we are not distinctly told.

Tuck), "it is not the crosier I fear, but the sceptre. Alas! that my sacrilegious fist should ever have been applied to the ear of the Lord's anointed!"

"Ha! ha!" said Richard, "sits the wind there? In truth I had forgotten the buffet, though mine ear sung after it for a whole day. But if the cuff was fairly given, I will be judged by the good men around, if it was not as well repaid—or, if thou thinkest I still owe thee aught, and will stand forth for another counterbuff"——

"By no means," replied Friar Tuck, "I had mine own returned, and with usury—may your Majesty ever pay your debts as fully!"

"If I could do so with cuffs," said the King, "my creditors should have little reason to complain of an empty exchequer."

"And yet," said the Friar, resuming his demure hypocritical countenance, "I know not what penance I ought to perform for that most sacrilegious blow!"——

"Speak no more of it, brother," said the King; "after having stood so many cuffs from Paynims and misbelievers, I were void of reason to quarrel with the buffet of a clerk so holy as he of Copmanhurst. Yet, mine honest Friar, I think it would be best both for the church and thyself that I should procure a licence to unfrock thee, and retain thee as a yeoman of our guard, serving in care of our person, as formerly in attendance upon the altar of Saint Dunstan."

"My Liege," said the Friar, "I humbly crave your pardon; and you would readily grant my excuse, did you but know how the sin of laziness has beset me, Saint Dunstan—may he be gracious to us!—stands quiet in his niche, though I should forget my orisons in killing a fat buck. I stay out of my cell sometimes a night, doing I wot not what, Saint Dunstan never complains; a quiet master he is, and a peaceful, as ever was made of wood. But to be yeoman in attendance on my sovereign the King—the honour is great, doubtless—yet, if I were but to step aside to comfort a widow in one corner, or to kill a deer in another, it would be, 'where is the dog priest?' says one. 'Who has seen the accursed Turk?' says another. 'The unfrocked villain destroys more venison than half the country besides,' says one keeper; 'and is hunting after every shy doe in the country!' quoth a second. In fine, good my Liege, I pray you to leave me as you found me; or, if in aught you desire to extend your benevolence to me, that I may be considered as the poor Clerk of Saint Dunstan's cell in Copmanhurst, to whom any small donation will be most thankfully acceptable."

"I understand thee," said the King, "and the Holy Clerk shall have a grant of vert and venison in my woods of Warncliffe. Mark, however, I will but assign thee three bucks every season! but if that do not prove an apology for thy slaying thirty, I am no Christian knight nor true king."

"Your Grace may be well assured," said the Friar, "that, with the grace of Saint Dunstan, I shall find the way of multiplying your most bounteous gift."

"I nothing doubt it, good brother," said the King; "and as venison is but dry food, our cellarer shall have orders to deliver to thee a butt of sack, a runlet of Malvoisie, and three hogsheads of ale of the first strike, yearly. If that will not quench thy thirst, thou must come to court, and become acquainted with my butler."

"But for Saint Dunstan?" said the Friar.

"A cope, a stole, and an altar-cloth shalt thou also have," continued the King, crossing himself. "But we may not turn our game into earnest, lest God punish us for thinking more on our follies than on his honour and worship."

"I will answer for my patron," said the priest, joyously.

"Answer for thyself, Friar," said King Richard, something sternly; but immediately stretching out his hand to the hermit, the latter, somewhat abashed, bent his knee, and saluted it. "Thou dost less honour to my extended palm than to my clenched fist," said the monarch; "thou didst only kneel to the one, and to the other didst prostrate thyself."

But the Friar, afraid perhaps of again giving offence by continuing the conversation in too jocose a style—a false step to be particularly guarded against by those who converse with monarchs—bowed profoundly, and fell into the rear.

At the same time, two additional personages appeared on the scene.

CHAPTER XLI

All hail to the lordlings of high degree,
Who live not more happy, though greater, than we!
    Our pastimes to see,
    Under every green tree,
In all the gay woodland, right welcome ye be.
                                        MACDONALD.

THE newcomers were Wilfred of Ivanhoe, on the Prior of Botolph's palfrey, and Gurth, who attended him, on the knight's own war horse. The astonishment of Ivanhoe was beyond bounds, when he saw his master besprinkled with blood and six or seven dead bodies lying around in the little glade in which the battle had taken place. Nor was he less surprised to see Richard surrounded by so many silvan attendants, the outlaws, as they seemed to be, of the forest, and a perilous retinue therefore for a prince. He hesitated whether to address the King as the Black Knight-errant, or in what other manner to demean himself towards him. Richard saw his embarrassment.

"Fear not, Wilfred," he said, "to address Richard Plantagenet as himself, since thou seest him in the company of true English hearts, although it may be they have been urged a few steps aside by warm English blood."

"Sir Wilfred of Ivanhoe," said the gallant outlaw, stepping forward, "my assurances can add nothing to those of our sovereign; yet, let me say somewhat proudly, that of men who have suffered much, he hath not truer subjects than those who now stand around him."

"I cannot doubt it, brave man," said Wilfred, "since thou art of the number. But what mean these marks of death and danger? these slain men, and the bloody armour of my Prince?"

"Treason hath been with us, Ivanhoe," said the King; "but, thanks to these brave men, treason hath met its meed. But, now I bethink me, thou too art a traitor," said Richard, smiling; "a most disobedient traitor; for were not our orders positive, that thou shouldst repose thyself at Saint Botolph's until thy wound was healed?"

"It is healed," said Ivanhoe, "it is not of more consequence than the scratch of a bodkin. But why, oh why, noble Prince, will you thus vex the hearts of your faithful servants, and expose your life by lonely journeys and rash adventures, as if it were of no more value than that of a mere knight-errant, who has no interest on earth but what lance and sword may procure him?"

"And Richard Plantagenet," said the King, "desires no more fame than his good lance and sword may acquire him—and Richard Plantagenet is prouder of achieving an adventure, with only his good sword, and his good arm to speed, than if he led to battle an host of an hundred thousand armed men."

"But your kingdom, my Liege," said Ivanhoe, "your kingdom is threatened with dissolution and civil war—your subjects menaced with every species of evil, if deprived of their sovereign in some of these dangers which it is your daily pleasure to incur, and from which you have but this moment narrowly escaped."

"Ho! ho! my kingdom and my subjects?" answered Richard, impatiently; "I tell thee, Sir Wilfred, the best of them are most willing to repay my follies in kind. For example, my very faithful servant, Wilfred of Ivanhoe, will not obey my positive commands, and yet reads his king a homily, because he does not walk exactly by his advice. Which of us has most reason to upbraid the other? Yet forgive me, my faithful Wilfred. The time I have spent, and am yet to spend in concealment, is, as I explained to thee at Saint Botolph's, necessary to give my friends and faithful nobles time to assemble their forces, that when Richard's return is announced, he should be at the head of such a force as enemies shall tremble to face, and thus subdue the meditated treason, without even unsheathing a sword. Estoteville and Bohun will not be strong enough to move forward to York for twenty-four hours. I must have news of Salisbury from the south; and of Beauchamp, in Warwickshire; and of Multon and Percy in the north. The Chancellor must make sure of London. Too sudden an appearance would subject me to dangers other than my lance and sword, though backed by the bow of bold Robin, or the quarter-staff of Friar Tuck, and the horn of the sage Wamba, may be able to rescue me from."

Wilfred bowed in submission, well knowing how vain it was to contend with the wild spirit of chivalry which so often impelled his master
upon dangers which he might easily have avoided, or rather, which it
was unpardonable in him to have sought out. The young knight sighed,
therefore, and held his peace; while Richard, rejoiced at having silenced
his counsellor, though his heart acknowledged the justice of the charge
he had brought against him, went on in conversation with Robin Hood.
"King of Outlaws," he said, "have you no refreshment to offer to your
brother sovereign? for these dead knaves have found me both in exercise and appetite."

"In troth," replied the outlaw, "for I scorn to lie to your grace, our
larger is chiefly supplied with"—— He stopped, and was somewhat
embarrassed.

"With venison, I suppose?" said Richard, gaily; "better food at need
there can be none; and truly, if a king will not remain at home and slay
his own game, methinks he should not brawl too loud if he finds it killed
to his hand."

"If your grace, then," said Robin, "will again honour with your presence one of Robin Hood's places of rendezvous, the venison shall not be
lacking; and a stoup of ale, and it may be a cup of reasonably good
wine, to relish it withal."

The outlaw accordingly led the way, followed by the buxom monarch,
more happy, probably, in this chance meeting with Robin Hood and his
foresters, than he would have been in again assuming his royal state, and
presiding over a splendid circle of peers and nobles. Novelty in society
and adventure were the zest of life to Richard Cœur-de-Lion, and it had
its highest relish when enhanced by dangers encountered and surmounted.
In the lion-hearted king, the brilliant, but useless character, of a knight
of romance, was in a great measure realised and revived; and the personal
glory which he acquired by his own deeds of arms, was far more dear to
his excited imagination, than that which a course of policy and wisdom
would have spread around his government. Accordingly, his reign was
like the course of a brilliant and rapid meteor, which shoots along the
face of Heaven, shedding around an unnecessary and portentous light,
which is instantly swallowed up by universal darkness; his feats of
chivalry furnishing themes for bards and minstrels, but affording none of
those solid benefits to his country on which history loves to pause, and
hold up as an example to posterity. But in his present company Richard
showed to the greatest imaginable advantage. He was gay, good-
humoured, and fond of manhood in every rank of life.

Beneath a huge oak-tree the silvan repast was hastily prepared for the
King of England, surrounded by men outlaws to his government, but
who now formed his court and his guard. As the flagon went round, the
rough foresters soon lost their awe for the presence of Majesty. The
song and the jest were exchanged—the stories of former deeds were told
with advantage: and at length, and while boasting of their successful

infraction of the laws, no one recollected they were speaking in presence of their natural guardian. The merry king, nothing heeding his dignity any more than his company, laughed, quaffed, and jested among the jolly band. The natural and rough sense of Robin Hood led him to be desirous that the scene should be closed ere anything should occur to disturb its harmony, the more especially that he observed Ivanhoe's brow clouded with anxiety. "We are honoured," he said to Ivanhoe, apart, "by the presence of our gallant sovereign; yet I would not that he dallied with time, which the circumstances of his kingdom may render precious."

"It is well and wisely spoken, brave Robin Hood," said Wilfred, apart; "and know, moreover, that they who jest with Majesty even in its gayest mood, are but toying with the lion's whelp, which, on slight provocation, uses both fangs and claws."

"You have touched the very cause of my fear," said the outlaw; "my men are rough by practice and nature, the King is hasty as well as good humoured; nor know I how soon cause of offence may arise, or how warmly it may be received—it is time this revel were broken off."

"It must be by your management then, gallant yeoman," said Ivanhoe; "for each hint I have essayed to give him serves only to induce him to prolong it."

"Must I so soon risk the pardon and favour of my sovereign?" said Robin Hood, pausing for an instant; "but by Saint Christopher it shall be so. I were undeserving his grace did I not peril it for his good. Here, Scathlock, get thee behind yonder thicket, and wind me a Norman blast on thy bugle, and without an instant's delay, on peril of your life."

Scathlock obeyed his captain, and in less than five minutes the revellers were startled by the sound of his horn.

"It is the bugle of Malvoisin," said the Miller, starting to his feet, and seizing his bow. The Friar dropped the flagon, and grasped his quarterstaff. Wamba stopt short in the midst of a jest, and betook himself to sword and target. All the others stood to their weapons.

Men of their precarious course of life change readily from the banquet to the battle; and, to Richard, the exchange seemed but a succession of pleasure. He called for his helmet and the most cumbrous parts of his armour, which he had laid aside; and while Gurth was putting them on, he laid his strict injunctions on Wilfred, under pain of his highest displeasure, not to engage in the skirmish which he supposed was approaching.

"Thou hast fought for me a hundred times, Wilfred,—and I have seen it. Thou shalt this day look on, and see how Richard will fight for his friend and liegeman."

In the meantime, Robin Hood had sent off several of his followers in different directions, as if to reconnoitre the enemy; and when he saw the company effectually broken up, he approached Richard, who was

now completely armed, and kneeling down on one knee, craved pardon
of his sovereign.

"For what, good yeoman?" said Richard, somewhat impatiently.
"Have we not already granted thee a full pardon for all transgressions?
Thinkest thou our word is a feather to be blown backward and forward
between us? Thou canst not have had time to commit any new offence
since that time?"

"Ay, but I have though," answered the yeoman, "if it be an offence
to deceive my prince for his own advantage. The bugle you have heard
was none of Malvoisin's, but blown by my direction, to break off the
banquet, lest it trenched upon hours of dearer import than to be thus
dallied with."

He then rose from his knee, folded his arms on his bosom, and in a
manner rather respectful than submissive, awaited the answer of the
King—like one who is conscious he may have given offence, yet is confident in the rectitude of his motive. The blood rushed in anger to the
countenance of Richard; but it was the first transient emotion, and his
sense of justice instantly subdued it.

"The King of Sherwood," he said, "grudges his venison and his wine-
flask to the King of England? It is well, bold Robin!—but when you
come to see me in merry London, I trust to be a less niggard host. Thou
art right, however, good fellow. Let us therefore to horse and away.
Wilfred has been impatient this hour. Tell me, bold Robin, hast thou
never a friend in thy band, who, not content with advising, will need
direct thy motions, and look miserable when thou dost presume to act
for thyself?"

"Such a one," said Robin, "is my lieutenant, Little John, who is even
now absent on an expedition as far as the borders of Scotland; and I
will own to your Majesty, that I am sometimes displeased by the freedom of his counsels—but, when I think twice, I cannot be long angry
with one who can have no motive for his anxiety save zeal for his master's service."

"Thou art right, good yeoman," answered Richard; "and if I had
Ivanhoe, on the one hand, to give grave advice, and recommend it by
the sad gravity of his brow, and thee, on the other, to trick me into
what thou thinkest my own good, I should have as little the freedom of
mine own will as any king in Christendom or Heathenesse. But come,
sirs, let us merrily on to Coningsburgh, and think no more on't."

Robin Hood assured them that he had detached a party in the direction of the road they were to pass, who would not fail to discover and
apprise them of any secret ambuscade; and that he had little doubt they
would find the ways secure, or, if otherwise, would receive such timely
notice of the danger as would enable them to fall back on a strong troop
of archers, with which he himself proposed to follow on the same route.

The wise and attentive precautions adopted for his safety touched
Richard's feelings, and removed any slight grudge which he might retain

on account of the deception the outlaw captain had practised upon him. He once more extended his hand to Robin Hood, assured him of his full pardon and future favour, as well as his firm resolution to restrain the tyrannical exercise of the forest rights and other oppressive laws, by which so many English yeomen were driven into a state of rebellion. But Richard's good intentions towards the bold outlaw were frustrated by the king's untimely death; and the Charter of the Forest was extorted from the unwilling hands of King John when he succeeded to his heroic brother. As for the rest of Robin Hood's career, as well as the tale of his treacherous death, they are to be found in those black-letter garlands, once sold at the low and easy rate of one halfpenny.

"Now cheaply purchased at their weight in gold."

The outlaw's opinion proved true; and the king, attended by Ivanhoe, Gurth, and Wamba, arrived, without any interruption, within view of the Castle of Coningsburgh, while the sun was yet in the horizon.

There are few more beautiful or striking scenes in England than are presented by the vicinity of this ancient Saxon fortress. The soft and gentle river Don sweeps through an amphitheatre, in which cultivation is richly blended with woodland, and on a mount, ascending from the river, well defended by walls and ditches, rises this ancient edifice, which, as its Saxon name implies, was, previous to the Conquest, a royal residence of the kings of England. The outer walls have probably been added by the Normans, but the inner keep bears token of very great antiquity. It is situated on a mount at one angle of the inner court, and forms a complete circle of perhaps twenty-five feet in diameter. The wall is of immense thickness, and is propped or defended by six huge external buttresses which project from the circle, and rise up against the sides of the tower as if to strengthen or to support it. These massive buttresses are solid when they arise from the foundation, and a good way higher up; but are hollowed out towards the top, and terminate in a sort of turrets communicating with the interior of the keep itself. The distant appearance of this huge building, with these singular accompaniments, is as interesting to the lovers of the picturesque, as the interior of the castle is to the eager antiquary, whose imagination it carries back to the days of the heptarchy. A barrow, in the vicinity of the castle, is pointed out as the tomb of the memorable Hengist; and various monuments, of great antiquity and curiosity, are shown in the neighbouring churchyard.[1]

When Cœur-de-Lion and his retinue approached this rude yet stately building, it was not, as at present, surrounded by external fortifications. The Saxon architect had exhausted his art in rendering the main keep defensible, and there was no other circumvallation than a rude barrier of palisades.

A huge black banner, which floated from the top of the tower, an-

[1] Note IX.—Castle of Coningsburgh.

nounced that the obsequies of the late owner were still in the act of being solemnised. It bore no emblem of the deceased's birth or quality, for armorial bearings were then a novelty among the Norman chivalry themselves, and were totally unknown to the Saxons. But above the gate was another banner, on which the figure of a white horse, rudely painted, indicated the nation and rank of the deceased, by the well-known symbol of Hengist and his Saxon warriors.

All around the castle was a scene of busy commotion; for such funeral banquets were times of general and profuse hospitality, which not only every one who could claim the most distant connexion with the deceased, but all passengers whatsoever, were invited to partake. The wealth and consequence of the deceased Athelstane occasioned this custom to be observed to the fullest extent.

Numerous parties, therefore, were seen ascending and descending the hill on which the castle was situated; and when the King and his attendants entered the open and unguarded gates of the external barrier, the space within presented a scene not easily reconciled with the cause of the assemblage. In one place cooks were toiling to roast huge oxen, and fat sheep; in another, hogsheads of ale were set abroach, to be drained at the freedom of all comers. Groups of every description were to be seen devouring the food and swallowing the liquor thus abandoned to their discretion. The naked Saxon serf was drowning the sense of his half-year's hunger and thirst, in one day of gluttony and drunkenness —the more pampered burgess and guild-brother was eating his morsel with gust, or curiously criticising the quantity of the malt and the skill of the brewer. Some few of the poorer Norman gentry might also be seen, distinguished by their shaven chins and short cloaks, and not less so by their keeping together, and looking with great scorn on the whole solemnity, even while condescending to avail themselves of the good cheer which was so liberally supplied.

Mendicants were of course assembled by the score, together with strolling soldiers returned from Palestine (according to their own account at least), pedlars were displaying their wares, travelling mechanics were enquiring after employment, and wandering palmers, hedge-priests, Saxon minstrels, and Welsh bards, were muttering prayers, and extracting mistuned dirges from their harps, crowds, and rotes.[1] One sent forth the praises of Athelstane in a doleful panegyric; another, in a Saxon genealogical poem, rehearsed the uncouth and harsh names of his noble ancestry. Jesters and jugglers were not awanting, nor was the occasion of the assembly supposed to render the exercise of their profession indecorous or improper. Indeed, the ideas of the Saxons on these occasions were as natural as they were rude. If sorrow was thirsty, there was drink—if hungry, there was food—if it sunk down upon and saddened

---

[1] The crowth, or crowd, was a species of violin. The rote a sort of guitar, or rather hurdy-gurdy, the strings of which were managed by a wheel, from which the instrument took its name.

the heart, here were the means supplied of mirth, or at least of amusement. Nor did the assistants scorn to avail themselves of those means of consolation, although, every now and then, as if suddenly recollecting the cause which had brought them together, the men groaned in unison, while the females, of whom many were present, raised up their voices and shrieked for very woe.

Such was the scene in the castle-yard at Coningsburgh when it was entered by Richard and his followers. The seneschal or steward deigned not to take notice of the groups of inferior guests who were perpetually entering and withdrawing, unless so far as was necessary to preserve order; nevertheless he was struck by the good mien of the monarch and Ivanhoe, more especially as he imagined the features of the latter were familiar to him. Besides, the approach of two knights, for such their dress bespoke them, was a rare event at a Saxon solemnity, and could not but be regarded as a sort of honour to the deceased and his family. And in his sable dress, and holding in his hand his white wand of office, this important personage made way through the miscellaneous assemblage of guests, thus conducting Richard and Ivanhoe to the entrance of the tower. Gurth and Wamba speedily found acquaintances in the courtyard, nor presumed to intrude themselves any farther until their presence should be required.

CHAPTER XLII

I found them winding of Marcello's corpse,
And there was such a solemn melody,
'Twixt doleful songs, tears and sad elegies,—
Such as old grandames, watching by the dead,
Are wont to outwear the night with.
Old Play.

THE mode of entering the great tower of Coningsburgh Castle is very peculiar, and partakes of the rude simplicity of the early times in which it was erected. A flight of steps, so deep and narrow as to be almost precipitous, leads up to a low portal in the south side of the tower, by which the adventurous antiquary may still, or at least could a few years since, gain access to a small stair within the thickness of the main wall of the tower, which leads up to the third story of the building—the two lower being dungeons or vaults, which neither receive air nor light, save by a square hole in the third story, with which they seem to have communicated by a ladder. The access to the upper apartments in the tower, which consists in all of four stories, is given by stairs which are carried up through the external buttresses.

By this difficult and complicated entrance, the good King Richard, followed by his faithful Ivanhoe, was ushered into the round apartment which occupies the whole of the third story from the ground. Wilfred, by the difficulties of the ascent, gained time to muffle his face in his

mantle, as it had been held expedient that he should not present himself
to his father until the King should give him the signal.

There were assembled in this apartment, around a large oaken table,
about a dozen of the most distinguished representatives of the Saxon
families in the adjacent counties. They were all old, or, at least, elderly
men; for the younger race, to the great displeasure of the seniors, had,
like Ivanhoe, broken down many of the barriers which separated for half
a century the Norman victors from the vanquished Saxons. The downcast and sorrowful looks of these venerable men, their silence and their
mournful posture, formed a strong contrast to the levity of the revellers
on the outside of the castle. Their grey locks and long full beards,
together with their antique tunics and loose black mantles, suited well
with the singular and rude apartment in which they were seated, and
gave the appearance of a band of ancient worshippers of Woden recalled
to life to mourn over the decay of their national glory.

Cedric, seated in equal rank among his countrymen, seemed yet, by
common consent, to act as chief of the assembly. Upon the entrance of
Richard (only known to him as the valorous Knight of the Fetterlock)
he arose gravely, and gave him welcome by the ordinary salutation, *Waes
hael,* raising at the same time a goblet to his head. The King, no stranger
to the customs of his English subjects, returned the greeting with the
appropriate words, *Drinc hael,* and partook of a cup which was handed
to him by the sewer. The same courtesy was offered to Ivanhoe, who
pledged his father in silence, supplying the usual speech by an inclination of his head, lest his voice should have been recognised.

When this introductory ceremony was performed, Cedric arose, and,
extending his hand to Richard, conducted him into a small and very rude
chapel, which was excavated, as it were, out of one of the external buttresses. As there was no opening, saving a very narrow loop-hole, the
place would have been nearly quite dark but for two flambeaux or
torches, which showed, by a red and smoky light, the arched roof and
naked walls, the rude altar of stone, and the crucifix of the same material.

Before this altar was placed a bier, and on each side of this bier
kneeled three priests, who told their beads, and muttered their prayers,
with the greatest signs of external devotion. For this service a splendid
soul-scat was paid to the convent of Saint Edmund's by the mother of
the deceased; and, that it might be fully deserved, the whole brethren,
saving the lame Sacristan, had transferred themselves to Coningsburgh,
where, while six of their number were constantly on guard in the performance of divine rites by the bier of Athelstane, the others failed not
to take their share of the refreshments and amusements which went on
at the castle. In maintaining this pious watch and ward, the good monks
were particularly careful not to interrupt their hymns for an instant, lest
Zernebock, the ancient Saxon Apollyon, should lay his clutches on the
departed Athelstane. Nor were they less careful to prevent any unhallowed layman from touching the pall, which, having been used at the

funeral of Saint Edmund, was liable to be desecrated, if handled by the profane. If, in truth, these attentions could be of any use to the deceased, he had some right to expect them at the hands of the brethren of Saint Edmund's, since, besides a hundred mancuses of gold paid down as the soul-ransom, the mother of Athelstane had announced her intention of endowing that foundation with the better part of the lands of the deceased, in order to maintain perpetual prayers for his soul, and that of her departed husband.

Richard and Wilfred followed the Saxon Cedric into the apartment of death, where, as their guide pointed with solemn air to the untimely bier of Athelstane, they followed his example in devoutly crossing themselves, and muttering a brief prayer for the weal of the departed soul.

This act of pious charity performed, Cedric again motioned them to follow him, gliding over the stone floor with a noiseless tread; and, after ascending a few steps, opened with great caution the door of a small oratory, which adjoined to the chapel. It was about eight feet square, hollowed, like the chapel itself, out of the thickness of the wall; and the loophole, which enlightened it, being to the west, and widening considerably as it sloped inward, a beam of the setting sun found its way into its dark recess, and showed a female of a dignified mien, and whose countenance retained the marked remains of majestic beauty. Her long mourning robes and her flowing wimple of black cypress, enhanced the whiteness of her skin, and the beauty of her light-coloured and flowing tresses, which time had neither thinned nor mingled with silver. Her countenance expressed the deepest sorrow that is consistent with resignation. On the stone table before her stood a crucifix of ivory, beside which was laid a missal having its pages richly illuminated, and its boards adorned with clasps of gold, and bosses of the same precious metal.

"Noble Edith," said Cedric, after having stood a moment silent, as if to give Richard and Wilfred time to look upon the lady of the mansion, "these are worthy strangers, come to take a part in thy sorrows. And this, in especial, is the valiant knight who fought so bravely for the deliverance of him for whom we this day mourn."

"His bravery has my thanks," returned the lady; "although it be the will of Heaven that it should be displayed in vain. I thank, too, his courtesy, and that of his companion, which hath brought them hither to behold the widow of Adeling, the mother of Athelstane, in her deep hour of sorrow and lamentation. To your care, kind kinsman, I intrust them, satisfied that they will want no hospitality which these sad walls can yet afford."

The guests bowed deeply to the mourning parent, and withdrew with their hospitable guide.

Another winding stair conducted them to an apartment of the same size with that which they had first entered, occupying indeed the story immediately above. From this room, ere yet the door was opened, proceeded a low and melancholy strain of vocal music. When they entered, they found themselves in the presence of about twenty matrons and maidens of distinguished Saxon lineage. Four maidens, Rowena leading the choir, raised a hymn for the soul of the deceased, of which we have only been able to decipher two or three stanzas:—

Dust unto dust,
To this all must;
The tenant hath resign'd
The faded form
To waste and worm—
Corruption claims her kind.

Through paths unknown
Thy soul hath flown,
To seek the realms of woe,
Where fiery pain
Shall purge the stain
Of actions done below.

In that sad place,
By Mary's grace,
Brief may thy dwelling be!
Till prayers and alms,
And holy psalms,
Shall set the captive free.

While this dirge was sung, in a low and melancholy tone, by the female choristers, the others were divided into two bands, of which one was engaged in bedecking, with such embroidery as their skill and taste could compass, a large silken pall, destined to cover the bier of Athelstane, while the others busied themselves in selecting, from baskets of flowers placed before them, garlands, which they intended for the same mournful purpose. The behaviour of the maidens was decorous, if not marked with deep affliction; but now and then a whisper or a smile called forth the rebuke of the severer matrons, and here and there might be seen a damsel more interested in endeavouring to find out how her mourning-robe became her, than in the dismal ceremony for which they were preparing. Neither was this propensity (if we must needs confess the truth) at all diminished by the appearance of two strange knights, which occasioned some looking up, peeping, and whispering. Rowena alone, too proud to be vain, paid her greeting to her deliverer with a graceful courtesy. Her demeanour was serious but not dejected; as it may be doubted whether thoughts of Ivanhoe, and of the uncertainty of his fate, did not claim as great a share in her gravity as the death of her kinsman.

To Cedric, however, who, as we have observed, was not remarkably clear-sighted on such occasions, the sorrow of his ward seemed so much deeper than any of the other maidens, that he deemed it proper to whisper the explanation—"She was the affianced bride of the noble Athelstane." It may be doubted whether this communication went a far way to increase Wilfred's disposition to sympathise with the mourners of Coningsburgh.

Having thus formally introduced the guests to the different chambers in which the obsequies of Athelstane were celebrated under different forms, Cedric conducted them into a small room, destined, as he informed them, for the exclusive accommodation of honourable guests, whose more slight connexion with the deceased might render them unwilling to join those who were immediately affected by the unhappy event. He assured them of every accommodation, and was about to withdraw when the Black Knight took his hand.

"I crave to remind you, noble Thane," he said, "that when we last parted, you promised, for the service I had the fortune to render you, to grant me a boon."

"It is granted ere named, noble Knight," said Cedric; "yet, at this sad moment"——

"Of that also," said the King, "I have bethought me—but my time is brief—neither does it seem to me unfit, that, when closing the grave on the noble Athelstane, we should deposit therein certain prejudices and hasty opinions."

"Sir Knight of the Fetterlock," said Cedric, colouring, and interrupting the King in his turn, "I trust your boon regards yourself and no other; for in that which concerns the honour of my house, it is scarce fitting that a stranger should mingle."

"Nor do I wish to mingle," said the King, mildly, "unless in so far as you will admit me to have an interest. As yet you have known me but as the Black Knight of the Fetterlock; know me now as Richard Plantagenet."

"Richard of Anjoù!" exclaimed Cedric, stepping backward with the utmost astonishment.

"No, noble Cedric—Richard of England! whose deepest interest, whose deepest wish, is to see her sons united with each other. And, how now, worthy Thane! hast thou no knee for thy prince?"

"To Norman blood," said Cedric, "it hath never bended."

"Reserve thine homage then," said the monarch, "until I shall prove my right to it by my equal protection of Normans and English."

"Prince," answered Cedric, "I have ever done justice to thy bravery and thy worth. Nor am I ignorant of thy claim to the crown through thy descent from Matilda, niece to Edgar Atheling, and daughter to Malcolm of Scotland. But Matilda, though of the royal Saxon blood, was not the heir to the monarchy."

"I will not dispute my title with thee, noble Thane," said Richard, calmly; "but I will bid thee look around thee, and see where thou wilt find another to be put into the scale against it."

"And hast thou wandered hither, Prince, to tell me so?" said Cedric. "To upbraid me with the ruin of my race, ere the grave has closed o'er the last scion of Saxon royalty?" His countenance darkened as he spoke. "It was boldly, it was rashly done!"

"Not so, by the holy rood!" replied the King; "it was done in the frank confidence which one brave man may repose in another, without a shadow of danger."

"Thou sayest well, Sir King—for King I own thou art, and wilt be, despite of my feeble opposition. I dare not take the only mode to prevent it, though thou hast placed the strong temptation within my reach!"

"And now to my boon," said the King, "which I ask not with one jot the less confidence, that thou hast refused to acknowledge my lawful sovereignty. I require of thee, as a man of thy word, on pain of being held faithless, man-sworn, and *nidering,* to forgive and receive to thy paternal affection the good knight, Wilfred of Ivanhoe. In this reconciliation thou wilt own I have an interest—the happiness of my friend, and the quelling of dissension among my faithful people."

"And this is Wilfred!" said Cedric, pointing to his son.

"My father!—my father!" said Ivanhoe, prostrating himself at Cedric's feet, "grant me thy forgiveness!"

"Thou hast it, my son," said Cedric, raising him up. "The son of Hereward knows how to keep his word, even when it has been passed to a Norman. But let me see thee use the dress and costume of thy English ancestry—no short cloaks, no gay bonnets, no fantastic plumage in my decent household. He that would be the son of Cedric must show himself of English ancestry. Thou art about to speak," he added, sternly, "and I guess the topic. The Lady Rowena must complete two years' mourning, as for a betrothed husband. All our Saxon ancestors would disown us were we to treat of a new union for her ere the grave of him she should have wedded—him, so much the most worthy of her hand by birth and ancestry—is yet closed. The ghost of Athelstane himself would burst his bloody cerements, and stand before us to forbid such dishonour to his memory."

It seemed as if Cedric's words had raised a spectre; for, scarce had he uttered them ere the door flew open, and Athelstane, arrayed in the garments of the grave, stood before them, pale, haggard, and like something arisen from the dead! [1]

The effect of this apparition on the persons present was utterly appalling. Cedric started back as far as the wall of the apartment would permit, and, leaning against it as one unable to support himself, gazed on the figure of his friend with eyes that seemed fixed, and a mouth which he appeared incapable of shutting. Ivanhoe crossed himself, re-

---

[1] The resuscitation of Athelstane has been much criticised, as too violent a breach of probability, even for a work of such fantastic character. It was a *tour-de-force,* to which the author was compelled to have recourse, by the vehement entreaties of his friend and printer, who was inconsolable on the Saxon being conveyed to the tomb.

peating prayers in Saxon, Latin, or Norman-French, as they occurred to his memory, while Richard alternately said, *Benedicite,* and swore, *Mort de ma vie!*

In the meantime, a horrible noise was heard below stairs, some crying, "Secure the treacherous monks!"—others, "Down with them into the dungeon!"—others, "Pitch them from the highest battlements!"

"In the name of God!" said Cedric, addressing what seemed the spectre of his departed friend, "if thou art mortal, speak!—if a departed spirit, say for what cause thou dost revisit us, or if I can do aught that can set thy spirit at repose. Living or dead, noble Athelstane, speak to Cedric!"

"I will," said the spectre, very composedly, "when I have collected breath, and when you give me time. Alive, saidst thou? I am as much alive as he can be who has fed on bread and water for three days, which seems three ages. Yes, bread and water, Father Cedric! By Heaven, and all saints in it, better food hath not passed my weasand for three live-long days, and by God's providence it is that I am now here to tell it."

"Why, noble Athelstane," said the Black Knight, "I myself saw you struck down by the fierce Templar towards the end of the storm at Torquilstone, and as I thought, and Wamba reported, your skull was cloven through the teeth."

"You thought amiss, Sir Knight," said Athelstane, "and Wamba lied. My teeth are in good order, and that my supper shall presently find. No thanks to the Templar though, whose sword turned in his hand, so that the blade struck me flatlings, being averted by the handle of the good mace with which I warded the blow; had my steel-cap been on, I had not valued it a rush, and had dealt him such a counter-buff as would have spoilt his retreat. But as it was, down I went, stunned, indeed, but unwounded. Others, of both sides, were beaten down and slaughtered above me, so that I never recovered my senses until I found myself in a coffin—(an open one, by good luck)—placed before the altar of the church of Saint Edmund's. I sneezed repeatedly—groaned—awakened, and would have arisen, when the Sacristan and Abbot, full of terror, came running at the noise, surprised, doubtless, and no way pleased to find the man alive whose heirs they had proposed themselves to be. I asked for wine—they gave me some, but it must have been highly medicated, for I slept yet more deeply than before, and wakened not for many hours. I found my arms swathed down—my feet tied so fast that mine ankles ache at the very remembrance—the place was utterly dark —the oubliette, as I suppose, of their accursed convent, and from the close, stifled, damp smell, I conceive it is also used for a place of sepulture. I had strange thoughts of what had befallen me, when the door of my dungeon creaked, and two villain monks entered. They would have persuaded me I was in purgatory, but I knew too well the pursy short-breathed voice of the Father Abbot. Saint Jeremy! how different from

that tone with which he used to ask me for another slice of the haunch!
—the dog has feasted with me from Christmas to Twelfth-night."

"Have patience, noble Athelstane," said the King, "take breath—
tell your story at leisure—beshrew me but such a tale is as well worth
listening to as a romance."

"Ay but, by the rood of Bromeholm, there was no romance in the matter!" said Athelstane. "A barley loaf and a pitcher of water—that *they*
gave me, the niggardly traitors, whom my father, and I myself, had enriched, when their best resources were the flitches of bacon and measures of corn, out of which they wheedled poor serfs and bondsmen in
exchange for their prayers—the nest of foul ungrateful vipers—barley
bread and ditch water to such a patron as I had been! I will smoke them
out of their nest, though I be excommunicated!"

"But in the name of Our Lady, noble Athelstane," said Cedric, grasping the hand of his friend, "how didst thou escape this imminent danger?
Did their hearts relent?"

"Did their hearts relent!" echoed Athelstane. "Do rocks melt with the
sun? I should have been there still had not some stir in the Convent,
which I find was their procession hitherward to eat my funeral feast,
when they well knew how and where I had been buried alive, summoned
the swarm out of their hive. I heard them droning out their death-psalms,
little judging they were sung in respect for my soul by those who were
thus famishing my body. They went, however, and I waited long for food
—no wonder—the gouty Sacristan was even too busy with his own
provender to mind mine. At length down he came, with an unstable step
and a strong flavour of wine and spices about his person. Good cheer had
opened his heart, for he left me a nook of pasty and a flask of wine,
instead of my former fare. I ate, drank, and was invigorated; when, to
add to my good luck, the Sacristan, too totty to discharge his duty of
turnkey fitly, locked the door beside the staple, so that it fell ajar. The
light, the food, the wine, set my invention to work. The staple to which
my chains were fixed was more rusted than I or the villain Abbot had
supposed. Even iron could not remain without consuming in the damps
of that infernal dungeon."

"Take breath, noble Athelstane," said Richard, "and partake of some
refreshment, ere you proceed with a tale so dreadful."

"Partake!" quoth Athelstane; "I have been partaking five times to-
day—and yet a morsel of that savoury ham were not altogether foreign
to the matter; and I pray you, fair sir, to do me reason in a cup of wine."

The guests, though still agape with astonishment, pledged their resuscitated landlord, who thus proceeded in his story:—He had indeed now
many more auditors than those to whom it was commenced, for Edith,
having given certain necessary orders for arranging matters within the
castle, had followed the dead-alive up to the strangers' apartment,
attended by as many of the guests, male and female, as could squeeze
into the small room, while others, crowding the staircase, caught up an

erroneous edition of the story, and transmitted it still more inaccurately
to those beneath, who again sent it forth to the vulgar without, in a fashion
totally irreconcilable to the real fact. Athelstane, however, went on as
follows, with the history of his escape:—

"Finding myself freed from the staple, I dragged myself up stairs as
well as a man loaded with shackles, and emaciated with fasting, might;
and after much groping about, I was at length directed, by the sound
of a jolly roundelay, to the apartment where the worthy sacristan, an it
so please ye, was holding a devil's mass with a huge beetle-browed, broad-
shouldered brother of the grey-frock and cowl, who looked much more
like a thief than a clergyman. I burst in upon them, and the fashion of
my grave-clothes, as well as the clanking of my chains, made me more
resemble an inhabitant of the other world than of this. Both stood aghast;
but when I knocked down the sacristan with my fist, the other fellow,
his pot-companion, fetched a blow at me with a huge quarter-staff."

"This must be our Friar Tuck, for a count's ransom," said Richard,
looking at Ivanhoe.

"He may be the devil, an he will," said Athelstane. "Fortunately he
missed the aim; and on my approaching to grapple with him, took to his
heels and ran for it. I failed not to set my own heels at liberty by means
of the fetter-key which hung amongst others at the sexton's belt; and I
had thoughts of beating out the knave's brains with the bunch of keys,
but gratitude for the nook of pasty and the flask of wine which the rascal
had imparted to my captivity, came over my heart; so, with a brace of
hearty kicks, I left him on the floor, pouched some baked meat, and a
leathern bottle of wine, with which the two venerable brethren had been
regaling, went to the stable, and found in a private stall mine own best
palfrey, which, doubtless, had been set apart for the holy Father Abbot's
particular use. Hither I came with all the speed the beast could compass
—man and mother's son flying before me wherever I came, taking me
for a spectre, the more especially as, to prevent my being recognised, I
drew the corpse-hood over my face. I had not gained admittance into my
own castle, had I not been supposed to be the attendant of a juggler who
is making the people in the castle-yard very merry, considering they are
assembled to celebrate their lord's funeral. I say the sewer thought I was
dressed to bear a part in the tregetour's mummery, and so I got admission,
and did but disclose myself to my mother, and eat a hasty morsel, ere I
came in quest of you, my noble friend."

"And you have found me," said Cedric, "ready to resume our brave
projects of honour and liberty. I tell thee, never will dawn a morrow so
auspicious as the next, for the deliverance of the noble Saxon race."

"Talk not to me of delivering anyone," said Athelstane; "it is well I am
delivered myself. I am more intent on punishing that villain abbot. He
shall hang on the top of this castle of Coningsburgh in his cope and stole;
and if the stairs be too strait to admit his fat carcass, I will have him
craned up from without."

"But, my son," said Edith, "consider his sacred office."

"Consider my three days' fast," replied Athelstane; "I will have their blood every one of them. Front-de-Bœuf was burnt alive for a less matter, for he kept a good table for his prisoners, only put too much garlic in his last dish of pottage. But these hypocritical, ungrateful slaves, so often the self-invited flatterers at my board, who gave me neither pottage nor garlic, more or less, they die, by the soul of Hengist!"

"But the pope, my noble friend," said Cedric——-

"But the devil, my noble friend," answered Athelstane; "they die, and no more of them. Were they the best monks upon earth, the world would go on without them."

"For shame, noble Athelstane," said Cedric; "forget such wretches in the career of glory which lies open before thee. Tell this Norman prince, Richard of Anjoù, that, lion-hearted as he is, he shall not hold undisputed the throne of Alfred while a male descendant of the Holy Confessor lives to dispute it."

"How!" said Athelstane, "is this the noble King Richard?"

"It is Richard Plantagenet himself," said Cedric; "yet I need not remind thee that, coming hither a guest of free-will, he may neither be injured nor detained prisoner—thou well knowest thy duty to him as his host."

"Ay, by my faith!" said Athelstane; "and my duty as a subject besides, for I here tender him my allegiance, heart and hand."

"My son," said Edith, "think on thy royal rights!"

"Think on the freedom of England, degenerate prince!" said Cedric.

"Mother and friend," said Athelstane, "a truce to your upbraidings. Bread and water and a dungeon are marvellous mortifiers of ambition, and I rise from the tomb a wiser man than I descended into it. One half of those vain follies were puffed into mine ear by that perfidious Abbot Wolfram, and you may now judge if he is a counsellor to be trusted. Since these plots were set in agitation, I have had nothing but hurried journeys, indigestions, blows and bruises, imprisonments and starvation; besides that they can only end in the murder of some thousands of quiet folk. I tell you, I will be king in my own domains, and nowhere else; and my first act of dominion shall be to hang the abbot."

"And my ward Rowena," said Cedric; "I trust you intend not to desert her?"

"Father Cedric," said Athelstane, "be reasonable. The Lady Rowena cares not for me. She loves the little finger of my kinsman Wilfred's glove better than my whole person. There she stands to avouch it. Nay, blush not, kinswoman, there is no shame in loving a courtly knight better than a country franklin, and do not laugh neither, Rowena, for grave-clothes and a thin visage are, God knows, no matter of merriment. Nay, an thou wilt needs laugh, I will find thee a better jest. Give me thy hand, or rather lend it me, for I but ask it in the way of friendship. Here, cousin Wilfred of Ivanhoe, in thy favour I renounce and abjure—— Hey! by

Saint Dunstan, our cousin Wilfred hath vanished! Yet, unless my eyes are still dazzled with the fasting I have undergone, I saw him stand there but even now."

All now looked around and enquired for Ivanhoe, but he had vanished. It was at length discovered that a Jew had been to seek him; and that, after very brief conference, he had called for Gurth and his armour, and had left the castle.

"Fair cousin," said Athelstane to Rowena, "could I think that this sudden disappearance of Ivanhoe was occasioned by other than the weightiest reason, I would myself resume"——

But he had no sooner let go her hand, on first observing that Ivanhoe had disappeared, than Rowena, who had found her situation extremely embarrassing, had taken the first opportunity to escape from the apartment.

"Certainly," quoth Athelstane, "women are the least to be trusted of all animals, monks and abbots excepted. I am an infidel, if I expected not thanks from her, and perhaps a kiss to boot. These cursed grave-clothes have surely a spell on them, every one flies from me. To you I turn, noble King Richard, with the vows of allegiance, which, as a liege-subject"——

But King Richard was gone also, and no one knew whither. At length it was learned that he had hastened to the courtyard, summoned to his presence the Jew who had spoken with Ivanhoe, and after a moment's speech with him, had called vehemently to horse, thrown himself upon a steed, compelled the Jew to mount another, and set off at a rate, which, according to Wamba, rendered the old Jew's neck not worth a penny's purchase.

"By my halidome!" said Athelstane, "it is certain that Zernebock h th possessed himself of my castle in my absence. I return in my gra ve-clothes, a pledge restored from the very sepulchre, and every one I speak to vanishes as soon as they hear my voice! But it skills not talking of it. Come, my friends, such of you as are left, follow me to the banquet-hall, lest any more of us disappear. It is, I trust, as yet tolerably furnished, as becomes the obsequies of an ancient Saxon noble; and should we tarry any longer, who knows but the devil may fly off with the supper?"

CHAPTER XLIII

Be Mowbray's sins so heavy in his bosom,
That they may break his foaming courser's back,
And throw the rider headlong in the lists,
A caitiff recreant!
Richard II.

OUR scene now returns to the exterior of the Castle, or Preceptory, of Templestowe, about the hour when the bloody die was to be cast for the life or death of Rebecca. It was a scene of bustle and life, as if the whole vicinity had poured forth its inhabitants to a village wake, or rural feast. But the earnest desire to look on blood and death is not peculiar to those dark ages; though in the gladiatorial exercise of single combat and general tourney, they were habituated to the bloody spectacle of brave men falling by each other's hands. Even in our own days, when morals are better understood, an execution, a bruising match, a riot, or a meeting of radical reformers, collects, at considerable hazard to themselves, immense crowds of spectators, otherwise little interested, except to see how matters are to be conducted, or whether the heroes of the day are, in the heroic language of insurgent tailors, flints or dunghills.

The eyes, therefore, of a very considerable multitude, were bent on the gate of the Preceptory of Templestowe, with the purpose of witnessing the procession; while still greater numbers had already surrounded the tiltyard belonging to that establishment. This enclosure was formed on a piece of level ground adjoining to the preceptory, which had been levelled with care, for the exercise of military and chivalrous sports. It occupied the brow of a soft and gentle eminence, was carefully palisaded around, and, as the Templars willingly invited spectators to be witnesses of their skill in feats of chivalry, was amply supplied with galleries and benches for their use.

On the present occasion, a throne was erected for the Grand Master at the east end, surrounded with seats of distinction for the Preceptors and Knights of the Order. Over these floated the sacred standard, called *Le Beau-seant*, which was the ensign, as its name was the battle-cry, of the Templars.

At the opposite end of the lists was a pile of faggots, so arranged around a stake, deeply fixed in the ground, as to leave a space for the victim whom they were destined to consume, to enter within the fatal circle, in order to be chained to the stake by the fetters which hung ready for that purpose. Beside this deadly apparatus stood four black slaves, whose colour and African features, then so little known in England, appalled the multitude, who gazed on them as on demons employed about their own diabolical exercises. These men stirred not, excepting now and then, under the direction of one who seemed their chief, to shift and replace the ready fuel. They looked not on the multitude. In fact, they seemed insensible of their presence, and of everything save the discharge of their own horrible duty. And when, in speech with each other, they expanded their blubber lips, and showed their white fangs, as if they grinned at the thoughts of the expected tragedy, the startled commons could scarcely help believing that they were actually the familiar spirits with whom the witch had communed, and who, her time being out, stood ready to assist in her dreadful punishment. They whispered to each other, and communicated all the feats which Satan had performed during that busy and unhappy period, not failing, of course, to give the devil rather more than his due.

"Have you not heard, Father Dennet," quoth one boor to another advanced in years, "that the devil has carried away bodily the great Saxon Thane, Athelstane of Coningsburgh?"

"Ay, but he brought him back though, by the blessing of God and Saint Dunstan."

"How's that?" said a brisk young fellow, dressed in a green cassock embroidered with gold, and having at his heels a stout lad bearing a harp upon his back, which betrayed his vocation. The minstrel seemed of no vulgar rank; for, besides the splendour of his gayly broidered doublet, he wore around his neck a silver chain, by which hung the *wrest*, or key, with which he tuned his harp. On his right arm was a silver plate, which, bearing, as usual, the cognisance or badge of the baron to whose family he belonged, had barely the word SHERWOOD engraved upon it. "How mean you by that?" said the gay minstrel, mingling in the conversation of the peasants; "I came to seek one subject for my rhyme, and, by'r Lady, I were glad to find two."

"It is well avouched," said the elder peasant, "that after Athelstane of Coningsburgh had been dead four weeks"——

"That is impossible," said the minstrel; "I saw him in life at the passage of arms at Ashby-de-la-Zouche."

"Dead, however, he was, or else translated," said the younger peasant; "for I heard the Monks of Saint Edmund's singing the death's hymn for him; and, moreover, there was a rich death-meal and dole at the Castle of Coningsburgh, as right was; and thither had I gone, but for Mabel Parkins, who"——

"Ay, dead was Athelstane," said the old man, shaking his head, "and the more pity it was, for the old Saxon blood"——

"But, your story, my masters—your story," said the minstrel, somewhat impatiently.

"Ay, ay—construe us the story," said a burly Friar, who stood beside them, leaning on a pole that exhibited an appearance between a pilgrim's staff and a quarter-staff, and probably acted as either when occasion served. "Your story," said the stalwart churchman; "burn not daylight about it, we have short time to spare."

"An please your reverence," said Dennet, "a drunken priest came to visit the sacristan at Saint Edmund's"——

"It does not please my reverence," answered the churchman, "that there should be such an animal as a drunken priest, or, if there were, that a layman should so speak him. Be mannerly, my friend, and conclude the holy man only wrapt in meditation, which makes the head dizzy and foot unsteady, as if the stomach were filled with new wine. I have felt it myself."

"Well, then," answered Father Dennet, "a holy brother came to visit the sacristan at Saint Edmund's—a sort of hedge-priest is the visitor, and kills half the deer that are stolen in the forest, who loves the tinkling of a pint-pot better than the sacring-bell, and deems a flitch of bacon worth ten of his breviary; for the rest, a good fellow and a merry, who will flourish a quarter-staff, draw a bow, and dance a Cheshire round with e'er a man in Yorkshire."

"That last part of thy speech, Dennet," said the minstrel, "has saved thee a rib or twain."

"Tush, man, I fear him not," said Dennet; "I am somewhat old and stiff, but when I fought for the bell and ram at Doncaster"——

"But the story—the story, my friend," again said the minstrel.

"Why, the tale is but this—Athelstane of Coningsburgh was buried at Saint Edmund's."

"That's a lie, and a loud one," said the Friar, "for I saw him borne to his own Castle of Coningsburgh."

"Nay, then, e'en tell the story yourself, my masters," said Dennet, turning sulky at these repeated contradictions; and it was with some difficulty that the boor could be prevailed on, by the request of his comrade and the minstrel, to renew his tale. "These two *sober* friars," said he at length, "since this reverend man will needs have them such, had continued drinking good ale, and wine, and what not, for the best part of a summer's day, when they were aroused by a deep groan, and a clanking of chains, and the figure of the deceased Athelstane entered the apartment, saying, 'Ye evil shepherds!' "——

"It is false," said the Friar, hastily, "he never spoke a word."

"So ho! Friar Tuck," said the minstrel, drawing him apart from the rustics; "we have started a new hare, I find."

"I tell thee, Allan-a-Dale," said the hermit, "I saw Athelstane of Coningsburgh as much as bodily eyes ever saw a living man. He had his shroud on, and all about him smelt of the sepulchre. A butt of sack will not wash it out of my memory."

"Pshaw!" answered the minstrel; "thou dost but jest with me!"

"Never believe me," said the Friar, "an I fetched not a knock at him with my quarter-staff that would have felled an ox, and it glided through his body as it might through a pillar of smoke!"

"By Saint Hubert," said the minstrel, "but it is a wondrous tale, and fit to be put in metre to the ancient tune, 'Sorrow came to the old Friar.' "

"Laugh, if ye list," said Friar Tuck; "but an ye catch me singing on such a theme, may the next ghost or devil carry me off with him headlong! No, no; I instantly formed the purpose of assisting at some good work, such as the burning of a witch, a judicial combat, or the like matter of godly service, and therefore am I here."

As they thus conversed, the heavy bell of the church of Saint Michael of Templestowe, a venerable building, situated in a hamlet at some distance from the preceptory, broke short their argument. One by one the sullen sounds fell successively on the ear, leaving but sufficient space for each to die away in distant echo, ere the air was again filled by repetition of the iron knell. These sounds, the signal of the approaching ceremony, chilled with awe the hearts of the assembled multitude, whose eyes were

now turned to the preceptory, expecting the approach of the Grand
Master, the champion, and the criminal.

At length the drawbridge fell, the gates opened, and a knight bearing
the great standard of the order, sallied from the castle, preceded by six
trumpets, and followed by the Knights Preceptors, two and two, the
Grand Master coming last, mounted on a stately horse, whose furniture
was of the simplest kind. Behind him came Brian de Bois-Guilbert, armed
cap-à-pie in bright armour, but without his lance, shield, and sword,
which were borne by his two esquires behind him. His face, though partly
hidden by a long plume which floated down from his barret-cap, bore a
strong and mingled expression of passion, in which pride seemed to contend with irresolution. He looked ghastly pale, as if he had not slept for
several nights, yet reined his pawing war-horse with the habitual ease
and grace proper to the best lance of the Order of the Temple. His general
appearance was grand and commanding; but, looking at him with
attention, men read that in his dark features from which they willingly
withdrew their eyes.

On either side rode Conrade of Mont-Fitchet, and Albert de Malvoisin,
who acted as godfathers to the champion. They were in their robes of
peace, the white dress of the order. Behind them followed other Companions of the Temple, with a long train of esquires and pages clad in
black, aspirants to the honour of being one day Knights of the Order.
After these neophytes came a guard of warders on foot, in the same sable
livery, amidst whose partisans might be seen the pale form of the accused,
moving with a slow but undismayed step towards the scene of her fate.
She was stript of all her ornaments, lest perchance there should be among
them some of those amulets which Satan was supposed to bestow upon
his victims, to deprive them of the power of confession even when under
the torture. A coarse white dress, of the simplest form, had been substituted for her Oriental garments; yet there was such an exquisite mixture of courage and resignation in her look, that even in this garb, and
with no other ornament than her long black tresses, each eye wept that
looked upon her, and the most hardened bigot regretted the fate that had
converted a creature so goodly into a vessel of wrath, and a waged slave
of the devil.

A crowd of inferior personages belonging to the preceptory followed
the victim, all moving with the utmost order, with arms folded, and
looks bent upon the ground.

This slow procession moved up the gentle eminence, on the summit of
which was the tilt-yard, and, entering the lists, marched once around
them from right to left, and when they had completed the circle, made
a halt. There was then a momentary bustle, while the Grand Master and
all his attendants, excepting the champion and his godfathers, dismounted from their horses, which were immediately removed out of the
lists by the esquires, who were in attendance for that purpose.

The unfortunate Rebecca was conducted to the black chair placed near the pile. On her first glance at the terrible spot where preparations were making for a death alike dismaying to the mind and painful to the body, she was observed to shudder and shut her eyes, praying internally doubtless, for her lips moved though no speech was heard. In the space of a minute she opened her eyes, looked fixedly on the pile as if to familiarise her mind with the object, and then slowly and naturally turned away her head.

Meanwhile, the Grand Master had assumed his seat; and when the chivalry of his order was placed around and behind him, each in his due rank, a loud and long flourish of the trumpets announced that the court were seated for judgment. Malvoisin, then, acting as godfather of the champion, stepped forward, and laid the glove of the Jewess, which was the pledge of battle, at the feet of the Grand Master.

"Valorous Lord, and reverend Father," said he, "here standeth the good knight, Brian de Bois-Guilbert, Knight Preceptor of the Order of the Temple, who, by accepting the pledge of battle which I now lay at your reverence's feet, hath become bound to do his devoir in combat this day, to maintain that this Jewish maiden, by name Rebecca, hath justly deserved the doom passed upon her in a Chapter of this most Holy Order of the Temple of Zion, condemning her to die as a sorceress; here, I say, he standeth, such battle to do, knightly and honourable, if such be your noble and sanctified pleasure."

"Hath he made oath," said the Grand Master, "that his quarrel is just and honourable? Bring forward the crucifix and the *Te igitur.*"

"Sir, and most reverend father," answered Malvoisin, readily, "our brother here present hath already sworn to the truth of his accusation in the hand of the good Knight Conrade de Mont-Fitchet; and otherwise he ought not to be sworn, seeing that his adversary is an unbeliever, and may take no oath."

This explanation was satisfactory, to Albert's great joy; for the wily knight had foreseen the great difficulty, or rather impossibility, of pre-vailing upon Brian de Bois-Guilbert to take such an oath before the assembly, and had invented this excuse to escape the necessity of his doing so.

The Grand Master, having allowed the apology of Albert Malvoisin, commanded the herald to stand forth and do his devoir. The trumpets then again flourished, and a herald, stepping forward, proclaimed aloud, —"Oyez, oyez, oyez.—Here standeth the good knight, Sir Brian de Bois-Guilbert, ready to do battle with any knight of free blood, who will sustain the quarrel allowed and allotted to the Jewess Rebecca, to try by champion, in respect of lawful essoine of her own body; and to such champion the reverend and valorous Grand Master here present allows a fair field, and equal partition of sun and wind, and whatever else apper-tains to a fair combat." The trumpets again sounded, and there was a dead pause of many minutes.

"No champion appears for the appellant," said the Grand Master. "Go, herald, and ask her whether she expects any one to do battle for her in this her cause." The herald went to the chair in which Rebecca was seated, and Bois-Guilbert suddenly turning his horse's head toward that end of the lists, in spite of hints on either side from Malvoisin and Mont-Fitchet, was by the side of Rebecca's chair as soon as the herald.

"Is this regular, and according to the law of combat?" said Malvoisin, looking to the Grand Master.

"Albert de Malvoisin, it is," answered Beaumanoir; "for in this appeal to the judgment of God, we may not prohibit parties from having that communication with each other, which may best tend to bring forth the truth of the quarrel."

In the meantime, the herald spoke to Rebecca in these terms:— "Damsel, the Honourable and Reverend the Grand Master demands of thee, if thou art prepared with a champion to do battle this day in thy behalf, or if thou dost yield thee as one justly condemned to a deserved doom?"

"Say to the Grand Master," replied Rebecca, "that I maintain my innocence, and do not yield me as justly condemned, lest I become guilty of mine own blood. Say to him, that I challenge such delay as his forms will permit, to see if God, whose opportunity is in man's extremity, will raise me up a deliverer; and when such uttermost space is passed, may His holy will be done!" The herald retired to carry this answer to the Grand Master.

"God forbid," said Lucas Beaumanoir, "that Jew or pagan should impeach us of injustice! Until the shadows be cast from the west to the eastward, will we wait to see if a champion shall appear for this unfortunate woman. When the day is so far passed, let her prepare for death."

The herald communicated the words of the Grand Master to Rebecca, who bowed her head submissively, folded her arms, and, looking up towards heaven, seemed to expect that aid from above which she could scarce promise herself from man. During this awful pause, the voice of Bois-Guilbert broke upon her ear—it was but a whisper, yet it startled her more than the summons of the herald had appeared to do.

"Rebecca," said the Templar, "dost thou hear me?"

"I have no portion in thee, cruel, hard-hearted man," said the unfortunate maiden.

"Ay, but dost thou understand my words?" said the Templar; "for the sound of my voice is frightful in mine own ears. I scarce know on what ground we stand, or for what purpose they have brought us hither. This listed space—that chair—these faggots—I know their purpose, and yet it appears to me like something unreal—the fearful picture of a vision, which appals my sense with hideous fantasies, but convinces not my reason."

"My mind and senses keep touch and time," answered Rebecca, "and tell me alike that these faggots are destined to consume my earthly body, and open a painful but a brief passage to a better world."

"Dreams, Rebecca,—dreams," answered the Templar; "idle visions, rejected by the wisdom of your own wiser Sadducees. Hear me, Rebecca," he said, proceeding with animation; "a better chance hast thou for life and liberty than yonder knaves and dotard dream of. Mount thee behind me on my steed—on Zamor, the gallant horse that never failed his rider. I won him in single fight from the Soldan of Trebizond—mount, I say, behind me—in one short hour is pursuit and inquiry far behind—a new world of pleasure opens to thee—to me a new career of fame. Let them speak the doom which I despise, and erase the name of Bois-Guilbert from their list of monastic slaves! I will wash out with blood whatever blot they may dare to cast on my scutcheon."

"Tempter," said Rebecca, "begone! Not in this last extremity canst thou move me one hair's-breadth from my resting place—surrounded as I am by foes, I hold thee as my worst and most deadly enemy—avoid thee, in the name of God!"

Albert Malvoisin, alarmed and impatient at the duration of their conference, now advanced to interrupt it.

"Hath the maiden acknowledged her guilt?" he demanded of Bois-Guilbert; "or is she resolute in her denial?"

"She is indeed *resolute*," said Bois-Guilbert.

"Then," said Malvoisin, "must thou, noble brother, resume thy place to attend the issue. The shades are changing on the circle of the dial. Come, brave Bois-Guilbert—come, thou hope of our holy order, and soon to be its head."

As he spoke in this soothing tone, he laid his hand on the knight's bridle, as if to lead him back to his station.

"False villain! what meanest thou by thy hand on my rein?" said Sir Brian, angrily. And shaking off his companion's grasp, he rode back to the upper end of the lists.

"There is yet spirit in him," said Malvoisin apart to Mont-Fitchet, "were it well directed—but, like the Greek fire, it burns whatever approaches it."

The judges had now been two hours in the lists, awaiting in vain the appearance of a champion.

"And reason good," said Friar Tuck, "seeing she is a Jewess—and yet, by mine order, it is hard that so young and beautiful a creature should perish without one blow being struck in her behalf! Were she ten times a witch, provided she were but the least bit of a Christian, my quarter-staff should ring noon on the steel cap of yonder fierce Templar, ere he carried the matter off thus."

It was, however, the general belief that no one could or would appear for a Jewess accused of sorcery; and the knights, instigated by Malvoisin, whispered to each other that it was time to declare the pledge of Rebecca forfeited. At this instant a knight, urging his horse to speed, appeared on the plain advancing towards the lists. A hundred voices exclaimed, "A champion! a champion!" And despite the prepossessions and prejudices of the multitude, they shouted unanimously as the knight rode into the tiltyard. The second glance, however, served to destroy the hope that his timely arrival had excited. His horse, urged for many miles to its utmost speed, appeared to reel from fatigue, and the rider, however undauntedly he presented himself in the lists, either from weakness, weariness, or both, seemed scarce able to support himself in the saddle.

To the summons of the herald, who demanded his rank, his name, and purpose, the stranger knight answered readily and boldly, "I am a good knight and noble, come hither to sustain with lance and sword the just and lawful quarrel of this damsel, Rebecca, daughter of Isaac of York; to uphold the doom pronounced against her to be false and truthless, and to defy Sir Brian de Bois-Guilbert as a traitor, murderer, and liar, as I will prove in this field with my body against his, by the aid of God, of Our Lady, and of Monseigneur Saint George, the good knight."

"The stranger must first show," said Malvoisin, "that he is good knight, and of honourable lineage. The Temple sendeth not forth her champions against nameless men."

"My name," said the knight, raising his helmet, "is better known, my lineage more pure, Malvoisin, than thine own. I am Wilfred of Ivanhoe."

"I will not fight with thee at present," said the Templar, in a changed and hollow voice. "Get thy wounds healed, purvey thee a better horse, and it may be I will hold it worth my while to scourge out of thee this boyish spirit of bravado."

"Ha! proud Templar," said Ivanhoe, "hast thou forgotten that twice didst thou fall before this lance? Remember the lists of Acre—remember the passage of arms at Ashby—remember thy proud vaunt in the halls of Rotherwood, and the gage of your gold chain against my reliquary, that thou wouldst do battle with Wilfred of Ivanhoe, and recover the honour thou hadst lost! By that reliquary, and the holy relic it contains, I will proclaim thee, Templar, a coward in every court in Europe—in every preceptory of thine order—unless thou do battle without further delay."

Bois-Guilbert turned his countenance irresolutely towards Rebecca, and then exclaimed, looking fiercely at Ivanhoe, "Dog of a Saxon! take thy lance, and prepare for the death thou hast drawn upon thee!"

"Does the Grand Master allow me the combat?" said Ivanhoe.

"I may not deny what thou hast challenged," said the Grand Master, "provided the maiden accepts thee as her champion. Yet I would thou wert in better plight to do battle. An enemy of our order hast thou ever been, yet would I have thee honourably met with."

"Thus—thus as I am, and not otherwise," said Ivanhoe; "it is the judgment of God—to his keeping I commend myself. Rebecca," said he, riding up to the fatal chair, "dost thou accept of me for thy champion?"

"I do," she said, "I do," fluttered by an emotion which the fear of death had been unable to produce, "I do accept thee as the champion whom Heaven hath sent me. Yet, no—no—thy wounds are uncured. Meet not that proud man—why shouldst thou perish also?"

But Ivanhoe was already at his post, and had closed his visor, and assumed his lance. Bois-Guilbert did the same; and his esquire remarked, as he clasped his visor, that his face which had, notwithstanding the variety of emotions by which he had been agitated, continued during the whole morning of an ashy paleness, was now become suddenly very much flushed.

The herald, then, seeing each champion in his place, uplifted his voice, repeating thrice—*Faites vos devoirs, preux chevaliers!* After the third cry, he withdrew to one side of the lists, and again proclaimed, that none, on peril of instant death, should dare, by word, cry, or action, to interfere with or disturb this fair field of combat. The Grand Master, who held in his hand the gage of battle, Rebecca's glove, now threw it into the lists, and pronounced the fatal signal words, *Laissez aller*.

The trumpets sounded, and the knights charged each other in full career. The wearied horse of Ivanhoe, and its no less exhausted rider, went down, as all had expected, before the well-aimed lance and vigorous steed of the Templar. This issue of the combat all had foreseen; but although the spear of Ivanhoe did but, in comparison, touch the shield of Bois-Guilbert, that champion, to the astonishment of all who beheld it, reeled in his saddle, lost his stirrups, and fell in the lists.

Ivanhoe, extricating himself from his fallen horse, was soon on foot, hastening to mend his fortune with his sword; but his antagonist arose not. Wilfred, placing his foot on his breast, and the sword's point to his throat, commanded him to yield him, or die on the spot. Bois-Guilbert returned no answer.

"Slay him not, Sir Knight," cried the Grand Master, "unshriven and unabsolved—kill not body and soul! We allow him vanquished."

He descended into the lists, and commanded them to unhelm the conquered champion. His eyes were closed—the dark red flush was still on his brow. As they looked on him in astonishment, the eyes opened—but they were fixed and glazed. The flush passed from his brow, and gave way to the pallid hue of death. Unscathed by the lance of his enemy, he had died a victim to the violence of his own contending passions.

"This is indeed the judgment of God," said the Grand Master, looking upwards—*"Fiat voluntas tua!"*

CHAPTER XLIV

So now 'tis ended, like an old wife's story.
WEBSTER.

WHEN the first moments of surprise were over, Wilfred of Ivanhoe demanded of the Grand Master, as judge of the field, if he had manfully and rightfully done his duty in the combat?

"Manfully and rightfully hath it been done," said the Grand Master;

"I pronounce the maiden free and guiltless. The arms and the body of the deceased knight are at the will of the victor."

"I will not despoil him of his weapons," said the Knight of Ivanhoe, "nor condemn his corpse to shame—he hath fought for Christendom— God's arm, no human hand, hath this day struck him down. But let his obsequies be private, as becomes those of a man who died in an unjust quarrel. And for the maiden"——

He was interrupted by a clattering of horses' feet, advancing in such numbers, and so rapidly, as to shake the ground before them; and the Black Knight galloped into the lists. He was followed by a numerous band of men-at-arms, and several knights in complete armour.

"I am too late," he said, looking around him. "I had doomed Bois· Guilbert for mine own property. Ivanhoe, was this well, to take on thee such a venture, and thou scarce able to keep thy saddle?"

"Heaven, my Liege," answered Ivanhoe, "hath taken this proud man for its victim. He was not to be honoured in dying as your will had designed."

"Peace be with him," said Richard, looking steadfastly on the corpse, "if it may be so—he was a gallant knight, and has died in his steel harness full knightly. But we must waste no time—Bohun, do thine office!"

A Knight stepped forward from the king's attendants, and, laying his hand on the shoulder of Albert de Malvoisin, said, "I arrest thee of high treason."

The Grand Master had hitherto stood astonished at the appearance of so many warriors. He now spoke.

"Who dares to arrest a Knight of the Temple of Zion within the girth of his own preceptory, and in the presence of the Grand Master? and by whose authority is this bold outrage offered?"

"I make the arrest," replied the knight, "I, Henry Bohun, Earl of Essex, Lord High Constable of England."

"And he arrests Malvoisin," said the King, raising his visor, "by the order of Richard Plantagenet, here present. Conrade Mont-Fitchet, it is well for thee thou art born no subject of mine. But for thee, Malvoisin, thou diest with thy brother Philip ere the world be a week older."

"I will resist thy doom," said the Grand Master.

"Proud Templar," said the King, "thou canst not—look up, and behold the Royal Standard of England floats over thy towers instead of thy Temple banner! Be wise, Beaumanoir, and make no bootless opposition. Thy hand is in the lion's mouth."

"I will appeal to Rome against thee," said the Grand Master, "for usurpation on the immunities and privileges of our order."

"Be it so," said the King; "but for thine own sake tax me not with usurpation now. Dissolve thy chapter, and depart with thy followers to thy next preceptory (if thou canst find one), which has not been made the scene of treasonable conspiracy against the King of England. Or, if thou wilt, remain to share our hospitality and behold our justice."

"To be a guest in the house where I should command?" said the Templar; "never! Chaplains, raise the Psalm, *Quare fremuerunt Gentes?* Knights, squires, and followers of the Holy Temple, prepare to follow the banner of *Beau-seant!*"

The Grand Master spoke with a dignity which confronted even that of England's king himself, and inspired courage into his surprised and dismayed followers. They gathered around him like the sheep around the watch-dog, when they hear the baying of the wolf. But they evinced not the timidity of the scared flock—there were dark brows of defiance, and looks which menaced the hostility they dared not to proffer in words. They drew together in a dark line of spears, from which the white cloaks of the knights were visible among the dusky garments of their retainers, like the lighter-coloured edges of a sable cloud. The multitude, who had raised a clamorous shout of reprobation, paused and gazed in silence on the formidable and experienced body to which they had unwarily bade defiance, and shrunk back from their front.

The Earl of Essex, when he beheld them pause in their assembled force dashed the rowels into his charger's sides, and galloped backwards and forwards to array his followers, in opposition to a band so formidable. Richard alone, as if he loved the danger his presence had provoked, rode slowly along the front of the Templars, calling aloud, "What, sirs! Among so many gallant knights, will none dare splinter a spear with Richard? Sirs of the Temple! your ladies are but sun-burned, if they are not worth the shiver of a broken lance!"

"The Brethren of the Temple," said the Grand Master, riding forward in advance of their body, "fight not on such idle and profane quarrel— and not with thee, Richard of England, shall a Templar cross lance in my presence. The pope and princes of Europe shall judge our quarrel, and whether a Christian prince has done well in buckling the cause which thou hast to-day adopted. If unassailed, we depart assailing no one. To thine honour we refer the armour and household goods of the order which we leave behind us, and on thy conscience we lay the scandal and offence thou hast this day given to Christendom."

With these words, and without waiting a reply, the Grand Master gave the signal of departure. Their trumpets sounded a wild march, of an Oriental character, which formed the usual signal for the Templars to advance. They changed their array from a line to a column of march, and moved off as slowly as their horses could step, as if to show it was only the will of their Grand Master, and no fear of the opposing and superior force, which compelled them to withdraw.

"By the splendour of Our Lady's brow!" said King Richard, "it is pity of their lives that these Templars are not so trusty as they are disciplined and valiant."

The multitude, like a timid cur which waits to bark till the object of its challenge has turned his back, raised a feeble shout as the rear of the squadron left the ground.

During the tumult which attended the retreat of the Templars, Rebecca saw and heard nothing—she was locked in the arms of her aged father, giddy, and almost senseless, with the rapid change of circumstances around her. But one word from Isaac at length recalled her scattered feelings.

"Let us go," he said, "my dear daughter, my recovered treasure—let us go to throw ourselves at the feet of the good youth."

"Not so," said Rebecca, "O no—no—no—I must not at this moment dare to speak to him. Alas! I should say more than——— No, my father, let us instantly leave this evil place."

"But, my daughter," said Isaac, "to leave him who hath come forth like a strong man with his spear and shield, holding his life as nothing, so he might redeem thy captivity; and thou, too, the daughter of a people strange unto him and his—this is service to be thankfully acknowledged."

"It is—it is—most thankfully—most devoutly acknowledged," said Rebecca. "It shall be still more so—but not now—for the sake of thy beloved Rachel, father, grant my request—not now!"

"Nay, but," said Isaac, insisting, "they will deem us more thankless than mere dogs!"

"But thou seest, my dear father, that King Richard is in presence, and that"———

"True, my best, my wisest Rebecca! Let us hence—let us hence! Money he will lack, for he has just returned from Palestine, and, as they say, from prison; and pretext for exacting it, should he need any, may arise out of my simple traffic with his brother John. Away, away, let us hence!"

And hurrying his daughter in his turn, he conducted her from the lists, and by means of conveyance which he had provided, transported her safely to the house of the Rabbi Nathan.

The Jewess, whose fortunes had formed the principal interest of the day, having now retired unobserved, the attention of the populace was transferred to the Black Knight. They now filled the air with "Long life to Richard with the Lion's Heart, and down with the usurping Templars!"

"Notwithstanding all this lip-loyalty," said Ivanhoe to the Earl of Essex, "it was well the King took the precaution to bring thee with him, noble Earl, and so many of thy trusty followers."

The Earl smiled and shook his head.

"Gallant Ivanhoe," said Essex, "dost thou know our master so well, and yet suspect him of taking so wise a precaution! I was drawing towards York, having heard that Prince John was making head there, when I met King Richard, like a true knight-errant, galloping hither to achieve in his own person this adventure of the Templar and the Jewess, with his own single arm. I accompanied him with my band, almost maugre his consent."

"And what news from York, brave Earl?" said Ivanhoe; "will the rebels bide us there?"

"No more than December's snow will bide July's sun," said the Earl; "they are dispersing; and who should come posting to bring us the news but John himself!"

"The traitor! the ungrateful insolent traitor!" said Ivanhoe; "did not Richard order him into confinement?"

"O! he received him," answered the Earl, "as if they had met after a hunting party; and, pointing to me and our men-at-arms, said, 'Thou seest, brother, I have some angry men with me—thou wert best go to our mother, carry her my duteous affection, and abide with her until men's minds are pacified.' "

"And this was all he said?" enquired Ivanhoe; "would not any one say that this Prince invites men to treason by his clemency?"

"Just," replied the Earl, "as the man may be said to invite death, who undertakes to fight a combat, having a dangerous wound unhealed."

"I forgive thee the jest, Lord Earl," said Ivanhoe; "but, remember, I hazarded but my own life—Richard, the welfare of his kingdom."

"Those," replied Essex, "who are specially careless of their own welfare are seldom remarkably attentive to that of others. But let us haste to the castle, for Richard meditates punishing some of the subordinate members of the conspiracy, though he has pardoned their principal."

From the judicial investigations which followed on this occasion, and which are given at length in the Wardour Manuscript, it appears that Maurice de Bracy escaped beyond seas, and went into the service of Philip of France; while Philip de Malvoisin, and his brother Albert, the Preceptor of Templestowe, were executed, although Waldemar Fitzurse, the soul of the conspiracy, escaped with banishment; and Prince John, for whose behoof it was undertaken, was not even censured by his good-natured brother. No one, however, pitied the fate of the two Malvoisins, who only suffered the death which they had both well deserved, by many acts of falsehood, cruelty, and oppression.

Briefly after the judicial combat, Cedric the Saxon was summoned to the court of Richard, which, for the purpose of quieting the counties that had been disturbed by the ambition of his brother, was then held at York. Cedric tushed and pshawed more than once at the message—but he refused not obedience. In fact, the return of Richard had quenched every hope that he had entertained of restoring a Saxon dynasty in England; for, whatever head the Saxons might have made in the event of a civil war, it was plain that nothing could be done under the undisputed dominion of Richard, popular as he was by his personal good qualities and military fame, although his administration was wilfully careless, now too indulgent, and now allied to despotism.

But, moreover, it could not escape even Cedric's reluctant observation that his project for an absolute union among the Saxons, by the marriage of Rowena and Athelstane, was now completely at an end, by the mutual dissent of both parties concerned. This was, indeed, an event which, in his ardour for the Saxon cause, he could not have anticipated, and even when the disinclination of both was broadly and plainly manifested, he could scarce bring himself to believe that two Saxons of royal descent should scruple, on personal grounds, at an alliance so necessary for the public weal of the nation. But it was not the less certain: Rowena had always expressed her repugnance to Athelstane, and now Athelstane was no less plain and positive in proclaiming his resolution never to pursue his addresses to the Lady Rowena. Even the natural obstinacy of Cedric sunk beneath these obstacles, where he, remaining on the point of junction, had the task of dragging a reluctant pair up to it, one with each hand. He made, however, a last vigorous attack on Athelstane, and he found that resuscitated sprout of Saxon royalty engaged, like country squires of our own day, in a furious war with the clergy.

It seems that, after all his deadly menaces against the Abbot of Saint Edmund's, Athelstane's spirit of revenge, what between the natural indolent kindness of his own disposition, what through the prayers of his mother Edith, attached, like most ladies (of the period) to the clerical order, had terminated in his keeping the abbot and his monks in the dungeons of Coningsburgh for three days on a meagre diet. For this atrocity the abbot menaced him with excommunication, and made out a dreadful list of complaints in the bowels and stomach, suffered by himself and his monks, in consequence of the tyrannical and unjust imprisonment they had sustained. With this controversy, and with the means he had adopted to counteract this clerical persecution, Cedric found the mind of his friend Athelstane so fully occupied that it had no room for another idea. And when Rowena's name was mentioned, the noble Athelstane prayed leave to quaff a full goblet to her health, and that she might soon be the bride of his kinsman Wilfred. It was a desperate case therefore. There was obviously no more to be made of Athelstane; or, as Wamba expressed it, in a phrase which has descended from Saxon times to ours, he was a cock that would not fight.

There remained betwixt Cedric and the determination which the lovers desired to come to, only two obstacles—his own obstinacy, and his dislike of the Norman dynasty. The former feeling gradually gave way before the endearments of his ward and the pride which he could not help nourishing in the fame of his son. Besides, he was not insensible to the honour of allying his own line to that of Alfred, when the superior claims of the descendant of Edward the Confessor were abandoned for ever. Cedric's aversion to the Norman race of kings was also much undermined,—first, by consideration of the impossibility of ridding England of the new dynasty, a feeling which goes far to create loyalty in the subject to the king *de facto;* and, secondly, by the personal attention of King Richard, who delighted in the blunt humour of Cedric, and, to use the language of the Wardour Manuscript, so dealt with the noble Saxon, that, ere he had been a guest at court for seven days, he had given his consent to the marriage of his ward Rowena and his son Wilfred of Ivanhoe.

The nuptials of our hero, thus formally approved by his father, were celebrated in the most august of temples, the noble Minster of York. The King himself attended, and from the countenance which he afforded on this and other occasions to the distressed and hitherto degraded Saxons, gave them a safer and more certain prospect of attaining their just rights, than they could reasonably hope from the precarious chance of a civil war. The Church gave her full solemnities, graced with all the splendour which she of Rome knows how to apply with such brilliant effect.

Gurth, gallantly apparelled, attended as esquire upon his young master whom he had served so faithfully, and the magnanimous Wamba, decorated with a new cap and a most gorgeous set of silver bells. Sharers of Wilfred's dangers and adversity, they remained, as they had a right to expect, the partakers of his more prosperous career.

But besides the domestic retinue, these distinguished nuptials were celebrated by the attendance of the high-born Normans, as well as Saxons, joined with the universal jubilee of the lower orders, that marked the marriage of two individuals as a pledge of the future peace and harmony betwixt two races, which, since that period, have been so completely mingled, that the distinction has become wholly invisible. Cedric lived to see this union approximate towards its completion; for as the two nations mixed in society and formed intermarriages with each other, the Normans abated their scorn, and the Saxons were refined from their rusticity. But it was not until the reign of Edward the Third that the mixed language, now termed English, was spoken at the court of London, and that the hostile distinction of Norman and Saxon seems entirely to have disappeared.

It was upon the second morning after this happy bridal, that the Lady Rowena was made acquainted by her handmaid Elgitha, that a damsel desired admission to her presence, and solicited that their parley might be without witness. Rowena wondered, hesitated, became curious, and ended by commanding the damsel to be admitted, and her attendants to withdraw.

She entered—a noble and commanding figure, the long white veil, in which she was shrouded, overshadowing rather than concealing the elegance and majesty of her shape. Her demeanour was that of respect, unmingled by the least shade either of fear, or of a wish to propitiate favour. Rowena was ever ready to acknowledge the claims, and attend to the feelings of others. She arose, and would have conducted her lovely visitor to a seat; but the stranger looked at Elgitha, and again intimated a wish to discourse with the Lady Rowena alone. Elgitha had no sooner retired with unwilling steps, than, to the surprise of the Lady of Ivanhoe, her fair visitant kneeled on one knee, pressed her hands to her forehead, and bending her head to the ground, in spite of Rowena's resistance, kissed the embroidered hem of her tunic.

"What means this, lady?" said the surprised bride; "or why do you offer to me a deference so unusual?"

"Because to you, Lady of Ivanhoe," said Rebecca, rising up and resuming the usual quiet dignity of her manner, "I may lawfully, and without rebuke, pay the debt of gratitude which I owe to Wilfred of Ivanhoe. I am—forgive the boldness which has offered to you the homage of my country—I am the unhappy Jewess for whom your husband hazarded his life against such fearful odds in the tiltyard of Templestowe."

"Damsel," said Rowena, "Wilfred of Ivanhoe on that day rendered back but in slight measure your unceasing charity towards him in his wounds and misfortunes. Speak, is there aught remains in which he or I can serve thee?"

"Nothing," said Rebecca, calmly, "unless you will transmit to him my grateful farewell."

"You leave England, then?" said Rowena, scarce recovering her surprise of this extraordinary visit.

"I leave it, lady, ere this moon again changes. My father hath a brother high in favour with Mohammed Boabdil, King of Granada— thither we go, secure of peace and protection, for the payment of such ransom as the Moslem exact from our people."

"And are you not then as well protected in England?" said Rowena. "My husband has favour with the King—the King himself is just and generous."

"Lady," said Rebecca, "I doubt it not—but the people of England are a fierce race, quarrelling ever with their neighbours or among themselves, and ready to plunge the sword into the bowels of each other. Such is no safe abode for the children of my people. Ephraim is an heartless dove —Issachar an over-laboured drudge, which stoops between two burdens. Not in a land of war and blood, surrounded by hostile neighbours, and distracted by internal factions, can Israel hope to rest during her wanderings."

"But you, maiden," said Rowena, "you surely can have nothing to fear. She who nursed the sick-bed of Ivanhoe," she continued, rising with enthusiasm, "she can have nothing to fear in England, where Saxon and Norman will contend who shall most do her honour."

"Thy speech is fair, lady," said Rebecca, "and thy purpose fairer; but it may not be—there is a gulf betwixt us. Our breeding, our faith, alike forbid either to pass over it. Farewell—yet, ere I go, indulge me one request. The bridal-veil hangs over thy face; deign to raise it, and let me see the features of which fame speaks so highly."

"They are scarce worthy of being looked upon," said Rowena; "but, expecting the same from my visitant, I remove the veil."

She took it off accordingly; and, partly from the consciousness of beauty, partly from bashfulness, she blushed so intensely that cheek, brow, neck, and bosom, were suffused with crimson. Rebecca blushed also, but it was a momentary feeling; and, mastered by higher emotions, past slowly from her features like the crimson cloud, which changes colour when the sun sinks beneath the horizon.

"Lady," she said, "the countenance you have deigned to show me will long dwell in my remembrance. There reigns in it gentleness and goodness; and if a tinge of the world's pride or vanities may mix with an expression so lovely, how should we chide that which is of earth for bearing some colour of its original? Long, long will I remember your features, and bless God that I leave my noble deliverer united with"——

She stopped short—her eyes filled with tears. She hastily wiped them, and answered to the anxious enquiries of Rowena, "I am well, lady—well. But my heart swells when I think of Torquilstone and the lists of Templestowe. Farewell. One, the most trifling part of my duty, remains undischarged. Accept this casket—startle not at its contents."

Rowena opened the small silver-chased casket, and perceived a carcanet, or necklace, with ear-jewels, of diamonds, which were obviously of immense value.

"It is impossible," she said, tendering back the casket. "I dare not accept a gift of such consequence."

"Yet keep it, lady," returned Rebecca. "You have power, rank, command, influence; we have wealth, the source both of our strength and weakness; the value of these toys, ten times multiplied, would not influence half so much as your slightest wish. To you, therefore, the gift is of little value, and to me, what I part with is of much less. Let me not think you deem so wretchedly ill of my nation as your commons believe. Think ye that I prize these sparkling fragments of stone above my liberty? or that my father values them in comparison to the honour of his only child? Accept them, lady—to me they are valueless. I will never wear jewels more."

"You are then unhappy!" said Rowena, struck with the manner in which Rebecca uttered the last words. "O, remain with us—the counsel of holy men will wean you from your erring law, and I will be a sister to you."

"No, lady," answered Rebecca, the same calm melancholy reigning in her soft voice and beautiful features; "that may not be. I may not change the faith of my fathers like a garment unsuited to the climate in which I seek to dwell, and unhappy, lady, I will not be. He, to whom I dedicate my future life, will be my comforter, if I do His will."

"Have you then convents, to one of which you mean to retire?" asked Rowena.

"No, lady," said the Jewess; "but among our people, since the time of Abraham downwards, have been women who have devoted their thoughts to Heaven, and their actions to works of kindness to men, tending the sick, feeding the hungry, and relieving the distressed. Among these will Rebecca be numbered. Say this to thy lord, should he chance to enquire after the fate of her whose life he saved."

There was an involuntary tremor in Rebecca's voice, and a tenderness of accent, which perhaps betrayed more than she would willingly have expressed. She hastened to bid Rowena adieu.

"Farewell," she said. "May He, who made both Jew and Christian, shower down on you His choicest blessings! The bark that wafts us hence will be under weigh ere we can reach the port."

She glided from the apartment, leaving Rowena surprised as if a vision had passed before her. The fair Saxon related the singular conference to her husband, on whose mind it made a deep impression. He lived long and happily with Rowena, for they were attached to each other by the bonds of early affection, and they loved each other the more, from the recollection of the obstacles which had impeded their union. Yet it would be enquiring too curiously to ask, whether the recollection of Rebecca's beauty and magnanimity did not recur to his mind more frequently than the fair descendant of Alfred might altogether have approved.

Ivanhoe distinguished himself in the service of Richard, and was graced with farther marks of the royal favour. He might have risen still higher, but for the premature death of the heroic Cœur-de-Lion before the Castle of Chaluz, near Limoges. With the life of a generous, but rash and romantic, monarch perished all the projects which his ambition and his generosity had formed; to whom may be applied, with a slight alteration, the lines composed by Jonson for Charles of Sweden—

> His fate was destined to a foreign strand,
> A petty fortress and an "humble" hand;
> He left the name at which the world grew pale,
> To point a moral, or adorn a TALE.

AUTHOR'S NOTES

I. p. 412.—THE RANGER OF THE FOREST, THAT CUTS THE FORECLAWS OFF OUR DOGS

A most sensible grievance of those aggrieved times were the Forest Laws. These oppressive enactments were the produce of the Norman Conquest, for the Saxon laws of the chase were mild and humane; while those of William, enthusiastically attached to the exercise of its rights, were to the last degree tyrannical. The formation of the New Forest bears evidence to his passion for hunting, where he reduced many a happy village to the condition of that one commemorated by my friend, Mr. William Stewart Rose,

> "Amongst the ruins of the church
> The midnight raven found a perch.
> A melancholy place;
> The ruthless Conqueror cast down,
> Woe worth the deed, that little town,
> To lengthen out his chase."

The disabling dogs, which might be necessary for keeping flocks and herds from running at the deer, was called *lawing,* and was in general use. The Charter of the Forest designed to lessen those evils, declares that inquisition, or view, for lawing dogs, shall be made every third year, and shall be then done by the view and testimony of lawful men, not otherwise; and they whose dogs shall be then found unlawed, shall give three shillings for mercy; and for the future, no man's ox shall be taken for lawing. Such lawing also shall be done by the assize commonly used, and which is, that three claws shall be cut off without the ball of the right foot. See on this subject the *Historical Essay on the Magna Charta of King John* (a most beautiful volume), by Richard Thomson.

II.—p. 416.—NEGRO SLAVES

The severe accuracy of some critics has objected to the complexion of the slaves of Brian de Bois-Guilbert, as being totally out of costume and propriety. I remember the same objection being made to a set of sable functionaries whom my friend, Mat Lewis, introduced as the guards and mischief-doing satellites of the wicked Baron, in his *Castle Spectre.* Mat treated the objection with great contempt, and averred in reply, that he made the slaves black in order to obtain a striking effect of contrast, and that, could he have derived a similar advantage from making his heroine blue, blue she should have been.

I do not pretend to plead the immunities of my order so highly as this; but neither will I allow that the author of a modern antique romance is obliged to confine himself to the introduction of those manners only which can be proved to have absolutely existed in times he is depicting, so that he restrain himself to such as are plausible and natural, and contain no obvious anachronism. In this point of view, what can be more natural, than that the Templars, who, we know, copied closely the luxuries of the Asiatic warriors, with whom they fought, should use the service of the enslaved Africans, whom the fate of war transferred to new masters? I am sure, if there are no precise proofs of their having done so, there is nothing, on the other hand, that can entitle us positively to conclude that they never did. Besides, there is an instance in romance.

John of Rampayne, an excellent juggler and minstrel, undertook to effect the escape of one Audulf de Bracy, by presenting himself in disguise at the court of the king, where he was confined. For this purpose, "he stained his hair and his whole body entirely as black as jet, so that nothing was white but his teeth," and succeeded in imposing himself on the king as an Ethiopian minstrel. He effected, by stratagem, the escape of the prisoner. Negroes, therefore, must have been known in England in the dark ages.[1]

III.—p. 529.—MINSTRELSY

The realm of France, it is well known, was divided betwixt the Norman and Teutonic race, who spoke the language in which the word Yes is pronounced as *oui;* and the inhabitants of the southern regions, whose speech bearing some affinity to the Italian, pronounced the same word *oc.* The poets of the former race were called *Minstrels,* and their poems *Lays:* those of the latter were termed *Troubadours,* and their compositions called *sirventes,* and other names. Richard, a professed admirer of the joyous science in all its branches, could imitate either the minstrel or troubadour. It is less likely that he should have been able to compose or sing an English Ballad; yet so much do we wish to assimilate Him of the Lion Heart to the band of warriors whom he led, that the anachronism, if there be one, may readily be forgiven.

IV.—p. 554.—BATTLE OF STAMFORD

A great topographical blunder occurred here in former editions. The bloody battle alluded to in the text, fought and won by King Harold, over his brother the rebellious Tosti, and an auxiliary force of Danes or Norsemen, was said, in the text, and a corresponding note, to have taken place at Stamford, in Leicestershire, and upon the river Welland. This is a mistake, into which the author has been led by trusting to his memory, and so confounding two places of the same name. The Stamford, Strangford, or Staneford, at which the battle really was fought, is a ford upon the river Derwent, at the distance of about seven miles from York, and situated in that large and opulent county. A long wooden bridge over the Derwent, the site of which, with one remaining buttress, is still shown to the curious traveller, was furiously contested. One Norwegian long defended it by his single arm, and was at length pierced with a spear thrust through the planks of the bridge from a boat beneath.

The neighbourhood of Stamford, on the Derwent, contains some memorials of the battle. Horseshoes, swords, and the heads of halberds, or bills, are often found there; one place is called the "Danes' well," another the "Battle flats." From a tradition that the weapon with which the Norwegian champion was slain, resembled a pear, or, as others say, that the trough or boat in which the soldier floated under the bridge to strike the blow, had such a shape, the country people usually begin a great market, which is held at Stamford, with an entertainment called the Pear-pie feast, which after all may be a corruption of the Spear-pie feast. For more particulars, Drake's *History of York* may be referred to. The author's mistake was pointed out to him, in the most obliging manner, by Robert Belt, Esq. of Bossal House. The battle was fought in 1066.

V.—p. 560.—THE RANGE OF IRON BARS ABOVE THAT GLOWING CHARCOAL

This horrid species of torture may remind the reader of that to which the Spaniards subjected Guatimozin, in order to extort a discovery of his concealed wealth. But, in fact, an instance of similar barbarity is to be found nearer home, and occurs in the annals of Queen Mary's time, containing so many other examples of atrocity. Every reader must recollect, that after the fall of the Catholic Church,

[1] "Dissertation on Romance and Minstrelsy," prefixed to Ritson's *Ancient Metrical Romances,* p. clxxxvii.

and the Presbyterian Church Government had been established by law, the rank, and especially the wealth, of the Bishops, Abbots, Priors, and so forth, were no longer vested in ecclesiastics, but in lay impropriators of the church revenues, or, as the Scottish lawyers called them, *titulars* of the temporalities of the benefice, though having no claim to the spiritual character of their predecessors in office.

Of these laymen, who were thus invested with ecclesiastical revenues, some were men of high birth and rank, like the famous Lord James Stewart, the Prior of St. Andrews, who did not fail to keep for their own use the rents, lands, and revenues of the church. But if, on the other hand, the titulars were men of inferior importance, who had been inducted into the office by the interest of some powerful person, it was generally understood that the new Abbot should grant for his patron's benefit such leases and conveyances of the church lands and tithes as might afford their protector the lion's share of the booty. This was the origin of those who were wittily termed Tulchan [1] Bishops, being a sort of imaginary prelate, whose image was set up to enable his patron and principal to plunder the benefice under his name.

There were other cases, however, in which men who had got grants of these secularised benefices, were desirous of retaining them for their own use, without having the influence sufficient to establish their purpose; and these became frequently unable to protect themselves, however unwilling to submit to the exactions of the feudal tyrant of the district.

Bannatyne, secretary to John Knox, recounts a singular course of oppression practised on one of those titular abbots, by the Earl of Cassilis in Ayrshire, whose extent of feudal influence was so wide that he was usually termed the King of Carrick. We give the fact as it occurs in Bannatyne's *Journal,* only premising that the journalist held his master's opinions, both with respect to the Earl of Cassilis as an opposer of the king's party, and as being a detester of the practice of granting church revenues to titulars, instead of their being devoted to pious uses, such as the support of the clergy, expense of schools, and the relief of the national poor. He mingles in the narrative, therefore, a well deserved feeling of execration against the tyrant who employed the torture, with a tone of ridicule towards the patient, as if, after all, it had not been ill bestowed on such an equivocal and amphibious character as a titular abbot. He entitles his narrative,

THE EARL OF CASSILIS' TYRANNY AGAINST A QUICK (*i.e.* LIVING) MAN

"Master Allan Stewart, friend to Captain James Stewart of Cardonall, by means of the Queen's corrupted court, obtained the Abbey of Crossraguel. The said Earl thinking himself greater than any king in those quarters, determined to have that whole benefice (as he hath divers others) to pay at his pleasure; and because he could not find sic security as his insatiable appetite required, this shift was devised. The said Mr. Allan being in company with the Laird of Bargany (also a Kennedy), was, by the Earl and his friends, enticed to leave the safeguard which he had with the laird, and come to make good cheer with the said Earl. The simplicity of the imprudent man was suddenly abused; and so he passed his time with them certain days, which he did in Maybole with Thomas Kennedie uncle to the said Earl: after which the said Mr. Allan passed, with quiet company, to visit the place and bounds of Crossraguel [his abbacy], of which the said Earl being surely advertised, determined to put in practice the tyranny which long before he had conceaved. And so, as king of the country, apprehended the said Mr. Allan, and carried him to the house of Denure, where for a season he was honourably treated (gif a prisoner can think any entertainment pleasing) ; but after that certain days were spent, and that the Earl could not obtain the feus of Crossraguel according to his awin appetite,

[1] A *Tulchan* is a calf's skin stuffed, and placed before a cow who has lost its calf, to induce the animal to part with her milk. The resemblance between such a Tulchan and a bishop named to transmit the temporalities of a benefice to some powerful patron is easily understood.

he determined to prove gif a collation could work that which neither dinner nor supper could do for a long time. And so the said Mr. Allan was carried to a secret chamber: with him passed the honourable Earl, his worshipful brother, and such as were appointed to be servants at that banquet. In the chamber there was a grit iron chimlay, under it a fire; other grit provision was not seen. The first course was,— 'My Lord Abbot' (said the Earl), 'it will please you confess here, that with your own consent you remain in my company, because ye durst not commit yourself to the hands of others.' The Abbot answered, 'Would you, my lord, that I should make a manifest lie for your pleasure? The truth is, my lord, it is against my will that I am here; neither yet have I any pleasure in your company.' 'But ye shall remain with me, nevertheless, at this time,' said the Earl. 'I am not able to resist your will and pleasure,' said the Abbot, 'in this place.' 'Ye must then obey me,' said the Earl,— and with that were presented unto him certain letters to subscribe, amongst which there was a five years' tack, and a nineteen years' tack, and a charter of feu of all the lands of Crossraguel, with all the clauses necessary for the Earl to haste him to hell. For gif adultery, sacrilege, oppression, barbarous cruelty, and theft heaped upon theft, deserve hell, the great King of Carrick can no more escape hell for ever, than the imprudent Abbot escaped the fire for a season as follows.

"After that the Earl spied repugnance, and saw that he could not come to his purpose by fair means, he commanded his cooks to prepare the banquet: and so first they flayed the sheep, that is, they took off the Abbot's cloathes even to his skin, and next they bound him to the chimney—his legs to the one end, and his arms to the other; and so they began to beet [i.e. feed] the fire sometimes to his buttocks, sometimes to his legs, sometimes to his shoulders and arms; and that the roast might not burn, but that it might rest in soppe, they spared not flambing with oil (basting as a cook bastes roasted meat); Lord, look thou to sic cruelty! And that the crying of the miserable man should not be heard, they closed his mouth that the voice might be stopped. It may be suspected that some partisan of the King's [Darnley's] murder was there. In that torment they held the poor man, till that often he cried for God's sake to dispatch him; for he had as meikle gold in his awin purse as would buy powder enough to shorten his pain. The famous King of Carrick and his cooks perceiving the roast to be eneuch, commanded it to be tane fra the fire, and the Earl himself began to grace in this manner:—'Benedicite, Jesus Maria, you are the most obstinate man that ever I saw; gif I had known that you had been so stubborn, I would not for a thousand crowns have handled you so; I never did so to man before you.' And yet he returned to the same practice within two days, and ceased not till that he obtained his formost purpose, that is, that he had got all his pieces subscryvit alsweill as ane half-roasted hand could do it. The Earl thinking himself sure enough so long as he had the half-roasted Abbot in his awin keeping, and yet being ashamed of his presence by reason of his former cruelty, left the place of Denure in the hands of certain of his servants, and the half-roasted Abbot to be kept there as prisoner. The Laird of Bargany, out of whose company the said Abbot had been enticed, understanding (not the extremity), but the retaining of the man, sent to the court, and raised letters of deliverance of the person of the man according to the order, which being disobeyed, the said Earl for his contempt was denounced rebel, and put to the horne. But yet hope was there none, neither to the afflicted to be delivered, neither yet to the purchaser [i.e. procurer] of the letters to obtain any comfort thereby; for in that time God was despised, and the lawful authority was contemned in Scotland, in hope of the sudden return and regiment of that cruel murderer of her awin husband, of whose lords the said Earl was called one; and yet, oftener than once, he was solemnly sworn to the King and to his Regent."

The Journalist then recites the complaint of the injured Allan Stewart, Commendator of Crossraguel, to the Regent and Privy Council, averring his having been carried, partly by flattery, partly by force, to the black vault of Denure, a strong fortalice, built on a rock overhanging the Irish channel. where its ruins are still visible. Here he stated he had been required to execute leases and conveyances of the whole churches and parsonages belonging to the Abbey of Crossraguel, which he utterly refused as an unreasonable demand, and the more so that he had already conveyed them to John Stewart of Cardonall, by whose interest he had been made Commendator. The complainant proceeds to state, that he was, after many menaces, stript, bound, and his limbs exposed to fire in the manner already described, till, compelled by excess of agony, he subscribed the charter and leases presented to him, of the contents of which he was totally ignorant. A few days afterwards, being again required to execute a ratification of these deeds before a notary and witnesses, and refusing to do so, he was once more subjected to the same torture, until his agony was so excessive that he exclaimed, "Fye on you, why do you not strike your whingers into me, or blow me up with a barrel of powder, rather than torture me thus unmercifully?" upon which the Earl commanded Alexander Richard, one of his attendants, to stop the patient's mouth with a napkin, which was done accordingly. Thus he was once more compelled to submit to their tyranny. The petition concluded with stating, that the Earl, under pretence of the deeds thus iniquitously obtained, had taken possession of the whole place and living of Crossraguel, and enjoyed the profits thereof for three years.

The doom of the Regent and Council shows singularly the total interruption of justice at this calamitous period, even in the most clamant cases of oppression. The Council declined interference with the course of the ordinary justice of the county (which was completely under the said Earl of Cassilis' control), and only enacted, that he should forbear molestation of the unfortunate Commendator, under the surety of two thousand pounds Scots. The Earl was appointed also to keep the peace towards the celebrated George Buchanan, who had a pension out of the same Abbacy, to a similar extent, and under the like penalty.

The consequences are thus described by the Journalist already quoted:

"The said Laird of Bargany perceiving that the ordiner justice could neither help the oppressed, nor yet the afflicted, applied his mind to the next remedy, and in the end, by his servants, took the house of Denure, where the poor Abbot was kept prisoner. The bruit flew fra Carrick to Galloway, and so suddenly assembled herd and hyre-man that pertained to the band of the Kennedies; and so within a few hours was the house of Denure environed again. The master of Cassilis was the frackast [*i.e.* the readiest or boldest] and would not stay, but in his heat would lay fire to the dungeon, with no small boasting that all enemies within the house should die.

"He was required and admonished by those that were within to be more moderate, and not to hazard himself so foolishly. But no admonition would help, till that the wind of an hacquebute blasted his shoulder, and then ceased he from further pursuit in fury. The Laird of Bargany had before purchest [obtained] of the authorities, letters, charging all faithful subjects to the King's Majesty, to assist him against that cruel tyrant and mansworn traitor, the Earl of Cassilis; which letters, with his private writings, he published, and shortly found sic concurrence of Kyle and Cunynghame with his other friends, that the Carrick company drew back fra the house: and so the other approached, furnished the house with more men, delivered the said Mr. Allan, and carried him to Ayr, where, publicly at the market cross of the said town, he declared how cruelly he was entreated, and how the murdered King suffered not sic torment as he did, excepting only he escaped the death: and, therefore, publickly did revoke all things that were done in that extremity, and especially he revoked the subscription of the three writings, to wit, of a fyve yeir tack and nineteen year tack, and of a charter of feu. And so the house remained, and remains (till this day, the 7th of February 1571), in the custody of the said Laird of Bargany and of his servants. And so cruelty was disappointed of proffeit present, and shall be eternallie punished, unless he earnestly repent. And this far for the cruelty committed, to give occasion unto others, and to such as hate the monstrous dealing of degenerate nobility, to look more diligently upon their behaviours, and to paint them forth unto the world, that they themselves may be ashamed of their own beastliness, and that the world may be advertised and admonished to abhor, detest, and avoid the company of all sic tyrants, who are not worthy of the society of men, but ought to be sent suddenly to the devil, with whom they must burn without end, for their contempt of God, and cruelty committed against his creatures. Let Cassilis and his brother be the first to be the example unto others. Amen. Amen." [1]

This extract has been somewhat amended or modernised in orthography, to render it more intelligible to the general reader. I have to add, that the Kennedies of Bargany, who interfered in behalf of the oppressed Abbot, were themselves a younger branch of the Cassilis family, but held different politics, and were powerful enough in this, and other instances, to bid them defiance.

The ultimate issue of this affair does not appear; but as the house of Cassilis are still in possession of the greater part of the feus and leases which belonged to Cross-raguel Abbey, it is probable the talons of the King of Carrick were strong enough, in those disorderly times, to retain the prey which they had so mercilessly fixed upon.

I may also add, that it appears by some papers in my possession, that the officers or Country Keepers on the border, were accustomed to torment their prisoners by binding them to the iron bars of their chimneys, to extort confession.

VI.—p. 640.—ULRICA'S DEATH SONG

It will readily occur to the antiquary, that these verses are intended to imitate the antique poetry of the Scalds—the minstrels of the old Scandinavians—the race, as the Laureate so happily terms them,

> "Stern to inflict and stubborn to endure,
> Who smiled in death."

The poetry of the Anglo-Saxons, after their civilisation and conversion, was of a different and softer character; but in the circumstances of Ulrica, she may be not unnaturally supposed to return to the wild strains which animated her forefathers during the time of Paganism and untamed ferocity.

VII.—p. 650.—RICHARD CŒUR-DE-LION

The interchange of a cuff with the jolly priest is not entirely out of character with Richard I., if romances read him aright. In the very curious romance on the subject of his adventures in the Holy Land, and his return from thence, it is recorded how he exchanged a pugilistic favour of this nature, while a prisoner in Germany. His opponent was the son of his principal warder, and was so imprudent as to give the challenge to this barter of buffets. The King stood forth like a true man, and received a blow which staggered him. In requital, having previously waxed his hand, a practice unknown, I believe, to the gentleman of the modern fancy, he returned the box on the ear with such interest as to kill his antagonist on the spot.—See, in Ellis's *Specimens of English Romance,* that of Cœur-de-Lion.

VIII.—p. 660.—HEDGE-PRIESTS

It is curious to observe, that in every state of society, some sort of ghostly consolation is provided for the members of the community, though assembled for purposes diametrically opposite to religion. A gang of beggars have their Patrico, and the banditti of the Apennines have among them persons acting as monks and priests, by whom they are confessed, and who perform mass before them. Unquestionably, such reverend persons, in such a society, must accommodate their manners and their morals to the community in which they live; and if they can occasionally obtain a degree of reverence for their supposed spiritual gifts, are, on most occasions, loaded

[1] Bannatyne's *Journal.*

with unmerciful ridicule, as possessing a character inconsistent with all around them.

Hence the fighting parson in the old play of Sir John Oldcastle, and the famous friar of Robin Hood's band. Nor were such characters ideal. There exists a monition of the Bishop of Durham against irregular churchmen of this class, who associated themselves with Border robbers, and desecrated the holiest offices of the priestly function, by celebrating them for the benefit of thieves, robbers, and murderers, amongst ruins and in caverns of the earth without regard to canonical form, and with torn and dirty attire, and maimed rites, altogether improper for the occasion.

IX.—p. 730.—CASTLE OF CONINGSBURGH

When I last saw this interesting ruin of ancient days, one of the very few remaining examples of Saxon fortification, I was strongly impressed with the desire of tracing out a sort of theory on the subject, which, from some recent acquaintance with the architecture of the ancient Scandinavians, seemed to me peculiarly interesting. I was, however, obliged by circumstances to proceed on my journey, without leisure to take more than a transient view of Coningsburgh. Yet the idea dwells so strongly in my mind, that I feel considerably tempted to write a page or two in detailing at least the outline of my hypothesis, leaving better antiquaries to correct or refute conclusions which are perhaps too hastily drawn.

Those who have visited the Zetland Islands are familiar with the description of castles called by the inhabitants Burghs; and by the Highlanders—for they are also to be found both in the Western Isles and on the mainland—Duns. Pennant has engraved a view of the famous Dun Dornadilla in Glenelg; and there are many others, all of them built after a peculiar mode of architecture, which argues a people in the most primitive state of society. The most perfect specimen is that upon the island of Mousa, near to the mainland of Zetland, which is probably in the same state as when inhabited.

It is a single round tower, the wall curving in slightly, and then turning outward again in the form of a dice-box, so that the defenders on the top might the better protect the base. It is formed of rough stones, selected with care, and laid in courses of circles, with much compactness, but without cement of any kind. The tower has never, to appearance, had roofing of any sort; a fire was made in the centre of the space which it encloses, and originally the building was probably little more than a wall drawn as a sort of screen around the great council fire of the tribe. But, although the means or ingenuity of the builders did not extend so far as to provide a roof, they supplied the want by constructing apartments in the interior of the walls of the tower itself. The circumvallation formed a double enclosure, the inner side of which was, in fact, two feet or three feet distant from the other, and connected by a concentric range of long flat stones, thus forming a series of concentric rings or stories of various heights, rising to the top of the tower. Each of these stories or galleries has four windows, facing directly to the points of the compass, and rising of course regularly above each other. These four perpendicular ranges of windows admitted air, and, the fire being kindled, heat, or smoke at least, to each of the galleries. The access from gallery to gallery is equally primitive. A path, on the principle of an inclined plane, turns round and round the building like a screw, and gives access to the different stories, intersecting each of them in its turn, and thus gradually rising to the top of the wall of the tower. On the outside there are no windows; and I may add, that an enclosure of a square, or sometimes a round form, gave the inhabitants of the Burgh an opportunity to secure any sheep or cattle which they might possess.

Such is the general architecture of that very early period when the Northmen swept the seas, and brought to their rude houses, such as I have described them, the plunder of polished nations. In Zetland there are several scores of these Burghs, occupying in every case, capes, headlands, islets, and similar places of advantage singularly well chosen. I remember the remains of one upon an island in a small lake near Lerwick, which at high tide communicates with the sea, the access to which is very ingenious, by means of a causeway or dike, about three or four inches under the surface of the water. This causeway makes a sharp angle in its approach to the Burgh. The inhabitants, doubtless, were well acquainted with this, but strangers, who might approach in a hostile manner, and were ignorant of the curve in the causeway, would probably plunge into the lake, which is six or seven feet in depth at the least. This must have been the device of some Vauban or Cohorn of those early times.

The style of these buildings evinces that the architect possessed neither the art of using lime or cement of any kind, nor the skill to throw an arch, construct a roof, or erect a stair; and yet, with all this ignorance, showed great ingenuity in selecting the situation of Burghs, and regulating the access to them, as well as neatness and regularity in the erection, since the buildings themselves show a style of advance in the arts scarcely consistent with the ignorance of so many of the principal branches of architectural knowledge.

I have always thought, that one of the most curious and valuable objects of antiquaries has been to trace the progress of society, by the efforts made in early ages to improve the rudeness of their first expedients, until they either approach excellence, or, as is most frequently the case, are supplied by new and fundamental discoveries, which supersede both the earlier and ruder system, and the improvements which have been ingrafted upon it. For example, if we conceive the recent discovery of gas to be so much improved and adapted to domestic use, as to supersede all other modes of producing domestic light; we can already suppose, some centuries afterwards, the heads of a whole Society of Antiquaries half turned by the discovery of a pair of patent snuffers, and by the learned theories which would be brought forward to account for the form and purpose of so singular an implement.

Following some such principle, I am inclined to regard the singular Castle of Coningsburgh—I mean the Saxon part of it—as a step in advance from the rude architecture, if it deserves the name, which must have been common to the Saxons as to other Northmen. The builders had attained the art of using cement, and of roofing a building,—great improvements on the original Burgh. But in the round keep, a shape only seen in the most ancient castles—the chambers excavated in the thickness of the walls and buttresses—the difficulty by which access is gained from one story to those above it, Coningsburgh still retains the simplicity of its origin, and shows by what slow degrees man proceeded from occupying such rude and inconvenient lodgings, as were afforded by the galleries of the Castle of Mousa, to the more splendid accommodations of the Norman castles, with all their stern and Gothic graces.

I am ignorant if these remarks are new, or if they will be confirmed by closer examination but I think, that, on a hasty observation, Coningsburgh offers means of curious study to those who may wish to trace the history of architecture back to the times preceding the Norman Conquest.

It would be highly desirable that a cork model should be taken of the Castle of Mousa, as it cannot be well understood by a plan.

The Castle of Coningsburgh is thus described:—

"The castle is large, the outer walls standing on a pleasant ascent from the river, but much overtopt by a high hill, on which the town stands, situated at the head of a rich and magnificent vale, formed by an amphitheatre of woody hills, in which flows the gentle Don. Near the castle is a barrow, said to be Hengist's tomb. The entrance is flanked to the left by a round tower, with a sloping base, and there are several similar in the outer wall; the entrance has piers of a gate, and on the east side the ditch and bank are double and very steep. On the top of the churchyard wall is a tombstone, on which are cut in high relief, two ravens, or such-like birds. On the south side of the churchyard lies an ancient stone, ridged like a coffin, on which is carved a man on horseback; and another man with a shield encountering a vast winged serpent, and a man bearing a shield behind him. It was probably one of the rude crosses not uncommon in churchyards in this county. The name of Coningsburgh, by which this castle goes in the old editions of the Britannia, would lead one to suppose it the residence of the Saxon kings. It afterwards belonged to King Harold. The Conqueror bestowed it on William de Warren, with all its privileges and jurisdiction, which are said to have extended over twenty-eight towns. At the corner of the area, which is of an irregular form, stands the great tower, or keep, placed on a small hill of its own dimensions, on which lies six vast projecting buttresses, ascending in a steep direction to prop and support the building, and continued upwards up the side as turrets. The tower within forms a complete circle, twenty-one feet in diameter, the walls fourteen feet thick. The ascent into the tower is by an exceeding deep flight of steep steps, four feet and a half wide, on the south side leading to a low doorway, over which is a circular arch crossed by a great transom stone. Within this door is the staircase which ascends straight through the thickness of the wall, not communicating with the room on the first floor, in whose centre is the opening to the dungeon. Neither of these lower rooms is lighted except from a hole in the floor of the third story; the room in which, as well as in that above it, is finished with compact smooth stonework, both having chimney-pieces, with an arch resting on triple clustered pillars. In the third story, or guard-chamber, is a small recess with a loop-hole, probably a bed-chamber, and in that floor above a niche for a saint or holy-water pot. Mr. King imagines this a Saxon castle of the first ages of the Heptarchy. Mr. Watson thus describes it. From the first floor to the second story (third from the ground) is a way by a stair in the wall five feet wide. The next staircase is approached by a ladder, and ends at the fourth story from the ground. Two yards from the door, at the head of this stair, is an opening nearly east, accessible by treading on the ledge of the wall, which diminishes eight inches each story; and this last opening leads into a room or chapel ten feet by twelve, and fifteen or sixteen high, arched with freestone, and supported by small circular columns of the same, the capitals and arches Saxon. It has an east window, and on each side in the wall, about four feet from the ground, a stone basin, with a hole and iron pipe to convey the water into or through the wall. This chapel is one of the buttresses, but no sign of it without, for even the window, though large within, is only a long narrow loop-hole, scarcely to be seen without. On the left side of this chapel is a small oratory, eight by six in the thickness of the wall, with a niche in the wall, and enlightened by a like loop-hole. The fourth stair from the ground, ten feet west from the chapel door, leads to the top of the tower through the thickness of the wall, which at top is but three yards. Each story is about fifteen feet high, so that the tower will be seventy-five feet from the ground. The inside forms a circle, whose diameter may be about twelve feet. The well at the bottom of the dungeon is piled with stones."—GOUGH's *Edition of Gamden's Britannia.* Second Edition, vol. iii. p. 267.

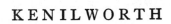

KENILWORTH

KENILWORTH

CHAPTER I

I am an innkeeper, and know my grounds,
And study them; Brain o' man, I study them.
I must have jovial guests to drive my ploughs,
And whistling boys to bring my harvests home,
Or I shall hear no flails thwack.

The New Inn.

IT is the privilege of tale-tellers to open their story in an inn, the free rendezvous of all travellers, and where the humour of each displays itself,
without ceremony or restraint. This is specially suitable when the scene
is laid during the old days of merry England, when the guests were in
some sort not merely the inmates, but the messmates and temporary
companions of mine Host, who was usually a personage of privileged
freedom, comely presence, and good-humour. Patronised by him, the
characters of the company were placed in ready contrast; and they
seldom failed, during the emptying of a six-hooped pot, to throw off
reserve, and present themselves to each other, and to their landlord, with
the freedom of old acquaintance.

The village of Cumnor, within three or four miles of Oxford, boasted,
during the eighteenth of Queen Elizabeth, an excellent inn of the old
stamp, conducted, or rather ruled, by Giles Gosling, a man of a goodly
person, and of somewhat round belly; fifty years of age and upwards,
moderate in his reckonings, prompt in his payments, having a cellar of
sound liquor, a ready wit, and a pretty daughter. Since the days of old
Harry Baillie of the Tabbard in Southwark, no one had excelled Giles
Gosling in the power of pleasing his guests of every description; and so
great was his fame, that to have been in Cumnor, without wetting a cup
at the bonny Black Bear, would have been to avouch one's-self utterly
indifferent to reputation as a traveller. A country fellow might as well
return from London, without looking in the face of majesty. The men
of Cumnor were proud of their Host, and their Host was proud of his
house, his liquor, his daughter, and himself.

It was in the court-yard of the inn which called this honest fellow
landlord, that a traveller alighted in the close of the evening, gave his
horse, which seemed to have made a long journey, to the hostler, and
made some enquiry, which produced the following dialogue betwixt the
myrmidons of the bonny Black Bear.

"What, ho! John Tapster."

"At hand, Will Hostler," replied the man of the spigot, showing himself in his costume of loose jacket, linen breeches, and green apron, half within and half without a door, which appeared to descend to an outer cellar.

"Here is a gentleman asks if you draw good ale," continued the hostler.

"Beshrew my heart else," answered the tapster, "since there are but four miles betwixt us and Oxford.—Marry, if my ale did not convince the heads of the scholars, they would soon convince my pate with the pewter flagon."

"Call you that Oxford logic?" said the stranger, who had now quitted the rein of his horse, and was advancing towards the inn-door, when he was encountered by the goodly form of Giles Gosling himself.

"Is it logic you talk of, Sir Guest?" said the host; "why, then, have at you with a downright consequence—

'The horse to the rack,
And to fire with the sack.'"

"Amen! with all my heart, my good host," said the stranger; "let it be a quart of your best Canaries, and give me your good help to drink it."

"Nay, you are but in your accidence yet, Sir Traveller, if you call on your host for help for such a sipping matter as a quart of sack—were it a gallon, you might lack some neighbourly aid at my hand, and yet call yourself a toper."

"Fear me not," said the guest, "I will do my devoir as becomes a man who finds himself within five miles of Oxford; for I am not come from the field of Mars to discredit myself amongst the followers of Minerva."

As he spoke thus, the landlord, with much semblance of hearty welcome, ushered his guest into a large low chamber, where several persons were seated together in different parties; some drinking, some playing at cards, some conversing, and some, whose business called them to be early risers on the morrow, concluding their evening meal, and conferring with the chamberlain about their night's quarters.

The entrance of a stranger procured him that general and careless sort of attention which is usually paid on such occasions, from which the following results were deduced:—The guest was one of those who, with a well-made person, and features not in themselves unpleasing, are nevertheless so far from handsome, that, whether from the expression of their features, or the tone of their voice, or from their gait and manner, there arises, on the whole, a disinclination to their society. The stranger's address was bold, without being frank, and seemed eagerly and hastily to claim for him a degree of attention and deference, which he feared would be refused, if not instantly vindicated as his right. His attire was a riding-cloak, which, when open, displayed a handsome jerkin overlaid with lace, and belted with a buff girdle, which sustained a broadsword and a pair of pistols.

"You ride well provided, sir," said the host, looking at the weapons as he placed on the table the mulled sack which the traveller had ordered.

"Yes, mine host; I have found the use on't in dangerous times, and I do not, like your modern grandees, turn off my followers the instant they are useless."

"Ay, sir?" said Giles Gosling; "then you are from the Low Countries, the land of pike and caliver?"

"I have been high and low, my friend, broad and wide, far and near; but here is to thee in a cup of thy sack—fill thyself another to pledge me; and, if it is less than superlative, e'en drink as you have brewed."

"Less than superlative?" said Giles Gosling, drinking of the cup, and smacking his lips with an air of ineffable relish,—"I know nothing of superlative, nor is there such a wine at the Three Cranes, in the Vintry, to my knowledge; but if you find better sack than that in the Sheres, or in the Canaries either, I would I may never touch either pot or penny more. Why, hold it up betwixt you and the light, you shall see the little motes dance in the golden liquor like dust in the sunbeam. But I would rather draw wine for ten clowns than one traveller.—I trust your honour likes the wine?"

"It is neat and comfortable, mine host; but to know good liquor, you should drink where the vine grows. Trust me, your Spaniard is too wise a man to send you the very soul of the grape. Why, this now, which you account so choice, were counted but as a cup of bastard at the Groyne, or at Port St. Mary's. You should travel, mine host, if you would be deep in the mysteries of the butt and pottle-pot."

"In troth, Signior Guest," said Giles Gosling, "if I were to travel only that I might be discontented with that which I can get at home, methinks I should go but on a fool's errand. Besides, I warrant you, there is many a fool can turn his nose up at good drink without ever having been out of the smoke of Old England; and so ever gramercy mine own fireside."

"This is but a mean mind of yours, mine host," said the stranger; "I warrant me, all your town's folk do not think so basely. You have gallants among you, I dare undertake, that have made the Virginia voyage, or taken a turn in the Low Countries at least. Come, cudgel your memory. Have you no friends in foreign parts that you would gladly have tidings of?"

"Troth, sir, not I," answered the host, "since ranting Robin of Drysandford was shot at the siege of the Brill. The devil take the caliver that fired the ball, for a blither lad never filled a cup at midnight! But he is dead and gone, and I know not a soldier, or a traveller, who is a soldier's mate, that I would give a peeled codling for."

"By the mass, that is strange. What! so many of our brave English hearts are abroad, and you, who seem to be a man of mark, have no friend, no kinsman, among them?"

"Nay, if you speak of kinsmen," answered Gosling, "I have one wild slip of a kinsman, who left us in the last year of Queen Mary; but he is better lost than found."

"Do not say so, friend, unless you have heard ill of him lately. Many a wild colt has turned out a noble steed.—His name, I pray you?"

"Michael Lambourne," answered the landlord of the Black Bear; "a son of my sister's—there is little pleasure in recollecting either the name or the connexion."

"Michael Lambourne!" said the stranger, as if endeavouring to recollect himself—"what, no relation to Michael Lambourne, the gallant cavalier who behaved so bravely at the siege of Venlo, that Grave Maurice thanked him at the head of the army? Men said he was an English cavalier, and of no high extraction."

"It could scarcely be my nephew," said Giles Gosling, "for he had not the courage of a hen-partridge for aught but mischief."

"O, many a man finds courage in the wars," replied the stranger.

"It may be," said the landlord; "but I would have thought our Mike more likely to lose the little he had."

"The Michael Lambourne whom I knew," continued the traveller, "was a likely fellow—went always gay and well attired, and had a hawk's eye after a pretty wench."

"Our Michael," replied the host, "had the look of a dog with a bottle at its tail, and wore a coat, every rag of which was bidding good-day to the rest."

"O, men pick up good apparel in the wars," replied the guest.

"Our Mike," answered the landlord, "was more like to pick it up in a frippery warehouse, while the broker was looking another way; and, for the hawk's eye you talk of, his was always after my stray spoons. He was tapster's boy here in this blessed house for a quarter of a year; and between misreckonings, miscarriages, mistakes, and misdemeanours, had he dwelt with me for three months longer, I might have pulled down sign, shut up house, and given the devil the key to keep."

"You would be sorry, after all," continued the traveller, "were I to tell you poor Mike Lambourne was shot at the head of his regiment at the taking of a sconce near Maestricht?"

"Sorry!—it would be the blithest news I ever heard of him, since it would ensure me he was not hanged. But let him pass—I doubt his end will never do such credit to his friends: were it so, I should say"—(taking another cup of sack)—"Here's God rest him, with all my heart."

"Tush, man," replied the traveller, "never fear but you will have credit by your nephew yet, especially if he be the Michael Lambourne whom I knew, and loved very nearly, or altogether, as well as myself. Can you tell me no mark by which I could judge whether they be the same?"

"Faith, none that I can think of," answered Giles Gosling, "unless that our Mike had the gallows branded on his left shoulder for stealing a silver caudle-cup from Dame Snort of Hogsditch."

"Nay, there you lie like a knave, uncle," said the stranger, slipping aside his ruff, and turning down the sleeve of his doublet from his neck and shoulder; "by this good day, my shoulder is as unscarred as thine own."

"What, Mike, boy—Mike!" exclaimed the host;—"and is it thou, in good earnest? Nay, I have judged so for this half hour; for I knew no other person would have ta'en half the interest in thee. But, Mike, an thy shoulder be unscathed as thou sayest, thou must own that Goodman Thong, the hangman, was merciful in his office, and stamped thee with a cold iron."

"Tush, uncle—truce with your jests. Keep them to season your sour ale, and let us see what hearty welcome thou wilt give a kinsman who has rolled the world around for eighteen years; who has seen the sun set where it rises, and has travelled till the west has become the east."

"Thou hast brought back one traveller's gift with thee, Mike, as I well see; and that was what thou least didst need to travel for. I remembered well, among thine other qualities, there was no crediting a word which came from thy mouth."

"Here's an unbelieving Pagan for you, gentlemen!" said Michael Lambourne, turning to those who witnessed this strange interview betwixt uncle and nephew, some of whom, being natives of the village, were no strangers to his juvenile wildness. "This may be called slaying a Cumnor fatted calf for me with a vengeance.—But, uncle, I come not from the husks and the swine-trough, and I care not for thy welcome or no welcome; I carry that with me will make me welcome, wend where I will."

So saying, he pulled out a purse of gold, indifferently well filled, the sight of which produced a visible effect upon the company. Some shook their heads, and whispered to each other, while one or two of the less scrupulous speedily began to recollect him as a school-companion, a townsman, or so forth. On the other hand, two or three grave sedate-looking persons shook their heads, and left the inn, hinting, that, if Giles Gosling wished to continue to thrive, he should turn his thriftless, godless nephew adrift again as soon as he could. Gosling demeaned himself as if he were much of the same opinion; for even the sight of the gold made less impression on the honest gentleman, than it usually doth upon one of his calling.

"Kinsman Michael," he said, "put up thy purse. My sister's son shall be called to no reckoning in my house for supper or lodging; and I reckon thou wilt hardly wish to stay longer, where thou art e'en but too well known."

"For that matter, uncle," replied the traveller, "I shall consult my own needs and conveniences. Meantime I wish to give the supper and sleeping cup to those good townsmen, who are not too proud to remember Mike Lambourne, the tapster's boy. If you will let me have entertainment for my money, so—if not, it is but a short two minutes' walk to the Hare and Tabor, and I trust our neighbours will not grudge going thus far with me."

"Nay, Mike," replied his uncle, "as eighteen years have gone over thy head, and I trust thou art somewhat amended in thy conditions, thou shalt not leave my house at this hour, and shalt e'en have whatever in reason you list to call for. But I would I knew that that purse of thine, which thou vapourest of, were as well come by as it seems well filled."

"Here is an infidel for you, my good neighbours!" said Lambourne, again appealing to the audience. "Here's a fellow will rip up his kinsman's follies of a good score of years standing—And for the gold, why, sirs, I have been where it grew, and was to be had for the gathering. In the New World have I been, man—in the Eldorado, where urchins play at cherry-pit with diamonds, and country wenches thread rubies for necklaces; instead of rowan-tree berries; where the pantiles are made of pure gold, and the paving-stones of virgin silver."

"By my credit. friend Mike," said young Laurence Goldthred, the cutting mercer of Abingdon, "that were a likely coast to trade to. And what may lawns, cypruses, and ribands fetch, where gold is so plenty?"

"O, the profit were unutterable," replied Lambourne, "especially when a handsome young merchant bears the pack himself; for the ladies of that clime are bona-robas, and being themselves somewhat sunburnt, they catch fire like tinder at a fresh complexion like thine, with a head of hair inclining to be red."

"I would I might trade thither," said the mercer, chuckling.

"Why, and so thou mayst," said Michael; "that is, if thou art the same brisk boy who was partner with me at robbing the Abbot's orchard—'tis but a little touch of alchymy to decoct thy house and land into ready money, and that ready money into a tall ship, with sails, anchors, cordage, and all things conforming; then clap thy warehouse of goods under hatches, put fifty good fellows on deck, with myself to command them, and so hoist topsails, and hey for the New World!"

"Thou hast taught him a secret, kinsman," said Giles Gosling, "to decoct, an that be the word, his pound into a penny, and his webs into a thread.—Take a fool's advice, neighbour Goldthred. Tempt not the sea, for she is a devourer. Let cards and cockatrices do their worst, thy father's bales may bide a banging for a year or two, ere thou comest to the Spital; but the sea has a bottomless appetite,—she would swallow the wealth of Lombard Street in a morning, as easily as I would a poached egg and a cup of clary;—and for my kinsman's Eldorado, never trust me if I do not believe he has found it in the pouches of some such gulls as thyself.—But take no snuff in the nose about it; fall to and welcome, for here comes the supper, and I heartily bestow it on all that will take share, in honour of my hopeful nephew's return, always trusting that he has come home another man—In faith, kinsman, thou art as like my poor sister as ever was son to mother."

"Not quite so like old Benedict Lambourne her husband, though," said the mercer, nodding and winking. "Dost thou remember, Mike, what thou saidst when the schoolmaster's ferule was over thee for striking up thy father's crutches?—it is a wise child, saidst thou, that knows its own father. Dr. Bricham laughed till he cried again, and his crying saved yours."

"Well, he made it up to me many a day after," said Lambourne; "and how is the worthy pedagogue?"

"Dead," said Giles Gosling, "this many a day since."

"That he is," said the clerk of the parish; "I sat by his bed the whilst —He passed away in a blessed frame, '*Morior—mortuus sum vel fui— mori*'—These were his latest words, and he just added, 'my last verb is conjugated.'"

"Well, peace be with him," said Mike, "he owes me nothing."

"No, truly," replied Goldthred; "and every lash which he laid on thee, he always was wont to say he spared the hangman a labour."

"One would have thought he left him little to do then," said the clerk; "and yet Goodman Thong had no sinecure of it with our friend, after all."

"*Voto a dios!*" exclaimed Lambourne, his patience appearing to fail him, as he snatched his broad slouched hat from the table and placed it on his head, so that the shadow gave the sinister expression of a Spanish bravo, to eyes and features which naturally boded nothing pleasant. "Harkee, my masters—all is fair among friends, and under the rose; and I have already permitted my worthy uncle here, and all of you, to use your pleasure with the frolics of my nonage. But I carry a sword and dagger, my good friends, and can use them lightly too upon oc- casion—I have learned to be dangerous upon points of honour ever since I served the Spaniard, and I would not have you provoke me to the degree of falling foul."

"Why, what would you do?" said the clerk.

"Ay, sir, what would you do?" said the mercer, bustling up on the other side of the table.

"Slit your throat, and spoil your Sunday's quavering, Sir Clerk," said Lambourne, fiercely; "cudgel you, my worshipful dealer in flimsy sarsenets, into one of your own bales."

"Come, come," said the host, interposing, "I will have no swaggering here.—Nephew, it will become you best to show no haste to take of- fence; and you, gentlemen, will do well to remember, that if you are in an inn, still you are the inn-keeper's guests, and should spare the honour of his family.—I protest your silly broils make me as oblivious as yourself; for yonder sits my silent guest as I call him, who hath been my two days' inmate, and hath never spoken a word, save to ask for his food and his reckoning—gives no more trouble than a very peasant

—pays his shot like a prince royal—looks but at the sum total of the reckoning, and does not know what day he shall go away. O, 'tis a jewel of a guest! and yet, hang-dog that I am, I have suffered him to sit by himself like a castaway in yonder obscure nook, without so much as asking him to take bite or sup along with us. It were but the right guerdon of my incivility, were he to set off to the Hare and Tabor before the night grows older."

With his white napkin gracefully arranged over his left arm, his velvet cap laid aside for the moment, and his best silver flagon in his right hand, mine host walked up to the solitary guest whom he mentioned, and thereby turned upon him the eyes of the assembled company.

He was a man aged betwixt twenty-five and thirty, rather above the middle size, dressed with plainness and decency, yet bearing an air of ease, which almost amounted to dignity, and which seemed to infer that his habit was rather beneath his rank. His countenance was reserved and thoughtful, with dark hair and dark eyes—the last, upon any momentary excitement, sparkled with uncommon lustre, but on other occasions had the same meditative and tranquil cast which was exhibited by his features. The busy curiosity of the little village had been employed to discover his name and quality, as well as his business at Cumnor; but nothing had transpired on either subject which could lead to its gratification. Giles Gosling, head-borough of the place, and a steady friend to Queen Elizabeth and the Protestant religion, was at one time inclined to suspect his guest of being a Jesuit, or seminary priest, of whom Rome and Spain sent at this time so many to grace the gallows in England. But it was scarce possible to retain such a prepossession against a guest who gave so little trouble, paid his reckoning so regularly, and who proposed, as it seemed, to make a considerable stay at the bonny Black Bear.

"Papists," argued Giles Gosling, "are a pinching, close-fisted race, and this man would have found a lodging with the wealthy squire at Bessellsley, or with the old Knight at Wootton, or in some other of their Roman dens, instead of living in a house of public entertainment, as every honest man and good Christian should. Besides, on Friday, he stuck by the salt beef and carrot, though there were as good spitch-cock'd eels on the board as ever were ta'en out of the Isis."

Honest Giles, therefore, satisfied himself that his guest was no Roman, and with all comely courtesy besought the stranger to pledge him in a draught of the cool tankard, and honour with his attention a small collation which he was giving to his nephew, in honour of his return, and, as he verily hoped, of his reformation. The stranger at first shook his head, as if declining the courtesy; but mine host proceeded to urge him with arguments founded on the credit of his house, and the construction which the good people of Cumnor might put upon such an unsocial humour.

"By my faith, sir," he said, "it touches my reputation that men should be merry in my house, and we have ill tongues amongst us at Cumnor, (as where be there not?) who put an evil mark on men who pull their hat over their brows as if they were looking back to the days that are gone, instead of enjoying the blithe sunshiny weather which God has sent us in the sweet looks of our sovereign mistress, Queen Elizabeth, whom Heaven long bless and preserve!"

"Why, mine host," answered the stranger, "there is no treason, sure, in a man's enjoying his own thoughts, under the shadow of his own bonnet? You have lived in the world twice as long as I have and you must know there are thoughts that will haunt us in spite of ourselves, and to which it is in vain to say, begone, and let me be merry."

"By my sooth," answered Giles Gosling, "if such troublesome thoughts haunt your mind, and will not get them gone for plain English, we will have one of Father Bacon's pupils from Oxford, to conjure them away with logic and with Hebrew—Or, what say you to laying them in a glorious red sea of claret, my noble guest? Come, sir, excuse my freedom. I am an old host, and must have my talk. This peevish humour of melancholy sits ill upon you—it suits not with a sleek boot, a hat of trim block, a fresh cloak, and a full purse. A pize on it, send it off to those who have their legs swathed with a hay-wisp, their heads thatched with a felt bonnet, their jerkins as thin as a cobweb, and their pouch without ever a cross to keep the fiend Melancholy from dancing on it. Cheer up, sir! or, by this good liquor, we will banish thee from the joys of blithesome company, into the mists of melancholy and the land of little-ease. Here be a set of good fellows willing to be merry; do not scowl on them like the devil looking over Lincoln."

"You say well, my worthy host," said the guest, with a melancholy smile, which, melancholy as it was, gave a very pleasant expression to his countenance—"You say well, my jovial friend; and they that are moody like myself, should not disturb the mirth of those who are happy —I will drink a round with your guests with all my heart, rather than be termed a mar-feast."

So saying, he arose and joined the company, who, encouraged by the precept and example of Michael Lambourne, and consisting chiefly of persons much disposed to profit by the opportunity of a merry meal at the expense of their landlord, had already made some inroads upon the limits of temperance, as was evident from the tone in which Michael enquired after his old acquaintances in the town, and the bursts of laughter with which each answer was received. Giles Gosling himself was somewhat scandalized at the obstreperous nature of their mirth, especially as he involuntarily felt some respect for his unknown guest. He paused, therefore, at some distance from the table occupied by these noisy revellers, and began to make a sort of apology for their license.

"You would think," he said, "to hear these fellows talk, that there was not one of them who had not been bred to live by Stand and Deliver; and yet to-morrow you will find them a set of as painstaking mechanics, and so forth, as ever cut an inch short of measure, or paid a letter of change in light crowns over a counter. The mercer there wears his hat awry, over a shagged head of hair, that looks like a curly water-dog's back, goes unbraced, wears his cloak on one side, and affects a ruffianly vapouring humour—when in his shop at Abingdon, he is, from his flat cap to his glistening shoes, as precise in his apparel as if he was named for mayor. He talks of breaking parks, and taking the highway, in such fashion that you would think he haunted every night betwixt Hounslow and London; when in fact he may be found sound asleep on his feather-bed, with a candle placed beside him on one side, and a Bible on the other, to fright away the goblins."

"And your nephew, mine host, this same Michael Lambourne, who is lord of the feast—is he, too, such an would-be ruffler as the rest of them?"

"Why, there you push me hard," said the host; "my nephew is my nephew, and though he was a desperate Dick of yore, yet Mike may have mended like other folks, you wot—And I would not have you think all I said of him, even now, was strict gospel—I knew the wag all the while, and wished to pluck his plumes from him—And now, sir, by what name shall I present my worshipful guest to these gallants?"

"Marry, mine host," replied the stranger, "you may call me Tressilian?"

"Tressilian?" answered mine host of the Bear; "a worthy name; and, as I think, of Cornish lineage; for what says the south proverb—

'By Pol, Tre, and Pen,
You may know the Cornish men.'

Shall I say the worthy Mr. Tressilian of Cornwall?"

"Say no more than I have given you warrant for, mine host, and so shall you be sure you speak no more than is true. A man may have one of those honourable prefixes to his name, yet be born far from Saint Michael's Mount."

Mine host pushed his curiosity no farther, but presented Mr. Tressilian to his nephew's company, who, after exchange of salutations, and drinking to the health of their new companion, pursued the conversation in which he found them engaged, seasoning it with many an intervening pledge.

CHAPTER II

Talk you of young Master Lancelot?
Merchant of Venice.

AFTER some brief interval, Master Goldthred, at the earnest instigation of mine host, and the joyous concurrence of his guest, indulged the company with the following morsel of melody:

"Of all the birds on bush or tree,
Commend me to the owl,
Since he may best ensample be
To those the cup that trowl.
For when the sun hath left the west,
He chooses the tree that he loves the best,
And he whoops out his song, and he laughs at his jest,
Then though hours be late, and weather foul,
We'll drink to the health of the bonny, bonny owl.

"The lark is but a bumpkin fowl,
He sleeps in his nest till morn;
But my blessing upon the jolly owl,
That all night blows his horn.
Then up with your cup till you stagger in speech,
And match me this catch till you swagger and screech,
And drink till you wink, my merry men each;
For though hours be late, and weather be foul,
We'll drink to the health of the bonny, bonny owl."

"There is savour in this, my hearts," said Michael, when the mercer had finished his song, "and some goodness seems left among you yet—but what a bead-roll you have read me of old comrades, and to every man's name tacked some ill-omened motto! And so Swashing Will of Wallingford hath bid us good-night?"

"He died the death of a fat buck," said one of the party, "being shot with a crossbow bolt, by old Thatcham, the Duke's stout park-keeper at Donnington Castle."

"Ay, ay, he always loved venison well," replied Michael, "and a cup of claret to boot—and so here's one to his memory. Do me right, my masters."

When the memory of this departed worthy had been duly honoured, Lambourne proceeded to enquire after Prance of Padworth.

"Pranced off—made immortal ten years since," said the mercer; "marry, sir, Oxford Castle and Goodman Thong, and the tenpenny-worth of cord, best know how."

"What, so they hung poor Prance high and dry? so much for loving to walk by moonlight—a cup to his memory, my masters—all merry fellows like moonlight. What has become of Hal with the Plume?—he who lived near Yattenden, and wore the long feather—I forget his name."

"What, Hal Hempseed?" replied the mercer, "why, you may remember he was a sort of a gentleman, and would meddle in state matters, and so he got into the mire about the Duke of Norfolk's affair these two or three years since, fled the country with a pursuivant's warrant at his heels, and has never since been heard of."

"Nay, after these baulks," said Michael Lambourne, "I need hardly enquire after Tony Foster; for when ropes, and crossbow shafts, and pursuivant's warrants, and such like gear, were so rife, Tony could hardly 'scape them."

"Which Tony Foster mean you?" said the innkeeper.

"Why, he they called Tony Fire-the-Fagot, because he brought a light to kindle the pile round Latimer and Ridley, when the wind blew out Jack Thong's torch, and no man else would give him light for love or money."

"Tony Foster lives and thrives," said the host.—"But, kinsman, I would not have you call him Tony Fire-the-Fagot, if you would not brook the stab."

"How! is he grown ashamed on't?" said Lambourne, "why, he was wont to boast of it, and say he liked as well to see a roasted heretic as a roasted ox."

"Ay, but, kinsman, that was in Mary's time," replied the landlord, "when Tony's father was Reeve here to the Abbot of Abingdon. But since that, Tony married a pure precisian, and is as good a Protestant, I warrant you, as the best."

"And looks grave, and holds his head high, and scorns his old companions," said the mercer.

"Then he hath prospered, I warrant him," said Lambourne; "for ever when a man hath got nobles of his own, he keeps out of the way of those whose exchequers lie in other men's purchase."

"Prospered, quotha!" said the mercer; "why, you remember Cumnor Place, the old mansion-house beside the churchyard?"

"By the same token, I robbed the orchard three times—what of that? —It was the old Abbot's residence when there was plague or sickness at Abingdon."

"Ay," said the host, "but that has been long over; and Anthony Foster hath a right in it, and lives there by some grant from a great courtier, who had the church-lands from the crown; and there he dwells, and has as little to do with any poor wight in Cumnor, as if he were himself a belted knight."

"Nay," said the mercer, "it is not altogether pride in Tony neither— there is a fair lady in the case, and Tony will scarce let the light of day look on her."

"How!" said Tressilian, who now for the first time interfered in their conversation, "did ye not say this Foster was married, and to a precisian?"

"Married he was, and to as bitter a precisian as ever eat flesh in Lent; and a cat-and-dog life she led with Tony, as men said. But she is dead, rest be with her, and Tony hath but a slip of a daughter; so it is thought he means to wed this stranger, that men keep such a coil about."

"And why so?—I mean, why do they keep a coil about her?" said Tressilian.

"Why, I wot not," answered the host, "except that men say she is as beautiful as an angel, and no one knows whence she comes, and every one wishes to know why she is kept so closely mewed up. For my part, I never saw her—you have, I think, Master Goldthred?"

"That I have, old boy," said the mercer. "Look you, I was riding hither from Abingdon—I passed under the east oriel window of the old mansion, where all the old saints and histories and suchlike are painted—It was not the common path I took, but one through the Park; for the postern-door was upon the latch, and I thought I might take the privilege of an old comrade to ride across through the trees, both for shading, as the day was somewhat hot, and for avoiding of dust, because I had on my peach-coloured doublet, pinked out with cloth of gold."

"Which garment," said Michael Lambourne, "thou wouldst willingly make twinkle in the eyes of a fair dame. Ah! villain, thou wilt never leave thy old tricks."

"Not so—not so," said the mercer, with a smirking laugh; "not altogether so—but curiosity, thou knowest, and a strain of compassion withal, —for the poor young lady sees nothing from morn to even but Tony Foster, with his scowling black brows, his bull's head, and his bandy legs."

"And thou wouldst willingly show her a dapper body, in a silken jerkin—a limb like a short-legged hen's, in a cordovan boot, and a round, simpering, what-d'ye-lack sort of a countenance, set off with a velvet bonnet, a Turkey feather, and a gilded brooch? Ah! jolly mercer, they who have good wares are fond to show them!—Come, gentles, let not the cup stand—here's to long spurs, short boots, full bonnets, and empty skulls!"

"Nay, now, you are jealous of me, Mike," said Goldthred; "and yet my luck was but what might have happened to thee, or any man."

"Marry confound thine impudence," retorted Lambourne; "thou wouldst not compare thy pudding face, and sarsenet manners, to a gentleman, and a soldier?"

"Nay, my good sir," said Tressilian, "let me beseech you will not interrupt the gallant citizen; methinks he tells his tale so well, I could hearken to him till midnight."

"It's more of your favour than of my desert," answered Master Goldthred; "but since I give you pleasure, worthy Master Tressilian, I shall proceed, maugre all the gibes and quips of this valiant soldier, who, peradventure, hath had more cuffs than crowns in the Low Countries.— And so, sir, as I passed under the great painted window, leaving my rein loose on my ambling palfrey's neck, partly for mine ease, and partly that I might have the more leisure to peer about, I hears me the lattice open; and never credit me, sir, if there did not stand there the person of as fair a woman as ever crossed mine eyes; and I think I have looked on as many pretty wenches, and with as much judgment, as other folks."

"May I ask her appearance, sir?" said Tressilian.

"O, sir," replied Master Goldthred, "I promise you, she was in gentlewoman's attire—a very quaint and pleasing dress, that might have served the Queen herself; for she had a forepart with body and sleeves, of ginger-coloured satin, which, in my judgment, must have cost by the yard some thirty shillings, lined with murrey taffeta, and laid down and guarded with two broad laces of gold and silver. And her hat, sir, was truly the best fashioned thing that I have seen in these parts, being of tawny taffeta, embroidered with scorpions of Venice gold, and having a border garnished with gold fringe;—I promise you, sir, an absolute and all-surpassing device. Touching her skirts, they were in the old pass-devant fashion."

"I did not ask you of her attire, sir," said Tressilian, who had shown some impatience during this conversation, "but of her complexion—the colour of her hair, her features."

"Touching her complexion," answered the mercer, "I am not so special certain; but I marked that her fan had an ivory handle, curiously inlaid;—and then again, as to the colour of her hair, why, I can warrant, be its hue what it might, that she wore above it a net of green silk, parcel twisted with gold."

"A most mercer-like memory," said Lambourne: "the gentleman asks him of the lady's beauty, and he talks of her fine clothes!"

"I tell thee," said the mercer, somewhat disconcerted, "I had little time to look at her; for just as I was about to give her the good time of day, and for that purpose had puckered my features with a smile——"

"Like those of a jackanape simpering at a chestnut," said Michael Lambourne.

—"Up started of a sudden," continued Goldthred, without heeding the interruption, "Tony Foster himself, with a cudgel in his hand——"

"And broke thy head across, I hope, for thine impertinence," said his entertainer.

"That were more easily said than done," answered Goldthred, indignantly; "no, no—there was no breaking of heads—it's true, he advanced his cudgel, and spoke of laying on, and asked why I did not keep the public road, and such like; and I would have knocked him over the pate handsomely for his pains, only for the lady's presence, who might have swooned, for what I know."

"Now, out upon thee for a faint-spirited slave!" said Lambourne; "what adventurous knight ever thought of the lady's terror, when he went to thwack giant, dragon, or magician, in her presence, and for her deliverance? But why talk to thee of dragons, who would be driven back by a dragon-fly. There thou hast missed the rarest opportunity!"

"Take it thyself, then, bully Mike," answered Goldthred.—"Yonder is the enchanted manor, and the dragon, and the lady, all at thy service, if thou darest venture on them."

"Why, so I would for a quartern of sack," said the soldier—"Or, stay --I am foully out of linen—wilt thou bet a piece of Hollands against these

five angels, that I go not up to the Hall to-morrow, and force Tony
Foster to introduce me to his fair guest?"

"I accept your wager," said the mercer; "and I think, though thou
hadst even the impudence of the devil, I shall gain on thee this bout.
Our landlord here shall hold stakes, and I will stake down gold till I
send the linen."

"I will hold stakes on no such matter," said Gosling. "Good now, my
kinsman, drink your wine in quiet, and let such ventures alone. I promise
you, Master Foster hath interest enough to lay you up in lavender
in the Castle at Oxford, or to get your legs made acquainted with the
town-stocks."

"That would be but renewing an old intimacy; for Mike's shins and
the town's wooden pinfold have been well known to each other ere now,"
said the mercer; "but he shall not budge from his wager, unless he means
to pay forfeit."

"Forfeit?" said Lambourne; "I scorn it. I value Tony Foster's wrath
no more than a shelled pea-cod; and I will visit his Lindabrides, by
Saint George, be he willing or no!"

"I would gladly pay your halves of the risk, sir," said Tressilian, "to
be permitted to accompany you on the adventure."

"In what would that advantage you, sir?" answered Lambourne.

"In nothing, sir," said Tressilian, "unless to mark the skill and valour
with which you conduct yourself. I am a traveller, who seeks for strange
rencounters and uncommon passages, as the knights of yore did after
adventures and feats of arms."

"Nay, if it pleasures you to see a trout tickled," answered Lambourne,
"I care not how many witness my skill. And so here I drink success to
my enterprise; and he that will not pledge me on his knees is a rascal,
and I will cut his legs off by the garters!"

The draught which Michael Lambourne took upon this occasion, had
been preceded by so many others, that reason tottered on her throne.
He swore one or two incoherent oaths at the mercer, who refused, reasonably enough, to pledge him to a sentiment which inferred the loss
of his own wager.

"Wilt thou chop logic with me," said Lambourne, "thou knave, with
no more brains than are in a skein of ravelled silk? by Heaven, I will
cut thee into fifty yards of galloon lace!"

But as he attempted to draw his sword for this doughty purpose,
Michael Lambourne was seized upon by the tapster and the chamberlain, and conveyed to his own apartment, there to sleep himself sober at
his leisure.

The party then broke up, and the guests took their leave; much more
to the contentment of mine host than of some of the company, who were
unwilling to quit good liquor, when it was to be had for free cost, so
long as they were able to sit by it. They were, however, compelled

to remove; and go at length they did, leaving Gosling and Tressilian in the empty apartment.

"By my faith," said the former, "I wonder where our great folks find pleasure, when they spend their means in entertainments, and in playing mine host without sending in a reckoning. It is what I but rarely practise; and whenever I do, by Saint Julian, it grieves me beyond measure. Each of these empty stoups now, which my nephew and his drunken comrades have swilled off, should have been a matter of profit to one in my line, and I must set them down a dead loss. I cannot, for my heart, conceive the pleasure of noise, and nonsense, and drunken freaks, and drunken quarrels, and smut, and blasphemy, and so forth, when a man loses money instead of gaining by it. And yet many a fair estate is lost in upholding such an useless course, and that greatly contributes to the decay of publicans; for who the devil do you think would pay for drink at the Black Bear, when he can have it for nothing at my Lord's or the Squire's?"

Tressilian perceived that the wine had made some impression even on the seasoned brain of mine host, which was chiefly to be inferred from his declaiming against drunkenness. As he himself had carefully avoided the bowl, he would have availed himself of the frankness of the moment, to extract from Gosling some further information upon the subject of Anthony Foster, and the lady whom the mercer had seen in his mansion-house; but his enquiries only set the host upon a new theme of declamation against the wiles of the fair sex, in which he brought, at full length the whole wisdom of Solomon to reinforce his own. Finally, he turned his admonitions, mixed with much objurgation, upon his tapsters and drawers, who were employed in removing the relics of the entertainment, and restoring order to the apartment; and at length, joining example to precept, though with no good success, he demolished a salver with half a score of glasses, in attempting to show how such service was done at the Three Cranes in the Vintry, then the most topping tavern in London. This last accident so far recalled him to his better self, that he retired to his bed, slept sound, and awoke a new man in the morning.

CHAPTER III

Nay, I'll hold touch—the game shall be play'd out,
It ne'er shall stop for me, this merry wager:
That which I say when gamesome, I'll avouch
In most sober mood, ne'er trust me else.
                                    The Hazard Table.

"AND how doth your kinsman, good mine host?" said Tressilian, when Giles Gosling first appeared in the public room, on the morning following the revel which we described in the last chapter. "Is he well, and will he abide by his wager?"

"For well, sir, he started two hours since, and has visited I know not what purlieus of his old companions; hath but now returned, and is at this instant breakfasting on new-laid eggs and muscadine; and for his wager, I caution you as a friend to have little to do with that, or indeed with aught that Mike proposes. Wherefore, I counsel you to a warm breakfast upon a culiss, which shall restore the tone of the stomach; and let my nephew and Master Goldthred swagger about their wager as they list."

"It seems to me, mine host," said Tressilian, "that you know not well what to say about this kinsman of yours; and that you can neither blame nor commend him without some twinge of conscience."

"You have spoken truly, Master Tressilian," replied Giles Gosling. "There is Natural Affection whimpering into one ear, 'Giles, Giles, why wilt thou take away the good name of thy own nephew? Wilt thou defame thy sister's son, Giles Gosling? wilt thou defoul thine own nest, dishonour thine own blood?' And then, again, comes Justice, and says, 'Here is a worthy guest as ever came to the bonny Black Bear; one who never challenged a reckoning,' (as I say to your face you never did, Master Tressilian—not that you have had cause,) 'one who knows not why he came, so far as I can see, or when he is going away; and wilt thou, being a publican, having paid scot and lot these thirty years in the town of Cumnor, and being at this instant head-borough, wilt thou suffer this guest of guests, this man of men, this six-hooped pot (as I may say) of a traveller, to fall into the meshes of thy nephew, who is known for a swasher and a desperate Dick, a carder and a dicer, a professor of the seven damnable sciences, if ever man took degrees in them?' No, by Heaven! I might wink, and let him catch such a small butterfly as Goldthred; but thou, my guest, shalt be forewarned, forearmed, so thou wilt but listen to thy trusty host."

"Why, mine host, thy counsel shall not be cast away," replied Tressilian; "however, I must uphold my share in this wager, having once passed my word to that effect. But lend me, I pray, some of thy counsel—This Foster, who or what is he, and why makes he such mystery of his female inmate?"

"Troth," replied Gosling, "I can add but little to what you heard last night. He was one of Queen Mary's Papists, and now he is one of Queen Elizabeth's Protestants; he was an on-hanger of the Abbot of Abingdon, and now he lives as master of the Manor-house. Above all, he was poor and is rich. Folk talk of private apartments in his old waste mansion-house, bedizened fine enough to serve the Queen, God bless her. Some men think he found a treasure in the orchard, some that he sold himself to the devil for treasure, and some say that he cheated the Abbot out of the church plate, which was hidden in the old Manor-house at the Reformation. Rich, however, he is, and God and his conscience, with the devil perhaps besides, only know how he came by it. He has sulky ways too, breaking off intercourse with all that are of the place, as if he had either some strange secret to keep, or held himself to be made of another clay than we are. I think it likely my kinsman and he will quarrel, if Mike thrust his acquaintance on him; and I am sorry that you, my worthy Master Tressilian, will still think of going in my nephew's company."

Tressilian again answered him, that he would proceed with great caution, and that he should have no fears on his account; in short, he bestowed on him all the customary assurances with which those who are determined on a rash action are wont to parry the advice of their friends.

Meantime, the traveller accepted the landlord's invitation, and had just finished the excellent breakfast, which was served to him and Gosling by pretty Cicely, the beauty of the bar, when the hero of the preceding night, Michael Lambourne, entered the apartment. His toilet had apparently cost him some labour, for his clothes, which differed from those he wore on his journey, were of the newest fashion, and put on with great attention to the display of his person.

"By my faith, uncle," said the gallant, "you made a wet night of it, and I feel it followed by a dry morning. I will pledge you willingly in a cup of bastard.—How, my pretty coz, Cicely! why, I left you but a child in the cradle, and there thou stand'st in thy velvet waistcoat, as tight a girl as England's sun shines on. Know thy friends and kindred, Cicely, and come hither, child, that I may kiss thee, and give thee my blessing."

"Concern not yourself about Cicely, kinsman," said Giles Gosling, "but e'en let her go her way, a' God's name; for although your mother were her father's sister, yet that shall not make you and her cater-cousins."

"Why, uncle," replied Lambourne, "think'st thou I am an infidel, and would harm those of mine own house?"

"It is for no harm that I speak, Mike," answered his uncle, "but a simple humour of precaution which I have. True, thou art as well gilded as a snake when he casts his old slough in the spring-time, but for all that, thou creepest not into my Eden. I will look after mine Eve, Mike, and so content thee.—But how brave thou be'st, lad! To look on thee now, and compare thee with Master Tressilian here, in his sad-coloured riding-suit, who would not say that thou wert the real gentleman, and he the tapster's boy?"

"Troth, uncle," replied Lambourne, "no one would say so but one of your country-breeding, that knows no better. I will say, and I care not who hears me, there is something about the real gentry that few men come up to that are not born and bred to the mystery. I wot not where the trick lies; but although I can enter an ordinary with as much audacity, rebuke the waiters and drawers as loudly, drink as deep a health, swear as round an oath, and fling my gold as freely about as any of the jingling spurs and white feathers that are around me,—yet, hang me if I can ever catch the true grace of it, though I have practised an hundred times. The man of the house sets me lowest at the board, and carves to me the last; and the drawer says,—'Coming, friend,' without any more reverence or regardful addition. But, hang it, let it pass; care killed a cat. I have gentry enough to pass the trick on Tony Fire-the-Fagot, and that will do for the matter in hand."

"You hold your purpose, then, of visiting your old acquaintance?" said Tressilian to the adventurer.

"Ay, sir," replied Lambourne; "when stakes are made, the game must be played; that is gamester's law, all over the world. You, sir, unless my memory fails me, (for I did steep it somewhat too deeply in the sack-butt,) took some share in my hazard?"

"I propose to accompany you in your adventure," said Tressilian, "if you will do me so much grace as to permit me; and I have staked my share of the forfeit in the hands of our worthy host."

"That he hath," answered Giles Gosling, "in as fair Harry-nobles as ever were melted into sack by a good fellow. So, luck to your enterprise, since you will needs venture on Tony Foster; but, by my credit, you had better take another draught before you depart, for your welcome at the Hall, yonder, will be somewhat of the driest. And if you do get into peril, beware of taking to cold steel; but send for me, Giles Gosling the head-borough, and I may be able to make something out of Tony yet, for as proud as he is."

The nephew dutifully obeyed his uncle's hint, by taking a second powerful pull at the tankard, observing, that his wit never served him so well as when he had washed his temples with a deep morning's draught; —and they set forth together for the habitation of Anthony Foster.

The village of Cumnor is pleasantly built on a hill, and in a wooded park closely adjacent was situated the ancient mansion occupied at this time by Anthony Foster, of which the ruins may be still extant. The park was then full of large trees, and in particular, of ancient and mighty oaks, which stretched their giant arms over the high wall surrounding the demense, thus giving it a melancholy, secluded, and monastic appearance. The entrance to the park lay through an old-fashioned gateway in the outer wall, the door of which was formed of two huge oaken leaves, thickly studded with nails, like the gate of an old town.

"We shall be finely holped up here," said Michael Lambourne, looking at the gateway and gate, "if this fellow's suspicious humour should refuse us admission altogether, as it is like may, in case this linsey-wolsey fellow of a mercer's visit to his premises has disquieted him. But, no," he added, pushing the huge gate, which gave way, "the door stands invitingly open; and here we are within the forbidden ground without other impediment than the passive resistance of a heavy oak door, moving on rusty hinges."

They stood now in an avenue overshadowed by such old trees as we have described, and which had been bordered at one time by high hedges of yew and holly. But these, having been untrimmed for many years, had run up into great bushes, or rather dwarf-trees, and now encroached, with their dark and melancholy boughs, upon the road which they once had screened. The avenue itself was grown up with grass, and, in one or two places, interrupted by piles of withered brushwood, which had been lopped from the trees cut down in the neighbouring park, and was here stacked for drying. Formal walks and avenues, which, at different points, crossed this principal approach, were, in like manner, choked up and interrupted by piles of brushwood and billets, and in other places by underwood and brambles. Besides the general effect of desolation which is so strongly impressed, whenever we behold the contrivances of man wasted and obliterated by neglect, and witness the marks of social life effaced gradually by the influence of vegetation, the size of the trees, and the outspreading extent of their boughs, diffused a gloom over the scene, even when the sun was at the highest, and made a proportional impression on the mind of those who visited it. This was felt even by Michael Lambourne, however alien his habits were to receiving any impressions, excepting from things which addressed themselves immediately to his passions.

"This wood is as dark as a wolf's mouth," said he to Tressilian, as they walked together slowly along the solitary and broken approach, and had just come in sight of the monastic front of the old mansion, with its shafted windows, brick walls, overgrown with ivy and creepirg shrubs, and twisted stalks of chimneys of heavy stone-work. "And yet," continued Lambourne, "it is fairly done on the part of Foster too; for since he chooses not visitors, it is right to keep his place in a fashion that will invite few to trespass upon his privacy. But had he been the Anthony I once knew him, these sturdy oaks had long since become the property of some honest woodmonger, and the manor-close here had looked lighter at midnight than it now does at noon, while Foster played fast and loose with the price, in some cunning corner in the purlieus of White-friars."

"Was he then such an unthrift?" asked Tressilian.

"He was," answered Lambourne, "like the rest of us, no saint, and no saver. But what I liked worst of Tony was, that he loved to take his pleasure by himself, and grudged, as men say, every drop of water that went past his own mill. I have known him deal with such measures of wine when he was alone, as I would not have ventured on with aid of the best toper in Berkshire;—that, and some sway towards superstition, which he had by temperament, rendered him unworthy the company of a good fellow. And now he has earthed himself here, in a den just befitting such a sly fox as himself."

"May I ask you, Master Lambourne," said Tressilian, "since your old companion's humour jumps so little with your own, wherefore you are so desirous to renew acquaintance with him?"

"And may I ask you, in return, Master Tressilian," answered Lambourne, "wherefore you have shown yourself so desirous to accompany me on this party?"

"I told you my motive," said Tressilian, "when I took share in your wager,—it was simple curiosity."

"La you there now!" answered Lambourne: "See how you civil and discreet gentlemen think to use us who live by the free exercise of our wits! Had I answered your question by saying that it was simple curiosity which led me to visit my old comrade Anthony Foster, I warrant you had set it down for an evasion, and a turn of my trade. But any answer, I suppose, must serve my turn."

"And wherefore should not bare curiosity," said Tressilian, "be a sufficient reason for my taking this walk with you?"

"O, content yourself, sir," replied Lambourne; "you cannot put the change on me so easy as you think, for I have lived among the quick-stirring spirits of the age too long, to swallow chaff for grain. You are a gentleman of birth and breeding—your bearing makes it good; of civil habits and fair reputation—your manners declare it, and my uncle avouches it; and yet you associate yourself with a sort of scant-of-grace, as men call me; and, knowing me to be such, you make yourself my companion in a visit to a man whom you are a stranger to,—and all out of mere curiosity, forsooth!—The excuse, if curiously balanced, would be found to want some scruples of just weight, or so."

"If your suspicions were just," said Tressilian, "you have shown no confidence in me to invite or deserve mine."

"O, if that be all," said Lambourne, "my motives lie above water. While this gold of mine lasts,"—taking out his purse, chucking it into the air, and catching it as it fell,—"I will make it buy pleasure, and when it is out, I must have more. Now, if this mysterious Lady of the Manor—this fair Lindabrides of Tony Fire-the-Fagot—be so admirable a piece as men say, why, there is chance that she may aid me to melt my nobles into groats; and, again, if Anthony be so wealthy a chuff as report speaks him, he may prove the philosopher's stone to me, and convert my groats into fair rose-nobles again."

"A comfortable proposal truly," said Tressilian; "but I see not what chance there is of accomplishing it."

"Not to-day, or perchance to-morrow," answered Lambourne; "I expect not to catch the old jack till I have disposed my ground-baits handsomely. But I know something more of his affairs this morning than I did last night, and I will so use my knowledge that he shall think it more perfect than it is.—Nay, without expecting either pleasure or profit, or both, I had not stepped a stride within this manor, I can tell you; for I promise you I hold our visit not altogether without risk.—But here we are, and we must make the best on't."

While he thus spoke, they had entered a large orchard which surrounded the house on two sides, though the trees, abandoned by the care of man, were overgrown and mossy, and seemed to bear little fruit. Those which had been formerly trained as espaliers, had now resumed their natural mode of growing, and exhibited grotesque forms, partaking of the original training which they had received. The greater part of the ground, which had once been parterres and flower-gardens, was suffered in like manner to run to waste, excepting a few patches which had been dug up, and planted with ordinary pot herbs. Some statues, which had ornamented the garden in its days of splendour, were now thrown down from their pedestals and broken in pieces, and a large summer-house, having a heavy stone front, decorated with carving, representing the life and actions of Samson, was in the same dilapidated condition.

They had just traversed this garden of the sluggard, and were within a few steps of the door of the mansion, when Lambourne had ceased speaking; a circumstance very agreeable to Tressilian, as it saved him the embarrassment of either commenting upon or replying to the frank avowal which his companion had just made of the sentiments and views which induced him to come hither. Lambourne knocked roundly and boldly at the huge door of the mansion, observing at the same time, he had seen a less strong one upon a county jail. It was not until they had knocked more than once, that an aged, sour-visaged domestic reconnoitred them through a small square hole in the door, well secured with bars of iron, and demanded what they wanted.

"To speak with Master Foster instantly on pressing business of the state," was the ready reply of Michael Lambourne.

"Methinks you will find difficulty to make that good," said Tressilian in a whisper to his companion, while the servant went to carry the message to his master.

"Tush," replied the adventurer; "no soldier would go on were he always to consider when and how he should come off. Let us once obtain entrance, and all will go well enough."

In a short time the servant returned, and drawing with a careful hand both bolt and bar, opened the gate, which admitted them through an archway into a square court, surrounded by buildings. Opposite to the arch was another door, which the serving-man in like manner unlocked, and thus introduced them into a stone-paved parlour, where there was but little furniture, and that of the rudest, and most ancient fashion. The windows were tall and ample, reaching almost to the roof of the room, which was composed of black oak; those opening to the quadrangle were obscured by the height of the surrounding buildings, and, as they were traversed with massive shafts of solid stone-work, and thickly painted with religious devices, and scenes taken from Scripture history, by no means admitted light in proportion to their size; and what did penetrate through them, partook of the dark and gloomy tinge of the stained glass.

Tressilian and his guide had time enough to observe all these particulars, for they waited some space in the apartment ere the present master of the mansion at length made his appearance. Prepared as he was to see an inauspicious and ill-looking person, the ugliness of Anthony Foster considerably exceeded what Tressilian had anticipated. He was

of middle stature, built strongly, but so clumsily as to border on deformity, and to give all his motions the ungainly awkwardness of a left-
legged and left-handed man. His hair, in arranging which men at that
time, as at present, were very nice and curious, instead of being carefully
cleaned and disposed into short curls, or else set up on end, as is represented in old paintings, in a manner resembling that used by fine gentlemen of our own day, escaped in sable negligence from under a furred
bonnet, and hung in elf-locks, which seemed strangers to the comb, over
his rugged brows, and around his very singular unprepossessing countenance. His keen dark eyes were deep set beneath broad and shaggy eyebrows, and as they were usually bent on the ground, seemed as if they
were themselves ashamed of the expression natural to them, and were
desirous to conceal it from the observation of men. At times, however,
when, more intent on observing others, he suddenly raised them, and
fixed them keenly on those with whom he conversed, they seemed to
express both the fiercer passions, and the power of mind which could at
will suppress or disguise the intensity of inward feeling. The features
which corresponded with these eyes and this form were irregular, and
marked so as to be indelibly fixed on the mind of him who had once seen
them. Upon the whole, as Tressilian could not help acknowledging to
himself, the Anthony Foster who now stood before them was the last
person, judging from personal appearance, upon whom one would have
chosen to intrude an unexpected and undesired visit. His attire was a
doublet of russet leather, like those worn by the better sort of country
folk, girt with a buff belt, in which was stuck on the right side a long
knife, or dudgeon dagger, and on the other a cutlass. He raised his eyes
as he entered the room, and fixed a keenly penetrating glance upon his
two visitors, then cast them down as if counting his steps, while he
advanced slowly into the middle of the room, and said, in a low and
smothered tone of voice, "Let me pray you, gentlemen, to tell me the
cause of this visit."

He looked as if he expected the answer from Tressilian; so true was
Lambourne's observation, that the superior air of breeding and dignity
shone through the disguise of an inferior dress. But it was Michael who
replied to him, with the easy familiarity of an old friend, and a tone
which seemed unembarrassed by any doubt of the most cordial reception.

"Ha! my dear friend and ingle, Tony Foster!" he exclaimed, seizing
upon the unwilling hand, and shaking it with such emphasis as almost to
stagger the sturdy frame of the person whom he addressed; "how fares
it with you for many a long year?—What! have you altogether forgotten
your friend, gossip, and playfellow, Michael Lambourne?"

"Michael Lambourne!" said Foster, looking at him a moment; then
dropping his eyes, and with little ceremony extricating his hand from
the friendly grasp of the person by whom he was addressed, "are you
Michael Lambourne?"

"Ay; sure as you are Anthony Foster," replied Lambourne.

" 'Tis well," answered his sullen host; "and what may Michael Lambourne expect from his visit hither?"

"*Voto a Dios*," answered Lambourne, "I expected a better welcome than I am like to meet, I think."

"Why, thou gallows-bird—thou jail-rat—thou friend of the hangman and his customers," replied Foster, "hast thou the assurance to expect countenance from any one whose neck is beyond the compass of a Tyburn tippet?"

"It may be with me as you say," replied Lambourne; "and suppose I grant it to be so for argument's sake, I were still good enough society for mine ancient friend Anthony Fire-the-Fagot, though he be, for the present, by some indescribable title, the master of Cumnor-Place."

"Hark you, Michael Lambourne," said Foster; "you are a gambler now, and live by the counting of chances—Compute me the odds that I do not, on this instant, throw you out of that window into the ditch there."

"Twenty to one that you do not," answered the sturdy visitor.

"And wherefore, I pray you?" demanded Anthony Foster, setting his teeth and compressing his lips, like one who endeavours to suppress some violent internal emotion.

"Because," said Lambourne, coolly, "you dare not for your life lay a finger on me. I am younger and stronger than you, and have in me a double portion of the fighting devil, though not, it may be, quite so much of the undermining fiend, that finds an underground way to his purpose—who hides halters under folk's pillows, and who puts ratsbane into their porridge, as the stage-play says."

Foster looked at him earnestly, then turned away, and paced the room twice, with the same steady and considerate pace with which he had entered it; then suddenly came back, and extended his hand to Michael Lambourne, saying, "Be not wroth with me, good Mike; I did but try whether thou hadst parted with aught of thine old and honourable frankness, which your enviers and backbiters called saucy impudence."

"Let them call it what they will," said Michael Lambourne, "it is the commodity we must carry through the world with us.—Uds daggers! I tell thee, man, mine own stock of assurance was too small to trade upon, I was fain to take in a ton or two more of brass at every port where I touched in the voyage of life; and I started overboard what modesty and scruples I had remaining, in order to make room for the stowage."

"Nay, nay," replied Foster, "touching scruples and modesty, you sailed hence in ballast.—But who is this gallant, honest Mike?—is he a Corinthian—a cutter like thyself?"

"I prithee, know Master Tressilian, bully Foster," replied Lambourne, presenting his friend in answer to his friend's question, "know him and honour him, for he is a gentleman of many admirable qualities; and though he traffics not in my line of business, at least so far as I know, he has, nevertheless, a just respect and admiration for artists of our class. He will come to in time, as seldom fails; but as yet he is only a Neophyte, only a Proselyte, and frequents the company of cocks of the game, as a puny fencer does the schools of the masters, to see how a foil is handled by the teachers of defence."

"If such be his quality, I will pray your company in another chamber, honest Mike, for what I have to say to thee is for thy private ear.— Meanwhile, I pray you, sir, to abide us in this apartment, and without leaving it—there be those in this house who would be alarmed by the sight of a stranger." [1]

Tressilian acquiesced, and the two worthies left the apartment together, in which he remained alone to await their return.

[1] See Note I.—Foster, Lambourne, and the Black Bear.

CHAPTER IV

> Not serve two masters?—Here's a youth will try it—
> Would fain serve God, yet give the devil his due;
> Says grace before he doth a deed of villainy,
> And returns his thanks devoutly when 'tis acted.
> *Old Play.*

THE room into which the Master of Cumnor-Place conducted his worthy visitant, was of greater extent than that in which they had at first conversed, and had yet more the appearance of dilapidation. Large oaken presses, filled with shelves of the same wood, surrounded the room, and had, at one time, served for the arrangement of a numerous collection of books, many of which yet remained, but torn and defaced, covered with dust, deprived of their costly clasps and bindings, and tossed together in heaps upon the shelves, as things altogether disregarded, and abandoned to the pleasure of every spoiler. The very presses themselves seemed to have incurred the hostility of those enemies of learning, who had destroyed the volumes with which they had been heretofore filled. They were, in several places, dismantled of their shelves, and otherwise broken and damaged, and were, moreover, mantled with cobwebs and covered with dust.

"The men who wrote these books," said Lambourne, looking round him, "little thought whose keeping they were to fall into."

"Nor what yeoman's service they were to do me," quoth Anthony Foster—"the cook hath used them for scouring his pewter, and the groom hath had nought else to clean my boots with this many a month past."

"And yet," said Lambourne, "I have been in cities where such learned commodities would have been deemed too good for such offices."

"Pshaw, pshaw," answered Foster, "they are Popish trash, every one of them,—private studies of the mumping old Abbot of Abingdon. The nineteenthly of a pure gospel sermon were worth a cart-load of such rakings of the kennel of Rome."

"Gad-a-mercy, Master Tony Fire-the-Fagot!" said Lambourne, by way of reply.

Foster scowled darkly at him, as he replied, "Hark ye, friend Mike; forget that name, and the passage which it relates to, if you would not have our newly-revived comradeship die a sudden and a violent death."

"Why," said Michael Lambourne, "you were wont to glory in the share you had in the death of the two old heretical bishops."

"That," said his comrade, "was while I was in the gall of bitterness and bond of iniquity, and applies not to my walk or my ways, now that I am called forth into the lists. Mr. Melchisedek Maultext compared my misfortune in that matter to that of the Apostle Paul, who kept the clothes of the witnesses who stoned Saint Stephen. He held forth on the matter three Sabbaths past, and illustrated the same by the conduct of an honourable person present, meaning me."

"I prithee peace, Foster," said Lambourne; "for I know not how it is, I have a sort of creeping comes over my skin when I hear the devil quote Scripture; and besides, man, how couldst thou have the heart to quit that convenient old religion, which you could slip off or on as easily as your glove? Do I not remember how you were wont to carry your con-science to confession, as duly as the month came round? and when thou hadst it scoured, and burnished, and whitewashed by the priest, thou wert ever ready for the worst villainy which could be devised, like a child who is always readiest to rush into the mire when he has got his Sunday's clean jerkin on."

"Trouble not thyself about my conscience," said Foster, "it is a thing thou canst not understand, having never had one of thine own. But let us rather to the point, and say to me, in one word, what is thy business with me, and what hopes have drawn thee hither?"

"The hope of bettering myself, to be sure," answered Lambourne, "as the old woman said, when she leapt over the bridge at Kingston. Look you, this purse has all that is left of as round a sum as a man would wish to carry in his slop-pouch. You are here well established, it would seem, and, as I think, well befriended, for men talk of thy being under some special protection—nay, stare not like a pig that is stuck, mon, thou canst not dance in a net and they not see thee? Now I know such pro-tection is not purchased for nought; you must have services to render for it, and in these I propose to help thee."

"But how if I lack no assistance from thee, Mike? I think thy modesty might suppose that were a case possible."

"That is to say," retorted Lambourne, "that you would engross the whole work, rather than divide the reward—but be not over-greedy, Anthony. Covetousness bursts the sack, and spills the grain. Look you, when the huntsman goes to kill a stag, he takes with him more dogs than one—He has the stanch lyme-hound to track the wounded buck over hill and dale, but he hath also the fleet gaze-hound to kill him at view. Thou art the lyme-hound, I am the gaze-hound, and thy patron will need the aid of both, and can well afford to requite it. Thou hast deep sagacity—an unrelenting purpose—a steady long-breathed malignity of nature, that surpasses mine. But then, I am the bolder, the quicker, the more ready, both at action and expedient. Separate, our properties are not so perfect; but unite them, and we drive the world before us. How sayst thou—shall we hunt in couples?"

"It is a currish proposal—thus to thrust thyself upon my private matters," replied Foster; "but thou wert ever an ill-nurtured whelp."

"You shall have no cause to say so, unless you spurn my courtesy," said Michael Lambourne; "but if so, keep thee well from me, Sir Knight, as the romance has it. I will either share your counsels or traverse them; for I have come here to be busy, either with thee or against thee."

"Well," said Anthony Foster, "since thou dost leave me so fair a choice, I will rather be thy friend than thine enemy. Thou art right; I *can* prefer thee to the service of a patron, who has enough of means to make us both, and an hundred more. And, to say truth, thou art well qualified for his service. Boldness and dexterity he demands—the justice-books bear witness in thy favour; no starting at scruples in his service—why, who ever suspected thee of a conscience?—an assurance he must have, who would follow a courtier—and thy brow is as impenetrable as a Milan visor. There is but one thing I would fain see amended in thee."

"And what is that, my most precious friend Anthony?" replied Lambourne; "for I swear by the pillow of the Seven Sleepers, I will not be slothful in amending it."

"Why, you gave a sample of it even now," said Foster. "Your speech twangs too much of the old stamp, and you garnish it ever and anon with singular oaths, that savour of Papistrie. Besides, your exterior man is altogether too deboshed and irregular to become one of his lordship's followers, since he has a reputation to keep up in the eye of the world. You must somewhat reform your dress, upon a more grave and composed fashion; wear your cloak on both shoulders, and your falling band unrumpled and well starched—You must enlarge the brim of your beaver, and diminish the superfluity of your trunk-hose—go to church, or, which will be better, to meeting, at least once a month—protest only upon your faith and conscience—lay aside your swashing look, and never touch the hilt of your sword, but when you would draw the carnal weapon in good earnest."

"By this light, Anthony, thou art mad," answered Lambourne, "and hast described rather the gentleman-usher to a puritan's wife, than the follower of an ambitious courtier! Yes, such a thing as thou wouldst make of me, should wear a book at his girdle instead of a poniard, and might just be suspected of manhood enough to squire a proud dame-citizen to the lecture at Saint Antonlin's, and quarrel in her cause with any flat-capp'd threadmaker that would take the wall of her. He must ruffle it in another sort that would walk to court in a nobleman's train."

"O, content you, sir," replied Foster, "there is a change since you knew the English world; and there are those who can hold their way through the boldest courses, and the most secret, and yet never a swaggering word, or an oath, or a profane word in their conversation."

"That is to say," replied Lambourne, "they are in a trading copartnery, to do the devil's business without mentioning his name in the firm?—Well, I will do my best to counterfeit, rather than lose ground in this new world, since thou sayest it is grown so precise. But, Anthony, what is the name of this nobleman, in whose service I am to turn hypocrite?"

"Aha! Master Michael, are you there with your bears?" said Foster, with a grim smile; "and is this the knowledge you pretend of my concernments?—How know you now there is such a person *in rerum natura*, and that I have not been putting a jape upon you all this time?"

"Thou put a jape on me, thou sodden-brained gull?" answered Lambourne, nothing daunted; "why, dark and muddy as thou think'st thyself, I would engage in a day's space to see as clear through thee and thy concernments, as thou call'st them, as through the filthy horn of an old stable lantern."

At this moment their conversation was interrupted by a scream from the next apartment.

"By the holy Cross of Abingdon," exclaimed Anthony Foster, forgetting his Protestantism in his alarm, "I am a ruined man!"

So saying, he rushed into the apartment whence the scream issued, followed by Michael Lambourne. But to account for the sounds which interrupted their conversation, it is necessary to recede a little way in our narrative.

It has been already observed, that when Lambourne accompanied Foster into the library, they left Tressilian alone in the ancient parlour. His dark eye followed them forth of the apartment with a glance of contempt, a part of which his mind instantly transferred to himself, for having stooped to be even for a moment their familiar companion. "These are the associates, Amy,"—it was thus he communed with himself,—"to which thy cruel levity—thine unthinking and most unmerited falsehood, has condemned him, of whom his friends once hoped far other things, and who now scorns himself as he will be scorned by others, for the baseness he stoops to for the love of thee! But I will not leave the pursuit of thee, once the object of my purest and most devoted affection, though to me thou canst henceforth be nothing but a thing to weep over —I will save thee from thy betrayer, and from thyself—I will restore thee to thy parent—to thy God. I cannot bid the bright star again sparkle in the sphere it has shot from, but——"

A slight noise in the apartment interrupted his reverie; he looked round, and in the beautiful and richly-attired female who entered at that instant by a side-door, he recognised the object of his search. The first impulse arising from this discovery, urged him to conceal his face with the collar of his cloak, until he should find a favourable moment of making himself known. But his purpose was disconcerted by the young lady, (she was not above eighteen years old,) who ran joyfully towards him, and, pulling him by the cloak, said playfully, "Nay, my sweet friend, after I have waited for you so long, you come not to my bower to play the masquer—You are arraigned of treason to true love and fond affection; and you must stand up at the bar, and answer it with face uncovered —how say you, guilty or not?"

"Alas, Amy!" said Tressilian, in a low and melancholy tone, as he suffered her to draw the mantle from his face. The sound of his voice, and still more the unexpected sight of his face, changed in an instant the lady's playful mood—She staggered back, turned as pale as death, and put her hands before her face. Tressilian was himself for a moment much overcome, but seeming suddenly to remember the necessity of using an opportunity which might not again occur, he said in a low tone, "Amy, fear me not."

"Why should I fear you?" said the lady, withdrawing her hands from her beautiful face, which was now covered with crimson,—"why should I fear you, Mr. Tressilian?—or wherefore have you intruded yourself into my dwelling, uninvited, sir, and unwished for?"

"Your dwelling, Amy!" said Tressilian. "Alas! is a prison your dwelling?—a prison, guarded by one of the most sordid of men, but not a greater wretch than his employer!"

"This house is mine," said Amy, "mine while I choose to inhabit it— If it is my pleasure to live in seclusion, who shall gainsay me?"

"Your father, maiden," answered Tressilian, "your broken-hearted father; who dispatched me in quest of you with that authority which he cannot exert in person. Here is his letter, written while he blessed his pain of body which somewhat stunned the agony of his mind."

"The pain!—is my father then ill?" said the lady.

"So ill," answered Tressilian, "that even your utmost haste may not restore him to health; but all shall be instantly prepared for your departure, the instant you yourself will give consent."

"Tressilian," answered the lady, "I cannot, I must not, I dare not leave this place. Go back to my father—tell him I will obtain leave to see him within twelve hours from hence. Go back, Tressilian—tell him I am well, I am happy—happy could I think he was so—tell him not to fear that I will come, and in such a manner that all the grief Amy has given him shall be forgotten—the poor Amy is now greater than she dare name.—Go, good Tressilian—I have injured thee too, but believe me I have power to heal the wounds I have caused—I robbed you of a childish heart, which was not worthy of you, and I can repay the loss with honours and advancement."

"Do you say this to me, Amy?—Do you offer me pageants of idle ambition, for the quiet peace you have robbed me of?—But be it so—I came not to upbraid, but to serve and to free you.—You cannot disguise it from me; you are a prisoner. Otherwise your kind heart—for it was

once a kind heart—would have been already at your father's bedside.—
Come—poor, deceived unhappy maiden!—all shall be forgot—all shall
be forgiven. Fear not my importunity for what regarded our contract—
it was a dream, and I have awaked—But come—your father yet lives
—Come, and one word of affection—one tear of penitence, will efface
the memory of all that has passed."

"Have I not already said, Tressilian," replied she, "that I will surely
come to my father, and that without farther delay than is necessary to
discharge other and equally binding duties?—Go, carry him the news—I
come as sure as there is light in heaven—that is, when I obtain permission."

"Permission?—permission to visit your father on his sick-bed, perhaps on his death-bed!" repeated Tressilian, impatiently; "and permission from whom?—From the villain, who, under disguise of friendship,
abused every duty of hospitality, and stole thee from thy father's roof!"

"Do him no slander, Tressilian!—He whom thou speakest of wears a
sword as sharp as thine—sharper, vain man—for the best deeds thou
hast ever done in peace or war, were as unworthy to be named with his,
as thy obscure rank to match itself with the sphere he moves in.—Leave
me! Go, do mine errand to my father, and when he next sends to me, let
him choose a more welcome messenger."

"Amy," replied Tressilian, calmly, "thou canst not move me by thy
reproaches.—Tell me one thing, that I may bear at least one ray of
comfort to my aged friend—This rank of his which thou dost boast—
dost thou share it with him, Amy?—Does he claim a husband's right to
control thy motions?"

"Stop thy base unmannered tongue!" said the lady; "to no question
that derogates from my honour, do I deign an answer."

"You have said enough in refusing to reply," answered Tressilian; "and
mark me, unhappy as thou art, I am armed with thy father's full authority
to command thy obedience, and I will save thee from the slavery of sin
and of sorrow, even despite of thyself, Amy."

"Menace no violence here!" exclaimed the lady, drawing back from
him, and alarmed at the determination expressed in his look and manner;
"threaten me not, Tressilian, for I have means to repel force."

"But not, I trust, the wish to use them in so evil a cause?" said
Tressilian. "With thy will—thine uninfluenced, free, and natural will,
Amy, thou canst not choose this state of slavery and dishonour—thou
hast been bound by some spell—entrapped by some deceit—art now
detained by some compelled vow.—But thus I break the charm—Amy, in
the name of thine excellent, thy broken-hearted father, I command thee
to follow me!"

As he spoke, he advanced and extended his arm, as with the purpose
of laying hold upon her. But she shrunk back from his grasp, and uttered
the scream which, as we before noticed, brought into the apartment
Lambourne and Foster.

The latter exclaimed, as soon as he entered, "Fire and fagot! what have we here?" Then addressing the lady, in a tone betwixt entreaty and command, he added, "Uds precious! madam, what make you here out of bounds?—Retire—retire—there is life and death in this matter.—And you, friend, whoever you may be, leave this house—out with you, before my dagger's hilt and your costard become acquainted—Draw, Mike, and rid us of the knave!"

"Not I, on my soul," replied Lambourne; "he came hither in my company, and he is safe from me by cutter's law, at least till we meet again.—But hark ye, my Cornish comrade, you have brought a Cornish flaw of wind with you hither, a hurricanoe as they call it in the Indies Make yourself scarce—depart—vanish—or we'll have you summoned before the Mayor of Halgaver, and that before Dudman and Ramhead meet." [1]

"Away, base groom!" said Tressilian—"And you, madam, fare you well—what life lingers in your father's bosom will leave him, at the news I have to tell."

He departed, the lady saying faintly as he left the room, "Tressilian, be not rash—say no scandal of me."

"Here is proper gear," said Foster. "I pray you go to your chamber, my lady, and let us consider how this is to be answered—nay, tarry not."

"I move not at your command, sir," answered the lady.

"Nay, but you must, fair lady," replied Foster; "excuse my freedom, but, by blood and nails, this is no time to strain courtesies—you *must* go to your chamber.—Mike, follow that meddling coxcomb, and, as you desire to thrive, see him safely clear of the premises, while I bring this headstrong lady to reason—Draw thy tool, man, and after him."

"I'll follow him," said Michael Lambourne, "and see him fairly out of Flanders—But for hurting a man I have drunk my morning's draught withal, 'tis clean against my conscience." So saying, he left the apartment.

Tressilian, meanwhile, with hasty steps, pursued the first path which promised to conduct him through the wild and overgrown park in which the mansion of Foster was situated. Haste and distress of mind led his steps astray, and instead of taking the avenue which led towards the village, he chose another, which, after he had pursued it for some time with a hasty and reckless step, conducted him to the other side of the demesne, where a postern-door opened through the wall, and led into the open country.

Tressilian paused an instant. It was indifferent to him by what road he left a spot now so odious to his recollections; but it was probable that the postern-door was locked, and his retreat by that pass rendered impossible.

"I must make the attempt, however," he said to himself; "the only means of reclaiming this lost—this miserable—this still most lovely and

[1] Two headlands on the Cornish coast. The expressions are proverbial.

most unhappy girl—must rest in her father's appeal to the broken laws of his country—I must haste to apprise him of this heart-rending intelligence."

As Tressilian, thus conversing with himself, approached to try some means of opening the door, or climbing over it, he perceived there was a key put into the lock from the outside. It turned round, the bolt revolved, and a cavalier, who entered, muffled in his riding-cloak, and wearing a slouched hat with a drooping feather, stood at once within four yards of him who was desirous of going out. They exclaimed at once, in tones of resentment and surprise, the one "Varney!" the other "Tressilian!"

"What make you here?" was the stern question put by the stranger to Tressilian, when the moment of surprise was past—"What make you here, where your presenc2 is neither expected nor desired?"

"Nay, Varney," replied Tressilian, "what make *you* here? Are you come to triumph over the innocence you have destroyed, as the vulture or carrion-crow comes to batten on the lamb, whose eyes it has first plucked out?—Or are you come to encounter the merited vengeance of an honest man?—Draw, dog, and defend thyself!"

Tressilian drew his sword as he spoke, but Varney only laid his hand on the hilt of his own, as he replied, "Thou art mad, Tressilian— I own appearances are against me, but by every oath a priest can make, or a man can swear, Mistress Amy Robsart hath had no injury from me; and in truth I were somewhat loath to hurt you in this cause—Thou know'st I can fight."

"I have heard thee say so, Varney," replied Tressilian; "but now, methinks, I would fain have some better evidence than thine own word."

"That shall not be lacking, if blade and hilt be but true to me," answered Varney; and drawing his sword with his right hand, he threw his cloak around his left, and attacked Tressilian with a vigour which, for a moment, seemed to give him the advantage of the combat. But this advantage lasted not long. Tressilian added to a spirit determined on revenge, a hand and eye admirably well adapted to the use of the rapier; so that Varney, finding himself hard pressed in his turn, endeavoured to avail himself of his superior strength, by closing with his adversary. For this purpose, he hazarded the receiving one of Tressilian's passes in his cloak, wrapt as it was around his arm, and ere his adversary could extricate his rapier thus entangled, he closed with him, shortening his own sword at the same time, with the purpose of dispatching him. But Tressilian was on his guard, and unsheathing his poniard, parried with the blade of that weapon the home-thrust which would otherwise have finished the combat, and, in the struggle which followed, displayed so much address, as might have confirmed the opinion that he drew his origin from Cornwall, whose natives are such masters in the art of wrestling, as, were the games of antiquity revived, might enable them to challenge all Europe to the ring. Varney, in his ill-advised attempt, received a fall so sudden and violent, that his sword flew several paces from his hand, and ere he could recover his feet, that of his antagonist was pointed to his throat.

"Give me the instant means of relieving the victim of thy treachery," said Tressilian, "or take the last look of your Creator's blessed sun!"

And while Varney, too confused or too sullen to reply, made a sudden effort to arise, his adversary drew back his arm, and would have executed his threat, but that the blow was arrested by the grasp of Michael Lambourne, who, directed by the clashing of swords, had come up just in time to save the life of Varney.

"Come, come, comrade," said Lambourne, "here is enough done, and more than enough—put up your fox, and let us be jogging—The Black Bear growls for us."

"Off, abject!" said Tressilian, striking himself free of Lambourne's grasp; "darest thou come betwixt me and mine enemy?"

"Abject! abject!" repeated Lambourne; "that shall be answered with cold steel whenever a bowl of sack has washed out memory of the morning's draught that we had together. In the meanwhile, do you see, shog—tramp—begone—we are two to one."

He spoke truth, for Varney had taken the opportunity to regain his weapon, and Tressilian perceived it was madness to press the quarrel farther against such odds. He took his purse from his side, and taking out two gold nobles, flung them to Lambourne; "There, caitiff, is thy morning wage—thou shalt not say thou hast been my guide unhired.—Varney, farewell—we shall meet where there are none to come betwixt us." So saying, he turned round and departed through the postern-door.

Varney seemed to want the inclination, or perhaps the power, (for his fall had been a severe one,) to follow his retreating enemy. But he glared darkly as he disappeared, and then addressed Lambourne; "Art thou a comrade of Foster's, good fellow?"

"Sworn friends, as the haft is to the knife," replied Michael Lambourne.

"Here is a broad piece for thee—follow yonder fellow, and see where he takes earth, and bring me word up to the mansion-house here. Cautious and silent, thou knave, as thou valuest thy throat."

"Enough said," replied Lambourne; "I can draw on a scent as well as a sleuth-hound."

"Begone, then," said Varney, sheathing his rapier; and, turning his back on Michael Lambourne, he walked slowly towards the house. Lambourne stopped but an instant to gather the nobles which his late companion had flung towards him so unceremoniously, and muttered to himself, while he put them up in his purse along with the gratuity of Varney, "I spoke to yonder gulls of Eldorado—By Saint Anthony, there is no Eldorado for men of our stamp equal to bonny Old England! It rains nobles, by Heaven—they lie on the grass as thick as dewdrops—you may have them for gathering. And if I have not my share of such glittering dewdrops, may my sword melt like an icicle!"

CHAPTER V

——He was a man
Versed in the world as pilot in his compass.
The needle pointed ever to that interest
Which was his loadstar, and he spread his sails
With vantage to the gale of others' passion.
The Deceiver—a Tragedy.

ANTHONY FOSTER was still engaged in debate with his fair guest, who treated with scorn every entreaty and request that she would retire to her own apartment, when a whistle was heard at the entrance-door of the mansion.

"We are fairly sped now," said Foster; "yonder is thy lord's signal, and what to say about the disorder which has happened in this household, by my conscience, I know not. Some evil fortune dogs the heels of that unhanged rogue Lambourne, and he has 'scaped the gallows against every chance, to come back and be the ruin of me!"

"Peace, sir," said the lady, "and undo the gate to your master.—My lord! my dear lord!" she then exclaimed, hastening to the entrance of the apartment; then added, with a voice expressive of disappointment: "Pooh! it is but Richard Varney."

"Ay, madam," said Varney, entering and saluting the lady with a respectful obeisance, which she returned with a careless mixture of negligence and of displeasure, "it is but Richard Varney; but even the first grey cloud should be acceptable, when it lightens in the east, because it announces the approach of the blessed sun."

"How! comes my lord hither to-night?" said the lady, in joyful, yet startled agitation; and Anthony Foster caught up the word, and echoed the question. Varney replied to the lady, that his lord purposed to attend her, and would have proceeded with some compliment, when, running to the door of the parlour, she called aloud: "Janet—Janet—come to my tiring-room instantly." Then returning to Varney, she asked if her lord sent any farther commendations to her.

"This letter, honoured madam," said he, taking from his bosom a small parcel wrapt in scarlet silk, "and with it a token to the Queen of his Affections." With eager speed the lady hastened to undo the silken string which surrounded the little packet, and failing to unloose readily the knot with which it was secured, she again called loudly on Janet: "Bring me a knife—scissors—aught that may undo this envious knot!"

"May not my poor poniard serve, honoured madam," said Varney, presenting a small dagger of exquisite workmanship, which hung in his Turkey-leather sword-belt.

"No, sir," replied the lady, rejecting the instrument which he offered —"Steel poniard shall cut no true-love knot of mine."

"It has cut many, however," said Anthony Foster, half aside, and looking at Varney. By this time the knot was disentangled without any other help than the neat and nimble fingers of Janet, a simply-attired pretty maiden, the daughter of Anthony Foster, who came running at the repeated call of her mistress. A necklace of orient pearl, the companion of a perfumed billet, was now hastily produced from the packet. The lady gave the one, after a slight glance, to the charge of her attendant, while she read, or rather devoured, the contents of the other.

"Surely, lady," said Janet, gazing with admiration at the neck-string of pearls, "the daughters of Tyre wore no fairer neck-jewels than these —And then the posy, 'For a neck that is fairer,'—each pearl is worth a freehold."

"Each word in this dear paper is worth the whole string, my girl— But come to my tiring-room, girl; we must be brave, my lord comes hither to-night.—He bids me grace you, Master Varney, and to me his wish is a law.—I bid you to a collation in my bower this afternoon, and you too, Master Foster. Give orders that all is fitting, and that suitable preparations be made for my lord's reception to-night." With these words she left the apartment.

"She takes state on her already," said Varney, "and distributes the favour of her presence, as if she were already the partner of his dignity. —Well—it is wise to practise beforehand the part which fortune prepares us to play—the young eagle must gaze at the sun, ere he soars on strong wing to meet it."

"If holding her head aloft," said Foster, "will keep her eyes from dazzling, I warrant you the dame will not stoop her crest. She will presently soar beyond reach of my whistle, Master Varney. I promise you, she holds me already in slight regard."

"It is thine own fault, thou sullen uninventive companion," answered Varney, "who know'st no mode of control, save downright brute force. —Canst thou not make home pleasant to her, with music and toys? Canst thou not make the out-of-doors frightful to her, with tales of goblins?—Thou livest here by the churchyard, and hast not even wit enough to raise a ghost, to scare thy females into good discipline."

"Speak not thus, Master Varney," said Foster; "the living I fear not, but I trifle not nor toy with my dead neighbours of the churchyard. I promise you, it requires a good heart to live so near it: worthy Master Holdforth, the afternoon's lecturer of Saint Antonlin's, had a sore fright there the last time he came to visit me."

"Hold thy superstitious tongue," answered Varney; "and while thou talk'st of visiting, answer me, thou paltering knave, how came Tressilian to be at the postern-door?"

"Tressilian!" answered Foster, "what know I of Tressilian?—I never heard his name."

"Why, villain, it was the very Cornish chough, to whom old Sir Hugh Robsart destined his pretty Amy, and hither the hot-brained fool has come to look after his fair runaway: there must be some order taken with him, for he thinks he hath wrong, and is not the mean hind that will sit down with it. Luckily he knows nought of my lord, but thinks he has only me to deal with. But how, in the fiend's name, came he hither?"

"Why, with Mike Lambourne, an you must know," answered Foster.

"And who is Mike Lambourne?" demanded Varney. "By Heaven! thou wert best set up a bush over thy door, and invite every stroller who passes by, to see what thou shouldst keep secret even from the sun and air."

"Ay! ay! this is a courtlike requital of my service to you, Master Richard Varney," replied Foster. "Didst thou not charge me to seek out for thee a fellow who had a good sword, and an unscrupulous conscience? and was I not busying myself to find a fit man—for, thank Heaven, my acquaintance lies not amongst such companions—when, as Heaven would have it, this tall fellow, who is in all his qualities the very flashing knave thou didst wish, came hither to fix acquaintance upon me in the plenitude of his impudence, and I admitted his claim, thinking to do you a pleasure—and now see what thanks I get for disgracing myself by converse with him!"

"And did he," said Varney, "being such a fellow as thyself, only lacking, I suppose, thy present humour of hypocrisy, which lies as thin over thy hard ruffianly heart as gold lacquer upon rusty iron—did he, I say, bring the saintly, sighing Tressilian in his train?"

"They came together, by Heaven!" said Foster; "and Tressilian—to speak Heaven's truth—obtained a moment's interview with our pretty moppet, while I was talking apart with Lambourne "

"Improvident villain! we are both undone," said Varney. "She has of late been casting many a backward look to her father's halls, whenever her lordly lover leaves her alone. Should this preaching fool whistle her back to her old perch, we were but lost men."

"No fear of that, my master," replied Anthony Foster; "she is in no mood to stoop to his lure, for she yelled out on seeing him as if an adder had stung her."

"That is good.—Canst thou not get from thy daughter an inkling of what passed between them, good Foster?"

"I tell you plain, Master Varney," said Foster, "my daughter shall not enter our purposes, or walk in our paths. They may suit me well enough, who know how to repent of my misdoings; but I will not have my child's soul committed to peril either for your pleasure or my lord's. I may walk among snares and pitfalls myself, because I have discretion, but I will not trust the poor lamb among them."

"Why, thou suspicious fool, I were as averse as thou art that thy baby-faced girl should enter into my plans, or walk to hell at her father's elbow. But indirectly thou mightest gain some intelligence of her?"

"And so I did, Master Varney," answered Foster; "and she said her lady called out upon the sickness of her father."

"Good!" replied Varney; "that is a hint worth catching, and I will work upon it. But the country must be rid of this Tressilian—I would have cumbered no man about the matter, for I hate him like strong poison—his presence is hemlock to me—and this day I had been rid of him, but that my foot slipped, when, to speak truth, had not thy comrade yonder come to my aid, and held his hand, I should have known by this time whether you and I have been treading the path to heaven or hell."

"And you can speak thus of such a risk!" said Foster. "You keep a stout heart, Master Varney—for me, if I did not hope to live many years, and to have time for the great work of repentance, I would not go forward with you."

"O! thou shalt live as long as Methuselah," said Varney, "and amass as much wealth as Solomon; and thou shalt repent so devoutly, that thy repentance shall be more famous than thy villainy,—and that is a bold word. But for all this, Tressilian must be looked after. Thy ruffian yonder is gone to dog him. It concerns our fortunes, Anthony."

"Ay, ay," said Foster, sullenly, "this it is to be leagued with one who knows not even so much of Scripture, as that the labourer is worthy of his hire. I must, as usual, take all the trouble and risk."

"Risk! and what is the mighty risk, I pray you?" answered Varney. "This fellow will come prowling again about your demesne or into your house, and if you take him for a house-breaker or a park-breaker, is it not most natural you should welcome him with cold steel or hot lead? Even a mastiff will pull down those who come near his kennel; and who shall blame him?"

"Ay, I have a mastiff's work and a mastiff's wage among you," said Foster. "Here have you, Master Varney, secured a good freehold estate out of this old superstitious foundation; and I have but a poor lease of this mansion under you, voidable at your honour's pleasure."

"Ay, and thou wouldst fain convert thy leasehold into a copyhold—the thing may chance to happen, Anthony Foster, if thou dost good service for it.—But softly, good Anthony—it is not the lending a room or two of this old house for keeping my lord's pretty paroquet—nay, it is not the shutting thy doors and windows to keep her from flying off, that may deserve it. Remember, the manor and tithes are rated at the clear annual value of seventy-nine pounds five shillings and fivepence halfpenny, besides the value of the wood. Come, come, thou must be conscionable; great and secret service may deserve both this and a better thing.—And now let thy knave come and pluck off my boots.—Get us some dinner, and a cup of thy best wine.—I must visit this mavis, brave in apparel, unruffled in aspect, and gay in temper."

They parted, and at the hour of noon, which was then that of dinner, they again met at their meal, Varney gaily dressed like a courtier of the time, and even Anthony Foster improved in appearance, as far as dress could amend an exterior so unfavourable.

This alteration did not escape Varney. When the meal was finished.

the cloth removed, and they were left to their private discourse—"Thou art gay as a goldfinch, Anthony," said Varney, looking at his host; "methinks, thou wilt whistle a jig anon—but I crave your pardon, that would secure your ejection from the congregation of the zealous butchers, the pure-hearted weavers, and the sanctified bakers of Abingdon, who let their ovens cool while their brains get heated."

"To answer you in the spirit, Master Varney," said Foster, "were—excuse the parable—to fling sacred and precious things before swine. So I will speak to thee in the language of the world, which he, who is King of the World, hath taught thee to understand, and to profit by in no common measure."

"Say what thou wilt, honest Tony," replied Varney; "for be it according to thine absurd faith, or according to thy most villainous practice, it cannot choose but be rare matter to qualify this cup of Alicant. Thy conversation is relishing and poignant, and beats caviare, dried neat's-tongue, and all other provocatives that give savour to good liquor."

"Well, then, tell me," said Anthony Foster, "is not our good lord and master's turn better served, and his ante-chamber more suitably filled, with decent, God-fearing men, who will work his will and their own profit quietly, and without worldly scandal, than that he should be manned, and attended, and followed by such open debauchers and ruffianly swordsmen, as Tidesly, Killigrew, this fellow Lambourne, whom you have put me to seek out for you, and other such, who bear the gallows in their face and murder in their right hand—who are a terror to peaceable men, and a scandal to my lord's service?"

"Oh, content you, good Master Anthony Foster," answered Varney; "he that flies at all manner of game must keep all kinds of hawks, both short and long-winged. The course my lord holds is no easy one, and he must stand provided at all points with trusty retainers to meet each sort of service. He must have his gay courtier, like myself, to ruffle it in the presence-chamber, and to lay hand on hilt when any speaks in disparagement of my lord's honour—"

"Ay," said Foster, "and to whisper a word for him into a fair lady's ear, when he may not approach her himself."

"Then," said Varney, going on without appearing to notice the interruption, "he must have his lawyers—deep subtle pioneers—to draw his contracts, his pre-contracts, and his post-contracts, and to find the way to make the most of grants of church-lands, and commons, and licenses for monopoly—And he must have physicians who can spice a cup or a caudle—And he must have his cabalists, like Dee and Allan, for conjuring up the devil—And he must have ruffling swordsmen, who would fight the devil when he is raised and at the wildest—And above all, without prejudice to others, he must have such godly, innocent, puritanic souls as thou, honest Anthony, who defy Satan, and do his work at the same time."

"You would not say, Master Varney," said Foster, "that our good lord and master, whom I hold to be fulfilled in all nobleness, would use such base and sinful means to rise, as thy speech points at?"

"Tush, man," said Varney, "never look at me with so sad a brow— you trap me not—nor am I in your power, as your weak brain may imagine, because I name to you freely the engines, the springs, the screws, the tackle, and braces, by which great men rise in stirring times.—Sayest thou our good lord is fulfilled of all nobleness?—Amen, and so be it—he has the more need to have those about him who are unscrupulous in his service, and who, because they know that his fall will overwhelm and crush them, must wager both blood and brain, soul and body, in order to keep him aloft; and this I tell thee, because I care not who knows it."

"You speak truth, Master Varney," said Anthony Foster; "he that is head of a party, is but a boat on a wave, that raises not itself, but is moved upward by the billow which it floats upon."

"Thou art metaphorical, honest Anthony," replied Varney; "that velvet doublet hath made an oracle of thee—we will have thee to Oxford to take the degrees in the arts.—And, in the meantime, hast thou arranged all the matters which were sent from London, and put the western chambers into such fashion as may answer my lord's humour?"

"They may serve a king on his bridal-day," said Anthony; "and I promise you that Dame Amy sits in them yonder, as proud and gay as if she were the Queen of Sheba."

" 'Tis the better, good Anthony," answered Varney; "we must found our future fortunes on her good liking."

"We build on sand then," said Anthony Foster; "for supposing that she sails away to court in all her lord's dignity and authority, how is she to look back upon me, who am her jailor, as it were, to detain her here against her will, keeping her a caterpillar on an old wall, when she would fain be a painted butterfly in a court garden?"

"Fear not her displeasure, man," said Varney. "I will show her that all thou hast done in this matter was good service, both to my lord and her; and when she chips the egg-shell and walks alone, she shall own we have hatched her greatness."

"Look to yourself, Master Varney," said Foster, "you may misreckon foully in this matter—She gave you but a frosty reception this morning, and, I think, looks on you, as well as me, with an evil eye."

"You mistake her, Foster—you mistake her utterly—To me she is bound by all the ties which can secure her to one who has been the means of gratifying both her love and ambition. Who was it that took the obscure Amy Robsart, the daughter of an impoverished and dotard knight—the destined bride of a moon-struck, moping enthusiast, like Edmund Tressilian, from her lowly fates, and held out to her in prospect, the brightest fortune in England, or perchance in Europe? Why, man, it was I—as I have often told thee—that found opportunity for their secret meetings—It was I who watched the wood while he beat for the deer—It was I who, to this day, am blamed by her family as the companion of her

flight, and were I in their neighbourhood, would be fain to wear a shirt of
better stuff than Holland linen, lest my ribs should be acquainted with
Spanish steel. Who carried their letters?—I. Who amused the old knight
and Tressilian?—I. Who planned her escape?—it was I. It was I, in
short, Dick Varney, who pulled this pretty little daisy from its lowly
nook, and placed it in the proudest bonnet in Britain."

"Ay, Master Varney," said Foster, "but it may be she thinks, that had
the matter remained with you, the flower had been stuck so slightly into
the cap, that the first breath of a changeable breeze of passion had blown
the poor daisy to the common."

"She should consider," said Varney, smiling, "the true faith I owed
my lord and master prevented me at first from counselling marriage—
and yet I did counsel marriage when I saw she would not be satisfied
without it—the sacrament, or the ceremony—which callest thou it,
Anthony?"

"Still she has you at feud on another score," said Foster; "and I tell
it you that you may look to yourself in time—She would not hide her
splendour in this dark lantern of an old monastic house, but would fain
shine a countess amongst countesses."

"Very natural, very right," answered Varney; "but what have I to
do with that?—she may shine through horn or through crystal at my
lord's pleasure, I have nought to say against it."

"She deems that you have an oar upon that side of the boat, Master
Varney," replied Foster, "and that you can pull it or no, at your good
pleasure. In a word, she ascribes the secrecy and obscurity in which she
is kept, to your secret counsel to my lord, and to my strict agency; and
so she loves us both as a sentenced man loves his judge and his jailor."

"She must love us better ere she leave this place, Anthony," answered
Varney. "If I have counselled for weighty reasons that she remain here
for a season, I can also advise her being brought forth in the full blow of
her dignity. But I were mad to do so, holding so near a place to my
lord's person, were she mine enemy. Bear this truth in upon her as occasion offers, Anthony, and let me alone for extolling you in her ear, and
exalting you in her opinion—*Ka me, ka thee*—it is a proverb all over
the world—The lady must know her friends, and be made to judge of
the power they have of being her enemies—meanwhile, watch her strictly,
but with all the outward observance that thy rough nature will permit.
'Tis an excellent thing that sullen look and bull-dog humour of thine;
thou shouldst thank God for it, and so should my lord; for when there is
aught harsh or hard-natured to be done, thou dost it as if it flowed from
thine own natural doggedness, and not from orders, and so my lord
escapes the scandal.—But, hark—some one knocks at the gate—Look
out at the window—let no one enter—this were an ill night to be interrupted."

"It is he whom we spoke of before dinner," said Foster, as he looked
through the casement; "it is Michael Lambourne."

"Oh, admit him, by all means," said the courtier, "he comes to give some account of his guest—it imports us much to know the movements of Edmund Tressilian—Admit him, I say, but bring him not hither— I will come to you presently, in the Abbot's library."

Foster left the room, and the courtier, who remained behind, paced the parlour more than once in deep thought, his arms folded on his bosom, until at length he gave vent to his meditations in broken words, which we have somewhat enlarged and connected, that his soliloquy may be intelligible to the reader.

" 'Tis true," he said, suddenly stopping, and resting his right hand on the table at which they had been sitting, "this base churl hath fathomed the very depth of my fear, and I have been unable to disguise it from him.—She loves me not—I would it were as true that I loved not her!—Idiot that I was, to move her in my own behalf, when wisdom bade me to be a true broker to my lord!—And this fatal error has placed me more at her discretion than a wise man would willingly be at that of the best piece of painted Eve's flesh of them all. Since the hour that my policy made so perilous a slip, I cannot look at her without fear, and hate, and fondness, so strangely mingled, that I know not whether, were it at my choice, I would rather possess or ruin her. But she must not leave this retreat until I am assured on what terms we are to stand. My lord's interest—and so far it is mine own—for if he sinks, I fall in his train—demands concealment of this obscure marriage—and besides I will not lend her my arm to climb to her chair of state, that she may set her foot on my neck when she is fairly seated. I must work an interest in her, either through love or through fear—and who knows but I may yet reap the sweetest and best revenge for her former scorn?—that were indeed a masterpiece of court-like art!—Let me but once be her counsel-keeper—let her confide to me a secret, did it but concern the robbery of a linnet's nest, and, fair Countess, thou art mine own!" He again paced the room in silence, stopped, filled, and drank a cup of wine, as if to compose the agitation of his mind; and muttering, "Now for a close heart and an open and unruffled brow," he left the apartment.

CHAPTER VI

The dews of summer night did fall,
The moon, sweet regent of the sky,
Silver'd the walls of Cumnor Hall,
And many an oak that grew thereby.[1]
Mickle.

Four apartments, which occupied the western side of the old quadrangle at Cumnor-Place, had been fitted up with extraordinary splendour. This had been the work of several days prior to that on which our story opened.

[1] This verse is the commencement of the ballad already quoted, as what suggested the novel.

Workmen sent from London, and not permitted to leave the premises until the work was finished, had converted the apartments in that side of the building, from the dilapidated appearance of a dissolved monastic house, into the semblance of a royal palace. A mystery was observed in all these arrangements: the workmen came thither and returned by night, and all measures were taken to prevent the prying curiosity of the villagers from observing or speculating upon the changes which were taking place in the mansion of their once indigent, but now wealthy neighbour, Anthony Foster. Accordingly, the secrecy desired was so far preserved, that nothing got abroad but vague and uncertain reports, which were received and repeated, but without much credit being attached to them.

On the evening of which we treat, the new and highly decorated suite of rooms were, for the first time, illuminated, and that with a brilliancy which might have been visible half-a-dozen miles off, had not oaken shutters, carefully secured with bolt and padlock, and mantled with long curtains of silk and of velvet, deeply fringed with gold, prevented the slightest gleam of radiance from being seen without.

The principal apartments, as we have seen, were four in number, each opening into the other. Access was given to them by a large scale staircase, as they were then called, of unusual length and height, which had its landing-place at the door of an antechamber, shaped somewhat like a gallery. This apartment the Abbot had used as an occasional council-room, but it was now beautifully wainscoted with dark foreign wood of a brown colour, and bearing a high polish, said to have been brought from the Western Indies, and to have been wrought in London with infinite difficulty, and much damage to the tools of the workmen. The dark colour of this finishing was relieved by the number of lights in silver sconces, which hung against the walls, and by six large and richly-framed pictures, by the first masters of the age. A massy oaken table, placed at the lower end of the apartment, served to accommodate such as chose to play at the then fashionable game of shovel-board; and there was at the other end an elevated gallery for the musicians or minstrels, who might be summoned to increase the festivity of the evening.

From this antechamber opened a banqueting room of moderate size, but brilliant enough to dazzle the eyes of the spectator with the richness of its furniture. The walls, lately so bare and ghastly, were now clothed with hangings of sky-blue velvet and silver; the chairs were of ebony, richly carved, with cushions corresponding to the hangings; and the place of the silver sconces which enlightened the antechamber, was supplied by a huge chandelier of the same precious metal. The floor was covered with a Spanish foot-cloth, or carpet, on which flowers and fruits were represented in such glowing and natural colours, that you hesitated to place the foot on such exquisite workmanship. The table, of old English oak, stood ready covered with the finest linen, and a large portable court-cupboard was placed with the leaves of its embossed folding-doors displayed, showing the shelves within, decorated with a full display of plate and porcelain. In the midst of the table stood a saltcellar of Italian workmanship—a beautiful and splendid piece of plate about two feet high, moulded into a representation of the giant Briareus, whose hundred hands of silver presented to the guests various sorts of spices, or condiments, to season their food withal.

The third apartment was called the withdrawing-room. It was hung with the finest tapestry, representing the fall of Phaeton; for the looms of Flanders were now much occupied on classical subjects. The principal seat of this apartment was a chair of state, raised a step or two from the floor, and large enough to contain two persons. It was surmounted by a canopy, which, as well as the cushions, side-curtains, and the very foot-cloth, was composed of crimson velvet, embroidered with seed-pearl. On the top of the canopy were two coronets, resembling those of an earl and countess. Stools covered with velvet, and some cushions disposed in the Moorish fashion, and ornamented with Arabesque needlework, supplied the place of chairs in this apartment, which contained musical instruments, embroidery frames, and other articles for ladies' pastime. Besides lesser lights, the withdrawing-room was illuminated by four tall torches of virgin wax, each of which was placed in the grasp of a statue, representing an armed Moor, who held in his left arm a round buckler of silver, highly polished, interposed betwixt his breast and the light, which was thus brilliantly reflected as from a crystal mirror.

The sleeping chamber belonging to this splendid suite of apartments, was decorated in a taste less showy, but not less rich, than had been displayed in the others. Two silver lamps, fed with perfumed oil, diffused at once a delicious odour and a trembling twilight-seeming shimmer through the quiet apartment. It was carpeted so thick, that the heaviest step could not have been heard, and the bed, richly heaped with down, was spread with an ample coverlet of silk and gold; from under which peeped forth cambric sheets, and blankets as white as the lambs which yielded the fleece that made them. The curtains were of blue velvet, lined with crimson silk, deeply festooned with gold, and embroidered with the loves of Cupid and Psyche. On the toilet was a beautiful Venetian mirror, in a frame of silver filigree, and beside it stood a gold posset-dish to contain the night-draught. A pair of pistols and a dagger, mounted with gold, were displayed near the head of the bed, being the arms for the night, which were presented to honoured guests, rather, it may be supposed, in the way of ceremony, than from any apprehension of danger. We must not omit to mention, what was more to the credit of the manners of the time, that in a small recess, illuminated by a taper, were disposed two hassocks of velvet and gold, corresponding with the bed furniture, before a desk of carved ebony. This recess had formerly been the private oratory of the Abbot, but the crucifix was removed, and instead, there were placed on the desk two Books of Common Prayer, richly bound, and embossed with silver. With this enviable sleeping apartment, which was so far removed from every sound, save that of the wind sighing among the oaks of the park, that Morpheus might have coveted it for his own proper repose, corresponded two wardrobes, or dressing-rooms as they are now termed, suitably furnished, and in a style of the same magnificence which we have already described. It ought to be added, that a part of the building in the adjoining wing was occupied by the kitchen and its offices, and served to accommodate the personal attendants of the great and wealthy nobleman, for whose use these magnificent preparations had been made.

The divinity for whose sake this temple had been decorated, was well worthy the cost and pains which had been bestowed. She was seated in the withdrawing-room which we have described, surveying, with the pleased eyes of natural and innocent vanity, the splendour which had been so suddenly created, as it were in her honour. For, as her own residence at Cumnor-Place formed the cause of the mystery observed in all the preparations for opening these apartments, it was sedulously arranged, that, until she took possession of them, she should have no means of knowing what was going forward in that part of the ancient building, or of exposing herself to be seen by the workmen engaged in the decorations. She had been, therefore, introduced on that evening to a part of the mansion which she had never yet seen, so different from all the rest, that it appeared, in comparison, like an enchanted palace. And when she first examined and occupied these splendid rooms, it was with the wild and unrestrained joy of a rustic beauty, who finds herself suddenly invested with a splendour which her most extravagant wishes had never imagined, and at the same time with the keen feeling of an affectionate heart, which knows that all the enchantment that surrounds her, is the work of the great magician Love.

The Countess Amy, therefore,—for to that rank she was exalted by her private but solemn union with England's proudest Earl,—had for a time flitted hastily from room to room, admiring each new proof of her lover and her bridegroom's taste, and feeling that admiration enhanced, as she recollected that all she gazed upon was one continued proof of his ardent and devoted affection.—"How beautiful are these hangings!— How natural these paintings, which seem to contend with life!—How richly wrought is that plate, which looks as if all the galleons of Spain had been intercepted on the broad seas to furnish it forth!—And oh, Janet!" she exclaimed repeatedly to the daughter of Anthony Foster, the close attendant, who, with equal curiosity, but somewhat less ecstatic joy, followed on her mistress's footsteps—"Oh, Janet! how much more delightful to think, that all these fair things have been assembled by his love, for the love of me! and that this evening—this very evening, which grows darker every instant, I shall thank him more for the love that has created such an unimaginable paradise, than for all the wonders it contains."

"The Lord is to be thanked first," said the pretty puritan, "who gave thee, lady, the kind and courteous husband, whose love has done so much for thee. I, too, have done my poor share. But if you thus run wildly from room to room, the toil of my crisping and my curling pins will vanish like the frost-work on the window when the sun is high."

"Thou sayest true, Janet," said the young and beautiful Countess, stopping suddenly from her tripping race of enraptured delight, and looking at herself from head to foot in a large mirror, such as she had never before seen, and which, indeed, had few to match it even in the Queen's palace—"Thou sayest true, Janet!" she answered, as she saw, with pardonable self-applause, the noble mirror reflect such charms as were seldom presented to its fair and polished surface; "I have more of the milkmaid than the countess, with these cheeks flushed with haste, and all these brown curls, which you laboured to bring to order, straying as wild as the tendrils of an unpruned vine—My falling ruff is chafed too, and shows the neck and bosom more than is modest and seemly— Come, Janet—we will practise state—we will go to the withdrawing-room, my good girl, and thou shalt put these rebel locks in order, and imprison within lace and cambric the bosom that beats too high."

They went to the withdrawing apartment accordingly, where the Countess playfully stretched herself upon the pile of Moorish cushions, half sitting, half reclining, half wrapt in her own thoughts, half listening to the prattle of her attendant.

While she was in this attitude, and with a corresponding expression betwixt listlessness and expectation on her fine and intelligent features, you might have searched sea and land without finding any thing half so expressive or half so lovely. The wreath of brilliants which mixed with her dark brown hair, did not match in lustre the hazel eye which a light brown eyebrow, pencilled with exquisite delicacy, and long eyelashes of the same colour, relieved and shaded. The exercise she had just taken, her excited expectation and gratified vanity, spread a glow over her fine features, which had been sometimes censured (as beauty as well as art has her minute critics) for being rather too pale. The milk-white pearls of the necklace which she wore, the same which she had just received as a true-love token from her husband, were excelled in purity by her teeth, and by the colour of her skin, saving where the blush of pleasure and self-satisfaction had somewhat stained the neck with a shade of light crimson.—"Now, have done with these busy fingers, Janet," she said to her handmaiden, who was still officiously employed in bringing her hair and her dress into order—"Have done, I say—I must see your father ere my lord arrives, and also Master Richard Varney, whom my lord has highly in his esteem—but I could tell that of him would lose him favour."

"O do not do so, good my lady!" replied Janet; "leave him to God, who punishes the wicked in his own time; but do not you cross Varney's path, for so thoroughly hath he my lord's ear, that few have thriven who have thwarted his courses."

"And from whom had you this, my most righteous Janet?" said the

Countess; "or why should I keep terms with so mean a gentleman as Varney, being, as I am, wife to his master and patron?"

"Nay, madam," replied Janet Foster, "your ladyship knows better than I—But I have heard my father say, he would rather cross a hungry wolf, than thwart Richard Varney in his projects—And he has often charged me to have a care of holding commerce with him."

"Thy father said well, girl, for thee," replied the lady, "and I dare swear meant well. It is a pity, though, his face and manner do little match his true purpose—for I think his purpose may be true."

"Doubt it not, my lady," answered Janet,—"Doubt not that my father purposes well, though he is a plain man, and his blunt looks may belie his heart."

"I will not doubt it, girl, were it only for thy sake; and yet he has one of those faces which men tremble when they look on—I think even thy mother, Janet—nay, have done with that poking-iron—could hardly look upon him without quaking."

"If it were so, madam," answered Janet Foster, "my mother had those who could keep her in honourable countenance. Why, even you, my lady, both trembled and blushed when Varney brought the letter from my lord."

"You are bold, damsel," said the Countess, rising from the cushions on which she sate half reclined in the arms of her attendant—"Know, that there are causes of trembling which have nothing to do with fear.—But, Janet," she added, immediately relapsing into the good-natured and familiar tone which was natural to her, "believe me I will do what credit I can to your father, and the rather that you, sweetheart, are his child.—Alas! alas!" she added, a sudden sadness passing over her fine features, and her eyes filling with tears, "I ought the rather to hold sympathy with thy kind heart, that my own poor father is uncertain of my fate, and they say lies sick and sorrowful for my worthless sake!—But I will soon cheer him—the news of my happiness and advancement will make him young again.—And that I may cheer him the sooner,"—she wiped her eyes as she spoke—"I must be cheerful myself—My lord must not find me insensible to his kindness, or sorrowful when he snatches a visit to his recluse, after so long an absence.—Be merry, Janet—the night wears on, and my lord must soon arrive.—Call thy father hither, and call Varney also—I cherish resentment against neither; and though I may have some room to be displeased with both, it shall be their own fault if ever a complaint against them reaches the Earl through my means.—Call them hither, Janet."

Janet Foster obeyed her mistress; and in a few minutes after, Varney entered the withdrawing-room with the graceful ease and unclouded front of an accomplished courtier, skilled, under the veil of external politeness, to disguise his own feelings, and to penetrate those of others. Anthony Foster plodded into the apartment after him, his natural gloomy vulgarity of aspect seeming to become yet more remarkable, from his clumsy attempt to conceal the mixture of anxiety and dislike with which he looked on her, over whom he had hitherto exercised so severe a control, now so splendidly attired, and decked with so many pledges of the interest which she possessed in her husband's affections. The blundering reverence which he made, rather *at* than *to* the Countess, had confession in it—It was like the reverence which the criminal makes to the judge, when he at once owns his guilt and implores mercy,—which is at the same time an impudent and embarrassed attempt at defence or extenuation, a confession of a fault, and an entreaty for lenity.

Varney, who, in right of his gentle blood, had pressed into the room before Anthony Foster, knew better what to say than he, and said it with more assurance and a better grace.

The Countess greeted him indeed with an appearance of cordiality, which seemed a complete amnesty for whatever she might have to complain of. She rose from her seat, and advanced two steps towards him, holding forth her hand as she said: "Master Richard Varney, you brought me this morning such welcome tidings, that I fear surprise and joy made me neglect my lord and husband's charge to receive you with distinction. We offer you our hand, sir, in reconciliation."

"I am unworthy to touch it," said Varney, dropping on one knee, "save as a subject honours that of a prince."

He touched with his lips those fair and slender fingers, so richly loaded with rings and jewels; then rising, with graceful gallantry, was about to hand her to the chair of state, when she said, "No, good Master Richard Varney, I take not my place there until my lord himself conducts me. I am for the present but a disguised Countess, and will not take dignity on me until authorized by him whom I derive it from."

"I trust, my lady," said Foster, "that in doing the commands of my lord your husband, in your restraint and so forth, I have not incurred your displeasure, seeing that I did but my duty towards your lord and mine; for Heaven, as holy writ saith, hath given the husband supremacy and dominion over the wife—I think it runs so, or something like it."

"I receive at this moment so pleasant a surprise, Master Foster," answered the Countess, "that I cannot but excuse the rigid fidelity which secluded me from these apartments, until they had assumed an appearance so new and so splendid."

"Ay, lady," said Foster, "it hath cost many a fair crown; and that more need not be wasted than is absolutely necessary, I leave you till my lord's arrival with good Master Richard Varney, who, as I think, hath somewhat to say to you from your most noble lord and husband.—Janet, follow me, to see that all be in order."

"No, Master Foster," said the Countess, "we will your daughter remains here in our apartment; out of ear-shot, however, in case Varney hath aught to say to me from my lord."

Foster made his clumsy reverence, and departed, with an aspect that seemed to grudge the profuse expense which had been wasted upon changing his house from a bare and ruinous grange to an Asiatic palace. When he was gone, his daughter took her embroidery frame, and went to establish herself at the bottom of the apartment, while Richard Varney, with a profoundly humble courtesy, took the lowest stool he could find, and placing it by the side of the pile of cushions on which the Countess had now again seated herself, sat with his eyes for a time fixed on the ground, and in profound silence.

"I thought, Master Varney," said the Countess, when she saw he was not likely to open the conversation, "that you had something to communicate from my lord and husband; so at least I understood Master Foster, and therefore I removed my waiting-maid. If I am mistaken, I will recall her to my side; for her needle is not so absolutely perfect in tent and cross-stitch, but what my superintendence is advisable."

"Lady," said Varney, "Foster was partly mistaken in my purpose. It was not *from* but *of* your noble husband, and my approved and most noble patron, that I am led, and indeed bound, to speak."

"The theme is most welcome, sir," said the Countess, "whether it be of or from my noble husband. But be brief, for I expect his hasty approach."

"Briefly then, madam," replied Varney, "and boldly, for my argument requires both haste and courage—You have this day seen Tressilian?"

"I have, sir, and what of that?" answered the lady somewhat sharply.

"Nothing that concerns me, lady," Varney replied with humility. "But, think you, honoured madam, that your lord will hear it with equal equanimity?"

"And wherefore should he not?—To me alone was Tressilian's visit embarrassing and painful, for he brought news of my good father's illness."

"Of your father's illness, madam!" answered Varney. "It must have been sudden then—very sudden; for the messenger whom I dispatched, at my lord's instance, found the good knight on the hunting field, cheering his beagles with his wonted jovial field-cry. I trust, Tressilian has but forged this news—He hath his reasons, madam, as you well know, for disquieting your present happiness."

"You do him injustice, Master Varney," replied the Countess, with animation,—"You do him much injustice. He is the freest, the most open, the most gentle heart that breathes. My honourable lord ever excepted, I know not one to whom falsehood is more odious than to Tressilian."

"I crave your pardon, madam," said Varney, "I meant the gentleman no injustice—I knew not how nearly his cause affected you. A man may, in some circumstances, disguise the truth for fair and honest purpose; for were it to be always spoken, and upon all occasions, this were no world to live in."

"You have a courtly conscience, Master Varney," said the Countess, "and your veracity will not, I think, interrupt your preferment in the world, such as it is.—But touching Tressilian—I must do him justice, for I have done him wrong, as none knows better than thou. Tressilian's conscience is of other mould—The world thou speakest of has not that which could bribe him from the way of truth and honour; and for living in it with a soiled fame, the ermine would as soon seek to lodge in the den of the foul polecat. For this my father loved him—For this I would have loved him—if I could—And yet in this case he had what seemed to him, unknowing alike of my marriage, and to whom I was united, such powerful reasons to withdraw me from this place, that I well trust he exaggerated much of my father's indisposition, and that thy better news may be the truer."

"Believe me they are, madam," answered Varney; "I pretend not to be a champion of that same naked virtue called truth, to the very outrance. I can consent that her charms be hidden with a veil, were it but for decency's sake. But you must think lower of my head and heart, than is due to one whom my noble lord deigns to call his friend, if you suppose I could wilfully and unnecessarily palm upon your ladyship a falsehood, so soon to be detected, in a matter which concerns your happiness."

"Master Varney," said the Countess, "I know that my lord esteems you, and holds you a faithful and a good pilot in those seas in which he has spread so high and so venturous a sail. Do not suppose, therefore, I meant hardly by you, when I spoke the truth in Tressilian's vindication —I am, as you well know, country-bred, and like plain rustic truth better than courtly compliment; but I must change my fashions with my sphere, I presume."

"True, madam," said Varney, smiling, "and though you speak now in jest, it will not be amiss that in earnest your present speech had some connexion with your real purpose.—A court-dame—take the most noble —the most virtuous—the most unimpeachable, that stands around our Queen's throne—would, for example, have shunned to speak the truth, or what she thought such, in praise of a discarded suitor, before the dependent and confidant of her noble husband."

"And wherefore," said the Countess, colouring impatiently, "should I not do justice to Tressilian's worth, before my husband's friend—before my husband himself—before the whole world?"

"And with the same openness," said Varney, "your ladyship will this night tell my noble lord your husband, that Tressilian has discovered your place of residence, so anxiously concealed from the world, and that he has had an interview with you?"

"Unquestionably," said the Countess. "It will be the first thing I tell him, together with every word that Tressilian said, and that I answered. I shall speak my own shame in this, for Tressilian's reproaches, less just than he esteemed them, were not altogether unmerited—I will speak, therefore, with pain, but I will speak, and speak all."

"Your ladyship will do your pleasure," answered Varney; "but methinks it were as well, since nothing calls for so frank a disclosure, to spare yourself this pain, and my noble lord the disquiet, and Master

Tressilian, since belike he must be thought of in the matter, the danger which is like to ensue."

"I can see nought of all these terrible consequences," said the lady, composedly, "unless by imputing to my noble lord unworthy thoughts, which I am sure never harboured in his generous heart."

"Far be it from me to do so," said Varney.—And then, after a moment's silence, he added, with a real or affected plainness of manner, very different from his usual smooth courtesy—"Come, madam, I will show you that a courtier dare speak truth as well as another, when it concerns the weal of those whom he honours and regards, ay, and although it may infer his own danger."—He waited as if to receive commands, or at least permission, to go on, but as the lady remained silent, he proceeded, but obviously with caution.—"Look around you," he said, "noble lady, and observe the barriers with which this place is surrounded, the studious mystery with which the brightest jewel that England possesses is secluded from the admiring gaze. See with what rigour your walks are circumscribed, and your movements restrained at the beck of yonder churlish Foster. Consider all this, and judge for yourself what can be the cause."

"My lord's pleasure," answered the Countess; "and I am bound to seek no other motive."

"His pleasure it is indeed," said Varney; "and his pleasure arises out of a love worthy of the object which inspires it. But he who possesses a treasure, and who values it, is oft anxious, in proportion to the value he puts upon it, to secure it from the depredations of others."

"What needs all this talk, Master Varney?" said the lady, in reply; "you would have me believe that my noble lord is jealous—Suppose it true, I know a cure for jealousy."

"Indeed, madam!" said Varney.

"It is," replied the lady, "to speak the truth to my lord at all times; to hold up my mind and my thoughts before him as pure as that polished mirror; so that when he looks into my heart, he shall only see his own features reflected there."

"I am mute, madam," answered Varney; "and as I have no reason to grieve for Tressilian, who would have my heart's blood were he able, I shall reconcile myself easily to what may befall the gentleman, in consequence of your frank disclosure of his having presumed to intrude upon your solitude.—You, who know my lord so much better than I, will judge, if he be like to bear the insult unavenged."

"Nay, if I could think myself the cause of Tressilian's ruin," said the Countess,—"I who have already occasioned him so much distress, I might be brought to be silent.—And yet what will it avail, since he was seen by Foster, and I think by some one else?—No, no, Varney, urge it no more. I will tell the whole matter to my lord; and with such pleading for Tressilian's folly, as shall dispose my lord's generous heart rather to serve than to punish him."

"Your judgment, madam," said Varney, "is far superior to mine, especially as you may, if you will, prove the ice before you step on it, by mentioning Tressilian's name to my lord, and observing how he endures it. For Foster and his attendant, they know not Tressilian by sight, and I can easily give them some reasonable excuse for the appearance of an unknown stranger."

The lady paused for an instant, and then replied, "If, Varney, it be indeed true that Foster knows not as yet that the man he saw was Tressilian, I own I were unwilling he should learn what nowise concerns him. He bears himself already with austerity enough, and I wish him not to be judge or privy-councillor in my affairs."

"Tush," said Varney, "what has the surly groom to do with your ladyship's concerns?—No more, surely, than the ban-dog which watches his court-yard. If he is in aught distasteful to your ladyship, I have interest enough to have him exchanged for a seneschal that shall be more agreeable to you."

"Master Varney," said the Countess, "let us drop this theme—when I complain of the attendants whom my lord has placed around me, it must be to my lord himself.—Hark! I hear the trampling of horse—He comes! he comes!" she exclaimed, jumping up in ecstasy.

"I cannot think it is he," said Varney; "or that you can hear the tread of his horse through the closely mantled casements."

"Stop me not, Varney—my ears are keener than thine—it is he!"

"But, madam!—but, madam!" exclaimed Varney, anxiously, and still placing himself in her way—"I trust that what I have spoken in humble duty and service, will not be turned to my ruin?—I hope that my faithful advice will not be bewrayed to my prejudice?—I implore that——"

"Content thee, man—content thee!" said the Countess, "and quit my skirt—you are too bold to detain me—Content thyself, I think not of thee."

At this moment the folding-doors flew wide open, and a man of majestic mien, muffled in the folds of a long dark riding-cloak, entered the apartment.

CHAPTER VII

——This is he
Who rides on the court-gale; controls its tides;
Knows all their secret shoals and fatal eddies;
Whose frown abases, and whose smile exalts.
He shines like any rainbow—and, perchance,
His colours are as transient.

Old Play.

THERE was some little displeasure and confusion on the Countess's brow, owing to her struggle with Varney's pertinacity; but it was exchanged for an expression of the purest joy and affection, as she threw herself into the arms of the noble stranger who entered, and clasping him to her bosom, exclaimed, "At length—at length thou art come!"

Varney discreetly withdrew as his lord entered, and Janet was about to do the same, when her mistress signed to her to remain. She took her place at the farther end of the apartment, and continued standing, as if ready for attendance.

Meanwhile the Earl, for he was of no inferior rank, returned his lady's caress with the most affectionate ardour, but affected to resist when she strove to take his cloak from him.

"Nay," she said, "but I will unmantle you—I must see if you have kept your word to me, and come as the great Earl men call thee, and not as heretofore like a private cavalier."

"Thou art like the rest of the world, Amy," said the Earl, suffering her to prevail in the playful contest; "the jewels, and feathers, and silk, are more to them than the man whom they adorn—many a poor blade looks gay in a velvet scabbard."

"But so cannot men say of thee, thou noble Earl," said his lady, as the cloak dropped on the floor, and showed him dressed as princes when they ride abroad; "thou art the good and well-tried steel, whose inly worth deserves, yet disdains, its outward ornaments. Do not think Amy can love thee better in this glorious garb, than she did when she gave her heart to him who wore the russet-brown cloak in the woods of Devon."

"And thou too," said the Earl, as gracefully and majestically he led his beautiful Countess towards the chair of state which was prepared for them both,—"thou too, my love, hast donned a dress which becomes thy rank, though it cannot improve thy beauty. What think'st thou of our court taste?"

The lady cast a sidelong glance upon the great mirror as they passed it by, and then said, "I know not how it is, but I think not of my own person, while I look at the reflection of thine. Sit thou there," she said, as they approached the chair of state, "like a thing for men to worship and to wonder at."

"Ay, love," said the Earl, "if thou wilt share my state with me."

"Not so," said the Countess; "I will sit on this footstool at thy feet, that I may spell over thy splendour, and learn, for the first time, how princes are attired."

And with a childish wonder, which her youth and rustic education rendered not only excusable but becoming, mixed as it was with a delicate show of the most tender conjugal affection, she examined and admired from head to foot the noble form and princely attire of him, who formed the proudest ornament of the court of England's Maiden Queen, renowned as it was for splendid courtiers, as well as for wise counsellors. Regarding affectionately his lovely bride, and gratified by her unrepressed admiration, the dark eye and noble features of the Earl expressed passions more gentle than the commanding and aspiring look which usually sate upon his broad forehead, and in the piercing brilliancy of his dark eye; and he smiled at the simplicity which dictated the questions she put to him concerning the various ornaments with which he was decorated.

"The embroidered strap, as thou callest it, around my knee," he said, "is the English Garter, an ornament which kings are proud to wear. See, here is the star which belongs to it, and here the Diamond George, the jewel of the Order. You have heard how King Edward and the Countess of Salisbury——"

"O, I know all that tale," said the Countess, slightly blushing, "and how a lady's garter became the proudest badge of English chivalry."

"Even so," said the Earl; "and this most honourable Order I had the good hap to receive at the same time with three most noble associates, the Duke of Norfolk, the Marquis of Northampton, and the Earl of Rutland. I was the lowest of the four in rank—but what then?—he that climbs a ladder must begin at the first round."

"But this other fair collar, so richly wrought, with some jewel like a sheep hung by the middle attached to it, what," said the young Countess, "does that emblem signify?"

"This collar," said the Earl, "with its double fusilles interchanged with these knobs, which are supposed to present flint-stones, sparkling with fire, and sustaining the jewel you enquire about, is the badge of the noble Order of the Golden Fleece, once appertaining to the House of Burgundy. It hath high privileges, my Amy, belonging to it, this most noble Order; for even the king of Spain himself, who hath now succeeded to the honours and demesnes of Burgundy, may not sit in judgment upon a knight of the Golden Fleece, unless by assistance and consent of the Great Chapter of the Order."

"And is this an Order belonging to the cruel king of Spain?" said the Countess. "Alas! my noble lord, that you will defile your noble English breast by bearing such an emblem! Bethink you of the most unhappy Queen Mary's days, when this same Philip held sway with her in England, and of the piles which were built for our noblest, and our wisest, and our most truly sanctified prelates and divines—And will you, whom men call the standard-bearer of the true Protestant faith, be contented to wear the emblem and mark of such a Romish tyrant as he of Spain?"

"O, content you, my love," answered the Earl; "we who spread our sails to gales of court favour, cannot always display the ensigns we love the best, or at all times refuse sailing under colours which we like not. Believe me, I am not the less good Protestant, that for policy I must accept the honour offered me by Spain, in admitting me to this his highest order of knighthood. Besides. it belongs properly to Flanders; and Egmont, Orange, and others, have pride in seeing it displayed on an English bosom."

"Nay, my lord, you know your own path best," replied the Countess. —"And this other collar, to what country does this fair jewel belong?"

"To a very poor one, my love," replied the Earl; "this is the Order of

Saint Andrew, revived by the last James of Scotland. It was bestowed on
me when it was thought the young widow of France and Scotland would
gladly have wedded an English baron; but a free coronet of England is
worth a crown matrimonial held at the humour of a woman, and owning
only the poor rocks and bogs of the north."

The Countess paused, as if what the Earl last said had excited some
painful but interesting train of thought; and, as she still remained silent,
her husband proceeded.

"And now, loveliest, your wish is gratified, and you have seen your
vassal in such of his trim array as accords with riding vestments; for
robes of state and coronets are only for princely halls."

"Well, then," said the Countess, "my gratified wish has, as usual, given
rise to a new one."

"And what is it thou canst ask that I can deny?" said the fond husband.

"I wished to see my Earl visit this obscure and secret bower," said
the Countess, "in all his princely array; and now, methinks, I long to sit
in one of his princely halls, and see him enter dressed in sober russet, as
when he won poor Amy Robsart's heart."

"That is a wish easily granted," said the Earl—"the sober russet shall
be donned to-morrow, if you will."

"But shall I," said the lady, "go with you to one of your castles, to
see how the richness of your dwelling will correspond with your peasant
habit?"

"Why, Amy," said the Earl, looking around, "are not these apartments decorated with sufficient splendour? I gave the most unbounded
order, and, methinks, it has been indifferently well obeyed—but if thou
canst tell me aught which remains to be done, I will instantly give
direction."

"Nay, my lord, now you mock me," replied the Countess; "the gaiety
of this rich lodging exceeds my imagination as much as it does my desert.
But shall not your wife, my love—at least one day soon—be surrounded
with the honour, which arises neither from the toils of the mechanic who
decks her apartment, nor from the silks and jewels with which your
generosity adorns her, but which is attached to her place among the
matronage, as the avowed wife of England's noblest Earl?"

"One day?" said her husband,—"Yes, Amy, my love, one day this
shall surely happen; and, believe me, thou canst not wish for that day
more fondly than I. With what rapture could I retire from labours of
state, and cares and toils of ambition, to spend my life in dignity and
honour on my own broad domains, with thee, my lovely Amy, for my
friend and companion! But, Amy, this cannot yet be; and these dear but
stolen interviews, are all I can give to the loveliest and the best beloved
of her sex."

"But *why* can it not be?" urged the Countess, in the softest tones of
persuasion,—"Why can it not immediately take place—this more perfect, this uninterrupted union, for which you say you wish, and which

he laws of God and man alike command?—Ah! did you but desire it half as much as you say, mighty and favoured as you are, who, or what, should bar your attaining your wish?"

The Earl's brow was overcast.

"Amy," he said, "you speak of what you understand not. We that toil in courts are like those who climb a mountain of loose sand—we dare make no halt until some projecting rock afford us a secure footing and resting-place—if we pause sooner, we slide down by our own weight, an object of universal derision. I stand high, but I stand not secure enough to follow my own inclination. To declare my marriage, were to be the artificer of my own ruin. But, believe me, I will reach a point, and that speedily, when I can do justice to thee and to myself. Meantime, poison not the bliss of the present moment, by desiring that which cannot at present be. Let me rather know whether all here is managed to thy liking. How does Foster bear himself to you?—in all things respectful, I trust, else the fellow shall dearly rue it."

"He reminds me sometimes of the necessity of this privacy," answered the lady, with a sigh; "but that is reminding me of your wishes, and therefore, I am rather bound to him than disposed to blame him for it."

"I have told you the stern necessity which is upon us," replied the Earl. "Foster is, I note, somewhat sullen of mood, but Varney warrants to me his fidelity and devotion to my service. If thou hast aught, however, to complain of the mode in which he discharges his duty, he shall abye it."

"O, I have nought to complain of," answered the lady, "so he discharges his task with fidelity to you; and his daughter Janet is the kindest and best companion of my solitude—her little air of precision sits so well upon her!"

"Is she indeed?" said the Earl; "she who gives you pleasure, must not pass unrewarded.—Come hither, damsel."

"Janet," said the lady, "come hither to my lord."

Janet, who, as we already noticed, had discreetly retired to some distance, that her presence might be no check upon the private conversation of her lord and lady, now came forward; and as she made her reverential curtsy, the Earl could not avoid smiling at the contrast which the extreme simplicity of her dress, and the prim demureness of her looks made, with a very pretty countenance and a pair of black eyes, that laughed in spite of their mistress's desire to look grave.

"I am bound to you, pretty damsel," said the Earl, "for the contentment which your service hath given to this lady." As he said this, he took from his finger a ring of some price, and offered it to Janet Foster, adding, "Wear this, for her sake and for mine."

"I am well pleased, my lord," answered Janet, demurely, "that my poor service hath gratified my lady, whom no one can draw nigh to without desiring to please; but we of the precious Master Holdforth's congregation, seek not, like the gay daughters of this world, to twine gold around our fingers, or wear stones upon our necks, like the vain women of Tyre and of Sidon."

"O, what! you are a grave professor of the precise sisterhood, pretty Mrs Janet," said the Earl, "and I think your father is of the same congregation in sincerity? I like you both the better for it; for I have been prayed for, and wished well to, in your congregations. And you may the better afford the lack of ornament, Mrs Janet, because your fingers are slender, and your neck white. But here is what neither papist nor puritan, latitudinarian nor precisian, ever boggles or makes mouths at. E'en take it, my girl, and employ it as you list."

So saying, he put into her hand five broad gold pieces of Philip and Mary.

"I would not accept this gold neither," said Janet, "but that I hope to find a use for it, which will bring a blessing on us all."

"Even please thyself, pretty Janet," said the Earl, "and I shall be well satisfied—And I prithee let them hasten the evening collation."

"I have bidden Master Varney and Master Foster to sup with us, my lord," said the Countess, as Janet retired to obey the Earl's commands; "has it your approbation?"

"What you do ever must have so, my sweet Amy," replied her husband; "and I am the better pleased thou hast done them this grace, because Richard Varney is my sworn man, and a close brother of my secret council; and for the present, I must needs repose much trust in this Anthony Foster."

"I had a boon to beg of thee, and a secret to tell thee, my dear lord," said the Countess, with a faltering accent.

"Let both be for to-morrow, my love," replied the Earl. "I see they open the folding-doors into the banqueting parlour, and as I have ridden far and fast, a cup of wine will not be unacceptable."

So saying he led his lovely wife into the next apartment, where Varney and Foster received them with the deepest reverences, which the first paid after the fashion of the court, and the second after that of the congregation. The Earl returned their salutation with the negligent courtesy of one long used to such homage; while the Countess repaid it with a punctilious solicitude, which showed it was not quite so familiar to her.

The banquet at which the company seated themselves, corresponded in magnificence with the splendour of the apartment in which it was served up, but no domestic gave his attendance. Janet alone stood ready to wait upon the company; and, indeed, the board was so well supplied with all that could be desired, that little or no assistance was necessary. The Earl and his lady occupied the upper end of the table, and Varney and Foster sat beneath the salt, as was the custom with inferiors. The latter, overawed perhaps by society to which he was altogether unused, did not utter a single syllable during the repast; while Varney, with great tact and discernment, sustained just so much of the conversation, as, without the appearance of intrusion on his part, prevented it from

languishing, and maintained the good-humour of the Earl at the highest
pitch. This man was indeed highly qualified by nature to discharge the
part in which he found himself placed, being discreet and cautious on
the one hand, and on the other, quick, keen-witted, and imaginative; so
that even the Countess, prejudiced as she was against him on many
accounts, felt and enjoyed his powers of conversation, and was more disposed than she had ever hitherto found herself, to join in the praises
which the Earl lavished on his favourite. The hour of rest at length arrived; the Earl and Countess retired to their apartment, and all was
silent in the castle for the rest of the night.

Early on the ensuing morning, Varney acted as the Earl's chamberlain
as well as his master of horse, though the latter was his proper office in
that magnificent household, where knights and gentlemen of good descent were well contented to hold such menial situations, as nobles themselves held in that of the sovereign. The duties of each of these charges
were familiar to Varney, who, sprung from an ancient but somewhat decayed family, was the Earl's page during his earlier and more obscure
fortunes, and, faithful to him in adversity, had afterwards contrived to
render himself no less useful to him in his rapid and splendid advance
to fortune; thus establishing in him an interest resting both on present
and past services, which rendered him an almost indispensable sharer
of his confidence.

"Help me to do on a plainer riding-suit, Varney," said the Earl, as he
laid aside his morning-gown, flowered with silk, and lined with sables,
"and put these chains and fetters there" (pointing to the collars of the
various Orders which lay on the table) "into their place of security--
my neck last night was wellnigh broke with the weight of them. I am half
of the mind that they shall gall me no more. They are bonds which knaves
have invented to fetter fools. How think'st thou, Varney?"

"Faith, my good lord," said his attendant, "I think fetters of gold are
like no other fetters—they are ever the weightier the welcomer."

"For all that, Varney," replied his master, "I am wellnigh resolved
they shall bind me to the court no longer. What can further service and
higher favour give me beyond the rank and large estate which I have
already secured?—What brought my father to the block, but that he
could not bound his wishes within right and reason?—I have, you know,
had mine own ventures and mine own escapes: I am wellnigh resolved to
tempt the sea no farther, but sit me down in quiet on the shore."

"And gather cockle-shells, with Dan Cupid to aid you," said Varney.

"How mean you by that, Varney?" said the Earl, somewhat hastily.

"Nay, my lord," said Varney, "be not angry with me. If your lordship
is happy in a lady so rarely lovely, that in order to enjoy her company
with somewhat more freedom, you are willing to part with all you have
hitherto lived for, some of your poor servants may be sufferers; but your
bounty hath placed me so high, that I shall ever have enough to main-

tain a poor gentleman in the rank befitting the high office he has held in your lordship's family."

"Yet you seem discontented when I propose throwing up a dangerous game, which may end in the ruin of both of us."

"I, my lord?" said Varney; "surely I have no cause to regret your lordship's retreat!—It will not be Richard Varney who will incur the displeasure of majesty, and the ridicule of the court, when the stateliest fabric that ever was founded upon a prince's favour melts away like a morning frost-work.—I would only have you yourself be assured, my lord, ere you take a step which cannot be retraced, that you consult your fame and happiness in the course you propose."

"Speak on, then, Varney," said the Earl; "I tell thee I have determined nothing, and will weigh all considerations on either side."

"Well, then, my lord," replied Varney, "we will suppose the step taken, the frown frowned, the laugh laughed, and the moan moaned. You have retired, we will say, to some one of your most distant castles, so far from court that you hear neither the sorrow of your friends, nor the glee of your enemies. We will suppose, too, that your successful rival will be satisfied (a thing greatly to be doubted) with abridging and cutting away the branches of the great tree which so long kept the sun from him, and that he does not insist upon tearing you up by the roots. Well; the late prime favourite of England, who wielded her general's staff and controlled her parliaments, is now a rural baron, hunting, hawking, drinking fat ale with country esquires, and mustering his men at the command of the High Sheriff——"

"Varney, forbear!" said the Earl.

"Nay, my lord, you must give me leave to conclude my picture.— Sussex governs England—the Queen's health fails—the succession is to be settled—a road is opened to ambition more splendid than ambition ever dreamed of.—You hear all this as you sit by the hob, under the shade of your hall-chimney—You then begin to think what hopes you have fallen from, and what insignificance you have embraced—and all that you might look babies in the eyes of your fair wife oftener than once a-fortnight."

"I say, Varney," said the Earl, "no more of this. I said not that the step, which my own ease and comfort would urge me to, was to be taken hastily, or without due consideration to the public safety. Bear witness to me, Varney; I subdue my wishes of retirement, not because I am moved by the call of private ambition, but that I may preserve the position in which I may best serve my country at the hour of need.—Order our horses presently—I will wear, as formerly, one of the livery cloaks, and ride before the portmantle.—Thou shalt be master for the day, Varney—neglect nothing that can blind suspicion. We will to horse ere men are stirring. I will but take leave of my lady, and be ready. I impose a restraint on my own poor heart, and wound one yet more dear to me; but the patriot must subdue the husband."

Having said this in a melancholy but firm accent, he left the dressing apartment.

"I am glad thou art gone," thought Varney, "or, practised as I am in the follies of mankind, I had laughed in the very face of thee! Thou mayst tire as thou wilt of thy new bauble, thy pretty piece of painted Eve's flesh there, I will not be thy hinderance. But of thine old bauble, ambi·tion, thou shalt not tire, for as you climb the hill, my lord, you must drag Richard Varney up with you; and if he can urge you to the ascent he means to profit by, believe me he will spare neither whip nor spur.—And for you, my pretty lady, that would be Countess outright, you were best not thwart my courses, lest you are called to an old reckoning on a new score. 'Thou shalt be master,' did he say?—By my faith, he may find that he spoke truer than he is aware of—And thus he, who, in the estimation of so many wise-judging men, can match Burleigh and Walsingham in policy, and Sussex in war, becomes pupil to his own menial; and all for a hazel eye and a little cunning red and white, and so falls ambition. And yet if the charms of mortal woman could excuse a man's politic pate for becoming bewildered, my lord had the excuse at his right hand on this blessed evening that has last passed over us. Well—let things roll as they may, he shall make me great, or I will make myself happy; and for that softer piece of creation, if she speak not out her interview with Tressilian, as well I think she dare not, she also must traffic with me for concealment and mutual support in spite of all this scorn.—I must to the stables.—Well, my lord, I order your retinue now; the time may soon come that *my* master of the horse shall order mine own.—What was Thomas Cromwell but a smith's son, and he died, my lord—on a scaffold, doubtless, but that, too, was in character—And what was Ralph Sadler, but the clerk of Cromwell, and he has gazed eighteen fair lordships,—*via!* I know my steerage as well as they!"

So saying, he left the apartment.

In the meanwhile the Earl had re-entered the bed-chamber, bent on taking a hasty farewell of the lovely Countess, and scarce daring to trust himself in private with her, to hear requests again urged, which he found it difficult to parry, yet which his recent conversation with his master of horse had determined him not to grant.

He found her in a white cymar of silk lined with furs, her little feet unstockinged and hastily thrust into slippers; her unbraided hair escaping from under her midnight coif, with little array but her own loveliness, rather augmented than diminished by the grief which she felt at the approaching moment of separation.

"Now, God be with thee, my dearest and loveliest!" said the Earl, scarce tearing himself from her embrace, yet again returning to fold her again and again in his arms, and again bidding farewell, and again returning to kiss and bid adieu once more. "The sun is on the verge of the blue horizon—I dare not stay.—Ere this I should have been ten miles from hence."

Such were the words, with which at length he strove to cut short their parting interview.

"You will not grant my request, then?" said the Countess. "Ah, false knight! did ever lady, with bare foot in slipper, seek boon of a brave knight, yet return with denial?"

"Any thing, Amy, any thing thou canst ask I will grant," answered the Earl—"always excepting," he said, "that which might ruin us both."

"Nay," said the Countess, "I urge not my wish to be acknowledged in the character which would make me the envy of England—as the wife, that is, of my brave and noble lord, the first as the most fondly beloved of English nobles.—Let me but share the secret with my dear father!—Let me but end his misery on my unworthy account—they say he is ill, the good old kind-hearted man!"

"*They* say?" asked the Earl, hastily; "who says? Did not Varney convey to Sir Hugh all we dare at present tell him concerning your happiness and welfare? and has he not told you that the good old knight was following, with good heart and health, his favourite and wonted exercise? Who has dared put other thoughts into your head?"

"O, no one, my lord, no one," said the Countess, something alarmed at the tone in which the question was put: "but yet, my lord, I would fain be assured by mine own eye-sight that my father is well."

"Be contented, Amy—thou canst not now have communication with thy father or his house. Were it not a deep course of policy to commit no secret unnecessarily to the custody of more than must needs be, it were sufficient reason for secrecy, that yonder Cornish man, yonder Trevanion, or Tressilian, or whatever his name is, haunts the old knight's house, and must necessarily know whatever is communicated there."

"My lord," answered the Countess, "I do not think it so. My father has been long noted a worthy and honourable man; and for Tressilian, if we can pardon ourselves the ill we have wrought him, I will wager the coronet I am to share with you one day, that he is incapable of returning injury for injury."

"I will not trust him, however, Amy," said her husband; "by my honour, I will not trust him—I would rather the foul fiend intermingle in our secret than this Tressilian!"

"And why, my lord?" said the Countess, though she shuddered slightly at the tone of determination in which he spoke; "let me but know why you think thus hardly of Tressilian?"

"Madam," replied the Earl, "my will ought to be a sufficient reason—If you desire more, consider how this Tressilian is leagued, and with whom. He stands high in the opinion of this Radcliffe, this Sussex, against whom I am barely able to maintain my ground in the opinion of our suspicious mistress; and if he had me at such advantage, Amy, as to become acquainted with the tale of our marriage, before Elizabeth were fitly prepared, I were an outcast from her grace for ever—a bankrupt at once in favour and in fortune, perhaps, for she hath in her a touch of her father Henry,—a victim, and it may be a bloody one, to her offended and jealous resentment."

"But why, my lord," again urged his lady, "should you deem thus injuriously of a man, of whom you know so little? What you do know of Tressilian is through me, and it is I who assure you that in no circumstances will he betray your secret. If I did him wrong in your behalf, my lord, I am now the more concerned you should do him justice.—You are offended at my speaking of him, what would you say had I actually myself seen him?"

"If you had," replied the Earl, "you would do well to keep that interview as secret as that which is spoken in a confessional. I seek no one's ruin; but he who thrusts himself on my secret privacy, were better look well to his future walk. The bear [1] brooks no one to cross his awful path."

"Awful, indeed!" said the Countess, turning very pale.

"You are ill, my love," said the Earl, supporting her in his arms; "stretch yourself on your couch again; it is but an early day for you to leave it.—Have you aught else, involving less than my fame, my fortune, and my life, to ask of me?"

"Nothing, my lord and love," answered the Countess, faintly; "something there was that I would have told you, but your anger has driven it from my recollection."

"Reserve it till our next meeting, my love," said the Earl fondly, and again embracing her; "and barring only these requests which I cannot and dare not grant, thy wish must be more than England and all its dependencies can fulfil, if it is not gratified to the letter."

Thus saying, he at length took farewell. At the bottom of the staircase he received from Varney an ample livery cloak and slouched hat, in which he wrapped himself so as to disguise his person, and completely conceal his features. Horses were ready in the courtyard for himself and Varney;—for one or two of his train, intrusted with the secret so far as to know or guess that the Earl intrigued with a beautiful lady at that mansion, though her name and quality were unknown to them, had already been dismissed over night.

Anthony Foster himself had in hand the rein of the Earl's palfrey, a stout and able nag for the road; while his old serving-man held the bridle of the more showy and gallant steed which Richard Varney was to occupy in the character of master.

As the Earl approached, however, Varney advanced to hold his master's bridle, and to prevent Foster from paying that duty to the Earl, which he probably considered as belonging to his own office. Foster scowled at an interference which seemed intended to prevent his paying his court to his patron, but gave place to Varney; and the Earl, mounting without farther observation, and forgetting that his assumed character of a domestic threw him into the rear of his supposed master, rode pen-

[1] The Leicester cognizance was the ancient device adopted by his father, when Earl of Warwick, the bear and ragged staff.

sively out of the quadrangle, not without waving his hand repeatedly in answer to the signals which were made by the Countess with her kerchief, from the windows of her apartment.

While his stately form vanished under the dark archway which led out of the quadrangle, Varney muttered, "There goes fine policy—the servant before the master!" then as he disappeared, seized the moment to speak a word with Foster. "Thou look'st dark on me, Anthony," he said, "as if I had deprived thee of a parting nod of my lord; but I have moved him to leave thee a better remembrance for thy faithful service. See here! a purse of as good gold as ever chinked under a miser's thumb and fore-finger. Ay, count them, lad," said he, as Foster received the gold with a grim smile, "and add to them the goodly remembrance he gave last night to Janet."

"How's this! how's this!" said Anthony Foster, hastily; "gave he gold to Janet?"

"Ay, man, wherefore not?—does not her service to his fair lady require guerdon?"

"She shall have none on't," said Foster; "she shall return it. I know his dotage on one face is as brief as it is deep. His affections are as fickle as the moon."

"Why, Foster, thou art mad—thou dost not hope for such good for- tune, as that my lord should cast an eye on Janet?—Who, in the fiend's name, would listen to the thrush when the nightingale is singing?"

"Thrush or nightingale, all is one to the fowler; and, Master Varney, you can sound the quailpipe most daintily to wile wantons into his nets. I desire no such devil's preferment for Janet as you have brought many a poor maiden to—Dost thou laugh?—I will keep one limb of my family, at least, from Satan's clutches, that thou mayst rely on—She shall re- store the gold."

"Ay, or give it to thy keeping, Tony, which will serve as well," answered Varney; "but I have that to say which is more serious.—Our lord is returning to court in an evil humour for us."

"How meanest thou?" said Foster. "Is he tired already of his pretty toy—his plaything yonder? He has purchased her at a monarch's ran- som, and I warrant me he rues his bargain."

"Not a whit, Tony," answered the master of the horse; "he dotes on her, and will forsake the court for her—then down go hopes, possessions, and safety—church-lands are resumed, Tony, and well if the holders be not called to account in Exchequer."

"That were ruin," said Foster, his brow darkening with apprehensions; "and all this for a woman!—Had it been for his soul's sake, it were some- thing; and I sometimes wish I myself could fling away the world that cleaves to me, and be as one of the poorest of our church."

"Thou art like enough to be so, Tony," answered Varney; "but I think the devil will give thee little credit for thy compelled poverty, and so thou losest on all hands. But follow my counsel, and Cumnor-Place shall be thy copyhold yet—Say nothing of this Tressilian's visit—not a word until I give thee notice."

"And wherefore, I pray you?" asked Foster, suspiciously.

"Dull beast!" replied Varney; "in my lord's present humour it were the ready way to confirm him in his resolution of retirement, should he know that his lady was haunted with such a spectre in his absence. He would be for playing the dragon himself over his golden fruit, and then, Tony, thy occupation is ended. A word to the wise—Farewell—I must follow him."

He turned his horse, struck him with the spurs, and rode off under the archway in pursuit of his lord.

"Would thy occupation were ended, or thy neck broken, damned pander!" said Anthony Foster. "But I must follow his beck, for his interest and mine are the same, and he can wind the proud Earl to his will. Janet shall give me those pieces though—they shall be laid out in some way for God's service, and I will keep them separate in my strong chest, till I can fall upon a fitting employment for them. No contagious vapour shall breathe on Janet—she shall remain pure as a blessed spirit, were it but to pray God for her father. I need her prayers, for I am at a hard pass—Strange reports are abroad concerning my way of life. The congregation look cold on me, and when Master Holdforth spoke of hypocrites being like a whited sepulchre, which within was full of dead men's bones, methought he looked full at me. The Romish was a comfortable faith; Lambourne spoke true in that. A man had but to follow his thrift by such ways as offered—tell his beads—hear a mass—confess, and be absolved. These puritans tread a harder and a rougher path; but I will try—I will read my Bible for an hour ere I again open mine iron chest."

Varney, meantime, spurred after his lord, whom he found waiting for him at the postern-gate of the park.

"You waste time, Varney," said the Earl; "and it presses. I must be at Woodstock before I can safely lay aside my disguise; and till then I journey in some peril."

"It is but two hours' brisk riding, my lord," said Varney; "for me, I only stopped to enforce your commands of care and secrecy on yonder Foster, and to enquire about the abode of the gentleman whom I would promote to your lordship's train, in the room of Trevors."

"Is he fit for the meridian of the antechamber, think'st thou?" said the Earl.

"He promises well, my lord," replied Varney, "but if your lordship were pleased to ride on, I could go back to Cumnor, and bring him to your lordship at Woodstock before you are out of bed."

"Why, I am asleep there, thou knowest, at this moment," said the Earl; "and I pray you not to spare horse-flesh, that you may be with me at my levee."

So saying, he gave his horse the spur, and proceeded on his journey, while Varney rode back to Cumnor by the public road, avoiding the park. The latter alighted at the door of the bonny Black Bear, and desired to speak with Master Michael Lambourne. That respectable character was not long of appearing before his new patron, but it was with downcast looks.

"Thou hast lost the scent," said Varney, "of thy comrade Tressilian. —I know it by thy hangdog visage. Is this thy alacrity, thou impudent knave?"

"Cogswounds!" said Lambourne, "there was never a trail so finely hunted. I saw him to earth at mine uncle's here—stuck to him like bees' wax—saw him at supper—watched him to his chamber, and presto—he is gone next morning, the very hostler knows not where!"

"This sounds like practice upon me, sir," replied Varney; "and if it prove so, by my soul you shall repent it!"

"Sir, the best hound will be sometimes at fault," answered Lambourne; "how should it serve me that this fellow should have thus evanished? You may ask mine host, Giles Gosling—ask the tapster and hostler—ask Cicely, and the whole household, how I kept eyes on Tressilian while he was on foot.—On my soul, I could not be expected to watch him like a sick nurse, when I had seen him fairly a-bed in his chamber. That will be allowed me, surely."

Varney did, in fact, make some enquiry among the household, which confirmed the truth of Lambourne's statement. Tressilian, it was unanimously agreed, had departed suddenly and unexpectedly, betwixt night and morning.

"But I will wrong no one," said mine host; "he left on the table in his lodging the full value of his reckoning, with some allowance to the servants of the house, which was the less necessary, that he saddled his own gelding, as it seems, without the hostler's assistance."

Thus satisfied of the rectitude of Lambourne's conduct, Varney began to talk to him upon his future prospects, and the mode in which he meant to bestow himself, intimating that he understood from Foster, he was not disinclined to enter into the household of a nobleman.

"Have you," said he, "ever been at court?"

"No," replied Lambourne; "but ever since I was ten years old, I have dreamt once a-week that I was there, and made my fortune."

"It may be your own fault if your dream comes not true," said Varney. "Are you needy?"

"Um!" replied Lambourne; "I love pleasure."

"That is a sufficient answer, and an honest one," said Varney. "Know you aught of the requisites expected from the retainer of a rising courtier?"

"I have imagined them to myself, sir," answered Lambourne; "as for example, a quick eye—a close mouth—a ready and bold hand—a sharp wit, and a blunt conscience."

"And thine, I suppose," said Varney, "has had its edge blunted long since?"

"I cannot remember, sir, that its edge was ever over keen," replied Lambourne. "When I was a youth, I had some few whimsies, but I rubbed them partly out of my recollection on the rough grindstone of the wars, and what remained I washed out in the broad waves of the Atlantic."

"Thou hast served, then, in the Indies?"

"In both East and West," answered the candidate for court-service, "by both sea and land; I have served both the Portugal and the Spaniard —both the Dutchman and the Frenchman, and have made war on our own account with a crew of jolly fellows, who held there was no peace beyond the Line." [1]

"Thou mayst do me, and my lord, and thyself, good service," said Varney, after a pause. "But observe, I know the world—and answer me truly, canst thou be faithful?"

"Did you not know the world," answered Lambourne, "it were my duty to say ay, without further circumstance, and to swear to it with life and honour, and so forth. But as it seems to me that your worship is one who desires rather honest truth than politic falsehood—I reply to you, that I can be faithful to the gallows' foot, ay, to the loop that dangles from it, if I am well used and well recompensed;—not otherwise."

"To thy other virtues thou canst add, no doubt," said Varney, in a jeering tone, "the knack of seeming serious and religious, when the moment demands it?"

"It would cost me nothing," said Lambourne, "to say yes—but, to speak on the square, I must needs say no. If you want a hypocrite, you may take Anthony Foster, who, from his childhood, had some sort of phantom haunting him, which he called religion, though it was that sort of godliness which always ended in being great gain. But I have no such knack of it."

"Well," replied Varney, "if thou hast no hypocrisy, hast thou not a nag here in the stable?"

"Ay, sir," said Lambourne, "that shall take hedge and ditch with my Lord Duke's best hunters. When I made a little mistake on Shooter's Hill, and stopped an ancient grazier whose pouches were better lined than his brain-pan, the bonny bay nag carried me sheer off, in spite of the whole hue and cry."

"Saddle him then, instantly, and attend me," said Varney. "Leave thy clothes and baggage under charge of mine host, and I will conduct thee to a service, in which, if thou do not better thyself, the fault shall not be fortune's, but thine own."

"Brave and hearty!" said Lambourne, "and I am mounted in an instant.—Knave, hostler, saddle my nag without the loss of one second,

[1] Sir Francis Drake, Morgan, and many a bold Buccanier of those days, were, in fact, little better than pirates.

as thou dost value the safety of thy noddle.—Pretty Cicely, take half this purse to comfort thee for my sudden departure."

"Gogsnouns!" replied the father, "Cicely wants no such token from thee.—Go away, Mike, and gather grace if thou canst, though I think thou goest not to the land where it grows."

"Let me look at this Cicely of thine, mine host," said Varney; "I have heard much talk of her beauty."

"It is a sunburnt beauty," said mine host, "well qualified to stand out rain and wind, but little calculated to please such critical gallants as yourself. She keeps her chamber, and cannot encounter the glance of such sunny-day courtiers as my noble guest."

"Well, peace be with her, my good host," answered Varney; "our horses are impatient—we bid you good day."

"Does my nephew go with you, so please you?" said Gosling.

"Ay, such is his purpose," answered Richard Varney.

"You are right—fully right," replied mine host—"you are, I say, fully right, my kinsman. Thou hast got a gay horse, see thou light not unaware upon a halter—or, if thou wilt needs be made immortal by means of a rope, which thy purpose of following this gentleman renders not unlikely, I charge thee to find a gallows as far from Cumnor as thou conveniently mayst; and so I commend you to your saddle."

The master of the horse and his new retainer mounted accordingly, leaving the landlord to conclude his ill-omened farewell, to himself and at leisure; and set off together at a rapid pace, which prevented conversation until the ascent of a steep sandy hill permitted them to resume it.

"You are contented, then," said Varney to his companion, "to take court service?"

"Ay, worshipful sir, if you like my terms as well as I like yours."

"And what are your terms?" demanded Varney.

"If I am to have a quick eye for my patron's interest, he must have a dull one towards my faults," said Lambourne.

"Ay," said Varney, "so they lie not so grossly open that he must needs break his shins over them."

"Agreed," said Lambourne. "Next, if I run down game, I must have the picking of the bones."

"That is but reason," replied Varney, "so that your betters are served before you."

"Good," said Lambourne; "and it only remains to be said, that if the law and I quarrel, my patron must bear me out, for that is a chief point."

"Reason again," said Varney, "if the quarrel hath happened in your master's service."

"For the wage and so forth, I say nothing," proceeded Lambourne; "it is the secret guerdon that I must live by."

"Never fear," said Varney; "thou shalt have clothes and spending money to ruffle it with the best of thy degree, for thou goest to a household where you have gold, as they say, by the eye."

"That jumps all with my humour," replied Michael Lambourne; "and it only remains that you tell me my master's name."

"My name is Master Richard Varney," answered his companion.

"But I mean," said Lambourne, "the name of the noble lord to whose service you are to prefer me."

"How, knave, art thou too good to call *me* master?" said Varney hastily; "I would have thee bold to others, but not saucy to me."

"I crave your worship's pardon," said Lambourne; "but you seemed familiar with Anthony Foster, now I am familiar with Anthony myself."

"Thou art a shrewd knave, I see," replied Varney. "Mark me—I do indeed propose to introduce thee into a nobleman's household; but it is upon my person thou wilt chiefly wait, and upon my countenance that thou wilt depend. I am his master of horse—Thou wilt soon know his name—it is one that shakes the council and wields the state."

"By this light, a brave spell to conjure with," said Lambourne, "if a man would discover hidden treasures!"

"Used with discretion, it may prove so," replied Varney; "but mark —if thou conjure with it at thine own hand, it may raise a devil who will tear thee in fragments."

"Enough said," replied Lambourne; "I will not exceed my limits."

The travellers then resumed the rapid rate of travelling which their discourse had interrupted, and soon arrived at the Royal Park of Woodstock. This ancient possession of the crown of England was then very different from what it had been when it was the residence of the fair Rosamond, and the scene of Henry the Second's secret and illicit amours; and yet more unlike to the scene which it exhibits in the present day, when Blenheim-House commemorates the victory of Marlborough, and no less the genius of Vanburgh, though decried in his own time by persons of taste far inferior to his own. It was, in Elizabeth's time, an ancient mansion in bad repair, which had long ceased to be honoured with the royal residence, to the great impoverishment of the adjacent village. The inhabitants, however, had made several petitions to the Queen to have the favour of the sovereign's countenance occasionally bestowed upon them; and upon this very business, ostensibly at least, was the noble lord, whom we have already introduced to our readers, a visitor at Woodstock.

Varney and Lambourne galloped without ceremony into the court-yard of the ancient and dilapidated mansion, which presented on that morning a scene of bustle which it had not exhibited for two reigns. Officers of the Earl's household, livery-men and retainers, went and came with all the insolent fracas which attaches to their profession. The neigh of horses and the baying of hounds were heard; for my lord, in his occupation of inspecting and surveying the manor and demesne, was of course provided with the means of following his pleasure in the chase or park, said to have been the earliest that was enclosed in England, and which was well stocked with deer that had long roamed there unmolested.

Several of the inhabitants of the village, in anxious hope of a favourable result from this unwonted visit, loitered about the court-yard, and awaited the great man's coming forth. Their attention was excited by the hasty arrival of Varney, and a murmur ran amongst them, "The Earl's master of the horse!" while they hurried to bespeak favour by hastily unbonneting, and proffering to hold the bridle and stirrup of the favoured retainer and his attendant.

"Stand somewhat aloof, my masters!" said Varney, haughtily, "and let the domestics do their office."

The mortified citizens and peasants fell back at the signal; while Lambourne, who had his eye upon his superior's deportment, repelled the services of those who offered to assist him, with yet more discourtesy— "Stand back, Jack peasant, with a murrain to you, and let these knave footmen do their duty!"

While they gave their nags to the attendants of the household, and walked into the mansion with an air of superiority which long practice and consciousness of birth rendered natural to Varney, and which Lambourne endeavoured to imitate as well as he could, the poor inhabitants of Woodstock whispered to each other, "Well-a-day—God save us from all such misproud princoxes! An the master be like the men, why, the fiend may take all, and yet have no more than his due."

"Silence, good neighbours!" said the Bailiff, "keep tongue betwixt teeth—we shall know more by and by.—But never will a lord come to Woodstock so welcome as bluff old King Harry! He would horsewhip a fellow one day with his own royal hand, and then fling him an handful of silver groats, with his own broad face on them, to 'noint the sore withal."

"Ay, rest be with him!" echoed the auditors; "it will be long ere this Lady Elizabeth horsewhip any of us."

"There is no saying," answered the Bailiff. "Meanwhile, patience, good neighbours, and let us comfort ourselves by thinking that we deserve such notice at her grace's hands."

Meanwhile, Varney, closely followed by his new dependent, made his way to the hall, where men of more note and consequence than those left in the court-yard awaited the appearance of the Earl, who as yet kept his chamber. All paid court to Varney, with more or less deference, as suited their own rank, or the urgency of the business which brought them to his lord's levee. To the general question of, "When comes my lord forth, Master Varney?" he gave brief answers, as, "See you not my boots? I am but just returned from Oxford, and know nothing of it," and the like, until the same query was put in a higher tone by a personage of more importance. "I will enquire of the chamberlain, Sir Thomas Copely," was the reply. The chamberlain, distinguished by his silver key, answered, that the Earl only awaited Master Varney's return to come down, but that he would first speak with him in his private chamber. Varney, therefore, bowed to the company, and took leave, to enter his lord's apartment.

There was a murmur of expectation which lasted a few minutes, and was at length hushed by the opening of the folding-doors at the upper end of the apartment, through which the Earl made his entrance, marshalled by his chamberlain and the steward of his family, and followed by Richard Varney. In his noble mien and princely features, men read nothing of that insolence which was practised by his dependents. His courtesies were, indeed, measured by the rank of those to whom they were addressed, but even the meanest person present had a share of his gracious notice. The enquiries which he made respecting the condition of the manor, of the Queen's rights there, and of the advantages and disadvantages which might attend her occasional residence at the royal seat of Woodstock, seemed to show that he had most earnestly investigated the matter of the petition of the inhabitants, and with a desire to forward the interest of the place.

"Now the Lord love his noble countenance," said the Bailiff, who had thrust himself into the presence-chamber; "he looks somewhat pale. I warrant him he hath spent the whole night in perusing our memorial. Master Toughyarn, who took six months to draw it up, said it would take a week to understand it; and see if the Earl hath not knocked the marrow out of it in twenty-four hours!"

The Earl then acquainted them that he should move their sovereign to honour Woodstock occasionally with her residence during her royal progresses, that the town and its vicinity might derive, from her countenance and favour, the same advantages as from those of her predecessors. Meanwhile, he rejoiced to be the expounder of her gracious pleasure, in assuring them that, for the increase of trade and encouragement of the worthy burgesses of Woodstock, her majesty was minded to erect the town into a Staple for wool.

This joyful intelligence was received with the acclamations not only of the better sort who were admitted to the audience-chamber, but of the commons who awaited without.

The freedom of the corporation was presented to the Earl upon knee by the magistrates of the place, together with a purse of gold pieces, which the Earl handed to Varney, who, on his part, gave a share to Lambourne, as the most acceptable earnest of his new service.

The Earl and his retinue took horse soon after to return to court, accompanied by the shouts of the inhabitants of Woodstock, who made the old oaks ring with re-echoing, "Long live Queen Elizabeth, and the noble Earl of Leicester!" The urbanity and courtesy of the Earl even threw a gleam of popularity over his attendants, as their haughty deportment had formerly obscured that of their master; and men shouted, "Long life to the Earl, and to his gallant followers!" as Varney and Lambourne, each in his rank, rode proudly through the streets of Woodstock.

CHAPTER VIII

Host. I will hear you, Master Fenton;
And I will, at least, keep your counsel.
                    Merry Wives of Windsor.

IT becomes necessary to return to the detail of those circumstances which accompanied, and indeed occasioned, the sudden disappearance of Tressilian from the sign of the Black Bear at Cumnor. It will be recollected that this gentleman, after his rencounter with Varney, had returned to Giles Gosling's caravansary, where he shut himself up in his own chamber, demanded pen, ink, and paper, and announced his purpose to remain private for the day: in the evening he appeared again in the public room, where Michael Lambourne, who had been on the watch for him, agreeably to his engagement to Varney, endeavoured to renew his acquaintance with him, and hoped he retained no unfriendly recollection of the part he had taken in the morning's scuffle.

But Tressilian repelled his advances firmly, though with civility— "Master Lambourne," he said, "I trust I have recompensed to your pleasure the time you have wasted on me. Under the show of wild bluntness which you exhibit, I know you have sense enough to understand me, when I say frankly, that the object of our temporary acquaintance having been accomplished, we must be strangers to each other in future."

"*Voto!*" said Lambourne, twirling his whiskers with one hand, and grasping the hilt of his weapon with the other; "if I thought that this usage was meant to insult me——"

"You would bear it with discretion, doubtless," interrupted Tressilian, "as you must do at any rate. You know too well the distance that is betwixt us, to require me to explain myself further—Good evening."

So saying, he turned his back upon his former companion, and entered into discourse with the landlord. Michael Lambourne felt strongly disposed to bully; but his wrath died away in a few incoherent oaths and ejaculations, and he sank unresistingly under the ascendency which superior spirits possess over persons of his habits and description. He remained moody and silent in a corner of the apartment, paying the most marked attention to every motion of his late companion, against whom he began now to nourish a quarrel on his own account, which he trusted to avenge by the execution of his new master Varney's directions. The hour of supper arrived, and was followed by that of repose, when Tressilian, like others, retired to his sleeping apartment.

He had not been in bed long, when the train of sad reveries, which supplied the place of rest in his disturbed mind, was suddenly interrupted by the jar of a door on its hinges, and a light was seen to glimmer in the apartment. Tressilian, who was as brave as steel, sprang from his bed at this alarm, and had laid hand upon his sword, when he was prevented from drawing it by a voice which said, "Be not too rash with your rapier, Master Tressilian—It is I, your host, Giles Gosling."

At the same time, unshrouding the dark lantern, which had hitherto only emitted an indistinct glimmer, the goodly aspect and figure of the landlord of the Black Bear was visibly presented to his astonished guest.

"What mummery is this, mine host?" said Tressilian; "have you supped as jollily as last night, and so mistaken your chamber? or is midnight a time for masquerading it in your guest's lodging?"

"Master Tressilian," replied mine host, "I know my place and my time as well as e'er a merry landlord in England. But here has been my hang-dog kinsman watching you as close as ever cat watched a mouse; and here have you, on the other hand, quarrelled and fought, either with him or with some other person, and I fear that danger will come of it."

"Go to, thou art but a fool, man," said Tressilian; "thy kinsman is beneath my resentment; and besides, why shouldst thou think I had quarrelled with any one whomsoever?"

"Oh! sir," replied the innkeeper, "there was a red spot on thy very cheek-bone, which boded of a late brawl, as sure as the conjunction of Mars and Saturn threatens misfortune—and when you returned, the buckles of your girdle were brought forward, and your step was quick and hasty, and all things showed your hand and your hilt had been lately acquainted."

"Well, good mine host, if I have been obliged to draw my sword," said Tressilian, "why should such a circumstance fetch thee out of thy warm bed at this time of night? Thou seest the mystery is all over."

"Under favour, that is what I doubt. Anthony Foster is a dangerous man, defended by strong court patronage, which hath borne him out in matters of very deep concernment. And, then, my kinsman—why, I have told you what he is; and if these two old cronies have made up their old acquaintance, I would not, my worshipful guest, that it should be at thy cost. I promise you, Mike Lambourne has been making very particular enquiries at my hostler, when and which way you ride. Now, I would have you think, whether you may not have done or said something for which you may be waylaid, and taken at disadvantage."

"Thou art an honest man, mine host," said Tressilian, after a moment's consideration, "and I will deal frankly with thee. If these men's malice is directed against me—as I deny not but it may—it is because they are the agents of a more powerful villain than themselves."

"You mean Master Richard Varney, do you not?" said the landlord; "he was at Cumnor-Place yesterday, and came not thither so private but what he was espied by one who told me."

"I mean the same, mine host."

"Then, for God's sake, worshipful Master Tressilian," said honest Gosling, "look well to yourself. This Varney is the protector and patron of Anthony Foster, who holds under him, and by his favour, some lease of yonder mansion and the park. Varney got a large grant of the lands of the Abbacy of Abingdon, and Cumnor-Place amongst others, from his master, the Earl of Leicester. Men say he can do every thing with him, though I hold the Earl too good a nobleman to employ him as some men talk of.—And then the Earl can do any thing (that is any thing right or fitting) with the Queen, God bless her; so you see what an enemy you have made to yourself."

"Well—it is done, and I cannot help it," answered Tressilian.

"Uds precious, but it must be helped in some manner," said the host. "Richard Varney—why, what between his influence with my lord, and his pretending to so many old and vexatious claims in right of the Abbot here, men fear almost to mention his name, much more to set themselves against his practices. You may judge by our discourses the last night. Men said their pleasure of Tony Foster, but not a word of Richard Varney, though all men judge him to be at the bottom of yonder mystery about the pretty wench. But perhaps you know more of that matter than I do, for women, though they wear not swords, are occasion for many a blade's exchanging a sheath of neat's leather for one of flesh and blood."

"I do indeed know more of that poor unfortunate lady than thou dost, my friendly host; and so bankrupt am I, at this moment, of friends and advice, that I will willingly make a counsellor of thee, and tell thee the whole history, the rather that I have a favour to ask when my tale is ended."

"Good Master Tressilian," said the landlord, "I am but a poor inn-keeper, little able to adjust or counsel such a guest as yourself. But as sure as I have risen decently above the world, by giving good measure and reasonable charges, I am an honest man; and as such, if I may not be able to assist you, I am, at least, not capable to abuse your confidence. Say away, therefore, as confidently as if you spoke to your father; and thus far at least be certain, that my curiosity, for I will not deny that which belongs to my calling, is joined to a reasonable degree of discretion."

"I doubt it not, mine host," answered Tressilian; and while his auditor remained in anxious expectation, he meditated for an instant how he should commence his narrative. "My tale," he at length said, "to be quite intelligible, must begin at some distance back.—You have heard of the battle of Stoke, my good host, and perhaps of old Sir Roger Robsart, who, in that battle, valiantly took part with Henry VII., the Queen's grandfather, and routed the Earl of Lincoln, Lord Geraldin and his wild Irish, and the Flemings whom the Duchess of Burgundy had sent over, in the quarrel of Lambert Simnel?"

"I remember both one and the other," said Giles Gosling, "it is sung of a dozen times a-week on my ale-bench below.—Sir Roger Robsart of Devon—O, ay,—'tis him of whom minstrels sing to this hour,—

'He was the flower of Stoke's red field,
When Martin Swart on ground lay slain;
In raging rout he never reel'd,
But like a rock did firm remain.' [1]

Ay, and then there was Martin Swart I have heard my grandfather talk of, and of the jolly Almains whom he commanded, with their slashed doublets and quaint hose, all frounced with ribands above the nether-stocks. Here's a song goes of Martin Swart, too, an I had but memory for it:—

'Martin Swart and his men,
Saddle them, saddle them,
Martin Swart and his men;
Saddle them well.' " [2]

"True, good mine host—the day was long talked of; but if you sing so loud, you will awake more listeners than I care to commit my confidence unto."

"I crave pardon, my worshipful guest," said mine host, "I was oblivious. When an old song comes across us merry old knights of the spigot, it runs away with our discretion."

"Well, mine host, my grandfather, like some other Cornishmen, kept a warm affection to the House of York, and espoused the quarrel of this Simnel, assuming the title of Earl of Warwick, as the county afterwards, in great numbers, countenanced the cause of Perkin Warbeck, calling himself the Duke of York. My grandsire joined Simnel's standard, and was taken fighting desperately at Stoke, where most of the leaders of that unhappy army were slain in their harness. The good knight to whom he rendered himself, Sir Roger Robsart, protected him from the immediate vengeance of the King, and dismissed him without ransom. But he was unable to guard him from other penalties of his rashness, being the heavy fines by which he was impoverished, according to Henry's mode of weakening his enemies. The good knight did what he might to mitigate the distresses of my ancestor; and their friendship became so strict, that my father was bred up as the sworn brother and intimate of the present Sir Hugh Robsart, the only son of Sir Roger, and the heir of his honest, and generous, and hospitable temper, though not equal to him in martial achievements."

"I have heard of Good Sir Hugh Robsart," interrupted the host, "many a time and oft. His huntsman and sworn servant, Will Badger, hath spoke of him an hundred times in this very house—a jovial knight

---

[1] This verse, or something similar, occurs in a long ballad, or poem, on Flodden-Field, reprinted by the late Henry Weber.
[2] This verse of an old song *actually* occurs in an old play, where the singer boasts,—
"Courteously I can both counter and knack
Of Martin Swart and all his merry-men."

he is, and hath loved hospitality and open housekeeping more than the present fashion, which lays as much gold lace on the seams of a doublet as would feed a dozen of tall fellows with beef and ale for a twelvemonth, and let them have their evening at the alehouse once a-week, to do good to the publican."

"If you have seen Will Badger, mine host," said Tressilian, "you have heard enough of Sir Hugh Robsart; and therefore I will but say, that the hospitality you boast of hath proved somewhat detrimental to the estate of his family, which is perhaps of the less consequence, as he has but one daughter to whom to bequeath it. And here begins my share in the tale. Upon my father's death, now several years since, the good Sir Hugh would willingly have made me his constant companion. There was a time, however, at which I felt the kind knight's excessive love for field-sports detained me from studies, by which I might have profited more; but I ceased to regret the leisure which gratitude and hereditary friend-ship compelled me to bestow on these rural avocations. The exquisite beauty of Mistress Amy Robsart, as she grew up from childhood to woman, could not escape one whom circumstances obliged to be so con-stantly in her company—I loved her, in short, mine host, and her father saw it."

"And crossed your true loves, no doubt?" said mine host; "it is the way in all such cases; and I judge it must have been so in your instance, from the heavy sigh you uttered even now."

"The case was different, mine host. My suit was highly approved by the generous Sir Hugh Robsart—it was his daughter who was cold to my passion."

"She was the more dangerous enemy of the two," said the innkeeper. "I fear me your suit proved a cold one."

"She yielded me her esteem," said Tressilian, "and seemed not unwill-ing that I should hope it might ripen into a warmer passion. There was a contract of future marriage executed betwixt us, upon her father's intercession; but to comply with her anxious request, the execution was deferred for a twelvemonth. During this period, Richard Varney ap-peared in the country, and, availing himself of some distant family con-nexion with Sir Hugh Robsart, spent much of his time in his company, until, at length, he almost lived in the family."

"That could bode no good to the place he honoured with his resi-dence," said Gosling.

"No, by the rood!" replied Tressilian. "Misunderstanding and misery followed his presence, yet so strangely, that I am at this moment at a loss to trace the gradations of their encroachments upon a family, which had, till then, been so happy. For a time Amy Robsart received the at-tentions of this man Varney with the indifference attached to common courtesies; then followed a period in which she seemed to regard him with dislike, and even with disgust; and then an extraordinary species of connexion appeared to grow up betwixt them. Varney dropped those airs of pretension and gallantry which had marked his former approaches; and Amy, on the other hand, seemed to renounce the ill-disguised disgust with which she had regarded them. They seemed to have more of privacy and confidence together, than I fully liked; and I suspected that they met in private, where there was less restraint than in our presence. Many circumstances, which I noticed but little at the time—for I deemed her heart as open as her angelic countenance—have since arisen on my memory, to convince me of their private understanding. But I need not detail them—the fact speaks for itself. She vanished from her father's house—Varney disappeared at the same time—and this very day I have seen her in the character of his paramour, living in the house of his sordid dependent Foster, and visited by him, muffled, and by a secret entrance."

"And this, then, is the cause of your quarrel? Methinks, you should have been sure that the fair lady either desired or deserved your inter‧ference."

"Mine host," answered Tressilian, "my father, such I must ever con‧sider Sir Hugh Robsart, sits at home struggling with his grief, or, if so far recovered, vainly attempting to drown, in the practice of his field-sports, the recollection that he had once a daughter—a recollection which ever and anon breaks from him under circumstances the most pathetic. I could not brook the idea that he should live in misery, and Amy in guilt; and I endeavoured to seek her out, with the hope of inducing her to return to her family. I have found her, and when I have either succeeded in my attempt, or have found it altogether unavailing, it is my purpose to embark for the Virginia voyage."

"Be not so rash, good sir," replied Giles Gosling; "and cast not yourself away because a woman—to be brief—*is* a woman, and changes her lovers like her suit of ribands, with no better reason than mere fantasy. And ere we probe this matter further, let me ask you what circumstances of suspicion directed you so truly to this lady's residence, or rather to her place of concealment?"

"The last is the better chosen word, mine host," answered Tressilian; "and touching your question, the knowledge that Varney held large grants of the demesnes formerly belonging to the Monks of Abingdon, directed me to this neighbourhood; and your nephew's visit to his old comrade, Foster, gave me the means of conviction on the subject."

"And what is now your purpose, worthy sir?—excuse my freedom in asking the question so broadly."

"I purpose, mine host," said Tressilian, "to renew my visit to the place of her residence to-morrow, and to seek a more detailed communi-cation with her than I have had to-day. She must indeed be widely changed from what she once was, if my words make no impression upon her."

"Under your favour, Master Tressilian," said the landlord, "you can follow no such course. The lady, if I understand you, has already re-jected your interference in the matter."

"It is but too true," said Tressilian; "I cannot deny it."

"Then, marry, by what right or interest do you process a compulsory interference with her inclination, disgraceful as it may be to herself and to her parents? Unless my judgment gulls me, those under whose protection she has thrown herself, would have small hesitation to reject your interference, even if it were that of a father or brother; but as a discarded lover, you expose yourself to be repelled with the strong hand, as well as with scorn. You can apply to no magistrate for aid or countenance; and you are hunting, therefore, a shadow in water, and will only (excuse my plainness) come by ducking and danger in attempting to catch it."

"I will appeal to the Earl of Leicester," said Tressilian, "against the infamy of his favourite.—He courts the severe and strict sect of puritans—He dared not, for the sake of his own character, refuse my appeal, even although he were destitute of the principles of honour and nobleness with which fame invests him. Or I will appeal to the Queen herself."

"Should Leicester," said the landlord, "be disposed to protect his dependent, (as indeed he is said to be very confidential with Varney,) the appeal to the Queen may bring them both to reason. Her majesty is strict in such matters, and (if it be not treason to speak it) will rather, it is said, pardon a dozen courtiers for falling in love with herself, than one for giving preference to another woman. Coragio then, my brave guest! for if thou layest a petition from Sir Hugh at the foot of the throne, bucklered by the story of thine own wrongs, the favourite Earl dared as soon leap into the Thames at the fullest and deepest, as offer to protect Varney in a cause of this nature.   But to do this with any chance of success, you must go formally to work; and, without staying here to tilt with the master of horse to a privy councillor, and expose yourself to the dagger of his camaradoes, you should hie you to Devonshire, get a petition drawn up for Sir Hugh Robsart, and make as many friends as you can to forward your interest at court."

"You have spoken well, mine host," said Tressilian, "and I will profit by your advice, and leave you to-morrow early."

"Nay, leave me to-night, sir, before to-morrow comes," said the landlord. "I never prayed for a guest's arrival more eagerly than I do to have you safely gone. My kinsman's destiny is most like to be hanged for something, but I would not that the cause were the murder of an honoured guest of mine. 'Better ride safe in the dark,' says the proverb, 'than in daylight with a cut-throat at your elbow.' Come, sir, I move you for your own safety. Your horse and all is ready, and here is your score."

"It is somewhat under a noble," said Tressilian, giving one to the host; "give the balance to pretty Cicely, your daughter, and the servants of the house."

"They shall taste of your bounty, sir," said Gosling, "and you should taste of my daughter's lips in graceful acknowledgment, but at this hour she cannot grace the porch to greet your departure."

"Do not trust your daughter too far with your guests, my good land-lord," said Tressilian.

"O, sir, we will keep measure; but I wonder not that you are jealous of them all.—May I crave to know with what aspect the fair lady at the Place yesterday received you."

"I own," said Tressilian, "it was angry as well as confused, and affords me little hope that she is yet awakened from her unhappy delusion."

"In that case, sir, I see not why you should play the champion of a wench that will none of you, and incur the resentment of a favourite's favourite, as dangerous a monster as ever a knight adventurer encountered in the old story books."

"You do me wrong in the supposition, mine host—gross wrong," said Tressilian; "I do not desire that Amy should ever turn thought upon me more. Let me but see her restored to her father, and all I have to do in Europe—perhaps in the world—is over and ended."

"A wiser resolution were to drink a cup of sack, and forget her," said the landlord. "But five-and-twenty and fifty look on those matters with different eyes, especially when one case of peepers is set in the skull of a young gallant, and the other in that of an old publican. I pity you, Master Tressilian, but I see not how I can aid you in the matter."

"Only thus far, mine host," replied Tressilian—"Keep a watch on the motions of those of the Place, which thou canst easily learn without suspicion, as all men's news fly to the ale-bench; and be pleased to communicate the tidings in writing to such person, and to no other, who shall bring you this ring as a special token—look at it—it is of value, and I will freely bestow it on you."

"Nay, sir," said the landlord, "I desire no recompense—but it seems an unadvised course in me, being in a public line, to connect myself in a matter of this dark and perilous nature. I have no interest in it."

"You, and every father in the land, who would have his daughter released from the snares of shame, and sin, and misery, have an interest deeper than aught concerning earth only could create."

"Well, sir," said the host, "these are brave words; and I do pity from my soul the frank-hearted old gentleman, who has minished his estate in good house-keeping for the honour of his country, and now has his daughter, who should be the stay of his age, and so forth, whisked up by such a kite as this Varney. And though your part in the matter is somewhat of the wildest, yet I will e'en be a madcap for company, and help you in your honest attempt to get back the good man's child, so far as being your faithful intelligencer can serve. And as I shall be true to you, I pray you to be trusty to me, and keep my secret; for it were bad for the custom of the Black Bear, should it be said the bear-warder interfered in such matters. Varney has interest enough with the justices to dismount my noble emblem from the post on which he swings so gallantly, to call in my license, and ruin me from garret to cellar."

"Do not doubt my secrecy, mine host," said Tressilian; "I will retain,

besides, the deepest sense of thy service, and of the risk thou dost run—
remember the ring is my sure token.—And now, farewell—for it was thy
wise advice that I should tarry here as short a time as may be."

"Follow me, then, Sir Guest," said the landlord, "and tread as gently
as if eggs were under your foot, instead of deal boards.—No man must
know when or how you departed."

By the aid of his dark lantern he conducted Tressilian, as soon as he
had made himself ready for his journey, through a long intricacy of
passages, which opened to an outer court, and from thence to a remote
stable, where he had already placed his guest's horse. He then aided
him to fasten on the saddle the small portmantle which contained his
necessaries, opened a postern-door, and with a hearty shake of the hand,
and a reiteration of his promise to attend to what went on at Cumnor-
Place, he dismissed his guest to his solitary journey.

CHAPTER IX

> Far in the lane a lonely hut he found,
> No tenant ventured on the unwholesome ground:
> Here smokes his forge, he bares his sinewy arm,
> And early strokes the sounding anvil warm;
> Around his shop the steely sparkles flew,
> As for the steed he shaped the bending shoe.
>
> GAY's *Trivia*.

As it was deemed proper by the traveller himself, as well as by Giles
Gosling, that Tressilian should avoid being seen in the neighbourhood
of Cumnor by those whom accident might make early risers, the landlord
had given him a route, consisting of various byways and lanes, which he
was to follow in succession, and which, all the turns and short-cuts duly
observed, was to conduct him to the public road to Marlborough.

But, like counsel of every other kind, this species of direction is much
more easily given than followed; and what betwixt the intricacy of the
way, the darkness of the night, Tressilian's ignorance of the country,
and the sad and perplexing thoughts with which he had to contend, his
journey proceeded so slowly, that morning found him only in the vale
of Whitehorse, memorable for the defeat of the Danes in former days,
with his horse deprived of a forefoot shoe, an accident which threatened
to put a stop to his journey, by laming the animal. The residence of a
smith was his first object of enquiry, in which he received little satisfaction from the dulness or sullenness of one or two peasants, early bound
for their labour, who gave brief and indifferent answers to his questions
on the subject. Anxious, at length, that the partner of his journey should
suffer as little as possible from the unfortunate accident, Tressilian dismounted, and led his horse in the direction of a little hamlet, where he
hoped either to find or hear tidings of such an artificer as he now wanted.
Through a deep and muddy lane, he at length waded on to the place,

which proved an assemblage of five or six miserable huts, about the doors of which one or two persons, whose appearance seemed as rude as that of their dwellings, were beginning the toils of the day. One cottage, however, seemed of rather superior aspect, and the old dame, who was sweeping her threshold, appeared something less rude than her neighbours. To her Tressilian addressed the oft-repeated question, whether there was a smith in this neighbourhood, or any place where he could refresh his horse? The dame looked him in the face with a peculiar expression, as she replied, "Smith! ay, truly is there a smith—what wouldst ha' wi' un, mon?"

"To shoe my horse, good dame," answered Tressilian; "you may see that he has thrown a fore-foot shoe."

"Master Holiday!" exclaimed the dame, without returning any direct answer—"Master Herasmus Holiday, come and speak to mon, and please you."

"*Favete linguis*," answered a voice from within; "I cannot now come forth, Gammer Sludge, being in the very sweetest bit of my morning studies."

"Nay, but, good now, Master Holiday, come ye out, do ye—Here's a mon would to Wayland Smith, and I care not to show him way to devil—his horse hath cast shoe."

"*Quid mihi cum caballo?*" replied the man of learning from within; "I think there is but one wise man in the hundred, and they cannot shoe a horse without him!"

And forth came the honest pedagogue, for such his dress bespoke him. A long, lean, shambling, stooping figure, was surmounted by a head thatched with lank black hair somewhat inclining to grey. His features had the cast of habitual authority, which I suppose Dionysius carried with him from the throne to the schoolmaster's pulpit, and bequeathed as a legacy to all of the same profession. A black buckram cassock was gathered at his middle with a belt, at which hung, instead of knife or weapon, a goodly leathern pen-and-ink-case. His ferula was stuck on the other side, like Harlequin's wooden sword; and he carried in his hand the tattered volume which he had been busily perusing.

On seeing a person of Tressilian's appearance, which he was better able to estimate than the country folks had been, the schoolmaster unbonneted, and accosted him with, "*Salve, domine, Intelligisne linguam Latinam?*"

Tressilian mustered his learning to reply, "*Linguæ Latinæ haud penitus ignarus, venia tua, domine eruditissime, vernaculam libentius loquor.*"

The Latin reply had upon the schoolmaster the effect which the mason's sign is said to produce on the brethren of the trowel. He was at once interested in the learned traveller, listened with gravity to his story of a tired horse and a lost shoe, and then replied with solemnity, "It may appear a simple thing, most worshipful, to reply to you that there dwells, within a brief mile of these *tuguria,* the best *faber ferrarius,* the most accomplished blacksmith, that ever nailed iron upon horse. Now, were I to say so, I warrant me you would think yourself *compos voti,* or, as the vulgar have it, a made man."

"I should at least," said Tressilian, "have a direct answer to a plain question, which seems difficult to be obtained in this country."

"It is a mere sending of a sinful soul to the evil un," said the old woman, "the sending a living creature to Wayland Smith."

"Peace, Gammer Sludge!" said the pedagogue; *"pauca verba,* Gammer Sludge; look to the furmity, Gammer Sludge; *curetur jentaculum,* Gammer Sludge; this gentleman is none of thy gossips." Then turning to Tressilian, he resumed his lofty tone, "And so, most worshipful, you would really think yourself *felix bis terque,* should I point out to you the dwelling of this same smith?"

"Sir," replied Tressilian, "I should in that case have all that I want at present—a horse fit to carry me forward—out of hearing of your learning." The last words he muttered to himself.

"O cæca mens mortalium!" said the learned man; "well was it sung by Junius Juvenalis, *'numinibus vota exaudita malignis!'"*

"Learned Magister," said Tressilian, "your erudition so greatly exceeds my poor intellectual capacity, that you must excuse my seeking elsewhere for information which I can better understand."

"There again now," replied the pedagogue, "how fondly you fly from him that would instruct you! Truly said Quintilian——"

"I pray sir, let Quintilian be for the present, and answer, in a word and in English, if your learning can condescend so far, whether there is any place here where I can have opportunity to refresh my horse, until I can have him shod?"

"Thus much courtesy, sir," said the schoolmaster, "I can readily render you, that although there is in this poor hamlet (*nostra paupera regna*) no regular *hospitium,* as my namesake Erasmus called it, yet, forasmuch as you are somewhat embued, or at least tinged as it were, with good letters, I will use my interest with the good woman of the house to accommodate you with a platter of furmity—an wholesome food for which I have found no Latin phrase—your horse shall have a share of the cowhouse, with a bottle of sweet hay, in which the good woman Sludge so much abounds, that it may be said of her cow, *fœnum habet in cornu;* and if it please you to bestow on me the pleasure of your company, the banquet shall cost you *ne semissem quidem,* so much is Gammer Sludge bound to me for the pains I have bestowed on the top and bottom of her hopeful heir Dickie, whom I have painfully made to travel through the accidence."

"Now, God yield ye for it, Master Herasmus," said the good Gammer, "and grant that little Dickie may be the better for his accident!—and for the rest, if the gentleman list to stay, breakfast shall be on the board in the wringing of a dishclout; and for horse-meat, and man's meat, I bear no such base mind as to ask a penny."

Considering the state of his horse, Tressilian, upon the whole, saw no better course than to accept the invitation thus learnedly made and hospitably confirmed, and take chance that when the good pedagogue had exhausted every topic of conversation, he might possibly condescend to tell him where he could find the smith they spoke of. He entered the hut accordingly, and sat down with the learned Magister Erasmus Holiday, partook of his furmity, and listened to his learned account of himself for a good half hour, ere he could get him to talk upon any other topic. The reader will readily excuse our accompanying this man of learning into all the details with which he favoured Tressilian, of which the following sketch may suffice.

He was born at Hogsnorton, where, according to popular saying, the pigs play upon the organ; a proverb which he interpreted allegorically, as having reference to the herd of Epicurus, of which litter Horace confessed himself a porker. His name of Erasmus, he derived partly from his father having been the son of a renowned washerwoman, who had held that great scholar in clean linen all the while he was at Oxford; a task of some difficulty, as he was only possessed of two shirts, "the one," as she expressed herself, "to wash the other." The vestiges of one of these *camiciæ*, as Master Holiday boasted, were still in his possession, having fortunately been detained by his grandmother to cover the balance of her bill. But he thought there was a still higher and overruling cause for his having had the name of Erasmus conferred on him, namely, the secret presentiment of his mother's mind, that, in the babe to be christened, was a hidden genius, which should one day lead him to rival the fame of the great scholar of Amsterdam. The schoolmaster's surname led him as far into dissertation as his Christian appellative. He was inclined to think that he bore the name of Holiday *quasi lucus a non lucendo,* because he gave such few holidays to his school. "Hence," said he, "the schoolmaster is termed, classically, *Ludi Magister,* because he deprives boys of their play." And yet, on the other hand, he thought it might bear a very different interpretation, and refer to his own exquisite art in arranging pageants, morris-dances, May-day festivities, and such like holiday delights, for which he assured Tressilian he had positively the purest and the most inventive brain in England; insomuch, that his cunning in framing such pleasures had made him known to many honourable persons, both in country and court, and especially to the noble Earl of Leicester—"And although he may now seem to forget me," he said, "in the multitude of state affairs, yet I am well assured, that had he some pretty pastime to array for entertainment of the Queen's Grace, horse and man would be seeking the humble cottage of Erasmus Holiday. *Parvo contentus,* in the meanwhile, I hear my pupils parse, and construe, worshipful sir, and drive away my time with the aid of the Muses. And I have at all times, when in correspondence with foreign scholars, subscribed myself Erasmus ab Die Fausto, and have enjoyed the distinction due to the learned under that title; witness the erudite Diedrichus Buckerschockius, who dedicated to me under that title his treatise on the letter *Tau*. In fine, sir, I have been a happy and distinguished man."

"Long may it be so, sir!" said the traveller; "but permit me to ask, in your own learned phrase, *Quid hoc ad Iphycli boves,* what has all this to do with the shoeing of my poor nag?"

"Festina lenter," said the man of learning, "we will persistently come to that point. You must know that some two or three years past, there came to these parts one who called himself Doctor Doboobie, although it may be he never wrote even *Magister artium,* save in right of his hungry belly. Or it may be, that if he had any degrees, they were of the devil's giving, for he was what the vulgar call a white witch—a cunning man, and such like.—Now, good sir, I perceive you are impatient; but if a man tell not his tale his own way, how have you warrant to think that he can tell it in yours?"

"Well, then, learned sir, take your way," answered Tressilian; "only let us travel at a sharper pace, for my time is somewhat of the shortest."

"Well, sir," resumed Erasmus Holiday, with the most provoking perseverance, "I will not say that this same Demetrius, for so he wrote himself when in foreign parts, was an actual conjurer, but certain it is, that he professed to be a brother of the mystical Order of the Rosy Cross, a disciple of Geber (*ex nomine cujus venit verbum vernaculum, gibberish*). He cured wounds by salving the weapon instead of the sore—told fortunes by palmistry—discovered stolen goods by the sieve and shears—gathered the right maddow and the male fern seed, through use of which men walk invisible—pretended some advances towards the panacea, or universal elixir, and affected to convert good lead into sorry silver."

"In other words," said Tressilian, "he was a quacksalver and common cheat; but what has all this to do with my nag, and the shoe which he has lost?"

"With your worshipful patience," replied the diffusive man of letters, "you shall understand that presently—*patientia* then, right worshipful, which word, according to our Marcus Tullius, is *'difficilium rerum diurna perpessio.'* This same Demetrius Doboobie, after dealing with the country, as I have told you, began to acquire fame *inter magnates,* among the prime men of the land, and there is likelihood he might have aspired to great matters, had not, according to vulgar fame, (for I aver not the thing as according with my certain knowledge,) the devil claimed his right, one dark night, and flown off with Demetrius, who was never seen or heard of afterwards. Now here comes the *medulla,* the very marrow, of my tale. This Doctor Doboobie had a servant, a poor snake, whom he employed in trimming his furnace, regulating it by just measure—compounding his drugs—tracing his circles—cajoling his patients, *et sic de cæteris.*—Well, right worshipful, the Doctor being removed thus strangely, and in a way which struck the whole country with terror, this poor Zany thinks to himself, in the words of Maro, *'Uno avulso, non deficit alter;'* and, even as a tradesman's apprentice sets himself up in his master's shop when he is dead, or hath retired from business, so doth this Wayland assume the dangerous trade of his defunct master. But although, most worshipful sir, the world is ever prone to listen to the pretensions of such unworthy men, who are, indeed, mere *saltim banqui* and *charlatani*, though usurping the style and skill of doctors of medicine, yet the pretensions of this poor Zany, this Wayland, were too gross to pass on them, nor was there a mere rustic, a villager, who was not ready to accost him in the sense of Persius, though in their own rugged words,—

> 'Diluis helleborum, certo compescere puncto
> Nescius examen? vetat hoc natura medendi;'

which I have thus rendered in a poor paraphrase of mine own,—

> Wilt thou mix hellebore, who doth not know
> How many grains should to the mixture go?
> The art of medicine this forbids, I trow.

Moreover, the evil reputation of the master, and his strange and doubtful end, or at least sudden disappearance, prevented any, excepting the most desperate of men, to seek any advice or opinion from the servant; wherefore, the poor vermin was likely at first to swarf for very hunger. But the devil that serves him, since the death of Demetrius or Doboobie, put him on a fresh device. This knave, whether from the inspiration of the devil, or from early education, shoes horses better than e'er a man betwixt us and Iceland; and so he gives up his practice on the bipeds, the two-legged and unfledged species called mankind, and betakes him entirely to shoeing of horses."

"Indeed! and where does he lodge all this time?" said Tressilian. "And does he shoe horses well?—show me his dwelling presently."

The interruption pleased not the Magister, who exclaimed, "*O, cœca mens mortalium!* though, by the way, I used that quotation before. But I would the classics could afford me any sentiment of power to stop those who are so willing to rush upon their own destruction. Hear but, I pray you, the conditions of this man," said he, in continuation, "ere you are so willing to place yourself within his danger——"

"A' takes no money for a's work," said the dame, who stood by, enraptured as it were with the fine words and learned apophthegms which glided so fluently from her erudite inmate, Master Holiday. But this interruption pleased not the Magister, more than that of the traveller.

"Peace," said he, "Gammer Sludge; know your place, if it be your will. *Sufflamina*, Gammer Sludge, and allow me to expound this matter to our worshipful guest.—Sir," said he, again addressing Tressilian, "this old woman speaks true, though in her own rude style; for certainly this *faber ferrarius*, or blacksmith, takes money of no one."

"And that is a sure sign he deals with Satan," said Dame Sludge; "since no good Christian would ever refuse the wages of his labour."

"The old woman hath touched it again," said the pedagogue; *"rem acu tetigit*—she hath pricked it with her needle's point.—This Wayland takes no money, indeed, nor doth he show himself to any one."

"And can this madman, for such I hold him," said the traveller, "know aught like good skill of his trade?"

"O, sir, in that let us give the devil his due—Mulciber himself, with all his Cyclops, could hardly amend him. But assuredly there is little wisdom in taking counsel or receiving aid from one, who is but too plainly in league with the author of evil."

"I must take my chance of that, good Master Holiday," said Tressilian, rising; "and as my horse must now have eaten his provender, I must needs thank you for your good cheer, and pray you to show me this man's residence, that I may have the means of proceeding on my journey."

"Ay, ay, do ye show him, Master Herasmus," said the old dame, who was, perhaps, desirous to get her house freed of her guest; "a' must needs go when the devil drives."

"Do manus," said the Magister, "I submit—taking the world to witness, that I have possessed this honourable gentleman with the full injustice which he has done and shall do to his own soul, if he becomes thus a trinketer with Satan. Neither will I go forth with our guest myself, but rather send my pupil.—*Ricarde! Adsis, nebulo."*

"Under your favour, not so," answered the old woman; "you may peril your own soul, if you list, but my son shall budge on no such errand; and I wonder at you, Dominie Doctor, to propose such a piece of service for little Dickie."

"Nay, my good Gammer Sludge," answered the preceptor, *"Ricardus* shall go but to the top of the hill, and indicate with his digit to the stranger the dwelling of Wayland Smith. Believe not that any evil can come to him, he having read this morning, fasting, a chapter of the Septuagint, and, moreover, having had his lesson in the Greek Testament."

"Ay," said his mother, "and I have sewn a sprig of witch's elm in the neck of un's doublet, ever since that foul thief has begun his practices on man and beast in these parts."

"And as he goes oft (as I hugely suspect) towards this conjurer for his own pastime, he may for once go thither, or near it, to pleasure us, and to assist this stranger.—*Ergo, heus, Ricarde! adsis, quœso, mi didascule."*

The pupil, thus affectionately invoked, at length came stumbling into the room; a queer, shambling, ill-made urchin, who, by his stunted growth, seemed about twelve or thirteen years old, though he was probably, in reality, a year or two older, with a carroty pate in huge disorder, a freckled sunburnt visage, with a snub nose, a long chin, and two peery grey eyes, which had a droll obliquity of vision, approaching to a squint, though perhaps not a decided one. It was impossible to look at the little man without some disposition to laugh, especially when Gammer Sludge, seizing upon and kissing him, in spite of his struggling and kicking in reply to her caresses, termed him her own precious pearl of beauty.

"*Ricarde*," said the preceptor, "you must forthwith (which is *profecto*) set forth so far as the top of the hill, and show this man of worship Wayland Smith's workshop."

"A proper errand of a morning," said the boy, in better language than Tressilian expected; "and who knows but the devil may fly away with me before I come back?"

"Ay, marry may un," said Dame Sludge, "and you might have thought twice, Master Dominie, ere you sent my dainty darling on arrow such errand. It is not for such doings I feed your belly and clothe your back, I warrant you!"

"Pshaw—*nugæ*, good Gammer Sludge," answered the preceptor; "I ensure you that Satan, if there be Satan in the case, shall not touch a thread of his garment; for Dickie can say his *pater* with the best, and may defy the foul fiend—*Eumenides, Stygiumque nefas.*"

"Ay, and I, as I said before, have sewed a sprig of the mountain-ash into his collar," said the good woman, "which will avail more than your clerkship, I wus; but for all that, it is ill to seek the devil or his mates either."

"My good boy," said Tressilian, who saw, from a grotesque sneer on Dickie's face, that he was more likely to act upon his own bottom than by the instruction of his elders, "I will give thee a silver groat, my pretty fellow, if you will but guide me to this man's forge."

The boy gave him a knowing side-look, which seemed to promise acquiescence, while at the same time he exclaimed, "I be your guide to Wayland Smith's! Why, man, did I not say that the devil might fly off with me, just as the kite there" (looking to the window) "is flying off with one of grandam's chicks?"

"The kite! the kite!" exclaimed the old woman in return, and forgetting all other matters in her alarm, hastened to the rescue of her chickens as fast as her old legs could carry her.

"Now for it," said the urchin to Tressilian; "snatch your beaver, get out your horse, and have at the silver groat you spoke of."

"Nay, but tarry, tarry," said the preceptor, "*Sufflamina, Ricarde!*"

"Tarry yourself," said Dickie, "and think what answer you are to make to granny for sending me post to the devil."

The teacher, aware of the responsibility he was incurring, bustled up in great haste to lay hold of the urchin, and to prevent his departure; but Dickie slipped through his fingers, bolted from the cottage, and sped him to the top of a neighbouring rising ground; while the preceptor, despairing, by well-taught experience, of recovering his pupil by speed of foot, had recourse to the most honied epithets the Latin vocabulary affords, to persuade his return. But to *mi anime, corculum meum,* and all such classical endearments, the truant turned a deaf ear, and kept frisking on the top of the rising ground like a goblin by moonlight, making signs to his new acquaintance, Tressilian, to follow him.

The traveller lost no time in getting out his horse, and departing to join his elfish guide, after half-forcing on the poor deserted teacher a recompense for the entertainment he had received, which partly allayed the terror he had for facing the return of the old lady of the mansion. Apparently this took place soon afterwards; for ere Tressilian and his guide had proceeded far on their journey, they heard the screams of a cracked female voice, intermingled with the classical objurgations of Master Erasmus Holiday. But Dickie Sludge, equally deaf to the voice of maternal tenderness and of magisterial authority, skipped on unconsciously before Tressilian, only observing, that "if they cried themselves hoarse, they might go lick the honey-pot, for he had eaten up all the honey-comb himself on yesterday even."

CHAPTER X

> There entering in, they found the goodman selfe
> Full busylie unto his work ybent,
> Who was to weet a wretched wearish elf,
> With hollow eyes and rawbone cheeks forspent,
> As if he had been long in prison pent.
>
> *The Faery Queene.*

"Are we far from the dwelling of the smith, my pretty lad?" said Tressilian to his young guide.

"How is it you call me?" said the boy, looking askew at him with his sharp grey eyes.

"I call you my pretty lad—is there any offence in that, my boy?"

"No—but were you with my grandam and Dominie Holiday, you might sing chorus to the old song of

> 'We three
> Tom-fools be.' "

"And why so, my little man?" said Tressilian.

"Because," answered the ugly urchin, "you are the only three ever called me pretty lad—Now my grandam does it because she is parcel blind by age, and whole blind by kindred—and my master, the poor Dominie, does it to curry favour, and have the fullest platter of furmity, and the warmest seat by the fire. But what *you* call me pretty lad for, you know best yourself."

"Thou art a sharp wag at least, if not a pretty one. But what do thy playfellows call thee?"

"Hobgoblin," answered the boy, readily; "but for all that, I would rather have my own ugly viznomy than any of their jolterheads, that have no more brains in them than a brick-bat."

"Then you fear not this smith, whom you are going to see?"

"Me fear him!" answered the boy; "if he were the devil folk think him, I would not fear him; but though there is something queer about him, he's no more a devil than you are, and that's what I would not tell to every one."

"And why do you tell it to me, then, my boy?" said Tressilian.

"Because you are another guess gentleman than those we see here every day," replied Dickie; "and though I am as ugly as sin, I would not have you think me an ass, especially as I may have a boon to ask of you one day."

"And what is that, my lad, whom I must not call pretty?" replied Tressilian.

"O, if I were to ask it just now," said the boy, "you would deny it me—but I will wait till we meet at court."

"At court, Richard! are you bound for court?" said Tressilian.

"Ay, ay, that's just like the rest of them," replied the boy; "I war-rant me you think, what should such an ill-favoured, scrambling urchin do at court? But let Richard Sludge alone; I have not been cock of the roost here for nothing. I will make sharp wit mend foul feature."

"But what will your grandam say, and your tutor, Dominie Holiday?"

"E'en what they like," replied Dickie; "the one has her chickens to reckon, and the other has his boys to whip. I would have given them the candle to hold long since, and shown this trumpery hamlet a fair pair of heels, but that Dominie promises I should go with him to bear share in the next pageant he is to set forth, and they say there are to be great revels shortly."

"And whereabout are they to be held, my little friend?" said Tressilian.

"Oh, at some castle far in the north," answered his guide—"a world's breadth from Berkshire. But our old Dominie holds that they cannot go forward without him; and it may be he is right, for he has put in order many a fair pageant. He is not half the fool you would take him for, when he gets to work he understands; and so he can spout verses like a play-actor, when, God wot, if you set him to steal a goose's egg, he would be drubbed by the gander."

"And you are to play a part in his next show?" said Tressilian, some-what interested by the boy's boldness of conversation, and shrewd esti-mate of character.

"In faith," said Richard Sludge, in answer, "he hath so promised me; and if he break his word, it will be the worse for him; for let me take the bit between my teeth, and turn my head downhill, and I will shake him off with a fall that may harm his bones—And I should not like much to hurt him neither," said he, "for the tiresome old fool has pain-fully laboured to teach me all he could.—But enough of that—here are we at Wayland Smith's forge-door."

"You jest, my little friend," said Tressilian; "there is nothing but a bare moor, and that ring of stones, with a great one in the midst, like a Cornish barrow."

"Ay, and that great flat stone in the midst, which lies across the top of these uprights," said the boy, "is Wayland Smith's counter, that you must tell down your money upon."

"What do you mean by such folly?" said the traveller, beginning to be angry with the boy, and vexed with himself for having trusted such a harebrained guide.

"Why," said Dickie, with a grin, "you must tie your horse to that upright stone that has the ring in't, and then you must whistle three times, and lay me down your silver groat on that other flat stone, walk out of the circle, sit down on the west side of that little thicket of bushes, and take heed you look neither to right nor to left for ten minutes, or so long as you shall hear the hammer clink, and whenever it ceases, say your prayers for the space you could tell a hundred, or count over a hundred, which will do as well,—and then come into the circle; you will find your money gone and your horse shod."

"My money gone to a certainty!" said Tressilian; "but as for the rest—Hark ye, my lad, I am not your schoolmaster; but if you play off your waggery on me, I will take a part of his task off his hands, and punish you to purpose."

"Ay, when you can catch me!" said the boy; and presently took to his heels across the heath, with a velocity which baffled every attempt of Tressilian to overtake him, loaded as he was with his heavy boots. Nor was it the least provoking part of the urchin's conduct, that he did not exert his utmost speed, like one who finds himself in danger or who is frightened, but preserved just such a rate as to encourage Tressilian to continue the chase, and then darted away from him with the swiftness of the wind, when his pursuer supposed he had nearly run him down, doubling at the same time, and winding, so as always to keep near the place from which he started.

This lasted until Tressilian, from very weariness, stood still, and was about to abandon the pursuit with a hearty curse on the ill-favoured urchin, who had engaged him in an exercise so ridiculous. But the boy, who had, as formerly, planted himself on the top of a hillock close in front, began to clap his long thin hands, point with his skinny fingers, and twist his wild and ugly features into an extravagant expression of laughter and derision, that Tressilian began half to doubt whether he had not in view an actual hobgoblin.

Provoked extremely, yet at the same time feeling an irresistible desire to laugh, so very odd were the boy's grimaces and gesticulations, the Cornish man returned to his horse, and mounted him with the purpose of pursuing Dickie at more advantage.

The boy no sooner saw him mount his horse, than he hollo'd out to him, that rather than he should spoil his white-footed nag, he would come to him, on condition he would keep his fingers to himself.

"I will make no conditions with thee, thou ugly varlet!" said Tressilian; "I will have thee at my mercy in a moment."

"Aha, Master Traveller," said the boy, "there is a marsh hard by would swallow all the horses of the Queen's guard—I will into it, and see where you will go then.—You shall hear the bittern bump, and the wild-drake quack, ere you get hold of me without my consent, I promise you."

Tressilian looked out, and, from the appearance of the ground behind the hillock, believed it might be as the boy said, and accordingly determined to strike up a peace with so light-footed and ready-witted an enemy—"Come down," he said, "thou mischievous brat!—Leave thy mopping and mowing, and come hither; I will do thee no harm, as I am a gentleman."

The boy answered his invitation with the utmost confidence, and danced down from his stance with a galliard sort of step, keeping his eye at the same time fixed on Tressilian's, who, once more dismounted, stood with his horse's bridle in his hand, breathless, and half-exhausted with his fruitless exercise, though not one drop of moisture appeared on the freckled forehead of the urchin, which looked like a piece of dry and discoloured parchment, drawn tight across the brow of a fleshless skull.

"And tell me," said Tressilian, "why you use me thus, thou mischievous imp? or what your meaning is by telling me so absurd a legend as you wished but now to put on me? Or rather show me, in good earnest, this smith's forge, and I will give thee what will buy thee apples through the whole winter."

"Were you to give me an orchard of apples," said Dickie Sludge, "I can guide thee no better than I have done. Lay down the silver token on the flat stone—whistle three times—then come sit down on the western side of the thicket of gorse; I will sit by you, and give you free leave to wring my head off, unless you hear the smith at work within two minutes after we are seated."

"I may be tempted to take thee at thy word," said Tressilian, "if you make me do aught half so ridiculous for your own mischievous sport—however, I will prove your spell.—Here, then, I tie my horse to this upright stone—I must lay my silver groat here, and whistle three times, sayst thou?"

"Ay, but thou must whistle louder than an unfledged ousel," said the boy, as Tressilian, having laid down his money, and half ashamed at the folly he practised, made a careless whistle—"You must whistle louder than that, for who knows where the smith is that you call for?—He may be in the King of France's stables for what I know."

"Why, you said but now he was no devil," replied Tressilian.

"Man or devil," said Dickie, "I see that I must summon him for you;" and therewithal he whistled sharp and shrill, with an acuteness of sound that almost thrilled through Tressilian's brain—"That is what I call whistling," said he, after he had repeated the signal thrice: "and now to cover, to cover, or Whitefoot will not be shod this day."

Tressilian, musing what the upshot of this mummery was to be, yet satisfied there was to be some serious result, by the confidence with which the boy had put himself in his power, suffered himself to be conducted to that side of the little thicket of gorse and brushwood which was farthest from the circle of stones, and there sat down; and as it occurred to him that, after all, this might be a trick for stealing his horse, he kept his hand on the boy's collar, determined to make him hostage for its safety.

"Now, hush and listen," said Dickie, in a low whisper; "you will soon hear the tack of a hammer that was never forged of earthly iron, for the stone it was made of was shot from the moon." And in effect Tressilian did immediately hear the light stroke of a hammer, as when a farrier is at work. The singularity of such a sound, in so very lonely a place, made him involuntarily start; but looking at the boy, and discovering, by the arch malicious expression of his countenance, that the urchin saw and enjoyed his light tremor, he became convinced that the whole was a concerted stratagem, and determined to know by whom, or for what purpose, the trick was played off.

Accordingly, he remained perfectly quiet all the time that the hammer continued to sound, being about the space usually employed in fixing a horse-shoe. But the instant the sound ceased, Tressilian, instead of interposing the space of time which his guide had required, started up with his sword in his hand, ran around the thicket, and confronted a man in a farrier's leathern apron, but otherwise fantastically attired in a bear-skin dressed with the fur on, and a cap of the same, which almost hid the sooty and begrimed features of the wearer—"Come back, come back!" cried the boy to Tressilian, "or you will be torn to pieces— no man lives that looks on him."—In fact, the invisible smith (now fully visible) heaved up his hammer, and showed symptoms of doing battle.

But when the boy observed that neither his own entreaties nor the menaces of the farrier, appeared to change Tressilian's purpose, but that, on the contrary, he confronted the hammer with his drawn sword, he exclaimed to the smith in turn, "Wayland, touch him not, or you will come by the worse!—the gentleman is a true gentleman, and a bold."

"So thou hast betrayed me, Flibbertigibbet?" said the smith; "it shall be the worse for thee!"

"Be who thou wilt," said Tressilian, "thou art in no danger from me, so thou tell me the meaning of this practice, and why thou drivest thy trade in this mysterious fashion."

The smith, however, turning to Tressilian, exclaimed, in a threatening tone, "Who questions the Keeper of the Crystal Castle of Light, the Lord of the Green Lion, the Rider of the Red Dragon?—Hence!— avoid thee, ere I summon Talpack with his fiery lance, to quell, crush, and consume!" These words he uttered with violent gesticulation, mouthing and flourishing his hammer.

"Peace, thou vile cozener, with thy gipsy cant!" replied Tressilian, scornfully, "and follow me to the next magistrate, or I will cut thee over the pate."

"Peace, I pray thee, good Wayland!" said the boy; "credit me, the swaggering vein will not pass here; you must cut boon whids."

"I think, worshipful sir," said the smith, sinking his hammer, and assuming a more gentle and submissive tone of voice, "that when so poor a man does his day's job, he might be permitted to work it out after his own fashion. Your horse is shod, and your farrier paid.—What need you cumber yourself further, than to mount and pursue your journey?"

"Nay, friend, you are mistaken," replied Tressilian; "every man has a right to take the mask from the face of a cheat and a juggler; and your mode of living raises suspicion that you are both."

"If you are so determined, sir," said the smith, "I cannot help myself save by force, which I were unwilling to use towards you, Master Tressilian; not that I fear your weapon, but because I know you to be a worthy, kind, and well-accomplished gentleman, who would rather help than harm a poor man that is in a strait."

"Well said, Wayland," said the boy, who had anxiously awaited the issue of their conference. "But let us to thy den, man, for it is ill for thy health to stand here talking in the open air."

"Thou art right, Hobgoblin," replied the smith; and going to the little thicket of gorse on the side nearest to the circle, and opposite to that at which his customer had so lately couched, he discovered a trap-door curiously covered with bushes, raised it, and, descending into the earth, vanished from their eyes. Notwithstanding Tressilian's curiosity, he had some hesitation at following the fellow into what might be a den of robbers, especially when he heard the smith's voice, issuing from the bowels of the earth, call out, "Flibbertigibbet, do you come last, and be sure to fasten the trap!"

"Have you seen enough of Wayland Smith now?" whispered the urchin to Tressilian, with an arch sneer, as if marking his companion's uncertainty.

"Not yet," said Tressilian, firmly; and shaking off his momentary irresolution, he descended into the narrow staircase, to which the entrance led, and was followed by Dickie Sludge, who made fast the trap-door behind him, and thus excluded every glimmer of daylight. The descent, however, was only a few steps, and led to a level passage of a few yards' length, at the end of which appeared the reflection of a lurid and red light. Arrived at this point, with his drawn sword in his hand, Tressilian found that a turn to the left admitted him and Hobgoblin, who followed closely, into a small square vault, containing a smith's forge, glowing with charcoal, the vapour of which filled the apartment with an oppressive smell, which would have been altogether suffocating, but that by some concealed vent the smithy communicated with the upper air. The light afforded by the red fuel, and by a lamp suspended in an iron chain,

served to show that, besides an anvil, bellows, tongs, hammers, a quantity of ready-made horse-shoes, and other articles proper to the profession of a farrier, there were also stoves, alembics, crucibles, retorts, and
other instruments of alchemy. The grotesque figure of the smith, and
the ugly but whimsical features of the boy, seen by the gloomy and
imperfect light of the charcoal fire and the dying lamp, accorded very
well with all this mystical apparatus, and in that age of superstition
would have made some impression on the courage of most men.

But nature had endowed Tressilian with firm nerves, and his education, originally good, had been too sedulously improved by subsequent
study to give way to any imaginary terrors; and after giving a glance
around him, he again demanded of the artist who he was, and by what
accident he came to know and address him by his name.

"Your worship cannot but remember," said the smith, "that about
three years since, upon Saint Lucy's Eve, there came a travelling juggler
to a certain hall in Devonshire, and exhibited his skill before a worshipful knight and a fair company—I see from your worship's countenance, dark as this place is, that my memory has not done me wrong."

"Thou hast said enough," said Tressilian, turning away, as wishing
to hide from the speaker the painful train of recollections which his
discourse had unconsciously awakened.

"The juggler," said the smith, "played his part so bravely, that the
clowns and clown-like squires in the company held his art to be little
less than magical; but there was one maiden of fifteen, or thereby, with
the fairest face I ever looked upon, whose rosy cheek grew pale, and
her bright eyes dim, at the sight of the wonders exhibited."

"Peace, I command thee, peace!" said Tressilian.

"I mean your worship no offence," said the fellow; "but I have cause
to remember how, to relieve the young maiden's fears, you condescended
to point out the mode in which these deceptions were practised, and to
baffle the poor juggler by laying bare the mysteries of his art, as ably
as if you had been a brother of his order.—She was indeed so fair a
maiden, that, to win a smile of her, a man might well——"

"Not a word more of her, I charge thee!" said Tressilian; "I do well
remember the night you speak of—one of the few happy evenings my
life has known."

"She is gone, then," said the smith, interpreting after his own fashion
the sigh with which Tressilian uttered these words—"She is gone, young,
beautiful, and beloved as she was!—I crave your worship's pardon—I
should have hammered on another theme—I see I have unwarily driven
the nail to the quick."

This speech was made with a mixture of rude feeling, which inclined
Tressilian favourably to the poor artisan, of whom before he was inclined
to judge very harshly. But nothing can so soon attract the unfortunate,
as real or seeming sympathy with their sorrows.

"I think," proceeded Tressilian, after a minute's silence, "thou wert in those days a jovial fellow, who could keep a company merry by song, and tale, and rebeck, as well as by thy juggling tricks—why do I find thee a laborious handicraftsman, plying thy trade in so melancholy a dwelling, and under such extraordinary circumstances?"

"My story is not long," said the artist; "but your honour had better sit while you listen to it." So saying, he approached to the fire a three-footed stool, and took another himself, while Dickie Sludge, or Flibberti-gibbet, as he called the boy, drew a cricket to the smith's feet and looked up in his face with features which, as illuminated by the glow of the forge, seemed convulsed with intense curiosity—"Thou too," said the smith to him, "shalt learn, as thou well deservest at my hand, the brief history of my life, and, in troth, it were as well tell it thee as leave thee to ferret it out, since Nature never packed a shrewder wit into a more ungainly casket.—Well, sir, if my poor story may pleasure you, it is at your command:—But will you not taste a stoup of liquor? I promise you that even in this poor cell I have some in store."

"Speak not of it," said Tressilian, "but go on with thy story, for my leisure is brief."

"You shall have no cause to rue the delay," said the smith, "for your horse shall be better fed in the meantime than he hath been this morning, and made fitter for travel."

With that the artist left the vault, and returned after a few minutes' interval. Here, also, we pause, that the narrative may commence in another chapter.

CHAPTER XI

I say, my lord can such a subtilty,
(But all his craft ye must not wot of me,
And somewhat help I yet to his working,)
That all the ground on which we ben riding,
Till that we come to Canterbury town,
He can all clean turnen so up so down,
And pave it all of silver and of gold.
        The Canon's Yeoman's Prologue—Canterbury Tales.

THE artist commenced his narrative in the following terms:—

"I was bred a blacksmith, and knew my art as well as e'er a black-thumb'd, leathern-apron'd, swart-faced knave of that noble mystery. But I tired of ringing hammer-tunes on iron stithies, and went out into the world, where I became acquainted with a celebrated juggler, whose fingers had become rather too stiff for legerdemain, and who wished to have the aid of an apprentice in his noble mystery. I served him for six years, until I was master of my trade—I refer myself to your worship, whose judgment cannot be disputed, whether I did not learn to ply the craft indifferently well?"

"Excellently," said Tressilian; "but be brief."

"It was not long after I had performed at Sir Hugh Robsart's, in your worship's presence," said the artist, "that I took myself to the stage, and have swaggered with the bravest of them all, both at the Black Bull, the Globe, the Fortune, and elsewhere; but I know not how—apples were so plenty that year, that the lads in the twopenny gallery never took more than one bite out of them, and threw the rest of the pippin at whatever actor chanced to be on the stage. So I tired of it—renounced my half share in the company—gave my foil to my comrade—my buskins to the wardrobe, and showed the theatre a clean pair of heels."

"Well, friend, and what," said Tressilian, "was your next shift?"

"I became," said the smith, "half partner, half domestic, to a man of much skill and little substance, who practised the trade of physicianer."

"In other words," said Tressilian, "you were Jack Pudding to a quacksalver."

"Something beyond that, let me hope, my good Master Tressilian," replied the artist; "and yet, to say truth, our practice was of an adventurous description, and the pharmacy which I had acquired in my first studies for the benefit of horses, was frequently applied to our human patients. But the seeds of all maladies are the same; and if turpentine, tar, pitch, and beef-suet, mingled with turmerick, gum-mastick, and one head of garlick, can cure the horse that hath been grieved with a nail, I see not but what it may benefit the man that hath been pricked with a sword. But my master's practice, as well as his skill, went far beyond mine, and dealt in more dangerous concerns. He was not only a bold adventurous practitioner in physic, but also, if your pleasure so chanced to be, an adept, who read the stars, and expounded the fortunes of mankind, genethliacally, as he called it, or otherwise. He was a learned distiller of simples, and a profound chemist—made several efforts to fix mercury, and judged himself to have made a fair hit at the philosopher's stone. I have yet a programme of his on that subject, which, if your honour understandeth, I believe you have the better, not only of all who read, but also of him who wrote it."

He gave Tressilian a scroll of parchment, bearing at top and bottom, and down the margin, the signs of the seven planets, curiously intermingled with talismanical characters, and scraps of Greek and Hebrew. In the midst were some Latin verses from a cabalistical author, written out so fairly, that even the gloom of the place did not prevent Tressilian from reading them. The tenor of the original ran as follows:—

"Si fixum solvas, faciasque volare solutum,
    Et volucrem figas, facient te vivere tutum;
    Si pariat ventum, valet auri pondere centum;
    Ventus ubi vult spirat—Capiat qui capere potest."

"I protest to you," said Tressilian, "all I understand of this jargon is, that the last words seem to mean 'Catch who catch can."

"That," said the smith, "is the very principle that my worthy friend

and master, Doctor Doboobie, always acted upon; until, being besotted
with his own imaginations, and conceited of his high chemical skill, he
began to spend, in cheating himself, the money which he had acquired
in cheating others, and either discovered or built for himself, I could
never know which, this secret elaboratory, in which he used to seclude
himself from both patients and disciples, who doubtless thought his long
and mysterious absences from his ordinary residence in the town of
Farringdon, were occasioned by his progress in the mystic sciences, and
his intercourse with the invisible world. Me also he tried to deceive; but
though I contradicted him not, he saw that I knew too much of his secrets
to be any longer a safe companion. Meanwhile, his name waxed famous,
or rather infamous, and many of those who resorted to him did so under
persuasion that he was a sorcerer. And yet his supposed advance in the
occult sciences, drew to him the secret resort of men too powerful to be
named, for purposes too dangerous to be mentioned. Men cursed and
threatened him, and bestowed on me, the innocent assistant of his studies,
the nickname of the Devil's foot-post, which procured me a volley of
stones as soon as ever I ventured to show my face in the street of the
village. At length, my master suddenly disappeared, pretending to me
that he was about to visit his elaboratory in this place, and forbidding
me to disturb him till two days were past. When this period had elapsed,
I became anxious, and resorted to this vault, where I found the fires
extinguished and the utensils in confusion, with a note from the learned
Doboobius, as he was wont to style himself, acquainting me that we
should never meet again, bequeathing me his chemical apparatus and the
parchment which I have just put into your hands, advising me strongly
to prosecute the secret which it contained, which would infallibly lead
me to the discovery of the grand magisterium."

"And didst thou follow this sage advice?" said Tressilian.

"Worshipful sir, no," replied the smith; "for, being by nature cautious,
and suspicious from knowing with whom I had to do, I made so many
perquisitions before I ventured even to light a fire, that I at length discovered a small barrel of gunpowder, carefully hid beneath the furnace,
with the purpose, no doubt, that as soon as I should commence the grand
work of the transmutation of metals, the explosion should transmute
the vault and all in it into a heap of ruins, which might serve at once for
my slaughter-house and my grave. This cured me of alchemy, and fain
would I have returned to the honest hammer and anvil; but who would
bring a horse to be shod by the Devil's post? Meantime, I had won the
regard of my honest Flibbertigibbet here, he being then at Farringdon
with his master, the sage Erasmus Holiday, by teaching him a few
secrets, such as please youth at his age; and after much counsel together,
we agreed, that since I could get no practice in the ordinary way, I
should try how I could work out business among these ignorant boors, by
practising upon their silly fears; and, thanks to Flibbertigibbet, who hath
spread my renown, I have not wanted custom. But it is won at too great

risk, and I fear I shall be at length taken up for a wizard, so that I seek but an opportunity to leave this vault when I can have the protection of some worshipful person against the fury of the populace, in case they chance to recognise me."

"And art thou," said Tressilian, "perfectly acquainted with the roads in this country?"

"I could ride them every inch by midnight," answered Wayland Smith, which was the name this adept had assumed.

"Thou hast no horse to ride upon," said Tressilian.

"Pardon me," replied Wayland; "I have as good a tit as ever yeoman bestrode; and I forgot to say it was the best part of the mediciner's legacy to me, excepting one or two of the choicest of his medical secrets, which I picked up without his knowledge and against his will."

"Get thyself washed and shaved, then," said Tressilian; "reform thy dress as well as thou canst, and fling away these grotesque trappings; and, so thou wilt be secret and faithful, thou shalt follow me for a short time, till thy pranks here are forgotten. Thou hast, I think, both address and courage, and I have matter to do that may require both."

Wayland Smith eagerly embraced the proposal, and protested his devotion to his new master. In a very few minutes he had made so great an alteration in his original appearance, by change of dress, trimming his beard and hair, and so forth, that Tressilian could not help remarking, that he thought he would stand in little need of a protector, since none of his old acquaintance were likely to recognise him.

"My debtors would not pay me money," said Wayland, shaking his head; "but my creditors of every kind would be less easily blinded. And, in truth, I hold myself not safe, unless under the protection of a gentle-man of birth and character, as is your worship."

So saying, he led the way out of the cavern. He then called loudly for Hobgoblin, who, after lingering for an instant, appeared with the horse furniture, when Wayland closed, and sedulously covered up the trap-door, observing, it might again serve him at his need, besides that the tools were worth somewhat. A whistle from the owner brought to his side a nag that fed quietly on the common, and was accustomed to the signal. While he accoutred him for the journey, Tressilian drew his own girths tighter, and in a few minutes both were ready to mount.

At this moment Sludge approached to bid them farewell.

"You are going to leave me, then, my old playfellow," said the boy: "and there is an end of all our game at bo-peep with the cowardly lub-bards whom I brought hither to have their broad-footed nags shod by the devil and his imps?"

"It is even so," said Wayland Smith; "the best friends must part, Flibbertigibbet; but thou, my boy, art the only thing in the Vale of Whitehorse which I shall regret to leave behind me."

"Well, I bid thee not farewell," said Dickie Sludge, "for you will be at these revels, I judge, and so shall I; for if Dominie Holiday take me not thither, by the light of day, which we see not in yonder dark hole, I will take myself there!"

"In good time," said Wayland; "but I pray you to do nought rashly."

"Nay, now you would make a child—a common child of me, and tell me of the risk of walking without leading strings. But before you are a mile from these stones, you shall know by a sure token, that I have more of the hobgoblin about me than you credit; and I will so manage, that, if you take advantage, you may profit by my prank."

"What dost thou mean, boy?" said Tressilian; but Flibbertigibbet only answered with a grin and a caper, and bidding both of them farewell, and, at the same time, exhorting them to make the best of their way from the place, he set them the example by running homeward with the same uncommon velocity with which he had baffled Tressilian's former attempts to get hold of him.

"It is in vain to chase him," said Wayland Smith; "for unless your worship is expert in lark-hunting, we should never catch hold of him— and besides, what would it avail? Better make the best of our way hence, as he advises."

They mounted their horses accordingly, and began to proceed at a round pace, as soon as Tressilian had explained to his guide the direction in which he desired to travel.

After they had trotted nearly a mile, Tressilian could not help observing to his companion, that his horse felt more lively under him than even when he mounted in the morning.

"Are you avised of that?" said Wayland Smith, smiling. "That is owing to a little secret of mine. I mixed that with an handful of oats which shall save your worship's heels the trouble of spurring these six hours at least. Nay, I have not studied medicine and pharmacy for nought."

"I trust," said Tressilian, "your drugs will do my horse no harm?"

"No more than the mare's milk which foaled him," answered the artist; and was proceeding to dilate on the excellence of his recipe, when he was interrupted by an explosion as loud and tremendous as the mine which blows up the rampart of a beleaguered city. The horses started, and the riders were equally surprised. They turned to gaze in the direction from which the thunder-clap was heard, and beheld, just over the spot they had left so recently, a huge pillar of dark smoke rising high into the clear, blue atmosphere. "My habitation is gone to wreck," said Wayland, immediately conjecturing the cause of the explosion—"I was a fool to mention the doctor's kind intentions towards my mansion before that limb of mischief Flibbertigibbet—I might have guessed he would long to put so rare a frolic into execution. But let us hasten on, for the sound will collect the country to the spot."

So saying, he spurred his horse, and Tressilian also quickening his speed, they rode briskly forward.

"This then, was the meaning of the little imp's token which he promised us?" said Tressilian: "had we lingered near the spot we had found it a love-token with a vengeance."

"He would have given us warning," said the smith; "I saw him look back more than once to see if we were off—'tis a very devil for mischief, yet not an ill-natured devil either. It were long to tell your honour how I became first acquainted with him, and how many tricks he played me. Many a good turn he did me too, especially in bringing me customers; for his great delight was to see them sit shivering behind the bushes when they heard the click of my hammer. I think Dame Nature, when she lodged a double quantity of brains in that misshapen head of his, gave him the power of enjoying other people's distresses, as she gave them the pleasure of laughing at his ugliness."

"It may be so," said Tressilian; "those who find themselves severed from society by peculiarities of form, if they do not hate the common bulk of mankind, are at least not altogether indisposed to enjoy their mishaps and calamities."

"But Flibbertigibbet," answered Wayland, "hath that about him which may redeem his turn for mischievous frolic; for he is as faithful when attached, as he is tricky and malignant to strangers; and, as I said before, I have cause to say so."

Tressilian pursued the conversation no farther; and they continued their journey towards Devonshire without farther adventure, until they alighted at an inn in the town of Marlborough, since celebrated for having given title to the greatest general (excepting one) whom Britain ever produced. Here the travellers received, in the same breath, an example of the truth of two old proverbs, namely, that *Ill news fly fast,* and that *Listeners seldom hear a good tale of themselves.*

The inn-yard was in a sort of combustion when they alighted; insomuch, that they could scarce get man or boy to take care of their horses, so full were the whole household of some news which flew from tongue to tongue, the import of which they were for some time unable to discover. At length, indeed, they found it respected matters which touched them nearly.

"What is the matter, say you, master?" answered, at length, the head hostler, in reply to Tressilian's repeated questions—"Why, truly, I scarce know myself. But here was a rider but now, who says that the devil hath flown away with him they called Wayland Smith, that won'd about three miles from the Whitehorse of Berkshire, this very blessed morning, in a flash of fire and a pillar of smoke, and rooted up the place he dwelt in, near that old cockpit of upright stones, as cleanly as if it had all been delved up for a cropping."

"Why, then," said an old farmer, "the more is the pity—for that Wayland Smith (whether he was the devil's crony or no I skill not) had a good notion of horse diseases, and it's to be thought the bots will spread in the country far and near, an Satan has not gien un time to leave his secret behind un."

"You may say that, Gaffer Grimesby," said the hostler in return; "I have carried a horse to Wayland Smith myself, for he passed all farriers in this country."

"Did you see him?" said Dame Alison Crane, mistress of the inn bearing that sign, and deigning to term *husband* the owner thereof, a mean-looking hop-o'-my-thumb sort of person, whose halting gait, and long neck and meddling henpecked insignificance, are supposed to have given origin to the celebrated old English tune of "My Dame hath a lame tame Crane."

On this occasion, he chirped out a repetition of his wife's question, "Didst see the devil, Jack Hostler, I say?"

"And what if I did see un, Master Crane?" replied Jack Hostler,—for, like all the rest of the household, he paid as little respect to his master as his mistress herself did.

"Nay, nought, Jack Hostler," replied the pacific Master Crane, "only if you saw the devil, methinks I would like to know what un's like?"

"You will know that one day, Master Crane," said his helpmate, "an ye mend not your manners, and mind your business, leaving off such idle palabras.—But truly, Jack Hostler, I should be glad to know myself what like the fellow was."

"Why, dame," said the hostler, more respectfully, "as for what he was like I cannot tell, nor no man else, for why I never saw un."

"And how didst thou get thine errand done," said Gaffer Grimesby, "if thou seedst him not?"

"Why, I had schoolmaster to write down ailment o' nag," said Jack Hostler; "and I went wi' the ugliest slip of a boy for my guide as ever man cut out o' lime-tree root to please a child withal."

"And what was it?—and did it cure your nag, Jack Hostler?"—was uttered and echoed by all who stood around.

"Why, how can I tell you what it was?" said the hostler; "simply it smelled and tasted—for I did make bold to put a pea's substance into my mouth—like hartshorn and savin mixed with vinegar—but then no hartshorn and savin ever wrought so speedy a cure—And I am dreading that if Wayland Smith be gone, the bots will have more power over horse and cattle."

The pride of art, which is certainly not inferior in its influence to any other pride whatever, here so far operated on Wayland Smith, that, notwithstanding the obvious danger of his being recognised, he could not help winking to Tressilian, and smiling mysteriously, as if triumphing in the undoubted evidence of his veterinary skill. In the meanwhile, the discourse continued.

"E'en let it be so," said a grave man in black, the companion of Gaffer Grimesby; "e'en let us perish under the evil God sends us, rather than the devil be our doctor."

"Very true," said Dame Crane; "and I marvel at Jack Hostler that he would peril his own soul to cure the bowels of a nag."

"Very true, mistress," said Jack Hostler, "but the nag was my master's; and had it been yours, I think ye would ha' held me cheap enow an I had feared the devil when the poor beast was in such a taking— For the rest let the clergy look to it. Every man to his craft, says the proverb; the parson to the prayer-book, and the groom to his curry-comb."

"I vow," said Dame Crane, "I think Jack Hostler speaks like a good Christian and a faithful servant, who will spare neither body nor soul in his master's service. However, the devil has lifted him in time, for a Constable of the Hundred came hither this morning to get old Gaffer Pinniewinks, the trier of witches, to go with him to the Vale of White-horse to comprehend Wayland Smith, and put him to his probation. I helped Pinniewinks to sharpen his pincers and his poking-awl, and I saw the warrant from Justice Blindas."

"Pooh—pooh—the devil would laugh both at Blindas and his warrant, constable and witch-finder to boot," said old Dame Crank, the papist laundress; "Wayland Smith's flesh would mind Pinniewinks' awl no more than a cambric ruff minds a hot piccadilloe-needle. But tell me, gentlefolks, if the devil ever had such a hand among ye, as to snatch away your smiths and your artists from under your nose, when the good Abbots of Abingdon had their own? By Our Lady, no!—they had their hallowed tapers, and their holy water, and their relics, and what not, could send the foulest fiends a-packing.—Go ask a heretic parson to do the like—But ours were a comfortable people."

"Very true, Dame Crank," said the hostler; "so said Simpkins of Simonburn when the curate kissed his wife,—'They are a comfortable people,' said he."

"Silence, thou foul-mouthed vermin," said Dame Crank; "is it fit for a heretic horse-boy like thee, to handle such a text as the Catholic clergy?"

"In troth no, dame," replied the man of oats; "and as you yourself are now no text for their handling, dame, whatever may have been the case in your day, I think we had e'en better leave un alone."

At this last exchange of sarcasm, Dame Crank set up her throat, and began a horrible exclamation against Jack Hostler, under cover of which Tressilian and his attendant escaped into the house.

They had no sooner entered a private chamber, to which Goodman Crane himself had condescended to usher them, and dispatched their worthy and obsequious host on the errand of procuring wine and refresh-ment, than Wayland Smith began to give vent to his self-importance.

"You see, sir," said he, addressing Tressilian, "that I nothing fabled in asserting that I possessed fully the mighty mystery of a farrier, or mareschal, as the French more honourably term us. These dog-hostlers, who, after all, are the better judges in such a case, know what credit they should attach to my medicaments. I call you to witness, worshipful Master Tressilian, that naught, save the voice of calumny and the hand of malicious violence, hath driven me forth from a station in which I held a place alike useful and honoured."

"I bear witness, my friend, but will reserve my listening," answered Tressilian, "for a safer time; unless, indeed, you deem it essential to your reputation, to be translated, like your late dwelling, by the assistance of a flash of fire. For you see your best friends reckon you no better than a mere sorcerer.

"Now, Heaven forgive them," said the artist, "who confound learned skill with unlawful magic! I trust a man may be as skillful, or more so, than the best chirurgeon ever meddled with horse-flesh, and yet may be upon the matter little more than other ordinary men, or at the worst no conjurer."

"God forbid else!" said Tressilian. "But be silent just for the present, since here comes mine host with an assistant, who seems something of the least."

Everybody about the inn, Dame Crank herself included, had been indeed so interested and agitated by the story they had heard of Wayland Smith, and by the new, varying, and more marvellous editions of the incident, which arrived from various quarters, that mine host, in his righteous determination to accommodate his guests, had been able to obtain the assistance of none of his household, saving that of a little boy, a junior tapster, of about twelve years old, who was called Sampson.

"I wish," he said, apologising to his guests, as he set down a flagon of sack, and promised some food immediately,—"I wish the devil had flown away with my wife and my whole family instead of this Wayland Smith, who, I dare say, after all said and done, was much less worthy of the distinction which Satan has done him."

"I hold opinion with you, good fellow," replied Wayland Smith; "and I will drink to you upon that argument."

"Not that I would justify any man who deals with the devil," said mine host, after having pledged Wayland in a rousing draught of sack, "but that—Saw ye ever better sack, my masters?—but that, I say, a man had better deal with a dozen cheats and scoundrel fellows, such as this Wayland Smith, than with a devil incarnate, that takes possession of house and home, bed and board."

The poor fellow's detail of grievances was here interrupted by the shrill voice of his helpmate, screaming from the kitchen, to which he instantly hobbled, craving pardon of his guests. He was no sooner gone than Wayland Smith expressed, by every contemptuous epithet in the language, his utter scorn for a nincompoop who stuck his head under his wife's apron-string; and intimated, that, saving for the sake of the horses which required both rest and food, he would advise his worshipful master Tressilian to push on a stage farther, rather than pay a reckoning to such a mean-spirited, crow-trodden, henpecked coxcomb, as Gaffer Crane.

The arrival of a large dish of good cow-heel and bacon, something soothed the asperity of the artist, which wholly vanished before a choice capon, so delicately roasted, that the lard frothed on it, said Wayland, like May-dew on a lily; and both Gaffer Crane and his good dame became, in his eyes, very painstaking, accommodating, obliging persons.

According to the manners of the times, the master and his attendant sat at the same table, and the latter observed, with regret, how little attention Tressilian paid to his meal. He recollected, indeed, the pain he had given by mentioning the maiden in whose company he had first seen him; but, fearful of touching upon a topic too tender to be tampered with, he chose to ascribe his abstinence to another cause.

"This fare is perhaps too coarse for your worship," said Wayland, as the limbs of the capon disappeared before his own exertions; "but had you dwelt as long I have done in yonder dungeon, which Flibbertigibbet has translated to the upper element, a place where I dared hardly broil my food, lest the smoke should be seen without, you would think a fair capon a more welcome dainty."

"If you are pleased, friend," said Tressilian, "it is well. Nevertheless, hasten thy meal if thou canst, for this place is unfriendly to thy safety, and my concerns crave travelling."

Allowing, therefore, their horses no more rest than was absolutely necessary for them, they pursued their journey by a forced march as far as Bradford, where they reposed themselves for the night.

The next morning found them early travellers. And, not to fatigue the reader with unnecessary particulars, they traversed without adventure the counties of Wiltshire and Somerset, and about noon of the third day after Tressilian's leaving Cumnor, arrived at Sir Hugh Robsart's seat, called Lidcote Hall, on the frontiers of Devonshire.

CHAPTER XII

Ah me! the flower and blossom of your house,
The wind hath blown away to other towers.
JOANNA BAILLIE's *Family Legend*.

THE ancient seat of Lidcote Hall was situated near the village of the same name, and adjoined the wild and extensive forest of Exmoor, plentifully stocked with game, in which some ancient rights belonging to the Robsart family, entitled Sir Hugh to pursue his favourite amusement of the chase. The old mansion was a low, venerable building, occupying a considerable space of ground, which was surrounded by a deep moat. The approach and drawbridge were defended by an octagonal tower, of ancient brick-work, but so clothed with ivy and other creepers, that it was difficult to discover of what materials it was constructed. The angles of this tower were each decorated with a turret, whimsically various in form and in size, and, therefore, very unlike the monotonous stone pepperboxes, which, in modern Gothic architecture, are employed for the same purpose. One of these turrets was square, and occupied as a clock-house. But the clock was now standing still; a circumstance peculiarly striking to Tressilian, because the good old knight, among other harmless peculiarities, had a fidgety anxiety about the exact measurement of time, very common to those who have a great deal of that commodity to dispose of, and find it lie heavy upon their hands,—just as we see shopkeepers amuse themselves with taking an exact account of their stock at the time there is least demand for it.

The entrance to the court-yard of the old mansion lay through an archway, surmounted by the foresaid tower, but the drawbridge was down, and one leaf of the iron-studded folding-doors stood carelessly open. Tressilian hastily rode over the drawbridge, entered the court, and began to call loudly on the domestics by their names. For some time he was only answered by the echoes and the howling of the hounds, whose kennel lay at no great distance from the mansion, and was surrounded by the same moat. At length Will Badger, the old and favourite attendant of the knight, who acted alike as squire of his body, and superintendent of his sports, made his appearance. The stout, weatherbeaten forester showed great signs of joy when he recognised Tressilian.

"Lord love you," he said, "Master Edmund, be it thou in flesh and fell?—Then thou mayst do some good on Sir Hugh, for it passes the wit of man, that is, of mine own, and the Curate's, and Master Mumblazen's, to do aught wi' un."

"Is Sir Hugh then worse since I went away, Will?" demanded Tressilian.

"For worse in body—no—he is much better," replied the domestic; "but he is clean mazed as it were—eats and drinks as he was wont—but sleeps not, or rather wakes not, for he is ever in a sort of twilight, that is neither sleeping nor waking. Dame Swineford thought it was like the dead palsy.—But no, no, dame, said I, it is the heart, it is the heart."

"Can ye not stir his mind to any pastimes?" said Tressilian.

"He is clean and quite off his sports," said Will Badger; "hath neither touched backgammon or shovel-board—nor looked on the big book of harrowtry wi' Master Mumblazen. I let the clock run down, thinking the missing the bell might somewhat move him, for you know, Master Edmund, he was particular in counting time; but he never said a word on't, so I may e'en set the old chime a towling again. I made bold to tread on Bungay's tail too, and you know what a round rating that would ha' cost me once a-day—but he minded the poor tyke's whine no more than a madge howlet whooping down the chimney—so the case is beyond me."

"Thou shalt tell me the rest within doors, Will.—Meanwhile let this person be ta'en to the buttery, and used with respect—He is a man of art."

"White art or black art, I would," said Will Badger, "that he had any art which could help us.—Here, Tom Butler, look to the man of art—and see that he steals none of thy spoons, lad," he added in a whisper to the butler, who showed himself at a low window, "I have known as honest a faced fellow have art enough to do that."

He then ushered Tressilian into a low parlour, and went, at his desire, to see in what state his master was, lest the sudden return of his darling pupil, and proposed son-in-law, should affect him too strongly. He returned immediately, and said that Sir Hugh was dozing in his elbow-chair, but that Master Mumblazen would acquaint Master Tressilian the instant he awaked.

"But it is chance if he knows you," said the huntsman, "for he has forgotten the name of every hound in the pack. I thought about a week since, he had gotten a favourable turn:—'Saddle me old Sorrel,' said he, suddenly, after he had taken his usual night-draught out of the great silver grace-cup, 'and take the hounds to Mount Hazelhurst to-morrow.' Glad men were we all, and out we had him in the morning, and he rode to cover as usual, with never a word spoken but that the wind was south, and the scent would lie. But ere we had uncoupled the hounds, he began to stare round him, like a man that wakes suddenly out of a dream— turns bridle and walks back to Hall again, and leaves us to hunt at leisure by ourselves, if we listed."

"You tell a heavy tale, Will," replied Tressilian; "but God must help us—there is no aid in man."

"Then you bring us no news of young Mistress Amy?—But what need I ask—your brow tells the story. Ever I hoped, that if any man could or would track her, it must be you. All's over and lost now. But if ever I have that Varney within reach of a flight-shot, I will bestow a forked shaft on him; and that I swear by salt and bread."

As he spoke, the door opened, and Master Mumblazen appeared; a withered, thin, elderly gentleman, with a cheek like a winter apple, and his grey hair partly concealed by a small high hat, shaped like a cone, or rather like such a strawberry-basket as London fruiterers exhibit at their windows. He was too sententious a person to waste words on mere salutation; so, having welcomed Tressilian with a nod and a shake of the hand, he beckoned him to follow to Sir Hugh's great chamber, which the good knight usually inhabited. Will Badger followed, unasked, anxious to see whether his master would be relieved from his state of apathy by the arrival of Tressilian.

In a long low parlour, amply furnished with implements of the chase, and with silvan trophies, by a massive stone chimney, over which hung a sword and suit of armour, somewhat obscured by neglect, sat Sir Hugh Robsart of Lidcote, a man of large size, which had been only kept within moderate compass by the constant use of violent exercise. It seemed to Tressilian that the lethargy, under which his old friend appeared to labour, had, even during his few weeks' absence, added bulk to his person; at least it had obviously diminished the vivacity of his eye, which, as they entered, first followed Master Mumblazen slowly to a large oaken desk, on which a ponderous volume lay open, and then rested, as if in uncertainty, on the stranger who had entered along with him. The Curate, a grey-headed clergyman, who had been a confessor in the days of Queen Mary, sat with a book in his hand in another recess in the apartment. He, too, signed a mournful greeting to Tressilian, and laid his book aside, to watch the effect his appearance should produce on the afflicted old man.

As Tressilian, his own eyes filling fast with tears, approached more and more nearly to the father of his betrothed bride, Sir Hugh's intelligence seemed to revive. He sighed heavily, as one who awakens from a state of stupor, a slight convulsion passed over his features, he opened his arms without speaking a word, and, as Tressilian threw himself into them, he folded him to his bosom.

"There is something left to live for yet," were the first words he uttered; and while he spoke, he gave vent to his feelings in a paroxysm of weeping, the tears chasing each other down his sunburnt cheeks and long white beard.

"I ne'er thought to have thanked God to see my master weep," said Will Badger; "but ncw I do, though I am like to weep for company."

"I will ask thee no questions," said the old Knight; "no questions—none, Edmund—thou hast not found her, or so found her, that she were better lost."

Tressilian was unable to reply, otherwise than by putting his hands before his face.

"It is enough—it is enough. But do not thou weep for her, Edmund. I have cause to weep, for she was my daughter,—thou hast cause to rejoice, that she did not become thy wife.—Great God! thou knowest best what is good for us—It was my nightly prayer that I should see Amy and Edmund wedded,—had it been granted, it had now been gall added to bitterness."

"Be comforted, my friend," said the Curate, addressing Sir Hugh, "it cannot be that the daughter of all our hopes and affections is the vile creature you would bespeak her."

"Oh, no," replied Sir Hugh, impatiently, "I were wrong to name broadly the base thing she is become—there is some new court name for it, I warrant me. It is honour enough for the daughter of an old De'nshire clown to be the leman of a gay courtier,—of Varney too,—of Varney whose grandsire was relieved by my father, when his fortune was broken, at the battle of—the battle of—where Richard was slain—out on my memory!—and I warrant none of you will help me——"

"The battle of Bosworth," said Master Mumblazen, "stricken between Richard Crookback and Henry Tudor, grandsire of the Queen that now is, *Primo Henrici Septimi;* and in the year one thousand four hundred and eighty-five, *post Christum natum.*"

"Ay, even so," said the old Knight, "every child knows it—But my poor head forgets all it should remember, and remembers only what it would most willingly forget. My brain has been at fault, Tressilian, almost ever since thou hast been away, and even yet it hunts counter."

"Your worship," said the good clergyman, "had better retire to your apartment, and try to sleep for a little space,—the physician left a composing draught,—and our Great Physician has commanded us to use earthly means, that we may be strengthened to sustain the trials he sends us."

"True, true, old friend," said Sir Hugh, "and we will bear our trials manfully—We have lost but a woman.—See, Tressilian,"—he drew from his bosom a long ringlet of glossy hair,—"see this lock!—I tell thee, Edmund, the very night she disappeared, when she bid me good even, as she was wont, she hung about my neck, and fondled me more than usual; and I, like an old fool, held her by this lock, until she took her scissors, severed it, and left it in my hand,—as all I was ever to see more of her!"

Tressilian was unable to reply, well judging what a complication of feelings must have crossed the bosom of the unhappy fugitive at that cruel moment. The clergyman was about to speak, but Sir Hugh interrupted him.

"I know what you would say, Master Curate,—after all, it is but a lock of woman's tresses,—and by woman, shame, and sin, and death, came into an innocent world—And learned Master Mumblazen, too, can say scholarly things of their inferiority."

"*C'est l'homme,*" said Master Mumblazen, "*qui se bast, et qui conseille.*"

"True," said Sir Hugh, "and we will bear us, therefore, like men who have both mettle and wisdom in us.—Tressilian, thou art as welcome as if thou hadst brought better news. But we have spoken too long dry-lipped.—Amy, fill a cup of wine to Edmund, and another to me." Then instantly recollecting that he called upon her who could not hear, he shook his head, and said to the clergyman, "This grief is to my bewildered mind what the Church of Lidcote is to our park: we may lose ourselves among the briers and thickets for a little space, but from the end of each avenue we see the old grey steeple and the grave of my forefathers. I would I were to travel that road to-morrow!"

Tressilian and the Curate joined in urging the exhausted old man to lay himself to rest, and at length prevailed. Tressilian remained by his pillow till he saw that slumber at length sunk down on him, and then returned to consult with the Curate what steps should be adopted in these unhappy circumstances.

They could not exclude from these deliberations Master Michael Mumblazen; and they admitted him the more readily, that besides what hopes they entertained from his sagacity, they knew him to be so great a friend to taciturnity, that there was no doubt of his keeping counsel. He was an old bachelor, of good family, but small fortune, and distantly related to the House of Robsart; in virtue of which connexion, Lidcote Hall had been honoured with his residence for the last twenty years.

His company was agreeable to Sir Hugh, chiefly on account of his profound learning, which, though it only related to heraldry and genealogy, with such scraps of history as connected themselves with these subjects, was precisely of a kind to captivate the good old knight; besides the convenience which he found in having a friend to appeal to, when his own memory, as frequently happened, proved infirm, and played him false concerning names and dates, which, and all similar deficiencies, Master Michael Mumblazen supplied with due brevity and discretion. And, indeed, in matters concerning the modern world, he often gave, in his enigmatical and heraldic phrase, advice which was well worth attending to, or, in Will Badger's language, started the game while others beat the bush.

"We have had an unhappy time of it with the good Knight, Master Edmund," said the Curate. "I have not suffered so much since I was torn away from my beloved flock, and compelled to abandon them to the Romish wolves."

"That was in *Tertio Mariæ*," said Master Mumblazen.

"In the name of Heaven," continued the Curate, "tell us, has your time been better spent than ours, or have you any news of that unhappy maiden, who, being for so many years the principal joy of this broken-down house, is now proved our greatest unhappiness? Have you not at least discovered her place of residence?"

"I have," replied Tressilian. "Know you Cumnor-Place, near Oxford?"

"Surely," said the clergyman; "it was a house of removal for the monks of Abingdon."

"Whose arms," said Master Michael, "I have seen over a stone chimney in the hall,—a cross-patoncé betwixt four martlets."

"There," said Tressilian, "this unhappy maiden resides, in company with the villain Varney. But for a strange mishap, my sword had revenged all our injuries, as well as hers, on his worthless head."

"Thank God, that kept thine hand from blood-guiltiness, rash young man!" answered the Curate. "Vengeance is mine, saith the Lord, and I will repay it. It were better study to free her from the villain's nets of infamy."

"They are called, in heraldry, *laquei amoris*, or *lacs d'amour*," said Mumblazen.

"It is in that I require your aid, my friends," said Tressilian; "I am resolved to accuse this villain, at the very foot of the throne, of falsehood, seduction, and breach of hospitable laws. The Queen shall hear me, though the Earl of Leicester, the villain's patron, stood at her right hand."

"Her Grace," said the Curate, "hath set a comely example of continence to her subjects, and will doubtless do justice on this inhospitable robber. But wert thou not better apply to the Earl of Leicester, in the first place, for justice on his servant? If he grants it, thou dost save the risk of making thyself a powerful adversary, which will certainly chance, if, in the first instance, you accuse his master of the horse, and prime favourite, before the Queen."

"My mind revolts from your counsel," said Tressilian. "I cannot brook to plead my noble patron's cause—the unhappy Amy's cause—before any one save my lawful Sovereign. Leicester, thou wilt say, is noble—be it so—he is but a subject like ourselves, and I will not carry my plaint to him, if I can do better. Still, I will think on what thou hast said,—but I must have your assistance to persuade the good Sir Hugh to make me his commissioner and fiduciary in this matter, for it is in his name I must speak, and not in my own. Since she is so far changed as to dote upon this empty profligate courtier, he shall at least do her the justice which is yet in his power."

"Better she died *cælebs* and *sine prole*," said Mumblazen, with more animation than he usually expressed, "than part, *per pale,* the noble coat of Robsart with that of such a miscreant!"

"If it be your object, as I cannot question," said the clergyman, "to save, as much as is yet possible, the credit of this unhappy young woman, I repeat, you should apply, in the first instance, to the Earl of Leicester. He is as absolute in his household as the Queen in her kingdom, and if he expresses to Varney that such is his pleasure, her honour will not stand so publicly committed."

"You are right, you are right," said Tressilian, eagerly, "and I thank you for pointing out what I overlooked in my haste. I little thought ever to have besought grace of Leicester; but I could kneel to the proud Dudley, if doing so could remove one shade of shame from this unhappy damsel. You will assist me then to procure the necessary powers from Sir Hugh Robsart?"

The Curate assured him of his assistance, and the herald nodded assent.

"You must hold yourselves also in readiness to testify, in case you are called upon, the open-hearted hospitality which our good patron exercised towards this deceitful traitor, and the solicitude with which he laboured to seduce his unhappy daughter."

"At first," said the clergyman, "she did not, as it seemed to me, much affect his company, but latterly I saw them often together."

"*Seiant* in the parlour," said Michael Mumblazen, "and *passant* in the garden."

"I once came on them by chance," said the priest, "in the South wood, in a spring evening—Varney was muffled in a russet cloak, so that I saw not his face,—they separated hastily, as they heard me rustle amongst the leaves, and I observed she turned her head and looked long after him."

"With neck *reguardant,*" said the herald—"and on the day of her flight, and that was on Saint Austen's Eve, I saw Varney's groom, attired in his liveries, hold his master's horse and Mistress Amy's palfrey, bridled and saddled *proper,* behind the wall of the churchyard."

"And now is she found mewed up in his secret place of retirement," said Tressilian. "The villain is taken in the manner, and I well wish he may deny his crime, that I may thrust conviction down his false throat! But I must prepare for my journey. Do you, gentlemen, dispose my patron to grant me such powers as are needful to act in his name."

So saying, Tressilian left the room.

"He is too hot," said the Curate; "and I pray to God that he may grant him the patience to deal with Varney as is fitting."

"Patience and Varney," said Mumblazen, "is worse heraldry than metal upon metal. He is more false than a siren, more rapacious than a griffin, more poisonous than a wyvern, and more cruel than a lion rampant."

"Yet I doubt much," said the Curate, "whether we can with propriety ask from Sir Hugh Robsart, being in his present condition, any deed deputing his paternal right in Mistress Amy to whomsoever——"

"Your reverence need not doubt that," said Will Badger, who entered as he spoke; "for I will lay my life he is another man when he wakes, then he has been these thirty days past."

"Ay, Will," said the Curate, "hast thou then so much confidence in Doctor Diddleum's draught?"

"Not a whit," said Will, "because master ne'er tasted a drop on't, seeing it was emptied out by the housemaid. But here's a gentleman, who came attending on Master Tressilian, has given Sir Hugh a draught that is worth twenty of yon un. I have spoken cunningly with him, and a better farrier, or one who hath a more just notion of horse and dog a.l-ment, I have never seen; and such a one would never be unjust to a Christian man."

"A farrier! you saucy groom—And by whose authority, pray?" said the Curate, rising in surprise and indignation; "or who will be warrant for this new physician?"

"For authority, an it like your reverence, he had mine; and for warrant, I trust I have not been five-and-twenty years in this house, without having right to warrant the giving of a draught to beast or body—I who can gie a drench, and a ball, and bleed, or blister, if need, to my very self."

The counsellors of the house of Robsart thought it meet to carry this information instantly to Tressilian, who as speedily summoned before him Wayland Smith, and demanded of him, (in private, however,) by what authority he had ventured to administer any medicine to Sir Hugh Robsart?

"Why," replied the artist, "your worship cannot but remember that I told you I had made more progress into my master's—I mean the learned Doctor Doboobie's—mystery than he was willing to own; and indeed half of his quarrel and malice against me was, that, besides that I got something too deep into his secrets, several discerning persons, and particularly a buxom young widow of Abingdon, preferred my prescriptions to his."

"None of thy buffoonery, sir," said Tressilian, sternly. "If thou hast trifled with us—much more, if thou hast done aught that may prejudice Sir Hugh Robsart's health, thou shalt find thy grave at the bottom of a tin-mine."

"I know too little of the great *arcanum* to convert the ore to gold," said Wayland, firmly. "But truce to your apprehensions, Master Tressilian—I understood the good Knight's case, from what Master William Badger told me; and I hope I am able enough to administer a poor dose of mandragorn, which, with the sleep that must needs follow, is all that Sir Hugh Robsart requires to settle his distraught brains."

"I trust thou dealest fairly with me, Wayland?" said Tressilian.

"Most fairly and honestly, as the event shall show," replied the artist. "What would it avail me to harm the poor old man for whom you are interested? you, to whom I owe it, that Gaffer Pinniewinks is not even now rending my flesh and sinews with his accursed pincers, and probing every mole in my body with his sharpened awl (a murrain on the hands which forged it!) in order to find out the witch's mark?—I trust to yoke myself as a humble follower to your worship's train, and I only wish to have my faith judged of by the result of the good Knight's slumbers."

Wayland Smith was right in his prognostication. The sedative draught which his skill had prepared, and Will Badger's confidence had administered, was attended with the most beneficial effects. The patient's sleep was long and healthful; and the poor old Knight awoke, humbled indeed in thought, and weak in frame, yet a much better judge of whatever was subjected to his intellect than he had been for some time past. He resisted for a while the proposal made by his friends, that Tressilian should undertake a journey to court, to attempt the recovery of his daughter, and the redress of her wrongs, in so far as they might yet be repaired. "Let her go," he said; "she is but a hawk that goes down the wind; I would not bestow even a whistle to reclaim her." But though he for some time maintained this argument, he was at length convinced it was his duty to take the part to which natural affection inclined him, and consent that such efforts as could yet be made should be used by Tressilian in behalf of his daughter. He subscribed, therefore, a warrant of attorney, such as the Curate's skill enabled him to draw up; for in those simple days the clergy were often the advisers of their flock in law, as well as in gospel.

All matters were prepared for Tressilian's second departure, within twenty-four hours after he had returned to Lidcote Hall; but one material circumstance had been forgotten, which was first called to the remembrance of Tressilian by Master Mumblazen. "You are going to court, Master Tressilian," said he; "you will please remember, that your blazonry must be *argent*, and *or*—no other tinctures will pass current." The remark was equally just and embarrassing. To prosecute a suit at court, ready money was as indispensable even in the golden days of Elizabeth as at any succeeding period; and it was a commodity little at the command of the inhabitants of Lidcote Hall. Tressilian was himself poor; the revenues of good Sir Hugh Robsart were consumed, and even anticipated, in his hospitable mode of living; and it was finally necessary that the herald who started the doubt should himself solve it. Master Michael Mumblazen did so by producing a bag of money, containing nearly three hundred pounds in gold and silver of various coinage, the savings of twenty years; which he now, without speaking a syllable upon the subject, dedicated to the service of the patron whose shelter and protection had given him the means of making this little hoard. Tressilian accepted it without affecting a moment's hesitation, and a mutual grasp of the hand was all that passed betwixt them, to express the pleasure which the one felt in dedicating his all to such a purpose, and that which the other received from finding so material an obstacle to the success of his journey so suddenly removed, and in a manner so unexpected.

While Tressilian was making preparations for his departure early the ensuing morning, Wayland Smith desired to speak with him; and, expressing his hope that he had been pleased with the operation of his medicine in behalf of Sir Hugh Robsart, added his desire to accompany him to court. This was indeed what Tressilian himself had several times thought of; for the shrewdness, alertness of understanding, and variety of resource, which this fellow had exhibited during the time they had travelled together, had made him sensible that his assistance might be of importance. But then Wayland was in danger from grasp of law; and of this Tressilian reminded him, mentioning something, at the same time, of the pincers of Pinniewinks, and the warrant of Master Justice Blindas. Wayland Smith laughed both to scorn.

"See you, sir!" said he, "I have changed my garb from that of a farrier to a serving-man; but were it still as it was, look at my mustaches—they now hang down—I will but turn them up, and dye them with a tincture that I know of, and the devil would scarce know me again."

He accompanied these words with the appropriate action; and in less than a minute, by setting up his mustaches and his hair, he seemed a different person from him that had but now entered the room. Still, however, Tressilian hesitated to accept his services, and the artist became proportionably urgent.

"I owe you life and limb," he said, "and I would fain pay a part of the debt, especially as I know from Will Badger on what dangerous service your worship is bound. I do not, indeed, pretend to be what is called a man of mettle, one of those ruffling tear-cats, who maintain their master's quarrel with sword and buckler. Nay, I am even one of those who hold the end of a feast better than the beginning of a fray. But I know that I can serve your worship better in such quest as yours, than any of these sword-and-dagger men, and that my head will be worth an hundred of their hands."

Tressilian still hesitated. He knew not much of this strange fellow, and was doubtful how far he could repose in him the confidence necessary to render him an useful attendant upon the present emergency. Ere

he had come to a determination, the trampling of a horse was heard in
the court-yard, and Master Mumblazen and Will Badger both entered
hastily into Tressilian's chamber, speaking almost at the same moment.

"Here is a serving-man on the bonniest grey tit I ever see'd in my
life," said Will Badger, who got the start;——"having on his arm a
silver cognizance, being a fire-drake holding in his mouth a brick-bat,
under a coronet of an Earl's degree," said Master Mumblazen, "and bearing a letter sealed of the same."

Tressilian took the letter, which was addressed "To the worshipful
Master Edmund Tressilian, our loving kinsman—These—ride, ride, ride,
—for thy life, for thy life, for thy life." He then opened it, and found
the following contents:—

"MASTER TRESSILIAN, OUR GOOD FRIEND AND COUSIN,

"We are at present so ill at ease, and otherwise so unhappily circumstanced, that we are desirous to have around us those of our friends on
whose loving kindness we can most especially repose confidence; amongst
whom we hold our good Master Tressilian one of the foremost and nearest, both in good will and good ability. We therefore pray you, with
your most convenient speed, to repair to our poor lodging, at Say's Court,
near Deptford, where we will treat farther with you of matters which we
deem it not fit to commit unto writing. And so we bid you heartily
farewell, being your loving kinsman to command,

"RATCLIFFE, EARL OF SUSSEX."

"Send up the messenger instantly, Will Badger," said Tressilian; and
as the man entered the room, he exclaimed, "Aha, Stevens, is it you?
how does my good lord?"

"Ill, Master Tressilian," was the messenger's reply, "and having therefore the more need of good friends around him."

"But what is my lord's malady?" said Tressilian, anxiously. "I heard
nothing of his being ill."

"I know not, sir," replied the man; "he is very ill at ease. The leeches
are at a stand, and many of his household suspect foul practice,—witchcraft, or worse."

"What are the symptoms?" said Wayland Smith, stepping forward
hastily.

"Anan?" said the messenger, not comprehending his meaning.

"What does he ail?" said Wayland; "where lies his disease?"

The man looked at Tressilian, as if to know whether he should answer
these enquiries from a stranger, and receiving a sign in the affirmative,
he hastily enumerated gradual loss of strength, nocturnal perspiration,
and loss of appetite, faintness, &c.

"Joined," said Wayland, "to a gnawing pain in the stomach, and a
low fever?"

"Even so," said the messenger, somewhat surprised.

"I know how the disease is caused," said the artist, "and I know the cause. Your master has eaten of the manna of Saint Nicholas. I know the cure too—my master shall not say I studied in his laboratory for nothing."

"How mean you?" said Tressilian, frowning; "we speak of one of the first nobles of England. Bethink you, this is no subject for buffoonery."

"God forbid!" said Wayland Smith. "I say that I know his disease, and can cure him. Remember what I did for Sir Hugh Robsart."

"We will set forth instantly," said Tressilian. "God calls us."

Accordingly, hastily mentioning this new motive for his instant departure, though without alluding to either the suspicions of Stevens, or the assurances of Wayland Smith, he took the kindest leave of Sir Hugh and the family at Lidcote Hall, who accompanied him with prayers and blessings, and, attended by Wayland and the Earl of Sussex's domestic, travelled with the utmost speed towards London.

CHAPTER XIII

> ——Ay, I know you have arsenic,
> Vitriol, sal-tartre, argaile, alkaly,
> Cinoper: I know all.—This fellow, Captain,
> Will come in time to be a great distiller,
> And give a say (I will not say directly,
> But very near) at the philosopher's stone.
> *The Alchemist.*

TRESSILIAN and his attendants pressed their route with all dispatch. He had asked the smith, indeed, when their departure was resolved on, whether he would not rather choose to avoid Berkshire, in which he had played a part so conspicuous? But Wayland returned a confident answer. He had employed the short interval they passed at Lidcote Hall in transforming himself in a wonderful manner. His wild and overgrown thicket of beard was now restrained to two small mustaches on the upper lip, turned up in a military fashion. A tailor from the village of Lidcote (well paid) had exerted his skill, under his customer's directions, so as completely to alter Wayland's outward man, and take off from his appearance almost twenty years of age. Formerly, besmeared with soot and charcoal—overgrown with hair, and bent double with the nature of his labour—disfigured too by his odd and fantastic dress, he seemed a man of fifty years old. But now, in a handsome suit of Tressilian's livery, with a sword by his side, and a buckler on his shoulder, he looked like a gay ruffling serving-man, whose age might be betwixt thirty and thirty-five, the very prime of human life. His loutish savage-looking demeanour seemed equally changed, into a forward, sharp, and impudent alertness of look and action.

When challenged by Tressilian, who desired to know the cause of a metamorphosis so singular and so absolute, Wayland only answered by singing a stave from a comedy, which was then new, and was supposed, among the more favourable judges, to augur some genius on the part of the author. We are happy to preserve the couplet, which ran exactly thus,—

> "Ban, ban, ca Caliban—
> Get a new master—Be a new man."

Although Tressilian did not recollect the verses, yet they reminded him that Wayland had once been a stage-player, a circumstance which, of itself, accounted indifferently well for the readiness with which he could assume so total a change of personal appearance. The artist himself was so confident of his disguise being completely changed, or of his having completely changed his disguise, which may be the more correct mode of speaking, that he regretted they were not to pass near his old place of retreat.

"I could venture," he said, "in my present dress, and with your worship's backing, to face Master Justice Blindas, even on a day of Quarter Sessions; and I would like to know what is become of Hobgoblin, who is like to play the devil in the world, if he can once slip the string, and leave his granny and his dominie.—Ay, and the scathed vault!" he said; "I would willingly have seen what havoc the explosion of so much gunpowder has made among Doctor Demetrius Doboobie's retorts and phials. I warrant me, my fame haunts the Vale of the Whitehorse long after my body is rotten; and that many a lout ties up his horse, lays down his silver groat, and pipes like a sailor whistling in a calm, for Wayland Smith to come and shoe his tit for him. But the horse will catch the founders ere the smith answers the call."

In this particular, indeed, Wayland proved a true prophet; and so easily do fables rise, that an obscure tradition of his extraordinary practice in farriery prevails in the Vale of Whitehorse even unto this day; and neither the tradition of Alfred's Victory, nor of the celebrated Pusey Horn, are better preserved in Berkshire than the wild legend of Wayland Smith.[1]

The haste of the travellers admitted their making no stay upon their journey, save what the refreshment of the horses required; and as many of the places through which they passed were under the influence of the Earl of Leicester, or persons immediately dependent on him, they thought it prudent to disguise their names, and the purpose of their journey. On such occasions the agency of Wayland Smith (by which name we shall continue to distinguish the artist, though his real name was Lancelot Wayland) was extremely serviceable. He seemed, indeed, to have a pleasure in displaying the alertness with which he could baffle investigations and amuse himself by putting the curiosity of tapsters and innkeepers on a false scent. During the course of their brief journey, three different and inconsistent reports were circulated by him on their account; namely, first, that Tressilian was the Lord Deputy of Ireland, come over

[1] See Note II.—Legend of Wayland Smith.

in disguise to take the Queen's pleasure concerning the great rebel Rory Oge Ma.:Carthy MacMahon; secondly, that the said Tressilian was an agent of Monsieur, coming to urge his suit to the hand of Elizabeth; thirdly, that he was the Duke of Medina, come over, incognito, to adjust the quarrel betwixt Philip and that princess.

Tressilian was angry, and expostulated with the artist on the various inconveniences, and, in particular, the unnecessary degree of attention to which they were subjected by the figments he thus circulated; but he was pacified (for who could be proof against such an argument?) by Wayland's assuring him that a general importance was attached to his own (Tressilian's) striking presence, which rendered it necessary to give an extraordinary reason for the rapidity and secrecy of his journey.

At length they approached the metropolis, where, owing to the more general recourse of strangers, their appearance excited neither observation nor inquiry, and finally they entered London itself.

It was Tressilian's purpose to go down directly to Deptford, where Lord Sussex resided, in order to be near the court, then held at Greenwich, the favourite residence of Elizabeth, and honoured as her birthplace. Still a brief halt in London was necessary; and it was somewhat prolonged by the earnest entreaties of Wayland Smith, who desired permission to take a walk through the city.

"Take thy sword and buckler, and follow me, then," said Tressilian; "I am about to walk myself, and we will go in company."

This he said, because he was not altogether so secure of the fidelity of his new retainer, as to lose sight of him at this interesting moment, when rival factions at the court of Elizabeth were running so high. Wayland Smith willingly acquiesced in the precaution, of which he probably conjectured the motive, but only stipulated, that his master should enter the shops of such chemists or apothecaries as he should point out, in walking through Fleet Street, and permit him to make some necessary purchases. Tressilian agreed, and obeying the signal of his attendant, walked successively into more than four or five shops, where he observed that Wayland purchased in each only one single drug, in various quantities. The medicines which he first asked for were readily furnished, each in succession, but those which he afterwards required were less easily supplied—and Tressilian observed, that Wayland more than once, to the surprise of the shopkeeper, returned the gum or herb that was offered to him, and compelled him to exchange it for the right sort, or else went on to seek it elsewhere. But one ingredient, in particular, seemed almost impossible to be found. Some chemists plainly admitted they had never seen it,—others denied that such a drug existed, excepting in the imagination of crazy alchemists,—and most of them attempted to satisfy their customer, by producing some substitute, which, when rejected by Wayland, as not being what he had asked for, they maintained possessed, in a superior degree, the self-same qualities. In general, they all displayed some curiosity concerning the purpose for which he wanted it. One old, meagre chemist, to whom the artist put the usual question, in terms which Tressilian neither understood nor could recollect, answered frankly, there was none of that drug in London, unless Yoglan the Jew chanced to have some of it upon hand.

"I thought as much," said Wayland. And as soon as they left the shop, he said to Tressilian, "I crave your pardon, sir, but no artist can work without his tools. I must needs go to this Yoglan's; and I promise you, that if this detains you longer than your leisure seems to permit, you shall, nevertheless, be well repaid, by the use I will make of this rare drug. Permit me," he added, "to walk before you, for we are now to quit the broad street, and we will make double speed if I lead the way."

Tressilian acquiesced, and, following the smith down a lane which turned to the left hand towards the river, he found that his guide walked on with great speed, and apparently perfect knowledge of the town, through a labyrinth of by-streets, courts, and blind alleys, until at length Wayland paused in the midst of a very narrow lane, the termination of which showed a peep of the Thames looking misty and muddy, which background was crossed saltier-ways, as Mr Mumblazen might have said, by the masts of two lighters that lay waiting for the tide. The shop under which he halted had not, as in modern days, a glazed window—but a paltry canvas screen surrounded such a stall as a cobbler now occupies, having the front open, much in the manner of a fishmonger's booth of the present day. A little old smock-faced man, the very reverse of a Jew in complexion, for he was very soft-haired as well as beardless, appeared, and with many courtesies asked Wayland what he pleased to want. He had no sooner named the drug, than the Jew started and looked surprised. "And vat might your vorship vant vith that drug, which is not named, mein God, in forty years as I have been chemist here?"

"These questions it is no part of my commission to answer," said Wayland; "I only wish to know if you have what I want, and having it, are willing to sell it?"

"Ay, mein God, for having it, that I have, and for selling it, I am a chemist, and sell every drug." So saying, he exhibited a powder, and then continued, "But it will cost much monies—Vot I ave cost its weight in gold—ay, gold well-refined—I vill say six times—It comes from Mount Sinai, where we had our blessed Law given forth, and the plant blossoms but once in one hundred year."

"I do not know how often it is gathered on Mount Sinai," said Wayland, after looking at the drug offered him with great disdain, "but I will wager my sword and buckler against your gaberdine, that this trash you offer me, instead of what I asked for, may be had for gathering any day of the week in the castle-ditch of Aleppo."

"You are a rude man," said the Jew; "and, besides, I ave no better than that—or if I ave, I will not sell it without order of a physician—or without you tell me vat you make of it."

The artist made brief answer in a language of which Tressilian could not understand a word, and which seemed to strike the Jew with the utmost astonishment. He stared upon Wayland like one who has suddenly recognised some mighty hero or dreaded potentate, in the person of an unknown and unmarked stranger. "Holy Elias!" he exclaimed, when he had recovered the first stunning effects of his surprise; and then passing from his former suspicious and surly manner to the very extremity of obsequiousness, he cringed low to the artist, and besought him to enter his poor house, to bless his miserable threshold by crossing it.

"Vill you not taste a cup vith the poor Jew, Zacharias Yoglan?—Vill you Tokay ave?—vill you Lachrymæ taste?—vill you——"

"You offend in your proffers," said Wayland; "minister to me in what I require of you, and forbear further discourse."

The rebuked Israelite took his bunch of keys, and opening with circumspection a cabinet which seemed more strongly secured than the other cases of drugs and medicines amongst which it stood, he drew out a little secret drawer, having a glass lid, and containing a small portion of a black powder. This he offered to Wayland, his manner conveying the deepest devotion towards him, though an avaricious and jealous expression which seemed to grudge every grain of what his customer was about to possess himself, disputed ground in his countenance, with the obsequious deference which he desired it should exhibit.

"Have you scales?" said Wayland.

The Jew pointed to those which lay ready for common use in the shop, but he did so with a puzzled expression of doubt and fear, which did not escape the artist.

"They must be other than these," said Wayland, sternly; "know you not that holy things lose their virtue if weighed in an unjust balance?"

The Jew hung his head, took from a steel-plated casket a pair of scales beautifully mounted, and said, as he adjusted them for the artist's use,—"With these I do mine own experiment—one hair of the high-priest's beard would turn them."

"It suffices," said the artist; and weighed out two drachms for himself of the black powder, which he very carefully folded up, and put into his pouch with the other drugs. He then demanded the price of the Jew, who answered, shaking his head and bowing,—

"No price—no, nothing at all from such as you.—But you will see the poor Jew again? you will look into his laboratory, where, God help him, he hath dried himself to the substance of the withered gourd of Jonah the holy prophet—You will have pity on him, and show him one little step on the great road?"

"Hush!" said Wayland, laying his finger mysteriously on his mouth, "it may be we shall meet again—thou hast already the *Schahmajm*, as thine own Rabbis call it—the general creation; watch, therefore, and pray, for thou must attain the knowledge of Alchahest Elixir, Samech, ere I may commune farther with thee." Then returning with a slight nod the reverential congees of the Jew, he walked gravely up the lane, followed by his master, whose first observation on the scene he had just witnessed was, that Wayland ought to have paid the man for his drug, whatever it was.

"I pay him?" said the artist; "May the foul fiend pay me if I do!—Had it not been that I thought it might displease your worship, I would have had an ounce or two of gold out of him, in exchange of the same just weight of brick-dust."

"I advise you to practise no such knavery while waiting upon me," said Tressilian.

"Did I not say," answered the artist, "that for that reason alone, I forebore him for the present?—Knavery, call you it?—why, yonder wretched skeleton hath wealth sufficient to pave the whole lane he lives in with dollars, and scarce miss them out of his own iron chest; yet he goes mad after the philosopher's stone—and besides, he would have cheated a poor serving-man, as he thought me at first, with trash that was not worth a penny—Match for match, quoth the devil to the collier; if his false medicine was worth my good crowns, my true brick-dust is as well worth his good gold."

"It may be so for aught I know," said Tressilian, "in dealing amongst Jews and apothecaries; but understand, that to have such tricks of leger-demain practised by one attending on me, diminishes my honour, and that I will not permit them. I trust thou hast made up thy purchases?"

"I have, sir," replied Wayland; "and with these drugs will I, this very day, compound the true orvietan, that noble medicine which is so seldom found genuine and effective within these realms of Europe, for want of that most rare and precious drug which I got but now from Yoglan."[1]

"But why not have made all your purchases at one shop?" said his master; "we have lost nearly an hour in running from one pounder of simples to another."

"Content you, sir," said Wayland. "No man shall learn my secret; and it would not be mine long, were I to buy all my materials from one chemist."

They now returned to their inn, (the famous Bell-Savage,) and while the Lord Sussex's servant prepared the horses for their journey, Wayland, obtaining from the cook the service of a mortar, shut himself up in a private chamber, where he mixed, pounded, and amalgamated the drugs which he had bought, each in its due proportion, with a readiness and address that plainly showed him well practised in all the manual operations of pharmacy.

By the time Wayland's electuary was prepared the horses were ready, and a short hour's riding brought them to the present habitation of

---

[1] Orvietan, or Venice treacle, as it was sometimes called, was understood to be a sovereign remedy against poison; and the reader must be contented, for the time he peruses these pages, to hold the same opinion, which was once universally received by the learned as well as the vulgar.

Lord Sussex, an ancient house, called Say's Court, near Deptford, which had long pertained to a family of that name, but had, for upwards of a century, been possessed by the ancient and honourable family of Evelyn. The present representative of that ancient house took a deep interest in the Earl of Sussex, and had willingly accommodated both him and his numerous retinue in his hospitable mansion. Say's Court was afterwards the residence of the celebrated Mr. Evelyn, whose "Silva" is still the manual of British planters; and whose life, manners, and principles, as illustrated in his Memoirs, ought equally to be the manual of English gentlemen.

CHAPTER XIV

This is rare news thou tell'st me, my good fellow;
There are two bulls fierce battling on the green
For one fair heifer—if the one goes down,
The dale will be more peaceful, and the herd,
Which have small interest in their brulziement
May pasture there in peace.

Old Play.

SAY'S COURT was watched like a beleaguered fort; and so high rose the suspicions of the times, that Tressilian and his attendants were stopped and questioned repeatedly by sentinels, both on foot and horseback, as they approached the abode of the sick Earl. In truth, the high rank which Sussex held in Queen Elizabeth's favour, and his known and avowed rivalry of the Earl of Leicester, caused the utmost importance to be attached to his welfare; for, at the period we treat of, all men doubted whether he or the Earl of Leicester might ultimately have the higher rank in her regard.

Elizabeth, like many of her sex, was fond of governing by factions, so as to balance two opposing interests, and reserve in her own hand the power of making either predominate, as the interest of the state, or perhaps as her own female caprice, (for to that foible even she was not superior,) might finally determine. To finesse—to hold the cards—to oppose one interest to another—to bridle him who thought himself highest in her esteem, by the fears he must entertain of another equally trusted, if not equally beloved, were arts which she used throughout her reign, and which enabled her, though frequently giving way to the weakness of favouritism, to prevent most of its evil effects on her kingdom and government.

The two nobles who at present stood as rivals in her favour, possessed very different pretensions to share it; yet it might be in general said, that the Earl of Sussex had been most serviceable to the Queen, while Leicester was most dear to the woman. Sussex was, according to the phrase of the times, a martialist; had done good service in Ireland, and in Scotland, and especially in the great northern rebellion, in 1569, which was quelled, in a great measure, by his military talents. He was, therefore, naturally surrounded and looked up to by those who wished to make arms their road to distinction. The Earl of Sussex, moreover, was of more ancient and honourable descent than his rival, uniting in his person the representations of the Fitz-Walters, as well as of the Rat-cliffes, while the scutcheon of Leicester was stained by the degradation of his grandfather, the oppressive minister of Henry VII, and scarce improved by that of his father, the unhappy Dudley, Duke of Nor-thumberland, executed on Tower-Hill, August 22, 1553. But in person, features, and address, weapons so formidable in the court of a female sovereign, Leicester had advantages more than sufficient to counter-balance the military services, high blood, and frank bearing of the Earl of Sussex; and he bore in the eye of the court and kingdom, the higher share in Elizabeth's favour, though (for such was her uniform policy) by no means so decidedly expressed as to warrant him against the final preponderance of his rival's pretensions. The illness of Sussex therefore happened so opportunely for Leicester, as to give rise to strange surmises among the public; while the followers of the one Earl were filled with the deepest apprehensions, and those of the other with the highest hopes of its probable issue. Meanwhile,—for in that old time, men never forgot the probability that the matter might be determined by length of sword,—the retainers of each noble flocked around their patron, appeared well armed in the vicinity of the court itself, and disturbed the ear of the sovereign by their frequent and alarming debates, held even within the precincts of her palace. This preliminary statement is necessary, to render what follows intelligible to the reader.[1]

On Tressilian's arrival at Say's Court, he found the place filled with the retainers of the Earl of Sussex, and of the gentlemen who came to attend their patron in his illness. Arms were in every hand, and a deep gloom on every countenance, as if they had apprehended an immediate and violent assault from the opposite faction. In the hall, however, to which Tressilian was ushered by one of the Earl's attendants, while another went to inform Sussex of his arrival, he found only two gentle-men in waiting. There was a remarkable contrast in their dress, appear-ance, and manners. The attire of the elder gentleman, a person as it seemed of quality and in the prime of life, was very plain and soldierlike, his stature low, his limbs stout, his bearing ungraceful, and his features of that kind which express sound common sense without a grain of vivacity or imagination. The younger, who seemed about twenty, or upwards, was clad in the gayest habit used by persons of quality at the period, wearing a crimson velvet cloak richly ornamented with lace and embroidery, with a bonnet of the same, encircled with a gold chain turned three times around it, and secured by a medal. His hair was adjusted very nearly like that of some fine gentlemen of our own time, that is, it was combed upwards, and made to stand as it were on end; and in his ears he wore a pair of silver ear-rings, having each a pearl of considerable size. The countenance of this youth, besides being regularly handsome and

[1] See Note III.—Leicester and Sussex.

accompanied by a fine person, was animated and striking in a degree that seemed to speak at once the firmness of a decided and the fire of an enterprising character, the power of reflection, and the promptitude of determination.

Both these gentlemen reclined nearly in the same posture on benches near each other; but each seeming engaged in his own meditations, looked straight upon the wall which was opposite to them, without speaking to his companion. The looks of the elder were of that sort which convinced the beholder, that, in looking on the wall, he saw no more than the side of an old hall hung around with cloaks, antlers, bucklers, old pieces of armour, partisans, and the similar articles which were usually the furniture of such a place. The look of the younger gallant had in it something imaginative; he was sunk in reverie, and it seemed as if the empty space of air betwixt him and the wall, were the stage of a theatre on which his fancy was mustering his own *dramatis personæ,* and treating him with sights far different from those which his awakened and earthly vision could have offered.

At the entrance of Tressilian both started from their musing, and bade him welcome; the younger, in particular, with great appearance of animation and cordiality.

"Thou art welcome, Tressilian," said the youth; "thy philosophy stole thee from us when this household had objects of ambition to offer—it is an honest philosophy, since it returns thee to us when there are only dangers to be shared."

"Is my lord, then, so greatly indisposed?" said Tressilian.

"We fear the very worst," answered the elder gentleman, "and by the worst practice."

"Fie," replied Tressilian, "my Lord of Leicester is honourable."

"What doth he with such attendants, then, as he hath about him?" said the younger gallant. "The man who raises the devil may be honest, but he is answerable for the mischief which the fiend does, for all that."

"And is this all of you, my mates," enquired Tressilian, "that are about my lord in his utmost straits?"

"No, no," replied the elder gentleman, "there are Tracy, Markham, and several more; but we keep watch here by two at once, and some are weary and are sleeping in the gallery above."

"And some," said the young man, "are gone down to the Dock yonder at Deptford, to look out such a hulk as they may purchase by clubbing their broken fortunes; and so soon as all is over, we will lay our noble lord in a noble green grave, have a blow at those who have hurried him thither, if opportunity suits, and then sail for the Indies with heavy hearts and light purses."

"It may be," said Tressilian, "that I will embrace the same purpose, so soon as I have settled some business at court."

"Thou business at court!" they both exclaimed at once; "and thou make the Indian voyage!"

"Why, Tressilian," said the younger man, "art thou not wedded, and beyond these flaws of fortune, that drive folks out to sea when their bark bears fairest for the haven?—What has become of the lovely Indamira that was to match my Amoret for truth and beauty?"

"Speak not of her!" said Tressilian, averting his face.

"Ay, stands it so with you?" said the youth, taking his hand very affectionately; "then, fear not I will again touch the green wound—But it is strange as well as sad news. Are none of our fair and merry fellowship to escape shipwreck of fortune and happiness in this sudden tempest? I had hoped thou wert in harbour, at least, my dear Edmund—But truly says another dear friend of thy name,

> 'What man that sees the ever whirling wheel
> Of Chance, the which all mortal things doth sway,
> But that thereby doth find and plainly feel,
> How Mutability in them doth play
> Her cruel sports to many men's decay.' "

The elder gentleman had risen from his bench, and was pacing the hall with some impatience, while the youth, with much earnestness and feeling, recited these lines. When he had done, the other wrapped himself in his cloak, and again stretched himself down, saying, "I marvel, Tressilian, you will feed the lad in this silly humour. If there were aught to draw a judgment upon a virtuous and honourable household like my lord's, renounce me if I think not it were this piping, whining, childish trick of poetry, that came among us with Master Walter Wittypate here and his comrades, twisting into all manner of uncouth and incomprehensible forms of speech, the honest plain English phrase which God gave us to express our meaning withal."

"Blount believes," said his comrade, laughing, "the devil woo'd Eve in rhyme, and that the mystic meaning of the Tree of Knowledge refers solely to the art of clashing rhymes, and meting out hexameters." [1]

At this moment the Earl's chamberlain entered, and informed Tressilian that his lord required to speak with him.

He found Lord Sussex dressed, but unbraced and lying on his couch, and was shocked at the alteration disease had made in his person. The Earl received him with the most friendly cordiality, and enquired into the state of his courtship. Tressilian evaded his enquiries for a moment, and turning his discourse on the Earl's own health, he discovered, to his surprise, that the symptoms of his disorder corresponded minutely with those which Wayland had predicated concerning it. He hesitated not, therefore, to communicate to Sussex the whole history of his attendant, and the pretensions he set up to cure the disorder under which he laboured. The Earl listened with incredulous attention until the name of Demetrius was mentioned, and then suddenly called to his secretary to bring him a certain casket which contained papers of importance. "Take

[1] See Note IV.—Sir Walter Raleigh.

out from thence," he said, "the declaration of the rascal cook whom we had under examination, and look heedfully if the name of Demetrius be not there mentioned."

The secretary turned to the passage at once, and read, "And said declarent, being examined, said, That he remembers having made the sauce to the said sturgeon-fish, after eating of which, the said noble Lord was taken ill; and he put the usual ingredients and condiments therein, namely——"

"Pass over his trash," said the Earl, "and see whether he had not been supplied with his materials by a herbalist called Demetrius."

"It is even so," answered the secretary. "And he adds, he has not since seen the said Demetrius."

"This accords with thy fellow's story, Tressilian," said the Earl; "call him hither."

On being summoned to the Earl's presence, Wayland Smith told his former tale with firmness and consistency.

"It may be," said the Earl, "thou art sent by those who have begun this work, to end it for them; but bethink, if I miscarry under thy medicine, it may go hard with thee."

"That were severe measure," said Wayland, "since the issue of medicine, and the end of life, are in God's disposal. But I will stand the risk. I have not lived so long under ground, to be afraid of a grave."

"Nay, if thou be'st so confident," said the Earl of Sussex, "I will take the risk too, for the learned can do nothing for me. Tell me how this medicine is to be taken."

"That will I do presently," said Wayland; "but allow me to condition that, since I incur all the risk of this treatment, no other physician shall be permitted to interfere with it."

"That is but fair," replied the Earl; "and now prepare your drug."

While Wayland obeyed the Earl's commands, his servants, by the artist's direction, undressed their master, and placed him in bed.

"I warn you," he said, "that the first operation of this medicine will be to produce a heavy sleep, during which time the chamber must be kept undisturbed; as the consequences may otherwise be fatal. I myself will watch by the Earl, with any of the gentlemen of his chamber."

"Let all leave the room, save Stanley and this good fellow," said the Earl.

"And saving me also," said Tressilian. "I too am deeply interested in the effects of this potion."

"Be it so, good friend," said the Earl; "and now for our experiment; but first call my secretary and chamberlain.

"Bear witness," he continued, when these officers arrived, "bear witness for me, gentlemen, that our honourable friend Tressilian is in no way responsible for the effects which this medicine may produce upon me, the taking it being my own free action and choice, in regard I believe it to be a remedy which God has furnished me by unexpected means, to recover me of my present malady. Commend me to my noble and princely Mistress; and say that I live and die her true servant, and wish to all about her throne the same singleness of heart and will to serve her, with more ability to do so than hath been assigned to poor Thomas Ratcliffe."

He then folded his hands, and seemed for a second or two absorbed in mental devotion, then took the potion in his hand, and, pausing, regarded Wayland with a look that seemed designed to penetrate his very soul, but which caused no anxiety or hesitation in the countenance or manner of the artist.

"Here is nothing to be feared," said Sussex to Tressilian; and swallowed the medicine without farther hesitation.

"I am now to pray your lordship," said Wayland, "to dispose yourself to rest as commodiously as you can; and of you, gentlemen, to remain as still and mute as if you waited at your mother's deathbed."

The chamberlain and secretary then withdrew, giving orders that all doors should be bolted, and all noise in the house strictly prohibited. Several gentlemen were voluntary watchers in the hall, but none remained in the chamber of the sick Earl, save his groom of the chamber, the artist, and Tressilian.—Wayland's Smith's predictions were speedily accomplished, and a sleep fell upon the Earl, so deep and sound, that they who watched his bedside began to fear, that, in his weakened state, he might pass away without awakening from his lethargy. Wayland Smith himself appeared anxious, and felt the temples of the Earl slightly, from time to time, attending particularly to the state of his respiration, which was full and deep, but at the same time easy and uninterrupted.

CHAPTER XV

You loggerheaded and unpolish'd grooms,
What, no attendants, no regard, no duty?
Where is the foolish knave I sent before?
Taming of the Shrew.

THERE is no period at which men look worse in the eyes of each other, or feel more uncomfortable, than when the first dawn of daylight finds them watchers. Even a beauty of the first order, after the vigils of a ball are interrupted by the dawn, would do wisely to withdraw herself from the gaze of her fondest and most partial admirers. Such was the pale, inauspicious, and ungrateful light, which began to beam upon those who kept watch all night, in the hall at Say's Court, and which mingled its cold, pale, blue diffusion with the red, yellow, and smoky beams of expiring lamps and torches. The young gallant, whom we noticed in our last chapter, had left the room for a few minutes, to learn the cause of a knocking at the outward gate, and on his return, was so struck with the forlorn and ghastly aspects of his companions of the watch, that he exclaimed, "Pity of my heart, my masters, how like owls you look! Methinks, when the sun rises, I shall see you flutter off with your eyes dazzled, to stick yourselves into the next ivy-tod or ruined steeple."

"Hold thy peace, thou gibing fool," said Blount; "hold thy peace. Is this a time for jeering, when the manhood of England is perchance dying within a wall's breadth of thee?"

"There thou liest," replied the gallant.

"How, lie!" exclaimed Blount, starting up, "lie! and to me?"

"Why, so thou didst, thou peevish fool," answered the youth; "thou didst lie on that bench even now, didst thou not? But art thou not a hasty coxcomb, to pick up a wry word so wrathfully? Nevertheless, loving and honouring my lord as truly as thou, or any one, I do say, that should Heaven take him from us, all England's manhood dies not with him."

"Ay," replied Blount, "a good portion will survive with thee, doubtless."

"And a good portion with thyself, Blount, and with stout Markham here, and Tracy, and all of us. But I am he will best employ the talent Heaven has given us all."

"As how, I prithee?" said Blount; "tell us your mystery of multiplying."

"Why, sirs," answered the youth, "ye are like goodly land, which bears no crop because it is not quickened by manure; but I have that rising spirit in me, which will make my poor faculties labour to keep pace with it. My ambition will keep my brain at work, I warrant thee."

"I pray to God it does not drive thee mad," said Blount; "for my part, if we lose our noble lord, I bid adieu to the court and to the camp both. I have five hundred foul acres in Norfolk, and thither will I, and change the court pantoufle for the country hobnail."

"O base transmutation!" exclaimed his antagonist; "thou hast already got the true rustic slouch—thy shoulders stoop, as if thine hands were at the stilts of the plough, and thou hast a kind of earthy smell about thee, instead of being perfumed with essence, as a gallant and courtier should. On my soul, thou hast stolen out to roll thyself on a hay mow! The only excuse will be to swear by thy hilt, that the farmer had a fair daughter."

"I pray thee, Walter," said another of the company, "cease thy raillery, which suits neither time nor place, and tell us who was at the gate just now."

"Doctor Masters, physician to her Grace in ordinary, sent by her special orders to enquire after the Earl's health," answered Walter.

"Ha! what!" exclaimed Tracy, "that was no slight mark of favour; if the Earl can but come through, he will match with Leicester yet. Is Masters with my lord at present?"

"Nay," replied Walter, "he is half way back to Greenwich by this time, and in high dudgeon."

"Thou didst not refuse him admittance?" exclaimed Tracy.

"Thou wert not, surely, so mad?" ejaculated Blount.

"I refused him admittance as flatly, Blount, as you would refuse a penny to a blind beggar; as obstinately, Tracy, as thou didst ever deny access to a dun."

"Why, in the fiend's name, didst thou trust him to go to the gate?" said Blount to Tracy.

"It suited his years better than mine," answered Tracy; "but he has undone us all now thoroughly. My lord may live or die, he will never have a look of favour from her Majesty again."

"Nor the means of making fortunes for his followers," said the young gallant, smiling contemptuously;—"there lies the sore point that will brook no handling. My good sirs, I sounded my lamentations over my lord somewhat less loudly than some of you; but when the point comes of doing him service, I will yield to none of you. Had this learned leech entered, thinkst thou not there had been such a coil betwixt him and Tressilian's mediciner, that not the sleeper only, but the very dead might have awakened? I know what larum belongs to the discord of doctors."

"And who is to take the blame of opposing the Queen's orders?" said Tracy: "for, undeniably, Doctor Masters came with her Grace's positive commands to cure the Earl."

"I, who have done the wrong, will bear the blame," said Walter.

"Thus, then, off fly the dreams of court favour thou hast nourished," said Blount; "and despite all thy boasted art and ambition, Devonshire will see thee shine a true younger brother, fit to sit low at the board, carve turn about with the chaplain, look that the hounds be fed, and see the squire's girths drawn when he goes a-hunting."

"Not so," said the young man, colouring, "not while Ireland and the Netherlands have wars, and not while the sea hath pathless waves. The rich West hath lands undreamed of, and Britain contains bold hearts to venture on the quest of them.—Adieu for a space, my masters. I go to walk in the court and look to the sentinels."

"The lad hath quicksilver in his veins, that is certain," said Blount, looking at Markham.

"He hath that both in brain and blood," said Markham, "which may either make or mar him. But, in closing the door against Masters, he hath done a daring and loving piece of service; for Tressilian's fellow hath ever averred, that to wake the Earl were death, and Masters would wake the Seven Sleepers themselves, if he thought they slept not by the regular ordinance of medicine."

Morning was well advanced, when Tressilian, fatigued and over-watched, came down to the hall with the joyful intelligence, that the Earl had awakened of himself, that he found his internal complaints much mitigated, and spoke with a cheerfulness, and looked round with a vivacity, which of themselves showed a material and favourable change had taken place. Tressilian at the same time commanded the attendance of one or two of his followers, to report what had passed during the night, and to relieve the watchers in the Earl's chamber.

When the message of the Queen was communicated to the Earl of Sussex, he at first smiled at the repulse which the physician had received from his zealous young follower, but instantly recollecting himself, he commanded Blount, his master of the horse, instantly to take boat, and go down the river to the Palace of Greenwich, taking young Walter and Tracy with him, and make a suitable compliment, expressing his grateful thanks to his Sovereign, and mentioning the cause why he had not been enabled to profit by the assistance of the wise and learned Doctor Masters.

"A plague on it," said Blount, as he descended the stairs, "had he sent me with a cartel to Leicester, I think I should have done his errand indifferently well. But to go to our gracious Sovereign, before whom all words must be lackered over either with gilding or with sugar, is such a confectionary matter as clean baffles my poor old English brain.—Come with me, Tracy, and come you too, Master Walter Wittypate, that art the cause of our having all this ado. Let us see if thy neat brain, that frames so many flashy fireworks, can help out a plain fellow at need with some of thy shrewd devices."

"Never fear, never fear," exclaimed the youth, "it is I will help you through—let me but fetch my cloak."

"Why, thou hast it on thy shoulders," said Blount,—"the lad is mazed."

"No, no, this is Tracy's old mantle," answered Walter; "I go not with thee to court unless as a gentleman should."

"Why," said Blount, "thy braveries are like to dazzle the eyes of none but some poor groom or porter."

"I know that," said the youth; "but I am resolved I will have my own cloak, ay, and brush my doublet to boot, ere I stir forth with you."

"Well, well," said Blount, "here is a coil about a doublet and a cloak —get thyself ready, a God's name!"

They were soon launched on the princely bosom of the broad Thames, upon which the sun now shone forth in all its splendour.

"There are two things scarce matched in the universe," said Walter to Blount,—"the sun in heaven, and the Thames on the earth."

"The one will light us to Greenwich well enough," said Blount, "and the other would take us there a little faster if it were ebb tide."

"And this is all thou think'st—all thou carest—all thou deem'st the use of the King of Elements, and the King of Rivers, to guide three such poor caitiffs, as thyself, and me, and Tracy, upon an idle journey of courtly ceremony!"

"It is no errand of my seeking, faith," replied Blount, "and I could excuse both the sun and the Thames the trouble of carrying me where I have no great mind to go; and where I expect but dog's wages for my trouble—and by my honour," he added, looking out from the head of the boat, "it seems to me as if our message were a sort of labour in vain; for see, the Queen's barge lies at the stairs, as if her Majesty were about to take water."

It was even so. The royal barge, manned with the Queen's watermen, richly attired in the regal liveries, and having the banner of England displayed, did indeed lie at the great stairs which ascended from the river, and along with it two or three other boats for transporting such part of her retinue as were not in immediate attendance on the royal person. The yeomen of the guard, the tallest and most handsome men which England could produce, guarded with their halberds the passage from the palace-gate to the river side, and all seemed in readiness for the Queen's coming forth, although the day was yet so early.

"By my faith, this bodes us no good," said Blount; "it must be some perilous cause puts her Grace in motion thus untimeously. By my counsel, we were best put back again, and tell the Earl what we have seen."

"Tell the Earl what we have seen!" said Walter; "why, what have we seen but a boat, and men with scarlet jerkins, and halberds in their hands? Let us do his errand, and tell him what the Queen says in reply."

So saying, he caused the boat to be pulled towards a landing-place at some distance from the principal one, which it would not, at that moment, have been thought respectful to approach, and jumped on shore, followed, though with reluctance, by his cautious and timid companions. As they approached the gate of the palace, one of the sergeant porters told them they could not at present enter, as her Majesty was in the act of coming forth. The gentlemen used the name of the Earl of Sussex; but it proved no charm to subdue the officer, who alleged in reply, that it was as much as his post was worth, to disobey in the least tittle the commands which he had received.

"Nay, I told you as much before," said Blount; "do, I pray you, my dear Walter, let us take boat and return."

"Not till I see the Queen come forth," returned the youth, composedly.

"Thou art mad, stark mad, by the mass!" answered Blount.

"And thou," said Walter, "art turned coward of the sudden. I have seen thee face half a score of shag-headed Irish kernes, to thy own share of them, and now thou wouldst blink and go back to shun the frown of a fair lady!"

At this moment the gates opened, and ushers began to issue forth in array, preceded and flanked by the band of Gentlemen Pensioners. After this, amid a crowd of lords and ladies, yet so disposed around her that she could see and be seen on all sides, came Elizabeth herself, then in the prime of womanhood, and in the full glow of what in a Sovereign was called beauty, and who would in the lowest rank of life have been truly judged a noble figure, joined to a striking and commanding physiognomy. She leant on the arm of Lord Hunsdon, whose relation to her by her mother's side often procured him such distinguished marks of Elizabeth's intimacy.

The young cavalier we have so often mentioned had probably never yet approached so near the person of his Sovereign, and he pressed forward as far as the line of warders permitted, in order to avail himself of the present opportunity. His companion, on the contrary, cursing his imprudence, kept pulling him backward, till Walter shook him off impatiently, and letting his rich cloak drop carelessly from one shoulder; a natural action, which served, however, to display to the best advantage his well-proportioned person. Unbonneting at the same time, he fixed his eager gaze on the Queen's approach, with a mixture of respectful curiosity, and modest yet ardent admiration, which suited so well with his fine features, that the warders, struck with his rich attire and noble countenance, suffered him to approach the ground over which the Queen was to pass, somewhat closer than was permitted to ordinary spectators. Thus the adventurous youth stood full in Elizabeth's eye,—an eye never indifferent to the admiration which she deservedly excited among her subjects, or to the fair proportions of external form which chanced to distinguish any of her courtiers. Accordingly, she fixed her keen glance on the youth, as she approached the place where he stood, with a look in which surprise at his boldness seemed to be unmingled with resentment, while a trifling accident happened which attracted her attention towards him yet more strongly. The night had been rainy, and just where the young gentleman stood, a small quantity of mud interrupted the Queen's passage. As she hesitated to pass on, the gallant, throwing his cloak from his shoulders, laid it on the miry spot, so as to ensure her stepping over it dry-shod. Elizabeth looked at the young man, who accompanied this act of devoted courtesy with a profound reverence, and a blush that overspread his whole countenance. The Queen was confused, and blushed in her turn, nodded her head, hastily passed on, and embarked in her barge without saying a word.

"Come along, Sir Coxcomb," said Blount; "your gay cloak will need the brush to-day, I wot. Nay, if you had meant to make a foot-cloth of your mantle, better have kept Tracy's old drab-de-bure, which despises all colours."

"This cloak," said the youth, taking it up and folding it, "shall never be brushed while in my possession."

"And that will not be long, if you learn not a little more economy— we shall have you in *cuerpo* soon, as the Spaniard says."

Their discourse was here interrupted by one of the Band of Pensioners.

"I was sent," said he, after looking at them attentively, "to a gentleman who hath no cloak, or a muddy one.—You, sir, I think," addressing the younger cavalier, "are the man; you will please to follow me."

"He is in attendance on me," said Blount; "on me, the noble Earl of Sussex's master of horse."

"I have nothing to say to that," answered the messenger; "my orders are directly from her Majesty, and concern this gentleman only."

So saying, he walked away, followed by Walter, leaving the others behind, Blount's eyes almost starting from his head with the excess of his astonishment. At length he gave vent to it in an exclamation—"Who the good jere would have thought this!" And shaking his head with a mysterious air he walked to his own boat, embarked, and returned to Deptford.

The young cavalier was, in the meanwhile, guided to the water-side by the Pensioner, who showed him considerable respect; a circumstance which, to persons in his situation, may be considered as an augury of no small consequence. He ushered him into one of the wherries which lay ready to attend the Queen's barge, which was already proceeding up the river, with the advantage of that flood-tide, of which, in the course of their descent, Blount had complained to his associates.

The two rowers used their oars with such expedition at the signal of the Gentleman Pensioner, that they very soon brought their little skiff under the stern of the Queen's boat, where she sate beneath an awning, attended by two or three ladies, and the nobles of her household. She looked more than once at the wherry in which the young adventurer was seated, spoke to those around her, and seemed to laugh. At length one of the attendants, by the Queen's order apparently, made a sign for the wherry to come alongside, and the young man was desired to step from his own skiff into the Queen's barge, which he performed with graceful agility at the fore part of the boat, and was brought aft to the Queen's presence, the wherry at the same time dropping into the rear. The youth underwent the gaze of Majesty, not the less gracefully that his self-possession was mingled with embarrassment. The muddied cloak still hung upon his arm, and formed the natural topic with which the Queen introduced the conversation.

"You have this day spoiled a gay mantle in our behalf, young man. We thank you for your service, though the manner of offering it was unusual and something bold."

"In a sovereign's need," answered the youth, "it is each liege-man's duty to be bold."

"God's pity! that was well said, my lord," said the Queen, turning to a grave person who sate by her, and answered with a grave inclination of the head, and something of a mumbled assent. "Well, young man, your gallantry shall not go unrewarded. Go to the wardrobe keeper, and he shall have orders to supply the suit which you have cast away in our service. Thou shalt have a suit, and that of the newest cut, I promise thee, on the word of a princess."

"May it please your Grace," said Walter, hesitating, "it is not for so humble a servant of your Majesty to measure out your bounties; but if it became me to choose——"

"Thou wouldst have gold, I warrant me," said the Queen, interrupting him; "fie, young man! I take shame to say, that, in our capital, such and so various are the means of thriftless folly, that to give gold to youth is giving fuel to fire, and furnishing them with the means of self-destruction. If I live and reign, these means of unchristian excess shall be abridged. Yet thou mayest be poor," she added, "or thy parents may be—It shall be gold, if thou wilt, but thou shalt answer to me for the use on't."

Walter waited patiently until the Queen had done, and then modestly assured her, that gold was still less in his wish than the raiment her Majesty had before offered.

"How, boy!" said the Queen, "neither gold nor garment? What is it thou wouldst have of me, then?"

"Only permission, madam—if it is not asking too high an honour—permission to wear the cloak which did you this trifling service."

"Permission to wear thine own cloak, thou silly boy!" said the Queen.

"It is no longer mine," said Walter; "when your Majesty's foot touched it, it became a fit mantle for a prince, but far too rich a one for its former owner."

The Queen again blushed; and endeavoured to cover, by laughing, a slight degree of not unpleasing surprise and confusion.

"Heard you ever the like, my lords? The youth's head is turned with reading romances—I must know something of him, that I may send him safe to his friends.—What art thou?"

"A gentleman of the household of the Earl of Sussex, so please your Grace, sent hither with his master of horse, upon a message to your Majesty."

In a moment the gracious expression which Elizabeth's face had hitherto maintained, gave way to an expression of haughtiness and severity.

"My Lord of Sussex," she said, "has taught us how to regard his messages, by the value he places upon ours. We sent but this morning the physician in ordinary of our chamber, and that at no usual time, understanding his lordship's illness to be more dangerous than we had before apprehended. There is at no court in Europe a man more skilled in this holy and most useful science than Doctor Masters, and he came from Us to our subject. Nevertheless, he found the gate of Say's Court defended by men with culverins, as if had been on the Borders of Scotland, not in the vicinity of our court; and when he demanded admittance in our name, it was stubbornly refused. For this slight of a kindness, which had but too much of condescension in it, we will receive, at present at least, no excuse; and some such we suppose to have been the purport of my Lord of Sussex's message."

This was uttered in a tone, and with a gesture, which made Lord Sussex's friends who were within hearing tremble. He to whom the speech was addressed, however, trembled not; but with great deference and humility, as soon as the Queen's passion gave him an opportunity, he replied:—"So please your most gracious Majesty, I was charged with no apology from the Earl of Sussex."

"With what were you then charged, sir?" said the Queen, with the impetuosity which, amid nobler qualities, strongly marked her character; "was it with a justification?—or, God's death! with a defiance?"

"Madam," said the young man, "my Lord of Sussex knew the offence approached towards treason, and could think of nothing save of securing the offender, and placing him in your Majesty's hands, and at your mercy. The noble Earl was fast asleep when your most gracious message reached him, a potion having been administered to that purpose by his physician; and his lordship knew not of the ungracious repulse your Majesty's royal and most comfortable message had received, until after he awoke this morning."

"And which of his domestics, then, in the name of Heaven, presumed to reject my message, without even admitting my own physician to the presence of him whom I sent him to attend?" said the Queen, much surprised.

"The offender, madam, is before you," replied Walter, bowing very low; "the full and sole blame is mine; and my lord has most justly sent me to abye the consequences of a fault, of which he is as innocent as a sleeping man's dreams can be of a waking man's actions."

"What! was it thou?—thou thyself, that repelled my messenger and my physician from Say's Court?" said the Queen. "What could occasion such boldness in one who seems devoted—that is, whose exterior bearing shows devotion—to his Sovereign?"

"Madam," said the youth,—who, notwithstanding an assumed appearance of severity, thought that he saw something in the Queen's face that resembled not implacability,—"we say in our country, that the physician is for the time the liege sovereign of his patient. Now, my noble master was then under dominion of a leech, by whose advice he hath greatly profited, who had issued his commands that his patient should not that night be disturbed, on the very peril of his life."

"Thy master hath trusted some false varlet of an empiric," said the Queen.

"I know not, madam, but by the fact, that he is now—this very morning—awakened much refreshed and strengthened, from the only sleep he hath had for many hours."

The nobles looked at each other, but more with the purpose to see what each thought of this news, than to exchange any remarks on what had happened. The Queen answered hastily, and without affecting to disguise her satisfaction, "By my word, I am glad he is better. But thou wert over bold to deny the access of my Doctor Masters. Know'st thou not the Holy Writ saith, 'in the multitude of counsel there is safety'?"

"Ay, madam," said Walter, "but I have heard learned men say, that the safety spoken of is for the physicians, not for the patient."

"By my faith, child, thou hast pushed me home," said the Queen, laughing; "for my Hebrew learning does not come quite at a call.—How say you, my Lord of Lincoln? Hath the lad given a just interpretation of the text?"

"The word *safety*, most gracious madam," said the Bishop of Lincoln, "for so hath been translated, it may be somewhat hastily, the Hebrew word, being——"

"My lord," said the Queen, interrupting him, "we said we had forgotten our Hebrew.—But for thee, young man, what is thy name and birth?"

"Raleigh is my name, most gracious Queen, the youngest son of a large but honourable family of Devonshire."

"Raleigh?" said Elizabeth, after a moment's recollection; "have we not heard of your service in Ireland?"

"I have been so fortunate as to do some service there, madam," replied Raleigh, "scarce, however, of consequence sufficient to reach your Grace's ears."

"They hear farther than you think of," said the Queen, graciously, "and have heard of a youth who defended a ford in Shannon against a whole band of wild Irish rebels, until the stream ran purple with their blood and his own."

"Some blood I may have lost," said the youth, looking down, "but it was where my best is due; and that is in your Majesty's service."

The Queen paused, and then said hastily, "You are very young, to have fought so well, and to speak so well. But you must not escape your penance for turning back Masters—the poor man hath caught cold on the river; for our order reached him when he was just returned from certain visits in London, and he held it matter of loyalty and conscience instantly to set forth again. So hark ye, Master Raleigh, see thou fail not to wear thy muddy cloak, in token of penitence, till our pleasure be farther known. And here," she added, giving him a jewel of gold, in the form of a chess-man, "I give thee this to wear at the collar."

Raleigh, to whom nature had taught intuitively, as it were, those courtly arts which many scarce acquire from long experience, knelt, and, as he took from her hand the jewel, kissed the fingers which gave it. He knew, perhaps, better than almost any of the courtiers who surrounded her, how to mingle the devotion claimed by the Queen, with the gallantry due to her personal beauty—and in this, his first attempt to unite them, he succeeded so well, as at once to gratify Elizabeth's personal vanity, and her love of power.[1]

His master, the Earl of Sussex, had the full advantage of the satisfaction which Raleigh had afforded Elizabeth on their first interview.

"My lords and ladies," said the Queen, looking around to the retinue by whom she was attended, "methinks, since we are upon the river, it were well to renounce our present purpose of going to the city, and surprise this poor Earl of Sussex with a visit. He is ill, and suffering doubtless under the fear of our displeasure, from which he hath been honestly cleared by the frank avowal of this malapert boy. What think ye? were it not an act of charity to give him such consolation as the

[1] See Note V.—Court favour of Sir Walter Raleigh.

thanks of a Queen, much bound to him for his loyal service, may perchance best minister?"

It may be readily supposed, that none to whom this speech was addressed, ventured to oppose its purport.

"Your Grace," said the Bishop of Lincoln, "is the breath of our nostrils." The men of war averred, that the face of the Sovereign was a whetstone to the soldier's sword; while the men of state were not less of opinion, that the light of the Queen's countenance was a lamp to the paths of her councillors; and the ladies agreed, with one voice, that no noble in England so well deserved the regard of England's Royal Mistress as the Earl of Sussex—the Earl of Leicester's right being reserved entire; so some of the more politic worded their assent—an exception to which Elizabeth paid no apparent attention. The barge had, therefore, orders to deposit its royal freight at Deptford, at the nearest and most convenient point of communication with Say's Court, in order that the Queen might satisfy her royal and maternal solicitude, by making personal enquiries after the health of the Earl of Sussex.

Raleigh, whose acute spirit foresaw and anticipated important consequences from the most trifling events, hastened to ask the Queen's permission to go in the skiff, and announce the royal visit to his master; ingeniously suggesting, that the joyful surprise might prove prejudicial to his health, since the richest and most generous cordials may sometimes be fatal to those who have been long in a languishing state.

But whether the Queen deemed it too presumptuous in so young a courtier to interpose his opinion unasked, or whether she was moved by a recurrence of the feeling of jealousy, which had been instilled into her, by reports that the Earl kept armed men about his person, she desired Raleigh, sharply, to reserve his counsel till it was required of him, and repeated her former orders, to be landed at Deptford, adding, "we will ourselves see what sort of household my Lord of Sussex keeps about him."

"Now the Lord have pity on us!" said the young courtier to himself. "Good hearts, the Earl hath many a one round him; but good heads are scarce with us—and he himself is too ill to give direction. And Blount will be at his morning meal of Yarmouth herrings and ale; and Tracy will have his beastly black puddings and Rhenish;—those thoroughpaced Welshmen, Thomas ap Rice and Evan Evans, will be at work on their leek porridge and toasted cheese—and she detests, they say, all coarse meats, evil smells, and strong wines. Could they but think of burning some rosemary in the great hall! but *vogue la galère,* all must now be trusted to chance. Luck hath done indifferent well for me this morning, for I trust I have spoiled a cloak, and made a court fortune—May she do as much for my gallant patron!"

The royal barge soon stopped at Deptford, and, amid the loud shouts of the populace, which her presence never failed to excite, the Queen, with a canopy borne over her head, walked, accompanied by her retinue, towards Say's Court, where the distant acclamations of the people gave the first notice of her arrival. Sussex, who was in the act of advising with Tressilian how he should make up the supposed breach in the Queen's favour, was infinitely surprised at learning her immediate approach—not that the Queen's custom of visiting her more distinguished nobility, whether in health or sickness, could be unknown to him; but the suddenness of the communication left no time for those preparations with which he well knew Elizabeth loved to be greeted, and the rudeness and confusion of his military household, much increased by his late illness, rendered him altogether unprepared for her reception.

Cursing internally the chance which thus brought her gracious visitation on him unaware, he hastened down with Tressilian, to whose eventful and interesting story he had just given an attentive ear.

"My worthy friend," he said, "such support as I can give your accusation of Varney, you have a right to expect, alike from justice and gratitude. Chance will presently show whether I can do aught with our Sovereign, or whether, in very deed, my meddling in your affair may not rather prejudice than serve you."

Thus spoke Sussex, while hastily casting around him a loose robe of sables, and adjusting his person in the best manner he could to meet the eye of his Sovereign. But no hurried attention bestowed on his apparel could remove the ghastly effects of long illness on a countenance which nature had marked with features rather strong than pleasing. Besides, he was low of stature, and, though broad-shouldered, athletic, and fit for martial achievements, his presence in a peaceful hall was not such as ladies love to look upon; a personal disadvantage, which was supposed to give Sussex, though esteemed and honoured by his Sovereign, considerable disadvantage when compared with Leicester, who was alike remarkable for elegance of manners, and for beauty of person.

The Earl's utmost dispatch only enabled him to meet the Queen as she entered the great hall, and he at once perceived there was a cloud on her brow. Her jealous eye had noticed the martial array of armed gentlemen and retainers with which the mansion-house was filled, and her first words expressed her disapprobation—"Is this a royal garrison, my Lord of Sussex, that it holds so many pikes and calivers? or have we by accident overshot Say's Court, and landed at our Tower of London?"

Lord Sussex hastened to offer some apology.

"It needs not," she said. "My lord, we intend speedily to take up a certain quarrel between your lordship and another great lord of our household, and at the same time to reprehend this uncivilized and dangerous practice of surrounding yourselves with armed, and even with ruffianly followers, as if, in the neighbourhood of our capital, nay in the very verge of our royal residence, you were preparing to wage civil war with each other. We are glad to see you so well recovered, my lord, though without the assistance of the learned physician whom we sent to you—Urge no excuse—we know how that matter fell out, and we have corrected for it the wild slip, young Raleigh.—By the way, my lord, we will speedily relieve your household of him, and take him into our own. Something there is about him which merits to be better nurtured than he is like to be amongst your very military followers."

To this proposal Sussex, though scarce understanding how the Queen came to make it, could only bow and express his acquiescence. He then entreated her to remain till refreshment could be offered, but in this he could not prevail. And, after a few compliments of a much colder and more commonplace character than might have been expected from a step so decidedly favourable as a personal visit, the Queen took her leave of Say's Court, having brought confusion thither along with her, and leaving doubt and apprehension behind.

CHAPTER XVI

> Then call them to our presence. Face to face,
> And frowning brow to brow, ourselves will hear
> The accuser and accused freely speak;—
> High-stomach'd are they both and full of ire,
> In rage deaf as the sea, hasty as fire.
>
> *Richard II.*

"I AM ordered to attend court to-morrow," said Leicester, speaking to Varney, "to meet, as they surmise, my Lord of Sussex. The Queen intends to take up matters betwixt us. This comes of her visit to Say's Court, of which you must needs speak so lightly."

"I maintain it was nothing," said Varney; "nay, I know from a sure intelligencer, who was within ear-shot of much that was said, that Sussex has lost rather than gained by that visit. The Queen said, when she stepped into the boat, that Say's Court looked like a guard-house, and smelt like an hospital. 'Like a cook's shop in Ram's Alley, rather,' said the Countess of Rutland, who is ever your lordship's good friend. And then my Lord of Lincoln must needs put in his holy oar, and say, that my Lord of Sussex must be excused for his rude and old-world house-keeping, since he had as yet no wife."

"And what said the Queen?" asked Leicester, hastily.

"She took him up roundly," said Varney, "and asked what my Lord Sussex had to do with a wife, or my Lord Bishop to speak on such a subject. 'If marriage is permitted,' she said, 'I nowhere read that it is enjoined.' "

"She likes not marriages, or speech of marriage, among churchmen," said Leicester.

"Nor among courtiers neither," said Varney; but, observing that Leicester changed countenance, he instantly added, "that all the ladies who were present had joined in ridiculing Lord Sussex's housekeeping, and in contrasting it with the reception her Grace would have assuredly received at my Lord of Leicester's."

"You have gathered much tidings," said Leicester, "but you have forgotten or omitted the most important of all. She hath added another to those dangling satellites, whom it is her pleasure to keep revolving around her."

"Your lordship meaneth that Raleigh, the Devonshire youth," said Varney, "the Knight of the Cloak, as they call him at court?"

"He may be Knight of the Garter one day, for aught I know," said Leicester, "for he advances rapidly—She hath cap'd verses with him, and such fooleries. I would gladly abandon, of my own free will, the part I have in her fickle favour; but I will not be elbowed out of it by the clown Sussex, or this new upstart. I hear Tressilian is with Sussex also, and high in his favour—I would spare him for considerations, but he will thrust himself on his fate—Sussex, too, is almost as well as ever in his health."

"My lord," replied Varney, "there will be rubs in the smoothest road, specially when it leads up hill. Sussex's illness was to us a god-send, from which I hoped much. He has recovered, indeed, but he is not now more formidable than ere he fell ill, when he received more than one foil in wrestling with your lordship. Let not your heart fail you, my lord, and all shall be well."

"My heart never failed me, sir," replied Leicester.

"No, my lord," said Varney; "but it has betrayed you right often. He that would climb a tree, my lord, must grasp by the branches, not by the blossom."

"Well, well, well!" said Leicester, impatiently; "I understand thy meaning—My heart shall neither fail me nor seduce me. Have my retinue in order—see that their array be so splendid as to put down not only the rude companions of Ratcliffe, but the retainers of every other nobleman and courtier. Let them be well armed withal, but without any outward display of their weapons, wearing them as if more for fashion's sake than for use. Do thou thyself keep close to me, I may have business for you."——

The preparations of Sussex and his party were not less anxious than those of Leicester.

"Thy Supplication, impeaching Varney of seduction," said the Earl to Tressilian, "is by this time in the Queen's hand—I have sent it through a sure channel. Methinks your suit should succeed, being, as it is, founded in justice and honour, and Elizabeth being the very muster of both. But, I wot not how—the gipsy" (so Sussex was wont to call his rival on account of his dark complexion) "hath much to say with her in these holiday times of peace—Were war at the gates, I should be one of her white boys; but soldiers, like their bucklers and Bilboa blades, get out of fashion in peace time, and satin sleeves and walking rapiers bear the bell. Well, we must be gay, since such is the fashion.—Blount, hast thou seen our household put into their new braveries?—But thou know'st as little of these toys as I do—thou wouldst be ready enow at disposing a stand of pikes."

"My good lord," answered Blount, "Raleigh hath been here, and taken that charge upon him—Your train will glitter like a May morning.— Marry, the cost is another question. One might keep an hospital of old soldiers at the charge of ten modern lackeys."

"We must not count cost to-day, Nicholas," said the Earl in reply; "I am beholden to Raleigh for his care—I trust, though, he has remembered that I am an old soldier, and would have no more of these follies than needs must."

"Nay, I understand nought about it," said Blount; "but here are your honourable lordship's brave kinsmen and friends coming in by scores to wait upon you to court, where, methinks, we shall bear as brave a front as Leicester, let him ruffle it as he will."

"Give them the strictest charges," said Sussex, "that they suffer no provocation short of actual violence to provoke them into quarrel—they have hot bloods, and I would not give Leicester the advantage over me by any imprudence of theirs."

The Earl of Sussex ran so hastily through these directions, that it was with difficulty Tressilian at length found opportunity to express his surprise that he should have proceeded so far in the affair of Sir Hugh Robsart as to lay his petition at once before the Queen—"It was the opinion of the young lady's friends," he said, "that Leicester's sense of justice should be first appealed to, as the offence had been committed by his officer, and so he had expressly told to Sussex."

"This could have been done without applying to me," said Sussex, somewhat haughtily. "*I*, at least, ought not to have been a counsellor when the object was a humiliating reference to Leicester; and I am surprised that you, Tressilian, a man of honour, and my friend, would assume such a mean course. If you said so, I certainly understood you not in a matter which sounded so unlike yourself."

"My lord," said Tressilian, "the course I would prefer, for my own sake, is that you have adopted; but the friends of this most unhappy lady——"

"O, the friends—the friends," said Sussex, interrupting him; "they must let us manage this cause in the way which seems best. This is the time and the hour to accumulate every charge against Leicester and his household, and yours the Queen will hold a heavy one. But at all events she hath the complaint before her."

Tressilian could not help suspecting that, in his eagerness to strengthen himself against his rival, Sussex had purposely adopted the course most likely to throw odium on Leicester, without considering minutely whether it were the mode of proceeding most likely to be attended with success. But the step was irrevocable, and Sussex escaped from farther discussing it by dismissing his company, with the command, "Let all be in order at eleven o'clock; I must be at court and in the presence by high noon precisely."

While the rival statesmen were thus anxiously preparing for their approaching meeting in the Queen's presence, even Elizabeth herself was not without apprehension of what might chance from the collision of two such fiery spirits, each backed by a strong and numerous body of followers, and dividing betwixt them, either openly or in secret, the hopes and wishes of most of her court. The band of Gentlemen Pensioners were all under arms, and a reinforcement of the yeomen of the guard was brought down the Thames from London. A royal proclamation was set forth, strictly prohibiting nobles of whatever degree, to approach the Palace with retainers or followers, armed with shot, or with long weapons; and it was even whispered, that the High Sheriff of Kent had secret instructions to have a part of the array of the county ready on the shortest notice.

The eventful hour, thus anxiously prepared for on all sides, at length approached, and, each followed by his long and glittering train of friends and followers, the rival Earls entered the Palace-yard of Greenwich at noon precisely.

As if by previous arrangement, or perhaps by intimation that such was the Queen's pleasure, Sussex and his retinue came to the Palace from Deptford by water, while Leicester arrived by land; and thus they entered the court-yard from opposite sides. This trifling circumstance gave Leicester a certain ascendency in the opinion of the vulgar, the appearance of his cavalcade of mounted followers showing more numerous and more imposing than those of Sussex's party, who were necessarily upon foot. No show or sign of greeting passed between the Earls, though each looked full at the other, both expecting perhaps an exchange of courtesies, which neither was willing to commence. Almost in the minute of their arrival the castle-bell tolled, the gates of the Palace were opened, and the Earls entered, each numerously attended by such gentlemen of their train, whose rank gave them that privilege. The yeomen and inferior attendants remained in the court-yard, where the opposite parties eyed each other with looks of eager hatred and scorn, as if waiting with impatience for some cause of tumult, or some apology for mutual aggression. But they were restrained by the strict commands of their leaders, and overawed, perhaps, by the presence of an armed guard of unusual strength.

In the meanwhile, the more distinguished persons of each train followed their patrons into the lofty halls and ante-chambers of the royal Palace, flowing on in the same current, like two streams which are com·pelled into the same channel, yet shun to mix their waters. The parties arranged themselves, as it were instinctively, on the different sides of the lofty apartments, and seemed eager to escape from the transient union which the narrowness of the crowded entrance had for an instant compelled them to submit to. The folding doors at the upper end of the long gallery were immediately afterwards opened, and it was announced in a whisper that the Queen was in her presence-chamber, to which these gave access. Both Earls moved slowly and stately towards the entrance; Sussex followed by Tressilian, Blount, and Raleigh, and Leicester by

Varney. The pride of Leicester was obliged to give way to court-forms, and with a grave and formal inclination of the head, he paused until his rival, a peer of older creation than his own, passed before him. Sussex returned the reverence with the same formal civility, and entered the presence-room. Tressilian and Blount offered to follow him, but were not permitted, the Usher of the Black Rod alleging in excuse, that he had precise orders to look to all admissions that day. To Raleigh, who stood back on the repulse of his companions, he said, "You, sir, may enter," and he entered accordingly.

"Follow me close, Varney," said the Earl of Leicester, who had stood aloof for a moment to mark the reception of Sussex; and, advancing to the entrance, he was about to pass on, when Varney, who was close behind him, dressed out in the utmost bravery of the day, was stopped by the usher, as Tressilian and Blount had been before him. "How is this, Master Bowyer?" said the Earl of Leicester. "Know you who I am, and that this is my friend and follower?"

"Your lordship will pardon me," replied Bowyer, stoutly; "my orders are precise, and limit me to a strict discharge of my duty."

"Thou art a partial knave," said Leicester, the blood mounting to his face, "to do me this dishonour, when you but now admitted a follower of my Lord of Sussex."

"My lord," said Bowyer, "Master Raleigh is newly admitted a sworn servant of her Grace, and to him my orders did not apply."

"Thou art a knave—an ungrateful knave," said Leicester; "but he that hath done, can undo—thou shalt not prank thee in thy authority long!"

This threat he uttered aloud, with less than his usual policy and discretion, and having done so, he entered the presence-chamber, and made his reverence to the Queen, who, attired with even more than her usual splendour, and surrounded by those nobles and statesmen whose courage and wisdom have rendered her reign immortal, stood ready to receive the homage of her subjects. She graciously returned the obeisance of the favourite Earl, and looked alternately at him and at Sussex, as if about to speak, when Bowyer, a man whose spirit could not brook the insult he had so openly received from Leicester, in the discharge of his office, advanced with his black rod in his hand, and knelt down before her.

"Why, how now, Bowyer?" said Elizabeth, "thy courtesy seems strangely timed!"

"My Liege Sovereign," he said, while every courtier around trembled at his audacity, "I come but to ask, whether, in the discharge of mine office, I am to obey your Highness's commands, or those of the Earl of Leicester, who has publicly menaced me with his displeasure, and treated me with disparaging terms, because I denied entry to one of his followers, in obedience to your Grace's precise orders?"

The spirit of Henry VIII. was instantly aroused in the bosom of his daughter, and she turned on Leicester with a severity which appalled him, as well as all his followers.

"God's death! my lord," such was her emphatic phrase, "what means this? We have thought well of you, and brought you near to our person; but it was not that you might hide the sun from our other faithful subjects. Who gave you license to contradict our orders, or control our officers? I will have in this court, ay, and in this realm, but one mistress, and no master. Look to it that Master Bowyer sustains no harm for his duty to me faithfully discharged; for, as I am Christian woman and crowned Queen, I will hold you dearly answerable.—Go, Bowyer, you have done the part of an honest man and a true subject. We will brook no mayor of the palace here."

Bowyer kissed the hand which she extended towards him, and withdrew to his post, astonished at the success of his own audacity. A smile of triumph pervaded the faction of Sussex; that of Leicester seemed proportionally dismayed, and the favourite himself, assuming an aspect of the deepest humility, did not even attempt a word in his own exculpation.

He acted wisely; for it was the policy of Elizabeth to humble, not to disgrace him, and it was prudent to suffer her, without opposition or reply, to glory in the exertion of her authority. The dignity of the Queen was gratified, and the woman began soon to feel for the mortification which she had imposed on her favourite. Her green eye also observed the secret looks of congratulation exchanged amongst those who favoured Sussex, and it was no part of her policy to give either party a decisive triumph.

"What I say to my Lord of Leicester," she said, after a moment's pause, "I say also to you, my Lord of Sussex. You also must needs ruffle in the court of England, at the head of a faction of your own?"

"My followers, gracious Princess," said Sussex, "have indeed ruffled in your cause, in Ireland, in Scotland, and against yonder rebellious Earls in the north. I am ignorant that——"

"Do you bandy looks and words with me, my lord?" said the Queen, interrupting him; "methinks you might learn of my Lord of Leicester the modesty to be silent, at least, under our censure. I say, my lord, that my grandfather and my father, in their wisdom, disbarred the nobles of this civilized land from travelling with such disorderly retinues; and think you, that because I wear a coif, their sceptre has in my hand been changed into a distaff? I tell you, no king in Christendom will less brook his court to be cumbered, his people oppressed, and his kingdom's peace disturbed, by the arrogance of overgrown power, than she who now speaks with you.—My Lord of Leicester, and you, my Lord of Sussex, I command you both to be friends with each other; or by the crown I wear, you shall find an enemy who will be too strong for both of you!"

"Madam," said the Earl of Leicester, "you who are yourself the fountain of honour, know best what is due to mine. I place it at your disposal, and only say, that the terms on which I have stood with my Lord of

Sussex have not been of my seeking; nor had he cause to think me his enemy, until he had done me gross wrong."

"For me, madam," said the Earl of Sussex, "I cannot appeal from your sovereign pleasure; but I were well content my Lord of Leicester should say in what I have, as he terms it, wronged him, since my tongue never spoke the word that I would not willingly justify either on foot or horseback."

"And for me," said Leicester, "always under my gracious Sovereign's pleasure, my hand shall be as ready to make good my words, as that of any man who ever wrote himself Ratcliffe."

"My lords," said the Queen, "these are no terms for this presence; and if you cannot keep your temper, we will find means to keep both that and you close enough. Let me see you join hands, my lords, and forget your idle animosities."

The two rivals looked at each other with reluctant eyes, each unwilling to make the first advance to execute the Queen's will.

"Sussex," said Elizabeth, "I entreat—Leicester, I command you."

Yet, so were her words accented, that the entreaty sounded like command, and the command like entreaty. They remained still and stubborn, until she raised her voice to a height which argued at once impatience and absolute command.

"Sir Henry Lee," she said, to an officer in attendance, "have a guard in present readiness, and man a barge instantly.—My Lords of Sussex and Leicester, I bid you once more to join hands—and, God's death! he that refuses shall taste of our Tower fare ere he sees our face again. I will lower your proud hearts ere we part, and that I promise, on the word of a Queen!"

"The prison," said Leicester, "might be borne, but to lose your grace's presence were to lose light and life at once.—Here, Sussex, is my hand."

"And here," said Sussex, "is mine in truth and honesty; but——"

"Nay, under favour, you shall add no more," said the Queen. "Why, this is as it should be," she added, looking on them more favourably, "and when you, the shepherds of the people, unite to protect them, it shall be well with the flock we rule over. For, my lords, I tell you plainly, your follies and your brawls lead to strange disorders among your servants.—My Lord of Leicester, you have a gentleman in your household, called Varney?"

"Yes, gracious madam," replied Leicester, "I presented him to kiss your royal hand when you were last at Nonsuch."

"His outside was well enough," said the Queen, "but scarce so fair, I should have thought, as to have caused a maiden of honourable birth and hopes to barter her fame for his good looks, and become his paramour. Yet so it is—this fellow of yours hath seduced the daughter of a good old Devonshire knight, Sir Hugh Robsart of Lidcote Hall, and she hath fled with him from her father's house like a castaway.—My Lord of Leicester, are you ill, that you look so deadly pale?"

"No, gracious madam," said Leicester; and it required every effort he could make to bring forth these few words.

"You are surely ill, my lord?" said Elizabeth, going towards him with hasty speech and hurried step, which indicated the deepest concern. "Call Masters—call our surgeon in ordinary—Where be these loitering fools? —We lose the pride of our court through their negligence.—Or is it possible, Leicester," she continued, looking on him with a very gentle aspect, "can fear of my displeasure have wrought so deeply on thee? Doubt not for a moment, noble Dudley, that we could blame *thee* for the folly of thy retainer—thee, whose thoughts we know to be far otherwise employed! He that would climb the eagle's nest, my lord, cares not who are catching linnets at the foot of the precipice."

"Mark you that?" said Sussex, aside to Raleigh. "The devil aids him surely! for all that would sink another ten fathom deep, seems but to make him float the more easily. Had a follower of mine acted thus——"

"Peace, my good lord," said Raleigh, "for God's sake, peace! Wait the change of the tide; it is even now on the turn."

The acute observation of Raleigh, perhaps, did not deceive him; for Leicester's confusion was so great, and, indeed, for the moment, so irresistibly overwhelming, that Elizabeth, after looking at him with a wondering eye, and receiving no intelligible answer to the unusual expressions of grace and affection which had escaped from her, shot her quick glance around the circle of courtiers, and reading, perhaps, in their faces, something that accorded with her own awakened suspicions, she said suddenly, "Or is there more in this than we see—or than you, my lord, wish that we should see? Where is this Varney? Who saw him?"

"An it please your Grace," said Bowyer, "it is the same against whom I this instance closed the door of the presence-room."

"An it please me?" repeated Elizabeth, sharply, not at that moment in the humour of being pleased with anything,—"It does *not* please me that he should pass saucily into my presence, or that you should exclude from it one who came to justify himself from an accusation."

"May it please you," answered the perplexed usher, "if I knew, in such case, how to bear myself, I would take heed——"

"You should have reported the fellow's desire to us, Master Usher, and taken our directions. You think yourself a great man, because but now we chid a nobleman on your account—yet, after all, we hold you but as the lead-weight that keeps the door fast. Call this Varney hither instantly —there is one Tressilian also mentioned in this petition—let them both come before us."

She was obeyed, and Tressilian and Varney appeared accordingly. Varney's first glance was at Leicester, his second at the Queen. In the looks of the latter, there appeared an approaching storm, and in the downcast countenance of his patron, he could read no directions in which way he was to trim his vessel for the encounter—he then saw Tressilian, and at once perceived the peril of the situation in which he was placed. But

Varney was as bold-faced and ready-witted as he was cunning and un-scrupulous,—a skilful pilot in extremity, and fully conscious of the advantages which he would obtain, could he extricate Leicester from his present peril, and of the ruin that yawned for himself, should he fail in doing so.

"Is it true, sirrah," said the Queen, with one of those searching looks which few had the audacity to resist, "that you have seduced to infamy a young lady of birth and breeding, the daughter of Sir Hugh Robsart of Lidcote Hall?"

Varney kneeled down, and replied, with a look of the most profound contrition, "There had been some love passages betwixt him and Mistress Amy Robsart."

Leicester's flesh quivered with indignation as he heard his dependent make this avowal, and for one moment he manned himself to step forward, and, bidding farewell to the court and the royal favour, confess the whole mystery of the secret marriage. But he looked at Sussex, and the idea of the triumphant smile which would clothe his cheek upon hearing the avowal, sealed his lips. "Not now, at least," he thought, "or in this presence, will I afford him so rich a triumph." And pressing his lips close together, he stood firm and collected, attentive to each word which Varney uttered, and determined to hide to the last the secret on which his court favour seemed to depend. Meanwhile, the Queen proceeded in her examination of Varney.

"Love passages!" said she, echoing his last words; "what passages, thou knave? and why not ask the wench's hand from her father, if thou hadst any honesty in thy love for her?"

"An it please your Grace," said Varney, still on his knees, "I dared not do so, for her father had promised her hand to a gentleman of birth and honour—I will do him justice, though I know he bears me ill will—one Master Edmund Tressilian, whom I now see in thy presence."

"Soh!" replied the Queen; "and what was your right to make the simple fool break her worthy father's contract, through your love *passages,* as your conceit and assurance terms them?"

"Madam," replied Varney, "it is in vain to plead the cause of human frailty before a judge to whom it is unknown, or that of love, to one who never yields to the passion"—He paused an instant, and then added, in a very low and timid tone, "which she inflicts upon all others."

Elizabeth tried to frown, but smiled in her own despite, as she answered, "Thou art a marvellously impudent knave—Art thou married to the girl?"

Leicester's feelings became so complicated and so painfully intense that it seemed to him as if his life was to depend on the answer made by Varney, who, after a moment's real hesitation, answered, "Yes."

"Thou false villain!" said Leicester, bursting forth into rage, yet unable to add another word to the sentence, which he had begun with such emphatic passion.

"Nay, my lord," said the Queen, "we will, by your leave, stand between this fellow and your anger. We have not yet done with him.—Knew your master, my Lord of Leicester, of this fair work of yours? Speak truth, I command thee, and I will be thy warrant from danger on every quarter."

"Gracious madam," said Varney, "to speak Heaven's truth, my lord was the cause of the whole matter."

"Thou villain, wouldst thou betray me?" said Leicester.

"Speak on," said the Queen, hastily, her cheek colouring, and her eyes sparkling, as she addressed Varney; "speak on—here no commands are heard but mine."

"They are omnipotent, gracious madam," replied Varney; "and to you there can be no secrets.—Yet I would not," he added, looking around him, "speak of my master's concerns to other ears."

"Fall back, my lords," said the Queen to those who surrounded her, "and do you speak on.—What hath the Earl to do with this guilty intrigue of thine?—See, fellow, that thou beliest him not!"

"Far be it from me to traduce my noble patron," replied Varney; "yet I am compelled to own that some deep, overwhelming, yet secret feeling, hath of late dwelt in my lord's mind, hath abstracted him from the cares of the household, which he was wont to govern with such religious strictness, and hath left us opportunities to do follies, of which the shame, as in this case, partly falls upon our patron. Without this, I had not had means or leisure to commit the folly which has drawn on me his displeasure; the heaviest to endure by me, which I could by any means incur,—saving always the yet more dreaded resentment of your Grace."

"And in this sense, and no other, hath he been accessory to thy fault?" said Elizabeth.

"Surely, madam, in no other," replied Varney; "but since somewhat hath chanced to him, he can scarce be called his own man. Look at him, madam, how pale and trembling he stands—how unlike his usual majesty of manner—yet what has he to fear from aught I can say to your Highness? Ah! madam, since he received that fatal packet!"

"What packet, and from whence?" said the Queen, eagerly.

"From whence, madam, I cannot guess; but I am so near to his person, that I know he has ever since worn, suspended around his neck, and next to his heart, that lock of hair which sustains a small golden jewel shaped like a heart—he speaks to it when alone—he parts not from it when he sleeps—no heathen ever worshipped an idol with such devotion."

"Thou art a prying knave to watch thy master so closely," said Elizabeth, blushing, but not with anger; "and a tattling knave to tell over again his fooleries.—What colour might the braid of hair be that thou pratest of?"

Varney replied, "A poet, madam, might call it a thread from the golden web wrought by Minerva; but, to my thinking, it was paler than even the purest gold—more like the last parting sunbeam of the softest day of spring."

"Why, you are a poet yourself, Master Varney," said the Queen, smiling; "but I have not genius quick enough to follow your rare metaphors— Look round these ladies—is there"—(she hesitated, and endeavoured to assume an air of great indifference)—"Is there here, in this presence, any lady, the colour of whose hair reminds thee of that braid? Methinks, without prying into my Lord of Leicester's amorous secrets, I would fain know what kind of locks are like the thread of Minerva's web, or the—what was it?—the last rays of the May-day sun."

Varney looked round the presence-chamber, his eye travelling from one lady to another, until at length it rested upon the Queen herself, but with an aspect of the deepest veneration. "I see no tresses," he said, "in this presence, worthy of such similes, unless where I dare not look on them."

"How, sir knave," said the Queen, "dare you intimate——"

"Nay, madam," replied Varney, shading his eyes with his hand, "it was the beams of the May-day sun that dazzled my weak eyes."

"Go to—go to," said the Queen; "thou art a foolish fellow"—and turning quickly from him she walked up to Leicester.

Intense curiosity, mingled with all the various hopes, fears, and passions, which influence court-faction, had occupied the presence-chamber during the Queen's conference with Varney, as if with the strength of an Eastern talisman. Men suspended every, even the slightest external motion, and would have ceased to breathe, had Nature permitted such an intermission of her functions. The atmosphere was contagious, and Leicester, who saw all around wishing or fearing his advancement or his fall, forgot all that love had previously dictated, and saw nothing for the instant but the favour or disgrace, which depended on the nod of Elizabeth and the fidelity of Varney. He summoned himself hastily, and prepared to play his part in the scene which was like to ensue, when, as he judged from the glances which the Queen threw towards him, Varney's communications, be they what they might, were operating in his favour. Elizabeth did not long leave him in doubt; for the more than favour with which she accosted him decided his triumph in the eyes of his rival, and of the assembled court of England—"Thou hast a prating servant of this same Varney, my lord," she said; "it is lucky you trust him with nothing that can hurt you in our opinion, for believe me, he would keep no counsel."

"From your Highness," said Leicester, dropping gracefully on one knee, "it were treason he should. I would that my heart itself lay before you, barer than the tongue of any servant could strip it."

"What, my lord," said Elizabeth, looking kindly upon him, "is there no one little corner over which you would wish to spread a veil? Ah! I see you are confused at the question, and your Queen knows she should not look too deeply into her servants' motives for their faithful duty, lest she see what might, or at least ought to, displease her."

Relieved by these last words, Leicester broke out into a torrent of expressions of deep and passionate attachment, which perhaps, at that moment, were not altogether fictitious. The mingled emotions which had at first overcome him, had now given way to the energetic vigour with which he had determined to support his place in the Queen's favour; and never did he seem to Elizabeth more eloquent, more handsome, more interesting, than while, kneeling at her feet, he conjured her to strip him of all his dower, but to leave him the name of her servant.—"Take from tne poor Dudley," he exclaimed, "all that your bounty has made him, and bid him be the poor gentleman he was when your Grace first shone · on him; leave him no more than his cloak and his sword, but let him still boast he has—what in word or deed he never forfeited—the regard of his adored Queen and mistress!"

"No, Dudley!" said Elizabeth, raising him with one hand, while she extended the other that he might kiss it; "Elizabeth has not forgotten that, whilst you were a poor gentleman, despoiled of your hereditary rank, she was as poor a princess, and that in her cause you then ventured all that oppression had left you—your life and honour.—Rise, my lord, and let my hand go!—Rise, and be what you have ever been, the grace of our court, and the support of our throne. Your mistress may be forced to chide your misdemeanours, but never without owning your merits.— And so help me God," she added, turning to the audience, who, with various feelings, witnessed this interesting scene,—"So help me God, gentlemen, as I think never sovereign had a truer servant than I have in this noble Earl!"

A murmur of assent rose from the Leicestrian faction, which the friends of Sussex dared not oppose. They remained with their eyes fixed on the ground, dismayed as well as mortified by the public and absolute triumph of their opponents. Leicester's first use of the familiarity to which the Queen had so publicly restored him, was to ask her commands concerning Varney's offence. "Although," he said, "the fellow deserves nothing from me but displeasure, yet, might I presume to intercede——"

"In truth, we had forgotten his matter," said the Queen; "and it was ill done of us, who owe justice to our meanest, as well as to our highest subject. We are pleased, my lord, that you were the first to recall the matter to our memory.—Where is Tressilian, the accuser?—let him come before us."

Tressilian appeared, and made a low and beseeming reverence. His person, as we have elsewhere observed, had an air of grace and even of nobleness, which did not escape Queen Elizabeth's critical observation. She looked at him with attention as he stood before her unabashed, but with an air of the deepest dejection.

"I cannot but grieve for this gentleman," she said to Leicester. "I have enquired concerning him, and his presence confirms what I heard, that he is a scholar and a soldier, well accomplished both in arts and arms. We women, my lord, are fanciful in our choice—I had said now, to judge by the eye, there was no comparison to be held betwixt your follower and this gentleman. But Varney is a well-spoken fellow, and, to speak truth, that goes far with us of the weaker sex.—Look you, Master Tressilian, a bolt lost is not a bow broken. Your true affection, as I will hold it to be, hath been, it seems, but ill requited; but you have scholarship, and you know there have been false Cressidas to be found, from the Trojan war downwards. Forget, good sir, this Lady Light o' Love—teach your affection to see with a wiser eye. This we say to you, more from the writings of learned men, than our own knowledge, being, as we are, far removed by station and will, from the enlargement of experience in such idle toys of humorous passion. For this dame's father, we can make his grief the less, by advancing his son-in-law to such station as may enable him to give an honourable support to his bride. Thou shalt not be forgotten thyself, Tressilian—follow our court, and thou shalt see that a true Troilus hath some claim on our grace. Think of what that archknave Shakspeare says—a plague on him, his toys come into my head when I should think of other matters—Stay, how goes it?

> 'Cressid was yours, tied with the bonds of heaven;
> These bonds of heaven are slipt, dissolved and loosed,
> And with another knot five fingers tied,
> The fragments of her faith are bound to Diomed.'

You smile, my lord of Southampton—perchance I make your player's verse halt through my bad memory—but let it suffice—let there be no more of this mad matter."

And as Tressilian kept the posture of one who would willingly be heard, though, at the same time, expressive of the deepest reverence, the Queen added with some impatience,—"What would the man have? The wench cannot wed both of you?—She has made her election—not a wise one perchance—but she is Varney's wedded wife."

"My suit should sleep there, most gracious Sovereign," said Tressilian, "and with my suit my revenge. But I hold this Varney's word no good warrant for the truth."

"Had that doubt been elsewhere urged," answered Varney, "my sword——"

"_Thy_ sword!" interrupted Tressilian, scornfully; "with her Grace's leave, my sword shall show——"

"Peace, you knaves, both!" said the Queen; "know you where you are?—This comes of your feuds, my lords," she added, looking towards Leicester and Sussex; "your followers catch your own humour, and must bandy and brawl in my court, and in my very presence, like so many Matamoros.—Look you, sirs, he that speaks of drawing swords in any other quarrel than mine or England's, by mine honour, I'll bracelet him with iron both on wrist and ankle!" She then paused a minute, and resumed in a milder tone, "I must do justice betwixt the bold and mutinous knaves notwithstanding.—My Lord of Leicester, will you warrant with your honour,—that is, to the best of your belief,—that your servant speaks truth in saying he hath married this Amy Robsart?"

This was a home-thrust, and had nearly staggered Leicester. But he had now gone too far to recede, and answered, after a moment's hesitation, "To the best of my belief—indeed on my certain knowledge—she is a wedded wife."

"Gracious madam," said Tressilian, "may I yet request to know, when and under what circumstances this alleged marriage——"

"Out, sirrah," answered the Queen; "*alleged* marriage!—Have you not the word of this illustrious Earl to warrant the truth of what his servant says? But thou art a loser—think'st thyself such at least—and thou shalt have indulgence—we will look into the matter ourself more at leisure.—My Lord of Leicester, I trust you remember we mean to taste the good cheer of your castle of Kenilworth on this week ensuing—we will pray you to bid our good and valued friend the Earl of Sussex to hold company with us there."

"If the noble Earl of Sussex," said Leicester, bowing to his rival with the easiest and with the most graceful courtesy, "will so far honour my poor house, I will hold it an additional proof of the amicable regard it is your Grace's desire we should entertain towards each other."

Sussex was more embarrassed—"I should," said he, "madam, be but a clog on your gayer hours, since my late severe illness."

"And have you been indeed so very ill?" said Elizabeth, looking on him with more attention than before; "you are in faith strangely altered, and deeply am I grieved to see it. But be of good cheer—we will our-selves look after the health of so valued a servant, and to whom we owe so much. Masters shall order your diet; and that we ourselves may see that he is obeyed, you must attend us in this progress to Kenilworth."

This was said so peremptorily, and at the same time with so much kindness, that Sussex, however unwilling to become the guest of his rival, had no resource but to bow low to the Queen in obedience to her commands, and to express to Leicester, with blunt courtesy, though mingled with embarrassment, his acceptance of his invitation. As the Earls exchanged compliments on the occasion, the Queen said to her High Treasurer, "Methinks, my lord, the countenances of these our two noble peers resemble that of the two famed classic streams, the one so dark and sad, the other so fair and noble—My old Master Ascham would have chid me for forgetting the author—It is Cæsar, as I think.—See what majestic calmness sits on the brow of the noble Leicester, while Sussex seems to greet him as if he did our will indeed, but not willingly."

"The doubt of your Majesty's favour," answered the Lord Treasurer, "may perchance occasion the difference, which does not—as what does? —escape your Grace's eye."

"Such doubt were injurious to us, my lord," replied the Queen. "We hold both to be near and dear to us, and will with impartiality employ both in honourable service for the weal of our kingdom. But we will break their farther conference at present.—My Lords of Sussex and Leicester, we have a word more with you. Tressilian and Varney are near your persons—you will see that they attend you at Kenilworth.—And as we shall then have both Paris and Menelaus within our call, so we will have the same fair Helen also, whose fickleness has caused this broil.— Varney, thy wife must be at Kenilworth, and forthcoming at my order. —My Lord of Leicester, we expect you will look to this."

The Earl and his follower bowed low, and raised their heads, without daring to look at the Queen, or at each other; for both felt at the instant as if the nets and toils which their own falsehood had woven, were in the act of closing around them. The Queen, however, observed not their confusion, but proceeded to say, "My Lords of Sussex and Leicester, we require your presence at the privy-council to be presently held, where matters of importance are to be debated. We will then take the water for our divertisement, and you, my lords, will attend us.—And that reminds us of a circumstance—Do you, Sir Squire of the Soiled Cassock," (distinguishing Raleigh by a smile,) "fail not to observe that you are to attend us on our progress. You shall be supplied with suitable means to reform your wardrobe."

And so terminated this celebrated audience, in which, as throughout her life, Elizabeth united the occasional caprice of her sex, with that sense and sound policy, in which neither man nor woman ever excelled her.

CHAPTER XVII

Well, then—our course is chosen—spread the sail—
Heave oft the lead, and mark the soundings well—
Look to the helm, good master—many a shoal
Marks this stern coast, and rocks, where sits the Siren,
Who, like ambition, lures men to their ruin.
                                        The Shipwreck.

DURING the brief interval that took place betwixt the dismissal of the audience and the sitting of the privy-council, Leicester had time to reflect that he had that morning sealed his own fate. "It was impossible for him now," he thought, "after having, in the face of all that was honourable in England, pledged his truth (though in an ambiguous phrase) for the statement of Varney, to contradict or disavow it, without exposing himself not merely to the loss of court-favour, but to the highest displeasure of the Queen, his deceived mistress, and to the scorn and contempt at once of his rival and of all his compeers." This certainty rushed at once on his mind, together with all the difficulties which he would necessarily be exposed to in preserving a secret, which seemed now equally essential to his safety, to his power, and to his honour. He was situated like one who walks upon ice, ready to give way around him, and whose only safety consists in moving onwards. by firm and unvacillating steps. The Queen's favour, to preserve which he had made such sacrifices, must now be secured by all means and at all hazards—it was the only plank which he could cling to in the tempest. He must settle himself, therefore, to the task of not only preserving, but augmenting the Queen's partiality—He must be the favourite of Elizabeth, or a man utterly shipwrecked in fortune and in honour. All other considerations must be laid aside for the moment, and he repelled the intrusive thoughts which forced on his mind the image of Amy, by saying to himself, there would be time to think hereafter how he was to escape from the labyrinth ultimately, since the pilot, who sees a Scylla under his bows, must not for the time think of the more distant dangers of Charybdis.

In this mood, the Earl of Leicester that day assumed his chair at the council table of Elizabeth; and when the hours of business were over, in this same mood did he occupy an honoured place near her, during her pleasure excursion on the Thames. And never did he display to more advantage his powers as a politician of the first rank, or his parts as an accomplished courtier.

It chanced that in that day's council matters were agitated touching the affairs of the unfortunate Mary, the seventh year of whose captivity in England was now in doleful currency. There had been opinions in favour of this unhappy princess laid before Elizabeth's council, and supported with much strength of argument by Sussex and others, who dwelt more upon the law of nations and the breach of hospitality, than, however softened or qualified, was agreeable to the Queen's ear. Leicester adopted the contrary opinion with great animation and eloquence, and described the necessity of continuing the severe restraint of the Queen of Scots, as a measure essential to the safety of the kingdom, and particularly of Elizabeth's sacred person, the lightest hair of whose head, he maintained, ought, in their lordships' estimation, to be matter of more deep and anxious concern, than the life and fortunes of a rival, who, after setting up a vain and unjust pretence to the throne of England, was now, even while in the bosom of her country, the constant hope and theme of encouragement to all enemies to Elizabeth, whether at home or abroad. He ended by craving pardon of their lordships, if in the zeal of speech he had given any offence, but the Queen's safety was a theme which hurried him beyond his usual moderation of debate.

Elizabeth chid him, but not severely, for the weight which he attached unduly to her personal interests; yet she owned, that since it had been the pleasure of Heaven to combine those interests with the weal of her subjects, she did only her duty when she adopted such measures of self-preservation as circumstances forced upon her; and if the council in their wisdom should be of opinion, that it was needful to continue some restraint on the person of her unhappy sister of Scotland, she trusted they would not blame her if she requested of the Countess of Shrewsbury to use her with as much kindness as might be consistent

with her safe keeping. And with this intimation of her pleasure, the
council was dismissed.

Never was more anxious and ready way made for "my Lord of
Leicester," than as he passed through the crowded ante-rooms to go
towards the river-side, in order to attend her Majesty to her barge—
never was the voice of the ushers louder, to "make room—make room
for the noble Earl"—never were these signals more promptly and reverently obeyed—never were more anxious eyes turned on him to obtain
a glance of favour, or even of mere recognition, while the heart of many
a humble follower throbbed betwixt the desire to offer his congratulations, and the fear of intruding himself on the notice of one so infinitely
above him. The whole court considered the issue of this day's audience,
expected with so much doubt and anxiety, as a decisive triumph on the
part of Leicester, and felt assured that the orb of his rival satellite, if
r ot altogether obscured by his lustre, must revolve hereafter in a dimmer and more distant sphere. So thought the court and courtiers, from
high to law; and they acted accordingly.

On the other hand, never did Leicester return the general greeting
with such ready and condescending courtesy, or endeavor more successfully to gather (in the words of one, who at that moment stood at no
great distance from him) "golden opinions from all sorts of men."

For all the favourite Earl had a bow, a smile at least, and often a
kind word. Most of these were addressed to courtiers, whose names have
long gone down the tide of oblivion; but some, to such as sound
strangely in our ears, when connected with the ordinary matters of
human life, above which the gratitude of posterity has long elevated
them. A few of Leicester's interlocutory sentences ran as follows:

"Poynings, good morrow, and how does your wife and fair daughter?
Why come they not to court?—Adams, your suit is naught—the Queen
will grant no more monopolies—but I may serve you in another matter.
My good Alderman Aylford, the suit of the City, affecting Queenhithe,
shall be forwarded as far as my poor interest can serve.—Master Edmund Spenser, touching your Irish petition, I would willingly aid you,
from my love to the Muses; but thou hast nettled the Lord Treasurer."

"My Lord," said the poet, "were I permitted to explain——"

"Come to my lodging, Edmund," answered the Earl—"not to-morrow, or next day, but soon.—Ha, Will Shakspeare—wild Will!—thou
hast given my nephew, Philip Sidney, love-powder—he cannot sleep
without thy Venus and Adonis under his pillow! He will have thee
hanged for the veriest wizard in Europe. Hark thee, mad wag, I have
not forgotten the matter of the patent, and of the bears."

The *player* bowed, and the Earl nodded and passed on—so that age
would have told the tale; in ours, perhaps, we might say the immortal
had done homage to the mortal. The next whom the favourite accosted,
was one of his own zealous dependents.

"How now, Sir Francis Denning," he whispered, in answer to his exulting salutation, "that smile hath made thy face shorter by one-third than when I first saw it this morning.—What, Master Bowyer, stand you back, and think you I bear malice? You did but your duty this morning; and if I remember aught of the passage betwixt us, it shall be in thy favour."

Then the Earl was approached, with several fantastic congees, by a person quaintly dressed in a doublet of black velvet, curiously slashed and pinked with crimson satin. A long cock's feather in the velvet bonnet, which he held in his hand, and an enormous ruff, stiffened to the extremity of the absurd taste of the times, joined with a sharp, lively, conceited expression of countenance, seemed to body forth a vain harebrained coxcomb, and small Wit; while the rod he held, and an assumption of formal authority, appeared to express some sense of official consequence, which qualified the natural pertness of his manner. A perpetual blush, which occupied rather the sharp nose than the thin cheek of this personage, seemed to speak more of "good life," as it was called, than of modesty; and the manner in which he approached to the Earl confirmed that suspicion.

"Good even to you, Master Robert Laneham," said Leicester, and seemed desirous to pass forward, without farther speech.

"I have a suit to your noble lordship," said the figure, boldly following him.

"And what is it, good master keeper of the council-chamber door?"

"*Clerk* of the council-chamber door," said Master Robert Laneham, with emphasis, by way of reply, and of correction.

"Well, qualify thine office as thou wilt, man," replied the Earl; "what wouldst thou have with me?"

"Simply," answered Laneham, "that your lordship would be, as heretofore, my good lord, and procure me license to attend the Summer Progress unto your lordship's most beautiful, and all-to-be unmatched Castle of Kenilworth."

"To what purpose, good Master Laneham?" replied the Earl; "bethink you, my guests must needs be many."

"Not so many," replied the petitioner, "but that your nobleness will willingly spare your old servitor his crib and his mess. Bethink you, my lord, how necessary is this rod of mine, to fright away all those listeners, who else would play at bo-peep with the honourable council, and be searching for keyholes and crannies in the door of the chamber, so as to render my staff as needful as a fly-flap in a butcher's shop."

"Methinks you have found out a fly-blown comparison for the honourable council, Master Laneham," said the Earl; "but seek not about to justify it. Come to Kenilworth, if you list; there will be store of fools there besides, and so you will be fitted."

"Nay, an there be fools, my lord," replied Laneham, with much glee, "I warrant I will make sport among them: for no greyhound loves to cote a hare, as I to turn and course a fool. But I have another singular favour to beseech of your honour."

"Speak it, and let me go," said the Earl; "I think the Queen comes forth instantly."

"My very good lord, I would fain bring a bed-fellow with me."

"How, you irreverent rascal!" said Leicester.

"Nay, my lord, my meaning is within the canons," answered his unblushing, or rather his everblushing petitioner. "I have a wife as curious as her grandmother, who eat the apple. Now, take her with me I may not, her Highness's orders being so strict against the officers bringing with them their wives in a progress, and so lumbering the court with womankind. But what I would crave of your lordship, is, to find room for her in some mummery, or pretty pageant, in disguise, as it were; so that, not being known for my wife, there may be no offence."

"The foul fiend seize ye both!" said Leicester, stung into uncontroll·able passion by the recollections which this speech excited—"Why stop you me with such follies?"

The terrified clerk of the chamber-door, astonished at the burst of resentment he had so unconsciously produced, dropped his staff of office from his hand, and gazed on the incensed Earl with a foolish face of wonder and terror, which instantly recalled Leicester to himself.

"I meant but to try if thou hadst the audacity which befits thine office," said he, hastily. "Come to Kenilworth, and bring the devil with thee, if thou wilt."

"My wife, sir, hath played the devil ere now, in a Mystery, in Queen Mary's time—but we shall want a trifle for properties."

"Here is a crown for thee," said the Earl,—"make me rid of thee—the great bell rings."

Master Robert Laneham [1] stared a moment at the agitation which he had excited, and then said to himself, as he stooped to pick up his staff of office, "The noble Earl runs wild humours to-day; but they who give crowns, expect us witty fellows to wink at their unsettled starts; and, by my faith, if they paid not for mercy, we would finger them tightly!"

Leicester moved hastily on, neglecting the courtesies he had hitherto dispensed so liberally, and hurrying through the courtly crowd, until he paused in a small withdrawing-room, into which he plunged to draw a moment's breath unobserved, and in seclusion.

"What am I now," he said to himself, "that am thus jaded by the words of a mean, weatherbeaten, goose-brained gull!—Conscience, thou art a bloodhound, whose growl wakes as readily at the paltry stir of a rat or mouse, as at the step of a lion.—Can I not quit myself, by one bold stroke, of a state so irksome, so unhonoured? What if I kneel to Elizabeth, and, owning the whole, throw myself on her mercy?"—

As he pursued this train of thought, the door of the apartment opened, and Varney rushed in.

[1] See Note VI.—Robert Laneham.

"Thank God, my lord, that I have found you!" was his exclamation.

"Thank the devil, whose agent thou art," was the Earl's reply.

"Thank whom you will, my lord," said Varney; "but hasten to the water-side. The Queen is on board, and asks for you."

"Go, say I am taken suddenly ill," replied Leicester; "for by Heaven, my brain can sustain this no longer!"

"I may well say so," said Varney, with bitterness of expression, "for your place, ay, and mine, who, as your master of the horse, was to have attended your lordship, is already filled up in the Queen's barge. The new minion, Walter Raleigh, and our old acquaintance, Tressilian, were called for to fill our places just as I hastened away to seek you."

"Thou art a devil, Varney," said Leicester, hastily; "but thou hast the mastery for the present—I follow thee."

Varney replied not, but led the way out of the palace, and towards the river, while his master followed him, as if mechanically; until, looking back, he said in a tone which savoured of familiarity at least, if not of authority, "How is this, my lord?—your cloak hangs on one side,—your hose are unbraced—permit me——"

"Thou art a fool, Varney, as well as a knave," said Leicester, shaking him off, and rejecting his officious assistance; "we are best thus, sir—when we require you to order our person, it is well, but now we want you not."

So saying, the Earl resumed at once his air of command, and with it his self-possession—shook his dress into yet wilder disorder—passed before Varney with the air of a superior and master, and in his turn led the way to the river-side.

The Queen's barge was on the very point of putting off; the seat allotted to Leicester in the stern, and that to his master of the horse on the bow of the boat, being already filled up. But on Leicester's approach, there was a pause, as if the bargemen anticipated some alteration in their company. The angry spot was, however, on the Queen's cheek, as, in that cold tone with which superiors endeavour to veil their internal agitation, while speaking to those before whom it would be derogation to express it, she pronounced the chilling words—"We have waited, my Lord of Leicester."

"Madam, and most gracious Princess," said Leicester, "you, who can pardon so many weaknesses which your own heart never knows, can best bestow your commiseration on the agitations of the bosom, which, for a moment, affect both head and limbs. I came to your presence, a doubting and an accused subject; your goodness penetrated the clouds of defamation, and restored me to my honour, and, what is yet dearer, to your favour—is it wonderful, though for me it is most unhappy, that my master of the horse should have found me in a state which scarce permitted me to make the exertion necessary to follow him to this place, when one glance of your Highness, although, alas! an angry one, has had power to do that for me, in which Esculapius might have failed?"

"How is this?" said Elizabeth hastily, looking at Varney; "hath your lord been ill?"

"Something of a fainting fit," answered the ready-witted Varney, "as your Grace may observe from his present condition. My lord's haste would not permit me leisure even to bring his dress into order."

"It matters not," said Elizabeth, as she gazed on the noble face and form of Leicester, to which even the strange mixture of passions by which he had been so lately agitated, gave additional interest, "make room for my noble lord—Your place, Master Varney, has been filled up; you must find a seat in another barge."

Varney bowed and withdrew.

"And you, too, our young Squire of the Cloak," added she, looking at Raleigh, "must, for the time, go to the barge of our ladies of honour. As for Tressilian, he hath already suffered too much by the caprice of women, that I should aggrieve him by my change of plan, so far as he is concerned."

Leicester seated himself in his place in the barge, and close to the Sovereign; Raleigh rose to retire, and Tressilian would have been so ill-timed in his courtesy as to offer to relinquish his own place to his friend, had not the acute glance of Raleigh himself, who seemed now in his native element, made him sensible, that so ready a disclamation of the royal favour might be misinterpreted. He sate silent, therefore, whilst Raleigh, with a profound bow, and a look of the deepest humiliation, was about to quit his place.

A noble courtier, the gallant Lord Willoughby, read, as he thought, something in the Queen's face which seemed to pity Raleigh's real or assumed semblance of mortification.

"It is not for us old courtiers," he said, "to hide the sunshine from the young ones. I will, with her Majesty's leave, relinquish for an hour that which her subjects hold dearest, the delight of her Highness's presence, and mortify myself by walking in star-light, while I forsake for a brief season, the glory of Diana's own beams. I will take place in the boat which the ladies occupy, and permit this young cavalier his hour of promised felicity."

The Queen replied, with an expression betwixt mirth and earnest, "If you are so willing to leave us, my lord, we cannot help the mortification. But, under favour, we do not trust you—old and experienced as you may deem yourself—with the care of our young ladies of honour. Your venerable age, my lord," she continued, smiling, "may be better assorted with that of my Lord Treasurer, who follows in the third boat, and whose experience even my Lord Willoughby's may be improved by."

Lord Willoughby hid his disappointment under a smile—laughed, was confused, bowed, and left the Queen's barge to go on board my Lord Burleigh's. Leicester, who endeavoured to divert his thoughts from all internal reflection, by fixing them on what was passing around, watched this circumstance among others. But when the boat put off from the shore

—when the music sounded from a barge which accompanied them— when the shouts of the populace were heard from the shore, and al. reminded him of the situation in which he was placed, he abstracted his thoughts and feelings by a strong effort from every thing but the neces-- sity of maintaining himself in the favour of his patroness, and exerted his talents of pleasing captivation with such success, that the Queen, alternately delighted with his conversation, and alarmed for his health, at length imposed a temporary silence on him, with playful yet anxious care, lest his flow of spirits should exhaust him.

"My lords," she said, "having passed for a time our edict of silence upon our good Leicester, we will call you to counsel on a gamesome matter, more fitted to be now treated of, amidst mirth and music, than in the gravity of our ordinary deliberations.—Which of you, my lords," said she, smiling, "know aught of a petition from Orson Pinnit, the keeper, as he qualifies himself, of our royal bears? Who stands godfather to his request?"

"Marry, with your Grace's good permission, that do I," said the Earl of Sussex.—"Orson Pinnit was a stout soldier before he was so mangled by the skenes of the Irish clan MacDonough, and I trust your Grace will be, as you always have been, good mistress to your good and trusty servants."

"Surely," said the Queen, "it is our purpose to be so, and in especial to our poor soldiers and sailors, who hazard their lives for little pay. We would give," she said, with her eyes sparkling, "yonder royal palace of ours to be an hospital for their use, rather than they should call their mistress ungrateful.—But this is not the question," she said, her voice, which had been awakened by her patriotic feelings, once more subsiding into the tone of gay and easy conversation; "for this Orson Pinnit's request goes something farther. He complains, that amidst the extreme delight with which men haunt the playhouses, and in especial their eager desire for seeing the exhibitions of one Will Shakspeare, (whom, I think, my lords, we have all heard something of,) the manly amusement of bear- baiting is falling into comparative neglect; since men will rather throng to see these roguish players kill each other in jest, than to see our royal dogs and bears worry each other in bloody earnest—What say you to this, my Lord of Sussex?"

"Why, truly, gracious madam," said Sussex, "you must expect little from an old soldier like me in favour of battles in sport, when they are compared with battles in earnest; and yet, by my faith, I wish Will Shakspeare no harm. He is a stout man at quarter-staff, and single falchion, though, as I am told, a halting fellow; and he stood, they say, a tough fight with the rangers of old Sir Thomas Lucy of Charlecot, when he broke his deer-park and kissed his keeper's daughter."

"I cry you mercy, my Lord of Sussex," said Queen Elizabeth, inter- rupting him; "that matter was heard in council, and we will not have this fellow's offence exaggerated—there was no kissing in the matter, and the defendant hath put the denial on record.—But what say you to his present practice, my lord, on the stage? for there lies the point, and not in any ways touching his former errors, in breaking parks, or the other follies you speak of."

"Why, truly, madam," replied Sussex, "as I said before, I wish the gamesome mad fellow no injury. Some of his whoreson poetry (I crave your Grace's pardon for such a phrase) has rung in mine ears as if the lines sounded to boot and saddle.—But then it is all froth and folly— no substance or seriousness in it, as your Grace has already well touched. What are half a dozen knaves, with rusty foils and tattered targets, making but a mere mockery of a stout fight, to compare to the royal game of bear-baiting, which hath been graced by your Highness's countenance, and that of your royal predecessors, in this your princely kingdom, famous for matchless mastiffs, and bold bearwards, over all Christendom? Greatly is it to be doubted that the race of both will decay, if men should throng to hear the lungs of an idle player belch forth nonsensical bombast, instead of bestowing their pence in encouraging the bravest image of war that can be shown in peace, and that is the sports of the Beargarden. There you may see the bear lying at guard with his red pinky eyes, watching the onset of the mastiff, like a wily captain, who maintains his defence that an assailant may be tempted to venture within his danger. And then comes Sir Mastiff, like a worthy champion, in full career at the throat of his adversary—and then shall Sir Bruin teach him the reward for those who, in their over-courage, neglect the policies of war, and, catching him in his arms, strain him to his breast like a lusty wrestler, until rib after rib crack like the shot of a pistolet. And then another mastiff, as bold, but with better aim and sounder judgment, catches Sir Bruin by the nether lip, and hangs fast, while he tosses about his blood and slaver, and tries in vain to shake Sir Talbot from his hold. And then"——

"Nay, by my honour, my lord," said the Queen, laughing, "you have described the whole so admirably, that, had we never seen a bear-baiting, as we have beheld many, and hope, with heaven's allowance, to see many more, your words were sufficient to put the whole Bear-garden before our eyes.—But come, who speaks next in this case?—My Lord of Leicester, what say you?"

"Am I then to consider myself as unmuzzled, please your Grace?" replied Leicester.

"Surely, my lord—that is, if you feel hearty enough to take part in our game," answered Elizabeth; "and yet, when I think of your cognizance of the bear and ragged staff, methinks we had better hear some less partial orator."

"Nay, on my word, gracious Princess," said the Earl, "though my brother Ambrose of Warwick and I do carry the ancient cognizance your Highness deigns to remember, I nevertheless desire nothing but fair play on all sides; or, as they say, 'fight dog, fight bear.' And in behalf of the players, I must needs say that they are witty knaves, whose rants and jests keep the minds of the commons from busying themselves with state affairs, and listening to traitorous speeches, idle rumours, and disloyal insinuations. When men are agape to see how Marlowe, Shakspeare, and other play artificers, work out their fanciful plots, as they call them, the mind of the spectators is withdrawn from the conduct of their rulers."

"We would not have the mind of our subjects withdrawn from the consideration of our own conduct, my lord," answered Elizabeth; "because the more closely it is examined, the true motives by which we are guided will appear the more manifest."

"I have heard, however, madam," said the Dean of St. Asaph's, an eminent Puritan, "that these players are wont, in their plays, not only to introduce profane and lewd expressions, tending to foster sin and harlotry, but even to bellow out such reflections on government, its origin and its object, as tend to render the subject discontented, and shake the solid foundations of civil society. And it seems to be, under your Grace's favour, far less than safe to permit these naughty foul-mouthed knaves to ridicule the godly for their decent gravity, and, in blaspheming heaven, and slandering its earthly rulers, to set at defiance the laws both of God and man."

"If we could think this were true, my lord," said Elizabeth, "we should give sharp correction for such offences. But it is ill arguing against the use of any thing from its abuse. And touching this Shakspeare, we think there is that in his plays that is worth twenty Bear-gardens; and that this new undertaking of his Chronicles, as he calls them, may entertain, with honest mirth, mingled with useful instruction, not only our subjects, but even the generation which may succeed to us."

"Your Majesty's reign will need no such feeble aid to make it remembered to the latest posterity," said Leicester. "And yet, in his way, Shakspeare hath so touched some incidents of your Majesty's happy government, as may countervail what has been spoken by his reverence the Dean of St. Asaph's. There are some lines, for example—I would my nephew, Philip Sidney, were here, they are scarce ever out of his mouth —they are spoken in a mad tale of fairies, love-charms, and I wot not what besides; but beautiful they are, however short they may and must fall of the subject to which they bear a bold relation—and Philip murmurs them, I think, even in his dreams."

"You tantalize us, my lord," said the Queen—"Master Philip Sidney is, we know, a minion of the Muses, and we are pleased it should be so. Valour never shines to more advantage than when united with the true taste and love of letters. But surely there are some others among our young courtiers who can recollect what your lordship has forgotten amid weightier affairs.—Master Tressilian, you are described to me as a worshipper of Minerva—remember you aught of these lines?"

Tressilian's heart was too heavy, his prospects in life too fatally blighted, to profit by the opportunity which the Queen thus offered to him of attracting her attention, but he determined to transfer the advantage to his more ambitious young friend; and, excusing himself on the score of want of recollection, he added, that he believed the beautiful verses, of which my Lord of Leicester had spoken, were in the remembrance of Master Walter Raleigh.

At the command of the Queen, that cavalier repeated, with accent and manner which even added to their exquisite delicacy of tact and beauty of description, the celebrated vision of Oberon:

> "That very time I saw, (but thou couldst not,)
> Flying between the cold moon and the earth,
> Cupid, all arm'd: a certain aim he took
> At a fair vestal, throned by the west;
> And loos'd his love-shaft smartly from his bow,
> As it should pierce a hundred thousand hearts:
> But I might see young Cupid's fiery shaft
> Quench'd in the chaste beams of the watery moon:
> And the imperial vot'ress passed on,
> In maiden meditation, fancy free."

The voice of Raleigh, as he repeated the last lines, became a little tremulous, as if diffident how the Sovereign to whom the homage was addressed might receive it, exquisite as it was. If this diffidence was affected, it was good policy; but if real, there was little occasion for it. The verses were not probably new to the Queen, for when was ever such elegant flattery long in reaching the royal ear to which it was addressed? But they were not the less welcome when repeated by such a speaker as Raleigh. Alike delighted with the matter, the manner, and the graceful form and animated countenance of the gallant young reciter, Elizabeth kept time to every cadence, with look and with finger. When the speaker had ceased, she murmured over the last lines as if scarce conscious that she was overheard, and as she uttered the words,

> "In maiden meditation, fancy free,"

she dropt into the Thames the supplication of Orson Pinnit, keeper of the royal bears, to find more favourable acceptance at Sheerness, or wherever the tide might waft it.

Leicester was spurred to emulation by the success of the young courtier's exhibition, as the veteran racer is roused when a high-mettled colt passes him on the way. He turned the discourse on shows, banquets, pageants, and on the character of those by whom these gay scenes were then frequented. He mixed acute observation with light satire in that just proportion which was free alike from malignant slander and insipid praise. He mimicked with ready accent the manners of the affected or the clownish, and made his own graceful tone and manner seem doubly such when he resumed it. Foreign countries—their customs—their manners—the rules of their courts—the fashions, and even the dress of their ladies, were equally his theme; and seldom did he conclude without conveying some compliment, always couched in delicacy, and expressed with propriety, to the Virgin Queen, her court and her government. Thus passed the conversation during this pleasure voyage, seconded by the rest of the attendants upon the royal person, in gay discourse, varied by remarks upon ancient classics and modern authors, and enriched by maxims of deep policy and sound morality, by the statesmen and sages who sate around, and mixed wisdom with the lighter talk of a female court.

When they returned to the palace, Elizabeth accepted, or rather selected, the arm of Leicester to support her, from the stairs where they landed, to the great gate. It even seemed to him, (though that might arise from the flattery of his own imagination,) that during this short passage, she leaned on him somewhat more than the slippiness of the way necessarily demanded. Certainly her actions and words combined to express a degree of favour, which, even in his proudest days, he had not till then attained. His rival, indeed, was repeatedly graced by the Queen's notice; but it was in a manner that seemed to flow less from spontaneous inclination, than as extorted by a sense of his merit. And, in the opinion of many experienced courtiers, all the favour she showed him was overbalanced, by her whispering in the ear of the Lady Derby, that "now she saw sickness was a better alchemist than she before wotted of, seeing it had changed my Lord of Sussex's copper nose into a golden one."

The jest transpired, and the Earl of Leicester enjoyed his triumph, as one to whom court favour had been both the primary and the ultimate motive of life, while he forgot in the intoxication of the moment, the perplexities and dangers of his own situation. Indeed, strange as it may appear, he thought less at that moment of the perils arising from his secret union, than of the marks of grace which Elizabeth from time to time showed to young Raleigh. They were indeed transient, but they were conferred on one accomplished in mind and body, with grace, gallantry, literature, and valour. An accident occurred in the course of the evening which riveted Leicester's attention to this object.

The nobles and courtiers who had attended the Queen on her pleasure expedition, were invited, with royal hospitality, to a splendid banquet in the hall of the palace. The table was not, indeed, graced by the presence of the Sovereign; for, agreeable to her idea of what was at once modest and dignified, the Maiden Queen, on such occasions, was wont to take in private, or with one or two favourite ladies, her light and temperate meal. After a moderate interval, the court again met in the splendid gardens of the palace; and it was while thus engaged, that the Queen suddenly asked a lady, who was near to her both in place and favour, what had become of the young Squire Lack-Cloak.

The Lady Paget answered, "she had seen Master Raleigh but two or three minutes since, standing at the window of a small pavilion or pleasure house, which looked out on the Thames, and writing on the glass with a diamond ring."

"That ring," said the Queen, "was a small token I gave him, to make amends for his spoiled mantle. Come, Paget, let us see what use he has made of it, for I can see through him already. He is a marvellously sharp-witted spirit."

They went to the spot, within sight of which, but at some distance, the young cavalier still lingered, as the fowler watches the net which he has set. The Queen approached the window, on which Raleigh had used her gift, to inscribe the following line:—

"Fain would I climb, but that I fear to fall."

The Queen smiled, read it twice over, once with deliberation to Lady Paget, and once again to herself. "It is a pretty beginning," she said, after the consideration of a moment or two; "but methinks the muse hath deserted the young wit, at the very outset of his task. It were good-natured—were it not, Lady Paget—to complete it for him? Try your rhyming faculties."

Lady Paget, prosaic from her cradle upwards, as ever any lady of the bedchamber before or after her, disclaimed all possibility of assisting the young poet.

"Nay, then, we must sacrifice to the Muses ourselves," said Elizabeth.

"The incense of no one can be more acceptable," said Lady Paget; "and your highness will impose such obligation on the ladies of Parnassus——"

"Hush, Paget," said the Queen, "you speak sacrilege against the immortal Nine—yet, virgins themselves, they should be exorable to a Virgin Queen—and therefore—let me see how runs his verse—

'Fain would I climb, but that I fear to fall.'

Might not the answer (for fault of a better) run thus—

'If thy mind fail thee, do not climb at all.' "

The dame of honour uttered an exclamation of joy and surprise at so happy a termination; and certainly a worse has been applauded, even when coming from a less distinguished author.

The Queen, thus encouraged, took off a diamond ring, and saying, "We will give this gallant some cause of marvel, when he finds his couplet perfected without his own interference," she wrote her own line beneath that of Raleigh.

The Queen left the pavilion—but retiring slowly, and often looking back, she could see the young cavalier steal, with the flight of a lapwing, towards the place where he had seen her make a pause;—"She staid but to observe," as she said, "that her train had taken;" and then, laughing at the circumstance with the Lady Paget, she took the way slowly towards the palace. Elizabeth, as they returned, cautioned her companion not to mention to any one the aid which she had given to the young poet— and Lady Paget promised scrupulous secrecy. It is to be supposed, that she made a mental reservation in favour of Leicester, to whom her ladyship transmitted without delay an anecdote, so little calculated to give him pleasure.

Raleigh, in the meanwhile, stole back to the window, and read, with a feeling of intoxication, the encouragement thus given him by the Queen in person to follow out his ambitious career, and returned to Sussex and his retinue, then on the point of embarking to go up the river, his heart beating high with gratified pride, and with hope of future distinction.

The reverence due to the person of the Earl prevented any notice being taken of the reception he had met with at court, until they had landed, and the household were assembled in the great hall at Say's Court; while that lord, exhausted by his late illness, and the fatigues of the day, had retired to his chamber, demanding the attendance of Wayland, his successful physician. Wayland, however, was nowhere to be found; and, while some of the party were, with military impatience, seeking him, and cursing his absence, the rest flocked around Raleigh, to congratulate him on his prospects of court favour.

He had the good taste and judgment to conceal the decisive circumstance of the couplet, to which Elizabeth had deigned to find a rhyme; but other indications had transpired, which plainly intimated that he had made some progress in the Queen's favour. All hastened to wish him joy on the mended appearance of his fortune: some from real regard, some, perhaps, from hopes that his preferment might hasten their own; and most from a mixture of these motives, and a sense that the countenance shown to any one of Sussex's household, was, in fact, a triumph to the whole. Raleigh returned the kindest thanks to them all, disowning, with becoming modesty, that one day's fair reception made a favourite, any more than one swallow a summer. But he observed that Blount did not join in the general congratulations and, somewhat hurt at his apparent unkindness, he plainly asked him the reason.

Blount replied with equal sincerity—"My good Walter, I wish thee as well as do any of these chattering gulls, who are whistling and whooping gratulations in thine ear, because it seems fair weather with thee. But I fear for thee, Walter," (and he wiped his honest eye,) "I fear for thee with all my heart. These court-tricks and gambols, and flashes of fine women's favour, are the tricks and trinkets that bring fair fortunes to farthings, and fine faces with witty coxcombs to the acquaintance of dull block and sharp axes."

So saying, Blount arose and left the hall, while Raleigh looked after him with an expression that blanked for a moment his bold and animated countenance.

Stanley just then entered the hall, and said to Tressilian, "My lord is calling for your fellow Wayland, and your fellow Wayland is just come hither in a sculler, and is calling for you, nor will he go to my lord till he sees you. The fellow looks as he were mazed, methinks—I would you would see him immediately."

Tressilian instantly left the hall, and causing Wayland Smith to be shown into a withdrawing apartment, and lights placed, he conducted the artist thither, and was surprised when he observed the emotion of his countenance.

"What is the matter with you, Smith?" said Tressilian; "have you seen the devil?"

"Worse, sir, worse," replied Wayland, "I have seen a basilisk. Thank God, I saw him first, for being so seen, and seeing not me, he will do the less harm."

"In God's name, speak sense," said Tressilian, "and say what you mean!"

"I have seen my old master," said the artist—"Last night, a friend whom I had acquired, took me to see the palace clock, judging me to be curious in such works of art. At the window of a turret next to the clock-house I saw my old master."

"Thou must needs have been mistaken," said Tressilian.

"I was not mistaken," said Wayland—"He that once hath his features by heart, would know him amongst a million. He was anticly habited; but he cannot disguise himself from me, God be praised, as I can from him. I will not, however, tempt Providence by remaining within his ken. Tarleton the player himself could not so disguise himself, but that, sooner or later, Doboobie would find him out. I must away to-morrow; for, as we stand together, it were death to me to remain within reach of him."

"But the Earl of Sussex?" said Tressilian.

"He is in little danger from what he has hitherto taken, provided he swallow the matter of a bean's size of the Orvietan, every morning fasting—but let him beware of a relapse."

"And how is that to be guarded against?" said Tressilian.

"Only by such caution as you would use against the devil," answered Wayland. "Let my lord's clerk of the kitchen kill his lord's meat himself, and dress it himself, using no spice but what he procures from the surest hands—Let the sewer serve it up himself, and let the master of my lord's household see that both clerk and sewer taste the dishes which the one dresses and the other serves. Let my lord use no perfumes which come not from well accredited persons; no unguents—no pomades. Let him, on no account, drink with strangers, or eat fruit with them, either in the way of nooning or otherwise. Especially, let him observe such caution if he goes to Kenilworth—the excuse of his illness, and his being under diet, will, and must, cover the strangeness of such practice."

"And thou," said Tressilian, "what dost thou think to make of thyself?"

"France, Spain, either India, East or West, shall be my refuge," said Wayland, "ere I venture my life by residing within ken of Doboobie, Demetrius, or whatever else he calls himself for the time."

"Well," said Tressilian, "this happens not inopportunely—I had business for you in Berkshire, but in the opposite extremity to the place where thou art known; and ere thou hadst found out this new reason for living private, I had settled to send thee thither upon a secret embassage."

The artist expressed himself willing to receive his commands, and Tressilian, knowing he was well acquainted with the outline of his business at court, frankly explained to him the whole, mentioned the agreement which subsisted betwixt Giles Gosling and him, and told what had that day been averred in the presence-chamber by Varney, and supported by Leicester.

"Thou seest," he added, "that, in the circumstances in which I am placed, it behoves me to keep a narrow watch on the motions of these unprincipled men, Varney and his complices, Foster and Lambourne, as well as on those of my Lord Leicester himself, who, I suspect, is partly a deceiver, and not altogether the deceived in that matter. Here is my ring, as a pledge to Giles Gosling—here is besides gold, which shall be trebled if thou serve me faithfully. Away down to Cumnor, and see what happens there."

"I go with double good-will," said the artist, "first, because I serve your honour, who has been so kind to me, and then, that I may escape my old master, who, if not an absolute incarnation of the devil, has, at least, as much of the demon about him, in will, word, and action, as ever polluted humanity.—And yet let him take care of me. I fly him now, as heretofore; but if, like the Scottish wild cattle,[1] I am vexed by frequent pursuit, I may turn on him in hate and desperation.—Will your honour command my nag to be saddled? I will but give the medicine to my lord, divided in its proper proportions, with a few instructions. His safety will then depend on the care of his friends and domestics— for the past he is guarded, but let him beware of the future."

Wayland Smith accordingly made his farewell visit to the Earl of Sussex, dictated instructions as to his regimen, and precautions concerning his diet, and left Say's Court without waiting for morning.

[1] A remnant of the wild cattle of Scotland are preserved at Chillingham Castle, near Wooler, in Northumberland, the seat of Lord Tankerville. They fly before strangers; but if disturbed and followed, they turn with fury on those who persist in annoying them.

CHAPTER XVIII

——————The moment comes—
It is already come—when thou must write
The absolute total of thy life's vast sum.
The constellations stand victorious o'er thee,
The planets shoot good fortune in fair junctions,
And tell thee, "Now's the time."
                    SCHILLER's *Wallenstein by* COLERIDGE.

WHEN Leicester returned to his lodging, after a day so important and so harassing, in which, after riding out more than one gale, and touching on more than one shoal, his bark had finally gained the harbour with banner displayed, he seemed to experience as much fatigue as a mariner after a perilous storm. He spoke not a word while his chamberlain exchanged his rich court-mantle for a furred night-robe, and when this officer signified that Master Varney desired to speak with his lordship, he replied only by a sullen nod. Varney, however, entered, accepting this signal as a permission, and the chamberlain withdrew.

The Earl remained silent and almost motionless in his chair, his head reclined on his hand, and his elbow resting on the table which stood beside him, without seeming to be conscious of the entrance, or of the presence, of his confidant. Varney waited for some minutes until he should speak, desirous to know what was the finally predominant mood of a mind, through which so many powerful emotions had that day taken their course. But he waited in vain, for Leicester continued still silent, and the confidant saw himself under the necessity of being the first to speak. "May I congratulate your lordship," he said, "on the deserved superiority you have this day attained over your most formidable rival?"

Leicester raised his head, and answered sadly, but without anger, "Thou, Varney, whose ready invention has involved me in a web of most mean and perilous falsehood, knowest best what small reason there is for gratulation on the subject."

"Do you blame me, my lord," said Varney, "for not betraying, on the first push, the secret on which your fortunes depended, and which you have so oft and so earnestly recommended to my safe keeping? Your lordship was present in person, and might have contradicted me and ruined yourself by an avowal of the truth; but surely it was no part of a faithful servant to have done so without your commands."

"I cannot deny it, Varney," said the Earl, rising and walking across the room; "my own ambition has been traitor to my love."

"Say, rather, my lord, that your love has been traitor to your greatness, and barred you from such a prospect of honour and power as the world cannot offer to any other. To make my honoured lady a countess, you have missed the chance of being yourself——"

He paused and seemed unwilling to complete the sentence.

"Of being myself *what?*" demanded Leicester; "speak out thy meaning, Varney."

"Of being yourself a KING, my lord," replied Varney; "and King of England to boot!—It is no treason to our Queen to say so. It would have chanced by her obtaining that which all true subjects wish her—a lusty, noble, and gallant husband."

"Thou ravest, Varney," answered Leicester. "Besides, our times have seen enough to make men loathe the Crown Matrimonial which men take from their wives' lap. There was Darnley of Scotland."

"He!" said Varney; "a gull, a fool, a thrice sodden ass, who suffered himself to be fired off into the air like a rocket on a rejoicing day. Had Mary had the hap to have wedded the noble Earl *once* destined to share her throne, she had experienced a husband of different metal; and her husband had found in her a wife as complying and loving as the mate of the meanest squire, who follows the hounds a-horseback, and holds her husband's bridle as he mounts."

"It might have been as thou sayst, Varney," said Leicester, a brief smile of self-satisfaction passing over his anxious countenance. "Henry Darnley knew little of women—with Mary, a man who knew her sex might have had some chance of holding his own. But not with Elizabeth, Varney—for I think God, when he gave her the heart of a woman, gave her the head of a man to control its follies.—No, I know her.—She will accept love-tokens, ay, and requite them with the like—put sugared sonnets in her bosom—ay, and answer them too—push gallantry to the very verge where it becomes exchange of affection—but she writes *nil ultra* to all which is to follow, and would not barter one iota of her own supreme power for all the alphabet of both Cupid and Hymen."

"The better for you, my lord," said Varney, "that is, in the case supposed, if such be her disposition; since you think you cannot aspire to become her husband. Her favourite you are, and may remain, if the lady at Cumnor-Place continues in her present obscurity."

"Poor Amy!" said Leicester, with a deep sigh; "she desires so earnestly to be acknowledged in presence of God and man!"

"Ay, but, my lord," said Varney, "is her desire reasonable?—that is the question.—Her religious scruples are solved—she is an honoured and beloved wife—enjoying the society of her husband at such times as his weightier duties permit him to afford her his company—What would she more? I am right sure that a lady so gentle and so loving would consent to live her life through in a certain obscurity—which is, after all, not dimmer than when she was at Lidcote Hall—rather than diminish the least jot of her lord's honours and greatness by a premature attempt to share them."

"There is something in what thou sayst," said Leicester; "and her appearance here were fatal—yet she must be seen at Kenilworth; Elizabeth will not forget that she has so appointed."

"Let me sleep on that hard point," said Varney; "I cannot else perfect the device I have on the stithy, which I trust will satisfy the Queen and please my honoured lady, yet leave this fatal secret where it is now buried.—Has your lordship further commands for the night?"

"I would be alone," said Leicester. "Leave me, and place my steel casket on the table.—Be within summons."

Varney retired—and the Earl, opening the window of his apartment, looked out long and anxiously upon the brilliant host of stars which glimmered in the splendour of a summer firmament. The words burst from him as at unawares—"I had never more need that the heavenly bodies should befriend me, for my earthly path is darkened and confused."

It is well known that the age reposed a deep confidence in the vain predictions of judicial astrology, and Leicester, though exempt from the general control of superstition, was not in this respect superior to his time; but, on the contrary, was remarkable for the encouragement which he gave to the professors of this pretended science. Indeed, the wish to pry into futurity, so general among the human race, is peculiarly to be found amongst those who trade in state mysteries, and the dangerous intrigues and cabals of courts. With heedful precaution to see that it had not been opened or its locks tampered with, Leicester applied a key to the steel casket, and drew from it, first, a parcel of gold pieces, which he put into a silk purse; then a parchment inscribed with planetary signs, and the lines and calculations used in framing horoscopes, on which he gazed intently for a few moments; and, lastly, took forth a large key, which, lifting aside the tapestry, he applied to a little concealed door in the corner of the apartment, and, opening it, disclosed a stair constructed in the thickness of the wall.

"Alasco," said the Earl, with a voice raised, yet no higher raised than to be heard by the inhabitant of the small turret to which the stair conducted—"Alasco, I say, descend."

"I come, my lord," answered a voice from above. The foot of an aged man was heard, slowly descending the narrow stair, and Alasco entered the Earl's apartment. The astrologer was a little man, and seemed much advanced in age, for his beard was long and white and reached over his black doublet down to his silken girdle. His hair was of the same venerable hue. But his eyebrows were as dark as the keen and piercing black eyes which they shaded, and this peculiarity gave a wild and singular cast to the physiognomy of the old man. His cheek was still fresh and ruddy, and the eyes we have mentioned resembled those of a rat, in acuteness, and even fierceness of expression. His manner was not without a sort of dignity; and the interpreter of the stars, though respectful, seemed altogether at his ease, and even assumed a tone of instruction and command, in conversing with the prime favourite of Elizabeth.

"Your prognostications have failed, Alasco," said the Earl, when they had exchanged salutations—"He is recovering."

"My son," replied the astrologer, "let me remind you, I warranted not his death—nor is there any prognostication that can be derived from the heavenly bodies, their aspects and their conjunctions, which is not liable to be controlled by the will of Heaven. *Astra regunt homines, sed regit astra Deus.*"

"Of what avail, then, is your mystery?" enquired the Earl.

"Of much, my son," replied the old man, "since it can show the natural and probable course of events, although that course moves in subordination to an Higher Power. Thus, in reviewing the horoscope which your lordship subjected to my skill, you will observe that Saturn, being in the sixth House in opposition to Mars, retrograde in the House of Life, cannot but denote long and dangerous sickness, the issue whereof is the will of Heaven, though death may probably be inferred—Yet, if I knew the name of the party, I would erect another scheme."

"His name is a secret," said the Earl; "yet, I must own, thy prognostication hath not been unfaithful. He has been sick, and dangerously so, not however to death. But hast thou again cast my horoscope as Varney directed thee, and art thou prepared to say what the stars tell of my present fortune?"

"My art stands at your command," said the old man; "and here, my son, is the map of thy fortunes, brilliant in aspect as ever beamed from those blessed signs whereby our life is influenced, yet not unchequered with fears, difficulties, and dangers."

"My lot were more than mortal were it otherwise," said the Earl; "proceed, father, and believe you speak with one ready to undergo his destiny in action and in passion, as may beseem a noble of England."

"Thy courage to do and to suffer, must be wound up yet a strain higher," said the old man. "The stars intimate yet a prouder title, yet a higher rank. It is for thee to guess their meaning, not for me to name it."

"Name it, I conjure you—name it, I command you," said the Earl, his eyes brightening as he spoke.

"I may not, and I will not," replied the old man. "The ire of princes is as the wrath of the lion. But mark, and judge for thyself. Here Venus, ascendant in the House of Life, and conjoined with Sol, showers down that flood of silver light, blent with gold, which promises power, wealth, dignity, all that the proud heart of man desires, and in such abundance, that never the future Augustus of that old and mighty Rome heard from his *Haruspices* such a tale of glory, as from this rich text my lord might read to my favourite son."

"Thou dost but jest with me, father," said the Earl, astonished at the strain of enthusiasm in which the astrologer delivered his prediction.

"Is it for him to jest who hath his eye on heaven, who hath his foot in the grave?" returned the old man, solemnly.

The Earl made two or three strides through the apartment, with his hand outstretched, as one who follows the beckoning signal of some phantom, waving him on to deeds of high import. As he turned, however, he caught the eye of the astrologer fixed on him, while an observing glance of the most shrewd penetration shot from under the penthouse of his shaggy dark eyebrows. Leicester's haughty and suspicious soul at once caught fire; he darted towards the old man from the further end of the lofty apartment, only standing still when his extended hand was within a foot of the astrologer's body.

"Wretch!" he cried, "if you dare to palter with me, I will have your skin stripped from your living flesh!—Confess thou hast been hired to deceive and betray me—that thou art a cheat, and I thy silly prey and booty!"

The old man exhibited some symptoms of emotion, but not more than the furious deportment of his patron might have extorted from innocence itself.

"What means this violence, my lord?" he answered, "or in what can I have deserved it at your hand?"

"Give me proof," said the Earl vehemently, "that you have not tampered with mine enemies."

"My lord," replied the old man, with dignity, "you can have no better proof than that which you yourself elected. In that turret I have spent the last twenty-four hours, under the key which has been in your own custody. The hours of darkness I have spent in gazing on the heavenly bodies with these dim eyes, and during those of light I have toiled this aged brain to complete the calculation arising from their combinations. Earthly food I have not tasted—earthly voice I have not heard—you are yourself aware I had not means of doing so—and yet I tell you—I who have been thus shut up in solitude and study—that within these twenty-four hours your star has become predominant in the horizon, and either the bright book of heaven speaks false, or there must have been a proportionate revolution in your fortunes upon earth. If nothing has happened within that space to secure your power, or advance your favour, then am I indeed a cheat, and the divine art, which was first devised in the plains of Chaldea, is a foul imposture."

"It is true," said Leicester, after a moment's reflection, "thou wert closely immured—and it is also true that the change has taken place in my situation which thou sayst the horoscope indicates."

"Wherefore this distrust, then, my son?" said the astrologer, assuming a tone of admonition; "the celestial intelligences brook not diffidence, even in their favourites."

"Peace, father," answered Leicester, "I have erred in doubting thee. Not to mortal man, nor to celestial intelligence—under that which is supreme—will Dudley's lips say more in condescension or apology. Speak rather to the present purpose—Amid these bright promises, thou hast said there was a threatening aspect—Can thy skill tell whence, or by whose means, such danger seems to impend?"

"Thus far only," answered the astrologer, "does my art enable me to answer your query. The infortune is threatened by the malignant and adverse aspect, through means of a youth,—and, as I think, a rival; but whether in love or in prince's favour, I know not; nor can I give farther indication respecting him, save that he comes from the western quarter."

"The western—ha!" replied Leicester, "it is enough—the tempest does indeed brew in that quarter!—Cornwall and Devon—Raleigh and Tressilian—one of them is indicated—I must beware of both.—Father, if I have done thy skill injustice, I will make thee a lordly recompense."

He took a purse of gold from the strong casket which stood before him. "Have thou double the recompense which Varney promised.—Be faithful—be secret—obey the directions thou shalt receive from my master of the horse, and grudge not a little seclusion or restraint in my cause—it shall be richly considered.—Here, Varney—conduct this venerable man to thine own lodging—tend him heedfully in all things, but see that he holds communication with no one."

Varney bowed, and the astrologer kissed the Earl's hand in token of adieu, and followed the master of the horse to another apartment, in which were placed wine and refreshments for his use.

The astrologer sat down to his repast, while Varney shut two doors with great precaution, examined the tapestry, lest any listener lurked behind it; and then sitting down opposite to the sage, began to question him.

"Saw you my signal from the court beneath?"

"I did," said Alasco, for by such name he was at present called, "and shaped the horoscope accordingly."

"And it passed upon the patron without challenge?" continued Varney.

"Not without challenge," replied the old man, "but it did pass; and I added, as before agreed, danger from a discovered secret, and a western youth."

"My lord's fear will stand sponsor to the one, and his conscience to the other, of these prognostications," replied Varney. "Sure never man chose to run such a race as his, yet continued to retain those silly scruples! I am fain to cheat him to his own profit. But touching your matters, sage interpreter of the stars, I can tell you more of your own fortune than plan or figure can show. You must be gone from hence forthwith."

"I will not," said Alasco, peevishly. "I have been too much hurried up and down of late—immured for day and night in a desolate turret-chamber—I must enjoy my liberty, and pursue my studies, which are of more import than the fate of fifty statesmen, and favourites, that rise and burst like bubbles in the atmosphere of a court."

"At your pleasure," said Varney, with a sneer which habit had rendered familiar to his features, and which forms the principal characteristic that painters have assigned to those of Satan—"At your pleasure," he said, "you may enjoy your liberty and your studies, until the daggers of Sussex's followers are clashing within your doublet, and against your ribs." The old man turned pale, and Varney proceeded. "Wot you not he hath offered a reward for the arch-quack and poison-vendor, Demetrius, who sold certain precious spices to his lordship's cook?—What! turn you pale, old friend? Does Hali already see an infortune in the House of Life!—Why, hark thee, we will have thee down to an old house of mine in the country, where thou shalt live with a hobnailed slave, whom thy alchemy may convert into ducats, for to such conversion alone is thy art serviceable."

"It is false, thou foul-mouthed railer," said Alasco, shaking with impotent anger; "it is well known that I have approached more nearly to projection than any hermetic artist who now lives. There are not six chemists in the world who possess so near an approximation to the grand arcanum——"

"Come, come," said Varney, interrupting him, "what means this, in the name of Heaven? Do we not know one another? I believe thee to be so perfect—so very perfect, in the mystery of cheating, that, having imposed upon all mankind, thou hast at length, in some measure, imposed upon thyself; and without ceasing to dupe others, hast become a species of dupe to thine own imagination. Blush not for it, man—thou art learned, and shalt have classical comfort:

'Ne quisquam Ajacem possit superare nisi Ajax.'

No one but thyself could have gulled thee—and thou hast gulled the whole brotherhood of the Rosy Cross beside—none so deep in the mystery as thou. But hark thee in thine ear; had the seasoning which spiced Sussex's broth wrought more surely, I would have thought better of the chemical science thou dost boast so highly."

"Thou art an hardened villain, Varney," replied Alasco; "many will do those things, who dare not speak of them."

"And many speak of them who dare not do them," answered Varney; "but be not wroth—I will not quarrel with thee—If I did, I were fain to live on eggs for a month, that I might feed without fear. Tell me at once, how came thine art to fail thee at this great emergency?"

"The Earl of Sussex's horoscope intimates," replied the astrologer, "that the sign of the ascendant being in combustion——"

"Away with your gibberish," replied Varney; "think'st thou it is the patron thou speak'st with?"

"I crave your pardon," replied the old man, "and swear to you, I know but one medicine that could have saved the Earl's life; and as no man living in England knows that antidote save myself,—moreover, as the ingredients, one of them in particular, are scarce possible to be come by, I must needs suppose his escape was owing to such a constitution of lungs and vital parts, as was never before bound up in a body of clay."

"There was some talk of a quack who waited on him," said Varney, after a moment's reflection. "Are you sure there is no one in England who has this secret of thine?"

"One man there was," said the doctor, "once my servant, who might have stolen this of me, with one or two other secrets of art. But content you, Master Varney, it is no part of my policy to suffer such interlopers to interfere in my trade. He pries into no mysteries more, I warrant you; for, as I well believe, he hath been wafted to heaven on the wing of a fiery dragon—Peace be with him!—But in this retreat of mine, shall I have the use of mine elaboratory?"

"Of a whole workshop, man," said Varney; "for a reverend father abbot, who was fain to give place to bluff King Hal, and some of his courtiers, a score of years since, had a chemist's complete apparatus, which he was obliged to leave behind him to his successors. Thou shalt there occupy, and melt, and puff, and blaze, and multiply, until the Green Dragon become a golden-goose, or whatever the newer phrase of the brotherhood may testify."

"Thou art right, Master Varney," said the alchemist, setting his teeth close, and grinding them together—"thou art right, even in thy very contempt of right and reason. For what thou sayst in mockery, may in sober verity chance to happen ere we meet again. If the most venerable sages of ancient days have spoken the truth—if the most learned of our own have rightly received it—if I have been accepted wherever I travelled, in Germany, in Poland, in Italy, and in the farther Tartary, as one to whom Nature has unveiled her darkest secrets—if I have acquired the most secret signs and passwords of the Jewish Cabala, so that the greyest beard in the synagogue would brush the steps to make them clean for me—if all this is so, and if there remains but one step—one little step—betwixt my long, deep, and dark, and subterranean progress, and that blaze of light which shall show Nature watching her richest and her most glorious productions in the very cradle—one step betwixt dependence and the power of sovereignty—one step betwixt poverty and such a sum of wealth as earth, without that noble secret, cannot minister from all her mines in the old or the new-found world—if this be all so, is it not reasonable that to this I dedicate my future life, secure, for a brief period of studious patience, to rise above the mean dependence upon favourites, and *their* favourites, by which I am now enthralled?"

"Now, bravo! bravo! my good father," said Varney, with the usual sardonic expression of ridicule on his countenance; "yet all this approximation to the philosopher's stone wringeth not one single crown out of my Lord Leicester's pouch, and far less out of Richard Varney's—*We* must have earthly and substantial services, man, and care not whom else thou canst delude with thy philosophical charlatanry."

"My son Varney," said the alchemist, "the unbelief, gathered around thee like a frost-fog, hath dimmed thine acute perception to that which is a stumbling-block to the wise, and which yet, to him who seeketh knowledge with humility, extends a lesson so clear, that he who runs may read. Hath not Art, think'st thou, the means of completing Nature's imperfect concoctions in her attempts to form the precious metals, even as by art we can perfect those other operations, of incubation, distillation, fermenta tion, and similar processes of an ordinary description, by which we extract life itself out of a senseless egg, summon purity and vitality out of muddy dregs, or call into vivacity the inert substance of a sluggish liquid?"

"I have heard all this before," said Varney, "and my heart is proof against such cant ever since I sent twenty good gold pieces, (marry, it was in the nonage of my wit,) to advance the grand magisterium, all which, God help the while, vanished *in fumo*. Since that moment, when I paid for my freedom, I defy chemistry, astrology, palmistry, and every other occult art, were it as secret as hell itself, to unloose the stricture of my purse-strings. Marry, I neither defy the manna of Saint Nicholas, nor can I dispense with it. Thy first task must be to prepare some when thou getst down to my little sequestered retreat yonder, and then make as much gold as thou wilt."

"I will make no more of that dose," said the alchemist, resolutely.

"Then," said the master of the horse, "thou shalt be hanged for what thou hast made already, and so were the great secret for ever lost to mankind.—Do not humanity this injustice, good father, but e'en bend to thy destiny, and make us an ounce or two of this same stuff, which cannot prejudice above one or two individuals, in order to gain lifetime to dis- cover the universal medicine, which shall clear away all mortal diseases at once. But cheer up, thou grave, learned, and most melancholy jack- anapes! Hast thou not told me, that a moderate portion of thy drug hath mild effects, no ways ultimately dangerous to the human frame, but which produces depression of spirits, nausea, headache, an unwillingness to change of place—even such a state of temper as would keep a bird from flying out of a cage, were the door left open?"

"I have said so, and it is true," said the alchemist; "this effect will it produce, and the bird who partakes of it in such proportion, shall sit for a season drooping on her perch, without thinking either of the free blue sky, or of the fair greenwood, though the one be lighted by the rays of the rising sun, and the other ringing with the newly awakened song of all the feathered inhabitants of the forest."

"And this without danger to life?" said Varney, somewhat anxiously.

"Ay, so that proportion and measure be not exceeded; and so that one who knows the nature of the manna be ever near to watch the symptoms, and succour in case of need."

"Thou shalt regulate the whole," said Varney; "thy reward shall be princely, if thou keep'st time and touch, and exceedest not the due pro- portion, to the prejudice of her health—otherwise thy punishment shall be as signal."

"The prejudice of *her* health!" repeated Alasco; "it is, then, a woman I am to use my skill upon?"

"No, thou fool," replied Varney, "said I not it was a bird—a reclaimed linnet, whose pipe might soothe a hawk when in mid stoop?—I see thine eye sparkle, and I know thy beard is not altogether so white as art has made it—*that*, at least, thou hast been able to transmute to silver. But mark me, this is no mate for thee. This caged bird is dear to one who brooks no rivalry, and far less such rivalry as thine, and her health must over all things be cared for. But she is in the case of being commanded down to yonder Kenilworth revels; and it is most expedient—most needful—most necessary, that she fly not thither. Of these necessities and their causes, it is not needful that she should know aught, and it is to be thought that her own wish may lead her to combat all ordinary reasons which can be urged for her remaining a housekeeper."

"That is but natural," said the alchemist, with a strange smile, which yet bore a greater reference to the human character, than the uninterested and abstracted gaze which his physiognomy had hitherto expressed, where all seemed to refer to some world distant from that which was existing around him.

"It is so," answered Varney; "you understand women well, though it may have been long since you were conversant among them.—Well, then, she is not to be contradicted—yet she is not to be humoured. Understand me—a slight illness, sufficient to take away the desire of removing from thence, and to make such of your wise fraternity as may be called in to aid, recommend a quiet residence at home, will, in one word, be esteemed good service, and remunerated as such."

"I am not to be asked to affect the House of Life?" said the chemist.

"On the contrary, we will have thee hanged if thou dost," replied Varney.

"And I must," added Alasco, "have opportunity to do my turn, and all facilities for concealment or escape, should there be detection?"

"All, all, and every thing, thou infidel in all but the impossibilities of alchemy.—Why, man, for what dost thou take me?"

The old man rose, and taking a light, walked towards the end of the apartment, where was a door that led to the small sleeping room destined for his reception during the night.—At the door he turned round, and slowly repeated Varney's question ere he answered it. "For what do I take thee, Richard Varney?—Why, for a worse devil than I have been myself. But I am in your toils, and I must serve you till my term be out."

"Well, well," answered Varney, hastily, "be stirring with grey light. It may be we shall not need thy medicine.—Do nought till I myself come down.—Michael Lambourne shall guide you to the place of your destination." [1]

When Varney heard the adept's door shut and carefully bolted within, he stepped towards it, and with similar precaution carefully locked it on the outside, and took the key from the lock, muttering to himself, "Worse than *thee*, thou poisoning quack-salver and witch-monger, who, if thou art not a bounden slave to the devil, it is only because he disdains such an apprentice!—I am a mortal man, and seek by mortal means the gratifica-

[1] See Note VII.—Dr. Julio.

tion of my passions, and advancement of my prospects—Thou art a vassal of hell itself.—So ho, Lambourne!" he called at another door, and Michael made his appearance with a flushed cheek and an unsteady step.

"Thou art drunk, thou villain!" said Varney to him.

"Doubtless, noble sir," replied the unabashed Michael, "we have been drinking all even to the glories of the day, and to my noble Lord of Leicester, and his valiant master of the horse.—Drunk! odds blades and poniards, he that would refuse to swallow a dozen healths on such an evening, is a base besognio, and a puckfoist, and shall swallow six inches of my dagger!"

"Hark ye, scoundrel," said Varney, "be sober on the instant—I command thee. I know thou canst throw off thy drunken folly, like a fool's coat, at pleasure; and if not, it were the worse for thee."

Lambourne drooped his head, left the apartment, and returned in two or three minutes with his face composed, his hair adjusted, his dress in order, and exhibiting as great a difference from his former self as if the whole man had been changed.

"Art thou sober now, and dost thou comprehend me?" said Varney, sternly.

Lambourne bowed in acquiescence.

"Thou must presently down to Cumnor-Place with the reverend man of art, who sleeps yonder in the little vaulted chamber. Here is the key, that thou mayst call him betimes. Take another trusty fellow with you. Use him well on the journey, but let him not escape you—pistol him if he attempt it, and I will be your warrant. I will give thee letters to Foster. The doctor is to occupy the lower apartments of the eastern quadrangle, with freedom to use the old elaboratory and its implements.—He is to have no access to the lady but such as I point out—only she may be amused to see his philosophical jugglery. Thou wilt await at Cumnor-Place my farther orders; and, as thou livest, beware of the ale-bench and the aquavitæ flask. Each breath drawn in Cumnor-Place must be kept severed from common air."

"Enough, my lord—I mean my worshipful master—soon, I trust, to be my worshipful knightly master. You have given me my lesson and my license;—I will execute the one, and not abuse the other. I will be in the saddle by daybreak."

"Do so, and deserve favour.—Stay—ere thou goest fill me a cup of wine—not out of that flask, sirrah," as Lambourne was pouring out from that which Alasco had left half finished, "fetch me a fresh one."

Lambourne obeyed, and Varney, after rinsing his mouth with the liquor, drank a full cup, and said, as he took up a lamp to retreat to his sleeping apartment, "It is strange—I am as little the slave of fancy as any one, yet I never speak for a few minutes with this fellow Alasco, but my mouth and lungs feel as if soiled with the fumes of calcined arsenic—pah!"

So saying, he left the apartment. Lambourne lingered, to drink a cup of the freshly opened flask. "It is from Saint-John's-Berg," he said, as he paused on the draught to enjoy its flavour, "and has the true relish of the violet. But I must forbear it now, that I may one day drink it at my own pleasure." And he quaffed a goblet of water to quench the fumes of the Rhenish wine, retired slowly towards the door, made a pause, and then, finding the temptation irresistible, walked hastily back, and took another long pull at the wine flask, without the formality of a cup.

"Were it not for this accursed custom," he said, "I might climb as high as Varney himself. But who can climb when the room turns round with him like a parish-top? I would the distance were greater, or the road rougher, betwixt my hand and mouth!—But I will drink nothing to-morrow, save water—nothing save fair water."

CHAPTER XIX

> *Pistol.* And tidings do I bring, and lucky joys,
> And happy news of price.
> *Falstaff.* I prithee now, deliver them like to a man
>   of this world.
> *Pistol.* A foutra for the world, and worldlings base!
> I speak of Africa, and golden joys.
> *Henry IV., Part 2.*

THE public room of the Black Bear at Cumnor, to which the scene of our story now returns, boasted, on the evening which we treat of, no ordinary assemblage of guests. There had been a fair in the neighbourhood, and the cutting mercer of Abingdon, with some of the other personages whom the reader has already been made acquainted with, as friends and customers of Giles Gosling, had already formed their wonted circle around the evening fire, and were talking over the news of the day.

A lively, bustling, arch fellow, whose pack and oaken *ellwand,* studded duly with brass points, denoted him to be of Autolycus's profession, occupied a good deal of the attention, and furnished much of the amusement, of the evening. The pedlars of those days, it must be remembered, were men of far greater importance than the degenerate and degraded hawkers of our modern times. It was by means of these peripatetic vendors that the country trade, in the finer manufactures used in female dress particularly, was almost entirely carried on; and if a merchant of this description arrived at the dignity of travelling with a pack-horse, he was a person of no small consequence, and company for the most substantial yeoman or Franklin whom he might meet in his wanderings.

The pedlar of whom we speak bore, accordingly, an active and unrebuked share in the merriment to which the rafters of the bonny Black Bear of Cumnor resounded. He had his smile with pretty Mistress Cicely, his broad laugh with mine host, and his jest upon dashing Master Goldthred, who, though indeed without any such benevolent intention on his own part, was the general butt of the evening. The pedlar and he were closely engaged in a dispute upon the preference due to the Spanish nether-stock over the black Gascoigne hose, and mine host had just winked to the guests around him, as who should say, "You will have mirth presently, my masters," when the trampling of horses was heard in the courtyard, and the hostler was loudly summoned, with a few of the newest oaths then in vogue, to add force to the invocation. Out tumbled Will Hostler, John Tapster, and all the militia of the inn, who had slunk from their posts in order to collect some scattered crumbs of the mirth which was flying about among the customers. Out into the yard sallied mine host himself also, to do fitting salutation to his new guests; and presently returned, ushering into the apartment his own worthy nephew, Michael Lambourne, pretty tolerably drunk, and having under his escort the astrologer. Alasco, though still a little old man, had, by altering his gown to a riding dress, trimming his beard and eyebrows, and so forth, struck at least a score of years from his apparent age, and might now seem an active man of sixty, or little upwards. He appeared at present exceedingly anxious, and had insisted much with Lambourne that they should not enter the inn, but go straight forward to the place of their destination. But Lambourne would not be controlled. "By Cancer and Capricorn," he vociferated, "and the whole heavenly host—besides all the stars that these blessed eyes of mine have seen sparkle in the southern heavens, to which these northern blinkers are but farthing candles, I will be unkindly for no one's humour—I will stay and salute my worthy uncle here.— Chesu! that good blood should ever be forgotten betwixt friends!—A gallon of your best, uncle, and let it go round to the health of the noble Earl of Leicester!—What! Shall we not collogue together, and warm the cockles of our ancient kindness?—Shall we not collogue, I say?"

"With all mine heart, kinsman," said mine host, who obviously wished to be rid of him; "but are you to stand shot to all this good liquor?"

This is a question has quelled many a jovial toper, but it moved not the purpose of Lambourne's soul. "Question my means, nuncle?" he said, producing a handful of mixed gold and silver pieces; "question Mexico and Peru—question the Queen's exchequer—God save her Majesty!— She is my good Lord's good mistress."

"Well, kinsman," said mine host, "it is my business to sell wine to those who can buy it—So, Jack Tapster, do me thine office.—But I would I knew how to come by money as lightly as thou dost, Mike."

"Why, uncle," said Lambourne, "I will tell thee a secret—Dost see this little old fellow here? as old and withered a chip as ever the devil put into his porridge—and yet, uncle, between you and me—he hath Potosi in that brain of his—'Sblood! he can coin ducats faster than I can vent oaths."

"I will have none of his coinage in my purse though, Michael," said mine host; "I know what belongs to falsifying the Queen's coin."

"Thou art an ass, uncle, for as old as thou art—Pull me not by the skirts, doctor, thou art an ass thyself to boot—so, being both asses, I tell ye I spoke but metaphorically."

"Are you mad?" said the old man; "is the devil in you?—can you not let us begone without drawing all men's eyes on us?"

"Sayst thou?" said Lambourne; "Thou art deceived now—no man shall see you an I give the word.—By Heavens, masters, an any one dare to look on this old gentleman, I will slash the eyes out of his head with my poniard!—So sit down, old friend, and be merry—these are mine ingles—mine ancient inmates, and will betray no man."

"Had you not better withdraw to a private apartment, nephew?" said Giles Gosling; "you speak strange matter," he added, "and there be intelligencers everywhere."

"I care not for them," said the magnanimous Michael—"intelligencers? pshaw!—I serve the noble Earl of Leicester—Here comes the wine—Fill round, Master Slinker, a carouse to the health of the flower of England, the noble Earl of Leicester! I say, the noble Earl of Leicester! He that does me not reason is a swine of Sussex, and I'll make him kneel to the pledge, if I should cut his hams and smoke them for bacon."

None disputed a pledge given under such formidable penalties; and Michael Lambourne, whose drunken humour was not of course diminished by this new potation, went on in the same wild way, renewing his acquaintance with such of the guests as he had formerly known, and experiencing a reception in which there was now something of deference, mingled with a good deal of fear; for the least servitor of the favourite Earl, especially such a man as Lambourne, was, for very sufficient reasons, an object both of the one and of the other.

In the meanwhile, the old man, seeing his guide in this uncontrollable humour, ceased to remonstrate with him, and sitting down in the most obscure corner of the room, called for a small measure of sack, over which he seemed, as it were, to slumber, withdrawing himself as much as possible from general observation, and doing nothing which could recall his existence to the recollection of his fellow-traveller, who by this time had got into close intimacy with his ancient comrade, Goldthred of Abingdon.

"Never believe me, bully Mike," said the mercer, "if I am not as glad to see thee as ever I was to see a customer's money!—Why, thou canst give a friend a sly place at a mask or a revel now, Mike; ay, or, I warrant thee, thou canst say in my lord's ear, when my honourable lord is down in these parts, and wants a Spanish ruff or the like—thou canst say in his ear, There is mine old friend, young Laurence Goldthred of Abingdon, has as good wares, lawn, tiffany, cambric, and so forth—ay, and is as pretty a piece of man's flesh, too, as is in Berkshire, and will ruffle it for your lordship with any man of his inches; and thou mayst say——"

"I can say a hundred d—d lies besides, mercer," answered Lambourne; "what, one must not stand upon a good word for a friend!"

"Here is to thee, Mike, with all my heart," said the mercer; "and thou canst tell one the reality of the new fashions too—Here was a rogue pedlar but now, was crying up the old-fashioned Spanish nether-stock over the Gascoigne hose, although thou seest how well the French hose set off the leg and knee, being adorned with parti-coloured garters and garniture in conformity."

"Excellent, excellent," replied Lambourne; "why, thy limber bit of a thigh, thrust through that bunch of slashed buckram and tiffany, shows like a housewife's distaff, when the flax is half spun off!"

"Said I not so?" said the mercer, whose shallow brain was now overflowed in his turn; "where then, where be this rascal pedlar?—there was a pedlar here but now, methinks—Mine host, where the foul fiend is this pedlar?"

"Where wise men should be, Master Goldthred," replied Giles Gosling; "even shut up in his private chamber, telling over the sales of to-day, and preparing for the custom of to-morrow."

"Hang him, a mechanical chuff!" said the mercer; "but for shame, it were a good deed to ease him of his wares,—a set of peddling knaves, who stroll through the land, and hurt the established trader. There are good fellows in Berkshire yet, mine host—your pedlar may be met withal on Maiden Castle."

"Ay," replied mine host, laughing, "and he who meets him may meet his match—the pedlar is a tall man."

"Is he?" said Goldthred.

"Is he?" replied the host; "ay, by cock and pie is he—the very pedlar he who raddled Robin Hood so tightly, as the song says,

> 'Now Robin Hood drew his sword so good,
>   The pedlar drew his brand,
> And he hath raddled him Robin Hood,
>   Till he neither could see nor stand.' "

"Hang him, foul scoyle, let him pass," said the mercer; "if he be such a one, there were small worship to be won upon him.—And now tell me, Mike—my honest Mike, how wears the Hollands you won of me?"

"Why, well, as you may see, Master Goldthred," answered Mike; "I will bestow a pot on thee for the handsel.—Fill the flagon, Master Tapster."

"Thou wilt win no more Hollands, I think, on such wager, friend Mike," said the mercer; "for the sulky swain, Tony Foster, rails at thee all to nought, and swears you shall ne'er darken his doors again, for that your oaths are enough to blow the roof off a Christian man's dwelling."

"Doth he say so, the mincing, hypocritical miser?" vociferated Lambourne;—"Why, then, he shall come down and receive my commands here, this blessed night, under my uncle's roof! And I will ring him such a black sanctus, that he shall think the devil hath him by the skirts for a month to come, for barely hearing me."

"Nay, now the pottle-pot is uppermost, with a witness!" said the mercer. "Tony Foster obey thy whistle!—Alas! good Mike, go sleep—go sleep."

"I tell thee what, thou thin-faced gull," said Michael Lambourne in high chafe, "I will wager thee fifty angels against the first five shelves of thy shop, numbering upward from the false light, with all that is on them, that I make Tony Foster come down to this public house, before we have finished three rounds."

"I will lay no bet to that amount," said the mercer, something sobered by an offer which intimated rather too private a knowledge, on Lambourne's part, of the secret recesses of his shop, "I will lay no such wager," he said; "but I will stake five angels against thy five, if thou wilt, that Tony Foster will not leave his own roof, or come to alehouse after prayer time, for thee, or any man."

"Content," said Lambourne.—"Here, uncle, hold stakes, and let one of your young bleed-barrels there—one of your infant tapsters, trip presently up to the Place, and give this letter to Master Foster, and say that I, his ingle, Michael Lambourne, pray to speak with him at mine uncle's castle here, upon business of grave import.—Away with thee, child, for it is now sun-down, and the wretch goeth to bed with the birds, to save mutton-suet—faugh!"

Shortly after this messenger was dispatched—an interval which was spent in drinking and buffoonery—he returned with the answer that Master Foster was coming presently.

"Won, won!" said Lambourne, darting on the stakes.

"Not till he comes, if you please," said the mercer, interfering.

"Why, 'sblood, he is at the threshold," replied Michael.—"What said he, boy?"

"If it please your worship," answered the messenger, "he looked out of window, with a musquetoon in his hand, and when I delivered your errand, which I did with fear and trembling, he said, with a vinegar aspect, that your worship might be gone to the infernal regions."

"Or to hell, I suppose," said Lambourne—"it is there he disposes of all that are not of the congregation."

"Even so," said the boy; "I used the other phrase as being the more poetical."

"An ingenious youth," said Michael; "shalt have a drop to wet thy poetical whistle—And what said Foster next?"

"He called me back," answered the boy, "and bid me say, you might come to him, if you had aught to say to him."

"And what next?" said Lambourne.

"He read the letter, and seemed in a fluster, and asked if your worship was in drink—and I said you were speaking a little Spanish, as one who had been in the Canaries."

"Out, you diminutive pint-pot, whelped of an overgrown reckoning!" replied Lambourne. "Out!—But what said he then?"

"Why," said the boy, "he muttered, that if he came not, your worship would bolt out what were better kept in; and so he took his old flat cap, and threadbare blue cloak, and, as I said before, he will be here incontinent."

"There is truth in what he said," replied Lambourne, as if speaking to himself—"My brain has played me its old dog's trick—but corragio—let him approach!—I have not rolled about in the world for many a day, to fear Tony Foster, be I drunk or sober.—Bring me a flagon of cold water, to christen my sack withal."

While Lambourne, whom the approach of Foster seemed to have recalled to a sense of his own condition, was busied in preparing to receive him, Giles Gosling stole up to the apartment of the pedlar, whom he found traversing the room in much agitation.

"You withdrew yourself suddenly from the company," said the landlord to the guest.

"It was time, when the devil became one among you," replied the pedlar.

"It is not courteous in you to term my nephew by such a name," said Gosling, "nor is it kindly in me to reply to it; and yet, in some sort, Mike may be considered as a limb of Satan."

"Pooh—I talk not of the swaggering ruffian," replied the pedlar, "it is of the other, who, for aught I know—But when go they? or wherefore come they?"

"Marry, these are questions I cannot answer," replied the host. "But look you, sir, you have brought me a token from worthy Master Tressilian—a pretty stone it is." He took out the ring, and looked at it, adding, as he put it into his purse again, that it was too rich a guerdon for any thing he could do for the worthy donor. He was, he said, in the public line, and it ill became him to be too inquisitive into other folk's concerns; he had already said, that he could hear nothing, but that the lady lived still at Cumnor-Place, in the closest seclusion, and, to such as by chance had a view of her, seemed pensive and discontented with her solitude. "But here," he said, "if you are desirous to gratify your master, is the rarest chance that hath occurred for this many a day. Tony Foster is coming down hither, and it is but letting Mike Lambourne smell another wine-flask, and the Queen's command would not move him from the ale-bench. So they are fast for an hour or so—Now, if you will don your pack, which will be your best excuse, you may, perchance, win the ear of the old servant, being assured of the master's absence, to let you try to get some custom of the lady, and then you may learn more of her condition than I or any other can tell you."

"True—very true," answered Wayland, for he it was; "an excellent device, but methinks something dangerous—for, say Foster should return?"

"Very possible indeed," replied the host.

"Or say," continued Wayland, "the lady should render me cold thanks for my exertions?"

"As is not unlikely," replied Giles Gosling. "I marvel, Master Tres-silian will take such heed of her that cares not for him."

"In either case I were foully sped," said Wayland; "and therefore I do not, on the whole, much relish your device."

"Nay, but take me with you, good master serving-man," replied mine host, "this is your master's business and not mine; you best know the risk to be encountered, or how far you are willing to brave it. But that which you will not yourself hazard, you cannot expect others to risk."

"Hold, hold," said Wayland; "tell me but one thing—Goes yonder old man up to Cumnor?"

"Surely, I think so," said the landlord; "their servant said he was to take their baggage thither, but the ale-tap has been as potent for him as the sack-spigot has been for Michael."

"It is enough," said Wayland, assuming an air of resolution—"I will thwart that old villain's projects—my affright at his baleful aspect begins to abate, and my hatred to arise. Help me on with my pack, good mine host—And look to thyself, old Albumazar—there is a malignant influ-ence in thy horoscope, and it gleams from the constellation Ursa Major."

So saying, he assumed his burden, and, guided by the landlord through the postern-gate of the Black Bear, took the most private way from thence up to Cumnor-Place.

CHAPTER XX

Clown. You have of these pedlars, that have
more in 'em than you'd think, sister.
Winter's Tale, Act IV., Scene 3.

In his anxiety to obey the Earl's repeated charges of secrecy, as well as from his own unsocial and miserly habits, Anthony Foster was more desirous, by his mode of housekeeping, to escape observation, than to resist intrusive curiosity. Thus, instead of a numerous household, to secure his charge, and defend his house, he studied, as much as possible, to elude notice, by diminishing his attendants; so that, unless when there were followers of the Earl, or of Varney, in the mansion, one old male domestic, and two aged crones, who assisted in keeping the Count-ess' apartments in order, were the only servants of the family.

It was one of these old women who opened the door when Wayland knocked, and answered his petition, to be admitted to exhibit his wares to the ladies of the family, with a volley of vituperation, couched in what is there called the *jowring* dialect. The pedlar found the means of check-ing this vociferation, by slipping a silver groat into her hand, and inti-mating the present of some stuff for a coif, if the lady would buy of his wares.

"God ield thee, for mine is aw in littocks—Slocket with thy pack into gharn, mon—Her walks in gharn." Into the garden she ushered the pedlar accordingly, and pointing to an old ruinous garden-house, said, "Yonder be's her, mon,—yonder be's her—Zhe will buy changes an zhe loikes stuffs."

"She has left me to come off as I may," thought Wayland, as he heard the hag shut the garden-door behind him. "But they shall not beat me, and they dare not murder me, for so little trespass, and by this fair twilight. Hang it, I will on—a brave general never thought of his retreat till he was defeated. I see two females in the old garden-house yonder— but how to address them?—Stay—Will Shakspeare, be my friend in need. I will give them a taste of Autolycus." He then sung, with a good voice, and becoming audacity, the popular playhouse ditty,—

> "Lawn as white as driven snow,
> Cyprus black as e'er was crow,
> Gloves as sweet as damask roses,
> Masks for faces and for noses."

"What hath fortune sent us here for an unwonted sight, Janet?" said the lady.

"One of those merchants of vanity, called pedlars," answered Janet, demurely, "who utters his light wares in lighter measures—I marvel old Dorcas let him pass."

"It is a lucky chance, girl," said the Countess; "we lead a heavy life here, and this may while off a weary hour."

"Ay, my gracious lady," said Janet; "but my father?"

"He is not *my* father, Janet, nor I hope my master," answered the lady—"I say, call the man hither—I want some things."

"Nay," replied Janet, "your ladyship has but to say so in the next packet, and if England can furnish them they will be sent.—There will come mischief on't—Pray, dearest lady, let me bid the man begone!"

"I will have thee bid him come hither," said the Countess;—"or stay, thou terrified fool, I will bid him myself, and spare thee a chiding."

"Ah, well-a-day, dearest lady, if that were the worst," said Janet, sadly, while the lady called to the pedlar, "Good fellow, step forward— undo thy pack—if thou hast good wares, chance has sent thee hither for my convenience, and thy profit."

"What may your ladyship please to lack?" said Wayland, unstrapping his pack, and displaying its contents with as much dexterity as if he had been bred to the trade. Indeed he had occasionally pursued it in the course of his roving life, and now commended his wares with all the volubility of a trader, and showed some skill in the main art of placing prices upon them.

"What do I please to lack?" said the lady, "why, considering I have not for six long months bought one yard of lawn or cambric, or one trinket, the most inconsiderable, for my own use, and at my own choice, the better question is, what hast thou got to sell? Lay aside for me that cambric partlet and pair of sleeves—and those roundells of gold fringe, drawn out with cyprus—and that short cloak of cherry-coloured fine cloth, garnished with gold buttons and loops.—Is it not of an absolute fancy, Janet?"

"Nay, my lady," replied Janet, "if you consult my poor judgment, it is, methinks, over gaudy for a graceful habit."

"Now, out upon thy judgment, if it be no brighter, wench," said the Countess; "thou shalt wear it thyself for penance sake; and I promise thee the gold buttons, being somewhat massive, will comfort thy father, and reconcile him to the cherry-coloured body. See that he snap them not away, Janet, and send them to bear company with the imprisoned angels, which he keeps captive in his strong-box."

"May I pray your ladyship to spare my poor father!" said Janet.

"Nay, but why should any one spare him that is so sparing of his own nature?" replied the lady.—"Well, but to our gear—That head garniture for myself, and that silver bodkin, mounted with pearl;—and take off two gowns of that russet cloth for Dorcas and Alison, Janet, to keep the old wretches warm against winter comes—And stay, hast thou no perfumes and sweet bags, or any handsome casting bottles of the newest mode?"

"Were I a pedlar in earnest, I were a made merchant," thought Wayland, as he busied himself to answer the demands which she thronged one on another, with the eagerness of a young lady who has been long secluded from such a pleasing occupation. "But how to bring her to a moment's serious reflection?" Then as he exhibited his choicest collection of essences and perfumes, he at once arrested her attention by observing, that these articles had almost risen to double value, since the magnificent preparations made by the Earl of Leicester to entertain the Queen and court at his princely Castle of Kenilworth.

"Ha!" said the Countess, hastily; "that rumour then is true, Janet."

"Surely, madam," answered Wayland; "and I marvel it hath not reached your noble ladyship's ears. The Queen of England feasts with the noble Earl for a week during the Summer's Progress; and there are many who will tell you England will have a king, and England's Elizabeth—God save her!—a husband, ere the Progress be over."

"They lie like villains!" said the Countess, bursting forth impatiently.

"For God's sake, madam, consider," said Janet, trembling with apprehension; "who would cumber themselves about pedlar's tidings?"

"Yes, Janet!" exclaimed the Countess; "right, thou hast corrected me justly. Such reports, blighting the reputation of England's brightest and noblest peer, can only find currency amongst the mean, the abject, and the infamous!"

"May I perish, lady," said Wayland Smith, observing that her violence directed itself towards him, "if I have done any thing to merit this strange passion!—I have said but what many men say."

By this time the Countess had recovered her composure, and endeavoured, alarmed by the anxious hints of Janet, to suppress all appearance of displeasure. "I were loath," she said, "good fellow, that our Queen should change the virgin style, so dear to us her people—think not of it." And, then, as if desirous to change the subject, she added, "And what is this paste, so carefully put up in the silver box?" as she examined the contents of a casket in which drugs and perfumes were contained in separate drawers.

"It is a remedy, madam, for a disorder of which I trust your ladyship will never have reason to complain. The amount of a small turkey-bean, swallowed daily for a week, fortifies the heart against those black vapours which arise from solitude, melancholy, unrequited affection, disappointed hope——"

"Are you a fool, friend?" said the Countess, sharply; "or do you think, because I have good-naturedly purchased your trumpery goods at your roguish prices, that you may put any gullery you will on me?—who ever heard that affections of the heart were cured by medicines given to the body?"

"Under your honourable favour," said Wayland, "I am an honest man, and I have sold my goods at an honest price—As to this most precious medicine, when I told its qualities, I asked you not to purchase it, so why should I lie to you? I say not it will cure a rooted affection of the mind, which only God and time can do; but I say, that this restorative relieves the black vapours which are engendered in the body of that melancholy which broodeth on the mind. I have relieved many with it, both in court and city, and of late one Master Edmund Tressilian, a worshipful gentleman in Cornwall, who, on some slight, received, it was told me, where he had set his affections, was brought into that state of melancholy which made his friends alarmed for his life."

He paused, and the lady remained silent for some time, and then asked, with a voice which she strove in vain to render firm and indifferent in its tone, "Is the gentleman you have mentioned perfectly recovered?"

"Passably, madam," answered Wayland; "he hath at least no bodily complaint."

"I will take some of the medicine, Janet," said the Countess. "I too have sometimes that dark melancholy which overclouds the brain."

"You shall not do so, madam," said Janet; "who shall answer that this fellow vends what is wholesome?"

"I will myself warrant my good faith," said Wayland; and, taking a part of the medicine, he swallowed it before them. The Countess now bought what remained, a step to which Janet, by farther objections, only determined her the more obstinately. She even took the first dose upon the instant, and professed to feel her heart lightened and her spirits augmented,—a consequence which, in all probability, existed only in her own imagination. The lady then piled the purchases she had made together, flung her purse to Janet, and desired her to compute the amount, and to pay the pedlar; while she herself, as if tired of the amusement she at first found in conversing with him, wished him good evening, and walked carelessly into the house, thus depriving Wayland of every opportunity to speak with her in private. He hastened, however, to attempt an explanation with Janet.

"Maiden," he said, "thou hast the face of one who should love her mistress. She hath much need of faithful service."

"And well deserves it at my hands," replied Janet; "but what of that?"

"Maiden, I am not altogether what I seem," said the pedlar, lowering his voice.

"The less like to be an honest man," said Janet.

"The more so," answered Wayland, "since I am no pedlar."

"Get thee gone then instantly, or I will call for assistance," said Janet; "my father must ere this be returned."

"Do not be so rash," said Wayland; "you will do what you may repent of. I am one of your mistress's friends; and she had need of more, not that thou shouldst ruin those she hath."

"How shall I know that?" said Janet.

"Look me in the face," said Wayland Smith, "and see if thou dost not read honesty in my looks."

And in truth, though by no means handsome, there was in his physiognomy the sharp, keen expression of inventive genius and prompt intellect, which, joined to quick and brilliant eyes, a well-formed mouth, and an intelligent smile, often gives grace and interest to features which are both homely and irregular. Janet looked at him with the sly simplicity of her sect, and replied, "Notwithstanding thy boasted honesty, friend, and although I am not accustomed to read and pass judgment on such volumes as thou hast submitted to my perusal, I think I see in thy countenance something of the pedlar—something of the picaroon."

"On a small scale, perhaps," said Wayland Smith, laughing. "But this evening, or to-morrow, will an old man come hither with thy father, who has the stealthy step of the cat, the shrewd and vindictive eye of the rat, the fawning wile of the spaniel, the determined snatch of the mastiff—of him beware, for your own sake and that of your mistress. See you, fair Janet, he brings the venom of the aspic under the assumed innocence of the dove. What precise mischief he meditates towards you I cannot guess, but death and disease have ever dogged his footsteps.—Say nought of this to thy mistress—my art suggests to me that in her state, the fear of evil may be as dangerous as its operation—But see that she takes my specific, for"—(he lowered his voice, and spoke low but impressively in her ear)—"it is an antidote against poison—Hark, they enter the garden!"

In effect, a sound of noisy mirth and loud talking approached the garden door, alarmed by which Wayland Smith sprung into the midst of a thicket of overgrown shrubs, while Janet withdrew to the garden-house that she might not incur observation, and that she might at the same time conceal, at least for the present, the purchases made from the supposed pedlar, which lay scattered on the floor of the summer-house.

Janet, however, had no occasion for anxiety. Her father, his old attendant, Lord Leicester's domestic, and the astrologer, entered the garden in tumult and in extreme perplexity, endeavouring to quiet Lambourne, whose brain had now become completely fired with liquor, and who was one of those unfortunate persons, who, being once stirred with the vinous stimulus, do not fall asleep like other drunkards, but remain partially influenced by it for many hours, until at length, by successive draughts, they are elevated into a state of uncontrollable frenzy. Like many men in this state also, Lambourne neither lost the power of motion, speech, or expression; but, on the contrary, spoke with unwonted emphasis and readiness, and told all that at another time he would have been most desirous to keep secret.

"What!" ejaculated Michael, at the full extent of his voice, "am I to have no welcome,—no carouse, when I have brought fortune to your old ruinous dog-house in the shape of a devil's ally, that can change slate-shivers into Spanish dollars?—Here, you Tony Fire-the-Fagot, papist, puritan, hypocrite, miser, profligate, devil, compounded of all men's sins, bow down and reverence him who has brought into thy house the very mammon thou worshippest!"

"For God's sake," said Foster, "speak low—come into the house—thou shalt have wine, or whatever thou wilt."

"No, old puckfoist, I will have it here," thundered the inebriated ruffian—"here, *al fresco,* as the Italian hath it.—No, no, I will not drink with that poisoning devil within doors, to be choked with the fumes of arsenic and quicksilver; I learned from villain Varney to beware of that."

"Fetch him wine, in the name of all the fiends!" said the alchemist.

"Aha! and thou wouldst spice it for me, old Truepenny, wouldst thou not? Ay, I should have copperas, and hellebore, and vitriol, and aquafortis, and twenty devilish materials, bubbling in my brain-pan, like a charm to raise the devil in a witch's cauldron. Hand me the flask thyself, old Tony Fire-the-Fagot—and let it be cool—I will have no wine mulled at the pile of the old burnt bishops—Or stay, let Leicester be king if he will—good—and Varney, villain Varney, grand vizier—why, excellent!—and what shall I be, then?—why, emperor—Emperor Lambourne!—I will see this choice piece of beauty that they have walled up here for their private pleasures—I will have her this very night to serve my wine-cup, and put on my nightcap. What should a fellow do with two wives, were he twenty times an Earl?—answer me that, Tony boy, you old reprobate hypocritical dog, whom God struck out of the book of life, but tormented with the constant wish to be restored to it—You old bishop-burning, blasphemous fanatic, answer me that?"

"I will stick my knife to the haft in him," said Foster, in a low tone, which trembled with passion.

"For the love of Heaven, no violence!" said the astrologer. "It cannot but be looked closely into.—Here, honest Lambourne, wilt thou pledge me to the health of the noble Earl of Leicester and Master Richard Varney?"

"I will, mine own Albumazar—I will, my trusty vendor of ratsbane— I would kiss thee, mine honest infractor of the Lex Julia (as they said at Leyden,) didst thou not flavour so damnably of sulphur, and such fiendish apothecary's stuff.—Here goes it, up seyes—to Varney and Leicester!—two more noble mounting spirits—and more dark-seeking, deep-diving, high-flying, malicious, ambitious miscreants—well, I say no more, but I will whet my dagger on his heart-spone, that refuses to pledge me! And so, my masters——"

Thus speaking, Lambourne exhausted the cup which the astrologer had handed to him, and which contained not wine, but distilled spirits. He swore half an oath, dropped the empty cup from his grasp, laid his hand on his sword without being able to draw it, reeled, and fell without sense or motion into the arms of the domestic, who dragged him off to his chamber and put him to bed.

In the general confusion, Janet regained her lady's chamber unobserved, trembling like an aspen leaf, but determined to keep secret from the Countess the dreadful surmises which she could not help entertaining from the drunken ravings of Lambourne. Her fears, however, though they assumed no certain shape, kept pace with the advice of the pedlar; and she confirmed her mistress in her purpose of taking the medicine which he had recommended, from which it is probable she would otherwise have dissuaded her. Neither had these intimations escaped the ears of Wayland, who knew much better how to interpret them. He felt much compassion at beholding so lovely a creature as the Countess, and whom he had first seen in the bosom of domestic happiness, exposed to the machinations of such a gang of villains. His indignation, too, had been highly excited, by hearing the voice of his old master, against whom he felt, in equal degree, the passions of hatred and fear. He nourished also a pride in his own art and resources; and, dangerous as the task was, he that night formed a determination to attain the bottom of the mystery, and to aid the distressed lady, if it were yet possible. From some words which Lambourne had dropped among his ravings, Wayland now, for the first time, felt inclined to doubt that Varney had acted entirely on his own account in wooing and winning the affections of this beautiful creature. Fame asserted of this zealous retainer, that he had accommodated his lord in former love intrigues; and it occurred to Wayland Smith, that Leicester himself might be the party chiefly interested. Her marriage with the Earl he could not suspect; but even the discovery of such a passing intrigue with a lady of Mistress Amy Robsart's rank, was a secret of the deepest importance to the stability of the favourite's power over Elizabeth. "If Leicester himself should hesitate to stifle such a rumour by very strange means," said he to himself, "he has those about him who would do him that favour without waiting for his consent. If I would meddle in this business, it must be in such guise as my old master uses when he compounds his manna of Satan, and that is with a close mask on my face. So I will quit Giles Gosling to-morrow, and change my course and place of residence as often as a hunted fox. I should like to see this little puritan, too, once more. She looks both pretty and intelligent, to have come of such a caitiff as Anthony Fire-the-Fagot."

Giles Gosling received the adieus of Wayland rather joyfully than otherwise. The honest publican saw so much peril in crossing the course of the Earl of Leicester's favourite, that his virtue was scarce able to support him in the task, and he was well pleased when it was likely to be removed from his shoulders; still, however, professing his good-will, and readiness, in case of need, to do Master Tressilian or his emissary any service, in so far as consisted with his character of a publican.

CHAPTER XXI

Vaulting ambition, that o'erleaps itself,
And falls on t'other side.
Macbeth.

THE splendour of the approaching revels at Kenilworth was now the conversation through all England; and every thing was collected at home or from abroad which could add to the gaiety or glory of the prepared reception of Elizabeth, at the house of her most distinguished favourite. Meantime, Leicester appeared daily to advance in the Queen's favour. He was perpetually by her side in council, willingly listened to in the moments of courtly recreation—favoured with approaches even to familiar intimacy—looked up to by all who had aught to hope at court—courted by foreign ministers with the most flattering testimonies of respect from their sovereigns—the *Alter Ego*, as it seemed, of the stately Elizabeth, who was now very generally supposed to be studying the time and opportunity for associating him, by marriage, into her sovereign power.

Amid such a tide of prosperity, this minion of fortune, and of the Queen's favour, was probably the most unhappy man in the realm which seemed at his devotion. He had the Fairy King's superiority over his friends and dependents, and saw much which they could not. The character of his mistress was intimately known to him; it was his minute and studied acquaintance with her humours, as well as her noble faculties, which, joined to his powerful mental qualities, and his eminent external accomplishments, had raised him so high in her favour; and it was that very knowledge of her disposition which led him to apprehend at every turn some sudden and overwhelming disgrace. Leicester was like a pilot possessed of a chart, which points out to him all the peculiarities of his navigation, but which exhibits so many shoals, breakers, and reefs of rocks, that his anxious eye reaps little more from observing them, than to be convinced that his final escape can be little else than miraculous.

In fact, Queen Elizabeth had a character strangely compounded of the strongest masculine sense, with those foibles which are chiefly supposed proper to the female sex. Her subjects had the full benefit of her virtues, which far predominated over her weaknesses; but her courtiers, and those about her person, had often to sustain sudden and embarrassing turns of caprice, and the sallies of a temper which was both jealous and despotic. She was the nursing-mother of her people, but she was also the true daughter of Henry VIII.; and though early sufferings and an excellent education had repressed and modified, they had not altogether destroyed, the hereditary temper of the "hard-ruled King."—"Her mind," said her witty god-son, Sir John Harrington, who had experienced both the smiles and the frowns which he describes, "was ofttime like the gentle air, that cometh from the western point in a summer's morn— 'twas sweet and refreshing to all around her. Her speech did win all affections. And again, she could put forth such alterations, when obedience was lacking, as left no doubting *whose* daughter she was. When she smiled, it was a pure sunshine, that every one did choose to bask in, if they could; but anon came a storm, from a sudden gathering of clouds, and the thunder fell, in a wondrous manner, on all alike." [1]

This variability of disposition, as Leicester well knew, was chiefly formidable to those who had a share in the Queen's affections, and who depended rather on her personal regard, than on the indispensable services which they could render to her councils and her crown. The favour of Burleigh, or of Walsingham, of a description far less striking than that by which he was himself upheld, was founded, as Leicester was well aware, on Elizabeth's solid judgment, not on her partiality; and was, therefore, free from all those principles of change and decay, necessarily incident to that which chiefly arose from personal accomplishments and female predilection. These great and sage statesmen were judged of by the Queen, only with reference to the measures they suggested, and the reasons by which they supported their opinions in council; whereas the success of Leicester's course depended on all those light and changeable gales of caprice and humour, which thwart or favour the progress of a lover in the favour of his mistress, and she, too, a mistress who was ever and anon becoming fearful lest she should forget the dignity, or compromise the authority, of the Queen, while she indulged the affections of the woman. Of the difficulties which surrounded his power, "too great to keep or to resign," Leicester was fully sensible;

[1] Nugæ Antiquæ, vol. i. pp. 355, 356-362.

and, as he looked anxiously round for the means of maintaining himself in his precarious situation, and sometimes contemplated those of descending from it in safety, he saw but little hope of either. At such moments, his thoughts turned to dwell upon his secret marriage, and its consequences; and it was in bitterness against himself, if not against his unfortunate Countess, that he ascribed to that hasty measure, adopted in the ardour of what he now called inconsiderate passion, at once the impossibility of placing his power on a solid basis, and the immediate prospect of its precipitate downfall.

"Men say," thus ran his thoughts, in these anxious and repentant moments, "that I might marry Elizabeth, and become King of England. All things suggest this. The match is carolled in ballads, while the rabble throw their caps up—It has been touched upon in the schools—whispered in the presence-chamber—recommended from the pulpit—prayed for in the Calvinistic churches abroad—touched on by statists in the very council at home—These bold insinuations have been rebutted by no rebuke, no resentment, no chiding, scarce even by the usual female protestations that she would live and die a virgin princess.—Her words have been more courteous than ever, though she knows such rumours are abroad—her actions more gracious—her looks more kind—nought seems wanting to make me King of England, and place me beyond the storms of court-favour, excepting the putting forth of mine own hand to take that crown imperial, which is the glory of the universe! And when I might stretch that hand out most boldly, it is fettered down by a secret and inextricable bond!—And here I have letters from Amy," he would say, catching them up with a movement of peevishness, "persecuting me to acknowledge her openly—to do justice to her and to myself—and I wot not what. Methinks I have done less than justice to myself already. And she speaks as if Elizabeth were to receive the knowledge of this matter with the glee of a mother hearing of the happy marriage of a hopeful son!—She, the daughter of Henry, who spared neither man in his anger, nor woman in his desire,—she to find herself tricked, drawn on with toys of passion to the verge of acknowledging her love to a subject, and he discovered to be a married man!—Elizabeth to learn that she had been dallied with in such fashion, as a gay courtier might trifle with a country wench—We should then see to our ruin *furens quid fœmina!*"

He would then pause, and call for Varney, whose advice was now more frequently resorted to than ever, because the Earl remembered the remonstrances which he had made against his secret contract. And their consultation usually terminated in anxious deliberation, how, or in what manner, the Countess was to be produced at Kenilworth. These communings had for some time ever ended in a resolution to delay the Progress from day to day. But at length a peremptory decision became necessary.

"Elizabeth will not be satisfied without her presence," said the Earl;

"whether any suspicion hath entered her mind, as my own apprehensions suggest, or whether the petition of Tressilian is kept in her memory by Sussex, or some other secret enemy, I know not; but amongst all the favourable expressions which she uses to me, she often recurs to the story of Amy Robsart. I think that Amy is the slave in the chariot, who is placed there by my evil fortune to dash and to confound my triumph, even when at the highest. Show me thy device, Varney, for solving the inextricable difficulty. I have thrown every such impediment in the way of these accursed revels as I could propound even with a shade of decency, but to-day's interview has put all to a hazard. She said to me kindly, but peremptorily, 'We will give you no farther time for preparations, my lord, lest you should altogether ruin yourself. On Saturday, the 9th of July, we will be with you at Kenilworth—We pray you to forget none of our appointed guests and suitors, and in especial this light-o'-love, Amy Robsart. We would wish to see the woman who could postpone yonder poetical gentleman, Master Tressilian, to your man, Richard Varney.'—Now, Varney, ply thine invention, whose forge hath availed us so often; for, sure as my name is Dudley, the danger menaced by my horoscope is now darkening around me."

"Can my lady be by no means persuaded to bear for a brief space the obscure character which circumstances impose on her?" said Varney, after some hesitation.

"How, sirrah! my Countess term herself *thy* wife!—that may neither stand with my honour nor with hers."

"Alas, my lord," answered Varney, "and yet such is the quality in which Elizabeth now holds her; and to contradict this opinion is to discover all."

"Think of something else, Varney," said the Earl, in great agitation; "this invention is naught—If I could give way to it, she would not; for I tell thee, Varney, if thou know'st it not, that not Elizabeth on the throne has more pride than the daughter of this obscure gentleman of Devon. She is flexible in many things, but where she holds her honour brought in question, she hath a spirit and temper as apprehensive as lightning, and as swift in execution."

"We have experienced that, my lord, else had we not been thus circumstanced," said Varney. "But what else to suggest I know not—Methinks she whose good fortune in becoming your lordship's bride gives rise to the danger, should do somewhat towards parrying it."

"It is impossible," said the Earl, waving his hand; "I know neither authority nor entreaties would make her endure thy name for an hour."

"It is somewhat hard, though," said Varney, in a dry tone; and, without pausing on that topic, he added, "Suppose some one were found to represent her? Such feats have been performed in the courts of as sharp-eyed monarchs as Queen Elizabeth."

"Utter madness, Varney," answered the Earl; "the counterfeit would be confronted with Tressilian, and discovery become inevitable."

"Tressilian might be removed from court," said the unhesitating Varney.

"And by what means?"

"There are many," said Varney, "by which a statesman in your situation, my lord, may remove from the scene one who pries into your affairs, and places himself in perilous opposition to you."

"Speak not to me of such policy, Varney," said the Earl, hastily; "which, besides, would avail nothing in the present case. Many others there be at court, to whom Amy may be known; and besides, on the absence of Tressilian, her father or some of her friends may be instantly summoned hither. Urge thine invention once more."

"My lord, I know not what to say," answered Varney; "but were I myself in such perplexity, I would ride post down to Cumnor-Place, and compel my wife to give her consent to such measures as her safety and mine required."

"Varney," said Leicester, "I cannot urge her to aught so repugnant to her noble nature, as a share in this stratagem—it would be a base requital for the love she bears me."

"Well, my lord," said Varney, "your lordship is a wise and honourable man, and skilled in those high points of romantic scruple, which are current in Arcadia, perhaps, as your nephew, Philip Sidney, writes. I am your humble servitor—a man of this world, and only happy that my knowledge of it, and its ways, is such as your lordship has not scorned to avail yourself of. Now I would fain know, whether the obligation lies on my lady or on you, in this fortunate union; and which has most reason to show complaisance to the other, and to consider that other's wishes, conveniences, and safety?"

"I tell thee, Varney," said the Earl, "that all it was in my power to bestow upon her, was not merely deserved, but a thousand times over-paid, by her own virtue and beauty; for never did greatness descend upon a creature so formed by nature to grace and adorn it."

"It is well, my lord, you are so satisfied," answered Varney, with his usual sardonic smile, which even respect to his patron could not at all times subdue—"you will have time enough to enjoy undisturbed the society of one so gracious and beautiful—that is, so soon as such confinement in the Tower be over, as may correspond to the crime of deceiving the affections of Elizabeth Tudor—A cheaper penalty, I presume, you do not expect."

"Malicious fiend!" answered Leicester, "do you mock me in my misfortune?—Manage it as thou wilt."

"If you are serious, my lord," said Varney, "you must set forth instantly, and post for Cumnor-Place."

"Do thou go thyself, Varney; the devil has given thee that sort of eloquence, which is most powerful in the worst cause. I should stand self-convicted of villainy, were I to urge such a deceit.—Begone, I tell thee—Must I entreat thee to mine own dishonour?"

"No, my lord," said Varney—"but if you are serious in intrusting me with the task of urging this most necessary measure, you must give me a letter to my lady, as my credentials, and trust to me for backing the advice it contains with all the force in my power. And such is my opinion of my lady's love for your lordship, and of her willingness to do that which is at once to contribute to your pleasure and your safety, that I am sure she will condescend to bear, for a few brief days, the name of so humble a man as myself, especially since it is not inferior in antiquity to that of her own paternal house."

Leicester seized on writing materials, and twice or thrice commenced a letter to the Countess, which he afterwards tore into fragments. At length he finished a few distracted lines, in which he conjured her, for reasons nearly concerning his life and honour, to consent to bear the name of Varney for a few days, during the revels at Kenilworth. He added, that Varney would communicate all the reasons which rendered this deception indispensable; and having signed and sealed these credentials, he flung them over the table to Varney, with a motion that he should depart, which his adviser was not slow to comprehend and to obey.

Leicester remained like one stupefied, till he heard the trampling of the horses, as Varney, who took no time even to change his dress, threw himself into the saddle, and, followed by a single servant, set off for Berkshire. At the sound, the Earl started from his seat, and ran to the window, with the momentary purpose of recalling the unworthy commission with which he had intrusted one, of whom he used to say, he knew no virtuous property save affection to his patron. But Varney was already beyond call—and the bright starry firmament, which the age considered as the Book of Fate, lying spread before Leicester when he opened the casement, diverted him from his better and more manly purpose.

"There they roll, on their silent, but potential course," said the Earl, looking around him, "without a voice which speaks to our ear, but not without influences which affect, at every change, the indwellers of this vile earthly planet. This, if astrologers fable not, is the very crisis of my fate! The hour approaches, of which I was taught to beware—the hour, too, which I was encouraged to hope for.—A King was the word—but how?—the crown matrimonial—all hopes of that are gone—let them go. The rich Netherlands have demanded me for their leader, and, would Elizabeth consent, would yield to me *their* crown.—And have I not such a claim, even in this kingdom? That of York, descending from George of Clarence to the House of Huntingdon, which, this lady failing, may have a fair chance—Huntingdon is of my house.—But I will plunge no deeper in these high mysteries. Let me hold my course in silence for a while, and in obscurity, like a subterranean river—the time shall come that I will burst forth in my strength, and bear all opposition before me."

While Leicester was thus stupefying the remonstrances of his own conscience, by appealing to political necessity for his apology, or losing himself amidst the wild dreams of ambition, his agent left town and tower behind him, on his hasty journey to Berkshire. *He* also nourished high hope. He had brought Lord Leicester to the point which he had desired, of committing to him the most intimate recesses of his breast, and of using him as the channel of his most confidential intercourse with his lady. Henceforward it would, he foresaw, be difficult for his patron either to dispense with his services, or refuse his requests, however unreasonable. And if this disdainful dame, as he termed the Countess, should comply with the request of her husband, Varney, her pretended husband, must needs become so situated with respect to her, that there was no knowing where his audacity might be bounded, perhaps not till circumstances enabled him to obtain a triumph, which he thought of with a mixture of fiendish feelings, in which revenge for her previous scorn was foremost and predominant. Again he contemplated the possibility of her being totally intractable, and refusing obstinately to play the part assigned to her in the drama at Kenilworth.

"Alasco must then do his part," he said—"Sickness must serve her Majesty as an excuse for not receiving the homage of Mrs Varney— ay, and a sore and wasting sickness it may prove, should Elizabeth continue to cast so favourable an eye on my lord of Leicester. I will not forego the chance of being favourite of a monarch for want of determined measures, should these be necessary.—Forward, good horse, forward—ambition, and haughty hope of power, pleasure, and revenge, strike their stings as deep through my bosom as I plunge the rowels in thy flanks—On, good horse, on—the devil urges us both forward."

CHAPTER XXII

Say that my beauty was but small,
　Among court ladies all despised,
Why didst thou rend it from that hall,
　Where, scornful Earl, 'twas dearly prized?

No more thou com'st with wonted speed,
　Thy once beloved bride to see;
But be she alive, or be she dead,
　I fear, stern Earl, 's the same to thee.
　　　　Cumnor-Hall, by WILLIAM JULIUS MICKLE.

THE ladies of fashion of the present, or of any other period, must have allowed, that the young and lovely Countess of Leicester had, besides her youth and beauty, two qualities which entitled her to a place amongst women of rank and distinction. She displayed, as we have seen in her interview with the pedlar, a liberal promptitude to make unnecessary purchases, solely for the pleasure of acquiring useless and showy trifles which ceased to please as soon as they were possessed; and she was, besides, apt to spend a considerable space of time every day in adorning her person, although the varied splendour of her attire could only attract the half satirical praise of the precise Janet, or an approving glance from the bright eyes which witnessed their own beams of triumph reflected from the mirror.

The Countess Amy had, indeed, to plead for indulgence in those frivolous tastes, that the education of the times had done little or nothing for a mind naturally gay and averse to study. If she had not loved to collect finery and to wear it, she might have woven tapestry or sewed embroidery, till her labours spread in gay profusion all over the walls and seats at Lidcote Hall; or she might have varied Minerva's labours with the task of preparing a mighty pudding against the time that Sir Hugh Robsart returned from the greenwood. But Amy had no natural genius either for the loom, the needle, or the receipt-book. Her mother had died in infancy; her father contradicted her in nothing; and Tressilian, the only one that approached her, who was able or desirous to attend to the cultivation of her mind, had much hurt his interest with her, by assuming too eagerly the task of a preceptor; so that he was regarded by the lively, indulged, and idle girl with some fear and much respect; but with little or nothing of that softer emotion which it had been his hope and his ambition to inspire. And thus her heart lay readily open, and her fancy became easily captivated by the noble exterior and graceful deportment, and complacent flattery of Leicester, even before he was known to her as the dazzling minion of wealth and power.

The frequent visits of Leicester at Cumnor, during the earlier part of their union, had reconciled the Countess to the solitude and privacy to which she was condemned; but when these visits became rarer and more rare, and when the void was filled up with letters of excuse, not always very warmly expressed, and generally extremely brief, discontent and suspicion began to haunt those splendid apartments which love had fitted up for beauty. Her answers to Leicester conveyed these feelings too bluntly, and pressed more naturally than prudently that she might be relieved from this obscure and secluded residence, by the Earl's acknowledgment of their marriage; and in arranging her arguments, with all the skill she was mistress of, she trusted chiefly to the warmth of the entreaties with which she urged them. Sometimes she even ventured to mingle reproaches, of which Leicester conceived he had good reason to complain.

"I have made her Countess," he said to Varney; "surely she might wait till it consisted with my pleasure that she should put on the coronet?"

The Countess Amy viewed the subject in directly an opposite light.

"What signifies," she said, "that I have rank and honour in reality, if I am to live an obscure prisoner, without either society or observance, and suffering in my character, as one of dubious or disgraced reputation? I care not for all those strings of pearl, which you fret me by warping into my tresses, Janet. I tell you, that at Lidcote Hall, if I put but a fresh rosebud among my hair, my good father would call me to him, that he might see it more closely; and the kind old curate would smile, and Master Mumblazen would say something about roses gules; and now I sit here, decked out like an image with gold and gems, and no one to see my finery but you, Janet. There was the poor Tressilian, too—but it avails not speaking of him."

"It doth not indeed, madam," said her prudent attendant; "and verily you make me sometimes wish you would not speak of him so often, or so rashly."

"It signifies nothing to warn me, Janet," said the impatient and incorrigible Countess; "I was born free, though I am now mewed up like some fine foreign slave, rather than the wife of an English noble. I bore it all with pleasure while I was sure he loved me; but, now, my tongue and heart shall be free, let them fetter these limbs as they will—I tell thee, Janet, I love my husband—I will love him till my latest breath—I cannot cease to love him, even if I would, or if he—which, God knows, may chance,—should cease to love me. But I will say, and loudly, I would have been happier than I now am, to have remained in Lidcote Hall; even although I must have married poor Tressilian, with his melancholy look, and his head full of learning, which I cared not for. He said, if I would read his favourite volumes, there would come a time that I should be glad of having done so—I think it is come now."

"I bought you some books, madam," said Janet, "from a lame fellow who sold them in the Market-place—and who stared something boldly at me, I promise you."

"Let me see them, Janet," said the Countess; "but let them not be of your own precise cast.—How is this, most righteous damsel?—'A Pair of Snuffers for the Golden Candlestick'—'A Handful of Myrrh and Hyssop to put a Sick Soul to Purgation'—'A Draught of Water from the Valley of Baca'—'Foxes and Firebrands'—What gear call you this, maiden?"

"Nay, madam," said Janet, "it was but fitting and seemly to put grace in your ladyship's way; but an you will none of it, there are play-books, and poet-books, I trow."

The Countess proceeded carelessly in her examination, turning over such rare volumes as would now make the fortune of twenty retail booksellers. Here was a "Boke of Cookery, imprinted by Richard Lant," and "Skelton's Books"—"The Passtime of the People"—"The Castle of Knowledge," &c. But neither to this lore did the Countess's heart incline, and joyfully did she start up from the listless task of turning over the leaves of the pamphlets, and hastily did she scatter them through the floor, when the rapid clatter of horses' feet, heard in the court-yard, called her to the window, exclaiming, "It is Leicester!—it is my noble Earl!—it is my Dudley!—Every stroke of his horse's hoof sounds like a note of lordly music!"

There was a brief bustle in the mansion, and Foster, with his downward look and sullen manner, entered the apartment to say, "That Master Richard Varney was arrived from my lord, having ridden all night, and craved to speak with her ladyship instantly."

"Varney?" said the disappointed Countess; "and to speak with me?—pshaw!—But he comes with news from Leicester—so admit him instantly."

Varney entered her dressing-apartment, where she sat arrayed in her native loveliness, adorned with all that Janet's art, and a rich and tasteful undress, could bestow. But the most beautiful part of her attire was her profuse and luxuriant light-brown locks, which floated in such a rich abundance around a neck that resembled a swan's, and over a bosom heaving with anxious expectation, which communicated a hurried tinge of red to her whole countenance.

Varney entered the room in the dress in which he had waited on his master that morning to court, the splendour of which made a strange contrast with the disorder arising from hasty riding during a dark night and foul ways. His brow bore an anxious and hurried expression, as one who has that to say of which he doubts the reception, and who hath yet posted on from the necessity of communicating his tidings. The Countess's anxious eye at once caught the alarm, as she exclaimed, "You bring news from my lord, Master Varney—Gracious Heaven! is he ill?"

"No, madam, thank Heaven!" said Varney. "Compose yourself, and permit me to take breath ere I communicate my tidings."

"No breath, sir," replied the lady, impatiently; "I know your theatrical arts. Since your breath hath sufficed to bring you hither, it may suffice to tell your tale, at least briefly, and in the gross."

"Madam," answered Varney, "we are not alone, and my lord's message was for your ear only."

"Leave us, Janet, and Master Foster," said the lady; "but remain in the next apartment, and within call."

Foster and his daughter retired, agreeably to the Lady Leicester's commands, into the next apartment, which was the withdrawing-room. The door which led from the sleeping-chamber was then carefully shut and bolted, and the father and daughter remained both in a posture of anxious attention, the first with a stern, suspicious, lowering cast of countenance, and Janet with folded hands, and looks which seemed divided betwixt her desire to know the fortunes of her mistress, and her prayers to Heaven for her safety. Anthony Foster seemed himself to have some idea of what was passing through his daughter's mind, for he crossed the apartment and took her anxiously by the hand, saying, "That is right—pray, Janet, pray,—we have all need of prayers, and some of us more than others. Pray, Janet,—I would pray myself, but I must listen to what goes on within—evil has been brewing, love—evil has been brewing. God forgive our sins; but Varney's sudden and strange arrival bodes us no good."

Janet had never before heard her father excite or even permit her attention to any thing which passed in their mysterious family, and now that he did so, his voice sounded in her ear—she knew not why— like that of a screech-owl denouncing some deed of terror and of woe. She turned her eyes fearfully towards the door, almost as if she expected some sounds of horror to be heard, or some sight of fear to display itself.

All, however, was as still as death, and the voices of those who spoke in the inner chamber were, if they spoke at all, carefully subdued to a tone which could not be heard in the next. At once, however, they were heard to speak, fast, thick, and hastily; and presently after the voice of the Countess was heard exclaiming, at the highest pitch to which indignation could raise it, "Undo the door, sir, I command you!—Undo the door!—I will have no other reply!" she continued, drowning with her vehement accents the low and muttered sounds which Varney was heard to utter betwixt whiles. "What ho! without there!" she persisted, accompanying her words with shrieks, "Janet, alarm the house!—Foster, break open the door—I am detained here by a traitor!—Use axe and lever, Master Foster—I will be your warrant!"

"It shall not need, madam," Varney was at length distinctly heard to say. "If you please to expose my lord's important concerns and your own to the general ear, I will not be your hindrance."

The door was unlocked and thrown open, and Janet and her father rushed in, anxious to learn the cause of these reiterated exclamations.

When they entered the apartment, Varney stood by the door grinding his teeth, with an expression in which rage, and shame, and fear, had each their share. The Countess stood in the midst of her apartment like a juvenile Pythoness, under the influence of the prophetic fury. The veins in her beautiful forehead started into swoln blue lines through the hurried impulse of her articulation—her cheek and neck glowed like scarlet—her eyes were like those of an imprisoned eagle, flashing red lightning on the foes which it cannot reach with its talons. Were it possible for one of the Graces to have been animated by a Fury, the countenance could not have united such beauty with so much hatred, scorn, defiance, and resentment. The gesture and attitude corresponded with the voice and looks, and altogether presented a spectacle which was at once beautiful and fearful; so much of the sublime had the energy of passion united with the Countess Amy's natural loveliness. Janet, as soon as the door was open, ran to her mistress; and more slowly, yet with more haste than he was wont, Anthony Foster went to Richard Varney.

"In the Truth's name, what ails your ladyship?" said the former.

"What, in the name of Satan, have you done to her?" said Foster to his friend.

"Who, I?—nothing," answered Varney, but with sunken head and sullen voice; "nothing but communicated to her her lord's commands, which, if the lady list not to obey, she knows better how to answer it than I may pretend to do."

"Now, by Heaven, Janet," said the Countess, "the false traitor lies in his throat! He must needs lie, for he speaks to the dishonour of my noble lord—he must needs lie doubly, for he speaks to gain ends of his own, equally execrable and unattainable."

"You have misapprehended me, lady," said Varney, with a sulky species of submission and apology; "let this matter rest till your passion be abated, and I will explain all."

"Thou shalt never have an opportunity to do so," said the Countess.— "Look at him, Janet. He is fairly dressed, hath the outside of a gentleman, and hither he came to persuade me it was my lord's pleasure—nay, more, my wedded lord's commands, that I should go with him to Kenilworth, and before the Queen and nobles, and in presence of my own wedded lord, that I should acknowledge him—*him* there—that very cloak-brushing, shoe-cleaning fellow—*him* there, my lord's lackey, for my liege lord and husband; furnishing against myself, great God! whenever I was to vindicate my right and my rank, such weapons as would hew my just claim from the root, and destroy my character to be regarded as an honourable matron of the English nobility!"

"You hear her, Foster, and you, young maiden, hear this lady," answered Varney, taking advantage of the pause which the Countess had made in her charge, more for lack of breath than for lack of matter— "You hear that her heat only objects to me the course which our good lord for the purpose to keep certain matters secret, suggests in the very letter which she holds in her hands."

Foster here attempted to interfere with a face of authority, which he thought became the charge intrusted to him. "Nay, lady, I must needs say you are over hasty in this—Such deceit is not utterly to be condemned when practised for a righteous end; and thus even the patriarch Abraham feigned Sarah to be his sister when they went down to Egypt."

"Ay, sir," answered the Countess; "but God rebuked that deceit even in the father of his chosen people, by the mouth of the heathen Pharaoh. Out upon you, that will read Scripture only to copy those things, which are held out to us as warnings, not as examples!"

"But Sarah disputed not the will of her husband, an it be your pleasure," said Foster, in reply; "but did as Abraham commanded, calling herself his sister, that it might be well with her husband for her sake, and that his soul might live because of her beauty."

"Now, so Heaven pardon me my useless anger," answered the Countess, "thou art as daring a hypocrite as yonder fellow is an impudent deceiver! Never will I believe that the noble Dudley gave countenance to so dastardly, so dishonourable a plan. Thus I tread on his infamy, if indeed it be, and thus destroy its remembrance for ever!"

So saying, she tore in pieces Leicester's letter, and stamped, in the extremity of impatience, as if she would have annihilated the minute fragments into which she had rent it.

"Bear witness," said Varney, collecting himself, "she hath torn my lord's letter, in order to burden me with the scheme of his devising; and although it promises nought but danger and trouble to me, she would lay it to my charge, as if I had any purpose of mine own in it."

"Thou liest, thou treacherous slave!" said the Countess, in spite of Janet's attempts to keep her silent, in the sad foresight that her vehemence might only furnish arms against herself,—"Thou liest!" she continued—"Let me go, Janet—Were it the last word I have to speak, he lies —he had his own foul ends to seek; and broader he would have displayed them, had my passion permitted me to preserve the silence which at first encouraged him to unfold his vile projects."

"Madam," said Varney, overwhelmed in spite of his effrontery, "I entreat you to believe yourself mistaken."

"As soon will I believe light darkness," said the enraged Countess. "Have I drank of oblivion? Do I not remember former passages, which, known to Leicester, had given thee the preferment of a gallows, instead of the honour of his intimacy?—I would I were a man but for five minutes! It were space enough to make a craven like thee confess his villainy. But go—begone!—Tell thy master, that when I take the foul course to which such scandalous deceits as thou hast recommended on his behalf must necessarily lead me, I will give him a rival something worthy of the name. He shall not be supplanted by an ignominious lackey, whose best fortune is to catch a gift of his master's last suit of clothes ere it is threadbare, and who is only fit to seduce a suburb-wench by the bravery of new roses in his master's old pantofles. Go, begone, sir—I scorn thee so much, that I am ashamed to have been angry with thee."

Varney left the room with a mute expression of rage, and was followed by Foster, whose apprehension, naturally slow, was overpowered by the eager and abundant discharge of indignation, which, for the first time, he had heard burst from the lips of a being, who had seemed till that moment too languid, and too gentle, to nurse an angry thought, or utter an intemperate expression. Foster, therefore, pursued Varney from place to place, persecuting him with interrogatories, to which the other replied not until they were in the opposite side of the quadrangle, and in the old library, with which the reader has already been made acquainted. Here he turned round on his persevering follower, and thus addressed him, in a tone tolerably equal; that brief walk having been sufficient to give one so habituated to command his temper, time to rally and recover his presence of mind.

"Tony," he said, with his usual sneering laugh, "it avails not to deny it. The Woman and the Devil, who, as thine oracle Holdforth will confirm to thee, cheated man at the beginning, have this day proved more powerful than my discretion. Yon termagant looked so tempting, and had the art to preserve her countenance so naturally, while I communicated my lord's message, that, by my faith, I thought I might say some little thing for myself. She thinks she hath my head under her girdle now, but she is deceived.—Where is Doctor Alasco?"

"In his laboratory," answered Foster; "it is the hour he is not spoken withal—we must wait till noon is past, or spoil his important—What said I, important?—I would say interrupt his divine studies."

"Ay, he studies the devil's divinity," said Varney,—"but when I want him, one hour must suffice as well as another. Lead the way to his pandemonium."

So spoke Varney, and with hasty and perturbed steps followed Foster, who conducted him through private passages, many of which were well-nigh ruinous, to the opposite side of the quadrangle, where, in a subterranean apartment, now occupied by the chemist Alasco, one of the Abbots of Abingdon, who had a turn for the occult sciences, had, much to the scandal of his convent, established a laboratory, in which, like other fools of the period, he spent much precious time, and money besides, in the pursuit of the grand arcanum.

Anthony Foster paused before the door, which was scrupulously secured within, and again showed a marked hesitation to disturb the sage in his operations. But Varney, less scrupulous, roused him, by knocking and voice, until at length, slowly and reluctantly, the inmate of the apartment undid the door. The chemist appeared, with his eyes bleared with the heat and vapours of the stove or alembic over which he brooded, and the interior of his cell displayed the confused assemblage of heterogeneous substances and extraordinary implements belonging to his profession. The old man was muttering, with spiteful impatience, "Am I for ever to be recalled to the affairs of earth from those of heaven?"

"To the affairs of hell," answered Varney, "for that is thy proper element.—Foster, we need thee at our conference."

Foster slowly entered the room. Varney, following, barred the door, and they betook themselves to secret council.

In the meanwhile, the Countess traversed the apartment, with shame and anger contending on her lovely cheek.

"The villain," she said, "the cold-blooded, calculating slave!—But I unmasked him, Janet—I made the snake uncoil all his folds before me, and crawl abroad in his naked deformity—I suspended my resentment, at the danger of suffocating under the effort, until he had let me see the very bottom of a heart more foul than hell's darkest corner.—And thou, Leicester, is it possible thou couldst bid me for a moment deny my wedded right in thee, or thyself yield it to another!—But it is impossible —the villain has lied in all.—Janet, I will not remain here longer—I fear him—I fear thy father—I grieve to say it, Janet—but I fear thy father, and, worst of all, this odious Varney. I will escape from Cumnor."

"Alas! madam, whither would you fly, or by what means will you escape from these walls?"

"I know not, Janet," said the unfortunate young lady, looking upwards, and clasping her hands together, "I know not where I shall fly, or by what means; but I am certain the God I have served will not abandon me in this dreadful crisis, for I am in the hands of wicked men."

"Do not think so, dear lady," said Janet; "my father is stern and strict in his temper, and severely true to his trust—but yet——"

At this moment, Anthony Foster entered the apartment, bearing in his hand a glass cup, and a small flask. His manner was singular; for, while approaching the Countess with the respect due to her rank, he had till this time suffered to become visible, or had been unable to suppress, the obdurate sulkiness of his natural disposition, which, as is usual with those of his unhappy temper, was chiefly exerted towards those over whom circumstances gave him control. But at present he showed nothing of that sullen consciousness of authority which he was wont to conceal under a clumsy affectation of civility and deference, as a ruffian hides his pistols and bludgeon under his ill-fashioned gaberdine. And yet it seemed as if his smile was more in fear than courtesy, and as if, while he pressed the Countess to taste of the choice cordial, which 3hould refresh her spirits after her late alarm, he was conscious of meditating some farther injury. His hand trembled also, his voice faltered, and his whole outward behaviour exhibited so much that was suspicious, that his daughter Janet, after she had stood looking at him in astonishment for some seconds, seemed at once to collect herself to execute some hardy resolution, raised her head, assumed an attitude and gait of determination and authority, and walking slowly betwixt her father and her mistress, took the salver from the hand of the former, and said in a low, but marked and decided tone, "Father, *I* will fill for my noble mistress, when such is her pleasure."

"Thou, my child?" said Foster, eagerly and apprehensively; "no, my child—it is not *thou* shalt render the lady this service."

"And why, I pray you," said Janet, "if it be fitting that the noble lady should partake of the cup at all?"

"Why—why?" said the seneschal, hesitating, and then bursting into passion as the readiest mode of supplying the lack of all other reason—"Why, because it is my pleasure, minion, that you should not!—Get you gone to the evening lecture."

"Now, as I hope to hear lecture again," replied Janet, "I will not go thither this night, unless I am better assured of my mistress's safety. Give me that flask, father";—and she took it from his reluctant hand, while he resigned it as if conscience-struck—"And now," she said, "father, that which shall benefit my mistress, cannot do *me* prejudice. Father, I drink to you."

Foster, without speaking a word, rushed on his daughter, and wrested the flask from her hand; then, as if embarrassed by what he had done, and totally unable to resolve what he should do next, he stood with it in his hand, one foot advanced and the other drawn back, glaring on his daughter with a countenance, in which rage, fear, and convicted villainy, formed a hideous combination.

"This is strange, my father," said Janet, keeping her eye fixed on his, in the manner in which those who have the charge of lunatics are said to overawe their unhappy patients; "will you neither let me serve my lady, nor drink to her myself?"

The courage of the Countess sustained her through this dreadful scene, of which the import was not the less obvious that it was not even hinted at. She preserved even the rash carelessness of her temper, and though her cheek had grown pale at the first alarm, her eye was calm and almost scornful. "Will *you* taste this rare cordial, Master Foster? Perhaps you will not yourself refuse to pledge us, though you permit not Janet to do so—Drink, sir, I pray you."

"I will not," answered Foster.

"And for whom, then, is the precious beverage reserved, sir?" said the Countess.

"For the devil, who brewed it!" answered Foster; and, turning on his heel, he left the chamber.

Janet looked at her mistress with a countenance expressive in the highest degree of shame, dismay, and sorrow.

"Do not weep for me, Janet," said the Countess, kindly.

"No, madam," replied her attendant, in a voice broken by sobs, "it is not for you I weep, it is for myself—it is for that unhappy man. Those who are dishonoured before man—those who are condemned by God, have cause to mourn—not those who are innocent!—Farewell, madam!" she said, hastily assuming the mantle in which she was wont to go abroad.

"Do you leave me, Janet?" said her mistress—"desert me in such an evil strait?"

"Desert you, madam!" exclaimed Janet; and, running back to her mistress, she imprinted a thousand kisses on her hand—"desert you!—may the Hope of my trust desert me when I do so!—No, madam; well you said the God you serve will open you a path for deliverance. There is a way of escape; I have prayed night and day for light, that I might see how to act betwixt my duty to yonder unhappy man, and that which I owe to you. Sternly and fearfully that light has now dawned, and I must not shut the door which God opens.—Ask me no more—I will return in brief space."

So speaking, she wrapped herself in her mantle, and saying to the old woman whom she passed in the outer-room, that she was going to evening prayer, she left the house.

Meanwhile her father had reached once more the laboratory, where he found the accomplices of his intended guilt.

"Has the sweet bird sipped?" said Varney, with half a smile; while the astrologer put the same question with his eyes, but spoke not a word.

"She has not, nor she shall not from my hands," replied Foster; "would you have me do murder in my daughter's presence?"

"Wert thou not told, thou sullen and yet faint-hearted slave," answered Varney, with bitterness, "that no *murder*, as thou call'st it, with that staring look and stammering tone, is designed in the matter? Wert thou not told, that a brief illness, such as woman puts on in very wantonness, that she may wear her night-gear at noon, and lie on a settle when she should mind her domestic business, is all here aimed at? Here is a learned man will swear it to thee, by the key of the Castle of Wisdom."

"I swear it," said Alasco, "that the elixir thou hast there in the flask will not prejudice life! I swear it by that immortal and indestructible quintessence of gold, which pervades every substance in nature, though its secret existence can be traced by him only, to whom Trismegistus renders the key of the Cabala."

"An oath of force," said Varney. "Foster, thou wert worse than a pagan to disbelieve it. Believe me, moreover, who swear by nothing but by my own word, that if you be not conformable, there is no hope, no, not a glimpse of hope, that this thy leasehold may be transmuted into a copyhold. Thus, Alasco will leave your pewter artillery untransmigrated, and I, honest Anthony, will still have thee for my tenant."

"I know not, gentlemen," said Foster, "where your designs tend to; but in one thing I am bound up,—that, fall back fall edge, I will have one in this place that may pray for me, and that one shall be my daughter. I have lived ill, and the world has been too weighty with me; but she is as innocent as ever she was when on her mother's lap, and she, at least, shall have her portion in that happy City, whose walls are of pure gold, and the foundations garnished with all manner of precious stones."

"Ay, Tony," said Varney, "that were a paradise to thy heart's content.—Debate the matter with him, Doctor Alasco; I will be with you anon."

So speaking, Varney arose, and, taking the flask from the table, he left the room.

"I tell thee, my son," said Alasco to Foster, as soon as Varney had left them, "that whatever this bold and profligate railer may say of the mighty science, in which, by Heaven's blessing, I have advanced so far, that I would not call the wisest of living artists my better or my teacher —I say, howsoever yonder reprobate may scoff at things too holy to be apprehended by men merely of carnal and evil thoughts, yet believe, that the city beheld by St. John, in that bright vision of the Christian Apocalypse, that New Jerusalem, of which all Christian men hope to partake, sets forth typically the discovery of the GRAND SECRET, whereby the most precious and perfect of nature's works are elicited out of her basest and most crude productions; just as the light and gaudy butterfly, the most beautiful child of the summer's breeze, breaks forth from the dungeon of a sordid chrysalis."

"Master Holdforth said nought of this exposition," said Foster, doubtfully; "and moreover, Doctor Alasco, the Holy Writ says, that the gold and precious stones of the Holy City are in no sort for those who work abomination, or who frame lies."

"Well, my son," said the Doctor, "and what is your inference from thence?"

"That those," said Foster, "who distil poisons, and administer them in secrecy, can have no portion in those unspeakable riches."

"You are to distinguish, my son," replied the alchemist, "betwixt that which is necessarily evil in its progress and in its end also, and that which, being evil, is, nevertheless, capable of working forth good. If, by the death of one person, the happy period shall be brought nearer to us, in which all that is good shall be attained, by wishing its presence—all that is evil escaped, by desiring its absence—in which sickness, and pain, and sorrow, shall be the obedient servants of human wisdom, and made to fly at the slightest signal of a sage,—in which that which is now richest and rarest shall be within the compass of every one who shall be obedient to the voice of wisdom,—when the art of healing shall be lost and absorbed in the one universal medicine,—when sages shall become monarchs of the earth, and death itself retreat before their frown,—if this blessed consummation of all things can be hastened by the slight circumstance, that a frail earthly body, which must needs partake corruption, shall be consigned to the grave a short space earlier than in the course of nature, what is such a sacrifice to the advancement of the holy Millennium?"

"Millennium is the reign of the Saints,"—said Foster, somewhat doubtfully.

"Say it is the reign of the Sages, my son," answered Alasco; "or rather the reign of Wisdom itself."

"I touched on the question with Master Holdforth last exercising night," said Foster; "but he says your doctrine is heterodox, and a damnable and false exposition."

"He is in the bonds of ignorance, my son," answered Alasco, "and as yet burning bricks in Egypt; or, at best, wandering in the dry desert of Sinai. Thou didst ill to speak to such a man of such matters. I will, however, give thee proof, and that shortly, which I will defy that peevish divine to confute, though he should strive with me as the magicians strove with Moses before King Pharaoh. I will do projection in thy presence, my son,—in thy very presence,—and thine eyes shall witness the truth."

"Stick to that, learned sage," said Varney, who at this moment entered the apartment; "if he refuse the testimony of thy tongue, yet how shall he deny that of his own eyes?"

"Varney!" said the adept—"Varney already returned! Hast thou——" he stopped short.

"Have I done mine errand, thou wouldst say," replied Varney—"I have!—And thou," he added, showing more symptoms of interest than he had hitherto exhibited, "art thou sure thou hast poured forth neither more nor less than the just measure?"

"Ay," replied the alchemist, "as sure as men can be in these nice proportions; for there is diversity of constitutions."

"Nay, then," said Varney, "I fear nothing. I know thou wilt not go a step farther to the devil than thou art justly considered for. Thou wert paid to create illness, and wouldst esteem it thriftless prodigality to do murder at the same price. Come, let us each to our chamber—We shall see the event to-morrow."

"What didst thou do to make her swallow it?" said Foster, shuddering.

"Nothing," answered Varney, "but looked on her with that aspect which governs madmen, women, and children. They told me, in Saint Luke's Hospital, that I have the right look for overpowering a refractory patient. The keepers made me their compliments on't; so I know how to win my bread, when my court-favour fails me."

"And art thou not afraid," said Foster, "lest the dose be disproportioned?"

"If so," replied Varney, "she will but sleep the sounder, and the fear of that shall not break my rest. Good-night, my masters."

Anthony Foster groaned heavily, and lifted up his hands and eyes. The alchemist intimated his purpose to continue some experiment of high import during the greater part of the night, and the others separated to their places of repose.

CHAPTER XXIII

> Now God be good to me in this wild pilgrimage!
> All hope in human aid I cast behind me.
> Oh, who would be a woman?—who that fool,
> A weeping, pining, faithful, loving woman?
> She hath hard measure still where she hopes kindest,
> And all her bounties only make ingrates.
>
> *Love's Pilgrimage.*

THE summer evening was closed, and Janet, just when her longer stay might have occasioned suspicion and enquiry in that jealous household, returned to Cumnor-Place, and hastened to the apartment in which she had left her lady. She found her with her head resting on her arms, and these crossed upon a table which stood before her. As Janet came in, she neither looked up nor stirred.

Her faithful attendant ran to her mistress with the speed of lightning, and rousing her at the same time with her hand, conjured the Countess, in the most earnest manner, to look up, and say what thus affected her. The unhappy lady raised her head accordingly, and looking on her attendant with a ghastly eye, and cheek as pale as clay, "Janet," she said, "I have drank it."

"God be praised!" said Janet, hastily—"I mean God be praised that it is no worse—the potion will not harm you.—Rise, shake this lethargy from your limbs, and this despair from your mind."

"Janet," repeated the Countess again, "disturb me not—leave me at peace—let life pass quietly—I am poisoned."

"You are not, my dearest lady," answered the maiden eagerly—"What you have swallowed cannot injure you, for the antidote has been taken before it, and I hastened hither to tell you that the means of escape are open to you."

"Escape!" exclaimed the lady, as she raised herself hastily in her chair, while light returned to her eye and life to her cheek; "but ah! Janet, it comes too late."

"Not so, dearest lady—Rise, take mine arm, walk through the apartment—Let not fancy do the work of poison!—So; feel you not now that you are possessed of the full use of your limbs?"

"The torpor seems to diminish," said the Countess, as, supported by Janet, she walked to and fro in the apartment; "but is it then so, and have I not swallowed a deadly draught? Varney was here since thou wert gone, and commanded me, with eyes in which I read my fate, to swallow yon horrible drug. Oh, Janet; it must be fatal; never was harmless draught served by such a cup-bearer!"

"He did not deem it harmless, I fear," replied the maiden; "but God confounds the devices of the wicked. Believe me, as I swear by the dear Gospel in which we trust, your life is safe from his practice. Did you not debate with him?"

"The house was silent," answered the lady—"thou gone—no other but he in the chamber—and he capable of every crime. I did but stipulate he would remove his hateful presence, and I drank whatever he offered.— But you spoke of escape, Janet; can I be so happy?"

"Are you strong enough to bear the tidings, and make the effort?" said the maiden.

"Strong!" answered the Countess—"Ask the hind, when the fangs of the deer-hound are stretched to gripe her, if she is strong enough to spring over a chasm. I am equal to every effort that may relieve me from this place."

"Hear me, then," said Janet. "One, whom I deem an assured friend of yours, has shown himself to me in various disguises, and sought speech of me, which,—for my mind was not clear on the matter until this evening—I have ever declined. He was the pedlar who brought you goods— the itinerant hawker who sold me books—whenever I stirred abroad I was sure to see him. The event of this night determined me to speak with him. He waits even now at the postern-gate of the park with means for your flight.—But have you strength of body?—Have you courage of mind?—Can you undertake the enterprise?"

"She that flies from death," said the lady, "finds strength of body— she that would escape from shame, lacks no strength of mind. The thoughts of leaving behind me the villain who menaces both my life and honour, would give me strength to rise from my deathbed."

"In God's name, then, lady," said Janet, "I must bid you adieu, and to God's charge I must commit you!"

"Will you not fly with me, then, Janet?" said the Countess, anxiously —"Am I to lose thee? Is this thy faithful service?"

"Lady, I would fly with you as willingly as bird ever fled from cage, but my doing so would occasion instant discovery and pursuit. I must remain, and use means to disguise the truth for some time—May Heaven pardon the falsehood, because of the necessity!"

"And am I then to travel alone with this stranger?" said the lady—"Bethink thee, Janet, may not this prove some deeper and darker scheme, to separate me perhaps from you, who are my only friend?"

"No, madam, do not suppose it," answered Janet readily; "the youth is an honest youth in his purpose to you; and a friend to Master Tressilian, under whose direction he is come hither."

"If he be a friend of Tressilian," said the Countess, "I will commit myself to his charge as to that of an angel sent from heaven; for than Tressilian, never breathed mortal man more free of whatever was base, false, or selfish. He forgot himself whenever he could be of use to others —Alas! and how was he requited!"

With eager haste they collected the few necessaries which it was thought proper the Countess should take with her, and which Janet, with speed and dexterity, formed into a small bundle, not forgetting to add such ornaments of intrinsic value as came most readily in her way, and particularly a casket of jewels, which she wisely judged might prove of service in some future emergency. The Countess of Leicester next changed her dress for one which Janet usually wore upon any brief journey, for they judged it necessary to avoid every external distinction which might attract notice. Ere these preparations were fully made, the moon had arisen in the summer heaven, and all in the mansion had betaken themselves to rest, or at least to the silence and retirement of their chambers.

There was no difficulty anticipated in escaping, whether from the house or garden, provided only they could elude observation. Anthony Foster had accustomed himself to consider his daughter as a conscious sinner might regard a visible guardian angel, which, notwithstanding his guilt, continued to hover around him, and therefore his trust in her knew no bounds. Janet commanded her own motions during the daytime, and had a master-key which opened the postern-door of the park, so that she could go to the village at pleasure, either upon the household affairs, which were entirely confided to her management, or to attend her devotions at the meeting-house of her sect. It is true, the daughter of Foster was thus liberally intrusted, under the solemn condition that she should not avail herself of these privileges, to do any thing inconsistent with the safe-keeping of the Countess; for so her residence at Cumnor-Place had been termed, since she began of late to exhibit impatience of the restrictions to which she was subjected. Nor is there reason to suppose, that any thing short of the dreadful suspicions which the scene of that evening had excited, could have induced Janet to violate her word, or deceive her father's confidence. But from what she had witnessed, she now conceived herself not only justified, but imperatively called upon, to make her lady's safety the principal object of her care, setting all other considerations aside.

The fugitive Countess with her guide traversed with hasty steps the broken and interrupted path, which had once been an avenue, now totally darkened by the boughs of spreading trees which met above their head, and now receiving a doubtful and deceiving light from the beams of the moon, which penetrated where the axe had made openings in the wood. Their path was repeatedly interrupted by felled trees, or the large boughs which had been left on the ground till time served to make them into fagots and billets. The inconvenience and difficulty attending these interruptions, the breathless haste of the first part of their route, the exhausting sensations of hope and fear, so much affected the Countess's strength, that Janet was forced to propose that they should pause for a few minutes to recover breath and spirits. Both therefore stood still beneath the shadow of a huge old gnarled oak-tree, and both naturally looked back to the mansion which they had left behind them, whose long dark front was seen in the gloomy distance, with its huge stacks of chimneys, turrets, and clock-house, rising above the line of the roof, and definedly visible against the pure azure blue of the summer sky. One light only twinkled from the extended and shadowy mass, and it was placed so low, that it rather seemed to glimmer from the ground in front of the mansion, than from one of the windows. The Countess's terror was awakened.—"They follow us!" she said, pointing out to Janet the light which thus alarmed her.

Less agitated than her mistress, Janet perceived that the gleam was stationary, and informed the Countess, in a whisper, that the light proceeded from the solitary cell in which the alchemist pursued his occult experiments.—"He is of those," she added, "who sit up and watch by night that they may commit iniquity. Evil was the chance which sent hither a man, whose mixed speech of earthly wealth and unearthly or superhuman knowledge, hath in it what does so especially captivate my poor father. Well spoke the good Master Holdforth—and, methought, not without meaning, that those of our household should find therein a practical use. 'There be those,' he said, 'and their number is legion, who will rather, like the wicked Ahab, listen to the dreams of the false prophet Zedekias, than to the words of him by whom the Lord has spoken.' And he further insisted—'Ah, my brethren, there be many Zedekiases among you—men that promise you the light of their carnal knowledge, so you will surrender to them that of your heavenly understanding. What are they better than the tyrant Naas, who demanded the right eye of those who were subjected to him?' And farther he insisted——"

It is uncertain how long the fair puritan's memory might have supported her in the recapitulation of Master Holdforth's discourse; but the Countess interrupted her, and assured her she was so much recovered that she could now reach the postern without the necessity of a second delay.

They set out accordingly, and performed the second part of their journey with more deliberation, and of course more easily, than the first hasty commencement. This gave them leisure for reflection; and Janet now, for the first time, ventured to ask her lady which way she proposed to direct her flight. Receiving no immediate answer,—for, perhaps, in the confusion of her mind, this very obvious subject of deliberation had not occurred to the Countess,—Janet ventured to add, "Probably to your father's house, where you are sure of safety and protection?"

"No, Janet," said the lady mournfully, "I left Lidcote Hall while my heart was light and my name was honourable, and I will not return thither till my lord's permission and public acknowledgment of our marriage restore me to my native home, with all the rank and honour which he has bestowed on me."

"And whither will you, then, madam?" said Janet.

"To Kenilworth, girl," said the Countess, boldly and freely. "I will see these revels—these princely revels—the preparation for which makes the land ring from side to side. Methinks, when the Queen of England feasts within my husband's halls, the Countess of Leicester should be no unbeseeming guest."

"I pray God you may be a welcome one!" said Janet, hastily.

"You abuse my situation, Janet," said the Countess, angrily, "and you forget your own."

"I do neither, dearest madam," said the sorrowful maiden; "but have you forgotten that the noble Earl has given such strict charges to keep your marriage secret, that he may preserve his court-favour? and can you think that your sudden appearance at his castle, at such a juncture, and in such a presence, will be acceptable to him?"

"Thou thinkest I would disgrace him?" said the Countess;—"nay, let go my arm, I can walk without aid, and work without counsel."

"Be not angry with me, lady," said Janet, meekly, "and let me still support you; the road is rough, and you are little accustomed to walk in darkness."

"If you deem me not so mean as may disgrace my husband," said the Countess, in the same resentful tone, "you suppose my Lord of Leicester capable of abetting, perhaps of giving aim and authority to, the base proceedings of your father and Varney, whose errand I will do to the good Earl."

"For God's sake, madam, spare my father in your report," said Janet; "let my services, however poor, be some atonement for his errors!"

"I were most unjust, dearest Janet, were it otherwise," said the Countess, resuming at once the fondness and confidence of her manner towards her faithful attendant. "No, Janet, not a word of mine shall do your father prejudice. But thou seest, my love, I have no desire but to throw myself on my husband's protection. I have left the abode he assigned for me, because of the villainy of the persons by whom I was surrounded —but I will disobey his commands in no other particular. I will appeal to him alone—I will be protected by him alone—To no other, than at his pleasure, have I or will I communicate the secret union which combines our hearts and our destinies. I will see him, and receive from his own lips the directions for my future conduct. Do not argue against my resolution, Janet; you will only confirm me in it—And to own the truth, I am resolved to know my fate at once, and from my husband's own mouth, and to seek him at Kenilworth is the surest way to attain my purpose."

While Janet hastily revolved in her mind the difficulties and uncertainties attendant on the unfortunate lady's situation, she was inclined to alter her first opinion, and to think, upon the whole, that since the Countess had withdrawn herself from the retreat in which she had been placed by her husband, it was her first duty to repair to his presence, and possess him with the reasons of such conduct. She knew what importance the Earl attached to the concealment of their marriage, and could not but own, that by taking any step to make it public without his permission, the Countess would incur, in a high degree, the indignation of her husband. If she retired to her father's house without an explicit avowal of her rank, her situation was likely greatly to prejudice her character; and if she made such an avowal, it might occasion an irreconcilable breach with her husband. At Kenilworth, again, she might plead her cause with her husband himself, whom Janet, though distrusting him more than the Countess did, believed incapable of being accessary to the base and desperate means which his dependants, from whose power the lady was now escaping, might resort to, in order to stifle her complaints of the treatment she had received at their hands. But at the worst, and were the Earl himself to deny her justice and protection, still at Kenilworth, if she chose to make her wrongs public, the Countess might have Tressilian for her advocate, and the Queen for her judge; for so much Janet had learned in her short conference with Wayland. She was, therefore, on the whole reconciled to her lady's proposal of going towards Kenilworth, and so expressed herself; recommending, however, to the Countess the utmost caution in making her arrival known to her husband.

"Hast thou thyself been cautious, Janet?" said the Countess; "this guide, in whom I must put my confidence, hast thou not intrusted to him the secret of my condition?"

"From me he has learned nothing," said Janet; "nor do I think that he knows more than what the public in general believe of your situation."

"And what is that?" said the lady.

"That you left your father's house—but I shall offend you again if I go on," said Janet, interrupting herself.

"Nay, go on," said the Countess; "I must learn to endure the evil report which my folly has brought upon me. They think, I suppose, that I have left my father's house to follow lawless pleasure—It is an error which will soon be removed,—indeed it shall, for I will live with spotless fame, or I shall cease to live.—I am accounted, then, the paramour of my Leicester?"

"Most men say of Varney," said Janet; "yet some call him only the convenient cloak of his master's pleasure; for reports of the profuse expense in garnishing yonder apartments have secretly gone abroad, and such doings far surpass the means of Varney. But this latter opinion is little prevalent; for men dare hardly even hint suspicion when so high a name is concerned, lest the Star-chamber should punish them for scandal of the nobility."

"They do well to speak low," said the Countess, "who would mention the illustrious Dudley as the accomplice of such a wretch as Varney.— We have reached the postern—Ah! Janet, I must bid thee farewell!— Weep not, my good girl," said she, endeavouring to cover her own reluctance to part with her faithful attendant under an attempt at playfulness, "and against we meet again, reform me, Janet, that precise ruff of thine for an open rabatine of lace and cut work, that will let men see thou hast a fair neck; and that kirtle of Philippine chency, with that bugle lace which befits only a chambermaid, into three-piled velvet and cloth of gold—thou wilt find plenty of stuffs in my chamber, and I freely bestow them on you. Thou must be brave, Janet; for though thou art now but the attendant of a distressed and errant lady, who is both nameless and fameless, yet, when we meet again, thou must be dressed as becomes the gentlewoman nearest in love and in service to the first Countess in England!"

"Now, may God grant it, dear lady!" said Janet;—"not that I may go with gayer apparel, but that we may both wear our kirtles over lighter hearts."

By this time the lock of the postern-door had, after some hard wrenching, yielded to the master-key; and the Countess, not without internal shuddering, saw herself beyond the walls which her husband's strict commands had assigned to her as the boundary of her walks. Waiting with much anxiety for their appearance, Wayland Smith stood at some distance, shrouding himself behind a hedge which bordered the high-road.

"Is all safe?" said Janet to him, anxiously, as he approached them with caution.

"All," he replied; "but I have been unable to procure a horse for the lady. Giles Gosling, the cowardly hilding, refused me one on any terms whatever; lest, forsooth, he should suffer—but no matter. She must ride on my palfrey, and I must walk by her side until I come by another horse. There will be no pursuit, if you, pretty Mistress Janet, forget not thy lesson."

"No more than the wise widow of Tekoa forgot the words which Joab put into her mouth," answered Janet. "To-morrow, I say that my lady is unable to rise."

"Ay, and that she hath aching and heaviness of the head—a throbbing at the heart, and lists not to be disturbed.—Fear not; they will take the hint, and trouble thee with few questions—they understand the disease."

"But," said the lady, "my absence must be soon discovered, and they will murder her in revenge.—I will rather return than expose her to such danger."

"Be at ease on my account, madam," said Janet; "I would you were as sure of receiving the favour you desire from those to whom you must make appeal, as I am that my father, however angry, will suffer no harm to befall me."

The Countess was now placed by Wayland upon his horse, around the saddle of which he had placed his cloak, so folded as to make her a commodious seat.

"Adieu, and may the blessing of God wend with you!" said Janet, again kissing her mistress's hand, who returned her benediction with a mute caress. They then tore themselves asunder, and Janet, addressing Wayland, exclaimed, "May Heaven deal with you at your need, as you are true or false to this most injured and most helpless lady!"

"Amen! dearest Janet," replied Wayland;—"and believe me, I will so acquit myself of my trust, as may tempt even your pretty eyes, saintlike as they are, to look less scornfully on me when we next meet."

The latter part of this adieu was whispered into Janet's ear; and, although she made no reply to it directly, yet her manner, influenced no doubt by her desire to leave every motive in force which could operate towards her mistress's safety, did not discourage the hope which Wayland's words expressed. She re-entered the postern-door, and locked it behind her, while, Wayland taking the horse's bridle in his hand, and walking close by its head, they began in silence their dubious and moonlight journey.

Although Wayland Smith used the utmost dispatch which he could make, yet this mode of travelling was so slow, that when morning began to dawn through the eastern mist, he found himself no farther than about ten miles distant from Cumnor. "Now, a plague upon all smooth-spoken hosts!" said Wayland, unable longer to suppress his mortification and uneasiness. "Had the false loon, Giles Gosling, but told me plainly two days since, that I was to reckon nought upon him, I had shifted better for myself. But your hosts have such a custom of promising whatever is called for, that it is not till the steed is to be shod you find they are out of iron. Had I but known, I could have made twenty shifts; nay, for that matter, and in so good a cause, I would have thought little to have prigged a prancer from the next common—it had but been sending back the brute to the head-borough. The farcy and the founders confound every horse in the stables of the Black Bear!"

The lady endeavoured to comfort her guide, observing, that the dawn would enable him to make more speed.

"True, madam," he replied; "but then it will enable other folk to take note of us, and that may prove an ill beginning of our journey. I had not cared a spark from anvil about the matter, had we been farther advanced on our way. But this Berkshire has been notoriously haunted ever since I knew the country, with that sort of malicious elves, who sit up late and rise early, for no other purpose than to pry into other folks' affairs. I have been endangered by them ere now. But do not fear," he added, "good madam; for wit, meeting with opportunity, will not miss to find a salve for every sore."

The alarms of her guide made more impression on the Countess's mind than the comfort which he judged fit to administer along with it. She looked anxiously around her, and as the shadows withdrew from the landscape, and the heightening glow of the eastern sky promised the speedy rise of the sun, expected at every turn that the increasing light would expose them to the view of the vengeful pursuers, or present some dangerous and insurmountable obstacle to the prosecution of their journey. Wayland Smith perceived her uneasiness, and, displeased with himself for having given her cause of alarm, strode on with affected alacrity, now talking to the horse as one expert in the language of the stable, now whistling to himself low and interrupted snatches of tunes, and now assuring the lady there was no danger; while at the same time he looked sharply around to see that there was nothing in sight which might give the lie to his words while they were issuing from his mouth. Thus did they journey on, until an unexpected incident gave them the means of continuing their pilgrimage with more speed and convenience.

CHAPTER XXIV

> *Richard.* A horse!—a horse!—my kingdom for a horse!
> *Catesby.* ———My lord, I'll help you to a horse.
> *Richard III.*

OUR travellers were in the act of passing a small thicket of trees close by the roadside, when the first living being presented himself whom they had seen since their departure from Cumnor-Place. This was a stupid lout, seemingly a farmer's boy, in a grey jerkin, with his head bare, his hose about his heels, and huge startups upon his feet. He held by the bridle what of all things they most wanted, a palfrey, namely, with a side-saddle, and all other garniture for a woman's mounting; and he hailed Wayland Smith with, "Zur, ye be zure the party?"

"Ay, that be I, my lad," answered Wayland, without an instant's hesitation; and it must be owned that consciences, trained in a stricter school of morality, might have given way to an occasion so tempting. While he spoke, he caught the rein out of the boy's hand, and almost at the same time helped down the Countess from his own horse, and aided her to mount on that which chance had thus presented for her acceptance. Indeed, so naturally did the whole take place, that the Countess, as it afterwards appeared, never suspected but that the horse had been placed there to meet them by the precaution of the guide, or some of his friends.

The lad, however, who was thus hastily dispossessed of his charge, began to stare hard, and scratch his head, as if seized with some qualms of conscience for delivering up the animal on such brief explanation.—"I be right zure thou be'st the party," said he, muttering to himself, "but thou shouldst ha zaid *Beans*, thou knaw'st."

"Ay, ay," said Wayland, speaking at a venture; "and thou *Bacon*, thou know'st."

"Noa, noa," said the lad; "bide ye—bide ye—it was *Peas* a should ha said."

"Well, well," answered Wayland, "peas be it, a God's name! though bacon were the better password."

And being by this time mounted on his own horse, he caught the rein of the palfrey from the uncertain hold of the hesitating young boor, flung him a small piece of money, and made amends for lost time by riding briskly off without farther parley. The lad was still visible from the hill up which they were riding, and Wayland, as he looked back, beheld him standing with his fingers in his hair as immovable as a guide-post, and his head turned in the direction in which they were escaping from him. At length, just as they topped the hill, he saw the clown stoop to lift up the silver groat which his benevolence had imparted.—"Now this is what I call a Godsend," said Wayland; "this is a bonny well-ridden bit of a going thing, and it will carry us so far till we get you as well mounted, and then we will send it back time enough to satisfy the Hue and Cry."

But he was deceived in his expectations; and fate, which seemed at first to promise so fairly, soon threatened to turn the incident, which he thus gloried in, into the cause of their utter ruin.

They had not ridden a short mile from the place where they left the lad, before they heard a man's voice shouting on the wind behind them, "Robbery! robbery!—Stop thief!" and similar exclamations, which Wayland's conscience readily assured him must arise out of the transaction to which he had been just accessary.

"I had better have gone barefoot all my life," he said; "it is the Hue and Cry, and I am a lost man. Ah! Wayland, Wayland, many a time thy father said horse-flesh would be the death of thee. Were I once safe among the horse-coursers in Smithfield, or Turnball Street, they should have leave to hang me as high as St. Paul's, if I e'er meddled more with nobles, knights, or gentlewomen!"

Amidst these dismal reflections, he turned his head repeatedly to see by whom he was chased, and was much comforted when he could only discover a single rider, who was, however, well mounted, and came after them at a speed which left them no chance of escaping, even had the lady's strength permitted her to ride as fast as her palfrey might have been able to gallop.

"There may be fair play betwixt us, sure," thought Wayland, "where

there is but one man on each side, and yonder fellow sits on his horse
more like a monkey than a cavalier. Pshaw! if it comes to the worst, it
will be easy unhorsing him. Nay, 'snails! I think his horse will take the
matter in his own hand, for he has the bridle betwixt his teeth. Oons,
what care I for him?" said he, as the pursuer drew yet nearer; "it is but
the little animal of a mercer from Abingdon, when all is over."

Even so it was, as the experienced eye of Wayland had descried at a
distance. For the valiant mercer's horse, which was a beast of mettle,
feeling himself put to his speed, and discerning a couple of horses riding
fast, at some hundred yards' distance before him, betook himself to the
road with such alacrity, as totally deranged the seat of his rider, who
not only came up with, but passed, at full gallop, those whom he had
been pursuing, pulling the reins with all his might, and ejaculating,
"Stop! stop!" an interjection which seemed rather to regard his own
palfrey, than what seamen call "the chase." With the same involuntary
speed, he shot ahead (to use another nautical phrase) about a furlong,
ere he was able to stop and turn his horse, and then rode back towards
our travellers, adjusting, as well as he could, his disordered dress, reset-
tling himself in the saddle, and endeavouring to substitute a bold and
martial frown, for the confusion and dismay which sate upon his visage
during his involuntary career.

Wayland had just time to caution the lady not to be alarmed, adding,
'This fellow is a gull, and I will use him as such."

When the mercer had recovered breath and audacity enough to con-
front them, he ordered Wayland, in a menacing tone, to deliver up
his palfrey.

"How?" said the smith, in King Cambyses' vein, "are we commanded
to stand and deliver on the King's highway? Then out, Excalibar, and
tell this knight of prowess, that dire blows must decide between us!"

"Haro and help, and hue and cry, every true man!" said the mercer,
"I am withstood in seeking to recover mine own!"

"Thou swear'st thy gods in vain, foul paynim," said Wayland, "for
I will through with mine purpose, were death at the end on't. Nevertheless, know, thou false man of frail cambric and ferrateen, that I am
he, even the pedlar, whom thou didst boast to meet on Maiden-castle-
moor, and despoil of his pack; wherefore betake thee to thy weapons
presently."

"I spoke but in jest, man," said Goldthred; "I am an honest shopkeeper and citizen, who scorns to leap forth on any man from behind
a hedge."

"Then, by my faith, most puissant mercer," answered Wayland, "I am
sorry for my vow, which was, that wherever I met thee, I would despoil
thee of thy palfrey, and bestow it upon my leman, unless thou couldst
defend it by blows of force. But the vow is passed and registered—and
all I can do for thee, is to leave the horse at Donnington, in the nearest
hostelry."

"But I tell thee, friend," said the mercer, "it is the very horse on which I was this day to carry Jane Thackham, of Shottesbrok, as far as the parish-church yonder, to become Dame Goldthred. She hath jumped out of the shot-window of old Gaffer Thackham's grange; and lo ye, yonder she stands at the place where she should have met the palfrey, with her camlet riding-cloak, and ivory-handled whip, like a picture of Lot's wife. I pray you, in good terms, let me have back the palfrey."

"Grieved am I," said Wayland, "as much for the fair damsel as for thee, most noble imp of muslin. But vows must have their course—thou wilt find the palfrey at the Angel yonder at Donnington. It is all I may do for thee, with a safe conscience."

"To the devil with thy conscience!" said the dismayed mercer— "Wouldst thou have a bride walk to church on foot?"

"Thou mayst take her on thy crupper, Sir Goldthred," answered Wayland; "it will take down thy steed's mettle."

"And how if you—if you forget to leave my horse, as you propose?" said Goldthred, not without hesitation, for his soul was afraid within him.

"My pack shall be pledged for it—yonder it lies with Giles Gosling, in his chamber with the damask'd leathern hangings, stuffed full with velvet, single, double, treble-piled—rash-taffeta, and parapa—shag, damask, and mocado, plush, and grogram——"

"Hold! hold!" exclaimed the mercer; "nay, if there be, in truth and sincerity, but the half of these wares—but if ever I trust bumpkin with bonny Bayard again!"

"As you list for that, good Master Goldthred, and so good morrow to you—and well parted," he added, riding on cheerfully with the lady, while the discountenanced mercer rode back much slower than he came, pondering what excuse he should make to the disappointed bride, who stood waiting for her gallant groom in the midst of the king's highway.

"Methought," said the lady, as they rode on, "yonder fool stared at me, as if he had some remembrance of me; yet I kept my muffler as high as I might."

"If I thought so," said Wayland, "I would ride back, and cut him over the pate—there would be no fear of harming his brains, for he never had so much as would make pap to a suckling gosling. We must now push on, however, and at Donnington we will leave the oaf's horse, that he may have no farther temptation to pursue us, and endeavour to assume such a change of shape as may baffle his pursuit, if he should persevere in it."

The travellers reached Donnington without farther alarm, where it became matter of necessity that the Countess should enjoy two or three hours' repose, during which Wayland disposed himself, with equal address and alacrity, to carry through those measures on which the safety of their future journey seemed to depend.

Exchanging his pedlar's gaberdine for a smock-frock, he carried the palfrey of Goldthred to the Angel Inn, which was at the other end of the village from that where our travellers had taken up their quarters. In the progress of the morning, as he travelled about his other business, he saw the steed brought forth and delivered to the cutting mercer himself, who, at the head of a valorous posse of the Hue and Cry, came to rescue, by force of arms, what was delivered to him without any other ransom than the price of a huge quantity of ale, drunk out by his assistents, thirsty, it would seem, with their walk, and concerning the price of which Master Goldthred had a fierce dispute with the head-borough, whom he had summoned to aid him in raising the country.

Having made this act of prudent, as well as just restitution, Wayland procured such change of apparel for the lady, as well as himself, as gave them both the appearance of country people of the better class; it being farther resolved, that, in order to attract the less observation, she should pass upon the road for the sister of her guide. A good, but not a gay horse, fit to keep pace with his own, and gentle enough for a lady's use, completed the preparations for the journey; for making which, and for other expenses, he had been furnished with sufficient funds by Tressilian. And thus, about noon, after the Countess had been refreshed by the sound repose of several hours, they resumed their journey, with the purpose of making the best of their way to Kenilworth, by Coventry and Warwick. They were not, however, destined to travel far, without meeting some cause of apprehension.

It is necessary to premise, that the landlord of the inn had informed them, that a jovial party, intended, as he understood, to present some of the masques or mummeries, which made a part of the entertainment with which the Queen was usually welcomed on the royal Progresses, had left the village of Donnington an hour or two before them, in order to proceed to Kenilworth. Now it had occurred to Wayland, that, by attaching themselves in some sort to this group, as soon as they should overtake them on the road, they would be less likely to attract notice, than if they continued to travel entirely by themselves. He communicated his idea to the Countess, who, only anxious to arrive at Kenilworth without interruption, left him free to choose the manner in which this was to be accomplished. They dressed forward their horses, therefore, with the purpose of overtaking the party of intended revellers, and making the journey in their company; and had just seen the little party, consisting partly of riders, partly of people on foot, crossing the summit of a gentle hill, at about half a mile's distance, and disappearing on the other side, when Wayland, who maintained the most circumspect observation of all that met his eye in every direction, was aware that a rider was coming up behind them on a horse of uncommon action, accompanied by a serving man, whose utmost efforts were unable to keep up with his master's trotting hackney, and who, therefore, was fain to follow him at a hand gallop. Wayland looked anxiously back at these horsemen, became considerably disturbed in his manner, looked back again, and became pale, as he said to the lady—"That is Richard Varney's trotting gelding—I would know him among a thousand nags—this is a worse business than meeting the mercer."

"Draw your sword," answered the lady, "and pierce my bosom with it, rather than I should fall into his hands!"

"I would rather by a thousand times," answered Wayland, "pass it through his body, or even mine own. But to say truth, fighting is not my best point, though I can look on cold iron like another, when needs must be. And, indeed, as for my sword,—(put on, I pray you)—it is a poor provant rapier, and I warrant you he has a special Toledo. He has a serving-man, too, and I think it is the drunken ruffian Lambourne, upon the horse on which men say—(I pray you heartily to put on)—he did the great robbery of the west country grazier. It is not that I fear either Varney or Lambourne in a good cause—(your palfrey will go yet faster if you urge him)—But yet—(nay, I pray you let him not break off into the gallop, lest they should see we fear them, and give chase—keep him only at the full trot)—But yet, though I fear them not, I would we were well rid of them, and that rather by policy than by violence. Could we once reach the party before us, we may herd among them, and pass unobserved, unless Varney be really come in express pursuit of us, and then, happy man be his dole!"

While he thus spoke, he alternately urged and restrained his horse, desirous to maintain the fleetest pace that was consistent with the idea of an ordinary journey on the road, but to avoid such rapidity of move-ment as might give rise to suspicion that they were flying.

At such a pace, they ascended the gentle hill we have mentioned, and, looking from the top, had the pleasure to see that the party which had left Donnington before them, were in the little valley or bottom on the other side, where the road was traversed by a rivulet, beside which was a cottage or two. In this place they seemed to have made a pause, which gave Wayland the hope of joining them, and becoming a part of their company, ere Varney should overtake them. He was the more anxious, as his companion, though she made no complaints, and expressed no fear, began to look so deadly pale, that he was afraid she might drop from her horse. Notwithstanding this symptom of decaying strength, she pushed on her palfrey so briskly, that they joined the party in the bottom of the valley, ere Varney appeared on the top of the gentle eminence which they had descended.

They found the company to which they meant to associate them-selves, in great disorder. The women, with dishevelled locks, and looks of great importance, ran in and out of one of the cottages, and the men stood around holding the horses, and looking silly enough, as is usual in cases where their assistance is not wanted.

Wayland and his charge paused, as if out of curiosity, and then grad-ually, without making any enquiries, or being asked any questions, they mingled with the group, as if they had always made part of it.

They had not stood there above five minutes, anxiously keeping as much to the side of the road as possible, so as to place the other travellers betwixt them and Varney, when Lord Leicester's master of the horse, followed by Lambourne, came riding fiercely down the hill, their horses' flanks and the rowels of their spurs showing bloody tokens of the rate at which they travelled. The appearance of the stationary group around the cottages, wearing their buckram suits in order to protect their masquing dresses, having their light carts for transporting their scenery, and carrying various fantastic properties in their hands for the more easy conveyance, let the riders at once into the character and purpose of the company.

"You are revellers," said Varney, "designing for Kenilworth?"

"*Recte quidem, Domine spectatissime,*" answered one of the party.

"And why the devil stand you here," said Varney, "when your utmost dispatch will but bring you to Kenilworth in time? The Queen dines at Warwick to-morrow, and you loiter here, ye knaves!"

"In very truth, sir," said a little diminutive urchin, wearing a vizard with a couple of sprouting horns of an elegant scarlet hue, having moreover a black serge jerkin drawn close to his body by lacing, garnished with red stockings, and shoes so shaped as to resemble cloven feet,—"In very truth, sir, and you are in the right on't. It is my father the Devil, who, being taken in labour, has delayed our present purpose, by increasing our company with an imp too many."

"The devil he has!" answered Varney, whose laugh, however, never exceeded a sarcastic smile.

"It is even as the juvenal hath said," added the masquer who spoke first; "our major devil, for this is but our minor one, is even now at *Lucina fer opem,* within that very *tugurium.*"

"By Saint George, or rather by the Dragon, who may be a kinsman of the fiend in the straw, a most comical chance!" said Varney. "How sayst thou, Lambourne, wilt thou stand godfather for the nonce?— if the devil were to choose a gossip, I know no one more fit for the office."

"Saving always when my betters are in presence," said Lambourne, with the civil impudence of a servant who knows his services to be so indispensable, that his jest will be permitted to pass muster.

"And what is the name of the devil or devil's dam, who has timed her turns so strangely?" said Varney. "We can ill afford to spare any of our actors."

"*Gaudet nomine Sibyllæ,*" said the first speaker, "she is called Sibyl Laneham, wife of Master Richard Laneham——"

"Clerk to the Council-chamber door," said Varney; "why, she is inexcusable, having had experience how to have ordered her matters better. But who were those, a man and a woman, I think, who rode so hastily up the hill before me even now?—do they belong to your company?"

Wayland was about to hazard a reply to this alarming enquiry, when the little diablotin again thrust in his oar.

"So please you," he said, coming close up to Varney, and speaking so as not to be overheard by his companions, "The man was our devil major, who has tricks enough to supply the lack of a hundred such as Dame Laneham; and the woman—if you please, is the sage person whose assistance is most particularly necessary to our distressed comrade."

"Oh, what, you have got the wise woman, then?" said Varney. "Why, truly, she rode like one bound to a place where she was needed—And you have a spare limb of Satan, besides, to supply the place of Mistress Laneham?"

"Ay, sir," said the boy, "they are not so scarce in this world as your honour's virtuous eminence would suppose—This master-fiend shall spit a few flashes of fire, and eruct a volume or two of smoke on the spot, if it will do you pleasure—you would think he had Ætna in his abdomen."

"I lack time just now, most hopeful imp of darkness, to witness his performance," said Varney; "but here is something for you all to drink the lucky hour—and so, as the play says, 'God be with your labour!'"

Thus speaking, he struck his horse with the spurs, and rode on his way.

Lambourne tarried a moment or two behind his master, and rummaged his pouch for a piece of silver, which he bestowed on the communicative imp, as he said, for his encouragement on his path to the infernal regions, some sparks of whose fire, he said, he could discover flashing from him already. Then having received the boy's thanks for his generosity, he also spurred his horse, and rode after his master as fast as the fire flashes from flint.

"And now," said the wily imp, sidling close up to Wayland's horse, and cutting a gambol in the air, which seemed to vindicate his title to relationship with the prince of that element, "I have told them who *you* are, do you in return tell me who *I* am?"

"Either Flibbertigibbet," answered Wayland Smith, "or else an imp of the devil in good earnest."

"Thou hast hit it," answered Dickie Sludge; "I am thine own Flibbertigibbet, man; and I have broken forth of bounds, along with my learned preceptor, as I told thee I would do, whether he would or not—But what lady hast thou got with thee? I saw thou wert at fault the first question was asked, and so I drew up for thy assistance. But I must know all who she is, dear Wayland.

"Thou shalt know fifty finer things, my dear ingle," said Wayland; "but a truce to thine enquiries just now; and since you are bound for Kenilworth, thither will I too, even for the love of thy sweet face and waggish company."

"Thou shouldst have said my waggish face and sweet company," said Dickie; "but how wilt thou travel with us—I mean in what character?"

"E'en in that thou hast assigned me, to be sure—as a juggler; thou know'st I am used to the craft," answered Wayland.

"Ay, but the lady?" answered Flibbertigibbet: "credit me, I think she *is* one, and thou art in a sea of troubles about her at this moment, as I can perceive by thy fidgeting."

"O, she, man!—she is a poor sister of mine," said Wayland—"she can sing and play o' the lute, would win the fish out o' the stream."

"Let me hear her instantly," said the boy; "I love the lute rarely; I love it of all things, though I never heard it."

"Then how canst thou love it, Flibbertigibbet?" said Wayland.

"As knights love ladies in old tales," answered Dickie—"on hearsay."

"Then love it on hearsay a little longer, till my sister is recovered from the fatigue of her journey," said Wayland;—muttering afterwards betwixt his teeth, "The devil take the imp's curiosity!—I must keep fair weather with him, or we shall fare the worse."

He then proceeded to state to Master Holiday his own talents as a juggler, with those of his sister as a musician. Some proof of his dexterity was demanded, which he gave in such a style of excellence, that, delighted at obtaining such an accession to their party, they readily acquiesced in the apology which he offered, when a display of his sister's talents was required. The new-comers were invited to partake of the refreshments with which the party were provided; and it was with some difficulty that Wayland Smith obtained an opportunity of being apart with his supposed sister during the meal, of which interval he availed himself to entreat her to forget for the present both her rank and her sorrows, and condescend, as the most probable chance of remaining concealed, to mix in the society of those with whom she was to travel.

The Countess allowed the necessity of the case, and when they resumed their journey, endeavoured to comply with her guide's advice, by addressing herself to a female near her, and expressing her concern for the woman whom they were thus obliged to leave behind them.

"O, she is well attended, madam," replied the dame whom she addressed, who, from her jolly and laughter-loving demeanour, might have been the very emblem of the Wife of Bath; "and my gossip Laneham thinks as little of these matters as any one. By the ninth day, an the revels last so long, we shall have her with us at Kenilworth, even if she should travel with her bantling on her back."

There was something in this speech which took away all desire on the Countess of Leicester's part to continue the conversation; but having broken the charm by speaking to her fellow-traveller first, the good dame, who was to play Rare Gillian of Croydon in one of the interludes, took care that silence did not again settle on the journey, but entertained her mute companion with a thousand anecdotes of revels, from the days of King Harry downwards, with the reception given them by the great folk, and all the names of those who played the principal characters; but ever concluding with "they would be nothing to the princely pleasures of Kenilworth."

"And when shall we reach Kenilworth?" said the Countess, with an agitation which she in vain attempted to conceal.

"We that have horses may, with late riding, get to Warwick to-night, and Kenilworth may be distant some four or five miles,—but then we must wait till the foot-people come up; although it is like my good Lord of Leicester will have horses or light carriages to meet them, and bring them up without being travel-toiled, which last is no good preparation, as you may suppose, for dancing before your betters—And yet, Lord help me, I have seen the day I would have tramped five leagues of lealand, and turned on my toe the whole evening after, as a juggler spins a pewter platter on the point of a needle. But age has clawed me somewhat in its clutch, as the song says; though, if I like the tune and like my partner, I'll dance the hays yet with any merry lass in Warwickshire, that writes that unhappy figure four with a round O after it."

If the Countess was overwhelmed with the garrulity of this good dame, Wayland Smith, on his part, had enough to do to sustain and parry the constant attacks made upon him by the indefatigable curiosity of his old acquaintance, Richard Sludge. Nature had given that arch youngster a prying cast of disposition, which matched admirably with his sharp wit; the former inducing him to plant himself as a spy on other people's affairs, and the latter quality leading him perpetually to interfere, after he had made himself master of that which concerned him not. He spent the livelong day in attempting to peer under the Countess's muffler, and apparently what he could there discern greatly sharpened his curiosity.

"That sister of thine, Wayland," he said, "has a fair neck to have been born in a smithy, and a pretty taper hand to have been used for twirling a spindle—faith, I'll believe in your relationship when the crow's egg is hatched into a cygnet."

"Go to," said Wayland, "thou art a prating boy, and should be breeched for thine assurance."

"Well," said the imp, drawing off, "all I say is,—remember you have kept a secret from me, and if I give thee not a Rowland for thine Oliver, my name is not Dickon Sludge!"

This threat, and the distance at which Hobgoblin kept from him for the rest of the way, alarmed Wayland very much, and he suggested to his pretended sister, that, on pretext of weariness, she should express a desire to stop two or three miles short of the fair town of Warwick, promising to rejoin the troop in the morning. A small village inn afforded them a resting-place; and it was with secret pleasure that Wayland saw the whole party, including Dickon, pass on, after a courteous farewell, and leave them behind.

"To-morrow, madam," he said to his charge, "we will, with your leave, again start early, and reach Kenilworth before the rout which are to assemble there."

The Countess gave assent to the proposal of her faithful guide; but, somewhat to his surprise, said nothing farther on the subject, which left Wayland under the disagreeable uncertainty whether or no she had formed any plan for her own future proceedings, as he knew her situation demanded circumspection, although he was but imperfectly acquainted with all its peculiarities. Concluding, however, that she must have friends within the castle, whose advice and assistance she could safely trust, he supposed his task would be best accomplished by conducting her thither in safety, agreeably to her repeated commands.

CHAPTER XXV

Hark, the bells summon, and the bugle calls,
But she the fairest answers not—the tide
Of nobles and of ladies throngs the halls,
But she the loveliest must in secret hide.
What eyes were thine, proud Prince, which in the gleam
Of yon gay meteors lost that better sense,
That o'er the glow-worm doth the star esteem,
And merit's modest blush o'er courtly insolence?
The Glass Slipper.

THE unfortunate Countess of Leicester had, from her infancy upwards, been treated by those around her with indulgence as unbounded as injudicious. The natural sweetness of her disposition had saved her from becoming insolent and ill-humoured; but the caprice which preferred the handsome and insinuating Leicester before Tressilian, of whose high honour and unalterable affection she herself entertained so firm an opinion—that fatal error, which ruined the happiness of her life, had its origin in the mistaken kindness that had spared her childhood the painful, but most necessary lesson, of submission and self-command. From the same indulgence, it followed that she had only been accustomed to form and to express her wishes, leaving to others the task of fulfilling them; and thus, at the most momentous period of her life, she was alike destitute of presence of mind, and of ability to form for herself any reasonable or prudent plan of conduct.

These difficulties pressed on the unfortunate lady with overwhelming force, on the morning which seemed to be the crisis of her fate. Overlooking every intermediate consideration, she had only desired to be at Kenilworth, and to approach her husband's presence; and now, when she was in the vicinity of both, a thousand considerations arose at once upon her mind, startling her with accumulated doubts and dangers, some real, some imaginary, and all exalted and exaggerated by a situation alike helpless, and destitute of aid and counsel.

A sleepless night rendered her so weak in the morning, that she was

altogether unable to attend Wayland's early summons. The trusty guide became extremely distressed on the lady's account, and somewhat alarmed on his own, and was on the point of going alone to Kenilworth, in the hope of discovering Tressilian, and intimating to him the lady's approach, when about nine in the morning he was summoned to attend her. He found her dressed, and ready for resuming her journey, but with a paleness of countenance which alarmed him for her health. She intimated her desire that the horses might be got instantly ready, and resisted with impatience her guide's request, that she would take some refreshment before setting forward. "I have had," she said, "a cup of water—the wretch who is dragged to execution needs no stronger cordial, and that may serve me which suffices for him—do as I command you." Wayland Smith still hesitated. "What would you have?" said she— "Have I not spoken plainly?"

"Yes, madam," answered Wayland; "but may I ask what is your farther purpose?—I only desire to know, that I may guide myself by your wishes. The whole country is afloat, and streaming towards the Castle of Kenilworth. It will be difficult travelling thither, even if we had the necessary passports for safe-conduct and free admittance— Unknown and unfriended, we may come by mishap.—Your ladyship will forgive my speaking my poor mind—Were we not better try to find out the masquers, and again join ourselves with them?"—The Countess shook her head, and her guide proceeded, "Then I see but one other remedy."

"Speak out, then," said the lady, not displeased, perhaps, that he should thus offer the advice which she was ashamed to ask! "I believe thee faithful—what wouldst thou counsel?"

"That I should warn Master Tressilian," said Wayland, "that you are in this place. I am right certain he would get to horse with a few of Lord Sussex's followers, and ensure your personal safety."

"And is it to *me* you advise," said the Countess, "to put myself under the protection of Sussex, the unworthy rival of the noble Leicester?" Then, seeing the surprise with which Wayland stared upon her, and afraid of having too strongly intimated her interest in Leicester, she added, "And for Tressilian, it must not be—mention not to him, I charge you, my unhappy name; it would but double *my* misfortunes, and involve *him* in dangers beyond the power of rescue." She paused; but when she observed that Wayland continued to look on her with that anxious and uncertain gaze, which indicated a doubt whether her brain was settled, she assumed an air of composure, and added, "Do thou but guide me to Kenilworth Castle, good fellow, and thy task is ended, since I will then judge what farther is to be done. Thou hast yet been true to me—here is something that will make thee rich amends."

She offered the artist a ring, containing a valuable stone. Wayland looked at it, hesitated a moment, and then returned it. "Not," he said, "that I am above your kindness, madam, being but a poor fellow, who have been forced, God help me! to live by worse shifts than the bounty of such a person as you. But, as my old master the farrier used to say to his customers, 'No cure no pay.' We are not yet in Kenilworth Castle, and it is time enough to discharge your guide, as they say, when you take your boots off. I trust in God your ladyship is as well assured of fitting reception when you arrive, as you may hold yourself certain of my best endeavours to conduct you thither safely. I go to get the horses; meantime, let me pray you once more, as your poor physician as well as guide, to take some sustenance."

"I will—I will," said the lady, hastily. "Begone, begone instantly!—It is in vain I assume audacity," said she, when he left the room; "even this poor groom sees through my affectation of courage, and fathoms the very ground of my fears."

She then attempted to follow her guide's advice by taking some food, but was compelled to desist, as the effort to swallow even a single morsel gave her so much uneasiness as amounted wellnigh to suffocation. A moment afterwards the horses appeared at the latticed window—the lady mounted, and found that relief from the free air and change of place, which is frequently experienced in similar circumstances.

It chanced well for the Countess's purpose that Wayland Smith, whose previous wandering and unsettled life had made him acquainted with almost all England, was intimate with all the by-roads, as well as direct communications, through the beautiful county of Warwick. For such and so great was the throng which flocked in all directions towards Kenilworth, to see the entry of Elizabeth into that splendid mansion of her prime favourite, that the principal roads were actually blocked up and interrupted, and it was only by circuitous by-paths that the travellers could proceed on their journey.

The Queen's purveyors had been abroad, sweeping the farms and villages of those articles usually exacted during a royal Progress, and for which the owners were afterwards to obtain a tardy payment from the Board of Green Cloth. The Earl of Leicester's household officers had been scouring the country for the same purpose; and many of his friends and allies, both near and remote, took this opportunity of ingratiating themselves, by sending large quantities of provisions and delicacies of all kinds, with game in huge numbers, and whole tuns of the best liquors, foreign and domestic. Thus the high-roads were filled with droves of bullocks, sheep, calves, and hogs, and choked with loaded wains, whose axle-trees cracked under their burdens of wine-casks and hogsheads of ale, and huge hampers of grocery goods, and slaughtered game, and salted provisions, and sacks of flour. Perpetual stoppages took place as these wains became entangled; and their rude drivers, swearing and brawling till their wild passions were fully raised, began to debate precedence with their waggon-whips and quarter-staves, which occasional riots were usually quieted by a purveyor, deputy-marshal's-man, or some other person in authority, breaking the heads of both parties.

Here were, besides, players and mummers, jugglers and showmen, of every description, traversing in joyous bands the paths which led to the Palace of Princely Pleasure; for so the travelling minstrels had termed Kenilworth in the songs which already had come forth in anticipation of the revels which were there expected. In the midst of this motley show, mendicants were exhibiting their real or pretended miseries, forming a strange, though common, contrast betwixt the vanities and the sorrows of human existence. All these floated along with the immense tide of population, whom mere curiosity had drawn together; and where the mechanic, in his leathern apron, elbowed the dink and dainty dame, his city mistress; where clowns, with hob-nailed shoes, were treading on the kibes of substantial burghers and gentlemen of worship; and where Joan of the dairy, with robust pace, and red sturdy arms, rowed her way onward, amongst those prim and pretty moppets, whose sires were knights and squires.

The throng and confusion was, however, of a gay and cheerful character. All came forth to see and to enjoy, and all laughed at the trifling inconveniences which at another time might have chafed their temper. Excepting the occasional brawls which we have mentioned among that irritable race the carmen, the mingled sounds which arose from the multitude were those of light-hearted mirth, and tiptoe jollity. The musicians preluded on their instruments—the minstrels hummed their songs—the licensed jester whooped betwixt mirth and madness, as he brandished his bauble—the morrice-dancers jangled their bells—the rustics halloo'd and whistled—men laughed loud, and maidens giggled shrill; while many a broad jest flew like a shuttle-cock from one party, to be caught in the air and returned from the opposite side of the road by another, at which it was aimed.

No inflictions can be so distressing to a mind absorbed in melancholy, as being plunged into a scene of mirth and revelry, forming an accompaniment so dissonant from its own feelings. Yet, in the case of the Countess of Leicester, the noise and tumult of this giddy scene distracted her thoughts, and rendered her this sad service, that it became impossible for her to brood on her own misery, or to form terrible anticipations of her approaching fate. She travelled on, like one in a dream, following implicitly the guidance of Wayland, who, with great address, now threaded his way through the general throng of passengers, now stood still until a favourable opportunity occurred of again moving forward, and frequently turning altogether out of the direct road, followed some circuitous by-path, which brought them into the highway again, after having given them the opportunity of traversing a considerable way with greater ease and rapidity.

It was thus he avoided Warwick, within whose Castle (that fairest monument of ancient and chivalrous splendour which yet remains uninjured by time) Elizabeth had passed the previous night, and where she was to tarry until past noon, at that time the general hour of dinner

throughout England, after which repast she was to proceed to Kenilworth. In the meanwhile, each passing group had something to say in
the Sovereign's praise, though not absolutely without the usual mixture
of satire which qualifies more or less our estimate of our neighbours,
especially if they chance to be also our betters.

"Heard you," said one, "how graciously she spoke to Master Bailiff
and the Recorder, and to good Master Griffin the preacher, as they
kneeled down at her coach-window?"

"Ay, and how she said to little Aglionby, 'Master Recorder, men
would have persuaded me that you were afraid of me, but truly I think,
so well did you reckon up to me the virtues of a sovereign, that I have
more reason to be afraid of you'—And then with what grace she took the
fair-wrought purse with the twenty gold sovereigns, seeming as though
she would not willingly handle it, and yet taking it withal."

"Ay, ay," said another, "her fingers closed on it pretty willingly
methought, when all was done; and methought, too, she weighed them
for a second in her hand, as she would say, I hope they be avoirdupois."

"She needed not, neighbour," said a third; "it is only when the corporation pay the accounts of a poor handicraft like me, that they put him off
with clipt coin.—Well, there is a God above all—Little Master Recorder,
since that is the word, will be greater now than ever."

"Come, good neighbour," said the first speaker, "be not envious—She
is a good Queen, and a generous—She gave the purse to the Earl of
Leicester."

"I envious?—beshrew thy heart for the word!" replied the handicraft—"But she will give all to the Earl of Leicester anon, methinks."

"You are turning ill, lady," said Wayland Smith to the Countess of
Leicester, and proposed that she should draw off from the road, and halt
till she recovered. But, subduing her feelings at this, and different
speeches to the same purpose, which caught her ear as they passed on,
she insisted that her guide should proceed to Kenilworth with all the
haste which the numerous impediments of their journey permitted.
Meanwhile, Wayland's anxiety at her repeated fits of indisposition, and
her obvious distraction of mind, was hourly increasing, and he became
extremely desirous, that, according to her reiterated requests, she should
be safely introduced into the Castle, where, he doubted not, she was
secure of a kind reception, though she seemed unwilling to reveal on
whom she reposed her hopes.

"An I were once rid of this peril," thought he, "and if any man shall
find me playing squire of the body to a damosel-errant, he shall have
leave to beat my brains out with my own sledge-hammer!"

At length the princely Castle appeared, upon improving which, and
the domains around, the Earl of Leicester had, it is said, expended sixty
thousand pounds sterling, a sum equal to half a million of our present
money.

The outer wall of this splendid and gigantic structure enclosed seven acres, a part of which was occupied by extensive stables, and by a pleasure garden, with its trim arbours and parterres, and the rest formed the large base-court, or outer yard, of the noble Castle. The lordly structure itself, which rose near the centre of this spacious enclosure, was composed of a huge pile of magnificent castellated buildings, apparently of different ages, surrounding an inner court, and bearing, in the names attached to each portion of the magnificent mass, and in the armorial bearings which were there blazoned, the emblems of mighty chiefs who had long passed away, and whose history, could Ambition have lent ear to it, might have read a lesson to the haughty favourite, who had now acquired and was augmenting the fair domain. A large and massive Keep, which formed the citadel of the Castle, was of uncertain though great antiquity. It bore the name of Cæsar, perhaps from its resemblance to that in the Tower of London so called. Some antiquaries ascribe its foundation to the time of Kenelph, from whom the Castle had its name, a Saxon king of Mercia, and others to an early era after the Norman Conquest. On the exterior walls frowned the scutcheon of the Clintons, by whom they were founded in the reign of Henry I., and of the yet more redoubted Simon de Montfort, by whom, during the Barons' wars, Kenilworth was long held out against Henry III. Here Mortimer, Earl of March, famous alike for his rise and his fall, had once gaily revelled in Kenilworth, while his dethroned sovereign, Edward II., languished in its dungeons. Old John of Gaunt, "time-honoured Lancaster," had widely extended the Castle, erecting that noble and massive pile which yet bears the name of Lancaster's Buildings; and Leicester himself had outdone the former possessors, princely and powerful as they were, by erecting another immense structure, which now lies crushed under its own ruins, the monument of its owner's ambition. The external wall of this royal Castle, was, on the south and west sides, adorned and defended by a lake partly artificial, across which Leicester had constructed a stately bridge, that Elizabeth might enter the Castle by a path hitherto untrodden, instead of the usual entrance to the northward, over which he had erected a gate-house, or barbican, which still exists, and is equal in extent, and superior in architecture, to the baronial castle of many a northern chief.

Beyond the lake lay an extensive chase, full of red deer, fallow deer, roes, and every species of game, and abounding with lofty trees, from amongst which the extended front and massive towers of the Castle were seen to rise in majesty and beauty. We cannot but add, that of this lordly palace, where princes feasted and heroes fought, now in the bloody earnest of storm and siege, and now in the games of chivalry, where beauty dealt the prize which valour won, all is now desolate. The bed of the lake is but a rushy swamp; and the massive ruins of the Castle only serve to show what their splendour once was, and to impress on the musing visitor the transitory value of human possessions, and the happiness of those who enjoy a humble lot in virtuous contentment.

It was with far different feelings that the unfortunate Countess of

Leicester viewed those grey and massive towers, when she first beheld them rise above the embowering and richly shaded woods, over which they seemed to preside. She, the undoubted wife of the great Earl, of Elizabeth's minion, and England's mighty favourite, was approaching the presence of her husband, and that husband's sovereign, under the protection, rather than the guidance, of a poor juggler; and though unquestioned Mistress of that proud Castle, whose lightest word ought to have had force sufficient to make its gates leap from their massive hinges to receive her, yet she could not conceal from herself the difficulty and peril which she must experience in gaining admission into her own halls.

The risk and difficulty, indeed, seemed to increase every moment, and at length threatened altogether to put a stop to her farther progress, at the great gate leading to a broad and fair road, which, traversing the breadth of the chase for the space of two miles, and commanding several most beautiful views of the Castle and lake, terminated at the newly constructed bridge, to which it was an appendage, and which was destined to form the Queen's approach to the Castle on that memorable occasion.

Here the Countess and Wayland found the gate at the end of this avenue, which opened on the Warwick road, guarded by a body of the Queen's mounted yeomen of the guard, armed in corslets richly carved and gilded, and wearing morions instead of bonnets, having their carbines resting with the butt-end on their thighs. These guards, distinguished for strength and stature, who did duty wherever the Queen went in person, were here stationed under the direction of a pursuivant, graced with the Bear and Ragged Staff on his arm, as belonging to the Earl of Leicester, and peremptorily refused all admittance, excepting to such as were guests invited to the festival, or persons who were to perform some part in the mirthful exhibitions which were proposed.

The press was of consequence great around the entrance, and persons of all kinds presented every sort of plea for admittance; to which the guards turned an inexorable ear, pleading, in return to fair words, and even to fair offers, the strictness of their orders, founded on the Queen's well-known dislike to the rude pressing of a multitude. With those whom such reasons did not serve, they dealt more rudely, repelling them without ceremony by the pressure of their powerful barbed horses, and good round blows from the stock of their carbines. These last manœuvres produced undulations amongst the crowd, which rendered Wayland much afraid that he might perforce be separated from his charge in the throng. Neither did he know what excuse to make in order to obtain admittance, and he was debating the matter in his head with great uncertainty, when the Earl's pursuivant, having cast an eye upon him, exclaimed, to his no small surprise, "Yeomen, make room for the fellow in the orange-tawny cloak—Come forward, Sir Coxcomb, and make haste. What, in the fiend's name, has kept you waiting? Come forward with your bale of woman's gear."

While the pursuivant gave Wayland this pressing yet uncourteous invitation, which, for a minute or two, he could not imagine was applied to him, the yeomen speedily made a free passage for him, while, only cautioning his companion to keep the muffler close around her face, he entered the gate leading her palfrey, but with such a drooping crest, and such a look of conscious fear and anxiety, that the crowd, not greatly pleased at any rate with the preference bestowed upon them, accompanied their admission with hooting, and a loud laugh of derision.

Admitted thus within the chase, though with no very flattering notice or distinction, Wayland and his charge rode forward, musing what difficulties it would be next their lot to encounter, through the broad avenue, which was sentinelled on either side by a long line of retainers, armed with swords and partisans, richly dressed in the Earl of Leicester's liveries, and bearing his cognizance of the Bear and Ragged Staff, each placed within three paces of his comrade, so as to line the whole road from the entrance into the park to the bridge. And, indeed, when the lady obtained the first commanding view of the Castle, with its stately towers rising from within a long sweeping line of outward walls, ornamented with battlements, and turrets, and platforms at every point of defence, with many a banner streaming from its walls, and such a bustle of gay crests, and waving plumes, disposed on the terraces and battlements, and all the gay and gorgeous scene, her heart, unaccustomed to such splendour, sank as if it died within her, and for a moment she asked herself, what she had offered up to Leicester to deserve to become the partner of this princely splendour. But her pride and generous spirit resisted the whisper which bade her despair.

"I have given him," she said, "all that woman has to give. Name and fame, heart and hand, have I given the lord of all this magnificence at the altar, and England's Queen could give him no more. He is my husband—I am his wife—Whom God hath joined, man cannot sunder. I will be bold in claiming my right; even the bolder, that I come thus unexpected, and thus forlorn. I know my noble Dudley well! He will be something impatient at my disobeying him, but Amy will weep, and Dudley will forgive her."

These meditations were interrupted by a cry of surprise from her guide Wayland, who suddenly felt himself grasped firmly round the body by a pair of long thin black arms, belonging to some one who had dropped himself out of an oak-tree, upon the croup of his horse, amidst the shouts of laughter which burst from the sentinels.

"This must be the devil, or Flibbertigibbet again!" said Wayland, after a vain struggle to disengage himself, and unhorse the urchin who clung to him; "Do Kenilworth oaks bear such acorns?"

"In sooth do they, Master Wayland," said his unexpected adjunct, "and many others, too hard for you to crack, for as old as you are, without my teaching you. How would you have passed the pursuivant at the upper gate yonder, had not I warned him our principal juggler was to follow us? and here have I waited for you, having clambered up into the tree from the top of our wain, and I suppose they are all mad for want of me by this time."

"Nay, then, thou art a limb of the devil in good earnest," said Wayland. "I give thee way, good imp, and will walk by thy counsel; only as thou art powerful, be merciful."

As he spoke, they approached a strong tower, at the south extremity of the long bridge we have mentioned, which served to protect the outer gateway of the Castle of Kenilworth.

Under such disastrous circumstances, and in such singular company, did the unfortunate Countess of Leicester approach, for the first time, the magnificent abode of her almost princely husband.

CHAPTER XXVI

Snug. Have you the lion's part written? pray
you, if it be, give it me, for I am slow of study.
Quince. You may do it extempore, for it is
nothing but roaring.

Midsummer-Night's Dream.

WHEN the Countess of Leicester arrived at the outer gate of the Castle of Kenilworth, she found the tower, beneath which its ample portal arch opened, guarded in a singular manner. Upon the battlements were placed gigantic warders, with clubs, battle-axes, and other implements of ancient warfare, designed to represent the soldiers of King Arthur; those primitive Britons, by whom, according to romantic tradition, the Castle had been first tenanted, though history carried back its antiquity only to the times of the Heptarchy. Some of these tremendous figures were real men, dressed up with vizards and buskins; others were mere pageants composed of pasteboard and buckram, which, viewed from beneath, and mingled with those that were real, formed a sufficiently striking representation of what was intended. But the gigantic porter who waited at the gate beneath, and actually discharged the duties of warder, owed none of his terrors to fictitious means. He was a man whose huge stature, thewes, sinews, and bulk in proportion, would have enabled him to enact Colbrand, Ascapart, or any other giant of romance, without raising himself nearer to heaven even by the altitude of a chopin. The legs and knees of this son of Anak were bare, as were his arms, from a span below the shoulders; but his feet were defended with sandals, fastened with cross straps of scarlet leather, studded with brazen knobs. A close jerkin of scarlet velvet, looped with gold, with short breeches of the same, covered his body and a part of his limbs; and he wore on his shoulders, instead of a cloak, the skin of a black bear. The head of this formidable person was uncovered, except by his shaggy black hair, which descended on either side around features of that huge, lumpish, and heavy cast, which are often annexed to men of very uncommon size, and which, notwithstanding some distinguished exceptions, have created a general prejudice against giants, as being a dull and sullen kind of persons. This tremendous warder was appropriately armed with a heavy club spiked with steel. In fine, he represented excellently one of those giants of popular romance, who figure in every fairy tale, or legend of knight-errantry.

The demeanour of this modern Titan, when Wayland Smith bent his attention to him, had in it something arguing much mental embarrassment and vexation; for sometimes he sat down for an instant on a massive stone bench, which seemed placed for his accommodation beside the gateway, and then ever and anon he started up, scratching his huge head, and striding to and fro on his post, like one under a fit of impatience and anxiety. It was while the porter was pacing before the gate in this agitated manner, that Wayland, modestly, yet as a matter of course, (not, however, without some mental misgiving), was about to pass him, and enter the portal arch. The porter, however, stopped his progress, bidding him, in a thundering voice, "Stand back!" and enforcing his injunction by heaving up his steel-shod mace, and dashing it on the ground before Wayland's horse's nose with such vehemence, that the pavement flashed fire, and the archway rang to the clamour. Wayland, availing himself of Dickie's hint, began to state that he belonged to a band of performers to which his presence was indispensable, that he had been accidentally detained behind, and much to the same purpose. But the warder was inexorable, and kept muttering and murmuring something betwixt his teeth, which Wayland could make little of; and addressing betwixt whiles a refusal of admittance, couched in language which was but too intelligible. A specimen of his speech might run thus.—"What, how now, my masters?" (to himself)—"Here's a stir—here's a coil."—(Then to Wayland)—"You are a loitering knave, and shall have no entrance."—(Again to himself)—"Here's a throng—here's a thrusting.—I shall ne'er get through with it—Here's a—humph—ha"—(To Wayland)—"Back from the gate, or I'll break the pate of thee"—(Once more to himself)—"Here's a—no—I shall never get through it."

"Stand still," whispered Flibbertigibbet into Wayland's ear; "I know where the shoe pinches, and will tame him in an instant."

He dropped down from the horse, and skipping up to the porter, plucked him by the tail of the bear-skin, so as to induce him to decline his huge head, and whispered something in his ear. Not at the command of the lord of some Eastern talisman did ever Afrite change his horrid frown into a look of smooth submission, more suddenly than the gigantic porter of Kenilworth relaxed the terrors of his look, at the instant Flibbertigibbet's whisper reached his ears. He flung his club upon the ground, and caught up Dickie Sludge, raising him to such a distance from the earth, as might have proved perilous had he chanced to let him slip.

"It is even so," he said, with a thundering sound of exultation—"it is even so, my little dandieprat—But who the devil could teach it thee?"

"Do not thou care about that," said Flibbertigibbet; "but——" he looked at Wayland and the lady, and then sunk what he had to say in a whisper, which needed not to be a loud one, as the giant held him for his convenience close to his ear. The porter then gave Dickie a warm caress, and set him on the ground with the same care which a careful housewife uses in replacing a cracked china cup upon her mantel-piece, calling out at the same time to Wayland and the lady, "In with you—in with you—and take heed how you come too late another day when I chance to be porter."

"Ay, ay, in with you," added Flibbertigibbet; "I must stay a short space with mine honest Philistine, my Goliath of Gath here; but I will be with you anon, and at the bottom of all your secrets, were they as deep and dark as the Castle dungeon."

"I do believe thou wouldst," said Wayland; "but I trust the secret will be soon out of my keeping, and then I shall care the less whether thou or any one knows it."

They now crossed the entrance tower, which obtained the name of the Gallery-tower, from the following circumstance:—The whole bridge, extending from the entrance to another tower on the opposite side of the lake, called Mortimer's Tower, was so disposed as to make a spacious tilt-yard, about one hundred and thirty yards in length, and ten in breadth, strewed with the finest sand, and defended on either side by strong and high palisades. The broad and fair gallery, destined for the ladies who were to witness the feats of chivalry presented on this area, was erected on the northern side of the outer tower, to which it gave name. Our travellers passed slowly along the bridge or tilt-yard, and arrived at Mortimer's Tower, at its farthest extremity, through which the approach led into the outer, or base court of the castle. Mortimer's Tower bore on its front the scutcheon of the Earl of March, whose daring ambition overthrew the throne of Edward II., and aspired to share his power with the "She-wolf of France," to whom the unhappy monarch was wedded. The gate, which opened under this ominous memorial, was guarded by many warders in rich liveries; but they offered no opposition to the entrance of the Countess and her guide, who, having passed by license of the principal porter of the Gallery-tower, were not, it may be supposed, liable to interruption from his deputies. They entered accordingly, in silence, the great outward court of the castle, having then full before them that vast and lordly pile, with all its stately towers, each gate open, as if in sign of unlimited hospitality, and the apartments filled with noble guests of every degree, besides dependants, retainers, domestics of every description, and all the appendages and promoters of mirth and revelry.

Amid this stately and busy scene, Wayland halted his horse, and looked upon the lady, as if waiting her commands what was next to be done, since they had safely reached the place of destination. As she remained silent, Wayland, after waiting a minute or two, ventured to ask her, in direct terms, what were her next commands. She raised her hand to her forehead, as if in the act of collecting her thoughts and resolution, while she answered him in a low and suppressed voice, like the murmurs of one who speaks in a dream—"Commands? I may indeed claim right to command, but who is there will obey me?"

Then suddenly raising her head, like one who has formed a decisive resolution, she addressed a gaily dressed domestic, who was crossing the court with importance and bustle in his countenance.—"Stop, sir," she said, "I desire to speak with the Earl of Leicester."

"With whom, an it please you?" said the man, surprised at the demand; and then looking upon the mean equipage of her who used towards him such a tone of authority, he added, with insolence, "Why, what Bess of Bedlam is this, would ask to see my lord on such a day as the present?"

"Friend," said the Countess, "be not insolent—my business with the Earl is most urgent."

"You must get some one else to do it, were it thrice as urgent," said the fellow.—"I should summon my lord from the Queen's royal presence to do *your* business, should I?—I were like to be thanked with a horsewhip. I marvel our old porter took not measure of such ware with his club, instead of giving them passage; but his brain is addled with getting his speech by heart."

Two or three persons stopped, attracted by the fleering way in which the serving-man expressed himself; and Wayland, alarmed both for himself and the lady, hastily addressed himself to one who appeared the most civil, and thrusting a piece of money into his hand, held a moment's counsel with him, on the subject of finding a place of temporary retreat for the lady. The person to whom he spoke, being one in some authority, rebuked the others for their incivility, and commanding one fellow to take care of the strangers' horses, he desired them to follow him. The Countess retained presence of mind sufficient to see that it was absolutely necessary she should comply with his request; and, leaving the rude lackeys and grooms to crack their brutal jests about light heads, light heels, and so forth, Wayland and she followed in silence the deputy-usher, who undertook to be their conductor.

They entered the inner court of the Castle by the great gateway, which extended betwixt the principal Keep, or Donjon, called Cæsar's Tower, and a stately building which passed by the name of King Henry's Lodging, and were thus placed in the centre of the noble pile, which presented on its different fronts magnificent specimens of every species of castellated architecture, from the Conquest to the reign of Elizabeth, with the appropriate style and ornaments of each.

Across this inner court also they were conducted by their guide to a small but strong tower, occupying the north-east angle of the building adjacent to the great hall, and filling up a space betwixt the immense range of kitchens and the end of the great hall itself. The lower part of this tower was occupied by some of the household officers of Leicester, owing to its convenient vicinity to the places where their duty lay; but in the upper storey, which was reached by a narrow winding stair, was a small octangular chamber, which, in the great demand for lodgings, had been on the present occasion fitted up for the reception of guests, though generally said to have been used as a place of confinement for some unhappy person who had been there murdered. Tradition called this prisoner Mervyn, and transferred his name to the tower. That it had been used as a prison was not improbable; for the floor of each storey was arched, the walls of tremendous thickness, while the space of the chamber did not exceed fifteen feet in diameter. The window, however, was pleasant, though narrow, and commanded a delightful view of what was called the *Pleasance;* a space of ground enclosed and decorated with arches, trophies, statues, fountains, and other architectural monuments, which formed one access from the castle itself into the garden. There was a bed in the apartment and other preparations for the reception of a guest, to which the Countess paid but slight attention, her notice being instantly arrested by the sight of writing materials placed on the table, (not very commonly to be found in the bedrooms of those days,) which instantly suggested the idea of writing to Leicester, and remaining private until she had received his answer.

The deputy-usher having introduced them into this commodious apartment, courteously asked Wayland, whose generosity he had experienced, whether he could do any thing farther for his service. Upon receiving a gentle hint, that some refreshment would not be unacceptable, he presently conveyed the smith to the buttery-hatch, where dressed provisions of all sorts were distributed, with hospitable profusion, to all who asked for them. Wayland was readily supplied with some light provisions, such as he thought would best suit the faded appetite of the lady, and did not omit the opportunity of himself making a hasty but hearty meal on more substantial fare. He then returned to the apartment in the turret, where he found the Countess, who had finished her letter to Leicester; and, in lieu of a seal and silken thread, had secured it with a braid of her own beautiful tresses, fastened by what is called a true-love knot.

"Good friend," said she to Wayland, "whom God hath sent to aid me at my utmost need, I do beseech thee, as the last trouble you shall take for an unfortunate lady, to deliver this letter to the noble Earl of Leicester. Be it received as it may," she said, with features agitated betwixt hope and fear, "thou, good fellow, shalt have no more cumber with me. But I hope the best; and if ever lady made a poor man rich, thou hast surely deserved it at my hand, should my happy days ever come round again. Give it, I pray you, into Lord Leicester's own hand, and mark how he looks on receiving it."

Wayland, on his part, readily undertook the commission, but anxiously prayed the lady, in his turn, to partake of some refreshment; in which he at length prevailed, more through importunity, and her desire to see him begone on his errand, than from any inclination the Countess felt to comply with his request. He then left her, advising her to lock her door on the inside, and not to stir from her little apartment—and went to seek an opportunity of discharging her errand, as well as of carrying into effect a purpose of his own, which circumstances had induced him to form.

In fact, from the conduct of the lady during the journey—her long fits of profound silence—the irresolution and uncertainty which appeared to pervade all her movements, and the obvious incapacity of thinking and acting for herself, under which she seemed to labour, Wayland had formed the not improbable opinion, that the difficulties of her situation had in some degree affected her understanding.

When she had escaped from the seclusion of Cumnor-Place, and the dangers to which she was there exposed, it would have seemed her most rational course to retire to her father's, or elsewhere, at a distance from the power of those by whom these dangers had been created. When, instead of doing so, she demanded to be conveyed to Kenilworth, Wayland had been only able to account for her conduct, by supposing that she meant to put herself under the tutelage of Tressilian, and to appeal to the protection of the Queen. But now, instead of following this natural course, she intrusted him with a letter to Leicester, the patron of Varney, and within whose jurisdiction at least, if not under his express authority, all the evils she had already suffered were inflicted upon her. This seemed an unsafe, and even a desperate measure, and Wayland felt anxiety for his own safety, as well as that of the lady, should he execute her commission, before he had secured the advice and countenance of a protector. He therefore resolved, before delivering the letter to Leicester, that he would seek out Tressilian, and communicate to him the arrival of the lady at Kenilworth, and thus at once rid himself of all farther responsibility, and devolve the task of guiding and protecting this unfortunate lady upon the patron who had at first employed him in her service.

"He will be a better judge than I am," said Wayland, "whether she is to be gratified in this humour of appeal to my Lord of Leicester, which seems like an act of insanity; and, therefore, I will turn the matter over on his hands, deliver him the letter, receive what they list to give me by way of guerdon, and then show the Castle of Kenilworth a pair of light heels; for, after the work I have been engaged in, it will be, I fear, neither a safe nor wholesome place of residence; and I would rather shoe colts on the coldest common in England, than share in their gayest revels."

CHAPTER XXVII

In my time I have seen a boy do wonders.
Robin, the red tinker, had a boy
Would ha' run through a cat-hole.
                                        The Coxcomb.

AMID the universal bustle which filled the Castle and its environs, it was no easy matter to find out any individual; and Wayland was still less likely to light upon Tressilian, whom he sought so anxiously, because, sensible of the danger of attracting attention, in the circumstances in which he was placed, he dared not make general enquiries among the retainers or domestics of Leicester. He learned, however, by indirect questions, that, in all probability, Tressilian must have been one of a large party of gentlemen in attendance on the Earl of Sussex, who had accompanied their patron that morning to Kenilworth, when Leicester had received them with marks of the most formal respect and distinction. He farther learned, that both Earls, with their followers, and many other nobles, knights, and gentlemen, had taken horse, and gone towards Warwick several hours since, for the purpose of escorting the Queen to Kenilworth.

Her Majesty's arrival, like other great events, was delayed from hour to hour; and it was now announced by a breathless post, that her Majesty, being detained by her gracious desire to receive the homage of her lieges who had thronged to wait upon her at Warwick, it would be the hour of twilight ere she entered the Castle. The intelligence released for a time those who were upon duty, in the immediate expectation of the Queen's appearance, and ready to play their part in the solemnities with which it was to be accompanied; and Wayland, seeing several horsemen enter the Castle, was not without hopes that Tressilian might be of the number. That he might not lose an opportunity of meeting his patron in the event of this being the case, Wayland placed himself in the base-court of the Castle, near Mortimer's Tower, and watched every one who went or came by the bridge, the extremity of which was protected by that building. Thus stationed, nobody could enter or leave the Castle without his observation, and most anxiously did he study the garb and countenance of every horseman, as, passing from under the opposite Gallery-tower, they paced slowly, or curvetted, along the tilt-yard, and approached the entrance of the base-court.

But while Wayland gazed thus eagerly to discover him whom he saw not, he was pulled by the sleeve by one by whom he himself would not willingly have been seen.

This was Dickie Sludge, or Flibbertigibbet, who, like the imp whose name he bore, and whom he had been accoutred in order to resemble, seemed to be ever at the ear of those who thought least of him. Whatever were Wayland's internal feelings, he judged it necessary to express pleasure at their unexpected meeting.

"Ta? is it thou, my miniken—my miller's thumb—my prince of caco-demons—my little mouse?"

"Ay," said Dickie, "the mouse which gnawed asunder the toils, just when the lion who was caught in them began to look wonderfully like an ass."

"Why, thou little hop-the-gutter, thou art as sharp as vinegar this afternoon! But tell me, how didst thou come off with yonder jolterheaded giant, whom I left thee with?—I was afraid he would have stripped thy clothes, and so swallowed thee, as men peel and eat a roasted chestnut."

"Had he done so," replied the boy, "he would have more brains in his guts than ever he had in his noddle. But the giant is a courteous monster, and more grateful than many other folk whom I have helped at a pinch, Master Wayland Smith."

"Beshrew me, Flibbertigibbet," replied Wayland, "but thou art sharper than a Sheffield whittle! I would I knew by what charm you muzzled yonder old bear."

"Ay, that is in your own manner," answered Dickie; "you think fine speeches will pass muster instead of good-will. However, as to this honest porter, you must know, that when we presented ourselves at the gate yonder, his brain was overburdened with a speech that had been penned for him, and which proved rather an overmatch for his gigantic faculties. Now this same pithy oration had been indited, like sundry others, by my learned magister, Erasmus Holiday, so I had heard it often enough to remember every line. As soon as I heard him blundering, and flounder-ing like a fish upon dry land, through the first verse, and perceived him at a stand, I knew where the shoe pinched, and helped him to the next word, when he caught me up in an ecstasy, even as you saw but now. I promised, as the price of your admission, to hide me under his bearish gaberdine, and prompt him in the hour of need. I have just now been getting some food in the Castle, and am about to return to him."

"That's right—that's right, my dear Dickie," replied Wayland; "haste thee, for Heaven's sake! else the poor giant will be utterly disconsolate for want of his dwarfish auxiliary—Away with thee, Dickie!"

"Ay, ay!" answered the boy—"Away with Dickie, when we have got what good of him we can.—You will not let me know the story of this lady, then, who is as much sister of thine as I am?"

"Why, what good would it do thee, thou silly elf?" said Wayland.

"O, stand ye on these terms?" said the boy; "well, I care not greatly about the matter,—only, I never smell out a secret, but I try to be either at the right or the wrong end of it, and so good evening to ye."

"Nay, but Dickie," said Wayland, who knew the boy's restless and intriguing disposition too well not to fear his enmity—"stay, my dear Dickie—part not with old friends so shortly!—Thou shalt know all I know of the lady one day."

"Ay!" said Dickie; "and that day may prove a nigh one.—Fare thee well, Wayland—I will to my large-limbed friend, who, if he have not so sharp a wit as some folk, is at least more grateful for the service which other folk render him. And so again, good evening to ye."

So saying, he cast a somerset through the gateway, and, lighting on the bridge, ran with the extraordinary agility which was one of his distinguishing attributes, towards the Gallery-tower, and was out of sight in an instant.

"I would to God I were safe out of this Castle again!" prayed Wayland, internally; "for now that this mischievous imp has put his finger in the pie, it cannot but prove a mess fit for the devil's eating. I would to Heaven Master Tressilian would appear!"

Tressilian, whom he was thus anxiously expecting in one direction, had returned to Kenilworth by another access. It was indeed true, as Wayland had conjectured, that, in the earlier part of the day he had accompanied the Earls on their cavalcade towards Warwick, not without hope that he might in that town hear some tidings of his emissary. Being disappointed in this expectation, and observing Varney amongst Leicester's attendants, seeming as if he had some purpose of advancing to, and addressing him, he conceived, in the present circumstances, it was wisest to avoid the interview. He, therefore, left the presence-chamber when the High-Sheriff of the county was in the very midst of his dutiful address to her Majesty; and, mounting his horse, rode back to Kenilworth, by a remote and circuitous road, and entered the castle by a small sally-port in the western wall, at which he was readily admitted as one of the followers of the Earl of Sussex, towards whom Leicester had commanded the utmost courtesy to be exercised. It was thus that he met not Wayland, who was impatiently watching his arrival, and whom he himself would have been, at least, equally desirous to see.

Having delivered his horse to the charge of his attendant, he walked for a space in the Pleasance and in the garden, rather to indulge in comparative solitude his own reflections, than to admire those singular beauties of nature and art which the magnificence of Leicester had there assembled. The greater part of the persons of condition had left the Castle for the present, to form part of the Earl's cavalcade; others, who remained behind, were on the battlements, outer walls, and towers, eager to view the splendid spectacle of the royal entry. The garden, therefore, while every other part of the Castle resounded with the human voice, was silent, but for the whispering of the leaves, the emulous warbling of the tenants of a large aviary, with their happier companions who remained denizens of the free air, and the plashing of the fountains, which, forced into the air from sculptures of fantastic and grotesque forms, fell down with ceaseless sound into the great basins of Italian marble.

The melancholy thoughts of Tressilian cast a gloomy shade on all the objects with which he was surrounded. He compared the magnificent scenes which he here traversed, with the deep woodland and wild moorland which surrounded Lidcote Hall, and the image of Amy Robsart glided like a phantom through every landscape which his imagination summoned up. Nothing is perhaps more dangerous to the future happiness of men of deep thought and retired habits, than the entertaining an early, long, and unfortunate attachment. It frequently sinks so deep into the mind, that it becomes their dream by night and their vision by day —mixes itself with every source of interest and enjoyment; and when blighted and withered by final disappointment, it seems as if the springs of the spirit were dried up along with it. This aching of the heart, this languishing after a shadow which has lost all the gaiety of its colouring, this dwelling on the remembrance of a dream from which we have been long roughly awakened, is the weakness of a gentle and generous heart, and it was that of Tressilian.

He himself at length became sensible of the necessity of forcing other objects upon his mind; and for this purpose he left the Pleasance, in order to mingle with the noisy crowd upon the walls, and view the preparation for the pageants. But as he left the garden, and heard the busy hum, mixed with music and laughter, which floated around him, he felt an uncontrollable reluctance to mix with society, whose feelings were in a tone so different from his own, and resolved, instead of doing so, to retire to the chamber assigned him, and employ himself in study until the tolling of the great castle-bell should announce the arrival of Elizabeth.

Tressilian crossed accordingly by the passage betwixt the immense range of kitchens and the great hall, and ascended to the third storey of Mervyn's Tower, and applying himself to the door of the small apartment which had been allotted to him, was surprised to find it was locked. He then recollected that the deputy-chamberlain had given him a master-key, advising him, in the present confused state of the Castle, to keep his door as much shut as possible. He applied this key to the lock, the bolt revolved, he entered, and in the same instant saw a female form seated in the apartment, and recognised that form to be Amy Robsart. His first idea was, that a heated imagination had raised the image on which it doted into visible existence; his second, that he beheld an apparition— the third and abiding conviction, that it was Amy herself, paler, indeed, and thinner than in the days of heedless happiness, when she possessed the form and hue of a wood-nymph, with the beauty of a sylph; but still Amy, unequalled in loveliness by aught which had ever visited his eyes.

The astonishment of the Countess was scarce less than that of Tressilian, although it was of shorter duration, because she had heard from Wayland that he was in the Castle. She had started up at his first entrance, and now stood facing him, the paleness of her cheeks having given way to a deep blush.

"Tressilian," she said, at length, "why come you here?"

"Nay, why come *you* here, Amy," returned Tressilian, "unless it be at length to claim that aid, which, as far as one man's heart and arm can extend, shall instantly be rendered to you?"

She was silent a moment, and then answered in a sorrowful, rather than an angry tone,—"I require no aid, Tressilian, and would rather be injured than benefited by any which your kindness can offer me. Believe me, I am near one whom law and love oblige to protect me."

"The villain, then, hath done you the poor justice which remained in his power," said Tressilian; "and I behold before me the wife of Varney?"

"The wife of Varney!" she replied, with all the emphasis of scorn; "With what base name, sir, does your boldness stigmatize the—the—the"—She hesitated, dropped her tone of scorn, looked down, and was confused and silent; for she recollected what fatal consequences might attend her completing the sentence with "the Countess of Leicester," which were the words that had naturally suggested themselves. It would have been a betrayal of the secret, on which her husband had assured her that his fortunes depended, to Tressilian, to Sussex, to the Queen, and to the whole assembled court. "Never," she thought, "will I break my promised silence. I will submit to every suspicion rather than that."

The tears rose to her eyes, as she stood silent before Tressilian; while, looking on her with mingled grief and pity, he said, "Alas! Amy, your eyes contradict your tongue. That speaks of a protector, willing and able to watch over you; but these tell me you are ruined, and deserted by the wretch to whom you have attached yourself."

She looked on him, with eyes in which anger sparkled through her tears, but only repeated the word "wretch!" with a scornful emphasis.

"Yes, *wretch!*" said Tressilian; "for were he aught better, why are you here, and alone in my apartment? why was not fitting provision made for your honourable reception?"

"In your apartment?" repeated Amy; "in *your* apartment? It shall instantly be relieved of my presence." She hastened towards the door; but the sad recollection of her deserted state at once pressed on her mind, and, pausing on the threshold, she added, in a tone unutterably pathetic, "Alas! I had forgot—I know not where to go——"

"I see—I see it all," said Tressilian, springing to her side, and leading her back to the seat, on which she sunk down—"you *do* need aid—you *do* need protection, though you will not own it; and you shall not need it long. Leaning on my arm, as the representative of your excellent and broken-hearted father, on the very threshold of the Castle-gate, you shall meet Elizabeth; and the first deed she shall do in the halls of Kenilworth, shall be an act of justice to her sex and her subjects. Strong in my good cause, and in the Queen's justice, the power of her minion shall not shake my resolution. I will instantly seek Sussex."

"Not for all that is under heaven!" said the Countess, much alarmed, and feeling the absolute necessity of obtaining time, at least, for consideration. "Tressilian, you were wont to be generous—Grant me one request, and believe, if it be your wish to save me from misery, and from madness, you will do more by making me the promise I ask of you, than Elizabeth can do for me with all her power!"

"Ask me any thing for which you can allege reason," said Tressilian; "but demand not of me——"

"O, limit not your boon, dear Edmund!" exclaimed the Countess—"you once loved that I should call you so—Limit not your boon to reason! for my case is all madness, and frenzy must guide the counsels which alone can aid me."

"If you speak thus wildly," said Tressilian, astonishment again overpowering both his grief and his resolution, "I must believe you indeed incapable of thinking or acting for yourself."

"Oh, no!" she exclaimed, sinking on one knee before him, "I am not mad—I am but a creature unutterably miserable, and, from circumstances the most singular, dragged on to a precipice by the arm of him who thinks he is keeping me from it—even by yours, Tressilian—by yours, whom I have honoured, respected—all but loved—and yet loved, too—loved, too, Tressilian—though not as you wished me."

There was an energy—a self-possession—an abandonment in her voice and manner—a total resignation of herself to his generosity, which, together with the kindness of her expressions to himself, moved him deeply. He raised her, and, in broken accents, entreated her to be comforted.

"I cannot," she said, "I will not be comforted, till you grant me my request! I will speak as plainly as I dare—I am now awaiting the commands of one who has a right to issue them—The interference of a third person—of you in especial, Tressilian, will be ruin—utter ruin to me. Wait but four-and-twenty hours, and it may be that the poor Amy may have the means to show that she values, and can reward, your disinterested friendship—that she is happy herself, and has the means to make you so—It is surely worth your patience, for so short a space?"

Tressilian paused, and weighing in his mind the various probabilities which might render a violent interference on his part more prejudicial than advantageous, both to the happiness and reputation of Amy; considering also that she was within the walls of Kenilworth, and could suffer no injury in a castle honoured with the Queen's residence, and filled with her guards and attendants,—he conceived, upon the whole, that he might render her more evil than good service, by intruding upon her his appeal to Elizabeth in her behalf. He expressed his resolution cautiously, however, doubting naturally whether Amy's hopes of extricating herself from her difficulties rested on any thing stronger than a blinded attachment to Varney, whom he supposed to be her seducer.

"Amy," he said, while he fixed his sad and expressive eyes on hers, which, in her ecstasy of doubt, terror, and perplexity, she cast up towards him, "I have ever remarked, that when others called thee girlish and wilful, there lay under that external semblance of youthful and self-willed folly, deep feeling and strong sense. In this I will confide, trusting your own fate in your own hands for the space of twenty-four hours, without any interference by word or act."

"Do you promise me this, Tressilian?" said the Countess. "Is it possible you can yet repose so much confidence in me? Do you promise, as you are a gentleman and a man of honour, to intrude in my matters, neither by speech nor action, whatever you may see or hear that seems to you to demand your interference?—Will you so far trust me?"

"I will, upon my honour," said Tressilian; "but when that space is expired——"

"When that space is expired," she said, interrupting him, "you are free to act as your judgment shall determine."

"Is there nought besides which I can do for you, Amy?" said Tressilian.

"Nothing," said she, "save to leave me,—that is, if—I blush to acknowledge my helplessness by asking it—if you can spare me the use of this apartment for the next twenty-four hours."

"This is most wonderful!" said Tressilian; "what hope or interest can you have in a castle, where you cannot command even an apartment?"

"Argue not, but leave me," she said; and added, as he slowly and unwillingly retired, "Generous Edmund! the time may come, when Amy may show she deserved thy noble attachment."

CHAPTER XXVIII

What, man, ne'er lack a draught, when the full can
Stands at thine elbow, and craves emptying!—
Nay, fear not me, for I have no delight
To watch men's vices, since I have myself
Of virtue nought to boast of.—I'm a striker,
Would have the world strike with me, pell-mell, all.
                    Pandæmonium.

TRESSILIAN, in strange agitation of mind, had hardly stepped down the first two or three steps of the winding staircase, when, greatly to his surprise and his displeasure, he met Michael Lambourne, wearing an impudent familiarity of visage, for which Tressilian felt much disposed to throw him down stairs; until he remembered the prejudice which Amy, the only object of his solicitude, was likely to receive from his engaging in any act of violence, at that time, and in that place.

He, therefore, contented himself with looking sternly upon Lambourne, as upon one whom he deemed unworthy of notice, and attempted to pass him in his way down stairs, without any symptom of recognition. But Lambourne, who, amidst the profusion of that day's hospitality, had not failed to take a deep, though not an overpowering cup of sack, was not in the humour of humbling himself before any man's looks. He stopped Tressilian upon the staircase without the least bashfulness or embarrassment, and addressed him as if they had been on kind and intimate terms;
—"What, no grudge between us, I hope, upon old scores, Master Tressilian?—nay, I am one who remember former kindness rather than later feud—I'll convince you that I meant honestly and kindly, ay, and comfortably by you."

"I desire none of your intimacy," said Tressilian—"keep company with your mates."

"Now, see how hasty he is!" said Lambourne; "and how these gentles, that are made questionless out of the porcelain clay of the earth, look down upon poor Michael Lambourne! You would take Master Tressilian now for the most maid-like, modest, simpering squire of dames, that ever made love when candles were long i' the stuff—snuff—call you it?—Why, you would play the saint on us, Master Tressilian, and forget that even now thou hast a commodity in thy very bedchamber, to the shame of my lord's castle, ha! ha! ha! Have I touched you, Master Tressilian?"

"I know not what you mean," said Tressilian, inferring, however, too surely, that this licentious ruffian must have been sensible of Amy's presence in his apartment; "but if," he continued, "thou art varlet of the chambers, and lackest a fee, there is one to leave mine unmolested."

Lambourne looked at the piece of gold, and put it in his pocket, saying —"Now, I know not but you might have done more with me by a kind word, than by this charming rogue. But after all, he pays well that pays with gold—and Mike Lambourne was never a make-bate, or a spoil-sport, or the like. E'en live and let others live, that is my motto—only, I would not let some folks cock their beaver at me neither, as if they were made of silver ore, and I of Dutch pewter. So if I keep your secret, Master Tressilian, you may look sweet on me at least; and were I to want a little backing or countenance, being caught, as you see the best of us may be, in a sort of peccadillo—why, you owe it me—and so e'en make your chamber serve you and that same bird in bower beside—it's all one to Mike Lambourne."

"Make way, sir," said Tressilian, unable to bridle his indignation; "you have had your fee."

"Um!" said Lambourne, giving place, however, while he sulkily muttered between his teeth, repeating Tressilian's words—"Make way—and you have had your fee—but it matters not, I will spoil no sport, as I said before; I am no dog in the manger—mind that."

He spoke louder and louder, as Tressilian, by whom he felt himself overawed, got farther and farther out of hearing.

"I am no dog in the manger—but I will not carry coals neither—mind that, my Master Tressilian; and I will have a peep at this wench, whom you have quartered so commodiously in your old haunted room—afraid of ghosts, belike, and not too willing to sleep alone. If *I* had done this now in a strange lord's castle, the word had been,—The porter's lodge for the knave! and,—Have him flogged—trundle him down stairs like a turnip!—Ay, but your virtuous gentlemen take strange privileges over us, who are downright servants of our senses. Well—I have my Master Tressilian's head under my belt by this lucky discovery, that is one thing certain; and I will try to get a sight of this Lindabrides of his, that is another."

CHAPTER XXIX

Now fare thee well, my master—if true service
Be guerdon'd with hard looks, e'en cut the tow-line,
And let our barks across the pathless flood
Hold different courses.

Shipwreck.

TRESSILIAN walked into the outer yard of the Castle, scarce knowing what to think of his late strange and most unexpected interview with Amy Robsart, and dubious if he had done well, being intrusted with the delegated authority of her father, to pass his word so solemnly to leave her to her own guidance for so many hours. Yet how could he have denied her request,—dependent as she had too probably rendered herself upon Varney? Such was his natural reasoning. The happiness of her future life might depend upon his not driving her to extremities, and since no authority of Tressilian's could extricate her from the power of Varney, supposing he was to acknowledge Amy to be his wife, what title had he to destroy the hope of domestic peace which might yet remain to her, by setting enmity betwixt them? Tressilian resolved, therefore, scrupulously to observe his word pledged to Amy, both because it had been given, and because, as he still thought, while he considered and reconsidered that extraordinary interview, it could not with justice or propriety have been refused.

In one respect, he had gained much towards securing effectual protection for this unhappy and still beloved object of his early affection. Amy was no longer mewed up in a distant and solitary retreat, under the charge of persons of doubtful reputation. She was in the Castle of Kenilworth, within the verge of the Royal Court for the time, free from all risk of violence, and liable to be produced before Elizabeth on the first summons. These were circumstances which could not but assist greatly the efforts which he might have occasion to use in her behalf.

While he was thus balancing the advantages and perils which attended her unexpected presence in Kenilworth, Tressilian was hastily and anxiously accosted by Wayland, who, after ejaculating, "Thank God, your worship is found at last!" proceeded with breathless caution to pour into his ear the intelligence, that the lady had escaped from Cumnor-Place.

"And is at present in this Castle," said Tressilian; "I know it, and I have seen her—Was it by her own choice she found refuge in my apartment?"

"No," answered Wayland; "but I could think of no other way of safely bestowing her, and was but too happy to find a deputy-usher who knew where you were quartered;—in jolly society truly, the hall on the one hand, and the kitchen on the other!"

"Peace, this is no time for jesting," answered Tressilian, sternly.

"I wot that but too well," said the artist, "for I have felt these three days as if I had an halter round my neck. This lady knows not her own mind—she will have none of your aid—commands you not to be named to her—and is about to put herself into the hands of my Lord Leicester. I had never got her safe into your chamber, had she known the owner of it."

"Is it possible?" said Tressilian. "But she may have hopes the Earl will exert his influence in her favour over his villainous dependant."

"I know nothing of that," said Wayland—"but I believe, if she is to reconcile herself with either Leicester or Varney, the side of the Castle of Kenilworth which will be safest for us will be the outside, from which we can fastest fly away. It is not my purpose to abide an instant after delivery of the letter to Leicester, which waits but your commands to find its way to him. See, here it is—but no—a plague on it—I must have left it in my dog-hole, in the hayloft yonder, where I am to sleep."

"Death and fury!" said Tressilian, transported beyond his usual patience; "thou hast not lost that on which may depend a stake more important than a thousand such lives as thine?"

"Lost it!" answered Wayland, readily; "that were a jest indeed! No, sir, I have it carefully put up with my night-sack, and some matters I have occasion to use—I will fetch it in an instant."

"Do so," said Tressilian; "be faithful, and thou shalt be well rewarded. But if I have reason to suspect thee, a dead dog were in better case than thou!"

Wayland bowed, and took his leave with seeming confidence and alacrity; but, in fact, filled with the utmost dread and confusion. The letter was lost, that was certain, notwithstanding the apology which he had made to appease the impatient displeasure of Tressilian. It was lost—it might fall into wrong hands—it would then, certainly, occasion a discovery of the whole intrigue in which he had been engaged; nor, indeed, did Wayland see much prospect of its remaining concealed, in any event. He felt much hurt, besides, at Tressilian's burst of impatience.

"Nay, if I am to be paid in this coin, for services where my neck is concerned, it is time I should look to myself. Here have I offended, for ought I know, to the death, the lord of this stately castle, whose word were as powerful to take away my life, as the breath which speaks it to blow out a farthing candle. And all this for a mad lady, and a melancholy gallant; who, on the loss of a four-nooked bit of paper, had his hand on his poignado, and swears death and fury!—Then there is the Doctor and Varney—I will save myself from the whole mess of them—Life is dearer than gold—I will fly this instant, though I leave my reward behind me."

These reflections naturally enough occurred to a mind like Wayland's, who found himself engaged far deeper than he had expected in a train of mysterious and unintelligible intrigues, in which the actors seemed hardly to know their own course. And yet, to do him justice, his personal fears were, in some degree, counterbalanced by his compassion for the deserted state of the lady.

"I care not a groat for Master Tressilian," he said; "I have done more than bargain by him, and have brought his errant-damozel within his reach, so that he may look after her himself; but I fear the poor thing is in much danger amongst these stormy spirits. I will to her chamber, and tell her the fate which has befallen her letter, that she may write another if she list. She cannot lack a messenger, I trow, where there are so many lackeys that can carry a letter to their lord. And I will tell her also that I leave the Castle, trusting her to God, her own guidance, and Master Tressilian's care and looking after.—Perhaps she may remember the ring she offered me—it was well earned, I trow; but she is a lovely creature, and—marry hang the ring! I will not bear a base spirit for the matter. If I fare ill in this world for my good nature, I shall have a better chance in the next.—So now for the lady, and then for the road."

With the stealthy step and jealous eye of the cat that steals on her prey, Wayland resumed the way to the Countess's chamber, sliding along by the side of the courts and passages, alike observant of all around him, and studious himself to escape observation. In this manner he crossed the outward and inward castle-yard, and the great arched passage, which, running betwixt the range of kitchen offices and the hall, led to the bottom of the little winding-stair that gave access to the chambers of Mervyn's Tower.

The artist congratulated himself on having escaped the various perils of the journey, and was in the act of ascending by two steps at once, when he observed that the shadow of a man, thrown from a door which stood ajar, darkened the opposite wall of the staircase. Wayland drew back cautiously, went down to the inner court-yard, spent about a quarter of an hour, which seemed at least quadruple its usual duration, in walking from place to place, and then returned to the tower, in hopes to find that the lurker had disappeared. He ascended as high as the suspicious spot —there was no shadow on the wall—he ascended a few yards farther— the door was still ajar, and he was doubtful whether to advance or retreat, when it was suddenly thrown wide open, and Michael Lambourne bolted out upon the astonished Wayland. "Who the devil art thou? and what seek'st thou in this part of the Castle? March into that chamber, and be hanged to thee!"

"I am no dog, to go at every man's whistle," said the artist, affecting a confidence which was belied by a timid shake in his voice.

"Sayst thou me so?—Come hither, Lawrence Staples."

A huge ill-made and ill-looked fellow, upwards of six feet high, appeared at the door, and Lambourne proceeded: "If thou be'st so fond of this tower, my friend, thou shalt see its foundations, good twelve feet below the bed of the lake, and tenanted by certain jolly toads, snakes, and so forth, which thou wilt find mighty good company. Therefore, once more I ask you in fair play, who thou art, and what thou seek'st here?"

If the dungeon-grate once clashes behind me, thought Wayland, I am a gone man. He therefore answered submissively, "He was the poor juggler whom his honour had met yesterday in Weatherly-bottom."

"And what juggling trick art thou playing in this tower? Thy gang," said Lambourne, "lie over against Clinton's buildings."

"I came here to see my sister," said the juggler, "who is in Master Tressilian's chamber, just above."

"Aha!" said Lambourne, smiling, "here be truths! Upon my honour, for a stranger, this same Master Tressilian makes himself at home among us, and furnishes out his cell handsomely, with all sorts of commodities. This will be a precious tale of the sainted Master Tressilian, and will be welcome to some folks, as a purse of broad pieces to me.—Hark ye, fellow," he continued, addressing Wayland, "thou shalt not give Puss a hint to steal away—we must catch her in her form. So, back with that pitiful sheep-biting visage of thine, or I will fling thee from the window of the tower, and try if your juggling skill can save your bones."

"Your worship will not be so hardhearted, I hope," said Wayland; "poor folk must live. I trust your honour will allow me to speak with my sister?"

"Sister on Adam's side, I warrant," said Lambourne; "or, if otherwise, the more knave thou. But sister or no sister, thou diest on point of fox, if thou comest a-prying to this tower once more. And now I think of it —uds daggers and death!—I will see thee out of the Castle, for this is a more main concern than thy jugglery."

"But, please your worship," said Wayland, "I am to enact Arion in the pageant upon the lake this very evening."

"I will act it myself, by Saint Christopher!" said Lambourne—"Orion, call'st thou him?—I will act Orion, his belt and his seven stars to boot. Come along, for a rascal knave as thou art—follow me!—Or stay—Lawrence, do thou bring him along."

Lawrence seized by the collar of the cloak the unresisting juggler, while Lambourne, with hasty steps, led the way to that same sallyport, or secret postern, by which Tressilian had returned to the Castle, and which opened in the western wall, at no great distance from Mervyn's Tower.

While traversing with a rapid foot the space betwixt the tower and the sallyport, Wayland in vain racked his brain for some device which might avail the poor lady, for whom, notwithstanding his own imminent danger, he felt deep interest. But when he was thrust out of the Castle, and informed by Lambourne, with a tremendous oath, that instant death would be the consequence of his again approaching it, he cast up his hands and eyes to heaven, as if to call God to witness he had stood to the uttermost in defence of the oppressed; then turned his back on the proud towers of Kenilworth, and went his way to seek a humbler and safer place of refuge.

Lawrence and Lambourne gazed a little while after Wayland, and then turned to go back to their tower, when the former thus addressed his companion: "Never credit me, Master Lambourne, if I can guess why thou hast driven this poor caitiff from the Castle, just when he was to bear a part in the show that was beginning, and all this about a wench."

"Ah, Lawrence," replied Lambourne, "thou art thinking of Black Joan Jugges of Slingdon, and hast sympathy with human frailty. But corragio, most noble Duke of the Dungeon and Lord of Limbo, for thou art as dark in this matter as thine own dominions of Little-ease. My most reverend Signior of the Low Countries of Kenilworth, know that our most notable master, Richard Varney, would give as much to have a hole in this same Tressilian's coat, as would make us some fifty midnight carousals, with the full leave of bidding the steward go snick up, if he came to startle us too soon from our goblets."

"Nay, an that be the case, thou hast right," said Lawrence Staples, the upper-warder, or, in common phrase, the first jailor, of Kenilworth Castle, and of the Liberty and Honour belonging thereto; "but how will you manage when you are absent at the Queen's entrance, Master Lambourne; for methinks thou must attend thy master there?"

"Why thou, mine honest prince of prisons, must keep ward in my absence—Let Tressilian enter if he will, but see thou let no one come out. If the damsel herself would make a break, an 'tis not unlike she may, scare her back with rough words—she is but a paltry player's wench after all."

"Nay, for that matter," said Lawrence, "I might shut the iron wicket upon her, that stands without the double door, and so force per force she will be bound to her answer without more trouble."

"Then Tressilian will not get access to her," said Lambourne, reflecting a moment. "But 'tis no matter—she will be detected in his chamber, and that is all one.—But confess, thou old bat's-eyed dungeon-keeper, that you fear to keep awake by yourself in that Mervyn's Tower of thine?"

"Why, as to fear, Master Lambourne," said the fellow, "I mind it not the turning of a key; but strange things have been heard and seen in that tower.—You must have heard, for as short time as you have been in Kenilworth, that it is haunted by the spirit of Arthur ap Mervyn, a wild chief taken by fierce Lord Mortimer, when he was one of the Lords Marchers of Wales, and murdered, as they say, in that same tower which bears his name?"

"O, I have heard the tale five hundred times," said Lambourne, "and how the ghost is always most vociferous when they boil leeks and stirabout, or fry toasted cheese, in the culinary regions. Santo Diavolo, man, hold thy tongue, I know all about it!"

"Ay, but thou dost not, though," said the turnkey, "for as wise as thou wouldst make thyself. Ah, it is an awful thing to murder a prisoner in his ward!—You, that may have given a man a stab in a dark street, know nothing of it. To give a mutinous fellow a knock on the head with the keys, and bid him be quiet, that's what I call keeping order in the ward; but to draw weapon and slay him, as was done to this Welsh lord, *that* raises you a ghost that will render your prison-house untenantable by any decent captive for some hundred years. And I have that regard for my prisoners, poor things, that I have put good squires and men of worship, that have taken a ride on the highway, or slandered my lord of Leicester, or the like, fifty feet under ground, rather than I would put them into that upper chamber yonder that they call Mervyn's Bower. Indeed, by good Saint Peter of the Fetters, I marvel my noble lord, or Master Varney, could think of lodging guests there; and if this Master Tressilian could get any one to keep him company, and in especial a pretty wench, why, truly, I think he was in the right on't."

"I tell thee," said Lambourne, leading the way into the turnkey's apartment, "thou art an ass.—Go bolt the wicket on the stair, and trouble not thy noddle about ghosts—Give me the wine stoup, man; I am somewhat heated with chafing with yonder rascal."

While Lambourne drew a long draught from a pitcher of claret, which he made use of without any cup, the warder went on, vindicating his own belief in the supernatural.

"Thou hast been few hours in this Castle, and hast been for the whole space so drunk, Lambourne, that thou art deaf, dumb, and blind. But we should hear less of your bragging, were you to pass a night with us at full moon, for then the ghost is busiest; and more especially when a rattling wind sets in from the north-west, with some sprinkling of rain, and now and then a growl of thunder. Body o' me, what crackings and clashings, what groanings and what howlings, will there be at such times in Mervyn's Bower, right as it were over our heads, till the matter of two quarts of distilled waters has not been enough to keep my lads and me in some heart!"

"Pshaw, man!" replied Lambourne, on whom his last draught, joined to repeated visitations of the pitcher upon former occasions, began to make some innovation, "thou speak'st thou know'st not what about spirits. No one knows justly what to say about them; and, in short, least said may in that matter be soonest amended. Some men believe in one thing, some in another—it is all matter of fancy. I have known them of all sorts, my dear Lawrence Lock-the-door, and sensible men too There's a great lord—we'll pass his name, Lawrence—he believes in the stars and the moon, the planets and their courses, and so forth, and that they twinkle exclusively for his benefit; when, in sober, or rather in drunken truth, Lawrence, they are only shining to keep honest fellows like me out of the kennel. Well, sir, let his humour pass, he is great enough to indulge it.—Then look ye, there is another—a very learned man, I promise you, and can vent Greek and Hebrew as fast as I can Thieves'-Latin —he has an humour of sympathies and antipathies—of changing lead into gold and the like—why, via, let that pass too, and let him pay those in transmigrated coin, who are fools enough to let it be current with them. —Then here comest thou thyself, another great man, though neither learned nor noble, yet full six feet high, and thou, like a purblind mole, must needs believe in ghosts and goblins, and such like.—Now, there is, besides, a great man—that is, a great little man, or a little great man, my dear Lawrence—and his name begins with V, and what believes he? Why, nothing, honest Lawrence—nothing in earth, heaven, or hell; and for my part, if I believe there is a devil, it is only because I think there must be some one to catch our aforesaid friend by the back 'when soul and body sever,' as the ballad says—for your antecedent will have a consequent—*raro antecedentem,* as Doctor Bircham was wont to say— But this is Greek to you now, honest Lawrence, and in sooth learning is dry work—Hand me the pitcher once more."

"In faith, if you drink more, Michael," said the warder, "you will be in sorry case either to play Arion or to wait on your master on such a solemn night; and I expect each moment to hear the great bell toll for the muster at Mortimer's Tower, to receive the Queen."

While Staples remonstrated, Lambourne drank; and then setting down the pitcher, which was nearly emptied, with a deep sigh, he said, in an undertone, which soon rose to a high one as his speech proceeded, "Never mind, Lawrence—if I be drunk, I know that shall make Varney uphold me sober. But, as I said, never mind, I can carry my drink discreetly. Moreover, I am to go on the water as Orion, and shall take cold unless I take something comfortable beforehand. Not play Orion! Let us see the best roarer that ever strained his lungs for twelve pence out-mouth me! What if they see me a little disguised?—Wherefore should any man be sober to-night? answer me that—It is matter of loyalty to be merry— and I tell thee, there are those in the Castle, who, if they are not merry when drunk, have little chance to be merry when sober—I name no names, Lawrence. But your pottle of sack is a fine shoeing-horn to pull on a royal humour, and a merry one. Huzza for Queen Elizabeth!—for the noble Leicester!—for the worshipful Master Varney!—and for Michael Lambourne, that can turn them all round his finger!"

So saying, he walked down stairs, and across the inner court.

The warder looked after him, shook his head, and, while he drew close and locked a wicket, which, crossing the staircase, rendered it impossible for any one to ascend higher than the storey immediately beneath Mervyn's Bower, as Tressilian's chamber was named, he thus soliloquised with himself—"It's a good thing to be a favourite—I wellnigh lost mine office, because one frosty morning Master Varney thought I smelled of aquavitæ; and this fellow can appear before him drunk as a wineskin, and yet meet no rebuke. But then he is a pestilent clever fellow withal, and no one can understand above one half of what he says."

CHAPTER XXX

Now bid the steeple rock—she comes, she comes!—
Speak for us, bells—speak for us, shrill-tongued tuckets.
Stand to thy linstock, gunner; let thy cannon
Play such a peal, as if a paynim foe
Came stretch'd in turban'd ranks to storm the ramparts.
We will have pageants too—but that craves wit,
And I'm a rough-hewn soldier.

                    The Virgin Queen—a Tragi-Comedy.

TRESSILIAN, when Wayland had left him, as mentioned in the last chapter, remained uncertain what he ought next to do, when Raleigh and
Blount came up to him arm in arm, yet, according to their wont, very
eagerly disputing together. Tressilian had no great desire for their
society in the present state of his feelings, but there was no possibility of
avoiding them; and indeed he felt that, bound by his promise not to
approach Amy, or take any step in her behalf, it would be his best course
at once to mix with general society, and to exhibit on his brow as little
as he could of the anguish and uncertainty which sat heavy at his heart.
He therefore made a virtue of necessity, and hailed his comrades with,
"All mirth to you, gentlemen. Whence come ye?"

"From Warwick, to be sure," said Blount; "we must needs home to
change our habits, like poor players, who are fain to multiply their persons to outward appearance by change of suits; and you had better do
the like, Tressilian."

"Blount is right," said Raleigh; "the Queen loves such marks of
deference, and notices, as wanting in respect, those who, not arriving
in her immediate attendance, may appear in their soiled and ruffled
riding-dress. But look at Blount himself, Tressilian, for the love of
laughter, and see how his villainous tailor hath apparelled him—in blue,
green, and crimson, with carnation ribands and yellow roses in his shoes!"

"Why, what wouldst thou have?" said Blount. "I told the cross-legged
thief to do his best, and spare no cost; and methinks these things are
gay enough—gayer than thine own—I'll be judged by Tressilian."

"I agree—I agree," said Walter Raleigh. "Judge betwixt us, Tressilian,
for the love of heaven!"

Tressilian, thus appealed to, looked at them both, and was immediately
sensible at a single glance, that honest Blount had taken upon the tailor's
warrant the pied garments which he had chosen to make, and was as
much embarrassed by the quantity of points and ribands which garnished
his dress, as a clown in his holiday clothes; while the dress of Raleigh
was a well-fancied and rich suit, which the wearer bore as a garb too well
adapted to his elegant person to attract particular attention. Tressilian
said, therefore, "That Blount's dress was finest, but Raleigh's the best
fancied."

Blount was satisfied with his decision. "I knew mine was finest," he
said; "if that knave Double-stitch had brought me home such a simple

doublet as that of Raleigh's, I would have beat his brains out with his own pressing-iron. Nay, if we must be fools, ever let us be fools of the first head, say I."

"But why gettest thou not on thy braveries, Tressilian?" said Raleigh.

"I am excluded from my apartment by a silly mistake," said Tressilian, "and separated for the time from my baggage. I was about to seek thee, to beseech a share of thy lodging."

"And welcome," said Raleigh; "it is a noble one. My Lord of Leicester has done us that kindness, and lodged us in princely fashion. If his courtesy be extorted reluctantly, it is at least extended far. I would advise you to tell your strait to the Earl's chamberlain—you will have instant redress."

"Nay, it is not worth while, since you can spare me room," replied Tressilian—"I would not be troublesome.—Has any one come hither with you?"

"O, ay," said Blount; "Varney and a whole tribe of Leicestrians, besides about a score of us honest Sussex folk. We are all, it seems, to receive the Queen at what they call the Gallery-tower, and witness some fooleries there; and then we're to remain in attendance upon the Queen in the Great Hall—God bless the mark—while those who are now waiting upon her Grace get rid of their slough, and doff their riding-suits. Heaven help me, if her Grace should speak to me, I shall never know what to answer!"

"And what has detained them so long at Warwick?" said Tressilian, unwilling that their conversation should return to his own affairs.

"Such a succession of fooleries," said Blount, "as were never seen at Bartholomew-fair. We have had speeches and players, and dogs and bears, and men making monkeys, and women moppets, of themselves— I marvel the Queen could endure it. But ever and anon came in something of 'the lovely light of her gracious countenance,' or some such trash. Ah! vanity makes a fool of the wisest. But, come, let us on to this same Gallery-tower,—though I see not what thou, Tressilian, canst do with thy riding-dress and boots."

"I will take my station behind thee, Blount," said Tressilian, who saw that his friend's unusual finery had taken a strong hold of his imagination; "thy goodly size and gay dress will cover my defects."

"And so thou shalt, Edmund," said Blount. "In faith I am glad thou think'st my garb well-fancied, for all Mr. Wittypate here; for when one does a foolish thing, it is right to do it handsomely."

So saying, Blount cocked his beaver, threw out his leg, and marched manfully forward, as if at the head of his brigade of pikemen, ever and anon looking with complaisance on his crimson stockings, and the huge yellow roses which blossomed on his shoes. Tressilian followed, wrapt in his own sad thoughts, and scarce minding Raleigh, whose quick fancy, amused by the awkward vanity of his respectable friend, vented itself in jests, which he whispered into Tressilian's ear.

In this manner they crossed the long bridge, or tilt-yard, and took their station, with other gentlemen of quality, before the outer gate of the Gallery, or Entrance-tower. The whole amounted to about forty persons, all selected as of the first rank under that of knighthood, and were disposed in double rows on either side of the gate, like a guard of honour, within the close hedge of pikes and partisans, which was formed by Leicester's retainers, wearing his liveries. The gentlemen carried no arms save their swords and daggers. These gallants were as gaily dressed as imagination could devise; and as the garb of the time permitted a great display of expensive magnificence, nought was to be seen but velvet and cloth of gold and silver, ribands, feathers, gems, and golden chains. In spite of his more serious subjects of distress, Tressilian could not help feeling, that he, with his riding-suit, however handsome it might be, made rather an unworthy figure among these "fierce vanities,"—and the rather because he saw that his dishabille was the subject of wonder among his own friends, and of scorn among the partisans of Leicester.

We could not suppress this fact, though it may seem something at variance with the gravity of Tressilian's character; but the truth is, that a regard for personal appearance is a species of self-love, from which the wisest are not exempt, and to which the mind clings so instinctively, that not only the soldier advancing to almost inevitable death, but even the doomed criminal who goes to certain execution, shows an anxiety to array his person to the best advantage. But this is a digression.

It was the twilight of a summer night, (9th July, 1575,) the sun having for some time set, and all were in anxious expectation of the Queen's immediate approach. The multitude had remained assembled for many hours, and their numbers were still rather on the increase. A profuse distribution of refreshments, together with roasted oxen, and barrels of ale set a-broach in different places of the road, had kept the populace in perfect love and loyalty towards the Queen and her favourite, which might have somewhat abated had fasting been added to watching. They passed away the time, therefore, with the usual popular amusements of whooping, hallooing, shrieking, and playing rude tricks upon each other, forming the chorus of discordant sounds usual on such occasions. These prevailed all through the crowded roads and fields, and especially beyond the gate of the Chase, where the greater number of the common sort were stationed; when, all of a sudden, a single rocket was seen to shoot into the atmosphere, and, at the instant, far heard over flood and field, the great bell of the Castle tolled.

Immediately there was a pause of dead silence, succeeded by a deep hum of expectation, the united voice of many thousands, none of whom spoke above their breath; or, to use a singular expression, the whisper of an immense multitude.

"They come now, for certain," said Raleigh. "Tressilian, that sound is grand. We hear it from this distance, as mariners, after a long voyage,

hear, upon their night-watch, the tide rush upon some distant and unknown shore."

"Mass!" answered Blount, "I hear it rather as I used to hear mine own
kine lowing from the close of Wittenswestlowe."

"He will assuredly graze presently," said Raleigh to Tressilian; "his
thought is all of fat oxen and fertile meadows—he grows little better
than one of his own beeves, and only becomes grand when he is provoked
to pushing and goring."

"We shall have him at that presently," said Tressilian, "if you spare
not your wit."

"Tush, I care not," answered Raleigh; "but thou too, Tressilian, hast
turned a kind of owl, that flies only by night; hast exchanged thy songs
for screechings, and good company for an ivy-tod."

"But what manner of animal art thou thyself, Raleigh," said Tressilian,
"that thou holdest us all so lightly?"

"Who, I?" replied Raleigh. "An eagle am I, that never will think of
dull earth while there is a heaven to soar in, and a sun to gaze upon."

"Well bragged, by Saint Barnaby!" said Blount; "but, good Master
Eagle, beware the cage, and beware the fowler. Many birds have flown as
high, that I have seen stuffed with straw, and hung up to scare kites.—
But hark, what a dead silence hath fallen on them at once!"

"The procession pauses," said Raleigh, "at the gate of the Chase,
where a sibyl, one of the *fatidicæ,* meets the Queen, to tell her fortune. I
saw the verses; there is little savour in them, and her Grace has been
already crammed full with such poetical compliments. She whispered to
me during the recorder's speech yonder, at Ford-mill, as she entered the
liberties of Warwick, how she was *'pertæsa barbaræ loquelæ.'* "

"The Queen whispered to *him!*" said Blount, in a kind of soliloquy;
"Good God, to what will this world come!"

His further meditations were interrupted by a shout of applause from
the multitude, so tremendously vociferous, that the country echoed for
miles round. The guards, thickly stationed upon the road by which the
Queen was to advance, caught up the acclamation, which ran like wildfire to the Castle, and announced to all within, that Queen Elizabeth had
entered the Royal Chase of Kenilworth. The whole music of the Castle
sounded at once, and a round of artillery, with a salvo of small arms, was
discharged from the battlements; but the noise of drums and trumpets,
and even of the cannon themselves, was but faintly heard amidst the
roaring and reiterated welcomes of the multitude.

As the noise began to abate, a broad glare of light was seen to appear
from the gate of the Park, and, broadening and brightening as it came
nearer, advanced along the open and fair avenue that led towards the
Gallery-tower; and which, as we have already noticed, was lined on
either hand by the retainers of the Earl of Leicester. The word was passed
along the line, "The Queen! The Queen! Silence, and stand fast!" Onward came the cavalcade, illuminated by two hundred thick waxen

torches, in the hands of as many horsemen, which cast a light like that of broad day all around the procession, but especially on the principal group, of which the Queen herself, arrayed in the most splendid manner, and blazing with jewels, formed the central figure. She was mounted on a milk-white horse, which she reined with peculiar grace and dignity; and in the whole of her stately and noble carriage, you saw the daughter of an hundred kings.

The ladies of the court, who rode beside her Majesty, had taken especial care that their own external appearance should not be more glorious than their rank and the occasion altogether demanded, so that no inferior luminary might appear to approach the orbit of royalty. But their personal charms, and the magnificence by which, under every prudential restraint, they were necessarily distinguished, exhibited them, as the very flower of a realm so far famed for splendour and beauty. The magnificence of the courtiers, free from such restraints as prudence imposed on the ladies, was yet more unbounded.

Leicester, who glittered like a golden image with jewels and cloth of gold, rode on her Majesty's right hand, as well in quality of her host, as of her Master of the Horse. The black steed which he mounted had not a single white hair on his body, and was one of the most renowned chargers in Europe, having been purchased by the Earl at large expense for this royal occasion. As the noble animal chafed at the slow pace of the procession, and, arching his stately neck, champed on the silver bits which restrained him, the foam flew from his mouth, and specked his well-formed limbs as if with spots of snow. The rider well became the high place which he held, and the proud steed which he bestrode; for no man in England, or perhaps in Europe, was more perfect than Dudley in horsemanship, and all other exercises belonging to his quality. He was bare-headed, as were all the courtiers in the train; and the red torch-light shone upon his long curled tresses of dark hair, and on his noble features, to the beauty of which even the severest criticism could only object the lordly fault, as it may be termed, of a forehead somewhat too high. On that proud evening, those features wore all the grateful solicitude of a subject, to show himself sensible of the high honour which the Queen was conferring on him, and all the pride and satisfaction which became so glorious a moment. Yet, though neither eye nor feature betrayed aught but feelings which suited the occasion, some of the Earl's personal attendants remarked that he was unusually pale, and they expressed to each other their fear that he was taking more fatigue than consisted with his health.

Varney followed close behind his master, as the principal esquire in waiting, and had charge of his lordship's black velvet bonnet, garnished with a clasp of diamonds, and surmounted by a white plume. He kept his eye constantly on his master; and, for reasons with which the reader is not unacquainted, was, among Leicester's numerous dependants, the one who was most anxious that his lord's strength and resolution should carry him successfully through a day so agitating. For although Varney was one of the few—the very few moral monsters, who contrive to lull to sleep the remorse of their own bosoms, and are drugged into moral insensibility by atheism, as men in extreme agony are lulled by opium, yet he knew that in the breast of his patron there was already awakened the fire that is never quenched, and that his lord felt, amid all the pomp and magnificence we have described, the gnawing of the worm that dieth not. Still, however, assured as Lord Leicester stood, by Varney's own intelligence, that his Countess laboured under an indisposition which formed an unanswerable apology to the Queen for her not appearing at Kenilworth, there was little danger, his wily retainer thought, that a man so ambitious would betray himself by giving way to any external weakness.

The train, male and female, who attended immediately upon the Queen's person, were of course of the bravest and the fairest—the highest born nobles and the wisest counsellors, of that distinguished reign, to repeat whose names were but to weary the reader. Behind came a long crowd of knights and gentlemen, whose rank and birth, however distinguished, were thrown into shade, as their persons into the rear of a procession, whose front was of such august majesty.

Thus marshalled, the cavalcade approached the Gallery-tower, which formed, as we have often observed, the extreme barrier of the Castle.

It was now the part of the huge porter to step forward; but the lubbard was so overwhelmed with confusion of spirit,—the contents of one immense black jack of double ale, which he had just drank to quicken his memory, having treacherously confused the brain it was intended to clear,—that he only groaned piteously, and remained sitting on his stone seat; and the Queen would have passed on without greeting, had not the gigantic warder's secret ally, Flibbertigibbet, who lay perdue behind him, thrust a pin into the rear of the short femoral garment which we elsewhere described.

The porter uttered a sort of yell, which came not amiss into his part, started up with his club, and dealt a sound douse or two on each side of him; and then, like a coach-horse pricked by the spur, started off at once into the full career of his address, and by dint of active prompting on the part of Dickie Sludge, delivered, in sounds of gigantic intonation, a speech which may be thus abridged;—the reader being to suppose that the first lines were addressed to the throng who approached the gateway; the conclusion, at the approach of the Queen, upon sight of whom, as struck by some heavenly vision, the gigantic warder dropped his club, resigned his keys, and gave open way to the goddess of the night, and all her magnificent train.

> "What stir, what turmoil, have we for the nones?
> Stand back, my masters, or beware your bones!
> Sirs, I'm a warder, and no man of straw,
> My voice keeps order, and my club gives law.

"Yet soft—nay, stay—what vision have we here?
What dainty darling's this—what peerless peer?
What loveliest face, that loving ranks unfold,
Like brightest diamond chased in purest gold?
Dazzled and blind, mine office I forsake,
My club, my key. My knee, my homage take,
Bright paragon; pass on in joy and bliss;—
Beshrew the gate that opes not wide at such a sight as this!" [1]

Elizabeth received most graciously the homage of the Herculean porter, and, bending her head to him in requital, passed through his guarded tower, from the top of which was poured a clamorous blast of warlike music, which was replied to by other bands of minstrelsy placed at different points on the Castle walls, and by others again stationed in the Chase; while the tones of the one, as they yet vibrated on the echoes, were caught up and answered by new harmony from different quarters.

Amidst these bursts of music, which, as if the work of enchantment, seemed now close at hand, now softened by distant space, now wailing so low and sweet as if that distance were gradually prolonged until only the last lingering strains could reach the ear, Queen Elizabeth crossed the Gallery-tower, and came upon the long bridge, which extended from thence to Mortimer's Tower, and which was already as light as day, so many torches had been fastened to the palisades on either side. Most of the nobles here alighted, and sent their horses to the neighbouring village of Kenilworth, following the Queen on foot, as did the gentlemen who had stood in array to receive her at the Gallery-tower.

On this occasion, as at different times during the evening, Raleigh addressed himself to Tressilian, and was not a little surprised at his vague and unsatisfactory answers; which, joined to his leaving his apartment without any assigned reason, appearing in an undress when it was likely to be offensive to the Queen, and some other symptoms of irregularity which he thought he discovered, led him to doubt whether his friend did not labour under some temporary derangement.

Meanwhile the Queen had no sooner stepped on the bridge than a new spectacle was provided; for as soon as the music gave signal that she was so far advanced, a raft, so disposed as to resemble a small floating island, illuminated by a great variety of torches, and surrounded by floating pageants formed to represent sea-horses, on which sat Tritons, Nereids, and other fabulous deities of the seas and rivers, made its appearance upon the lake, and, issuing from behind a small heronry where it had been concealed, floated gently towards the farther end of the bridge.

On the islet appeared a beautiful woman, clad in a watchet-coloured

[1] This is in imitation of Gascoigne's verses spoken by the Herculean porter, as mentioned in the text. The original may be found in the republication of the Princely Pleasures of Kenilworth, by the same author, in the History of Kenilworth, already quoted. Chiswick, 1821.

silken mantle, bound with a broad girdle, inscribed with characters like the phylacteries of the Hebrews. Her feet and arms were bare, but her wrists and ankles were adorned with gold bracelets of uncommon size. Amidst her long silky black hair, she wore a crown or chaplet of artificial mistletoe, and bore in her hand a rod of ebony tipped with silver. Two Nymphs attended on her, dressed in the same antique and mystical guise.

The pageant was so well managed, that this Lady of the Floating Island, having performed her voyage with much picturesque effect, landed at Mortimer's Tower with her two attendants, just as Elizabeth presented herself before that outwork. The stranger then, in a well-penned speech, announced herself as that famous Lady of the Lake, renowned in the stories of King Arthur, who had nursed the youth of the redoubted Sir Lancelot, and whose beauty had proved too powerful both for the wisdom and the spells of the mighty Merlin. Since that early period she had remained possessed of her crystal dominions, she said, despite the various men of fame and might by whom Kenilworth had been successively tenanted. The Saxons, the Danes, the Normans, the Saintlowes, the Clintons, the Mountforts, the Mortimers, the Plantagenets, great though they were in arms and magnificence, had never, she said, caused her to raise her head from the waters which hid her crystal palace. But a greater than all these great names had now appeared, and she came in homage and duty to welcome the peerless Elizabeth to all sport, which the Castle and its environs, which lake or land, could afford.

The Queen received this address also with great courtesy, and made answer in raillery, "We thought this lake had belonged to our own dominions, fair dame; but since so famed a lady claims it for hers, we will be glad of some other time to have further communing with you touching our joint interests."

With this gracious answer the Lady of the Lake vanished and Arion, who was amongst the maritime deities, appeared upon his dolphin. But Lambourne, who had taken upon him the part in the absence of Wayland, being chilled with remaining immersed in an element to which he was not friendly, having never got his speech by heart, and not having, like the porter, the advantage of a prompter, paid it off with impudence, tearing off his vizard, and swearing, "Cogs bones! he was none of Arion or Orion either, but honest Mike Lambourne, that had been drinking her Majesty's health from morning till midnight, and was come to bid her heartily welcome to Kenilworth Castle."

This unpremeditated buffoonery answered the purpose probably better than the set speech would have done. The Queen laughed heartily, and swore (in her turn) that he had made the best speech she had heard that day. Lambourne, who instantly saw his jest had saved his bones, jumped on shore, gave his dolphin a kick, and declared he would never meddle with fish again, except at dinner.

At the same time that the Queen was about to enter the Castle, that memorable discharge of fireworks by water and land took place, which

Master Laneham, formerly introduced to the reader, has strained all his eloquence to describe.

"Such," says the Clerk of the Council-chamber, "was the blaze of burning darts, the gleams of stars coruscant, the streams and hail of fiery sparks, lightnings of wildfire, and flight-shot of thunderbolts, with continuance, terror, and vehemency, that the heavens thundered, the waters surged, and the earth shook; and for my part, hardy as I am, it made me very vengeably afraid."[1]

CHAPTER XXXI

Nay, this is matter for the month of March,
When hares are maddest. Either speak in reason,
Giving cold argument the wall of passion,
Or I break up the court.
                    Beaumont and Fletcher.

It is by no means our purpose to detail minutely all the princely festivities of Kenilworth, after the fashion of Master Robert Laneham, whom we quoted in the conclusion of the last chapter. It is sufficient to say, that under discharge of the splendid fireworks which we have borrowed Laneham's eloquence to describe, the Queen entered the base-court of Kenilworth, through Mortimer's Tower, and moving on through pageants of heathen gods and heroes of antiquity, who offered gifts and compliments on the bended knee, at length found her way to the great hall of the Castle, gorgeously hung for her reception with the richest silken tapestry, misty with perfumes, and sounding to strains of soft and delicious music. From the highly carved oaken roof hung a superb chandelier of gilt bronze, formed like a spread eagle, whose outstretched wings supported three male and three female figures, grasping a pair of branches in each hand. The hall was thus illuminated by twenty-four torches of wax. At the upper end of the splendid apartment was a state canopy, overshadowing a royal throne, and beside it was a door, which opened to a long suite of apartments, decorated with the utmost magnificence for the Queen and her ladies, whenever it should be her pleasure to be private.

The Earl of Leicester having handed the Queen up to her throne, and seated her there, knelt down before her, and kissing the hand which she

[1] See Laneham's Account of the Queen's Entertainment at Killingworth Castle, in 1575, a very diverting tract, written by as great a coxcomb as ever blotted paper. (See vol. xxii. p. 312.) The original is extremely rare, but it has been twice reprinted; once in Mr. Nichol's very curious and interesting collection of the Progresses and Public Processions of Queen Elizabeth, vol. i.; and more lately in a beautiful antiquarian publication termed *Kenilworth Illustrated,* printed at Chiswick, for Meridew of Coventry, and Radcliffe of Birmingham. It contains reprints of Laneham's Letter, Gascoigne's Princely Progress, and other scarce pieces, annotated with accuracy and ability. The author takes the liberty to refer to this work as his authority for the account of the festivities.

held out, with an air in which romantic and respectful gallantry was happily mingled with the air of loyal devotion, he thanked her, in terms of the deepest gratitude, for the highest honour which a sovereign could render to a subject. So handsome did he look when kneeling before her, that Elizabeth was tempted to prolong the scene a little longer than there was, strictly speaking, necessity for; and ere she raised him, she passed her hand over his head, so near, as almost to touch his long curled and perfumed hair, and with a movement of fondness, that seemed to intimate she would, if she dared, have made the motion a slight caress.[1]

She at length raised him, and, standing beside the throne, he explained to her the various preparations which had been made for her amusement and accommodation, all of which received her prompt and gracious approbation. The Earl then prayed her Majesty for permission, that he himself, and the nobles who had been in attendance upon her during the journey, might retire for a few minutes, and put themselves into a guise more fitting for dutiful attendance, during which space, those gentlemen of worship, (pointing to Varney, Blount, Tressilian, and others), who had already put themselves into fresh attire, would have the honour of keeping her presence-chamber.

"Be it so, my lord," answered the Queen; "you could manage a theatre well, who can thus command a double set of actors. For ourselves, we will receive your courtesies this evening but clownishly, since it is not our purpose to change our riding attire, being in effect something fatigued with a journey, which the concourse of our good people hath rendered slow, though the love they have shown our person hath, at the same time, made it delightful."

Leicester, having received this permission, retired accordingly, and was followed by those nobles who had attended the Queen to Kenilworth in person. The gentlemen who had preceded them, and were of course dressed for the solemnity, remained in attendance. But being most of them of rather inferior rank, they remained at an awful distance from the throne which Elizabeth occupied. The Queen's sharp eye soon distinguished Raleigh amongst them, with one or two others who were personally known to her, and she instantly made them a sign to approach, and accosted them very graciously. Raleigh, in particular, the adventure of whose cloak, as well as the incident of the verses, remained on her mind, was very graciously received; and to him she most frequently applied for information concerning the names and rank of those who were

---

[1] To justify what may be considered as a high-coloured picture, the author quotes the original of the courtly and shrewd Sir James Melville, being then Queen Mary's envoy at the Court of London.

"I was required," says Sir James, "to stay till I had seen him made Earle of Leicester, and Baron of Denbigh, with great solemnity; herself (Elizabeth) helping to put on his ceremonial, he sitting on his knees before her, keeping a great gravity and a discreet behaviour; but she could not refrain from putting her hand to his neck to kittle (i.e. tickle) him, smilingly, the French Ambassador and I standing beside her."—MELVILLE's *Memoirs. Bannatyne Edition,* p. 120.

in presence. These he communicated concisely, and not without some traits of humorous satire, by which Elizabeth seemed much amused. "And who is yonder clownish fellow?" she said, looking at Tressilian, whose soiled dress on this occasion greatly obscured his good mien.

"A poet, if it please your Grace," replied Raleigh.

"I might have guessed that from his careless garb," said Elizabeth. "I have known some poets so thoughtless as to throw their cloaks into gutters."

"It must have been when the sun dazzled both their eyes and their judgment," answered Raleigh.

Elizabeth smiled, and proceeded,—"I asked that slovenly fellow's name, and you only told me his profession."

"Tressilian is his name," said Raleigh, with internal reluctance, for he foresaw nothing favourable to his friend from the manner in which she took notice of him.

"Tressilian!" answered Elizabeth. "O, the Menelaus of our romance. Why, he has dressed himself in a guise that will go far to exculpate his fair and false Helen. And where is Farnham, or whatever his name is— my Lord of Leicester's man, I mean—the Paris of this Devonshire tale?"

With still greater reluctance Raleigh named and pointed out to her Varney, for whom the tailor had done all that art could perform in making his exterior agreeable; and who, if he had not grace, had a sort of tact and habitual knowledge of breeding, which came in place of it.

The Queen turned her eye from the one to the other—"I doubt," she said, "this same poetical Master Tressilian, who is too learned, I warrant me, to remember what presence he was to appear in, may be one of those of whom Geoffrey Chaucer says wittily, the wisest clerks are not the wisest men. I remember that Varney is a smooth-tongued varlet. I doubt this fair runaway hath had reasons for breaking her faith."

To this Raleigh durst make no answer, aware how little he should benefit Tressilian by contradicting the Queen's sentiments, and not at all certain, on the whole, whether the best thing that could befall him, would not be that she should put an end at once by her authority to this affair, upon which it seemed to him Tressilian's thoughts were fixed with unavailing and distressing pertinacity. As these reflections passed through his active brain, the lower door was opened, and Leicester, accompanied by several of his kinsmen, and of the nobles who had embraced his faction, re-entered the Castle-hall.

The favourite Earl was now apparelled all in white, his shoes being of white velvet; his understocks (or stockings) of knit silk; his upper stocks of white velvet, lined with cloth of silver, which was shown at the slashed part of the middle thigh; his doublet of cloth of silver, the close jerkin of white velvet, embroidered with silver and seed-pearl, his girdle and the scabbard of his sword of white velvet with golden buckles; his poniard and sword hilted and mounted with gold; and over all, a rich loose robe of white satin, with a border of golden embroidery a foot in breadth. The collar of the Garter, and the azure Garter itself around his knee, completed the appointments of the Earl of Leicester; which were so well matched by his fair stature, graceful gesture, fine proportion of body, and handsome countenance, that at that moment he was admitted by all who saw him, as the goodliest person whom they had ever looked upon. Sussex and the other nobles were also richly attired, but, in point of splendour and gracefulness of mien, Leicester far exceeded them all.

Elizabeth received him with great complacency. "We have one piece of royal justice," she said, "to attend to. It is a piece of justice, too, which interests us as a woman, as well as in the character of mother and guardian of the English people."

An involuntary shudder came over Leicester, as he bowed low, expressive of his readiness to receive her royal commands; and a similar cold fit came over Varney, whose eyes (seldom during that evening removed from his patron) instantly perceived, from the change in his looks, slight as that was, of what the Queen was speaking. But Leicester had wrought his resolution up to the point which, in his crooked policy, he judged necessary; and when Elizabeth added—"It is of the matter of Varney and Tressilian we speak—is the lady in presence, my lord?" His answer was ready:—"Gracious madam, she is not."

Elizabeth bent her brows and compressed her lips. "Our orders were strict and positive, my lord," was her answer——

"And should have been obeyed, good my liege," replied Leicester, "had they been expressed in the form of the lightest wish. But—Varney, step forward—this gentleman will inform your Grace of the cause why the lady" (he could not force his rebellious tongue to utter the words—*his wife*) "cannot attend on your royal presence."

Varney advanced, and pleaded with readiness, what indeed he firmly believed, the absolute incapacity of the party (for neither did he dare, in Leicester's presence, term her his wife) to wait on her Grace.

"Here," said he, "are attestations from a most learned physician, whose skill and honour are well known to my good Lord of Leicester; and from an honest and devout Protestant, a man of credit and substance, one Anthony Foster, the gentleman in whose house she is at present bestowed, that she now labours under an illness which altogether unfits her for such a journey as betwixt this Castle and the neighbourhood of Oxford."

"This alters the matter," said the Queen, taking the certificates in her hand, and glancing at their contents—"Let Tressilian come forward.— Master Tressilian, we have much sympathy for your situation, the rather that you seem to have set your heart deeply on this Amy Robsart, or Varney. Our power, thanks to God, and the willing obedience of a loving people, is worth much, but there are some things which it cannot compass. We cannot, for example, command the affections of a giddy young girl, or make her love sense and learning better than a courtier's fine doublet;

and we cannot control sickness, with which it seems this lady is afflicted, who may not, by reason of such infirmity, attend our court here, as we had required her to do. Here are the testimonials of the physician who hath her under his charge, and the gentleman in whose house she resides, so setting forth."

"Under your Majesty's favour," said Tressilian, hastily, and, in his alarm for the consequence of the imposition practised on the Queen, forgetting, in part at least, his own promise to Amy, "these certificates speak not the truth."

"How, sir!" said the Queen,—"Impeach my Lord of Leicester's veracity! But you shall have a fair hearing. In our presence the meanest of our subjects shall be heard against the proudest, and the least known against the most favoured; therefore you shall be heard fairly, but beware you speak not without a warrant! Take these certificates in your own hand; look at them carefully, and say manfully if you impugn the truth of them, and upon what evidence."

As the Queen spoke, his promise and all its consequences rushed on the mind of the unfortunate Tressilian, and while it controlled his natural inclination to pronounce that a falsehood which he knew from the evidence of his senses to be untrue, gave an indecision and irresolution to his appearance and utterance, which made strongly against him in the mind of Elizabeth, as well as of all who beheld him. He turned the papers over and over, as if he had been an idiot, incapable of comprehending their contents. The Queen's impatience began to become visible.—"You are a scholar, sir," she said, "and of some note, as I have heard; yet you seem wondrous slow in reading text hand—How say you, are these certificates true or no?"

"Madam," said Tressilian, with obvious embarrassment and hesitation, anxious to avoid admitting evidence which he might afterwards have reason to confute, yet equally desirous to keep his word to Amy, and to give her, as he had promised, space to plead her own cause in her own way—"Madam—Madam, your Grace calls on me to admit evidence which ought to be proved valid by those who found their defence upon them."

"Why, Tressilian, thou art critical as well as poetical," said the Queen, bending on him a brow of displeasure; "methinks these writings, being produced in the presence of the noble Earl to whom this Castle pertains, and his honour being appealed to as the guarantee of their authenticity, might be evidence enough for thee. But since thou lists to be so formal— Varney, or rather my Lord of Leicester, for the affair becomes yours," (these words, though spoken at random, thrilled through the Earl's marrow and bones,) "what evidence have you as touching these certificates?"

Varney hastened to reply, preventing Leicester,—"So please your Majesty, my young Lord of Oxford, who is here in presence, knows Master Anthony Foster's hand and his character."

The Earl of Oxford, a young unthrift, whom Foster had more than once accommodated with loans on usurious interest, acknowledged, on this appeal, that he knew him as a wealthy and independent franklin, supposed to be worth much money, and verified the certificate produced to be his handwriting.

"And who speaks to the Doctor's certificates?" said the Queen. "Alasco, methinks, is his name."

Masters, her Majesty's physician, (not the less willingly that he remembered his repulse from Say's Court, and thought that his present testimony might gratify Leicester, and mortify the Earl of Sussex and his faction,) acknowledged he had more than once consulted with Doctor Alasco, and spoke of him as a man of extraordinary learning and hidden acquirements, though not altogether in the regular course of practice. The Earl of Huntingdon, Lord Leicester's brother-in-law, and the old Countess of Rutland, next sang his praises, and both remembered the thin beautiful Italian hand in which he was wont to write his receipts, and which corresponded to the certificate produced as his.

"And now, I trust, Master Tressilian, this matter is ended," said the Queen. "We will do something ere the night is older to reconcile old Sir Hugh Robsart to the match. You have done your duty something more than boldly; but we were no woman had we not compassion for the wounds which true love deals; so we forgive your audacity, and your uncleansed boots withal, which have wellnigh over-powered my Lord of Leicester's perfumes."

So spoke Elizabeth, whose nicety of scent was one of the characteristics of her organisation, as appeared long afterwards when she expelled Essex from her presence, on a charge against his boots similar to that which she now expressed against those of Tressilian.

But Tressilian had by this time collected himself, astonished as he had at first been by the audacity of the falsehood so feasibly supported, and placed in array against the evidence of his own eyes. He rushed forward, kneeled down, and caught the Queen by the skirt of her robe. "As you are Christian woman," he said, "madam, as you are crowned Queen, to do equal justice among your subjects—as you hope yourself to have fair hearing (which God grant you) at that last bar at which we must all plead, grant me one small request! Decide not this matter so hastily. Give me but twenty-four hours' interval, and I will, at the end of that brief space, produce evidence which will show to demonstration, that these certificates, which state this unhappy lady to be now ill at ease in Oxfordshire, are false as hell!"

"Let go my train, sir!" said Elizabeth, who was startled at his vehemence, though she had too much of lion in her to fear; "the fellow must be distraught—that witty knave, my godson Harrington, must have him into his rhymes of Orlando Furioso!—And yet, by this light, there is something strange in the vehemence of his demand.—Speak, Tressilian; what wilt thou do if, at the end of these four-and-twenty hours, thou canst not confute a fact so solemnly proved as this lady's illness?"

"I will lay down my head on the block," answered Tressilian.

"Pshaw!" replied the Queen. "God's light! thou speak'st like a fool. What head falls in England but by just sentence of English law?—I ask thee, man—if thou hast sense to understand me—wilt thou, if thou shalt fail in this improbable attempt of thine, render me a good and sufficient reason why thou dost undertake it?"

Tressilian paused, and again hesitated; because he felt convinced, that if, within the interval demanded, Amy should become reconciled to her husband, he would in that case do her the worst of offices by again ripping up the whole circumstances before Elizabeth, and showing how that wise and jealous princess had been imposed upon by false testimonials. The consciousness of this dilemma renewed his extreme embarrassment of look, voice, and manner; he hesitated, looked down, and on the Queen repeating her question with a stern voice and flashing eye, he admitted with faltering words, "That it might be—he could not positively—that is, in certain events—explain the reasons and grounds on which he acted."

"Now, by the soul of King Henry," said the Queen, "this is either moonstruck madness, or very knavery!—Seest thou, Raleigh, thy friend is far too Pindaric for this presence. Have him away, and make us quit of him, or it shall be the worse for him; for his flights are too unbridled for any place but Parnassus, or Saint Luke's Hospital. But come back instantly thyself, when he is placed under fitting restraint.—We wish we had seen the beauty which could make such havoc in a wise man's brain."

Tressilian was again endeavouring to address the Queen, when Raleigh, in obedience to the orders he had received, interfered, and, with Blount's assistance, half led, half forced him out of the presence-chamber, where he himself indeed began to think his appearance did his cause more harm than good.

When they had attained the antechamber, Raleigh entreated Blount to see Tressilian safely conducted into the apartments allotted to the Earl of Sussex's followers, and, if necessary, recommended that a guard should be mounted on him.

"This extravagant passion," he said, "and, as it would seem, the news of the lady's illness, has utterly wrecked his excellent judgment. But it will pass away if he be kept quiet. Only let him break forth again at no rate; for he is already far in her Highness's displeasure, and should she be again provoked, she will find for him a worse place of confinement, and sterner keepers."

"I judged as much as that he was mad," said Nicholas Blount, looking down upon his own crimson stockings and yellow roses, "whenever I saw him wearing yonder damned boots, which stunk so in her nostrils—I will but see him stowed, and be back with you presently.—But, Walter, did the Queen ask who I was?—methought she glanced an eye at me."

"Twenty—twenty eye-glances she sent, and I told her all how thou wert a brave soldier, and a—— But, for God's sake, get off Tressilian!"

"I will—I will," said Blount; "but methinks this court-haunting is no such bad pastime, after all. We shall rise by it, Walter, my brave lad. Thou said'st I was a good soldier, and a—What besides, dearest Walter?"

"An all unutterable—codshead.—For God's sake begone!"

Tressilian, without further resistance or expostulation, followed, or rather suffered himself to be conducted by Blount to Raleigh's lodgings, where he was formally installed into a small truckle-bed, placed in a wardrobe, and designed for a domestic. He saw but too plainly, that no remonstrances would avail to procure the help or sympathy of his friends, until the lapse of the time for which he had pledged himself to remain inactive, should enable him either to explain the whole circumstances to them, or remove from him every pretext or desire of farther interference with the fortunes of Amy, by her having found means to place herself in a state of reconciliation with her husband.

With great difficulty, and only by the most patient and mild remonstrances with Blount, he escaped the disgrace and mortification of having two of Sussex's stoutest yeomen quartered in his apartment. At last, however, when Nicholas had seen him fairly deposited in his truckle-bed, and had bestowed one or two hearty kicks, and as hearty curses, on the boots, which, in his lately acquired spirit of foppery, he considered as a strong symptom, if not the cause, of his friend's malady, he contented himself with the modified measure of locking the door on the unfortunate Tressilian; whose gallant and disinterested efforts to save a female who had treated him with ingratitude, thus terminated, for the present, in the displeasure of his Sovereign, and the conviction of his friends that he was little better than a madman.

CHAPTER XXXII

The wisest Sovereigns err like private men,
And royal hand has sometimes laid the sword
Of chivalry upon a worthless shoulder,
Which better had been branded by the hangman.
What then?—Kings do their best—and they and we
Must answer for the intent, and not the event.
Old Play.

"It is a melancholy matter," said the Queen, when Tressilian was withdrawn, "to see a wise and learned man's wit thus pitifully unsettled. Yet this public display of his imperfection of brain plainly shows us that his supposed injury and accusation were fruitless; and therefore, my Lord of Leicester, we remember your suit formerly made to us in behalf of your faithful servant Varney, whose good gifts and fidelity, as they are useful to you, ought to have due reward from us, knowing well that your lordship, and all you have, are so earnestly devoted to our service. And we render Varney the honour more especially, that we are a guest, and we fear a chargeable and troublesome one, under your lordship's roof;

and also for the satisfaction of the good old Knight of Devon, Sir Hugh Robsart, whose daughter he hath married; and we trust the especial mark of grace which we are about to confer, may reconcile him to his son-in-law.—Your sword, my Lord of Leicester."

The Earl unbuckled his sword, and, taking it by the point, presented on bended knee the hilt to Elizabeth.

She took it slowly, drew it from the scabbard, and while the ladies who stood around turned away their eyes with real or affected shuddering, she noted with a curious eye the high polish and rich damasked ornaments upon the glittering blade.

"Had I been a man," she said, "methinks none of my ancestors would have loved a good sword better. As it is with me, I like to look on one, and could, like the Fairy of whom I have read in some Italian rhymes— were my godson Harrington here, he could tell me the passage [1]—even trim my hair, and arrange my head-gear, in such a steel mirror as this is.— Richard Varney, come forth, and kneel down. In the name of God and Saint George, we dub thee knight! Be Faithful, Brave, and Fortunate.— Arise, Sir Richard Varney."

Varney rose and retired, making a deep obeisance to the Sovereign who had done him so much honour.

"The buckling of the spur, and what other rites remain," said the Queen, "may be finished to-morrow in the chapel; for we intend Sir Richard Varney a companion in his honours. And as we must not be partial in conferring such distinction, we mean on this matter to confer with our cousin of Sussex."

That noble Earl, who since his arrival at Kenilworth, and indeed since the commencement of this Progress, had found himself in a subordinate situation to Leicester, was now wearing a heavy cloud on his brow—a circumstance which had not escaped the Queen, who hoped to appease his discontent, and to follow out her system of balancing policy by a

---

[1] The incident alluded to occurs in the poem of Orlando Innamorato of Boiardo, libro ii. canto 4, stanza 25.

"Non era per ventura," etc.

It may be rendered thus:—

> As then, perchance, unguarded was the tower,
>   So enter'd free Anglanté's dauntless knight.
> No monster and no giant guard the bower
>   In whose recess reclined the fairy light,
> Robed in a loose cymar of lily white,
>   And on her lap a sword of breadth and might,
> In whose gold blade, as in a mirror bright,
>   Like maid that trims her for a festal night,
> The fairy deck'd her hair, and placed her coronet aright.

Elizabeth's attachment to the Italian school of poetry was singularly manifested on a well-known occasion. Her godson, Sir John Harrington, having offended her delicacy by translating some of the licentious passages of the Orlando Furioso, she imposed on him, as a penance, the task of rendering the *whole* poem into English.

mark of peculiar favour, the more gratifying as it was tendered at a moment when his rival's triumph appeared to be complete.

At the summons of Queen Elizabeth, Sussex hastily approached her person; and being asked on which of his followers, being a gentleman and of merit, he would wish the honour of knighthood to be conferred, he answered, with more sincerity than policy, that he would have ventured to speak for Tressilian, to whom he conceived he owed his own life, and who was a distinguished soldier and scholar, besides a man of unstained lineage, "only," he said, "he feared the events of that night——" And then he stopped.

"I am glad your lordship is thus considerate," said Elizabeth; "the events of this night would make us, in the eyes of our subjects, as mad as this poor brain-sick gentleman himself—for we ascribe his conduct to no malice—should we choose this moment to do him grace."

"In that case," said the Earl of Sussex, somewhat discountenanced, "your Majesty will allow me to name my master of the horse. Master Nicholas Blount, a gentleman of fair estate and ancient name, who has served your Majesty both in Scotland and Ireland, and brought away bloody marks on his person, all honourably taken and requited."

The Queen could not help shrugging her shoulders slightly even at this second suggestion; and the Duchess of Rutland, who read in the Queen's manner that she had expected Sussex would have named Raleigh, and thus would have enabled her to gratify her own wish, while she honoured his recommendation, only waited the Queen's assent to what he had proposed, and then said, that she hoped, since these two high nobles had been each permitted to suggest a candidate for the honours of chivalry, she, in behalf of the ladies in presence, might have a similar indulgence.

"I were no woman to refuse you such a boon," said the Queen, smiling.

"Then," pursued the Duchess, "in the name of these fair ladies present, I request your Majesty to confer the rank of knighthood on Walter Raleigh, whose birth, deeds of arms, and promptitude to serve our sex with sword or pen, deserve such distinction from us all."

"Gramercy, fair ladies," said Elizabeth, smiling, "your boon is granted, and the gentle squire Lack-Cloak shall become the good knight Lack-Cloak, at your desire. Let the two aspirants for the honour of chivalry step forward."

Blount was not as yet returned from seeing Tressilian, as he conceived, safely disposed of; but Raleigh came forth, and, kneeling down, received at the hand of the Virgin Queen that title of honour, which was never conferred on a more distinguished or more illustrious object.

Shortly afterwards Nicholas Blount entered, and, hastily apprized by Sussex, who met him at the door of the hall, of the Queen's gracious purpose regarding him, he was desired to advance towards the throne. It is a sight sometimes seen, and it is both ludicrous and pitiable, when an honest man of plain common sense is surprised, by the coquetry of a pretty woman, or any other cause, into those frivolous fopperies which only sit well upon the youthful, the gay, and those to whom long practice has rendered them a second nature. Poor Blount was in this situation. His head was already giddy from a consciousness of unusual finery, and the supposed necessity of suiting his manners to the gaiety of his dress; and now this sudden view of promotion altogether completed the conquest of the newly inhaled spirit of foppery over his natural disposition, and converted a plain, honest, awkward man, into a coxcomb of a new and most ridiculous kind.

The knight-expectant advanced up the hall, the whole length of which he had unfortunately to traverse, turning out his toes with so much zeal, that he presented his leg at every step with its broadside foremost, so that it greatly resembled an old-fashioned table-knife with a curved point, when seen sideways. The rest of his gait was in correspondence with this unhappy amble; and the implied mixture of bashful fear, and self-satisfaction, was so unutterably ridiculous, that Leicester's friends did not suppress a titter, in which many of Sussex's partisans were unable to resist joining, though ready to eat their nails with mortification. Sussex himself lost all patience, and could not forbear whispering into the ear of his friend, "Curse thee! canst thou not walk like a man and a soldier?" an interjection which only made honest Blount start and stop, until a glance at his yellow roses and crimson stockings restored his self-confidence, when on he went at the same pace as before.

The Queen conferred on poor Blount the honour of knighthood with a marked sense of reluctance. That wise Princess was fully aware of the propriety of using great circumspection and economy in bestowing these titles of honour, which the Stewarts, who succeeded to her throne, distributed with an imprudent liberality, which greatly diminished their value. Blount had no sooner arisen and retired, than she turned to the Duchess of Rutland. "Our woman wit," she said, "dear Rutland, is sharper than that of those proud things in doublet and hose. Seest thou, out of these three knights, thine is the only true metal to stamp chivalry's imprint upon?"

"Sir Richard Varney, surely—the friend of my Lord of Leicester—surely _he_ has merit," replied the Duchess.

"Varney has a sly countenance, and a smooth tongue," replied the Queen. "I fear me, he will prove a knave—but the promise was of ancient standing. My Lord of Sussex must have lost his own wits, I think, to recommend to us first a madman like Tressilian, and then a clownish fool like this other fellow. I protest, Rutland, that while he sat on his knees before me, mopping and mowing as if he had scalding porridge in his mouth, I had much ado to forbear cutting him over the pate, instead of striking his shoulder."

"Your Majesty gave him a smart _accolade_," said the Duchess; "we who stood behind heard the blade clatter on his collar-bone, and the poor man fidgeted too as if he felt it."

"I could not help it, wench," said the Queen, laughing; "but we will have this same Sir Nicholas sent to Ireland or Scotland, or somewhere, to rid our court of so antic a chevalier; he may be a good soldier in the field, though a preposterous ass in a banqueting hall."

The discourse became then more general, and soon after there was a summons to the banquet.

In order to obey this signal, the company were under the necessity of crossing the inner court of the Castle, that they might reach the new-buildings, containing the large banqueting-room, in which preparations for supper were made upon a scale of profuse magnificence, corresponding to the occasion.

The livery cupboards were loaded with plate of the richest description, and the most varied; some articles tasteful, some perhaps grotesque, in the invention and decoration, but all gorgeously magnificent, both from the richness of the work and value of the materials. Thus the chief table was adorned by a salt, ship-fashion, made of mother-of-pearl, garnished with silver and divers warlike ensigns, and other ornaments, anchors, sails, and sixteen pieces of ordnance. It bore a figure of Fortune, placed on a globe, with a flag in her hand. Another salt was fashioned of silver, in form of a swan in full sail. That chivalry might not be omitted amid this splendour, a silver Saint George was presented, mounted and equipped in the usual fashion in which he bestrides the dragon. The figures were moulded to be in some sort useful. The horse's tail was managed to hold a case of knives, while the breast of the dragon presented a similar accommodation for oyster knives.[1]

In the course of the pass from the hall of reception to the banqueting-room, and especially in the court-yard, the new-made knights were assailed by the heralds, pursuivants, minstrels, etc., with the usual cry of *Largesse, largesse, chevaliers très hardis!* an ancient invocation, intended to awaken the bounty of the acolytes of chivalry towards those whose business it was to register their armorial bearings, and celebrate the deeds by which they were illustrated. The call was of course liberally and courteously answered by those to whom it was addressed. Varney gave his largesse with an affectation of complaisance and humility. Raleigh bestowed his with the graceful ease peculiar to one who has attained his own place, and is familiar with its dignity. Honest Blount gave what his tailor had left him of his half-year's rent, dropping some pieces in his hurry, then stooping down to look for them, and then distributing them amongst the various claimants, with the anxious face and mien of the parish beadle dividing a dole among paupers.

The donations were accepted with the usual clamour and *vivats* of applause common on such occasions; but as the parties gratified were chiefly dependents of Lord Leicester, it was Varney whose name was repeated with the loudest acclamations. Lambourne, especially, distinguished himself by his vociferations of "Long life to Sir Richard Var-

[1] See Note VIII.—Furniture of Kenilworth.

ney!—Health and honour to Sir Richard!—Never was a more worthy knight dubbed!"—then, suddenly sinking his voice, he added,—"since the valiant Sir Pandarus of Troy,"—a winding-up of his clamorous applause, which set all men a-laughing who were within hearing of it.

It is unnecessary to say any thing farther of the festivities of the evening, which were so brilliant in themselves, and received with such obvious and willing satisfaction by the Queen, that Leicester retired to his own apartment, with all the giddy raptures of successful ambition. Varney, who had changed his splendid attire, and now waited on his patron in a very modest and plain undress, attended to do the honours of the Earl's *coucher*.

"How! Sir Richard," said Leicester, smiling, "your new rank scarce suits the humility of this attendance."

"I would disown that rank, my lord," said Varney, "could I think it was to remove me to a distance from your lordship's person."

"Thou art a grateful fellow," said Leicester; "but I must not allow you to do what would abate you in the opinion of others."

While thus speaking, he still accepted, without hesitation, the offices about his person, which the new-made knight seemed to render as eagerly as if he had really felt, in discharging the task, that pleasure which his words expressed.

"I am not afraid of men's misconstruction," he said, in answer to Leicester's remark, "since there is not—(permit me to undo the collar)— a man within the Castle, who does not expect very soon to see persons of a rank far superior to that which, by your goodness, I now hold, rendering the duties of the bedchamber to you, and accounting it an honour."

"It might, indeed, so have been"—said the Earl, with an involuntary sigh; and then presently added, "My gown, Varney—I will look out on the night. Is not the moon near to the full?"

"I think so, my lord, according to the calendar," answered Varney.

There was an abutting window, which opened on a small projecting balcony of stone, battlemented as is usual in Gothic castles. The Earl undid the lattice, and stepped out into the open air. The station he had chosen commanded an extensive view of the lake, and woodlands beyond, where the bright moonlight rested on the clear blue waters, and the distant masses of oak and elm trees. The moon rode high in the heavens, attended by thousands and thousands of inferior luminaries. All seemed already to be hushed in the nether world, excepting occasionally the voice of the watch, (for the yeomen of the guard performed that duty wherever the Queen was present in person,) and the distant baying of the hounds, disturbed by the preparations amongst the grooms and prickers for a magnificent hunt, which was to be the amusement of the next day.

Leicester looked out on the blue arch of heaven, with gestures and a countenance expressive of anxious exultation, while Varney, who remained within the darkened apartment, could, (himself unnoticed,) with a secret satisfaction, see his patron stretch his hands with earnest gesticulation towards the heavenly bodies.

"Ye distant orbs of living fire," so ran the muttered invocation of the ambitious Earl, "ye are silent while you wheel your mystic rounds, but Wisdom has given to you a voice. Tell me, then, to what end is my high course destined! Shall the greatness to which I have aspired be bright, pre-eminent, and stable as your own; or am I but doomed to draw a brief and glittering train along the nightly darkness, and then to sink down to earth, like the base refuse of those artificial fires with which men emulate your rays?"

He looked on the heavens in profound silence for a minute or two longer, and then again stepped into the apartment, where Varney seemed to have been engaged in putting the Earl's jewels into a casket.

"What said Alasco of my horoscope?" demanded Leicester. "You already told me, but it has escaped me, for I think but lightly of that art."

"Many learned and great men have thought otherwise," said Varney; "and, not to flatter your lordship, my own opinion leans that way."

"Ay, Saul among the prophets?" said Leicester—"I thought thou wert sceptical in all such matters as thou couldst neither see, hear, smell, taste, or touch, and that thy belief was limited by thy senses."

"Perhaps, my lord," said Varney, "I may be misled on the present occasion, by my wish to find the predictions of astrology true. Alasco says, that your favourite planet is culminating, and that the adverse influence—he would not use a plainer term—though not overcome, was evidently combust, I think he said, or retrograde."

"It is even so," said Leicester, looking at an abstract of astrological calculations which he had in his hand; "the stronger influence will prevail, and, as I think, the evil hour pass away.—Lend me your hand, Sir Richard, to doff my gown—and remain an instant, if it is not too burdensome to your knighthood, while I compose myself to sleep. I believe the bustle of this day has fevered my blood, for it streams through my veins like a current of molten lead—remain an instant, I pray you—I would fain feel my eyes heavy ere I closed them."

Varney officiously assisted his lord to bed, and placed a massive silver night-lamp, with a short sword, on a marble table which stood close by the head of the couch. Either in order to avoid the light of the lamp, or to hide his countenance from Varney, Leicester drew the curtain, heavy with entwined silk and gold, so as completely to shade his face. Varney took a seat near the bed, but with his back towards his master, as if to intimate that he was not watching him, and quietly waited till Leicester himself led the way to the topic by which his mind was engrossed.

"And so, Varney," said the Earl, after waiting in vain till his dependant should commence the conversation, "men talk of the Queen's favour towards me?"

"Ay, my good lord," said Varney; "of what can they else, since it is so strongly manifested?"

"She is indeed my good and gracious mistress," said Leicester after another pause; "but it is written, 'Put not thy trust in Princes.' "

"A good sentence and a true," said Varney, "unless you can unite their interest with yours so absolutely, that they must needs sit on your wrist like hooded hawks."

"I know what thou meanest," said Leicester, impatiently, "though thou art to-night so prudentially careful of what thou sayst to me— Thou wouldst intimate, I might marry the Queen if I would?"

"It is your speech, my lord, not mine," answered Varney; "but whose soever be the speech, it is the thought of ninety-nine out of an hundred men throughout broad England."

"Ay, but," said Leicester, turning himself in his bed, "the hundredth man knows better. Thou, for example, knowest the obstacle that cannot be overleaped."

"It must, my lord, if the stars speak true," said Varney, composedly.

"What! talk'st thou of them," said Leicester, "that believest not in them or in aught else?"

"You mistake, my lord, under your gracious pardon," said Varney; "I believe in many things that predict the future. I believe, if showers fall in April, that we shall have flowers in May; that if the sun shines, grain will ripen; and I believe in much natural philosophy to the same effect, which, if the stars swear to me, I will say the stars speak the truth. And in like manner, I will not disbelieve that which I see wished for and expected on earth, solely because the astrologers have read it in the heavens."

"Thou art right," said Leicester, again tossing himself on his couch— "Earth does wish for it. I have had advices from the reformed churches of Germany—from the Low Countries—from Switzerland, urging this as a point on which Europe's safety depends. France will not oppose it—The ruling party in Scotland look to it as their best security—Spain fears it, but cannot prevent it—and yet thou knowest it is impossible."

"I know not that, my lord," said Varney, "the Countess is indisposed."

"Villain!" said Leicester, starting up on his couch, and seizing the sword which lay on the table beside him, "go thy thoughts that way?— thou wouldst not do murder!"

"For whom, or what, do you hold me, my lord?" said Varney, assuming the superiority of an innocent man subjected to unjust suspicion. "I said nothing to deserve such a horrid imputation as your violence infers. I said but that the Countess was ill. And Countess though she be—lovely and beloved as she is, surely your lordship must hold her to be mortal? She may die, and your lordship's hand become once more your own."

"Away! away!" said Leicester; "let me have no more of this."

"Good night, my lord," said Varney, seeming to understand this as a command to depart; but Leicester's voice interrupted his purpose.

"Thou 'scapest me not thus, Sir Fool," said he; "I think thy knighthood has addled thy brains—Confess thou hast talked of impossibilities, as of things which may come to pass."

"My lord, long live your fair Countess," said Varney; "but neither your love nor my good wishes can make her immortal. But God grant she live long to be happy herself, and to render you so! I see not but you may be King of England notwithstanding."

"Nay, now, Varney, thou art stark-mad," said Leicester.

"I would I were myself within the same nearness to a good estate of freehold," said Varney. "Have we not known in other countries, how a left-handed marriage might subsist betwixt persons of differing degree?— ay, and be no hinderance to prevent the husband from conjoining himself afterwards with a more suitable partner?"

"I have heard of such things in Germany," said Leicester.

"Ay, and the most learned doctors in foreign universities justify the practice from the Old Testament," said Varney. "And after all, where is the harm? The beautiful partner, whom you have chosen for true love, has your secret hours of relaxation and affection. Her fame is safe— her conscience may slumber securely—You have wealth to provide royally for your issue, should heaven bless you with offspring. Meanwhile you may give to Elizabeth ten times the leisure, and ten thousand times the affection, that ever Don Philip of Spain spared to her sister Mary; yet you know how she doted on him though so cold and neglectful. It requires but a close mouth and an open brow, and you keep your Eleanor and your fair Rosamond far enough separate.—Leave me to build you a bower to which no jealous Queen shall find a clew."

Leicester was silent for a moment, then sighed, and said, "It is impossible.—Good-night, Sir Richard Varney—yet stay—Can you guess what meant Tressilian by showing himself in such careless guise before the Queen to-day?—to strike her tender heart, I should guess, with all the sympathies due to a lover, abandoned by his mistress, and abandoning himself."

Varney, smothering a sneering laugh, answered, "He believed Master Tressilian had no such matter in his head."

"How!" said Leicester; "what mean'st thou? There is ever knavery in that laugh of thine, Varney."

"I only meant, my lord," said Varney, "that Tressilian has taken the sure way to avoid heart-breaking. He hath had a companion—a female companion—a mistress—a sort of player's wife or sister, as I believe,— with him in Mervyn's Bower, where I quartered him for certain reasons of my own."

"A mistress!—mean'st thou a paramour?"

"Ay, my lord; what female else waits for hours in a gentleman's chamber?"

"By my faith, time and space fitting, this were a good tale to tell," said Leicester. "I ever distrusted those bookish, hypocritical, seeming-virtuous scholars. Well—Master Tressilian makes somewhat familiar with my house—if I look it over, he is indebted to it for certain recollections. I would not harm him more than I can help. Keep eye on him, however, Varney."

"I lodged him for that reason," said Varney, "in Mervyn's Tower, where he is under the eye of my very vigilant, if he were not also my very drunken, servant, Michael Lambourne, whom I have told your Grace of."

"Grace!" said Leicester; "what mean'st thou by that epithet?"

"It came unawares, my lord; and yet it sounds so very natural, that I cannot recall it."

"It is thine own preferment that hath turned thy brain," said Leicester, laughing; "new honours are as heady as new wine."

"May your lordship soon have cause to say so from experience," said Varney; and, wishing his patron good night, he withdrew.

CHAPTER XXXIII

Here stands the victim—there the proud betrayer,
E'en as the hind pull'd down by strangling dogs
Lies at the hunter's feet—who courteous proffers
To some high dame, the Dian of the chase,
To whom he looks for guerdon, his sharp blade,
To gash the sobbing throat.
The Woodsman.

WE are now to return to Mervyn's Bower, the apartment, or rather the prison, of the unfortunate Countess of Leicester, who for some time kept within bounds her uncertainty and her impatience. She was aware that, in the tumult of the day, there might be some delay ere her letter could be safely conveyed to the hands of Leicester, and that some time more might elapse ere he could extricate himself from the necessary attendance on Elizabeth, to come and visit her in her secret bower. "I will not expect him," she said, "till night—he cannot be absent from his royal guest, even to see me. He will, I know, come earlier if it be possible, but I will not expect him before night."—And yet all the while she did expect him; and, while she tried to argue herself into a contrary belief, each hasty noise, of the hundred which she heard, sounded like the hurried step of Leicester on the staircase, hasting to fold her in his arms.

The fatigue of body which Amy had lately undergone, with the agitation of mind natural to so cruel a state of uncertainty, began by degrees strongly to affect her nerves, and she almost feared her total inability to maintain the necessary self-command through the scenes which might lie before her. But, although spoiled by an over-indulgent system of education, Amy had naturally a mind of great power, united with a frame

which her share in her father's woodland exercises had rendered uncom-
monly healthy. She summoned to her aid such mental and bodily resources; and not unconscious how much the issue of her fate might depend
on her own self-possession, she prayed internally for strength of body
and for mental fortitude, and resolved, at the same time, to yield to no
nervous impulse which might weaken either.

Yet when the great bell of the Castle, which was placed in Cæsar's
Tower, at no great distance from that called Mervyn's, began to send
its pealing clamour abroad, in signal of the arrival of the royal procession,
the din was so painfully acute to ears rendered nervously sensitive by
anxiety, that she could hardly forbear shrieking with anguish, in answer
to every stunning clash of the relentless peal.

Shortly afterwards, when the small apartment was at once enlightened
by the shower of artificial fires with which the air was suddenly filled,
and which crossed each other like fiery spirits, each bent on his own
separate mission, or like salamanders executing a frolic dance in the
region of the Sylphs, the Countess felt at first as if each rocket shot close
by her eyes, and discharged its sparks and flashes so nigh that she could
feel a sense of the heat. But she struggled against these fantastic terrors,
and compelled herself to rise, stand by the window, look out, and gaze
upon a sight, which at another time would have appeared to her at once
captivating and fearful. The magnificent towers of the Castle were enveloped in garlands of artificial fire, or shrouded with tiaras of pale smoke.
The surface of the lake glowed like molten iron, while many fireworks,
(then thought extremely wonderful, though now common,) whose flame
continued to exist in the opposing element, dived and rose, hissed and
roared, and spouted fire, like so many dragons of enchantment, sporting
upon a burning lake.

Even Amy was for a moment interested by what was to her so new a
scene. "I had thought it magical art," she said, "but poor Tressilian
taught me to judge of such things as they are. Great God! and may not
these idle splendours resemble my own hoped for happiness,—a single
spark, which is instantly swallowed up by surrounding darkness,—a
precarious glow, which rises but for a brief space into the air, that its
fall may be the lower? O, Leicester! after all—all that thou hast said—
hast sworn—that Amy was thy love, thy life, can it be that thou art
the magician at whose nod these enchantments arise, and that she sees
them, as an outcast, if not a captive?"

The sustained, prolonged, and repeated bursts of music, from so many
different quarters, and at so many varying points of distance, which
sounded as if not the Castle of Kenilworth only, but the whole country
around, had been at once the scene of solemnizing some high national festival, carried the same oppressive thought still closer to her heart, while
some notes would melt in distant and falling tones, as if in compassion
for her sorrows, and some burst close and near upon her, as if mocking
her misery, with all the insolence of unlimited mirth. "These sounds,"

she said, "are mine—mine, because they are HIS; but I cannot say,—Be still, these loud strains suit me not;—and the voice of the meanest peasant that mingles in the dance, would have more power to modulate the music, than the command of her who is mistress of all!"

By degrees the sounds of revelry died away, and the Countess withdrew from the window at which she had sate listening to them. It was night, but the moon afforded considerable light in the room, so that Amy was able to make the arrangement which she judged necessary. There was hope that Leicester might come to her apartment as soon as the revel in the Castle had subsided; but there was also risk she might be disturbed by some unauthorised intruder. She had lost confidence in the key, since Tressilian had entered so easily, though the door was locked on the inside; yet all the additional security she could think of, was to place the table across the door, that she might be warned by the noise, should any one attempt to enter. Having taken these necessary precautions, the unfortunate lady withdrew to her couch, stretched herself down on it, mused in anxious expectation, and counted more than one hour after midnight, till exhausted nature proved too strong for love, for grief, for fear, nay even for uncertainty, and she slept.

Yes, she slept. The Indian sleeps at the stake, in the intervals between his tortures; and mental torments, in like manner, exhaust by long continuance the sensibility of the sufferer, so that an interval of lethargic repose must necessarily ensue, ere the pangs which they inflict can again be renewed.

The Countess slept, then, for several hours, and dreamed that she was in the ancient house at Cumnor-Place, listening for the low whistle with which Leicester often used to announce his presence in the court-yard, when arriving suddenly on one of his stolen visits. But on this occasion, instead of a whistle, she heard the peculiar blast of a bugle-horn, such as her father used to wind on the fall of the stag, and which huntsmen then called a *mort*. She ran, as she thought, to a window that looked into the court-yard, which she saw filled with men in mourning garments. The old Curate seemed about to read the funeral service. Mumblazen, tricked out in an antique dress, like an ancient herald, held aloft a scutcheon, with its usual decorations of skulls, cross-bones, and hour-glasses, surrounding a coat-of-arms, of which she could only distinguish that it was surmounted with an Earl's coronet. The old man looked at her with a ghastly smile, and said, "Amy, are they not rightly quartered?" Just as he spoke, the horns again poured on her ear the melancholy yet wild strain of the mort, or death-note, and she awoke.

The Countess awoke to hear a real bugle-note, or rather the combined breath of many bugles, sounding not the *mort*, but the jolly *reveille*, to remind the inmates of the Castle of Kenilworth, that the pleasures of the day were to commence with a magnificent stag-hunting in the neighbouring Chase. Amy started up from her couch, listened to the sound, saw the first beams of the summer morning already twinkle through the lattice of her window, and recollected, with feelings of giddy agony, where she was, and how circumstanced.

"He thinks not of *me*," she said—"he will not come nigh me! A Queen is his guest, and what cares he in what corner of his huge Castle a wretch like me pines in doubt, which is fast fading into despair?" At once a sound at the door, as of some one attempting to open it softly, filled her with an ineffable mixture of joy and fear; and, hastening to remove the obstacle she had placed against the door, and to unlock it, she had the precaution to ask, "Is it thou, my love?"

"Yes, my Countess," murmured a whisper in reply.

She threw open the door, and exclaiming, "Leicester!" flung her arms around the neck of the man who stood without, muffled in his cloak.

"No—not quite Leicester," answered Michael Lambourne, for he it was, returning the caress with vehemence,—"not quite Leicester, my lovely and most loving Duchess, but as good a man."

With an exertion of force, of which she would at another time have thought herself incapable, the Countess freed herself from the profane and profaning grasp of the drunken debauchee, and retreated into the midst of her apartment, where despair gave her courage to make a stand.

As Lambourne, on entering, dropped the lap of his cloak from his face, she knew Varney's profligate servant; the very last person, excepting his detested master, by whom she would have wished to be discovered. But she was still closely muffled in her travelling dress, and as Lambourne had scarce ever been admitted to her presence at Cumnor-Place, her person, she hoped, might not be so well known to him as his was to her, owing to Janet's pointing him frequently out as he crossed the court, and telling stories of his wickedness. She might have had still greater confidence in her disguise, had her experience enabled her to discover that he was much intoxicated; but this could scarce have consoled her for the risk which she might incur from such a character, in such a time, place, and circumstances.

Lambourne flung the door behind him as he entered, and folding his arms, as if in mockery of the attitude of distraction into which Amy had thrown herself, he proceeded thus: "Hark ye, most fair Callipolis—or most lovely Countess of clouts, and divine Duchess of dark corners—if thou takest all that trouble of skewering thyself together, like a trussed fowl, that there may be more pleasure in the carving, even save thyself the labour. I love thy first frank manner the best—like thy present as little"—(he made a step towards her, and staggered)—"as little as—such a damned uneven floor as this, where a gentleman may break his neck if he does not walk as upright as a posture-master on the tight-rope."

"Stand back!" said the Countess; "do not approach nearer to me on thy peril!"

"My peril!—and stand back!—Why, how now, madam? Must you have a better mate than honest Mike Lambourne? I have been in America, girl, where the gold grows, and have brought off such a load on't——"

"Good friend," said the Countess, in great terror at the ruffian's determined and audacious manner, "I prithee begone, and leave me."

"And so I will, pretty one, when we are tired of each other's company—not a jot sooner."—He seized her by the arm, while, incapable of further defence, she uttered shriek upon shriek. "Nay, scream away if you like it," said he, still holding her fast; "I have heard the sea at the loudest, and I mind the squalling woman no more than a miauling kitten—Damn me!—I have heard fifty or a hundred screaming at once, when there was a town stormed."

The cries of the Countess, however, brought unexpected aid, in the person of Lawrence Staples, who had heard her exclamations from his apartment below, and entered in good time to save her from being discovered, if not from more atrocious violence. Lawrence was drunk also, from the debauch of the preceding night; but fortunately his intoxication had taken a different turn from that of Lambourne.

"What the devil's noise is this in the ward?" he said—"What! man and woman together in the same cell? that is against rule. I will have decency under my rule, by Saint Peter of the Fetters!"

"Get thee down stairs, thou drunken beast," said Lambourne; "seest thou not the lady and I would be private?"

"Good sir, worthy sir!" said the Countess, addressing the jailor, "do but save me from him, for the sake of mercy!"

"She speaks fairly," said the jailor, "and I will take her part. I love my prisoners; and I have had as good prisoners under my key, as they have had in Newgate or the Compter. And so, being one of my lambkins, as I say, no one shall disturb her in her pen-fold. So, let go the woman, or I'll knock your brains out with my keys."

"I'll make a blood-pudding of thy midriff first," answered Lambourne, laying his left hand on his dagger, but still detaining the Countess by the arm with his right—"So have at thee, thou old ostrich, whose only living is upon a bunch of iron keys!"

Lawrence raised the arm of Michael, and prevented him from drawing his dagger; and as Lambourne struggled and strove to shake him off, the Countess made a sudden exertion on her side, and slipping her hand out of the glove on which the ruffian still kept hold, she gained her liberty, and escaping from the apartment, ran down stairs; while, at the same moment, she heard the two combatants fall on the floor with a noise which increased her terror. The outer wicket offered no impediment to her flight, having been opened for Lambourne's admittance; so that she succeeded in escaping down the stair, and fled into the Pleasance, which seemed to her hasty glance the direction in which she was most likely to avoid pursuit.

Meanwhile, Lawrence and Lambourne rolled on the floor of the apartment, closely grappled together. Neither had, happily, opportunity to draw their daggers; but Lawrence found space enough to dash his heavy keys across Michael's face, and Michael, in return, grasped the turnkey so felly by the throat, that the blood gushed from nose and mouth; so that they were both gory and filthy spectacles, when one of the other officers of the household, attracted by the noise of the fray, entered the room, and with some difficulty effected the separation of the combatants.

"A murrain on you both," said the charitable mediator, "and especially on you, Master Lambourne! What the fiend lie you here for, fighting on the floor, like two butchers' curs in the kennel of the shambles?"

Lambourne arose, and, somewhat sobered by the interposition of a third party, looked with something less than his usual brazen impudence of visage; "We fought for a wench, an thou must know," was the reply.

"A wench! Where is she?" said the officer.

"Why, vanished, I think," said Lambourne looking around him; "unless Lawrence hath swallowed her. That filthy paunch of his devours as many distressed damsels and oppressed orphans, as e'er a giant in King Arthur's history: they are his prime food; he worries them body, soul, and substance."

"Ay, ay! It's no matter," said Lawrence, gathering up his huge ungainly form from the floor; "but I have had your betters, Master Michael Lambourne, under the little turn of my forefinger and thumb; and I shall have thee, before all's done, under my hatches. The impudence of thy brow will not always save thy shin-bones from iron, and thy foul thirsty gullet from a hempen cord."—The words were no sooner out of his mouth, when Lambourne again made at him.

"Nay, go not to it again," said the sewer, "or I will call for him shall tame you both, and that is Master Varney—Sir Richard, I mean—he is stirring, I promise you—I saw him cross the court just now."

"Did'st thou, by G—!" said Lambourne, seizing on the basin and ewer which stood in the apartment; "Nay, then, element, do thy work—I thought I had enough of thee last night, when I floated about for Orion, like a cork on a fermenting cask of ale."

So saying, he fell to work to cleanse from his face and hands the sign of the fray, and get his apparel into some order.

"What hast thou done to him?" said the sewer, speaking aside to the jailor; "his face is fearfully swelled."

"It is but the imprint of the key of my cabinet—too good a mark for his gallows-face. No man shall abuse or insult my prisoners; they are my jewels, and I lock them in safe casket accordingly.—And so, mistress, leave off your wailing—Hey! why surely there was a woman here!"

"I think you are all mad this morning," said the sewer; "I saw no woman here, nor no man neither in a proper sense, but only two beasts rolling on the floor."

"Nay, then I am undone," said the jailor; "the prison's broken, that is all. Kenilworth prison is broken," he continued, in a tone of maudlin lamentation, "which was the strongest jail betwixt this and the Welsh marches—ay, and a house that has had knights, and earls, and kings sleeping in it, as secure as if they had been in the Tower of London. It is broken, the prisoners fled, and the jailor in much danger of being hanged!"

So saying he retreated down to his own den to conclude his lamentations, or to sleep himself sober. Lambourne and the sewer followed him close, and it was well for them, since the jailor, out of mere habit, was about to lock the wicket after him; and had they not been within the reach of interfering, they would have had the pleasure of being shut up in the turret-chamber, from which the Countess had been just delivered.

That unhappy lady, as soon as she found herself at liberty, fled, as we have already mentioned, into the Pleasance. She had seen this richly ornamented space of ground from the window of Mervyn's Tower; and it occurred to her, at the moment of her escape, that, among its numerous arbours, bowers, fountains, statues, and grottoes, she might find some recess, in which she could lie concealed until she had an opportunity of addressing herself to a protector, to whom she might communicate as much as she dared of her forlorn situation, and through whose means she might supplicate an interview with her husband.

"If I could see my guide," she thought, "I would learn if he had delivered my letter. Even did I but see Tressilian, it were better to risk Dudley's anger, by confiding my whole situation to one who is the very soul of honour, than to run the hazard of further insult among the insolent menials of this ill-ruled place. I will not again venture into an enclosed apartment. I will wait, I will watch—amidst so many human beings, there must be some kind heart which can judge and compassionate what mine endures."

In truth, more than one party entered and traversed the Pleasance. But they were in joyous groups of four or five persons together, laughing and jesting in their own fulness of mirth and lightness of heart.

The retreat which she had chosen gave her the easy alternative of avoiding observation. It was but stepping back to the farthest recess of a grotto, ornamented with rustic work and moss-seats, and terminated by a fountain, and she might easily remain concealed, or at her pleasure discover herself to any solitary wanderer, whose curiosity might lead him to that romantic retirement. Anticipating such an opportunity, she looked into the clear basin, which the silent fountain held up to her like a mirror, and felt shocked at her own appearance, and doubtful at the same time, muffled and disfigured as her disguise made her seem to herself, whether any female (and it was from the compassion of her own sex that she chiefly expected sympathy) would engage in conference with so suspicious an object. Reasoning thus like a woman, to whom external appearance is scarcely in any circumstances a matter of unimportance, and like a beauty, who had some confidence in the power of her own charms, she laid aside her travelling cloak and capotaine hat, and placed them beside her, so that she could assume them in an instant, ere one could penetrate from the entrance of the grotto to its extremity, in case the intrusion of Varney or of Lambourne should render such disguise necessary. The dress which she wore under these vestments was somewhat of a theatrical cast, so as to suit the assumed personage of one of the females who was to act in the pageant. Wayland had found the means of arranging it thus upon the second day of their journey, having experienced the service arising from the assumption of such a character on the preceding day. The fountain, acting both as a mirror and ewer, afforded Amy the means of a brief toilette, of which she availed herself as hastily as possible; then took in her hand her small casket of jewels, in case she might find them useful intercessors, and retiring to the darkest and most sequestered nook, sat down on a seat of moss, and awaited till fate should give her some chance of rescue, or of propitiating an intercessor.

CHAPTER XXXIV

Have you not seen the partridge quake,
Viewing the hawk approaching nigh?
She cuddles close beneath the brake,
Afraid to sit, afraid to fly.
Prior.

It chanced upon that memorable morning, that one of the earliest of the huntress train, who appeared from her chamber in full array for the Chase, was the Princess for whom all these pleasures were instituted, England's Maiden Queen. I know not if it were by chance, or out of the befitting courtesy due to a mistress by whom he was so much honoured, that she had scarcely made one step beyond the threshold of her chamber, ere Leicester was by her side, and proposed to her, until the preparations for the Chase had been completed, to view the Pleasance, and the gardens which it connected with the Castleyard.

To this new scene of pleasures they walked, the Earl's arm affording his Sovereign the occasional support which she required, where flights of steps, then a favourite ornament in a garden, conducted them from terrace to terrace, and from parterre to parterre. The ladies in attendance, gifted with prudence, or endowed perhaps with the amiable desire of acting as they would be done by, did not conceive their duty to the Queen's person required them, though they lost not sight of her, to approach so near as to share, or perhaps disturb, the conversation betwixt the Queen and the Earl, who was not only her host, but also her most trusted, esteemed, and favoured servant. They contented themselves with admiring the grace of this illustrious couple, whose robes of state were now exchanged for hunting suits, almost equally magnificent.

Elizabeth's silvan dress, which was of a pale blue silk, with silver lace and *aiguillettes,* approached in form to that of the ancient Amazons; and was, therefore, well suited at once to her height, and to the dignity of her mien, which her conscious rank and long habits of authority had rendered in some degree too masculine to be seen to the best advantage in ordinary female weeds. Leicester's hunting suit of Lincoln-green, richly embroidered with gold, and crossed by the gay baldric, which sustained a bugle-horn, and a wood-knife instead of a sword, became its master, as did his other vestments of court, or of war. For such were the perfections of his form and mien, that Leicester was always supposed to be seen to the greatest advantage in the character and dress which for the time he represented or wore.

The conversation of Elizabeth and the favourite Earl has not reached us in detail. But those who watched at some distance (and the eyes of courtiers and court ladies are right sharp) were of opinion, that on no occasion did the dignity of Elizabeth, in gesture and motion, seem so decidedly to soften away into a mien expressive of indecision and tenderness. Her step was not only slow, but even unequal, a thing most unwonted in her carriage; her looks seemed bent on the ground, and there was a timid disposition to withdraw from her companion, which external gesture in females often indicates exactly the opposite tendency in the secret mind. The Duchess of Rutland, who ventured nearest, was even heard to aver, that she discerned a tear in Elizabeth's eye, and a blush on her cheek; and still further, "She bent her looks on the ground to avoid mine," said the Duchess; "she who, in her ordinary mood, could look down a lion." To what conclusion these symptoms led is sufficiently evident; nor were they probably entirely groundless. The progress of a private conversation, betwixt two persons of different sexes, is often decisive of their fate, and gives it a turn very different perhaps from what they themselves anticipated. Gallantry becomes mingled with conversation, and affection and passion come gradually to mix with gallantry. Nobles, as well as shepherd swains, will, in such a trying moment, say more than they intended; and Queens, like village maidens, will listen longer than they should.

Horses in the meanwhile neighed, and champed the bits with impatience in the base-court; hounds yelled in their couples, and yeomen, rangers, and prickers, lamented the exhaling of the dew, which would prevent the scent from lying. But Leicester had another chase in view, or, to speak more justly towards him, had become engaged in it without premeditation, as the high-spirited hunter which follows the cry of the hounds that have crossed his path by accident. The Queen—an accomplished and handsome woman—the pride of England, the hope of France and Holland, and the dread of Spain, had probably listened with more than usual favour to the mixture of romantic gallantry with which she always loved to be addressed; and the Earl had, in vanity, in ambition, or in both, thrown in more and more of that delicious ingredient, until his importunity became the language of love itself.

"No, Dudley," said Elizabeth, yet it was with broken accents—"No, I must be the mother of my people. Other ties, that make the lowly maiden happy, are denied to her Sovereign—No, Leicester, urge it no more—Were I as others, free to seek my own happiness—then, indeed—

but it cannot—cannot be.—Delay the chase—delay it for half an hour —and leave me, my lord."

"How, leave you, madam!" said Leicester,—"Has my madness offended you?"

"No, Leicester, not so!" answered the Queen, hastily; "but it is madness, and must not be repeated. Go—but go not far from hence—and meantime let no one intrude on my privacy."

While she spoke thus, Dudley bowed deeply, and retired with a slow and melancholy air. The Queen stood gazing after him, and murmured to herself—"Were it possible—were it *but* possible!—but no—no—Elizabeth must be the wife and mother of England alone."

As she spoke thus, and in order to avoid some one whose step she heard approaching, the Queen turned into the grotto in which her hapless, and yet but too successful, rival lay concealed.

The mind of England's Elizabeth, if somewhat shaken by the agitating interview to which she had just put a period, was of that firm and decided character which soon recovers its natural tone. It was like one of those ancient druidical monuments, called Rocking-stones. The finger of Cupid, boy as he is painted, could put her feelings in motion, but the power of Hercules could not have destroyed their equilibrium. As she advanced with a slow pace towards the inmost extremity of the grotto, her countenance, ere she had proceeded half the length, had recovered its dignity of look, and her mien its air of command.

It was then the Queen became aware, that a female figure was placed beside, or rather partly behind, an alabaster column, at the foot of which arose the pellucid fountain, which occupied the inmost recess of the twilight grotto. The classical mind of Elizabeth suggested the story of Numa and Egeria, and she doubted not that some Italian sculptor had here represented the Naiad, whose inspirations gave laws to Rome. As she advanced, she became doubtful whether she beheld a statue, or a form of flesh and blood. The unfortunate Amy, indeed, remained motionless, betwixt the desire which she had to make her condition known to one of her own sex, and her awe for the stately form which approached her, and which, though her eyes had never before beheld, her fears instantly suspected to be the personage she really was. Amy had arisen from her seat with the purpose of addressing the lady, who entered the grotto alone, and, as she at first thought, so opportunely. But when she recollected the alarm which Leicester had expressed at the Queen's knowing aught of their union, and became more and more satisfied that the person whom she now beheld was Elizabeth herself, she stood with one foot advanced and one withdrawn, her arms, head, and hands, perfectly motionless, and her cheek as pallid as the alabaster pedestal against which she leaned. Her dress was of pale sea-green silk, little distinguished in that imperfect light, and somewhat resembled the drapery of a Grecian Nymph, such an antique disguise having been thought the more secure, where so many masquers and revellers were assembled; so that the Queen's doubt of her being a living form was well justified by all contingent circumstances, as well as by the bloodless cheek and the fixed eye.

Elizabeth remained in doubt, even after she had approached within a few paces, whether she did not gaze on a statue so cunningly fashioned, that by the doubtful light it could not be distinguished from reality. She stopped, therefore, and fixed upon this interesting object her princely look with so much keenness, that the astonishment which had kept Amy immovable gave way to awe, and she gradually cast down her eyes, and drooped her head under the commanding gaze of the Sovereign. Still, however, she remained in all respects, saving this slow and profound inclination of the head, motionless and silent.

From her dress, and the casket which she instinctively held in her hand, Elizabeth naturally conjectured that the beautiful but mute figure which she beheld was a performer in one of the various theatrical pageants which had been placed in different situations to surprise her with their homage, and that the poor player, overcome with awe at her presence, had either forgot the part assigned her, or lacked courage to go through it. It was natural and courteous to give her some encouragement; and Elizabeth accordingly said, in a tone of condescending kindness,—"How now, fair Nymph of this lovely grotto—art thou spellbound and struck with dumbness by the charms of the wicked enchanter whom men term Fear?—We are his sworn enemy, maiden, and can reverse his charm. Speak, we command thee."

Instead of answering her by speech, the unfortunate Countess dropped on her knee before the Queen, let her casket fall from her hand, and clasping her palms together, looked up in the Queen's face with such a mixed agony of fear and supplication, that Elizabeth was considerably affected.

"What may this mean?" she said; "this is a stronger passion than befits the occasion. Stand up, damsel—what wouldst thou have with us?"

"Your protection, madam," faltered forth the unhappy petitioner.

"Each daughter of England has it while she is worthy of it," replied the Queen; "but your distress seems to have a deeper root than a forgotten task. Why, and in what, do you crave our protection?"

Amy hastily endeavoured to recall what she were best to say, which might secure herself from the imminent dangers that surrounded her, without endangering her husband; and plunging from one thought to another, amidst the chaos which filled her mind, she could at length, in answer to the Queen's repeated enquiries, in what she sought protection, only falter out, "Alas! I know not."

"This is folly, maiden," said Elizabeth, impatiently; for there was something in the extreme confusion of the suppliant, which irritated her curiosity, as well as interested her feelings. "The sick man must tell his malady to the physician, nor are WE accustomed to ask questions so oft, without receiving an answer."

"I request—I implore," stammered forth the unfortunate Countess,— "I beseech your gracious protection—against—against one Varney." She

choked wellnigh as she uttered the fatal word, which was instantly caught
up by the Queen.

"What, Varney—Sir Richard Varney—the servant of Lord Leicester?
—What, damsel, are you to him, or he to you?"

"I—I—was his prisoner—and he practised on my life—and I broke
forth to—to——"

"To throw thyself on my protection, doubtless," said Elizabeth. "Thou
shalt have it—that is, if thou art worthy; for we will sift this matter to
the uttermost.—Thou art," she said, bending on the Countess an eye
which seemed designed to pierce her very inmost soul,—"thou art Amy,
daughter of Sir Hugh Robsart of Lidcote Hall?"

"Forgive me—forgive me—most gracious Princess!" said Amy, dropping once more on her knee, from which she had arisen.

"For what should I forgive thee, silly wench?" said Elizabeth; "for
being the daughter of thine own father? Thou art brain-sick, surely. Well,
I see I must wring the story from thee by inches—Thou didst deceive
thine old and honoured father—thy look confesses it—cheated Master
Tressilian—thy blush avouches it—and married this same Varney?"

Amy sprung on her feet, and interrupted the Queen eagerly, with, "No,
madam, no—as there is a God above us, I am not the sordid wretch you
would make me! I am not the wife of that contemptible slave—of that
most deliberate villain! I am not the wife of Varney! I would rather be
the bride of Destruction!"

The Queen, overwhelmed in her turn by Amy's vehemence, stood silent
for an instant, and then replied, "Why, God ha' mercy, woman!—I see
thou canst talk fast enough when the theme likes thee. Nay, tell me,
woman," she continued, for to the impulse of curiosity was now added that
of an undefined jealousy that some deception had been practised on her,
—"tell me, woman—for by God's day, I will know—whose wife, or
whose paramour, art thou? Speak out, and be speedy—Thou wert better
dally with a lioness than with Elizabeth."

Urged to this extremity, dragged as it were by irresistible force to the
verge of the precipice, which she saw but could not avoid,—permitted not
a moment's respite by the eager words and menacing gestures of the
offended Queen, Amy at length uttered in despair, "The Earl of Leicester
knows it all."

"The Earl of Leicester!" said Elizabeth, in utter astonishment—"The
Earl of Leicester!" she repeated with kindling anger,—"Woman, thou
art set on to this—thou dost belie him—he takes no keep of such things
as thou art. Thou art suborned to slander the noblest lord, and the
truest-hearted gentleman, in England! But were he the right hand of
our trust, or something yet dearer to us, thou shalt have thy hearing, and
that in his presence. Come with me—come with me instantly!"

As Amy shrunk back with terror, which the incensed Queen interpreted
as that of conscious guilt, Elizabeth rapidly advanced, seized on her
arm, and hastened with swift and long steps out of the grotto, and along

the principal alley of the Pleasance, dragging with her the terrified Countess, whom she still held by the arm, and whose utmost exertions could but just keep pace with those of the indignant Queen.

Leicester was at this moment the centre of a splendid group of lords and ladies, assembled together under an arcade, or portico, which closed the alley. The company had drawn together in that place, to attend the commands of her Majesty when the hunting-party should go forward, and their astonishment may be imagined, when, instead of seeing Elizabeth advance towards them with her usual measured dignity of motion, they beheld her walking so rapidly, that she was in the midst of them ere they were aware; and then observed, with fear and surprise, that her features were flushed betwixt anger and agitation, that her hair was loosened by her haste of motion, and that her eyes sparkled as they were wont when the spirit of Henry VIII. mounted highest in his daughter. Nor were they less astonished at the appearance of the pale, extenuated, half dead, yet still lovely female, whom the Queen upheld by main strength with one hand, while with the other she waved aside the ladies and nobles who pressed towards her, under the idea that she was taken suddenly ill. "Where is my Lord of Leicester?" she said, in a tone that thrilled with astonishment all the courtiers who stood around—"Stand forth, my Lord of Leicester!"

If, in the midst of the most serene day of summer, when all is light and laughing around, a thunderbolt were to fall from the clear blue vault of heaven, and rend the earth at the very feet of some careless traveller, he could not gaze upon the smouldering chasm, which so unexpectedly yawned before him, with half the astonishment and fear which Leicester felt at the sight that so suddenly presented itself. He had that instant been receiving, with a political affectation of disavowing and misunderstanding their meaning, the half uttered, half intimated congratulations of the courtiers upon the favour of the Queen, carried apparently to its highest pitch during the interview of that morning; from which most of them seemed to augur, that he might soon arise from their equal in rank to become their master. And now, while the subdued yet proud smile with which he disclaimed those inferences was yet curling his cheek, the Queen shot into the circle, her passions excited to the uttermost; and, supporting with one hand, and apparently without an effort, the pale and sinking form of his almost expiring wife, and pointing with the finger of the other to her half dead features, demanded in a voice that sounded to the ears of the astounded statesman like the last dread trumpet-call, that is to summon body and spirit to the judgment-seat, "Knowest thou this woman?"

As, at the blast of that last trumpet, the guilty shall call upon the mountains to cover them, Leicester's inward thoughts invoked the stately arch which he had built in his pride, to burst its strong conjunction, and overwhelm them in its ruins. But the cemented stones, architrave and battlement, stood fast; and it was the proud master himself, who, as if some actual pressure had bent him to the earth, kneeled down before Elizabeth, and prostrated his brow to the marble flag-stones, on which he stood.

"Leicester," said Elizabeth, in a voice which trembled with passion, "could I think thou hast practised on me—on me thy Sovereign—on me thy confiding, thy too partial mistress, the base and ungrateful deception which thy present confusion surmises—by all that is holy, false lord, that head of thine were in as great peril as ever was thy father's!"

Leicester had not conscious innocence, but he had pride to support him. He raised slowly his brow and features, which were black and swoln with contending emotions, and only replied, "My head cannot fall but by the sentence of my peers—to them I will plead, and not to a princess who thus requites my faithful service!"

"What! my lords," said Elizabeth, looking around, "we are defied, I think—defied in the Castle we have ourselves bestowed on this proud man!—My Lord Shrewsbury, you are marshal of England, attach him of high treason!"

"Whom does your Grace mean?" said Shrewsbury, much surprised, for he had that instant joined the astonished circle.

"Whom should I mean, but that traitor Dudley, Earl of Leicester!—Cousin of Hunsdon, order out your band of gentlemen pensioners, and take him into instant custody.—I say, villain, make haste!"

Hunsdon, a rough old noble, who, from his relationship to the Boleyns, was accustomed to use more freedom with the Queen than almost any other dared to do, replied bluntly, "And it is like your Grace might order me to the Tower to-morrow, for making too much haste. I do beseech you to be patient."

"Patient—God's life!" exclaimed the Queen,—"name not the word to me—thou know'st not of what he is guilty!"

Amy, who had by this time in some degree recovered herself, and who saw her husband, as she conceived, in the utmost danger from the rage of an offended Sovereign, instantly (and alas! how many women have done the same) forgot her own wrongs, and her own danger, in her apprehensions for him, and throwing herself before the Queen, embraced her knees, while she exclaimed, "He is guiltless, madam—he is guiltless—no one can lay aught to the charge of the noble Leicester!"

"Why, minion," answered the Queen, "didst not thou, thyself, say that the Earl of Leicester was privy to thy whole history?"

"Did I say so?" repeated the unhappy Amy, laying aside every consideration of consistency, and of self-interest; "O, if I did, I foully belied him. May God so judge me, as I believe he was never privy to a thought that would harm me!"

"Woman!" said Elizabeth, "I will know who has moved thee to this; or my wrath—and the wrath of kings is a flaming fire—shall wither and consume thee like a weed in the furnace."

As the Queen uttered this threat, Leicester's better angel called his pride to his aid, and reproached him with the utter extremity of meanness which would overwhelm him for ever, if he stooped to take shelter under the generous interposition of his wife, and abandoned her, in return for her kindness, to the resentment of the Queen. He had already raised his head, with the dignity of a man of honour, to avow his marriage, and proclaim himself the protector of his Countess, when Varney, born, as it appeared, to be his master's evil genius, rushed into the presence, with every mark of disorder on his face and apparel.

"What means this saucy intrusion?" said Elizabeth.

Varney, with the air of a man altogether overwhelmed with grief and confusion, prostrated himself before her feet, exclaiming, "Pardon, my Liege, pardon!—or at least let your justice avenge itself on me, where it is due; but spare my noble, my generous, my innocent patron and master!"

Amy, who was yet kneeling, started up as she saw the man whom she deemed most odious place himself so near her, and was about to fly towards Leicester, when, checked at once by the uncertainty and even timidity which his looks had reassumed as soon as the appearance of his confidant seemed to open a new scene, she hung back, and, uttering a faint scream, besought of her Majesty to cause her to be imprisoned in the lowest dungeon of the Castle—to deal with her as the worst of criminals—"but spare," she exclaimed, "my sight and hearing, what will destroy the little judgment I have left—the sight of that unutterable and most shameless villain!"

"And why, sweetheart?" said the Queen, moved by a new impulse; "what hath he, this false knight, since such thou accountest him, done to thee?"

"Oh, worse than sorrow, madam, and worse than injury—he hath sown dissension where most there should be peace. I shall go mad if I look longer on him!"

"Beshrew me, but I think thou art distraught already," answered the Queen.—"My Lord Hunsdon, look to this poor distressed young woman, and let her be safely bestowed, and in honest keeping, till we require her to be forthcoming."

Two or three of the ladies in attendance, either moved by compassion for a creature so interesting, or by some other motive, offered their service to look after her; but the Queen briefly answered, "Ladies, under favour, no.—You have all (give God thanks) sharp ears and nimble tongues— our kinsman Hunsdon has ears of the dullest, and a tongue somewhat rough, but yet of the slowest.—Hunsdon, look to it that none have speech of her."

"By Our Lady!" said Hunsdon, taking in his strong sinewy arms the fading and almost swooning form of Amy, "she is a lovely child; and though a rough nurse, your Grace hath given her a kind one. She is safe with me as one of my own ladybirds of daughters."

So saying, he carried her off, unresistingly and almost unconsciously;

his war-worn locks and long grey beard mingling with her light-brown tresses, as her head reclined on his strong square shoulder. The Queen followed him with her eye—she had already, with that self-command which forms so necessary a part of a Sovereign's accomplishments, suppressed every appearance of agitation, and seemed as if she desired to banish all traces of her burst of passion from the recollection of those who had witnessed it. "My Lord of Hunsdon says well," she observed, "he is indeed but a rough nurse for so tender a babe."

"My Lord of Hunsdon," said the Dean of St. Asaph, "I speak it not in defamation of his more noble qualities, hath a broad license in speech, and garnishes his discourse somewhat too freely with the cruel and superstitious oaths, which savour both of profaneness and of old papistrie."

"It is the fault of his blood, Mr. Dean," said the Queen, turning sharply round upon the reverend dignitary as she spoke; "and you may blame mine for the same distemperature. The Boleyns were ever a hot and plain-spoken race, more hasty to speak their mind than careful to choose their expressions. And, by my word—I hope there is no sin in that affirmation—I question if it were much cooled by mixing with that of Tudor."

As she made this last observation, she smiled graciously, and stole her eyes almost insensibly round to seek those of the Earl of Leicester, to whom she now began to think she had spoken with hasty harshness upon the unfounded suspicion of a moment.

The Queen's eye found the Earl in no mood to accept the implied offer of conciliation. His own looks had followed, with late and rueful repentance, the faded form which Hunsdon had just borne from the presence; they now reposed gloomily on the ground, but more—so at least it seemed to Elizabeth—with the expression of one who has received an unjust affront, than of him who is conscious of guilt. She turned her face angrily from him, and said to Varney, "Speak, Sir Richard, and explain these riddles—thou hast sense and the use of speech, at least, which elsewhere we look for in vain."

As she said this, she darted another resentful glance towards Leicester, while the wily Varney hastened to tell his own story.

"Your Majesty's piercing eye," he said, "has already detected the cruel malady of my beloved lady; which, unhappy that I am, I would not suffer to be expressed in the certificate of her physician, seeking to conceal what has now broken out with so much the more scandal."

"She is then distraught?" said the Queen—"indeed we doubted not of it—her whole demeanour bears it out. I found her moping in a corner of yonder grotto; and every word she spoke—which indeed I dragged from her as by the rack—she instantly recalled and forswore. But how came she hither? Why had you her not in safe-keeping?"

"My gracious Liege," said Varney, "the worthy gentleman under whose charge I left her, Master Anthony Foster, has come hither but now, as fast as man and horse can travel, to show me of her escape, which was managed with the art peculiar to many who are afflicted with this malady. He is at hand for examination."

"Let it be for another time," said the Queen. "But, Sir Richard, we envy you not your domestic felicity; your lady railed on you bitterly, and seemed ready to swoon at beholding you."

"It is the nature of persons in her disorder, so please your Grace," answered Varney, "to be ever most inveterate in their spleen against those, whom, in their better moments, they hold nearest and dearest."

"We have heard so, indeed," said Elizabeth, "and give faith to the saying."

"May your Grace then be pleased," said Varney, "to command my unfortunate wife to be delivered into the custody of her friends?"

Leicester partly started; but, making a strong effort, he subdued his emotion, while Elizabeth answered sharply, "You are something too hasty, Master Varney; we will have first a report of the lady's health and state of mind from Masters, our own physician, and then determine what shall be thought just. You shall have license, however, to see her, that if there be any matrimonial quarrel betwixt you—such things we have heard do occur, even betwixt a loving couple—you may make it up, without further scandal to our court, or trouble to ourselves."

Varney bowed low, and made no other answer.

Elizabeth again looked towards Leicester, and said, with a degree of condescension which could only arise out of the most heartfelt interest, "Discord, as the Italian poet says, will find her way into peaceful convents, as well as into the privacy of families; and we fear our own guards and ushers will hardly exclude her from courts. My Lord of Leicester, you are offended with us, and we have right to be offended with you. We will take the lion's part upon us, and be the first to forgive."

Leicester smoothed his brow, as by an effort, but the trouble was too deep-seated that its placidity should at once return. He said, however, that which fitted the occasion, "that he could not have the happiness of forgiving, because she who commanded him to do so, could commit nᵣ injury towards him."

Elizabeth seemed content with this reply, and intimated her pleasuɪ that the sports of the morning should proceed. The bugles sounded—thᴜ hounds bayed—the horses pranced—but the courtiers and ladies sought the amusements to which they were summoned with hearts very different from those which had leaped to the morning's *reveille*. There was doubt, and fear, and expectation on every brow, and surmise and intrigue in every whisper.

Blount took an opportunity to whisper into Raleigh's ear, "This storm came like a levanter in the Mediterranean."

"*Varium et mutabile*"—answered Raleigh, in a similar tone.

"Nay, I know nought of your Latin," said Blount; "but I thank God Tressilian took not the sea during that hurricane. He could scarce have missed shipwreck, knowing as he does so little how to trim his sails to a court gale."

"Thou wouldst have instructed him?" said Raleigh.

"Why, I have profited by my time as well as thou, Sir Walter," replied honest Blount. "I am knight as well as thou, and of the earlier creation."

"Now, God further thy wit," said Raleigh; "but for Tressilian, I would I knew what were the matter with him. He told me this morning he would not leave his chamber for the space of twelve hours or thereby, being bound by a promise. This lady's madness, when he shall learn it, will not, I fear, cure his infirmity. The moon is at the fullest, and men's brains are working like yeast. But hark! they sound to mount. Let us to horse, Blount; we young knights must deserve our spurs."

CHAPTER XXXV

————Sincerity,
Thou first of virtues! let no mortal leave
Thy onward path, although the earth should gape,
And from the gulf of hell Destruction cry,
To take dissimulation's winding way.

Douglas.

It was not till after a long and successful morning's sport, and a prolonged repast which followed the return of the Queen to the Castle, that Leicester at length found himself alone with Varney, from whom he now learned the whole particulars of the Countess's escape, as they had been brought to Kenilworth by Foster, who, in his terror for the consequences, had himself posted thither with the tidings. As Varney, in his narrative, took especial care to be silent concerning those practices on the Countess's health which had driven her to so desperate a resolution, Leicester, who could only suppose that she had adopted it out of jealous impatience, to attain the avowed state and appearance belonging to her rank, was not a little offended at the levity with which his wife had broken his strict commands, and exposed him to the resentment of Elizabeth.

"I have given," he said, "to this daughter of an obscure Devonshire gentleman, the proudest name in England. I have made her sharer of my bed and of my fortunes. I ask but of her a little patience, ere she launches forth upon the full current of her grandeur, and the infatuated woman will rather hazard her own shipwreck and mine, will rather involve me in a thousand whirlpools, shoals, and quicksands, and compel me to a thousand devices which shame me in mine own eyes, than tarry for a little space longer in the obscurity to which she was born.—So lovely, so delicate, so fond, so faithful—yet to lack in so grave a matter the prudence which one might hope from the veriest fool—it puts me beyond my patience."

"We may post it over yet well enough," said Varney, "if my lady will be but ruled, and take on her the character which the time commands."

"It is but too true, Sir Richard," said Leicester, "there is indeed no other remedy. I have heard her termed thy wife in my presence, without contradiction. She must bear the title until she is far from Kenilworth."

"And long afterwards, I trust," said Varney; then instantly added, "For I cannot but hope it will be long after ere she bear the title of Lady Leicester—I fear me it may scarce be with safety during the life of this Queen. But your lordship is best judge, you alone knowing what passages have taken place betwixt Elizabeth and you."

"You are right, Varney," said Leicester; "I have this morning been both fool and villain; and when Elizabeth hears of my unhappy marriage, she cannot but think herself treated with that premeditated slight which women never forgive. We have once this day stood upon terms little short of defiance; and to those, I fear, we must again return."

"Is her resentment, then, so implacable?" said Varney.

"Far from it," replied the Earl; "for, being what she is in spirit and in station, she has even this day been but too condescending, in giving me opportunities to repair what she thinks my faulty heat of temper."

"Ay," answered Varney; "the Italians say right—in lovers' quarrels, the party that loves most is always most willing to acknowledge the greater fault.—So then, my lord, if this union with the lady could be concealed, you stand with Elizabeth as you did?"

Leicester sighed, and was silent for a moment, ere he replied.

"Varney, I think thou art true to me, and I will tell thee all. I do *not* stand where I did. I have spoken to Elizabeth—under what mad impulse I know not—on a theme which cannot be abandoned without touching every female feeling to the quick, and which yet I dare not and cannot prosecute. She can never, never forgive me, for having caused and witnessed those yieldings to human passion."

"We must do something, my lord," said Varney, "and that speedily."

"There is nought to be done," answered Leicester, despondingly; "I am like one that has long toiled up a dangerous precipice, and when he is within one perilous stride of the top, finds his progress arrested when retreat has become impossible. I see above me the pinnacle which I cannot reach—beneath me the abyss into which I must fall, as soon as my relaxing grasp and dizzy brain join to hurl me from my present precarious stance."

"Think better of your situation, my lord," said Varney—"let us try the experiment in which you have but now acquiesced. Keep we your marriage from Elizabeth's knowledge, and all may yet be well. I will instantly go to the lady myself—She hates me, because I have been earnest with your lordship, as she truly suspects, in opposition to what she terms her rights. I care not for her prejudices—She *shall* listen to me; and I will show her such reasons for yielding to the pressure of the times, that I doubt not to bring back her consent to whatever measures these exigencies may require."

"No, Varney," said Leicester; "I have thought upon what is to be done, and I will myself speak with Amy."

It was now Varney's turn to feel, upon his own account, the terrors which he affected to participate solely on account of his patron. "Your lordship will not yourself speak with the lady?"

"It is my fixed purpose," said Leicester; "fetch me one of the livery-cloaks; I will pass the sentinel as thy servant. Thou art to have free access to her."

"But, my lord——"

"I will have no *buts*," replied Leicester; "it shall be even thus, and not otherwise. Hunsdon sleeps, I think, in Saintlowe's Tower. We can go thither from these apartments by the private passage, without risk of meeting any one. Or what if I do meet Hunsdon? he is more my friend than enemy, and thick-witted enough to adopt any belief that is thrust on him. Fetch me the cloak instantly."

Varney had no alternative save obedience. In a few minutes Leicester was muffled in the mantle, pulled his bonnet over his brows, and followed Varney along the secret passage of the Castle which communicated with Hunsdon's apartments, in which there was scarce a chance of meeting any inquisitive person, and hardly light enough for any such to have satisfied their curiosity. They emerged at a door where Lord Hunsdon had, with military precaution, placed a sentinel, one of his own northern retainers as it fortuned, who readily admitted Sir Richard Varney and his attendant, saying only, in his northern dialect, "I would, man, thou couldst make the mad lady be still yonder; for her moans do sae dirl through my head, that I would rather keep watch on a snow-drift, in the waste of Catlowdie."

They hastily entered, and shut the door behind them.

"Now, good devil, if there be one," said Varney, within himself, "for once help a votary at a dead pinch, for my boat is amongst the breakers!"

The Countess Amy, with her hair and her garments dishevelled, was seated upon a sort of couch, in an attitude of the deepest affliction, out of which she was startled by the opening of the door. She turned hastily round, and, fixing her eye on Varney, exclaimed, "Wretch! art thou come to frame some new plan of villainy?"

Leicester cut short her reproaches by stepping forward, and dropping his cloak, while he said, in a voice rather of authority than of affection, "It is with me, madam, you have to commune, not with Sir Richard Varney."

The change effected on the Countess's look and manner was like magic. "Dudley!" she exclaimed, "Dudley! and art thou come at last?" And with the speed of lightning she flew to her husband, clung around his neck, and, unheeding the presence of Varney, overwhelmed him with caresses, while she bathed his face in a flood of tears; muttering, at the same time, but in broken and disjointed monosyllables, the fondest expressions which Love teaches his votaries.

Leicester, as it seemed to him, had reason to be angry with his lady for transgressing his commands, and thus placing him in the perilous situation in which he had that morning stood. But what displeasure could keep its ground before these testimonies of affection from a being so lovely, that even the negligence of dress, and the withering effects of fear, grief, and fatigue, which would have impaired the beauty of others, rendered hers but the more interesting! He received and repaid her caresses with fondness, mingled with melancholy, the last of which she seemed scarcely to observe, until the first transport of her own joy was over; when, looking anxiously in his face, she asked if he was ill.

"Not in my body, Amy," was his answer.

"Then I will be well too,—O Dudley! I have been ill!—very ill, since we last met!—for I call not this morning's horrible vision a meeting. I have been in sickness, in grief, and in danger—But thou art come, and all is joy, and health, and safety!"

"Alas! Amy," said Leicester, "thou hast undone me!"

"I, my lord?" said Amy, her cheek at once losing its transient flush of joy—"how could I injure that which I love better than myself?"

"I would not upbraid you, Amy," replied the Earl; "but are you not here contrary to my express commands—and does not your presence here endanger both yourself and me?"

"Does it, does it indeed!" she exclaimed, eagerly; "then why am I here a moment longer? O, if you knew by what fears I was urged to quit Cumnor-Place!—but I will say nothing of myself—only that if it might be otherwise, I would not willingly return *thither;*—yet if it concern your safety——"

"We will think, Amy, of some other retreat," said Leicester; "and you shall go to one of my Northern Castles, under the personage—it will be but needful, I trust, for a very few days—of Varney's wife."

"How, my Lord of Leicester!" said the lady, disengaging herself from his embraces; "is it to your wife you give the dishonourable counsel to acknowledge herself the bride of another—and of all men, the bride of that Varney?"

"Madam, I speak it in earnest—Varney is my true and faithful servant, trusted in my deepest secrets. I had better lose my right hand than his service at this moment. You have no cause to scorn him as you do."

"I could assign one, my lord," replied the Countess; "and I see he shakes even under that assured look of his. But he that is necessary as your right hand to your safety, is free from any accusation of mine. May he be true to you; and that he may be true, trust him not too much or too far. But it is enough to say, that I will not go with him unless by violence, nor would I acknowledge him as my husband, were all——"

"It is a temporary deception, madam," said Leicester, irritated by her opposition, "necessary for both our safeties, endangered by you through female caprice, or the premature desire to seize on a rank to which I gave you title, only under condition that our marriage, for a time, should continue secret. If my proposal disgust you, it is yourself has brought it on both of us. There is no other remedy—you must do what your own impatient folly hath rendered necessary—I command you."

"I cannot put your commands, my lord," said Amy, "in balance with those of honour and conscience. I will NOT, in this instance, obey you. You may achieve your own dishonour, to which these crooked policies naturally tend, but I will do nought that can blemish mine. How could you again, my lord, acknowledge me as a pure and chaste matron, worthy to share your fortunes, when, holding that high character, I had strolled the country the acknowledged wife of such a profligate fellow as your servant Varney?"

"My lord," said Varney interposing, "my lady is too much prejudiced against me, unhappily, to listen to what I can offer; yet it may please her better than what she proposes. She has good interest with Master Edmund Tressilian, and could doubtless prevail on him to consent to be her companion to Lidcote Hall, and there she might remain in safety until time permitted the development of this mystery."

Leicester was silent, but stood looking eagerly on Amy, with eyes which seemed suddenly to glow as much with suspicion as displeasure.

The Countess only said, "Would to God I were in my father's house!—When I left it, I little thought I was leaving peace of mind and honour behind me."

Varney proceeded with a tone of deliberation. "Doubtless this will make it necessary to take strangers into my lord's counsels; but surely the Countess will be warrant for the honour of Master Tressilian, and such of her father's family——"

"Peace, Varney," said Leicester; "by Heaven I will strike my dagger into thee, if again thou namest Tressilian as a partner of my counsels!"

"And wherefore not?" said the Countess; "unless they be counsels fitter for such as Varney, than for a man of stainless honour and integrity.—My lord, my lord, bend no angry brows on me—it is the truth, and it is I who speak it. I once did Tressilian wrong for your sake—I will not do him the further injustice of being silent when his honour is brought in question. I can forbear," she said, looking at Varney, "to pull the mask off hypocrisy, but I will not permit virtue to be slandered in my hearing."

There was a dead pause. Leicester stood displeased, yet undetermined, and too conscious of the weakness of his cause; while Varney, with a deep and hypocritical affectation of sorrow, mingled with humility, bent his eyes on the ground.

It was then that the Countess Amy displayed, in the midst of distress and difficulty, the natural energy of character, which would have rendered her, had fate allowed, a distinguished ornament of the rank which she held. She walked up to Leicester with a composed step, a dignified air, and looks in which strong affection essayed in vain to shake the firmness of conscious truth and rectitude of principle. "You have spoke your mind, my lord," she said, "in these difficulties, with which, unhappily, I have found myself unable to comply. This gentleman—this person, I would say—has hinted at another scheme, to which I object not but as it displeases you. Will your lordship be pleased to hear what a young and timid woman, but your most affectionate wife, can suggest in the present extremity?"

Leicester was silent, but bent his head towards the Countess, as an intimation that she was at liberty to proceed.

"There hath been but one cause for all these evils, my lord," she proceeded, "and it resolves itself into the mysterious duplicity with which you have been induced to surround yourself. Extricate yourself at once, my lord, from the tyranny of these disgraceful trammels. Be like a true English gentleman, knight, and earl, who holds that truth is the foundation of honour, and that honour is dear to him as the breath of his nostrils. Take your ill-fated wife by the hand, lead her to the footstool of Elizabeth's throne—Say, that in a moment of infatuation, moved by supposed beauty, of which none perhaps can now trace even the remains, I gave my hand to this Amy Robsart.—You will then have done justice to me, my lord, and to your own honour; and should law or power require you to part from me, I will oppose no objection—since I may then with honour hide a grieved and broken heart in those shades from which your love withdrew me. Then—have but a little patience, and Amy's life will not long darken your brighter prospects."

There was so much of dignity, so much of tenderness, in the Countess's remonstrance, that it moved all that was noble and generous in the soul of her husband. The scales seemed to fall from his eyes, and the duplicity and tergiversation of which he had been guilty stung him at once with remorse and shame.

"I am not worthy of you, Amy," he said, "that could weigh aught which ambition has to give against such a heart as thine. I have a bitter penance to perform, in disentangling, before sneering foes and astounded friends, all the meshes of my own deceitful policy.—And the Queen—but let her take my head, as she has threatened."

"Your head, my lord!" said the Countess; "because you used the freedom and liberty of an English subject in choosing a wife? For shame; it is this distrust of the Queen's justice, this apprehension of danger, which cannot but be imaginary, that, like scarecrows, have induced you to forsake the straightforward path, which, as it is the best, is also the safest."

"Ah, Amy, thou little knowest!" said Dudley; but, instantly checking himself, he added, "Yet she shall not find in me a safe or easy victim of arbitrary vengeance.—I have friends—I have allies—I will not, like Norfolk, be dragged to the block, as a victim to sacrifice. Fear not, Amy; thou shalt see Dudley bear himself worthy of his name. I must instantly communicate with some of those friends on whom I can best rely; for, as things stand, I may be made prisoner in my own Castle."

"O, my good lord," said Amy, "make no faction in a peaceful state! There is no friend can help us so well as our own candid truth and honour. Bring but these to our assistance, and you are safe amidst a whole army of the envious and malignant. Leave these behind you, and all other defence will be fruitless. Truth, my noble lord, is well painted unarmed."

"But Wisdom, Amy," answered Leicester, "is arrayed in panoply of proof. Argue not with me on the means I shall use to render my confession—since it must be called so—as safe as may be; it will be fraught with enough of danger, do what we will.—Varney, we must hence.— Farewell, Amy, whom I am to vindicate as mine own, at an expense and risk of which thou alone couldst be worthy! You shall soon hear farther from me."

He embraced her fervently, muffled himself as before, and accompanied Varney from the apartment. The latter, as he left the room, bowed low, and, as he raised his body, regarded Amy with a peculiar expression, as if he desired to know how far his own pardon was included in the reconciliation which had taken place betwixt her and her lord. The Countess looked upon him with a fixed eye, but seemed no more conscious of his presence, than if there had been nothing but vacant air on the spot where he stood.

"She has brought me to the crisis," he muttered—"She or I are lost. There was something—I wot not if it was fear or pity—that prompted me to avoid this fatal crisis. It is now decided—She or I must *perish*."

While he thus spoke, he observed, with surprise, that a boy, repulsed by the sentinel, made up to Leicester, and spoke with him. Varney was one of those politicians, whom not the slightest appearances escape without enquiry. He asked the sentinel what the lad wanted with him, and received for answer, that the boy had wished him to transmit a parcel to the mad lady, but that he cared not to take charge of it, such communication being beyond his commission. His curiosity satisfied in that particular, he approached his patron, and heard him say—"Well, boy, the packet shall be delivered."

"Thanks, good Master Serving-man," said the boy, and was out of sight in an instant.

Leicester and Varney returned with hasty steps to the Earl's private apartment, by the same passage which had conducted them to Saint-lowe's Tower.

CHAPTER XXXVI

———I have said
This is an adulteress—I have said with whom:
More, she's a traitor, and Camillo is
A federary with her, and one that knows
What she should shame to know herself.
Winter's Tale.

THEY were no sooner in the Earl's cabinet, than, taking his tablets from his pocket, he began to write, speaking partly to Varney, and partly to himself:—"There are many of them close bounden to me, and especially those in good estate and high office; many who, if they look back towards my benefits, or forward towards the perils which may befall themselves, will not, I think, be disposed to see me stagger unsupported. Let me see—Knollis is sure, and through his means Guernsey and Jersey—Horsey commands in the Isle of Wight—My brother-in-law, Huntingdon, and Pembroke, have authority in Wales—Through Bedford I lead the Puritans, with their interest, so powerful in all the boroughs—My brother of Warwick is equal, wellnigh, to myself, in wealth, followers, and dependencies—Sir Owen Hopton is at my devotion; he commands the Tower of London, and the national treasure deposited there—My father and grandfather needed never to have stooped their heads to the block, had they thus forecast their enterprises.—Why look you so sad, Varney? I tell thee, a tree so deep-rooted is not easily to be torn up by the tempest."

"Alas! my lord," said Varney, with well-acted passion, and then resumed the same look of despondency which Leicester had before noted.

"Alas!" repeated Leicester, "and wherefore alas, Sir Richard? Doth your new spirit of chivalry supply no more vigorous ejaculation, when a noble struggle is impending? Or, if *alas* means thou wilt flinch from the conflict, thou mayst leave the Castle, or go join mine enemies, whichever thou thinkest best."

"Not so, my lord," answered his confidant; "Varney will be found fighting or dying by your side. Forgive me, if, in love to you, I see more fully than your noble heart permits you to do, the inextricable difficulties with which you are surrounded. You are strong, my lord, and powerful; yet, let me say it without offence, you are so only by the reflected light of the Queen's favour. While you are Elizabeth's favourite, you are all, save in name, like an actual sovereign. But let her call back the honours she has bestowed, and the Prophet's gourd did not wither more suddenly. Declare against the Queen, and I do not say that in the wide nation, or in this province alone, you would find yourself instantly deserted and outnumbered; but I will say, that even in this very Castle, and in the midst of your vassals, kinsmen, and dependants, you would be a captive, nay, a sentenced captive, should she please to say the word. Think upon Norfolk, my lord,—upon the powerful Northumberland,—the splendid Westmoreland;—think on all who have made head against this sage Princess. They are dead, captive, or fugitive. This is not like other thrones, which can be overturned by a combination of powerful nobles; the broad foundations which support it are in the extended love and affections of the people. You might share it with Elizabeth if you would; but neither yours, nor any other power, foreign or domestic, will avail to overthrow, or even to shake it."

He paused, and Leicester threw his tablets from him with an air of reckless despite. "It may be as thou sayst," he said; "and, in sooth, I care not whether truth or cowardice dictate thy forebodings. But it shall not be said I fell without a struggle.—Give orders that those of my retainers who served under me in Ireland be gradually drawn into the main Keep, and let our gentlemen and friends stand on their guard, and go armed, as if they expected an onset from the followers of Sussex. Possess the townspeople with some apprehension; let them take arms, and be ready, at a signal given, to overpower the Pensioners and Yeomen of the Guard."

"Let me remind you, my lord," said Varney, with the same appearance of deep and melancholy interest, "that you have given me orders to prepare for disarming the Queen's guard. It is an act of high treason, but you shall nevertheless be obeyed."

"I care not," said Leicester, desperately;—"I care not. Shame is behind me, Ruin before me; I must on."

Here there was another pause, which Varney at length broke with the following words: "It is come to the point I have long dreaded. I must either witness, like an ungrateful beast, the downfall of the best and kindest of masters, or I must speak what I would have buried in the deepest oblivion, or told by any other mouth than mine."

"What is that thou sayst, or wouldst say?" replied the Earl; "we have no time to waste on words, when the time calls us to action."

"My speech is soon made, my lord—would to God it were as soon answered! Your marriage is the sole cause of the threatened breach with your Sovereign, my lord, is it not?"

"Thou knowest it is!" replied Leicester. "What needs so fruitless a question?"

"Pardon me, my lord," said Varney; "the use lies here. Men will wager their lands and lives in defence of a rich diamond, my lord; but were it not first prudent to look if there is no flaw in it?"

"What means this?" said Leicester, with eyes sternly fixed on his dependant; "of whom dost thou dare to speak?"

"It is——of the Countess Amy, my lord, of whom I am unhappily bound to speak; and of whom I *will* speak, were your lordship to kill me for my zeal."

"Thou mayst happen to deserve it at my hand," said the Earl; "but speak on, I will hear thee."

"Nay, then, my lord, I will be bold. I speak for my own life as well as for your lordship's. I like not this lady's tampering and trickstering with this same Edmund Tressilian. You know him, my lord. You know he had formerly an interest in her, which it cost your lordship some pains to supersede. You know the eagerness with which he has pressed on the suit against me in behalf of this lady, the open object of which is to drive your lordship to an avowal of what I must ever call your most unhappy marriage, the point to which my lady also is willing, at any risk, to urge you."

Leicester smiled constrainedly. "Thou meanest well, good Sir Richard, and wouldst, I think, sacrifice thine own honour, as well as that of any other person, to save me from what thou think'st a step so terrible. But, remember,"—he spoke these words with the most stern decision,—"you speak of the Countess of Leicester."

"I do, my lord," said Varney; "but it is for the welfare of the Earl of Leicester. My tale is but begun. I do most strongly believe that this Tressilian has, from the beginning of his moving in her cause, been in connivance with her ladyship the Countess."

"Thou speak'st wild madness, Varney, with the sober face of a preacher. Where, or how, could they communicate together?"

"My lord," said Varney, "unfortunately I can show that but too well. It was just before the supplication was presented to the Queen, in Tressilian's name, that I met him, to my utter astonishment, at the postern-gate, which leads from the demesne at Cumnor-Place."

"Thou met'st him, villain! and why didst thou not strike him dead?" exclaimed Leicester.

"I drew on him, my lord, and he on me; and had not my foot slipped, he would not, perhaps, have been again a stumbling-block in your lordship's path."

Leicester seemed struck dumb with surprise. At length he answered, "What other evidence hast thou of this, Varney, save thine own assertion?—for, as I will punish deeply, I will examine coolly and warily. Sacred Heaven! but no—I will examine coldly and warily—coldly and warily." He repeated these words more than once to himself, as if in the very sound there was a sedative quality; and again compressing his lips, as if he feared some violent expression might escape from them, he asked again, "What farther proof?"

"Enough, my lord," said Varney, "and to spare. I would it rested with me alone, for with me it might have been silenced for ever. But my servant, Michael Lambourne, witnessed the whole, and was, indeed, the means of first introducing Tressilian into Cumnor-Place; and therefore I took him into my service, and retained him in it, though something of a debauched fellow, that I might have his tongue always under my own command." He then acquainted Lord Leicester how easy it was to prove the circumstance of their interview true, by evidence of Anthony Foster, with the corroborative testimonies of the various persons at Cumnor, who had heard the wager laid, and had seen Lambourne and

Tressilian set off together. In the whole narrative, Varney hazarded nothing fabulous, excepting that, not indeed by direct assertion, but by inference, he led his patron to suppose that the interview betwixt Amy and Tressilian at Cumnor-Place had been longer than the few minutes to which it was in reality limited.

"And wherefore was I not told of all this," said Leicester, sternly. "Why did all of ye—and in particular thou, Varney—keep back from me such material information?"

"Because, my lord," replied Varney, "the Countess pretended to Foster and to me, that Tressilian had intruded himself upon her; and I concluded their interview had been in all honour, and that she would at her own time tell it to your lordship. Your lordship knows with what unwilling ears we listen to evil surmises against those whom we love; and I thank Heaven, I am no make-bate or informer, to be the first to sow them."

"You are but too ready to receive them, however, Sir Richard," replied his patron. "How know'st thou that this interview was not in all honour, as thou hast said? Methinks the wife of the Earl of Leicester might speak for a short time with such a person as Tressilian, without injury to me, or suspicion to herself."

"Questionless, my lord," answered Varney; "had I thought otherwise, I had been no keeper of the secret. But here lies the rub—Tressilian leaves not the place without establishing a correspondence with a poor man, the landlord of an inn in Cumnor, for the purpose of carrying off the lady. He sent down an emissary of his, whom I trust soon to have in right sure keeping under Mervyn's Tower. Killigrew and Lambsbey are scouring the country in quest of him. The host is rewarded with a ring for keeping counsel—your lordship may have noted it on Tressilian's hand—here it is. This fellow, this agent, makes his way to the Place as a pedlar, holds conferences with the lady, and they make their escape together by night—rob a poor fellow of a horse by the way, such was their guilty haste; and at length reach this Castle, where the Countess of Leicester finds refuge—I dare not say in what place."

"Speak, I command thee," said Leicester; "speak, while I retain sense enough to hear thee."

"Since it must be so," answered Varney, "the lady resorted immediately to the apartment of Tressilian, where she remained many hours, partly in company with him and partly alone. I told you Tressilian had a paramour in his chamber—I little dreamed that paramour was——"

"Amy, thou wouldst say," answered Leicester; "but it is false, false as the smoke of hell! Ambitious she may be—fickle and impatient—'tis a woman's fault; but false to me!—never, never.—The proof—the proof of this!" he exclaimed, hastily.

"Carrol, the Deputy Marshal, ushered her thither by her own desire, on yesterday afternoon—Lambourne and the warder both found her there at an early hour this morning."

"Was Tressilian there with her?" said Leicester, in the same hurried tone.

"No, my lord. You may remember," answered Varney, "that he was that night placed with Sir Nicholas Blount, under a species of arrest."

"Did Carrol, or the other fellows, know who she was?" demanded Leicester.

"No, my lord," replied Varney; "Carrol and the warder had never seen the Countess, and Lambourne knew her not in her disguise; but, in seeking to prevent her leaving the cell, he obtained possession of one of her gloves, which, I think, your lordship may know."

He gave the glove, which had the Bear and Ragged Staff, the Earl's impress, embroidered upon it in seed-pearls.

"I do, I do recognise it," said Leicester. "They were my own gift. The fellow of it was on the arm which she threw this very day around my neck!"—He spoke this with violent agitation.

"Your lordship," said Varney, "might yet further enquire of the lady herself, respecting the truth of these passages."

"It needs not—it needs not," said the tortured Earl; "it is written in characters of burning light, as if they were branded on my very eye-balls! I see her infamy—I can see nought else; and,—gracious Heaven!— for this vile woman was I about to commit to danger the lives of so many noble friends—shake the foundation of a lawful throne—carry the sword and torch through the bosom of a peaceful land—wrong the kind mistress who made me what I am—and would, but for that hell-framed marriage, have made me all that man can be! All this I was ready to do for a woman, who trinkets and traffics with my worst foes!— And thou, villain, why didst thou not speak sooner?"

"My lord," said Varney, "a tear from my lady would have blotted out all I could have said. Besides, I had not these proofs until this very morning, when Anthony Foster's sudden arrival, with the examinations and declarations, which he had extorted from the innkeeper Gosling, and others, explained the manner of her flight from Cumnor-Place, and my own researches discovered the steps which she had taken here."

"Now, may God be praised for the light he has given! so full, so satis-factory, that there breathes not a man in England who shall call my proceeding rash, or my revenge unjust.—And yet, Varney, so young, so fair, so fawning, and so false! Hence, then, her hatred to thee, my trusty, my well-beloved servant, because you withstood her plots, and endangered her paramour's life!"

"I never gave her any other cause of dislike, my lord," replied Varney; "but she knew that my counsels went directly to diminish her influence with your lordship; and that I was, and have been, ever ready to peril my life against your enemies."

"It is too, too apparent," replied Leicester; "yet, with what an air of magnanimity she exhorted me to commit my head to the Queen's mercy, rather than wear the veil of falsehood a moment longer! Methinks the angel of truth himself can have no such tones of high-souled impulse. Can it be so, Varney?—Can falsehood use thus boldly the language of truth?—Can infamy thus assume the guise of purity?—Varney, thou hast been my servant from a child—I have raised thee high—can raise thee higher. Think, think for me! Thy brain was ever shrewd and piercing—May she not be innocent? prove her so, and all I have yet done for thee shall be as nothing—nothing—in comparison of thy recompense!"

The agony with which his master spoke had some effect even on the hardened Varney, who, in the midst of his own wicked and ambitious designs, really loved his patron as well as such a wretch was capable of loving anything; but he comforted himself, and subdued his self-reproaches, with the reflection, that if he inflicted upon the Earl some immediate and transitory pain, it was in order to pave his way to the throne, which, were this marriage dissolved by death or otherwise, he deemed Elizabeth would willingly share with his benefactor. He therefore persevered in his diabolical policy; and, after a moment's consideration, answered the anxious queries of the Earl with a melancholy look, as if he had in vain sought some exculpation for the Countess; then, suddenly raising his head, he said, with an expression of hope, which instantly communicated itself to the countenance of his patron,—"Yet wherefore, if guilty, should she have perilled herself by coming hither? Why not rather have fled to her father's, or elsewhere?—though that, indeed, might have interfered with her desire to be acknowledged as Countess of Leicester."

"True, true, true!" exclaimed Leicester, his transient gleam of hope giving way to the utmost bitterness of feeling and expression; "thou art not fit to fathom a woman's depth of wit, Varney. I see it all. She would not quit the estate and title of the wittol who had wedded her. Ay, and if in my madness I had started into rebellion, or if the angry Queen had taken my head, as she this morning threatened, the wealthy dower which law would have assigned to the Countess Dowager of Leicester, had been no bad windfall to the beggarly Tressilian. Well might she goad me on to danger, which could not end otherwise than profitably to her.—Speak not for her, Varney! I will have her blood!"

"My lord," replied Varney, "the wildness of your distress breaks forth in the wildness of your language."

"I say, speak not for her!" replied Leicester; "she has dishonoured me—she would have murdered me—all ties are burst between us. She shall die the death of a traitress and adulteress, well merited both by the laws of God and man! And—what is this casket," he said, "which was even now thrust into my hand by a boy, with the desire I would convey it to Tressilian, as he could not give it to the Countess? By Heaven! the words surprised me as he spoke them, though other matters chased them from my brain; but now they return with double force.—It is her casket of jewels!—Force it open, Varney; force the hinges open with thy poniard."

"She refused the aid of my dagger once," thought Varney, as he unsheathed the weapon, "to cut the string which bound a letter, but now it shall work a mightier ministry in her fortunes."

With this reflection, by using the three-cornered stiletto-blade as a wedge, he forced open the slender silver hinges of the casket. The Earl no sooner saw them give way, than he snatched the casket from Sir Richard's hand, wrenched off the cover, and tearing out the splendid contents, flung them on the floor in a transport of rage, while he eagerly searched for some letter or billet, which should make the fancied guilt of his innocent Countess yet more apparent. Then stamping furiously on the gems, he exclaimed, "Thus I annihilate the miserable toys for which thou hast sold thyself, body and soul, consigned thyself to an early and timeless death, and me to misery and remorse for ever!— Tell me not of forgiveness, Varney—She is doomed!"

So saying, he left the room, and rushed into an adjacent closet, the door of which he locked and bolted.

Varney looked after him, while something of a more human feeling seemed to contend with his habitual sneer. "I am sorry for his weakness," he said, "but love has made him a child. He throws down and treads on these costly toys—with the same vehemence would he dash to pieces this frailest toy of all, of which he used to rave so fondly. But that taste also will be forgotten when its object is no more. Well, he has no eye to value things as they deserve, and that nature has given to Varney. When Leicester shall be a sovereign, he will think as little of the gales of passion, through which he gained that royal port, as ever did sailor in harbour, of the perils of a voyage. But these tell-tale articles must not remain here—they are rather too rich vails for the drudges who dress the chamber."

While Varney was employed in gathering together and putting them into a secret drawer of a cabinet that chanced to be unlocked, he saw the door of Leicester's closet open, the tapestry pushed aside, and the Earl's face thrust out, but with eyes so dead, and lips and cheeks so bloodless and pale, that he started at the sudden change. No sooner did his eyes encounter the Earl's, than the latter withdrew his head, and shut the door of the closet. This manœuvre Leicester repeated twice, without speaking a word, so that Varney began to doubt whether his brain was not actually affected by his mental agony. The third time, however, he beckoned, and Varney obeyed the signal. When he entered, he soon found his patron's perturbation was not caused by insanity, but by the fellness of purpose which he entertained, contending with various contrary passions. They passed a full hour in close consultation; after which the Earl of Leicester, with an incredible exertion, dressed himself, and went to attend his royal guest.

CHAPTER XXXVII

You have displaced the mirth, broke the good meeting
With most admired disorder.

                                                    Macbeth.

IT was afterwards remembered, that during the banquets and revels
which occupied the remainder of this eventful day, the bearing of
Leicester and Varney were totally different from their usual demeanour.
Sir Richard Varney had been held rather a man of counsel and of action,
than a votary of pleasure. Business, whether civil or military, seemed
always to be his proper sphere; and while in festivals and revels, although
he well understood how to trick them up and present them, his own
part was that of a mere spectator; or, if he exercised his wit, it was
in a rough, caustic, and severe manner, rather as if he scoffed at the
exhibition and the guests, than shared the common pleasure.

But upon the present day his character seemed changed. He mixed
among the younger courtiers and ladies, and appeared for the moment
to be actuated by a spirit of light-hearted gaiety, which rendered him
a match for the liveliest. Those who had looked upon him as a man
given up to graver and more ambitious pursuits, a bitter sneerer and
passer of sarcasms at the expense of those, who, taking life as they find
it, were disposed to snatch at each pastime it presents, now perceived
with astonishment that his wit could carry as smooth an edge as their
own, his laugh be as lively, and his brow as unclouded. By what art of
damnable hypocrisy he could draw this veil of gaiety over the black
thoughts of one of the worst of human bosoms, must remain unintelligible
to all but his compeers, if any such ever existed; but he was a man of
extraordinary powers, and those powers were unhappily dedicated in
all their energy to the very worst of purposes.

It was entirely different with Leicester. However habituated his mind
usually was to play the part of a good courtier, and appear gay, assiduous, and free from all care but that of enhancing the pleasure of the
moment, while his bosom internally throbbed with the pangs of unsatis-
fied ambition, jealousy, or resentment, his heart had now a yet more
dreadful guest, whose workings could not be overshadowed or suppressed; and you might read in his vacant eye and troubled brow, that
his thoughts were far absent from the scenes in which he was compelling
himself to play a part. He looked, moved, and spoke, as if by a succession of continued efforts; and it seemed as if his will had in some
degree lost the promptitude of command over the acute mind and goodly
form of which it was the regent. His actions and gestures, instead of
appearing the consequence of simple volition, seemed, like those of an
automaton, to wait the revolution of some internal machinery ere they
could be performed; and his words fell from him piecemeal, interrupted,
as if he had first to think what he was to say, then how it was to be said,
and as if, after all, it was only by an effort of continued attention that

he completed a sentence without forgetting both the one and the other.

The singular effects which these distractions of mind produced upon the behaviour and conversation of the most accomplished courtier of England, as they were visible to the lowest and dullest menial who approached his person, could not escape the notice of the most intelligent princess of the age. Nor is there the least doubt, that the alternate negligence and irregularity of his manner, would have called down Elizabeth's severe displeasure on the Earl of Leicester, had it not occurred to her to account for it, by supposing that the apprehension of that displeasure which she had expressed towards him with such vivacity that very morning, was dwelling upon the spirits of her favourite, and, spite of his efforts to the contrary, distracted the usual graceful tenor of his mien, and the charms of his conversation. When this idea, so flattering to female vanity, had once obtained possession of her mind, it proved a full and satisfactory apology for the numerous errors and mistakes of the Earl of Leicester; and the watchful circle around observed with astonishment, that, instead of resenting his repeated negligence, and want of even ordinary attention, (although these were points on which she was usually extremely punctilious,) the Queen sought, on the contrary, to afford him time and means to recollect himself, and deigned to assist him in doing so, with an indulgence which seemed altogether inconsistent with her usual character. It was clear, however, that this could not last much longer, and that Elizabeth must finally put another and more severe construction on Leicester's uncourteous conduct, when the Earl was summoned by Varney to speak with him in a different apartment.

After having had the message twice delivered to him, he rose, and was about to withdraw, as it were, by instinct—then stopped, and turning round, entreated permission of the Queen to absent himself for a brief space upon matters of pressing importance.

"Go, my lord," said the Queen; "we are aware our presence must occasion sudden and unexpected occurrences, which require to be provided for on the instant. Yet, my lord, as you would have us believe ourself your welcome and honoured guest, we entreat you to think less of our good cheer, and favour us with more of your good countenance, than we have this day enjoyed; for, whether prince or peasant be the guest, the welcome of the host will always be the better part of the entertainment. Go, my lord; and we trust to see you return with an unwrinkled brow, and those free thoughts which you are wont to have at the disposal of your friends."

Leicester only bowed low in answer to this rebuke, and retired. At the door of the apartment he was met by Varney, who eagerly drew him apart, and whispered in his ear, "All is well!"

"Has Masters seen her?" said the Earl.

"He has, my lord; and as she would neither answer his queries, nor allege any reason for her refusal, he will give full testimony that sh labours under a mental disorder, and may be best committed to the charge of her friends. The opportunity is therefore free, to remove her as we proposed."

"But Tressilian?" said Leicester.

"He will not know of her departure for some time," replied Varney; "it shall take place this very evening, and to-morrow he shall be cared for."

"No, by my soul," answered Leicester; "I will take vengeance on him with mine own hand!"

"You, my lord, and on so inconsiderable a man as Tressilian!—No, my lord, he hath long wished to visit foreign parts. Trust him to me—I will take care he returns not hither to tell tales."

"Not so, by Heaven, Varney!" exclaimed Leicester.—"Inconsiderable do you call an enemy, that hath had power to wound me so deeply, that my whole after life must be one scene of remorse and misery?—No; rather than forego the right of doing myself justice with my own hand on that accursed villain, I will unfold the whole truth at Elizabeth's footstool, and let her vengeance descend at once on them and on myself."

Varney saw with great alarm that his lord was wrought up to such a pitch of agitation, that if he gave not way to him, he was perfectly capable of adopting the desperate resolution which he had announced, and which was instant ruin to all the schemes of ambition which Varney had formed for his patron and for himself. But the Earl's rage seemed at once uncontrollable and deeply concentrated; and while he spoke, his eyes shot fire, his voice trembled with excess of passion, and the light foam stood on his lip.

His confidant made a bold and successful effort to obtain the mastery of him even in this hour of emotion.—"My lord," he said, leading him to a mirror, "behold your reflection in that glass, and think if these agitated features belong to one who, in a condition so extreme, is capable of forming a resolution for himself."

"What, then, wouldst thou make me?" said Leicester, struck at the change in his own physiognomy, though offended at the freedom with which Varney made the appeal. "Am I to be thy ward, thy vassal,—the property and subject of my servant?"

"No, my lord," said Varney, firmly, "but be master of yourself, and of your own passion. My lord, I, your born servant, am ashamed to see how poorly you bear yourself in the storm of fury. Go to Elizabeth's feet, confess your marriage—impeach your wife and her paramour of adultery—and avow yourself, amongst all your peers, the wittol who married a country girl, and was cozened by her and her book-learned gallant.—Go, my lord—but first take farewell of Richard Varney, with all the benefits you ever conferred on him. He served the noble, the lofty, the high-minded Leicester, and was more proud of depending on him, than he would be of commanding thousands. But the abject lord who stoops to every adverse circumstance, whose judicious resolves are scattered like chaff before every wind of passion, him Richard Varney serves not. He is as much above him in constancy of mind, as beneath him in rank and fortune."

Varney spoke thus without hypocrisy, for, though the firmness of mind which he boasted was hardness and impenetrability, yet he really felt the ascendency which he vaunted; while the interest which he actually felt in the fortunes of Leicester, gave unusual emotion to his voice and manner.

Leicester was overpowered by his assumed superiority; it seemed to the unfortunate Earl as if his last friend was about to abandon him. He stretched his hand towards Varney, as he uttered the words, "Do not leave me—What wouldst thou have me do?"

"Be thyself, my noble master," said Varney, touching the Earl's hand with his lips, after having respectfully grasped it in his own; "be yourself, superior to those storms of passion which wreck inferior minds. Are you the first who has been cozened in love? The first whom a vain and licentious woman has cheated into an affection, which she has afterwards scorned and misused? And will you suffer yourself to be driven frantic, because you have not been wiser than the wisest men whom the world has seen? Let her be as if she had not been—let her pass from your memory, as unworthy of ever having held a place there. Let your strong resolve of this morning, which I have both courage, zeal, and means enough to execute, be like the fiat of a superior being, a passionless act of justice. She hath deserved death—let her die!"

While he was speaking, the Earl held his hand fast, compressed his lips hard, and frowned, as if he laboured to catch from Varney a portion of the cold, ruthless, and dispassionate firmness which he recommended. When he was silent, the Earl still continued to grasp his hand, until, with an effort at calm decision, he was able to articulate, "Be it so—she dies! —But one tear might be permitted."

"Not one, my lord," interrupted Varney, who saw by the quivering eye and convulsed cheek of his patron, that he was about to give way to a burst of emotion,—"Not a tear—the time permits it not—Tressilian must be thought of——"

"That indeed is a name," said the Earl, "to convert tears into blood. Varney, I have thought on this, and I have determined—neither entreaty nor argument shall move me—Tressilian shall be my own victim."

"It is madness, my lord; but you are too mighty for me to bar your way to your revenge. Yet resolve at least to choose fitting time and opportunity, and to forbear him until those shall be found."

"Thou shalt order me in what thou wilt," said Leicester, "only thwart me not in this."

"Then, my lord," said Varney, "I first request of you to lay aside the wild, suspected, and half-frenzied demeanour, which hath this day drawn the eyes of all the court upon you; and which, but for the Queen's partial indulgence, which she hath extended towards you in a degree far beyond her nature, she had never given you the opportunity to atone for."

"Have I indeed been so negligent?" said Leicester, as one who awakes from a dream; "I thought I had coloured it well; but fear nothing, my mind is now eased—I am calm. My horoscope shall be fulfilled; and that it may be fulfilled, I will tax to the highest every faculty of my mind. Fear me not, I say—I will to the Queen instantly—not thine own looks and language shall be more impenetrable than mine.—Hast thou aught else to say?"

"I must crave your signet-ring," said Varney, gravely, "in token to those of your servants whom I must employ, that I possess your full authority in commanding their aid."

Leicester drew off the signet-ring, which he commonly used, and gave it to Varney with a haggard and stern expression of countenance, adding only, in a low, half-whispered tone, but with terrific emphasis, the words, "What thou dost, do quickly."

Some anxiety and wonder took place, meanwhile, in the Presence-hall, at the prolonged absence of the noble Lord of the Castle, and great was the delight of his friends, when they saw him enter as a man, from whose bosom, to all human seeming, a weight of care had been just removed. Amply did Leicester that day redeem the pledge he had given to Varney, who soon saw himself no longer under the necessity of maintaining a character so different from his own, as that which he had assumed in the earlier part of the day, and gradually relapsed into the same grave, shrewd, caustic observer of conversation and incident, which constituted his usual part in society.

With Elizabeth, Leicester played his game as one, to whom her natural strength of talent, and her weakness in one or two particular points, were well known. He was too wary to exchange on a sudden the sullen personage which he had played before he retired with Varney; but, on approaching her, it seemed softened into a melancholy, which had a touch of tenderness in it, and which, in the course of conversing with Elizabeth, and as she dropped in compassion one mark of favour after another to console him, passed into a flow of affectionate gallantry, the most assiduous, the most delicate, the most insinuating, yet at the same time the most respectful, with which a Queen was ever addressed by a subject. Elizabeth listened, as in a sort of enchantment; her jealousy of power was lulled asleep; her resolution to forsake all social or domestic ties, and dedicate herself exclusively to the care of her people, began to be shaken, and once more the star of Dudley culminated in the court-horizon.

But Leicester did not enjoy this triumph over nature, and over conscience, without its being embittered to him, not only by the internal rebellion of his feelings against the violence which he exercised over them, but by many accidental circumstances, which in the course of the ban-

quet, and during the subsequent amusements of the evening, jarred upon
that nerve, the least vibration of which was agony.

The courtiers were, for example, in the great hall, after having left
the banqueting-room, awaiting the appearance of a splendid masque,
which was the expected entertainment of this evening, when the Queen
interrupted a wild career of wit, which the Earl of Leicester was running
against Lord Willoughby, Raleigh, and some other courtiers, by saying—
"We will impeach you of high treason, my lord, if you proceed in this
attempt to slay us with laughter. And here comes a thing may make us
all grave at his pleasure, our learned physician Masters, with news belike
of our poor suppliant, Lady Varney—nay, my lord, we will not have you
leave us, for this being a dispute betwixt married persons, we do not hold
our own experience deep enough to decide thereon, without good counsel.
—How now, Masters, what think'st thou of the runaway bride?"

The smile with which Leicester had been speaking, when the Queen
interrupted him, remained arrested on his lips, as if it had been carved
there by the chisel of Michael Angelo, or of Chantrey; and he listened
to the speech of the physician with the same immovable cast of countenance.

"The Lady Varney, gracious Sovereign," said the court physician
Masters, "is sullen, and would hold little conference with me touching
the state of her health, talking wildly of being soon to plead her own
cause before your own presence, and of answering no meaner person's
enquiries."

"Now, the heavens forfend!" said the Queen; "we have already suffered
from the misconstructions and broils which seem to follow this poor
brain-sick lady wherever she comes.—Think you not so, my lord?" she
added, appealing to Leicester, with something in her look that indicated
regret, even tenderly expressed, for their disagreement of that morning.
Leicester compelled himself to bow low. The utmost force he could exert
was inadequate to the farther effort of expressing in words his acquiescence in the Queen's sentiment.

"You are vindictive," she said, "my lord; but we will find time and
place to punish you. But once more to this same trouble-mirth, this Lady
Varney—What of her health, Masters?"

"She is sullen, madam, as I already said," replied Masters, "and
refuses to answer interrogatories, or be amenable to the authority of the
mediciner. I conceive her to be possessed with a delirium, which I incline
to term rather *hypochondria* than *phrenesis;* and I think she were best
cared for by her husband in his own house, and removed from all this
bustle of pageants, which disturbs her weak brain with the most fantastic
phantoms. She drops hints as if she were some great person in disguise—
some Countess or Princess perchance. God help them, such are often the
hallucinations of these infirm persons!"

"Nay, then," said the Queen, "away with her with all speed. Let
Varney care for her with fitting humanity; but let them rid the castle of

her forthwith. She will think herself lady of all, I warrant you. It is pity so fair a form, however, should have an infirm understanding —What think you, my lord?"

"It is a pity indeed," said the Earl, repeating the words like a task which was set him.

"But, perhaps," said Elizabeth, "you do not join with us in our opinion of her beauty; and indeed we have known men prefer a statelier and more Juno-like form, to that drooping fragile one, that hung its head like a broken lily. Ay, men are tyrants, my lord, who esteem the animation of the strife above the triumph of an unresisting conquest, and, like sturdy champions, love best those women who can wage contest with them.—I could think with you, Rutland, that, give my Lord of Leicester such a piece of painted wax for a bride, he would have wished her dead ere the end of the honeymoon."

As she said this, she looked on Leicester so expressively, that, while his heart revolted against the egregious falsehood, he did himself so much violence as to reply in a whisper, that Leicester's love was more lowly than her Majesty deemed, since it was settled where he could never command, but must ever obey.

The queen blushed, and bid him be silent; yet looked as if she expected that he would not obey her commands. But at that moment the flourish of trumpets and kettle-drums from a high balcony which overlooked the hall, announced the entrance of the masquers, and relieved Leicester from the horrible state of constraint and dissimulation in which the result of his own duplicity had placed him.

The masque which entered consisted of four separate bands, which followed each other at brief intervals, each consisting of six principal persons and as many torch-bearers, and each representing one of the various nations by which England had at different times been occupied.

The aboriginal Britons, who first entered, were ushered in by two ancient Druids, whose hoary hair was crowned with a chaplet of oak, and who bore in their hands branches of mistletoe. The masquers who followed these venerable figures were succeeded by two Bards, arrayed in white, and bearing harps, which they occasionally touched, singing at the same time certain stanzas of an ancient hymn to Belus, or the Sun. The aboriginal Britons had been selected from amongst the tallest and most robust young gentlemen in attendance on the court. Their masks were accommodated with long shaggy beards and hair; their vestments were of the hides of wolves and bears; while their legs, arms, and the upper parts of their bodies, being sheathed in flesh-coloured silk, on which were traced in grotesque lines representations of the heavenly bodies, and of animals and other terrestrial objects, gave them the lively appearance of our painted ancestors, whose freedom was first trenched upon by the Romans.

The sons of Rome, who came to civilize as well as to conquer, were next produced before the princely assembly; and the manager of the revels had correctly imitated the high crest and military habits of that celebrated people, accommodating them with the light yet strong buckler, and the short two-edged sword, the use of which had made them victors of the world. The Roman eagles were borne before them by two standard-bearers, who recited a hymn to Mars, and the classical warriors followed with the grave and haughty step of men who aspired at universal conquest.

The third quadrille represented the Saxons, clad in the bearskins which they had brought with them from the German forests, and bearing in their hands the redoubtable battle-axes which made such havoc among the natives of Britain. They were preceded by two Scalds, who chanted the praises of Odin.

Last came the knightly Normans, in their mailshirts and hoods of steel, with all the panoply of chivalry, and marshalled by two Minstrels, who sung of war and ladies' love.

These four bands entered the spacious hall with the utmost order, a short pause being made, that the spectators might satisfy their curiosity as to each quadrille before the appearance of the next. They then marched completely round the hall, in order the more fully to display themselves, regulating their steps to organs, shalms, hautboys, and virginals, the music of the Lord Leicester's household. At length the four quadrilles of masquers, ranging their torch-bearers behind them, drew up in their several ranks, on the two opposite sides of the hall, so that the Romans confronting the Britons, and the Saxons the Normans, seemed to look on each other with eyes of wonder, which presently appeared to kindle into anger, expressed by menacing gestures. At the burst of a strain of martial music from the gallery the masquers drew their swords on all sides, and advanced against each other in the measured steps of a sort of Pyrrhic, or military dance, clashing their swords against their adversaries' shields, and clattering them against their blades as they passed each other in the progress of the dance. It was a very pleasant spectacle to see how the various bands, preserving regularity amid motions which seemed to be totally irregular, mixed together, and then disengaging themselves, resumed each their own original rank as the music varied.

In this symbolical dance were represented the conflicts which had taken place among the various nations which had anciently inhabited Britain.

At length, after many mazy evolutions, which afforded great pleasure to the spectators, the sound of a loud-voiced trumpet was heard, as if it blew for instant battle, or for victory won. The masquers instantly ceased their mimic strife, and collecting themselves under their original leaders, or presenters, for such was the appropriate phrase, seemed to share the anxious expectation which the spectators experienced concerning what was next to appear.

The doors of the hall were thrown wide, and no less a person entered than the fiend-born Merlin, dressed in a strange and mystical attire,

suited to his ambiguous birth and magical power. About him and behind
him fluttered or gambolled many extraordinary forms, intended to represent the spirits who waited to do his powerful bidding; and so much did
this part of the pageant interest the menials and others of the lower class
then in the Castle, that many of them forgot even the reverence due to
the Queen's presence, so far as to thrust themselves into the lower part of
the hall.

The Earl of Leicester, seeing his officers had some difficulty to repel
these intruders, without more disturbance than was fitting where the
Queen was in presence, arose and went himself to the bottom of the hall;
Elizabeth, at the same time, with her usual feeling for the common people,
requesting that they might be permitted to remain undisturbed to witness
the pageant. Leicester went under this pretext; but his real motive was
to gain a moment to himself, and to relieve his mind, were it but for one
instant, from the dreadful task of hiding, under the guise of gaiety and
gallantry, the lacerating pangs of shame, anger, remorse, and thirst for
vengeance. He imposed silence by his look and sign upon the vulgar
crowd, at the lower end of the apartment; but, instead of instantly returning to wait on her Majesty, he wrapped his cloak around him, and mixing
with the crowd, stood in some degree an undistinguished spectator of the
progress of the masque.

Merlin, having entered, and advanced into the midst of the hall, summoned the presenters of the contending bands around him by a wave of
his magical rod, and announced to them, in a poetical speech, that the
isle of Britain was now commanded by a Royal Maiden, to whom it was
the will of fate that they should all do homage, and request of her to
pronounce on the various pretensions which each set forth to be esteemed
the pre-eminent stock, from which the present natives, the happy subjects of that angelical Princess, derived their lineage.

In obedience to this mandate, the bands, each moving to solemn music,
passed in succession before Elizabeth; doing her, as they passed, each
after the fashion of the people whom they represented, the lowest and
most devotional homage, which she returned with the same gracious
courtesy that had marked her whole conduct since she came to Kenilworth.

The presenters of the several masques, or quadrilles, then alleged, each
in behalf of his own troop, the reasons which they had for claiming pre-
eminence over the rest; and when they had been all heard in turn, she
returned them this gracious answer: "That she was sorry she was not
better qualified to decide upon the doubtful question which had been
propounded to her by the direction of the famous Merlin, but that it
seemed to her that no single one of these celebrated nations could claim
pre-eminence over the others, as having most contributed to form the
Englishman of her own time, who unquestionably derived from each of
them some worthy attribute of his character. Thus," she said, "the
Englishman had from the ancient Briton his bold and tameless spirit of

freedom,—from the Roman his disciplined courage in war, with his love of letters and civilisation in time of peace,—from the Saxon his wise and equitable laws,—and from the chivalrous Norman his love of honour and courtesy, with his generous desire for glory."

Merlin answered with readiness, that it did indeed require that so many choice qualities should meet in the English, as might render them in some measure the muster of the perfections of other nations, since that alone could render them in some degree deserving of the blessings they enjoyed under the reign of England's Elizabeth.

The music then sounded, and the quadrilles, together with Merlin and his assistants, had begun to remove from the crowded hall, when Leicester, who was, as we have mentioned, stationed for the moment near the bottom of the hall, and consequently engaged in some degree in the crowd, felt himself pulled by the cloak, while a voice whispered in his ear, "My lord, I do desire some instant conference with you."

CHAPTER XXXVIII

How is't with me, when every noise appals me?
Macbeth.

"I DESIRE some conference with you." The words were simple in themselves, but Lord Leicester was in that alarmed and feverish state of mind, when the most ordinary occurrences seem fraught with alarming import; and he turned hastily round to survey the person by whom they had been spoken. There was nothing remarkable in the speaker's appearance, which consisted of a black silk doublet and short mantle, with a black vizard on his face; for it appeared he had been among the crowd of masks who had thronged into the hall in the retinue of Merlin, though he did not wear any of the extravagant disguises by which most of them were distinguished.

"Who are you, or what do you want with me?" said Leicester, not without betraying, by his accents, the hurried state of his spirits.

"No evil, my lord," answered the mask, "but much good and honour, if you will rightly understand my purpose. But I must speak with you more privately."

"I can speak with no nameless stranger," answered Leicester, dreading he knew not precisely what from the request of the stranger; "and those who are known to me, must seek another and a fitter time to ask an interview."

He would have hurried away, but the mask still detained him.

"Those who talk to your lordship of what your own honour demands, have a right over your time, whatever occupations you may lay aside in order to indulge them."

"How! my honour? Who dare impeach it?" said Leicester.

"Your own conduct alone can furnish grounds for accusing it, my lord, and it is that topic on which I would speak with you."

"You are insolent," said Leicester, "and abuse the hospitable license of the time, which prevents me from having you punished. I demand your name?"

"Edmund Tressilian of Cornwall," answered the mask. "My tongue has been bound by a promise for four-and-twenty hours,—the space is passed, —I now speak, and do your lordship the justice to address myself first to you."

The thrill of astonishment which had penetrated to Leicester's very heart at hearing that name pronounced by the voice of the man he most detested, and by whom he conceived himself so deeply injured, at first rendered him immovable, but instantly gave way to such a thirst for revenge as the pilgrim in the desert feels for the water-brooks. He had but sense and self-government enough left to prevent his stabbing to the heart the audacious villain, who, after the ruin he had brought upon him, dared, with such unmoved assurance, thus to practise upon him farther. Determined to suppress for the moment every symptom of agitation, in order to perceive the full scope of Tressilian's purpose, as well as to secure his own vengeance, he answered in a tone so altered by restrained passion as scarce to be intelligible,—"And what does Master Edmund Tressilian require at my hand?"

"Justice, my lord," answered Tressilian, calmly but firmly.

"Justice," said Leicester, "all men are entitled to—You, Master Tressilian, are peculiarly so, and be assured you shall have it."

"I expect nothing less from your nobleness," answered Tressilian; "but time presses, and I must speak with you to-night—May I wait on you in your chamber?"

"No," answered Leicester, sternly, "not under a roof, and that roof mine own—We will meet under the free cope of heaven."

"You are discomposed or displeased, my lord," replied Tressilian; "yet there is no occasion for distemperature. The place is equal to me, so you allow me one half hour of your time uninterrupted."

"A shorter time will, I trust, suffice," answered Leicester—"Meet me in the Pleasance, when the Queen has retired to her chamber."

"Enough," said Tressilian, and withdrew; while a sort of rapture seemed for the moment to occupy the mind of Leicester.

"Heaven," he said, "is at last favourable to me, and has put within my reach the wretch who has branded me with this deep ignominy—who has inflicted on me this cruel agony. I will blame fate no more, since I am afforded the means of tracing the wiles by which he means still farther to practise on me, and then of at once convicting and punishing his villainy. To my task—to my task!—I will not sink under it now,—since midnight, at farthest, will bring me vengeance."

While these reflections thronged through Leicester's mind, he again made his way amid the obsequious crowd, which divided to give him

passage, and resumed his place, envied and admired, beside the person of
his Sovereign. But, could the bosom of him thus admired and envied,
have been laid open before the inhabitants of that crowded hall, with all
its dark thoughts of guilty ambition, blighted affection, deep vengeance,
and conscious sense of meditated cruelty, crossing each other like spectres
in the circle of some foul enchantress,—which of them, from the most
ambitious noble in the courtly circle, down to the most wretched menial,
who lived by shifting of trenchers, would have desired to change characters with the favourite of Elizabeth, and the Lord of Kenilworth!

New tortures awaited him as soon as he had rejoined Elizabeth.

"You come in time, my lord," she said, "to decide a dispute between
us ladies. Here has Sir Richard Varney asked our permission to depart
from the Castle with his infirm lady, having, as he tells us, your lordship's
consent to his absence, so he can obtain ours. Certes, we have no will to
withhold him from the affectionate charge of this poor young person—
but you are to know that Sir Richard Varney hath this day shown himself so much captivated with these ladies of ours, that here is our Duchess
of Rutland says, he will carry his poor insane wife no farther than the
lake, plunge her in, to tenant the crystal palaces that the enchanted
nymph told us of, and return a jolly widower, to dry his tears, and to
make up the loss among our train. How say you, my lord?—We have seen
Varney under two or three different guises—you know what are his proper
attributes—think you he is capable of playing his lady such a knave's
trick?"

Leicester was confounded, but the danger was urgent, and a reply
absolutely necessary. "The ladies," he said, "think too lightly of one of
their own sex, in supposing she could deserve such a fate, or too ill of
ours, to think it could be inflicted upon an innocent female."

"Hear him, my ladies," said Elizabeth; "like all his sex, he would
excuse their cruelty by imputing fickleness to us."

"Say not *us*, madam," replied the Earl; "we say that meaner women,
like the lesser lights of heaven, have revolutions and phases, but who
shall impute mutability to the sun, or to Elizabeth?"

The discourse presently afterwards assumed a less perilous tendency,
and Leicester continued to support his part in it with spirit, at whatever
expense of mental agony. So pleasing did it seem to Elizabeth, that the
Castle bell had sounded midnight ere she retired from the company, a
circumstance unusual in her quiet and regular habits of disposing of
time. Her departure was of course the signal for breaking up the company, who dispersed to their several places of repose, to dream over
the pastimes of the day, or to anticipate those of the morrow.

The unfortunate Lord of the Castle, and founder of the proud festival,
retired to far different thoughts. His direction to the valet who attended
him, was to send Varney instantly to his apartment. The messenger returned after some delay, and informed him that an hour had elapsed since

Sir Richard Varney had left the Castle, by the postern-gate, with three other persons, one of whom was transported in a horse-litter.

"How came he to leave the Castle after the watch was set?" said Leicester; "I thought he went not till daybreak."

"He gave satisfactory reasons, as I understand," said the domestic, "to the guard, and, as I hear, showed your lordship's signet——"

"True—true," said the Earl; "yet he has been hasty—Do any of his attendants remain behind?"

"Michael Lambourne, my lord," said the valet, "was not to be found when Sir Richard Varney departed, and his master was much incensed at his absence. I saw him but now saddling his horse to gallop after his master."

"Bid him come hither instantly," said Leicester; "I have a message to his master."

The servant left the apartment, and Leicester traversed it for some time in deep meditation—"Varney is over zealous," he said, "over pressing—He loves me, I think—but he hath his own ends to serve, and he is inexorable in pursuit of them. If I rise he rises, and he hath shown himself already but too eager to rid me of this obstacle which seems to stand betwixt me and sovereignty. Yet I will not stoop to bear this disgrace. She shall be punished, but it shall be more advisedly. I already feel, even in anticipation, that over-haste would light the flames of hell in my bosom. No—one victim is enough at once, and that victim already waits me."

He seized upon writing materials, and hastily traced these words:—
"Sir Richard Varney, we have resolved to defer the matter intrusted to your care, and strictly command you to proceed no farther in relation to our Countess, until our further order. We also command your instant return to Kenilworth, as soon as you have safely bestowed that with which you are intrusted. But if the same-placing of your present charge shall detain you longer than we think for, we command you, in that case, to send back our signet-ring by a trusty and speedy messenger, we having present need of the same. And requiring your strict obedience in these things, and commending you to God's keeping, we rest your assured good friend and master,

"R. LEICESTER.

"Given at our Castle of Kenilworth, the tenth of July, in the year of Salvation one thousand five hundred and seventy-five."

As Leicester had finished and sealed this mandate, Michael Lambourne, booted up to mid-thigh, having his riding-cloak girthed around him with a broad belt, and a felt-cap on his head, like that of a courier, entered his apartment, ushered in by the valet.

"What is thy capacity of service?" said the Earl.

"Equerry to your lordship's master of the horse," answered Lambourne, with his customary assurance.

"Tie up thy saucy tongue, sir," said Leicester; "the jests that may suit Sir Richard Varney's presence, suit not mine. How soon wilt thou overtake thy master?"

"In one hour's riding, my lord, if man and horse hold good," said Lambourne, with an instant alteration of demeanour, from an approach to familiarity to the deepest respect. The Earl measured him with his eye from top to toe.

"I have heard of thee," he said; "men say thou art a prompt fellow in thy service, but too much given to brawling and to wassail to be trusted with things of moment."

"My lord," said Lambourne, "I have been soldier, sailor, traveller, and adventurer; and these are all trades in which men enjoy to-day, because they have no surety of to-morrow. But though I may misuse mine own leisure, I have never neglected the duty I owe my master."

"See that it be so in this instance," said Leicester, "and it shall do thee good. Deliver this letter speedily and carefully into Sir Richard Varney's hands."

"Does my commission reach no farther?" said Lambourne.

"No," answered Leicester, "but it deeply concerns me that it be carefully as well as hastily executed."

"I will spare neither care nor horse-flesh," answered Lambourne, and immediately took his leave.

"So, this is the end of my private audience, from which I hoped so much!" he muttered to himself, as he went through the long gallery, and down the back staircase. "Cogsbones! I thought the Earl had wanted a cast of mine office in some secret intrigue, and it all ends in carrying a letter! Well, his pleasure shall be done, however, and as his lordship well says, it may do me good another time. The child must creep ere he walk, and so must your infant courtier. I will have a look into this letter, however, which he hath sealed so sloven-like."—Having accomplished this, he clapped his hands together in ecstasy, exclaiming "The Countess —the Countess!—I have the secret that shall make or mar me.—But come forth, Bayard," he added, leading his horse into the court-yard, "for your flanks and my spurs must be presently acquainted."

Lambourne mounted, accordingly, and left the Castle by the postern-gate, where his free passage was permitted, in consequence of a message to that effect left by Sir Richard Varney.

As soon as Lambourne and the valet had left the apartment, Leicester proceeded to change his dress for a very plain one, threw his mantle around him, and, taking a lamp in his hand, went by the private passage of communication to a small secret postern-door which opened into the court-yard, near to the entrance of the Pleasance. His reflections were of a more calm and determined character than they had been at any late period, and he endeavoured to claim, even in his own eyes, the character of a man more sinned against than sinning.

"I have suffered the deepest injury," such was the tenor of his medita tions, "yet I have restricted the instant revenge which was in my power, and have limited it to that which is manly and noble. But shall the union which this false woman has this day disgraced, remain an abiding fetter on me, to check me in the noble career to which my destinies invite me? No—there are other means of disengaging such ties, without unloosing the cords of life. In the sight of God, I am no longer bound by the union she has broken. Kingdoms shall divide us—oceans roll betwixt us, and their waves, whose abysses have swallowed whole navies, shall be the sole depositaries of the deadly mystery."

By such a train of argument did Leicester labour to reconcile his conscience to the prosecution of plans of vengeance, so hastily adopted, and of schemes of ambition, which had become so woven in with every purpose and action of his life, that he was incapable of the effort of relinquishing them; until his revenge appeared to him to wear a face of justice, and even of generous moderation.

In this mood, the vindictive and ambitious Earl entered the superb precincts of the Pleasance, then illumined by the full moon. The broad yellow light was reflected on all sides from the white freestone, of which the pavement, balustrades, and architectural ornaments of the place, were constructed; and not a single fleecy cloud was visible in the azure sky, so that the scene was nearly as light as if the sun had but just left the horizon. The numerous statues of white marble glimmered in the pale light, like so many sheeted ghosts just arisen from their sepulchres, and the fountains threw their jets into the air, as if they sought that their waters should be brightened by the moonbeams, ere they fell down again upon their basins in showers of sparkling silver. The day had been sultry, and the gentle night-breeze, which sighed along the terrace of the Pleasance, raised not a deeper breath than the fan in the hand of youthful beauty. The bird of summer night had built many a nest in the bowers of the adjacent garden, and the tenants now indemnified themselves for silence during the day, by a full chorus of their own unrivalled warblings, now joyous, now pathetic, now united, now responsive to each other, as if to express their delight in the placid and delicious scene to which they poured their melody.

Musing on matters far different from the fall of waters, the gleam of moonlight, or the song of the nightingale, the stately Leicester walked slowly from the one end of the terrace to the other, his cloak wrapped around him, and his sword under his arm, without seeing any thing resembling the human form.

"I have been fooled by my own generosity," he said, "if I have suffered the villain to escape me—ay, and perhaps to go to the rescue of the Adulteress, who is so poorly guarded."

These were his thoughts, which were instantly dispelled, when, turning to look back towards the entrance, he saw a human form advancing slowly from the portico, and darkening the various objects with its shadow, as passing them successively, in its approach towards him.

"Shall I strike ere I again hear his detested voice?" was Leicester's thought, as he grasped the hilt of the sword. "But no! I will see which way his vile practice tends. I will watch, disgusting as it is, the coils and mazes of the loathsome snake, ere I put forth my strength and crush him."

His hand quitted the sword-hilt, and he advanced slowly towards Tressilian, collecting, for their meeting, all the self-possession he could command, until they came front to front with each other.

Tressilian made a profound reverence, to which the Earl replied with a haughty inclination of the head, and the words, "You sought secret conference with me, sir—I am here and attentive."

"My lord," said Tressilian, "I am so earnest in that which I have to say, and so desirous to find a patient, nay a favourable, hearing, that I will stoop to exculpate myself from whatever might prejudice your lordship against me. You think me your enemy?"

"Have I not some apparent cause?" answered Leicester, perceiving that Tressilian paused for a reply.

"You do me wrong, my lord. I am a friend, but neither a dependant nor partisan, of the Earl of Sussex, whom courtiers call your rival; and it is some considerable time since I ceased to regard either courts, or court-intrigues, as suited to my temper or genius."

"No doubt, sir," answered Leicester; "there are other occupations more worthy a scholar, and for such the world holds Master Tressilian— Love has his intrigues as well as ambition."

"I perceive, my lord," replied Tressilian, "you give much weight to my early attachment for the unfortunate young person of whom I am about to speak, and perhaps think I am prosecuting her cause out of rivalry, more than a sense of justice."

"No matter for my thoughts, sir," said the Earl; "proceed. You have as yet spoken of yourself only; an important and worthy subject doubtless, but which, perhaps, does not altogether so deeply concern me, that I should postpone my repose to hear it. Spare me further prelude, sir, and speak to the purpose, if indeed you have aught to say that concerns me. When you have done, I, in my turn, have something to communicate."

"I will speak, then, without farther prelude, my lord," answered Tressilian; "having to say that which, as it concerns your lordship's honour, I am confident you will not think your time wasted in listening to. I have to request an account from your lordship of the unhappy Amy Robsart, whose history is too well known to you. I regret deeply that I did not at once take this course, and make yourself judge between me and the villain by whom she is injured. My lord, she extricated herself from an unlawful and most perilous state of confinement, trusting to the effects of her own remonstrance upon her unworthy husband, and extorted from me a promise, that I would not interfere in her behalf until she had used her own efforts to have her rights acknowledged by him."

"Ha," said Leicester, "remember you to whom you speak?"

"I speak of her unworthy husband, my lord," repeated Tressilian, "and my respect can find no softer language. The unhappy young woman is withdrawn from my knowledge, and sequestered in some secret place of this Castle,—if she be not transferred to some place of seclusion better fitted for bad designs. This must be reformed, my lord—I speak it as authorized by her father,—and this ill-fated marriage must be avouched and proved in the Queen's presence, and the lady placed without restraint, and at her own free disposal. And, permit me to say, it concerns no one's honour that these most just demands of mine should be complied with, so much as it does that of your lordship."

The Earl stood as if he had been petrified, at the extreme coolness with which the man, whom he considered as having injured him so deeply, pleaded the cause of his criminal paramour, as if she had been an innocent woman, and he a disinterested advocate; nor was his wonder lessened by the warmth with which Tressilian seemed to demand for her the rank and situation which she had disgraced, and the advantages of which she was doubtless to share with the lover who advocated her cause with such effrontery. Tressilian had been silent for more than a minute ere the Earl recovered from the excess of his astonishment; and, considering the pre-possessions with which his mind was occupied, there is little wonder that his passion gained the mastery of every other consideration. "I have heard you, Master Tressilian," said he, "without interruption, and I bless God that my ears were never before made to tingle by the words of so frontless a villain. The task of chastising you is fitter for the hangman's scourge than the sword of a nobleman, but yet—— Villain, draw and defend thyself!"

As he spoke the last words, he dropped his mantle on the ground, struck Tressilian smartly with his sheathed sword, and instantly drawing his rapier, put himself into a posture of assault. The vehement fury of his language at first filled Tressilian, in his turn, with surprise equal to what Leicester had felt when he addressed him. But astonishment gave rise to resentment, when the unmerited insults of his language were followed by a blow, which immediately put to flight every thought save that of instant combat. Tressilian's sword was instantly drawn, and though perhaps somewhat inferior to Leicester in the use of the weapon, he understood it well enough to maintain the contest with great spirit, the rather that of the two he was for the time the more cool, since he could not help imputing Leicester's conduct either to actual frenzy, or to the influence of some strong delusion.

The rencontre had continued for several minutes, without either party receiving a wound, when of a sudden voices were heard beneath the portico, which formed the entrance of the terrace, mingled with the steps of men advancing hastily. "We are interrupted," said Leicester to his antagonist; "follow me."

At the same time a voice from the portico said, "The jackanape is right—they are tilting here."

Leicester, meanwhile, drew off Tressilian into a sort of recess behind one of the fountains, which served to conceal them, while six of the yeomen of the Queen's guard passed along the middle walk of the Pleasance, and they could hear one say to the rest, "We shall never find them to-night amongst all these squirting funnels, squirrel-cages, and rabbit-holes; but if we light not on them before we reach the farther end, we will return, and mount a guard at the entrance, and so secure them till morning."

"A proper matter," said another, "the drawing of swords so near the Queen's presence, ay, and in her very palace as 'twere!—Hang it, they must be some poor drunken game-cocks fallen to sparring—'twere pity almost we should find them—the penalty is chopping of a hand, is it not?—'twere hard to lose hand for handling a bit of steel, that comes so natural to one's gripe."

"Thou art a brawler thyself, George," said another; "but take heed, for the law stands as thou sayest."

"Ay," said the first, "an the act be not mildly construed; for thou know'st 'tis not the Queen's Palace, but my lord of Leicester's."

"Why, for that matter, the penalty may be as severe," said another; "for an our gracious Mistress be Queen, as she is, God save her, my Lord of Leicester is as good as King."

"Hush! thou knave!" said a third; "how know'st thou who may be within hearing?"

They passed on, making a kind of careless search, but seemingly more intent on their own conversation than bent on discovering the persons who had created the nocturnal disturbance.

They had no sooner passed forward along the terrace, than Leicester, making a sign to Tressilian to follow him, glided away in an opposite direction, and escaped through the portico undiscovered. He conducted Tressilian to Mervyn's Tower, in which he was now again lodged; and then, ere parting with him, said these words, "If thou hast courage to continue and bring to an end what is thus broken off, be near me when the court goes forth to-morrow—we shall find a time, and I will give you a signal when it is fitting."

"My lord," said Tressilian, "at another time I might have enquired the meaning of this strange and furious inveteracy against me. But you have laid that on my shoulder which only blood can wash away; and were you as high as your proudest wishes ever carried you, I would have from you satisfaction for my wounded honour."

On these terms they parted, but the adventures of the night were not yet ended with Leicester. He was compelled to pass by Saintlowe's Tower, in order to gain the private passage which led to his own chamber, and in the entrance thereof he met Lord Hunsdon half clothed, and with a naked sword under his arm.

"Are you awakened, too, with this 'larum, my Lord of Leicester?" said the old soldier. " 'Tis well—By gog's-nails, the nights are as noisy as the day in this Castle of yours. Some two hours since, I was waked by the screams of that poor brain-sick Lady Varney, whom her husband was forcing away. I promise you, it required both your warrant and the Queen's to keep me from entering into the game, and cutting that Varney of yours over the head; and now there is a brawl down in the Pleasance, or what you call the stone terrace-walk, where all yonder gimcracks stand?"

The first part of the old man's speech went through the Earl's heart like a knife; to the last he answered that he himself had heard the clash of swords, and had come down to take order with those who had been so insolent so near the Queen's presence.

"Nay, then," said Hunsdon, "I will be glad of your lordship's company."

Leicester was thus compelled to turn back with the rough old lord to the Pleasance, where Hunsdon heard from the yeomen of the guard, who were under his immediate command, the unsuccessful search they had made for the authors of the disturbance; and bestowed for their pains some round dozen of curses on them, as lazy knaves and blind whoresons. Leicester also thought it necessary to seem angry that no discovery had been effected; but at length suggested to Lord Hunsdon, that after all it could only be some foolish young men, who had been drinking healths pottle-deep, and who would be sufficiently scared by the search which had taken place after them. Hunsdon, who was himself attached to his cup, allowed that a pint-flagon might cover many of the follies which it had caused. "But," he added, "unless your lordship will be less liberal in your housekeeping, and restrain the overflow of ale, and wine, and wassail, I foresee it will end in my having some of these good fellows into the guard-house, and treating them to a dose of the strappado— And with this warning, good-night to you."

Joyful at being rid of his company, Leicester took leave of him at the entrance of his lodging, where they had first met, and entering the private passage, took up the lamp which he had left there, and by its expiring light found the way to his own apartment.

CHAPTER XXXIX

> Room! room! for my horse will wince
> If he comes within so many yards of a prince;
> For to tell you true, and in rhyme,
> He was foal'd in Queen Elizabeth's time;
> When the great Earl of Lester
> In his castle did feast her.
> *Masque of Owls.*—BEN JONSON.

THE amusement with which Elizabeth and her court were next day to be regaled, was an exhibition by the true-hearted men of Coventry, who were to represent the strife between the English and the Danes, agreeably to a custom long preserved in their ancient borough, and warranted for truth by old histories and chronicles. In this pageant, one party of the townsfolk presented the Saxons and the other the Danes, and set forth, both in rude rhymes and with hard blows, the contentions of these two fierce nations, and the Amazonian courage of the English women, who, according to the story, were the principal agents in the general massacre of the Danes, which took place at Hocktide, in the year of God 1012. This sport, which had been long a favourite pastime with the men of Coventry, had, it seems, been put down by the influence of some zealous clergymen, of the more precise cast, who chanced to have considerable influence with the magistrates. But the generality of the inhabitants had petitioned the Queen that they might have their play again, and be honoured with permission to represent it before her Highness. And when the matter was canvassed in the little council, which usually attended the Queen for dispatch of business, the proposal, although opposed by some of the stricter sort, found favour in the eyes of Elizabeth, who said that such toys occupied, without offence, the minds of many, who, lacking them, might find worse subjects of pastime; and that their pastors, however commendable for learning and godliness, were somewhat too sour in preaching against the pastimes of their flocks, and so the pageant was permitted to proceed.

Accordingly, after a morning repast, which Master Laneham calls an ambrosial breakfast, the principal persons of the court, in attendance upon her Majesty, pressed to the Gallery-tower, to witness the approach of the two contending parties of English and Danes; and after a signal had been given, the gate which opened in the circuit of the Chase was thrown wide, to admit them. On they came, foot and horse; for some of the ambitious burghers and yeomen had put themselves into fantastic dresses, imitating knights, in order to resemble the chivalry of the two different nations. However, to prevent fatal accidents, they were not permitted to appear on real horses, but had only license to accoutre themselves with those hobbyhorses, as they are called, which anciently formed the chief delight of a morrice-dance, and which still are exhibited on the stage, in the grand battle fought at the conclusion of Mr. Bayes's tragedy. The infantry followed in similar disguises. The whole exhibition was to be considered as a sort of anti-masque, or burlesque of the more stately pageants, in which the nobility and gentry bore part in the show, and, to the best of their knowledge, imitated with accuracy the personages whom they represented. The Hocktide play was of a different character, the actors being persons of inferior degree, and their habits the better fitted for the occasion, the more incongruous and ridiculous that they were in themselves. Accordingly their array, which the progress of our tale allows us no time to describe, was ludicrous enough, and their weapons, though sufficiently formidable to deal sound blows, were long alder-poles instead of lances, and sound cudgels for swords; and for fence, both cavalry and infantry, were well equipped with stout head pieces and targets, both made of thick leather.

Captain Coxe, that celebrated humorist of Coventry, whose library of ballads, almanacks, and penny histories, fairly wrapped up in parchment, and tied round for security with a piece of whipcord, remains still the envy of antiquaries, being himself the ingenious person under whose direction the pageant had been set forth, rode valiantly on his hobbyhorse before the bands of English, high-trussed, saith Laneham, and brandishing his long sword, as became an experienced man of war, who had fought under the Queen's father, bluff King Henry, at the siege of Boulogne. This chieftain was, as right and reason craved, the first to enter the lists, and, passing the Gallery at the head of his myrmidons, kissed the hilt of his sword to the Queen, and executed at the same time a gambade, the like whereof had never been practised by two-legged hobbyhorse. Then passing on with all his followers of cavaliers and infantry, he drew them up with martial skill at the opposite extremity of the bridge, or tilt-yard, until his antagonists should be fairly prepared for the onset.

This was no long interval; for the Danish cavalry and infantry, no way inferior to the English in number, valour and equipment, instantly arrived, with the northern bagpipe blowing before them in token of their country, and headed by a cunning master of defence, only inferior to the renowned Captain Coxe, if to him, in the discipline of war. The Danes, as invaders, took their station under the Gallery-tower, and opposite to that of Mortimer; and, when their arrangements vere completely made, a signal was given for the encounter.

Their first charge upon each other was rather moderate, for either party had some dread of being forced into the lake. But as reinforcements came up on either side, the encounter grew from a skirmish into a blazing battle. They rushed upon one another, as Master Laneham testifies, like rams inflamed by jealousy, with such furious encounter, that both parties were often overthrown, and the clubs and targets made a most horrible clatter. In many instances, that happened which had been dreaded by the more experienced warriors, who began the day of strife. The rails which defended the ledges of the bridge had been, perhaps on purpose, left but slightly fastened, and gave way under the pressure of those who thronged to the combat, so that the hot courage of many of the combatants received a sufficient cooling. These incidents might have occasioned more serious damage than became such an affray, for many of the champions who met with this mischance could not swim, and those who could were encumbered with their suits of leathern and of paper armour; but the case had been provided for, and there were several boats in readiness to pick up the unfortunate warriors, and convey them to the dry land, where, dripping and dejected, they comforted themselves with the hot ale and strong waters which were liberally allowed to them, without showing any desire to re-enter so desperate a conflict.

Captain Coxe alone, that paragon of Black-Letter Antiquaries, after twice experiencing, horse and man, the perilous leap from the bridge into the lake, equal to any extremity to which the favourite heroes of chivalry, whose exploits he studied in an abridged form, whether Amadis, Belianis, Bevis, or his own Guy of Warwick, had ever been subjected to—Captain Coxe, we repeat, did alone, after two such mischances, rush again into the heat of conflict, his bases and the foot-cloth of his hobby-horse dropping water, and twice reanimated by voice and example the drooping spirits of the English; so that at length their victory over the Danish invaders became, as was just and reasonable, complete and decisive. Worthy he was to be rendered immortal by the pen of Ben Jonson, who, fifty years afterwards, deemed that a masque, exhibited at Kenilworth, could be ushered in by none with so much propriety, as by the ghost of Captain Coxe, mounted upon his redoubted hobbyhorse.

These rough rural gambols may not altogether agree with the reader's preconceived idea of an entertainment presented before Elizabeth, in whose reign letters revived with such brilliancy, and whose court, governed by a female, whose sense of propriety was equal to her strength of mind, was no less distinguished for delicacy and refinement, than her councils for wisdom and fortitude. But whether from the political wish to seem interested in popular sports, or whether from a spark of old Henry's rough masculine spirit, which Elizabeth sometimes displayed, it is certain the Queen laughed heartily at the imitation, or rather the burlesque of chivalry, which was presented in the Coventry play. She called near her person the Earl of Sussex and Lord Hunsdon, partly perhaps to make amends to the former, for the long and private audiences, with which she had indulged the Earl of Leicester, by engaging him in conversation upon a pastime, which better suited his taste than those pageants that were furnished forth from the stores of antiquity. The disposition which the Queen showed to laugh and jest with her military leaders, gave the Earl of Leicester the opportunity he had been watching for withdrawing from the royal presence, which to the court around, so well had he chosen his time, had the graceful appearance of leaving his rival free access to the Queen's person, instead of availing himself of his right as her landlord, to stand perpetually betwixt others, and the light of her countenance.

Leicester's thoughts, however, had a far different object from mere courtesy; for no sooner did he see the Queen fairly engaged in conversation with Sussex and Hunsdon, behind whose back stood sir Nicholas Blount, grinning from ear to ear at each word which was spoken, than, making a sign to Tressilian, who, according to appointment, watched his motions at a little distance, he extricated himself from the press, and walking towards the Chase, made his way through the crowds of ordinary spectators, who, with open mouth, stood gazing on the battle of the English and the Danes. When he had accomplished this, which was a work of some difficulty, he shot another glance behind him to see that Tressilian had been equally successful, and as soon as he saw him also free from the crowd, he led the way to a small thicket, behind which stood a lackey, with two horses ready saddled. He flung himself on the one, and made signs to Tressilian to mount the other, who obeyed without speaking a single word.

Leicester then spurred his horse, and galloped without stopping until he reached a sequestered spot, environed by lofty oaks, about a mile's distance from the Castle, and in an opposite direction from the scene to which curiosity was drawing every spectator. He there dismounted, bound his horse to a tree, and only pronouncing the words, "Here there is no risk of interruption," laid his cloak across his saddle, and drew his sword.

Tressilian imitated his example punctually, yet could not forbear saying, as he drew his weapon, "My lord, as I have been known to many as one who does not fear death, when placed in balance with honour, methinks I may, without derogation, ask, wherefore, in the name of all that is honourable, your lordship has dared to offer me such a mark of disgrace, as places us on these terms with respect to each other?"

"If you like not such marks of my scorn," replied the Earl, "betake yourself instantly to your weapon, lest I repeat the usage you complain of."

"It shall not heed, my lord," said Tressilian. "God judge betwixt us! and your blood, if you fall, be on your own head."

He had scarce completed the sentence, when they instantly closed in combat.

But Leicester, who was a perfect master of defence among all other exterior accomplishments of the time, had seen, on the preceding night, enough of Tressilian's strength and skill, to make him fight with more caution than heretofore, and prefer a secure revenge to a hasty one. For some minutes they fought with equal skill and fortune, till, in a desperate lunge which Leicester successfully put aside, Tressilian exposed himself at disadvantage; and, in a subsequent attempt to close, the Earl forced his sword from his hand, and stretched him on the ground. With a grim smile he held the point of his rapier within two inches of the throat of his fallen adversary, and placing his foot at the same time upon his breast, bid him confess his villainous wrongs towards him, and prepare for death.

"I have no villainy nor wrong towards thee to confess," answered Tressilian, "and am better prepared for death than thou. Use thine advantage as thou wilt, and may God forgive you! I have given you no cause for this."

"No cause!" exclaimed the Earl, "no cause!—but why parley with such a slave?—Die a liar, as thou hast lived!"

He had withdrawn his arm for the purpose of striking the fatal blow, when it was suddenly seized from behind.

The Earl turned in wrath to shake off the unexpected obstacle, but was surprised to find that a strange-looking boy had hold of his sword-arm, and clung to it with such tenacity of grasp, that he could not shake him off without a considerable struggle, in the course of which Tressilian had opportunity to rise and possess himself once more of his weapon. Leicester again turned towards him with looks of unabated ferocity, and the combat would·have recommenced with still more desperation on both sides, had not the boy clung to Lord Leicester's knees, and in a shrill tone implored him to listen one moment ere he prosecuted this quarrel.

"Stand up, and let me go," said Leicester, "or, by Heaven, I will pierce thee with my rapier!—What hast thou to do to bar my way to revenge?"

"Much—much!" exclaimed the undaunted boy; "since my folly has been the cause of these bloody quarrels between you, and perchance of worse evils. O, if you would ever again enjoy the peace of an innocent mind, if you hope again to sleep in peace and unhaunted by remorse, take so much leisure as to peruse this letter, and then do as you list."

While he spoke in this eager and earnest manner, to which his singular features and voice gave a goblin-like effect, he held up to Leicester a packet, secured with a long tress of woman's hair, of a beautiful light-brown colour. Enraged as he was, nay, almost blinded with fury to see his destined revenge so strangely frustrated, the Earl of Leicester could not resist this extraordinary supplicant. He snatched the letter from his hand—changed colour as he looked on the superscription—undid, with faltering hand, the knot which secured it—glanced over the contents, and, staggering back, would have fallen, had he not rested against the trunk of a tree, where he stood for an instant, his eyes bent on the letter, and his sword-point turned to the ground, without seeming to be conscious of the presence of an antagonist, towards whom he had shown little mercy, and who might in turn have taken him at advantage. But for such revenge Tressilian was too noble-minded—he also stood still in surprise, waiting the issue of this strange fit of passion, but holding his weapon ready to defend himself in case of need, against some new and sudden attack on the part of Leicester, whom he again suspected to be under the influence of actual frenzy. The boy, indeed, he easily recognized as his old acquaintance Dickon, whose face, once seen, was scarcely to be forgotten; but how he came thither at so critical a moment, why his interference was so energetic, and, above all, how it came to produce so powerful an effect upon Leicester, were questions which he could not solve.

But the letter was of itself powerful enough to work effects yet more wonderful. It was that which the unfortunate Amy had written to her husband, in which she alleged the reasons and manner of her flight from, Cumnor-Place, informed him of her having made her way to Kenilworth to enjoy his protection, and mentioned the circumstances which had compelled her to take refuge in Tressilian's apartment, earnestly requesting he would, without delay, assign her a more suitable asylum. The letter concluded with the most earnest expressions of devoted attachment, and submission to his will in all things, and particularly respecting her situation and place of residence, conjuring him only that she might not be placed under the guardianship or restraint of Varney.

The letter dropped from Leicester's hand when he had perused it. "Take my sword," he said, "Tressilian, and pierce my heart, as I would but now have pierced yours!"

"My lord," said Tressilian, "you have done me great wrong; but something within my breast ever whispered that it was by egregious error."

"Error, indeed!" said Leicester, and handed him the letter; "I have been made to believe a man of honour a villain, and the best and purest of creatures a false profligate.—Wretched boy, why comes this letter now, and where has the bearer lingered?"

"I dare not tell you, my lord," said the boy, withdrawing, as if to keep beyond his reach;—"but here comes one who was the messenger."

Wayland at the same moment came up; and, interrogated by Leicester, hastily detailed all the circumstances of his escape with Amy,—the fatal practices which had driven her to flight,—and her anxious desire to throw herself under the instant protection of her husband,—pointing out the evidence of the domestics of Kenilworth, "who could not," he observed, "but remember her eager enquiries after the Earl of Leicester on her first arrival."

"The villains!" exclaimed Leicester; "but O, that worst of villains, Varney!—and she is even now in his power!"

"But not, I trust in God," said Tressilian, "with any commands of fatal import?"

"No, no, no!" exclaimed the Earl, hastily.—"I said something in madness—but it was recalled, fully recalled, by a hasty messenger; and she is now—she must now be safe."

"Yes," said Tressilian, "she *must* be safe, and I *must* be assured of her safety. My own quarrel with you is ended, my lord; but there is another to begin with the seducer of Amy Robsart, who has screened his guilt under the cloak of the infamous Varney."

"The *seducer* of Amy!" replied Leicester, with a voice like thunder; "say her husband!—her misguided, blinded, most unworthy husband!—She is as surely Countess of Leicester as I am belted Earl. Nor can you, sir, point out that manner of justice which I will not render her at my own free will. I need scarce say, I fear not your compulsion."

The generous nature of Tressilian was instantly turned from consideration of any thing personal to himself, and centred at once upon Amy's welfare. He had by no means undoubting confidence in the fluctuating resolutions of Leicester, whose mind seemed to him agitated beyond the government of calm reason; neither did he, not withstanding the assurances he had received, think Amy safe in the hands of his dependents. "My lord," he said, calmly, "I mean you no offence, and am far from seeking a quarrel. But my duty to Sir Hugh Robsart compels me to carry this matter instantly to the Queen, that the Countess's rank may be acknowledged in her person."

"You shall not need, sir," replied the Earl, haughtily; "do not dare to interfere. No voice but Dudley's shall proclaim Dudley's infamy—To Elizabeth herself will I tell it, and then for Cumnor-Place with the speed of life and death!"

So saying, he unbound his horse from the tree, threw himself into the saddle, and rode at full gallop towards the Castle.

"Take me before you, Master Tressilian," said the boy, seeing Tressilian mount in the same haste—"my tale is not all told out, and I need your protection."

Tressilian complied, and followed the Earl, though at a less furious rate. By the way the boy confessed, with much contrition, that in resentment at Wayland's evading all his enquiries concerning the lady, after Dickon conceived he had in various ways merited his confidence, he had purloined from him, in revenge, the letter with which Amy had intrusted him for the Earl of Leicester. His purpose was to have restored it to him that evening, as he reckoned himself sure of meeting with him, in consequence of Wayland's having to perform the part of Arion, in the pageant. He was indeed something alarmed when he saw to whom the letter was addressed; but he argued that, as Leicester did not return to Kenilworth until that evening, it would be again in the possession of the proper messenger, as soon as, in the nature of things, it could possibly be delivered. But Wayland came not to the pageant, having been in the interim expelled by Lambourne from the Castle, and the boy, not being able to find him, or to get speech of Tressilian, and finding himself in possession of a letter addressed to no less a person than the Earl of Leicester, became much afraid of the consequences of his frolic. The caution, and indeed the alarm, which Wayland had expressed respecting Varney and Lambourne, led him to judge, that the letter must be designed for the Earl's own hand, and that he might prejudice the lady, by giving it to any of the domestics. He made an attempt or two to obtain an audience of Leicester, but the singularity of his features, and the meanness of his appearance, occasioned his being always repulsed by the insolent menials whom he applied to for that purpose. Once, indeed, he had nearly succeeded, when, in prowling about, he found in the grotto the casket which he knew to belong to the unlucky Countess, having seen it on her journey; for nothing escaped his prying eye. Having strove in vain to restore it either to Tressilian or the Countess, he put it into the hands, as we have seen, of Leicester himself, but unfortunately he did not recognise him in his disguise.

At length, the boy thought he was on the point of succeeding, when the Earl came down to the lower part of the hall but just as he was about to accost him, he was prevented by Tressilian. As sharp in ear as in wit, the boy heard the appointment settled betwixt them, to take place in the Pleasance, and resolved to add a third to the party, in hopes that, either in coming or in returning, he might find an opportunity of delivering the letter to Leicester; for strange stories began to flit among the domestics, which alarmed him for the lady's safety. Accident, however, detained Dickon a little behind the Earl, and, as he reached the arcade, he saw them engaged in combat; in consequence of which he hastened to alarm the guard, having little doubt, that what bloodshed took place betwixt them, might arise out of his own frolic. Continuing to lurk in the portico, he heard the second appointment, which Leicester, at parting, assigned to Tressilian, and was keeping them in view during the encounter of the Coventry men, when, to his surprise, he recognised Wayland in the crowd, much disguised, indeed, but not sufficiently so to escape the prying glance of his old comrade. They drew aside out of the crowd to explain their situation to each other. The boy confessed to Wayland what we have above told, and the artist, in return, informed him, that his deep anxiety for the fate of the unfortunate lady had brought him back to the neighbourhood of the Castle, upon his learning that morning at a village about ten miles distant, that Varney and Lambourne, whose violence he dreaded, had both left Kenilworth over-night.

While they spoke, they saw Leicester and Tressilian separate themselves from the crowd, dogged them until they mounted their horses, when the boy, whose speed of foot has been before mentioned, though he could not possibly keep us with them, yet arrived, as we have seen, soon enough to save Tressilian's life. The boy had just finished his tale when they reached the Gallery-tower.

CHAPTER XL

High o'er the eastern steep the sun is beaming,
And darkness flies with her deceitful shadows;—
So truth prevails o'er falsehood.

Old Play.

As Tressilian rode along the bridge lately the scene of so much riotous sport, he could not but observe that men's countenances had singularly changed during the space of his brief absence. The mock fight was over, but the men, still habited in their masquing suits, stood together in groups, like the inhabitants of a city who have been just startled by some strange and alarming crew.

When he reached the base-court, appearances were the same—domestics, retainers, and under officers, stood together and whispered, bending their eyes towards the windows of the great hall, with looks which seemed at once alarmed and mysterious.

Sir Nicholas Blount was the first person of his own particular acquaintance Tressilian saw, who left him no time to make enquiries, but greeted him with, "God help thy heart, Tressilian, thou art fitter for a

clown than a courtier—thou canst not attend, as becomes one who follows her Majesty.—Here you are called for, wished for, waited for—no
man but you will serve the turn; and hither you come with a misbegotten brat on thy horse's neck, as if thou wert dry nurse to some suckling
devil, and wert just returned from airing."

"Why, what is the matter?" said Tressilian, letting go the boy, who
sprung to ground like a feather, and himself dismounting at the same
time.

"Why, no one knows the matter," replied Blount; "I cannot smell it
out myself, though I have a nose like other courtiers. Only, my Lord of
Leicester has galloped along the bridge, as if he would have rode over all
in his passage, demanded an audience of the Queen, and is closeted even
now with her, and Burleigh and Walsingham—and you are called for—
but whether the matter be treason or worse, no one knows."

"He speaks true, by Heaven!" said Raleigh, who that instant appeared; "you must immediately to the Queen's presence."

"Be not rash, Raleigh," said Blount, "remember his boots—For
Heaven's sake, go to my chamber, dear Tressilian, and don my new
bloom-coloured silken hose—I have worn them but twice."

"Pshaw!" answered Tressilian; "do thou take care of this boy, Blount;
be kind to him, and look he escapes you not—much depends on him."

So saying, he followed Raleigh hastily, leaving honest Blount with
the bridle of his horse in one hand, and the boy in the other. Blount gave
a long look after him.

"Nobody," he said, "calls me to these mysteries,—and he leaves me
here to play horse-keeper and child-keeper at once. I could excuse the
one, for I love a good horse naturally; but to be plagued with a bratchet
whelp.—Whence come ye, my fair-favoured little gossip?"

"From the Fens," answered the boy.

"And what didst thou learn there, forward imp?"

"To catch gulls, with their webbed feet and yellow stockings," said
the boy.

"Umph!" said Blount, looking down on his own immense roses,—
"Nay, then the devil take him asks thee more questions."

Meantime Tressilian traversed the full length of the great hall, in
which the astonished courtiers formed various groups, and were whispering mysteriously together, while all kept their eyes fixed on the door,
which led from the upper end of the hall into the Queen's withdrawing
apartment. Raleigh pointed to the door—Tressilian knocked, and was
instantly admitted. Many a neck was stretched to gain a view into the
interior of the apartment; but the tapestry which covered the door on
the inside was dropped too suddenly to admit the slightest gratification
of curiosity.

Upon entrance, Tressilian found himself, not without a strong palpitation of heart, in the presence of Elizabeth, who was walking to and fro
in a violent agitation. which she seemed to scorn to conceal, while two or

three of her most sage and confidential counsellors exchanged anxious looks with each other, but delayed speaking till her wrath had abated. Before the empty chair of state in which she had been seated, and which was half pushed aside by the violence with which she had started from it, knelt Leicester, his arms crossed, and his brows bent on the ground, still and motionless as the effigies upon a sepulchre. Beside him stood the Lord Shrewsbury, then Earl Marshal of England, holding his baton of office—the Earl's sword was unbuckled, and lay before him on the floor.

"Ho, sir!" said the Queen, coming close up to Tressilian, and stamping on the floor with the action and manner of Henry himself; "*you* knew of this fair work—*you* are an accomplice in this deception which has been practised on us—*you* have been a main cause of our doing injustice?" Tressilian dropped on his knees before the Queen, his good sense showing him the risk of attempting any defence at that moment of irritation. "Art dumb, sirrah!" she continued; "thou know'st of this affair—dost thou not?"

"Not, gracious madam, that this poor lady was Countess of Leicester."

"Nor shall any one know her for such," said Elizabeth. "Death of my life! Countess of Leicester!—I say Dame Amy Dudley—and well if she have not cause to write herself widow of the traitor Robert Dudley."

"Madam," said Leicester, "do with me what it may be your will to do—but work no injury on this gentleman—he hath in no way deserved it."

"And will he be the better for thy intercession," said the Queen, leaving Tressilian, who slowly arose, and rushing to Leicester, who continued kneeling,—"the better for thy intercession, thou doubly false—thou doubly forsworn?—of thy intercession, whose villainy hath made me ridiculous to my subjects, and odious to myself?—I could tear out mine eyes for their blindness!"

Burleigh here ventured to interpose.

"Madam," he said, "remember that you are a Queen—Queen of England—mother of your people. Give not way to this wild storm of passion."

Elizabeth turned round to him, while a tear actually twinkled in her proud and angry eye. "Burleigh," she said, "thou art a statesman—thou dost not, thou canst not, comprehend half the scorn—half the misery, that man has poured on me!"

With the utmost caution—with the deepest reverence, Burleigh took her hand at the moment he saw her heart was at the fullest, and led her aside to an oriel window, apart from the others.

"Madam," he said, "I am a statesman, but I am also a man—a man already grown old in your councils, who have not and cannot have a wish on earth but your glory and happiness—I pray you to be composed."

"Ah, Burleigh," said Elizabeth, "thou little knowest—" here her tears fell over her cheeks in despite of her.

"I do—I do know, my honoured sovereign. O beware that you lead not others to guess that which they know not!"

"Ha!" said Elizabeth, pausing as if a new train of thought had suddenly shot across her brain. "Burleigh, thou art right—thou art right—anything but disgrace—anything but a confession of weakness—anything rather than seem the cheated—slighted—'Sdeath! to think on it is distraction!"

"Be but yourself, my Queen," said Burleigh; "and soar far above a weakness which no Englishman will ever believe his Elizabeth could have entertained, unless the violence of her disappointment carries a sad conviction to his bosom."

"What weakness, my lord?" said Elizabeth, haughtily; "would you too insinuate that the favour in which I held yonder proud traitor, derived its source from aught"—But here she could no longer sustain the proud tone which she had assumed, and again softened as she said, "But why should I strive to deceive even thee, my good and wise servant!"

Burleigh stooped to kiss her hand with affection, and—rare in the annals of courts—a tear of true sympathy dropped from the eye of the minister on the hand of his Sovereign.

It is probable that the consciousness of possessing this sympathy, aided Elizabeth in supporting her mortification, and suppressing her extreme resentment; but she was still more moved by fear that her passion should betray to the public the affront and the disappointment, which, alike as a woman and a Queen, she was so anxious to conceal. She turned from Burleigh, and sternly paced the hall till her features had recovered their usual dignity, and her mien its wonted stateliness of regular motion.

"Our Sovereign is her noble self once more," whispered Burleigh to Walsingham; "mark what she does, and take heed you thwart her not."

She then approached Leicester, and said, with calmness, "My Lord Shrewsbury, we discharge you of your prisoner.—My Lord of Leicester, rise and take up your sword—a quarter of an hour's restraint, under the custody of our Marshal, my lord, is, we think, no high penance for months of falsehood practised upon us. We will now hear the progress of this affair."—She then seated herself in her chair, and said, "You, Tressilian, step forward, and say what you know."

Tressilian told his story generously, suppressing as much as he could what affected Leicester, and saying nothing of their having twice actually fought together. It is very probable that, in doing so, he did the Earl good service; for had the Queen at that instant found any thing on account of which she might vent her wrath upon him, without laying open sentiments of which she was ashamed, it might have fared hard with him. She paused when Tressilian had finished his tale.

"We will take that Wayland," she said, "into our own service, and place the boy in our Secretary-office for instruction, that he may in future use discretion towards letters. For you, Tressilian, you did wrong in not communicating the whole truth to us, and your promise not to do so was both imprudent and undutiful. Yet, having given your word to this unhappy lady, it was the part of a man and a gentleman to keep it; and on the whole, we esteem you for the character you have sustained in this matter.—My Lord of Leicester, it is now your turn to tell us the truth, an exercise to which you seem of late to have been too much a stranger."

Accordingly, she extorted, by successive questions, the whole history of his first acquaintance with Amy Robsart—their marriage—his jealousy —the causes on which it was founded, and many particulars besides. Leicester's confession, for such it might be called, was wrenched from him piecemeal, yet was upon the whole accurate, excepting that he totally omitted to mention that he had, by implication, or otherwise, assented to Varney's designs upon the life of his Countess. Yet the consciousness of this was what at that moment lay nearest to his heart; and although he trusted in great measure to the very positive counter-orders which he had sent by Lambourne, it was his purpose to set out for Cumnor-Place, in person, as soon as he should be dismissed from the presence of the queen, who, he concluded, would presently leave Kenilworth.

But the Earl reckoned without his host. It is true, his presence and his communications were gall and wormwood to his once partial mistress. But, barred from every other and more direct mode of revenge, the Queen perceived that she gave her false suitor torture by these enquiries, and dwelt on them for that reason, no more regarding the pain which she herself experienced, than the savage cares for the searing of his own hands by grasping the hot pincers with which he tears the flesh of his captive enemy.

At length, however, the haughty lord, like a deer that turns to bay, gave intimation that his patience was failing. "Madam," he said, "I have been much to blame—more than even your just resentment has expressed. Yet, madam, let me say, that my guilt, if it be unpardonable, was not unprovoked; and that, if beauty and condescending dignity could seduce the frail heart of a human being, I might plead both, as the causes of my concealing this secret from your Majesty."

The Queen was so much struck by this reply, which Leicester took care should be heard by no one but herself, that she was for the moment silenced, and the Earl had the temerity to pursue his advantage. "Your Grace, who has pardoned so much, will excuse my throwing myself on your royal mercy for those expressions, which were yester-morning ac-counted but a light offence."

The Queen fixed her eyes on him while she replied, "Now, by Heaven, my lord, thy effrontery passes the bounds of belief, as well as patience! But it shall avail thee nothing.—What, ho! my lords, come all and hear the news—My Lord of Leicester's stolen marriage has cost me a husband, and England a King. His lordship is patriarchal in his tastes—one wife at a time was insufficient, and he designed us the honour of his left hand. Now, is not this too insolent,—that I could not grace him with a few marks of court-favour, but he must presume to think my hand and crown at his disposal?—You, however, think better of me; and I can pity this ambitious man, as I could a child, whose bubble of soap has burst between his hands. We go to the presence-chamber—My Lord of Leicester, we command your close attendance on us."

All was eager expectation in the hall, and what was the universal astonishment, when the Queen said to those next her, "The revels of Kenilworth are not yet exhausted, my lords and ladies—we are to solemnize the noble owner's marriage."

There was a universal expression of surprise.

"It is true, on our royal word," said the Queen; "he hath kept this a secret even from us, that he might surprise us with it at this very place and time. I see you are dying of curiosity to know the happy bride— It is Amy Robsart, the same who, to make up the May-game yesterday, figured in the pageant as the wife of his servant Varney."

"For God's sake, madam," said the Earl, approaching her with a mixture of humility, vexation, and shame in his countenance, and speaking so low as to be heard by no one else, "take my head, as you threatened in your anger, and spare me these taunts! Urge not a falling man—tread not on a crushed worm."

"A worm, my lord?" said the Queen, in the same tone; "nay, a snake is the nobler reptile, and the more exact similitude—the frozen snake you wot of, which was warmed in a certain bosom——"

"For your own sake—for mine, madam," said the Earl—"while there is yet some reason left in me——"

"Speak aloud, my lord," said Elizabeth, "and at farther distance, so please you—your breath thaws our ruff. What have you to ask of us?"

"Permission," said the unfortunate Earl, humbly, "to travel to Cumnor-Place."

"To fetch home your bride belike?—Why, ay,—that is but right—for, as we have heard, she is indifferently cared for there. But, my lord, you go not in person—we have counted upon passing certain days in this castle of Kenilworth, and it were slight courtesy to leave us without a landlord during our residence here. Under your favour, we cannot think to incur such disgrace in the eyes of our subjects. Tressilian shall go to Cumnor-Place instead of you, and with him some gentleman who hath been sworn of our chamber, lest my Lord of Leicester should be again jealous of his old rival.—Whom wouldst thou have to be in commission with thee, Tressilian?"

Tressilian, with humble deference, suggested the name of Raleigh.

"Why, ay," said the Queen; "so God ha' me, thou hast made a good choice. He is a young knight besides, and to deliver a lady from prison is an appropriate first adventure.—Cumnor-Place is little better than a prison, you are to know, my lord and ladies. Besides, there are certain faitours there whom we would willingly have in fast keeping. You will furnish them, Master Secretary, with the warrant necessary to secure the bodies of Richard Varney and the foreign Alasco, dead or alive. Take a sufficient force with you, gentlemen—bring the lady here in all honour—lose no time, and God be with you!"

They bowed, and left the presence.

Who shall describe how the rest of that day was spent at Kenilworth? The Queen, who seemed to have remained there for the sole purpose of mortifying and taunting the Earl of Leicester, showed herself as skilful in that female art of vengeance, as she was in the science of wisely governing her people. The train of state soon caught the signal, and, as he walked among his own splendid preparations, the Lord of Kenilworth, in his own Castle, already experienced the lot of a disgraced courtier, in the slight regard and cold manners of alienated friends, and the ill-concealed triumph of avowed and open enemies. Sussex, from his natural military frankness of disposition, Burleigh and Walsingham, from their penetrating and prospective sagacity, and some of the ladies, from the compassion of their sex, were the only persons in the crowded court who retained towards him the countenance they had borne in the morning.

So much had Leicester been accustomed to consider court-favours as the principal object of his life, that all other sensations were, for the time, lost in the agony which his haughty spirit felt at the succession of petty insults and studied neglects to which he had been subjected; but when he retired to his own chamber for the night, that long fair tress of hair which had once secured Amy's letter, fell under his observation, and with the influence of a counter-charm, awakened his heart to nobler and more natural feelings. He kissed it a thousand times; and while he recollected that he had it always in his power to shun the mortifications which he had that day undergone, by retiring into a dignified and even princelike seclusion, with the beautiful and beloved partner of his future life, he felt that he could rise above the revenge which Elizabeth had condescended to take.

Accordingly, on the following day, the whole conduct of the Earl displayed so much dignified equanimity; he seemed so solicitous about the accommodations and amusements of his guests, yet so indifferent to their personal demeanour towards him; so respectfully distant to the Queen, yet so patient of her harassing displeasure, that Elizabeth changed her manner to him, and, though cold and distant, ceased to offer him any direct affront. She intimated also with some sharpness to others around her, who thought they were consulting her pleasure in showing a neglectful conduct to the Earl, that while they remained at Kenilworth, they ought to show the civility due from guests to the Lord of the Castle. In short, matters were so far changed in twenty-four hours, that some of the more experienced and sagacious courtiers foresaw a strong possibility of Leicester's restoration to favour, and regulated their demeanour towards him, as those who might one day claim merit for not having deserted him in adversity. It is time, however, to leave these intrigues, and follow Tressilian and Raleigh on their journey.

The troop consisted of six persons; for, besides Wayland, they had in company a royal pursuivant and two stout serving-men. All were well armed, and travelled as fast as it was possible with justice to their horses, which had a long journey before them. They endeavoured to procure some tidings as they rode along of Varney and his party, but could hear none, as they had travelled in the dark. At a small village about twelve miles from Kenilworth, where they gave some refreshment to their horses, a poor clergyman, the curate of the place, came out of a small cottage, and entreated any of the company who might know aught of surgery, to look in for an instant on a dying man.

The empiric Wayland undertook to do his best, and as the curate conducted him to the spot, he learned that the man had been found on the highroad, about a mile from the village, by labourers, as they were going to their work on the preceding morning, and the curate had given him shelter in his house. He had received a gun-shot wound which seemed to be obviously mortal, but whether in a brawl or from robbers they could not learn, as he was in a fever and spoke nothing connectedly. Wayland entered the dark and lowly apartment, and no sooner had the curate drawn aside the curtain, than he knew in the distorted features of the patient the countenance of Michael Lambourne. Under pretence of seeking something which he wanted, Wayland hastily apprized his fellow-travellers of this extraordinary circumstance; and both Tressilian and Raleigh, full of boding apprehensions, hastened to the curate's house to see the dying man.

The wretch was by this time in the agonies of death, from which a much better surgeon than Wayland could not have rescued him, for the bullet had passed clear through his body. He was sensible, however, at least in part, for he knew Tressilian, and made signs that he wished him to stoop over his bed. Tressilian did so, and after some inarticulate murmurs, in which the names of Varney and Lady Leicester were alone distinguishable, Lambourne bade him "make haste, or he would come too late." It was in vain Tressilian urged the patient for further information; he seemed to become in some degree delirious, and when he again made a signal to attract Tressilian's attention, it was only for the purpose of desiring him to inform his uncle, Giles Gosling of the Black Bear, "that he had died without his shoes after all." A convulsion verified his words a few minutes after, and the travellers derived nothing from having met with him, save the obscure fears concerning the fate of the Countess, which his dying words were calculated to convey, and which induced them to urge their journey with the utmost speed, pressing horses in the Queen's name, when those which they rode became unfit for service.

CHAPTER XLI

The death-bell thrice was heard to ring,
   An aerial voice was heard to call;
And thrice the raven flapp'd its wing,
   Around the towers of Cumnor-Hall.
                                   Mickle.

WE are now to return to that part of our story where we intimated that
Varney, possessed of the authority of the Earl of Leicester, and of the
Queen's permission to the same effect, hastened to secure himself against
discovery of his perfidy, by removing the Countess from Kenilworth
Castle. He had proposed to set forth early in the morning, but reflecting
that the Earl might relent in the interim, and seek another interview
with the Countess, he resolved to prevent, by immediate departure, all
chance of what would probably have ended in his detection and ruin. For
this purpose he called for Lambourne, and was exceedingly incensed to
find that his trusty attendant was abroad on some ramble in the neighbouring village, or elsewhere. As his return was expected Sir Richard
commanded that he should prepare himself for attending him on an
immediate journey, and follow him in case he returned after his departure.

In the meanwhile, Varney used the ministry of a servant called Robin
Tider, one to whom the mysteries of Cumnor-Place were already in some
degree known, as he had been there more than once in attendance on the
Earl. To this man, whose character resembled that of Lambourne, though
he was neither quite so prompt nor altogether so profligate, Varney gave
command to have three horses saddled, and to prepare a horse-litter, and
have them in readiness at the postern-gate. The natural enough excuse of
his lady's insanity, which was now universally believed, accounted for
the secrecy with which she was to be removed from the Castle, and he
reckoned on the same apology in case the unfortunate Amy's resistance
or screams should render such necessary. The agency of Anthony Foster
was indispensable, and that Varney now went to secure.

This person, naturally of a sour unsocial disposition, and somewhat
tired, besides, with his journey from Cumnor to Warwickshire, in order
to bring the news of the Countess's escape, had early extricated himself
from the crowd of wassailers, and betaken himself to his chamber, where
he lay asleep, when Varney, completely equipped for travelling, and with
a dark lantern in his hand, entered his apartment. He paused an instant
to listen to what his associate was murmuring in his sleep, and could
plainly distinguish the words, "*Ave Maria—ora pro nobis*—No—it runs
not so—deliver us from evil—Ay, so it goes."

"Praying in his sleep," said Varney; "and confounding his old and
new devotions—He must have more need of prayer ere I am done with
him.—What ho! holy man—most blessed penitent!—Awake—awake!
The devil has not discharged you from service yet."

As Varney at the same time shook the sleeper by the arm, it changed the current of his ideas, and he roared out, "Thieves!—thieves! I will die in defence of my gold—my hard-won gold, that has cost me so dear. —Where is Janet?—Is Janet safe?"

"Safe enough, thou bellowing fool!" said Varney; "art thou not ashamed of thy clamour?"

Foster by this time was broad awake, and, sitting up in his bed, asked Varney the meaning of so untimely a visit. "It augurs nothing good," he added.

"A false prophecy, most sainted Anthony," returned Varney; "it augurs that the hour is come for converting thy leasehold into copyhold —What sayst thou to that?"

"Had'st thou told me this in broad day," said Foster, "I had rejoiced —but at this dead hour, and by this dim light, and looking on thy pale face, which is a ghastly contradiction to thy light words, I cannot but rather think of the work that is to be done, than the guerdon to be gained by it."

"Why, thou fool, it is but to escort thy charge back to Cumnor-Place."

"Is that indeed all?" said Foster; "thou look'st deadly pale, and thou art not moved by trifles—is that indeed all?"

"Ay, that—and maybe a trifle more," answered Varney.

"Ah, that trifle more!" said Foster; "still thou look'st paler and paler."

"Heed not my countenance," said Varney, "you see it by this wretched light. Up and be doing, man—Think of Cumnor-Place—thine own proper copyhold—Why, thou mayst found a weekly lectureship, besides endow-ing Janet like a baron's daughter.—Seventy pounds and odd."

"Seventy-nine pounds, five shillings and fivepence half-penny, besides the value of the wood," said Foster; "and I am to have it all as copy-hold?"

"All, man—squirrels and all—no gipsy shall cut the value of a broom —no boy so much as take a bird's nest, without paying thee a quittance. —Ay, that is right—don thy matters as fast as possible—horses and every thing are ready, all save that accursed villain Lambourne, who is out on some infernal gambol."

"Ay, Sir Richard," said Foster, "you would take no advice. I ever told you that drunken profligate would fail you at need. Now I could have helped you to a sober young man."

"What, some slow-spoken, long-breathed brother of the congregation? —Why, we shall have use for such also, man—Heaven be praised, we shall lack labourers of every kind.—Ay, that is right—forget not your pistols—Come now, and let us away."

"Whither?" said Anthony.

"To my lady's chamber—and, mind—she *must* along with us. Thou art not a fellow to be startled by a shriek?"

"Not if Scripture-reason can be rendered for it; and it is written, 'wives, obey your husbands.' But will my lord's commands bear us out if we use violence?"

"Tush, man! here is his signet," answered Varney; and, having thus silenced the objections of his associate, they went together to Lord Hunsdon's apartments, and, acquainting the sentinel with their purpose, as a matter sanctioned by the Queen and the Earl of Leicester, they entered the chamber of the unfortunate Countess.

The horror of Amy may be conceived, when, starting from a broken slumber, she saw at her bedside Varney, the man on earth she most feared and hated. It was even a consolation to see that he was not alone, though she had so much reason to dread his sullen companion.

"Madam," said Varney, "there is no time for ceremony. My Lord of Leicester, having fully considered the exigencies of the time, sends you his orders immediately to accompany us on our return to Cumnor-Place. See, here is his signet, in token of his instant and pressing commands."

"It is false!" said the Countess; "thou hast stolen the warrant,—thou, who art capable of every villainy, from the blackest to the basest!"

"It is TRUE, madam," replied Varney; "so true, that if you do not instantly arise, and prepare to attend us, we must compel you to obey our orders."

"Compel!—thou darest not put it to that issue, base as thou art," exclaimed the unhappy Countess.

"That remains to be proved, madam," said Varney, who had determined on intimidation as the only means of subduing her high spirit; "if you put me to it, you will find me a rough groom of the chamber."

It was at this threat that Amy screamed so fearfully, that had it not been for the received opinion of her insanity, she would quickly have had Lord Hunsdon and others to her aid. Perceiving, however, that her cries were vain, she appealed to Foster in the most affecting terms, conjuring him, as his daughter Janet's honour and purity was dear to him, not to permit her to be treated with unwomanly violence.

"Why, madam, wives must obey their husbands,—there's Scripture warrant for it," said Foster; "and if you will dress yourself, and come with us patiently, there's no one shall lay finger on you while I can draw a pistol-trigger."

Seeing no help arrive, and comforted even by the dogged language of Foster, the Countess promised to arise and dress herself, if they would agree to retire from the room. Varney at the same time assured her of all safety and honour while in their hands, and promised, that he himself would not approach her, since his presence was so displeasing. Her husband, he added, would be at Cumnor-Place within twenty-four hours after they had reached it.

Somewhat comforted by this assurance, upon which, however, she saw little reason to rely, the unhappy Amy made her toilette by the assistance of the lantern, which they left with her when they quitted the apartment.

Weeping, trembling, and praying, the unfortunate lady dressed herself,—with sensations how different from the days in which she was wont to decorate herself in all the pride of conscious beauty! She endeavoured to delay the completing her dress as long as she could, until, terrified by the impatience of Varney, she was obliged to declare herself ready to attend them.

When they were about to move, the Countess clung to Foster with such an appearance of terror at Varney's approach, that the latter protested to her, with a deep oath, that he had no intention whatever of even coming near her. "If you do but consent to execute your husband's will in quietness, you shall," he said, "see but little of me. I will leave you undisturbed to the care of the usher whom your good taste prefers."

"My husband's will!" she exclaimed. "But it is the will of God, and let that be sufficient to me.—I will go with Master Foster as unresistingly as ever did a literal sacrifice. He is a father at least; and will have decency, if not humanity. For thee, Varney, were it my latest word, thou art an equal stranger to both."

Varney replied only, she was at liberty to choose, and walked some paces before them to show the way; while, half leaning on Foster, and half carried by him, the Countess was transported from Saintlowe's Tower to the postern-gate, where Tider waited with the litter and horses.

The Countess was placed in the former without resistance. She saw with some satisfaction, that while Foster and Tider rode close by the litter, which the latter conducted, the dreaded Varney lingered behind, and was soon lost in darkness. A little while she strove, as the road winded round the verge of the lake, to keep sight of those stately towers which called her husband lord, and which still, in some places, sparkled with lights, where wassailers were yet revelling. But when the direction of the road rendered this no longer possible, she drew back her head, and, sinking down in the litter, recommended herself to the care of Providence.

Besides the desire of inducing the Countess to proceed quietly on her journey, Varney had it also in view to have an interview with Lambourne, by whom he every moment expected to be joined, without the presence of any witnesses. He knew the character of this man, prompt, bloody, resolute, and greedy, and judged him the most fit agent he could employ in his further designs. But ten miles of their journey had been measured ere he heard the hasty clatter of horse's hoofs behind him, and was overtaken by Michael Lambourne.

Fretted as he was with his absence, Varney received his profligate servant with a rebuke of unusual bitterness. "Drunken villain," he said, "thy idleness and debauched folly will stretch a halter ere it be long; and, for me, I care not how soon!"

This style of objurgation, Lambourne, who was elated to an unusual degree, not only by an extraordinary cup of wine, but by the sort of confidential interview he had just had with the Earl, and the secret of which he had made himself master, did not receive with his wonted humility. "He would take no insolence of language," he said, "from the best knight that ever wore spurs. Lord Leicester had detained him on some business of import, and that was enough for Varney, who was but a servant like himself."

Varney was not a little surprised at his unusual tone of insolence; but, ascribing it to liquor, suffered it to pass as if unnoticed, and then began to tamper with Lambourne, touching his willingness to aid in removing out of the Earl of Leicester's way an obstacle to a rise, which would put it in his power to reward his trusty followers to their utmost wish. And upon Michael Lambourne's seeming ignorant what was meant, he plainly indicated "the litter-load, yonder," as the impediment which he desired should be removed.

"Look you, Sir Richard, and so forth," said Michael, "some are wiser than some, that is one thing, and some are worse than some, that's another. I know my lord's mind on this matter better than thou, for he hath trusted me fully in the matter. Here are his mandates, and his last words were, Michael Lambourne—for his lordship speaks to me as a gentleman of the sword, and useth not the words drunken villain, or such like phrases, of those who know not how to bear new dignities,— Varney, says he, must pay the utmost respect to my Countess—I trust to you for looking to it, Lambourne, says his lordship, and you must bring back my signet from him peremptorily."

"Ay," replied Varney, "said he so, indeed? You know all, then?"

"All—all—and you were as wise to make a friend of me while the weather is fair betwixt us."

"And was there no one present," said Varney, "when my lord so spoke?"

"Not a breathing creature," replied Lambourne. "Think you my lord would trust any one with such matters, save an approved man of action like myself?"

"Most true," said Varney; and, making a pause, he looked forward on the moonlight road. They were traversing a wide and open heath. The litter being at least a mile before them, was both out of sight and hearing. He looked behind, and there was an expanse, lighted by the moonbeams, without one human being in sight. He resumed his speech with Lambourne: "And will you turn upon your master, who has introduced you to this career of courtlike favour—whose apprentice you have been, Michael—who has taught you the depths and shallows of court intrigue?"

"Michael not me!" said Lambourne; "I have a name will brook a *master* before it as well as another; and as to the rest, if I have been an apprentice, my indenture is out, and I am resolute to set up for myself."

"Take thy quittance first, thou fool!" said Varney; and with a pistol, which he had for some time held in his hand, shot Lambourne through the body.

The wretch fell from his horse, without a single groan; and Varney, dismounting, rifled his pockets, turning out the lining, that it might appear he had fallen by robbers. He secured the Earl's packet, which was his chief object, but he also took Lambourne's purse, containing some gold pieces, the relics of what his debauchery had left him, and, from a singular combination of feelings, carried it in his hand only the length of a small river, which crossed the road, into which he threw it as far as he could fling. Such are the strange remnants of conscience, which remain after she seems totally subdued, that this cruel and remorseless man would have felt himself degraded had he pocketed the few pieces belonging to the wretch whom he had thus ruthlessly slain.

The murderer reloaded his pistol, after cleansing the lock and barrel from the appearances of late explosion, and rode calmly after the litter, satisfying himself that he had so adroitly removed a troublesome witness to many of his intrigues, and the bearer of mandates which he had no intentions to obey, and which, therefore, he was desirous it should be thought had never reached his hand.

The remainder of the journey was made with a degree of speed, which showed the little care they had for the health of the unhappy Countess. They paused only at places where all was under their command, and where the tale they were prepared to tell of the insane Lady Varney would have obtained ready credit, had she made an attempt to appeal to the compassion of the few persons admitted to see her. But Amy saw no chance of obtaining a hearing from any to whom she had an opportunity of addressing herself, and, besides, was too terrified of the presence of Varney, to violate the implied condition, under which she was to travel free from his company. The authority of Varney, often so used, during the Earl's private journeys to Cumnor, readily procured relays of horses where wanted, so that they approached Cumnor-Place upon the night after they left Kenilworth.

At this period of the journey, Varney came up to the rear of the litter, as he had done before repeatedly during their progress, and asked, "What does she?"

"She sleeps," said Foster; "I would we were home—her strength is exhausted."

"Rest will restore her," answered Varney. "She shall soon sleep sound and long—we must consider how to lodge her in safety."

"In her own apartments, to be sure," said Foster. "I have sent Janet to her aunt's, with a proper rebuke, and the old women are truth itself —for they hate this lady cordially."

"We will not trust them, however, friend Anthony," said Varney; "we must secure her in that stronghold where you keep your gold."

"My gold!" said Anthony, much alarmed; "why, what gold have I? —God help me, I have no gold—I would I had."

"Now, marry hang thee, thou stupid brute—who thinks of or cares for, thy gold?—If I did, could I not find an hundred better ways to come at it?—In one word, thy bedchamber, which thou hast fenced so curiously, must be her place of seclusion; and thou, thou hind, shalt press her pillows of down.—I dare to say the Earl will never ask after the rich furniture of these four rooms."

This last consideration rendered Foster tractable, he only asked permission to ride before, to make matters ready, and, spurring his horse, he posted before the litter, while Varney falling about threescore paces behind it, remained only attended by Tider.

When they had arrived at Cumnor-Place, the Countess asked eagerly for Janet, and showed much alarm when informed that she was no longer to have the attendance of that amiable girl.

"My daughter is dear to me, madam," said Foster, gruffly; "and I desire not that she should get the court-tricks of lying and 'scaping—somewhat too much of that has she learned already, an it please your ladyship."

The Countess, much fatigued and greatly terrified by the circumstances of her journey, made no answer to this insolence, but mildly expressed a wish to retire to her chamber.

"Ay, ay," muttered Foster, " 'tis but reasonable; but, under favour, you go not to your gewgaw toyhouse yonder—you will sleep to-night in better security."

"I would it were in my grave," said the Countess; "but that mortal feelings shiver at the idea of soul and body parting."

"You, I guess, have no chance to shiver at that," replied Foster. "My lord comes hither to-morrow, and doubtless you will make your own ways good with him."

"But does he come hither?—does he indeed, good Foster?"

"O ay, good Foster!" replied the other. "But what Foster shall I be to-morrow, when you speak of me to my lord—though all I have done was to obey his own orders?"

"You shall be my protector—a rough one indeed—but still a protector," answered the Countess. "O, that Janet were but here!"

"She is better where she is," answered Foster—"one of you is enough to perplex a plain head—but will you taste any refreshment?"

"O no, no—my chamber—my chamber. I trust," she said, apprehensively, "I may secure it on the inside?"

"With all my heart," answered Foster, "so I may secure it on the outside"; and taking a light, he led the way to a part of the building where Amy had never been, and conducted her up a stair of great height, preceded by one of the old women with a lamp. At the head of the stair, which seemed of almost immeasurable height, they crossed a short wooden gallery, formed of black oak, and very narrow, at the farther end of which was a strong oaken door, which opened and admitted them into the miser's apartment, homely in its accommodations in the very last degree, and, except in name, little different from a prison-room.

Foster stopped at the door, and gave the lamp to the Countess, without either offering or permitting the attendance of the old woman who had carried it. The lady stood not on ceremony, but taking it hastily, barred the door, and secured it with the ample means provided on the inside for that purpose.

Varney, meanwhile, had lurked behind on the stairs, but hearing the door barred, he now came up on tiptoe, and Foster, winking to him, pointed with self-complacence to a piece of concealed machinery in the wall, which, playing with much ease and little noise, dropped a part of the wooden gallery, after the manner of a drawbridge, so as to cut off all communication between the door of the bedroom, which he usually inhabited, and the landing-place of the high winding-stair which ascended to it. The rope by which this machinery was wrought was generally carried within the bedchamber, it being Foster's object to provide against invasion from without; but now that it was intended to secure the prisoner within, the cord had been brought over to the landing-place, and was there made fast, when Foster, with much complacency, had dropped the unsuspected trap-door.

Varney looked with great attention at the machinery, and peeped more than once down the abyss which was opened by the fall of the trap-door. It was dark as pitch, and seemed profoundly deep, going, as Foster informed his confederate in a whisper, nigh to the lowest vault of the Castle. Varney cast once more a fixed and long look down into this sable gulf, and then followed Foster to the part of the manor-house most usually inhabited.

When they arrived in the parlour which we have mentioned, Varney requested Foster to get them supper, and some of the choicest wine. "I will seek Alasco," he added; "we have work for him to do, and we must put him in good heart."

Foster groaned at this intimation, but made no remonstrance. The old woman assured Varney that Alasco had scarce eaten or drunken since her master's departure, living perpetually shut up in the laboratory, and talking as if the world's continuance depended on what he was doing there.

"I will teach him that the world hath other claims on him," said Varney, seizing a light, and going in quest of the alchemist. He returned, after a considerable absence, very pale, but yet with his habitual sneer on his cheek and nostril—"Our friend," he said, "has exhaled."

"How! what mean you?" said Foster—"Run away—fled with my forty pounds, that should have been multiplied a thousand fold? I will have Hue and Cry!"

"I will tell thee a surer way," said Varney.

"How! which way?" exclaimed Foster; "I will have back my forty pounds—I deemed them as surely a thousand times multiplied—I will have back my in-put, at the least."

"Go hang thyself, then, and sue Alasco in the Devil's Court of Chancery, for thither he has carried the cause."

"How!—what dost thou mean—is he dead?"

"Ay, truly is he," said Varney; "and properly swoln already in the face and body—He had been mixing some of his devil's medicines, and the glass mask which he used constantly had fallen from his face, so that the subtle poison entered the brain, and did its work."

"*Sancta Maria!*" said Foster;—"I mean, God in His mercy preserve us from covetousness and deadly sin!—Had he not had projection, think you? Saw you no ingots in the crucibles?"

"Nay, I looked not but at the dead carrion," answered Varney; "an ugly spectacle—he was swoln like a corpse three days exposed on the wheel—Pah? give me a cup of wine."

"I will go," said Foster, "I will examine myself——" He took the lamp, and hastened to the door, but there hesitated, and paused. "Will you not go with me?" said he to Varney.

"To what purpose?" said Varney; "I have seen and smelled enough to spoil my appetite. I broke the window, however, and let in the air—it reeked of sulphur, and such like suffocating steams, as if the very devil had been there."

"And might it not be the act of the Demon himself?" said Foster, still hesitating; "I have heard he is powerful at such times, and with such people."

"Still, if it *were* that Satan of thine," answered Varney, "who thus jades thy imagination, thou art in perfect safety, unless he is a most unconscionable devil indeed. He hath had two good sops of late."

"How, *two* sops—what mean you?" said Foster—"what mean you?"

"You will know in time," said Varney;—"and then this other banquet —but thou wilt esteem Her too choice a morsel for the fiend's tooth— she must have her psalms, and harps, and seraphs."

Anthony Foster heard, and came slowly back to the table; "God! Sir Richard, and must that then be done?"

"Ay, in very truth, Anthony, or there comes no copyhold in thy way," replied his inflexible associate.

"I always foresaw it would land there!" said Foster; "but how, Sir Richard, how?—for not to win the world would I put hands on her."

"I cannot blame thee," said Varney; "I should be reluctant to do that myself—we miss Alasco and his manna sorely; ay, and the dog Lambourne."

"Why, where tarries Lambourne?" said Anthony.

"Ask no questions," said Varney, "thou wilt see him one day, if thy creed is true.—But to our graver matter.—I will teach thee a spring, Tony, to catch a pewit—yonder trap-door—yonder gimcrack of thine, will remain secure in appearance, will it not, though the supports are withdrawn beneath?"

"Ay, marry, will it," said Foster; "so long as it is not trodden on."

"But were the lady to attempt an escape over it," replied Varney, "her weight would carry it down?"

"A mouse's weight would do it," said Foster.

"Why, then, she dies in attempting her escape, and what could you or

I help it, honest Tony? Let us to bed, we will adjust our project to-morrow."

On the next day, when evening approached, Varney summoned Foster to the execution of their plan. Tider and Foster's old man-servant were sent on a feigned errand down to the village, and Anthony himself, as if anxious to see that the Countess suffered no want of accommodation, visited her place of confinement. He was so much staggered at her mildness and patience with which she seemed to endure her confinement, that he could not help earnestly recommending to her not to cross the threshold of her room on any account whatever, until Lord Leicester should come, "Which," he added, "I trust in God, will be very soon." Amy patiently promised that she would resign herself to her fate, and Foster returned to his hardened companion with his conscience half-eased of the perilous load that weighed on it. "I have warned her," he said; "surely in vain is the snare set in the sight of any bird!"

He left, therefore, the Countess's door unsecured on the outside, and under the eye of Varney, withdrew the supports which sustained the falling trap, which, therefore, kept its level position merely by a slight adhesion. They withdrew to wait the issue on the ground-floor adjoining, but they waited long in vain. At length Varney, after walking long to and fro, with his face muffled in his cloak, threw it suddenly back, and exclaimed, "Surely never was a woman fool enough to neglect so fair an opportunity of escape!"

"Perhaps she is resolved," said Foster, "to await her husband's return."

"True!—most true," said Varney, rushing out, "I had not thought of that before.'"

In less than two minutes, Foster, who remained behind, heard the tread of a horse in the court-yard and then a whistle similar to that which was the Earl's usual signal;—the instant after the door of the Countess's chamber opened, and in the same moment the trap-door gave way. There was a rushing sound—a heavy fall—a faint groan—and all was over.

At the same instant, Varney called in at the window, in an accent and tone which was an indescribable mixture betwixt horror and raillery, "Is the bird caught?—is the deed done?"

"O God, forgive us!" replied Anthony Foster.

"Why, thou fool," said Varney, "thy toil is ended, and thy reward secure. Look down into the vault—what seest thou?"

"I see only a heap of white clothes, like a snowdrift," said Foster. "O God, she moves her arm!"

"Hurl something down on her.—Thy gold chest, Tony—it is an heavy one."

"Varney, thou art an incarnate fiend!" replied Foster;—"There needs nothing more—she is gone!"

"So pass our troubles," said Varney, entering the room; "I dreamed not I could have mimicked the Earl's call so well."

"Oh, if there be judgment in Heaven, thou hast deserved it," said

Foster, "and wilt meet it!—Thou hast destroyed her by means of her best affections—It is a seething of the kid in the mother's milk!"

"Thou art a fanatical ass," replied Varney; "let us now think how the alarm should be given,—the body is to remain where it is."

But their wickedness was to be permitted no longer;—for, even while they were at this consultation, Tressilian and Raleigh broke in upon them, having obtained admittance by means of Tider and Foster's servant, whom they had secured at the village.

Anthony Foster fled on their entrance; and, knowing each corner and pass of the intricate old house, escaped all search. But Varney was taken on the spot; and, instead of expressing compunction for what he had done, seemed to take a fiendish pleasure in pointing out to them the remains of the murdered Countess, while at the same time he defied them to show that he had any share in her death. The despairing grief of Tressilian, on viewing the mangled and yet warm remains of what had lately been so lovely and so beloved, was such, that Raleigh was compelled to have him removed from the place by force, while he himself assumed the direction of what was to be done.

Varney, upon a second examination, made very little mystery either of the crime or of its motives; alleging, as a reason for his frankness, that though much of what he confessed could only have attached to him by suspicion, yet such suspicion would have been sufficient to deprive him of Leicester's confidence, and to destroy all his towering plans of ambition. "I was not born," he said, "to drag on the remainder of life a degraded outcast,—nor will I so die, that my fate shall make a holiday to the vulgar herd."

From these words it was apprehended he had some design upon himself, and he was carefully deprived of all means by which such could be carried into execution. But like some of the heroes of antiquity, he carried about his person a small quantity of strong poison, prepared probably by the celebrated Demetrius Alasco. Having swallowed this potion over-night, he was found next morning dead in his cell; nor did he appear to have suffered much agony, his countenance presenting, even in death, the habitual expression of sneering sarcasm, which was predominant while he lived. "The wicked man," saith the Scripture, "hath no bonds in his death."

The fate of his colleague in wickedness was long unknown. Cumnor-Place was deserted immediately after the murder; for, in the vicinity of what was called the Lady Dudley's Chamber, the domestics pretended to hear groans, and screams, and other supernatural noises. After a certain length of time, Janet, hearing no tidings of her father, became the uncontrolled mistress of his property, and conferred it with her hand upon Wayland, now a man of settled character, and holding a place in Elizabeth's household. But it was after they had been both dead for some years, that their eldest son and heir, in making some researches about Cumnor-Hall, discovered a secret passage, closed by an iron door, which, opening from behind the bed in the Lady Dudley's Chamber, descended to a sort of cell, in which they found an iron chest containing a quantity of gold, and a human skeleton stretched above it. The fate of Anthony Foster was now manifest. He had fled to this place of concealment, forgetting the key of the spring-lock; and being barred from escape, by the means he had used for preservation of that gold, for which he had sold his salvation, he had there perished miserably. Unquestionably the groans and screams heard by the domestics were not entirely imaginary, but were those of this wretch, who, in his agony, was crying for relief and succour.

The news of the Countess's dreadful fate put a sudden period to the pleasures of Kenilworth. Leicester retired from court, and for a considerable time abandoned himself to his remorse. But as Varney in his last declaration had been studious to spare the character of his patron, the Earl was the object rather of compassion than resentment. The Queen at length recalled him to court; he was once more distinguished as a statesman and favourite, and the rest of his career is well known to history. But there was something retributive in his death, if, according to an account very generally received, it took place from his swallowing a draught of poison, which was designed by him for another person.[1]

Sir Hugh Robsart died very soon after his daughter, having settled his estate on Tressilian. But neither the prospect of rural independence, nor the promises of favour which Elizabeth held out to induce him to follow the court, could remove his profound melancholy. Wherever he went, he seemed to see before him the disfigured corpse of the early and only object of his affection. At length, having made provision for the maintenance of the old friends and old servants who formed Sir Hugh's family at Lidcote Hall, he himself embarked with his friend Raleigh for the Virginia expedition, and, young in years but old in grief, died before his day in that foreign land.

Of inferior persons it is only necessary to say, that Blount's wit grew brighter as his yellow roses faded; that, doing his part as a brave commander in the wars, he was much more in his element than during the short period of his following the court; and that Flibbertigibbet's acute genius raised him to favour and distinction, in the employment both of Burleigh and Cecil.

[1] See Note IX.—Death of the Earl of Leicester.

NOTES

Note I. p. 797.—FOSTER, LAMBOURNE, AND THE BLACK BEAR

IF faith is to be put in epitaphs, Anthony Foster was something the very reverse of the character represented in the novel. Ashmole gives this description of his tomb. I copy from the "Antiquities of Berkshire," vol. i. p. 143.

"In the north wall of the chancel at Cumnor church, is a monument of grey marble, whereon, in brass plates, are engraved a man in armour, and his wife in the habit of her times, both kneeling before a fald-stoole, together with the figures of three sons kneeling behind their mother. Under the figure of the man is this inscription:—

> ANTONIUS FORSTER, generis generosa propago,
> Cumneræ Dominus, Bercheriensis erat.
> Armiger, Armigero prognatus patre Ricardo,
> Qui quondam Iphlethæ Salopiensis erat.
> Quatuor ex isto fluxerunt stemmate nati,
> Ex isto Antonius stemmate quartus erat.
> Mente sagax, animo precellens, corpore, promptus;
> Eloquii dulcis, ore disertus erat.
> In factis probitas; fuit in sermone venustas,
> In vultu gravitas, relligione fides,
> In patriam pietas, in egenos grata voluntas,
> Accedunt relliquis annumeranda bonis.
> Si quod cuncta rapit, rapuit non omnia Lethum,
> So quod Mors rapuit, vivida fama dedit.

> .   .   .   .   .

"These verses following are writ at length, two by two, in praise of him:—

> Argute resonas Cithare pretendere chordas
> Novit, et Aonia concrepuisse Lyra.
> Gaudebat terre teneras defigere plantas;
> Et mira pulchras construere arte domos
> Composita varias lingua formare loquelas
> Doctus, et edocta scribere multa manu.

"The arms over it thus:—

> Quart. { I. 3 *Hunter's Horns* stringed.
> { II. 3 *Pinions* with their points upwards.

"The crest is a *Stag* Couchant, vulnerated through the neck by a broad arrow; on his side is a *Martlett* for a difference."

From this monumental inscription it appears, that Anthony Foster, instead of being a vulgar, low-bred, puritanical churl, was in fact a gentleman of birth and consideration, distinguished for his skill in the arts of music and horticulture, as also in languages. In so far, therefore, the Anthony Foster of the romance has nothing but the name in common with the real individual. But notwithstanding the charity, benevolence, and religious faith imputed by the monument of grey marble to its tenant, tradition, as well as secret history, name him as the active agent in the death of the Countess; and it is added, that from being a jovial and convivial gallant, as we may infer from some expressions in the epitaph, he sunk, after the fatal deed, into a man of gloom and retired habits, whose looks and manners indicated that he suffered under the pressure of some atrocious secret.

The name of Lambourne is still known in the vicinity, and it is said some of the clan partake the habits, as well as name, of the Michael Lambourne of the romance, A man of this name lately murdered his wife, outdoing Michael in this respect, who only was concerned in the murder of the wife of another man.

I have only to add, that the jolly Black Bear has been restored to his predomi-nance over bowl and bottle, in the village of Cumnor.

Note II. p. 886.—Legend of Wayland Smith

The great defeat, given by Alfred to the Danish invaders, is said, by Mr. Gough, to have taken place near Ashdown, in Berkshire. "The burial place of Baereg, the Danish chief, who was slain in this fight, is distinguished by a parcel of stones, less than a mile from the hill, set on edge, enclosing a piece of ground somewhat raised. On the east side of the southern extremity, stand three squarish flat stones, of about four or five feet over either way, supporting a fourth, and now called by the vulgar Wayland Smith, from an idle tradition about an invisible smith replacing lost horse-shoes there."—Gough's edition of Camden's "Britannia," vol. i. p. 221.

The popular belief still retains memory of this wild legend, which, connected as it is with the site of a Danish sepulchre, may have arisen from some legend concern-ing the northern Duergar, who resided in the rocks, and were cunning workers in steel and iron. It was believed that Wayand Smith's fee was sixpence, and that, unlike other workmen, he was offended if more was offered. Of late his offices have again been called to memory; but fiction has in this, as in other cases, taken the liberty to pillage the stores of oral tradition. This monument must be very ancient, for it has been kindly pointed out to me that it is referred to in an ancient Saxon charter, as a landmark. The monument has been of late cleared out, and made con-siderably more conspicuous.

Note III. p. 892.—Leicester and Sussex

Naunton gives us numerous and curious particulars of the jealous struggle which took place between Ratcliffe, Earl of Sussex, and the rising favourite Leicester. The former, when on his deathbed, predicted to his followers, that, after his death, the gipsy (so he called Leicester, from his dark complexion) would prove too many for them.

Note IV. p. 894.—Sir Walter Raleigh

Among the attendants and adherents of Sussex, we have ventured to introduce the celebrated Raleigh, in the dawn of his court favour.

In Aubrey's correspondence there are some curious particulars of Sir Walter Raleigh. "He was a tall, handsome, bold man; but his næve was that he was damnably proud. Old Sir Robert Harley of Brampton Brian Castle, who knew him, would say, it was a great question who was the proudest, Sir Walter, or Sir Thomas Overbury; but the difference that was, was judged in Sir Thomas's side. In the great parlour at Downton, at Mr. Raleigh's, is a good piece, an original of Sir Walter, in a white satin doublet, all embroidered with rich pearls, and a mighty rich chain of great pearls about his neck. The old servants have told me that the real pearls were near as big as the painted ones. He had a most remarkable aspect, an exceeding high forehead, long-faced, and sour-eyelided." A rebus is added, to this purpose:—

> The enemy to the stomach, and the word of disgrace,
> Is the name of the gentleman with the bold face.

Sir Walter Raleigh's beard turned up naturally, which gave him an advantage over the gallants of the time, whose mustaches received a touch of the barber's art to give them the air then most admired.—*See* AUBREY's *Correspondence,* vol. ii., part ii., p. 500.

Note V. p. 905.—COURT FAVOUR OF SIR WALTER RALEIGH

The gallant incident of the cloak is the traditional account of this celebrated statesman's rise at court. None of Elizabeth's courtiers knew better than he how to make his court to her personal vanity, or could more justly estimate the quantity of flattery which she could condescend to swallow. Being confined in the Tower for some offence, and understanding the Queen was about to pass to Greenwich in her barge, he insisted on approaching the window, that he might see, at whatever distance, the Queen of his Affections, the most beautiful object which the earth bore on its surface. The Lieutenant of the Tower (his own particular friend) threw himself between his prisoner and the window; while Sir Walter, apparently influenced by a fit of unrestrainable passion, swore he would not be debarred from seeing his light, his life, his goddess! A scuffle ensued, *got up* for effect's sake, in which the Lieutenant and his captive grappled and struggled with fury—tore each other's hair,—and at length drew daggers, and were only separated by force. The Queen being informed of this scene exhibited by her frantic adorer, it wrought, as was to be expected, much in favour of the captive Paladin. There is little doubt that his quarrel with the Lieutenant was entirely contrived for the purpose which it produced.

Note VI. p. 926.—ROBERT LANEHAM

Little is known of Robert Laneham, save in his curious letter to a friend in London, giving an account of Queen Elizabeth's entertainments at Kenilworth, written in a style of the most intolerable affectation, both in point of composition and orthography. He describes himself as a *bon vivant,* who was wont to be jolly and dry in the morning, and by his good-will would be chiefly in the company of the ladies. He was, by the interest of Lord Leicester, Clerk of the Council Chamber door, and also keeper of the same. "When council sits," says he, "I am at hand. If any makes a babbling, *Peace,* say I. If I see a listener or a pryer in at the chinks or lockhole, I am presently on the bones of him. If a friend comes, I make him sit down by me on a form or chest. The rest may walk, a God's name!" There has been seldom a better portrait of the pragmatic conceit and self-importance of a small man in office.

Note VII. p. 947.—DR. JULIO

The Earl of Leicester's Italian physician, Julio, was affirmed by his contemporaries to be a skilful compounder of poisons, which he applied with such frequency, that the Jesuit Parsons extols ironically the marvellous good luck of this great favourite, in the opportune deaths of those who stood in the way of his wishes. There is a curious passage on the subject:—

"Long after this, he fell in love with the Lady Sheffield, whom I signified before, and then also had he the same fortune to have her husband dye quickly, with an extreme rheume in his head (as it was given out), but as others say, of an artificiall catarre, that stopped his breath.

"The like good chance had he in the death of my Lord of Essex (as I have said before), and that at a time most fortunate for his purpose; for when he was coming home from Ireland, with intent to revenge himselfe upon my Lord of Leicester for begetting his wife with childe in his absence (the childe was a daughter, and brought up by the Lady Shandoes, W. Knooles his wife), my Lord of Leicester hearing thereof, wanted not a friend or two to accompany the deputy, as among other a couple of the Earles own servants, Crompton (if I misse not his name) yeoman of his bottles, and Lloid his secretary, entertained afterward by my Lord of Leicester, and so he dyed in the way, of an extreme fluxe, caused by an Italian receipe, as all his friends are well assured, the maker whereof was a chyrurgeon (as it is beleeved) that then was newly come to my Lord from Italy,—a cunning man and sure in operation, with whom, if the good Lady had been sooner acquainted, and used his help, she should not have needed to sitten so pensive at home, and fearefull of her husband's former returne out of the same country.... Neither must you marvaile though all these died in divers manners of outward diseases, for this is the excellency of the Italian art, for which this chyrurgian and Dr. Julio were entertained so carefully, who can make a man dye in what manner or show of sicknesse you will— by whose instructions, no doubt; but his lordship is now cunning, especially adding also to these the counsell of his Doctor Bayly, a man also not a little studied (as he seemeth) in his art; for I heard him once myselfe, in a publique act in Oxford, and that in presence of my Lord of Leicester (if I be not deceived), maintain, that poyson might be so tempered and given as it should not appear presently, and yet should kill the party afterward, at what time should be appointed; which argument belike pleased well his lordship, and therefore was chosen to be discussed in his audience, if I be not deceived of his being that day present. So, though one dye of a flux, and another of a catarre, yet this importeth little to the matter, but showeth rather the great cunning and skill of the artificer."—PARSONS' *Leicester's Commonwealth*, p. 23.

It is unnecessary to state the numerous reasons why the Earl is represented in the tale as being rather the dupe of villains than the unprincipled author of their atrocities. In the latter capacity, which a part at least of his contemporaries imputed to him, he would have made a character too disgustingly wicked, to be useful for the purposes of fiction.

I have only to add, that the union of the poisoner, the quacksalver, the alchemist, and the astrologer, in the same person, was familiar to the pretenders to the mystic sciences.

Note VIII. p. 1046.—FURNITURE OF KENILWORTH

In revising this work for the present edition, I have had the means of making some accurate additions to my attempt to describe the princely pleasures of Kenilworth, by the kindness of my friend William Hamper, Esq., who had the goodness to communicate to me an inventory of the furniture of Kenilworth in the days of the magnificent Earl of Leicester. I have adorned the text with some of the splendid articles mentioned in the inventory, but antiquaries, especially, will be desirous to see a more full specimen than the story leaves room for.

EXTRACTS FROM KENILWORTH INVENTORY, A.D. 1584

A Salte, ship-fashion, of the mother of perle, garnished with silver and divers workes, warlike-ensignes, and ornaments, with xvj peeces of ordinance, whereof ij on wheles, two anckers on the foreparte, and on the stearne the image of Dame Fortune standing on a globe with a flag in her hand. Pois xxxij oz.

A gilt salte like a swann, mother of perle. Pois xxx oz. iij quarters.

A George on horseback, of wood, painted and gilt, with a case for knives in the tayle of the horse, and a case for oyster knives in the brest of the Dragon.

A green barge-cloth, embrother'd with white lions and beares.

A performing pann, of silver. Pois xix oz.

In the halle. Tabells, long and short, vj. Forms, long and short, xiiij.

HANGINGS

(These are minutely specified, and consisted of the following subjects in tapestry, and gilt and red leather.)

Flowers, beasts, and pillars arched. Forest worke. Historie Storie of Susanna, the Prodigall Childe, Saule, Tobie, Hercules, Lady Fame, Hawking and Hunting, Jezabell, Judith and Holofernes, David, Abraham, Sampson, Hippolitus, Alexander the Great, Naaman the Assyrian, Jacob, &c.

Bedsteds, with their Furniture

(These are magnificent and numerous. I shall copy, *verbatim*, the description of what appears to have been one of the best.)

A bedsted of wallnut-tree, toppe fashion, the pillers redd and varnished, the ceelor, tester, and single vallance of crimson sattin, paned with a broad border of bone lace of goïde and silver. The tester richlie embrothered with my Lo. armes in a garland of hoppes, roses, and pomegranetts, and lyned with buckerom. Fyve curteins of crimson sattin to the same bedsted, garnished with buttons and loops of crimson silk and golde, containing xiiij bredths of sattin, and one yarde iij quarters deepe. The celor, vallance, and curtains lyned with crymson taffata sarsenet.

A crymson sattin counterpointe, quilted and embr. with a golde twiste, and lyned with redd sarsenet, being in length iij yards good, and in breadth iij scant.

A chaise of crymson sattin, suteable.

A fayre quilte of crymson sattin, vj breadths, iij yards 3 quarters naile deepe, all lozenged over with silver twiste, in the midst a cinquefoile within a garland of ragged staves, fringed round aboute with a small fringe of crymson silke, lyned throughe with white fustian.

Fyve plumes of coolered feathers, garnished with bone lace and spangells of goulde and silver, standing in cups * knitt all over with goulde, silver, and crymson silk.

A carpett for a cupboarde of crymson sattin, embrothered with a border of goulde twiste, about iij parts of it fringed with silk and goulde, lyned with bridges † sattin, in length ij yards, and ij bredths of sattin.

(There were eleven down beds and ninety feather beds, besides thirty-seven mattresses.)

Chayres, Stooles, and Cushens

(These were equally splendid with the beds, &c. I shall here copy that which stands at the head of the list.)

A chaier of crimson velvet, the seate and backe partlie embrothered, with R. L. in cloth of goulde, the beare and ragged staffe in clothe of silver, garnished with lace and fringe of goulde, silver, and crimson silck. The frame covered with velvet, bounde aboute the edge with goulde lace, and studded with gilt nailes.

A square stoole and a foote stoole, of crimson velvet, fringed and garnished suteable.

A long cushen of crimson velvet, embr. with the ragged staffe in a wreathe of goulde, with my Lo. posie *"Droyte et Loyall"* written in the same, and the letter R. L. in clothe of goulde, being garnished with lace, fringe, buttons, and tassels of gold, silver and crimson silck, lyned with crimson taff, being in length 1 yard quarter.

A square cushen, of the like velvet, embr. suteable to the long cushen.

Carpets

(There were 10 velvet carpets for tables and windows, 49 Turkey carpets for floors, and 32 cloth carpets. One of each I will now specify.)

A carpett of crimson velvet, richly embr. with my Lo. posie, beares and ragged staves, &c., of clothe of goulde and silver, garnished upon the seames and aboute with golde lace, fringed accordinglie, lyned with crimson taffata sarsenette, being 3 breadths of velvet, one yard 3 quarters long.

A great Turquoy carpett, the grounde blew, with a list of yelloe at each end, being in length x yards, in bredthe iiij yards and quarter.

* Probably on the centre and four corners of the bedstead. Four bears and ragged staves occupied a similar position on another of these sumptuous pieces of furniture.
† *i.e.* Bruges.

A long carpett of blew clothe, lyned with bridges sattin, fringed with blew silck and goulde, in length vj yards lack a quarter, the whole bredth of the clothe.

PICTURES

(Chiefly described as having curtains.)

The Queene's Majestie (2 great tables). 3 of my Lord. St. Jerome. Lo. of Arundell. Lord Mathevers. Lord of Pembroke. Counte Egmondt. The Queene of Scots. King Philip. The Baker's Daughters. The Duke of Feria. Alexander Magnus. Two Yonge Ladies. Pompæa Sabina. Fred. D. of Saxony. Emp. Charles. K. Philip's Wife. Prince of Orange and his Wife. Marq. of Berg and his Wife. Counte de Horne. Count Holstrate. Monsr. Brederode. Duke Alva. Cardinal Grandville. Duches of Parma. Henriè of Pembrooke and his young Countess. Countis of Essex. Occacion and Repentance. Lord Mowntacute. Sir Jas. Crofts. Sir Wr. Mildmay. Sir Wm. Pickering. Edwin Abp. of York.

A tabell of an historie of men, women, and children, molden in wax.

A little foulding table of ebanie, garnished with white bone, wherein are written verses with lres. of goulde.

A table of my Lord's armes.

Fyve of the plannetts, painted in frames.

Twentie-three cardes, * or maps of countries.

INSTRUMENTS

(I shall give two specimens.)

An instrument of organs, regalls, and virginalls, covered with crimson velvet, and garnished with goulde lace.

A fair pair of double virginalls.

CABONETTS

A cabonnett of crimson sattin, richlie embr. with a device of hunting the stagg, in goulde, silver, and silck, with iiij glasses in the topp thereof, xvj cupps of flowers made of goulde, silver, and silck, in a case of leather, lyned with greene sattin of bridges.

(Another of purple velvet. A desk of red leather.)

A CHESS BORDE of ebanie, with checkars of christall and other stones, layed with silver, garnished with beares and ragged staves, and cinquefoiles, of silver. The xxxij men likewyse of christall and other stones sett, the one sort in silver white, the other gilte, in a case gilded and lyned with green cotton.

(Another of bone and ebanie. A pair of tabells of bone.)

A GREAT BRASON CANDLESTICK to hang in the roofe of the howse, verie fayer and curiouslye wrought, with xxiiij branches, xij greate and xij of lesser size, 6 rowlers and ij wings for the spreade eagle, xxiiij socketts for candells, xij greater and xij of a lesser sorte, xxiiij sawcers, or candlecupps, of like proporcion to put under the socketts, iij images of men and iij of weomen, of brass, verie finely and artificiallie done.

These specimens of Leicester's magnificence may serve to assure the reader that it scarce lay in the power of a modern author to exaggerate the lavish style of expense displayed in the princely pleasures of Kenilworth.

Note IX. p. 1127.—DEATH OF THE EARL OF LEICESTER

In a curious manuscript copy of the information given by Ben Jonson to Drummond of Hawthornden, as abridged by Sir Robert Sibbald, Leicester's death is

---

* *i.e.* Charts.

ascribed to poison administered as a cordial by his countess, to whom he had given it, representing it to be a restorative in any faintness, in the hope that she herself might be cut off by using it. It may be here added, that the following satirical epitaph on Leicester occurs in Drummond's Collections, but is evidently not of his composition:—

EPITAPH ON THE ERLE OF LEISTER.

Here lies a valiant warriour,
    Who never drew a sword;
Here lies a noble courtier,
    Who never kept his word;
Here lies the Erle of Leister,
    Who govern'd the estates,
Whom the earth could never living love,
And the just Heaven now hates.

GLOSSARY

A', *he.*

ABYE, *suffer.*

ANGEL, *an English gold coin, worth about ten shillings, impressed with the figure of an angel.*

A's, *his.*

BASTARD, *inferior liquor.*

BESHREW, *ill befall.*

BLITHER, *pleasanter, happier.*

BONA-ROBAS, *strumpets.*

BOTS, *worms in a horse's stomach.*

BRATCHET-WHELP, *young brat.*

BRAVERIES, *fineries, holiday attire.*

BRUILZIEMENT, *a quarrel, broil.*

CAITIFF, *a mean, despicable fellow.*

CALIVER, *a species of musket.*

CAMLET, *a kind of stuff made out of camel's hair.*

CAPOTAINE HAT, *a species of hood.*

CARTEL, *a note of defiance, challenge.*

CAUDLE-CUP, *a cup of heated wine with other ingredients.*

CERTES, *faith, in truth.*

CHERRY-PIT, *a game played with cherry-stones.*

CLARY, *claret.*

COCKATRICE, *a fabulous serpent, said to be produced from a cock's egg brooded by a serpent.*

CODLING, *an immature apple.*

CORRAGIO, *courage.*

COSTARD, *the head.*

COZENOR, *a cheat.*

CULLIS, *a fine strong broth.*

CUT BOON WHIDS, *give good words.*

DAMOZEL-ERRANT, *unprotected female.*

DEBOSHED, *debauched.*

DECOCT, *boil down.*

ELL-WAND, *yard-stick.*

FOOT-CLOTH, *covering for a horse, reaching almost to the ground.*

FOUNDERS, *lameness, caused by inflammation in the foot of a horse.*

GAZEHOUND, *a hound that pursues by sight rather than by the scent.*

GEAR, *goods, dress, belongings.*

GRAMERCY, *great thanks.*

GROAT, *an old English coin, worth about fourpence.*

GUERDON, *reward.*

GULL, *dupe, one easily befooled.*

HEADBOROUGH, *a county town where a Sheriff-court is held.*

HOWLET, *a small owl.*

JOLTERHEADS, *dunces, blockheads.*

JUVENAL, *youth, juvenile.*

LEECH, *physician.*

LINSEY-WOLSEY, *stuff made of linen and wool mixed.*

LINSTOCK, *the staff to hold the match for firing a cannon.*

LOON, *rascal.*

MAR-FEAST, *one who refuses to drink in company.*

MAVIS, *the throstle, or song-thrush.*

MOPPET, *dear little girl.*

MUFFLER, *a covering for the lower part of the face.*

MULLED SACK, *spiced sherry, or canary wine.*

MURRAIN, *cattle-plague.*

MUSCADINE, *wine made from the muscatel or muscadel, a rich, juicy grape.*

NETHER-STOCKS, *stockings.*

NOBLE, *a gold coin, worth 6s. 8d. sterling.*

ORVIETAN, *Venice treacle, supposed to be a sovereign remedy against poison.*

PALABRAS, *words.*

PANTILES, *tiles with hollow surfaces.*

PANTOFLES, *slippers.*

PARLOUS, *perilous.*

PEDAGOGUE, *tutor.*

POSSET, *a beverage consisting of milk curdled by wine.*

POTTLE-POT, *vessel containing a pottle, or four pints.*

PRIGGED A PRANCER, *stole a horse.*

PUISSANT, *powerful, forcible.*

PURSUIVANT, *a State messenger.*

ROOD, *cross.*

ROWAN-TREE, *mountain-ash.*

SACK, *hot spiced wine of sherry or canary.*

SALLYPORT, *secret postern.*

SCOT AND LOT, *parish payments according to the tenant's means.*

SHOG, *jog, move off.*

SHOVEL-BOARD, *a game.*

SIRRAH, *Sir!* (an expression of reproach or contempt).

SLOUGH, *bespatterings of mud.*

STITHIES, *anvils.*

THWACK, *strike.*

TIRING-ROOM, *dressing-room.*

TIT, *small horse.*

TOKAY, *wine made of white grapes at Tokay, Hungary.*

TROW, *believe, consider.*

TUCKETS, *flourishes.*

TYBURN TIPPET, *hangman's rope.*

TYKE, *dog, snarling fellow.*

UN, *him.*

VIZNOMY, *visage.*

WAIN, *waggon.*

WATCHET-COLOURED, *blue.*

WHITE WITCH, *a cunning man.*

WOT, *know.*

WOTTED, *knew.*

WOU'D, *lived.*

The Best of the World's Best Books
COMPLETE LIST OF TITLES IN
THE MODERN LIBRARY